Nora Roberts is the *New York Times* bestselling author of more than 190 novels. Under the pen-name J. D. Robb, she is author of the *New York Times* bestselling futuristic suspense series, which features Lieutenant Eve Dallas and Roarke. There are more than 300 million copies of her books in print, and she has had more than 150 *New York Times* bestsellers.

Visit her website at www.nora-roberts.co.uk

By Nora Roberts:

Homeport
The Reef
River's End
Carolina Moon
The Villa
Midnight Bayou
Three Fates
Birthright
Northern Lights
Blue Smoke
Montana Sky
Angels Fall
High Noon
Divine Evil
Tribute
Sanctuary

Three Sisters Island Trilogy:
Dance Upon the Air
Heaven and Earth
Face the Fire

Chesapeake Bay Quartet:
Sea Swept
Rising Tides
Inner Harbour
Chesapeake Blue

The Key Trilogy:
Key of Light
Key of Knowledge
Key of Valour

In the Garden Trilogy:
Blue Dahlia
Black Rose
Red Lily

The Irish Trilogy:
Jewels of the Sun
Tears of the Moon
Heart of the Sea

The Circle Trilogy:
Morrigan's Cross
Dance of the Gods
Valley of Silence

The Dream Trilogy:
Daring to Dream
Holding the Dream
Finding the Dream

The Sign of Seven Trilogy:
Blood Brothers
The Hollow
The Pagan Stone

As J. D. Robb:

Naked in Death
Glory in Death
Immortal in Death
Rapture in Death
Ceremony in Death
Vengeance in Death
Holiday in Death
Conspiracy in Death
Loyalty in Death
Witness in Death
Judgement in Death
Betrayal in Death
Seduction in Death
Reunion in Death
Purity in Death
Portrait in Death
Imitation in Death
Divided in Death
Visions in Death
Survivor in Death
Origin in Death
Memory in Death
Born in Death
Innocent in Death
Creation in Death
Strangers in Death

By Nora Roberts and J. D. Robb:

Remember When

NORA ROBERTS

Dance Upon the Air

PIATKUS

PIATKUS

First published in the US in 2001 by G. P. Putnam's Sons
First published in Great Britain in 2001 by Piatkus Books
Reprinted 2001 (twice), 2002 (three times), 2003, 2004 (three times), 2005, 2006, 2007, 2008, 2009

All characters and events in this publication, other than those clearly in the public domain, are fictitious and any resemblance to real persons, living or dead, is purely coincidental.

A CIP catalogue record for this book is available from the British Library

ISBN 978-0-7499-3277-0

Printed and bound in Great Britain by
CPI Mackays, Chatham, ME5 8TD

Papers used by Piatkus Books are natural, renewable and recyclable products made from wood grown in sustainable forests and certified in accordance with the rules of the Forest Stewardship Council.

Piatkus Books
An imprint of
Little, Brown Book Group
100 Victoria Embankment
London EC4Y 0DY

An Hachette Livre UK Company
www.hachettelivre.co.uk

www.piatkus.co.uk

To the Broads, the Brats, the Brawn,
and the Babes,
For the fun and the friendships

It is sweet to dance to violins
When Love and Life are Fair:
To dance to flutes, to dance to lutes
Is delicate and rare:
But it is not sweet with nimble feet
To dance upon the air!

—Oscar Wilde

Prologue

Salem Village, Massachusetts
June 22, 1692

In the dark green shadows of the deep woods, an hour before moonrise, they met in secret. Soon the longest day would become the shortest night of the solstice.

There would be no celebration, no rite of thanksgiving for the light, the warmth, on this Sabbat of Litha. This midsummer was a time of ignorance, and of death.

The three who met, met in fear.

"Have we all we need?" The one known here as Air pulled her hood closer so that not a single pale lock of hair could be seen in the light of the dying day.

"What we have shall do." Earth laid her parcel on the ground. The part of her that wanted to weep and to rage over what had been done, over what was to come, was buried deep. With her head bent, her thick brown hair fell forward free.

"Is there no other way for us?" Air touched a hand to Earth's shoulder, and both looked at the third.

She stood, slim and straight. There was sorrow in her eyes, but behind it lived a firm purpose. She who was Fire threw back her hood in a gesture of defiance. Curling waves of red spilled out.

"It is because of our way there is no other. They will hunt us down like thieves and brigands, murder us, as they have already murdered a poor innocent."

"Bridget Bishop was not a witch." Earth spoke bitterly as she rose to her feet.

"No, and so she told the court of oyer and terminer. So she swore. Yet they hanged her. Murdered over the lies of a few young girls and the ravings of the fanatics who smell brimstone in every breath of air."

"But there have been petitions." Air linked her fingers together like a woman preparing to pray. Or plead. "Not everyone supports the court, or this terrible persecution."

"Too little," Earth murmured. "And far too late."

"It will not end with one death. I have seen it." Fire closed her eyes, saw again the horrors to come. "Our protection cannot outlast the hunt. They will find us, and they will destroy us."

"We have done nothing." Air dropped her hands to her sides. "No harm."

"What harm did Bridget Bishop do?" Fire countered. "What harm have any of the others accused and waiting trial done to the people of Salem Town? Sarah Osborne died in a Boston prison. For what crime?"

Temper lanced through her, hot and keen, and was

ruthlessly rejected. Even now she refused to let power be stained by anger and hate.

"The blood is up in these Puritans," she continued. "These *pioneers*. Fanatics they are, and they will bring a wave of death before sanity returns."

"If we could help."

"We cannot stop it, sister."

"No." Fire nodded at Earth. "All we can do is survive. So we leave this place, the home we made here, the lives we might have led here. And make another."

Gently, she cupped Air's face in her hands. "Grieve not for what can never be, but celebrate what can. We are the Three, and we will not be vanquished in this place."

"We will be lonely."

"We will be together."

And in that last flicker of the day they cast the circle—one by two by three. Fire ringed around the earth, and the wind lifted the flames high.

Inside the magic circle they formed another, joining hands.

Accepting now, Air lifted her face to the sky. "As night takes the day, we offer this light. We are true to the Way and stand for the right. Truth here is done, a circle of one."

Earth, defiant, raised her voice. "This hour is our last upon this ground. Present, future, past, we will not be found. Strength not rue, a circle of two."

"We offered our craft with harm to none, but the hunt for our blood has already begun. We will make our place away from here." Fire lifted joined hands high. "Away from death, away from fear. Power lives free, a circle of three."

The wind kicked, the earth trembled. And the magic fire speared through the night. Three voices rose, in unison.

"Away from hate let this land be torn. Lift it from fear, from death and scorn. Carve rock, carve tree, carve hill and stream. Carry us with it on midsummer moonbeam. Out past the cliff and out past the shore, to be severed from this land forever more. We take our island out to the sea. As we will, so mote it be."

And a great roar sounded in the forest, a swirling torrent of wind, a wild leap of fire. While those who hunted what they never understood slept in their righteous beds, an island rose up toward sky, circled madly toward sea.

Settled safe and serene on quiet waves. And took its first breath of life on that shortest night.

One

THREE SISTERS ISLAND
JUNE, 2001

She kept staring straight ahead as the knuckle of land, bumpy and green with distance, began revealing its secrets. The lighthouse, of course. What was an offshore New England island without its stalwart spear? This one, pure and dazzling white, rose on a craggy cliff. Just as it should, Nell thought.

There was a stone house near it, fog-gray in the sharp summer sunlight, with peaked roofs and gables and what she hoped was a widow's walk circling the top story.

She'd seen paintings of the Light of the Sisters and the house that stood so strong and firm beside it. It was the one she'd seen in the little shop on the mainland, the one that had sent her impulsively to the car ferry.

She'd been following impulse and instinct for six months, just two months after her meticulous and hard-worked plan had freed her.

Every moment of those first two months had been

terror. Then, gradually, terror had eased to anxiety, and a different kind of fear, almost like a hunger, that she would lose what she had found again.

She had died so she could live.

Now she was tired of running, of hiding, of losing herself in crowded cities. She wanted a home. Wasn't that what she'd always wanted? A home, roots, family, friends. The familiar that never judged too harshly.

Maybe she would find some part of that here, on this spit of land cradled by the sea. Surely she could get no farther away from Los Angeles than this pretty little island—not unless she left the country altogether.

If she couldn't find work on the island, she could still take a few days there. A kind of vacation from flight, she decided. She would enjoy the rocky beaches, the little village, she would climb the cliffs and roam the thick wedge of forest.

She'd learned how to celebrate and cherish every moment of being. It was something she would never, ever forget again.

Delighted with the scatter of clapboard cottages tucked back from the dock, she leaned on the rail of the ferry, let the wind blow through her hair. It was back to its natural sun-drenched blond. When she'd run, she'd hacked it short as a boy's, gleefully snipping off the long, tumbling curls, then dying it deep brown. Over the past months, she'd changed the color periodically—bright red, coal black, a soft sable brown. She still kept it fairly short and very straight.

It said something, didn't it, that she'd finally been able to let it be. Something about reclaiming herself, she thought.

Evan had liked it long, with a riot of curls. At times he had dragged her by it, across the floor, down the stairs. Using it like chains.

No, she would never wear it long again.

A shudder ran through her, and she glanced quickly over her shoulder, scanning the cars, the people. Her mouth went dry, her throat hot as she searched for a tall, slim man with gilded hair and eyes as pale and hard as glass.

He wasn't there, of course. He was three thousand miles away. She was dead to him. Hadn't he told her a hundred times that the only way she would be free of him was in death?

Helen Remington had died so Nell Channing could live.

Furious with herself for going back, even for a moment in her mind, Nell tried to calm herself. She breathed in slowly. Salt air, water. Freedom.

As her shoulders relaxed again, a tentative smile played around her mouth. She stayed at the rail, a small woman with short, sunny hair that danced cheerfully around a delicate face. Her mouth, unpainted and soft, curved up and teased out the hint of dimples in her cheeks. Pleasure brought a rosy glow to her skin.

She wore no makeup, another deliberate act. There was a part of her that was still hiding, still hunted, and she did whatever she could to pass unnoticed.

Once she had been considered a beauty, and had groomed herself accordingly. She'd dressed as she'd been told to dress, wearing sleek, sexy, sophisticated clothes selected by a man who claimed to love her above all things. She'd known the feel of silk against her skin, what it was to casually clasp diamonds around her throat. Helen Remington had known all the privileges of great wealth.

And for three years had lived in fear and misery.

Nell wore a simple cotton shirt over faded jeans. Her feet were comfortable in cheap white sneakers. Her only jewelry was an antique locket that had been her mother's.

Some things were too precious to leave behind.

As the ferry slowed to dock, she walked back to her car. She would arrive on Three Sisters with one small bag of belongings, a rusted secondhand Buick, and $208 to her name.

She couldn't have been happier.

Nothing, she thought as she parked the car near the docks and began to wander on foot, could have been farther from the pleasure palaces and glitz of Beverly Hills. And nothing, she realized, had ever called more truly to her soul than this little postcard village. Houses and shops were both tidy and prim with their colors faded by sea salt and sun. Cobblestone streets were curvy and whistle-clean as they climbed the hilly terrain or arrowed back to the docks.

Gardens were lovingly tended, as if weeds were illegal. Dogs barked behind picket fences and children rode bikes of cherry red and electric blue.

The docks themselves were a study in industry. Boats and nets and ruddy-cheeked men in tall rubber boots. She could smell fish and sweat.

She hiked up the hill from the docks and turned to look back. From there she could see the tour boats plugging along in the bay, and the little sickle slash of sand beach where people spread out on towels or bobbed in the energetic surf. A little red tram with white letters that read THREE SISTERS TOURS was rapidly filling up with day-trippers and their cameras.

Fishing and tourism, she supposed, were what kept the island afloat. But that was economics. It stood against sea, storms, and time, surviving and flourishing at its own pace. That, she thought, was courage.

It had taken her too long to find her own.

High Street speared across the hill. Shops and restaurants and what she supposed were island businesses lined it. One of the restaurants should be her first stop, she thought. It was possible she could hook a job as a waitress or short-order cook, at least for the summer season. If she could find work, she could hunt up a room.

She could stay.

In a few months, people would know her. They'd wave as she walked by, or call out her name. She was so tired of being a stranger, of having no one to talk to. No one who cared.

She stopped to study the hotel. Unlike the other buildings it was stone instead of wood. Its three stories with elaborate gingerbread, iron balconies, and peaked roofs were undeniably romantic. The name suited it, she decided. The Magick Inn.

It was a good bet that she'd find work there. Waitressing in the dining room, or as part of the housekeeping staff. A job was the first order of business.

But she couldn't make herself go inside, deal with it. She wanted time first, a little time before she settled down to the practical.

Flighty, Evan would have said. You're much too flighty and foolish for your own good, Helen. Thank God you have me to take care of you.

Because his voice played all too clearly in her ears, because the words nipped at the confidence she'd slowly rebuilt, she turned deliberately away and walked in the opposite direction.

She would get a damn job when she was ready to, but for now she was going to wander, to play tourist, to explore. When she was finished roaming High Street, she'd go back to her car and drive all over the island. She wouldn't even stop at the Island Tourist Board to get a map.

Following her nose, she hitched up her backpack and crossed the street. She passed craft shops, gift shops, loitered at the windows. She enjoyed pretty things that sat on shelves without purpose. One day, when she settled again, she'd make a home just as she pleased, full of clutter and fun and color.

An ice cream shop made her smile. There were round glass tables and white iron chairs. A family of four sat at one, laughing as they spooned up whipped cream and confetti-colored sprinkles. A boy wearing a white cap and apron stood behind the counter, and a girl in snug cutoff jeans flirted with him as she considered her choices.

Nell sketched the picture in her mind and walked on.

The bookstore stopped her, made her sigh. Her home would be full of books, too, but not rare first editions never meant to be opened and read. She'd have old, scarred books, shiny new paperbacks all in a jumble of stories. In fact, that was one thing she could start now. A paperback novel wouldn't add much weight to her pack if she had to move on.

She looked up from the display in the window to

the Gothic lettering spilling across the glass. Café Book. Well, that was perfect. She would hunt through the stacks, find something fun to read, and look through it over a cup of coffee.

She stepped inside to air that was fragrant with flowers and spice, and heard music played on pipes and harps. Not only the hotel was magic, Nell thought the minute she crossed the threshold.

Books, in a banquet of colors and shapes, lined deep blue shelves. Overhead, tiny pricks of light showered down from the ceiling like stars. The checkout counter was an old oak cabinet, deeply carved with winged faeries and crescent moons.

A woman with dark, choppy hair sat on a high stool behind it, idly paging through a book. She glanced up and adjusted silver-framed reading glasses.

"Morning. Can I help you?"

"I'm just going to look around, if that's all right."

"Enjoy. Let me know if I can help you find anything."

As the clerk went back to her book, Nell roamed. Across the room two generous chairs faced a stone hearth. On the table between stood a lamp fashioned from a figurine of a robed woman with her arms lifted high. Other shelves held trinkets, statues of colored stone, crystal eggs, dragons. She wandered through, passing books on one side, rows of candles on the other.

At the rear, stairs curved to the second floor. She climbed and found more books, more trinkets, and the café.

Half a dozen tables of glossy wood were arranged near the front window. Along the side was a glass display and counter boasting an impressive array of pastries, sandwiches, and a kettle of that day's soup. The prices were on the high side, but not unreasonable. Nell thought she might have some soup to go with her coffee.

Moving closer, she heard the voices from the open door behind the counter.

"Jane, this is ridiculous, and totally irresponsible."

"It is not. It's Tim's big chance, and it's a way off this damn island. We're taking it."

"The possibility of an audition for a play that may or may not be produced Off Broadway is *not* a big chance. Neither one of you will have a job. You won't—"

"We're going, Mia. I told you I'd work till noon today, and I worked till noon."

"You told me that less than twenty-four hours ago."

There was impatience in the voice—a low, lovely voice. Unable to help herself, Nell edged closer.

"How the hell am I going to keep the café up without anyone to cook?"

"It's all about you, isn't it? You can't even wish us luck."

"Jane, I'll wish you a miracle, because that's what it's going to take. No, wait—don't go off in a huff."

Nell caught movement in the doorway and stepped to the side. But she didn't move out of earshot.

"Be careful. Be happy. Oh, damn it. Blessed be, Jane."

"Okay." There was a loud sniffle. "I'm sorry, really, I'm sorry for leaving you in the lurch this way. But Tim needs to do this, and I need to be with Tim. So . . . I'll miss you, Mia. I'll write."

Nell managed to duck behind shelves just as a weeping woman raced out of the back and ran down the stairs.

"Well, isn't this just fine."

Nell peeked out, blinked in automatic admiration.

The woman who stood in the doorway was a vision. Nell couldn't think of another word for her. She had a mass of hair the color of autumn leaves. Reds and golds spilled over the shoulders of a long blue dress that left her arms bare to the silver bracelets that winked bright on each wrist. Her eyes, sparking with temper, were gray as smoke and dominated a flawless face. Slashing cheekbones, a full, wide mouth painted siren red. Skin like . . . Nell had heard skin compared to alabaster, but this was the first time she'd seen it.

She was tall, willow-slim and perfect.

Nell glanced toward the café tables to see if any of the customers who loitered there were as awestruck as she herself. But no one seemed to notice the woman or the temper swirling around her like water on the boil.

She inched out to get a better look, and those gray eyes shifted. Pinned her.

"Hello. Can I help you?"

"I was . . . I thought . . . I'd like a cup of cappuccino and a bowl of soup. Please."

Annoyance flashed in Mia's eyes and nearly sent Nell back behind the shelves. "I can handle the soup. We have lobster bisque today. I'm afraid the espresso machine is beyond my current capabilities."

Nell looked at the beautiful copper-and-brass machine, felt a little tingle. "I could make it myself."

"You know how to work this thing?"

"Yes, actually, I do."

Considering, Mia gestured and Nell scurried behind the counter.

"I could make you one while I'm at it."

"Why not?" Brave little rabbit, Mia mused, as she watched Nell take over the machine. "Just what sent you to my door? Backpacking?"

"No. Oh." Nell flushed, remembering her pack. "No, just exploring a little. I'm looking for a job, and a room."

"Ah."

"Excuse me, I know it was rude, but I overheard your . . . conversation. If I understand it correctly, you're in a bit of a jam. I can cook."

Mia watched the steam rise, listened to the hiss. "Can you?"

"I'm a very good cook." Nell offered Mia the frothing coffee. "I've done catering, I've worked in a bakery, and I've waitressed. I know how to prepare food and how to serve it."

"How old are you?"

"Twenty-eight."

"Do you have a criminal record?"

A giggle nearly burst out of Nell's throat. For a moment it danced lively in her eyes. "No. I'm tediously honest, a dependable worker and a creative cook."

Don't babble, don't babble! she ordered herself, but she couldn't seem to stop. "I need the job because I'd like to live on the island. I'd like a job here because I enjoy books and I liked the, well, the feel of your shop as soon as I walked in."

Intrigued, Mia angled her head. "And what did you feel?"

"Possibilities."

Excellent answer, Mia mused. "Do you believe in possibilities?"

Nell considered. "Yes. I've had to."

"Excuse me?" A couple stepped up to the counter. "We'd like to have two iced mochas and two of those éclairs."

"Of course. Just a moment." Mia turned back to Nell. "You're hired. Apron's in the back. We'll work out the details later today." She sipped her cappuccino. "Well done," she added and stepped out of the way. "Oh—what's your name?"

"I'm Nell. Nell Channing."

"Welcome to Three Sisters, Nell Channing."

Mia Devlin ran Café Book the way she ran her life. With a style born out of instinct, and largely for her personal amusement. She was a crafty businesswoman who enjoyed making a profit. But always on her own terms.

What bored her, she ignored. What intrigued her, she pursued.

At the moment, Nell Channing intrigued her.

If Nell had been exaggerating her skills, Mia would have fired her as quickly as she'd hired her, and with no regret. She may have, if the spirit moved her, helped Nell secure a job elsewhere. But that wouldn't have taken much time, or interfered with her business.

She'd have taken that step only because something

about Nell had tugged at her the instant those big blue eyes met hers.

Injured innocence. That had been Mia's first impression, and she trusted her first impressions implicitly. Competence as well, Mia thought, though the confidence was a little shaky.

Still, once Nell had suited up and started work at the café, she'd steadied in that area, too.

Mia observed her through the afternoon, noted that she handled the food orders, the customers, the cash register, and the baffling mystery of the espresso machine smoothly.

They'd need to spruce her up a bit, Mia decided. They were casual on the island, but the ancient jeans were a bit too laid-back for Mia's personal taste.

Satisfied for the moment, Mia walked back into the café kitchen. It impressed her that the counters and appliances were clean. Jane had never managed to be a tidy cook, even though most of the baked goods had been prepared by her off-site.

"Nell?"

Taken by surprise, Nell jolted and spun around from the stove, where she'd been scrubbing burners. Her cheeks flushed as she looked at Mia and the young woman beside her.

"Didn't mean to startle you. This is Peg. She works the counter from two to seven."

"Oh. Hello."

"Hi. Jeez, I can't believe Jane and Tim are just *leaving*. New York City!" Peg sounded a bit envious. She was little and perky, with a mop of curly hair bleached nearly white. "Jane made awesome blueberry muffins."

"Yes, well, Jane and her muffins aren't here anymore. I need to talk to Nell now, so you're in charge of the café."

"No problem. Catch you later, Nell."

"Why don't we use my office? We'll get to those details. We're open from ten to seven, summer hours. In the winter we cut back and close at five. Peg prefers the afternoon shift. She likes to party and isn't a morning person. In any case, since we start serving at ten, I'll need you here in the morning."

"That's okay with me." She followed Mia up another flight of steps. She hadn't paid attention, Nell realized. She hadn't known the shop had three floors. A few months before, she would never have missed that detail. She'd have checked out the space, the exits.

Relaxing didn't mean getting sloppy, she reminded herself. She had to be ready, at any time, to run again.

They passed a large storeroom, lined with bookshelves and stacked with boxes, then went through a doorway into Mia's office.

The antique cherry desk suited her, Nell thought. She imagined Mia surrounded by the rich and the beautiful. There were flowers here, and thriving plants, little bits of crystal and polished rocks in bowls. Along with the stylish furnishings were a top-of-the-line computer, a fax, filing cabinets, and shelves for publishers' catalogs. Mia gestured to a chair and took the one behind the desk for herself.

"You had a few hours in the café, so you've seen the type of fare we offer. There's a specialty sandwich each day, the day's soup, a small selection of alternate sandwiches. Two or three varieties of cold salads. Pastries, cookies, muffins, biscotti. In the past

I left the menu choices up to the cook. Are you comfortable with that?"

"Yes, ma'am."

"Please, I'm barely a year older than you. It's Mia. Until we're sure this is going to work, I'd prefer you make up the next day's menu for my approval." She took a legal pad out of the drawer, passed it across the desk. "Why don't you write down what you have in mind for tomorrow?"

Panic wanted to crawl through her, tremble in her fingers. Nell took a deep breath, waited until her mind was blank and clear, then began to write. "This time of year, I think we should keep the soups light. Herbed consommé. Tortellini salad, a white bean, and a shrimp. I'd do a spiced-chicken pita for the sandwich, and a vegetarian selection, but I'd have to see what's in season. I can make you tarts, again depending on what looks good fruit-wise. The éclairs are popular—I can duplicate those. A six-layer chocolate-and-cream torte. Awesome blueberry muffins, as well as walnut. You're low on hazelnut biscotti. Cookies? Chocolate chip is never wrong. Macadamia. Instead of a third cookie, I'd offer brownies. I make an irresistible triple-fudge brownie."

"How much can you prepare on-site?"

"All of it, I guess. But if you're going to serve the pastries and muffins starting at ten, I'll need to start about six."

"If you had your own kitchen?"

"Oh, well." What a lovely fantasy that was. "I'd prep some of the menu the night before, bake fresh in the morning."

"Um-hmm. How much money do you have, Nell Channing?"

"Enough."

"Don't be prickly," Mia advised breezily. "I can advance you a hundred dollars. Going against a salary, to start, of seven an hour. You'll log your shopping, cooking hours daily. You'll charge what you need, food-wise, to the store's account. I'll want the receipts, again daily."

When Nell opened her mouth to speak, Mia simply lifted one slim, coral-tipped finger. "Wait. You'll be expected to serve and to clear tables when there's a rush, and to assist customers in the book section on your level during lulls. You get two half-hour breaks, Sundays off, and a fifteen percent employee discount on purchases, not including food or drink—which unless you turn out to be a glutton, will be part of your perks. With me so far?"

"Yes, but I—"

"Good. I'm here every day. If you have a question or problem you can't handle, get me. If I'm not available, go to Lulu. She's usually at the counter on the main floor, and she knows everything. You look quick enough to catch on; if you don't know an answer, don't be afraid to ask. Now, you're looking for a place to stay."

"Yes." It was like being swept away by a fast, unexpected wind. "I hope to—"

"Come with me." Mia pulled a set of keys out of a drawer, pushed away from the desk and clipped out—she wore gorgeous, needle-thin heels, Nell noted.

Once they were on the main level, she walked

straight toward a rear door. "Lulu!" she called out. "Back in ten."

Feeling clumsy and foolish, Nell followed her through the back exit and into a small garden paved with stepping-stones. A huge black cat sunned itself on one of them and blinked open one luminous gold eye as Mia stepped nimbly over.

"That's Isis. She won't trouble you."

"She's beautiful. Is the garden your work?"

"Yes. No place is a home without flowers. Oh, I didn't ask—do you have transportation?"

"Yes, I have a car. It can loosely be called transportation."

"That's handy. You won't have far to go, but it'd be troublesome to cart your goods on foot every day." At the edge of the lot she turned left, kept up her brisk pace, passed the backs of shops, across from neatly kept houses.

"Ms.—I'm sorry, I don't know your last name."

"It's Devlin, but I told you to call me Mia."

"Mia, I'm grateful for the job. For the chance. And I can promise you, you won't be sorry. But . . . can I ask where we're going?"

"You need a place." She turned a corner, stopped and gestured. "That should do it."

Across the narrow side street sat a little yellow house, like a cheerful sunbeam at the edge of a tiny grove of stunted trees. The shutters were white, as was the narrow strip of porch. There were flowers there, too, in a happy dance of bright summer colors.

It sat back from the road on a neat square of lawn with trees tucking it into shade and dappled sunlight.

"Is this your house?" Nell asked.

"Yes. For the moment." Jingling the keys, Mia walked up the flagstone path. "I bought it last spring."

Had been compelled to, Mia remembered. An investment, she'd told herself. Though she, a businesswoman down to the bone, had done nothing so far about renting it out. She'd waited, just as, she understood, the house had waited.

She unlocked the front door, stepped back. "It's been blessed."

"Excuse me?"

Mia only nodded. "Welcome."

The furnishings were sparse. A simple sofa that desperately needed re-covering, a deep-cushioned chair, a scatter of tables.

"Bedrooms on either side, though the one to the left is more suited to an office or study. The bathroom's minute, but charming, and the kitchen's been modernized and should do very well. It's straight back. I've worked on the gardens, but they need more care. There's no AC, but the furnace works. Still, you'll be glad the fireplace works as well come January."

"It's wonderful." Unable to resist, Nell wandered, poking her head in the main bedroom where a pretty bed with a white iron headboard stood. "Like a fairy cottage. You must love living here."

"I don't live here. You do."

Nell turned back, slowly. There was Mia, in the center of the little room, her hands cupped together with the keys in her palm. Light beamed through the two front windows and seemed to set her hair to flame.

"I don't understand."

"You need a place, I have a place. I live on the

cliffs. I prefer it there. This is your place, for now. Don't you feel it?"

She only knew she felt happy, and full of nerves at the same time. And that the moment she'd stepped into the house, she'd wanted to stretch and settle, very much like the cat in the sunshine.

"I can stay here?"

"Life's been hard, hasn't it?" Mia murmured. "That you'd tremble at good fortune. You'll pay rent, for nothing that comes free holds its value. We'll work the terms out of your salary. Settle in. You'll have to come back and sign forms and so on. But that can wait for the morning. Island Market is your best source for the ingredients you'll need for tomorrow's menu. I'll let them know you're coming, so you can charge to the store account. Any pots, pans, whatever are your expense, but I'll float that until the end of the month. I expect to see you, and your creations, by nine-thirty sharp."

She stepped over and dropped the keys into Nell's limp hand. "Any questions?"

"Too many to know where to begin. I don't know how to thank you."

"Don't waste your tears, little sister," Mia replied. "They're too precious. You'll work hard for what you make here."

"I can't wait to get started." Nell held out her hand. "Thank you, Mia."

Their hands touched, clasped. A spark snapped out, blue as flame and quickly gone. With a half laugh, Nell jerked back. "Must be a lot of static, or something, in the air."

"Or something. Well, welcome home, Nell." Turning, Mia started for the door.

"Mia." Emotion gathered in her throat, ached there. "I said this was like a fairy cottage. You must be my fairy godmother."

Mia's smile was dazzling, and her laughter low and rich as warmed cream. "You'll find out soon enough I'm far from it. I'm just a practical witch. Don't forget to bring me the receipts," she added and quietly closed the door behind her.

Two

The village, Nell decided, was a bit like Briga- doon as seen by Nathaniel Hawthorne. She'd taken some time to explore before she'd gone to the market. For months she'd told herself she was safe. She was free. But for the first time, wandering the pretty streets with their quaint houses, breathing in the sea air, listening to the sharp New England voices, she *felt* safe. And free.

No one knew her, but they would. They would know Nell Channing, the clever cook who lived in the little cottage in the wood. She would make friends here, and a life. A future. Nothing from the past would touch her here.

One day she would be as much a part of the island as the narrow post office with its faded gray wood or the tourist center cobbled together by old clinker bricks, and the long, sturdy dock where fishermen brought their daily catch.

To celebrate she bought a wind chime fashioned of

stars that she saw in a shop window. It was her first purchase for pleasure in nearly a year.

She spent her first night on the island in the lovely bed, hugging her happiness to her as she listened to the stars ring and the sea breathe.

She was up before sunrise, eager to begin. While the day's soup simmered, she rolled out pastry dough. She'd spent every penny she had, including most of the advance and a good portion of her next month's salary on kitchen tools. It didn't matter. She would have the best and produce the best. Mia Devlin, her benefactor, would never have cause to regret taking her on.

Everything in the kitchen was precisely as she wanted it. Not as she'd been told it must be. When she had time, she would make a run to the island's garden center for herbs. Some she would plant outside the windowsill. All cluttered together the way she liked things to be. Nothing, absolutely nothing, in her home would be uniform and precise and stylishly sleek. She wouldn't have acres of marble or seas of glass or towering urns of terrifyingly exotic flowers without warmth or scent. There wouldn't be . . .

She stopped herself. It was time to stop reminding herself of what wouldn't be, and plan what would be. Yesterday would hound her until she firmly closed the door on it and shot the bolt.

While the sun came up, turning the east-facing windows to flame, she slid the first batch of tarts into the oven. She remembered the rosy-cheeked woman who had helped her at the market. Dorcas Burmingham—such a fine Yankee name, Nell thought. And full of welcome and curiosity. The curiosity would have shut

Nell down once, turned her inward. But she'd been able to chat, to answer some questions breezily and avoid others.

Tarts cooled on the rack and muffins went into the oven. As the kitchen filled with light, Nell sang to welcome the day.

Lulu folded her arms over her skinny chest. It was, Mia knew, her way of trying to look intimidating. As Lulu barely inched up to five feet, weighed ninety pounds soaking wet, and had the face of a woeful pixie, it took work for her to look intimidating.

"You don't know anything about her."

"I know she's alone, looking for work, and in the right place at the right time."

"She's a stranger. You don't just hire a stranger, *and* lend her money, give her a house, without at least doing a background check. Not one reference, Mia. Not one. For all you know, she's a psychopath running from the law."

"You've been reading true crime books again, haven't you?"

Lulu scowled, an expression that on her harmless face approximated a pained smile. "There are bad people in the world."

"Yes, there are." Mia printed out the mail-order requests that had come through her computer. "Without them we'd have no balance, no challenge. She's running from something, Lu, but not the law. And fate pointed her here. It brought her to me."

"And sometimes fate's a backstabber."

"I'm well aware of that." With the printouts in hand, Mia walked out of the office, Lulu on her heels. Only the fact that Lulu Cabot had essentially raised her prevented Mia from telling her to mind her own business. "And you should know I can protect myself."

"You take in strays, your guard goes down."

"She's not a stray, she's a seeker. There's a difference. I felt something from her," Mia added as she started downstairs to fill the orders. "When she's more comfortable I'll look closer."

"At least get a reference."

Mia lifted a brow as she heard the back door open. "I just got one. She's prompt. Don't poke at her, Lulu," Mia ordered as she handed the printouts over. "She's also tender yet. Well, good morning, Nell."

"Good morning." Arms full of covered trays, Nell breezed in. "I pulled my car around back. That's all right, isn't it?"

"That's just fine. Need a hand?"

"Oh, no, thanks. I have everything stacked in the car."

"Lulu, this is Nell. You can get acquainted later."

"Nice to meet you, Lulu. I'll just start setting things up."

"You go right ahead." Mia waited until Nell climbed the stairs. "Looks dangerous, doesn't she?"

Lulu set her jaw. "Looks can be deceiving."

Moments later Nell jogged downstairs again. She wore a plain white T-shirt tucked into her jeans. The little gold locket lay against it like a charm. "I started a first pot of coffee. I'll bring some down next trip, but I don't know how you like it."

"Black for me, sweet and light for Lu. Thanks."

"Um . . . would you mind not going up to the café until I've finished? I'd really like you to see the whole presentation. So just . . ." She backed toward the door, face flushed, as she spoke. "Wait. Okay?"

"Eager to please," Mia commented as she and Lulu filled the orders. "Eager to work. Yes, definite psychopathic tendencies. Call the cops."

"Shut up."

Twenty minutes later, breathless, jangled with pleasure and nerves, Nell came downstairs again. "Can you come up now? I still have time to change things around if it doesn't suit you. Oh, could you come, too, Lulu? Mia said you know everything about the shop, so you'd know if it doesn't look the way it should."

"Hmph." Grudgingly Lulu stopped ringing up the mail orders. "Café's not my department." But with a shrug, she followed Mia and Nell upstairs.

The display case was brimming with glossy pastries, wide-topped muffins and scones popping with golden currants. A tall torte gleamed under a sleek chocolate frosting and laces of whipped cream. Cookies as big as a man's palm covered two delicate white sheets of baker's paper. Wafting out of the kitchen was the scent of soup simmering.

On the chalkboard, written in a fine and careful hand, were the day's specials. The glass had been polished to a gleam, the coffee was irresistibly fragrant, and a pale blue canning jar filled with cinnamon sticks stood on the counter.

Mia walked up and down the display, like a general inspecting troops, while Nell stood struggling not to wring her hands.

"I didn't put the salads and the soup out yet. I thought if I waited till around eleven for that, people would be more apt to go for the pastries. There're more tarts in the back, and the brownies. I didn't put them out because, well, I think people want them more if it doesn't look as if you're oversupplied. And the brownies are more lunch and afternoon items. I put the torte out now, hoping customers might think about it and end up coming back into the shop again later for a slice. But I can rearrange things if you'd rather—"

She broke off when Mia lifted a finger. "Let's sample one of those tarts."

"Oh. Sure. Just let me get one from the back." She darted into the kitchen, then back out again with a tart in a little paper doily.

Saying nothing, Mia broke it in two, handed half to Lulu. As she took the first bite, her lips curved. "How's that for a reference?" she murmured, then turned back to Nell. "If you keep looking so nervous, customers are going to think something's wrong with the food. Then they won't order it, and they'll miss something very special. You have a gift, Nell."

"You like it?" Nell let out a relieved sigh. "I sampled one of everything this morning. I'm half sick," she said as she pressed a hand to her stomach. "I wanted everything to be just right."

"And so it is. Now relax, because once word gets out we've got a genius in the kitchen, you're going to be very busy."

Nell didn't know if word got out, but she was soon too busy for nerves. By ten-thirty she was brewing another pot of coffee and resupplying trays. Every time her cash register rang, it was a separate little thrill. And when she bagged up a half a dozen muffins for a customer who claimed she'd never tasted better, Nell had to order herself not to spring into a dance.

"Thanks. Come back soon." Beaming, she turned to the next customer.

That was Zack's first impression of her. A pretty blonde wearing a white apron and a mile-wide smile with winking dimples. It gave him a quick and pleasant little jolt, and his own grin flashed in response.

"I heard about the muffins, but I didn't hear about the smile."

"Smile's free. The muffins'll cost you."

"I'll take one. Blueberry. And a large black coffee to go. I'm Zack. Zack Todd."

"Nell." She scooped up one of the to-go cups. She didn't have to shoot him a sidelong glance. Experience had taught her to read a face fast and remember it. His was still in her mind as she filled the cup.

Tanned, with faint lines fanning out from sharp green eyes. A firm jaw with an intriguing diagonal scar scoring it. Brown hair, a little long, with a bit of curl that was already sun-streaked in June. A narrow face with a long, straight nose, a mouth that smiled easily and showed a slightly crooked incisor.

It struck her as an honest face. Easygoing, friendly. She set the coffee on the counter, casting him another glance as she plucked a muffin from the tray.

He had broad shoulders and good arms. His shirt was rolled up at the sleeves and faded from sun and water. The hand that curled around the coffee cup was big and wide. She tended to trust big hands on a man. It was the slender, manicured ones that could strike so lethally.

"Just one?" she said as she bagged his muffin.

"One'll do me for now. Word is you just got to the island yesterday."

"Good timing for me." She rang up his order, pleased when he opened the bag and sniffed.

"Good timing all around if this tastes as good as it smells. Where'd you come in from?"

"Boston."

He cocked his head. "Doesn't sound like Boston. Your accent," he explained when she simply stared at him.

"Oh." She took his money with a steady hand, made change. "Not originally. A little town in the Midwest—outside of Columbus. I moved around a lot, though." Her smile stayed in place as she handed him his change and receipt. "I guess that's why I don't sound like I'm from anywhere in particular."

"Guess so."

"Hey, Sheriff."

Zack glanced over his shoulder, nodded. "Morning, Miz Macey."

"You get 'round to talking to Pete Stahr about that dog of his?"

"Heading that way now."

"Dog as soon roll in dead fish as he would in roses. Then what's he do but run right through my hanging wash. Had to do the lot of it again. I like dogs same as the next."

"Yes, ma'am."

"But Pete's got to keep that hound on a leash."

"I'll have a word with him this morning. You ought to get yourself one of these muffins, Miz Macey."

"I just came in for a book." But she looked at the display, her lips pursing in her wide face. "Do look tasty, don't they? You'd be the new girl."

"Yes." Nell's throat was raw and hot. She feared her voice sounded the same. "I'm Nell. Can I get you anything?"

"Maybe I'll just have a sit-down with a cup of tea and one of those tarts. I've got a weak spot for a good fruit tart. None of those fancy teas, mind. Give me good orange pekoe. You tell that Pete to keep his dog out of my wash," she added to Zack. "Else he'll be doing my laundry."

"Yes, ma'am." He smiled at Nell again, kept his eyes on her face deliberately as he'd noted how quickly it had paled when Gladys Macey had called him sheriff. "Nice meeting you, Nell."

She gave him a little nod. Kept her hands busy, he noticed, but not quite steady.

Just what, he wondered, would a pretty young woman like that have to fear from the law? Then again, he thought as he walked downstairs, some people were just naturally skittish when it came to cops.

He scanned the main level, spotted Mia stocking shelves in the mystery section. Either way, Zack decided, it wouldn't hurt to ask a few casual questions.

"Busy in here today."

"Mmm." She slid paperbacks into slots without looking around. "I expect it to get busier. Season's just underway, and I have my new secret weapon in the café."

"Just met her. You're renting her the yellow cottage."

"That's right."

"You check her employment record, references?"

"Now, Zack." Mia did turn now. In her heels she was nearly eye to eye with him, and she gave his cheek a sassy pat. "We've been friends a long time. Long enough for me to tell you to mind your own business. I don't want you going up to my café and interrogating my staff."

"Okay, I'll just haul her down to the station house and get out my rubber hose."

She chuckled, then leaned over and gave him a peck on the cheek. "You brute. Don't worry about Nell. She isn't looking for trouble."

"Got twitchy when she found out I was sheriff."

"Honey, you're so handsome you make all the girls twitchy."

"Never worked on you," he countered.

"A lot you know. Now go away, let me run my business."

"I'm going. Have to do my sworn duty and scold Pete Stahr over his smelly dog."

"Sheriff Todd, you're so brave." She batted her lashes. "What would we islanders do without you and your stalwart sister protecting us?"

"Ha, ha. Ripley's due in on the noon ferry. Any sooner, I'd stick her with dog detail."

"Is a week up already?" Mia grimaced and went back to shelving. "Oh, well, nothing good lasts forever."

"I'm not getting in the middle of you two again. I'd sooner deal with Pete's dog."

She laughed at him, but once he'd gone she looked toward the steps, thought of Nell, and wondered.

She made it a point to go upstairs late in the morning. Nell had already put out the salads and the soup, subtly shifting the mode toward the lunch crowd. The salads, Mia noted, looked fresh and appealing, and the scent of the soup was going to tempt anyone who walked into the store.

"How's it going?"

"Fine. We've finally hit a little lull." Nell wiped her hands on her apron. "Brisk business this morning. The muffins won the race, but the tarts came in a close second."

"You're officially on break," Mia told her. "I'll take care of anyone who comes in, unless they want something that requires the use of that monster machine."

In the kitchen, Mia slid onto a stool, crossed her legs. "Stop by my office after your shift. We'll get the employment forms signed."

"Okay. I've been thinking about tomorrow's menu."

"We'll discuss that then, too. Why don't you get yourself a cup of coffee and relax?"

"I'm already hyped enough." But Nell did open the fridge, removed a small bottle of water. "I'll stick with this."

"You've settled into the house all right?"

"It was easy. I can't remember ever sleeping better, or waking better. With the windows open, I can just hear the surf. It's like a lullaby. And did you see the sunrise this morning? Spectacular."

"I'll take your word for it. I tend to avoid sunrise. It insists on coming so early in the day." She held out her hand and surprised Nell into passing the bottle of water to her for a sip. "I heard you met Zack Todd."

"Did I?" Nell immediately picked up a cloth, began buffing the stove. "Oh. Sheriff Todd. Yes, he had coffee, black, and a blueberry muffin to go."

"There's been a Todd on the island for centuries, and Zachariah's one of the best of the lot. Kind," Mia said deliberately. "Caring, and decent without being a pain in the ass about it."

"Is he your . . ." The word "boyfriend" just didn't seem to apply with a woman like Mia. "Are you and he involved?"

"Romantically? No." Mia held the bottle back out to Nell. "He's entirely too good for me. Though I did have a mild crush on him when I was fifteen or sixteen. After all, he's a prime specimen. You must have noticed."

"I'm not interested in men."

"I see. Is that what you're running from? A man?" When Nell didn't respond, Mia slid to her feet. "Well, if and when you're inclined to talk about it, I'm an excellent listener, with a sympathetic ear."

"I appreciate all you've done for me, Mia. I just want to do my job."

"Fair enough." The bell dinged, signaling someone had come to the counter. "No, you're on break," Mia reminded her before Nell could hurry out of the kitchen. "I'll take the counter for a while. And don't look so sad, little sister. You've no one to answer to now but yourself."

Oddly soothed, Nell stayed where she was. She could hear the low ripple of Mia's voice as she spoke to the customers. The store music was flutes now and something fluid. She could close her eyes and imagine herself here, just here, the next day. The next year. Comfortable and comforted. Productive and happy.

There was no reason to be sad or afraid, no cause to be concerned about the sheriff. He'd have no purpose in paying attention to her, looking into her background. And if he did, what would he find? She'd been careful. She'd been thorough.

No, she was no longer running away. She'd run to. And she was staying.

She finished off her water, started out of the kitchen just as Mia turned around. The clock in the square began to bong the noon hour, in slow, ponderous tones.

The floor beneath her feet seemed to tremble, and the light went brilliant and bright. Music swelled inside her head, like a thousand harp strings plucked in unison. The wind—she could have sworn she felt a hot wind flow over her face and lift her hair. She smelled candle wax and fresh earth.

The world shuddered and spun, then righted itself in a blink of time, as if it had never moved. She shook her head to clear it and found herself staring into Mia's deep gray eyes.

"What was that? An earthquake?" Even as she said it, Nell saw that no one else in the store looked concerned. People milled, sat, chatted, sipped. "I thought . . . I felt . . ."

"Yes, I know." Though Mia's voice was quiet, there was an edge to it Nell hadn't heard before. "Well, that explains it."

"Explains what?" Shaken, Nell gripped Mia's wrist. And felt something like power rocket up her arm.

"We'll talk about it. Later. Now the noon ferry's

in." And Ripley was back, she thought. They, the three, were all on-island now. "We'll be busy. Serve your soup, Nell," she said gently, and walked away.

Mia wasn't often taken by surprise, and she didn't care for it. The strength of what she'd felt and experienced along with Nell had been more intense, more intimate, than she'd expected. And that annoyed her. She should have been prepared. She of all people knew, believed, and understood what twist fate had taken so many years before. And what twist it could take now.

Still, believing in fate didn't mean a woman simply stood there and let it run her down. Actions could and would be taken. But she had to think, to sort things out.

What in the goddess's name was she supposed to do to make things right when she would be bound to a stubborn twit of a woman who consistently denied her power and a scared rabbit on the run who didn't know she had any?

She closed herself in her office, paced. She rarely turned to magic here. It was her place of business, and she deliberately kept it separate and earthbound. But there were exceptions, she told herself, to every rule.

So thinking, she took her crystal globe from the shelf, set it on her desk. It amused her to see it there, along with her two-line phone and computer. Still, magic respected progress, even if progress didn't always respect magic.

Laying her hands on either side of the globe, she cleared her mind.

"Show me what I have to see. This island holds the sisters three, and we will shape our destiny. Visions in glass come clear to me. As I will, so mote it be."

The globe shimmered and swirled. And cleared. In its depths, like figures in water, she saw herself, Nell, and Ripley. A circle formed in the shadows of the woods, and a fire burning. The trees were aflame as well, but with color struck by autumn. Light poured out from a full moon like water shimmering.

A new shadow formed in the trees and became a man. Beautiful and golden with eyes that burned.

The circle broke. Even as Nell ran, the man struck out. She shattered like glass, a thousand pieces scattering. And the skies opened to lightning, blasted with thunder, and all Mia could see in the glass was a torrent of water as the woods, and the island they lived on, tumbled into the sea.

Mia stepped back, planted her hands on her hips. "Isn't that always the way?" she said in disgust. "A man ruins everything. Well, we'll see about that." She put the globe back on the shelf. "We'll just see about that."

By the time Nell knocked on her door, Mia was just finishing up some paperwork. "Right on time," she said as she logged off the computer. "That's a pretty habit of yours. I need you to fill out these forms." She gestured to the neat stack on the desk.

"I've dated them yesterday. How's the lunch crowd moving?"

"Smoothly enough." Nell sat. Her palms no longer sweated when she filled out forms. Name, date of birth, Social Security number. Those basic facts and figures were hers. She'd seen to it personally. "Peg dives right in. I made up tomorrow's menu."

"Mmm." Mia took the folded paper Nell pulled out of her pocket, read it over while Nell filled in the form. "It looks good. More adventurous than Jane's tended to be."

"Too adventurous?"

"No, just more. So . . . what will you do with the rest of your day?" Mia briefly looked at the first completed form. "Nell, no middle initial, Channing?"

"Take a walk on the beach, do some gardening. Maybe explore the woods around the cottage."

"There's a small stream where columbine grows wild this time of year, and in the deeper shade jack-in-the-pulpits and ferns. The kind that make you think the faeries hide in them."

"You don't strike me as the kind of person who looks for shy faeries."

Mia's lips curved. "We don't know each other well yet. Three Sisters is alive with legend and lore, and the woods have all manner of secrets. Do you know the story of the Three Sisters?"

"No."

"I'll tell you one day when there's time for tales and stories. But for now you should be out in the light and air."

"Mia, what happened before? At noon?"

"You tell me. What do you think happened?"

"It felt like an earth tremor, but not. The light changed, and so did the air. Like a . . . blast of energy."

It sounded foolish when she said it, but she pushed on. "You felt it too. But no one else did. No one else felt anything out of the ordinary."

"Most people expect the ordinary, and that's what they get."

"If that's a riddle, I don't know how to solve it." Impatient, Nell shoved to her feet. "You weren't surprised by it—a little irritated but not surprised."

Mia sat back, intrigued, and lifted a brow. "True enough. You read people very well."

"Survival skill."

"And sharply honed," Mia added. "What happened? I suppose you could call it a connection. What happens when three positive charges occupy the same space at the same time?"

Nell shook her head. "I have no idea."

"Neither do I. But it'll be interesting to find out. Like recognizes like, don't you think? I recognized you."

Nell's blood went cold and burned under her skin. "I don't know what you mean."

"Not who you are, or were," Mia said gently. "But what. You can trust me to respect that, and your privacy. I won't pry into your yesterdays, Nell. I'm more interested in the tomorrows."

Nell opened her mouth. She nearly, very nearly, let it pour out. Everything she'd escaped from, everything that haunted her. But to do so put her fate in the hands of another. That was something she would never do again.

"Tomorrow I'll serve a summer vegetable soup and a chicken, zucchini, and ricotta sandwich. That's as complicated as it's going to get."

"That's as good a start as any. Enjoy your afternoon." Mia waited until Nell reached the door. "Nell? As long as you're still afraid, he wins."

"I don't give a damn about winning," Nell replied. Then she stepped out quickly and closed the door behind her.

Three

Nell found the stream, and the wild columbine—like little drops of sun in the green shade. Sitting on the soft floor of the forest, listening to the stream gurgle and the birds chirp, she found her peace again.

This was her place. She was as sure of that as she'd been of any single thing in all her life. She belonged here as she'd belonged nowhere else.

Even as a child she'd felt displaced. Not by her parents, she thought, running her fingers over her locket. Never by them. But home had been wherever her father was stationed, and until his orders changed. There'd been no single place for childhood, no pretty spot for memories to take root and bloom.

Her mother had had the gift of making a home wherever they were, and for however long. But it wasn't the same as knowing you would wake up to the same view out of your bedroom window day after day.

And that was a yearning Nell had carried with her always.

Her mistake had been in believing she could soothe that yearning with Evan, when she should have known it was something she had to find for herself.

Perhaps she had, now. Here in this place.

That's what Mia had meant. *Like recognizing like.* They both belonged on the island. Maybe, in some lovely way, they belonged to it. It was as simple as that.

Still, Mia was an intuitive woman, and an oddly powerful one. She sensed secrets. Nell could only hope she was as good as her word and wouldn't pry. If anyone started digging through the layers, she would have to leave. No matter how much she belonged, she couldn't stay.

It wasn't going to happen.

Nell got to her feet, stretching up her arms to the thin sunbeams, and turned slow circles. She wouldn't *let* it happen. She was going to trust Mia. She was going to work for her and live in the little yellow cottage and wake each morning with a giddy, glorious sense of freedom.

In time, she thought as she began to walk back toward her house, she and Mia might become real friends. It would be fascinating to have a friend that vivid, that clever.

What was it like to be a woman like Mia Devlin? she wondered. To be someone so utterly beautiful, so sublimely confident? A woman like that would never have to question herself, to remake herself, to worry that whatever she did, or could do, would never be good enough.

What a marvelous thing.

Still, while a woman might be born beautiful, confidence could be learned. It could be won. And wasn't there amazing satisfaction from winning those small battles? Every time you did, you went back to war better armed.

Enough dawdling, enough introspection, she thought and quickened her pace. She was going to blow the last of her advance at the garden center.

If that wasn't confidence, she decided, what was?

They let her open an account. Another debt to Mia, Nell thought as she drove back across the island. She worked for Mia Devlin, so she was looked upon kindly, she was trusted, she was allowed to take away merchandise on the strength of her signature on a tally.

A kind of magic, she supposed, that existed only in small towns. She'd struggled not to take advantage, and had still ended up with half a dozen flats. And pots, and soil. And a silly stone gargoyle who would guard what she planted.

Eager to begin, she parked in front of the cottage and hopped out. The minute she opened the back door of the car, she was immersed in her small, fragrant jungle.

"We're going to have such fun, and I'm going to take wonderful care of all of you."

Feet planted firmly, she stretched inside to lift the first tray.

Hell of a view, Zack thought as he stopped across the street. A small, shapely female bottom in snug, faded jeans. If a man didn't spend a minute appreciating that, he was a sorry individual.

He got out of his cruiser, leaned against the door, and watched her take out a flat of pink and white petunias. "Pretty picture."

She jerked, nearly bobbled the tray. He noted that, just as he noted the alarm shoot into her eyes. But he straightened lazily, strolled across the street.

"Let me give you a hand."

"That's all right. I've got it."

"And a lot more. Gonna be busy." He reached past her, took out two more flats. "Where're you going with them?"

"Just around the back for now. I haven't decided where I'm putting everything yet. But really, you don't have to—"

"Smells good. What've you got here?"

"Herbs. Rosemary, basil, tarragon, and so on." The quickest way to be rid of him, she decided, was to let him cart the trays around. So she started across the yard. "I'm going to put in an herb bed outside the kitchen, maybe add a few vegetables when I have time."

"Planting flowers is planting roots, my mother always says."

"I intend to do both. Just on the stoop'll be fine. Thank you, Sheriff."

"You've got a couple more in the front seat."

"I can—"

"I'll fetch them. Did you think to get any soil?"

"Yes, in the trunk."

He smiled easily, held out his hand. "I need the keys."

"Oh. Well." Trapped, she dug in her pocket. "Thanks."

When he strolled off, she clasped her hands together. It was all right. He was just being helpful. Not every man, not every cop, was a danger. She knew better than that.

He came back loaded, and the sight of him, a huge bag of soil slung over one shoulder and a flat of pink geraniums and white impatiens in his big hands, made her laugh.

"I got too much." She took the flowers from him. "I only meant to get herbs, and before I knew it . . . I couldn't seem to stop."

"That's what they all say. I'll get your pots and tools."

"Sheriff." It had once been natural to her to repay kindness with kindness. She wanted it to be natural again. "I made some lemonade this morning. Would you like a glass?"

"I'd appreciate it."

All she had to do was remind herself to relax, to be herself. She filled two glasses with ice and poured in the tart lemonade. He was already back when she came out. Something about the way he looked, big and male, standing in the middle of pink and white flowers, gave her a quick little jolt.

Attraction. Even as she recognized the sensation she reminded herself it wasn't anything she could or wanted to feel again.

"I appreciate the pack mule services."

"Welcome." He took the glass, draining half of it while that little jolt became a twitchy dance in her belly.

He lowered the glass. "This is the real thing. Can't think the last time I had fresh lemonade. You're a real find, aren't you?"

"I just like to fuss in the kitchen." She bent, picked up her new garden spade.

"You didn't buy any gloves."

"No, I didn't think of it."

She wanted him to drink his lemonade and scat, Zack thought, but was too polite to say so. Because he knew that, he sat on the little stoop outside the kitchen door, made himself comfortable. "Mind if I sit a minute? It's been a long day. Don't let me stop you from getting started, though. It's pleasant to watch a woman in the garden."

She'd wanted to sit on the stoop, she thought. To sit there in the sunshine and imagine what she would do with the flowers and herbs. Now all she could do was begin.

She started with the pots, reminding herself if she didn't like the results, she could always redo them.

"Did you, um, talk to the man with the dog?"

"Pete?" Zack asked, sipped at his lemonade. "I think we came to an understanding, and peace settles over our little island once more."

There was humor in the way he said it, and a lazy satisfaction as well. It was hard not to appreciate both.

"It must be interesting, being the sheriff here. Knowing everyone."

"It has its moments." She had small hands, he noticed as he watched her work. Quick, clever fingers. She kept her head bent, her eyes averted. Shyness, he decided, coupled with what seemed to him to be a rusty sense of socializing. "A lot of it's refereeing, or dealing with summer people who're vacationing too hard. Mostly it's running herd on about three thousand people. Between me and Ripley it's simple enough."

"Ripley?"

"My sister. She's the other island cop. Todds have been island cops for five generations. That's looking real nice," he said, gesturing toward her work-in-progress with his glass.

"Do you think?" She sat back on her heels. She'd mixed some of everything into the pot, stuck in some of the vinca. It didn't look haphazard as she'd feared it might. It looked cheerful. And so did her face when she lifted it. "It's my first."

"I'd say you've got a knack. Ought to wear a hat, though. Fair skin like yours is going to burn if you stay out long."

"Oh." She rubbed the back of her hand over her nose. "Probably."

"Guess you didn't have a garden in Boston."

"No." She filled the second pot with soil. "I wasn't there very long. It wasn't my place."

"I know what you mean. I've spent some time on the mainland. Never felt home. Your folks still in the Midwest?"

"My parents are dead."

"I'm sorry."

"So am I." She tucked a geranium into the new pot. "Is this conversation, Sheriff, or an inquiry?"

"Conversation." He picked up a plant that was just out of her reach and held it. A cautious woman, he decided. In his experience cautious people usually had a reason. "Any point in me inquiring?"

"I'm not wanted for anything, never been arrested. And I'm not looking for trouble."

"That about covers it." He handed her the plant. "It's a small island, Miz Channing. Mostly friendly. Curiosity comes along with it, though."

"I suppose." She couldn't afford to alienate him, she reminded herself. She couldn't afford to alienate anyone. "Look, I've been traveling for a while now, and I'm tired of it. I came here looking for work and a quiet place to live."

"Looks like you found both." He got to his feet. "I appreciate the lemonade."

"You're welcome."

"That's a pretty job you're doing. You've got a knack for it, all right. Afternoon, Miz Channing."

"Afternoon, Sheriff."

As he walked back to his car he tallied up what he'd learned about her. She was alone in the world, wary of cops, prickly about questions. She was a woman of simple tastes and skittish nerves. And for reasons he couldn't quite fathom, she just didn't quite add up for him.

He glanced at her car as he crossed to his own, scanned the license plate. The Massachusetts tag looked brand spanking new. Wouldn't hurt to run it, he thought. Just to settle his mind.

His gut told him Nell Channing might not have been looking for trouble, but she wasn't a stranger to it.

Nell served apple turnovers and lattes to the young couple by the window and then cleared an adjoining table. A trio of women were browsing the stacks, and she suspected they'd be lured into the café section before long.

With her hands full of mugs, she loitered by the window. The ferry was arriving from the mainland, chased by gulls that circled and dived. Buoys bobbed in a sea that was soft and green today. A white pleasure boat, sails fat with wind, skimmed along the surface.

Once she'd sailed on another sea, in another life. It was one of the few pleasures she took from that time. The feel of flying over the water, rising on waves. Odd, wasn't it, that the sea had always called to her? It had changed her life. And had taken it.

Now, this new sea had given her another life.

Smiling at the thought, she turned and bumped solidly into Zack. Even as he took her arm to steady her, she was jerking back. "I'm sorry. Did I spill anything on you? I'm clumsy, I wasn't watching where—"

"No harm done." He hooked the fingers of one hand through two mug handles and, careful not to touch her again, took them from her. "I was in your way. Nice boat."

"Yes." She sidestepped, hurried back to the counter, behind it. She *hated* having anyone come up behind her. "But I'm not getting paid to watch boats. Can I get you anything?"

"Take a breath, Nell."

"What?"

"Take a breath." He said it gently as he set the mugs on the counter. "Get yourself steady again."

"I'm fine." Resentment pricked through her. She clanged mugs together as she scooped them off the counter. "I didn't expect to have anyone hulking around behind me."

His lips twitched. "That's better. I'll take one of those turnovers and a large coffee to go. Did you finish your planting?"

"Nearly." She didn't want to talk to him, so she busied herself with the coffee. She didn't want to have the island cop making friendly conversation and watching her out of those sharp green eyes.

"Maybe you can make use of this when you're finishing up and tending to your flowers." He laid a bag on the counter.

"What is it?"

"Garden tool." He counted out his money, set that on the counter as well.

She wiped her hands on her apron, scowled. But curiosity pushed her into opening the bag. Baffled humor lit her eyes as she studied the perfectly ridiculous rolled-brim straw hat. Foolish fake flowers danced around the crown.

"This is the silliest hat I've ever seen."

"Oh, there were sillier," he assured her. "But it'll keep the sun from burning your nose."

"It's very considerate of you, but you shouldn't—"

"Around here it's called being neighborly." The beeper on his belt signaled. "Well, back to work."

She managed to wait until he was halfway down the steps before she snatched the hat and dashed into the kitchen to try it on in the reflection of the stove hood.

Ripley Todd poured herself another cup of coffee and sipped it while looking out the front window of the station house. It had been a quiet morning, and that was just the way she liked it.

But there was something in the air. She was doing her best to ignore it, but *something* was in the air. It was easier to tell herself it was overstimulation from the week she'd spent in Boston.

Not that she hadn't enjoyed herself. She had. The law enforcement workshops and seminars had interested her, given her food for thought. She liked police work, the routine and detail of it. But the demands and chaos of the city wore on her, even in that short a time.

Zack would've said it was simply that she didn't like people overmuch. Ripley would've been the last one to argue with him about that.

She caught sight of him now, heading down the street. It would, she estimated, take him a good ten minutes to make the half block. People stopped him, always had a word to say.

More, she thought, people just liked being around him. He had a kind of . . . she didn't want to use the word "aura." It was too Mia-like. Air, she decided. Zack just had the kind of air about him that made people feel better about things. They knew if they took their troubles to him, he'd have the answer, or take the time to find it.

Zack was a sociable creature, Ripley mused. Affable and patient and consistently fair. No one would accuse her of being any of those things.

Maybe that was why they made a good team.

Since he was heading in, she opened the front door to the summer air and street sounds, the way he liked it best. She brewed a fresh pot of coffee and was just pouring him a cup when he finally arrived.

"Frank and Alice Purdue had a baby girl—eight pounds, five ounces, at nine this morning. Calling her Belinda. The Younger boy, Robbie, fell out of a tree, broke his arm. Missy Hachin's cousin in Bangor bought a brand-new Chevrolet sedan."

As he spoke, Zack took the offered coffee, sat at his desk, propped up his feet. And grinned. The ceiling fan was squeaking again. He'd really meant to see to that.

"So, what's new with you?"

"Speeder on the north coast road," Ripley told him. "Don't know where they thought they were going in such a hurry. I explained that the cliffs and the light and so on had been in place for a few centuries and weren't likely to move away in an afternoon." She plucked a fax out of his in box. "And this came in for you. Nell Channing. That's the new cook at Mia's place, right?"

"Umm-hmm." He scanned the motor vehicle report. No traffic violations. She still carried an Ohio driver's license, due for renewal in just over two years. The car was registered in her name. He'd been right about the new tags. She'd had them less than a week. Before that, the car had carried Texas tags.

Interesting.

Ripley scooted onto the corner of the desk they shared and sampled his coffee since he wasn't drinking it. "Why'd you run her?"

"Curious. She's a curious woman."

"Curious how?"

He started to answer, then shook his head. "Why don't you drop into the café for lunch, check her out yourself. I'd be interested in your impression."

"Maybe I will." Frowning, Ripley glanced at the open door. "I think a storm's coming in."

"It's clear as glass out there, honey."

"Something's coming," she said half to herself, then grabbed her baseball cap. "I'll take a walk around, maybe stop in the café and take a look at our newest resident."

"Take your time. I'll do the afternoon beach patrol."

"You're welcome to it." Ripley slid on her sunglasses and strode out.

She liked her village, the order of it. As far as Ripley was concerned, everything had a place and that's just where it should stay. She didn't mind the vagaries of sea and weather—that was just another natural order of things.

June meant a fresh influx of tourists and summer people, temperatures moving from warm to hot, beach bonfires and smoking grills.

It also meant excess partying, the routine drunk and disorderly, the occasional lost child, and the inevitable lovers' spats. But the tourists who celebrated, drank, wandered, and squabbled brought summer dollars to the island that kept it afloat during the frigid gales of winter.

She would cheerfully—well, perhaps not too cheerfully—suffer the problems of strangers for a few months in order to preserve Three Sisters.

This nine square miles of rock and sand and soil was all the world she needed.

Overbaked people were staggering up from the beach toward the village for lunch. She could never figure out what possessed a human being to flop itself down and broil like a trout in the sun. Besides the discomfort, the sheer boredom of it would have driven her wild inside an hour.

Ripley wasn't one to lie down if she could stand.

Not that she didn't enjoy the beach. She jogged along the surf every morning, summer and winter. When weather permitted, she finished off her run with a swim. When it didn't, she often ducked into the hotel and took advantage of its indoor pool.

But she preferred the sea.

As a result she had a tight, athletic body that was most often clad in khakis and T-shirts. Her skin was tanned like her brother's, her eyes the same vivid green. She wore her straight brown hair long and most often pulled through the back of her baseball cap.

Her features were an odd mix—a wide, slightly top-heavy mouth, a small nose, and dark, arching brows. Her looks had made her feel awkward as a child, but Ripley liked to think she'd grown into them, and grown out of worrying about them.

She strolled into Café Book, waved at Lulu, and headed for the stairs. With luck, she could get a look at this Nell Channing and avoid Mia altogether.

She was still three steps from the café level when she saw her luck wasn't going to hold.

Mia was behind the counter, looking slick as always in some floaty floral dress. Her hair was tied back and still managed to explode around her face.

The woman working beside her looked tidy, nearly prim in comparison.

Ripley immediately preferred Nell.

She jammed her thumbs into her back pockets and swaggered toward the counter.

"Deputy Todd." Mia angled her head, looked down her nose. "What could possibly bring you here?"

Ignoring Mia, Ripley studied Nell. "I'll have today's special soup and sandwich."

"Nell, this is Ripley, Zack's unfortunate sister. As she's come in for lunch we can safely assume hell has frozen over."

"Kiss ass, Mia. Nice to meet you, Nell. I'll have a lemonade to go with that."

"Yes. All right." Nell shifted her gaze from face to face. "Right away," she murmured and ducked into the kitchen to put the sandwich together.

"Heard you scooped her up right off the ferry," Ripley continued.

"More or less." Mia ladled the soup. "Don't poke at her, Ripley."

"Why would I?"

"Because you're you." Mia set the soup on the counter. "Notice anything odd when you stepped off the ferry yesterday?"

"No." Ripley replied too quickly.

"Liar," Mia said quietly as Nell came back with the sandwich.

"Can I take this to a table for you, Deputy Todd?"

"Yeah, thanks." Ripley tugged money out of her pocket. "Why don't you ring me up, Mia?"

Ripley timed it, sliding into a chair just as Nell set the food down. "Looks great."

"I hope you enjoy it."

"I'm sure I will. Where'd you learn to cook?"

"Here and there. Can I get you anything else?"

Ripley held up a finger, spooned up soup and sampled. "Nope. This is great. Really. Hey, did you make all those pastries yourself?"

"Yes."

"A lot of work."

"It's what I'm paid for."

"Right. Don't let Mia work you too hard. She's pushy."

"On the contrary," Nell said in a voice that chilled. "She's incredibly generous, incredibly kind. Enjoy your lunch."

Loyal, Ripley decided as she continued to eat. She couldn't fault Nell for that. Polite, too, even if she was a bit stiff about it. As if, Ripley thought, she wasn't quite used to dealing with people.

Nervous. She'd visibly cringed at the relatively mild byplay between Ripley and Mia. Well, Ripley decided with a shrug, some people couldn't handle conflict, even when it had nothing to do with them.

All in all, she thought Nell Channing was harmless. And a hell of a good cook.

The meal put her in such a good mood that she took the time to go by the counter on her way out. It was easier to decide to do so since Mia was occupied elsewhere.

"Well, now you've done it."

Nell froze. She deliberately kept her face blank, her hands loose. "I beg your pardon?"

"Now I'm going to have to start coming in here

regularly, something I've managed to avoid for years. Lunch was great."

"Oh. Good."

"You may have noticed, Mia and I aren't exactly chummy."

"It's none of my business."

"You live on the island, everybody's business is your business. But don't worry, we manage to stay out of each other's way for the most part. You won't get squeezed in the middle. I'm going to take a couple of those chocolate chip cookies for later."

"You save if you buy three."

"Twist my arm. Three, then. I'll give one to Zack and be a hero."

Relaxed now, Nell bagged the cookies, rang up the bill. But when she took the money from Ripley and their hands touched, the bright shock had her gasping.

Ripley glared, one long, frustrated stare. Snagging her cookies, she strode toward the stairs.

"Deputy—" Clenching her hand tight, Nell called after her. "You forgot your change."

"Keep it." She bit the words off as she stomped down the stairs. There was Mia at the bottom, hands folded, brow lifted. Ripley simply snarled and kept going.

A storm was coming. Though the sky stayed clear and the sea calm, a storm was coming. Its violence roared through Nell's dreams and tossed her helplessly into the past.

The huge white house sat on a verdant carpet of lawn. Inside, its edges were sharp, its surfaces hard. Colors were pale—sands and taupes and grays.

But for the roses he bought her, always bought her, that were the color of blood.

The house was empty. But it seemed to be waiting.

In sleep she turned her head away, resisted. She didn't want to go into that place. Not ever again.

But the door opened, the tall white door that opened into the long, wide foyer. White marble, white wood, and the cold, cold sparkle of crystal and chrome.

She watched herself walk in—long, pale hair sweeping past the shoulders of a sleek white dress that sent off an icy glitter. Her lips were red, like the roses.

He came in with her, close behind. Always so close behind. His hand was there, lightly on the small of her back. She could still feel it there if she let herself.

He was tall, slim. Like a prince in his evening black with his hair a gold helmet. She had fallen in love with the fairy-tale look of him, and she had believed his promises of happy-ever-after. And hadn't he taken her to this palace, this white palace in this fantasy land, and given her everything a woman could want?

How many times had he reminded her of that?

She knew what happened next. She remembered the glittery white dress, remembered how tired and relieved she was that the evening was over, and that it had gone well. She'd done nothing to upset him, to embarrass him, to annoy him.

Or so she'd thought.

Until she'd turned to say something about how nice an evening it had been, and had seen his expression.

He'd waited until they were home, until they were alone, to make the transformation. It was one of his best skills.

And she remembered the fear that had clutched her belly even as she scrambled to think of what she'd done.

Did you enjoy yourself, Helen?

Yes, it was a lovely party. But a long one. Would you like me to fix you a brandy before we go to bed?

You enjoyed the music?

Very much. Music? Had she said something inappropriate about the music? She could be so stupid about such things. Barely, she repressed a shudder as he reached out to toy with her hair. *It was wonderful to be able to dance outside, near the gardens.*

She stepped back, hoping to turn toward the stairs, but his hand fisted in her hair, held her in place. *Yes, I noticed how much you enjoyed dancing, especially with Mitchell Rawlings. Flirting with him. Flaunting yourself. Humiliating me in front of my friends, my clients.*

Evan, I wasn't flirting. I was only—

The backhanded slap sent her sprawling, the bright shock of pain blinding her. When she would have rolled into a protective ball, he dragged her across the marble floor by the hair.

How many times has he had his hands on you?

She denied, she wept, he accused. Until he grew weary of it and left her to crawl away and sob in a corner.

But this time, in this dream, she crawled off into

the shadows of the forest, where the air was soft and the ground warm.

And there, where the stream gurgled over its smooth rocks, she slept.

Then awoke to the cannon-blast of thunder and the jagged rip of lightning. Awoke to terror. She was running through the woods now, her white dress a sparkling beacon. Her blood pumped, the blood of the hunted. Trees crashed behind her, and the ground heaved under her feet and boiled with mist.

Still she ran, her breath tearing out of her throat and ending in whimpers. There were screams in the wind, and not all of them hers. Fear ruled until there was nothing else inside her, no reason, no sense, no answer.

The wind slapped at her with sharp and gleeful hands, and clawing fingers of brush tore her dress to shreds.

She was climbing, scrabbling like a lizard along the rock. Through the dark the beam from the lighthouse slashed like a silver blade, and below, the wild violence of the sea churned.

She kicked and cried and climbed. But she didn't look back, couldn't force herself to look around and face what pursued her.

Instead, choosing flight over fight, she leaped from the rocks, spun and spun in the wind on her plunge toward the water. And the cliffs, the light, the trees all tumbled in after her.

Four

*On her first day off, Nell rearranged the fur*niture—what there was of it. She watered her flowers and herbs, did the wash, and baked a loaf of brown bread.

It was still shy of nine o'clock when she cut the first slice for her breakfast.

Evan had hated her early-rising habit, and had complained that that was the reason she was dull at parties. Now, in her little cottage near the sea, there was no one to criticize, no need to creep about. She had her windows open wide, and the whole day belonged just to her.

Still munching on bread and with a heel of the loaf in the pocket of her shorts, she took herself off for a long walk on the beach.

The boats were out, bobbing and gliding over the water. The sea was a soft, dreamy blue with frisky waves that rolled up lacy on the sand. Gulls winged over it, white-breasted in their graceful dance on the air. The music of them, the long, shrill cries, pierced the low, endless rumble of the surf.

She turned in a little dance of her own. Then she tugged the bread from her pocket and tore it into small pieces, tossing it high to watch the gulls circle and dive.

Alone, she thought, lifting her face to the sky. But not lonely. She doubted she would ever be lonely again.

At the sound of church bells she turned to look back at the village, at the pretty white steeple. She glanced down at her shorts with the frayed hem, her sandy sneakers. Hardly dressed for services, she decided. But she could worship in her own way, and offer a prayer of thanksgiving.

While the bells rang and echoed, she sat near the edge of the water. Here was peace, she thought, and joy. She would never, never take either for granted. She would remember to give something back every day. Even if it was just a heel of bread for the gulls. She would tend what she planted. She would remember to be kind, and never forget to offer a helping hand.

She would keep her promises and expect nothing more than the chance to lead a good life that hurt no one.

She would earn what she'd been given, and treasure it.

She would take pleasure in the simple things, she decided. Starting right now.

Rising, she began to collect shells, tucking them in her pockets at first. When the pockets were full, she tugged off her shoes and used them. She reached the far end of the beach, where rocks jutted out of the sand and began to tumble toward the sea. Here there were palm-size stones worn cobble smooth. She picked one, then another, wondering if she could fashion an edging for her little herb bed.

A movement to her left had her wrapping her fingers tight around the stone and turning quickly. Her heart continued to beat in hard jerks as she watched Zack coming down a zigzag of wooden steps.

"Morning."

"Good morning." In automatic defense, she glanced back, uneasy to realize how far from the village proper she'd wandered. The beach was no longer empty, but the scattered people were some distance away.

"Nice day for a long walk on the beach," he commented, leaning against the handrail to study her. "You've sure had one."

He'd watched her, from her dance with the gulls. It was a shame, he thought, how quickly her face could go from radiant to guarded.

"I didn't realize how far I'd come."

"Nothing's really that far on an island this size. It's going to be a hot one," he said easily. "Beach'll be crowded before noon. It's nice to get a little time on it before it's full of towels and bodies."

"Yes, well . . ."

"Come on up."

"What?"

"Come on up. To the house. I'll give you a bag for those shells and stones."

"Oh, that's all right. I don't really need—"

"Nell—is it cops in general, men in general, or me in particular that worry you?"

"I'm not worried."

"Prove it." He stayed where he was, but held out a hand.

She kept her eyes on his. He had good eyes. Smart ones, but patient too. Slowly she stepped forward and lifted her hand to his.

"What do you plan to do with your shells?"

"Nothing." Her pulse was galloping, but she made herself climb the sandy steps with him. "Well, nothing brilliant. Just scatter them around, I suppose."

His hand held hers loosely, but even so she could tell it was hard and rough. He wore no rings, no watch on his wrist.

No pampering, she thought. No adornments.

Like her, he was barefoot, and his jeans were ripped at the knee, frayed at the hem. With his sun-streaked hair and tawny skin, he looked more beach bum than sheriff. It tamped down some of her anxiety.

At the landing they turned, walked along a gentle slope. Below, on the far side of the rocks, was a sunny inlet where a small red boat bobbed lazily at a rickety pier.

"Everything's a picture," she said quietly.

"Have you done any sailing?"

"Yes. A little," she said quickly. "Is that your boat?"

"She's mine."

There was a sudden wild splashing of water, and a sleek, dark head appeared, cruising around the rocks. As Nell stared, a huge black dog leaped onto the shore and shook herself madly.

"Her, too," Zack stated. "Mine, that is. Are you all right with dogs? Tell me now. I can hold her off and give you a fair head start."

"No, I like dogs." Then she blinked, looked back at him. "What do you mean, head start?"

He didn't bother to answer, just grinned as the dog leaped up the slope in powerful bounds. She jumped on Zack, tail wagging and spewing water, and licked his face. On two short, deep barks she bunched her muscles and would have given Nell the same treatment if Zack hadn't blocked her.

"This is Lucy. She's friendly, but mannerless. Down, Lucy."

Lucy got down, her entire body wagging now. Then, obviously unable to control her joy and affection, she leaped on Zack again.

"She's two," he explained, firmly pushing her down and shoving her butt to the ground with his hand. "Black Lab. I'm told they mellow out some when they're older."

"She's beautiful." Nell stroked Lucy's head, and at the first touch the dog collapsed on the ground and rolled over, belly up.

"No pride, either," Zack began, then looked surprised when Nell just hunkered down and sent Lucy into ecstasy by rubbing her belly with both hands.

"You don't need pride when you're beautiful, do you, Lucy? Oh, there's nothing like a big, beautiful dog, is there? I always—oh!"

In a delirium of pleasure, Lucy rolled, scrambled, and knocked Nell flat on her back. Zack was fast, but not quite fast enough to keep her from being leaped on and licked.

"Jesus, Lucy. No! Hey, I'm sorry." Zack shoved at the dog and lifted Nell to her feet one-handed. "You okay? Did she hurt you?"

"No. I'm fine." She'd had the wind knocked out of her, but that was only part of the reason for breathlessness. He was brushing at her while the dog sat, head down, tail cautiously thumping. He was, Nell noted, frustrated and concerned. But not angry.

"You didn't hit your head, did you? Damn dog weighs almost as much as you do. Banged your elbow a little," he added, then realized she was actually giggling. "What's so funny?"

"Nothing, really. It's just sweet the way she's pretending to look ashamed. She's obviously terrified of you."

"Yeah, I take a bat to her twice a week whether she needs it or not." He ran his hands lightly up and down Nell's arms. "Sure you're okay?"

"Yes." It struck her then that they were now standing very close, almost embracing. And that his hands were on her, and her skin was much too warm from them. "Yes," she said again and took a deliberate step in retreat. "No harm done."

"You're sturdier than you look." There were long, lean muscles in those arms, he noted. He'd already admired the ones in her legs. "Come on inside," he said. "Not you," he added, pointing at the dog. "You're banished."

He scooped Nell's shoes up from the ground and walked toward a wide porch. Curious, and unable to think of an excuse not to follow, Nell went through the screened door he opened and into a big, bright, messy kitchen.

"It's the maid's decade off." Comfortable in his own clutter, he set her shoes on the floor and went to the refrigerator. "Can't offer you homemade lemonade, but we've got some iced tea."

"That's fine, thanks. It's a wonderful kitchen."

"We use it mostly for heating up takeout."

"That's a shame." There were acres of granite-toned counters, and wonderful rough-hewn cabinets with leaded-glass fronts. A generous double sink with a window over it offered a view of the inlet and the sea.

Plenty of storage and work space, she mused. With a little organization and a bit of imagination, it would be a marvelous . . .

We? He'd said "we," she realized. Was he married? She'd never thought of that, never considered the possibility. Not that it mattered, of course, but . . .

He'd flirted with her. She may have been out of practice and short on experience, but she knew when a man was flirting.

"You've got a lot of thoughts going on inside that head at one time." Zack held out a glass. "Want to share any of them?"

"No. That is, I was just thinking what a nice room this is."

"It was a lot more presentable when my mother was in charge of it. Now that it's just Ripley and me, the kitchen doesn't get a lot of attention."

"Ripley. Oh. I see."

"You were wondering if I was married, or maybe living here with someone who wasn't my sister. That's nice."

"It's none of my business."

"I didn't say it was, just said it was nice. I'd take you through the house, but it's probably in worse shape than the kitchen. And you've got a tidy soul. We'll go this way." He took her hand again, pulled her back outside.

"Where? I really should be getting back."

"It's Sunday, and we've hit our day off together. I've got something you'll like," he continued and tugged her across the porch.

It wrapped around the house, edged the side where there was a scrubby garden and a couple of gnarled trees. Weather-worn steps led up to a second-story porch that faced the sea.

He kept his hand over hers and led her up them.

Air and sun washed over her, made her think how easy it would be to stretch out in the wooden chaise and let the day rock away.

A telescope stood by the rail, along with a stone troth that had yet to be planted.

"You're right." She stepped to the rail, leaned out and breathed. "I do like it."

"You look west, you can see the mainland when it's clear enough."

"You don't have your telescope pointed west."

At the moment all his attention was on her very pretty set of legs. "I guess I don't."

"What do you look at?"

"Whatever strikes my fancy at the time."

She glanced over as she moved away. He was staring at her now—long, speculative looks, and they both knew it. "It'd be tempting to stay out here all day," she said as she turned the corner and looked out on the village. "Watch the comings and the goings."

"I watched you this morning, feeding the gulls." He leaned on the rail, a man at home, and drank his tea. "I woke up thinking, 'You know, I'm going to find a reason to drop by the yellow cottage today, get another look at Nell Channing,' then I came out here with my morning coffee, and there you were. So I didn't have to make up a reason to get another look at you."

"Sheriff—"

"It's my day off," he reminded her. He started to lift his hand to touch her hair, but when she edged back he simply slid it into his pocket. "Since it is, why don't we spend a couple hours of it on the water? We can go for a sail."

"I can't. I have to . . ."

"You don't have to hunt up excuses. Some other time."

"Yes." The knot that had formed in her belly loosened. "Some other time. I really should go. Thanks for the drink, and the view."

"Nell—" He took her hand again, kept his fingers light when hers jerked. "There's a line between making a woman a little nervous and scaring her. That's a line I wouldn't want to cross. When you get to know me a little better, you'll believe that," he added.

"Right now I'm working on getting to know myself a little better."

"Fair enough. I'll get you a bag for your shells and stones."

He made a point of going into the café every morning. A cup of coffee, a muffin, a few words. To Zack's way of thinking, she'd get used to seeing him, talking to him, and the next time he worked it around so they were alone together, she wouldn't feel compelled to check for running room.

He was perfectly aware that Nell wasn't the only one who noticed his new morning habit. Zack didn't mind the teasing comments, the sly winks and chuckles. Island life had a rhythm, and whenever anything new added a beat, everyone felt it.

He sipped Nell's truly excellent coffee while he stood on the dock listening to Carl Macey bitch about lobster poachers.

"Three blessed days this week trap's been empty, and they ain't troubling to close it after them, neither. I've got the suspicion it's them college boys renting the Boeing place. Ayah." He spat. "That's who's doing it. I catch 'em at it, I'm gonna give them rich college brats something to remember."

"Well, Carl, the fact is, it sounds like summer people, and sounds like kids on top of it. Why don't you let me have a talk with them?"

"Got no call interfering with a man's livelihood that way."

"No, but they wouldn't be thinking of it like that."

"They'd better start thinking." The weathered face went grim. "I went up to see Mia Devlin, asked her to put a spell on my traps."

Zack winced. "Now, Carl—"

"Better than me peppering their skinny white asses with buckshot now, ain't it? I swear that's next in line."

"Let me handle this."

"I'm telling you, ain't I?" Scowling, Carl bobbed his head. "No harm in covering all my bases. Besides,

I got a look at the new mainlander while I was up to the bookstore." Carl's pug-homely, wrinkled face folded into a snicker. "See why you're such a regular customer there these days. Ayah. Big blue eyes like that sure start a man's day off on the right foot."

"They can't hurt. You keep your shotgun in your gun cabinet, Carl. I'll take care of things."

He headed back to the station house first, for his list of summer people. The Boeing place was an easy enough walk, but he decided to take the cruiser to make it more official.

The summer rental was a block back from the beach, with a generous screened porch on the side. Beach towels and swim trunks hung drooping from a nylon line strung inside the screen. The picnic table on the porch was heaped with beer cans and the remnants of last night's meal.

They hadn't had the sense, Zack thought with a shake of his head, to ditch the evidence. Scraped-out lobster shells lay upended on the table like giant insects. Zack dug his badge out of his pocket and pinned it on. Might as well get in their faces with it.

He knocked, and kept right on knocking until the door opened. The boy who opened the door was about twenty. Squinting against the sun, his hair a wild disarray, he wore brightly striped boxer shorts and a golden summer tan.

He said, "Ugh."

"Sheriff Todd, Island Police. Mind if I come inside?"

"Whafor? Timzit?"

Hungover, big-time, Zack decided, and translated.

"To talk to you. It's about ten-thirty. Your friends around?"

"Somewhere? Problem? Christ." The boy swallowed, winced, then stumbled through the living room past the breakfast counter and to the sink, where he turned the water on full. And stuck his head under the faucet.

"Some party, huh?" Zack said when he surfaced, dripping.

"Guess." He snagged paper towels, rubbed his face dry. "We get too loud?"

"No complaints. What's your name, son?"

"Josh, Josh Tanner."

"Well, Josh, why don't you rouse your pals? I don't want to take up a lot of your time."

"Yeah, well. Okay."

He waited, listened. There was some cursing, a few thuds, water running. A toilet flushed.

The three young men who trooped back in with Josh looked plenty the worse for wear. They stood, in various states of undress, until one flopped down on a chair and smirked.

"What's the deal?"

All attitude, Zack calculated. "And you'd be?"

"Steve Hickman."

Boston accent, Zack concluded. Upper-class one, almost Kennedyesque. "Okay, Steve, here's the deal. Lobster poaching carries a thousand-dollar fine. Reason for that is that while it's a kick to sneak out and empty the traps, boil up a couple, some people depend on the catch for their living. An evening's entertainment to you is money out of their pocket."

As he lectured, Zack saw the boys shift uncomfortably. The one who'd answered the door was flushing guiltily and keeping his eyes averted.

"What you had out there on the porch last night would've run you about forty down at the market. So you look up a man by the name of Carl Macey at the docks, give him forty, and that'll be the end of it."

"I don't know what you're talking about. Does this Macey put a brand on his lobsters?" Steve smirked again, scratched his belly. "You can't prove we poached anything."

"True enough." Zack glanced around the room, skimmed faces. Nerves, a little shame. "This place rents for what, about twelve hundred a week in full season, and the boat you've rented puts another two-fifty onto that. Add entertainment, food, beer. You guys're shelling out 'round about a grand apiece for a week here."

"And pumping it into the island economy," Steve said with a thin smile. "Pretty stupid to hassle us over a couple of allegedly poached lobsters."

"Maybe. Even more stupid not to come up with ten bucks each to smooth things over. You think about that. It's a small island," Zack said as he started for the door. "Word gets around."

"Is that a threat? Threatening civilians could result in a litigious action."

Zack glanced back, shook his head. "I bet you're pre-law, aren't you?" He strolled out, back to his cruiser. It wouldn't take him long to hit the right spots in the village and make his point.

Ripley walked down High Street and met Zack in front of the Magick Inn. "Lobster Boy's credit card got hung up at the pizza place," she began. "Seems the circuits were down or whatever and he had to dig for cash to pay for lunch."

"That so?"

"Yeah. And you know, every video they wanted to rent was already out."

"Hell of a thing."

"And I hear all the jet skis were already reserved or out of order today."

"That's a shame."

"And continuing in a series of bizarre coincidences, the AC in their rental just up and died."

"And it's a hot one today, too. Supposed to be muggy tonight. Bound to be uncomfortable sleeping."

"You're a mean son of a bitch, Zachariah." Ripley rose on her toes and gave him a quick, smacking kiss on the mouth. "That's why I love you."

"I'm going to have to get meaner. That Hickman boy's a tough nut. The other three'll fold fast enough, but he'll take some more persuading." Zack swung an arm around Ripley's shoulder. "So, are you going into the café for some lunch?"

"I might be. Why?"

"I thought you could do me a little favor, since you love me and everything."

The long whip of her ponytail bobbed as she turned her head to look up at him. "If you want me to talk Nell into dating you, just forget it."

"I can get my own dates, thanks."

"Batting zero so far."

"I'm still on deck," he countered. "What I was hoping is that you'd tell Mia we're handling the lobster boys, and not to . . . do anything."

"What do you mean, 'do anything'? What does she have to do with it?" Ripley stopped, her temper flaring. "Damn it."

"Don't get riled. It's just that Carl said he'd talked to her. I'd just as soon it not get around that our resident witch is cooking up a spell. Or whatever."

To keep Ripley in check, Zack tightened his grip on her shoulders. "I'd go in myself and have a word with her, but the lobster boys should be coming along in a few minutes. I want to be standing here, looking smug and authoritative."

"I'll talk to her."

"You play nice, Rip. And remember it was Carl who went to her."

"Yeah, yeah, yeah." She shook off his arm and marched across the street.

Witches and spells. It was all a bunch of nonsense, idiotic hooey, she thought as she breezed down the sidewalk. A man like Carl Macey ought to know better. Stirring up a bunch of silliness. It was all right for the tourists to buy all the Three Sisters lore—it was one of the things that brought them over from the mainland. But it burned her butt when it was one of her own.

And Mia encouraged it, too. Just by being Mia.

Ripley swung into Café Book and scowled over at Lulu, who was ringing up a customer. "Where is she?"

"Upstairs. Pretty busy today."

"Yeah, she's a busy little bee," Ripley muttered and headed up.

She spotted Mia with a customer in the cookbook

section. Ripley bared her teeth. Mia fluttered her lashes. Simmering with impatience, Ripley strode into the café, waited her turn, then snapped out an order for coffee.

"No lunch today?" Flushed with the bustle of the noon crowd, Nell poured out from a fresh pot.

"Lost my appetite."

"That's too bad." Mia cooed from behind Ripley. "The lobster salad's particularly good today."

Ripley merely jerked a thumb, then marched behind the counter and into the kitchen. She jammed her hands on her hips when Mia strolled in after her.

"Zack and I are handling the problem. I want you to stay out of it."

A bowl of top cream was less smooth than Mia's voice. "I wouldn't dream of interfering with the law of the land."

"Excuse me." Nell hesitated, cleared her throat. "Sandwiches. I need to make them up."

"Go right ahead." Mia gestured. "I imagine Deputy Fife and I are nearly done."

"Just save the smart-ass comments."

"I do. I store them up just for you."

"I don't want you doing anything, and I want you to tell Carl you didn't do anything."

"Too late." Enjoying herself, Mia smiled brilliantly. "It's already done. A very simple spell—even someone with your fumbling abilities could have managed it."

"Cancel it."

"No. Why does it concern you? You claim not to believe in the Craft."

"I don't. But I know how rumors work around here. If anything happens to those boys—"

"Don't insult me." All humor fled from Mia's voice. "You know very well I'd do nothing to harm them, or anyone. You know, that's the heart of it. That's what you're afraid of. Afraid that if you opened yourself to what's inside you again, you wouldn't be able to control it."

"I'm not afraid of anything. And you're not pulling me in that way." She pointed at Nell, who was struggling to keep very busy with sandwiches. "You've got no right pulling her in, either."

"I don't make the pattern, Ripley. I just recognize it. And so do you."

"It's a waste of time talking to you." Ripley stormed out of the kitchen.

Mia let out a little sigh, her only sign of distress. "Conversations with Ripley never seem particularly productive. You mustn't let it worry you, Nell."

"It has nothing to do with me."

"I can feel your anxiety all the way over here. People argue, often bitterly. They don't all solve the conflict with fists. Here, now." She moved behind Nell and rubbed her shoulders. "Let the worry go. Tension's bad for the digestion."

At the touch Nell felt a trickle of warmth melt away the ice that had balled in her belly. "I guess I like both of you. I hate to see you dislike each other."

"I don't dislike Ripley. She annoys me, frustrates me, but I don't dislike her. You wonder what we were talking about, but you won't ask, will you, little sister?"

"No. I don't like questions."

"I'm fascinated by them. We need to talk, you and I." Mia stepped back, waited for Nell to pick up the completed order and turn. "I have things to do this evening. Tomorrow, then. I'll buy you a drink. Let's make it early. Five at the Magick Inn. The lounge. It's called the Coven. You can leave your questions at home if you like," Mia said as she started out. "I'll bring the answers anyway."

Five

It went pretty much as Zack had expected. The Hickman kid had to flex his muscles. The other three had folded, and Zack expected Carl to get his money from them the next morning. But Hickman had to prove he was smarter, braver, and far superior to some dinky island sheriff.

From his place on the dock, Zack watched the rented boat putt along toward the lobster traps. He was already on the wrong side of the law, Zack mused, nibbling on sunflower seeds. Boating after dark without running lights. That would cost him.

But it was nothing to the grand that the little defiance was going to cost the college boy's father.

He expected the kid was going to give him some trouble when he hauled him in. Which meant they'd both be spending a few hours in the station house that night. One of them behind bars.

Well, lessons learned, Zack decided, lowering his

binoculars and reaching down for his flashlight as the boy began to haul up a pot.

The scream was high and girlish, and gave Zack a hell of a jolt. He switched on his light, shot the bright beam of it across the water. A light fog crept over the surface, so that the boat seemed to bob in smoke. The boy stood, the trap gripped in both hands, the look on his face as he stared into it one of sheer horror.

Before Zack could call out, the boy flung the trap high and wide. Even as it splashed into the water, he was tumbling in.

"Oh, well, hell," Zack muttered, peeved at the prospect of ending his workday soaking wet. He stepped to the end of the dock, scooped up a life preserver. The kid was doing more screaming than swimming, but he was making some progress toward shore.

"Here you go, Steve." Zack tossed the preserver in. "Head this way. I don't want to have to come in after you."

"Help me." The boy flailed, swallowed water, choked. But he managed to grab the flotation. "They're eating my face!"

"Almost there." Zack knelt down, held out a hand. "Come on up. You're still in one piece."

"My head! My head!" Steve slipped and slithered onto the dock, then lay there on his belly, shuddering. "I saw my head in the trap. They were eating my face!"

"Your head's still on your shoulders, son." Zack hunkered down. "Catch your breath. Had yourself a hallucination, that's all. Been drinking a bit, haven't you? That, and some guilt got to you."

"I saw . . . I saw." He sat up, laid shaking hands on

his face to make certain all his parts were there, then began to shake in stupendous relief.

"Fog, dark, water. It's a tricky kind of situation, especially on a couple bottles of beer. You're going to feel a lot better when you give Carl that forty dollars. In fact, why don't we go get you cleaned up, get your wallet, and go by his place now? You'll sleep better for it."

"Yeah. Sure. Right. Okay."

"That's fine." Zack helped him to his feet. "I'll take care of getting the boat back, don't you worry."

That Mia, Zack thought as he led the unprotesting boy away from the water. You had to give her credit for creativity.

It took a while to calm the boy down, then to calm four boys down once he'd taken Steve back to the rental. Then there was Carl to deal with, and the boat. Which was probably why Zack ended up nodding off at the station house just before three A.M.

He woke two hours later, stiff as a board and annoyed with himself. Ripley, he decided as he stumbled out to his cruiser, was taking the first shift.

He meant to drive straight home, but he'd gotten into the habit of swinging past the yellow cottage at the end of his shift. Just to make sure everything was as it should be.

He made the turn before he realized it, and saw the lights in her windows. Concern as much as curiosity made him pull over and get out of the car.

Because the kitchen light was on, he went to the

back door. He was lifting his hand to knock when he saw her standing on the other side of the screen, a long, smooth-bladed knife gripped in both hands.

"If I tell you I was just in the neighborhood, you won't gut me with that, will you?"

Her hands began to tremble, and her breath exploded out of her as she dropped the knife on the table with a clatter.

"I'm sorry I scared you. I saw your light as I was . . . hey, hey." When she swayed, he bolted through the door, gripping both her arms and lowering her into a chair. "Sit. Breathe. Head down. Jesus, Nell. I'm sorry." He stroked her hair, patted her back, and wondered whether she would just keel over on the floor if he jumped up to get her a glass of water.

"It's all right. I'm all right. I heard the footsteps. In the dark. It's so quiet here, you can hear everything, and I heard you coming toward the house."

She'd wanted to run like a rabbit in the other direction and keep going. She didn't remember picking up the knife, hadn't known she could.

"I'm going to get you some water."

"No, I'm all right." Mortified now, she realized, but all right. "I just wasn't expecting anyone to come to the door."

"Guess not. It's still shy of five-thirty." He sat back on his heels when she lifted her head again. Color was coming back, he noted with relief. "What're you doing up?"

"I'm usually up by—" She jumped like a spring as the oven timer buzzed. "God! God!" With a half laugh she pounded a fist on her heart. "I'm going to be lucky to survive till sunrise at this rate. My muffins," she said and got up quickly to take them out of the oven, slide the next batch in.

"I didn't realize you started so early."

He could see, now that he looked around, that she'd been at it a while. There was something simmering on the stove and smelling like glory. A huge bowl of batter sat on the counter. Another bowl, covered with a cloth, was beside the stove. Still one more was on the table, where she'd obviously been mixing something before he'd scared ten years off her life.

Ingredients were lined up, as organized as a marching band.

"I didn't realize you worked so late." She calmed herself by cutting shortening into the flour for her pastry dough.

"I don't usually. I had a little project to finish up last night, and when it was all said and done, dropped off in my office chair. Nell, if you don't give me a cup of that coffee I'm going to start crying. It'll embarrass us both."

"Oh. Sorry. Um."

"You just keep on with what you're doing there. Cups?"

"Cabinet to the right of the sink."

"Want me to top yours off?"

"I suppose."

He poured a cup, filled hers as it sat by the sink. "You know, I don't think these muffins look quite right."

With the bowl tucked in the crook of her arm, she turned. Her face was a study of alarm and insult. "What do you mean?"

"Just don't look quite the thing. Why don't you let

me test one for you?" He gave her a quick, boyish grin that had her lips twitching.

"Oh, for heaven's sake. Why don't you just ask for one?"

"More fun this way. No, don't bother. I can get it myself." He plucked one out of the pan, burned the tips of his fingers. As he tossed the muffin from hand to hand to cool it, the scent told him it was going to be worth it. "I've sure got a soft spot for your blueberry muffins, Nell."

"Mr. Bigelow, Lancefort Bigelow, prefers my cream puffs. He said if I'd make them for him every day, he'd marry me and we'd move to Bimini."

Still grinning, Zack broke the muffin in half, treated himself to the fragrant steam. "That's pretty stiff competition."

Bigelow, a confirmed bachelor, was ninety.

He watched her stir the dough, form it into a ball. Then she emptied the muffin pan, set them to cool on a rack while she refilled the cups. When the timer buzzed again, she shifted trays, went back to roll out her pastry dough.

"You've got yourself a real system," he commented. "Where'd you learn to bake?"

"My mother—" She broke off, realigned her thoughts. It was too easy in the quiet kitchen, with all these homey smells, to get overly comfortable and reveal too much. "My mother liked to bake," she said. "And I picked up recipes and techniques here and there."

He didn't want her to stiffen up, so he let it pass. "Do you ever make those cinnamon rolls? You know the ones with that sticky white icing?"

"Mmm."

"I make them sometimes."

"Really." She began to cut the dough for tarts and glanced back at him. He looked so . . . male, she thought, leaning back on the counter with his ankles crossed and a mug of coffee in his hand. "I didn't know you cooked."

"Sure, now and then. You buy these tubes down at the market. Then you take them home, rap them against the counter and peel the bun things out, cook them, and squirt icing on the top. Nothing to it."

It made her laugh. "I'll have to try that sometime." She went to the refrigerator, took out her bowl of filling.

"I'll give you some pointers on it." He drained his cup, set it in the sink. "I guess I'd better get home, and get out of your way. Thanks for the coffee."

"You're welcome."

"And the muffin. It was just fine."

"That's a relief." She stood at the table, methodically spooning filling into the center of her rounds of dough. When he stepped toward her, she tensed a little, but continued to work.

"Nell?"

She looked up, and filling slopped out of her spoon when he put his hand on her cheek.

"I sure hope this doesn't put you off," he said, and leaning down, he laid his lips on hers.

She didn't move a muscle. Couldn't. Her eyes stayed open, locked on his. Watching, as a deer might watch when pinned in the crosshairs.

His lips were warm. She registered that. And softer than they looked. He didn't touch her. She imagined she'd have leaped out of her skin if he'd laid his hands on her now.

But it was only his mouth, light and easy on hers.

He'd prepared himself for her to be annoyed, or disinterested. He hadn't expected her to be scared. That was what he felt from her, a rigid anxiety that could easily bloom into fear. So he didn't touch her as he wanted to, not even a gentle brush of fingers down her arms.

If she'd stepped back, he'd have done nothing to stop her. But her absolute stillness was its own defense. It was he who stepped back, and kept it light despite a gnawing in the gut that was more than a stir of desire for her—it was a cold fury for whoever had hurt her.

"Seems I have a soft spot for more than your muffins." He tucked his thumbs in his front pockets. "See you later."

He strolled out, hoping the kiss and the ease of his leaving would give her something to think about.

He wasn't going to get any sleep. Resigned to it, he thrilled Lucy by taking her for an early-morning swim in the inlet. The romp, and her sheer foolishness, worked off a good portion of his stiffness, and his frustration.

He watched Ripley finish her run on the beach and dive into the surf. Dependable as sunrise, he thought as she cut through the waves. Maybe he didn't always know what went on in her head, or how it got there, but he rarely had to worry about Ripley Todd.

She could handle herself.

Lucy ran out to meet her as she started back, and the two wet females had a wrestle and a race. They both joined him on the upper porch, Lucy to flop down in delighted exhaustion, and Ripley sucking on a bottle of water.

"Mom called last night." Ripley flopped down herself, on one of the deck chairs. "They made it to the Grand Canyon. They're sending us six million pictures that Dad took with his digital. I'm afraid to start the download."

"Sorry I missed the call."

"I told them you were on a stakeout," she said with her tongue in her cheek. "They got a kick out of the lobster caper. Any updates?"

"Oh, yeah."

He sat on the arm of the Adirondack chair, and filled her in.

She turned her face up to the sky and hooted. "I *knew* I should've gone with you. Idiot drunk putz. Lobster Boy, not you."

"I figured. He wasn't that drunk, Rip."

She lifted a hand, waved it at him. "Don't start that. I'm in too good a mood for you to spoil it by mentioning Mia and her double, double, toil and trouble routine."

"Suit yourself."

"I usually do. I'm going to get a shower. I'll take the first shift. You must be wiped."

"I'm okay. Listen . . ." But he trailed off, trying to think how to put what he wanted to say.

"Listening."

"I went by the yellow cottage on the way home. Nell's lights were on, so I stopped in."

"Aha," Ripley teased.

"Gutter-face. I had a cup of coffee and a muffin."

"Gee, Zack, I'm sorry to hear that."

Normally he'd have laughed. Instead he rose, paced to the rail. "You stop in and see her most every day. You're friendly, right?"

"I guess we're friendly enough. It's hard not to like her."

"Women tend to confide stuff to their female friends, don't they?"

"Probably. You want me to ask her if she likes you enough to go to the school dance with you?" She started to snicker, but stopped when he turned around and saw his face. "Hey, sorry. I didn't know it was serious. What's up?"

"I think she's been abused."

"Man." Ripley stared down at her water bottle. "That's tough."

"Some son of a bitch messed with her, I'm sure of it. Whether or not she's had counseling or gotten help, it seems to me she could use a . . . you know, a girl-friend. Somebody she could talk to about it."

"Zack, you know I'm no good at that kind of thing. You are."

"I've got the wrong equipment to be Nell's girl-friend, Rip. Just . . . just see if you can spend some time with her. Go out on the boat, or go shopping or . . ." He gestured vaguely. "Paint each other's toe-nails."

"Excuse me?"

"Give me a break. I don't know what you people do in your mysterious caves when men aren't around."

"We have pillow fights in our underwear."

He brightened because she wanted him to. "Really? I was afraid that was a myth. So, be a friend, okay?"

"Are you starting to get a thing for her?"

"Yeah. So?"

"So, I guess I'll be a friend."

Nell walked into the Coven at precisely five. It was not, as she'd feared, a dark, eerie place, but rather cozy. The light was faintly blue and added a soft tint to the white flowers in the center of each table.

The tables themselves were round, with deep chairs and small sofas circling them. At the glossy bar the glasses sparkled. Nell had no more than chosen a table when a young waitress in trim, unrelieved black set a silver bowl of mixed snacks in front of her.

"Can I get you a drink?"

"I'm waiting for someone. Maybe just a mineral water for now. Thanks."

The only other patrons were a couple poring over an Island Tours brochure while they sipped white wines and nibbled from a cheese plate. The music was low, and very like what Mia tended to play in the bookstore. Nell tried to relax in her chair, wishing she'd brought a book.

Ten minutes later, Mia breezed in, the long skirt swirling around her long legs. She carried a book, and lifted her free hand in a wave toward the bar. "A glass of Cabernet, Betsy."

"First glass is on Carl Macey." Betsy shot Mia a wink. "He gave me orders."

"Tell him I enjoyed it." She sat down across from Nell. "Did you drive over?"

"No, I walked."

"Do you drink alcoholic beverages?"

"Now and then."

"Have one now. What's your pleasure?"

"The Cabernet'll be fine. Thanks."

"Two, Betsy. Damn, I love these things." She began to pick through the snack bowl. "Especially the little cheese ones that look like Chinese symbols. So, I brought you a book. A gift." Mia nudged the book toward Nell. "I thought you'd like to read about where you've chosen to live."

"Yes, I've been meaning to. *The Three Sisters: Legends and Lore*," she said, reading the cover. "Thank you."

"You're settling in now, getting your feet under you. I should tell you first that I couldn't be happier with your work."

"I'm glad to hear it. I love working at the café, the store. I couldn't have tailor-made a job I'd like more."

"Oh, you're Nell." Catching the comment as she served the wine, Betsy beamed. "You're always gone when I get to the café. I try to zip in before I open the bar. Great cookies."

"Thanks."

"You hear from Jane, Mia?"

"Just today. Tim got his audition, and they're hopeful. They're paying the rent by working at a bakery in Chelsea."

"I hope they're happy."

"So do I."

"I'll leave you two alone. Let me know if you need anything."

"So." Mia lifted her glass, tapped it to Nell's. "*Slainte.*"

"I'm sorry?"

"A Gaelic toast. Cheers." Mia brought the glass to her lips, watching Nell over the rim. "What do you know about witches?"

"Which sort? Like Elizabeth Montgomery on *Bewitched* or the ones who wear crystals and burn candles and sell little bottles of love potion?"

Mia laughed, crossed her legs. "Actually, I wasn't thinking of Hollywood or pseudo-Wiccans."

"I didn't mean to be insulting. I know there are people who take the matter very seriously. A kind of religion. That should be respected."

"Even if they are kooks," Mia said with a hint of a smile.

"No. You're not a kook. I understand . . . Well, you mentioned it that first day, then your conversation with Ripley yesterday."

"Good. Then we've established that I'm a witch." Mia sipped again. "You're a sweet one, Nell. There you are, trying very hard to discuss this intelligently, soberly, when you're thinking I'm—let's say—eccentric. We'll table that for the moment and go back in history so I can lay some groundwork for you. You know of the witch trials in Salem."

"Sure. A few hysterical young girls, fanatical Puritans. Mob mentality. Burn the witch."

"Hang," Mia corrected. "Nineteen people—all innocents—were hanged in 1692. One was pressed to death when he refused to declare himself innocent or guilty. Others died in prison. There have been witch-hunts throughout time. Here, in Europe, in every corner of the world. Even when most stopped believing, or admitting to a belief, in witchcraft, there were hunts. Nazism, McCarthyism, the KKK, and so on. Nothing more than fanatics, with power, pushing their own agendas and finding enough weak minds to do the dirty work."

And don't, Mia thought, taking a breath, get me started. "But today we're concerned with one microcosm of history."

She leaned back, tapped a finger lightly on the book. "The Puritans came here, searching, they said, for religious freedom. Of course, many of them were only looking for a place to force their beliefs and their fears on others. And in Salem, they persecuted and murdered blindly, so blindly that not one of the nineteen souls they took was the soul of a witch."

"Prejudice and fear are never clear-sighted."

"Well said. There were three among them. Women who'd chosen this place to live their lives and live their craft. Powerful women who had helped the sick and the sorry. They knew, these three, that they could no longer stay where they would, sooner or later, be accused and condemned. So the Isle of Three Sisters was created."

"Created?"

"It's said that they met in secret and cast a spell. And part of the land was torn away from the mainland. We're living on what they took from that time and that place. A sanctuary. A haven. Isn't that what you came for, Nell?"

"I came for work."

"And found it. They were known as Air and Earth and Fire. For some years they lived quietly and at peace. And alone. It was loneliness that weakened them. The one known as Air wished for love."

"We all do," Nell said quietly.

"Perhaps. She dreamed of a prince, golden and handsome, who would sweep her away to some lovely place where they would live happily and have children to comfort her. She was careless with her wish, as women can be when they yearn. He came for her, and she saw only that he was golden and handsome. She went away with him, left her haven. She tried to be a good and dutiful wife, and bore her children, loved them. But it wasn't enough for him. Under the gold, he was dark. She grew to fear him, and he fed on her fear. One night, mad with that hunger, he killed her for being what she was."

"That's a sad story." Nell's throat was dry, but she didn't lift her glass.

"There's more, but that's enough for now. Each had a sad story, and a tragic end. And each left a legacy. A child who would bear a child who would bear a child, and so on. There would come a time, it was said, when a descendant from each of the sisters would be on the island at the same time. Each would have to find a way to redeem and break the pattern set three hundred years ago. If not, the island would topple into the sea. Lost as Atlantis."

"Islands don't topple into the sea."

"Islands aren't created by three women, usually," Mia countered. "If you believe the first, the second isn't much of a stretch."

"You believe it." Nell nodded. "And that you're one of the descendants."

"Yes. As you are."

"I'm no one."

"That's him talking, not you. I'm sorry." Instantly contrite, Mia reached out and gripped Nell's hand before she could rise. "I said I wouldn't pry, and I won't. But it annoys me to hear you say you're no one. To hear you mean it. Forget all the rest for now if you must, but don't forget who and what you are. You're an intelligent woman with spine enough to make a life for herself. With a gift—magic in the kitchen. I admire you."

"I'm sorry." Struggling to settle again, Nell reached for her wine. "I'm speechless."

"You had the courage to strike out on your own. To come to a strange place and make yourself part of it."

"Courage had nothing to do with it."

"You're wrong. He didn't break you."

"He did." Despite herself, Nell's eyes filled. "I just took the pieces and ran away."

"Took the pieces, escaped and rebuilt. Can't you be proud of that?"

"I can't explain what it was like."

"You don't have to. But you will, eventually, have to recognize your own power. You'll never feel complete until you do."

"I'm only looking for a normal life."

"You can't forget the possibilities." Mia held out a hand, palm up. Waited.

Unable to resist, Nell reached out, laid her palm against Mia's. And felt the heat, a painless burn of power. "It's in you. I'll help you find it. I'll teach you," Mia stated as Nell stared dumbfounded at the shimmer of light between their palms. "When you're ready."

Ripley scanned the beach scene and saw nothing out of the ordinary. Someone's toddler was having a tantrum, and the high-pitched cranky sound of No! No! No! blasted the air.

Somebody missed his nap, she thought.

People were scattered over the sand, staking out their territory with towels, blankets, umbrellas, totes, coolers, portable stereos. Nobody just went to the beach anymore, she mused. They packed for a day on the sand the way they packed to go to Europe.

It never failed to amuse her. Every day couples and groups would haul their possessions out of their rentals and hotel rooms and set up their temporary nests on the shore. And every day they would pack everything up again and haul it, along with a good bit of sand, back again.

Holiday nomads. The Bedouins of summer.

Leaving them to it, she headed up to the village. She carried nothing but her police issue, a Swiss Army knife, and a few dollars. Life was simpler that way.

She turned on High Street, intending to spend those few dollars on a quick meal. She was off duty, as much as either she or Zack was ever off duty, and was looking forward to a cold beer and a hot pizza.

When she spotted Nell standing in front of the hotel, looking dazed, she hesitated. It was as good a time as any, she supposed, to make that friendly overture.

"Hey, Nell."

"What? Oh. Hello, Ripley."

"You look a little lost."

"No." She knew just where she was, Nell thought. At the moment, it was the only thing she was absolutely sure of. "Just a little distracted."

"Long day, huh? Listen, I'm about to grab some dinner. A little early, but I'm starved. Why don't we split a pizza? My treat."

"Oh." She continued to blink, like someone coming out of a dream.

"The Surfside makes the best pizza on the island. Well, it's the only pizza place on the island, but still . . . How're things going at the café?"

"Good." There was really nothing to do but fall into step. She couldn't think clearly and would have sworn that her fingers still tingled. "I love working there."

"You've classed up the place," Ripley commented, and angled her head to get a look at the book Nell carried. "Reading up on island voodoo?"

"Voodoo? Oh." With a nervous laugh, Nell tucked the book under her arm. "I guess if I'm living here, I ought to know . . . things."

"Sure." Ripley pulled open the door of the pizzeria. "The tourists love all that island mystique crap. When we hit the solstice, we'll be flooded with New Agers. Hey, Bart!"

Ripley gave the man behind the counter a salute and grabbed an empty booth.

It may have been early, but the place was jammed.

The jukebox was blaring, and the two video games tucked back in a small alcove shot out noise and light.

"Bart and his wife, Terry, run the place." Ripley shifted, stretched her legs out on the bench. "They've got your calzones, your pasta, and yadda yadda," she said, tossing Nell a laminated menu. "But it's really all about the pizza. You up for that?"

"Sure."

"Great. Anything you don't like on it?"

Nell scanned the menu. Why couldn't she *think*? "No."

"Even better. We'll get a large, loaded. What we don't eat, I'll take home to Zack. He'll pick off the mushrooms and onions and be grateful."

She slid out of the booth again. "Want a beer?"

"No. No, thanks. Just water."

"Coming up."

Seeing no point in waiting for table service, Ripley walked up to the counter, placed the order. Nell watched the way she joked with the long, thin man behind the counter. The way she hooked her sunglasses in the collar of her shirt. The way she stretched gorgeously toned and tanned arms out for the drinks. The way her dark hair bobbed as she turned to walk back to the booth.

The noise receded, like echoes in a dream, until it was a wash of white sound under a rising roar. Like waves cresting. As Ripley sat across from her again, Nell saw her mouth moving, but heard nothing. Nothing at all.

Then, like a door flung open, it all swarmed back.

". . . right up through Labor Day," Ripley finished, and reached for her beer.

"You're the third." Nell gripped her tingling hands together on the table.

"Huh?"

"The third. You're the third sister."

Ripley opened her mouth, then closed it again in a long, thin line. "Mia." She ground the two syllables together, then gulped down half her beer. "Don't start with me."

"I don't understand."

"There's nothing *to* understand. Just drop it." She slapped the glass back on the table, leaned forward. "Here's the deal. Mia can think, believe, whatever she wants. She can behave however she wants as long as she doesn't break the law. I don't have to buy into it. If you want to, that's your business. But I'm here for pizza and a beer."

"I don't know what I buy into. It makes you angry. It just confuses me."

"Look, you strike me as a sensible woman. Sensible women don't go around claiming to be witches descended from a trio of witches who carved an island out of a chunk of Massachusetts."

"Yes, but—"

"No buts. There's reality and there's fantasy. Let's stick with reality, because anything else is going to put me off my pizza. So, are you going to go out with my brother?"

"Go . . ." Confused, Nell pushed a hand through her hair. "Could you rewind that question?"

"Zack's working up to asking you out. You interested? Before you answer, let me say he's had all his shots, practices good personal hygiene, and though he has some annoying habits, he's reasonably well adjusted. So, think about that. I'll get the pizza."

Nell blew out a breath, sat back. She had, she decided, entirely too much to think about in one short evening.

Six

Ripley was right about the solstice. Café Book was so busy Mia had taken on two part-time clerks for the shop and added another behind the café counter.

The run on the vegetarian dishes over a two-day period kept Nell in a constant state of panic.

"We're running low on eggplant and alfalfa," she said as Peg came on shift. "I thought I'd calculated . . . Hell." She yanked off her apron. "I'm going to run down to the market, get what I can. I may have to substitute, change the menu for the rest of the day."

"Hey, whatever. Don't sweat it."

Easy for you to say, Nell thought as she rushed downstairs. She'd run out of hazelnut muffins by noon, and there was no way the chocolate chunk cookies were going to last the day at the rate they were disappearing. It was her responsibility to make certain everything in the café ran as Mia expected it to run. If she made a mistake—

In her rush to the back door, she all but ran over Lulu.

"I'm sorry. I'm sorry. I'm such an idiot. Are you all right?"

"I'll live." Lulu brushed fussily at her shirt. The girl had put in a good three weeks' work, but that didn't mean Lulu was ready to trust her. "Slow down. Just because you're off shift doesn't mean you have to run out of the place like it's on fire."

"No, I'm sorry. Is Mia—would you tell Mia I'm sorry, and that I'll be right back?"

She bolted out the door and didn't stop running until she was in the produce section of Island Market. Panic and dread churned in her stomach. How could she have been so *stupid*? Buying supplies was an essential part of her job. Hadn't she been told to expect larger crowds over the solstice weekend? A moron could have done a better job planning for it.

The pressure in her chest was making her head light, but she forced herself to think, to study her choices, to select. She filled her basket quickly, waiting in agony in the checkout line as the minutes ticked away.

Dorcas chatted at her, and Nell managed to make some responses while all the while her brain was screaming: Hurry!

She gathered the three heavy bags and, cursing herself for not thinking to bring her car, began to carry them as quickly as she could manage back to the shop.

"Nell! Nell, wait a minute." Shaking his head when she didn't respond, Zack jogged across the street. "Let me give you a hand with those."

It amazed her she didn't jump straight out of her

sneakers as he reached out, took two of the bags. "I can get them. I can do it. I'm in a hurry."

"You'll move faster if you're not weighed down. Supplies for the café?"

"Yes. Yes." She was nearly running again. She could get another salad put together. Ten minutes, fifteen tops. And prep the ingredients for sandwiches. Then she could deal with the sweets. If she could get started right away, there might not be any gap.

"I guess you're pretty busy." He didn't like the look on her face. It was so grim, so set. Like someone about to go to war.

"I should've anticipated. There's no excuse for it."

She shoved through the back door of the shop, bolted up the stairs. By the time he got to the kitchen, she was already unbagging.

"Thank you. I can take care of it now. I know what to do."

She moved like a dervish, Zack thought, her eyes glassy and face pale.

"I thought you got off at two, Nell."

"Two?" She didn't bother to look up, but continued to chop, grate, mix. "No. I made a mistake. I have to fix it. Everything's going to be all right. It's going to be fine. No one's going to be upset or inconvenienced. I should have planned better. I will next time. I promise."

"Need two sandwich specials and a veggie pita—Jeez, Nell," Peg murmured as she stepped to the doorway.

Zack put a hand on her arm. "Get Mia," he said quietly.

"Two specials and a veggie. Okay. Okay." Nell set

the bean-and-cucumber salad aside, hauled out the sandwich ingredients. "I bought some more eggplant, so we'll be fine. Just fine."

"No one's upset, Nell. You don't need to worry. Why don't you sit down a minute?"

"I only need a half hour. Twenty minutes. None of the guests will be disturbed." She picked up the orders, spun around, then jerked to a halt as Mia came in. "It's all right. Really, it's all right. We'll have plenty of everything."

"I'll take those." Peg eased by, slipped the orders out of Nell's hand. "They look great."

"I'm just putting together a new salad." There were bands around her chest, around her head. Tightening, tightening. "It won't take any time at all. Then I'll take care of the rest. I'll take care of it. Don't be angry."

"No one's angry, Nell. I think you should take a break now."

"I don't need one. I'll just finish." In desperation, she grabbed a bag of nuts. "I know I should've planned better, and I'm terribly sorry, but I'll make sure everything's perfect."

He couldn't stand it, couldn't stand to see her standing there, trembling now, her face white. "Hell with this," Zack spat, and stepped toward her.

"Don't!" She stumbled back, dropping the bag, flinging her arms up as if to guard her face from a blow. The moment she did, shame smothered panic.

"Oh, baby." Zack's voice was ripe with sympathy. She could do nothing but turn away from it.

"I want you to come with me now." Mia moved to her, took her hand. "All right? Come with me now."

Miserably embarrassed, helplessly shaken, Nell let herself be led away. Zack jammed his hands in his pockets and felt useless.

"I don't know what got into me." The fact was, the last hour was largely a blur.

"I'd say you had a big, whopping panic attack. Now sit down." Mia walked across her office, opened what Nell had taken to be a file drawer. Instead she saw a mini-fridge stocked with small bottles of water and juice.

"You don't have to talk to me," Mia said as she stepped over, gave Nell an opened bottle of water. "But you should think about talking to someone."

"I know." Rather than drinking, Nell rubbed the chilled bottle over her face. It was beyond ridiculous, she thought now, falling to pieces over eggplant. "I thought I was over it. That hasn't happened in a really long time. Months. We were so busy, and supplies were running low. It got bigger and bigger in my mind until I thought if I didn't get some more eggplant, the world was going to end." She drank now, deeply. "Stupid."

"Not stupid if you were used to being punished for something just that petty in the past."

Nell lowered the bottle. "He's not here. He can't hurt me."

"Can't he? Little sister, he's never stopped hurting you."

"If that's true, it's my problem. I'm not a dishrag anymore, I'm not a punching bag or a doormat."

"Good to hear."

She pressed her fingers to her temple. She had to let something out, she realized. Lift something off, or she'd break again. "We had a party once and ran out of martini olives. It was the first time he hit me."

Mia's face registered no shock, no judgment. "How long did you stay with him?"

There was no censure in the question, no slick surface of pity or underlying smugness. Because the question was asked in a brisk and practical tone, Nell responded in kind. "Three years. If he finds me, he'll kill me. I knew that when I left. He's an important man. Wealthy, connected."

"He's looking for you?"

"No, he thinks I'm dead. Nearly nine months now. I'd rather be dead than live the way I was living. That sounds melodramatic, but—"

"No, it doesn't. The employment forms you filled out for me? Are they safe?"

"Yes. My grandmother's maiden name. I broke some laws. Computer hacking, false statement, forged documents to get new identification, a driver's license, Social Security number."

"Computer hacking?" Lifting a brow, Mia smiled. "Nell, you surprise me."

"I'm good with computers. I used to—"

"You don't have to tell me."

"It's all right. I helped run a business, a catering business, with my mother a long time ago. I used a computer for records, invoices, what have you. Since I was going to keep the books, the records, I took some courses. When I started planning to run, I did a lot of research. I knew I'd only get one chance.

God. I've never been able to talk to anyone about it. I never thought I could."

"Do you want to tell me the rest?"

"I'm not sure. It gets stuck somewhere. Right about here," she said, tapping a fist on her chest.

"If you decide you want to, come up to the house tonight. I'll show you my gardens. My cliffs. Meanwhile, take a breather, take a walk, take a nap."

"Mia, I'd like to finish in the café. Not because I'm upset or worried. I'd just like to finish."

"All right."

The drive up the coast was breathtaking. The curving road with its sudden, unexpected twists. The steady roar of the water, the rush of wind. The memories it brought back should have disturbed her, left her shaken. Instead as Nell pushed her poor rust-bucket of a car for speed, she felt exhilarated. As if she were leaving all her excess weight on the twisted road behind her.

Maybe it was the sight of that tall white tower against the summer sky and the broody stone house beside it. They looked like something out of a storybook. Old and sturdy and wonderfully secret.

The painting she'd seen on the mainland hadn't done them justice. Oil and canvas hadn't been able to translate the sweep of the wind, the texture of the rocks, the gnarled humps of trees.

And, she thought as she rounded the last turn, the painting hadn't had Mia, standing between two vivid flows of flowers in a blue dress with her miles of red hair rioting in the wind.

Nell parked her sad car behind Mia's shiny silver convertible.

"I hope you don't take this the wrong way," Nell called out.

"I always take things the right way."

"I was just thinking, if I were a man, I'd promise you anything."

When Mia only laughed, Nell tipped back her head and tried to take in all the house at once—the dour stone, the fanciful gables, the romance of the widow's walk.

"It's wonderful. It suits you."

"It certainly does."

"But so far from everything, everyone. You're not lonely here?"

"I enjoy my own company. Are you afraid of heights?"

"No," Nell answered. "No, I'm not."

"Have a look at the headland. It's spectacular."

Nell walked with her, between the house and the tower, out to the rugged jag of cliffs that jutted over the ocean. Even here there were flowers, tough little blooms that fought their way through cracks or blossomed along the scruffy tufts of wild grass.

Below, the waves thrashed and fumed, hurling themselves against the base of the cliffs, rearing back to slap again. Beyond, the water turned a deep, deep blue and stretched forever.

"When I was a girl I would sit here, and wonder at all this. Sometimes I still do."

Nell turned her head, studied Mia's profile. "Did you grow up here?"

"Yes. In this house. It's always been mine. My parents were for the sea, and now they sail it. They're currently in the South Pacific, I think. We were always more a couple and a child than a family. They never quite adjusted to me, nor I to them, for that matter. Though we got along well enough."

With a little shrug, she turned away. "The light's been here nearly three hundred years, sending out its beam to guide ships and seamen. Still, there've been wrecks, and it's said—as one would expect it to be said of such places—that on some nights, when the wind is right, one can hear the desperate calls of the drowned."

"Not a comforting bedtime story."

"No. The sea isn't always kind."

Still she was drawn to it, compelled to stand and watch its whims, its charm and its violence. Fire, drawn to Water.

"The house came before," she added. "It was the first house built on the island."

"Conjured by magic in the moonlight," Nell added. "I read the book."

"Well, magic or mortar, it stands. The gardens are my joy, and I've indulged myself there." She gestured.

Nell looked back toward the house, blinked. The rear was a fantasy of blooms, shapes, arbors, paths. The juxtaposition between raw cliffs and lush fairyland almost made her dizzy.

"My God, Mia! It's amazing, spectacular. Like a painting. Do you do all the work yourself?"

"Mmm. Now and then I'll dragoon a strong back,

but for the most part I can handle it. It relaxes me," she said as they walked toward the first tangle of hedges. "And gratifies me."

There seemed to be dozens of secret places, unexpected turns. An iron trellis buried under wisteria, a sudden stream of pure white blossoms curling through like a satin ribbon. A tiny pool where water lilies drifted and reeds speared up around a statue of a goddess.

There were stone fairies and fragrant lavender, marble dragons and trailing nasturtium. Cheerfully blooming herbs tumbled through a rock garden and spilled toward a cushion of moss covered with starry flowers.

"No wonder you're not lonely here."

"Exactly." Mia led the way down a crooked path to a small stone island. The table there was stone as well, and stood on the base of a laughing winged gargoyle. "We're having champagne, to celebrate the solstice."

"I've never met anyone like you."

Mia lifted the bottle out of a gleaming copper pail. "I should hope not. I insist on being unique." She poured two glasses, sat, then stretched out her legs and wiggled the painted toes of her bare feet. "Tell me how you died, Nell."

"I drove off a cliff." She took her glass, drank deep. "We lived in California. Beverly Hills and Monterey. It seemed at first like being a princess in a castle. He swept me off my feet."

She couldn't sit, so she wandered the little island and drew in the scent of the flowers. She heard the tinkle of bells and saw that Mia had the same starry wind chime she'd bought for herself on her first day.

"My father was in the military. We moved around a lot, and that was hard. But he was wonderful. So handsome, and brave and strong. I suppose he was strict, but he was never unkind. I loved being with him. He couldn't always be with us, and we missed him. I loved seeing him come back, in his uniform, and the way his face would light up when my mother and I went to meet him. He was killed in the Gulf War. I still miss him."

She drew a deep breath. "It wasn't easy for my mother, but she got through it. That's when she started the catering business. She called it A Moveable Feast. Hemingway."

"Clever," Mia acknowledged. "Classy."

"She was both. She's always been a terrific cook and loved to entertain. She taught me . . . it was something we liked doing together."

"A bond between you," Mia commented. "A lovely and strong one."

"Yes. We moved to Chicago, and she built up an impressive reputation while I went to college, took care of the books, and pitched in whenever I could manage it around classes. When I was twenty-one, I started working with her full-time. We expanded and developed an elite list of clients. That's how I met Evan, at a party in Chicago we were catering. A very important party for very important people. I was twenty-four. He was ten years older, and everything I wasn't. Sophisticated, brilliant, cultured."

Mia held up a finger. "Why do you say that? You're a traveled, educated woman with an enviable skill."

"I didn't feel like any of those things when I was with him." Nell sighed. "In any case, I didn't move in the same circles. I cooked for the rich, the high-powered, the glamorous. I didn't share the table with them. He made me feel . . . grateful that he would pay attention to me. As if it were some fabulous compliment. I just realized that." She shook her head.

"He flirted with me, and it was exciting. He sent me two dozen roses the next day. It was always red roses. He asked me out, and took me to the theater, to parties, to fabulous restaurants. He stayed in Chicago for two weeks, made it clear he was staying, reorganizing his schedule, putting off his clients, his work, his life, for me. I was meant for him," Nell whispered, rubbing arms that were suddenly chilled.

"We were meant for each other. Then, when he told me that, it was thrilling. Later, not so very much later, it was terrifying. He said things to me that seemed romantic then. We'd always be together. We'd never be apart. He would never let me go. He dazzled me, and when he asked me to marry him, I didn't think twice. My mother had reservations, asked me to give it some time, but I wouldn't listen. We eloped, and I went back to California with him. The press called it the romance of the decade."

"Ah. Yes." Mia nodded as Nell turned back. "It clicks. You looked different then. More like a pampered kitten."

"I looked the way he told me to look, and behaved the way he told me to behave. At first that seemed fine. He was older, wiser, and I was new in his world. He made it seem reasonable, just as he made it seem . . . instructional when he would tell me I was slow or dull. He knew best, so if he ordered me to change my dress for another before I was permitted to go out, he was only looking out for my interests—and our image. It was very subtle at first, those digs, those demands. And whenever I pleased him, I was given a little treat. Like a puppy being trained. Here, you performed very well for company last night, have a diamond bracelet. God, it disgusts me how easily I was manipulated."

"You were in love."

"I did love him. The man I thought he was. And he was so clever, so relentless. The first time he hit me, it was a horrible shock, but it never occurred to me that I didn't deserve it. I'd been so well trained. It got worse after that, but slowly, bit by bit. My mother was killed, hardly a year after I left. Drunk driver," Nell said, her voice thickening.

"And you were alone then. I'm so sorry."

"He was so kind, so supportive. He made all the arrangements, canceled his appointments for a week to take me to Chicago. He did everything a loving husband could do. And the day we got home, he went wild. He waited until we were home, back in that house, and he'd sent all the servants away. Then he knocked me down, he raved, and slapped. He never used his fists on me, always an open hand. I think it was somehow more degrading. He accused me of having an affair with one of the mourners. A man who'd been a good friend of my parents. A kind and decent man whom I thought of as an uncle.

"Well." Surprised that her glass was empty, she walked back to the table, poured another. There were birds singing, a pretty chippering among the flowers.

"We don't need a blow-by-blow account. He abused me, I took it."

She lifted her glass, drank, steadied herself again. "I went to the police once. He had a lot of friends on the force, a lot of influence. They didn't take me seriously. Oh, I had some bruises, but nothing life-threatening. He found out, and he explained to me in ways I'd understand that if I ever humiliated him like that again, he'd kill me. I got away once, but he found me. He told me I belonged to him, and that he would never let me go. He told me that when his hands were around my throat. That if I ever tried to leave him, he'd find me, and he'd kill me. No one would ever know. And I believed him."

"But you did leave him."

"I planned it for six months, step by step, always careful not to upset him, not to give him cause to suspect. We entertained, we traveled, we slept together. We were the picture of the perfect affluent couple. He still hit me. There was always something I didn't do quite right, but I would always apologize. I pilfered cash whenever I could and hid it in a box of tampons. Pretty safe bet he wouldn't look there. I got a fake driver's license, and I hid that too. And then I was ready.

"He had a sister in Big Sur. She was having a lavish tea party. Very female. I was expected to go. That morning, I complained of a headache, which, of course, annoyed him. I was just making excuses, he said. A number of his clients would be there, and I just wanted to embarrass him by not showing up. So I said I'd go. Naturally I'd go. I would just take some aspirin and be fine. But I knew my reluctance would ensure him letting me out of the house."

She'd gotten clever, too, Nell thought now. At deceit, at pretense.

"I wasn't even frightened then. He went off to play golf, and I put what I needed in the trunk of the car. I stopped on the way and put on a black wig. I picked up the secondhand bike I'd bought the week before, and put it in the trunk. I stopped again before I got to the party, hid the bike at a spot I'd picked out. I drove down Highway 1, and I went to tea."

Nell sat down, spoke calmly while Mia sat in silence. "I made sure that a number of people noted I wasn't feeling very well. Barbara, his sister, even suggested I lie down for a bit. I waited until most of the guests had left, then I thanked her for a lovely time. She was worried about me. I looked pale. I brushed her off, and I got back in the car."

Her voice was calm, almost flat. She was just a woman telling a mildly distasteful story. One that had happened to someone else.

That's what she told herself.

"It was dark now. I needed it to be. I called Evan on my cell phone to tell him I was on my way. He always insisted on that. I got to the stretch of the road where I'd hidden the bike, and there were no other cars. I knew it could be done. Had to be. I took off my seat belt. I didn't think. I'd practiced it in my head a thousand times, so I didn't let myself think. I opened the door, still driving, swerving, going faster. I aimed for the edge. If I didn't make it, well, I was no worse off. I jumped. It was like flying. The car soared over the edge, just soared like a bird, then it crashed on the rocks, horrible sound, and it tumbled and rolled and fell into the water. I ran, back to where I had the bike and the bag. I pulled off my beautiful suit and put on old jeans and a sweatshirt, the wig. I still wasn't afraid."

No, she hadn't been afraid, not then. But now, as she relived it, her voice began to hitch. It hadn't happened to someone else after all.

"I rode down the hills, and up and down. When I got to Carmel, I went into the bus station and I paid cash for a one-way ticket to Las Vegas. When I was on the bus, and it started to move out of the station, I was afraid. Afraid he would come and stop the bus. And I would lose. But he didn't. In Vegas I got on a bus for Albuquerque, and in Albuquerque I bought a paper and read about the tragic death of Helen Remington."

"Nell." Mia reached out, closed a hand over Nell's. She doubted that Nell was aware she'd been crying for the last ten minutes. "I've never met anyone like you, either."

Nell lifted her glass and, as tears spilled down her cheeks, toasted. "Thanks."

At Mia's insistence, she spent the night. It seemed sensible after several glasses of champagne and an emotional purge to let herself be led to a big four-poster. Without protest, she slipped on a borrowed silk nightshirt, climbed between soft linen sheets, and fell instantly asleep.

And woke in the moonlit dark.

It took her a moment to orient herself, to remember where she was and what had awakened her. Mia's guest room, she thought groggily. And people were singing.

No, not singing. Chanting. It was a lovely, melodious sound, just on the edges of her hearing. Drawn to it, she rose and, still logy with sleep, moved directly to the terrace doors.

She pushed them open to a warm, whipping wind and stepped out into the pearl-white light of a three-quarter moon. The scent of flowers seemed to rise up and surround her until her head spun with it as it had with wind.

The heartbeat of the sea was fast, almost a rage, and her own raced to keep pace.

Then she saw Mia, dressed in a robe that gleamed silver in the moonlight, step out of the woods where trees swayed like dancers.

She walked to the cliffs, the silver of her gown, the flame of her hair, whirling. There, high on the rocks, she faced the sea and lifted her arms to star and moon.

The air filled with voices, and the voices seemed filled with joy. With her eyes dazzled with wonder, stinging with tears she didn't understand, Nell watched as light, shimmering beams of it, slid down from the sky to brush the tips of Mia's fingers, the ends of her flying hair.

For a moment it seemed she was like a candle, straight, slim, incandescent, lighting the edge of the world.

Then there was only the sound of the surf, the pearl-white light of the waning moon, and a woman standing alone on a cliff.

Mia turned, walked back toward the house. Her head lifted, and her eyes met Nell's. Held. Held.

She smiled quietly, moved into the shadow of the house. And was gone.

Seven

It was still dark when Nell tiptoed down to Mia's kitchen. The house was huge, and took some maneuvering. Though she wasn't sure what time Mia rose for the day, she brewed a pot of coffee for her hostess and wrote a note of thanks before she left.

They would have to talk, Nell thought as she drove home in the softening light of pre-dawn. About a number of things. And they would, she decided, as soon as she could figure out where to begin.

She could almost convince herself that what she'd seen in the moonlight had been nothing more than a champagne-induced dream. Almost. But it was too clear in her mind to be a dream.

Light spilling out of stars like liquid silver. A rising wind full of song. A woman glowing like a torch.

Such things should be fantasy. But they weren't . . . if they were real and she had a part in them, she needed to know what it all meant.

For the first time in nearly four years she felt absolutely steady, absolutely calm. For now, that was enough.

By noon she was too busy to think about more than the job at hand. There was a paycheck in her pocket, and a day off around the corner.

"Iced hazelnut cappuccino, large." The man who ordered leaned on the counter as Nell began to work. She judged him as mid-thirties, health-club fit, and a mainlander.

It pleased her that she could already, with very decent accuracy, spot a mainlander. And feel the slightly smug reaction of an islander.

"So, how much aphrodisiac do you put in those cookies?" he asked her.

She glanced at him. "I'm sorry?"

"Ever since I tasted your oatmeal raisin, I haven't been able to get you out of my mind."

"Really? I could've sworn I put all the aphrodisiac in the macadamia nut."

"In that case I'll take three," he said. "I'm Jim, and you've seduced me with your baked goods."

"Then you'd better stay away from my three-bean salad. It'll ruin you for all other women."

"If I buy all the three-bean salad, will you marry me and have my children?"

"Well, I would, Jim, but I've taken a sacred oath to stay free to bake for all the world." She capped his coffee, bagged it. "Do you really want those cookies?"

"You bet. How about a clambake? Some friends

and I are sharing a house. We're going to do in some clams tonight."

"Tonight a clambake, tomorrow a house in the suburbs and a cocker spaniel." She rang him up, took his money with a smile. "Better safe than sorry. But thanks."

"You're breaking my heart," he said, and sighing heavily, he walked away.

"Oh, man, he is so cute." Peg craned her neck to keep him in sight until he'd gone downstairs. "You're really not interested?"

"No." Nell took off her apron, rolled her shoulders.

"Then you wouldn't mind if I gave him a shot?"

"Be my guest. There's plenty of bean salad in the fridge. Oh, and Peg? Thanks for being understanding about yesterday."

"Hey, everybody gets weird now and then. See you Monday."

See you Monday, Nell thought. It was just that simple. She was a member of the team, she had friends. She had deflected an overture from an attractive man without getting the jitters.

In fact, she enjoyed it, the way she used to enjoy such things. The day might come when she didn't feel compelled to deflect.

One day she might go to a clambake with a man and some of his friends. Talk, laugh, enjoy the companionship. Light, casual friendships. She could do that. There couldn't be any serious relationships in her future even if she could learn to handle one emotionally.

She was, after all, still legally married.

But now, just now, that fact was more of a safety net than the nightmare it had been. She was free to be whoever she wanted to be, but not free enough to be bound again, not to any man.

She decided to treat herself to an ice cream cone, and a detour to the beach. People called her by name as she passed, and that was a quiet thrill.

As she crossed the sand, she spotted Pete Stahr and his infamous dog. Both looked sheepish as Zack stood beside them, hands on hips.

He never wore a hat as he'd advised her to do when gardening. As a result his hair was lighter at the tips and almost always disordered from the ocean breeze. He rarely wore his badge either, she noted, but the gun rode in the holster at his hip almost casually.

It occurred to her that if he had stopped by the café and asked her to go to a clambake, she might not have brushed him off.

When the dog lifted his paw hopefully, Zack shook his head, pointed to the leash that Pete held. Once the leash was secured, man and dog walked off, heads hung low.

Zack turned, the sun bouncing off his dark glasses. And she knew instinctively that he was looking at her. Nell braced herself and went to him.

"Sheriff."

"Nell. Pete let his dog off the leash again. Mutt smells like a fish house. Ice cream's dripping."

"It's hot." Nell licked at the cone and decided to get it over with. "About yesterday—"

"Feeling better?"

"Yes."

"Good. Gonna share any of that?"

"What? Oh. Sure." She held out the cone, felt a little tingle in the blood when he licked just above her fingertips. Funny, she thought, she hadn't gotten any tingles from the cute guy with the clambake. "You're not going to ask?"

"Not as long as you'd rather I didn't." Yes, he'd looked at her. And had seen the deliberate squaring of her shoulders before she started toward him. "Why don't you walk with me a while? There's a nice breeze off the water."

"I was wondering . . . what does Lucy do all day when you're out upholding the law?"

"This and that. Dog chores."

That tickled a laugh out of her. "Dog chores?"

"Sure. Some days a dog's got to hang around the house, roll in the grass, and think long thoughts. Other times, she comes on in to the office with me, when she's in the mood. Swims, chews up my shoes. I'm thinking about buying her a brother or sister."

"I was thinking about getting a cat. I'm not sure I'd be able to train a puppy. A cat would be easier. I saw a notice on the board in the market for free kittens."

"The Stubens girl's cat. They've still got one or two left, last I heard. Their place is over on Bay. White saltbox, blue shutters."

She nodded, stopped. Impulse, she reminded herself, had served her well so far. Why stop following it? "Zack, I'm going to try out a new recipe tonight. Tuna and linguini with sun-dried tomatoes and feta. I could use a guinea pig."

He lifted her hand, took another taste of her dripping ice cream. "Well, it happens I don't have any pressing plans for tonight, and as sheriff I do what I can to serve the needs of the community. What time?"

"Is seven all right with you?"

"Works for me."

"Fine, I'll see you then. Bring an appetite," she said as she hurried away.

"Count on it," he said, and tipped down his dark glasses to watch her dash back toward the village.

At seven, the appetizers were ready, and the wine was chilling. Nell had bought a secondhand table and planned to spend part of her day off scraping and painting it. But for now she covered the scarred wood and peeling green paint with a sheet.

It stood on her back lawn, along with the two old chairs she'd picked up for a song. They weren't particularly pretty at the moment, but they had potential. And they were hers.

She'd set the table with two plates, two bowls, and wineglasses—all purchases from the island thrift shop. Nothing matched, but she thought the result was cheerful and charming.

And as far from the formal china and heavy silver of her past as possible.

Her garden was coming along well, and the tomato and pepper plants, the squash and zucchini, would all be put in the following morning.

She was very close to broke again, and completely content.

"Well, now, doesn't that look sweet?"

Nell turned to see Gladys Macey standing on the edge of her lawn, gripping an enormous white purse.

"Just as pretty as a picture."

"Mrs. Macey. Hello."

"Hope you don't mind me dropping by this way. I'd've called, but you haven't got a phone."

"No, of course not. Um, can I get you something to drink?"

"No, no, don't you fuss. I've come by on business."

"Business?"

"Yes, indeed." Her tidy helmet of black hair barely moved as she gave a sharp nod. "Carl and I got our thirtieth anniversary coming up last part of July."

"Congratulations."

"You can say that again. Two people stick it out for three decades, it's saying something. Since it is, I want a party, and I just finished telling Carl he's not getting out of putting on a suit for it, either. I was wondering if you'd take care of putting the refreshments together for me."

"Oh. Well."

"I want a catered affair," Gladys said definitely. "And I want it spiffy. When my girl got married, two years ago last April, we hired a caterer from the mainland. Too snippy for my taste, and too dear for Carl's, but we didn't have much to choose from. I don't figure you're going to get snippy with me or charge me a king's ransom for a bowl of cold shrimp."

"Mrs. Macey, I appreciate you thinking of me, but I'm not set up to cater."

"Well, you got time, don't you? I've got a list here of how many people and the kind of business I'm thinking of." She pulled a file folder out of the enormous purse, pushed it into Nell's hand. "I want to have it right at my house, and I've got my mother's good china and so forth. You just look over what I've put together there, and we'll talk about it tomorrow. You come on by the house tomorrow afternoon."

"I'd certainly like to help you. Maybe I can . . ." She looked down at the folder, saw that Gladys had marked it "Thirtieth Anniversary" and had added a heart with her initials and Carl's in the center.

Touched, she tucked the folder under her arm. "I'll see what I can do."

"You're a nice girl, Nell." Gladys glanced over her shoulder at the sound of a car, lifted her eyebrows as she recognized Zack's cruiser. "And you've got good taste. You come on by tomorrow, and we'll talk this out. Have a nice dinner now."

She strolled toward her car, stopping to say a few words to Zack. She gave him a pat on the cheek, noted the flowers in his hand. By the time she was behind the wheel, she was planning who she'd call first to spread the news that Zachariah Todd was sparking the little Channing girl.

"I'm a little late. Sorry. We had a fender bender in the village. Put me behind."

"It's all right."

"I thought you might like these for your garden."

She smiled at the pot of Shasta daisies. "They're perfect. Thanks." She took them, set them beside her kitchen stoop. "I'll get the wine and the appetizers."

He walked into the kitchen behind her. "Something smells great."

"Once I got started, I tried out a couple of different recipes. You've got your work cut out for you."

"I'm up for it. Now what's this?" He crouched down, stroked a finger over the smoke-gray kitten circled on a pillow in the corner.

"That's Diego. We're living together."

The kitten mewed, stretched, then began to bat at Zack's shoelaces. "You've been busy. Cooking, buying furniture, getting a roommate." Scooping up Diego, he turned toward her. "Nobody's going to find any moss on you, Nell."

He stood there, big and handsome, with a gray kitten nuzzling at his shoulder.

He'd brought her white daisies in a plastic pot.

"Oh, damn." She set her tray of appetizers down again, took a breath. "I might as well get this over with. I don't want you to get the wrong impression about dinner, and . . . things. I'm very attracted to you, but I'm not in a place where I can act on my feelings. It's only fair to tell you that up front. There are good reasons for it, but I'm not willing to get into them. So, if you'd rather just go, no hard feelings."

He listened soberly, rubbing a finger between the kitten's silky ears. "I appreciate you spelling that out for me. Seems a shame to waste all this food, though." He plucked a stuffed olive from the tray, popped it into his mouth. "I'll just hang around, if it's all the same to you. Why don't I take the wine outside?"

He picked up the bottle and, still carrying Diego, bumped the screened door with his hip. "Oh, and in the interest of fair play, I'll tell you I'll be nudging you out of that place you're in."

With that said, he held the door open. "You want to bring those on out?"

"I'm not as easy a nudge as you might think."

"Honey, there's nothing easy about you."

She picked up the tray, sailed by him. "I take that as a compliment."

"It was meant as one. Now, why don't we have some wine, relax, and you can tell me what Gladys Macey was after."

When they were seated, she poured the wine, and he settled the kitten in his lap. "I thought, being sheriff, you'd know all there is to know about what's going on."

"Well." He leaned over the tray, selected a gnocchi. "I can deduce, seeing as I'm a trained observer. There's a file on your counter, marked with Gladys's handwriting, which leads me to believe she's planning on an anniversary party. And, as I'm sitting here, heading straight toward heaven with whatever the hell it is I just put in my mouth—and knowing Gladys is a shrewd lady—I'd suppose she's wanting you to cater it. How'd I do?"

"Dead on."

"Are you going to do it?"

"I'm going to think about it."

"You'd do a great job." He plucked another selection from the tray, examined it suspiciously. "Any mushrooms in this thing? I hate mushrooms."

"No. We're fungi-free tonight. Why would I do a good job?"

"I said great job." He popped it in his mouth. Some creamy cheese and herbs in a thin and flaky pastry. "Because you cook like a magician, you look like an angel, and you're as organized as a computer. You get things done, and you've got style. How come you're not eating any of this?"

"I want to see if you live first." When he only grinned and kept eating, she sat back and sipped her wine. "I'm a good cook. Put me in a kitchen, and I rule the world. I'm presentable, but I don't look like an angel."

"I'm the one looking at you."

"I'm organized," she continued, "because I keep my life simple."

"Which is another way of saying you're not going to complicate it with me."

"There you go, dead on again. I'm going to get the salad."

Zack waited until her back was turned before he let his amusement show. "Easy enough to ruffle her feathers," he said to Diego, "when you know where to scratch. Let me tell you something I've learned over the years about women. Keep changing the rhythm, and they'll never know what to expect next."

When Nell came back out, Zack launched into the story of the pediatrician from Washington and the stockbroker from New York who'd bumped fenders outside the pharmacy on High Street.

He made her laugh, put her gently at ease again. Before she knew it, she was telling him about various kitchen feuds in restaurants where she'd worked.

"Temperaments and sharp implements," she said. "A dangerous combination. I once had a line chef threaten me with an electric whisk."

Because dusk was falling, he lit the squat red candle she'd set on the table. "I had no idea there was so much danger and intrigue behind those swinging doors."

"And sexual tension," she added, twirling linguini onto her fork. "Smoldering looks over simmering pots of stock, broken hearts shattering in the whipping cream. It's a hotbed."

"Food's got all that sensuality. Flavor, texture, scent. This tuna's getting me pretty worked up."

"So, the dish passes the audition."

"It's great." Candlelight suited her, he thought. It put little gold lights in those deep blue pools. "Do you make this stuff up, or collect recipes, what?"

"Both, I like to experiment. When my mother . . ." She trailed off, but Zack merely picked up the wine bottle, topped off their glasses. "She liked to cook," Nell said simply. "And entertain."

"My mother—well, we'll just say the kitchen wasn't her best room. I was twenty before I realized a pork chop wasn't supposed to bounce if you dropped it. She lived on an island most of her life, but as far as she was concerned tuna came out of a can. She's hell with numbers, though."

"Numbers."

"Certified public accountant—retired now. She and my dad bought themselves one of those big tin cans on wheels and hit the great American highway about a year ago. They're having a terrific time."

"That's nice." And so was the unmistakable affection in his voice. "Do you miss them?"

"I do. I'm not going to say I miss my mother's cooking, but I miss their company. My father used to sit out on the back porch and play the banjo. I miss that."

"The banjo." It sounded so charming. "Do you play?"

"No. I never could get my fingers to cooperate."

"My father played the piano. He used to—" She stopped herself again, realigning her thoughts as she rose. "I could never get my fingers to cooperate either. Strawberry shortcake for dessert. Can you manage it?"

"I can probably choke some down, just to be polite. Let me give you a hand."

"No." She waved him down before he could rise. "I've got it. It'll just take me . . ." She glanced down as she cleared his plate, saw Diego sprawled belly-up in apparent ecstasy in his lap. "Have you been sneaking that cat food from the table?"

"Me?" All innocence, Zack picked up his wineglass. "I don't know what makes you think that."

"You'll spoil him, *and* make him sick." She started to reach down, scoop up the kitten, then realized that considering Diego's location, the move was just a tad too personal. "Put him down a while so he can run around and work off that tuna before I take him inside."

"Yes, ma'am."

She had the coffee on and was about to slice the cake when he came through the door with the serving bowl.

"Thanks. But guests don't clear."

"They did in my house." He looked at the cake, all fluffy white and succulent red. And back at her. "Honey, I've got to tell you, that's a work of art."

"Presentation's half the battle," she said, pleased. She went still when he laid his hand over the back of hers. Nearly relaxed again when he simply moved hers to widen the size of the slice.

"I'm a big patron of the arts."

"At this rate Diego's not the only one who's going to be sick." But she cut him a piece twice the size of her own. "I'll bring the coffee."

"I should tell you something else," he began as he picked up the plates, then held the door for her again. "I plan on touching you. A lot. Maybe you could work on getting used to it."

"I don't like being handled."

"I didn't plan to start out that way." He walked to the table, set down the cake plates, and sat. "Though handling, on both sides, can have some satisfying results. I don't put marks on women, Nell. I don't use my hands that way."

"I'm not going to talk about that," she answered curtly.

"I'm not asking you to. I'm talking about me, and you, and the way things are now."

"Things aren't any way now—like that."

"They're going to be." He scooped up some cake, sampled it. "God, woman, you sell this on the open market, you'd be a millionaire inside of six months."

"I don't need to be rich."

"Got your back up again," he observed and kept right on eating. "I don't mind that. Some men look for a woman who'll buckle under, tow the line, whatever." He shrugged, speared a fat strawberry. "Now, me, I wonder why. It seems that would get boring fast for both parties involved. No spark there, if you know what I mean."

"I don't need sparks either."

"Everybody does. People who set them off each other every time they turn around, though, well, that would just wear you out." Something told her he didn't wear out—or wear down—easily.

"But if you don't light a spark now and again," he went on, "you miss the sizzle that comes with it. If you cooked without spice or seasoning, you'd come up with something you could eat, but it wouldn't satisfy."

"That's very clever. But there are some of us who stay healthier on a bland diet."

"My great-uncle Frank." Zack gestured with his fork before he dived into the cake again. "Ulcers. Some said it came from pure meanness, and it's hard to argue. He was a hardheaded, miserly Yankee. Never married. He preferred curling up in bed with his ledgers rather than a woman. Lived to be ninety-eight."

"And the moral of the story?"

"Oh, I wasn't thinking of morals. Just Great-uncle Frank. We'd go to dinner at my grandmother's the third Sunday of every month when I was a boy. She made the best damn pot roast—you know, the kind circled around with the little potatoes and carrots? My mother didn't inherit Gran's talent with a pot roast. But, anyway, Great-uncle Frank would come and eat rice pudding while the rest of us gorged. The man scared the hell out of me. I can't look at a bowl of rice pudding to this day without getting the shakes."

It must be some kind of magic, she decided, that made it so impossible not to relax around him. "I think you're making half that up."

"Not a single word. You can look him up in the registry at the Island Methodist Church. Francis Morris Bigelow. Gran, she married a Ripley, but was a Bigelow by birth and older sister to Frank. She lived to just past her hundredth birthday herself. We tend to be long-lived in my family, which is why most of us don't settle down to marriage and family until into our thirties."

"I see." Since he'd polished off his cake, Nell nudged hers toward him and wasn't the least bit surprised when he took a forkful. "I'd always thought New England Yankees were a taciturn breed. You know—ayah, nope, maybe."

"We like to talk in my family. Ripley can be short-winded, but then she isn't overly fond of people as a species. This is the best meal I've had since Sunday dinner at my gran's."

"That is the ultimate compliment."

"We'd finish it off exactly right if we were to take a walk on the beach."

She couldn't think of a reason to say no. Maybe she didn't want to.

The light was fading, going deep at the edges. A needle-thin and needle-bright swath of light swept over the horizon, and a blush of pink gleamed in the west. The tide had gone out, leaving a wide avenue of dark, damp sand that was cool underfoot. The surf teased it, foaming out in ribbons while narrow-bodied birds with legs like stilts pecked for their supper.

Others strolled the beach. Almost all couples now, Nell noted. Hand-in-hand or arm-in-arm. As a precaution, she'd tucked her own hands in her pockets after she'd pried off her shoes and rolled up her jeans.

Here and there were stockpiles of driftwood that would be bonfires when full dark fell. She wondered what it would be like to sit by the flames with a group of friends. To laugh and talk of nothing important.

"Haven't seen you go in yet."

"In?"

"The water," Zack explained.

She didn't own a bathing suit, but saw no reason to say so. "I've waded in a couple of times."

"Don't swim?"

"Of course I can swim."

"Let's go."

He scooped her up so fast her heart stuck between her chest and her throat. She could barely manage to breathe, much less scream. Before full panic had a chance to bloom, she was in the water.

Zack was laughing, spinning her away from an oncoming wave to take the brunt of it himself. She was sliding, rolling, fighting to gain her feet when he simply nipped her at the waist and righted her.

"Can't live on Three Sisters without being baptized." Tossing his wet hair back, he pulled her farther out.

"It's freezing."

"Balmy," he corrected. "Your blood's just thin yet. Here comes a good-size one. You'd better hold on to me."

"I don't want to—" Whatever she did or didn't want, the sea had its own ideas. The wave hit, knocked her off her feet, and had her legs tangling with his.

"You idiot." But she was laughing as she surfaced. When the air hit her skin, she quickly dunked neck-deep again. "The sheriff's supposed to have more sense than to jump in the ocean fully dressed."

"I'd've stripped down, but we haven't known each

other long enough." He rolled over on his back, floating lazily. "The first stars are coming out. There's nothing like it. Nothing in the world like it. Come on."

The sea rocked her, made her feel weightless as she watched the color of the sky change. As the tone deepened bit by bit, stars winked to life.

"You're right, there's nothing like it. But it's still freezing."

"You just need a winter on the island to thicken your blood up." He took her hand, a quiet connection as they drifted an armspan apart. "I've never spent more than three months at a time off-island, and that was for college. Had three years of that, and couldn't take it anymore. I knew what I wanted anyway. And that's what I've got."

The rhythm of the waves, the sweep of the sky. The quiet flow of his voice coming out of the dark.

"It's a kind of magic, isn't it?" She sighed as the cool, moist breeze whispered over her face. "To know what you want, to just know. And to get it."

"Magic doesn't hurt. Work helps. So does patience and all kinds of things."

"I know what I want now, and I'm getting it. That's magic to me."

"The island's never been short on that commodity. Comes from being founded by witches, I suppose."

Surprise tinged her voice. "Do you believe in that sort of thing?"

"Why wouldn't I? Things are, whether people believe in them or not. There were lights in the sky last night that weren't stars. A person could look the other way, but they'd still have been there."

He planted his feet again, lifting her until she stood facing him with the water fuming at waist level. Night had drifted in, and the lights of the stars sprinkled over the surface of the water.

"You can turn away from something like this." He skimmed her wet hair away from her face, left his hands resting there. "But it's still going to be there."

She pressed a hand against his shoulder as his mouth lowered to hers. She meant to turn away, told herself to turn away, to where everything was safe and ordered and simple.

But the spark he'd spoken of snapped inside her, warm and bright. She curled her fingers into his wet shirt and let herself feel.

Alive. Cold where the air whisked over her skin. Hot in the belly where desire began to build. Testing herself, she leaned into him, parted her lips under his.

He took his time, as much for himself as for her. Sampling, savoring. She tasted of the sea. Smelled of it. For a moment, in the star-drenched surf, he let himself drown.

He eased back, let his hands run over her shoulders, down her arms before he linked his fingers with hers. "Not so complicated." He kissed her again, lightly, though the lightness cost him. "I'll walk you home."

Eight

"*Mia, can I talk to you?*"

With ten minutes until opening, Nell hurried down from the café. Lulu was already ringing up mail orders and shot her a typically suspicious look while Mia continued to put the finishing touches on a new display.

"Of course. What's on your mind?"

"Well, I . . ." The store was small enough, and empty enough, that Lulu would hear every word. "I thought we could go up to your office for a minute."

"Here's fine. Don't let Lulu's sour face put you off." Mia built a small tower out of new summer releases. "She's worried you're going to ask me for a loan, and naturally I'm such a soft touch—along with my soft head—I'll let you rob me blind so I'll die penniless and alone in some filthy gutter. Isn't that right, Lu?"

Lulu merely sniffed and jabbed keys on the cash register.

"Oh, no, it's not about money. I'd never ask for—after you've been so—damn it." Nell fisted her hands in her hair, tugged until the pain stiffened her spine. Deliberately now, she turned to face Lulu.

"I understand you're protective of Mia, and you have no reason to trust me. I came out of nowhere, with nothing, and haven't been here a month. But I'm not a thief, and I'm not a user. I've carried my weight here, and I'm going to keep carrying it. And if Mia asked me to try serving sandwiches while standing on one foot and singing 'Yankee Doodle Dandy,' I'd give it my best shot. Because I came out of nowhere, with nothing, and she gave me a chance."

Lulu sniffed again. "Wouldn't mind seeing that myself. Likely bring in fresh trade, too. Never said you didn't carry your weight," she added. "But that doesn't mean I won't keep a watch on you."

"Fine with me. I understand."

"All this sentimental bonding." Mia dabbed at her lashes. "It's ruining my mascara." She stepped back from her display, nodded in approval. "Now what do you need to talk to me about, Nell?"

"Mrs. Macey is having an anniversary party next month. She'd like to have a fancy catered affair."

"Yes, I know." Mia turned to straighten stock on the shelves. "She'll drive you a bit crazy with changes and suggestions and questions, but you can handle it."

"I didn't agree to . . . We just discussed it yesterday. I didn't realize you'd heard she asked already. I wanted to talk to you first."

"It's a small island, word gets around. You don't need to talk to me about an outside catering job, Nell."

She made a mental note to order more ritual candles. There'd been a run on them during the solstice, and they were running unacceptably low on Passion and on Prosperity. Which just showed, she supposed, where many people's priorities lay.

"Your free time is your time," she added.

"I just wanted to tell you that if I did the job for her, it wouldn't interfere with my work here."

"I should hope not, particularly since I'm giving you a raise." She glanced at her watch. "Time to open, Lu."

"You're giving me a raise?"

"You've earned it. I hired you at a probationary salary. You're officially off probation." She unlocked the door, walked over to turn on the music system. "How was your dinner with Zack the other night?" Mia asked with amusement. "A small island, as I said."

"It was fine. It was just a friendly dinner."

"Good-looking boy," Lulu said. "Quality, too."

"I'm not trying to lure him into temptation."

"Something wrong with you, then." Lulu tipped down her silver frames and peered over them. It was a look she was particularly proud of. "If I were a few years younger, I'd be setting out lures. Got a great pair of hands on him. Bet he knows how to use them."

"No doubt," Mia said mildly. "But you're embarrassing our Nell. Now where was I? Gladys's anniversary, check. Raise, check. Dinner with Zack, check." She paused, tapped a fingertip against her lips. "Ah, yes. Nell, I wanted to ask. Do you have a religious or political objection to cosmetics or jewelry?"

She could find nothing more constructive to do than huff out her breath. "No."

"That's a relief. Here." She took off the silver dangles on her ears, handed them to Nell. "Wear these. If anyone asks where you got them, they come from All That Glitters, two doors down. We like to promote other merchants. I'll want them back at the end of your shift. Tomorrow you might try a little blush, maybe some lipstick, eyeliner."

"I don't have any."

"I'm sorry." Mia held up a hand, laid the other on her heart, and staggered to the counter for support. "I feel a little faint. Did you say you don't own *any* lipstick?"

The corner of Nell's mouth turned up and brought out a hint of dimples. "I'm afraid not."

"Lulu, we have to help this woman. It's our duty. Emergency supplies. Hurry."

Lips quivering with what might have been a smile, Lulu hauled a large cosmetic bag out from under the counter. "She's got good skin."

"A blank canvas, Lu. A blank canvas. Come with me," she ordered Nell.

"The café—the regulars will be coming in any second."

"I'm fast, and I'm good. Let's move." She grabbed Nell's hand, hauled her upstairs and into the rest room.

Ten minutes later, Nell was serving her first customers and wearing silver earrings, peach-toned lipstick, and expertly smudged slate eyeliner.

There was something, she decided, very comforting about feeling female again.

She took the catering job and crossed her fingers. When Zack asked if she'd like to go for an evening sail, she said yes and felt powerful.

When a customer asked if she could bake a cake in the shape of a ballerina for a birthday party, she said absolutely. And spent her fee on a pair of earrings.

As word spread, she found herself agreeing to provide picnic-style food for a party of twenty for July Fourth and ten box lunches for a private day sailor.

At her kitchen table, Nell spread out notes, files, menus. Somehow she was becoming her own cottage industry. Which, she thought, looking around, seemed perfectly apt.

She glanced up at the brisk knock on the door, and happily welcomed Ripley in.

"Got a minute?"

"Sure. Sit down. Do you want anything?"

"I'm fine." Ripley sat, then picked up Diego when he sniffed at her shoes. "Meal planning?"

"I've got to organize these catering jobs. If I had a computer . . . Well, eventually. I'd sell my soul for a professional blender. And both feet for a commercial-grade food processor. But for now, we make do."

"Why don't you use the computer at the bookstore?"

"Mia's already doing enough."

"Whatever. Listen, I've got this date for the Fourth. A date with potential," she added. "Casual because Zack and I are more or less on duty right through the night. Fireworks and beer sometimes make people a little too festive for their own good."

"I can't wait to see the fireworks. Everyone says they're spectacular."

"Yeah, we do a hell of a job on them. The thing is, this guy—he's a security consultant on the mainland—he's been hitting on me, and I decided to let him land one."

"Ripley, that's so romantic, I can barely catch my breath."

"He's really built, too," Ripley continued as she scratched Diego's ears, "so the after-fireworks fireworks potential is fairly high, if you get me. I've been in a downswing sexwise. Anyway, we talked about having this night picnic deal, and somehow I got stuck with doing the food. Since I think I'd like to jump this guy's bones, I don't want to poison him first."

"A romantic picnic for two." Nell made notes. "Vegetarian or carnivore?"

"Carnivore. Not too fancy, okay?" Ripley plucked a grape from the bowl of fruit on the table, popped it in her mouth. "I don't want him more interested in the food than me."

"Check. Pickup or delivery?"

"This is so cool." Cheerful, she popped another grape. "I can pick it up. Can we keep it under fifty?"

"Under fifty. Tell him to pick up a nice crisp white wine. Now if you had a picnic hamper . . ."

"We've got one somewhere."

"Perfect. Bring that by and we'll pack it up. You'll be set, foodwise. The bone-jumping portion of the evening is up to you."

"I can handle that. You know, if you want, I can ask around, see if anybody's got a secondhand computer they want to sell."

"That would be great. I'm glad you came by." She rose, got out two glasses. "I was afraid you were annoyed with me."

"No, not with you. That particular subject annoys me. It's a bunch of bullshit, just like . . ." She scowled through the screened door. "Well, speak of the devil."

"I try not to. Why borrow trouble?" Mia sailed in, laid a note on the counter. "Phone message for you, Nell. Gladys and her newest party brainstorm."

"I'm sorry. You don't have time to run over here this way. I'll speak to her again and I promise I'll see about getting a phone."

"Don't worry about it. I wanted a walk or I'd have left it for tomorrow. And I'll have a glass of that lemonade."

"She needs a computer," Ripley said flatly. "She won't use the one at the store because she doesn't want to hassle you."

"Ripley. Mia, I'm perfectly fine working this way."

"She can certainly use the computer at the store when it's free," Mia said to Ripley. "And she doesn't need you running interference between her and me."

"She wouldn't if you weren't trying to push your psychic hooey on her."

" 'Psychic hooey' sounds like the name of a second-rate rock band and has nothing to do with what I am. But even that's better than blind, stubborn denial. Knowledge is always better than ignorance."

"You want ignorance?" Ripley said, getting to her feet.

"Stop! Stop it." Jittering inside, Nell put herself between them. "This is ridiculous. Do you two always go at each other this way?"

"Yes." Mia picked up a glass, sipped delicately. "We enjoy it, don't we, Deputy?"

"I'd enjoy popping you one more, but then I'd have to arrest myself."

"Try it." Mia angled her chin. "I promise not to press charges."

"Nobody hits anybody. Not in my house."

Instantly contrite, Mia set down her glass, rubbed a hand down Nell's arm. It was rigid as steel. "I'm sorry, little sister. Ripley and I irritate each other, a long-standing habit. But we shouldn't put you in the middle. We shouldn't put her in the middle," Mia said to Ripley. "It isn't fair."

"Something we agree on. How about this? If we run into each other here, it's a neutral zone. You know, like Romulan space. No warfare."

"Romulan Neutral Zone. I've always admired your grip on popular culture. Agreed." She even picked up the second glass, passed it to Ripley. "There. You see, Nell, you're a good influence on us already." She handed the third glass to Nell. "To positive influences."

Ripley hesitated, cleared her throat. "Okay, okay, what the hell. Positive influences."

And standing in a loose circle, they tapped glasses. They rang like a bell, one bright peal as a shower of light fountained up from that connection of second-hand kitchenware.

Mia smiled slowly as Nell let out a laughing gasp.

"Damn it," Ripley muttered, and gulped down lemonade. "I hate that."

Celebrants streamed to the island for the Fourth. Red, white, and blue flags snapped from the rails of the ferries as they chugged to the mainland and back. Banners and bunting swagged the eaves of the storefronts on High Street, waving cheerfully as tourists and islanders alike jammed the streets and beaches.

For Nell it was anything but a holiday, but that didn't prevent her celebrational mood as she delivered orders. She not only had a job she loved, she had a business she could be proud of.

Independence Day, she thought. She was going to make it hers.

For the first time in nine months, she began to plan for a future that included bank accounts, mail delivery, and personal possessions that couldn't be stuffed into a duffel or backpack at a moment's notice.

A normal, functioning life, she thought as she paused by the display window of Beach Where. The mannequin was wearing breezy summer slacks with bold blue and white stripes and a gauzy white top that scooped low at the breasts. Strappy white sandals as fun as they were impractical adorned its feet.

Nell bit her lip. Her pay was burning a hole in the pocket of her ancient jeans. That had always been her problem, she reminded herself. If she had ten dollars, she could find a way to spend nine of it.

She'd learned how to save and scrimp and resist. How to make five dollars stretch like elastic.

But she hadn't had anything new, anything pretty, in so long. And Mia had been hinting, not quite so gently of late, that she should spruce up a bit on the job.

Plus, she had to make some sort of a showing of herself for the catering sideline. If she was going to be a businesswoman, she should dress the part. On the island that meant casual. Still, casual could mean attractive.

On the other hand, it would be more practical, more sensible, to save the money and invest it in kitchen tools. She needed a food processor more than she needed sandals.

"Are you going to listen to the good angel or the bad angel?"

"Mia." Vaguely embarrassed at being caught daydreaming over a pair of shoes, Nell laughed. "You startled me."

"Great sandals. On sale, too."

"They are?"

Mia tapped the glass just below the Sale sign. "My favorite four-letter word. I smell possibilities, Nell. Let's shop."

"Oh, but I really shouldn't. I don't need anything."

"You really do need work." Mia tossed back her hair, took Nell's elbow in a firm grip, much like a mother with a stubborn child. "Shopping for shoes has nothing to do with need, and everything to do with lust. Do you know how many pair of shoes I own?"

"No."

"Neither do I," she said as she strong-armed Nell into the shop. "Isn't that wonderful? They have those slacks in a candy-cane pink. They'd look fabulous on you. Size six?"

"Yes. But I really need to save for a good food processor." Despite herself she reached out to finger the material of the slacks that Mia pulled off the rack. "They're so soft."

"Try them with this." A brief hunt turned up what Mia considered the perfect top, a clingy white halter. "Don't forget to lose the bra. You've got little feet. Six there, too?"

"Yes, actually." Nell took a discreet peek at the price tags. Even with the sale it was more than she'd spent on herself in months. She was stuttering protests as Mia shoved her behind a dressing room curtain.

"Trying doesn't mean buying," she whispered to herself over and over as she stripped down to her practical cotton panties.

Mia was right about the pink, she thought as she slipped into the slacks. The bright color was an instant mood lifter. But the halter, well, that was another matter. It felt . . . decadent to wear something so close-fitting without a bra. And the back—she turned to look over her shoulder. There basically wasn't a back.

Evan would never have allowed her to wear something so revealing and casually suggestive.

Even as the thought popped into her mind, Nell cursed herself.

"Okay, back up and erase," she ordered herself.

"How you doing in there?"

"Fine. Mia, it's an adorable outfit, but I don't think . . ."

Before she could finish, Mia whisked open the curtain and stood, the sandals in one hand while she tapped her lip with the finger of her free hand. "Perfect. Girl-next-door sexy, casual, chic. Add the shoes. I saw this little bag. Just the thing. Be right back."

It was like being marched through a campaign by a veteran general, Nell thought. And she, a mere foot soldier, couldn't seem to do anything but follow orders.

Twenty minutes later, her habitual jeans, T-shirt, and sneakers were tucked into a shopping bag. What was left of her cash was stuffed into a palm-size purse that she wore cross-body and at the hip of her new slacks, which flapped softly around her legs in the frisky breeze.

"How do you feel?"

"Guilty. Great." Unable to resist, Nell wiggled her toes in her new sandals.

"That'll do. Now, let's buy some earrings to go with it."

Nell abandoned all resistance. Independence Day, she reminded herself. She fell for the rose quartz drops the minute she saw them.

"What is it about earrings that makes you feel so confident?"

"Body adornments show that we're aware of our bodies and expect others to be aware as well. Now, let's take a walk on the beach and get some reaction."

Nell fingered the pale pink stones swinging from her ears. "Can I ask you a question?"

"Go ahead."

"I've been here a month now, and in all that time I haven't seen you with anyone. A date, I mean. A male companion."

"I'm not interested in anyone at the moment." Mia held the flat of her hand above her brow to skim the beach. "Yes, there was someone. Once. But that was another phase of my life."

"Did you love him?"

"Yes, I did. Very much."

"I'm sorry. I shouldn't pry."

"It's no secret," Mia said lightly. "And the wound's long healed. I like being on my own, in control of my destiny, and all the little day-to-day decisions and choices. Coupling requires a certain amount of unselfishness. I'm a selfish creature by nature."

"That's not true."

"Generosity has levels." Mia began to walk, lifting her face to the breeze. "And it's not synonymous with altruism. I do what suits me, which stems from self-interest. I don't find that something to apologize for."

"I've had personal acquaintance with the selfish. You may do what suits you, Mia, but you'd never deliberately hurt anyone. I've watched you with people. They trust you because they know they can."

"Not causing harm is a responsibility that comes from what I've been given. You're the same."

"I don't see how that can be. I've been powerless."

"And because of it you have empathy for those in pain and those who despair. Nothing happens to us without purpose, little sister. What we do because of it, what we do about it, is the key to who and what we are."

Nell looked out to sea, to the boats gliding, the jet skiers racing, the swimmers gleefully riding the waves. She could turn away, she thought, from what she was being told and what would be asked of her. She could have a calm and normal life here.

Or she could have more.

"The night I stayed at your house, the night of the

solstice, when I saw you on the cliffs I told myself I was dreaming."

Mia didn't turn, just continued to look calmly out over the ocean. "Is that what you want to believe?"

"I'm not entirely sure. I dreamed of this place. Even when I was a child, I had dreams. For a long time I ignored them, or blocked them out. When I saw the painting—the cliffs, the lighthouse, your house—I had to come here. It was like finally being allowed to come home."

She looked back at Mia. "I used to believe in fairy tales. Then I learned better. The hard way."

And so, Mia thought, had she. No man had ever lifted his hand to her, but there were other ways to bruise and scar. "Life isn't a fairy tale, and the gift carries a price."

A shudder raced up Nell's spine. Easier, she thought, to turn away. Safer, to run away.

A boat out to sea let off a sky rocket. The gleeful shriek of sound ended on a burst of light that showered little specks of gold as it shattered. A delighted roar went up from the beach. She heard a child call out in wonder.

"You said you would teach me."

Mia let out a breath she hadn't been aware she was holding. So much rested on this. "And so I will."

They turned together to watch the next rocket soar.

"Are you going to stay to watch the fireworks?" Nell asked her.

"No, I can see them from my cliffs. And it's less frantic. Besides, I hate being a fifth wheel."

"Fifth wheel?"

"Ladies." Zack strolled up. It was one of the rare

times he had his badge pinned to his shirt. "I'm going to have to ask you to move along. Two beautiful women standing on the beach creates a safety hazard."

"Isn't he cute?" Mia reached up to cup his face and give him a noisy kiss. "When I was in third grade, I planned to marry him and live in a sand castle."

"You might've clued me in on it."

"You were sweet on Hester Burmingham."

"No, I just had lustful feelings for her shiny red Schwinn. The Christmas I turned twelve, I got one of my own from Santa, and Hester ceased to exist in my little world."

"Men are bastards."

"Maybe, but I've still got the bike, and Hester's got twin girls and a minivan. Happy ending all around."

"Hester still checks out your butt when you're walking away," Mia told him, delighted when his mouth dropped open. "And on that note, I take my leave. Enjoy the fireworks."

"That woman always manages to get the last word," Zack muttered. "By the time a man untangles his tongue, she's gone. And speaking of getting a man's tongue tangled, you look great."

"Thanks." She held her arms out to the side. "I splurged."

"In all the right places. Let me cart that for you." He slipped the shopping bag out of her hand.

"I need to take it home, and see to some things."

"I can walk in that direction for a bit. I was hoping to see you around today. I heard you've been busy, delivering potato salad all over the island."

"I must've made twenty gallons of it, and enough fried chicken to deplete the poultry population for the next three months."

"Don't suppose you've got any left."

Her dimples winked. "I might."

"It's been hard to find time to eat—traffic control, beach patrol. I had to sit on a couple of kids who thought it'd be fun to toss firecrackers in trash cans and watch them blow up. I've confiscated enough firecrackers, roman candles, and bottle rockets to start my own insurrection. And all that on two hot dogs."

"That doesn't seem fair."

"No, it doesn't. I spotted a couple of your box lunches. Looked to me like there was apple pie in there."

"You have good vision. I could probably hunt up a few drumsticks, scrape together a pint of potato salad. I might even be able to manage a slab of apple pie and donate it to a hardworking public servant."

"Might even be tax deductible. I've got to supervise the fireworks display." He stopped at the end of the street. "We usually get it started right around nine." He set her shopping bag down to run his hands up her bare arms. "Things start thinning out around nine-thirty, nine-forty-five. I lost the toss with Ripley, so I've got to take the last patrol, cruise around the island to make sure nobody's set their house on fire. Maybe you'd like to take a drive."

"I might."

His fingers danced up and down her back. "Do me a favor? Put your hands on my shoulders. I'd like you to have a grip on me when I kiss you this time."

"Zack—" She took two careful breaths. "I'd like you to have a grip on me this time, too."

He wrapped his arms around her. She circled his neck. For a moment they stood, lips a breath apart while her system shivered with anticipation.

Mouths brushed, retreated, brushed again. It was she who moaned, she who crushed her lips to his on a hot spurt of hunger.

She hadn't let herself want. Even when he'd stirred those dormant needs to life, she'd been careful not to want. Until now.

She wanted the strength of him, the press of that hard, male body. She wanted the ripe flavor of him and the heat.

The silky dance of tongues, the teasing nip of teeth, the edgy thrill of feeling a heart pound against her own. She let out a little gasp of pleasure when he changed the angle of the kiss.

And dived in again.

She set off aches in him that throbbed like pulse beats. Quiet sounds of need hummed in her throat and burned in his blood. Her skin was like hot satin, and the feel of it under his hands sent erotic images through his brain—desires, demands that belonged to the dark.

Dimly he heard another rocket burst, and the shouts of approval from the beach behind them.

He could have her inside her cottage in two minutes. Naked and under him in three.

"Nell." Breathless, churning toward desperate, he broke the kiss.

And she smiled at him. Her eyes were dark, filled with trust and pleasure.

"Nell," he said again, and lowered his forehead to

hers. There were times when you took, he knew. And times when you waited. "I've got to make my rounds."

"All right."

He picked up her bag, handed it to her. "You'll come back?"

"Yes. I'll come back." She was floating on air as she spun around and headed for her cottage.

Nine

"*Power," Mia told Nell, "carries with it responsibility*, a respect for tradition. It must be tempered with compassion, hopefully intelligence, and an understanding of human flaws. It is never to be used carelessly, though there is room for humor. Above all, it must never be used to harm."

"How did you know you were . . . How did you know what you were?"

"A witch." Mia sat back on her heels. She was weeding her garden. She was wearing a shapeless dress of grass green with deep pockets in the skirt, thin floral gardening gloves, and a wide-brimmed straw hat. At the moment, she couldn't have looked less like the witch she professed to be.

"You can say the word. It's not illegal. We're not the pointed-hat-wearing, broomstick-riding cacklers that much of fiction drew us to be. We're people—housewives, plumbers, businesswomen. How we live is a personal choice."

"Covens?"

"Another personal choice. I've never been much of a joiner myself. And most who form groups or study the Craft are just looking for a pastime, or an answer. There's nothing wrong with that. Calling yourself a witch and holding rituals is one thing, being one is another."

"How do you know the difference?"

"How do I answer you, Nell?" She leaned forward again, neatly snipping off deadheads. "There's something inside you, burning. A song in your head, a whisper in your ear. You know these things as well as I do. You just didn't recognize them."

The deadhead went along with her weeds into a basket.

"When you peel an apple, haven't you ever thought if you could finish it without breaking the chain, you'd have a wish granted or gather good luck? Snapped a wishbone? Crossed your fingers? Little charms," Mia said, sitting back again, "old traditions."

"It can't be as simple as that."

"As simple as a wish, as complex as love. As dangerous, potentially, as a lightning bolt. Power is risk. It's also joy."

She picked up one of the deadheads, cupped it gently in her hands. Opening them again, she offered Nell a sunny yellow blossom.

Delighted, fascinated, Nell twirled it in her fingers. "If you can do this, why do you let any of them die?"

"There's a cycle, a natural order. It's to be respected. Change is necessary." She rose, picked up her basket of weeds and dead flowers, and carried it to a composter. "Without it there'd be no progress, no rebirth, no anticipation."

"One flower blooms off to make room for another."

"A lot of the Craft is philosophy. Would you like to try something more practical?"

"Me?"

"Yes, a simple spell. A stir of the air, I think, considering. Besides, it's a warm day, and a breeze would be welcome."

"You want me to . . ." Nell made a circling motion with her finger. "Stir the air?"

"It's a matter of technique. You need to focus. Feel the air moving over your face, your body. See it in your mind, rippling, turning. You can hear it, the music of it."

"Mia."

"No. Put doubts aside and think of those possibilities. Focus. It's a simple goal. It's all around you. You only have to stir it. Take it in your hands," she said, lifting her own, "and say the words. 'Air is breath and breath is air. Stir it round from here to there. Spin a breeze and spin it lightly.' As you will, Nell, so mote it be. Say the words, one times three."

Mesmerized, Nell repeated them. Felt the faintest flutter across her cheek. Said them again and saw Mia's hair lift. On the third count, Mia's voice joined hers.

The wind spun around them, a private carousel of air, cool and fragrant with a happy little hum. The same hum sounded inside her as Nell turned, circling round and round, her short cap of hair dancing.

"It feels wonderful! You did it."

"I gave it the last nudge." Mia laughed as her dress

billowed out. "But you got it started. Very well done for your first time. Now quiet it again. Use your mind. Visualize it going still. That's it. Good. You picture things well."

"I've always liked to draw moments in my head," Nell said, breathless now. "You know, images that appeal or that I want to remember. It's sort of like that. Wow, I'm dizzy." She sat straight down on the ground. "I felt a tingling inside, not unpleasant. Almost like you do when you're thinking—really thinking—about sex."

"Magic is sexy." Mia dropped down beside her. "Especially when you hold the power. Have you been doing a lot of thinking about sex?"

"I didn't give it a thought for eight months." Steadier now, Nell shook back her hair. "I wasn't sure I'd ever want to be with a man again. Since the Fourth, I've been doing a lot of thinking about sex. The kind of thinking that makes you very itchy."

"Well, I've been there. Why don't you do something about it? Scratch the itch?"

"I thought, I'd assumed, that after the fireworks last week, Zack and I would end up in bed. But after we drove around and he finished his patrol, he took me home. Kissed me good night at the door, the kind of kiss that lifts the top of your head off and spins it around. Then he went home."

"I don't suppose it occurred to you to drag him inside, toss him on the floor, and rip his clothes off."

The idea made Nell chuckle. "I can't do things like that."

"A minute ago you didn't think you could conjure a breeze either. You have the power, little sister.

Zachariah Todd is the kind of man who's willing to put that power in your hands, to give you the choice of time and place. If there was a man like that I was attracted to, and who was attracted to me, I'd do something about that power."

She felt the tingle again, the stir inside her this time. "I wouldn't know how to begin."

"Visualize, little sister," Mia said wickedly. "Visualize."

Zack couldn't think of a better way to spend a Sunday morning than skinny-dipping with the girl he loved. The water was cool, the sun warm, and the inlet private enough to allow for such activities.

They discussed taking a sail later, and the adoration in her beautiful brown eyes told him she'd follow him anywhere. He stroked her, sent her into a wiggle of delight before they swam companionably through the crisp and quiet water.

When a man had a female so uncomplicatedly devoted, Zack figured, he had it all.

Then she gave a yip of excitement, splashed a stream of water in his face, and headed to shore. Zack watched his boon companion desert him for the woman standing on the rough bank.

Lucy bounded onto the bank and straight into Nell, knocking her back two full steps and drenching her with seawater and doggie kisses.

Zack listened to Nell's laughter, watched her scrub her hands enthusiastically over Lucy's wet fur. Maybe a man who had a pretty dog didn't have quite everything, he decided.

"Hey. How's it going?"

"It's going good." Shoulders, she thought. The man had amazing shoulders. "How's the water?"

"Close to perfect. Come on in, see for yourself."

"Thanks, but I don't have a suit with me."

"Me either." He flashed a grin. "Which is why I didn't follow Lucy's example."

"Oh." Her gaze shot down, then immediately back up to hover six inches over his head. "Well. Ha."

Visualize, Mia had told her. But this didn't seem quite the appropriate time.

"I promise not to look. You're already wet."

"All the same, I think I'll stay out here."

Lucy dived back in, retrieved a mangled rubber ball. After scrabbling back to shore again, she deposited it neatly at Nell's feet.

"Wants to play," Zack told her. And so did he.

Obliging, Nell picked up the ball and tossed it. Before it hit the surface, Lucy was leaping in pursuit.

"Pretty good arm. We've got a softball game coming up in a couple of weeks if you're interested." He drifted closer to the bank as he spoke.

Nell scooped up the ball Lucy retrieved, heaved it again. "Maybe. I was thinking about trying out another recipe."

"Is that so?"

"The catering's turning into an actual enterprise. If I want to expand on it, I need to be able to offer a variety of dishes."

"I'm a strong believer in capitalism, so anything I can do to help."

She looked down. He had such a nice face, she thought. She would just concentrate on that and wouldn't think about the rest of him. Right now. "I appreciate that, Sheriff. I've been playing it by ear so far, but I think it's time to put together an actual list, with pricing and services. If I do all that, formalize it, I have to apply for a business license."

That wouldn't be a problem, she assured herself. She was clear.

"It's going to keep you busy."

"I like being busy. There's nothing worse than not being able to do anything with your time or your interests." She shook her head. "And don't I sound dull and boring?"

No, but she had sounded grim. "How do you feel about recreation?"

"I approve of recreation." Her eyebrows lifted as he hooked a hand lightly around her ankle. "And just what is that?"

"I call it the long arm of the law."

"You're too nice to pull me in after I've come over here to offer to feed you."

"No, I'm not." He gave her foot a playful little tug. "But I'm willing to give you a chance to strip first."

"That's considerate of you."

"My mother raised me right. Come on in and play, Nell." He glanced back at Lucy, who was busy paddling around with the ball in her mouth. "We've got a chaperone."

Why not? she thought. She wanted to be with him. Even more, she wanted to be the kind of woman who *could* be with him. A woman confident and open enough to do something fun and foolish like tossing off her clothes and diving in.

The grin she sent him was quick and careless. As she toed off her shoes, he treaded water. "I changed my mind. I'm going to watch," he warned her. "I'd tell you I wouldn't peek, but I'd be lying."

"Do you lie?"

"Not if I can help it." His gaze lowered as she gripped the hem of her T-shirt. "So I'm not going to tell you I'll keep my hands off you once you get in here. I want you wet and naked, Nell. I just plain want you."

"If I wanted you to keep your hands off me, I wouldn't be here." She took a deep breath, started to peel off her shirt.

"Sheriff Todd! Sheriff Todd!"

"There is no God," Zack grumbled as the lovely glimpse of creamy flesh vanished under Nell's hastily tugged-down shirt. "Out here," he called. "Is that you, Ricky?" To Nell, he said, "It'll only take me two, three minutes to drown him. Just stand by."

"Yes, sir, Sheriff."

A towheaded boy of about ten scrambled across the rocky slope, his freckled face pink with excitement. He gave Nell a hasty nod. "Ma'am. Sheriff, my mom said I was to come right over and tell you. The tenants in the Abbott rental are having a big fight. There's screaming and crashing and cursing and everything."

"Is that Dale Abbott's or Buster's place?"

"Buster's, Sheriff. The one right across from ours. Mom says it sounds like the man in there's beating the woman something fierce."

"I'm on my way. Go on back. Go straight home and in the house."

"Yes, sir."

Nell stayed where she was. She saw a blur of tanned, muscled body as Zack levered himself out of the water. "Sorry, Nell."

"No, you need to go. You need to help her." It felt as though there were a thin glaze over her brain as she watched him hitch on jeans. "Hurry."

"I'll be back as soon as I can."

He left her there, hated leaving her there with her hands gripping each other tightly, and bolted up the steps to get a shirt.

He was at the Abbott rental in under four minutes. A handful of people edged the street while the sounds of shouting and breaking glasses poured out of the house. A man Zack didn't recognize jogged up to him as he approached the deck stairs.

"You're the sheriff. I'm Bob Delano, renting the place next door. I tried seeing what I could do, but the doors're locked. I thought about breaking one in, but they said you were on the way."

"I'll take care of it, Mr. Delano. Maybe you could keep those people back."

"Sure. I've seen that guy, Sheriff. Big sonofabitch. You want to watch yourself."

"I appreciate it. Get on back now." Zack pounded a fist on the door. Though he'd have preferred to have Ripley with him, he hadn't risked waiting for her to answer his beeper call. "This is Sheriff Todd. I want you to open the door, and open it now." Something shattered inside, and a woman began to wail. "If this door isn't open in five seconds, I'm kicking it in."

The man came to the door. Delano was right. He was one big sonofabitch. Six-four, maybe, and a good two seventy-five. He looked hungover and mad as piss.

"What the hell do you want?"

"I want you to step back, sir, and keep your hands where I can see them."

"You got no right coming in here. I'm renting this place paid in full."

"Your rental agreement doesn't give you leave to destroy property. Now back up."

"You're not coming in here without a warrant."

"Bet?" Zack said softly. His hand shot out, lightning-quick, gripped the man's wrist, and twisted. "Now, you want to take a swing at me," he continued in the same mild tone, "we'll add resisting arrest and assaulting an officer to the mix. More paperwork, but I get paid for it."

"By the time my lawyer's done, I'm going to own this fucking island."

"You're welcome to call him—from down at the station house." Zack cuffed him and looked around with relief as he heard Ripley pounding up the stairs.

"Sorry. I was all the way over on Broken Shell. What's this? Domestic dispute?"

"And then some. This is my deputy," Zack informed his prisoner. "Take my word, she can clean your clock. Put him in the back of the cruiser, Ripley. Get his particulars, read him his rights."

"What's your name, sir?"

"Fuck you."

"Okay, Mr. Fuck You, you're under arrest for . . ." She glanced back at Zack, who was already moving through the broken glass and crockery to the woman sitting on the floor, holding her face in her hands and sobbing.

"Destruction of private property, disturbing the peace, assault."

"You got that? Now unless you want me to kick your ass in front of all these nice people, we'll just walk to the cruiser and take a little drive. You have the right to remain silent," she continued, giving him a helpful shove to get him going.

"Ma'am." She was late thirties, Zack estimated. Probably pretty when her lip wasn't split and her brown eyes weren't blackened. "I need you to come with me. I'll take you to a doctor."

"I don't need a doctor." She curled into herself. Zack noted shallow cuts on her arms, gifts from flying glass. "What's going to happen to Joe?"

"We'll talk about that. Can you tell me your name?"

"Diane, Diane McCoy."

"Let me help you up, Ms. McCoy."

Diane McCoy sat hunched in a chair with an ice bag held to her left eye. She continued to refuse medical assistance. After offering her a cup of coffee, Zack pulled his own chair from behind his desk, hoping the move would put her more at ease.

"Ms. McCoy, I want to help you."

"I'm okay. We'll pay for the damages. You just have the rental agency make up a list and we'll pay for it."

"That's something we'll need to see to. I want you to tell me what happened."

"We just had a fight, that's all. People do. You didn't need to lock Joe up. If there's a fine, we'll pay it."

"Ms. McCoy, you're sitting there with your lip bleeding, your eye black, and cuts and bruises all over your arms. Your husband assaulted you."

"It wasn't like that."

"What was it like?"

"I asked for it."

Even as Ripley let out a vicious stream of air across the room, Zack leveled a warning glance. "You asked him to hit you, Ms. McCoy? To knock you down, to bloody your lip?"

"I aggravated him. He's under a lot of pressure." The words tumbled out, slurred a bit from her swollen lip. "This is supposed to be a vacation, and I shouldn't've nagged at him that way."

She must have sensed Ripley's furious disapproval as she turned her head, stared defiantly. "Joe works hard, fifty weeks a year. The least I can do is leave him alone on his vacation."

"It seems to me," Ripley countered, "the least he could do is keep from punching you in the face on your vacation."

"Ripley, get Ms. McCoy a glass of water." And shut up. He didn't have to say the last with his mouth, when his expression said it so clearly. "What started the trouble, Ms. McCoy?"

"I guess I got up on the wrong side of the bed. Joe was up late, drinking. A man's entitled to sit in front of the TV with a few beers on his vacation. He left the place a mess—beer cans, spilled chips all over the rug. It irritated me, and I started on him the minute he was awake. If I'd shut up when he told me to, none of this would've happened."

"And not shutting up when you were told gave him the right to use his fists on you, Ms. McCoy?"

She powered up. "What happens between a husband and wife is nobody's business but theirs. We shouldn't have broken things, and we'll pay for them. I'll clean the place up myself."

"Ms. McCoy, they have counseling programs back in Newark," Zack began, "and shelters for women who need them. I can make some calls, get you some information."

Her eyes might have been swollen, but they could still flash fury. "I don't need any information. You can't keep Joe locked up if I don't press charges, and I won't."

"You're wrong there. I can keep him locked up for disturbing the peace. And the property owners can press charges."

"You'll just make it worse." Tears began to fall. She took the paper cup Ripley offered her and gulped at the water. "Don't you see? You'll just make it worse. He's a good man. Joe's a good man, he's just got a short fuse is all. I said we'd pay. I'll write you a check. We don't want any trouble. I'm the one who made him mad. I threw things at him, too. You're going to have to lock me up along with him. What's the point?"

What was the point? Zack thought later. He hadn't been able to reach her, and he wasn't egotistical enough to think he was the first to try. He couldn't help when help was rejected. The McCoys were caught in a cycle that was bound to end badly.

And all he could do was remove the cycle from his island.

It took half the day to straighten out the mess. A check for two thousand satisfied the rental company. A cleaning crew was already in place by the time the McCoys had packed up. Zack waited, saying nothing as Joe McCoy loaded suitcases and coolers into the back of a late-model Grand Cherokee.

The couple got in from opposite sides. Diane wore big sunglasses to hide the damage. They both ignored Zack as he got into the cruiser and followed them to the ferry.

He stayed there, watching, until the Jeep and the people inside it were no more than a dot on their way to the mainland.

He hadn't expected that Nell would have waited for him, and decided it was just as well. He was too depressed and far too angry to talk to her. Instead he sat in the kitchen with Lucy, nursed a beer. He was considering indulging in a second when Ripley came in.

"I don't get it. I just don't *get* women like that. The guy's got a hundred fifty pounds on her, but it's *her* fault he bashed her face. And she believed it."

She got out a beer for herself, jerking the bottle at him as she twisted off the cap.

"Maybe she needs to."

"Oh, like hell, Zack. Like hell." Still simmering, she dropped into the chair across from him. "She's healthy, she's got a brain. What does she gain hooking herself to a guy who uses her for a punching bag when the mood strikes him? If she'd pressed charges, we could've held him long enough for her to pack her bags and get gone. We should've held him anyway."

"She wouldn't have left. It wouldn't have made one damn bit of difference."

"Okay, you're right. I know it. It just burns me, that's all." She sipped her beer, watching him. "You're thinking about Nell. You figure it was like that for her?"

"I don't know what it was like for her. She doesn't talk about it."

"Have you asked?"

"If she wanted to tell me, she would."

"Well, don't snap my head off." Ripley propped her feet on the chair beside her. "I'm asking you because I know you, big brother. If you've got a thing for her, and the thing turns into a *big* thing, you're never going to be square with it unless you have the story. Without the story, you can't help, and when you can't help, it drives you nuts. You're brooding right now because you couldn't help—to your satisfaction—a woman you'd never seen before and won't see again. It's that Good Samaritan gene of yours."

"Isn't there someone else on the island you can go annoy?"

"No, because I love you best. Now, instead of having another beer, why don't you take Luce and go for a sail? Still plenty of daylight yet, and it'll clear your head and improve your disposition. You're just no fun to be around when you're broody."

"Maybe I will."

"Good. Go. Odds of a second crisis in one day are slim to none, but I'll take a cruise around, just in case."

"Okay." He got up and after a moment's hesitation leaned down and kissed the top of her head. "I love you best, too."

"Don't I know it." She waited until he got to the door. "You know, Zack, whatever Nell's story is, there's one key difference between her and Diane McCoy. Nell got gone."

Ten

On Monday the incident at the Abbott rental was the talk of the village. Everyone had had time to form an opinion, particularly those who hadn't witnessed the event.

"Buster said they'd busted up every blessed knick-knack in the place. I'll have some of that lobster salad, Nell, honey," Dorcas Burmingham said, then went straight back to gossiping with her companion. She and Biddy Devlin, Mia's third cousin once removed and the proprietor of Surfside Treasures, had a standing lunch date at the café every Monday at twelve-thirty.

"I heard Sheriff Todd had to forcibly remove the man from the premises," Biddy expounded. "At *gun-point*."

"Oh, Biddy, no such thing. I talked to Gladys Macey, who had it straight from Anne Potter who sent for the sheriff in the first place that Zack had his gun holstered right along. Can I have an iced mocha with that salad, Nell?"

"Domestic disputes are one of the most dangerous calls for a policeman," Biddy informed her. "I read that somewhere. My, that soup smells divine, Nell. I don't believe I've ever had gazpacho before, but I'm going to have to try a cup, and one of your brownies."

"I'll bring your lunch out to you," Nell offered, "if you'd like to get a table."

"Oh, that's all right, we'll wait for it." Dorcas waved the offer away. "You've got enough to do. Anyway, I heard that even though that brute bloodied that poor woman's lip and blackened her eye, she stuck by him. Wouldn't press charges."

"It's a crying shame is what it is. Odds are her father beat on her mother, so she grew up seeing such things and thinking that's just what happens. It's a cycle. That's what the statistics say. Abuse spawns abuse. I'll wager you, if that woman had grown up in a loving home, she wouldn't be living with a man who treated her that way."

"Ladies, that'll be thirteen eighty-five." Nell's head throbbed like a bad tooth, and her nerve endings stretched thin as hair strands while the two women went through their weekly routine of whose turn it was to pay.

It was always playful, and usually it amused Nell. But now she wanted them gone. She wanted to hear no more about Diane McCoy.

What did they know about it? she thought bitterly. These two comfortable women with their comfortable lives? What did they know about fear and helplessness?

It wasn't always a cycle. She wanted to scream it. It wasn't always a pattern. She'd had a loving home, with parents who'd been devoted to each other, and to her. There had been arguments, irritation, annoyances. While voices may have been raised, fists never had.

She had never been struck in her life before Evan Remington.

She wasn't a goddamn statistic.

By the time the women headed off to a table, thin, sharp-edged bands of steel had locked themselves around Nell's temples. She turned blindly to the next customer and found Ripley studying her.

"You look a little shaky, Nell."

"Just a headache. What can I get you today?"

"Why don't you get yourself an aspirin? I'll wait."

"No, it's fine. The fruit-and-cabbage salad's good. It's a Scandinavian recipe. I've had positive feedback on it."

"Okay, I'm game. I'll take an iced tea with it. Those two," she added, nodding toward Biddy and Dorcas. "They chatter like a couple of parrots. It'd give anybody a headache. I guess everybody's been yakking about the trouble yesterday."

"Well." She wanted a dark room, an hour's quiet. "Big news."

"Zack did everything he could to help that woman. She didn't want to be helped. Not everyone does."

"Not everyone knows what to do with an offer of help, or who they can trust to give it."

"Zack can be trusted." Ripley laid her money on

the counter. "Maybe he plays it low key, that's his way. But when push comes to shove, he stands up. You ought to do something for that headache, Nell," she added, and took her lunch to a table.

She didn't have time to do more about it than swallow a couple of aspirin. Peg was late, rushing in full of apologies and with a sparkle in her eye that told Nell a man had been responsible for her tardiness.

As Nell had an appointment with Gladys Macey to—please, God—finalize the menu for the anniversary party, she had to rush home, gather her notes and files.

The headache had escalated to nightmare territory by the time she knocked on Gladys's door.

"Nell, I've told you, you don't have to knock. You just call out and walk in," Gladys said and pulled her inside. "I'm just so excited about this. I watched this program on the Home and Garden channel just the other day. Got me all sorts of ideas to talk over with you. I think we ought to string those little white lights through my trees, and put those luminaries—with little hearts on the bags—along the walk and the patio. What do you think?"

"Mrs. Macey, I think you should have whatever you want. I'm really just the caterer."

"Now, honey, I think of you as my party coordinator. Let's sit down in the living room."

The room was spotlessly clean, as if dust was a sin against nature. Every stick of furniture matched, with the pattern in the sofa picked up in the valance of the window treatments and the narrow border of wallpaper that ran just under the ceiling.

There were two identical lamps, two identical chairs, two identical end tables. The rug matched the curtains, the curtains matched the throw pillows.

All the wood was honey maple, including the cabinet of the big-screen TV, which was currently running a Hollywood gossip program.

"I've got a weakness for that kind of show. All those famous people. I love seeing what clothes they're wearing. You just sit down," Gladys ordered. "Make yourself comfortable. I'm going to get us a nice cold Coke, then we'll roll up our sleeves and dive right in."

As she had the first time she'd toured Gladys's house for pre-party plans, Nell found herself bemused. Every room was tidy as a church pew and as rigidly organized as a furniture showroom floor. Magazines were fanned precisely on the coffee table, and offset by an arrangement of silk flowers in the exact tones of mauve and blues as the upholstery.

The fact that the house managed to be friendly said more, to Nell's mind, about the occupants than the decor.

Nell sat, opened her files. She knew Gladys would bring the tea in pale green glasses that matched her everyday dishes and would set them on blue coasters.

There was, she thought, a comfort in knowing that.

She began to read over her notes, then felt her stomach hitch at the chirpy voice of the program host.

"Last night's gala brought out the glitter and the glamour. Evan Remington, power broker extraordinaire and attorney to the stars, looked as sensational as one of his own clients in Hugo Boss. Though Remington denies rumors of a romance between him and his companion for the evening, the delectable Natalie Winston—who simmered in a beaded sheath by Valentino—sources in the know say differently.

"Remington was widowed only last September when his wife, Helen, apparently lost control of her car while driving back to their home in Monterey. Her Mercedes sedan crashed over the cliffs on Highway 1. Her body, sadly, was never recovered. *Hollywood Beat* is happy to see Evan Remington back in stride after this tragic event."

Nell was on her feet, her breath short and shallow. Evan's face seemed to fill the wide screen, every handsome line, every strand of golden hair.

She could hear his voice, clear and terrifyingly calm. *Do you think I can't see you, Helen? Do you think I'll let you go?*

"I didn't mean to take so long, but I thought you might appreciate someone else's baking for a change. I just made this pound cake yesterday. Carl packed away nearly half of it. I can't think where that man puts it. Why, if I ate a fraction of what he—"

Tray in hand, Gladys stopped, her happy chatter shifting instantly to surprised concern when she saw Nell's face. "Honey, you're so pale. What's wrong?"

"I'm sorry. I'm sorry, I'm not feeling well." Panic was an icy poker jabbing through her belly. "Headache. I don't think I can do this now."

"Of course not. Poor thing. Don't you worry. I'm going to drive you home and tuck you right into bed."

"No, no. I'd rather walk. Fresh air. I'm so sorry,

Mrs. Macey." Nell fumbled with her files, almost sobbing when they slipped through her trembling fingers. "I'll call you. Reschedule."

"I don't want you to think a thing of it. Nell, sweetheart, you're shaking."

"I just need to go home." With a last terrified glance at the television screen, she bolted for the door.

She forced herself not to run. When you ran, people noticed you, and they wondered. They asked questions. Fitting in, that was essential. Blending. Doing nothing to draw attention. But even as she ordered herself to breathe slow and steady, the air wheezed in her lungs, clogged there until she was gulping for it.

Do you think I'll let you go?

Sweat ran cold and clammy on her skin, and she smelled her own fear. The edges of her vision blurred as she shot a single wild look over her shoulder. The minute she was through the door of her cottage, the nausea hit, a bright bite of pain.

She stumbled to the bathroom, was hideously ill. When she was empty, she lay on the narrow floor and waited for the shaking to pass.

When she could stand again, she peeled off her clothes, leaving them in a heap as she stepped into the shower. She ran the hot water, as hot as she could bear, imagining the spray penetrating her skin until it warmed her icy bones.

Wrapped in a towel, she crawled into bed, pulled the covers over her head, and let herself slide into oblivion.

Diego climbed agilely up the bedskirt, stretched out alongside her. And lay still and silent as a sentry.

She wasn't sure how long she slept, but she woke as if from a long illness that had left her body heavy and tender and her stomach raw. She was tempted simply to roll back into sleep and stay there. But that would solve nothing.

It was doing that got her through, and always had.

She sat on the edge of the bed, like an old woman testing bone and balance. The image of Evan's face could float back into her mind if she let it. So she closed her eyes, let it form.

That, too, was a kind of test.

She could look at him, would look at him. Remember what had been, and what had changed. To deal, she reminded herself, with what had happened.

For comfort, she gathered the kitten into her lap and rocked.

She had run again. After almost a year, the sight of him on a television screen had terrorized her to the point of blind flight. Had made her ill and stripped away every bit of the hard-won armor she'd built until she'd been a quivering, quaking mass of panic.

Because she had allowed it. She let him have that hold on her. No one could change that but herself. She'd found the courage to run, Nell told herself. Now she had to find the courage to stand.

Until she could think of him, until she could say his name without fear, she wasn't free.

She held the picture of him in her mind, imagined it breaking apart, her will a hammer against glass. "Evan Remington," she whispered, "you can't touch me now. You can't hurt me. You're over, and I'm just beginning."

The effort exhausted her, but she set Diego on the floor, then pushed herself to her feet, dragged on a sweatshirt and shorts. She would go back to work, design and evaluate her menu. It was time to figure out how to set up an office of sorts in the little bedroom.

If Gladys Macey wanted a party coordinator, that's just what she was going to get.

She had dropped the file when she bolted into the cottage, and now she gathered up all the scattered notes, magazine clippings, and carefully written menu selections and carried them into the kitchen. She was mildly surprised to see that the sun still shone.

It felt as if she'd slept for hours.

The clock on the stove told her it was barely six. Time enough to reevaluate the Macey job proposal, to create a comprehensive list of menu and service selections for what she was going to call Sisters Catering.

She would take Mia up on the offer of the store computer and design a look for her handouts, her business cards. She had to calculate a budget, set up books.

No one was going to take her seriously unless she took herself seriously first.

But when she put her files down and looked around, she wondered why the prospect of putting on water for coffee seemed so far out of her scope.

The knock on the front door had her spinning around. Her first thought when she saw Zack through the screen was, not now. Not yet. She hadn't had time to gather herself back to what she needed to be.

But he was already opening the door, already studying her across the short distance from the front of the cottage to the back. "Are you all right, Nell?"

"Yes."

"You don't look all right."

She could imagine how she looked. "I wasn't feeling well earlier." Self-conscious, she scooped a hand through her hair. "I had a headache, and so I took a nap. I'm fine now."

Hollow-eyed and pale, and far from fine, was Zack's judgment. He couldn't back off and leave her alone any more than he could have left a stray pup on the side of the road.

Diego gave him an opening, pouncing out of a corner to attack his shoes. Zack picked up the kitten, ruffling his fur as he walked to Nell. "You take anything?"

"Yes."

"Eat anything?"

"No. I don't need a nurse, Zack. It was just a headache."

Just a headache didn't send a woman bolting out of someone's house as if the devil were on her heels. Which was exactly how Gladys had described it. "You look pretty rough, honey, so I'm going to fix you the traditional Todd family restorer."

"I appreciate it, but I was going to work for a while."

"Go ahead." He handed her the kitten, moved past her to the refrigerator. "I'm not much in the kitchen, but I can manage this—just like my mother did when one of us wasn't feeling right. Got any jelly?"

It was right in front of his face, she thought crossly. What was it about men that struck them blind the minute they opened a refrigerator door? "Second shelf."

"I don't—oh, yeah. We always used grape, but strawberry should work. Go ahead and work. Don't mind me."

Nell set Diego by his dish of food. "What are you fixing?"

"Scrambled eggs and rolled-over jelly sandwiches."

"Rolled-over jelly sandwiches." Too tired to argue, she sat. "Sounds perfect. Mrs. Macey called you, didn't she?"

"No. I did run into her, though. She mentioned you were upset about something."

"I wasn't upset. I had a headache. The skillet's in the bottom cabinet, left."

"I'll find what I need. Place isn't big enough to hide much."

"Do you make scrambled eggs and rolled-over jelly sandwiches for everyone on the island when they have a headache?"

"That would depend. I'm making it for you because you tug at me, Nell. Have since I first met you. And when I walk in here and see you looking like something that's been flattened by a passing steamroller, it troubles me."

She said nothing when he cracked eggs, dumped in milk and too much salt. He was a good man, she believed. A kind and decent one. And she had no right tugging at him.

"Zack, I'm not going to be able to give you what you want, what you're looking for. I know yesterday I indicated I could—that I would. I shouldn't have."

"How do you know what I'm looking for, what I

want?" He stirred the eggs in the bowl. "And whatever it is, it's my problem, isn't it?"

"It isn't fair for me to give you the impression there can be anything between us."

"I'm a big boy." He put enough butter in the skillet to make her wince. "I don't expect everything to be fair. And the fact is, there's already something between us. You pretending otherwise doesn't change it." He turned around as the butter melted. "The fact that we haven't slept together doesn't change it either. We would have yesterday, if I hadn't gotten that call."

"It would've been a mistake."

"If life wasn't full of mistakes, it'd be a mighty tedious process. If all I wanted was a roll in the sheets, I'd've gotten you there."

"You're probably right—that's my point."

"Right about the mistakes or the sex?" he asked and began slathering jelly on bread.

She decided that even if she had the answer, it wouldn't matter. Kind, decent, he was. And also stubborn as a mule. "I'll make coffee."

"Don't do coffee with this. Calls for tea. And I'll make it."

He filled the kettle, set it on the stove. Poured the eggs into the heated skillet in a sizzling rush.

"Now you're angry."

"I walked in half angry, and one look at you took care of part two. Funny thing, though, I can be pissed off at a woman and hold myself back from knocking her around. That's the kind of amazing self-control I have."

Nell drew a calming breath, folded her hands on the table. "I'm well aware that not every man deals with temper with physical violence. That's the kind of amazing intelligence I have."

"Good for us." He rooted around until he found teabags, an herbal blend he felt more suited to fancy china cups than the solid stoneware mugs she had available.

He scooped eggs onto plates, found forks, and tore off paper towels in lieu of napkins.

He'd said he wasn't much in the kitchen, Nell thought as he set a plate in front of her and went back to dunk the teabags in the mugs. But even here he had an appeal. He never wasted a move, she noted, and wondered if it came from grace or practicality.

Either way, it worked.

He sat across from her, let Diego climb adventurously up the leg of his jeans and knead his thigh. "Eat."

She forked up a bite, sampled. "They're better than they should be, considering you used a pound of salt per egg."

"I like salt."

"Don't feed the cat at the table." She sighed, ate. It was so blessedly normal, sitting like this, eating oversalted eggs and strawberry jelly squished in a piece of folded bread.

"I'm not the mess I used to be," she said. "But I still have moments. Until I don't, I'm not prepared to complicate my life, or anyone else's."

"That's sensible."

"I'm going to concentrate on my work."

"A person's got to have priorities."

"There are things I want to do, things I need to learn. For myself."

"Uh-huh." He polished off his eggs, sat back with his tea. "Ripley said you're scouting for a computer. The rental agency's looking to upgrade a couple of theirs. You could probably get a fair deal. You might want to stop by, ask for Marge. She manages the place."

"Thanks. I'll check it out tomorrow. Why aren't you mad anymore?"

"Who said I'm not?"

"I know how to read mad."

He studied her face. She had some color back now, but she looked exhausted. "I bet you do. Not much point in it." He took his plate to the sink, rinsed it off. "I might brood some later. I've got a real knack for that, according to my sister."

"I used to be a champion sulker." Satisfied that they were back on an even keel, she picked up her plate. "I might see if I can get back into that. You were right about the traditional Todd meal. It did the trick."

"Never misses. Still, grape jelly's better for it."

"I'll stock some, just in case."

"Good. I'm going to let you get back to work. In a minute."

He yanked her against him, jerked her up to her toes, covered her mouth with his in a hot, possessive kiss. The blood seemed to rush to her head, then poured out of it again, leaving her dizzy, weak and achy.

One strangled moan escaped before she was back on the flat of her feet and gripping the edge of the counter for balance.

"Nothing sensible about that," Zack said, "but it's

real. You're going to have to shuffle it into your list of priorities. Don't work too late."

He strolled out, letting the screened door slap comfortably shut behind him.

In her dream that night there was a circle. A thin line upon the earth as silver as starlight. Within that sphere there were three women, robed in white. Their voices flowed like music, though the words were strange to her. As they sang, spears of light sprang up from the circle, shimmering bars of silver against the black curtain of night.

She saw a cup, a knife with a carved handle, and sprigs of herbs as green as summer.

From the cup they drank, one by one. And she tasted wine, sweet and light, on her tongue. The dark-haired one drew symbols on the ground with the blade of the knife.

And she smelled earth, fresh and dark.

As they circled, chanted, a pure gold flame spurted in the center. The heat of it warmed her skin.

Then they rose up, above the gold of the fire, above the cool silver of the spears of light, as if they danced on the air.

And she knew the freedom and the joy as the wind kissed her cheeks.

Eleven

Closed in Mia's office, Nell sweated over facts, figures, reality, and possibilities.

She liked the possibilities best, as they included a secondhand computer with all the capabilities she required, an attractive sales kit, professional business cards, a cozy yet functional home office, and a commercial-grade food processor.

The fact was, she needed all of these things, and several more, in order to create a viable, reasonably profitable business.

Her figures proved she could make this her reality if she settled for a reality without any frills—which included food, drink, and clothing—for approximately twelve months.

As she saw it, her choices were to live like a mole for about a year, or to do without the professional tools that would help her build her business.

Living like a mole wasn't so bad, she mused. She'd done essentially that for months before she'd come to the island. If she hadn't weakened and frittered away money on wind chimes and sandals and earrings, she wouldn't have remembered how much fun it was to fritter away money in the first place.

Now it had to stop.

By her calculations she could, provided Marge at Island Realty was patient enough, scrape up the money for the computer within three weeks. She would need several hundred more, of course, for the printer, the phone line, the business license, the office supplies. Once she was set up, she could design and generate the sales kits and menus right on the desktop.

With a sigh, she sat back, combed her hands through her hair. She'd left out the uniform. She could hardly cater the Macey affair in jeans and a T-shirt, or a sexy little halter. She needed good black slacks, a crisp white shirt, sensible but classy black shoes.

She looked up when Mia walked in.

"Hi. I'll get out of your way."

"No need." Mia waved her back. "I just need to check something in the September catalog." She plucked it off a shelf, flipped through while watching Nell over the pages. "Financial worries?"

"Why do you ask?"

"Vibes."

"They're not worries so much as obstacles of varying heights. I hate admitting I'm taking on too much too fast."

"And why is that? Not hating it, but why do you say you're taking on too much?" Mia asked as she sat, stretched out like a cat on a hearth rug.

"A few side jobs, some boxed lunches, one major party, and here I am designing logos and business cards, trying to squeeze out money for a computer when I can easily keep things organized in a spiral notebook. I need to rein myself in."

"There's little that's more boring than reining in," Mia stated. "When I started this place, most people didn't think I could make it fly. A small community, a seasonal tourist trade. Bookstores and fancy coffee were for cities and snazzy suburbs. They were wrong. I knew what I wanted, and what I was capable of achieving. So do you."

"In another six months or a year," Nell agreed. "But I'm getting ahead of myself."

"Why wait? You need capital, but you can't risk going to the bank for a business loan. So many pesky questions about credit history, employment history, and so on."

Mia inclined her head when Nell sighed. She enjoyed hitting the center of the target with the first arrow. "As careful as you've been, you may have left a hole," Mia continued, "and you're too smart to take chances there."

"I thought about it," Nell admitted. "If I opened myself up that way, I'd never relax. Nell Channing doesn't have a credit history, and it'll take me time to establish one."

"Which is one of the obstacles to that capital. There are spells, of course. But I dislike doing spells for financial gain. It seems so . . . crass."

"It doesn't seem so crass when I'm trying to stretch my budget to buy basic office equipment."

Pursing her lips, Mia tapped the tips of her fingers together. "I had an acquaintance who was in a bit of a financial squeeze. She worked a spell asking that her current money worries be cleared. And won fifty thousand in the lottery the next week."

"Really?"

"Really. She was able to pay her debts and treat herself to a week at the Doral Spa in Miami. Fabulous place, by the way. When she returned, her car broke down, her roof sprang a leak, her basement flooded, and she received an audit notice from the IRS. In the end, she'd done nothing more than trade one set of worries for another, though she did get that week at the spa, which can't be discounted."

Nell acknowledged the humor in Mia's words with a small grin. "I hear you. Magic isn't a crutch to be used for convenience."

"You're a quick study, little sister. So, let's talk business." Mia toed off her pretty heels, curled up her legs. "I'm in the market for an investment."

"Mia, I can't tell you how much I appreciate that, but—"

"You want to do it yourself, and blah, blah, blah." With a flick of the wrist, Mia swatted Nell's protest aside. "Please, let's behave like grown-ups."

"Are you trying to irritate or intimidate me into accepting a loan?"

"I don't generally try to irritate or intimidate, though I've been told I'm good at both. And I didn't say anything about a loan. We're discussing an investment."

She uncurled lazily and got a bottle of water for each of them out of her mini-fridge. "I would consider a loan, I suppose, for your start-up costs. Say, ten thousand, payable over a period of sixty months at twelve percent interest."

"I don't need ten thousand," Nell said, giving the bottle cap an annoyed twist. "And twelve percent is ridiculous."

"A bank would charge less, but I'm not a bank and I wouldn't ask those pesky questions."

Mia's lips curved, red and shapely over the mouth of the bottle. "But I prefer an investment. I'm a businesswoman who likes profit. You have a skill, a marketable one, which has already proven itself of interest on the island. With working capital, you can establish a viable business, which, I feel, will enhance rather than compete with my own. I've some ideas on that, actually, but we can get into that later. I make a ten K investment, become your silent partner, for a reasonable compensation of, say, eight percent of gross profits."

"I don't need ten." It had been a very long time, Nell thought as she tapped her fingers on the desk, since she'd negotiated fees, contracts. Amazing how quickly it came back.

Ten thousand would be welcome and would eliminate the sweat and worry. But if you avoided the sweat and worry, she thought, you eliminated the glow of satisfaction that came when you succeeded.

"Five will do," she decided. "For six percent, of net."

"Five, then, for seven, net."

"Done."

"Excellent. I'll have my lawyer draw up a contract."

"I'll open an account for the business at the bank."

"Would it be less sticky if I took care of that, and the license application?"

"I'll do it. I have to take a stand sometime."

"Little sister, you took one months ago. But I leave it to you. Nell," she said as she opened the door, "we're going to kick ass."

She worked like a demon, preparing, planning, implementing. Her kitchen was a hotbed of experimentation, rejections, and successes. Her little office was the scene of hours of late-evening sessions where, on her secondhand computer and printer, she became her own desktop publisher, producing menus, flyers, business cards, invoices, and stationery, all with the inscription "Sisters Catering" and the logo she'd designed of three women standing in a circle, hands clasped.

And every one listed Nell Channing as proprietor and carried her new phone number.

When she finished putting her first sales kit together, she took it, along with the best bottle of champagne she could afford, and drove to Mia's to leave them on her doorstep.

They were in business.

On the day of the Macey party, Nell stood in Gladys's kitchen and surveyed the scene. She'd been working on-site since four, and had thirty minutes before the guests were due to arrive.

For the first time since Nell had begun the setup for the party, she finally had a moment's peace and quiet. If Gladys made it through the evening without fainting from excitement and anxiety, it would be a miracle.

Every inch of the kitchen was organized to Nell's specifications. In precisely ten minutes, she would begin setting out the appetizers. As the guest list had expanded to more than a hundred, she had used all her powers of persuasion to convince Gladys to forgo the formal, sit-down meal in favor of fun, interesting food stations set up at strategic points throughout the house and on the patio.

She'd seen to the floral arrangements herself, and had personally helped Carl deal with the fairy lights and luminaries. There were candles in rented silver holders, and paper napkins that, at Nell's suggestion, carried a heart with the happy couple's initials inside.

It still touched her the way Gladys's eyes had filled when she'd seen them.

Satisfied the kitchen was ready for the battle to come, she went out to check on the rest of the field, and her troops.

She'd hired Peg to help serve, and Betsy from the Magick Inn to tend the bar. She herself would fill in in both areas whenever she could leave the kitchen unattended.

"It looks great," she announced and moved to the patio doors. The evening promised to be clear. Both she and Gladys had suffered untold agonies over the possibility of rain.

Nell tugged down the black vest she'd added to her uniform selection. "One more time. Peg, you circulate, trying to make a complete circuit every fifteen minutes. When your tray's empty, or nearly so, you head back to the kitchen. If I'm not there to refill, you'll arrange the next selection the way I showed you."

"I practiced it a zillion times."

"I know." Nell gave her an encouraging pat on the arm. "Betsy, I'll try to keep up with the empties and discards. If I run behind, or you're running low on anything, just give me a sign."

"Check. And everything looks great."

"So far, so good." And she was determined it would only get better. "Carl Junior's in charge of the music, so I'm not going to worry about it. Let's get this show on the road. Peg, vegetable crudites, station one."

It was more than just a party to Nell—it was a new beginning. As she lit the last of the candles, she thought of her mother, and the first official catering job they'd worked together.

"I've made a circle, Mom," she murmured. "And I'm going to make it shine." Touching the flame to wick, with her mother in her mind, Nell made that vow.

She glanced over and beamed as Gladys Macey came out of the master bedroom. "You look beautiful."

"Nervous as a bride." She fluffed at her hair. "I went into Boston for this getup. Not too fussy, is it?"

The cocktail suit was a pale mint green with a sparkle of beads glittering on the lapels and cuffs.

"It's gorgeous, and so are you. And there's nothing for you to be nervous about. All you have to do is enjoy yourself."

"Are you sure there's going to be enough cocktail shrimp?"

"I'm sure."

"I just don't know what people are going to think of that chicken in peanut sauce."

"They'll love it."

"What about—"

"Gladys, stop haranguing the girl." Scowling, dragging at the knot of his tie, Carl stepped out. "Let her do her job."

"Mr. Macey, you make a picture." Unable to resist, Nell reached over and straightened his tie herself.

"Made me buy a new suit."

"And you look very handsome in it," Nell assured him.

"Done nothing but complain about it since he got home from work."

Well used to their squabbling by now, Nell smiled. "Personally, I like a man who's not too comfortable in suits and ties. It's very sexy."

At Nell's statement Carl's face went bright pink. "Don't know why we couldn't have had a barbecue and a couple of kegs."

Before Gladys could snap back at him, Nell lifted a tray of appetizers. "I think you're going to have a wonderful time, starting right now."

Manners forced Carl to take one of the fancy salmon bites. The minute it hit his tongue, he pursed his lips. "Got a nice flavor to it," he admitted. "Guess it'd go down nice with a beer."

"You step right into the living room and Betsy will fix you up. I think I hear the first guests arriving."

"Oh, my! Oh, my goodness." Patting her hair again, Gladys shot quick looks everywhere. "I meant to see if everything was as it should be before—"

"Everything's exactly as it should be. You greet your guests, leave the rest to me."

It took less than fifteen minutes for the initial party stiffness to unbend. Music began to pump, conversation began to roll, and as Nell made her circuit with the chicken kabobs, she saw that she'd been right. People loved them.

It was fun to see the familiar island residents in their festive best, knotted into conversational groups or wandering out to the patio. She kept her ears open for comments about the food and the atmosphere, and felt a quick tingle with each positive remark. But best of all was seeing her client glow like a candle.

Within an hour the house was jammed, and she was working at top speed.

"They're going through these trays like starving hordes," Peg told her as she scrambled into the kitchen. "You'd think every one of them fasted a week before tonight."

"It'll slow down after the dancing starts." Moving quickly, Nell refilled the tray.

"Station . . . hell, I can never remember the numbers. The meatballs are about half gone. You said I should tell you."

"I'll take care of it. Is anything not going over?"

"Not that I've seen." Peg hefted the tray. "The way it's moving, I'd say this crowd would eat the paper napkins if you put sauce on them."

Amused, Nell took out the miniature egg rolls she had warming in the oven. As she arranged them on a tray, Ripley strolled in.

"Some party."

"It's great, isn't it?"

"Yeah, swank."

"You look pretty swank yourself," Nell commented.

Ripley looked down at her basic black dress. It was short, satisfactorily clingy, and had the advantage of being able to go to a party or, with a blazer, double as meeting attire.

"I got this number in black and in white. Figure that covers the bases as far as dresses go." She glanced around, saw absolute order, heard the hum of the dishwasher, smelled the scent of spice. "How do you keep everything organized in here?"

"I'm brilliant."

"Seems like." Ripley plucked up one of the egg rolls, popped it into her mouth. "Food's fabulous," she said with her mouth full. "I never told you, but that picnic deal you fixed for me was really great."

"Oh, yeah? How did that work out?"

"Just dandy, thanks," Ripley replied.

Her smug smile transformed into a scowl when Mia stepped in.

"I wanted to extend my compliments." She spotted the egg rolls. "Ah, a new offering." She took one, bit in. "Lovely. Hello, Ripley. I barely recognized you in your girl attire. How did you decide whether to wear the black or the white this evening?"

"Up yours."

"Don't start. I haven't time to referee."

"Don't worry." Ripley snagged one more egg roll. "I can't waste the energy on Hecate here. Gladys's nephew from Cambridge just arrived and is looking just fine. I'm going to go hit on him."

"It's so comforting to know some things never change."

"Don't touch anything," Nell ordered, then hurried out with the tray.

"So . . ." Because she preferred being away from the crowd of people, but still wanted to eat, Ripley eased up the lid on a covered tray. "Nell seems okay."

"Why wouldn't she?"

"Don't play dumb, Mia. It doesn't suit that cat face of yours." Ripley helped herself to a couple of frosted, heart-shaped cookies. "I don't need a scrying mirror to see she's had a rough time. A woman like her doesn't pop up on the island with nothing to her name but a backpack and a secondhand Buick unless she's on the run. Zack figures some guy knocked her around."

When Mia said nothing, Ripley leaned back on the counter, nibbled. "Look, I like her, and my brother's gone over her. I'm not looking to hassle her, but maybe to help if she needs it."

"With or without your badge?"

"Either or both. It seems to me she's putting down stakes here, not just working for you, but starting this catering deal. She's starting a life on Three Sisters. That makes her one of mine."

"Give me one of those." Mia held out her hand, waited until Ripley gave her a cookie. "What are you asking me, Ripley?"

"If Zack's right, and if he is, if someone's going to come after her."

"Whatever Nell's told me in confidence has to be respected."

Loyalty, Ripley was forced to admit, was never a question with Mia. It was more a religion. "I'm not asking you to break a confidence."

Mia nipped into the cookie. "You just can't say it, can you?"

"Oh, kiss ass." Ripley slapped the lid back on the tray, started to storm out. But there was something about the way Nell had been, flushed and happy, as she worked in the miraculously ordered kitchen, that pulled at her.

She spun back. "Tell me what you've seen. I want to help her."

"Yes, I know." Mia finished the cookie, dusted the crumbs from her fingers. "There's a man. He hunts and he haunts her. He's the physical reality of her every fear, doubt, worry. If he comes here, if he finds her, she'll need both of us. And she'll need the courage to take her own power and use it."

"What's his name?"

"I can't tell you that. It wasn't shown to me."

"But you know it."

"What she gave to me I can't pass on to you. I can't break her trust." The worry in Mia's eyes crawled into Ripley's belly. "If I could, and did, his name would make no difference. This is her path, Ripley. We can guide and support, instruct and assist. But in the end, it'll be her choice. You know the legend as well as I."

"I'm not getting into that." Ripley pushed the subject away with a sharp gesture. "I'm talking about someone's safety. A friend's safety."

"So am I. But I'm also talking about a friend's destiny. If you really want to help her, you could start by taking responsibility for your own." With that, Mia walked out.

"Responsibility, my butt." Ripley was annoyed enough to pry up the lid for one more cookie.

She knew what her responsibilities were. She was obliged to see to the safety of the residents and visitors of Three Sisters Island. To keep order and uphold the law.

Beyond that, her responsibilities were nobody's business but hers. And it wasn't responsible to go around practicing mumbo jumbo and clinging to some stupid legend that was as much nonsense now as it had been three centuries before.

She was the island deputy, not part of some mystic trio of saviors. And she wasn't destined to mete out some nebulous psychic justice.

Now she'd lost her appetite, and her desire to hit on Gladys Macey's nephew. Served her right for wasting time with Mia Devlin.

Disgusted, she stalked out of the kitchen. The first thing she saw as she moved back toward the party was Zack. He was in the middle of things, where he always seemed to be when it came to people. They were drawn to him. But even as he stood in the middle of a group who chattered at him, she could see that his gaze and his mind were aimed elsewhere.

It was all for Nell.

Now, Ripley watched her brother as he watched Nell circulate with her fancy little egg rolls. There was no doubt about it.

The man was completely over the moon.

While she could resist and ignore Mia's talk of destinies and responsibilities when it came to herself, when it came to a newly formed and still evolving friendship, it was an entirely different matter. Especially if it involved her brother.

There was nothing she wouldn't have done for Zack, even if it meant linking hands with Mia.

She was going to have to pay close attention to the situation, reevaluate periodically. Do some hard, uncomfortable thinking.

"He's on the edge," Mia whispered in her ear. "The shimmering edge just before the breathless tumble."

"I've got eyes, don't I?"

"Do you know what happens when he falls?"

Ripley took the wineglass out of Mia's hand, drank half of it. "Why don't you tell me?"

"He'll lay down his life for her, without an instant's hesitation. He's the most admirable man I know." She took the glass back, sipped. "That, at least, is a point of absolute agreement between us."

Because she knew it, Ripley weakened. "I want a protective spell. I want you to take care of that."

"I've already done what I can. In the end, it has to be a circle of three."

"I can't think about this now. I'm not going to talk about it now."

"All right. Why don't we just stand here and watch a strong and admirable man fall in love? Moments this pure shouldn't be wasted." Mia laid a hand on Ripley's shoulder, a casual link. "She doesn't see it. Even as it passes over her like a breath of warm air, she isn't whole enough to know it."

With a sigh that may have held the barest whiff of envy, Mia looked down into her wine. "Come on. I'll buy you a drink."

Zack bided his time. He talked with the other guests, danced with the ladies, shared a celebratory beer with Carl. He listened with apparent interest to village complaints and scrutinized the alcohol intake of anyone who held car keys.

He watched Nell serve food, chat with the guests, replenish pots staying warm over little cans of sterno. What he observed, he thought, was a blooming.

He started to ask if he could lend her a hand, then realized it was laughable. Not only did he have no clue what needed to be done, but she so obviously needed no one's help.

As the crowd thinned out, he drove a few celebrants home himself, to be on the safe side. It was nearly midnight before he felt his own duties were dispatched and he could hunt Nell up in the kitchen.

Empty trays were stacked neatly on Gladys's marbled white counter. Serving bowls were nested. The sink was filled with soapy water that sent up little fingers of steam, and Nell was systematically loading the dishwasher.

"When's the last time you were off your feet?"

"I lost track." She slid plates into slots. "But the fact that they're killing me makes me incredibly happy."

"Here." He held out a glass of champagne. "I thought you deserved this."

"I certainly do." She took a quick sip before she set it aside. "All these weeks of planning, and it's done. And I have five, count them, five appointments for jobs next week. Did you know Mary Harrison's daughter is getting married next spring?"

"I heard that. To John Bigelow. Cousin of mine."

"I have a shot at catering it."

"I vote you put those meatballs of yours on the menu. They were really tasty."

"I'll make a note of it." It felt so good to be able to plan ahead. Not just a day or a week, but months ahead. "Did you see the way Gladys and Carl danced together?"

She straightened, pressing hard on the aching small of her back. "Thirty years, and they were dancing on the patio, looking at each other like it was the first time. It was the best moment of the night for me. Do you know why?"

"Why?"

She turned to him. "Because them dancing together, them looking at each other the way they were, was what this was all about. Not decorations or pretty lights or cocktail shrimp. It was about people making a connection, and believing in it. In each other. What would have happened if either one of them, all those years ago, had stepped back or turned away? They'd have missed dancing on the patio, and everything in between."

"I never got to dance with you." He reached out, skimmed his fingers over her cheek. "Nell—"

"There you are!" Eyes damp and brilliant, Gladys rushed in. "I was afraid you'd slipped out."

"No, indeed. I need to finish up here, then do a run-through of the house to make sure I have everything back in order."

"You certainly do not. You've done enough, more

than I expected. I never had such a party, not in my whole life. Why, people will be talking about it for years."

She took Nell's shoulders, kissed both her cheeks. "I was a pest, and I know it." Then she hugged Nell breathless. "Oh, this was such a treat, and I'm not waiting three decades to do it again. Now, I want you to go home and get off your feet."

She pressed a crisp hundred-dollar bill into Nell's hand. "This is for you."

"Mrs. Macey, you're not supposed to tip me. Peg and—"

"I've taken care of them. You're going to hurt my feelings if you don't take this and go buy yourself something pretty. Now I want you to scat. Anything else needs to be done, it'll wait until tomorrow. Sheriff, you help our Nell out to her car with her trays."

"I'll do that."

"This was better than my wedding," Gladys said as she started to the door. She turned back briefly, winked. "Now let's see if we can improve on my wedding night."

"Looks like Carl's in for a surprise." Zack hefted a stack of trays. "We'd better move along, give the young couple some privacy."

"I'm right behind you."

It took three trips between them, with Carl pushing a bottle of champagne into Nell's hands as he nudged them along.

"Here's your hat, what's your hurry?" Zack chuckled as he loaded Nell's trunk.

"Where's your car?"

"Hmm? Oh, Ripley used it to take the last couple

of semi-impaired guests home. Most people walked, which helped out."

Nell let herself look at him. He was wearing a suit, but had already rid himself of the tie. She could see the faint bulge where he'd stuffed it in his pocket.

He'd opened his collar, so she could see the clean, tanned line of his throat.

There was a faint smile on his lips as he watched the lights in the Macey house wink out, one at a time. His profile wasn't perfect. His hair hadn't been styled. And the way he stood, his thumbs tucked in the front pockets of his suit pants, was relaxed rather than posed.

When the shimmer of desire came, she didn't try to close it off. Instead she took a step forward.

"I've only had half a glass of champagne. I'm unimpaired, thinking clearly, and my reflexes are perfect."

He turned his head toward her. "As sheriff, I'm glad to know it."

Still watching him, she drew her keys out of her pocket, held them dangling. "Come home with me. You drive."

The twinkle in his eyes turned to razor-sharp intensity. "I'm not going to ask if you're sure." He took the keys. "I'm just going to tell you to get in the car."

Her knees felt a bit wobbly, but she walked to the door, slid in while he got behind the wheel.

When he yanked her across the seat, ravished her mouth, she forgot all about wobbly knees and did her best to crawl into his lap.

"Hold on, just hold on. Christ Jesus." He stabbed the keys into the ignition. The engine whimpered to life, and he swung the protesting car into a tight U-turn. It shimmied in protest, making Nell giggle nervously.

"If this heap falls apart before we get there, we'll have to run for it. Zack—" She flipped off the seat belt she'd automatically snapped on, and slithered over to bite his ear. "I feel like I'm going to explode."

"Did I ever mention I'm particularly partial to women wearing little black vests?"

"No. Really?"

"I just found out tonight." Reaching out, he snagged the vest by the center vee, tugged her back against him. Understandably distracted, he took the turn too sharp and bumped the wheels over the curb.

"One more minute," he panted. "Just one more minute."

With a squeal of brakes and a violent jerk, he stopped in front of Nell's cottage. He managed, barely, to turn off the ignition before he reached for her. Dragging her across his lap, he found her mouth with his again. And let his hands do as they pleased.

Need spurted through her, hot and welcome. Riding on it, she tugged at his jacket, arched against his hands. And thrilled at the first scrape of callus over her flesh.

"Inside." He felt as randy and impatient as a teenager, and as fumbling as he fought to open the car door. "We have to get inside."

He whipped her out, his breathing already ragged as they continued to fight with each other's clothes. They stumbled, and buttons popped off his shirt. As he half carried her toward the cottage, her delighted laughter rang in his head.

"Oh! I love your hands! I want them all over me."

"I'll take care of that. Goddamn it, what's wrong with this door?" Even as he vented his frustration by rapping his hip hard against it, it flew open.

They ended up in a heap on the floor, half in, half out.

"Right here. Right here." She chanted it while her fingers worked busily at his belt.

"Wait. Just a—let me close the—" He managed to roll, scoot, and kick the door shut.

The room was all moonlight and shadows. The floor was as hard as brick. Neither of them noticed as they tore at clothes, rolled and tugged. He caught glimpses, beautiful, erotic images of pale skin, soft curves, delicate lines.

He wanted to look. He wanted to wallow.

He had to take.

When her shirt caught at her wrists by the cuffs, he gave up, gave in and lowered his mouth to her breast.

She vibrated beneath him, a volcano on the brink of erupting. Flashes of white-hot heat, curls of keen-edged longing raced through her system until she was raw and ready.

She arched under him, more demand than offer, her nails biting restlessly into his back. The world was spinning, faster and faster, as if she'd leaped upon some mad carousel and all that kept her earthbound was the glorious weight of his body on hers.

"Right now." She gripped his hips, opened for him. "Right now!"

He plunged, letting his body take over, letting his mind go. There was nothing but the relentless fury to mate. She closed around him, a hot, wet fist, and he felt her tighten, stretching like a bow beneath him before she let out a cry that rang with triumph.

Her climax ripped through him like madness.

Pleasure geysered through her, flooding senses, swamping reason. Flying free, she wrapped herself around him, clinging tight to take him with her.

And with her sheer joy, drove him over the edge.

Twelve

His ears were ringing. Or maybe it was just the sound of his heart banging against his ribs like a fist on piano keys. Either way, he couldn't get his mind clear or his body to move. He'd have worried about temporary paralysis if he could've worked up the energy to worry about anything.

"Okay," he managed and breathed in. "All right." And out again. "I guess I tripped."

"Me, too." She was flattened under him, in the perfect position to nuzzle at his throat.

"Did you get banged up anywhere?"

"No. You broke my fall." She gave the strong line of that throat a little scrape with her teeth. "Such a hero."

"Yeah. You bet."

"I rushed you. I hope you don't mind."

"It's a little hard to complain just at the moment." He found the energy to roll over, dragging her with him so she was cushioned against him. "But I'm hoping you'll give me a chance to show off my style and finesse."

She lifted her head, shook her hair back, and just grinned down at him.

"What?"

"I was just thinking how much I like your style. Every time I caught a glimpse of you tonight during the party, I just wanted to lick my lips. Big, handsome Sheriff Todd standing around in a suit he wished he didn't have to wear, nursing one lonely beer all evening so he could drive people home safe, and watching me with those patient green eyes until I was so turned on I'd have to go back to the kitchen just to calm down again."

"Is that right?" He ran his hands down her arms, amused when he hit the cuffs of her shirt. Carefully he began to unbutton them. "Do you know what I was thinking when I was watching you?"

"Not exactly."

"I was thinking how you looked like a dancer, all grace and competence. And I tried not to think what you might have on under that starched white shirt and sexy little vest."

Once he'd freed her wrists, he ran his hands back up her arms. "You've got such a fine, streamlined shape to you, Nell. It's been driving me crazy for weeks."

"I don't know how to explain how it makes me feel to know that. To feel steady enough to want that." She threw her head back, her arms up. "Oh, God! I feel so alive. I don't want it ever to stop."

She leaned down again, kissed him hard, then

scrambled to her feet. "I want that champagne. I want to get drunk and make love with you all night."

"I can get behind that idea." He sat up, then his eyes widened as she pulled open the door. "What're you doing?"

"Getting the champagne out of the car."

"Let me get my pants on, and I'll get it. Nell!" Stupefied, he sprang to his feet as she raced outside, naked as a jaybird. "Well, for God's sake!" He grabbed his pants, carrying them with him to the doorway. "Get back in here before I have to haul you in for indecent exposure."

"There's nobody to see." It felt fabulous, and exactly right to stand naked in the cool night air, to feel it caress the skin so recently heated by passion. With the grass tickling her feet, she threw her arms out to the side and turned in circles. "Come on out, it's a beautiful night. Moon and stars and the sound of the sea."

She looked impossibly alluring, the gold of her hair silvered by starlight, her milky skin shimmering with it, and her face lifted to the sky.

Then her gaze met his across the little patch of lawn with a power so intense it stole his breath. For a moment he would have sworn the whole of her sparkled.

"There's something in the air here," she said, turning her hands up, palms cupped as if she could catch the breath of the night. "I feel it inside me, beating like a pulse. And when I feel that, it seems I could do anything."

With her palm still cupped, she held out her hand to him. "Will you come kiss me in the moonlight?"

He couldn't resist, and didn't try, but walked to her, took her outstretched hand. With the sky sprinkling light over them, he lowered his mouth to hers in a kiss that warmed rather than burned.

The tenderness of it crept into her heart. When he lifted her into his arms, she cradled her head on his shoulder, knowing she was safe and welcome there.

He carried her inside, through the little cottage and to the old bed that shifted quietly under their weight.

Later, he told himself as he lost himself in her, he would think about how he felt to find himself falling in love with a witch.

She awoke before dawn from one of the snatches of sleep they'd allowed each other. She felt his warmth, and his weight. The ease of it, the sheer and steady normality of him, was both comfort and arousal.

She drew his face for herself in her mind, feature by feature. When she had it complete, she held it there as she slipped out of bed to start her day.

She showered, dressed in shorts and a sleeveless shirt. Quietly, she picked up the clothes they'd scattered in the living room and all but floated into the kitchen.

She'd never experienced desire like that before, not the kind that sprang like an animal inside you and swallowed you whole.

She hoped to have the experience again.

And the tenderness that had come later, the insatiable thirst for more, the dark, breathless groping. All of it.

Nell Channing had a lover. And he was sleeping in her bed.

He wanted her, and that was a thrill. He wanted her for who she was, and not who he could mold her to be. And that was a balm.

Blissful, she brewed coffee, and while its scent perfumed the air she worked up a dough for cinnamon buns, another for bread. While she worked she sang to herself and watched the new day put roses in the sky.

Once her garden was watered, and she'd sipped at her first cup of coffee, she slid a batch of buns into the oven. With her mug in one hand, a pencil in the other, she began to toy with her menu for the coming week.

"What're you doing?"

She jumped like a rabbit at the sleep-roughened sound of his voice, and the coffee slopped over onto the paper. "Did I wake you? I'm sorry. I tried to be quiet."

He held up a hand. "Nell, don't do that. It pisses me off." His voice was thick with sleep, and despite herself dread curled in her stomach as he stepped toward her.

"There's one thing I'm going to ask you." He picked up her mug, drank to clear his mind and voice. "Don't ever mix me up with him. If you'd waked me up and it annoyed me, I would say so. But the fact is I woke up because you weren't there and I missed you."

"Some habits are hard to break, no matter how much you try."

"Well, keep trying." He said it lightly, moved over

to the stove to pour a full mug for himself. "You got something baking already?" He sniffed the air. "Mother of God." He breathed it, reverently. "Cinnamon buns?"

Her dimples flickered. "And if they are?"

"I'll be your slave."

"You're so easy, Sheriff." She got a hot mitt out of the drawer. "Why don't you sit down? I'll give you breakfast, and we can discuss what I expect from my slave."

On Monday morning Nell breezed into Café Book loaded with boxes of baked goods, called out a cheery hello, and swung upstairs.

At the front counter, Lulu stopped ringing up weekend mail orders, her lips twitching as Mia turned from stocking shelves.

"Somebody," Mia said, "got lucky this weekend."

"You going up to squeeze her for details?"

"Please." Mia tucked in another book, brushed lint from her skirt. "Do dryads dance in the woods?"

Amused, Lulu cackled. "Well, don't forget to fill me in."

Mia walked into the café, and through the homey, irresistible scent of cinnamon buns. "Busy weekend," she commented, scanning the morning's offerings.

"You bet."

"And a terrific party Saturday night. Hell of a job, little sister."

"Thanks." Nell lined up her muffins before pouring the first of the morning coffee for Mia. "I've got several meetings this week with potential clients that came out of it."

"Congratulations. But . . ." Mia drew in the scent of her coffee. "I don't think future catering jobs are what has you glowing today. Let me try one of those buns there."

Casually, she walked around to the rear of the counter while Nell selected the bun. "You definitely have the look of a woman who spent her weekend doing more than baking."

"I did some gardening. My tomato plants are coming right along."

"Mmm-hmm." She brought the fragrant bun to her lips, took a neat bite. "I'm imagining Sheriff Todd was just as tasty as this. Give. We open in ten."

"I shouldn't talk about it. It's rude, isn't it?"

"Absolutely not. It's required and expected. Have a little sympathy, will you? I haven't engaged in sexual activities for a considerable time, so I'm entitled to a few vicarious thrills. You look so damn happy."

"I am. It was wonderful." Nell did a quick little dance, then grabbed a bun for herself. "Outrageous. He has such . . . stamina."

"Oh. Mmm." Mia ran her tongue over her lips. "Don't stop now."

"I think we broke several standing records."

"Now you're bragging, but that's all right. You're among friends."

"You know the best part?"

"I'm hoping you'll tell me, and all the other parts as well."

"He didn't, doesn't, treat me like I'm fragile or needy or, I don't know . . . wounded. So I don't feel fragile or needy or wounded when I'm with him. The first time, we barely made it into the house, and ended up on the floor tearing at each other's clothes. It was so *normal.*"

"We could all use a bit of that kind of normal now and then. He's a great kisser, isn't he?"

"Oh, boy, and when he . . ." Trailing off, Nell paled.

"I was fifteen," Mia explained as she bit into the cinnamon bun again. "He gave me a ride home from a party, and we satisfied our mutual curiosity with a couple of very long, very intense lip-locks. While I won't insult your intelligence and claim it was like kissing my brother, I will say we didn't suit and have chosen to be friends. But they were really fine kisses."

She licked icing off her finger. "So I have some small idea just how delightful your weekend was."

"I'm glad I didn't know that before. I might have been intimidated."

"Aren't you sweet? So, what are you going to do about Zachariah Todd?"

"Enjoy him."

"Perfect answer." For the moment. "He has really good hands, too, doesn't he?" Mia commented as she strolled away.

"Now you're going to have to shut up."

Laughing, Mia started down the steps. "I'm opening the doors."

And so, she thought, little sister, are you.

It wouldn't have surprised Mia to know that Zack was undergoing personal interrogation over coffee and buns as well.

"Didn't see you around much this weekend."

"Had stuff to do. And didn't I bring you a present?"

Ripley worked her way enthusiastically through the first bun. "Um. Good," she managed to slur. "Guess the stuff had to do with the island's best cook, which I cleverly deduced since you've got a bag holding half a dozen buns."

"Down to four now." He enjoyed one of his own while he slogged through paperwork at his desk. "John Macey still hasn't paid these parking tickets. He needs a goose."

"I'll goose him. So, you and Nell got down to the mattress rhumba?"

Zack gave her a single withering look. "You've got such a mushy, romantic heart, Rip. I don't know how you get through life with it weighing you down."

"Avoiding the question's usually answering the question in the affirmative. Cop 101. How'd it go?"

"Do I ask you about your sex life?"

She waved a finger, signaling a pause in the conversation while she swallowed. "Yes."

"Only because I'm older and wiser."

"Yeah, right." She snagged a second bun, not only because they were incredible but because she knew it would annoy him. "If we let you slide on the older and wiser bull, then we'll agree I'm younger and more cynical. Are you going to do a deeper run on her background?"

"No." Deliberately he opened a drawer, dropped the bag of buns inside, shut it.

"If you're serious about her, and knowing you, you are, you need a handle on it, Zack. She didn't drop out of the sky onto Three Sisters."

"She took the ferry," he said coolly. "What's your problem with her? I thought you liked her."

"I do. A lot, as it happens." She eased a hip onto the corner of his desk. "But for reasons that often escape me, I like you a lot, too. You've got a soft spot for the troubled and wounded, Zack, and sometimes, through no fault of their own, the troubled and wounded can bite right through the soft parts."

"Have you ever known me not to be able to take care of myself?"

"You're in love with her." When he blinked, stared, she pushed off the desk, paced restlessly around the office area. "What, am I blind and stupid? I've known you all my life, and I know every move, every tone, every expression on that dopey face of yours. You're in love with her, and you don't even know who she is."

"She's exactly who and what I've wanted my whole life."

Ripley stopped in the act of kicking the desk, and her eyes went soft and helpless. "Aw, damn it, Zack. Why'd you have to go and say something like that?"

"Because it's true. It's the way it is for us Todds, isn't it? We go along, go alone, then *pow*, it hits and it's all over. I've been hit, and I like it."

"Okay, let's just back up a little." Determined to stand up for him whether he wanted it or not, she slapped her palms on the desk, leaned over. "She's got trouble. She's managed to break free of it, at least temporarily, but it's there. He may come after her, Zack. If I hadn't been worried about you, I'd never have asked Mia about it. Rather saw my tongue in half with a rusty kitchen knife. But I did ask her, and she's not clear on it."

"Honey, what you said before about knowing me, that's true. Now what do you think my reaction is to what you just said?"

She hissed out a breath. "If he comes after her, he'll have to get through you."

"Close enough. Shouldn't you be out on patrol, or would you rather take the paperwork portion of our day?"

"I'd rather eat lice." She put on her cap, yanked the tail of her hair through the back. "Look, I'm glad you found someone who suits you. I'm even more glad I like her. But there's more to Nell Channing than a nice woman with a murky past who can bake like a team of angels."

"You mean she's a witch," he said easily. "Yeah, I figured that out. I've got no particular problem with it." So saying, he went back to the keyboard, chuckling to himself when Ripley slammed the door behind her.

"The goddess doesn't require sacrifice," Mia said. "She's a mother. Like a mother, she requires respect, love, discipline, and wants happiness for her children."

The evening was cool. Mia could already scent the

end of summer. Soon her woods would change from green and lush to wild color. She'd already seen the woolly caterpillars, watched the busy squirrel hoarding nuts. Signals, she thought, of a long, cold winter.

But for now, her roses bloomed, and the most tender of her herbs trailed fragrantly among her garden stones.

"Magic springs from the elements, and from the heart. But its rituals are best served with tools, even visual aids, if you will. Any craft depends on certain routines and implements."

She walked through her garden to her kitchen door, opened it for Nell. "I have some for you."

The room was as fragrant as the garden. Hanks of herbs dried on hooks. Pots of flowers that Mia had chosen for indoor company stood on the long line of smooth counter. What could only be described as a cauldron sat on the stove, simmering away with the strong sweetness of heliotrope.

"What are you cooking?"

"Oh, just a little charm for someone who has a job interview later in the week. She's nervous." Mia passed a hand through the steam. "Heliotrope for success, sunflower for career, a bit of hazel to assist in communication—and this and that. I'll empower some suitable crystals for her that she can carry in a pouch in her purse."

"Will she get the job?"

"That's up to her. The Craft doesn't promise us everything we desire, nor is it a crutch for weak spines to lean on. Now, your tools," she continued, gesturing to the table.

She'd selected them carefully, with an image of Nell in her mind.

"You should, once you're home, cleanse them. No one should touch them without your permission. They require your energy. The wand is made from a birch branch pruned from a living tree on the winter solstice. The crystal on its tip is clear quartz. It was a gift to me from the one who trained me."

It was lovely, slim and smooth, and felt almost silky when Nell trailed a finger over it. "You can't give me something that was a gift."

"It was meant to be passed on. You'll want to have others, too; copper is good. This is your broom," she continued, lifting a brow as Nell stifled a laugh.

"Sorry, I just never thought . . . a broom?"

"You won't be riding on it. Hang it at the door of your home for protection, use it to sweep out negative energy. A cup—again, one day you'll want to select your own, but for now this will serve. I bought it at Island Market, glassware section. Sometimes the simple works best. The pentacle is from a maple bur. It must always stand upright. The athame isn't used for physical cutting, but for directing energy."

She didn't touch it, but told Nell to do so.

"Some prefer swords, but I don't think you will," she added as Nell explored the carved handle with a fingertip. "The blade's dull, and meant to be. The bolline, on the other hand, is meant to cut in the physical. The handle's curved, which will give you a good grip for harvesting your herbs and plants, carving wands, inscribing candles, and so on. There are those, kitchen witches, who use it to cut food. The choice is yours, of course."

"Of course," Nell agreed.

"I assume you can handle the purchase and selection of your own cauldron. Cast iron's best. You can find an incense burner that appeals to you at one of the gift shops, and the incense as well—cones and sticks are more accessible locally. When you've time you can make your own incense powder. You'll need some straw baskets, some swatches of silk. Do you want to write this down?"

Nell blew out a breath. "Maybe I'd better."

"Candles," Mia continued after handing Nell a pad and pencil. "I'll explain the purpose of colors and symbols. I have some crystals for you, but you'll want more, of your own selection. A couple dozen canning jars, with lids, a mortar and pestle, sea salt. I have a Tarot deck you can borrow, and some wooden boxes, though I'll want them back as well. This will get you started."

"It's more involved than I thought. Before—the day in the garden—all I did was stand there."

"There are things you'll be able to do with your mind and heart, and others that require things—as an extension of power, and as a respect for tradition. Now that you have a computer, you'll want to keep a record of spells."

"A record of spells, on my computer?"

"Why not be practical and efficient? Nell, have you spoken to Zack about any of this?"

"No."

"Are you worried about his reaction?"

She touched the wand again, and wondered. "That's part of it, but before we even get there, I don't know how I'd begin to tell him. I haven't resolved it completely for myself."

"Fair enough. What you share or don't is your choice, just as what you give or what you take."

"With Ripley feeling the way she does, I thought he might feel the same. I guess I don't want to hit any hitches so soon."

"Who could blame you? Let's take a walk."

"I really should be getting back. It's nearly dark."

"He'll wait." Mia opened a carved box, took out her wand. The tip was a round of quartz as smoky as her eyes. "Take yours. It's time you learned how to cast a circle. We'll keep it simple," she promised, nudging Nell through the door. "And after what I have in mind, I can almost guarantee the sex will be sensational."

"It's not all sex," Nell began. "But that's a definite plus."

As they walked toward the woods, a light mist swirled to hug the ground. Long shadows spilled out of the trees, black lines over pale gray.

"The weather's changing," Mia said. "The last weeks of summer always make me melancholy. It's odd, because I love the autumn, the smells and the colors of it, that slice in the air when you step out first thing in the morning."

You're lonely. Nell nearly said it before she checked her tongue. How could such a statement help but sound smug and self-satisfied coming from a woman who'd just taken a lover?

"Maybe a holdover from childhood," she suggested. "End of summer means back to school." She followed Mia down a well-beaten path, through mist and shadow. "I always hated those first couple of weeks of school, not so much if my father had a second year on the same base, but at those times when I was the new kid and everyone else was already picked off in groups."

"How did you handle it?"

"I learned how to talk to people, to make friends even though they were transient. Lived in my own head a lot. I guess some of that made me a perfect target for Evan. He promised to love, honor, and cherish, forever. I really wanted forever with someone."

"And now?"

"Now I just want to carve out my own space, and stick."

"Something else we have in common. This is one of my spaces."

They stepped into a clearing where the mist was white from the quiet light of the rising moon. The full ball of it shimmered between the trees, teased the dark summer leaves, spilled through at the edges of a stand of three stones. From the branches that ringed the clearing hung hanks of herbs. The glitter of strung crystals rang gently together in the light wind.

And the sound of the wind, the stones, the nearby sea, was music.

There was a primitive, *essential* feel to the place.

"It's beautiful here," Nell began, "and . . . I want to say eerie, but not in a frightening way. You almost expect to see ghosts, or headless horsemen. And if you did, it would seem absolutely natural, not frightening at all."

She turned, her steps shredding the mist like gray

silk, and caught the scents of verbena, rosemary, and sage carried on the breeze from the tree branches.

Caught something else as well—a quiet hum that was almost like music.

"This is where you were the night of the solstice, before you came out to stand on the cliffs."

"This ground is hallowed," Mia told her. "It's said the sisters stood here, three hundred years and more past, and worked their spell to create their haven. Whether they did or not, I've always been drawn here. We'll cast the circle together. It's a basic ritual."

Mia drew her ritual knife from her pocket and began. Fascinated, Nell repeated the words, the gestures, and found herself unsurprised when a thin ring of light glowed through the smoke of the mist.

"We call on Air, on Earth, on Water and Fire to guard our circle and grant our desire. Here protect and witness this rite. Open our minds to the magic of night."

Mia laid down her knife, her wand, nodded to Nell after her chant was repeated. "You can cast your own circle in your own way, with your own words when you're ready. I hope you don't mind, but I prefer working skyclad when weather permits."

With this Mia slipped off her dress and folded it neatly while Nell gaped. "Oh, well, I don't really—"

"It's not required." At ease with her nakedness, Mia picked up her wand again. "I generally prefer it, particularly for this ritual."

There was a tattoo—a birthmark? Nell wondered. A small pentagram shape against the milk-white skin of her thigh.

"What ritual?"

"We'll draw down the moon. Some—most—usually do this when there's serious work to be done, but I sometimes need, or like, the extra burst of energy. To begin, open yourself. Mind, breath, heart, loin. Trust yourself. Every woman is ruled by the moon, just as the sea is. Hold your wand in your right hand."

Mirroring Mia's gestures, Nell lifted her arms, slowly raising them high, then clasping her wand with both hands.

"On this night, in this hour, we call upon Luna's power. Merge with us light into light." Slowly, the wands were turned, aimed at hearts. "Woman and goddess glowing bright. Power and joy pour down from thee. As we will, so mote it be."

She felt it, cool and fluid and strong, a flood of energy and light inside her. Pulsing, as that white ball of moon seemed to pulse as it rose gracefully above the trees. She could all but see it, blue-edged silver spurts of light that spun down and into her.

With the power came a rush of joy. It came out of Nell in a laughing gasp as Mia lowered her wand.

"Sometimes it's just lovely being a girl, isn't it? We'll close the circle now. I believe, little sister, you'll find an appropriate outlet for all that fresh energy."

When she was alone, Mia put her own energy to use working a protective spell. Nell had a great deal of natural power, largely untapped. She could and would help her explore it, control it, and refine it. But there was something more immediate preying on her mind now.

Within the circle, within the woods, she'd seen something Nell had not. She'd watched the single dark cloud slide over the heart of the moon.

Thirteen

The last weeks of summer passed in a blur. Days were filled with work, with plans for the jobs she'd won and proposals for more.

Once the weather turned she would lose the summer-people aspect of her business. So she would be the clever ant, Nell decided, who carefully prepared for winter.

She'd solicit jobs for holiday parties, for Super Bowl Sunday, for cabin fever victims. The islanders were growing so accustomed to calling her for their events, small and large, it would become strange to do otherwise.

Nights were nearly always spent with Zack—taking advantage of the final burst of warmth with candlelight dinners alfresco, evening sails made brisk from the chill rising from the water, long, luxurious love-making in the cozy nest of her bed.

Once she lit red candles for passion. They seemed to work exceptionally well.

At least two evenings a week she worked with Mia on what she thought of as her ritual lessons.

And at dawn she was baking in her kitchen.

The life she'd always looked for was all around her, and more. She had a power inside her that ran like silver. And love that glowed warm gold.

There were times she caught him watching her, quietly, patiently. The waiting look. Each time she did, there was a tug of guilt, a ripple of unease. And each time that she took the coward's way and ignored it, she disappointed both of them.

She could rationalize it. She was happy, and entitled to a time of peace and pleasure. Only a year before, she'd risked her life, and would have forfeited it, rather than live trapped and afraid.

For so many months following, she'd been alone, constantly on the move, wary of every sound. She awakened night after night in cold sweats from dreams she couldn't face even in the dark.

If she'd locked that time in a box and buried the key, who had a better right?

It was the now that mattered, and she was giving Zack all she could of the now.

As summer slipped into fall she was convinced of it, and of the solidity of her haven on Three Sisters.

With her latest kitchen catalogs and her new subscription to *Saveur* under her arm, Nell walked out of the post office and headed down High Street toward the market. The summer people had been replaced by tourists eager to view New England foliage at its peak.

She couldn't blame them. Wedges of the island were covered with a brilliant patchwork of flaming color. Every morning she studied the changes from her own kitchen window, dreaming into her own woods as the leaves took on fire. There were times she walked the beach in the evening just to see the slow roll of fog tumble in, swallow water, cloak the buoys, and muffle the long, monotonous *bongs*.

Mornings, a fine, glassy frost might glitter on the ground only to melt under the strengthening sun until it beaded on the grass like tears on lashes.

Rains swept in, pounded the beaches, the cliffs, then swept out again until it seemed to her that the whole of the world sparkled like something under a glass dome.

She was under that dome, Nell thought. Safe and secure and away from the world that raged beyond sea and inlet.

With the brisk wind sneaking up her sweater, she waved at familiar faces, paused briefly at the crosswalk to check traffic, then jogged carelessly into the market for the pork chops she intended to make for dinner.

Pamela Stevens, on an impromptu visit to the island with her husband, Donald, gave a little cry of surprise and rolled down the window of their rented BMW sedan.

"I'm not stopping at any of these shops, Pamela, no matter how quaint they are, until I find the right place to park."

"I've just seen a ghost." Pamela dropped back on the seat, laid a hand over her heart.

"It's witches around here, Pamela, not ghosts."

"No, no, Donald. Helen Remington. Evan Remington's wife. I'd swear I've just seen her ghost."

"Don't know why in God's name she would come

all the way out here to haunt anybody. Can't even find a damn parking lot."

"I'm not joking. The woman could've been her double, except for the hair and the clothes. Helen wouldn't have been caught dead in that frightful sweater." She craned her neck to try to keep the market in sight. "Pull over, Donald. I've just got to go back and get a closer look."

"As soon as I find a parking place."

"It looked just like her," Pamela repeated. "So odd, and it gave me such a jolt. Poor Helen. I was one of the last people who spoke to her before that terrible accident."

"And so you said, a hundred times for six months after she drove off the cliff."

"Something like that stays with you." Bristling, Pamela straightened in her seat, sent her nose in the air. "I was very fond of her. She and Evan were a beautiful couple. She was so young and pretty, with everything to live for. When something tragic like that happens, it reminds you that lives can change with the snap of a finger."

*By the time Pamela managed to drag her hus-*band back to the market, Nell was unpacking her single bag of groceries and trying to decide between couscous and a spicy new sauce she wanted to try out on red potato wedges.

She decided to decide later, and flipping on the portable stereo Zack had left at her cottage, she settled down with Alanis Morissette and her issue of *Saveur*.

While she crunched on an apple from the basket on her table, she pulled over her notepad and began to scribble ideas sparked from an article on artichokes.

She moved from there to a feature on Australian wines and noted the writer's opinion of the best values.

The sound of footsteps didn't jolt her now, but gave her a warm feeling as she glanced over to watch Zack come in.

"A little early for the upholder of law and order to call it a day, isn't it?"

"I swapped some time with Ripley."

"What's in the box?"

"A present."

"For me?" Shoving her notebook aside, she got up, stepped hurriedly to the counter. Her mouth fell open. Love and lust tangled and burned inside her.

"A food processor. Commercial grade, top of the line." With reverent hands, she stroked the box the way some women might stroke mink. "Oh, my God."

"According to my mother, if a man gives a woman anything that plugs into an electric socket for a gift, he'd better be fully paid up on his life insurance. But I didn't think that rule applied here."

"It's the best on the market. I've wanted it forever."

"I've seen you ogling it in the catalog a few times." He caught her when she launched herself into his arms to cover his face with kisses. "I guess I'm not going to need that life insurance."

"I love it, I love it, I *love* it." She finished with a hard, smacking kiss, then leaped down to attack the box. "But it's outrageously expensive. I shouldn't let you give me an outrageously expensive present right out of the blue. But I'm going to because I can't stand the idea of not having it."

"It's rude to turn down a gift, and anyway, it's not out of the blue. A day early, but I didn't think that mattered. Happy birthday."

"My birthday's in April, but I'm not arguing because . . ."

She caught herself. The pulse began to throb in her temples, hot and hard. Helen Remington's birthday was in April. Nell Channing's was listed clearly on all identification as September nineteenth.

"I don't know what I was thinking. Slipped my mind." Because her palms sprang with damp, she wiped them hastily on her jeans. "I've been so busy, I forgot about my birthday."

All of his pleasure of giving her the gift curdled, left a sour ball in his belly. "Don't do that. Keeping things to yourself is one thing. Lying to my face is another."

"I'm sorry." She bit down hard on her lip, tasted shame.

"So am I." Because he wanted her to look at him, he cupped her chin, lifted it.

"I keep waiting for you to take the step, Nell, but you don't. You sleep with me, and you don't hold anything back there. You talk to me about what you hope to do tomorrow, and you listen when I talk to you. But there're no yesterdays."

He'd tried not to dwell on that, tried to tell himself, as he'd told Ripley, that it wasn't important. But now, slapped in the face with it, he couldn't pretend.

"You let me into your life from the day you stepped onto the island."

It was true, perfectly true. What point would there be in denying it? "For me, my life started from there. Nothing before then matters anymore."

"If it didn't, you wouldn't have to lie to me."

Panic wanted to climb into her throat. She countered it with a snap of temper. "What difference does it make if my birthday's tomorrow, or a month from now, or six months ago? Why does it have to matter?"

"What matters is you don't trust me. That's hard on me, Nell, because I'm in love with you."

"Oh, Zack, you can't—"

"I'm in love with you," he repeated, taking her arms to hold her still. "And you know it."

And of course, that was perfectly true as well. "But I don't know what to do about it. I don't know what to do with what I feel for you. Trusting that, trusting you, it's not that simple. Not for me."

"You want me to accept that, but you don't want to tell me why it's not that simple. Play fair, Nell."

"I can't." A tear spilled over, shimmered down her cheek. "I'm sorry."

"If that's the way it is, we're both fooling ourselves."

He let her go and walked away.

Knocking on Zack's front door was one of the hardest things Nell had ever done. She'd spent so much time stepping back from anger. Now she would have to face it, head on. And with little defense. This was a turmoil she'd caused, and only she could resolve it.

She walked to the front of the house because it seemed more formal than strolling across the beach and up the stairs to the back. Before she knocked, she rubbed her fingers over the turquoise stone she'd slipped into her pocket to aid her verbal communication.

Though she wasn't convinced such things worked, she didn't see how it could make her situation any worse.

She lifted her hand, cursed herself as she lowered it again. There was an old rocker on the front porch, and a pot of geraniums that were frost-burned and pathetic. She wished she'd seen them before the weather had turned so she could have urged Zack to carry them inside.

And she was stalling.

She squared her shoulders, knocked.

Was torn between relief and despair when no one answered.

Just as she'd given up and turned away, the door swung open.

Ripley stood in leggings cropped just below the knee and a T-shirt marked with a vee of sweat between her breasts. She gave Nell one long, cool stare, then leaned on the doorjamb.

"Wasn't sure I heard anyone knock. I was lifting, and had the music up."

"I was hoping to talk to Zack."

"Yeah, I figured. You pissed him off good. It takes work to do that. Me, I've had years of practice, but you must have an innate talent for it."

Nell slipped her hand in her pocket, fingered the stone. She would have to get through the shield to get to the target. "I know he's angry with me, and he has a right to be. Don't I have a right to apologize?"

"Sure, but if you do it with choking little sobs and flutters, you're going to piss me off. I'm a lot meaner than Zack."

"I don't intend to cry and flutter." Nell's own temper bubbled up as she stepped forward. "And I don't think Zack would appreciate you getting in the middle of this. I know I don't."

"Good for you." Satisfied, Ripley shifted to let Nell in. "He's up on the back deck, brooding through his telescope and drinking a beer. But before you go up and say whatever you have to say to him, I'm going to tell you something. He could've looked into your background, picked the pieces apart. I would have. But he's got standards, personal standards, so he didn't."

The guilt that had settled on her since he'd walked out her door took on more weight. "He would've considered that rude."

"Right. I don't mind being rude. So you square this with him, or deal with me."

"Understood."

"I like you, and I respect someone who takes care of business. But when you mess with a Todd, you don't get off free. Fair warning."

Ripley turned toward the stairs leading to the second floor. "Help yourself to a beer on the way through the kitchen. I've got to finish my reps."

Nell skipped the beer, though she'd have relished a tall glass of ice water to ease the burn in her throat. She walked through the comfortably untidy living room, through the equally untidy kitchen, and took the outside steps up to the deck.

He sat in a big chair faded to gray by the weather, a bottle of Sam Adams nestled between his thighs and his scope tilted starward.

He knew she was there but didn't acknowledge her. The scent of her was peaches and nerves.

"You're angry with me, and I deserve it. But you're too fair not to listen."

"I might work my way up to fair by tomorrow. You'd be smarter to wait."

"I'll risk it." She wondered if he knew how much it meant—how much he meant—that she would risk it. "I lied. I've lied often and I've lied well, and I'd do it again. The choice was between honesty and survival. For me, it still is, so I'm not going to tell you everything you need to know. Everything you deserve to know. I'm sorry."

"If two people don't trust each other, they've got no business being together."

"That's easy for you to say, Zack."

When he shifted his gaze from the stars to hers, and the heat of it scorched her, she stepped closer. Her heart throbbed. She didn't fear that he would strike her. But she did fear that he'd never want to touch her again.

"No, damn it, it is easy for you. You've got your place here. You've always had it, and you don't have to question it, or fight for it."

"If I've got a place," he said in careful, measured tones, "I've had to earn it. The same as anyone."

"That's different, because you started on a foundation, a solid one, and built from there. These past few months I've been working to earn a place here. I have earned it. But it's different."

"Okay, maybe it is. But you and I started on the same ground, Nell, when it comes to what we were making together."

Were making, she thought. Not are making. If this was his line she could stand where she was, keep on her side of it, or take the first step over.

It wasn't any harder, she decided, than driving off a cliff.

"I was with a man, for three years, I was with a man who hurt me. Not just the slaps and the shoves. Those kinds of bruises don't last. But others do."

She had to let out a little breath to ease the pressure in her chest. "He systematically chipped away at my confidence, my self-esteem, my courage and my choices, and he did it so skillfully they were gone before I realized what was happening. It's not easy to rebuild those things, and I'm still working on it. Coming here, just walking over here tonight took everything I've managed to store up. I shouldn't have gotten involved with you, and I didn't intend to. But something about being here, and about being with you, made me feel normal again."

"That's the start of a fine speech. Why don't you sit down and just talk to me."

"I did what I had to do to get away from him. I'm not going to apologize for it."

"I'm not asking you to."

"I'm not going into the details." She turned away, leaned on the rail and stared out at the night-dark sea. "I'll tell you it was like living in a pit that got deeper and deeper and colder and colder. Whenever I tried to crawl out, he was right there."

"But you found a way."

"I won't go back. Whatever I have to do, wherever I have to run, I won't go back. So I've lied, and deceived. I've broken the law. And I've hurt you." She turned back. "The only thing I'm sorry for is the last."

She said it defiantly, almost furiously as she stood with her back to the rail and her hands in white-knuckled fists.

Terror and courage, he thought, dragging at each other inside her. "Did you think I wouldn't understand?"

"Zack." She lifted her hands, dropped them. "*I* still don't understand. I wasn't a doormat when I met him, I wasn't a victim waiting to be exploited. I came from a solid, steady family, as functional as any family manages to be. I was educated, independent, helping to run a business. There'd been men in my life before, nothing really serious, but normal, healthy relationships. Then there I was, manipulated and abused. And trapped."

Oh, baby, he thought, as he had when she'd fallen to pieces in the café kitchen. "Why are you still blaming yourself for it?"

The question broke her rhythm. For a moment she could only stare at him, baffled. "I don't know." She walked over to sit in the chair beside him.

"It'd be a good next step to stop doing that." He said it easily, taking a sip of his beer. There was still temper inside him, dregs of it for Nell, but a new and ripe well of it for the man—the faceless, nameless entity—who'd scarred her.

He thought he might work that off later by pounding the hell out of Ripley's punching bag.

"Why don't you tell me about your family?" he suggested and offered her the beer. "You know my mother can't cook worth a damn and my father likes to take snapshots with his new toy. You know they grew up here on the island, got married, and had a couple of kids. And you've had personal acquaintance with my sister."

"My father was in the Army. He was a lieutenant colonel."

"An Army brat." Since she shook her head at the beer, he took another pull himself. "Saw some of the world, didn't you?"

"Yeah, we moved around a lot. He always liked getting new orders. Something new to handle, I suppose. He was a good man, very steady, with a wonderful, warm laugh. He liked old Marx Brothers movies and Reese's peanut butter cups. Oh, God."

Grief caught her by the throat, choked off her voice, dug raw wounds in her stomach.

"He's been gone so long, I don't know how it could seem like yesterday."

"When you love somebody, it's always there. I still think about my grandmother now and again." He took Nell's hand, held it loosely. "When I do, I can smell her. Lavender water and peppermint. She died when I was fourteen."

How was it he could understand, and so exactly? That, she thought, was the magic of him. "My father was killed in the Gulf War. I thought he was invincible. He'd always seemed to be. Everyone said he was a good soldier, but I remember he was a good father.

He would always listen if I needed to tell him something. He was honest and fair, and had this code of honor, a personal one that meant more than all the rules and regulations. He . . . God." She turned her head to study Zack's face. "It just hit me, how much you're like him. He would have approved of you, Sheriff Todd."

"I'm sorry I never got the chance to meet him." He turned the scope toward her. "Why don't you take a look, see what you can find up there?"

She lowered her head toward the viewer, scanned the stars. "You've forgiven me."

"Let's say we've made some progress."

"Good thing for me. Otherwise Ripley was going to kick my ass."

"And she's a hell of an ass-kicker, too."

"She loves you. I always wanted a brother or a sister. My mother and I were tight, and I guess we got tighter after we lost my father. But I always wanted a sister. You'd've liked my mother. She was tough and smart and full of fun. Started her own business from the ground up after she was widowed. And she made it work."

"Sounds like someone else I know."

Her lips curved. "My father always said I took after her. Zack, who I am now is who I was before. The three years between, they were the aberration. You wouldn't recognize the person I became during that lost time. I barely do."

"Maybe you had to go through it to get where you are now."

"Maybe." The light through the scope haloed as her eyes misted. "I feel like I was always headed here. All those moves when I was growing up. I'd look around and think: No, this isn't it. Not yet. The day I crossed over on the ferry, and I saw the island floating on the water, I knew. This is my place."

He lifted their joined hands, kissed the back of hers. "The day I saw you behind the counter in the café, I knew."

The thrill rocketed up her arm, and straight into her heart. "I've got baggage, Zack. I've got complications. More than I can tell you. You matter to me more than I thought anyone ever could. I don't want to mess up your life with my problems."

"From where I'm sitting, Nell, it's too late to worry about that. I'm in love with you."

Another long thrill rippled through her. "There's so much you don't know, and any one piece of it could change your mind."

"You don't think much of my wherewithal."

"Oh, yes, I do. Okay." She pulled her hand away, rose. She faced crises better on her feet. "There's something else I can tell you, and I don't expect you to understand or accept it."

"You're a kleptomaniac."

"No."

"An agent for a clandestine splinter group."

She managed to laugh. "No. Zack—"

"Wait, I get one more. You're one of those *Star Trek* addicts who can recite all the dialogue in every episode."

"No, only in the first season of the original."

"Well, that's all right, then. Okay, I give up."

"I'm a witch."

"Oh, well, I know that."

"I'm not using that as a euphemism for temperament," she said impatiently. "I mean it literally. Spells and charms and that sort of thing. A witch."

"Yeah, I got that the night you were dancing naked on your front lawn and glowing like a candle. Nell, I've lived on Three Sisters all my life. Do you expect me to be stupefied, or to do that crossed-fingers thing to ward off evil?"

Unsure if she was relieved or disappointed by his reaction, she frowned at him. "I guess I expected you to be something."

"It gave me a moment," he admitted. "But then, living with Rip sort of tones down the jolt. Of course she hasn't had anything to do with that kind of thing for years now. If you were to tell me you'd put some sort of love spell on me, I might be a little irked."

"Of course I didn't. I wouldn't even know how. I'm just . . . learning."

"An apprentice witch, then." Amused at both of them, he got to his feet. "I imagine Mia'll whip you into shape before long."

Did nothing surprise the man? "A couple of nights ago, I drew down the moon."

"What the hell does that mean? No, never mind, I don't have much of a head for the metaphysical. I'm a simple man, Nell." He ran his hands up and down her arms in the way he had that managed to arouse and soothe at the same time.

"No, you're not."

"Simple enough to know I'm standing here with a pretty woman and wasting the moonlight." He lowered his mouth to hers, drew her up and into a sumptuous kiss.

When her head fell back in surrender, and her arms wound around his neck, he circled her toward the glass door.

"I want to take you to bed. My bed. I want to love you—the Army brat who takes after her mother." He slid the door open, drew her inside. "I do love you."

Here, she thought as they lowered to the bed, was truth. And here was compassion. He would give these to her, as much as desire, as much as need. When he touched her, those thrills, those soft and fluid aches, were welcome.

The yearning she'd felt for home was satisfied.

Slow and sweet she moved with him. Freely, she opened for him, baring her heart as well as her body.

Her skin hummed under the brush of his fingers. The long, liquid pull inside her made her sigh. When her mouth met his again, she poured all she had into the kiss. What she couldn't give him in words, she could give him here, with her heart. With her body.

He skimmed his lips over her shoulder, tracing the shape of it, marveling at the firmness of muscle, the delicacy of bone. The taste of her intoxicated him, a flavor he'd come to crave as much as the next breath of air.

He found her breast, pleasured them both with lips and teeth and tongue until her heart began to beat under his mouth like the endless pulse of the sea. And as that beat quickened, she rose beneath him with a single breathless gasp.

Without hurry, he moved down her. A skim of fingers, a brush of lips. Felt her begin to tremble while his own blood pounded in sharp, anvil strikes of need.

Her hands groped, then fisted desperately in the

sheets when he lifted her hips and used his mouth on her. With a kind of ruthless patience, he shot her screaming to peak.

Her breath was sobbing now, her skin slick and damp as she rolled with him over the tangled sheets. Heat spiked, seemed to throb in the air, under her skin until her body felt like a furnace stoked too high.

"Zack—"

"Not yet. Not yet."

He was wild for her, for the taste of flesh, the urgency of her hands. In the pale splash of moonlight through the glass, her body seemed unearthly, white marble erotically hot to the touch and glimmering with the healthy sweat of lust.

When he fixed his teeth on her neck, it felt like feeding. Her mouth was wild, her body plunging. Then she cried out again, shocked pleasure, when his fingers drove her relentlessly over the edge.

Beyond control, beyond reason, she moved like lightning. She would have sworn the bed spun, in fast, dizzy circles, as she straddled him. Panting, she took him, rode him, drove him as he had driven her. Curved down to him, she ravished his mouth, then flung herself back, arms bowed behind her head, and flew as power whipped through her.

He reached for her, his fingers sliding helplessly down her busy hips. His blood was a rage, his mind a torrent. For a moment, all he could see was her eyes, flame-blue and vivid as jewels.

He reared up, pressed his lips to her heart, and shattered.

Fourteen

Ripley stopped her cruiser and watched Nell unpack her car. The sun had gone down, and with the cold snap that had slapped the island with a wicked northeast punch, any tourists were snuggled into the hotel sipping hot drinks.

Most of the natives would be sensibly settled in front of the television or finishing up dinner. She was looking forward to engaging in both those activities herself.

But she hadn't managed a one-on-one with Nell since the evening she'd come to the door.

"You're either getting a very late start or a really early one," Ripley called out.

Nell hefted the box and hunched inside the fleece-lined jacket she'd mail-ordered from the mainland. "A second start. The book club that Mia runs is back from its summer break. First meeting's tonight."

"Oh, yeah." Ripley got out of the car. She was wearing an ancient and well-loved bomber jacket and hiking boots. Her summer-weight ball cap had been replaced by one of plain black wool. "Need a hand?"

"I wouldn't turn one down." Happy that she sensed no lingering animosity, Nell gestured with her elbow to the second box. "Refreshments for the meeting. Are you going?"

"Not a chance."

"Don't like to read?"

"No, I like to read, I just don't like groups. Groups are made up of members," she explained. "And members are almost always people. So there you go."

"People you know," Nell pointed out.

"Which gives my stand a firmer base. This group's a bunch of hens who'll spend as much time pecking at the latest gossip as they will discussing whatever book they used as an excuse to get out of the house for the evening."

"How do you know that if you don't belong to the club?"

"Let's just say I have a sixth sense about these things."

"All right." Nell adjusted the balance of her box as they walked toward the rear entrance. Despite the weather, Mia's salvia hung on, as red and sassy as July. "Is that why you don't accept the Craft? Because it's like joining a group?"

"That would be reason enough. Added to that, I don't like being told I have to fall in line with something that started three hundred years before I was born."

A blast of wind blew her ponytail into a thick, dark whip. She ignored it, and the cold fingers that tried to sneak under her jacket. "I figure whatever needs to be dealt with can and should be dealt with without cackling over a cauldron, and I don't like having people wondering if I'm going to come flying by on my broom wearing a pointy black hat."

"I can't argue with the first two reasons." Nell opened the door, stepped into the welcome warmth. "But the second two don't hold. I've never once heard Mia cackle, over a cauldron or otherwise, and I've never seen anyone look at her as if they expected her to jump on a broom."

"Wouldn't surprise me if she did." Ripley strode into the main store, nodded at Lulu. "Lu."

"Rip." Lulu continued setting up the folding chairs. "Joining us tonight?"

"Are they holding the Ice Capades in hell?"

"Not that I've heard." She sniffed the air. "Do I smell gingerbread?"

"Got it in one," Nell told her. "Is there any special way you want the refreshments set up?"

"You're the expert there. Mia's upstairs yet. If she doesn't like the way you've done it, she'll tell you."

Nell carried the box to the table that was already waiting. She'd made some pricks in Lulu's shell, but had yet to crack all the way through. It was, she admitted, becoming a personal challenge.

"Do you think I can stay for some of the discussion?"

Lulu peered narrowly over the tops of her glasses. "You read the book?"

Damn. Nell took out the plate of gingerbread first, hoping the scent would sweeten her chances. "Well, no. I didn't know about the club until last week, and—"

"A person's got an hour a day that can be put to reading. I don't care how busy they are."

"Oh, stop being such a bitch, Lulu."

Nell's jaw dropped at Ripley's command, but the sidelong look she risked showed her Lulu's reaction was a happy grin.

"I can't. It goes down to the bone. You can stay if this one stays." She jerked a thumb at Ripley.

"I'm not interested in hanging out with a bunch of females chattering about a book and who's sleeping with who, who shouldn't be. Besides, I haven't had my dinner."

"Café's open another ten minutes," Lulu told her. "Split pea and ham soup was good today. And it'll do you good to spend some time with females. Explore your inner woman."

Ripley snorted. But the idea of the soup—in fact, any food that she wasn't obliged to fix herself—held tremendous appeal. "My inner woman doesn't need any exploration. She's lean and mean. But I'll check out the soup."

She sauntered toward the steps. "I might stay for the first twenty minutes," she called back. "But if I do, I want first crack at that gingerbread."

"Lulu?" Nell arranged star-shaped cookies on a glass plate.

"What?"

"I'll call you a bitch if it'll help bring us closer as people willing to explore our inner woman."

Lulu gave a snort of her own. "You've got a quick mouth on you when you want to. You carry your weight and you keep your word. That goes a way with me."

"I also make superior gingerbread."

Lulu walked over, picked up a slice. "I'll be the judge of that. See that you read October's book before the next discussion."

Nell's dimples flickered. "I will."

Upstairs, Ripley annoyed Peg by demanding a bowl of soup minutes before closing.

"I've got a date, so if you don't finish this before my time's up, you'll just have to wash the bowl yourself."

"I can dump it in the sink the same as you would, for Nell to deal with in the morning. Give me a hot chocolate to go with it. Are you still stepping out with Mick Burmingham?"

"That's right. We're snugging in and having a video festival. We're watching *Scream One*, *Two*, and *Three*."

"Very sexy. If you want to take off, I won't snitch to Mia."

Peg didn't hesitate. "Thanks." She whipped off her apron. "I'm gone."

Appreciating the fact that the café was empty, Ripley settled down to enjoy her soup in blissful solitude. Nothing could have spoiled her pleasure more quickly than hearing the click of Mia's heels on the floor barely one minute later.

"Where's Peg?"

"I cut her loose. Hot date."

"I don't appreciate you giving my employees permission to leave early. The café doesn't close for another four minutes, and it's part of her job description to clean the case, counters, and kitchen after that time."

"Well, I booted her along, so you can kick my ass instead of hers." Intrigued, Ripley continued to spoon up soup as she studied Mia.

It was a rare event to see the cool Ms. Devlin heated up, and jittery. She was twisting the chain of the amulet she wore around her neck, continued to worry it as she strode over to the display counter and hissed.

"There are health regulations about cleanliness in food services. Since you were so generous to Peg, you can damn well scrub this up yourself."

"In a pig's eye," Ripley muttered, but felt a tug of guilt that threatened to spoil her appetite. "What bug crawled up your butt?"

"I have a business to run here, and it takes more than stalking around the village looking cocky, which is your specialty."

"Oh, get fucked, Mia. It'll improve your humor."

Mia rounded back. "Unlike you, fucking isn't my answer to every whim and itch."

"You want to play the ice maiden because Sam Logan dumped you, that's your . . ." Ripley trailed off, despising herself even as the hot color in Mia's face drained. "Sorry. Out of line. Way out of line."

"Forget it."

"When I sucker punch somebody, I apologize. Even if you did come in here looking for a fight. In fact, I'll not only apologize, I'll ask you what's wrong."

"What the hell do you care?"

"Normally, I don't. But normally I don't see you spooked. What's the deal?"

They'd been friends once, and good ones. As close as any sisters. Because of that it was harder for Mia to sit, to open up, than it would have been if Ripley had been a stranger.

But the matter was more important than feuds or grudges. She sat across from Ripley, leveled her gaze. "There's blood on the moon."

"Oh, for—"

Before Ripley could finish, Mia's hand shot out, gripped her wrist. "Trouble, bad trouble is coming. A dark force. You know me well enough to be sure I wouldn't say it, wouldn't tell you, of all people, unless I was sure."

"And you know me well enough to know what I think of portents and omens." But there was a cold chill working up her spine.

"It's coming, after the leaves finish dying, before the first snow. I'm sure of that, too, but I can't see what it is, or where it comes from. Something's blocking it."

It disturbed Ripley when Mia's eyes went that deep, that dark. It seemed you could see a thousand years in them. "Any trouble comes to the island, Zack and I will handle it."

"It'll take more. Ripley, Zack loves Nell and you love him. They're at the center of this. I feel it. If you don't flex, something will break. Something none of us can put right again. I can't do whatever needs to be done alone, and Nell isn't ready yet."

"I can't help you that way."

"Won't."

"Can't or won't comes out to the same thing."

"Yes, it does," Mia said as she got to her feet. There

wasn't temper sparking her eyes; that would have been easy to fight. There was weariness. "Deny what you are, lose what you are. I sincerely hope you don't regret it."

Mia went downstairs to greet her book club and deal with the business at hand.

Alone, Ripley rested her chin on her fist. It was a guilt trip, that was all. When Mia wasn't shooting out spiteful little darts, she heaped on layers of sticky guilt. Ripley wasn't falling for it. If there was a red haze over the moon, it was due to some atmospheric quirk and had nothing to do with her.

She would leave the omens and portents to Mia since she enjoyed them so much.

She shouldn't have dropped in tonight, shouldn't have put herself in a position where Mia could try to pin her. All they did was annoy each other. It had been that way for more than a decade.

But not always.

They'd been friends, next to inseparable friends, until they'd teetered on the cusp of adulthood. Ripley remembered her mother had called them twins of the heart. They'd shared everything, and maybe that was the problem.

It was natural for interests to diverge when people grew up, natural for childhood friends to drift apart. Not that she and Mia had drifted, she admitted. It had been more like a sword slash down the center of their friendship. Abrupt and violent.

But she'd had the right to go her own way. She'd *been* right to go her own way. And she wasn't going back now just because Mia was jittery over some atmospheric hitch.

Even if Mia was right and trouble was coming, it would be dealt with through the rules and obligations of the law, and not with spellbinding.

She had put away her childish things, the toys and the tools she had no further interest in. That had been sensible, mature. When people looked at her now, they saw Ripley Todd, deputy, a dependable, responsible woman who did her job; they didn't see some flaky island priestess who would brew them a potion to beef up their sex lives.

Irritated because even her thoughts sounded defensive and nasty, she gathered up her dishes and took them into the kitchen. There was just enough guilt still pricking at her to oblige her to rinse the dishes, load them in the dishwasher, scrub out the sink.

That, she decided, paid her debt.

She could hear the voices, all female, flowing back from the front of the store where the book club gathered. She could smell the incense Mia lit, a scent for protection. Ripley snuck out the back. A fleet of steamrollers couldn't have pushed her forward and into that noisy clutch of women now.

Just outside the back door she saw the fat black candle burning, a charm to repel evil. She would have sneered at it, but her gaze was drawn up.

The waning globe of the moon was shrouded in a thin and bloody mist.

Unable to work up that sneer, she jammed her hands in her jacket pockets and stared down at her own boots as she walked to her car.

When the last of the book club members were out the door, Mia flipped the locks. Nell was already clearing plates and napkins while Lulu closed the register.

"That was fun!" Stoneware rang gaily as Nell stacked coffee cups. "And so interesting. I've never discussed a book that way. Whenever I read one, I just think, well, I liked it or I didn't, but I never talked about why. And I promise to read next month's selection so I'll have something to contribute."

"I'll see to the dishes, Nell. You must be tired."

"I'm not." Nell lifted a loaded tray. "There was so much energy in here tonight. I feel like I just lapped it up."

"Isn't Zack waiting for you?"

"Oh, not tonight. I told him I was going to crash the party."

Lulu waited until Nell was upstairs. "What's wrong?" she asked Mia.

"I'm not entirely sure." To keep her hands busy, Mia began folding the chairs. "That's what concerns me most. Something's coming, and I can't pin it down. It's all right for tonight." She glanced up the stairs as she carted chairs to the storeroom. "She's all right for tonight."

"She's the center." Lulu stored her own haul of chairs. "I guess I felt that all along, and didn't cut her much of a break. But the fact is, that's a sweet girl who works hard. Does somebody want to hurt her?"

"Someone already has, and I don't intend to let him do it again. I'll try a foretelling, but I need to prepare for it. I need to clear my mind. There's time. I can't tell how much, but it'll have to be enough."

"Will you tell her?"

"Not just yet. She'll have her own preparations, her own cleansing to do. She's in love, and that makes her strong. She'll need to be."

"What makes you strong, Mia?"

"Purpose. Love never worked for me."

"I heard he's in New York."

Mia shrugged, a deliberate gesture. She knew who Lulu meant, and it irritated her to have Sam Logan tossed at her twice in one night. "It's a big city," she said flatly. "He'll have plenty of company. I want to finish and go home. I need sleep."

"Idiot man," Lulu muttered under her breath. There were too many idiot men in the world, to her way of thinking. And most of them ended up bumping up against stubborn women.

Spells were, Nell decided, really just a kind of recipe. And there she was on solid ground. A recipe required time, care, and quality ingredients in proper proportions for success. Add a bit of imagination and it became a personal dish.

She set aside time between jobs and book work to study the spell book Mia had lent her. She imagined Mia would be amused by the idea of viewing it as a kind of metaphysical cookbook, but she didn't think she would be offended.

Time also had to be carved out for meditation, visualization, for gathering and creating her own tools so that she'd have what she liked to consider a well-supplied witch's pantry.

But now she intended to reward herself with her first solo practice session.

"Love spells, banishing spells, protection spells," she chanted as she flipped through. "Binding spells, money spells, healing spells."

Something for everybody, she thought, and remembered Mia's warning about being careful what she wished for. A careless or selfish wish could boomerang in unpleasant, or certainly unexpected, ways.

She would keep it simple, choosing something that involved no one and couldn't inadvertently cause harm or trouble.

She used her broom first, sweeping the negative energy away, then she set it by the kitchen door to prevent any reentry. With Diego ribboning between her legs, she chose her candles, inscribed them with the appropriate symbols. Deciding that she could use all the help she could get, she selected crystals to bolster the energy. She arranged them, and the pot of frost-burned geraniums she'd taken from Zack's front porch.

Expelled a breath, drew in fresh.

She referred back to the healing spell Mia had written out on parchment in India ink and, closing her eyes, adjusted the words in her mind to suit her purpose.

"Here goes," she whispered.

"This damaged bloom I seek to heal, from its withered petals fresh beauty reveal. Um . . . its blooming time was too soon done, its color brings pleasure to all and harm to no one. Set the flower within it free. As I will, so mote it be."

She bit her lip, waited. The geranium sat stubbornly

wilted in its pot. Nell bent over, looking close for some little sign of green.

She straightened again. "Shoot. I guess I'm not ready to solo."

But maybe she should try again. She needed to visualize, to *see* the plant lush and full and blooming. She needed to smell leaves and petals, channel her energy. Or was it the plant's energy? In any case, giving up after one try made her a pretty wimpy witch.

She closed her eyes again, started to process, then yelped at the brisk knock on her back door. She spun around so quickly, she booted Diego halfway across the little room, which caused him to plop down and begin to wash himself as if that was what he'd intended all along.

Chuckling, Nell opened the door to Ripley.

"I was cruising by, saw the candlelight. Are you having power trouble?" Even as she asked, she looked past Nell and saw the ritual candles on the table. "Oh."

"Practicing, and from the results, I need a lot more. Come on in."

"I don't want to interrupt." Since the night of the book club meeting she'd made a point to stop by, or at least cruise by, every evening. "Isn't that the dead plant from our front porch?"

"It's not dead yet, but it's close. I asked Zack if I could try to bring it back."

"Working spells on dead geraniums? Man, you slay me."

"I figured if I made any mistakes, it couldn't hurt anything. Do you want some tea? I brewed some just a while ago."

"Well, maybe. Zack said to let you know he'd be

by when he finished up. We had a D and D—drunk and disorderly," she explained. "Underage minor. He's just about sicked up all of the six-pack he swiped from his parents' refrigerator. Zack's walking him home."

"Anyone I know?"

"The Stubens boy, the oldest. His girlfriend dumped him yesterday, so he decided to cry in his daddy's beer. Since the result was him getting sick as three dogs, I think he'll look for another way to ease his broken heart next time out. What's that smell?"

"I've got a pork loin roasting. You're welcome to stay for dinner."

"I'd just as soon not sit here and watch you two make googly eyes at each other. But I wouldn't mind you sending a doggie bag home with Zack."

"Happy to." She handed Ripley a cup of tea. "But we don't make googly eyes at each other."

"Do so."

Nell got a plate of tiny appetizers out of the fridge.

"Man, do you guys eat like this every night?" Ripley asked.

"I practice on Zack."

"Lucky bastard." Ripley helped herself to a little wedge of bruschetta. "Anything he doesn't go for, you can send on to me. I'll let you know if it's any good."

"That's generous of you. Try a stuffed mushroom. Zack won't touch them."

"Doesn't know what he's missing," Ripley announced after one bite. "The catering deal's moving along pretty well, huh?"

"It is." But Nell dreamed of a convection oven and a Sub-Zero refrigerator. Impossible and impractical in her cozy cottage kitchen, she reminded herself. And, for the moment, out of Sisters Catering's financial grasp. "I'm doing sandwiches and cake for a christening on Saturday."

"The new Burmingham baby."

"Right. And Lulu's sister and family from Baltimore are coming in next week. Lulu wants to wow them. There's some sibling rivalry there." Nell jerked a thumb toward the oven. "I'm making this pork loin, so I wanted to try it out first."

"That's going some for Lu. She squeezes a penny until Lincoln weeps."

"We worked out a deal, a barter. She's knitting me a couple of sweaters. I can use them with winter coming."

"We've got a warm spell coming. We'll snag a bit of Indian summer before it hits."

"I hope you're right."

"So . . ." Ripley bent down, picked up Diego. "How's Mia doing?"

"She's fine. She seems a little distracted lately." Nell lifted her eyebrows. "Why do you ask?"

"No reason. I guess she's busy making plans for Halloween. She really gets into it."

"We're going to decorate the store the week of the first. I'm warned that every kid on the island hits Café Book for trick or treat."

"Who can resist candy from the witch? I'd better go." She gave Diego a quick scratch as she set him down. "Zack'll be along any minute. I can take that pot out of your way if you . . ." She trailed off as she glanced over.

A glory of crimson petals covered healthy green stalks. "Well, well, son of a bitch."

"I did it! It worked. Oh! Oh!" In one leap Nell was at the table, her nose buried in blooms. "I can't believe it. I mean, I wanted to believe it, but I didn't really think I could manage it. Not by myself. Isn't it lovely?"

"Yeah, it's okay."

She knew what it was like, the rush of power, that bright thrill. The pleasures, both small and huge. Ripley felt an echo of it now as Nell lifted the pot high and circled.

"It's not all flowers and moonbeams, Nell."

"What happened?" Nell lowered the pot, cradled it like a baby. "What happened to make you resent what you have?"

"I don't resent it. I just don't want it."

"I've been powerless. This is better."

"What's better isn't being able to make flowers bloom. It's being able to take care of yourself. You didn't need a spell book to figure out how to do that."

"One doesn't have to be exclusive of the other."

"Maybe not. But life's a hell of a lot easier when they are." She walked to the door, opened it. "Don't leave your candles unattended."

By the time Zack arrived, Nell had the table cleared and set. The kitchen was fragrant with her roast and the aftermath of her candles.

She liked hearing him come to the kitchen door, those long strides. The way he stopped and wiped his feet on the mat. The rush of brisk air he let in when he opened the door. And the easy smile he gave her as he kept on walking until his mouth covered hers.

"Later than I expected."

"It's all right. Ripley stopped by and told me you would be."

"Then I guess I don't need these." He took the bouquet of carnations from behind his back.

"No, but I do." She gathered them up. "Thanks. I thought we'd try this Australian wine I read about, if you want to open it."

"Fine." He turned to shrug out of his jacket and hang it on the kitchen peg. His gaze hit the pot of geraniums she'd set on the side counter. It gave him a little jolt, but after the briefest hesitation, he went on and pegged his jacket. "I don't guess you did that with fertilizer."

"No." She linked her fingers together around the carnation stems. "I didn't. Does it bother you?"

"Not bother. But talking about it, even knowing about it's different than seeing it." At home in her kitchen, he pulled open a drawer for a corkscrew. "In any case, you don't have to smooth out every ripple with me."

"I love you, Zack."

He stood, the corkscrew in one hand, the bottle of wine in the other. And suddenly couldn't move. Emotions overwhelmed him.

"It's been hard waiting for you to say that to me."

"I couldn't say it before."

"Why now?"

"Because you brought me carnations. Because I don't have to smooth out every ripple with you. Because when I hear you coming up to my door everything inside me lifts and sighs. And because love is the most vital magic. I want to give mine to you."

He set the wine and corkscrew aside carefully, stepped over to her. Gently, he stroked his hands across her cheeks, into her hair. "I've waited my whole life for you." Tenderly, he kissed her forehead, her cheeks. "I want to spend the rest of it with you."

She ignored the clutch in her belly and concentrated on the joy. "Let's give each other the now. Every minute's precious." She laid her head on his shoulder. "Every minute counts."

Fifteen

Evan Remington wandered the palatial rooms of his Monterey home. Bored, restless, he studied his possessions. Each one had been selected with care, either by him personally or by a decorator following explicit instructions.

He had always known precisely what he preferred, and precisely what he wanted. He'd always made certain to obtain it. Whatever the cost, whatever the effort.

Everything that surrounded him reflected his taste, a taste admired by associates, peers, and those whose goal it was to fall into either category.

And everything dissatisfied him.

He considered an auction. He could find some currently trendy charity and generate some nice press while he disposed of items he no longer wanted. He could let it leak that he was disposing of those items because they held too many painful memories of his dead wife.

The lovely, lost Helen.

He even considered selling the house. The fact was, it did remind him of her. It wasn't a problem in Los Angeles. She hadn't died in Los Angeles.

Since her accident, he had seldom come to Monterey. It was rare for him to stay more than a few days, and he always came alone. He didn't consider the servants. They fell along the same lines as the furnishings to him. Necessary and efficient.

The first time he'd come back, he'd been raw with grief. He'd wept like a madman while lying across the bed he'd last shared with her, clinging to the nightgown she'd worn. Breathing in the scent of her.

His love was consuming, and his pain threatened to eat him alive.

She had *belonged* to him.

When the torrent had passed, he'd wandered the house like a ghost, touching what she had touched, hearing her voice echo in his ears, catching a whiff of her scent everywhere. As if it was inside him.

He'd spent an hour in her closet, caressing her clothes. And forgetting the night he had locked her in there when she'd been late coming home.

He wallowed in her, and when he could stand the confinement of the house no longer, he'd driven to the site of her death. And had stood, a solitary figure, weeping on the cliffs.

His doctor prescribed medication and rest. His friends encircled him with sympathy.

He began to enjoy it.

Within a month, he'd forgotten he had insisted that Helen make the trip to Big Sur that day. In his mind, in the cradle of his memory, he saw himself entreating her not to attend, to stay home and rest until she was well again.

Of course, she hadn't listened. She had never listened.

Grief turned to fury, a raging flood of anger that he drowned with liquor and solitude. She'd betrayed him, going out against his wishes, insisting on attending some frivolous party rather than respecting her husband's request.

She had left him unforgivably alone.

But even rage passes. The hole it left in him he filled with a fantasy of her, of their marriage, even of himself. He heard people speak of them as a perfect couple, cruelly parted by tragedy.

He read it, thought it. Believed it.

He wore one of her earrings on a chain next to his heart and let the affectation leak to a suitable media source. It was said Gable did the same when he'd lost Lombard.

He kept her clothes in her closets, her books on the shelves, her perfumes in their bottles. He had an angel of white marble erected for her in the cemetery where no body lay. Every week, a dozen red roses were placed at its feet.

To keep himself sane, he threw himself into his work. He began to sleep again, without so many dreams in which Helen came to him. Gradually, at the urging of friends, he began to go out again socially.

But the women eager to comfort the widower didn't interest him. He dated only because it kept him in the press. He bedded a few of the women only because there would be talk otherwise, of an unflattering sort.

Sex had never driven him. Control had.

He had no wish ever to marry again. There would never be another Helen. They had been destined for each other. She'd been meant for him, meant to be molded and formed by him. If he'd had to punish her occasionally—well, discipline was part of the formation. He'd had to teach her.

Finally, in their last few weeks together, he had believed she had learned. It had been a rare thing for her to make a mistake, in public or private. She'd deferred to him as a wife was meant to defer to a husband, and had made certain that he was pleased with her.

He remembered, or convinced himself that he remembered, that he'd been about to reward her with a trip to Antigua. She had been fascinated by the ocean, his Helen. And had told him, during those first heady weeks of love and discovery, how she sometimes dreamed of living on an island.

In the end, the sea had taken her.

Because he could feel the depression rolling into him like a fog, he poured a glass of mineral water and took one of his pills.

No, he wouldn't sell the house, he decided in one of his lightning mood changes. He would open it. He would give one of the lavish, A-list parties, the kind he and Helen had hosted so often and so successfully.

It would feel as if she were there beside him, as she was meant to be.

When the phone rang, he ignored it and continued to stand, gently rubbing an etched gold hoop earring through the fine linen of his shirt.

"Sir? Ms. Reece is on the phone. She'd like to speak with you if you're available."

Saying nothing, Evan held out a hand for the portable phone. He never glanced at the uniformed maid who gave it to him, but slid open the terrace door and stepped outside in the balm of breeze to speak to his sister.

"Yes, Barbara?"

"Evan, I'm glad you were in. Deke and I were hoping you'd join us at the club this afternoon. We can have a set of tennis, lunch by the pool. I hardly see my baby brother these days."

He started to refuse. His sister's country club circle held little interest for him. But he reconsidered quickly, knowing how well Barbara planned entertainment. And how much of the annoyance of the details she would willingly take from his hands.

"I'd like that. I want to speak to you anyway." He glanced at his Rolex. "Why don't I meet you there. Eleven-thirty?"

"Absolutely perfect. Prepare yourself. I've been working on my backhand."

His tennis game was off. Barbara had broken his serve yet again and was prancing around like a fool in her designer tennis skirt. Of course, *she* had time to fritter around any fucking day of the week, making time with some slick-fingered tennis pro while her asshole husband practiced his putting.

He, on the other hand, was a busy man, with a demanding business and high-powered clients who whined like babies if he didn't give them his full attention.

He didn't have time for goddamn games.

He bulleted one over the net, gritted his teeth audibly when Barbara hustled and returned it. Sweat dampened his face, ran down his back. And his mouth peeled back in a snarl as he raced over the court.

It was a look Nell would have recognized. One she would have feared.

Barbara recognized it as well and instinctively bungled a return. "You're killing me," she called out, and shook her head as she took her time going back to position.

Evan had always been temperamental, she thought. It was hard for him not to win, not to get his way. It always had been. As a child his retribution had come in one of two forms. Icy silence that could bore holes in steel. Or quick, hot violence.

You're older, her mother had said, always. *Be a good girl, be a good sister. Let the baby win.*

It was such an old and ingrained habit, she barely registered her decision to blow the next return as well. And after all, the afternoon would be so much more pleasant if he won the match. Why cause contention over a tennis game?

So, burying her own competitive spirit, she took a dive, surrendering the game.

His expression changed almost instantly.

"Good game, Evan. I never could keep up with you."

She sent him an indulgent smile as they positioned themselves for the next. Boys hate to lose to girls, she thought. It was another of her mother's homilies.

And what were men but big boys?

By the time it was over and he'd won the match,

he was in a fine mood. He felt loose and limber and affectionate. He swung an arm over Barbara's shoulders, bussed her cheek. "Your backhand still needs some work."

There was a little bubble of annoyance in her throat, automatically swallowed. "Yours is lethal." She picked up her bag. "And since you humiliated me, you get to buy lunch. I'll meet you on the lounge terrace. Thirty minutes."

She kept him waiting, always a minor irritation. But it pleased him to see how attractive she was, how well presented. He detested sloppy attire or unkempt hair on a woman, and Barbara never disappointed him.

She was four years his senior, but could have passed for thirty-five. Her skin was pampered and taut, her hair sleek and glossy, and her figure trim.

She joined him under the shade of the umbrella, smelling subtly of her favored White Diamonds.

"I'm going to console myself with a champagne cocktail." She crossed legs garbed in thin raw silk. "Between that and sitting with the most handsome man in the club, my mood should immediately improve."

"And I was just thinking what a beautiful woman I have for a sister."

Her face lit up. "You always say the sweetest things."

It was true, she thought. He did. When he won. It made her all the more pleased that she'd tanked the match.

"Let's not wait for Deke," she said, still beaming at him. "Lord knows when he'll finish his game."

She ordered her cocktail and a Cobb salad, moaning dramatically when Evan selected shrimp scampi. "Oh, I hate you for your metabolism. You never gain an ounce. I'm going to have a bite of yours, then curse you when I'm tortured tomorrow by my personal trainer."

"A little more discipline, Barbara, and you'd keep your figure without paying someone to make you sweat."

"Believe me, she's worth every penny. The sadist." With a contented sigh, she sat back, careful to keep her face out of the sun. "Tell me, darling, what did you want to talk to me about?"

"I'm going to give a party, at the Monterey house. It's time to . . ."

"Yes." She leaned forward again to cover his hand with hers, squeezed. "Yes, it is time. I'm so glad to see you looking well again, Evan, to hear you making plans. You went through such a horrible time."

Tears welled, and her affection for him was such that she blinked them back thinking not of her mascara but of his sensibilities.

He detested public scenes.

"You've begun to move on in the past few months. That's healthy. Helen would have wanted that."

"You're right, of course." He eased his hand away as their drinks were served.

He didn't like being touched. Casually, of course, was one thing. In the business world, hugs and kisses were just another tool. But he detested being touched with intensity.

"I haven't entertained, not really, since it happened. Business affairs, of course, but . . . Helen and I planned every detail of our parties together. She handled so much of it—the invitations, the menu—all subject to my approval, of course. I was hoping I could impose on you to help me."

"Of course I will. You just tell me what you have in mind, and when. I went to a party just last week, very lavish and fun. I'll steal some ideas. It was Pamela and Donald. Pamela's often a pain in the neck, but she does know how to throw a party. Speaking of her, I feel I should tell you—and I hope it doesn't upset you. I'm afraid you'll hear it from someone else."

"What is it?"

"Pamela's been nattering, you know how she is."

Evan could barely picture the woman. "About what?"

"She and Donald took a holiday out east a couple of weeks ago. Cape Cod, primarily, though she talked him into driving about and staying at a few bed-and-breakfasts like nomads. She claims while they were out there, sightseeing in some little village or other, she saw a woman who looked just like Helen."

Evan's hand vised on his glass. "What do you mean?"

"She cornered me at her party, went on and on about it. Claimed that at first glance she thought she'd seen a ghost. In fact, she was so insistent about how this . . . apparition might have been poor Helen's double, she asked me if Helen had a sister. I told her no, of course. I imagine she caught a glimpse of some fine-boned blonde about Helen's age and enhanced the whole thing in her mind. The way she's going on about it, I didn't want you to hear some rumor that would cause you any pain."

"The woman's an idiot."

"Well, she's certainly imaginative," Barbara said. "Now that we've gotten that out of the way, tell me how many people you're planning to invite."

"Two hundred, two-fifty," he said absently. "Just where did Pamela claim to see this ghost of hers?"

"Oh, some island off the East Coast. I'm not even sure of the name, as I was busy trying to change the subject. Something about sisters. Formal or casual?"

"What?"

"The party, honey. Formal or casual?"

"Formal," he murmured, and let his sister's voice buzz in his head like bees.

Lulu lived in a saltbox two blocks back from High Street. It stood out from its more conservative neighbors with its lipstick-red shutters and porch. On that red porch was a glider splattered and streaked with a rainbow of paint in a mad pattern that rivaled a Jackson Pollock canvas.

A purple gazing ball stood on the thin swath of lawn and shaded a gargoyle who squatted, permanently sticking out his tongue at passersby.

A winged dragon of iridescent green flew on the roof as a weather vane, along with a wildly striped wind sock. In the short driveway sat a dignified late-model sedan in practical black, and Lulu's Day-Glo orange VW, circa 1971.

Love beads, from the same era, dangled from the rearview mirror.

Following instructions, Nell parked on the street

one house down, then hauled her delivery to the back door. Lulu swung it open before Nell could knock.

"I'll give you prompt." And with this, Lulu grabbed Nell's arm just above the elbow and yanked her inside. "I sent the lot of them out for a walk and don't figure they'll be back for twenty minutes. More, if I'm lucky. Syl's been a pain in my butt since she was born."

"Your sister."

"My parents insist she is, but I have my doubts." Lulu poked her head in the box the minute Nell set it down on the center island. "The idea that I share blood with that pompous, narrow-minded, pissy little twerp gives me the willies. I'm eighteen months older, so we went through the sixties at close to the same pace. Difference is, she remembers them, which says it all."

"Ah." Nell tried to imagine Lulu as a freewheeling, free-loving hippie, and found it wasn't that much of a stretch. For the family dinner, she'd donned a sweatshirt that announced she was all out of estrogen and had a gun.

Fair warning, Nell decided.

"Um. Still, it's nice that you sometimes get together like this."

"She just comes out here, once every damn year, to lord it over me. According to the Gospel of Sylvia, a woman isn't a woman unless she has a husband and children, chairs some crappy committee, and knows how to make an emergency centerpiece out of twine, spit, and an empty tuna can."

"We're going to do a hell of a lot better than that." Nell busied herself by putting the roast in the oven, turning it to warm. "I made it au jus, so you just spoon that over, and serve it with the side dishes. The autumn salad goes first. Tell them to leave room for the pumpkin cheesecake."

"That'll totally amaze her." Lulu poured another glass of the wine she was tippling to get through the event. "I had a husband."

She said it so fiercely, so viciously that Nell turned to stare. "Oh?"

"Don't know what made me do it legal. I wasn't knocked up or anything. Stupid. I guess I did it to prove I could still rebel. He was no good, just as useless as he was handsome. It turned out his idea of marriage was having someplace to go after he'd finished boinking whatever floozie caught his fancy that particular night."

"I'm sorry."

"No need to be sorry. Live and learn. I kicked his ass out in nineteen-eighty-five. The only time it bothers me is when Syl comes around gloating about her husband, who's no more than a paper pusher, and has a spare tire you could ride on to Cleveland, her kids, who are a couple of snotty teenagers in two-hundred dollar track shoes, and the joys of her life in the suburbs. I'd rather be shot dead than live in some cookie-cutter house in the 'burbs."

Since either the wine or the situation with Syl was making Lulu loquacious, Nell took advantage. "So, you didn't grow up here together?"

"Hell, no. We grew up in Baltimore. I took off when I was seventeen, went straight to Haight-Ashbury. I lived in a commune in Colorado for a while, traveled, experienced. When I came here, I wasn't yet twenty. I've been here over thirty-two years now. God."

The idea of that had her knocking back the wine and pouring more.

"Mia's grandmother gave me a job doing this and that for her, then when Mia came along, her mother hired me to mind her when she needed minding. Carly Devlin's a nice enough person, but the fact was she didn't have much interest in raising a child."

"So you did. I didn't realize." No wonder, Nell thought, she was so protective of Mia. "Whatever your sister thinks, you've got a daughter at the heart of it."

"Damn right." She gave a little nod, then set down her glass. "Do whatever you need to do here. I'll be right back." She started out, turned back. "If Syl the Pill comes back before I do, just tell her how you work at the bookstore and stopped in to ask me something about work."

"No problem." Keeping tabs on the time, Nell organized the meal, slipping the salad and the dressing in the refrigerator, sliding the scalloped potatoes and the herbed green beans in with the roast.

She peeked into the dining room, saw the table had yet to be set, and hunted out dishes and linens.

"First half of your payment," Lulu announced as she came back in with a wrinkled shopping bag.

"Thanks. Listen, I didn't know what dishes you wanted, but I think these'll work well. It's family, and they're casual and cheerful."

"Good thing, as that's all I've got."

Lulu waited while Nell dipped into the shopping bag, then smiled smugly at the gasp of pleasure. "Oh, oh, Lulu!"

It was a simple design, a mock turtleneck that could and would be worn with everything. But the color was a deep, rich blue and the material was as soft as a cloud.

"I never expected anything like this." Already, Nell was holding it up, rubbing her cheek against the shoulder. "It's absolutely wonderful."

"You wear too many neutrals." Pleasing herself, Lulu tugged and fussed, then stood back to admire the result. "They wash the color out of your face. This brings it in, goes with your coloring. I started on the second one, nice tunic length in a good strong red."

"I don't know how to thank you. I can't wait to try it on and—"

"They're back," Lulu hissed, and immediately began shoving Nell toward the door. "Go! Get."

"You need to toss the salad just before—"

"Yes, yes. Go!"

Nell clutched her new sweater as Lulu slammed the door in her face.

"Serving," she finished and chuckled all the way to the car.

The minute she got home she stripped off her sweatshirt and slid into the magnificent sweater. Unable to get a satisfactory view from top to bottom, she dragged a chair in front of the mirror and stood on it.

There'd been a time when she'd had dozens of sweaters—cashmere, silk, the softest cottons, the thinnest wools. None of them brought her the sheer joy of this one, handmade by a friend.

Or close enough to a friend, she thought. And payment for a job well done.

She took it off again, folded it lovingly in a drawer.

She would wear it to work on Monday. For now the sweatshirt was a better choice. She had messy work to do.

Her trio of pumpkins waited on a bed of newspapers on her kitchen table. She'd already used a portion of the largest for Lulu's dessert. It only waited to be carved into the appropriate design.

She would make pumpkin bread, she thought, as she began on the second. And pie, cookies. The hulls would serve as decorations on her front porch. Big, fat, scary pumpkins to entertain the neighbors and children.

She was up to her elbows in pumpkin meat and seeds when Zack strolled in the door. "I get to do the third one." He came up behind her, wrapping his arms tight, nuzzling her neck. "I'm a jack-o'-lantern master."

"The things you learn about people."

"Want me to dump the guts for you?"

"Dump them? How would I make a pie?"

"With a can." His brow furrowed as he watched her slide chunks of pumpkin into a large bowl. "You mean you actually use that stuff?"

"Of course. Where do you think they get the stuff *in* the cans?"

"I never thought about it. Pumpkin factory." He picked up the knife to start on the third while Nell washed her hands.

"You've obviously led a very sheltered life, Sheriff Todd."

"If that's so, I can't think of anyone I'd rather have corrupt me. How about when we finish this, we take a drive to the windward side, sit in my cruiser and break a few laws."

"Love to." She came back with a Magic Marker and began to draw a hideous face on the first pumpkin. "Everything quiet in the village?"

"It tends to be on Sundays this time of year. Did you get Lulu all set?"

"I did. I didn't realize she'd been married once."

"Long time ago. Some drifter who worked on the docks for a bit, I'm told. Seems to me I heard it didn't last six months. I guess it soured her on men, because I've never known her to take up with one since."

"She worked for Mia's grandmother, then her mother."

"That's right. Lu's kept the reins on Mia as long as I can remember. In fact, thinking about it, Lu's the only one Mia's let hold the reins for very long. Mia had a thing going with Sam Logan—his family owns the hotel. It didn't work out, and he left the island, Jesus, it's been ten years, maybe more."

"Oh, I see." Sam Logan, Nell thought. The man Mia had loved once.

"Sam and I hung out together some, back when we were younger," Zack went on as he hollowed out the pumpkin. "We've lost touch. But I remember that when Sam and Mia were seeing each other, Lulu watched him like a hawk."

He grinned, remembering it, then pulled the knife out of the heart of the pumpkin.

Nell saw it gleam in the overhead light, she saw it drip. She saw, as a rushing wind filled her head, the blood that stained his shirt, his hands, and pooled like a red river on the floor at his feet.

She made no sound at all as she slid bonelessly from the chair.

"Hey, hey, hey. Come on, Nell, come on back now."

His voice was dim, as if they were both underwater. Something cool slid over her face. She seemed to rise from fathoms deep, slowly toward the surface. As her eyes opened, she saw a white mist that rolled away, layer by gauzy layer, until she saw his face.

"Zack!" In terror, she grabbed at him, yanking his shirt to check for wounds. Her fingers felt fat and fumbling.

"Hold on." He might have laughed at the way she pulled at his buttons if her face hadn't been deathly white. "Lie back down, get your breath."

"Blood. So much blood."

"Ssh." His first reaction when she'd fainted had been panic, and he'd dealt with it as he always did. By doing what came next. He'd picked her up, carried her to the couch, and revived her. Now the penetrating fear she exuded tied knots in his belly.

"I bet you haven't eaten enough to keep a bird alive today, have you? Somebody who cooks as much as you do should learn how to eat regular meals. I'm going to get you a glass of water, something to eat. If you're not feeling steady then, I'm calling the doctor."

"I'm not sick. I'm not hurt. You were bleeding." Her hands shook as they ran over him. "There was blood all over your shirt, your hands, the floor. The knife. I saw . . ."

"I'm not bleeding, honey. Not so much as a nick."

He lifted his hands, turning them to prove it. "Just a trick of the light, that's all."

"It wasn't." She locked her arms around him, held on ferociously. "I saw it. Don't touch the knife anymore. Don't touch it."

"Okay." He kissed the top of her head, stroked her hair. "I won't. Everything's all right, Nell."

She closed her hand around her locket, ran a charm for protection through her head. "I want you to wear this." Steadier now, she eased back and slipped the chain over her head. "All the time. Don't take it off."

He looked at the carved heart at the end of the chain and had a normal man's reaction. "I appreciate that, Nell. Really I do. But that's a girl thing."

"Wear it under your shirt," she said impatiently. "No one has to see it. I want you to wear it night and day." She looped it over his head even as he grimaced. "I want you to promise me you will."

Anticipating his next protest, Nell framed his face with her hands. "It belonged to my mother. It's the only thing of hers I still have. The only thing I brought away with me. Please do this for me, Zack. Promise me you won't take it off, not for any reason."

"All right. I'll promise that if you promise me you'll eat something."

"We'll have pumpkin soup. You'll like it."

That night, while she slept, she ran wildly through the woods, unable to find her way in the dark of the moon.

The scent of blood and death chased her.

Sixteen

Nell put it all out of her mind, or tried to, and went to work. She served coffee and muffins, joked with regulars. She wore her new blue sweater and stirred the pumpkin soup she had simmering for the lunch crowd.

She replenished the stack of business cards Mia had suggested that she put beside the café's cash register.

It was all so normal, almost breezy. Except she reached for the locket she no longer wore a dozen times through the morning. Each time she did, the image of Zack covered with blood flashed through her mind.

He'd had to go to the mainland that morning, and the idea of him being off-island was one more fear. He could be attacked on the street, mugged. Left to lie bleeding and dying.

By the end of her shift she'd concluded she hadn't done enough, and needed help.

She found Mia helping a customer with a selection of children's books. She waited, mentally wringing her hands, until the choices were made and the customer headed to checkout.

"I know you're busy, but I need to talk to you."

"All right. Let me get my jacket. We'll take a walk."

She was back moments later with a suede jacket tossed over her short dress. Both were the color of butternut squash that made her hair glint like a mane of fire.

She waved at Lulu as she walked out the front door. "Taking my lunch break. Great sweater," she added as they stepped outside. "Lulu's work, isn't it?"

"Yes."

"You've jumped a hurdle. She wouldn't have made you something that fine if she hadn't decided to accept you. Congratulations."

"Thanks. I . . . did you want to get some lunch?"

"No." Mia shook her hair back, breathed deep. There were times, rare times, when she felt locked inside the bookstore. When she needed space desperately. "I want to walk."

Ripley had been right about Indian summer. The cold snap had given way to balmy days of warmth and moist breezes that carried the scents of both sea and forest. The sky was clouded up, and against that dull pewter the trees rose like flaming beacons. The ocean mirrored the sky, and its kicky waves foretold a storm brewing.

"It'll rain within the hour," Mia predicted. "And look." She gestured out to sea. Seconds later, as if she'd ordered it, a pale jag of lightning cracked the steel mirror of sky. "Storm's coming. I love a good storm. The air goes electric and the energy of it pumps into your blood. Makes me restless, though. I want my cliffs in a storm."

Mia slipped out of her lovely shoes, hooked them on her fingers, and stepped barefoot into the sand. "The beach is almost empty," she pointed out. "It's a good place to walk, and for you to tell me what's troubling you."

"I had a . . . I don't know if it was a vision. I don't know what it was. It frightens me."

Mia slid her free arm through Nell's and kept the pace easy. "Tell me."

When she finished, Mia kept walking. "Why did you give him your locket?"

"It was all I could think of. An impulse. The thing that mattered most to me, I suppose."

"You were wearing it when you died. You brought it with you into your new life. This symbol of where you came from, this connection to your mother. Your talisman. Strong magic. He'll wear it because you asked him to, and that makes it stronger yet."

"It's a locket, Mia. Something my father bought my mother for Christmas one year. It's not particularly valuable."

"You know better than that. Its value is its meaning to you, and the love you have for your parents, the love you've given to Zack."

"Is it enough? I don't see how it can be. I know what it meant, Mia." And this was the terror that stretched like a beast inside her. "In the vision his face was gray, and the blood—there was so much blood. In the vision, he was dead." She made herself say it again. "He was dead. Isn't there something you can do?"

She'd already done all she could think of, all she felt within her power. "What do you think I can do that you haven't?"

"I don't know. So much more. Was it a premonition?"

"Is that what you believe?"

"Yes. Yes." Even thinking of it stopped her breath. "It was so clear. He's going to be killed, and I don't know how."

"What we see are possibilities, potentials, Nell. Nothing is absolute. Nothing, good or bad, is guaranteed. You were given this vision, and you acted to protect."

"Isn't there a way to stop whoever will try to hurt him? A spell?"

"Spells aren't a cure for every circumstance, or shouldn't be. And remember, what you send out can come back to you or yours, threefold. Attack one thing, unleash another."

She didn't say what went through her mind. Stop the knife, Mia thought grimly, and you may load a gun.

"A storm's coming," she repeated. "And more than the lightning is going to slash through the sky this afternoon."

"You know something."

"I *feel* something. I can't see it clearly. Perhaps it's not for me to see." That was a frustration, this barrier. And the knowledge that she, so long a solitary witch, couldn't do what needed to be done alone. "I'll help you all I can, that I can promise."

Even as she worried it wouldn't be enough, she saw Ripley standing on the edge of the sand. "Call Ripley down. She'll come for you. Tell her what you've told me."

Nell didn't have to call, only to turn and look. In her practical chinos and sensible boots, Ripley strode toward them. "You're going to get wet if you stay out here much longer."

"Thunder," Mia said, and a dull rumbling of it rolled above the sea. "Some lightning." And it burst like a firewall toward the west. "But no rain for a half hour or so."

"You forecasting the weather now, Glinda?" Ripley said pleasantly. "You ought to get yourself a job on TV."

"Don't. Not now." Nell expected the sky to break open any second, but she didn't care. "I'm worried about Zack."

"Yeah? Me, too. I've got to worry when my brother starts wearing girlie jewelry. But I have to thank you for giving me the opportunity to razz him."

"Did he tell you why he's wearing it?"

"No. And I hesitate to repeat just what he did say to me in such polite company. But it got our day off to a fine start."

"I had a vision," Nell began.

"Oh, perfect." In disgust, Ripley started to turn away, stopping when Nell gripped her arm. "I like you, Nell, but you're going to piss me off."

"Let her go, Nell. She's afraid to listen."

"I'm not afraid of anything." And it burned her butt that Mia knew exactly which button to push. "Go ahead, tell me what you saw in the crystal ball."

"I wasn't looking at a crystal ball. I was looking at Zack," Nell said, and told her.

No matter how hard she denied it, how carelessly she shrugged, Ripley was shaken down to the toes. "Zack can take care of himself." She paced away, and back again. "Look, in case you haven't noticed, he's a capable, thoroughly trained officer of the law. He carries a weapon, and knows how to use it when and if he has to. If he makes the job look easy, it's because he knows how to handle whatever comes along. I'd trust him with my life."

"I think Nell's asking if she can trust you with his."

"I've got a badge, I've got a weapon, and a solid right cross. That's how I handle things," Ripley said furiously. "If someone comes after Zack, you can bet your ass they'll have to go through me."

"One times three, Ripley." Deliberately, Mia laid a hand on her arm. "In the end, that's what it'll take."

"I'm not going to do it."

Mia nodded. They were standing in a circle under the angry sky. "You already are."

Instinctively, Ripley stepped back, broke the connection. "Don't look for me," she said. "Not this way." She turned her back on them and the rising wind and, kicking at the sand, she walked back to the village.

"She'll think about this, and struggle with it. As her head's made of granite, it's going to take longer than I like. But for the first time in years, she's wavering." Mia gave Nell a comforting pat on the shoulder. "She won't risk Zack."

They went back to the bookstore, and had no sooner stepped inside when the rain fell in a torrent.

*Nell burned the candles in her trio of jack-o'-*lanterns not just to decorate now, but for their original purpose. She set them on her porch to frighten away evil.

Between the knowledge gleaned from the books Mia had lent her and her own instincts, she set about making her cottage as safe a haven as she could manage.

She swept away negative energy, lit candles for tranquility and protection. She laid red jasper and small pots of sage on the windowsills and moonstones and sprigs of rosemary under the pillows on her bed.

She made a pot of chicken soup.

It simmered while the rain lashed, and her little cottage became a cozy cocoon.

But she couldn't relax in it. She paced from window to window, door to door. She looked for busywork and couldn't find it. She forced herself to sit in her office, to complete a job proposal. But after ten minutes she was up again, her concentration as fractured as the lightning-struck sky.

Giving up, she called the station house. Surely Zack was back from the mainland by now. She would speak to him, hear his voice. Then she'd feel better.

But it was Ripley who answered and told her in a voice as cold as a slap that Zack hadn't returned, that he would be back when he got back.

Now her worry doubled. The storm took on the proportions of a tempest for her. The howl of the wind was no longer musical but full of teeth and threats.

The rain was a smothering curtain and the lightning a weapon hurled.

Dark pressed against the windows as if it would break the glass and burst in. The power she'd learned to accept, even to embrace, began to waver like a candle flame under hot breath.

A thousand scenarios raced through her mind, each more horrible than the last. In the end, unable to bear it, she grabbed her jacket. She would go down to the docks, wait for the ferry. Will him to come.

She wrenched open the door in a blast of lightning. In the blind dark that followed, she saw the shadow move toward her. She opened her mouth to scream, then through the scent of rain and wet earth and the sting of ozone, she caught the scent of her lover.

"Zack!" She leaped at him, nearly sending the two of them tumbling off the stoop as he caught both her and his balance. "I've been so worried."

"And now you're wet." He carried her into the house. "I picked a hell of a day to go off-island. Bitch of a ferry ride back." He set her on her feet, then stripped off his soaking jacket. "I'd've called, but I couldn't get my cell phone to connect. That'll be the last ferry coming or going tonight, in this weather."

He dragged a hand through his hair, scattered rain.

"You're soaked to the bone." And because his shirt was wet, she saw, with relief, the faint outline of the locket just above his heart. "And cold," she added when she took his hand.

"I've got to admit, I've been dreaming about a hot shower the last half hour."

And would have had one by now, he thought, if

Ripley hadn't met him at the front door, interrogated him, then told him Nell had called in a panic.

"Go take one now. Then you can have a bowl of hot soup."

"Definitely the best offer I've had all day." He cupped her face in his hands. "I'm sorry you worried. You shouldn't have."

"Now I'm not. Go on, before you catch cold."

"Islanders are hardier stock than that." But he kissed her lightly on the forehead and went straight for the shower.

He left his clothes in a sopping heap on the bathroom floor, turned the spray on hot, and let out a grateful sigh when he stepped in.

The little room, and the tub in it, hadn't been designed for a man of six-one. The nozzle was aimed straight at his throat, and if he wasn't careful he rapped his elbow against the wall whenever he moved his arms.

But he'd developed a routine during the time he'd been with Nell.

Bracing his hands on the front wall, he bent over so the spray sluiced over his head and back. Since she tended to use fragrant and feminine soaps and shampoos, he'd casually placed some of his own on the ledge above the lip of the tub.

Neither of them had mentioned these additions—or the change of clothing he'd left on the shelf of her closet.

They didn't talk about the fact that they rarely spent a night apart. Other people did, he knew. He saw the winks and was becoming accustomed to having his name and hers roll off people's tongues together as if they were one word.

But they hadn't spoken of it. Maybe it was a kind of superstition, he thought, not to speak out loud what you were most afraid to lose.

Or maybe it was just another kind of cowardice.

He wasn't sure it mattered, but he was sure it was time to take another step forward.

He'd taken one himself, the biggest step he'd ever taken, on the mainland that afternoon.

He had to admit he felt good about it. He'd felt a little jittery, but that had passed quickly enough. Even the hideous ride back from the mainland hadn't managed to dampen his mood.

The sounds on the other side of the curtain surprised him enough to make him move too quickly. The rap of his elbow against the wall echoed in the little room, and was followed, viciously, by a stream of curses.

"Are you all right?" Torn between amusement and sympathy, Nell pressed her lips together tight and kept his wet bundle of clothes crammed against her chest.

He wrenched off the spray and whipped the curtain back. "This room is a hazard. I've a good mind to check the code and . . . what are you doing with those?"

"Well, I—" She broke off, baffled when he all but leaped naked out of the tub and snatched them back from her. "I was just going to toss them in the dryer."

"I'll take care of it later. I've got a change around here." He dumped them on the floor again, ignoring her wince as they hit with a wet plop behind him.

"At least hang them up. They'll just mildew lying in a pile like that."

"Okay, okay." He grabbed a towel, ran it roughly over his hair. "Did you just come in here to pick up after me?"

"Actually, yes." Now her gaze traveled down, slowly, over the damp chest where her locket glittered, the flat belly, the narrow hips he swagged in the towel. "But right at the moment, I'm not thinking tidy."

"Is that so?" One look from her did more to warm his blood than an ocean of hot water. "What are you thinking?"

"I'm thinking the very best thing to do with a man who has just come in from a storm is tuck him into bed. Come with me."

He let her take his hand and draw him through to the bedroom. "Are we going to play doctor? Because I think I could get really sick if it was worth my while."

She chuckled, then tossed back the quilt. "In."

"Yes, ma'am."

Before he could twitch off the towel, she did it for him. But when he grabbed for her, she evaded, then gave him a nudge onto the bed.

"You may know," she began and, picking up matches, walked around the room lighting candles, "that in lore and legend witches often served as healers."

Candlelight swayed, and it shimmered. "I'm starting to feel really healthy."

"I'll be the judge of that."

"I'm counting on it."

She turned to him. "Do you know what I've never done for anyone?"

"No, but I'm riveted."

She slowly lifted the hem of her sweater. She remembered the day she'd stood, poised like this, on the sunny back of his inlet.

"I want you to watch me." Inch by inch, she peeled the sweater up her body. "And want me."

If he'd been struck blind, he would have seen her, skin glowing in delicate light.

She slipped out of her shoes in a kind of graceful dance. Her simple white bra cut low and sweet over the subtle curve of her breasts. She lifted her hand to the center clasp, watched his eyes follow the move, then she deliberately left it fastened and trailed her fingertips down her midriff to the hook of her slacks.

His pulse began to thrum as the fabric slithered over her hips, down her legs. When it pooled at her feet, she stepped out with that same fluid ease.

"Why don't you let me do the rest?"

Her lips curved and she stepped closer, but not close enough. She'd never set out to seduce a man before, and wasn't ready to surrender the power.

She could imagine his hands on her as she ran her own up her body, as his breath rushed out of his lungs.

With that faint and knowing smile on her face, she flicked open her bra, let it slide away. Her breasts already felt full, and tender. She peeled the panties over her hips, stepped free of them. She was already wet.

"I want to take you," she whispered. "Slowly. I want you to take me." She eased onto the bed on hands and knees to straddle him. "Slowly." She seemed to melt over him. "As if there'll never be an end to it."

Her lips were warm and soft on his. Seeking. The taste of him slid through her system like a drug. When he rolled to take more, to deepen it, she went with him. But not in surrender.

She ran her fingertips lightly up and down his back, finding pleasure in the ridge of muscle, the ripple of it as she aroused him.

She let herself float on sensation as he gave her, and took from her, the gradual glide she'd demanded. Candlelight shifted, then the flames ran straight and true as spears and filled the air with fragrance.

They rose together, danced on that scented air. They knelt on the bed, centered on it, torso to torso and mouth to mouth.

If it was a spell, he'd have stayed bound eternally without question, without struggle. Witch or woman, a blend of both, she was his.

He watched the way his hand looked against her skin, dark to light, rough to fragile. The way her breasts could be cupped in his palms, and how the tips hardened under the brush of his thumb.

They touched, and tasted. A brush, a sip, a lazy caress, a long, slow drink.

When at last he slipped inside her, the gentle rise and fall was like waves of silk. Magic shimmered as they watched each other, as for each, for that moment, no one else existed. Beat to beat, with an intimacy that was more than mating, that abounded past needs and outraced passion.

It welled in her heart, overflowed in a spill like gold.

Her lips curved again as he lowered his mouth to hers. Their hands joined, fingers linking as they slid off the world together.

When she lay curled to his side, her palm over the steady beat of his heart, it seemed nothing could touch them. Her haven, she thought, was safe, as they were safe inside it.

All of her fears and worries, that creeping dread, seemed foolish now.

They were simply a man and a woman in love, lying in a warm bed and listening to the last of a storm pass overhead.

"I wonder if I'll ever learn how to manipulate objects."

"Honey, you manipulate just fine," he chuckled.

"No." She gave him a playful slap. "I mean moving things from one point to another. If I could, I'd chant the proper incantation and so on, and we'd have chicken soup in bed."

"It doesn't work like that. Does it?" he asked.

"I bet it does for Mia, if she wants it enough. But for lowly students such as me, it takes getting up, going into the kitchen and doing it all the old-fashioned way."

She turned her head to give his shoulder a pecking kiss, then rolled away.

"Why don't you stay here and I'll get the soup?"

She tossed a look over her shoulder as she walked to the closet for the robe she'd finally gotten around to buying. "Clever of you to suggest that after I was already up."

"I thought so. And since you caught me, I'll throw some clothes on and come out and give you a hand."

"Fine. Bring out that wet heap in the bathroom while you're at it."

Wet heap? It took him a minute to remember, so she was already out of the room when he leaped out of bed and snatched up his sodden pants from the floor. Digging in the pocket, he let out a breath as his fingers closed around a small box.

She had a round loaf of bread on a cutting board and was ladling up wide bowls of soup when he came in. She looked so pretty, so at home in her soft pink robe, he thought, her feet bare, her hair a little mussed.

"Nell, why don't we let that cool a minute?"

"We'll need to. Do you want some wine?"

"In a minute." Odd, he thought he'd be nervous, at least a little. Instead he was rock calm. He laid his hands on her shoulders, turned her, then ran them down to her elbows. "I love you, Nell."

"I—"

It was as far as she got before his lips silenced hers.

"I thought of different ways to do this. Taking you for a drive one night, or a walk on the beach next full moon. Or for a fancy dinner at the hotel. But this is the right way for us, the right place, and the right time."

The little flutter in her stomach was a warning. But she couldn't step back. She couldn't move at all.

"I thought of different ways to ask you, what words might suit best, and how I should say them. But the only ones that come to me right now are I love you, Nell. Marry me."

The breath that she had been holding released as joy and grief waged a helpless war inside her. "Zack. We've been together such a short time."

"We can wait a while to get married if you want, though I don't see the point in it."

"Why can't we just leave things the way they are?"

Of all the reactions he'd been expecting, the hitch of fear in her voice hadn't been among them. "Because we need a place of our own, a life of our own, not pieces of yours and mine."

"Marriage is just a legality. That's all." She turned away, reached blindly into the cupboard for glasses.

"For some people." He said it quietly. "Not for you or me. We're basic, Nell. When basic people fall in love, and mean it, they get married, start a family. I want to share my life with you, make children with you, grow old with you."

Tears threatened. Everything he said was what she wanted, so deep in her heart that it was into her soul. "You're moving too fast."

"I don't think so." He took the box from his pocket. "I bought this today because we've already started our life together, Nell. It's time to see where it takes us."

Her fingers curled into her palms as she looked down. He'd bought her a sapphire, a rich, warm stone set in a simple band of gold. He'd have known she would need warmth and simplicity.

Evan had chosen a diamond, a brilliant square in platinum that had sat on her finger like ice.

"I'm sorry. Zack, I'm so sorry. I can't marry you."

He felt the slice through his heart, but he never flinched as he watched her face. "Do you love me, Nell?"

"Yes."

"Then I deserve to know why you won't make a promise to me, and take one from me."

"You're right." She struggled to steady herself. "I can't marry you, Zack, because I'm already married."

Nothing she could have said would have stunned him more. "Married? You're *married*? For God's sake, Nell, we've been together for months."

"I know." It wasn't just shock she saw now. It wasn't just anger. He stared at her as if she were a stranger. "I left him, you see. More than a year ago."

He struggled over the first hurdle. The fact that she'd been married and hadn't told him. But he couldn't make it over the second. That she was married still.

"Left him, but didn't divorce him."

"No, I couldn't. I—"

"And you let me touch you, you slept with me, let me fall in love with you, knowing you weren't free."

"Yes." It was so cold, suddenly so cold in the little kitchen that it penetrated her bones. "I don't have any excuses for it."

"I won't ask when you were planning to tell me. Obviously you weren't." He closed the box with a snap, jammed it back in his pocket. "I don't sleep with other men's wives, Nell. A word from you, one goddamn word from you, and we wouldn't have gotten to this point."

"I know. It's my fault." As his anger grew, hardened his face, she felt the strength she'd rebuilt draining away like the color in her cheeks.

"You think that makes up for it?" he shot back, as temper and misery careened inside him. "You think taking the blame for it cleans the fucking slate on this?"

"No."

"Goddamn it." He spun away from her and caught the way she flinched at the move. "I'll yell when I need to yell. You're only making me madder standing there like you're waiting for a punch. I'm not going to hit you. Not now, not ever. And it's insulting for you to stand there wondering if I will."

"You don't know what it's like."

"No, I don't, because you won't tell me." He reined himself in as much as he could, though temper was still sparking. "Or you tell me just enough to keep things running smooth until the next time."

"Maybe that's true. But I told you I couldn't tell you everything. That I wasn't going to go into the details."

"This isn't a damn detail. You're still married to the man who did this to you."

"Yes."

"Are you planning on ending the marriage?"

"No."

"Well, that's plain enough." He snatched up his boots, his jacket.

"I can't let him find out where I am. I can't let him find me."

He started to yank the door open, then stood there a moment, his hand on the knob. "Did you ever stop and think, just once did you ever stop and look at me and know I'd do whatever needed to be done for you? I'd have done it, Nell, for a stranger, because it's my job. How could you not know I'd do it for you?"

She did know, she thought as he walked away from her. It was only one of the things that frightened her. Unable to cry, she sat miserably in the house she had made safe, and empty.

Seventeen

"I've lost him. I've ruined it."

Nell sat in Mia's great, gorgeous cavern of a living room, in front of an ox-roasting fire sipping a cup of healing cinnamon tea. Isis stretched her lean, warm body over her lap like a cozy blanket.

None of it lifted her mood.

"Damaged it, perhaps. And nothing's lost that can be found again."

"I can't fix this, Mia. Everything he said to me is true. I didn't want to think about it, to see it, but it's true. I had no right to let things get as serious as they did."

"I don't happen to have a hair shirt handy, but I imagine we can make something up." At Nell's shocked stare, Mia lifted one shoulder elegantly. "It's not that I don't sympathize with both of you, because I do. But the fact is, Nell, you fell in love, both of you. And both of you dealt with it the way you needed to deal with it. You brought each other something that not everyone is given. That's nothing to regret."

"I don't regret loving him, or being loved by him. I regret a lot of things, but not that."

"All right, then. You need to take the next step."

"There is no next step. I can't marry Zack because I'm legally tied to someone else. And even if Evan decides to divorce me in absentia or whatever, I still couldn't marry Zack. My identification is false."

"Details."

"Not to him."

"Yes, you're right." She tapped her pretty fingernails on the side of her cup as she considered. "Some things Zack would see, because he's Zack, as black and white. I'm sorry I didn't think this far ahead and warn you of that. I know him," Mia continued as she rose to stretch. "I didn't anticipate that he'd move toward legal binding so quickly. I'm jaded when it comes to love."

She poured more tea, pondered while she roamed the room and sipped.

There were two sofas, both in deep hunter green, that begged for a body to sink down and sink in. They were scattered with jewel-toned pillows, all in soft fabrics. Texture was essential to luxury, and when at leisure, Mia insisted on luxury.

The room was populated with antiques, because she preferred the old to the new unless it was in business equipment. The rugs on the wide-planked chestnut floor were satisfactorily faded. There were flowers everywhere, in priceless crystal or in cheerful colored bottles of no special value.

Some of the candles she surrounded herself with in every room were lit. The white ones, for peace.

"You've hurt him, Nell, on two levels. One by not falling into his arms in utter delight when he proposed." She stopped, lifting one brow. "I told you I was jaded in this area, but nonetheless, when a man asks a woman to marry him, he's not going to be pleased when she says 'No, thank you.' "

"I'm not a complete idiot, Mia."

"No, darling. I'm sorry." Contrite, though secretly amused at the biting tone, Mia stopped behind the sofa and stroked Nell's hair. "Of course you're not. And I should have said three levels, the second being his sense of honor. He has just discovered himself poaching on what he would consider another man's territory."

"Oh, really. I'm not a damn rabbit."

"Zack would see himself breaking a code. The third level is that he would certainly have done so anyway, *if* he'd known. If you'd told him the circumstances. He could adjust his line there, because he loves you and wants you, and because he would be relieved that you'd escaped from a horrible situation. But the fact that you didn't tell him, that you let him go into this, let him fall in love with you blind, is going to be hard for him to swallow."

"Why can't he see that my marriage to Evan means nothing? I'm not Helen Remington anymore."

"Do you want comfort or truth?" Mia asked flatly.

"I can't have both. It may as well be truth."

"You lied to him, and by lying you put him in an untenable position. More, you told him you didn't intend to end the marriage."

"I can't—"

"Wait. You won't end it, and without an end there can't be a beginning. This is purely your choice, Nell, and no one can or should take it from you. But you've blocked Zack from being able to stand for you. To stand with you or, more to his liking, I imagine, to step in front of you and face your demon. Nell."

She sat again, taking Nell's hands. "Do you think he wears a badge for amusement, for the pathetic pay, for the power?"

"No. But he doesn't understand what Evan can do, what he's capable of. Mia, there's a madness inside him. A kind of cold, deliberate madness that I can't begin to explain."

"People tend to think the word 'evil' is overdramatic," Mia said, "when actually, it's extremely simple."

"Yes." A few knots untangled. She should have known by now that she didn't have to explain to Mia. "And he doesn't understand that I can't bear the idea of seeing Evan again, of hearing his voice. I think I'd break this time. I think it would shatter me."

"You're stronger than that."

Nell shook her head. "He . . . shrinks me. I don't know if you can understand what I mean."

"Yes, I do. Do you want a spell, a charm, to bolster yourself? To shield yourself from one man so you can have the other?" Mia reached over, stroked Isis along her sleek back. The cat raised her head, exchanged what seemed to be a telling look with her mistress, then curled up.

"There are things that can be done," Mia said, briskly now. "To protect, to center yourself, to enhance your own energies. But beneath it all, Nell, the power's inside you. For now . . ."

She slipped the silver chain and its silver disk over her head. "You gave Zack your talisman, so I'll give you one of mine. It was my great-grandmother's."

"I can't take it from you."

"On lend," Mia said, slipping the chain over Nell's head. "She was a very canny witch, my great-grandmama. Married well. Made a killing on the stock market, and kept it, for which I continue to be grateful. I wouldn't like being poor. She acted as doctor on the island before we had one with a medical degree living here. She treated warts, delivered babies, stitched up gashes, and nursed half the population through a dangerous run of influenza among other things."

"It's lovely. What does the carving mean?"

"It's an old language, similar to what was written on the ogham stones in ancient Ireland. It means courage. And now that you're wearing my courage, I'll give you my advice. Sleep. Let him wrestle with his feelings while you examine your own. When you go to him—and as much as he loves you he won't come back to you—be clear in your mind what it is you want, and what you're willing to do for it."

"You're being an asshole, Zack."

"Okay. Now will you shut up?"

Ripley considered never shutting up a sister's privilege. "Listen, I know she screwed up. But don't you want to know why?" She slapped her hands on his desk, leaning down so she could get in his face in a satisfactory manner. "Don't you want to push, dig, maneuver until she tells you why she's still married?"

"She had plenty of time to tell me if she wanted to." Zack concentrated on his computer. His business on the mainland hadn't just been buying a ring; he had also testified in a court case. Now that it was done, he could update his file.

Ripley made a sound somewhere between a groan and a scream. "You make me crazy. I don't know how you don't make yourself crazy. You're in love with a married woman."

He spared her a withering glance. "That fact is very clear in my mind right about now. Go do your patrol."

"Look, it's obvious she doesn't want the other guy. She ditched him. Also obvious is that she's moony about you and vice versa. Nell's been here, what, five months? And from all appearances she's digging in for the duration. Whatever came before is over."

"She's legally married. That doesn't spell over for me."

"Yeah, yeah, Dudley Do-Right." The fact that she admired his code of honor didn't mean it couldn't exasperate her. "So let it ride for a while. Just let things go as they've been going. Why the hell do you have to marry her, anyway? Oh, wait, I forgot who I'm talking to. But if you want my advice—"

"I don't. I really don't."

"Fine. Stew in your own juice, then." She grabbed her jacket, then immediately tossed it down again. "I'm sorry. I can't stand to see you hurting."

Because he knew that, he gave up on pretending to update files, rubbed his hands over his face. "I can't make a life with someone who has another life that she hasn't finished. I can't take a woman to bed who's legally married to another man. And I can't love someone the way I love Nell and not want, not expect, marriage, home, and children. I can't do those things, Rip."

"No, you can't." She came to him then, wrapping her arms around his neck from the back, resting her chin on top of his head. "Maybe I could." Though she couldn't imagine loving anyone enough to make the choice. "But I understand you can't. What I don't understand is why if you love her, and you want her, you can't sit her down and make her explain it. You deserve to know."

"I'm not going to make her do anything, not only because I don't work that way but because I have a feeling the man she's married to did plenty of making her."

"Zack." Ripley turned her head so that her cheek rested on his hair. "Did it ever occur to you that she's afraid to divorce him?"

"Yeah." His stomach did a quick, nasty pitch. "I came around to that about three o'clock in the morning. If it's true, I've got plenty of feelings to punch into that bag. But it doesn't change what is. She's married, she didn't tell me. She doesn't trust me enough to be there for her, whatever it takes."

He reached up, closed his hand around hers.

That's how Nell saw them when she opened the door, holding on to each other. And she saw the beam of blame shoot out of Ripley's eyes even as the shutters came down on Zack's.

"I need to speak with you. Alone. Please."

Instinctively Ripley tightened her grip, but Zack gave her hand a squeeze. "Ripley was just heading out on patrol."

"Yeah, sure, toss me out just when it's getting good." She was shrugging into her jacket, contemplating that *this* was what it felt like when people said you could cut the tension with a knife, when Betsy poked her head in the door.

"Sheriff—Hi, Nell, Ripley. Sheriff, Bill and Ed Sutter are starting to mix it up out in front of the hotel. It looks like it could get messy."

"I'll take care of it."

"No." Zack got up at Ripley's statement. "We'll take care of it."

The Sutter brothers vacillated between staunch family loyalty and hating each other like poison. Since they were both bullheaded and built like the same animal, he thought it best not to let Ripley get into a two-on-one situation. He gave Nell a brief glance as he walked outside. "You'll have to wait."

So cold, she thought, rubbing her arms. It was hard to accept ice from a man who had such warmth. He wasn't going to make this easy. Oddly enough, even after the worst of it the evening before, she'd convinced herself that he would.

He would let her talk. He would sympathize, understand, hold her.

Standing alone in the station house, Nell watched that little fantasy crack in two and disappear.

Here she was, swallowing her pride, risking her peace of mind and well-being, and all he could do was spare her a single icy look.

Well, then, maybe she should just let bad enough alone.

Stung, she pulled open the door. Two steps out and she could not only see the commotion up the street, she could hear it. Freezing in place, she hugged herself and watched it play out.

One big man with short-cropped hair belly-slammed another big man with short-cropped hair. Curses were flying. An interested crowd was gathering at a safe distance, and some of them appeared to be taking sides by hooting and calling out names.

Zack and Ripley were already wading in, muscling the men apart. Nell couldn't hear what they were saying, but while it quieted the crowd, it didn't appear to have much impact on the Sutter brothers.

They were all but snapping at each other's faces.

Nell cringed, closed in when she saw the first fist strike. There was a lot of shouting now, and she heard it like the pounding of the surf. A lot of motion that seemed lost in a fast blur.

Zack had one man's arm, Ripley the other's. Both had their handcuffs out. Bumping, shoving. Curses and clipped warnings.

Then one brother swung viciously at the other, missed his mark and plowed his fist into Zack's face.

She watched Zack's head snap back, heard the crowd gasp as one voice. Everyone went so still, it seemed like a film stopped in a freeze-frame.

She was already rushing across the street as motion and voices started again.

"Well, goddamn it, Ed, you're under arrest." Zack snapped the cuffs in place as Ripley did the same. "And for good measure, the same goes for you, Bill.

Couple of hotheaded peckerbrains. You people go on about your business now," he ordered as he muscled Ed around.

He caught sight of Nell, standing on the sidewalk like a deer caught in the headlights, and cursed again.

"Come on, Sheriff, you know I wasn't aiming at you."

"Doesn't matter a damn to me who you were aiming at." Not when he tasted blood in his mouth. "You just assaulted an officer."

"He started it."

"Like hell," Bill shot back as Ripley walked him briskly along. "But I'm sure as hell going to finish it when I get the chance."

"You and what army?"

"Just shut up," Ripley ordered. "Couple of forty-year-old delinquents."

"Ed's the one who punched him. What're you hauling me in for?"

"You're a damn public nuisance. If the two of you want to butt heads, do it in the privacy of one of your homes and keep it off the streets."

"You're not going to put us in jail." Calmer now as he saw his fate, Ed turned his head to appeal. "Come on now, Zack, you know my wife'll skin me if you lock me up. It was just family business, after all."

"Not when it's on my street, and not when it involves my goddamn face." His jaw throbbed like a bitch. He marched Ed straight into the station house and back to one of the two tiny holding cells. "You're going to have some time to cool off before I get around to calling your wife. Whether she cares enough to come down and make your bail is up to her."

"Same goes," Ripley told Bill cheerfully as she uncuffed him and nudged him into a cell.

Once the cell doors were shut and locked, she dusted her hands. "I'll write up the report. I type slower than you do. I'll call the wives, too, though I suspect they'll hear about this before I even start on the paperwork."

"Yeah." Disgusted, Zack swiped the back of his hand over his mouth and smeared blood.

"You're going to want some ice on that jaw. Lip, too. Ed Sutter's got a fist the size of Idaho. Hey, Nell, why don't you take our hero to your place and give him some ice?"

Unaware that she'd come in, Zack turned slowly and stared at Nell as she stood in the open doorway.

"Yes. All right."

"There's ice in the back. I can take care of it."

"You'd be better off putting some distance between yourself and Ed," Ripley advised. "Until you're sure you're not going to unlock that cell and punch him back."

"Maybe."

His eyes weren't cold anymore, Nell noted. They were hot green glass. She moistened her lips. "Ice'll help keep the swelling down. And . . . some rosemary tea might help the ache."

"Fine. Great." His head was already ringing, why not finish it off? "Two-hundred-and-fifty-dollar fine, for both of them," he snapped at Ripley. "Or twenty days. They don't like the sound of that, fill out a formal arrest warrant, and they can deal with the court."

"Yes, sir." Ripley beamed as Zack stalked out.

Wasn't this great? she thought. The whole thing had really brightened her mood.

They walked to the cottage in silence. Nell no longer knew what to say or how to say it. This furiously angry man was every bit as much a stranger as the icy cold one had been. There was no doubt in her mind that he didn't particularly want to deal with her right now. She knew just how long it could take to regain equilibrium after a blow to the face.

Still, he'd taken a fist at short range, and other than the head, and temper snap, he'd had little reaction.

People were always saying someone was tougher than he looked. It seemed to be true about Zachariah Todd.

She opened the cottage door and, still saying nothing, walked back to the kitchen and began to make an ice pack out of a plastic bag wrapped in a thin cloth.

"Appreciate it. I'll get the dishcloth back to you."

She'd already lifted the kettle to make tea. She blinked at him. "Where are you going?"

"To walk off what I can of this mad."

Seeing no choice, she set the kettle down again. "I'll go with you."

"You don't want to be with me right now, and I don't want to be with you."

It was quite a discovery to learn that there were times a slap was preferable to words. "That can't be helped. We have things to talk about, and the longer it's put off the harder it'll be."

She opened the kitchen door, waited. "Let's try the woods. We can consider it neutral territory."

He hadn't bothered with a jacket, and the rain that

had swept in the night before had left cool temperatures in its wake. He didn't seem to mind. She glanced up at him as they headed into her little wedge of forest.

"That ice isn't going to do any good if you don't use it."

He pressed it to his aching jaw and felt mildly ridiculous.

"In the summer when I came here I wondered what it would be like to walk through the trees in autumn, with all the color and the first bites of cold. I'd missed the cold, the change of seasons, when I lived in California."

She let out a little breath, drew one in. "I lived in California for three years. Los Angeles primarily, though we spent a lot of time in the house in Monterey. I preferred it there, but I learned not to let him know that or he'd have found ways to cancel trips north. He liked to find little ways to punish me."

"You married him."

"I did. He was handsome and romantic and clever and rich. I thought, Why, here comes my prince and we'll live happily ever after. I was dazzled and flattered and in love. He worked very hard to make me fall in love with him. There's no point in going into all the details. You've guessed some of them anyway. He was cruel, in little ways, in big ones. He made me feel small. Small, smaller, smallest, until I all but disappeared. When he hit me . . . the first time it was a shock. No one had ever hit me before. I should've left, right that minute. Or tried. He would never have let me, but I should've tried. But I'd only been married a few months, and somehow he made me feel I'd deserved it. For being stupid. Or clumsy. Or forgetful. For all manner of things. He trained me like a dog. I'm not proud of that."

"Did you get help?"

It was so quiet in the woods. She could hear, in that quiet, every step she and Zack took over the ground already strewn with fallen leaves.

"Not at first. I knew about abuse, intellectually. I'd read articles, stories. But that didn't apply to me. I wasn't part of that cycle. I'd come from a good, stable home. I'd married an intelligent, successful man. I lived in a big, beautiful house. I had servants."

She slipped a hand into her pocket. She'd made a magic bag for courage, and had tied it with seven careful knots. Letting her fingers worry it helped calm her nerves.

"It was just that I kept making mistakes, that was all. I thought that once I learned, everything would be fine again. But it only got worse, and I couldn't keep deluding myself. One night he dragged me upstairs by my hair. I had long hair then," she explained. "I thought he would kill me. I thought he would beat me and rape me, then kill me. He didn't. He didn't do any of those things. But I realized he could have, and I wouldn't have been able to stop him. I went to the police, but he's an influential man. He has connections. I had a few bruises, but nothing major. They didn't do anything."

Knowing that burned a hole through him. "They should have. They should've taken you to a shelter."

"As far as they were concerned, I was a rich, spoiled trophy wife causing trouble. It doesn't matter," she said wearily. "They could have taken me anywhere.

He'd have found me. I ran once, and he found me. And I paid for it. He made it clear to me, he made sure I understood one vital point: I belonged to him, and I would never get away. Wherever I went, he'd find me. He loved me."

It sent a violent chill through her to say it. She stopped, turned to face Zack. "His version of love, beyond rules, beyond bounds. Selfish, cold and obsessive and powerful. He would see me dead before he'd let me go. That's not an exaggeration."

"I believe you. But you got away."

"Because he thinks I'm dead." She told him, her voice clear and empty of emotion, what she had done to break the chains.

"Jesus Christ, Nell." He threw the ice bag to the ground. "It's a miracle you didn't kill yourself."

"Either way, I was getting away. I was coming here. I believe, completely believe, that the minute that car went over the cliff, I started coming here. And to you."

Because he wanted, too strongly, to touch her and wasn't yet sure if it would be a caress or a furious shake, he jammed his hands in his pockets. "I had a right to know, when things changed between us. I had a right to know."

"I didn't expect things to change between us."

"But they damn well did. And if you didn't know where we were heading, then you *are* stupid."

"I'm not stupid." Her voice took on an edge. "Maybe I was wrong, but I'm not stupid. I didn't expect to fall in love with you, I didn't *want* to fall in love with you, or even get involved with you. You pursued me."

"It doesn't make any difference how it happened.

The fact is, it did. You know where you stood and why, but you didn't let me know."

"I'm a liar," she said evenly. "I'm a cheat, I'm a bitch. But don't you ever call me stupid again."

"Jesus Christ." At his wits' end, he stalked away, lifted his gaze to the sky.

"I won't be demeaned, not by anyone. Not ever again. I won't be belittled, and I won't be brushed aside until it's convenient for you to pay attention again."

Curious, he turned his head, stared at her. "Is that what you think this is?"

"I'm *telling* you how it is. I did a lot of thinking since you walked out of the house yesterday. I'm not going to whimper and slide into the corner just because you're annoyed with me. That insults both of us."

"Well, three cheers."

"Oh, go to hell."

He turned completely around and stepped toward her. The dread curled in her stomach, her palms went clammy, but she stood her ground.

"It's a hell of a time to pick a fight with me, especially when you're wrong."

"I'm only wrong if I'm standing where you are. Standing here, I did what I had to do. I wish I hadn't hurt you, but I can't go back and change that."

"No, you can't. So we go from here. Did you leave out anything else I should know?"

"The woman who drove off that cliff was named Helen Remington. Mrs. Evan Remington. I don't answer to that name anymore. It's not who I am."

"Remington." He said it softly. She could all but

see him flipping through some mental data file. "Hollywood type."

"That's right."

"You got about as far away from that as you could manage."

"That's right, too. I'll never go back. I've found the life I want here."

"With or without me?"

For the first time since she'd begun her story, her stomach clutched. "That's up to you."

"No, it's not. You already know what I want. Now it's what you want."

"I want you. You know that."

"Then you have to finish what you started. You have to end it. File for divorce."

"I can't. Haven't you heard anything I've said?"

"Every word, and more that you didn't say." Part of him wanted to soothe her, to draw her close, shelter her. To tell her none of it mattered now.

But it did.

"You can't live your whole life wondering, looking over your shoulder, or pretending three years away. Neither can I. For one thing, it's going to start eating at you, and for another, the world's a small place. You'll never be sure he won't find you. If he does, or if you're afraid he has, are you going to run again?"

"It's been more than a year since I left. He can't find me if he thinks I'm dead."

"You'll never be sure. You have to end it, but you don't have to end it alone. I won't let him touch you. This isn't his turf," he said, lifting her face with a finger under her chin. "It's mine."

"You're underestimating him."

"I don't think so. I know I'm not underestimating myself, or Ripley, or Mia. Or a lot of people on the island who would go out of their way for you."

"I don't know if I can do what you're asking. For more than a year I've focused on doing everything I could to make certain he doesn't find out I'm alive, he doesn't find out where I am. I don't know if I've got it in me to step out again. I need to think. I need you to give me time to think."

"All right. Tell me what you decide." He stooped to get the ice bag. The ice was mostly melted. As he didn't care a great deal about the pain in his jaw, he opened it, spilled out the contents. "If you don't want to marry me, Nell, I'll accept that. But after you think all this through, I need you to tell me what you decide there, too."

"I love you. I don't have to think that through."

He stared at her, standing in the quiet woods where the leaves rioted color and the air still carried the faintest scent of yesterday's rain.

He held out a hand for hers. "I'll walk you home."

Eighteen

Ripley gave Zack her most pitiful look. And whined. She saved up her whines to add to the impact when she whipped one out.

"But I don't wanna go to Mia's."

Living with her for nearly thirty years made him immune to such tactics. Though he had to give her big points for delivery.

"When you were a kid you practically lived at Mia's."

"Then, now. See the difference? Why can't you go?"

"Because I have a penis. I'll restrain myself and not ask if you see the difference. Be a pal, Rip."

She spun in a circle, her version of drumming her heels on the floor. "If Nell's going to be hanging out at Mia's tonight, then Mia can keep an eye on her. Jesus, Zack, don't be such a mommy. The asshole in L.A. doesn't even know she's alive yet."

"If I'm being overprotective we'll just all have to

live with it. I don't want her driving to the cliffs alone at night." The thought of her car flying over cliffs three thousand miles away left a ball of ice in his gut. "Until this thing is resolved, I want to keep an eye on her."

"So keep *your* eye on her. You're the ones trying to decide if you're going to be long-suffering, star-crossed lovers, or Ward and June Cleaver."

He let the insult pass, as it was her way of starting a pissing match so she could storm out and get out of doing what he asked. "I'll never figure how it is I know more about women than you do, when you're of the same species."

"Watch it, slick."

He supposed he hadn't let the insult pass after all. "She doesn't need me hovering over her. She doesn't need a man, even such a sterling example of manhood as myself, crowding her. She's got tough decisions to make. I'm trying to keep a little distance, without making an issue of keeping a little distance, until she's made them."

"Gee, you sure do think a lot."

The simple fact was, he was putting her in a hell of a pinch. He wanted her to keep an eye on Nell, and Ripley wanted to keep an eye on Zack. She hadn't had an easy moment in the two days since he'd told her Nell's story.

Blood on the moon, she thought. Nell's vision of Zack covered with blood. A sociopathic, potentially homicidal husband, and Ripley's own disturbing dreams. She hated knowing she was dipping into omen territory, but . . . hell, it didn't bode well.

"What are you going to be doing while I'm babysitting the love of your life at Witch Central?"

There was something else he'd learned in nearly thirty years of knowing her. He could always count on Ripley. "Taking both our evening patrols, buying some takeout, and going home to a lonely dinner."

"If you think that makes me feel sorry for you, think again. I'd trade places with you in a heartbeat." She walked to the door. "I'll go by Nell's, tell her I want to tag along tonight. I want you to watch your back."

"Excuse me?"

"I don't want to talk about it. I'm just saying."

"I'll watch my back."

"And buy some beer. You drank the last bottle."

She slammed the door because . . . just because.

Mia set out fresh charms. Every day, it seemed, the air got a little heavier. As if something was dragging it down. She glanced outside. It was already dark. There was so much night at the end of October, so many hours until dawn.

There were things it wasn't wise to speak of at night, or even think. Night could be an open window.

She burned incense of sage to counter negativity, fastened on earrings of amethyst to strengthen her intuition. She'd been tempted to slip some rosemary under her pillow, to help chase away her troubled dreams. But she needed to see, needed to look.

She added jasper to the chain around her neck, a strengthener of energy, a reliever of stress.

It was the first time in years she could recall being so constantly hounded by stress.

Tonight wasn't the time for it, she reminded herself. She was going to take Nell to the next step, and such things should be joyful.

She fingered the magic bag in her pocket, filled with crystals and herbs, and, as she'd taught Nell, tied with seven knots. She detested being so edgy, as if waiting and waiting for disaster to strike.

Foolish, really, when she'd been preparing for disaster, and how to divert it, all her life.

She heard the car, saw the streak of lights slash across her front windows. As she walked to the door, she visualized pouring the stress into a small silver box, locking it.

So she appeared to be her usual calm self as she opened the door. Until she saw Ripley.

"Slumming, Deputy?"

"Didn't have anything better to do." She was surprised to see Mia in a long black dress. Mia rarely wore black. The one thing Ripley had to admit, the woman wasn't often obvious. "Special occasion?"

"As it happens. I don't have any objections to you being here, if Nell wants you. But don't interfere."

"You don't interest me enough to interfere."

"Is this argument going to take long?" Nell asked pleasantly. "I was hoping for a glass of wine."

"I think we're done. Come in, and welcome. We'll take the wine with us."

"With us? Where are we going?"

"To the circle. You've brought what I told you?"

"Yes." Nell patted the large leather pouch she wore.

"Good. I'll get what I need, then we'll go."

Ripley wandered around freely enough while Mia got ready. She had always liked the cliff house. Loved it. The big, crowded rooms, the odd corners, the thick carved doors and glossy floors.

She'd have gotten by happily enough with one room and a cot, but she had to admit Mia's place had style. And class. As far as atmosphere went, you couldn't top it.

Class, style, and atmosphere aside, it was always comfortable. A place where you knew you could sink into a chair and put your feet up.

A place, she recalled, where she had once run as free and as welcome as a pet puppy. It was a hell of a note to realize, all at once, how much she'd missed it. Missed it all.

"You still use the gable room?" Ripley asked casually while Mia selected a red wine from the rack.

When Mia glanced back their eyes met. Shared memories. "Yes. Some of your things are still there," she said as she wrapped three glasses in white linen.

"I don't want them."

"They're still there, in any case. Since you're here, you can carry this bag." She gestured, then picked up the second that held the wine and glasses.

She opened the back door, and Isis streaked through. It surprised Nell, as the cat generally couldn't be bothered to join them.

"It's a special night." Mia threw up the hood of the cloak she swirled over her shoulders. Black again, with a lining of deep wine-red. "She knows it. It's nearly Samhain. Nell needs to practice lighting the balefire."

Ripley's head snapped up. "Moving a little fast, aren't you?"

Mia merely studied the moon as they walked. It was down to a thumbnail and would soon be full dark. Around that sliver of white she could see a haze blacker, thicker than the sky.

"No."

Annoyed that Mia had made her uneasy yet again, Ripley shrugged. "Halloween. Lifting the dead. The night boils with evil spirits and only the brave or foolish walk in the dark."

"Nonsense," Mia said lightly. "And there's no point in taking that route to try to scare Nell."

"The end of the third and last harvest of the year." Nell breathed deep of the night. "A time for remembering the dead, for celebrating the eternal cycle. Also the night when the veil between life and death is said to be its thinnest. Hardly a negative time, but one of reaffirmation and fun. And, of course, Mia's birthday."

"The big three-oh this time, too," said Ripley.

"Don't be so smug." There was a little bite in Mia's voice, a not entirely playful nip. "You'll be hitting it yourself in six weeks."

"Yeah, but you'll always be older than me."

Isis was already in the clearing, sitting still as a sphinx in the center.

"We have some candles for working light. You can put them on the stones, Ripley, and light them."

"No." She shoved her hands, very deliberately, into the pockets of her bomber jacket. "Carting your bag of tricks is one thing. I won't participate."

"Oh, for pity sakes. You'll hardly spoil your magic

celibacy by lighting one or two candles." But Mia snatched the bag from her and stalked to the stones.

"I'll do it," Nell insisted. "There's no point in either of you being angry, when you're each doing what you want."

"Why are you so angry?" Ripley kept her voice down, crouched as Mia came back to select what she needed from her bags. "I usually have to work a lot harder to get under your skin."

"Maybe my skin's thinner these days."

"You look tired."

"I am tired. Something's coming. It's pushing, and pushing closer. I don't know how much longer I can hold it back, or even if I'm meant to. There'll be blood."

She gripped Ripley's wrist, held her still. "And pain. Terror and grief. And I'm afraid that without the circle there'll be death."

"If you're so sure of this, afraid of this, why haven't you sent for someone? You know others."

"It's not for others, and you know it." She glanced back toward Nell. "Maybe she's strong enough."

Mia straightened, tossed back her hood. "Nell. We'll cast the circle."

Whatever she'd expected to feel, Ripley hadn't expected the yearning that ribboned through her as she watched the basic ritual, as the familiar words echoed in her head.

She'd given it up, she reminded herself. She'd set it aside.

She watched wand and athame glimmer. She had always preferred the sword.

Her mouth pursed in consideration as Mia lit candles with a wooden match. Even as she opened her mouth to speak, to question, Mia sent her a quieting look.

Fine, your way as usual, Ripley thought, and kept her comments to herself.

"Earth, wind, fire, water—elements, hear this call from your daughters. While the moon above does ride, within the magic circle rise."

With her head thrown back and her arms raised, Mia waited. And the wind lifted, all but sang, the candle flames speared, ruler-straight despite the swirl of humming air. Under her feet, the earth trembled lightly, and in her cauldron, fragrant liquid began to bubble.

As Mia lowered her arms again, each subsided.

Nell had yet to get her breath back. Over the past months, she'd seen and done and been told the fantastic. But until tonight she hadn't been treated to such a vivid display.

"Power awaits," Mia told her, and held out a hand.

When Nell clasped it, she found Mia's skin warm, nearly hot.

"It waits in you. Your link is air, and calling to it comes most easily to you. But there are four. Tonight, you'll make fire."

"The balefire, yes. But we didn't bring wood."

With a little chuckle, Mia stepped back. "We won't need it. Center yourself. Clear your mind. This fire does not burn. This fire does no harm. It lights the dark and glows from charm. When you make its golden tower, you will know your strength and power. And once begun, bring harm to none."

"It's too soon for her," Ripley said from outside the circle.

"Quiet. You're not to interfere. Look at me, Nell. You can trust me, and yourself. Watch. And see."

"Hold on to your hats," Ripley muttered, and stepped a bit further back, just in case.

Mia opened her hands, empty hands. Spread her fingers. Turning them over, she held her arms out as if reaching.

There was a spark, electric blue. Then another, then a dozen, then too many to count. They sizzled, like fire on water, turned the air within the circle to deep sapphire.

And there, where the bare ground had been, rose a bright and gilded pillar of flame.

Nell's legs simply folded until her butt hit the ground with a solid thump. Nothing that was going through her mind, had she been able to capture any of the scattered pieces of her thoughts, could have made its way out of her mouth.

"Told you." Ripley sighed, shook her head.

"Quiet!" Mia spun away from the fire, held out a hand to help Nell to her feet. "You've seen me do magic before, little sister. You've done magic yourself."

"Not like that."

"It's a basic skill."

"Basic? Mia, really. You made *fire*. Out of nothing."

"What she means is it's along the lines of losing your virginity. It's kind of a jolt," Ripley said helpfully. "It might be less pleasurable than you expect the first time around, but after a while, you get better at it."

"Close enough." Mia agreed. "Now center yourself, Nell. You know how. Clear your mind. Visualize, gather the power. Make your fire."

"I can't possibly—"

Mia cut her off with a lifted hand. "How do you know unless you try? Concentrate." She stepped behind Nell, laid her hands on Nell's shoulders. "There's light inside you, and heat, energy. You know it. Bring it together. Feel it. It's like a tingling in the belly, and it rises toward the heart. It spreads up, fills you."

Gently, she put her hands under Nell's arms, lifting them. "It runs under your skin, like a river, flows down your arms, to your fingertips. Let it come. It's time."

While they worked, Ripley watched. There was something lovely about it in a strange way. Something like watching Mia balance Nell on her first two-wheeler, offering encouragement, keeping pace, building confidence.

The first time wasn't easy on student or teacher, she knew. Nell's face was sheened with the sweat of effort. The muscles in her arms trembled.

The clearing, never completely silent, seemed to vibrate. The air here, never completely still, sighed.

There was a faint and fitful spark. When Nell would have leaped back, Mia was there, holding her in place, her quiet and steady encouragement like a chant.

Another spark, stronger.

Ripley watched Mia step back, leaving her little sister wobbling on two wheels, solo. Despising the weakness, Ripley felt tears, pure sentiment, gather in her eyes. And a little spurt of pride as Nell's fire shimmered to life.

For the first time since she'd begun, Nell felt the

beat of her own heart, the rise and fall of her own chest. Power, bright as silver, pumped through her blood.

"It's better than losing your virginity. It's beautiful, and bright," she whispered. "Nothing will ever be the same for me again."

She turned, full of joy. But Mia was no longer looking at her, but at Ripley.

"We need three."

Furious, Ripley refused to let the tears fall. "You won't get the third from me."

Mia had seen the tears, and understood them. She also understood Ripley. "Very well." To Nell she said, "She probably can't do it anymore."

"Don't tell me what I can't do," Ripley piped up.

"It'd be hard for her to find that out, especially after watching you do so well, after such a short time."

"And stop talking like I'm not here. I hate that."

"Why *are* you here?" Mia asked with annoyance. "Nell and I can make the third together." Which had been Mia's plan before she'd seen Ripley at the door. "We certainly don't need you and your pathetic, rusty attempts. She was never as good as me," she said to Nell. "It always infuriated her that what came so easily to me was such an effort for her."

"I was every bit as good as you."

"Hardly."

"Better."

Ah, Mia thought. Ripley never could turn down a challenge. "Prove it."

Weakened by sentiment, stirred by longing, and bristling with the dare, Ripley stepped into the circle.

No, Nell thought. She swaggered.

She didn't hold out her arms as Mia had, but seemed to throw them, and the fire that burst from their tips, onto the ground.

The minute she did, she hissed like a snake. "You did that on purpose."

"Perhaps, but so did you. And look here, the sky did not fall. You made the choice, Ripley. I couldn't have pushed you into it unless you'd wanted it."

"This doesn't change anything. It's one time only."

"If you say so, but you might as well have some wine while you're here." Mia studied the trio of flames as she picked up the bottle. Ripley's was bigger than hers, a result of temper. But not, Mia thought with satisfaction, nearly as elegant.

And, pouring the wine, she felt a fire inside herself. That was hope.

They had another glass when they returned to Mia's house.

Restless now, Ripley wandered from window to window. Jingling the change in her pocket. Mia ignored her. For as long as she'd known her, Ripley had never been a quiet soul. And at the moment, Mia understood there was a considerably testy war going on inside of her.

"Have you decided how you're going to handle your situation with Zack?"

Nell glanced up at her. She sat on the floor, mesmerized by the fire. "No. Part of me hopes that Evan will divorce me, take it out of my hands. And the rest of me knows that's not the core of the problem."

"If you don't stand up to bullies, they tromp all over you."

Nell admired Ripley. Strong, wiry, and ready, she thought. "Knowing that and acting on it are two different things. Evan would never have taken a piece out of someone like you."

Ripley lifted a shoulder. "So, take it back."

"She will when she's ready," Mia countered. "You of all people should know that it's impossible to push one person's beliefs, ideas, or standards on another. Or to erase someone else's fear."

"She's upset with me because I hurt Zack. I can't blame you."

"He's a big boy." Ripley shrugged, then sat on the arm of the couch. "What are you going to do about him—Zack, that is—in the meantime?"

"Do?"

"Yeah, do. Are you just going to let him slide through his brooding phase—which is what comes after the pissed-off phase with him and, let me tell you, is a lot harder to live with. I figure we've gotten to be pals, more or less, since you've been here. Do a pal a favor and snap him out of it before I have to smother him in his sleep."

"We've talked."

"I don't mean talk. I mean action. Is she really that much of a sweetie?" Ripley asked Mia.

"Apparently. Ripley, in her own delicate way, is suggesting that you lure Zack back to bed and soothe away your troubles with a bout or two of hot jungle sex. Which is her answer to all manner of pesky annoyances, including hangnails."

"Bite me. Mia's given up sex, which explains why she's such a bitch."

"I haven't given it up, I'm simply more selective than a cat in heat."

"It isn't about sex." Making the statement, making it firm and fast, was Nell's only solution to fending off another argument.

Ripley snorted. "Yeah, sure, right."

Mia sighed. "It pains me, more than I can say, to agree with Ripley. Even partially. Certainly your relationship with Zack isn't, as all of Ripley's are, based on sex. But it's a vital part of it, an expression of your feelings, a celebration of them, and your intimacy."

"You can put flowers on it, it's still sex." Ripley gestured with her glass. "However high-minded Zack is, he's still a guy. Being around you and not getting laid—"

"Ripley, please."

"Not having intimacy," she said in a prissy tone after Mia's reprimand, "is going to make him edgy. If he's going to deal with your L.A. asshole, he should be in top form."

"He's been very careful to keep me at a distance, in that area."

"Then close the distance, in that area," Ripley said simply. "Here's what we do. You drop me off at your place. I'll bunk there tonight. You go over to the house and take care of business. You've been hanging out with him long enough to know what buttons to push."

"That's sneaky, deceitful, and manipulative."

Ripley cocked her head at Nell. "What's your point?"

Despite herself, Nell laughed. "Maybe I will go over. To *talk*," she added.

"Whatever you want to call it." Ripley polished off her wine. "Maybe you could take these glasses and things back into the kitchen, get your stuff together."

"Sure." She rose, began to gather the glasses. "I'll just be a minute."

"Take your time."

Mia waited until Nell was out of the room. "It won't take her long, so say what you didn't want to say in front of her."

"What I did tonight doesn't change anything."

"That's redundant."

"Just shut up." She paced again. She'd opened herself—only for a short time, but that's all that had been needed. She'd felt that heaviness in the air, the pressure. "Okay, trouble's coming. I'm not going to pretend I don't feel it, and I'm not going to pretend I haven't tried to figure a way to deal with it. Maybe I could, but I won't bet Zack on it. I'm going to sign up for this, Mia." She turned back. "But just for this."

Mia didn't rub it in. In fact, it didn't occur to her to do so. "We'll light the balefires at midnight on Samhain eve. We'll meet at ten on the Sabbat. Zack already wears Nell's talisman, but I'd protect your house if I were you. Do you remember how?"

"I know what to do," Ripley snapped. "Once this passes, things go back the way they were. This is—"

"Yes, I know," Mia retorted. "A one-time-only."

Zack had given up on paperwork, given up on his telescope, and pretty much given up on the idea that he could will himself to sleep. He was trying to bore himself to sleep now, by reading one of Ripley's gun magazines.

Lucy was sprawled beside the bed in a deep sleep that he envied. Every now and then her legs would twitch as she chased dream gulls or swam in her dream inlet. But she lifted her head, one sharp motion, let out a soft, warning woof seconds before Zack heard the front door open.

"Relax, girl. It's just Ripley."

At the sound of the name, Lucy was up and scrambling for the door, where she stood wagging her entire body.

"Forget it. It's too late to play."

The knock on the bedroom door had Lucy barking joyfully and Zack cursing. "What?"

Lucy whipped herself into happy circles as the door opened, then she leaped enthusiastically on Nell.

Zack shot up in bed. "Lucy, down! Sorry. I thought it was Rip." He nearly threw back the covers, then remembered he was buck naked. "Is something wrong?"

"No. Nothing." She bent over to pet Lucy, wondering which of them was more embarrassed, and decided it was a tie. "I just wanted to see you. Talk to you."

He peeked at the clock, noted it was coming onto midnight. "Why don't you go downstairs? I'll be right there."

"No." He wasn't going to treat her like a guest. "This is fine." She came over, sat on the side of the bed. He still wore the locket, and that meant something. "I made fire tonight."

He studied her face. "Okay."

"No." She laughed a little, and scratched Lucy's head. "I made it. Not with wood and a match. With magic."

"Oh." There was a tickling inside his chest. "I don't know what I'm supposed to say to that. Congratulations? Or . . . wow?"

"It made me feel strong, and excited. And . . . complete. I wanted to tell you. It made me feel something like I do when I'm with you. When you touch me. You don't want to touch me because I have a legal tie to someone else."

"It doesn't stop the want, Nell."

She nodded, let the relief of that come. "You won't touch me because I have a legal tie to someone else. But the fact is, Zack, the only man I have a real tie to is you. When I ran, I told myself I would never tie myself to another man. Never risk that again. Then there was you. I have magic in me." She lifted a hand, fisted, to her heart. "And it's amazing and thrilling and sweet. Still, it's nothing—nothing, Zack—to what I have in me for you."

Any defense, any rational reason he may have had quite simply crumbled. "Nell."

"I miss you. Just being with you. I'm not asking you to make love with me. I was going to. I was going to try to seduce you."

He skimmed his fingers through her hair. "What changed your mind?"

"I don't want to ever lie to you again, even in a harmless way. And I won't use one set of your feelings against another set. I just want to be with you, Zack, just be. Don't tell me to go."

He drew her down until her head was cradled on his shoulder, and he felt her long, long sigh of contentment echo his own.

Nineteen

It wasn't easy for an important, successful man to get away by himself for a few days. It was a complicated and tedious business to reschedule meetings, postpone appointments, inform clients, alert staff.

There was a whole world of people dependent upon him.

More tedious yet was making travel arrangements personally rather than using the services of an assistant.

But after careful thought, Evan decided there was nothing else to be done. No one was to know where he was, or what he was doing. Not his staff, not his clients, not the press. Naturally, he could be reached via cell phone if there was a crisis of any sort. Otherwise, until he'd done what he set out to do, he would remain incommunicado.

He had to know.

He hadn't been able to get the information his sister had so casually passed on to him out of his mind.

Helen's double. Helen's ghost.

Helen.

He would wake up at night in a cold sweat from images of Helen, *his* Helen, walking along some picturesque beach. Alive. Laughing at him. Giving herself to any man who crooked his finger.

It couldn't be borne.

The terrible grief he'd felt upon her death was turning slowly, inexorably, into a cold and killing rage.

Had she tricked him? Had she somehow planned and executed the faking of her own death?

He hadn't thought her smart enough, certainly not brave enough, to try to leave him, much less succeed. She *knew* the consequences. He had made them perfectly clear.

Till death do us part.

Obviously she couldn't have done so alone. She'd had help. A man, a lover. A woman, especially a woman like Helen, could never have devised such a scheme on her own. How many times had she sneaked off to lie with some wife-stealing bastard, working out the details of her deception?

Laughing and fucking, plotting and planning.

Oh, there would be payment made.

He could calm himself again, continue about his business and his life without an outward ripple. He could nearly convince himself again that Pamela's claims were nonsense. She was, after all, a woman. And women, by nature, were given to flights of fancy and foolishness.

Ghosts didn't exist. And there was only one Helen Remington. The Helen who had been meant for him.

But at times in that big, glamorous house in Beverly Hills, he thought he heard ghosts whispering, or caught the bright sound of his dead wife's taunting laughter.

What if she wasn't dead?

He had to know. He had to be careful, and clever.

"Ferry's loading."

His eyes, pale as water, blinked. "I beg your pardon?"

The ferry worker stopped blowing on his take-out cup of coffee and instinctively stepped back from that blank stare. It was, he would think later, like staring into an empty sea.

"Ferry's loading," he repeated. "You're going to Three Sisters, ain't ya?"

"Yes." The smile that spread over the handsome face was worse than the eyes. "Yes, I am."

According to legend, the one known as Air had left her island to go with the man who promised to love her, to care for her. And when he'd broken those promises and turned her life into a misery she had done nothing. She'd borne children in sorrow, raised them in fear. Had bowed, and had broken.

Had died.

Her last act had been to send her children back to the Sisters for protection. But she had done nothing, even with her powers, to protect or save herself.

So the first link in the chain of a curse was forged.

Nell thought of the story again. Of the choices and mistakes, and of destiny. She kept it clear in her head as she walked down the street of what had become her home. What she intended to keep as her home.

When she walked in, Zack was delivering a blistering lecture to a young boy she didn't recognize. Automatically, she started to step out again, but Zack merely held up a finger and never broke rhythm.

"You're not only going straight over to Mrs. Demeara's and clean up every last scrap of pumpkin guts and apologize for being a moron, but you're going to pay a fine for possession of illegal explosives and willful destruction of property—five hundred dollars."

"Five hundred dollars!" The boy, thirteen at the outside, Nell calculated, lifted a head that had been sunk low. "Jeez, Sheriff Todd, I ain't got five hundred dollars. My mom's going to kill me as is."

Zack merely raised his eyebrows and looked merciless. "Did I say I was finished?"

"No, sir," the boy mumbled, and went back to looking so hangdog that Nell wanted to go pat his head.

"You can work off the fine by cleaning the station house. Twice a week, three dollars an hour."

"Three? But it'll take me . . ." The boy had smartened up enough to shut up. "Yes, sir. You weren't finished."

His lips wanted to twitch, but Zack kept them in a firm, hard line. "I've got some odd chores around my place, too. Saturdays."

And oh, Zack thought, that one stung. There was no crueler fate than being imprisoned by chores on a Saturday.

"Same rate. You can start there this Saturday, and in here Monday after school. If I hear you're in any more trouble like this, your mother's going to have to stand in line to skin you. Clear?"

"Yes, Uncle Zack . . . um, I mean, yes, sir, Sheriff."

"Beat it."

He beat it, nearly spinning the air into a funnel as he raced past Nell.

"Uncle Zack?"

"Second cousins, really. It's an honorary term."

"What did he do to earn the hard labor?"

"Stuck an ash can, that's a firecracker, in his history teacher's pumpkin. It was a damn big pumpkin, too. Blew that shit all over hell and back again."

"Now you're sounding proud of him."

He pokered up, as best he could. "You're mistaken. Idiot boy could've blown his fingers off, which is what I nearly did at about the same age when I blew my science teacher's pumpkin to hell and back. Which is beside the point, especially when we'll be in for similar Halloween pranks tomorrow if I don't make an example now."

"I think you did the job." She walked over, sat down. "Have you got time for another matter, Sheriff?"

"I could probably carve out time." It surprised him that she hadn't leaned over to kiss him, and that she sat so straight, so still, so solemn. "What's the matter?"

"I'm going to need some help, and some advice. On the law, I suppose. I've generated false identification, and I've put false information on official forms, signing them with a name that isn't legally mine. I think faking my own death is illegal, too. At least there must be something about life insurance fraud. There were probably policies."

He didn't take his eyes off hers. "I think a lawyer would be able to handle that for you, and that when all facts are known, there'll be no charges brought. What are you telling me, Nell?"

"I want to marry you. I want to live my life with you, and make those children with you. To do that, I have to end this, so I will. I need to know what I'm going to have to do, and if I'll have to go to jail."

"You're not going to jail. Do you think I'd let that happen?"

"It's not up to you, Zack."

"The false papers and so on aren't going to put anyone's sense of justice up. The fact is . . ." He'd given this angle a great deal of thought. "The fact is, Nell, once you tell the story you're going to be a hero."

"No. I'm no one's hero."

"Do you know the statistics on spousal abuse?" He pulled open his bottom drawer, took out a file and dropped it on his desk. "I've put some data together on it. You might want to have a look at it sometime."

"It was different for me."

"It's different for everybody, every time. The fact that you came from a good home and you lived in a big, fancy house doesn't change anything. A lot of people who think it's different for them or that there's nothing they can do to change their situation are going to look at you, hear what you did. Some of them might take a step they might not have taken because of you. That makes you a hero."

"Diane McCoy. It still bothers you that you couldn't help her. That she wouldn't let you help her."

"There are a lot of Diane McCoys out there."

She nodded. "All right. But even if public sentiment falls on my side, there are still legalities."

"We'll handle them, one at a time. As far as the insurance, they'll get their money back. We'll pay it back if we have to. We'll do what we have to do together."

When she heard that, a weight lifted. "I don't know where to start."

He rose, came around to her, crouched at her feet. "I want you to do this for me. That's selfish, but I can't help it. But I want you to do it for yourself, too. Be sure."

"I'll be Nell Todd. I'll have a name I want."

She saw his expression alter, the deepening of emotion in his gaze, and knew she had never been more sure of anything. "I'm afraid of him, and I can't help that either. But I think I realize I'll never stop until this is done. I want to live with you. I want to sit out on the porch at night and look at the stars. I want that beautiful ring you bought me on my finger. I want so many things with you I thought I'd never have. I'm scared, and I want to stop being scared."

"I know a lawyer in Boston. We'll call him, and we'll start."

"Okay." She let out a breath. "Okay."

"There's one thing I can take care of right now." He straightened, walked over and opened a drawer in his desk. Her heart gave a lovely little flutter when she saw the box in his hand. "I've been carting this around with me, putting it in here, or in my dresser at home. Let's put it where it belongs."

She got to her feet, held out her hand. "Yes, let's."

Her stomach was jumping when she left to walk back to the bookstore. But there was anticipation tangled with the nerves. And every time she looked down at the deep blue stone on her finger, anticipation won.

She walked in, sent a wave to Lulu, and practically floated upstairs to Mia's office.

"I need to tell you."

Mia turned from her keyboard. "All right. I could spoil your moment by saying congratulations and I know you'll be very happy together, but I won't."

"You saw my ring."

"Little sister, I saw your face." However jaded she considered herself about love, the sight of it warmed her heart. "But I want to see the ring." She leaped up, snatched Nell's left hand. "A sapphire." She couldn't stop the sigh. "It's a love gift. As a ring it sends out healing, and can also be used as protection against evil. Beyond all that, it's a doozy." She kissed Nell on either cheek. "I'm happy for you."

"We talked to a lawyer, someone Zack knows in Boston. My lawyer now. He's going to help me with the complications, and with the divorce. He's going to file a restraining order against Evan. I know it's only a piece of paper."

"It's a symbol. There's power in that."

"Yeah. In a day or two, once he's got everything in

place, he'll contact Evan. So he'll know. With or without a restraining order, he'll come, Mia. I know he will."

"You may be right." Was this what she'd been feeling, the dread, the building of pressure?

The last leaves had died, and the first snow had yet to fall.

"But you're prepared, and you're not alone. Zack and Ripley will meet every ferry that comes here after he's been contacted. If you don't plan to move in with Zack right away, then you'll stay with me. Tomorrow's the Sabbat. Ripley's agreed to participate. When the circle's joined, he can't break it. That I can promise you."

She intended to tell Ripley next, if she could find her. But the minute Nell stepped outside, she was stricken with a wave of nausea that rolled thick and greasy through her belly. She staggered a little, sweat popping out on her skin. With no choice, she leaned back against the wall of the building and waited for it to pass.

When the worst of it eased, she regulated her breathing. The jitters, she told herself. Everything was going to start happening now, and happening very fast. There'd be no turning back. There would be questions, and press, and stares, murmurs even from people she'd come to know.

It was natural to be a little queasy.

She looked down at her ring again, the hopeful glint of it, and the lingering dregs of sickness passed.

She would find Ripley later, she decided. Right now she was going to buy a bottle of champagne and the makings for a good Yankee pot roast.

Evan drove off the ferry and onto Three Sisters as Nell leaned weakly against the wall of the bookstore. He surveyed the docks, disinterested. The beach, unimpressed. Following the instructions he'd been given, he drove to High Street and pulled up in front of the Magick Inn.

A hole-in-the-wall in a town suitable for middle-class Currier and Ives buffs, he judged. He got out of the car, studied the street, just as Nell turned the corner into the market.

He walked inside, and checked in.

He'd booked a suite, but found no charm in the coffered ceilings, the lovingly preserved antiques. He detested the fussiness of such rooms, preferring the streamlined, the modern. The art, if one could call it that, ran to misty watercolors and seascapes. The mini-bar didn't hold his favored brand of mineral water.

And the view? He could see nothing but beach and water, noisy gulls and what he supposed were fishing boats run by locals.

Dissatisfied, he walked to the parlor. From there he could see the curve of the land and the sudden sharp jut of cliffs where the lighthouse stood. He noted the stone house as well and wondered what type of idiot would choose to live in such an isolated spot.

Then he found himself squinting. There seemed to be some sort of light dappling through the trees. A trick of the eye, he decided, already bored.

In any case, he had hardly come for the scenery, thank the Lord. He'd come to look for Helen or to satisfy himself that what was left of her was still at the bottom of the Pacific. On an island this size, he was sure he could get the task done in a day.

He unpacked, meticulously hanging his clothes so that each garment was aligned precisely one inch from the next. He set out his toiletries, including his triple-milled soap. He never used the amenities offered in hotels. Even the idea of it revolted him.

And last, he set the framed photograph of his wife on the bureau. He leaned over, kissed the curved bow of her mouth through the glass.

"If you're here, darling Helen, I'll find you."

On his way out, he made a reservation for dinner. The only meal he found acceptable to eat in a hotel room was breakfast.

He stepped out, turned left, just as Nell, with her two bags of groceries, swung around the end of the block to the right, toward home.

It was, Nell was sure, the happiest morning of her life. The sky was silver, with sweeps and rises of rose and gold and deep red. Her lawn was carpeted with leaves that would crunch merrily underfoot and had left the trees bare and spooky. Which was perfect for an island Halloween.

She had a man sleeping in her bed who had shown his appreciation for a good pot roast in a very satisfactory way.

Muffins were baking, the wind was shivering, and she was prepared to face her demons.

She would be leaving her little cottage behind soon,

and that she would miss. But the idea of setting up housekeeping with Zack made up for it.

They would spend Christmas together, she thought. Maybe even be married by then if all the legal tangles could be unraveled.

She wanted to be married outside, in the air. It was impractical, but it was what she wanted. She would wear a long dress, of velvet. Blue velvet. And carry a spray of white flowers. The people she had come to know would all be there to bear witness.

While she daydreamed, the cat meowed piteously.

"Diego." She bent down, stroked him. He was no kitten now but a sleek young cat. "I forgot to feed you. I'm very scattered of brain today," she told him. "I'm in love, and I'm getting married. You'll come to live with us in our house by the sea, and make friends with Lucy."

She got out his kibble, filling his bowl while he wound excitedly through her legs.

"A woman who talks to her cat could be considered strange."

Nell didn't jump, which pleased both of them. Instead she rose and walked to Zack, who stood in the doorway. "He might be my familiar. But I'm told that'll be up to him. Good morning, Sheriff Todd."

"Good morning, Ms. Channing. Can I buy a cup of coffee and a muffin?"

"Payment first."

He came to her, wrapped her up in a long, deep kiss. "That do it?"

"Oh, yeah. Just let me give you your change." She drew him down again, lingered over the taste of him. "I'm so happy."

At precisely eight-thirty, Evan sat down to a breakfast of sweetened coffee, fresh orange juice, an egg-white omelette, and two slices of whole wheat toast.

He'd already made use of the hotel health club, such as it was. He had only glanced at the pool. He disliked using public swimming pools, but had considered it until he'd seen it was already being used. A long, lean brunette was streaking through the water. As if she was in a race, he'd thought.

He'd only caught glimpses of her face as she turned it rhythmically in and out of the water in time with her strokes.

And he didn't see, as he dismissed her and walked away, her sudden loss of pace. The way she pulled up in the water as if gathering for attack. How she shoved her goggles, treading water as she looked around for what had felt like an enemy.

He'd showered in his room, dressed in a pale gray sweater and dark slacks. He glanced at his watch, ready to be annoyed if his meal should be above one minute late.

But it arrived, just as requested. He didn't chat with the waiter. He never did such foolish things. The man was paid to deliver food, not to fraternize with guests.

He enjoyed his breakfast, surprised that he could find no fault with it, as he read the morning paper and listened to the news on the parlor television.

He considered how best to do what he'd come to do. Walking through the village as he'd done yesterday, driving around the island as he planned to do today, might not be enough. Still, it wouldn't do to ask people if they knew anyone of Helen's description. People never minded their own business, and there would be questions. Speculation. Attention.

If, by some chance, Helen was alive and here, the less attention paid to him, the better.

If she were, what would she do? She had no skills. How could she earn a living without him to provide for her? Unless, of course, she'd used her body to entice yet another man. Women were, at the center, whores.

He had to sit back and wait for the fury to pass. It was difficult to think in logical steps through anger. However justified.

He would find her, he reassured himself. If she was alive, he would find her. He would simply know. And that took him to what would be done when and if he did.

There was no question that she would have to be punished. For distressing him, for deceiving him, for attempting to break free of the promises she'd made to him. The inconvenience, the embarrassment of it all couldn't be calculated.

He would take her back to California, of course, but not right away. They would need to go somewhere quiet, somewhere private first, so he could remind her of those promises. So he could remind her who was in charge.

They would say she'd been thrown from the car. That she'd struck her head or some such thing. She'd had amnesia and had wandered away from the scene of the accident.

The press would love it, Evan decided. They would eat it up.

They would work out the details of the story once they were settled in that private, quiet place.

If none of that was possible, if she tried to refuse him, to run again, to go crying to the police as she'd done before, he would have to kill her.

He made the decision as coolly as he had decided what to have for breakfast.

Her choices were just as simple, in his opinion. Live—or die.

At the knock on his door, Evan folded the paper precisely, walked over to answer.

"Good morning, sir," the young maid said cheerfully. "You requested housekeeping service between nine and ten."

"That's right." He checked his watch, noted it was nine-thirty. He had lingered over his thoughts longer than he'd planned.

"I hope you're enjoying your stay. Would you like me to start in the bedroom?"

"Yes."

He sat with his last cup of coffee, watched a report on a fresh hot spot in Eastern Europe that couldn't have interested him less. It was too early to call the coast and see if there was anything he needed to know. But he could call New York. He had a deal cooking there, and it wouldn't hurt to stir the pot.

He went into the bedroom to retrieve his memo book and found the maid, her arms full of fresh linen, staring at the framed photograph of Helen.

"Is there a problem?"

"What?" She flushed. "No, sir. I'm sorry."

She moved quickly to make the bed.

"You were looking at this photograph very intently. Why is that?"

"She's a lovely woman." His voice was sending skitters up her spine. She wanted to get the suite clean and get out.

"Yes, she is. My wife, Helen. The way you looked at the photograph, I thought perhaps you might have met her at some time or other."

"Oh, no, sir, I doubt it. It's just that she reminded me of someone."

He had to consciously stop his teeth from grinding. "Oh?"

"She really looks a lot like Nell—except Nell doesn't have all that beautiful hair or that look of . . . I don't know, polish, I guess you'd say."

"Really?" His blood began to sizzle, but he kept his voice mild now, almost friendly. "That's interesting. My wife would be fascinated to know there's a woman who looks that much like her."

Nell. Helen's mother had called her Nell. A simple, inelegant name. He had always disliked it.

"Does she live on the island, this Nell?"

"Oh, sure. She's lived here since early summer, in the yellow cottage. Runs the café at the bookstore—does catering, too. Cooks like a dream. You should try the café for lunch. There's a soup-and-sandwich special every day, and you can't beat it."

"I might do that," he said, very softly.

Nell strolled through the back door of Café Book, called out a casual greeting to Lulu, then continued upstairs.

Once she was there, she moved like lightning.

Just under two minutes later, she called down in a voice she tried to infuse with frustrated apology. “Mia, I’m sorry, but could you come up here a minute?”

“Ought to be able to set up on her own by now,” Lulu mumbled and earned a slanted look from the boss.

“You ought to be able to give her a break by now,” Mia returned and started upstairs.

Nell stood by one of the café tables, where a pretty frosted cake glittered under the lighted birthday candles. Also on the table were a small wrapped box and three flutes frothy with mimosas.

“Happy birthday.”

The sweetness of the gesture made up for being caught off guard, as she rarely was. Mia’s smile bloomed—absolute delight. “Thank you. Cake?” She lifted a brow as she picked up a flute. “Mimosas, *and* presents. It almost makes it worth turning thirty.”

“Thirty.” Coming up behind her, Lulu snorted. “Still a baby. When you hit fifty, we’ll talk.” She held out another wrapped box, a larger one. “Happy birthday.”

“Thanks. Well, what first?”

“Wish first,” Nell ordered, “and blow out the candles.”

It had been a long time since she’d made anything as simple as a wish, but she did so now, then swept her breath over the candles.

“You have to cut the first piece.” Nell handed her a cake knife.

"All right. Then I want my presents." Mia cut, then picked up the large box and tore in.

The throw was soft as water, the color of midnight sky. Scattered over it were the symbols of the zodiac. "Oh, Lu, it's fabulous!"

"Keep you warm."

"It's beautiful." Nell stroked the throw. "I tried to imagine it when Lulu described it, but it's so much more."

"Thank you." Mia turned, rubbed her cheek over Lulu's before kissing it.

Though pleased color pinched Lulu's cheeks, she waved Mia away. "Go on, open Nell's before she bursts."

"It's just that they made me think of you," Nell began as Mia set the throw aside to open the little box. Inside were earrings, a dangle of silver stars twinkling against tiny globes of moonstone.

"They're wonderful." Mia held them up to the light before she kissed Nell. "And perfect, particularly today," she added, holding out her arms.

She was wearing black again, but the sleek sweep of the dress was picked out in tiny silver stars and moons. "I couldn't resist it for Halloween, and now these . . ." She made quick work of slipping off the earrings she'd put on that morning and replacing them with Nell's. "Just top it off."

"Okay, then." Lulu raised her glass. "To hitting the big three-oh."

"Oh, Lulu, don't spoil it." But Mia laughed as she clicked glasses. "I want cake." She lifted her little silver watch that dangled from one of her chains. "We're going to open just a few minutes late today."

It wasn't difficult to find the yellow cottage. Evan drove past it, slowing his car to study the small house tucked among the trees. Little better than a shack, was his opinion, and the insult of it nearly choked him.

She would live in that hovel rather than in the beautiful homes he'd provided for her.

He had to fight the urge to go to the café, to drag her out and into the street. Public scenes, he reminded himself, were not the way to deal with a deceitful wife.

Such things required privacy.

He drove back to the village, parked his car, then went back on foot. His blood was already bubbling. Careful study showed him that none of the neighboring houses were close enough to worry him. Still, he strolled into the trees first, circled around. Stood in their shadows watching the house.

When nothing moved, nothing stirred, he crossed to the back door.

There was a wave of something—something strong and fretful. It seemed to push against him, as if to bar him from the door. For a moment it laid what might have been fear over his skin, and he actually found himself stepping back, off the stoop.

Fury bubbled, burned away that fear. While the stars hanging from the eaves chimed madly in a sudden gust of wind, he shoved through what seemed like a wall of solid air and gripped the doorknob.

She didn't even lock the house, he thought in disgust as he let himself in. See how careless she was, how foolish?

He saw the cat and nearly snarled. He detested animals. Filthy creatures. They stared at each other for one long moment, then Diego streaked away.

Evan scanned the kitchen, then began to walk through the cottage. He wanted to see how his dead wife had been living this past year.

He could hardly wait to see her again.

Twenty

She started to head home half a dozen times that afternoon, but there was so much fun in the village. Most of the merchants had decked themselves out in costumes to celebrate the day. There were demons selling hardware and fairies ringing up produce.

She had a late lunch with Ripley, and an impromptu meeting with Dorcas about catering a Christmas party.

And it seemed that every second person she passed stopped her to congratulate her on her engagement.

She belonged. To the village, she thought. To Zack. And finally, finally, she belonged to herself.

She swung by the station house to make a date with Zack to hand out the goody bags she'd already made up for the ghosts and goblins expected at dusk.

"I might be a little late. Have to run herd on some of the older kids," Zack told her. "I've already dealt with a couple of teenagers who tried to convince me the twelve rolls of toilet paper they were buying were for their mothers."

"How did you get the toilet paper for rolling houses when you were a kid?"

"I stole it out of the bathroom closet at home, like anyone with half a brain."

Her dimples deepened. "Any more exploding pumpkins?"

"No, I think the word got out on that." He cocked his head. "You sure look chipper today."

"I am chipper today." She stepped forward, wrapped her arms around his neck.

He'd just gotten his arms around her when his phone rang. "Hold that thought," he told her, and answered.

"Sheriff's office. Yeah, Mrs. Stubens. Hmm?" He stopped lowering his hip to the corner of the desk and stood straight again. "Is anybody hurt? Good. No, just stay right there, I'm on my way. Nancy Stubens," he told Nell as he strode over to the coat rack for his jacket. "Teaching her boy how to drive. He ran straight into the Bigelows' parked Honda Civic."

"But is he all right?"

"Yeah, I'll just go sort things out for them. It might take a while. That Honda was brand-new."

"You know where to find me."

She walked out with him, felt a nice steady glow when he leaned down to kiss her good-bye. Then they walked in opposite directions.

She'd gone half a block when Gladys Macey hailed her.

"Nell! Hold on." Puffing a little at the effort to

catch up, Gladys patted her heart. "Let me see that ring I'm hearing so much about."

Before Nell could offer her hand, Gladys was grabbing it, bending over close to get a good, long look. "Should have known that Todd boy would do a good job." She gave a nod of approval, then looked up at Nell. "You got a winner there, and I don't mean the ring."

"I know it."

"I watched him grow up. Once he got some man on him, if you know what I mean, I used to wonder what sort of woman would catch his fancy. I like knowing it's you. I've got a fondness for you."

"Mrs. Macey." Undone, Nell hugged her. "Thank you."

"You'll be good for him." She patted Nell's back. "And he'll be good for you. I know you've had some troubles." She simply nodded as Nell drew back. "You had something in your eyes when you came here. It's not there much anymore."

"I left all that behind. I'm happy."

"It shows. Have you set the date?"

"No, not yet." Nell thought of lawyers, of conflict. Of Evan. She would deal with it, she told herself. With all of it. "As soon as we can."

"I want a front-row seat at the wedding."

"You'll have one. And all the champagne you can drink at our thirtieth anniversary party."

"I'll hold you to it. Well, I've got to get on. Monsters'll come knocking at the door before long, and I don't want my windows soaped. You tell that man of yours I said he did well."

"I will." That man of hers, Nell thought as she began to walk again. What a wonderful phrase.

She quickened her steps. She was going to have to hurry to beat dusk.

She went to the front of the cottage, glancing around a bit self-consciously. Secure that she was alone in the lowering light, she held her arms out toward her jack-o'-lanterns, breathed in, focused.

It took some work, a hard slap of effort, and a match would certainly have been quicker. But it wouldn't have given her the same rush as watching the candles spurt flame and the pumpkins glow from the fire in her mind.

Boy! She let out her breath on a quick laugh. Boy, oh boy, that was so *cool.*

It wasn't just the magic, she decided. It was the knowing—who and what she was. It was finding her strength, her purpose, and her heart. Taking back control so that she could share it with a man who believed in her.

Whatever happened tomorrow, or a year from tomorrow, she was now and always Nell.

She danced up the steps and into the front door.

"Diego! I'm home. You wouldn't believe the day I've had. Absolutely the best day."

She twirled into the kitchen, flipping on the light. She put on the kettle for tea before beginning to fill a big wicker basket with her goody bags.

"I hope we get a lot of kids. It's been years since I've done trick or treat. I can't wait." She opened a cupboard. "Oh, for heaven's sake! I left my car at the bookstore. What was I thinking?"

"You always were absentminded."

The mug she reached for slipped like water out of her hand, smashed on the counter, shattered on the floor. A roaring filled her ears as she turned.

"Hello, Helen." Evan walked slowly toward her. "It's so good to see you."

She couldn't say his name, could make no sound at all. She prayed it was another vision, a hallucination. But he reached out, and those slender fingers brushed her cheek.

She went cold to the marrow.

"I've missed you. Did you think I wouldn't come?" Those fingers slid around the back of her neck now and brought on a hideous wave of nausea. "Wouldn't find you? Haven't I told you, Helen, so many times, that nothing would ever keep us apart?"

She only closed her eyes when he bent, brushed his mouth over hers. "What have you done to your hair?" His hand fisted it, tugged viciously. "You know how I love your hair. Did you cut it off to displease me?"

A tear slithered down her cheek as she shook her head. His voice, his touch, seemed to drain everything she was away and leave her as she'd been.

She felt Nell fading away.

"It does displease me, Helen. You've caused me a great deal of trouble. A great deal. You've stolen a year of our lives."

His fingers tightened, went biting cruel as he jerked her chin up. "Look at me, you stupid little bitch. Look at me when I speak to you."

Her eyes opened and all she could see were his, those clear, empty pools.

"You'll have to pay for it, you know that. More

than a year erased. And all the while you've been living in this miserable little shack, laughing at me, working as a waitress, serving people. Trying to start your pitiful little business, kitchen business. Humiliating me."

His hand slid from her cheek to her throat, squeezed. "I'm going to forgive you after a time, Helen. After a time, because I know you're slow, and just a bit stupid. Have you nothing to say to me, my love? Nothing to say after this long separation?"

Her lips were cold, felt as if they might crack. "How did you find me?"

He smiled then, and made her shudder. "I told you I'd always find you, wherever you went, whatever you did." He gave her a hard shove that jammed her back into the counter. The pain registered in kind of an absent way, like a memory.

"Do you know what I found here, in your little nest, Helen? Helen, my whore? Men's clothing. How many men have you slept with, slut?"

The kettle began to shriek, but neither of them heard.

"Did you find yourself some strapping local fisherman, let him put his fumbling, workingman's hands all over you? All over what belongs to me?"

Zack. It was her first clear thought. Clear enough that her swimming eyes registered bright fear.

"There's no fisherman," she said and barely cried out when he slapped her.

"Liar. You know how I detest liars."

"There's no—" The tears escaped at the next slap. But it snapped her back to who she was. She was Nell Channing, and she would fight. "Keep away from me.

Keep away." She grabbed for the knife block, but he was quicker. He'd always been quicker.

"Is this what you want?" He drew the long, jagged-edged blade free, turned it in the light an inch from her nose. She braced herself. She thought: So, he'll kill me after all.

Instead he reared back, smashing the side of her face with a vicious backhanded slap that sent her flying. She crashed into the table, striking her head against the edge of the thick wood. The world went bright, went dark.

She didn't feel her body hit the floor.

Mia treated a young space explorer. The book-store was one of the most popular spots on Halloween. She had dancing skeletons, grinning pumpkins, flying ghosts, and, of course, a coven of witches. Her usual store music had been replaced with howls and shrieks and rattling chains.

She was having the time of her life.

She served a cowboy ghoul a cup of punch from a cauldron as the dry ice packed beneath it sent out curls of smoke.

His eyes were huge as he watched her. "Are you gonna ride on your broomstick tonight?"

"Of course." She bent down. "What kind of a witch would I be otherwise?"

"The witch who chased Dorothy was a bad witch."

"She was a very bad witch," Mia agreed. "I happen to be a very good one."

"She was ug–ly, and had a green face. You're pretty," he giggled and slurped his punch.

"Thank you very much. You, on the other hand, are very scary." She handed him a bag of candy. "I hope you won't trick me."

"Huh-uh. Thanks, lady." He dropped the bag in his begging sack, then ran off to find his mother.

Amused, Mia started to straighten. The pain came fast, bright, like a spear of light through the temple. She saw a man with pale eyes and bright hair, and the gleam of the blade.

"Call Zack." She rushed to the door, calling out to a startled Lulu. "There's trouble. Nell's in trouble. Call Zack."

She raced into the street, swung around a group of costumed children and nearly plowed into Ripley. "Nell."

"I know it." Ripley's head was still ringing. "We have to hurry."

She came to slowly, her vision fractured, her head screaming. There was absolute silence. She rolled, moaning, and managed to get to her hands and knees. Nausea sent her curling into a ball again.

The kitchen was dark now, lit only by the faint glow of a candle in the center of the table.

He sat there, in one of her kitchen chairs. She could see his shoes, the gleam of them, the perfect crease in his slacks, and she wanted to weep.

"Why do you make me punish you, Helen? I can

only think you must enjoy it." He nudged her with his shoe. "Is that it?"

She started to crawl away. Just a moment, she prayed. Give me one moment to breathe, and I can find my strength again.

He simply pressed his foot into her back.

"We're going to go somewhere where we can be alone. Where we can discuss all this foolishness, all this trouble you've caused me."

He frowned a little. How was he to get her away? He hadn't meant to put marks on her, not where they could be noticed. She had pushed him to it.

"We'll walk to my car," he decided. "You'll wait there for me while I pack and check out."

She shook her head. She knew it was useless, but she shook her head, then began to cry quietly when she felt Diego brush against her legs.

"You'll do exactly as I say." He tapped the tip of the knife against the table. "If you don't, you'll leave me no choice. People already believe you're dead, Helen. Beliefs can easily become reality."

His head snapped up as he heard a sound outside the door. "Perhaps the fisherman's come calling," he whispered, and rose, turning the knife in his hand.

Zack opened the door, hesitating, cursing as the phone on his belt rang. The break in stride saved his life.

He caught a blur of movement, a glimpse of the blade hacking down. He twisted, going for his weapon with a cross-body draw. The knife ripped through his shoulder instead of burying itself in his heart.

Nell screamed, gained her feet, only to have her head spin and send her staggering. In the dark kitchen, she could see the two silhouettes struggle. A weapon, she thought, biting her lip to keep from passing out again.

The bastard would *not* take what was hers. He would *not* harm what she loved.

She stumbled for the knife block, but it was gone.

She turned back, prepared to leap, to use teeth and nails. And saw Evan standing over Zack's body, the knife dripping in his hand.

"Oh, my God, no! No!"

"Your knight in shining armor, Helen? Is this the man you've been fucking behind my back? He's not dead yet. I have a right to kill him for trying to steal my wife."

"Don't." She drew in a breath, released it. Struggled to gather herself and find her core of strength. "I'll go with you. I'll do anything you want."

"You will, anyway," Evan commanded.

"He doesn't matter." She began to edge around the counter, saw Diego crouched, teeth bared. "He doesn't matter to either of us. It's me you want, isn't it? You came all this way for me."

He would go after her. If she could get out the door, he'd go after her and leave Zack. It took all her will to keep herself from throwing herself down over Zack, to shield him. If she did, if she so much as looked at him now, they were both dead.

"I knew you would," she continued, every muscle trembling as she watched Evan lower the knife to his side. "I always knew."

Evan took one step toward her, and the cat leaped like a tiger on his back. With his howl of rage in her ears, Nell ran.

She veered toward the street, toward the village, but even as she glanced back, he was coming through the door. She would never make it.

So, it would be the two of them, after all. Putting her faith in the fates, she dived into the trees.

Zack pulled himself to his knees as Evan bolted out the door. The pain was like hot teeth gnawing at his shoulder. Blood dripped from his fingers as he got to his feet.

Then he thought of Nell and forgot the pain.

He was flying out the door just as the trees swallowed her and the man who pursued her.

"Zack!"

He paused only to flick a terrified glance at his sister and Mia. "He's after her. He's got a knife, and she doesn't have much lead."

Ripley bit down on the worry. His shirt was soaked with blood. She nodded, drew her weapon as he did. "Whatever you've got," she said to Mia, "we use."

She plunged into the woods behind her brother.

In the dark of the moon, the night was blind. She ran like a wild thing, tearing through brush, leaping over fallen branches. If she could lose him, get him deep enough in and lose him, she could circle back to Zack.

She prayed with every beat of her heart that he was alive.

She could hear Evan behind her, close, too close. Her breath was coming in gasps, tattered by fear, but his was a steady determined beat.

Dizziness swept over her, urged her to drop to her knees. She fought it off, nearly stumbled. She would not lose now.

Then his body slammed into hers and sent her sprawling.

She rolled, kicked, her only thought to get free of him. Then froze when he yanked her head back by her short cap of hair and pressed the knife tip to her throat.

Her body emptied, went limp as a doll's. "Why don't you just do it," she said wearily. "Just end it."

"You ran from me." There was as much bafflement as rage in his voice. "You ran."

"And I'll keep running. Until you kill me, I'll keep running. I'd rather be dead than live with you. I've already died once, so do it. I've stopped being afraid of you."

She felt the blade bite. At the sound of running feet he dragged her up.

Even with a knife at her throat, she felt joy when she saw Zack.

Alive. The dark stain on his shirt glimmered in the faint starlight. But he was alive, and nothing mattered more.

"Let her go." Zack took his stance, supporting his gun hand with his weak one. "Drop the knife and step away from her."

"I'll slit her throat. She's mine, and I won't hesitate." Evan's eyes passed from Zack's to Ripley's to Mia's as they stood in a half circle.

"Hurt her, and you're dead. You won't walk away from here."

"You've no right to interfere between a husband and wife." There was something almost reasonable in his voice, something sane under the madness. "Helen is my wife. Legally, morally, eternally." He jerked her head back another inch with the blade. "Throw your guns down and walk away. This is my business."

"I can't get a clear shot," Ripley said under her breath. "Not enough light to be sure."

"It's not the way. Put the gun down, Ripley." Mia stretched out her hand.

"The hell with that." Her finger itched on the trigger. The bastard, was all she could think as she saw Nell's exposed throat, smelled her brother's blood.

"Ripley," Mia said again, soft, insistent under the sharp, clipped orders from Zack to drop the knife. To step away.

"Damn it, damn it. You better be right."

Zack didn't hear them. They'd ceased to exist for him. His only reality was Nell.

"I'll do more than kill you." Zack held the gun rock steady and his voice was calm as a lake. "If you cut her, so much as nick her, I'll take you apart, piece by piece. I'll put bullets in your knees, in your balls, in your gut. I'll stand over you and watch while you bleed out."

The color that rage brought to Evan's face drained away. He believed what he saw in Zack's eyes. Believed the pain and death he saw there, and was afraid. His hands trembled on the handle of the knife, but he didn't move. "She belongs to me."

Ripley's hand gripped Mia's. Nell felt the punch

of energy they created, felt the hot waves of love and terror that rolled off Zack as he stood bleeding for her.

And felt, as she had never felt, fear from the man who gripped her.

Her name was Nell Channing, now and always. And the man behind her was less than nothing.

She closed her hand over the pendant Mia had given her. It vibrated. "I belong to myself." Power trickled back into her, a slow pool. "I belong to me." And faster. "And to you," she said, her eyes locked on Zack's. "He's done hurting me now."

She lifted her other hand, laid it on Evan's wrist, lightly. "Let me go, Evan, and you'll walk away. We'll put all of this behind us. It's your chance. The last chance."

His breath hissed at her ear. "You stupid bitch. Do you think I'll ever let you go?"

"And your choice." There was pity in her voice. "Your last."

The chant was in her head, rising, as if it had only been waiting for her to free it.

She wondered how she could have been so afraid of him.

"What you've done to all and me, turns back to you, one times three. From you this night I'll forever be free. As I will, so mote it be."

Her skin glowed like sunlight, her pupils dark as stars. The knife trembled, whispered along her skin, away, then fell. She heard the choking gasp, the high whine that couldn't reach a scream as Evan collapsed behind her.

She didn't spare him a glance.

"Don't shoot him," she said quietly to Zack. "Don't kill him like this. It wouldn't be good for you."

Because she could see the intent, she walked to Zack as Evan began to moan. "It wouldn't be good for us. He's nothing now." She laid a hand over Zack's heart, felt its wild beat. "He's what he made himself."

Evan lay on the ground, twitching as if something vile slithered under his skin. His face was bone white.

Zack lowered the gun, wrapped his good arm around Nell. He held her there a moment as she reached out, clasping hands with Mia, and linking them all.

"Stay with them," Zack told her. "I'll deal with him. I won't kill him. He'll suffer more if he lives."

Ripley watched her brother walk toward the writhing man, take out his handcuffs. He needed to do this last thing, she thought, and she needed to let him. "He gets two minutes to secure and Mirandize that smear of slime, then I want him taken to the clinic. I don't know how bad he's hurt."

"I'll take him." Nell looked down at the blood, Zack's blood, on her hand, curled her fist over it, and felt life pump. "I'll stay with him."

"Courage"—Mia reached out, touched the pendant—"breaks the spell. Love weaves another." She pulled Nell into her arms for a fierce hug. "You did well, little sister." She turned toward Ripley. "And you found your fate."

Early on the Feast of the Saints, long after the balefires were charmed away, before dawn broke the sky, Nell sat in the kitchen of the yellow cottage, her hand resting loosely in Zack's.

She needed to come back, to be there, to tidy away what had happened and what might have happened. She'd swept away the negative forces that had lingered and had lit candles and incense.

"I wish you'd stayed overnight at the clinic."

She turned her hand under Zack's, squeezed. "I could say the same."

"I've got a few stitches, you've got the concussion."

"Mild," she reminded him, "and twenty-three stitches is more than a few."

Twenty-three stitches, he thought. A long, nasty gash. The doctor had called it a miracle that no muscle or tendons had been severed.

Zack called it magic. Nell's magic.

She reached out to touch the fresh white bandage, then trailed her fingers over the gold locket. "You didn't take it off."

"You asked me not to. It got hot," he told her, and brought her gaze back to his. "An instant before he cut me. I could see, in my head, in that quick blur, the blade going toward my heart, then being deflected. As if it hit a shield. I thought I imagined it. But I didn't."

"We were stronger than he was." Nell brought their joined hands to her cheek. "I was afraid, drowning in fear from the minute I heard his voice. It took away everything I'd built, everything I'd learned about myself. He paralyzed me, sucked out my will. That was his power over me. But it began to come back, and when he hurt you, it flooded back. But I couldn't think, not clearly. Hitting my head was part of it, I suppose."

"You ran to save me."

"And you followed to save me. We're a couple of heroes."

He touched her face, gently. There were bruises on it that he felt throb in his own. "He's never going to hurt you again. I'll go in and relieve Ripley at dawn, and contact the prosecutor's office on the mainland. A couple of attempted-murder charges will keep him locked up, no matter how fancy his lawyers are."

"I'm not afraid of him anymore. He looked pathetic in the end, eaten up by his own cruelty. Terrified of it. His madness is staring back at him now. He'll never be able to hide it again."

He could still see Evan Remington's colorless eyes, wide and wild in a face white as bone. "A padded room's as good as a cell."

She got to her feet to pour more tea. But when she came back to the table, Zack wrapped an arm around her, pressed his face into her body.

"It's going to take a while for me to get the picture of you with a knife to your throat out of my head."

She stroked his hair. "We have a lifetime to put others in its place. I want to marry you, Sheriff Todd. I want to start that lifetime very soon."

She slid into his lap, sighing as she rested her head on his good shoulder. Through the window she could see the first streaks of color announcing dawn, the pale burn across the sky.

Laying a hand on his heart, she timed its beats to her own. And knew the truest magic was there.

Turn the page for a preview of

HEAVEN AND EARTH

The second book in Nora Roberts's all-new Three Sisters Island trilogy

He didn't look so very different from the other passengers on the ferry. His long, black coat flapped in the wind. His hair, an ordinary sort of dark blond, flew around his face and had no particular style.

He'd remembered to shave and had only nicked himself twice, just under the strong line of his jaw. His face—and it was a good one—was hidden behind one of his cameras as he snapped pictures of the island using a long lens.

His skin still held the tropical tan he'd picked up in Borneo. Against it, his eyes were the luminous golden brown of honey just bottled. His nose was straight and narrow, his face a bit thin.

The hollows in his cheeks tended to deepen when he lost himself in work for long periods and forgot regular meals. It gave him an intriguing starving-scholar look.

His mouth smiled easily, sensually.

He was somewhat tall, somewhat lanky.

And somewhat clumsy.

He had to grip the rail to keep a shudder of the ferry from pitching him over it. He'd been leaning out too far, of course. He knew that, but anticipation often made him forget the reality of the moment.

He steadied himself again, dipped into his coat pocket for a stick of gum.

He came out with an ancient lemon drop, a couple of crumpled sheets of notepaper, a ticket stub—which baffled him, as he couldn't quite remember when he'd last been to the movies—and a lens cap he'd thought he'd lost.

He made do with the lemon drop and watched the island.

He'd consulted with a shaman in Arizona, visited a man who claimed to be a vampire in the mountains of Hungary, been cursed by a brujo after a regrettable incident in Mexico. He'd lived among ghosts in a cottage in Cornwall and had documented the rights and rituals of a necromancer in Romania.

For nearly twelve years, MacAllister Booke had studied, recorded, and witnessed the impossible. He'd interviewed witches, ghosts, lycanthropes, alien abductees, and psychics. Ninety-eight percent of them were delusional or con artists. But the remaining two percent . . . well, that kept him going.

He didn't just believe in the extraordinary. He'd made it his life's work.

The idea of spending the next few months on a chunk of land that legend claimed had been torn from the mainland of Massachusetts by a trio of witches and settled as a sanctuary was fascinating to him.

He'd researched Three Sisters Island extensively

and had dug up every scrap of information he could find on Mia Devlin, the current island witch. She hadn't promised him an interview or access to any of her work. But he hoped to persuade her.

A man who had talked himself into a ceremony held by neo-Druids should be able to convince a solitary witch to let him watch her work a few spells.

Besides, he imagined they could make a trade. He had something he was sure would interest her, and anyone else who was tied into the three-hundred-year-old curse.

He lifted his camera again, adjusting the framing to capture the spear of the white lighthouse, the brooding ramble of the old stone house, both clinging to the high cliffs. He knew Mia lived there, high above the village, close to the thick slice of forest.

Just as he knew she owned the village bookstore and ran it successfully. A practical witch, who, by all appearances, knew how to live, and live well, in both worlds.

He could hardly wait to meet her face-to-face.

The blast of the horn warned him to prepare for docking. He walked back to his Land Rover, put his camera in its case on the passenger seat.

The lens cap in his pocket was, once again, forgotten.

While he had these last few minutes to himself, he updated some notes, then added to the day's journal entry.

The ferry ride was pleasant. The day's clear and cold. I was able to take a number of pictures from different vantage points, though I'll need to rent a boat for views of the windward side of the island.

Geographically, topographically, there's nothing unusual about Three Sisters Island. Its area is approximately nine square miles, and its year-round inhabitants—largely in the fishing or the retail and tourist trade—number less than three thousand. It has a small sand beach, numerous inlets, coves, and shale beaches. It is partially forested, and the indigenous fauna include white-tail deer, rabbit, raccoon. Typical seabirds for this area, as well as owls, hawks, and palliated woodpeckers in the forested regions.

There is one village. The majority of the residents live in the village proper or within a half-mile radius, though there are some houses and rental units farther afield.

There is nothing about the island's appearance that would indicate it is a source of paranormal activity. But I've found that appearances are unreliable documentary tools.

I'm eager to meet Mia Devlin and begin my study.

He felt the slight bump of the ferry's docking, but didn't look up.

Docked, Three Sisters Island, January 6, 2002. Glanced at his watch. *12:03 P.M. EST.*

*The village streets were storybook tidy, the traf*fic light. Mac drove through, circled, logging various spots on his tape recorder. He could find an ancient Mayan ruin in the jungle with a map scribbled on a crushed napkin, but he had a habit of forgetting more pedestrian locations. Bank, post office, market. Ah, pizzeria, hot damn!

He found a parking place without trouble only a stop down from Café Book. He liked the look of the place immediately—the display window, the view of the sea. He fished around for his briefcase, tossed the mini-recorder inside, just in case, and climbed out.

He liked the look of the store even more on the inside. The cheerful fire in a stone hearth, the big checkout counter carved with moons and stars. Seventeenth century, he decided, and suitable for a museum. Mia Devlin had taste as well as talent.

He started to cross to it and the little gnomelike woman sitting on a high stool behind it. A movement, a flash of color caught his attention. Mia stepped out of the stacks and smiled.

"Good afternoon. Can I help you?"

His first clear thought was, Wow.

"I'm, ah, hmm. I'm looking for Ms. Devlin. Mia Devlin."

"And you've found her." She walked toward him, held out a hand. "MacAllister Booke?"

"Yeah." Her hand was long and narrow. Rings sparkled on it like jewels on white silk. He was afraid to squeeze too hard.

"Welcome to Three Sisters. Why don't you come upstairs? I'll buy you a cup of coffee, or perhaps some lunch. We're very proud of our café."

"Ah . . . I wouldn't mind some lunch. I've heard good things about your café."

"Perfect. I hope your trip in was uneventful."

Up till now, he thought. "It was fine, thanks." He followed her up the stairs. "I like your store."

"So do I. I hope you'll make use of it during your stay on the island. This is my friend, and the artist of our café, Nell Todd. Nell, Dr. Booke."

"Nice to meet you."

She showed her dimples and leaned over the counter to shake his hand.

"Dr. Booke has just arrived from the mainland, and I imagine he could use some lunch. On the house, Dr. Booke. Just tell Nell what you'd like."

"I'll take the sandwich special, and a large cappuccino, thanks. Do you do the baking, too?"

"That's right. I recommend the apple brown betty today."

"I'll try it."

"Mia?" Nell asked.

"Just a cup of the soup and the jasmine tea."

"Coming up. I'll bring your orders out."

"I can see I'm not going to have to worry about my next meal while I'm here," Mac commented as they took a window table.

"Nell also owns and runs Sisters Catering. She delivers."

"Good to know." He blinked twice, but her face—the sheer glory of it—didn't dim. "Okay, I just have to get this out, and I hope you're not offended. You're the most beautiful woman I've ever seen in my life."

"Thank you." She sat back. "And I'm not the least bit offended."

"Good. I don't want things to start off on the wrong foot, since I'm hoping to work with you."

"And as I explained over the phone, I don't . . . work for audiences."

"I'm hoping you'll change your mind after you get to know me better."

He had a potent smile, she decided. Charmingly crooked, deceptively harmless. "We'll see about that. As for your interest in the island itself, and its history, you won't lack for data. The majority of the permanent residents here are from families who've lived on Sisters for generations."

"Todd, for instance," he said, glancing back toward the counter.

"Nell married a Todd, just a little under two weeks ago, in fact. Zachariah Todd, our sheriff. While she's . . . new to the island, the Todds have, indeed, lived here for generations."

He knew who Nell was. The former wife of Evan Remington. A man who had once wielded considerable power and influence in the entertainment industry. A man who had been found to be a violent abuser. And who was now deemed legally insane and under lock and key.

It had been Sheriff Todd who'd arrested him, right here on Three Sisters, after what were reputed to be strange events on Halloween night.

The Sabbat of Samhain.

It was something Mac intended to explore in more depth.

Even as he started to bring it up, something in Mia's expession warned him to bide his time there.

"Looks great. Thanks," he said instead to Nell as she served their lunch.

"Enjoy. Mia, is tonight still good for you?"

"Absolutely."

"I'll come up about seven, then. Let me know if you need anything else, Dr. Booke."

"Nell's just back from her honeymoon," Mia said in a quiet voice when she was alone with him again. "I don't think questions about certain areas of her life are appropriate just now."

"All right."

"Are you always so cooperative, Dr. Booke?"

"Mac. Probably not. But I don't want to make you mad right off the bat." He bit into his sandwich. "Good," he managed. "Really good."

She leaned forward, toyed with her soup. "Lulling the natives into complacency?"

"You're really good, too. Do you have psychic abilities?"

"Don't we all on some level? Didn't one of your papers explore the development of what you called the neglected sixth sense?"

"You've read my work."

"I have. What I am, Mac, isn't something I neglect. Neither is it something I exploit or allow to be exploited. I agreed to rent you the cottage, and to talk with you when the mood strikes me, because of one simple thing."

"Okay. What?"

"You have a brilliant and, more important, a flexible mind. I admire that. As far as trusting that, time will tell." She glanced over and gestured. "And here comes a bright enough, and very inflexible, mind. Deputy Ripley Todd."

Mac looked over, saw the attractive brunette stride on long legs to the café counter, lean on it, chat with

Nell. "Ripley's another common surname on the island."

"Yes, she's Zack's sister. Their mother was a Ripley. They have long ties, on both sides of their family, to the Sisters. Very long ties," Mia repeated. "If you're looking for a cynic to weigh in on your research, Ripley's your girl."

Unable to resist, Mia caught Ripley's attention and motioned her over.

Ordinarily Ripley would merely have sneered and walked in the opposite direction. But a strange face on the island usually bore checking out.

A good-looking guy, she thought as she strolled over. In a bookish kind of way. As soon as the thought hit, her brows drew together. Bookish. Mia's doctor of freakology.

"Dr. MacAllister Booke, Deputy Ripley Todd."

"Nice to meet you." He got to his feet, surprising Ripley with his length as he unfolded himself from the chair. Most of his height, she judged, was leg.

"I didn't know they gave out degrees for the study of crapola."

"Isn't she adorable?" Mia beamed. "I was just telling Mac that he should interview you for your narrow, closed mind. After all, it wouldn't take much time."

"Yawn." Ripley hooked her thumbs in her pockets and studied Mac's face. "I don't think I'd have much to say that you'd want to hear. Mia's the goddess of woo-woo stuff around here. You have any questions about the practicalities of day-to-day life on the island, you can usually find me or the sheriff around."

"Appreciate it. Oh, I've only got a master's in crapola. Haven't finished my thesis on that one yet."

Her lips twitched. "Cute. That your Rover out front?"

"Yes." Had he left the keys in it again? he wondered, already patting pockets. "Is there a problem?"

"No. Nice ride. I'm going to grab some lunch."

"She isn't abrasive and annoying on purpose," Mia said when Ripley walked away. "She was born that way."

"It's okay." He sat again, picked up his meal where he'd left off. "I get a lot of that kind of thing." He nodded at Mia. "I imagine you do, too."

"Now and then. You're awfully well adjusted and affable, aren't you, Dr. MacAllister Booke?"

"Afraid so. It's pretty boring."

"I don't think so." Mia picked up her tea, studied him over the rim. "No, I don't think so at all."

HIGH NOON

Nora Roberts

Those closest to you can do the most harm

Phoebe MacNamara first comes face to face with Duncan Swift high up on a rooftop, as she tries to stop one of his ex-employees from jumping. As Savannah's chief hostage negotiator, Phoebe is talented, courageous and willing to risk her life to save others – and Duncan is determined to keep this intriguing woman in his life.

But Phoebe has made enemies too. When she is viciously assaulted and sent threatening messages, she realises that someone is out to destroy her – both professionally and personally. With Duncan by her side, Phoebe must discover just who is pursuing her, before it's too late . . .

'Women are addicted to her contemporary novels as chocoholics are to Godiva . . . Roberts is a superstar'
New York Times

978-0-7499-3898-7

SANCTUARY

Nora Roberts

Safe from harm – or the most dangerous place of all?

Photographer Jo Ellen Hathaway thought she'd escaped the house called Sanctuary long ago. She'd spent her loneliest years there, after the sudden, unexplained disappearance of her mother. But now someone is sending her pictures; strange, candid close-ups, culminating in the most shocking portrait of all – a photo of her mother, dead.

Jo decides she must return to Sanctuary to face her past. While her presence stirs up old family resentments, Jo finds solace with architect Nathan Delaney – who is also battling his own demons.

But a sinister presence is still watching the Hathaway family with interest. It seems Sanctuary may be the most dangerous place of all . . .

'Exciting, romantic, great fun'
Cosmopolitan

978-0-7499-3824-6

Nora Roberts is the *New York Times* bestselling author of more than 190 novels. Under the pen name J. D. Robb, she is the author of the *New York Times* bestselling futuristic suspense series, which features Lieutenant Eve Dallas and Roarke. There are more than 300 million copies of her books in print, and she has had more than 150 *New York Times* bestsellers.

Visit her website at www.nora-roberts.co.uk

By Nora Roberts:

Homeport
The Reef
River's End
Carolina Moon
The Villa
Midnight Bayou
Three Fates
Birthright
Northern Lights
Blue Smoke
Angels Fall
High Noon
Divine Evil
Tribute
Sanctuary

Three Sisters Island Trilogy:
Dance Upon the Air
Heaven and Earth
Face the Fire

Chesapeake Bay Quartet:
Sea Swept
Rising Tides
Inner Harbour
Chesapeake Blue

The Key Trilogy:
Key of Light
Key of Knowledge
Key of Valour

In the Garden Trilogy:
Blue Dahlia
Black Rose
Red Lily

The Irish Trilogy:
Jewels of the Sun
Tears of the Moon
Heart of the Sea

The Circle Trilogy:
Morrigan's Cross
Dance of the Gods
Valley of Silence

The Dream Trilogy:
Daring to Dream
Holding the Dream
Finding the Dream

The Sign of Seven Trilogy:
Blood Brothers
The Hollow
The Pagan Stone

As J.D. Robb:

Naked in Death
Glory in Death
Immortal in Death
Rapture in Death
Ceremony In Death
Vengeance in Death
Holiday in Death
Conspiracy in Death
Loyalty in Death
Witness in Death
Judgment in Death
Betrayal in Death
Seduction in Death
Reunion In Death
Purity in Death
Portrait in Death
Imitation in Death
Divided in Death
Visions in Death
Survivor in Death
Origin in Death
Born in Death
Memory in Death
Innocent in Death
Creation in Death
Strangers in Death

By Nora Roberts and J.D. Robb
Remember When

River's End

Nora Roberts

PIATKUS

First published in the US in 1999 by G. P. Putnam's Sons
First published in Great Britain in 1999 by Piatkus Books
Reprinted 2000 (twice), 2001 (three times), 2002 (three times),
2003 (twice), 2005, 2006 (three times), 2007, 2008, 2009

A CIP catalogue record for this book
is available from the British Library

ISBN 978-0-7499-3159-9

Typeset in Times by Phoenix Photosetting, Chatham, Kent
Printed and bound in Great Britain by
CPI Mackays, Chatham, ME5 8TD

Papers used by Piatkus Books are natural, renewable and recyclable products made from wood grown in sustainable forests and certified in accordance with the rules of the Forest Stewardship Council.

Piatkus Books
An imprint of
Little, Brown Book Group
100 Victoria Embankment
London EC4Y 0DY

An Hachette Livre UK Company
www.hachettelivre.co.uk

www.piatkus.co.uk

To Mom and Pop
Thanks for being mine.

River's End

The woods are lovely, dark and deep.
But I have promises to keep,
And miles to go before I sleep,
And miles to go before I sleep.

—Robert Frost

She forgot whether she was hunter or hunted, only knew [illegible] some [illegible] against the [illegible]

[illegible]

Prologue

The monster was back. The smell of him was blood. The sound of him was terror.

She had no choice but to run, and this time to run toward him.

The lush wonder of forest that had once been her haven, that had always been her sanctuary, spun into a nightmare. The towering majesty of the trees was no longer a grand testament to nature's vigor, but a living cage that could trap her, conceal him. The luminous carpet of moss was a bubbling bog that sucked at her boots. She ripped through ferns, rending their sodden fans to slimy tatters, skidded over a rotted log and destroyed the burgeoning life it nursed.

Green shadows slipped in front of her, beside her, behind her, seemed to whisper her name.

Livvy, my love. Let me tell you a story.

Breath sobbed out of her lungs, set to grieving by fear and loss. The blood that still stained her fingertips had gone ice-cold.

Rain fell, a steady drumming against the windswept canopy, a sly trickle over lichen-draped bark. It soaked into the greedy ground until the whole world was wet and ripe and somehow hungry.

She forgot whether she was hunter or hunted, only knew through some deep primal instinct that movement was survival.

She would find him, or he would find her. And somehow it would be finished. She would not end as a coward. And if there was any light in the world, she would find the man she loved. Alive.

She curled the blood she knew was his into the palm of her hand and held it like hope.

Fog snaked around her boots, broke apart at her long, reckless strides. Her heartbeat battered her ribs, her temples, her fingertips in a feral, pulsing rhythm.

She heard the crack overhead, the thunder snap of it, and leaped aside as a branch, weighed down by water and wind and time, crashed to the forest floor.

A little death that meant fresh life.

She closed her hand over the only weapon she had and knew she would kill to live.

And through the deep green light haunted by darker shadows, she saw the monster as she remembered him in her nightmares.

Covered with blood, and watching her.

Olivia

A simple child that light draws its breath,
And feels its life in every limb,
What should it know of death?

—William Wordsworth

[illegible]

[illegible] told the best stories, wonderfully silly ones with
pink giraffes and two-headed cows. But he'd gotten sick, and the
[illegible] made him do bad things and say bad words [illegible]
[illegible] wasn't like [illegible]. He'd had to go away [illegible]
[illegible] had told her [illegible] to go away until [illegible]
[illegible] That's why he could only come to see her sometimes
[illegible] by Aunt Annie or Uncle David had to stay [illegible] the
whole time.

[illegible]

Chapter One

Beverly Hills, 1979

Olivia was four when the monster came. It shambled into dreams that were not dreams and ripped away with bloody hands the innocence monsters covet most.

On a night in high summer, when the moon was bright and full as a child's heart and the breeze was softly perfumed with roses and jasmine, it stalked into the house to hunt, to slaughter, to leave behind the indifferent dark and the stink of blood.

Nothing was the same after the monster came. The lovely house with its many generous rooms and acres of glossy floors would forever carry the smear of his ghost and the silver-edged echo of Olivia's lost innocence.

Her mother had told her there weren't any monsters. They were only pretend, and her bad dreams only dreams. But the night she saw the monster, heard it, smelled it, her mother couldn't tell her it wasn't real.

And there was no one left to sit on the bed, to stroke her hair and tell her pretty stories until she slipped back into sleep.

Her daddy told the best stories, wonderfully silly ones with pink giraffes and two-headed cows. But he'd gotten sick, and the sickness had made him do bad things and say bad words in a loud, fast voice that wasn't like Daddy's at all. He'd had to go away. Her mother had told her he'd had to go away until he wasn't sick anymore. That's why he could only come to see her sometimes, and Mama or Aunt Jamie or Uncle David had to stay right in the room the whole time.

Once, she'd been allowed to go to Daddy's new house on the

beach. Aunt Jamie and Uncle David had taken her, and she'd been fascinated and delighted to watch through the wide glass wall as the waves lifted and fell, to see the water stretch and stretch into forever where it bumped right into the sky.

Then Daddy wanted to take her out on the beach to play, to build sand castles, just the two of them. But her aunt had said no. It wasn't allowed. They'd argued, at first in those low, hissing voices adults never think children could hear. But Olivia had heard and, hearing, had sat by that big window to stare harder and harder at the water. And as the voices got louder, she made herself *not* hear because they hurt her stomach and made her throat burn.

And she would *not* hear Daddy call Aunt Jamie bad names, or Uncle David say in a rough voice, *Watch your step, Sam. Just watch your step. This isn't going to help you.*

Finally, Aunt Jamie had said they had to go and had carried her out to the car. She'd waved over her aunt's shoulder, but Daddy hadn't waved back. He'd just stared, and his hands had stayed in fists at his sides.

She hadn't been allowed to go back to the beach house and watch the waves again.

But it had started before that. Weeks before the beach house, more weeks before the monster came.

It had all happened after the night Daddy had come into her room and awakened her. He'd paced her room, whispering to himself. It was a hard sound, but when she'd stirred in the big bed with its white lace canopy she hadn't been afraid. Because it was Daddy. Even when the moonlight spilled through the windows onto his face, and his face looked mean and his eyes too shiny, he was still her daddy.

Love and excitement had bounced in her heart.

He'd wound up the music box on her dresser, the one with the Blue Fairy from *Pinocchio* that played 'When You Wish upon a Star'.

She sat up in bed and smiled sleepily. 'Hi, Daddy. Tell me a story.'

'I'll tell you a story.' He'd turned his head and stared at his daughter, the small bundle of tousled blond hair and big brown eyes. But he'd only seen his own fury. 'I'll tell you a goddamn story, Livvy my love. About a beautiful whore who learns how to lie and cheat.'

'Where did the horse live, Daddy?'

'What horse?'

'The beautiful one.'

He'd turned around then, and his lips had peeled back in a snarl. 'You don't listen! You don't listen any more than she does. I said *whore* goddamn it!'

Olivia's stomach jumped at his shout, and there was a funny metal sting in her mouth she didn't recognize as fear. It was her first real taste of it. 'What's a whore?'

'Your mother. Your fucking mother's a whore.' He swept his arm over the dresser, sending the music box and a dozen little treasures crashing to the floor.

In bed, Olivia curled up and began to cry.

He was shouting at her, saying he was sorry. *Stop that crying right now!* He'd buy her a new music box. When he'd come over to pick her up, he'd smelled funny, like a room did after a grown-up party and before Rosa cleaned.

Then Mama came rushing in. Her hair was long and loose, her nightgown glowing white in the moonlight.

'Sam, for God's sake, what are you doing? There, Livvy, there, baby, don't cry. Daddy's sorry.'

The vicious resentment all but smothered him as he looked at the two golden heads close together. The shock of realizing his fists were clenched, that they wanted, *yearned* to pound, nearly snapped him back. 'I told her I was sorry.'

But when he started forward, intending to apologize yet again, his wife's head snapped up. In the dark, her eyes gleamed with a fierceness that bordered on hate. 'Stay away from her.' And the vicious threat in her mother's voice had Olivia wailing.

'Don't you tell me to stay away from my own daughter. I'm sick and tired, sick and damn tired of orders from you, Julie.'

'You're stoned again. I won't have you near her when you've been using.'

Then all Olivia could hear were the terrible shouts, more crashing, the sound of her mother crying out in pain. To escape she crawled out of bed and into her closet to bury herself among her mountain of stuffed toys.

Later, she learned that her mother had managed to lock him out of the room, to call the police on her Mickey Mouse phone. But that night, all she knew was that Mama had crawled into the closet with her, held her close and promised everything would be all right.

That's when Daddy had gone away.

Memories of that night could sneak into her dreams. When they did, and she woke, Olivia would creep out of bed and into her mother's room down the hall. Just to make sure she was there. Just to see if maybe Daddy had come home because he was all better again.

Sometimes they were in a hotel instead, or another house. Her mother's work meant she had to travel. After her father got sick, Olivia always, always went with her. People said her mother was a star, and it made Olivia giggle. She knew stars were the little lights up in heaven, and her mother was right here.

Her mother made movies, and lots and lots of people came to see her pretend to be somebody else. Daddy made movies, too, and she knew the story about how they'd met when they were both pretending to be other people. They'd fallen in love and gotten married, and they'd had a baby girl.

When Olivia missed her father, she could look in the big leather book at all the pictures of the wedding when her mother had been a princess in a long white dress that sparkled and her father had been the prince in his black suit.

There was a big silver-and-white cake, and Aunt Jamie had worn a blue dress that made her look almost as pretty as Mama. Olivia imagined herself into the pictures. She would wear a pink dress and flowers in her hair, and she would hold her parents' hands and smile. In the pictures, everyone smiled and was happy.

Over that spring and summer, Olivia often looked at the big leather book.

The night the monster came, Olivia heard the shouting in her sleep. It made her whimper and twist. Don't hurt her, she thought. Don't hurt my mama. Please, please, please, Daddy.

She woke with a scream in her head, with the echo of it on the air. And wanted her mother.

She climbed out of bed, her little feet silent on the carpet. Rubbing her eyes, she wandered down the hallway where the light burned low.

But the room with its big blue bed and pretty white flowers was empty. Her mother's scent was there, a comfort. All the magic bottles and pots stood on the vanity. Olivia amused herself for a little while by playing with them and pretending she was putting on the colors and smells the way her mother did.

One day she'd be beautiful, too. Like Mama. Everyone said so. She sang to herself while she preened and posed in the tall mirror, giggling as she imagined herself wearing a long white dress, like a princess.

She tired of that and, feeling sleepy again, shuffled out to find her mother.

As she approached the stairs, she saw the lights were on downstairs. The front door was open, and the late-summer breeze fluttered her nightgown.

She thought there might be company, and maybe there would be cake. Quiet as a mouse, she crept down the stairs, holding her fingers to her lips to stop a giggle.

And heard the soaring music of her mother's favorite, *Sleeping Beauty*.

The living room spilled from the central hall, flowing out with high arched ceilings, oceans of glass that opened the room to the gardens her mother loved. There was a big fireplace of deep blue lapis and floors of sheer white marble. Flowers speared and spilled from crystal vases, and silver urns and lamps had shades the colors of precious jewels.

But tonight, the vases were broken, shattered on the tiles with their elegant and exotic flowers trampled and dying. The glossy ivory walls were splattered with red, and tables the cheerful maid Rosa kept polished to a gleam were overturned.

There was a terrible smell, one that seemed to paint the inside of Olivia's throat with something vile and had her stomach rippling.

The music crescendoed, a climactic sweep of sobbing strings.

She saw glass winking on the floor like scattered diamonds and streaks of red smearing the white floor. Whimpering for her mother, she stepped in. And she saw.

Behind the corner of the big sofa, her mother lay sprawled on her side, one hand flung out, fingers spread wide. Her warm blond hair was wet with blood. So much blood. The white robe she'd worn was red with it, and ripped to ribbons.

She couldn't scream, couldn't scream. Her eyes rounded and bulged in her head, her heart bumped painfully against her ribs, and a trickle of urine slipped down her legs. But she couldn't scream.

Then the monster that crouched over her mother, the monster with hands red to the wrists, with wet red streaks over his face, over his clothes, looked up. His eyes were wild, shiny as the glass that sparkled on the floor.

'Livvy,' her father said. 'God, Livvy.'

And as he stumbled to his feet, she saw the silver-and-red gleam of bloody scissors in his hand.

Still she didn't scream. But now she ran. The monster was real, the monster was coming, and she had to hide. She heard a long, wailing call, like the howl of a dying animal in the woods.

She went straight to her closet, burrowed among the stuffed toys. There her mind hid as well. She stared blindly at the door, sucked quietly on her thumb and barely heard the monster as he howled and called and searched for her.

Doors slammed like gunshots. The monster sobbed and screamed, crashing through the house as it called her name. A wild bull with blood on his horns.

Olivia, a doll among dolls, curled up tight and waited for her mother to come and wake her from a bad dream.

That's where Frank Brady found her. He might have overlooked her huddled in with all the bears and dogs and pretty dolls. She didn't move, didn't make a sound. Her hair was a golden blond, shiny as rain to her shoulders; her face a colorless oval, dominated by huge amber eyes under brows as dark as mink pelt.

Her mother's eyes, he thought with grim pity. Eyes he'd looked into dozens of times on the movie screen. Eyes he'd studied less than an hour ago and found filmed and lifeless.

The eyes of the child looked at him, looked through him. Recognizing shock, he crouched down, resting his hands on his knees rather than reaching for her.

'I'm Frank.' He spoke quietly, kept his eyes on hers. 'I'm not going to hurt you.' Part of him wanted to call out for his partner, or one of the crime scene team, but he thought a shout might spook her. 'I'm a policeman.' Very slowly, he lifted a hand to tap the badge that hung from his breast pocket. 'Do you know what a policeman does, honey?'

She continued to stare, but he thought he caught a flicker in her eyes. Awareness, he told himself. She hears me. 'We help people. I'm here to take care of you. Are these all your dolls?' He smiled at her and picked up a squashy Kermit the Frog. 'I know this guy. He's on *Sesame Street*. Do you watch that on TV? My boss is just like Oscar the Grouch. But don't tell him I said so.'

When she didn't respond, he pulled out every Sesame Street character he could remember, making comments, letting Kermit hop on his knee. The way she watched him, eyes wide and terrifyingly blank, ripped at his heart.

'You want to come out now? You and Kermit?' He held out a hand, waited.

Hers lifted, like a puppet's on a string. Then, when the contact was made, she tumbled into his arms, shivering now with her face buried against his shoulder.

He'd been a cop for ten years, and still his heart ripped.

'There now, baby. You're okay. You'll be all right.' He stroked a hand down her hair, rocking for a moment.

'The monster's here.' She whispered it.

Frank checked his motion then, cradling her, got to his feet. 'He's gone now.'

'Did you chase him away?'

'He's gone.' He glanced around the room, found a blanket and tucked it around her.

'I had to hide. He was looking for me. He had Mama's scissors. I want Mama.'

God. Dear God, was all he could think.

At the sound of feet coming down the hall, Olivia let out a low keening sound and tightened her grip around Frank's neck. He murmured to her, patting her back as he moved toward the door.

'Frank, there's – you found her.' Detective Tracy Harmon studied the little girl wrapped around his partner and raked a hand through his hair. 'The neighbor said there's a sister. Jamie Melbourne. Husband's David Melbourne, some kind of music agent. They only live about a mile from here.'

'Better notify them. Honey, you want to go see your Aunt Jamie?'

'Is my mama there?'

'No. But I think she'd want you to go.'

'I'm sleepy.'

'You go on to sleep, baby. Just close your eyes.'

'She see anything?' Tracy murmured.

'Yeah.' Frank stroked her hair as her eyelids drooped. 'Yeah, I think she saw too damn much. We can thank Christ the bastard was too blitzed to find her. Call the sister. Let's get the kid over there before the press gets wind of this.'

He came back. The monster came back. She could see him creeping through the house with her father's face and her mother's scissors. Blood slid down the snapping blades like thin, glossy ribbons. In her father's voice he whispered her name, over and over again.

Livvy, Livvy love. Come out. Come out and I'll tell you a story.

And the long sharp blades in his hands hissed open and closed as he shambled toward the closet.

'No, Daddy! No, no, no!'

'Livvy. Oh honey, it's all right. I'm here. Aunt Jamie's right here.'

'Don't let him come. Don't let him find me.' Wailing, Livvy burrowed into Jamie's arms.

'I won't. I won't. I promise.' Devastated, Jamie pressed her face into the fragile curve of her niece's neck. She rocked both of them in the delicate half-light of the bedside lamp until Olivia's shivers stopped. 'I'll keep you safe.'

She rested her cheek on the top of Olivia's head and let the tears come. She didn't allow herself to sob, though hot, bitter sobs welled and pressed into her throat. The tears were silent, sliding down her cheeks to dampen the child's hair.

Julie. Oh God, oh God, Julie.

She wanted to scream out her sister's name. To rave it. But there was the child, now going limp with sleep in her arms, to consider.

Julie would have wanted her daughter protected. God knew, she had tried to protect her baby.

And now Julie was dead.

Jamie continued to rock, to soothe herself now as Olivia slept in her arms. That beautiful, bright woman with the wickedly husky laugh, the giving heart and boundless talent, dead at the age of thirty-two. Killed, the two grim-faced detectives had told her, by the man who had professed to love her to the point of madness.

Well, Sam Tanner was mad, Jamie thought as her hands curled

into brutal fists. Mad with jealousy, with drugs, with desperation. Now he'd destroyed the object of his obsession.

But he would never, never touch the child.

Gently, Jamie laid Olivia back in bed, smoothed the blankets over her, let her fingertips rest for a moment on the blond hair. She remembered the night Olivia had been born, the way Julie had laughed between contractions.

Only Julie MacBride, Jamie thought, could make a joke out of labor. The way Sam had looked, impossibly handsome and nervous, his blue eyes brilliant with excitement and fear, his black hair tousled so that she'd smoothed it with her own fingers to soothe him.

Then he'd brought that beautiful little girl up to the viewing glass, and there'd been tears of love and wonder in his eyes.

Yes, she remembered that, and remembered thinking as she smiled at him through that glass that they were perfect. The three of them, perfect together. Perfect for one another.

It had seemed so.

She walked to the window, stared out at nothing. Julie's star had been on the rise, and Sam's already riding high. They'd met on the set of a movie, fell wildly in love and were married within four months while the press raved and simpered over them.

She'd worried, Jamie admitted. It was all so fast, so Hollywood. But Julie had always known exactly what she wanted, and she'd wanted Sam Tanner. For a while, it had seemed as happy-ever-after as the stories Julie told her daughter at bedtime.

But this fairy tale had ended in a nightmare – blocks away, only blocks away while she'd slept, Jamie thought, squeezing her eyes shut as a sob clawed at her throat.

The sudden flash of lights had her jumping back, her heart pumping fast. David, she realized, and turned quickly to the bed to be certain Olivia slept peacefully. Leaving the light on low, she hurried out. She was coming down the stairs as the door opened and her husband walked in.

He stood there for a long moment, a tall man with broad shoulders. His hair of deep brown was mussed, his eyes, a quiet mix of gray and green, full of fatigue and horror. Strength was what she'd always found in him. Strength and stability. Now he looked sick and shaken, his usual dusky complexion pasty, a muscle jumping in his firm, square jaw.

'God, Jamie. Oh, sweet God.' His voice broke, and somehow that made it worse. 'I need a drink.' He turned away, walked unsteadily into the front salon.

She had to grip the railing for balance before she could order her legs to move, to follow him. 'David?'

'I need a minute.' His hands shook visibly as he took a decanter of whisky from the breakfront, poured it into a short glass. He braced one hand on the wood, lifted the glass with the other and drank it down like medicine. 'Jesus, God, what he did to her.'

'Oh, David.' She broke. The control she'd managed to cling to since the police had come to the door shattered. She simply sank to the floor in a spasm of sobs and shudders.

'I'm sorry, I'm sorry.' He rushed to her and gathered her against him. 'Oh, Jamie, I'm so sorry.'

They stayed there, on the floor in the lovely room, as the light turned pearly with dawn. She wept in harsh, racking gasps until he wondered that her bones didn't shatter from the power of it.

The gasps turned to moans that were her sister's name, then the moans to silence.

'I'll take you upstairs. You need to lie down.'

'No, no, no.' The tears had helped. Jamie told herself they'd helped though they left her feeling hollowed-out and achy. 'Livvy might wake up. She'll need me. I'll be all right. I have to be all right.'

She sat back, scrubbing her hands over her face to dry it. Her head throbbed like an open wound, her stomach was a mass of cramps. But she got to her feet. 'I need you to tell me. I need you to tell me everything.' When he shook his head, her chin came up. 'I have to know, David.'

He hesitated. She looked so tired, so pale and so fragile. Where Julie had been long and willowy, Jamie was small and fine-boned. Both had carried a look of delicacy that he knew was deceptive. He'd often joked that the MacBride sisters were tough broads, bred to climb mountains and tramp through woods.

'Let's get some coffee. I'll tell you everything I know.'

Like her sister, Jamie had refused live-in staff. It was her house, by God, and she wouldn't sacrifice her privacy. The day maid wouldn't be in for another two hours, so she brewed the coffee herself while David sat at the counter and stared out the window.

They didn't speak. In her head she ran over the tasks she would have to face that day. The call to her parents would be the worst, and she was already bracing for it. Funeral arrangements would have to be made – carefully, to ensure as much dignity and privacy as possible. The press would be salivating. She would make sure the television remained off as long as Olivia was in the house.

She set two cups of coffee on the counter, sat. 'Tell me.'

'There isn't much more than Detective Brady already told us,' David began. 'There wasn't any forced entry. She let him in. She was, ah, dressed for bed, but hadn't been to bed. It looked as though she'd been in the living room working on clippings. You know how she liked to send your folks clippings.'

He rubbed both hands over his face, then picked up his coffee. 'They must have argued. There were signs of a fight. He used the scissors on her.' Horror bloomed in his eyes. 'Jamie, he must have lost his mind.'

His gaze came to hers, held. When he reached for her hand, she curled her fingers around his tightly. 'Did he – was it quick?'

'I don't – I've never seen – he went wild.' He closed his eyes a moment. She would hear, in any case. There would be leaks, there would be media full of truth and lies. 'Jamie, she was . . . he stabbed her repeatedly, and slashed her throat.'

The color drained from her face, but her hand stayed firm in his. 'She fought back. She must have fought him. Hurt him.'

'I don't know. They have to do an autopsy. We'll know more after that. They think Olivia saw some of it, saw something, then hid from him.' He drank coffee in the faint hope it would settle his jittery stomach. 'They want to talk to her.'

'She can't be put through that.' This time she jerked back, yanking her hand free. 'She's a baby, David. I won't have them put her through that. They know he did it,' she said with a fierce and vicious bitterness. 'I won't have my sister's child questioned by the police.'

David let out a long breath. 'He's claiming he found Julie that way. That he came in and found her already dead.'

'Liar.' Her eyes fired, and color flooded back into her face, harsh and passionate. 'Murdering bastard. I want him dead. I want to kill him myself. He made her life a misery this past year, and now he's killed her. Burning in hell isn't enough.'

She whirled away, wanting to pound something, tear something to pieces. Then stopped short when she saw Olivia staring at her from the doorway with wide eyes.

'Livvy.'

'Where's Mama?' Her bottom lip trembled. 'I want my mama.'

'Livvy.' As temper drained into grief, and grief into helplessness, Jamie bent down and picked her up.

'The monster came and hurt Mama. Is she all right now?'

Over the child's head, Jamie's desperate eyes met her husband's. He held out a hand, and she walked over so the three of them stood wrapped together.

'Your mother had to go away, Livvy.' Jamie closed her eyes as she pressed a kiss to Olivia's head. 'She didn't want to, but she had to.'

'Is she coming back soon?'

There was a ripple in Jamie's chest, like a wave breaking on rock. 'No, honey. She's not coming back.'

'She always comes back.'

'This time she can't. She had to go to heaven and be an angel.'

Olivia knuckled her eyes. 'Like a movie?'

As her legs began to tremble, Jamie sat, cradling her sister's child. 'No, baby, not like a movie this time.'

'The monster hurt her and I ran away. So she won't come back. She's mad at me.'

'No, no, Livvy.' Praying for wisdom, Jamie eased back, cupped Olivia's face in her hands. 'She wanted you to run away. She wanted you to be a smart girl, and run away and hide. To be safe. That was what she wanted most of all. If you hadn't, she'd have been very sad.'

'Then she'll come back tomorrow.' Tomorrow was a concept she knew only as later, another time, soon.

'Livvy.' With a nod to his wife, David slid the child onto his lap, relieved when she laid her head against his chest and sighed. 'She can't come back, but she'll be watching you from up in heaven.'

'I don't want her to be in heaven.' She began to cry now, soft, sniffling sobs. 'I want to go home and see Mama.'

When Jamie reached for her, David shook his head. 'Let her cry it out,' he murmured.

Jamie pressed her lips together, nodded. Then she rose to go up to her bedroom and call her parents.

Chapter Two

The press stalked, a pack of rabid wolves scenting heart blood. At least that was how Jamie thought of them as she barricaded her family behind closed doors. To be fair, a great many of the reporters were shocked and grieving and broadcast the story with as much delicacy as the circumstances allowed.

Julie MacBride had been well loved – desired, admired and envied – but loved all the same.

But Jamie wasn't feeling particularly fair. Not when Olivia sat like a doll in the guest room or wandered downstairs as thin and pale as a ghost. Wasn't it enough that the child had lost her mother in the most horrible of ways? Wasn't it enough that she, herself, had lost her sister, her twin, her closest friend?

But she had lived in the glittery world of Hollywood with its seductive shadows for eight years now. And she knew it was never enough.

Julie MacBride had been a public figure, a symbol of beauty, talent, sex with the girl-next-door spin, a country girl turned glamorous movie princess who'd married the reigning prince and lived with him in their polished castle in Beverly Hills.

Those who paid their money at the box office, who devoured glossy articles in *People* or absurdities in the tabloids, considered her theirs. Julie MacBride of the quick and brilliant smile and smoky voice.

But they didn't know her. Oh, they thought they did, with their exposés, their interviews and glossy articles. Julie had certainly been open and honest in most of them. That was her way, and she'd never taken her success for granted. It had always thrilled and delighted her. But no matter how much print and tape and film they'd run on the actress, they'd never really understood the woman herself: her sense of fun and foolishness, her love of the forest and mountains of Washington State where she'd grown up, her absolute loyalty to family, her unshakable love and devotion to her daughter.

And her tragic and undying love for the man who'd killed her.

That was what Jamie found hardest to accept. She'd let him in, was all she could think. In the end, she'd gone with her heart and had opened the door to the man she loved, even knowing he'd stopped being that man.

Would she have done the same? They'd shared a great deal, more than sisters, more than friends. Part of it came from being twins, certainly, but added to that was their shared childhood in the deep woods. The hours, the days, the evenings they'd spent exploring together. Learning, loving the scents and sounds and secrets of the forest. Following tracks, sleeping under the stars. Sharing their dreams as naturally as they had once shared the womb.

Now it was as if something in Jamie had died as well. The kindest part, she thought. The freshest and most vulnerable part. She doubted she would ever be whole again. Knew she would never be the same again.

Strong, she could be strong. Would have to be. Olivia depended on her; David would need her. She knew he'd loved Julie, too, had thought of her as his own sister. And her parents as his own.

She stopped pacing to glance up the stairs. They were here now, up with Olivia in her room. They would need her, too. However sturdy they were, they would need their remaining child to help them get through the next weeks.

When the doorbell rang, she jumped, then closed her eyes. She who had once considered herself fearless was shaking at shadows and whispers. She drew a breath in, let it out slowly.

David had arranged for guards, and the reporters were ordered not to come onto the property. But over that long, terrible day one slipped through now and then. She wanted to ignore the bell. To let it ring and ring and ring. But that would disturb Olivia, upset her parents.

She marched toward the door intending to rip off the reporter's skin, then through the etched-glass panels beside the wood she recognized the detectives who had come in the dark of the morning to tell her Julie was dead.

'Mrs. Melbourne. I'm sorry to disturb you.'

It was Frank Brady who spoke, and he whom Jamie focused on. 'Detective Brady, isn't it?'

'Yes, may we come in?'

'Of course.' She stepped back. Frank noted that she had enough control to keep behind the door, not to give the camera crews a shot at her. It had been her control he'd noted, and admired, the night before.

She'd rushed out of the house, he recalled, even before they'd fully braked at the entrance. But the minute she'd seen the girl in his arms, she'd seemed to snap back, to steady. She'd taken charge of her niece, bundling her close, carrying her upstairs.

He studied her again as she led them into the salon.

He knew now that she and Julie MacBride had been twins, with Jamie the elder by seven minutes. Yet there wasn't as much resemblance as he might have expected. Julie MacBride had owned a blazing beauty – despite delicate features and that golden coloring, it had flamed out and all but burned the onlooker.

The sister had quieter looks, hair more brown than blond that was cut in a chin-length swing and worn sleek, eyes more chocolate than gold and lacking that sensuous heavy-lidded shape. She was about five-three, Frank calculated, probably about a hundred and ten pounds on slender bones where her sister had been a long-stemmed five-ten.

He wondered if she'd been envious of her sister, of that perfection of looks and the excess of fame.

'Can I get you anything? Coffee?'

It was Tracy who answered, judging that she needed to do something normal before getting down to business. 'I wouldn't mind some coffee, Mrs. Melbourne. If it's not too much trouble.'

'No . . . we seem to have pots going day and night. I'll see to it. Please sit down.'

'She's holding up,' Tracy commented when he was alone with his partner.

'She's got a way to go.' Frank flicked open the curtains a slit to study the mob of press at the edge of the property. 'This one's going to be a zoo, a long-running one. It's not every day America's princess gets cut to ribbons inside her own castle.'

'By the prince,' Tracy added. He tapped his pocket where he kept his cigarettes – then thought better of it. 'We'll get maybe one more shot at him before he pulls it together and calls for a lawyer.'

'Then we'd better make it a bull's-eye.' Frank let the curtain close and turned as Jamie came back into the room with a tray of coffee.

He sat when she did. He didn't smile. Her eyes told him she didn't require or want pleasantries and masks. 'We appreciate this, Mrs. Melbourne. We know this is a bad time for you.'

'Right now it seems it'll never be anything else.' She waited while Tracy added two heaping spoonfuls of sugar to his mug. 'You want to talk to me about Julie.'

'Yes, ma'am. Were you aware that your sister placed a nine-one-one call due to a domestic disturbance three months ago?'

'Yes.' Her hands were steady as she lifted her own mug. 'Sam came home in an abusive state of mind. Physically abusive this time.'

'This time?'

'He'd been verbally, emotionally abusive before.' Her voice was brisk and clear. She refused to let it quaver. 'Over the last year and a half that I know of.'

'Is it your opinion Mr. Tanner has a problem with drugs?'

'You know very well Sam has a habit.' Her eyes stayed level on Frank's. 'If you haven't figured that out, you're in the wrong business.'

'Sorry, Mrs. Melbourne. Detective Brady and I are just trying to touch all the bases. We have to figure you'd know your sister's husband, his routines. Maybe she talked to you about their personal problems.'

'She did, of course. Julie and I were very close. We could talk about anything.' For a moment, Jamie looked away, struggling to keep it all steady. Voice, hands, eyes. 'I think it started a couple of years ago, social cocaine.' She smiled, but it was thin and hard. 'Julie hated it. They argued about it. They began to argue over a great many things. His last two movies didn't do as well as expected, critically or financially. Actors can be a tender species. Julie was worried because Sam became edgy, argumentative. But as much as she tried to smooth things over, her own career was soaring. He resented that, began to resent her.'

'He was jealous of her,' Frank prompted.

'Yes, when he should have been proud. They began to go out more, parties, clubs. He felt he needed to be seen. Julie supported him in that, but she was a homebody. I know it's difficult to equate the image, the beauty, glamour, with a woman who was happiest at home, in her garden, with her daughter, but that was Julie.'

Her voice cracked. She cleared it, sipped more coffee and continued. 'She was working on the feature with Lucas Manning, *Smoke and Shadows*. It was a demanding, difficult role. Very physical. Julie couldn't afford to work twelve or fourteen hours, come home, then polish herself up for night after night on the town. She wanted time to relax, time with Olivia. So Sam started going out on his own.'

'There were some rumors about your sister and Manning.'

Jamie shifted her gaze to Tracy, nodded. 'Yes, there usually are when two very attractive people fire up the screen. People romanticize, and they enjoy gossip. Sam hounded her about other men, and Lucas in particular most recently. The rumors were groundless. Julie considered Lucas a friend and a marvelous leading man.'

'How did Sam take it?' Frank asked her.

She sighed now and set down her mug, but didn't rub at the ache behind her eyes. 'If it had been three or four years ago, he'd have laughed it off, teased her about it. Instead he hounded her, sniped at her. He accused her of trying to run his life, of encouraging other men, then of being with other men. Lucas was his prime target. It hurt Julie very much.'

'Some women would turn to a friend, to another man under that kind of pressure.' Frank watched her steadily as her eyes flared, her mouth tightened.

'Julie took her marriage seriously. She loved her husband. Enough, as it turned out, to stick by him until he killed her. And if you want to turn this around and make her seem cheap and ordinary—'

'Mrs. Melbourne.' Frank lifted a hand. 'If we want to close this case, to get justice for your sister, we need to ask. We need all the pieces.'

She ordered herself to breathe, slowly in, slowly out, and poured more coffee she didn't want. 'The pieces are simple. Her career was moving up, and his was shaky. The shakier it got, the more he did drugs and the more he turned the blame on her. She called the police that night last spring because he attacked her in their daughter's room and she was afraid for Livvy. She was afraid for all of them.'

'She filed for divorce.'

'That was a difficult decision for her. She wanted Sam to get help, to go into counseling, and she used the separation as a hammer. Most of all, she wanted to protect her daughter. Sam had become unstable. She wouldn't risk her child.'

'Yet it appears she opened the door to him on the night of her death.'

'Yes.' Jamie's hand shook now. Once. She set the coffee down and folded both hands in her lap. 'She loved him. Despite everything, she loved him and believed if he could beat the drugs they'd get back together. She wanted more children. She wanted her husband back. She was careful to keep the separation out of the press. Beyond the family, the only people who knew of it were the lawyers. She'd hoped to keep it that way as long as possible.'

'Would she have opened the door to him when he was under the influence of drugs?'

'That's what happened, isn't it?'

'I'm just trying to get a picture,' Frank told her.

'She must have. She wanted to help him, and she believed she could handle him. If it hadn't been for Livvy, I don't think she'd have filed papers.'

But her daughter had been in the house that night, Frank thought. In the house, and at risk. 'You knew them both very well.'

'Yes.'

'In your opinion, is Sam Tanner capable of killing your sister?'

'The Sam Tanner Julie married would have thrown himself in front of a train to protect her.' Jamie picked up her coffee again, but it didn't wash away the bitterness that coated her throat. 'The one you have in custody is capable of anything. He killed my sister. He mutilated her, ripping her apart like an animal. I want him to die for it.'

She spoke coolly, but her eyes were ripe and hot with hate. Frank met that violent gaze, nodded. 'I understand your feelings, Mrs. Melbourne.'

'No, no, detective. You couldn't possibly.'

Frank let it go as Tracy shifted in his chair. 'Mrs. Melbourne,' Frank began. 'It would be very helpful if we were able to speak with Olivia.'

'She's four years old.'

'I realize that. But the fact is, she's a witness. We need to know what she saw, what she heard.' Reading both denial and hesitation on her face, he pressed. 'Mrs. Melbourne, I don't want to cause you or your family any more pain, and I don't want to upset the child. But she's part of this. A key part.'

'How can you ask me to put her through that, to make her talk about it?'

'It's in her head. Whatever she saw or heard is already there. We need to ask her what that was. She knows me from that night. She felt safe with me. I'll be careful with her.'

'God.' Jamie lifted her hands, pressed her fingers to her eyes and tried to think clearly. 'I have to be there. I have to stay with her, and you'll stop if I say she's had enough.'

'That's fine. She'll be more comfortable with you there. You have my word, I'll make it as easy as I can. I have a kid of my own.'

'I doubt he's ever witnessed a murder.'

'No, ma'am, but his father's a cop.' Frank sighed a little as he rose. 'They know more than you want them to.'

'Maybe they do.' She wouldn't know, she thought as she led them out and up the stairs. David hadn't wanted children, and since she hadn't been sure she did either, she'd been content to play doting aunt to her sister's daughter.

Now she would have to learn. They would all have to learn.

At the door to the bedroom, she motioned the two detectives back. She opened it a crack, saw that her parents were sitting on the floor with Olivia, putting a child's puzzle together.

'Mom. Could you come here a minute?'

The woman who stepped out had Jamie's small build, but seemed tougher, more athletic. The tan and the sun-bleached tips of her brown hair told Frank she liked the outdoors. He gauged her at early fifties and imagined she passed for younger when her face wasn't drawn and etched with grief. Her soft blue eyes, bloodshot and bruised-looking, skimmed over Frank's face, then his partner's.

'This is my mother, Valerie MacBride. Mom, these are the

detectives who . . . They're in charge,' Jamie finished. 'They need to talk to Livvy.'

'No.' Val's body went on alert as she pulled the door closed behind her. 'That's impossible. She's just a baby. I won't have it. I won't have anyone reminding her of what happened.'

'Mrs. MacBride—' But even as Frank spoke, she was turning on him.

'Why didn't you protect her? Why didn't you keep that murdering bastard away from her? My baby's dead.' She covered her face with her hands and wept silently.

'Please wait here,' Jamie murmured and put her arms around her mother. 'Come lie down, Mom. Come on now.'

When Jamie came back, her face was pale and showed signs of weeping. But her eyes were dry now. 'Let's get this over with.' She squared her shoulders, opened the door.

The man who looked up had folded his long legs Indian style. His hair was a beautiful mix of gold and silver around a narrow face that was tanned and handsome. The eyes of deep amber he'd passed to his younger daughter, and to her daughter, were fanned with lines and widely set under dark brows.

His hand, long and wide-palmed, reached out to lie on Olivia's shoulder in an instinctive gesture of protection as he studied the men behind Jamie.

'Dad.' Jamie forced her lips into a smile. 'This is Detective Brady and Detective Harmon. My father, Rob MacBride.'

Rob rose, and though he offered his hand to each detective in turn, he kept himself between them and his granddaughter. 'What's this about, Jamie?'

'They need to talk to Livvy.' She pitched her voice low and gripped his hand before he could protest. 'They need to,' she repeated, squeezing. 'Please, Dad, Mom's upset. She's lying down in your room. I'm going to stay here. I'll be right here with Livvy the whole time. Go talk to Mom. Please . . .' Because her voice threatened to break, she took a moment. 'Please, we have to get through this. For Julie.'

He bent, rested his brow against hers. Just stood that way for a moment, his body bowed, his hand in hers. 'I'll talk to your mother.'

'Where are you going, Grandpop? We haven't finished the puzzle.'

He glanced back, fighting the tears that wanted to swim into his eyes. 'I'll be back, Livvy love. Don't grow up while I'm gone.'

She giggled at that, but her thumb had found its way into her mouth as she stared up at Frank.

She knew who he was – the policeman with long arms and green eyes. His face looked tired and sad. But she remembered he had a nice voice and gentle hands.

'Hi, Livvy.' Frank crouched down. 'Do you remember me?'

She nodded and spoke around her thumb. 'You're Frank the policeman. You chased the monster away. Is it coming back?'

'No.'

'Can you find my mama? She had to go to heaven and she must be lost. Can you go find her?'

'I wish I could.' Frank sat on the floor, folded his legs as her grandfather had.

Tears welled into her eyes, trembled on her lashes and cut at Frank's heart like tiny blades. 'Is it because she's a star? Stars have to be in heaven.'

He heard Jamie's low sound of despair behind him, quickly controlled as she stepped forward. But he needed the child's trust now, so he laid a hand on her cheek and went with instinct. 'Sometimes, when we're really lucky, very special stars get to stay with us for a while. When they have to go back, it makes us sad. It's all right to be sad. Did you know the stars are there, even in the daytime?'

'You can't see them.'

'No, but they're there, and they can see us. Your mother's always going to be there, looking out for you.'

'I want her to come home. We're going to have a party in the garden with my dolls.'

'Do your dolls like parties?'

'Everybody likes parties.' She picked up the Kermit she'd brought with her from home. 'He eats bugs.'

'That's a frog for you. Does he like them plain or with chocolate syrup?'

Her eyes brightened at that. 'I like *everything* with chocolate syrup. Do you have a little girl?'

'No, but I have a little boy, and he used to eat bugs.'

Now she laughed and her thumb popped back out of her mouth. 'He did not.'

'Oh yes. I was afraid he'd turn green and start hopping.' Idly, Frank picked up a puzzle piece, fit it into place. 'I like puzzles. That's why I became a policeman. We work on puzzles all the time.'

'This is Cinderella at the ball. She has a be-u-tiful dress and a pumpkin.'

'Sometimes I work on puzzles in my head, but I need help with the pieces to make the picture in there. Do you think you can help me, Livvy, by telling me about the night I met you?'

'You came to my closet. I thought you were the monster, but you weren't.'

'That's right. Can you tell me what happened before I came and found you?'

'I hid there for a long, long time, and he didn't know where I was.'

'It's a good hiding place. Did you play with Kermit that day, or with puzzles?'

'I played with lots of things. Mama didn't have to work and we went swimming in the pool. I can hold my breath under the water for an ever, because I'm like a fish.'

He tugged her hair, peeked at her neck. 'Yep, there are the gills.'

Her eyes went huge. 'Mama says she can see them, too! But I can't.'

'You like to swim?'

'It's the most fun of anything. I have to stay in the little end, and I can't go in the water unless Mama or Rosa or a big person's there. But one day I can.'

'Did you have friends over that day, to play?'

'Not that day. Sometimes I do.' She pursed her lips and industriously fit another piece of her puzzle into place. 'Sometimes Billy or Cherry or Tiffy come, but that day Mama and me played, and we took a nap and we had some cookies Rosa made. And Mama read her script and she laughed and she talked on the phone: "Lou, I love it!"' Livvy recited in such a smooth and adult tone, Frank blinked at her. '"I *am* Carly. It's about damn time I got my teeth into a romantic comedy with wit. Make the deal."'

'Ah . . .' Frank struggled between surprise and admiration while Livvy tried to set another piece of her puzzle in place.

'That's really good. You have a good memory.'

'Daddy says I'd be a parrot if I had wings. I 'member lots of things.'

'I bet you do. Do you know what time you went to bed?'

'I'm 'posed to go to bed at eight o'clock. Chickens go broody at eight. Mama told me the story about the lady with long, long hair who lived in the tower.'

'Later you woke up. Were you thirsty?'

'No.' She lifted her thumb to her mouth again. 'I had a bad dream.'

'My Noah has bad dreams, too. When he tells me about them, he feels better.'

'Is Noah your little boy? How old is he?'

'He's ten now. Do you want to see his picture?'

'Uh-huh.' She scooted closer as Frank took out his wallet and flipped through. Cocking her head, she studied the school photo of a boy with untidy brown hair and a wide grin. 'He's pretty. Maybe he can come over to play.'

'Maybe. Sometimes he has bad dreams about space aliens.'

Forgive me, Noah, Frank thought with some amusement as he replaced his wallet, for sharing your darkest secret. 'When he tells me about them, he feels better. You want to tell me about your bad dream?'

'People are yelling. I don't like when Mama and Daddy fight. He's sick and he has to get well, and we have to keep wishing really, really hard for him to get all better so he can come home.'

'In your dream you heard your mother and father yelling?'

'People are yelling, but I can't hear what they say. I don't want to. I want them to stop. I want my mama to come. Somebody screams, like in the movies that Rosa watches. They scream and scream, and I wake up. I don't hear anything, 'cause it was just a dream. I want Mama.'

'Did you go to find her?'

'She wasn't in bed. I wanted to get in bed with her. She doesn't mind. Then I . . .'

She broke off and gave a great deal of attention to her puzzle.

'It's all right, Livvy. You can tell me what happened next.'

'I'm not supposed to touch the magic bottles. I didn't break any.'

'Where are the magic bottles?'

'On Mama's little table with the mirror. I can have some when I get bigger, but they're toys for big girls. I just played with them for a minute.'

She sent Frank such an earnest look, he had to smile. 'That's all right then. What did you do next?'

'I went downstairs. The lights were on, and the door was open. It was warm outside. Maybe somebody came to see us, maybe we can have cake.' Tears began to stream down her cheeks. 'I don't want to say now.'

'It's okay, Livvy. You can tell me. It's okay to tell me.'

And it was. She could look into his green eyes and it was all right to say. 'It smells bad, and things are broken, and they're red and wet and nasty. The flowers are on the floor and there's glass. You don't walk near glass in your bare feet 'cause it hurts. I don't want to step in it. I see Mama, and she's lying down on the floor, and the red and the wet is all over her. The monster's with her. He has her scissors in his hand.'

She held up her own, fingers curled tight and a glazed look in her eye. '"Livvy. God, Livvy,"' she said in a horrible mimic of her father's voice. 'I ran away, and he kept calling. He was breaking things and looking for me and crying. I hid in the closet.' Another tear trembled and fell. 'I wet my pants.'

'That's all right, honey. That doesn't matter.'

'Big girls don't.'

'You're a very big girl. And very brave and smart.' When she gave him a watery smile, he prayed he wouldn't have to put her through that night again.

He drew her attention back to her puzzle, made some foolish comment about talking pumpkins that had her giggling. He didn't want her parting thought of him to be of fear and blood and madness.

Still, when he turned at the door to glance back, Olivia's eyes were on him, quietly pleading, and holding that terrifyingly adult expression only the very young can manage.

As he started downstairs, he found his thoughts running with Jamie Melbourne's. He wanted Sam Tanner's blood.

'You were very good with her.' Jamie's control had almost reached the end of its strength. She wanted to curl up and weep as her mother was. To mire herself in chores and duties as her husband was. Anything, anything but reliving this over again as she had through Olivia's words.

'She's a remarkable girl.'

'Takes after her mother.'

He stopped then, turned and looked at Jamie squarely. 'I'd say she's got some of her aunt in her.'

There was a flicker of surprise over her face, then a sigh. 'She had nightmares last night, and I'll catch her just staring off into space with that – that vacant look in her eyes. Sucking her thumb. She stopped sucking her thumb before she was a year old.'

'Whatever comforts. Mrs. Melbourne, you've got a lot on your mind, and a lot more to deal with. You're going to want to think about counseling, not just for Olivia, but for all of you.'

'Yes, I'll think about it. Right now, I just have to get through the moment. I want to see Sam.'

'That's not a good idea.'

'I want to see the man who murdered my sister. I want to look him in the eye. That's my therapy, Detective Brady.'

'I'll see what I can do. I appreciate your time and cooperation. And again, we're sorry for your loss.'

'See that he pays.' She opened the door, braced herself against the calls and shouts of the press, of the curious, crowded in the street.

'We'll be in touch' was all Frank said.

Jamie closed the door, leaned heavily against it. She lost track of how long she stood there, eyes closed, head bent, but she jerked straight when a hand fell on her shoulder.

'Jamie, you need some rest.' David turned her into his arms. 'I want you to take a pill and lie down.'

'No, no pills. I'm not having my mind or my feelings clouded.' But she laid her head on his shoulder and some of the pressure eased out of her chest. 'The two detectives were just here.'

'You should have called me.'

'They wanted to talk to me, and to Livvy.'

'Livvy?' He pulled her back to stare at her. 'For God's sake, Jamie, you didn't let them interrogate that child?'

'It wasn't like that, David.' Resentment wanted to surface, but she was too tired for it. 'Detective Brady was very gentle with her, and I stayed the whole time. They needed to know what she'd seen. She's the only witness.'

'The hell with that. They have him cold. He was there, he had the weapon. He was fucking stoned as he's been half the time the last year.'

At Jamie's quick warning look toward the stairs, he sucked in a breath, let it out slowly. Calm, he reminded himself. They all had to stay calm to get through this. 'They have all the evidence they need to put him away for the rest of his miserable life,' he finished.

'Now they have Livvy's statement that she saw him, she heard him.' She lifted a hand to her head. 'I don't know how it works, I don't know what happens next. I can't think about it.'

'I'm sorry.' He gathered her close again. 'I just don't want you or Livvy, or any of us, to suffer more than we have to. I want you to call me before you let them talk to her again. I think we need to consult a child psychologist to make sure it isn't damaging to her.'

'Maybe you're right. She likes Detective Brady, though. You can tell she feels safe with him. I upset my mother.' For a moment, she burrowed against David's throat. 'I need to go up to her.'

'All right. Jamie.' He slid his hands down her arms, linked fingers with her. 'They're going to release Julie's body day after tomorrow. We can hold the memorial service the following day, if you're ready for it. I've started making the arrangements.'

'Oh, David.' Pathetically grateful, she shuddered back a sob. 'You didn't have to do that. I was going to make calls later today.'

'I know what you want for her. Let me take care of this for all of us, Jamie. I loved her, too.' He brought her hands to his lips, pressed a kiss to her fingers.

'I know.'

'I have to do something. Details are what I do best. I, ah, I've been working on a press release. There has to be one.' He ran his hands up her arms again, back down in a gesture of comfort. 'It's more your area than mine, but I figured simple was best. I'll run it by you before it's confirmed. But as for the rest . . . just let me take care of it.'

'I don't know what I'd do without you, David. I don't know what I'd do.'

'You'll never have to find out.' He kissed her, softly. 'Go up to your mother, and promise me you'll try to get some rest.'

'Yes, I will.'

He waited until she walked upstairs, then went to the door, stared out the glass panels at the figures sweltering outside in the high summer heat.

And though of vultures over fresh kill.

Chapter Three

She didn't want to take a nap. She wasn't sleepy. But Olivia tried, because Aunt Jamie had asked her to, and lay in the bed that wasn't hers.

It was a pretty room with little violets climbing up the walls and white curtains with tiny white dots on them that made everything soft and filmy when you looked through them. She always slept in this room when she came to visit.

But it wasn't home.

She'd told Grandma she wanted to go home, that she could come, too. They could have a tea party in the garden until Mama got home.

But Grandma's eyes had gotten bright and wet, and she'd hugged Olivia so hard it almost hurt.

So she hadn't said anything more about going home.

When she heard the murmur of voices down the hall, behind the door of the room where her grandparents were staying. Olivia climbed out of bed and tiptoed from the room. Aunt Jamie had said, when Olivia asked, that Grandma and Grandpop were taking naps, too. But if they were awake, maybe they could go out and play. Grandma and Grandpop liked to be outside best of all. They could play ball or go swimming or climb a tree.

Grandpop said there were trees that reached right up and brushed the sky in Washington. Olivia had been there to visit when she was a tiny baby and again when she'd been two, so she couldn't remember very well. She thought Grandpop could find a sky-brushing tree for her so she could climb all the way up and call her mother. Mama would hear if she could just get closer to heaven.

When she opened the door, she saw her grandmother crying, her aunt sitting beside her holding her hands. It made her stomach hurt to see Grandma cry, and it made her afraid when she saw her grandpop's face. It was so tight and his eyes were too dark and mean. His voice, when he spoke, was quiet but hard, as if he were trying to break the words instead of say them. It made Olivia cringe back to make herself small.

'It doesn't matter why he did it. He's crazy, crazy with jealousy and drugs. What matters is he killed her, he took her away from us. He'll pay for it, every day of his miserable life, he'll pay. It'll never be enough.'

'We should've made her come home.' Tears continued to slide down Grandma's cheeks. 'When she told us she and Sam were having trouble, we should have told her to bring Livvy and come home for a while. To get her bearings.'

'We didn't know he'd gotten violent, didn't know he'd hurt her.' Grandpa's fists balled at his sides. 'If I'd known, I'd have come down here and dealt with the son of a bitch myself.'

'We can't go back, Dad.' Jamie spoke wearily, for some of that responsibility was hers. She had known and said nothing. Julie had asked her to say nothing. 'If we could, I know I'd be able to see a hundred different things I could do to change it, to stop it. But I can't, and we have to face the now. The press—'

'Fuck the press.'

From her peep through the doorway, Olivia widened her eyes. Grandpop never said the bad word. She could only goggle as her aunt nodded calmly.

'Well, Dad, before much longer they might look to fuck us. That's the way of it. They'll canonize Julie, or make her a whore. Or they'll do both. We have to, for Livvy's sake, take as much control as we can. There'll be speculation and stories about her marriage and relationship with Sam – speculation about other men. Particularly Lucas Manning.'

'Julie was not a cheat.' Grandma's voice rose, snapped.

'I know that, Mom. But that's the kind of game that's played.'

'She's dead,' Grandpop said flatly. 'Julie's dead. How much worse can it get?'

Slowly, Olivia backed up from the door. She knew what dead meant. Flowers got dead when they were all brown and stiff and you had to throw them away. Tiffy's old dog, Casey, had died and they'd dug a hole in the yard and put him inside, covered him up with dirt and grass.

Dead meant you couldn't come back.

She kept moving away from the door while the breath got hot and thick in her chest, while flashes of blood and broken glass, of monsters and snapping scissors raced through her head.

Then that breath burst out, burning over her heart as she started to run. And she started to scream.

'Mama's not dead. Mama's not dead and in a hole in the yard. She's coming back. She's coming back soon.'

She kept running, away from the shouts of her name, down the steps, down the hall. At the front door, she fought with the knob while tears flooded her cheeks. She had to get outside. She had to find a tree, a sky-brushing tree, so she could climb up and call Mama home.

She fought it open and raced out. There were crowds of people, and she didn't know where to go. Everyone was shouting, at once, like a big wave of sound crashing over her head, hurting her ears. She pressed her hands to them, crying, calling for her mother.

A dozen cameras greedily captured the shot. Ate the moment and her grief and her fear.

Someone shouted for them to leave her alone, she's just a baby. But the reporters surged forward, caught in the frenzy. Sun shot off lenses, blinded her. She saw shadows and shapes, a blur of strange faces. Voices boomed out questions, commands.

Look this way, Olivia! Over here.
Did your father try to hurt you?
Did you hear them fighting?
Look at me, Olivia. Look at the camera.

She froze like a fawn in the crosshairs, eyes dazed and wild. Then she was being scooped up from behind, her face pressed into the scent and shape of her aunt.

'I want Mama, I want Mama.' She could only whisper it while Aunt Jamie held her tight.

'She's just a child.' Unable to stop herself, Jamie lifted her voice to a shout. 'Damn you, God damn every one of you, she's only a child.'

She turned back toward the house and shook her head fiercely before her husband and her parents could step out. 'No, stay inside. Don't give them any more. Don't give them another thing.'

'I'll take her upstairs.' Grandma's eyes were dry now. Dry and cold and calm. 'You're right, Jamie. We deal with them now.' She pressed her lips to Olivia's hair as she started upstairs. For her, Olivia was the now.

This time Olivia slept, deep in the exhaustion of terror and misery, while her grandmother watched over her. That, Val decided, was her job now.

In less soothing surroundings, Frank Brady thought of the child he'd seen that morning. He kept the image of her, those wide brown eyes holding trustingly to his, while he did his job.

Sam Tanner was the now for Frank.

Despite the hours in prison and the fact that his system was jumping for a hit, Sam's looks had suffered little. It appeared as though he'd been prepped for the role of the afflicted lover, shocked and innocent and suffering, but still handsome enough to make the female portion of the audience long to save him.

His hair was dark, thick and untidy. His eyes, a brilliant Viking blue, were shadowed. His love affair with cocaine had cost him some weight, but that only added a romantic, hollowed-out look to his face.

His lips tended to tremble. His hands were never still.

They'd taken away his bloody clothes and given him a washed-out gray shirt and slacks that bagged on him. They'd kept his belt and his shoelaces. He was on suicide watch, but had only begun to notice the lack of privacy. The full scope of his situation was still buried under the fog of shock and withdrawal from his drug of choice.

The interrogation room had plain beige walls and the wide expanse of two-way glass. There was a single table, three chairs. His tended to wobble if he tried to lean back. A water fountain in the corner dispensed stingy triangular cups of lukewarm water, and the air was stuffy.

Frank sat across from him, saying nothing. Tracy leaned against the wall and examined his own fingernails. The silence and overheated room had sweat sliding greasily down Sam's back.

'I don't remember any more than I told you before.' Unable to stand the quiet, Sam let the words tumble out. He'd been so sure when they'd finished talking to him the first time, they'd let him go. Let him go so he could find out what they'd done with Julie, with Olivia.

Oh God, Julie. Every time he thought of her, he saw blood, oceans of blood.

Frank only nodded, his eyes patient. 'Why don't you tell me what you told me before? From the beginning.'

'I *keep* telling you. I went home—'

'You weren't living there anymore, were you, Mr. Tanner?' This from Tracy, and just a little aggressive.

'It's still my home. The separation was just temporary, just until we worked some problems out.'

'Right.' Tracy kept studying his fingernails. 'That's why your wife filed papers, got sole custody of the kid, why you had limited visitation and bought that palace on the beach.'

'It was just formality.' Color washed in and out of Sam's face. He was desperate for a hit, just one quick hit to clear his head, sharpen his focus. Why didn't people understand how hard it was to *think*, for Christ's sake. 'And I bought the Malibu house as an investment.'

When Tracy snorted, Frank lifted a hand. They'd been partners for six years and had their rhythm down as intimately as lovers. 'Give the guy a chance to tell it, Tracy. You keep interrupting, you'll throw him off. We're just trying to get all the details, Mr. Tanner.'

'Okay, okay. I went home.' He rubbed his hands on his thighs, hating the rough feel of the bagging trousers. He was used to good material, expertly cut. By God, he thought as he continued to pick and pluck at his pant legs, he'd earned the best.

'Why did you go home?'

'What?' He blinked, shook his head. 'Why? I wanted to talk to Julie. I needed to see her. We just needed to straighten things out.'

'Were you high, Mr. Tanner?' Frank asked it gently, almost friend to friend. 'It'd be better if you were up-front about that kind of thing. Recreational use . . .' He let his shoulders lift and fall. 'We're not going to push you on that, we just need to know your state of mind.'

He'd denied it before, denied it right along. It was the kind of thing that could ruin you with the public. People in the business, well, they understood how things were. But cocaine didn't play well at the box office.

But a little coke between friends? Hell, that wasn't a big deal. Not a big fucking deal, as he was forever telling Julie when she nagged him. If she'd just . . .

Julie, he thought again, and pressed his fingers to his eyes. Was she really dead?

'Mr. Tanner?'

'What?' The eyes that had women all over the world sighing blinked. They were bloodshot, bruised and blank.

'Were you using when you went to see your wife?' Before he could deny it again, Frank leaned forward. 'Before you answer, I'm going to tell you that we searched your car and found your stash. Now we're not going to give you grief about possession. As long as you're up-front.'

'I don't know what you're talking about.' He scrubbed the back of his hand over his mouth. 'Anybody could have put that there. You could've planted it, for all I know.'

'You saying we planted evidence?' Tracy moved fast, a lightning strike of movement. He had Sam by the collar and half out of the chair. 'Is that what you're saying?'

'Easy, take it easy. Come on now.' Frank lifted both hands. 'Mr. Tanner's just confused. He's upset. You didn't mean to say we'd planted drugs in your car, did you?'

'No, I—'

'Because that's serious business, Mr. Tanner. A very serious accusation. It won't look good for you, especially since we have a number of people who'll testify you like a little nose candy now and then. Just a social thing,' Frank continued as Tracy let out a snort of disgust and went back to leaning on the wall. 'We don't have to make a big deal out of that. Unless you do. Unless you try saying we planted that coke when we know it was yours. When I can look at you right now and see you could use a little just to smooth the edges a bit.'

Face earnest, Frank leaned forward. 'You're in a hell of a fix here, Sam. A hell of a fix. I admire your work, I'm a big fan. I'd like to cut you a break, but you're not helping me or yourself by lying about the drugs. Just makes it worse.'

Sam worried his wedding ring, turning it around and around on his finger. 'Look, maybe I had a couple of hits, but I was in control. I was in control.' He was desperate to believe it. 'I'm not an addict or anything, I just took a couple of hits to clear my head before I went home.'

'To talk to your wife,' Frank prompted. 'To straighten things out.'

'Yeah, that's right. I needed to make her understand we should get back together, get rid of the lawyers and fix things. I missed her and Livvy. I wanted our life back. Goddamn it, I just wanted our life back.'

'I don't blame you for that. Beautiful wife and daughter. A man would be crazy to give it all up easy. You wanted to straighten out your troubles, so you went over there, and talked to her.'

'That's right, I – no, I went over and I found her. I found her. Oh, Jesus Christ.' He closed his eyes then, covered his face. 'Oh God, Julie. There was blood, blood everywhere, broken glass, the lamp I bought her for her birthday. She was lying there in the blood and the glass. I tried to pick her up. The scissors were in her back. I pulled them out.'

Hadn't he? He thought he'd pulled them out, but couldn't quite remember. They'd been in his hand, hot and slick with blood.

'I saw Livvy, standing there. She started running away.'

'You went after her,' Frank said quietly.

'I think – I must have. I think I went a little crazy. Trying to find her, trying to find who'd done that to Julie. I don't remember. I called the police.' He looked back at Frank. 'I called the police as soon as I could.'

'How long?' Tracy pushed away from the wall, stuck his face close to Sam's. 'How long did you go through the house looking for that little girl, with scissors in your hand, before you broke down and called the cops?'

'I don't know. I'm not sure. A few minutes, maybe. Ten, fifteen.'

'Lying bastard!'

'Tracy—'

'He's a fucking lying bastard, Frank. He'd've found that kid, she'd be in the morgue next to her mother.'

'No. No.' Horror spiked in his voice. 'I'd never hurt Livvy.'

'That's not what your wife thought, is it, Tanner?' Tracy jabbed a finger into Sam's chest. 'She put it in writing that she was afraid for you to be alone with the kid. You're a cokehead, and a sorry son of a bitch, and I'll tell you just how it went down. You thought about her in that big house, locking you out, keeping you away from her and your kid because she couldn't stand the sight of you. Maybe you figure she's spreading her legs for another man. Woman who looks like that, there's going to be other men. And you got yourself all coked up and drove over there to show her who was boss.'

'No, I was just going to talk to her.'

'But she didn't want to talk to you, did she, Tanner? She told you to get out, didn't she? Told you to go to hell. Maybe you knocked her around a little first, like you did the other time.'

'It was an accident. I never meant to hurt her. We were arguing.'

'So you picked up the scissors.'

'No.' He tried to draw back, tried to clear the images blurring in his head. 'We were in Livvy's room. Julie wouldn't have scissors in Livvy's room.'

'You were downstairs and you saw them on the table, sitting there, shiny, sharp. You grabbed them and you cut her to pieces because she was done with you. If you couldn't have her, no one was going to have her. That's what you thought, isn't it, Tanner? The bitch deserved to die.'

'No, no, no, I couldn't have done that. I couldn't have.' But he remembered the feel of the scissors in his hands, the way his fingers had wrapped around them, the way blood had dripped down the blade. 'I loved her. I loved her.'

'You didn't mean to do it, did you, Sam?' Frank picked up the ball, sliding back into the seat, his voice gentle, his eyes level. 'I know how it is. Sometimes you love a woman so much it makes you crazy. When they don't listen, don't hear what you're saying, don't understand what you need, you have to find a way to make them. That's all it was, wasn't it? You were trying to find a way to make her listen, and she wouldn't. You lost your temper. The drugs, they played a part in that. You just didn't have control of yourself. You argued, and the scissors were just there. Maybe she came at you. Then it just happened, before you could stop it. Like the other time when you didn't mean to hurt her. It was a kind of accident.'

'I don't know.' Tears were starting to swim in his eyes. 'I had the scissors, but it was after. It had to be after. I pulled them out of her.'

'Livvy saw you.'

Sam's face went blank as he stared at Frank. 'What?'

'She saw you. She heard you, Sam. That's why she came downstairs. Your four-year-old daughter's a witness. The murder weapon has your prints all over it. Your bloody footprints are all over the house. In the living room, the hall, going up the stairs. There are bloody fingerprints on the doorjamb of your little girl's bedroom. They're yours. There was no one else there, Sam, no burglar like you tried to tell us yesterday. No intruder. There was no sign of a break-in, nothing was stolen, your wife wasn't raped. There were three people in the house that night. Julie, Livvy and you.'

'There had to be someone else.'

'No, Sam. No one else.'

'My God, my God, my God.' Shaking, he laid his head on the table and sobbed like a child.

When he had finished sobbing, he confessed.

Frank read the signed statement for the third time, got up, walked around the tiny coffee room and settled for the nasty dregs in the pot. With the cup half full of what even the desperate would call sludge, he sat at the table and read the confession again.

When his partner came in, Frank spoke without looking up. 'This thing's got holes, Tracy. It's got holes you could drive that old Caddy you love so much through without scraping the paint.'

'I know it.' Disgusted, Tracy set a fresh pot on to brew, then went to the scarred refrigerator to steal someone's nicely ripened Bartlett pear. He bit in, grunted with satisfaction, then sat. 'But the guy's whacked, Frank. Jonesing, jittery. And he was flying that night. He's never going to remember it step-by-step.'

He swiped at pear juice dribbling down his chin. 'We know he did it. We got the physical evidence, motive, opportunity. We place him at the scene. Hell, we got a witness. Now we got a confession. We did our job, Frank.'

'Yeah, but it doesn't sit right in the gut. Not all the way right. See here where he says he broke the music box, the kid's Disney music box. There was no music box. He's getting the two nights confused, blending them into one.'

'He's a fucking cokehead,' Tracy said impatiently. 'His story about coming in after a break-in doesn't wash. She let him in – her sister confirmed it was something she'd do. This guy ain't no Richard Kimble, pal. No one-armed man, no TV show. He picked up the scissors, jammed them into her back while she was turned. She goes down – no defensive wounds – then he just keeps hacking at her while she's trying to crawl away. We got the blood trail, the ME's report. We know how it went down. Makes me sick.'

He pitched the pear core into the trash, then scraped his chair back to get fresh coffee.

'I've been working bodies for seven years now,' Frank murmured. 'It's one of the worst I've seen. A man does that to a woman, he's got powerful feelings for her.' He sighed himself, rubbed his tired eyes. 'I'd like a cleaner statement, that's all. Some high-dollar lawyer's going to dance through those holes before this is done.'

With a shake of his head, he rose. 'I'm going home, see if I remember what my wife and kid look like.'

'Lawyer or no lawyer,' Tracy said as Frank started out, 'Sam Tanner's going down for this, and he'll spend the rest of his worthless life in a cage.'

'Yeah, he will. And that little girl's going to have to live with that. That's what makes me sick, Tracy. That's what eats through my gut.'

He thought about it on the drive home, through the impossible traffic on the freeway, down the quiet street where the houses, all tiny and tidy like his own, were jammed close together with patches of lawn gasping from the lack of rain.

Olivia's face was lodged in his mind, the rounded cheeks of childhood, the wounded, too-adult eyes under striking dark brows. And the whisper of the first words she'd spoken to him:

The monster's here.

Then he pulled into the short driveway beside his little stucco house, and it was all so blessedly normal. Noah had left his bike crashed on its side in the yard, and his wife's impatiens were wilting because she'd forgotten to water them, again. God knew why she planted the things. She killed them with the regularity of a garden psychopath. Her ancient VW Bug was already parked, emblazoned with the bumper stickers and decals of her various causes. Celia Brady collected causes the way some women collected recipes.

He noted that the VW was leaking oil again, swore without any real heat and climbed out of his car.

The front door burst open, then slammed like a single gunshot. His son raced out, a compact bullet with shaggy brown hair, bruised knees and holey sneakers.

'Hey, Dad! We just got back from protesting whale hunting. Mom's got these records with whales singing on them. Sounds like alien invaders.'

Frank winced, knowing he'd be listening to whale song for the next several days. 'I don't suppose we've got dinner?'

'We picked up the Colonel on the way home. I talked her into it. Man, all that health food lately, a guy could starve.'

Frank stopped, laid a hand on his son's shoulder. 'You're telling me we have fried chicken in the house? Don't toy with me, Noah.'

Noah laughed, his dark green eyes dancing. 'A whole bucket. Minus the piece I swiped on the way home. Mom said we'd go for it because you'd need some comfort food.'

'Yeah.' It was good to have a woman who loved you enough to know you. Frank sat down on the front stoop, loosened his tie and draped an arm around Noah's shoulders when the boy sat beside him. 'I guess I do.'

'The TV's had bulletins and stuff all the time about that movie star. Julie MacBride. We saw you and Tracy going into that big house, and they showed pictures of the other house, the bigger one where she got killed. And just now, right before you got home? There was this little girl, the daughter. She came running out of the house. She looked really scared.'

Noah hadn't been able to tear his eyes from the image, even when those huge terrified eyes seemed to stare right into his and plead with him for help.

'Gee, Dad, they got right up in her face, and she was crying and screaming and holding her hands over her ears, until somebody came and took her back inside.'

'Oh, Christ.' Frank braced his elbows on his knees, put his face into his hands. 'Poor kid.'

'What are they going to do with her, if her mother's dead and her father's going to jail and all?'

Frank blew out a breath. Noah always wanted to know the whats and the whys. They didn't censor him – that had been Celia's stand, and Frank had come around to believing her right. Their boy was bright, curious, and knew right from wrong. He was a cop's son, Frank thought, and he had to learn that there were bad guys, and they didn't always pay.

'I don't know for sure. She has family who love her. They'll do the best they can.'

'On the TV, they said she was in the house when it happened. Was she?'

'Yes.'

'Wow.' Noah scratched at a scab on his knee, frowned. 'She looked really scared,' he murmured. Noah did understand bad guys existed, that they didn't always pay. And that being a child didn't mean you were safe from them. But he couldn't understand what it would be like to be afraid of your own father.

'She'll be all right.'

'Why did he do it, Dad?' Noah looked up into his father's face. He almost always found the answers there.

'We may never know for certain. Some will say he loved her too much, others will say he was crazy. That it was drugs or jealousy or rage. The only one who'll ever really know is Sam Tanner. I'm not sure he understands why himself.'

Frank gave Noah's shoulders a quick squeeze. 'Let's go listen to whales sing and eat chicken.'

'And mashed potatoes.'

'Son, you might just see a grown man cry.'

Noah laughed again and trooped inside with his father. But he, too, loved enough to understand. And he was sure he would hear his father pacing the floor that night, as he did when his job troubled him most.

Chapter Four

Confession may be good for the soul, but in Sam Tanner's case it was also good for snapping reality into sharp focus. Less than an hour after he wrote his tearful statement admitting the brutal and drug-hazed murder of his wife, he exercised his civil rights.

He called the lawyer he'd claimed had only complicated his marital problems and demanded representation. He was panicked and ill and had by this point forgotten half of what he'd confessed.

So it was a lawyer who specialized in domestic law who first claimed the confession had been given under duress, ordered his client to stick to his right to remain silent and called out the troops.

Charles Brighton Smith would head the defense team. He was a sixty-one-year-old fox with a dramatic mane of silver hair, canny blue eyes and a mind like a laser. He embraced high-profile cases with gusto and loved nothing better than a tumultuous court battle with a media circus playing in the center ring.

Before he flew into L.A., he'd already begun assembling his team of researchers, clerks, litigators, experts, psychologists and jury profilers. He'd leaked his flight number and arrival time and was prepared – and elegantly groomed – for the onslaught of press when he stepped off the plane.

His voice was rich and fruity, drawing up through the diaphragm like an opera singer's. His face was stern and carefully composed to show concern, wisdom and compassion as he made his sweeping opening statement.

'Sam Tanner is an innocent man, a victim of this tragedy. He's lost the woman he loved in the most brutal of fashions, and now that horror has been compounded by the police in their rush to close the case. We hope to correct this injustice swiftly so that Sam can deal with his grief and go home to his daughter.'

He took no questions, made no other comments. He let his bodyguards plow through the crowd and lead him to the waiting limo. When he settled inside, he imagined the media would be rife with sound bites from his entrance.

And he was right.

After seeing the last news flash of Smith's Los Angeles arrival, Val MacBride shut off the television with a snap. It was all a game to them, she thought. To the press, the lawyers, the police, the public. Just another show to bump ratings, to sell newspapers and magazines, to get their picture on the covers or on the news.

They were using her baby, her poor murdered baby.

Yet it couldn't be stopped. Julie had chosen to live in the public eye, and had died in it.

Now they would use that, the lawyers. That public perception would be twisted and exploited to make a victim out of the man who'd killed her. He would be a martyr. And Olivia was just one more tool.

That, Val told herself, she could stop.

She went quietly from the room, stopping only to peek in on Olivia. She saw Rob, sprawled on the floor with their grandchild, his head close to her as they colored together.

It made her want to smile and weep at the same time. The man was solid as a rock, she thought with great gratitude. No matter how hard you leaned on him, he stayed straight.

She left them to each other and went to find Jamie.

The house was built on the straight, clean lines of a T. In the left notch Jamie had her office. When she'd come to Los Angeles eight years before to act as her sister's personal assistant, she'd lived and worked out of the spare room in Julie's dollhouse bungalow in the hills.

Val remembered worrying a bit about both of them then, but their calls and letters and visits home had been so full of fun and excitement she'd tried not to smother the light with nagging and warnings. They'd lived in that house together for two years, until Julie had met and married Sam. And less than six months afterward, Jamie had been engaged to David. A man who managed rock and roll bands, of all things, she'd thought at the time. But he'd turned out to be as steady as her own Rob.

She'd considered her girls safe then, safe and happy and settled with good men. How could she have been so wrong?

She pushed that thought away as useless and knocked lightly on Jamie's office door before opening it.

The room had Jamie's sense of style and organization. Ordinarily the sleek vertical blinds would have been open to the sunlight and the view of the pool and flowers. But the paparazzi and their telescopic lenses had the house under siege. The blinds were shut tight, the lamps on though it was midafternoon.

We're like hostages, Val thought as her daughter sent her a harried smile and continued to talk on her desk phone.

Val sat in the simple button-backed chair across from the desk and waited.

Jamie looked tired, she noticed, and nearly sighed when she realized how little attention she'd paid over the last few days to the child she had left.

As her heart stuttered, Val closed her eyes, took several quiet breaths. She needed to focus on the matter at hand and not get mired in her grief.

'I'm sorry, Mom.' Jamie hung up the phone, pushed both hands through her hair. 'There's so much to do.'

'I haven't been much help.'

'Oh, yes, you have. I don't know how we'd manage without you and Dad. Livvy – I can't handle this and give her the attention she needs right now. David's shouldered a lot of the load.'

She rose and went to the small refrigerator for a bottle of water. Her system had begun to revolt at the gallons of coffee she'd gulped down. In the center of her forehead was a constant, dull headache no medication seemed to touch.

'But he has his own work,' she continued as she poured two glasses. 'I've had people offer to field some of the calls and cables and notes, but . . .'

'This is for family,' Val finished.

'Yes.' Jamie handed her mother a glass, eased her hip on the desk. 'People are leaving flowers at the gate of Julie's house. I needed to make arrangements for them to be taken to hospitals. Lucas Manning, bless him, is helping me with that. The letters are just starting to come in, and though Lou, Julie's agent, is going to help handle them, I think we're going to be snowed under in another week or two.'

'Jamie—'

'We already have a mountain of condolences from people in the business, people she knew or worked with. And the phone calls—'

'Jamie,' Val said more firmly. 'We have to talk about what happens next.'

'This is what happens next for me.'

'Sit down.' When the phone rang, Val shook her head. 'Let it go, Jamie, and sit down.'

'All right. All right.' Giving in, Jamie sat, let her head fall back.

'There's going to be a trial,' Val began, and this had Jamie sitting up again.

'There's no point in thinking about that now.'

'It has to be thought of. Sam's fancy new lawyer's already on TV, prancing and posing. Some people are hot to say he couldn't have done it. He's a hero, a victim, a figure of tragedy. More will say it before it's over.'

'You shouldn't listen.'

'No, and I don't intend to anymore.' Val's voice went fierce. 'I don't intend to take any chances that Livvy will hear any of it, will be exposed to any of it or be used as she was the other day when she got outside. I want to take her home, Jamie. I want to take her back to Washington as soon as possible.'

'Take her home?' For a moment, Jamie's mind went completely blank. 'But this is her home.'

'I know you love her. We all do.' Val set her glass aside to take her daughter's hand. 'Listen to me, Jamie. That little girl can't stay here, closed up in this house like a prisoner. She can't even go outside. We can't risk her going to her window without knowing some photographer will zoom in and snap her picture. She can't live like that. None of us can.'

'It'll pass.'

'When? How? Maybe, maybe it would have eased up a little, but not now that there's going to be a trial. She won't be able to start preschool in the fall, or play with her friends without bodyguards, without having people look at her, stare, point, whisper. And some won't bother to whisper. I don't want her to face that. I don't think you do either.'

'Oh God, Mom.' Torn to bits again, Jamie rose. 'I want to raise her. David and I talked about it.'

'How can you do that here, honey? With all the memories, all the publicity, all the risks. She needs to be protected from that but not locked in a house, however lovely, in the center of it all. Are you and David willing to give up your home, your work, your lifestyle, to take her away, to devote your time to her? Your father and I can give her a safe place. We can cut her off from the press.' She took a deep breath. 'And I intend to see a lawyer myself, right away, to start custody proceedings. I won't have that man getting near her, ever again. It's what's right for her, Jamie. It's what Julie would want for her.'

What about me? Jamie wanted to scream it. What about what I need, what I want? She was the one who soothed Livvy's nightmares, who comforted and rocked and sat with her in the long dark hours. 'Have you talked to Dad about this?' Her voice was dull now, her face turned away.

'We discussed it this morning. He agrees with me. Jamie, it's what's best. You and David could come, spend as much time as you like. She'll always be yours, too, but not here, Jamie. Not here.'

Frank pushed away from his desk, surprised when he saw Jamie Melbourne. She took off her dark glasses as she crossed the squad room, then passed them restlessly from hand to hand.

'Detective Brady, I'd like to speak with you if you have a moment.'

'Of course. We'll go in the coffee room.' He tried a smile. 'But I'm not recommending the coffee.'

'No, I'm trying to stay away from it just now.'

'Do you want to speak with Detective Harmon?'

'It's not necessary to pull both of you away from your work.' She moved into the cramped little room. 'I came on impulse. Not an easy feat,' she added as she walked to the stingy window. At least it was a window, she thought. At least she could look outside. 'There are still reporters. Not as many, but a number of them camped out. I think I ran over that snippy one from Channel Four.'

'Never liked him anyway.'

She leaned her hands on the windowsill and laughed. Then couldn't stop. The bubble of sound had burst a hole in her dam of control. Her shoulders shook and the laugh turned to sobs. She held on to the sill, rocking back and forth until Frank drew her gently into a chair, gave her a box of tissues and held her hand.

He said nothing, just waited for her to empty out.

'I'm sorry, I'm sorry.' Frantically she pulled tissue after tissue out of the box. 'This isn't what I came here to do.'

'If you don't mind my saying so, Mrs. Melbourne, it's about time you let that go. The longer you hold it in, the bigger it gets.'

'Julie was the emotional one. She felt everything in big soaring waves.' Jamie blew her nose. 'And she was one of those women who looked gorgeous when she cried.' She mopped her raw and swollen eyes. 'You could have hated her for that.' She sat back. 'I buried my sister yesterday. I keep trying to take a step back from that now that it's done, but it won't stop coming into my head.'

She let out a long breath. 'My parents want to take Olivia back to Washington. They want to apply for full custody and take her away.' She pulled out another tissue, then began to fold it neatly, precisely, into squares. 'Why am I telling you? I was going to tell David, cry on his shoulder, then I found myself going into the garage, getting into the car. I guess I needed to tell someone who wasn't so involved, yet wasn't really separate. You won.'

'Mrs. Melbourne—'

'Why don't you call me Jamie now that I've cried all over you? I'd certainly be more comfortable calling you Frank.'

'Okay, Jamie. You're facing the worst anybody faces, and things are coming at you from all directions at once. It's hard to see.'

'You think my mother's right, about Livvy.'

'I can't speak for your family.' He got up, poured some water. 'As a parent,' he continued, offering the paper cup, 'I think I'd want my kid as far away from this mess as possible, at least temporarily.'

'Yes, my head knows that.' But her heart, her heart didn't know how much more it could take. 'Yesterday morning, before the service, I took Livvy out in the backyard. It's screened by trees, it seemed safe enough. I wanted to try to talk to her, to try to help her understand. This morning there was a picture of the two of us out there in the paper. I never even saw the photographer. I don't want that for her.'

She drew in a deep breath. 'I want to see Sam.'

Frank sat again. 'Don't do that to yourself.'

‘I’ll have to see him in court. I’ll have to look him in the face, day after day during the trial. I need to see him now, before it begins. I need to do that before I let Livvy go.’

‘I don’t know if he’ll agree to it. His lawyers are keeping him on a short leash.’

‘He’ll see me.’ She got to her feet. ‘He won’t be able to stop himself. His ego won’t let him.’

He took her because he decided she’d find a way to do what she felt she had to do with or without his help.

She said nothing as they dealt with security and protocol. Nothing when they entered the visitors’ area with its long counters and glass partitions. Frank showed her to a stool. ‘I have to back off here. I can’t have any contact with him without his lawyer at this point. I’ll be right outside.’

‘I’ll be fine. Thank you.’

She’d braced herself so she didn’t jolt at the harsh sound of the buzzer. A door opened, and Sam was led in.

She’d wanted him to be pale, to look ill and gray and battered. How could he, she thought as her hands fisted in her lap, how could he look so perfect, so carelessly handsome? The hard lights didn’t detract from his appearance, nor the faded, ill-fitting prison clothes. If anything, they added to the appeal.

When he sat, offered her a long, pain-filled stare out of those deep blue eyes, she all but expected to hear a director call out *Cut! Print!*

She kept her gaze level and reached for the phone. He mirrored the move on the other side of the glass. She heard him clear his throat.

‘Jamie, I’m so glad you came. I’ve been going out of my mind. Julie.’ He closed his eyes. ‘Oh God, Julie.’

‘You killed her.’

His eyes flew open. She read the shock in them, and the hurt. Oh, she thought, oh yes, he was good.

‘You can’t believe that. Sweet Jesus, Jamie, you of all people know how much we loved each other. I’d never hurt her. Never.’

‘You’ve done nothing but hurt her for more than a year now, with your jealousy, your accusations, your drugs.’

‘I’m going into rehab. I know I’ve got a problem, and if I’d listened to her, if I'd only listened, I'd have been there that night and she'd still be alive.'

'You were there that night, and that's why she's dead.'

'No. No.' He pressed a hand to the glass as if he could pass through it and reach her. 'I found her. You have to listen to me, Jamie—'

'No, I don't.' She felt the calm slide over her, into her. 'No, Sam, I don't. But you have to listen to me. I pray every day, every hour, every minute of every day that you'll suffer, that you'll pay for what you've done. It'll never be enough, no matter what they do to you, it'll never be enough, but I'll dream of you, Sam, in a cage for the rest of your life. That'll help me get through.'

'They'll let me out.' Panic and nausea spewed into his throat, burned there. 'The cops don't have dick, all they want is headlines. And when I get out, I'm taking Livvy and I'm starting over.'

'Livvy's as dead to you as Julie. You'll never see her again.'

'You can't keep my own daughter away from me.' Rage leaped into his eyes, with glimmers of hate at the edges. 'I'll get out, and I'll take back what's mine. You were always jealous of Julie. Always knew you were second best. You wanted what she had, but you won't get it.'

She said nothing, let him rave. His voice was an ugly buzz in her ear. She never took her eyes off his face, never flinched at the violence she saw there, or the vileness of the names he called her.

And when he'd run out, when his breath was heaving and his fists clenched, she spoke calmly. 'This is your life now, Sam. Look around you. Walls and bars. If they ever let you out, if they ever unlock the cage, you'll walk out an old man. Old and broken and ruined. Nothing but a blip on a film clip running on late-night television. They won't even remember your name. They won't even know who you are.'

She smiled then, for the first time, and it was fierce and bright. 'And neither will Olivia.'

She hung up the phone, ignoring him when he beat on the glass, watching coolly as the guard came over to restrain him. He was shouting, she could see his mouth moving, see the angry color flood his face as the guard muscled him toward the door.

When they closed the door behind him, when she knew the lock had snicked into place, she let out a long breath. And felt the beginnings of peace.

The minute she arrived home, David rushed into the foyer. His arms came around her, clutched her tight. 'My God, Jamie, where were you? I was frantic.'

'I'm sorry. There was something I needed to do.' She drew back, touched his cheek. 'I'm fine.'

He studied her for a minute, then his eyes cleared. 'Yes, I can see that. What happened?'

'I got something out of my system.' She kissed him, then drew away. Eventually she'd tell him what she'd done, Jamie thought. But not now. 'I need to talk to Livvy.'

'She's upstairs. Jamie, your father and I talked. I know they want to take her north, away from this.'

She pressed her lips together. 'You agree with them.'

'I'm sorry, honey, but yes, I do. It's going to be ugly here, for God knows how long. I think you should go, too.'

'You know I can't. I'll be needed at the trial, and even if they didn't need me,' she continued before he could speak, 'I'd have to see it through. I'd have to, David, for myself as much as for Julie.' She gave his arm an absent squeeze. 'Let me talk to Livvy.'

She climbed the steps slowly. It hurt, she thought. Every step was painful. It was amazing, really, just how much pain the human heart could take. She opened the door to the pretty room she'd decorated specifically for her niece's visits.

And saw the curtains drawn, the lights blazing in the middle of the day. Just another kind of prison, she thought as she stepped inside.

Her mother sat on the floor with Livvy, playing with an elaborate plastic castle and dozens of little people. Val glanced up, kept her eyes on Jamie's, her hand on Livvy's shoulder.

The gesture told Jamie just how torn her mother was, so she managed to fix on a smile as she moved forward.

'Well, what's all this?'

'Uncle David bought me a castle.' Sheer delight bubbled in Olivia's voice. 'There's a king and a queen and a princess and a dragon and *everything*.'

'It's beautiful.' God bless you, David, Jamie thought and settled onto the floor. 'Is this the queen?'

‘Uh-huh. Her name’s Magnificent. Right, Grandma?’

‘That’s right, baby. And here’re King Wise and Princess Delightful.’

While Olivia played, Jamie laid a hand over her mother’s. ‘I wonder if you could go down and see if there’s fresh coffee.’

‘Of course.’ Understanding, Val turned her hand up so their palms met.

When they were alone, Jamie sat quietly, watching.

‘Livvy, do you remember the forest? Grandma’s house up in the woods, all the big trees and the streams and the flowers?’

‘I went there when I was a baby, but I don’t remember. Mama said we’d go back sometime and she’d show me her best places.’

‘Would you like to go there, to Grandma’s house?’

‘To visit?’

‘To live. I bet you could have the same room your mother had when she was a little girl. It’s a big old house, right in the forest. Everywhere you look there are trees, and when the wind blows, they sigh and shiver and moan.’

‘Is it magic?’

‘Yes, a kind of magic. The sky’s very blue, and inside the forest, the light is green and the ground’s soft.’

‘Will Mama come?’

Yes, Jamie thought, it was amazing how much pain the heart could take and go on beating. ‘Part of her never left, part of her’s always there. You’ll see the places we played when we were girls. Grandma and Grandpop will take very good care of you.’

‘Is it far, far away?’

‘Not so very far. I’ll come visit you.’ She drew Olivia onto her lap. ‘As often as I can. We’ll walk in the woods and wade in the streams until Grandma calls us home for cookies and hot chocolate.’

Olivia turned her face into Jamie’s shoulder. ‘Will the monster find me there?’

‘No.’ Jamie’s arms tightened. ‘You’ll always be safe there. I promise.’ But not all promises can be kept.

Chapter Five

Olympic Rain Forest, 1987

In the summer of Olivia's thirteenth year, she was a tall, gangly girl with a wild mane of hair the color of bottled honey. Eyes nearly the same shade were long lidded under dark, slashing brows. She'd given up her dreams of being a princess in a castle for other ambitions. They'd run from explorer to veterinarian to forest ranger, which was her current goal.

The forest, with its green shadows and damp smells, was her world, one she rarely left. She was most often alone there, but never lonely. Her grandfather taught her how to track, how to stalk a deer and elk with a camera. How to sit quietly as minutes became hours to watch the majestic journey of a buck or the grace of a doe and fawn.

She'd learned to identify the trees, the flowers, the moss and the mushrooms, though she'd never developed a proficient hand at drawing them as her grandmother had hoped.

She spent quiet days fishing with her grandmother, and there had learned patience. She'd taken on a share of the chores of the lodge and campground the MacBrides had run in Olympic for two generations, and there had learned responsibility.

She was allowed to roam the woods, to wade in the streams, to climb the hills. But never, never to go beyond their borders alone.

And from this, she learned freedom had limits.

She'd left Los Angeles eight years before and had never been back. Her memories of the house in Beverly Hills were vague flickers of high ceilings and shining wood, pretty colors and a pool with bright blue water surrounded by flowers.

During the first months she'd lived in the big house in the forest, she'd asked when they would go back to where she lived or when her mother would come for her, where her father was. But whenever she asked questions, her grandmother's mouth would clamp tight and her eyes would go shiny and dark.

From that, Olivia learned to wait.

Then she learned to forget.

She grew tall, and she grew tough. The fragile little girl who hid in closets became little more than a memory, and one that ghosted into dreams. Living in the present was another lesson she learned, and learned well.

With her chores at the campground over for the day, Olivia wandered down the path toward home. The afternoon was hers now, as much a reward as the salary her grandmother banked for her twice monthly in town. She thought about fishing, or hiking up to high ground to dream over the lake, but felt too restless for such sedentary activities. She'd have enjoyed a swim even this early in the season, but it was one of her grandmother's hard-and-fast rules not to swim alone.

Olivia broke it from time to time and was always careful to dry her hair completely before coming home.

Grandma worried, she thought now. Too much, too often and about nearly everything. If Olivia sneezed, she'd race to the phone to call the doctor unless Grandpop stopped her. If Olivia was ten minutes late coming home, her grandmother was out on the porch calling.

Once she'd nearly called Search and Rescue because Olivia had stayed at the campground playing with other children and forgotten to come home until dark.

It made Olivia roll her eyes to think of it. She'd never get lost in the forest. It was home, and she knew every twist and turn as well as she knew the rooms in her own house. She knew Grandpop had said as much because she'd heard them arguing about it more than once. Whenever they did, Grandma would be better for a few days, but then it would start again.

She moved through the gentle green light and soft shadows of the forest and into the clearing where the MacBride house had stood for generations.

The mica in the old stone glinted in the quiet sunlight. When it rained, the hidden colors in the rock, the browns and reds and greens, would come out and gleam. The windows sparkled, always there to let in the light or the comforting gloom. It was three levels, each stacked atop the other at a different angle with decks jutting out everywhere to stitch it all together. Flowers and ferns and wild rhododendrons hugged the foundation, then sprawled out in a hodgepodge garden her grandfather babied like a beloved child.

Huge pansies with purple and white faces spilled out of stone pots, and an enormous bed of impatiens, sassy and pink, danced along the edge of the lower deck.

She'd spent many satisfying hours with her grandfather and his flowers. Her hands in the dirt and her head in the clouds.

She started down the stone walkway, varying giant and baby steps to avoid all the cracks. She skipped up the steps, spun into a quick circle, then pulled open the front door.

She had only to step inside to realize the house was empty. She called out anyway, from habit, as she walked through the living room with its big, ragged sofas and warm yellow walls.

She sniffed, pleased to catch the scent of fresh cookies. Only sighed a little when she reached the kitchen and discovered they were oatmeal.

'Why can't they be chocolate-chip,' she muttered, already digging into the big glass jar that held them. 'I could eat a million chocolate-chip cookies.'

She settled for the oatmeal, eating fast and greedily as she read the note on the refrigerator.

Livvy. I had to run into town, to go to the market. Your Aunt Jamie and Uncle David are coming to visit. They'll be here tonight.

'Yes!' Olivia let out a whoop and scattered crumbs. 'Presents!'

To celebrate, she reached for a third cookie, then muttered a quiet 'damn' under her breath at the rest of the message.

Stay at home, honey, so you can help me with the groceries when I get back. You can tidy up your room – if you can find it. Stop eating all the cookies. Love, Grandma

'Sheesh.' With true regret, Olivia put the top back on the jar.

Now she was stuck in the house. Grandma might be *hours* shopping. What was she supposed to do all day? Feeling put upon, she clumped up the back stairs. Her room wasn't that bad. It just had her stuff, that was all. Why did it matter so much if it was put away when she'd only want to get it out again?

Her various projects and interests were scattered around. Her rock collection, her drawings of wildlife and plants with the scientific names painstakingly lettered beneath. The chemistry set she'd been desperate for the previous Christmas was shoved on a shelf and ignored, except for the microscope which held a prominent position on her desk.

There was a shoebox crammed with what she considered specimens – twigs, dead bugs, bits of ferns, hair, scrapings of tobacco and scraps of bark.

The clothes she'd worn yesterday were in a heap on the floor. Precisely where she'd stepped out of them. Her bed was unmade and in a tangle of blankets and sheets – exactly the way it had been when she'd leaped out of it at dawn.

It all looked perfectly fine to Olivia. But she marched over to the bed, dragged the covers up, slapped the pillows a couple of times. She kicked discarded shoes under the bed, tossed clothes in the direction of the hamper or the closet. She blew away dust and eraser bits from the surface of her desk, stuffed pencil stubs in the glass jar, pushed papers in the drawer and considered it a job well done.

She thought about curling up on her windowseat to dream and sulk for a while. The trees were stirring, the tops of the soaring Douglas firs and western hemlocks sighing and shifting in the incoming breeze. The western sky had taken on the bruised and fragile look of an incoming storm. She could sit and watch it roll in, see if she could spot the line of rain before it fell.

Better, much better, would be to go outside, to smell it, to lift her face up and draw in the scent of rain and pine. An alone smell, she always thought. The better to be absorbed in solitude.

She nearly did just that, was already turning toward the tall glass doors that led to the deck off her room. But all the boxes and games and puzzles jammed on her shelves pricked her conscience. Her grandmother had been asking her to sort through and straighten out the mess for weeks. Now, with Aunt Jamie coming – and surely bringing presents with her – there was bound to be a lecture on the care and appreciation of your possessions.

Heaving a long-suffering sigh, Olivia snatched down old, neglected board games and jigsaw puzzles and made a teetering stack. She'd take them up to the attic, she decided, then her room would be practically perfect.

Carefully she went up the stairs and opened the door. When the light flashed on, she glanced around, looking for the best place to store her castoffs in the huge cedar-scented space. Old lamps, not quite ready to be shipped off to Good Will, stood bare of bulbs and shades in a corner where the roofline dipped low. A child-size rocking chair and baby furniture that looked ancient to Olivia were neatly stacked against one wall along with storage boxes and chests. Pictures that had once graced the walls of the house or the lodge were ghosted in dust covers. A creaky wooden shelf her grandfather had made in his wood shop held a family of dolls and stuffed animals.

Val MacBride, Olivia knew, didn't like to throw things away either. Possessions ended up being transferred to the attic or to the lodge or simply recycled within the house.

Olivia carried her boxes to the toy shelf and stacked them on the floor beside it. More out of boredom than interest, she poked into some of the drawers, pondered baby clothes carefully wrapped in tissue and scattered with cedar chips to keep them sweet. In another was a blanket, all pink and white with soft satin edgings. She fingered it as it stirred some vague memory. But her stomach got all hot and crampy, so she closed the drawer again.

Technically she wasn't supposed to come to the attic without permission, and she was never allowed to open drawers or chests or boxes. Her grandmother said that memories were precious, and when she was older she could take them out. It was always when she was older, Olivia thought. It was never, never now.

She didn't see why it was such a big deal. It was just a bunch of old junk, and she wasn't a kid anymore. It wasn't as if she'd break something or lose it.

Anyway, she didn't really care.

The rain started to patter on the roof, like fingers lightly drumming on a table. She glanced toward the little window that faced the front of the clearing. And saw the chest.

It was a cherrywood chest with a domed lid and polished-brass fittings. It was always kept deep under the overhang, and always locked. She noticed such things. Her grandfather said she had eyes like a cat, which had made her giggle when she'd been younger. Now it was something she took pride in.

Today, the chest wasn't shoved back under the roofline, and neither was it locked. Grandma must have put something away,

Olivia thought and strolled casually over as if she weren't particularly interested.

She knew the story about Pandora's box and how the curious woman had opened it and set free all the ills upon the world. But this wasn't the same thing, she told herself as she knelt in front of it. And since it wasn't locked, what was the harm in opening it up and taking a peek inside?

It was probably just full of sentimental junk or musty old clothes or pictures turning yellow.

But her fingers tingled – in warning or anticipation – as she lifted the heavy lid.

The scent struck her first and made her breath come fast and hard.

Cedar, from the lining. Lavender. Her grandfather had a sweep of it planted on the side of the house. But under those, something else. Something both foreign and familiar. Though she couldn't identify it, the waft of it had her heart beating fast, like a quick, impatient knocking in her chest.

The tingling in her fingers became intense, making them shake as she reached inside. There were videos, labeled only with dates and stored in plain black dust covers. Three thick photo albums, boxes of varying sizes. She opened one very like the box her grandparents used to store their old-fashioned Christmas balls.

There, resting in foam for protection, were half a dozen decorative bottles.

'The magic bottles,' she whispered. It seemed the attic was suddenly filled with low and beautiful laughter, flickering images, exotic scents.

On your sixteenth birthday, you can choose the one you like best. But you mustn't play with them, Livvy. They might break. You could cut your hand or step on glass.

Mama leaned over, her soft hair falling over the side of her face. Laughing, her eyes full of fun, she sprayed a small cloud of perfume on Olivia's throat.

The scent. Mama's perfume. Scrambling up to her knees again, Olivia leaned into the chest, breathed long and deep. And smelled her mother.

Setting the box aside, she reached in for the first photo album. It was heavy and awkward, so she laid it across her lap. There were no pictures of her mother in the house. Olivia remembered there had been, but they'd disappeared a long time before. The album was full of them, pictures of her mother when she'd been a young girl, pictures of her with Jamie, and with her parents. Smiling, laughing, making faces at the camera.

Pictures in front of the house and in the house, at the campground and at the lake. Pictures with Grandpop when his hair had been more gold than silver, and with Grandma in a fancy dress.

There was one of her mother holding a baby. 'That's me,' Olivia whispered. 'Mama and me.' She turned the next page and the next, all but devouring each photo, until they abruptly stopped. She could see the marks on the page where they'd been removed.

Impatient now, she set it aside and reached for the next.

Not family photos this time but newspaper clippings, magazine articles. Her mother on the cover of *People* and *Newsweek* and *Glamour*. Olivia studied these first, looking deep, absorbing every feature. She had her mother's eyes. She'd known that, remembered that, but to see it so clearly, to look with her own into them, the color, the shape, the slash of dark eyebrows.

Excitement, grief, pleasure swirled through her in a tangled mass as she stroked a finger over each glossy image. She'd been so beautiful, so perfect.

Then her heart leaped again as she paged through and found a series of pictures of her mother with a dark-haired man. He was handsome, like a poet, she thought as her adolescent heart sighed. There were pictures of them in a garden, and in a big room with dozens of glittering lights, on a sofa with her mother snuggled into his lap with their faces close and their smiles for each other.

Sam Tanner. It said his name was Sam Tanner. Reading it, she began to shiver. Her stomach cramped, a dozen tight fists that twisted.

Daddy. It was Daddy. How could she have forgotten? It was Daddy, holding hands with Mama, or with his arm around her shoulders.

Holding scissors bright with blood.

No, no, that couldn't be. It was a dream, a nightmare. Imagination, that was all.

She began to rock, pressing her hands to her mouth as the images began to creep in. Panic, burning fingers of it, had her by the throat, squeezing until her breath came in strangled gasps.

Broken glass sparkling on the floor in the lights. Dying flowers. The warm breeze through the open door.

It wasn't real. She wouldn't let it be real.

Olivia pushed the book aside and lifted out the last with hands that trembled. There'd be other pictures, she told herself. More pictures of her parents smiling and laughing and holding each other.

But it was newspapers again, with big headlines that seemed to scream at her.

JULIE MACBRIDE MURDERED
SAM TANNER ARRESTED
FAIRY TALE ENDS IN TRAGEDY

There were pictures of her father, looking dazed and unkempt. More of her aunt, her grandparents, her uncle. And of her, she saw with a jolt. Of her years before with her eyes wild and blank and her hands pressed to her ears.

JULIE'S CHILD, ONLY WITNESS TO MOTHER'S SLAYING

She shook her head in denial, ripping quickly through the pages now. There, another face that awakened memories. His name was Frank, she thought. He chased the monster away. He had a little boy and he'd liked puzzles.

A policeman. Soft, hunted sounds trembled in her throat. He'd carried her out of the house, the house where the monster had come. Where all the blood was.

Because her mother was dead. Her mother was dead. She knew that, of course she knew that. But we don't talk about it, she reminded herself, we never talk about it because it makes Grandma cry.

She ordered herself to close the book, to put it all away again, back in the chest, back in the dark. But she was already turning the pages, searching the words and pictures.

Drugs. Jealousy. Obsession.

Tanner Confesses!

Tanner Retracts Confession. Proclaims His Innocence.

Four-Year-Old Daughter Chief Witness.

The Tanner trial took one more dramatic turn today as the

videotaped testimony of Tanner's daughter, four-year-old Olivia, was introduced. The child was questioned in the home of her maternal aunt, Jamie Melbourne, and videotaped with permission of her grandparents, acting as guardians. Previously Judge Sato ruled that the taped statement could be introduced as evidence, sparing the minor the trauma of a court appearance.

She remembered, she remembered it all now. They'd sat in Aunt Jamie's living room. Her grandparents had been there, too. A woman with red hair and a soft voice had asked her questions about the night the monster had come. Grandma had promised it would be the last time she would have to talk about it, the very last time.

And it was.

The woman had listened and asked more questions. Then a man had talked to her, a man with a careful smile and careful eyes. She'd thought since it was the last time, she'd be able to go back home. That it would all go away.

But she'd come to Washington instead, to the big house in the forest.

Now, she knew why.

Olivia turned more pages, narrowed her eyes against tears until they were stinging dry. And with her jaw tight and her eyes clear, read another flurry of headlines.

SAM TANNER CONVICTED

GUILTY! JURY CONVICTS TANNER

TANNER SENTENCED TO LIFE

'You killed my mother, you bastard.' She said it with all the hate a young girl could muster. 'I hope you're dead, too. I hope you died screaming.'

With steady hands, she closed the book, carefully replaced it along with the others in the chest. She shut the lid, then rose to go turn off the lights. She walked down the stairs, through the empty house to the back porch.

Sitting there, she stared out into the rain.

She didn't understand how she could have buried everything that had happened, how she could have locked it up the way her grandmother locked the boxes and books in the chest.

But she knew she wouldn't do so again. She would remember, always. And she would find out more, find out everything she could about the night her mother died, about the trial, about her father.

She understood she couldn't ask her family. They thought she was still a child, one who needed to be protected. But they were wrong. She'd never be a child again.

She heard the sound of the Jeep rumbling up the lane through the rain. Olivia closed her eyes and concentrated. A part of her hardened, then wondered if she'd inherited acting skills from either of her parents. She tucked the hate, the grief and the anger into a corner of her heart. Sealed it inside.

Then she stood up, a smile ready for her grandmother when the Jeep braked at the end of the drive.

'Just who I wanted to see.' Val tossed up the hood of her jacket as she stepped out of the Jeep. 'We're loaded here, Livvy. Get a jacket and give me a hand, will you?'

'I don't need a jacket. I won't melt.' She stepped out into the rain. The steady drum of it was a comfort. 'Are we having spaghetti and meatballs for dinner?'

'For Jamie's first night home?' Val laughed and passed Olivia a grocery bag. 'What else?'

'I'd like to make it.' Olivia shifted the bag, then reached in for another.

'You – really?'

Olivia jerked a shoulder and headed into the house. The door slapped shut behind her, then opened again as Val pushed in with more bags. 'What brought this on? You always say cooking is boring.'

That had been when she'd been a kid, Olivia thought. Now was different. 'I have to learn sometime. I'll get the rest, Grandma.' She started out, then turned back. The anger was inside her, didn't want to stay locked up. It wanted to leap out, she realized, and slice at her grandmother. And that was wrong. Deliberately, she walked over and gave Val a fierce hug. 'I want to learn to cook like you.'

While Val blinked in stunned pleasure, Olivia hurried outside for the rest of the bags. What had gotten into the girl? Val wondered as she unpacked fresh tomatoes and lettuce and peppers. Just that morning she'd whined about fixing a couple of pieces of toast, all but danced with impatience to get outside. Now she wanted to spend her free afternoon cooking.

When Olivia came back in, Val lifted her eyebrows. 'Livvy, did you get in trouble at the campground?'

'No.'

'Are you after something? That fancy new backpack you've had your eye on?'

Olivia sighed, shoved the damp hair out of her eyes. 'Gran, I want to learn how to cook spaghetti. It's not a big deal.'

'I just wondered about the sudden interest.'

'If I don't know how to cook, I can't be independent. And if I'm going to learn, I'd might as well learn right.'

'Well.' Pleased, Val nodded. 'My girl's growing up on me.' She reached over, brushed Olivia's cheek with her fingertips. 'My pretty little Livvy.'

'I don't want to be pretty.' Some of the fire of that buried anger smoked into her eyes. 'I want to be smart.'

'You can be both.'

'I'd rather work on smart.'

Changes, Val thought. You couldn't stop them, could never hold a moment. 'All right. Let's get this stuff put away and get started.'

With patience Val explained what ingredients they'd use and why, which of the herbs they'd add from the kitchen garden and how their flavors would blend. If she noticed that Olivia paid almost fierce attention to every detail, she was more amused than concerned.

If she could have heard her granddaughter's thoughts, she might have wept.

Did you teach my mother how to make the sauce? Olivia wondered. Did she stand here with you when she was my age at this same stove and learn how to brown garlic in olive oil? Did she smell the same smells and hear the rain beating on the roof?

Why won't you tell me about her? How will I know who she was if you don't? How will I know who I am?

Then Val laid a hand on her shoulder. 'That's good, honey. That's fine. You've got a real knack.'

Olivia stirred the herbs into the slow simmer of the sauce. And for now, let the rest go.

Chapter Six

Because the first night Jamie and David came to visit was always treated as a special occasion, the family ate in the dining room with its long oak table set with white candles in silver holders, fresh flowers in crystal vases and Great-Grandma Capelli's good china.

Food was abundant, as was conversation. As always, the meal spun out for two hours while the candles burned down and the sun that had peeked out of the clouds began to slide behind the trees.

'Livvy, that was just wonderful.' Jamie groaned and leaned back to pat her stomach. 'So wonderful, I haven't left room for any tiramisù.'

'I have.' Rob twinkled, giving Olivia's hair a tug. 'I'll just shake the spaghetti into my hollow leg. She's got your hand with the sauce, Val.'

'My mother's, more like. I swear it was better than mine. I was beginning to wonder if our girl would ever do more than fry fish over a campfire.'

'Blood runs true,' Rob commented and winked at his granddaughter. 'That Italian was bound to pop out sooner or later. The MacBride side was never known for its skill in the kitchen.'

'What are they known for, Dad?'

He laughed, wiggled his brows at Jamie. 'We're lovers, darling.'

Val snorted, slapped his arm, then rose. 'I'll clear,' Jamie said, starting to get up.

'No.' Val pointed a finger at her daughter. 'You don't catch KP on your first night. Livvy's relieved, too. Rob and I will clean this up, then maybe we'll all have room for coffee and dessert.'

'Hear that, Livvy?' David leaned over to murmur in her ear. 'You cook, you don't scrub pots. Pretty good deal.'

'I'm going to start cooking regularly.' She grinned at him. 'It's a lot more fun than doing dishes. Do you want to take a hike tomorrow, Uncle David? We can use my new backpack.'

Olivia slanted her grandmother a look, struggling not to smirk.

'You spoil her, David,' Val stated as she stacked dishes. 'She wasn't going to get that backpack until her birthday this fall.'

'Spoil her?' His face bland, David poked a finger into Olivia's ribs and made her giggle. 'Nah, she's not even ripe yet. Plenty of time yet before she spoils. Do you mind if I switch on the TV in the other room? I've got a client doing a concert on cable. I promised I'd catch it.'

'You go right on,' Val told him. 'Put your feet up and get comfortable. I'll bring coffee in shortly.'

'Want to come up and talk to me while I unpack?' Jamie asked her niece.

'Could we take a walk?' Olivia had been waiting for the right moment. It seemed everyone had conspired to make it now. 'Before it gets dark?'

'Sure.' Jamie stood, stretched. 'Let me get a jacket. It'll do me good to work off some of that pasta. Then I won't feel guilty if I don't make it over to the health club at the lodge tomorrow.'

'I'll tell Grandma. Meet you out back.'

Even in summer, the nights were cool. The air smelled of rain and wet roses. The long days of July held the light even while a ghost moon rose in the eastern sky. Still, Jamie fingered the flashlight in her pocket. They would need it in the forest. It was the forest she wanted. She would feel safe there, safe enough to say what she needed to say and ask what she needed to ask.

'It's always good to be home.' Jamie took a deep breath and smiled at her father's garden.

'Why don't you live here?'

'My work's in L.A. So's David's. But we both count on coming up here a couple of times a year. When I was a girl, your age, I suppose, I thought this was the whole world.'

'But it's not.'

'No.' Jamie angled her head as she looked over at Olivia. 'But it's one of the best parts. I hear you're a big help at the campground and the lodge. Grandpop says he couldn't do without you.'

'I like working there. It's not like work.' Olivia scuffed a boot in the dirt and angled away from the house toward the trees. 'Lots of people come. Some of them don't know *anything*. They don't even know the difference between a Douglas fir and a hemlock, or they wear expensive designer boots and get blisters. They think the more you pay for something the better it is, and that's just stupid.' She slanted Jamie a look. 'A lot of them come from Los Angeles.'

'Ouch.' Amused, Jamie rubbed her heart. 'Direct hit.'

'There're too many people down there, and cars and smog.'

'That's true enough.' All that felt very far away, Jamie realized, when you stepped into the deep woods, smelled the pine, the soft scent of rot, felt the carpet of cones and needles under your feet. 'But it can be exciting, too. Beautiful homes, wonderful palm trees, shops, restaurants, galleries.'

'Is that why my mother went there? So she could shop and go to restaurants and have a beautiful home?'

Jamie stopped short. The question had snapped out at her, an unexpected backhanded slap that left her dazed. 'I – she . . . Julie wanted to be an actress. It was natural for her to go there.'

'She wouldn't have died if she'd stayed home.'

'Oh, Livvy.' Jamie started to reach out, but Olivia stepped back.

'You have to promise not to say anything to anyone. Not to Grandma or Grandpop or Uncle David. Not to anyone.'

'But, Livvy—'

'You *have* to promise.' Panic snuck into her voice, tears into her eyes. 'If you promise you won't say anything, then you won't.'

'All right, baby.'

'I'm not a baby.' But this time Olivia let herself be held. 'Nobody ever talks about her, and all her pictures got put away. I can't remember unless I try really hard. Then it gets all mixed up.'

'We just didn't want you to hurt. You were so little when she died.'

'When he killed her.' Olivia drew back. Her eyes were dry now and glinting in the dim light. 'When my father killed her. You have to say it out loud.'

'When Sam Tanner killed her.'

The pain reared up, hideously fresh. Giving in to it, Jamie sat beside a nurse log, breathed out slowly. The ground was damp, but it didn't seem to matter.

'Not talking about it doesn't mean we don't love her, Livvy. Maybe it means we loved her too much. I don't know.'

'Do you think about her?'

'Yes.' Jamie reached out a hand, clasping Olivia's firmly. 'Yes, I do. We were very close. I miss her every day.'

With a nod, Olivia sat beside her, idly played her light on the ground. 'Do you think about him?'

Jamie shut her eyes. Oh God, what should she do, how should she handle this? 'I try not to.'

'But do you?'

'Yes.'

'Is he dead, too?'

'No.' Nerves jittering, Jamie rubbed a hand over her mouth. 'He's in prison.'

'Why did he kill her?'

'I don't know. I just don't know. It doesn't do any good to wonder, Livvy, because it'll never make sense. It'll never be right.'

'He used to tell me stories. He used to carry me on his back. I remember. I'd forgotten, but I remember now.'

She continued to play the light, dancing it over the rotting log that nurtured seedlings she recognized as hemlock and spruce, the rosettes of tree moss that tumbled over it, the bushy tufts of globe lichen that tangled with it. It kept her calm, seeing what she knew, putting a name to it.

'Then he got sick and went away. That's what Mama told me, but it wasn't really true. It was drugs.'

'Where are you hearing these things?'

'Are they true?' She looked away from the log, the flourishing life. 'Aunt Jamie, I want to know what's true.'

'Yes, they're true. I'm sorry they happened to you, to Julie, to me, to all of us. We can't change it, Livvy. We just have to go on and do the best we can.'

'Is what happened why I can never come visit you? Why Grandma teaches me instead of my going to school with other kids? Why my name's MacBride instead of Tanner?'

Jamie sighed. She heard an owl hoot and a rustle in the brush. Hunters and hunted, she thought. Only looking to survive the night. 'We decided it was best for you not to be exposed to the publicity, to the gossip, the speculations. Your mother was famous. People were interested in her life, in what happened. In you. We wanted to get you away from all that. To give you a chance, the chance Julie would have wanted for you to have a safe, happy childhood.'

'Grandma locked it all away.'

'Mom – Grandma . . . It was so hard on her, Livvy. She lost her daughter.' The one she couldn't help but love best. 'You helped get her through it. Can you understand that?' She gripped Olivia's hand again. 'She needed you as much as you needed her. She's centered her life on you these last years. Protecting you was so important – and maybe by doing that she protected herself, too. You can't blame her for it.'

'I don't want to. But it's not fair to ask me to forget everything. I can't talk to her or Grandpop.' The tears wanted to come again. Her eyes stung horribly as she forced them back. 'I need to remember my mother.'

'You're right. You're right.' Jamie draped an arm around Olivia's shoulders and hugged. 'You can talk to me. I won't tell anyone else. And we'll both remember.'

Content with that, Olivia laid her head on Jamie's shoulder. 'Aunt Jamie, do you have tapes of the movies my mother was in?'

'Yes.'

'One day I want to see them. We'd better go back in.' She rose, her eyes solemn as she looked at Jamie. 'Thanks for telling me the truth.'

What a shock it was, Jamie thought, to expect a child and see a woman. 'I'll make you another promise right here, Livvy. This is a special place for me, a place where if you make a promise, you have to keep it. I'll always tell you the truth, no matter what.'

'I promise, too.' Olivia held out her hand. 'No matter what.'

They walked out, hands linked. At the edge of the clearing, Olivia looked up. The sky had gone a deep, soft blue. The moon, no longer a ghost, cut its white slice out of the night. 'The first stars are out. They're there, even in the daytime, even when you can't see them. But I like to see them. That's Mama's star.' She pointed up to the tiny glimmer near the tail of the crescent moon. 'It comes out first.'

Jamie's throat closed, burned. 'She'd like that. She'd like that you thought of her, and weren't sad.'

'Coffee's on!' Val called through the door. 'I made you a latte, Livvy. Extra foam.'

'We're coming. She's happy you're here, so I get latte.' Olivia's smile was so sudden, so young, it nearly broke Jamie's heart. 'Let's get our share of tiramisù before Grandpop hogs it all.'

'Hey, for tiramisù, I'd take my own father down without a qualm.'

'Race you.' Olivia darted off like a bullet, blond hair flying.

It was that image – the long blond hair swinging, the girlish dare, the swift race through the dark – that Jamie carried with her through the evening. She watched Olivia scoop up dessert, stage a mock battle with her grandfather over his serving, nag David for details about his meeting Madonna at a party. And she wondered if Olivia was mature enough, controlled enough, to tuck all her thoughts and emotions away or if she was simply young enough to cast them aside in favor of sweets and attention.

As much as she'd have preferred it to be the latter, she decided Olivia had inherited some of Julie's skills as an actress.

There was a weight on her heart as she prepared for bed in the room that had been hers as a girl. Her sister's child was looking to her now, as she had during those horrible days eight years before. Only this time, she wasn't such a little girl and wouldn't be satisfied with cuddles and stories.

She wanted the truth, and that meant Jamie would have to face parts of the truth she'd tried to forget.

She'd dealt with the unauthorized biographies, the documentaries, the television movie, the tabloid insanity and rumors dealing with her sister's life and her death. They still cropped up from time to time. The young, beautiful actress, cut down in her prime by the man she loved. In a town that fed itself on fantasy and gossip, grim fairy tales could often take on the sheen of legends.

She'd done her best to discourage it. She gave no interviews to the press, cut no deals, endorsed no projects. In this way she protected her parents, the child. And herself.

Still, every year, a new wave of Julie MacBride stories sprang up. Every year, she thought, leaning on the pedestal sink and staring at her own face in the mirror, on the anniversary of her death.

So she fled home every summer, escaped it for a few days, let herself be tucked away as she'd let Olivia be tucked away.

They were entitled to their privacy, weren't they? She sighed, rubbed her eyes. Just as Olivia was entitled to talk about the mother she'd lost. Somehow, she had to see to it that they managed to have both.

She straightened, pushed the hair back from her face. She'd let her hairdresser talk her into a perm and some subtle highlighting around her face. She had to admit, he'd been right. It gave her a softer, younger look. Youth wasn't just a matter of vanity, she thought. It was a matter of business.

She was beginning to see lines creeping around her eyes, those nasty little reminders of age and wear and tear. Sooner or later, she'd have to consider a tuck. She'd mentioned it to David, and he'd just laughed.

Lines? What lines? I don't see any lines.

Men, she thought now, but they'd both known his response had pleased her.

Still, it didn't mean she could afford to neglect her skin. She took the time to smooth on her night cream, using firm, upward strokes along her throat, dabbing on the eye cream with her pinkies. Then she added a trail of perfume between her breasts in case her husband was feeling romantic.

He often was.

Smiling to herself, she went back into the bedroom where she'd left the light burning for David. He hadn't come up yet, so she closed the door quietly, then moved to the cheval glass. She removed her robe and took inventory.

She worked out like a fiend three days a week with a personal trainer she secretly called the Marquessa de Sade. But it paid off. Perhaps her breasts would no longer qualify as perky, but the rest of her was nice and tight. As long as she could pump and sweat, there'd be no need for nips and tucks anywhere but her eyes.

She understood the value of keeping herself attractive – in her public relations work and in her marriage. The actors and entertainers she and David worked with seemed to get younger every time she blinked. Some of his clients were beautiful and desirable women, *young* women. Succumbing to temptation, Jamie knew, was more often the rule rather than the exception in the life she and David lived.

She also knew she was lucky. Nearly fourteen years, she mused. The length of their marriage was a not-so-minor miracle in Hollywood. They'd had bumps and dips, but they'd gotten through them.

She'd always been able to depend on him, and he on her. And the other not-so-minor miracle was that they loved each other.

She slipped back into her robe, belting it as she walked to the deck doors and threw them open to the night. She stepped out, to listen to the wind sigh through the trees. To look for Julie's star.

'How many times did we sit out on nights like this and dream? We'd whisper together when we were supposed to be in bed. And we'd plan. Such big, shiny plans. I've got so much I dreamed of, so much I wouldn't have had if you hadn't had the big dreams first. I might never have met David if not for you. Would never have had the courage to start my own company. So many things I wouldn't have done, wouldn't have seen if I hadn't followed after you.'

She leaned on the rail, closing her eyes as the wind toyed with her hair, the hem of her robe, shivered along her bare skin. 'I'll make sure Livvy dreams big, too. That nothing stops her from grabbing hold of what she needs most. And I'm sorry, Julie. I'm sorry I had a part in trying to make her forget you.'

She stepped back, rubbing her arms as the air turned chilly. But she stayed outside, watching the stars until David found her.

'Jamie?' When she turned, his eyes warmed. 'You look beautiful. I was afraid you'd gone to bed while I puffed cigars and told lies with your father.'

'No, I wanted to wait for you.' She stepped into his arms, nestled her head on his shoulder. 'I waited just for this.'

'Good. You've been quiet tonight. Are you all right?'

'Hmm. Just a little lost in thoughts.' Too many she couldn't share with him. A promise had been given. 'Tomorrow it'll be eight years. Sometimes it seems like a lifetime ago, and others like yesterday. It means so much to me, David, that you come with me every year. That you understand why I have to be here. I know how hard it is for you to juggle your schedule to carve out these few days.'

'Jamie, she mattered to all of us. And you . . .' He drew her back to kiss her. 'You matter most.'

With a smile, she laid her hand on his cheek. 'I must. I know how much you love tramping through the woods and spending an afternoon fishing.'

He grimaced. 'Your mother's taking me out on the river tomorrow.'

'My hero.'

'I think she knows I hate fishing and makes me go out every summer to pay her back for stealing her daughter.'

'Well then, the least her daughter can do is make it worth your while.'

'Oh yeah?' His hands were already sliding down to mold her bottom through the thin robe. 'How?'

'Come with me. I'll show you.'

Olivia dreamed of her mother and whimpered in her sleep. They huddled together in a closet filled with animals who stared with glassy eyes. She shivered in the dark, holding tight, so tight because the monster raged outside the door. He was calling her name, roaring it out while he stomped on the floor.

She buried her face against her mother's breast, pressed her hands over her ears as something crashed close, so close to where she tried to disappear.

Then the door burst open and the closet bloomed with light. In the light she saw the blood, all over her hands, all over her mother's hair. And Mama's eyes were like the eyes of the animals. Glassy and staring.

'I've been looking for you,' Daddy said, and snapped the scissors that shined and dripped.

As she tossed in sleep, others dreamed of Julie.

Images of a lovely young girl laughing in the kitchen as she learned to make red sauce like her grandmother's. Of a much-loved companion who raced through the woods with her pale hair flying. Of a lover who sighed in the night. A woman of impossible beauty dancing in a white dress on her wedding day.

Of death, so terrible, so stark it couldn't be remembered in the light.

And those who dreamed of her wept.

Even her killer.

*

It was still dark when Val knocked briskly on the bedroom door. 'Up and at 'em, David. Coffee's on and the fish are biting.'

With a pitiful moan, David rolled over, buried his head under the pillow. 'Oh, my God.'

'Ten minutes. I'll pack your breakfast.'

'The woman's not human. She can't be.'

With a sleepy laugh, Jamie nudged him toward the edge of the bed. 'Up and at 'em, fish boy.'

'Tell her I died in my sleep. I'm begging you.' He pushed the pillow off his head and managed to bring his wife's silhouette into focus. She smiled when his hand closed warmly over her breast. 'Go catch fish, and if you're very good, I'll reward you tonight.'

'Sex doesn't buy everything,' he said with some dignity, then crawled out of bed. 'But it buys me.' He tripped over something in the dark, cursed, then limped to the bathroom while his wife snickered.

She was sound asleep when he came back, gave her an absent kiss and stumbled out.

Light was filtering through the windows when the shakes and whispers woke her. 'Huh? What?'

'Aunt Jamie? Are you awake?'

'Not until I've had my coffee.'

'I brought you some.'

Jamie pried one eye open, focused blearily on her niece. She sniffed once, caught the scent and sighed. 'You are my queen.'

With a laugh, Olivia sat on the side of the bed as Jamie struggled up. 'I made it fresh. Grandma and Uncle David are gone, and Grandpop left for the lodge. He said he had paperwork to do, but he just likes to go over there and talk to people.'

'You got his number.' Eyes closed, Jamie took the first sip. 'So what are you up to?'

'Well . . . Grandpop said that I could have the day off if you wanted to go for a hike. I could take you on one of the easy trails. It's sort of practice for being a guide. I can't really be one until I'm sixteen, even though I know all the trails better than mostly anyone.'

Jamie opened one eye again. Olivia had a bright smile on her face and a plea in her eye. 'You've got my number, too, don't you?'

‘I can use my new backpack. I’ll make sandwiches and stuff while you’re getting dressed.’

‘What kind of sandwiches?’

‘Ham and Swiss.’

‘Sold. Give me twenty minutes.’

‘All right!’ Olivia darted out of the room, leaving Jamie to take the first two of that twenty minutes to settle back and enjoy her coffee.

It was warm and bright, with a wild blue sky of high summer. A perfect day, Jamie decided, to think of what is rather than what had been.

She flexed her feet in her ancient and reliable boots and studied her niece. Olivia had her hair tucked up in a fielder’s cap with the *River’s End Lodge and Campground* logo emblazoned on the crown. Her T-shirt was faded, the over-shirt unbuttoned and frayed at the cuffs. Her boots looked worn and comfortable, the backpack brightly blue.

She had a compass and a knife sheath hooked to her belt.

She looked, Jamie realized, supremely competent.

‘Okay, what’s your spiel?’

‘My spiel?’

‘Yeah, I’ve hired you to guide me on the trail today, to show me the ropes, to make my hiking experience a memorable one. I know nothing. I’m an urban hiker.’

‘Urban hiker?’

‘That’s right. Rodeo Drive’s my turf, and I’ve come here to taste nature. I want my money’s worth.’

‘Okay.’ Olivia squared her shoulders, cleared her throat. ‘Today we’re going to hike the John MacBride Trail. This trail is an easy two-point-three-mile hike that loops through the rain forest, then climbs for a half a mile to the lake area, which offers magnificent views. Um . . . More experienced hikers often choose to continue the hike from that point on one of the more difficult trails, but this choice gives the visitor . . . um, the chance to experience the rain forest as well as the lake vistas. How was that?’

‘Not bad.’

It was, Olivia thought, almost word for word from one of the books on sale at the lodge gift shop. All she’d done was to focus on bringing the page into her head and basically reading it off.

But she'd fix that. She'd learn to personalize her guides. She'd learn to be the best there was.

'Okay. As your guide, and the representative of River's End Lodge and Campground, I'll be providing your picnic lunch and explanations of the flora and fauna we see on our tour. I'll be happy to answer any questions.'

'You're a natural. Ready when you are.'

'Neat. The trailhead begins here, at the original site of the first MacBride homestead. John and Nancy MacBride traveled west from Kansas in 1853 and settled here on the edges of the Quinault rain forest.'

'I thought rain forests were in the tropics,' Jamie said and fluttered her lashes at Olivia as they moved toward the trees.

'The Quinault Valley holds one of the few temperate rain forests in the world. We have mild temperatures and a lot of rainfall.'

'The trees are so *tall*! What are they?'

'The overstory of trees is Sitka spruce; you can identify them by the flaky bark. And Douglas fir. They grow really tall and straight. When they get old, the bark's dark brown and has those deep groves in it. Then there's western hemlock. It's not usually a canopy tree, and it's shade-tolerant so it's understory. It doesn't grow as fast as the Douglas fir. You see the cones, all over the place?' Olivia stooped to pick one up. 'This one's a Doug-fir, see the three points? There'll be lots of them inside the forest, but you won't see saplings because they're not shade-tolerant. The animals like them, and bears like to eat their bark.'

'Bears! *Eek!*'

'Oh, Aunt Jamie.'

'Hey, I'm your city-slicker client, remember?'

'Right. You don't have to worry about bear if you take simple safety precautions,' Olivia parroted. 'The black bear lives in this area. The biggest problem with them is they like to steal food, so you've got to use proper storage for food and garbage. You never, never leave food or dirty dishes unattended in your campsite.'

'But you have food in your backpack. What if the bears smell it and come after us?'

‘I have the food wrapped in double plastic, so they won’t. But if a bear comes around, you should make lots of noise. You need to be calm, give them room so they can go away.’

They stepped out of the clearing and into the trees. Almost immediately the light turned soft and green with only a few stray shimmers of sun sneaking through the canopy of trees. Those thin fingers were pale, watery and lovely. The ground was littered with cones, thick with moss and ferns. The green covered the world in subtly different shapes, wildly different textures.

A thrush called out and darted by, barely ruffling the air.

‘It looks prehistoric.’

‘I guess it is. I think it’s the most beautiful place in the world.’

Jamie laid her hand on Olivia’s shoulder. ‘I know.’ And a safe place, Jamie thought. A wise place for a child to go. ‘Tell me what I’m seeing as we go, Livvy. Make it come alive for me.’

They walked at an easy pace, with Olivia doing her best to use a tour guide’s voice and rhythm. But the forest always captured her. She wondered why it had to be explained at all when you could just see.

The light was so soft it was as if she could feel it on her skin, the air so rich with scent it almost made her head reel. Pine and damp and the dying logs that were the life source for new trees. The deceptively fragile look of the moss that spilled and spread and climbed everywhere. The sounds – the crunch of boots over needles and cones, the stirring of small animals that darted here and there on the day’s business, the call of birds, the sudden surprising gurgle of water in a little stream. They all came together for her in their own special kind of silence.

It was her cathedral, more magnificent and certainly more holy to her than any of the pictures she’d seen of the glorious buildings in Rome or Paris. This ground lived and died every day.

She pointed out a ring of mushrooms that added splashes of white and yellow, the lichens that upholstered the great trunks of trees, the papery seeds spilled by the grand Sitka spruce, the complicated tangle of vine maples that insisted on growing close to the trail.

They wound between nurse logs, shaggy with moss and sprouts, brushed through feathery crops of ferns and spotted, thanks to Olivia’s sharp eye, an eagle lording it over the branches high overhead.

'Hardly anyone uses this trail,' Olivia said, 'because the first part of it's private. But the public trails start to loop there now, and you begin to see people.'

'Don't you like to see people, Livvy?'

'Not so much in the forest.' She offered a sheepish smile. 'I like to think it's mine, and no one will ever change it. See? Listen.' She held up a hand, closed her eyes.

Intrigued, Jamie did the same. She heard the faint tinkle of music, could just make out the slick twang of country and western.

'People take away the magic,' Olivia said solemnly, then started up the upward slant of the trail.

As they climbed, Jamie began to pick up more sounds. A voice, a child's laugh. Where the trees thinned, sunlight sprinkled in until that soft green twilight was gone.

The lakes spread out in the distance, sparkling with sun, dotted with boats. And the great mountains speared up against the sky while the dips and valleys and gorges cut through with curves and slashes.

Warmer now, she sat and tugged off her overshirt to let the sun play on her arms. 'There's all kinds of magic.' She smiled when Olivia shrugged off her pack. 'You don't have to be alone for it to work.'

'I guess not.' Carefully, Olivia unpacked the food, the thermos, then, sitting Indian style, offered Jamie her binoculars. 'Maybe you can see Uncle David and Grandma.'

'Maybe Uncle David dived overboard and swam home.' With a laugh, Jamie lifted the field glasses. 'Oh, there are swans. I love the way they look. Just gliding along. I should've brought my camera. I don't know why I never think of it.'

She lowered the glasses to pick up one of the sandwiches Olivia had cut into meticulously even halves. 'It's always beautiful here. Whatever the season, whatever the time of day.'

She glanced down, noticed that Olivia was watching her steadily. It gave her a little chill to see that measuring look in a child's eyes. 'What is it?'

'I have to ask you for a favor. You won't want to do it, but I thought about it a lot, and it's important. I need you to get me an address.' Olivia pressed her lips together, then blew out a breath. 'It's for the policeman, the one who took me to your house that night. His name is Frank. I remember him, but not very well. I want to write to him.'

'Livvy, why? There's nothing he can tell you that I can't. It can't be good for you to worry so much about this.'

'It has to be better to know things than to wonder. He was nice to me. Even if I can only write and tell him I remember he was nice to me, I'd feel better. And . . . he was there that night, Aunt Jamie. You weren't there. It was just me until he came and found me. I want to talk to him.'

She turned her head to stare out at the lakes. 'I'll tell him my grandparents don't know I'm writing. I won't tell lies. But I need to try. I only remember his name was Frank.'

Jamie closed her eyes, felt her heart sink a little. 'Brady. His name is Frank Brady.'

Chapter Seven

Frank Brady turned the pale-blue envelope over in his hands. His name and the address of the precinct had been handwritten, neat and precise and unmistakably childlike, as had the return address in the corner.

Olivia MacBride.

Little Livvy Tanner, he mused, a young ghost out of the past.

Eight years. He'd never really put that night, those people, that case aside. He'd tried. He'd done his job, justice had followed through as best it could, and the little girl had been whisked away by family who loved her.

Closed, finished, over. Despite the stories on Julie MacBride that cropped up from time to time, the gossip, the rumors, the movies that ran on late-night television, it was done. Julie MacBride would be forever thirty-two and beautiful, and the man who'd killed her wouldn't see the outside of a cage for another decade or more.

Why the hell would the kid write to him after all this time? he wondered. And why the hell didn't he just open the letter and find out?

Still, he hesitated, frowning at the envelope while phones shrilled around him and cops moved in and out of the bull pen. He found himself wishing his own phone would ring so he could set the letter aside, pick up a new case. Then with a quiet oath, he tore the envelope open, spread out the single sheet of matching stationery and read:

> *Dear Detective Brady,*
>
> *I hope you remember me. My mother was Julie MacBride, and when she was killed you took me to my aunt's house. You came to see me there, too. I didn't really understand then*

about murder or that you were investigating. You made me feel safe, and you told me how the stars were there even in the daytime. You helped me then. I hope you can help me now.

I've been living with my grandparents in Washington State. It's beautiful here and I love them very much. Aunt Jamie came to visit this week, and I asked her if she could give me your address so I could write to you. I didn't tell my grandparents because it makes them sad. We never talk about my mother, or what my father did.

I have questions that nobody can answer but you. It's awfully important to me to know the truth, but I don't want to hurt my grandmother. I'm twelve years old now, but she doesn't understand that when I think about that night and try to remember it gets mixed up and that makes it worse. Will you talk to me?

I thought maybe if you wanted to take a vacation you could even come here. I remember you had a son. You said he ate bugs and had bad dreams sometimes about alien invaders, but he's older now so I guess he doesn't anymore.

Christ, Frank thought with a stunned laugh. The kid had a memory like an elephant.

There's lots to do up here. Our lodge and campground is really nice, and I could even send you our brochures. You can go fishing or hiking or boating. The lodge has a swimming pool and nightly entertainment. We're also close to some of the most beautiful beaches in the Northwest.

Even as Frank felt his lips twitch at her sales pitch, he scanned the rest.

Please come. I have no one else to talk to.
Your truly,
Olivia

'Jesus.' He folded the letter, slipped it back in its envelope and into his jacket pocket. But he wasn't able to tuck Olivia out of his mind so easily.

*

He carried both the letter and the memory of the girl with him all day. He decided he'd write her a gentle response, keep it light – sympathetic but noncommittal. He could tell her how Noah was starting college in the fall, and how he'd been named Most Valuable Player in his basketball tournament. Chatty, easy. He'd use his work and his family commitments as an excuse not to go up to see her.

What good would it do to go to Washington and talk to her? It would only upset everyone involved. He couldn't possibly take on a responsibility like that. Her grandparents were good people.

He'd done a background check on them when they'd filed for custody. Just tying up loose ends, he told himself now as he'd told himself then. And maybe in the first couple of years he'd done a few more checks – just to make sure the kid was settling in all right.

Then he'd closed the book. He meant it to stay closed.

He was a cop, he reminded himself as he turned down the street toward home. He wasn't a psychologist, a social worker, and his only connection to Olivia was murder.

It couldn't possibly help her to talk to him.

He pulled into the drive behind a bright blue Honda Civic. It had replaced his wife's VW four years before. Both bumpers were crowded with stickers. His wife might have given up her beloved Bug, but she hadn't given up her causes.

Noah's bike had been upgraded to a secondhand Buick the boy pampered like a lover. He'd be loading it up and driving it off to college in a matter of weeks. The thought of that struck Frank as it always did – like an arrow to the heart.

The flowers that danced around the door thrived, due to Noah's attention. God knew where he'd gotten the green thumb, Frank thought as he climbed out of the car. Once the boy was away at school, both he and Celia would kill the blooms within a month.

He stepped in the front door to the sound of Fleetwood Mac. His heart sank. Celia liked to cook to Fleetwood Mac, and if she'd decided to cook it meant that Frank would be sneaking into the kitchen in the middle of the night, searching out his well-hidden stashes of junk food.

The living room was tidy – another bad sign. The fact that there were no newspapers or shoes scattered around meant Celia had gotten off early from her job at the women's shelter and was feeling domestic.

He and Noah suffered when Celia shifted into a domestic mode. There would be a home-cooked meal that had much more to do with nutrition than taste, a tidy house where he'd never be able to find anything and very likely freshly folded laundry. Which meant half his socks would be missing.

Things ran much more smoothly in the Brady household when Celia left the domestic chores to her men.

When Frank stepped into the kitchen, his worst fears were confirmed. Celia stood happily stirring something at the stove. There was a fresh loaf of some kind of tree-bark bread on the counter beside an enormous yellow squash.

But she looked so damn pretty, he thought, with her bright hair pulled back in a smooth ponytail, her narrow, teenage-boy hips bumping to the beat and her long, slim feet bare.

She carried a look of competent innocence that he'd always thought disguised a boundless determination. There was nothing Celia Brady wanted to accomplish that she didn't manage to do.

Just, he thought, as she'd managed him one way or another since she'd been a twenty-year-old coed and he the twenty-three-year-old rookie who'd arrested her during a protest against animal testing.

The first two weeks of their relationship they'd spent arguing. The second two weeks they'd spent in bed. She'd refused to marry him, so they'd fought about that. But he had his own share of determination. During the year they'd lived together, he'd worn her down.

Unexpectedly he came up behind her and hugged her tight. 'I love you, Celia.'

She turned in his arms and gave him a quick kiss. 'You're still eating the black beans and squash. It's good for you.'

He figured he'd live through it – and he had mini-pizzas buried in the depths of the freezer. 'I'll eat it, and I'll still love you. I'm a tough guy. Where's Noah?'

'Out shooting hoops with Mike. He's got a date with Sarah later.'

'Again?'

Celia had to smile. 'She's a very nice girl, Frank. And with him going off to college in a few weeks, they want to spend as much time together as they can.'

'I just wish he wasn't so hung up on this one girl. He's only eighteen.'

'Frank, after a half term in college, Sarah won't be more than a vague memory. Now, what's really wrong?'

He didn't bother to sigh, but took the beer she held out to him. 'Do you remember the MacBride case?'

'Julie MacBride?' Celia's eyebrows lifted. 'Of course. It was the biggest high-profile case of your career, and you still get sad if one of her movies comes on TV. But what about the MacBride case? You closed it years ago. Sam Tanner's in prison.'

'The little girl.'

'Yes, I remember. she broke your heart.' Celia rubbed his arm. 'Softie.'

'Her grandparents got custody, took her up to Washington State. They own a place up there, lodge, campground on the Olympic Peninsula. Attached to the national forest.'

'The Olympic National Forest?' Celia's eyes went bright. 'Oh, that's beautiful country. I hiked up that way the summer I graduated from high school. They've really kept the greedy bloodsuckers at bay.'

To Celia greedy bloodsuckers were anyone who wanted to chop down a tree, demolish an old building, hunt rabbits or pour concrete over farmland.

'Tree hugger.'

'Ha ha. If you had any idea how much damage can be done by loggers who don't have the foresight to—'

'Don't start, Cee, I'm already eating beans and squash.'

She pouted a moment, then shrugged a shoulder and started to rise. Since putting her back up hadn't been part of his strategy, he reached in his pocket for the letter. 'Just read this, and tell me what you think.'

'So now you're interested in what I think.' But after reading the first couple lines, she sat again, and the light of battle in her eyes melted into compassion. 'Poor little thing,' she murmured. 'She's so sad. And so brave.'

She smoothed her fingers over the letter, then handed it back to Frank before she went back to stir her pot. 'You know, Frank, a family vacation before Noah heads off to college would be good for all of us. And we haven't been camping since he was three and you took an oath never to spend another night sleeping on the ground.'

Half the weight the letter had put on his shoulders slid off. 'I really do love you, Celia.'

Olivia did her best to behave normally, to tuck the nerves and excitement away so her grandparents wouldn't notice. Inside, she was breathless and jittery, and her head ached a little, but she did her morning chores and managed to eat a little lunch so no one would comment on her lack of appetite.

The Bradys would be there soon.

She'd been relieved when her grandfather had been called to the campground right after lunch to handle some little snag. It hadn't been hard to make excuses to stay behind instead of going with him, though she'd felt guilty about being less than honest.

The guilt had her working twice as hard as she might have on cleaning the terrace outside the lodge dining room and weeding the gardens that bordered it.

It was also the perfect spot from which to watch arrivals and departures.

Olivia weeded the nasturtiums that tumbled over the low stone wall in cheery yellows and oranges, deadheaded the bright white Shasta daisies behind them and kept one eye on the turn toward Reception.

Her hands sweated inside her garden gloves, which she'd worn only because she wanted to be adult and shake hands with the Brady family without having grime on her fingers and under her fingernails. She wanted Frank to see that she was grown-up enough to understand about her mother, about her father.

She didn't want him to see a scared little girl who needed to be protected from monsters.

She was going to learn to chase the monsters away herself, Olivia thought. Then, despite her plans, she absently swiped a hand over her cheek and smeared it with soil.

She'd brushed her hair and smoothed it into a neat ponytail that she'd slipped through the opening in the back of her red cap. She wore jeans and a River's End T-shirt. Both had been clean that morning, and though she'd tried to keep them that way, the knees of her jeans were soiled now.

That would only prove that she'd been working, she told herself. That she was responsible.

They should be here by now, she thought. They had to be here soon, they just had to. Otherwise her grandfather might come back. He might recognize Frank Brady. He probably would. Grandfather remembered everyone and everything. Then he'd find ways to keep her from talking to Frank, to keep her from asking questions. All the planning, the care, the hopes she had would be for nothing if they didn't get there soon.

A couple strolled out onto the terrace, sat at one of the little iron tables. One of the staff would come out to serve them drinks or snacks, Olivia knew. Then she'd lose the solitude.

Olivia worked her way along the border, half listening as the woman read about the trails in her guidebook. Planning tomorrow's hike, debating whether to take one of the long ones and order one of the picnic lunches the lodge provided.

Ordinarily Olivia might have stopped working long enough to recommend just that plan, to give her own description of the trail the woman seemed to favor. The guests enjoyed the personal touch, and her grandparents encouraged her to share her knowledge of the area with them. But she had too much on her mind for chit-chat and continued to work steadily down the edge of the terrace until she was nearly out of sight.

She saw the big old car bumping up the drive, but noted immediately that the man driving it was too young to be Frank Brady. He had a pretty face – what she could see of it, as he wore a cap and sunglasses. His hair spilled out of the cap, wavy and sun-streaked brown.

The woman in the passenger seat was pretty, too. His mother, Olivia guessed, though she didn't look very old either. Maybe she was his aunt, or his big sister.

She ran through the reservations in her head, trying to remember if they had a couple coming in that day, then she spotted another figure sprawled in the backseat.

Her heart began to thud in her chest, the answering echo a dull beat in her head. Slowly she got to her feet as the car coasted around the last turn and parked.

She knew him right away. Olivia didn't consider it at all strange that her bleary memory of his face shot into sharp focus the minute Frank stepped out of the car. She remembered perfectly now, the color of his eyes, the sound of his voice, the way his hand had felt, big and gentle on her cheek.

Her aching head spun, once, sickly, as he turned his head and saw her. She felt her knees tremble, but she pulled off her gloves and stuck them in her back pocket. Her mouth was dust dry, but she forced a polite smile on her face and started forward.

So did he.

For Olivia, at that moment, the woman and the young man who got out of the car faded into the background. As did the wall of great trees, the searing blue sky above them, the flutter of butterflies, the chatter of birds.

She saw only him, as she'd seen only him the night he'd opened the closet door.

'I'm Olivia,' she said in a voice that sounded very far away to her own ears. 'Thank you for coming, Detective Brady.' She held out her hand.

How many times, Frank wondered, would this one little girl break his heart? She stood so poised, her eyes so solemn, her smile so polite. And her voice shook.

'It's nice to see you again, Olivia.' He took her hand in his, held it. 'Livvy. Don't they call you Livvy anymore?'

'Yes.' Her smile warmed, just a little. 'Did you have a nice trip?'

'Very nice. We decided to drive, so we needed my son's car. It's the only one big enough to be comfortable for that long. Celia?'

He reached out, then slipped his arm around his wife's shoulders. It was a gesture Olivia noticed. She liked to study the way people were together. The woman fit easily against him, and her smile was friendly. Her eyes sympathetic.

'This is Celia, my wife.'

'Hello, Livvy. What a beautiful place. You know I camped in your campgrounds once, when I was Noah's age. I've never forgotten this area. Noah, this is Livvy MacBride, her family owns the lodge.'

He glanced over, nodded – polite but distant. 'Hey' was all he said as he tucked his hands in his back pockets. Behind the dark glasses, he took in every feature of her face.

She was taller than he expected. Gangly. He reminded himself his image of her was stuck on the little girl with her hands clamped over her ears and her face wild with fear and grief.

He'd never forgotten how she'd looked. He'd never forgotten her.

'Noah's a man of few words these days,' Celia said soberly, but the way her eyes laughed had Olivia smiling again.

'You can leave your car here if you want while you check in. All the lake-view units were booked, but you have a really nice view of the forest. It's one of the family units on the ground floor and has its own patio.'

'It sounds wonderful. I remember taking pictures of the lodge all those years ago.' To put Olivia at ease, Celia laid a hand on her shoulder and turned to study the building. 'It looks as if it grew here, like the trees.'

It was grand and old and dignified. Three stories, with the main section under a steeply pitched roof. Windows were generous, to offer the guests stunning views. The wood had weathered to a soft brown and, with the deep green trim, seemed as much a part of the forest as the giant trees that towered over it.

Pathways were fashioned of stone with small evergreens and clumps of ferns and wildflowers scattered throughout. Rather than manicured, the ground looked appealingly wild and untouched.

'It's not intrusive at all. Whoever built it understood the importance of working with nature instead of beating it back.'

'My great-grandfather. He did the original building, then he and his brother and my grandfather added on to it. He named it, too.' Olivia resisted the urge to rub her damp palms on her jeans. 'There's no river that ends here or anything. It's a metaphor.'

'For finding rest and shelter at the end of a journey,' Celia suggested and made Olivia smile.

'Yeah, exactly. That's what he wanted to do. It was really just an inn at first, and now it's a resort. But we want that same restful atmosphere and are dedicated to preserving the area and seeing to it that the lodge adds to rather than detracts from the purity of the forest and lakes.'

'You're talking her language.' Frank winked. 'Celia's a staunch conservationist.'

'So is anyone with brains,' Olivia said automatically and had Celia nodding in approval.

'We're going to get along just fine. Why don't you show me

around the lodge while these big strong men deal with the luggage?'

Olivia glanced back at Frank as Celia led her off. Impatience all but shimmered around her, but she did as she was asked and opened one half of the great double doors.

'I never made it inside during my other trip,' Celia was saying. 'I was on a pretty tight budget, and I was busy turning my nose up at any established creature comforts. I was one of the first hippies.'

Olivia stopped, blinked. 'Really? You don't look like a hippy.'

'I only wear my love beads on special occasions now – like the anniversary of Woodstock.'

'Was Frank a hippy, too?'

'Frank?' Celia threw back her head and laughed in sheer delight. 'Oh no, not Mister Conservative. That man was born a cop – and a Republican. Well,' she said with a sigh, 'what can you do? Oh, but this is lovely.'

She turned a half circle in the main lobby, admiring the floors and walls of natural pine and fir, the great stone fireplace filled in the warmth of August with fresh flowers rather than flames. Chairs and sofas in soft earth tones were arranged in cozy groups.

Several guests were enjoying coffee or wine while they sat and contemplated the views or studied their guidebooks.

There was Native American art in paintings and wall hangings and rugs, and copper pails that held generous bouquets of fresh flowers or greenery.

It seemed more like a sprawling living room than a lobby, which, Celia imagined, had been just the intention.

The front desk was a polished wood counter manned by two clerks in crisp white shirts and hunter green vests. Daily activities were handwritten on an old slate board, and a stoneware bowl of pastel-colored mints sat on the counter.

'Welcome to River's End.' The female clerk had a quick grin for Olivia before she turned a welcoming smile on Celia. 'Will you be staying with us?'

'Yes, Celia Brady and family. My husband and son are getting our luggage.'

'Yes, Mrs. Brady, we're happy to have you.' While she spoke, the clerk tapped her fingers over the keyboard below the counter. 'I hope you had a pleasant trip.'

'Very.' Celia noted the name tag pinned to the vest. 'Thank you, Sharon.'

'And you'll be staying with us for five nights. You have our family package, which includes breakfast for three every morning, any one of our guided tours . . .'

Olivia tuned out Sharon's welcome address and explanation and looked toward the door. Her stomach began to flutter again as Frank came in with Noah behind him. They were loaded down with luggage and backpacks.

'I can help you with that. Sharon, I can show the Bradys to their rooms and tell them where everything is.'

'Thanks, Livvy. You can't do better than with a MacBride as your guide, Mrs. Brady. Enjoy your stay.'

'It's this way.' Struggling not to hurry, Olivia led the way down a hallway off the lobby, turned right. 'The health club is to the left and complimentary to guests. You can reach the pool through there or by going out the south entrance.'

She rattled off information, meal service times, room service availability, lounge hours, rental information for canoes, fishing gear, bikes.

At the door to their rooms, she stood back, and despite nerves found herself pleased when Celia let out a little gasp of pleasure.

'It's great! Just great! Oh, Frank, look at that view. It's like being in the middle of the forest.' She moved immediately to the patio doors and flung them open. 'Why do we live in the city?'

'It has something to do with employment,' Frank said dryly.

'The master bedroom is in here, and the second bedroom there.'

'I'll go dump my stuff.' Noah headed off to the other end of the sitting room.

'You'll want to unpack, get settled in.' Olivia linked her hands together, pulled them apart. 'Is there anything I can get you, or any questions . . . I – there are some short, easy trails if you want to do any exploring this afternoon.'

'Frank, why don't you play scout?' Celia smiled, unable to resist the plea in Olivia's eyes. 'Noah and I will probably laze by the pool for a bit. Livvy can show you around now and you can stretch your legs.'

'Good idea. Do you mind, Livvy?'

'No. No, I don't mind. We can go right out this way.' She

gestured to the patio doors. 'There's an easy half-mile loop; you don't even need any gear.'

'Sounds perfect.' He kissed Celia, ran a hand down her arm. 'See you in a bit.'

'Take your time.' She walked to the door after them, watched the girl lead the man toward the trees.

'Mom?'

She didn't turn, kept watching until the two figures slipped into the shadows of the forest. 'Hmmm?'

'Why didn't you tell me?'

'Tell you what, Noah?'

'That's Julie MacBride's kid, isn't it?'

Celia turned now to where Noah stood in the doorway of his room, his shoulder nonchalantly propped against the frame, his eyes alert and just a bit annoyed.

'Yes. Why?'

'We didn't come up here to play in the woods and go fishing. Dad hates fishing, and his idea of a vacation is lying in the hammock in the backyard.'

She nearly laughed. It was exactly true. 'What's your point?'

'He came up to see the kid. Does that mean something new's come up on the Julie MacBride murder?'

'No. It's nothing like that. I didn't know you had any interest in that business, Noah.'

'Why wouldn't I?' He pushed away from the doorway and picked up one of the bright red apples in a blue bowl on the table. 'It was Dad's case, and a big one. People still talk about it. And he thinks about it.' Noah jerked his chin in the direction his father had taken. 'Even if he doesn't talk about it. What's the deal, Mom?'

Celia lifted her shoulders, let them fall. 'The girl – Olivia – wrote to him. She has some questions. I don't think her grandparents have told her very much, and I don't think they know she wrote your father. So, let's give the two of them a little room.'

'Sure.' Noah bit into the apple, and his gaze drifted toward the window where the tall young girl had led the man toward the trees. 'I was just wondering.'

Chapter Eight

The trees closed them in, like giant bars in an ancient prison. Frank had expected a kind of openness and charm, and instead found himself uneasily walking through a strange world where the light glowed eerily green and nature came in odd, primitive shapes.

Even the sounds and smells were foreign, potent and ripe. Dampness clung to the air. He'd have been more comfortable in a dark alley in East L.A.

He caught himself glancing over his shoulder and wishing for the comforting weight of his weapon.

'You ever get lost in here?' he asked Olivia.

'No, but people do sometimes. You should always carry a compass, and stay on the marked trails if you're a novice.' She tipped up her face to study his. 'I guess you're an urban hiker.'

He grinned at the term. 'You got that right.'

She smiled, and the humor made her eyes glow. 'Aunt Jamie said that's what she is now. But you can get lost in the city, too, can't you?'

'Yeah. Yeah, you can.'

She looked away now, slowing her pace. 'It was nice of you to come. I didn't think you would. I wasn't sure you'd even remember me.'

'I remember you, Livvy.' He touched her arm lightly, felt the stiffness and control a twelve-year-old shouldn't have. 'I've thought about you, wondered how you were.'

'My grandparents are great. I love living here. I can't imagine living anywhere else. People come here for vacation, but I get to live here all the time.' She said it all very fast, as if she needed to get out everything good before she turned a corner.

'You have a nice family,' she began.

'Thanks. I think I'll probably keep them.'

Her smile came and went quickly. 'I have a nice family, too. But I . . . That's a nurse log,' she pointed out as nerves crept back into her voice. 'When a tree falls, or branches do, the forest makes use of them. Nothing's wasted here. That's a Douglas fir, and you can see the sprouts of western hemlock growing out of it, and the spread of moss, the ferns and mushrooms. When something dies here, it gives other things a chance to live.'

She looked up at him again, her eyes a shimmering amber behind a sheen of tears. 'Why did my mother die?'

'I can't answer that, Livvy. I can never really answer the why, and it's the hardest part of my job.'

'It was a waste, wasn't it? A waste of something good and beautiful. She was good and beautiful, wasn't she?'

'Yes, yes she was.'

With a nod, she began to walk again and didn't speak until she was certain she'd fought back the tears. 'But my father wasn't. He couldn't have been good and beautiful, not really. But she fell in love with him, and she married him.'

'Your father had problems.'

'Drugs,' she said flatly. 'I read about it in newspapers my grandmother has put away in our attic. He took drugs and he killed her. He couldn't have loved her. He couldn't have loved either of us.'

'Livvy, life isn't always that simple, that black-and-white.'

'If you love something, you take care of it. You protect it. If you love enough, you'd die to protect it.' She spoke softly, but her voice was fierce. 'He says he didn't do it. But he did. I saw him. I can still see him if I let myself.' She pressed her lips together. 'He would have killed me, too, if I hadn't gotten away.'

'I don't know.' How did he answer this child, with her quiet voice and old eyes. 'It's possible.'

'You talked to him. After.'

'Yes. That's part of my job.'

'Is he crazy?'

Frank opened his mouth, closed it again. There were no pat answers here. 'The court didn't think so.'

'But did you?'

Frank let out a sigh. He could see how they'd circled around now, see parts of the roofline, the glint of the windows of the inn. 'Livvy, I think he was weak, and the drugs played into that weakness. They made him believe things that weren't true and do things that weren't right. Your mother separated from him to protect you as much, probably more, than herself. And, I think, hoping it would push him into getting help.'

But it didn't, Olivia thought. It didn't make him get help, it didn't protect anyone.

'If he wasn't living there anymore, why was he in the house that night?'

'The evidence indicated she let him in.'

'Because she still loved him.' She shook her head before Frank could answer. 'It's all right. I understand. Will they keep him in jail forever?'

There are so few forevers, Frank thought. 'He was given a sentence of twenty years to life, the first fifteen without possibility of parole.'

Her eyes narrowed in a frown of concentration. Fifteen years was longer than she'd been alive, but it wasn't enough. 'Does that mean he can just get out in seven more years? Just like that, after what he did?'

'No, not necessarily. The system ...' How could he possibly explain the twists and turns of it to a child? 'He'll go before a panel, like a test.'

'But the people on the panel don't know. They weren't there. It won't matter to them.'

'Yes, it will matter. I can go.' And he would, Frank decided, and speak for the child. 'I'm allowed to go and address the panel because I was there.'

'Thank you.' The tears wanted to come back, so she held out a hand to shake his. 'Thank you for talking to me.'

'Livvy.' He took her hand, then touched his free one to her cheek. 'You can call or write me anytime you want.'

'Really?'

'I'd like it if you did.'

The tears stopped burning, her nerves smoothed out. 'Then I will. I'm really glad you came. I hope you and your family have a good time. If you want, I can sign you up for one of the guided hikes while you're here, or I can show you which trails you can take on your own.'

Going with instinct, Frank smiled at her. 'We'd like that, but only if we can hire you as guide. We want the best.'

She studied him with calm and sober eyes. 'Skyline Trail's only thirty-one miles.' When his mouth fell open, she smiled a little. 'Just kidding. I know a nice day hike if you like to take pictures.'

'What's your definition of a nice day hike?'

Her grin flashed, quick and surprising. 'Just a couple of miles. You'll see beaver and osprey. The lodge can make up a boxed lunch if you want a picnic.'

'Sold. How about tomorrow?'

'I'll check with my grandfather, but it should be all right. I'll come by about eleven-thirty.' She glanced down at his scuffed hightops. 'You'd be better off with boots, but those are okay if you don't have them. I'll see you tomorrow.'

'Livvy?' he called when she turned back toward the trees. 'Should I buy a compass?'

She tossed a quick smile over her shoulder. 'I won't let you get lost.'

She walked into the trees, going fast now until she was sure no one could see. Then she stopped, hugging herself hard, rocking, letting the tears spill out.

They were hot and stinging; her chest ached with them as it hitched. But after they'd fallen, after she was able to breathe again, to scrub her face dry with her hands, she felt better.

And at age twelve, Olivia decided what she would do with and how she would live her life. She would learn all there was to learn about the forest, the lakes, the mountains that were her home. She would live and she would work in the place she loved, the place where her mother had grown up.

She would, over time, find out more about her mother. And about the man who killed her. She would love the first with all her heart. Just as she would hate the second.

And she would never, never fall in love the way her mother had.

She would become her own woman. Starting now.

She stopped to wash her face in the stream, then sat quietly until she was sure all traces of tears and tattered emotions were gone. Her grandparents were to be protected – that was another promise she made herself. She would see to it that nothing she did ever caused them pain.

So when she walked into the clearing and saw her grandfather weeding his flowers, she crossed to him, knelt beside him with a smile. 'I just did this over at the lodge. The gardens look really nice there.'

'You got my green thumb, kiddo.' He winked at her. 'We won't talk about the color of your grandmother's.'

'She does okay with houseplants. A family just checked into the lodge. A couple and their son.' Casually, Olivia uprooted a weed. She didn't want to lie to him, but she thought it wisest to skirt around the bare truth. 'The mother said she'd hiked around here when she was a teenager, but I don't think the other two know a bush from a porcupine. Anyway, they'd like me to go out with them tomorrow, just a short hike. I thought I'd take them to Irely Lake, along the river so they could take pictures.'

He sat back on his heels, the line of worry already creasing his forehead. 'I don't know, Livvy.'

'I'd like to do it. I know the way, and I want to start learning even more about running the lodge and campground, more about the trails and even the backcountry areas. I've gone along on guided hikes before, and I want to see if I can do one by myself. It's just down to Irely. If I do a good job, I could start training to guide other hikes during the summer and maybe give talks and stuff for kids. When I'm older, I could even do overnights, and be a naturalist like they have in the park. Only I'd be better, because I grew up here. Because it's home.'

He reached out to skim his knuckles over her cheek. He could see Julie in her eyes, Julie, when she'd been a young girl and telling him of her dreams to be a great actress. Her dream had taken her away from him. Olivia's would keep her close.

'You're still young enough to change your mind a dozen times.'

'I won't. But anyway, I won't know if I'm good or if it's really what I want until I try. I want to try, just a little bit, tomorrow.'

'Just down to Irely?'

'I showed the father the loop trail from the inn before I left. He kept talking about getting lost.' She shared an easy chuckle with Rob. 'I think Irely's about all he can handle.'

Knowing she'd won, she got up, brushed off her jeans. 'I'm going to go see if Grandma needs any help with dinner.' Then she stopped, leaned down to wrap her arms around Rob's neck. 'I'm going to make you proud of me.'

'I am proud of you, baby.'

She hugged tighter. 'Just wait,' she whispered, then darted inside.

Olivia was exactly on time. She'd decided that would be important to how she lived her life from now on. She would always be prompt; she would always be prepared.

She arrived early at the lodge to collect the boxed lunch for the hike. It would be her job to carry the supplies. She was young and strong, she thought as she stowed them in her backpack. She would get older, and she would get stronger.

She shouldered the pack, adjusted the straps.

She had her compass, her knife, bottled water, spare plastic bags to seal up any trash or garbage, her camera, a notepad and pencils, a first-aid kit.

She'd spent three hours the night before reading, studying, absorbing information and history. She was going to see to it that the Bradys had an entertaining, and an educational, afternoon.

When she walked around to the patio entrance of the unit, she saw Noah sitting in one of the wooden chairs. He was wearing headphones and tapping his fingers restlessly on the arm of the chair. His legs were long, clad in ripped jeans and stretched out to cross at the ankles of high-top Nikes.

He wore sunglasses with very dark lenses. It occurred to her she'd yet to see him without them. His hair was damp as if he'd recently come from the shower or the pool. It was casually slicked back and drying in the sun.

She thought he looked like a rock star.

Shyness wanted to swallow her, but she straightened her shoulders. If she was going to be a guide, she had to learn to get over being shy around boys and everyone else. 'Hi.'

His head moved a little, his fingers stopped tapping. She realized he'd probably had his eyes closed behind those black lenses and hadn't even seen her.

'Yeah, hi.' He reached down to turn off the cassette that was singing in his ears. 'I'll get the troops.'

When he stood up, she had to tip back her head to keep her eyes on his face. 'Did you try the pool?'

'Yeah.' He gave her a grin and had the woman's heart still sleeping in the child's breast stirring. 'Water's cold.' He opened the patio door. 'Hey, the trailblazer's here.' There was a muffled response from behind the bedroom door before he turned back to Olivia. 'You might as well sit down. Mom's never ready on time.'

'There's no hurry.'

'Good thing.'

Deciding it was more polite to sit since he'd asked her to, she lowered herself to the stone patio. She fell into a silence that was part shyness and part simple inexperience.

Noah studied her profile. She interested him because of her connection to his father and to Julie MacBride and, he admitted, because of her connection to murder. Murder fascinated him.

He would have asked her about it if he hadn't been certain both his parents would have skinned him for it. He might have risked that, but he remembered the image of the small child with her hands over her ears and tears flooding her cheeks.

'So . . . what do you do around here?'

Her gaze danced in his direction, then away. 'Stuff.' She felt the heat climb into her cheeks at the foolishness of the answer.

'Oh yeah, stuff. We never do that in California.'

'Well, I do chores, help out at the campground and here at the lodge. I hike and fish. I'm learning about the history of the area, the flora and fauna, that sort of thing.'

'Where do you go to school?'

'My grandmother teaches me at home.'

'At home?' He tipped down his sunglasses so she got a glimpse of deep green eyes. 'Some deal.'

'She's pretty strict,' Olivia mumbled, then leaped to her feet in relief when Frank stepped out.

'Celia's coming. I figured I should go get our lunch.'

'I have it.' Olivia shifted her pack. 'Cold fried chicken, potato salad, fruit and pound cake. Sal, that's the chef, he makes the best.'

'You shouldn't carry all that,' Frank began, but she stepped back.

'It's part of my job.' Then she looked past him, saw Celia and felt shy again. 'Good morning, Mrs. Brady.'

'Good morning. I saw a deer out my window this morning. She stepped through the fog like something out of a fairy tale. By the time I snapped out of it and dug out my camera, she was gone.'

'You'll probably see more. The blacktail is common in the

forest. You might catch sight of a Roosevelt elk, too.'

Celia tapped the camera hanging from a strap around her neck as she stepped out. 'This time, I'm prepared.'

'If you're ready, we'll get started.' Olivia had already, subtly she hoped, checked out their shoes and clothes and gear. It would do well enough for the short, easy hike. 'You can stop me anytime you want to take pictures or rest or ask questions. I don't know how much you know about Olympic, or the rain forest,' she began as she started the walk.

She'd practiced her presentation that morning as she'd dressed and led into it very much as she had when her aunt had played tourist for her.

When she mentioned bear, Celia didn't squeal as Jamie had, but sighed. 'Oh, I'd love to see one.'

'Jeez, Mom, you would.'

Celia laughed and hooked an arm around Noah's neck. 'Hopeless city boys, Livvy. Both of them. You've got your work cut out for you with these two.'

'That's okay, it's good practice.'

She identified trees for them, but got the feeling only Celia was particularly interested. Though Noah did seem to perk up when she spotted an eagle for him high in the moss- and lichen-draped trees. But when she cut over to the river and the world opened up a bit, all three of her charges seemed to get into the spirit.

'This is the Quinault,' Olivia told them. 'It runs to the coast. The Olympic Range rings the interior.'

'God, it's beautiful. It takes your breath away.' Celia had her camera up, busily framing and snapping. 'Look at the way the mountains stand against the sky, Frank. White and green and gray against that blue. It's like taking a picture of a painting.'

Olivia scrambled around in her head for what she knew about the mountains. 'Ah, Mount Olympus is actually less than eight thousand feet at its peak, but it rises from the rain forest at almost sea level, so it looks bigger. It has, I think it's six, glaciers. We're on the western slopes of the range.'

She led them along the river, pointing out the clever dams the beavers built, the stringlike petals of wild goldthread, the delicate white of marsh marigold. They passed other hikers on the trail, singles and groups.

Celia stopped often for pictures, and her men posed with

patience if not enthusiasm. When Olivia managed to catch a red-legged frog, Celia took pictures of that as well, laughing in delight when it let out its long feeble croak.

Then she surprised Olivia by stroking a long finger over the frog's back. Hardly any of the women Olivia knew wanted to pet frogs. When she released it, she and Celia smiled at each other in perfect unity.

'Your mother's found a soul sister,' Frank muttered to Noah.

Olivia was about to point out an osprey nest when a toddler raced down the trail, evading the young parents who called and rushed after him.

He tripped and came to a skidding halt on knees and elbows almost at Olivia's feet. And wailed like a thousand bagpipes.

She started to bend down, but Noah was faster and had the boy scooped up, jiggling him cheerfully. 'Uh-oh. Wipeout.'

'Scotty! Oh, honey, I told you not to run!' The frantic mother grabbed for him, then looked back at her out-of-breath husband. 'He's bleeding. He's scraped his knees.'

'Damn it. How bad? Let's see, buddy.'

As the boy screamed and sobbed, Olivia slipped off her pack. 'You'll need to wash his cuts. I have some bottled water and a first-aid kit.'

She went to work so efficiently, Frank signaled Celia back.

'You'll have to hold him still,' Olivia said. 'I can't clean it if he's kicking.'

'I know it hurts, honey, I know. We're going to make it all better.' The mother kissed Scotty's cheeks. 'Here, let me clean off the cuts. Thanks so much.' She took the cloth Olivia had dampened and struggled with her husband to keep the child still long enough to see the damage.

'Just scrapes. Knocked the bark off, buddy.' The father kept his voice light, but his face was very pale as his wife cleaned the blood away.

Olivia handed over antiseptic, and one glance at the little bottle had Scotty switching from wails to ear-piercing screams.

'Hey, you know what you need.' Noah pulled a candy bar out of his back pocket, waved it in front of Scotty's face. 'You need to spoil your lunch.'

Scotty eyed the chocolate bar through fat tears. His lips

trembled, but instead of a screech he let out a pitiful whimper. 'Candy.'

'You bet. You like candy? This is pretty special candy. It's only for brave boys. I bet you're brave.'

Scotty sniffled, reached out, too intent on the bar to notice his mother quickly bandaging his knees. ''kay'.

'Here you go, then.' Noah held it out, then tugged it just out of reach with a grin. 'I forgot. I can only give this candy to somebody named Scotty.'

'I'm Scotty.'

'No kidding? Then this must be yours.'

'Thanks. Thanks so much.' The mother shifted the now-delighted child to her hip and shoved back her hair with her free hand. 'You're lifesavers.'

Olivia glanced up from where she was repacking her first-aid kit. 'You should make sure you pick up one of these if you're going to do much hiking. The River's End Lodge gift shop carries them, or you can get them in town.'

'First on my list. Along with emergency chocolate. Thanks again.' She looked over to Frank and Celia. 'You've got great kids.'

Olivia started to speak, then ducked her head and said nothing. But not so quickly that Celia hadn't seen the look of unhappiness. 'You two make a good team,' she said cheerfully. 'And that little adventure worked up my appetite. When's lunch, Liv?'

Olivia looked up, blinked. Liv, she thought. It sounded strong and sure and smart. 'There's nice area just a little farther down. We might get lucky and see a couple of beavers instead of just their dams.'

She picked her spot, a shady area just off the trail where they could sit and watch the water, or gaze off toward the mountains. The air was warm, the sky clear in one of those perfect summer days the peninsula could offer.

Olivia nibbled at her chicken and held herself back just a little. She wanted to watch the Bradys together. They seemed so easy, so meshed. Later, when she was older and looked back on that comfortable hour, she would call it a rhythm. They had a rhythm of movement, of speech, of silences. Little bits of humor that were intimately their own, tossed-off comments, teasing, body language.

And she would realize, remembering, that however much she and her grandparents loved one another, they didn't have quite that same connection.

A generation stood between them. Her mother's life, and her death.

But just then all she knew was that she felt a tug of longing, an ache of envy. It made her ashamed. 'I'm going to walk down a little more.' She got up, ordering herself to do so casually. 'I'll see if I can spot some beavers. If I do, I'll come back and get you.'

'Poor little thing,' Celia murmured when Olivia walked down the trail. 'She's lonely. I don't even think she knows how lonely she is.'

'Her grandparents are good people, Celia.'

'I'm sure they are. But where are the other kids? The ones her age she should be playing with on a beautiful day like this?'

'She doesn't even go to school,' Noah put in. 'She told me her grandmother teaches her at home.'

'They've put her in a bubble. A spectacular one,' Celia added as she looked around, 'but it's still closed.'

'They're afraid. They have reason to be.'

'I know, but what will they do when she starts to beat her wings against the bubble? And what will she do if she doesn't?'

Noah got to his feet. 'I think I'll walk down, too. Never seen a beaver.'

'He has a kind heart,' Celia commented, smiling after him.

'Yeah, and he also has a curious mind. I hope he doesn't try to pump her.'

'Give him some credit, Frank.'

'If I didn't, I'd be going to look for beavers, too, instead of taking a nap.' With that, he stretched out and laid his head in his wife's lap.

Noah found her sitting on the bank of the river, very quiet and very still. It made a picture in his mind – very much like, yet so very different from, the one he had of her as a small child running from grief.

Here she simply sat, her cap over her butterscotch hair, her back straight as a die, staring out over water that ran fast and bright and clear.

She wasn't running from grief this time, he thought. She was learning to live with it.

It was sort of her personal river's end, he supposed.

Her head turned quickly at his approach. She kept her gaze steady on his face, those rich eyes of hers solemn, as he moved to her and sat down.

'They come to play here,' she told him in a low voice. 'They don't mind people too much. They get used to them. But you have more luck if you don't make a lot of noise and movement.'

'I guess you spend a lot of time just hanging around.'

'There's always something to see or do.' She kept scanning the river. He made her feel odd in a way she couldn't decide was pleasant or not. She only knew it was different from anything she'd felt before. A kind of drumming just under her heart. 'I guess it's nothing like Los Angeles.'

'Nothing at all.' At that point in his life, L.A. *was* the world. 'It's okay, though. Mom's big on nature and shit. You know, save the whales, save the spotted owl, save the whatever. She gets into it.'

'If more people did, we wouldn't need to save them in the first place.'

She spoke with just enough heat to make him smile. 'Yeah, that's what she says. I got no problem with it. Mostly I like my nature in the city park, with a basketball hoop.'

'I bet you've never even been fishing.'

'Why should I?' He sent her a quick flash of a grin that had the drumming inside her picking up its beat. 'I can walk right into McDonald's and buy a fish sandwich.'

'Yuck.'

'Hey, you want yuck? Sticking a defenseless worm on some hook and drowning it so you can pull up some flopping, slimy fish.' The fact that she smiled a little, that her eyes shimmered with a mild and adult kind of humor, pleased him. 'That's disgusting.'

'That's skill,' she corrected, almost primly, but she was looking at him now, instead of at the river. 'Isn't it crowded in the city, and full of noise and traffic and smog and stuff?'

'Sure.' He leaned back comfortably on his elbows. 'That's why I love it. Something's always happening.'

'Something's always happening here, too. Look.' Forgetting her shyness, she laid a hand on his leg.

A pair of beavers swam cheerfully upriver, their slick heads skimming the surface, ripples shimmying over the water in widening pools around them. Then, like a dream, a heron rose up over the opposite bank and glided with a majestic flap of wings across the river, so close its shadow flowed over them.

'Bet you never saw that in the city.'

'Guess not.'

He amused himself with the beavers. They were really pretty cute, he decided, circling, splashing, flipping over to swim on their backs.

'You know about my mother.'

Noah looked over sharply. She was facing the water again, her face set, her jaw tight. There were a dozen questions he'd wanted to ask if he found the opportunity, but now that she'd opened the door he found he couldn't.

She was just a kid.

'Yeah. It's rough.'

'Have you ever seen any of her movies?'

'Sure. Lots of them.'

Olivia pressed her lips together. She had to know. Someone had to tell her. He would. She hoped he'd treat her like a grown-up instead of someone who needed constant protecting. 'Was she wonderful in them?'

'Haven't you ever seen one?' When she shook her head, he shifted, not sure how to answer. The best answer, his mother often said, was the simple truth. 'She was really good. I mostly like action flicks, you know, but I've watched hers on TV. Man, she was beautiful.'

'I don't mean how she looked.' Her voice snapped out, surprising him into staring. 'I mean how she *was*. Was she a good actress?'

'Sure. Really good. She made you believe. I guess that's what it's all about.'

Olivia's shoulders relaxed. 'Yes.' She nodded. 'She left here because she wanted to act. I just wanted to know if she was good. "She made you believe".' Olivia murmured it, then tucked that single statement into her heart. 'Your father ... he came here because I asked him to. He's a great man. You should know that. You have parents who care about things, about people. You should never forget that.'

She got to her feet. 'I'll go get them so they can see the beavers before we head back.'

Noah sat where he was. He hadn't asked her the questions in his head, but she'd answered one of them. How did it feel to be the daughter of someone famous who'd died in a violent way.

It felt lousy. Just lousy.

Noah

It takes two to speak the truth—
one to speak, and another to hear.

—Henry David Thoreau

Chapter Nine

Washington State University, 1993

There was nothing to be nervous about. Noah reminded himself of that as he checked the address of the trim two-story house. He'd been planning this trip, this connection for a long time. And that, he supposed as he parked his rental car at the curb in the quiet tree-lined neighborhood, was exactly why he was nervous.

Maybe he sensed his life could change today, that seeing Olivia MacBride again could alter the course he was on. He was willing to take that new direction. There was no gain without risk, after all. That's where the damp palms and jumpy belly came from.

It was nothing personal.

He combed back his hair by using the fingers of his hands in two quick rakes. He'd thought about getting a trim before coming here, but hell, he was on vacation.

More or less.

Two weeks away from the newspaper, where his struggle to make a name for himself as a crime reporter wasn't as satisfying as he'd thought it would be. Politics, print space, editors and advertising concerns got in the way of stories he wanted to tell.

And he wanted to tell them his way.

That was why he was here. To write the one story he'd never been able to forget, and to tell it his way.

Julie MacBride's murder.

One of the keys to it lived on the second floor of this pretty house that had been converted into four apartments. They and others like it had been designed to accommodate the overflow from the college campus. For those who could afford separate housing, he thought. Who could pay the price for privacy. And who wanted it badly enough – who didn't look for the pace and companionship, the bursts of energy in college life.

Personally, he'd loved his years on campus at UCLA. Maybe the first semester had been mostly a blur of parties, girls and drunken late-night philosophical discussions only the young could understand. But he'd buckled down after that.

He'd wanted his degree in journalism. And his parents would have killed him if he'd washed out.

Those two incentives had worked for him in equal measure.

And what, he wondered, was Olivia's incentive?

If after nearly three years on the job he'd learned he wasn't a reporter at heart, he was still a good one. He'd done his research. He knew Olivia MacBride was majoring in natural resource science, that her grades were a straight four point oh. He knew she'd spent one year, her freshman year, on campus in a dorm. And that she'd moved out and into her own apartment the following fall.

He knew she belonged to no clubs or sororities and was monitoring two extra classes while shouldering an eighteen-credit load during her spring semester.

That told him she was focused, dedicated and probably a little more than obsessive about her studies.

But there were things he couldn't research through computers, through transcripts. It didn't tell him what she wanted, what she hoped for.

What she felt about her parents.

To know all that, he needed to know her. To write the book that fermented in the back of his heart and his mind, he had to get inside her head.

The two images of her that burned brightest in his mind were of the child's tear-stained face and the young girl's solemn eyes. As he walked into the house, noted the hallway cutting the space precisely in two, he wondered what he would see now.

He climbed the steps, noted the small plaque that identified apartment 2-B. No name, he thought. Just the number. The MacBrides still guarded their privacy like the last gold coin in an empty sack.

'Here goes nothing,' he muttered, and pressed the buzzer.

He had a couple of basic plans of approach in mind, believing it best to be flexible until he gauged his ground. Then she opened the door and every plan, every practical thought ran out of his mind like water from a tipped bowl. Slow and steady and completely.

She wasn't beautiful, certainly not if you measured her by her mother's staggering image. It was almost impossible to do otherwise when you saw the eyes, rich golden brown under slashing dark brows.

She was tall and slim, but with an efficient toughness to her build he found surprisingly, almost ridiculously sexy. Her hair had darkened since he'd seen her last, but was shades lighter than her eyes and drawn back in a smooth ponytail that left her face unframed.

The child's face had refined, sharpened and taken on the edge of young womanhood Noah always thought of as faintly feline.

She wore jeans, a WSU sweatshirt, no shoes and a vaguely annoyed expression.

He found himself standing, staring foolishly, unable to do anything but grin at her.

She cocked one of those killer eyebrows, and a surprising kick of lust joined his sheer pleasure at seeing her again. 'If you're looking for Linda, she's across the hall. Two-A.'

She said it as though she said it often and in a voice that was throatier than he remembered.

'I'm not looking for Linda. I'm looking for you.' And the thought crossed his mind that he always had been. That was so absurd, he dismissed it immediately. 'And you just put a huge hole in my ego by not remembering me.'

'Why should I remember . . .?' She trailed off, focusing those fascinating eyes on him as she hadn't when she'd thought he was just another of the nuisance men who flocked around her across-the-hall neighbor. And as she did, her lips parted, those eyes warmed. 'You're Noah. Noah Brady. Frank's son.' Her gaze shifted from his, over his shoulder. 'Is he—'

'No, it's just me. Got a minute?'

'Yes. Yes, of course. Come in.' Flustered, she stepped back. She'd been deep into the writing of a paper on the root symbiosis of fungus. Now she went from being buried in science to flying back over time, into memories.

And into the lovely little crush she'd had on him when she'd been twelve.

'I can make some coffee, or I probably have something cold.'

'Either's fine.' He took the first-time visitor's circling scan of the tidy room, the organized desk with its humming computer, the soft cream walls, the deep blue sofa. The space was compact, creatively arranged and comfortably simple. 'Nice place.'

'Yes, I like it.' Relished, hoarded the blissful thrill of living alone for the first time in her life.

She didn't fuss, fluttering around as some women were prone to, apologizing for the mess even when there wasn't one. She simply stood there, looking at him as if she didn't know quite where to begin.

He looked back and wondered the same thing himself.

'Ah . . . I'll just be a minute.'

'No rush.'

He followed her into the kitchen, flustering her again. It was hardly more than a passageway, with stove, refrigerator and sink lining one side and stingy counter space between.

Despite the limited space, he managed to wander around. When he stood at the window, they were close enough to bump shoulders. She rarely let a man get close. 'Coke or coffee?' she asked when she'd pulled open the fridge and taken a quick survey.

'Coke's fine. Thanks.'

He would have taken the can from her, but she was already reaching for a glass.

For God's sake, Olivia, she scolded herself, open your mouth and speak. 'What are you doing in Washington?'

'I'm on vacation.' He smiled at her, and the drumming that had been under her heart six years before started up as if it had never stopped. 'I work for the *L.A. Times*.' She smelled of soap and shampoo, and something else, something subtle. Vanilla, he realized, like the candles his mother liked.

'You're a reporter.'

'I always wanted to write.' He took the glass from her. 'I didn't realize it until I was in college, but that's what I wanted.' And because he felt her wariness slide between them like a band of smoke, he smiled again and decided there was no hurry about telling her what he'd come for. 'I had a couple of weeks coming, and the friend I was going to flake out at the beach with for a few days couldn't get away after all. So I decided to head north.'

'You're not up here on assignment, then.'

'No.' That was the truth, absolutely true, he told himself. 'I'm on my own. I decided to look you up, since you're the only person I know in the entire state of Washington. How do you like college?'

'Oh, very much.' Making a deliberate effort to relax, she led him back into the living room. 'I miss home off and on, but classes keep me busy.'

She sat on the couch, assuming he'd take the chair, but he sat beside her and companionably stretched out his legs. 'What are you working on?' He nodded toward the computer.

'Fungus.' She laughed, took a nervous sip of her drink. He was wonderful to look at, the untidy sun-streaked brown of his hair, the deep green eyes that reminded her of home, the easy sensuality of his smile.

She remembered she'd once thought he looked like a rock star. He still did.

'I'm a natural resource science major.'

He started to tell her he knew, stopped himself. Too many explanations, he thought, and ignored the little whisper of guilt in his ear. 'It fits.'

'Like a glove,' she agreed. 'How are your parents?'

'They're great. You told me once I should appreciate them. I do.' He shifted, his eyes meeting hers, holding hers, until the blood that had always remained calm and cool around men heated. 'More, I guess, since I moved out, got my own place. That distance of the adult child, you know?'

'Yes, I do.'

'Do you still work at the lodge?'

'Summers, over breaks.' Do other men look at me this way? she wondered. Wouldn't she have noticed if one had ever looked at her as if her face were all that mattered? 'I – did you ever learn to fish?'

'No.' He grinned again and his fingers trailed lightly over the back of her hand.

'So it's still fish sandwiches at McDonald's?'

'They never miss. But I can occasionally do better. How about dinner?'

'Dinner?'

'As in eating, the evening meal. Even a natural resource science major must have heard of the ritual evening meal. Why don't you have yours with me tonight?'

Her ritual evening meal usually consisted of whatever she had time to toss together in her miniature kitchen or, failing that, what she picked up on the way home from a late class.

Besides, she had a paper to finish, a test to study for, a lab project to prepare for. And he had the most beautiful green eyes. 'That would be nice.'

'Good. I'll pick you up at seven. Got a favorite place?'

'Place? Oh, no, no, not really.'

'Then I'll surprise you.' He got up, giving her hand an absentminded squeeze as she rose to lead him to the door. 'Don't fill up on fungus,' he told her, and grinned one last time before he left.

Olivia quietly closed the door, quietly turned to lean back against it. She let out a long breath, told herself she was being ridiculous, that she was too old to indulge in silly crushes. Then for the first time in longer than she could remember, she had a purely frivolous thought:

What in God's name was she going to wear?

He'd bring up the subject of her father, of the book, during dinner. Gently, Noah told himself. He wanted her to have time to consider it, to understand what he hoped to do and the vital part she'd play in it.

It couldn't be done without her cooperation. Without her family's. Without, he thought, as he stuck his hands in his pockets and climbed the steps to her apartment again, Sam Tanner.

She wasn't a kid anymore. She'd be sensible. And when she understood his motivations, the results he wanted to accomplish, how could she refuse? The book he wanted to craft wouldn't just be about murder, about blood and death, but about people. The human factor. The motivations, the mistakes, the steps. The heart, he thought.

This kind of story began and ended with the heart. That's what he had to make her understand.

He was connected to it, and had been if not from the minute his father had answered the call to go to the house in Beverly Hills, then from the instant he himself had seen the image of the child on his living-room television screen.

He didn't just want to write about it. He had to.

He'd be straight with her about that.

Before he could push the buzzer of 2-B, the door of 2-A opened.

'Well, hello.'

And this, he thought, must be Linda. The smile was a knee-jerk reaction to the smoldering brunette with laser blue eyes. His blood ran just a few beats faster, as the little red dress painted over female curves meant it to.

He knew her type and appreciated it. Just as he appreciated the way she moved, the metronome sway of hips, as she stepped out into the hall, crossing to him on ice-pick heels the same hot sex color as the dress.

'Can you give me a hand with this? I'm just . . . all thumbs tonight.'

She dangled a thin gold bracelet from her fingertips, breathed in and out slow and deep, just in case he hadn't noticed the really lovely breasts straining against the slick red.

'Sure.' There was nothing more flattering to the male ego than an obvious woman. He took the bracelet, circled it around her wrist and enjoyed the way she shifted her body closer, angled in to tip her face back and look into his.

'If Liv's had you tucked away, it's no wonder she never goes out.'

He fastened the bracelet and wallowed in the come-and-get-me fragrance pumping off Linda's skin. 'Doesn't she?'

'All work and all work, that's our Liv.' She laughed and gave a skilled shake of her head that tossed her luxuriant dark curls. 'Me, I like to play.'

'I bet you do.' He still had Linda's wrist in his hand, and the friendly grin on his face, when the door behind him opened.

He forgot Linda had ever been born. He forgot the book. He very nearly forgot his name.

Olivia was anything but obvious. She stood in the doorway, wearing a dress of quiet blue that covered a lot more area than Linda's red. And made him wonder just what was under all that soft material. She'd left her hair loose so that it fell straight as rain and gave him a glimpse of glints of gold at her ears.

He already knew he'd have to get close, very close, to catch her scent. Her lips were unpainted, her eyes cool.

No, she was definitely not a kid anymore, he thought, thankfully.

'You look great.'

She only lifted her eyebrows, skimmed her gaze over Linda. 'I'll just get a jacket.'

She pivoted, walked back into her apartment on long, wonderful hiker's legs.

There was no reason to be angry, she told herself as she snatched up her jacket and bag. No reason for this grinding sense of disappointment. She wouldn't have known he was flirting with Linda if she hadn't been watching for his car like a love-struck teenager. If she hadn't scurried over to the door to look out the Judas hole and watch him come toward the door.

There was no point in feeling let down because she had agonized for two hours over the right dress, the right hairstyle. It was her own problem. Her own responsibility.

She turned back toward the door and bumped right into him.

'Sorry. Let me help you with that.' He was close now, and drew in her scent as he took the jacket from her. It was perfect for her. Just perfect.

'I didn't mean to interrupt.'

'Interrupt what?' He slipped the jacket on for her and indulged himself in a sniff at her hair.

'You and Linda?'

'Who? Oh.' He laughed, taking Olivia's hand and walking to the door. 'Not exactly shy, is she?'

'No.'

'Did you finish your paper?'

'Yes, barely.'

'Good. You can tell me all about fungus.'

It made her laugh. He held her hand all the way down to the car, then he skimmed his fingers over her hair, brushing it back just as she started to climb in.

Her heart stumbled, and fell right at his feet.

He'd found an Italian place just casual enough not to intimidate. Tiny white candles flickered on soft, salmon-colored cloths. Conversation was muted and punctuated with laughter. The air was ripe with good, rich scents.

He was easy to talk to. He was the first man, outside of family, she'd ever had dinner with who seemed actually interested in her studies and her plans to use them. Then she remembered his mother.

'Is your mother still involved with causes?'

'She and her congressmen are on a first-name basis. She never lets up. I think the current focus is the plight of the mustang. Are you going to let me taste that?'

'What?' She'd just lifted a forkful of portobello mushroom. 'Oh. Sure.'

When she would have put the bite on his plate, he simply took her wrist, guided her hand toward his mouth. Heat washed into her belly as his eyes watched hers over the fork.

'It's terrific.'

'Ah, there is a wide variety of edible mushrooms in the rain forest.'

'Yeah. Maybe I'll make it back up there one of these days and you can show me.'

'I'm – we're hoping to add a naturalist center to the lodge. There'd be lectures and talks on how to identify the edibles.'

'Edible fungus – it never sounds as appetizing as it is.'

'Actually, the mushroom isn't the fungus. It's a fruiting body of the fungus organism. Like an apple from the apple tree.'

'No kidding?'

'When you see a fairy ring, it's the fruit of the continuous body of the fungus that grows in the soil, expanding year after year and —' She caught herself. 'And you can't possibly care.'

'Hey, I like to know what I'm eating. Why do they call them fairy rings?'

She blinked at him. 'I suppose because that's what they look like.'

'Are there fairies in your forest, Liv?'

'I used to think so. When I was little, I'd sit there, in the green light, and think if I was very quiet, I'd see them come out and play.'

'And you never did?'

'No.' So she'd given up fairy tales. Science was reliable. 'But I saw deer and elk and marten and bear. They're magical enough for me.'

'And beaver.'

She smiled, relaxing back as the waiter cleared, then served the main course. 'Yes. There's still a dam where I took your family that day.'

She sampled her angel-hair pasta with its generous chunks of tomato and shrimp. 'They always give you more than you could possibly eat.'

'Says who?' He dug into his manicotti, with shells bursting with cheese and spices.

It amazed her that he managed not only to do justice to his meal but also to put away a good portion of hers. Then still had room to order dessert and cappuccino.

'How can you eat like that and not weigh three hundred pounds?' she wanted to know.

'Metabolism.' He grinned as he scooped up a spoonful of the whipped-cream-and-chocolate concoction on his plate. 'Same with my dad. Drives my mother crazy. Here, try this. It's amazing.'

'No, I can't –' But he already had the spoon to her lips, and she opened them automatically. The rich glory of it melted on her tongue. '*Hmm*, well. Yes.'

He had to pull himself back a little. Her response, the half-closed eyes, the just-parted lips made him think of sex. Made him realize he wanted his mouth on hers, so all those tastes would mingle.

'Let's take a walk.' He scribbled a tip and his signature on the bill, pocketed his credit card. Air, he told himself; he needed a little air to clear her and his fantasies out of his head.

But they were still there when he drove her home, when he walked her to her door, when she turned and smiled at him.

She saw it now, clear and dark in his eyes. Desire for her, the anticipation of that first kiss. A tremble shivered up the center of her body.

'This was nice.' Could you possibly be more inane, Liv? she asked herself. 'Thanks.'

'What are you doing tomorrow?'

'Tomorrow?' Her mind went as blank as glass. 'I have classes.'

'No, tomorrow night.'

'There's . . .' Studying, another paper, extra lab work. 'Nothing.'

'Good. Seven, then.'

Now, she thought, he would kiss her now. And she'd probably implode. 'All right.'

''Night, Liv.' He only ran his hand down her arm, over the back of hers, then walked away.

Chapter Ten

He took her to McDonald's, and she laughed until her sides burned.

She fell in love with him over fish sandwiches and fries, under glaringly bright lights and through the noisy chatter of children.

She forgot the vow she'd made as a child that she would never, never love anyone so much she'd be vulnerable to him. That she would never hook her heart to a man and give him the power to break it, and her.

She simply rode that wonderful, that wild and windy crest of first love.

She told him what she hoped to do, describing the naturalist center she'd already designed in her mind and had shared with no one but family.

The biggest dream in her life was easy to share with him. He listened, he watched her face. What she wanted seemed to matter to him.

Because she fascinated him, he put aside all the work he'd done that day – the sketchy outline for the book, the notes, the more detailed plans for interviews – and just enjoyed her.

He told himself there was plenty of time. He had the best part of two weeks, after all. What was wrong with taking the first few days with her?

He wondered if the center she spoke of with such passion was her way of opening the bubble his mother had described or just another way to expand its boundaries and stay inside.

'It'll be a lot of work.'

'It's not work when you're doing what you love.'

That he understood. His assignments at the paper had become a grind, but every time he opened himself up to the book, dived into the research, pored over his notes and files, it was a thrill. 'Then you can't let anything stop you.'

'No.' Her eyes were alive with the energy of it. 'Just a few more years, and I'm going to make it happen.'

'Then I'll come see it.' His hand closed over hers on the white plastic table. And you, he thought.

'I hope so.' And because she did, because she found she could, she turned her hand over and linked her fingers with his.

They talked about music, about books, about everything couples talk about when they're desperate to find every shared interest and explore it.

When he discovered she had not only never been to a basketball game, but had never watched one on television, he looked totally, sincerely shocked.

'You've got a huge hole in your education here, Liv.' He had her hand again as they walked to his car. 'I'm sending you copies of my tapes of the Lakers.'

'They would be a basketball team.'

'They, Olivia, would be gods. Okay.' He settled behind the wheel. 'We've managed to introduce you to the cultural delights of fast food; we have the only true sport heading your way. What's next?'

'I don't know how to thank you for helping me this way.'

'It's the least I can do.'

He already knew what was next, as he'd spent part of his day scoping out the area around the college. He had a pretty good idea it wasn't only fish sandwiches and sports Olivia had missed.

He took her dancing.

The club was loud, crowded and perfect. He'd already decided if he was alone with her he wouldn't be able to stop himself from moving too fast.

He was an observer, a measurer of people. It had taken only one evening with her for him to realize she was every bit as lonely as the young girl he remembered on the banks of the river. And that she was completely untouched.

There were rules. He believed strongly in rules, in rights and wrongs and in consequences. She wasn't ready for the needs she stirred up inside him.

He wasn't sure he was ready for them himself.

He saw her dazzled and wary look when they shoved their way through the crowd. Amused by it, delighted by her, he leaned close to her ear.

'Mass humanity at ritual. You could do a paper.'

'I'm a naturalist.'

'Baby, this is nature.' He found them a table, jammed in with other tables, leaned forward to shout over the driving scream of music. 'Male, female, basic courtship rituals.'

She glanced toward the tiny dance floor where dozens of couples managed to squeeze in together and writhe. 'I don't think that qualifies as courtship.'

But it was interesting enough to watch. She'd always avoided places like this. Too many people in too small a space. It tended to create pressure in her chest, to release little flutters of panic in her throat. But she didn't feel uneasy tonight, bumped up against Noah, his hand lightly covering hers on the table.

He ordered a beer, and she opted for sparkling water. By the time the waitress had managed to swerve, shuffle and elbow her way through with their order, Olivia was relaxed.

The music was loud, and not particularly good, but it meshed nicely with that drumming under her heart. A kind of primitive backbeat to her own longings.

Since she couldn't hear her own thoughts, she forgot them and just watched.

Courtship. She supposed Noah was right, after all. The plumage – in this case leather and denim, bold colors or basic black. The repeated movements that signaled a demand to be noticed by the opposite sex, a sexual invitation, a willingness to mate. Eye contact, the flirtation glance toward, then away, then back again.

She found herself smiling. Hadn't she seen the ritual, in various forms, in countless species?

She said essentially this to Noah, speaking almost against his ear to be heard, and felt his rumble of laughter before he turned his face and she saw his smile.

Just as she realized how incredibly stupid she must have sounded, he tugged her to her feet.

'Are we leaving?'

'No, we're joining.'

Now the panic came, fast and hard to fill her chest. 'No, I can't.'

She tried to pull her hand free as he headed for the dance floor. 'I don't dance.'

'Everyone dances.'

'No, really.' Her skin went hot all over, burning from the inside out. 'I don't know how.'

They were on the edge of the dance floor, surrounded, closed in, and his hands were on her hips. His face was close. 'Just move.' His body did just that against hers, and turned the panic into a different, deeper, far more intimate fear. 'It doesn't matter how.'

He guided her hips, side to side, shifted so that they moved in a small circle. The music was fast, driven by a frenzied riff on an electric guitar and the vocalist's roar. Beside them someone let out a wild laugh. Someone bumped her hard from behind and brought her up against Noah, curves to angles, heat to heat.

Her hands gripped his shoulders now. Her face was flushed, her eyes, dark and wide, on his, her lips parted as the breath rushed in and out.

Through all the scents – the clash of perfume, sweat, spilled beer – he smelled only her. Fresh and quiet, like a meadow.

'Olivia.' She couldn't hear his voice, but watched in dazed amazement as her name formed on his lips. It seemed that the only thing inside her now was the warm, sweet longing.

'The hell with it.' He had to have her, if only one taste. His arms wrapped tight around her waist, urging her up to her toes. He felt the quick intake of her breath, and the tremble that followed it. And hesitated, hesitated, drawing out the moment, the now, the ache and the anticipation until they were both reeling from it.

Then he brushed his mouth over hers, soft, smooth. Nibbled her in, patient pleasure. Slid into her silkily, as if he'd always belonged there.

He heard her moan, low and long, over the thunder in his own blood. Slow, easy, he ordered himself. Sweet God. He wanted to dive, to devour, to demand more and still more as the surprisingly sharp, stunningly sexy taste of her flooded through him.

Her body was pressed against his, slender and strong. Her arms had locked around his neck, holding on. Holding him. Her mouth was full, and just shy enough to speak of innocence.

Just a little more, he thought and changed the angle of the kiss to take it.

The music crashed around them, building to a frenzy of

guitars, a feral pounding of drums, a shouting stream of voices.

And she floated, drifted, glided. She imagined herself a single white feather, weightless, spinning slowly, endlessly, through the soft green light of the forest. Her heart swelled and its beat quieted to a thick, dull thud. The muscles in her stomach loosened and dipped. As she skimmed her fingers into his hair, tipped her head back in surrender, she could have wept from the discovery.

This, she thought, is life. Is beginnings. Is everything.

'Olivia.' He said her name again, ended the kiss while he still had the power to do so, then just nudged her head to the curve of his shoulder.

The band ripped into another number, pumping the crowd to a fever pitch.

While they swayed together in the mêlée, Noah wondered what the hell he was going to do now.

He kissed her again at her door, and this time she felt little licks of heat from him, quick riffs of frustration that were oddly thrilling. Then he was closing the door between them and leaving her staring blankly at the solid panel of wood.

She pressed a hand to her heart. It was beating fast, and wasn't that wonderful? This was what it was like to be in love, to be wanted. She held the feeling close, closing her eyes, savoring it. Then her lids flew open again.

She should have asked him in. What was wrong with her? Why was she such an idiot around men? He'd wanted her, she was sure of it. She wanted him. Finally there was someone who made her feel.

She flung open her door, raced down the steps, and burst outside just as his car pulled away from the curb. She watched the red taillights wink away and wondered why she could never quite match her pace to anyone else's.

He worked through the morning. And thought about calling her a dozen times. Then he shut down his laptop and changed into sweat shorts. The punishing workout he subjected himself to in the hotel's gym helped purge some of the guilt and frustration.

He needed to change directions, he decided as he did a third set of curls with free weights. He should never have gone this far down this road with Olivia.

He puffed out short breaths, added another rep while sweat ran satisfactorily down his back.

He'd have bet a year's pay that she was a virgin. He had no right to touch her. However horrible an experience she'd been through, she'd lived the first eighteen years of her life completely sheltered. Like some princess in an enchanted forest in a fairy tale. He was years older – not the six that separated them chronologically, but in experience. He had no right to take advantage of that.

As he switched to flies, the practical side of his mind reminded him she was also smart, strong and capable. She was ambitious and her eyes were as ancient as a goddess's. Those were traits she owned that appealed to him every bit as much as the shyness she tried to hide.

He hadn't taken advantage of her. She'd responded, she'd all but melted against him, goddamn it. She had to feel something of what he felt. That bond, that connection, the absolute rightness of it.

Then he circled back around and berated himself for thinking with his glands.

That had to stop. He'd call her, ask her if they could meet for coffee later. Something simple. Then he'd tell her about the book he was preparing to write. He'd explain things carefully, how he was going to contact everyone involved in the case. That he'd started with her because she'd been the reason the idea had formed in his mind in the first place.

He wondered if the seed had been planted the first time he'd seen her.

He set the weights aside, mopped his face with a towel. He'd call her as soon as he'd gone up to his room and showered. And he'd do what he now realized he should have done as soon as she'd opened her apartment door to him.

Feeling better, looser, he bypassed the elevator and took the stairs to the ninth floor.

And jolted to a halt when he saw her standing in front of his door, digging through an oversized purse.

'Liv?'

'God!' She nearly stumbled back, then stared at him. 'You startled me.' She kept her hands buried in her bag until she was sure they wouldn't shake. 'I was just about to write you a note and slip it under your door.'

She sent him a smile and stood there looking neat and fresh in jeans and a boxy jacket. When he didn't respond, she shifted uneasily. 'I hope you don't mind that I came by.'

'No, sorry.' He couldn't afford to let her dazzle him again. 'I just wasn't expecting you. I was down in the gym.'

'Really? I would never have guessed.'

His quick grin had the worst of the tension smoothing out of her stomach. He dug his keycard out of his pocket, slid it into the door. 'Come on in. And you can tell me instead of writing a note.'

'I had some time between classes.' That was a lie. She was, for the first time in her college career, skipping class. How could she be expected to concentrate on wildlife ecology when she was planning to ask him to take her to bed?

Oh God, how could she possibly tell him why she'd come? How would she begin?

'Time enough for coffee?'

'I . . . yes. I was going to invite you to dinner – a home-cooked meal.'

'Oh yeah? Much better than coffee.' He tried to think. He could talk to her more privately at her apartment. She'd be more comfortable there. She was obviously nervous now, standing in his cramped hotel room, with her hands locked together while she flicked uneasy glances toward the bed.

So they'd get out. All he had to do was keep his hands off her in the mean-time.

'I need to clean up a little,' he told her.

'Ah . . .' He looked wonderful, damp from his workout, the muscles in his arms toned and tough. She remembered how strong they'd been when they'd banded around her. 'I just have to pick up a few things at the market.'

'Tell you what. Give me a chance to take a shower, and we'll both go to the market. Then I can watch you cook.'

'All right.'

He grabbed jeans from the back of a chair, hunted up a shirt. 'There's a very miserly honor bar under the TV. Help yourself. We've got cable,' he added as he dug socks and underwear out of a drawer. 'Just have a seat. Give me ten minutes.'

'Take your time.' The minute he closed the door to the bathroom, she lowered herself to the edge of the bed. Her knees were shaking.

Good Lord, how was she going to manage this and not make a complete fool of herself? Marketing, they were going marketing. She wanted to giggle wildly. She'd just come from the drugstore where she'd had to gather every fiber of her courage to walk to the counter and buy condoms.

Now they lay in her purse, weighing like lead. Not because of the heft of the decision she'd made, but because of the fear that she'd misread what she'd seen in his eyes the night before. What she'd tasted when he'd kissed her.

She had intended to ask him to dinner, but that would have been after. After she'd knocked on his door, after he'd opened it and she'd smiled and stepped to him, slipped her arms around him, kissed him.

She'd imagined it so perfectly that when she'd knocked and he hadn't answered, she'd been completely baffled, and now nothing was going as she'd scripted it in her head.

She'd come here to offer herself, to tell him she wanted him to be the one. She'd imagined more – the way his eyes would focus on her face, so deep, so intense, until her vision blurred and his mouth would cover hers.

The way he'd pick her up – even the quick rushing feel in her stomach the sweep of that would cause. How he'd carry her to the bed.

She let out a breath and got up to pace. Of course she'd built up the room differently in her mind. It had been larger, with prettier colors, a soft spread over the bed, a mountain of pillows.

She'd added candlelight.

This room was small, with colors of gray and faded rose. Bland, she thought, as so many hotel rooms were. But it didn't matter. She closed her eyes and listened to the water drumming in the shower.

What would he do if she went in, if she quietly stripped, stepped into the steam and spray with him? Would their bodies come together then? Wet and hot and ready.

She didn't have the courage for it. Sighing, she walked to the honor bar, perused the selections without interest, wandered to the desk where he'd set up his computer and piles of disorganized notes and files.

She'd wait until he came out. She was better at dealing with matters, both small and vital, in a clear, face-to-face fashion. She wasn't the sultry seductress and never would be.

Would that disappoint him?

Annoyed with herself, she shook her head. She had to stop second-guessing him, criticizing herself. When he came back out again, she would simply let him know she wanted him, and see what happened next.

Idly, she tidied his notes, tapping edges together. She liked the fact that he'd brought work with him. She respected the ambition, the dedication, the energy. It was important to respect someone you loved.

He hadn't talked very much about his work, she thought now, then rolled her eyes. Because she'd been too busy babbling about herself. She'd ask him about it, she decided. About what he liked best in his work, how it felt to see his words in print and know that people read them.

She thought it must be a wonderful, satisfying feeling, and smiled over it as she stacked his notes.

The name MacBride, scrawled in black ink on a yellow legal pad caught her eye, had her frowning, lifting the sheet of paper.

Within seconds, her blood had gone cold and she was riffling through his work without a thought for his privacy.

Noah rubbed a towel over his hair and worked out exactly what he would say to Olivia. Once they'd come to an agreement on professional terms, they'd work on the personal ones. He could go to River's End and spend some time with her that summer. To do the interviews, certainly. But to be with her. He'd never known a woman he was so compelled to *be* with.

He'd have to arrange for more time off from the newspaper. Or just fucking quit, he thought, staring at his own face in the steamy mirror. Of course he'd have to figure out how the hell he was going to live until the book was written and sold. But he'd work that out.

He never doubted it would sell. He was meant to write books, and he was damn sure he was meant to write this one.

And he was beginning to think, not entirely easily, that he was meant to be with Olivia.

None of that would happen until he took the first step.

He took one, into the bedroom, and heard the world crash around his ears. She was standing by his desk, his papers in her hands, and a look of iced fury in those amber eyes.

'You son of a bitch.' She said it quietly, but the words ripped the air like a scream. 'You scheming, calculating bastard.'

'Just a minute.'

'Don't touch me.' She slapped him back with the words even as he started toward her. 'Don't think about touching me. You're here on your own, not as a reporter. Fucking liar, it was all for a story.'

'No.' He stepped to the side to block her before she could stride to the door. 'Just wait. I'm not here for the paper.'

She still held his notes and, looking him dead in the eye, crumpled them in her hand and tossed them in his face.

'Just how big a fool do you think I am?'

'I don't.' He grabbed her arms. He expected her to struggle, to claw and spit and scratch. Instead she went rigid. She turned off. He could see in her eyes the way she simply shut off. A little desperate, he gave her a quick, light shake.

'Listen, goddamn it. It's not for the paper. I want to write a book. I should have told you, I meant to tell you. Then . . . Jesus, Liv, you know what happened. The minute I looked at you everything got confused. I wanted to spend some time with you. I needed to. That's a first for me. Every time I looked at you . . . I just went under.'

'You used me.' She'd be cold, she'd stay cold. Nothing he could say, nothing he could do could penetrate the wall of ice. She wouldn't permit it. She wouldn't let herself fall into that trap again.

'If I did, I'm sorry. I let what I felt for you get in the way of what was right. Last night, walking away from you was the hardest thing I've ever done. I wanted you so much it ached right down to the bone.'

'You'd have slept with me to get information for your book.' Stay cold, she ordered herself. Pain couldn't cut through ice.

'No.' It ripped at his guts that she would think it, that she would believe it. 'You have to know better than that. What happened between us had nothing to do with the book. It was about you and me. I wanted you, Liv, from the minute you opened your door, but I couldn't touch you until I'd explained everything. I was going to talk to you about it tonight.'

'Were you?' There was a snap of amusement in her voice –

frigid amusement that cut like frosted razors. 'That's very convenient, Noah. Take your hands off me.'

'You have to listen to me.'

'No, I don't. I don't have to listen to you. I don't have to look at you. I don't have to think about you ever again once I'm out of this room. So I'll finish this, here and now. Pay attention.'

She pushed his hands away, and her eyes were level, a burning gold. 'This is my life, not yours. My business, no one else's. I won't cooperate with your goddamn book, and neither will my family. I'll see to it. And if I find out you've tried to contact anyone I care about, anyone who matters to me, I'll do everything I can to make you suffer.'

She shoved him back. 'Stay away from me and mine, Brady. If you call me again, if you contact me again, I'll ask my aunt to use every bit of her influence to see you're fired from the *Times*. And if you've done your research, you know just how much influence she has.'

The threat taunted his own temper, had him yanking it back. 'I've hurt you. I'm sorry. I didn't realize what I'd feel for you, how huge it could be. I didn't plan what happened here, between us.'

'As far as I'm concerned, nothing happened between us. I despise you and everyone like you. Keep away from me.' She snatched up her bag, shoved by him to the door. 'I once told you that your father was a great man. He is. Beside him, Noah, you're very small.'

She didn't even bother to slam the door. He watched it close with a quiet click.

She didn't run, but she wanted to. Her chest was full and heavy, her eyes stinging with tears she refused to shed. He'd used her; he'd betrayed her. She'd let herself love, she'd let herself trust, and what she'd gotten had been lies.

He'd never wanted her. He'd wanted her mother, her father. He'd wanted the blood and the grief. She would never, never give them to him.

She would never give her trust to anyone again.

She wondered if her mother had felt anything like this when she'd known the man she'd loved was a lie. If she'd felt this emptiness, this sick sadness, this burning betrayal.

Olivia let rage coat over misery and promised herself she'd never think of Noah Brady again.

Chapter Eleven

Venice, California, 1999

Noah Brady figured his life was just about perfect. Thanks to the critical and popular success of his first book, he had his trim little bungalow on the beach and the financial resources to live pretty much as he liked.

He loved his work – the intensity and punch of writing true crime with the bent of sliding into the mind and heart of those who chose murder as a solution, or as recreation. It was much more satisfying than the four years he'd worked as a reporter, forced to accept assignments and to gear his style to fit the newspaper.

God knew it paid better, he thought, as he jogged the last of his daily three-mile run along the beach.

Not that he was in it for the money, but the money sure as hell didn't hurt.

Now with his second book just hitting the bookstores, the reviews and sales solid, he figured it didn't get much better.

He was young, healthy, successful and blissfully unattached – since he'd recently untangled himself from a relationship that had started off intriguing, sexy and fun and had degenerated into mildly annoying.

Who'd have though that Caryn, self-described party girl and wannabe actress, would have morphed into a clinging, suffocating female who whined and sulked every time he wanted an evening on his own?

He knew he'd been in trouble when more and more of her things started taking up permanent residence in his closet and drawers. When her makeup began making itself at home on his bathroom counter. He'd come dangerously close to living with her mostly by default. No, not default, *his* fault, Noah corrected, because he'd been so preoccupied with the research and writing on his next book he'd barely noticed.

Which, of course, is what pissed her off enough to send her into a raging, tearful snit when she'd tossed accusations of selfishness and neglect at him while she'd tossed her things into a tote bag the size of Kansas. She'd broken two lamps – one nearly over his head, but he'd been quicker – had upended his prized gloxinia into a mess of soil, broken leaves and shattered pottery. Then she'd walked out on him, flipping back her long, straight California blond hair.

As he'd stood, just a little dazed in the middle of the debris, she'd shot him a killing look out of brimming blue eyes and had told him he could reach her at Marva's when he was man enough to apologize.

Noah decided he was man enough to be relieved when the door slammed behind her.

That hadn't stopped her from leaving messages on his machine that ranged from snotty to weepy to raging. He didn't know what was wrong with her. She was a stunningly beautiful woman in a town that worshiped beautiful women. She was hardly going to spend time alone if she wanted a man to play with.

It never occurred to him that she might have been in love with him. Or at least believed herself to be.

His mother would have said that was typical of him. He was able to see inside strangers, victims, witnesses, the guilty and the innocent with uncanny insight and interest. But when it came to personal relationships, he barely skimmed the surface.

He'd wanted to once, and the results had been disastrous. For Olivia, and for him.

It had taken him months to get over those three days he'd spent with her. To get over her. In time he'd managed to convince himself it had been the book after all, the thirst to write it, that had tilted his feelings for her into something he'd nearly thought was love.

She'd simply interested him, and attracted him, and because of that – and inexperience – he'd handled the entire situation badly. He'd found ways to put that aside, just as he'd put the idea of that particular book aside. He'd found other women, and other murders.

When he thought of Olivia, it was with regret, guilt and a wondering about what might have been.

So he tried not to think of it.

He jogged toward the tidy, two-story bungalow the color of buttermilk. The sun splattered over the red-tile roof, shot out from the windows. It might have been late March, but southern California was experiencing a sultry heat wave that delighted him.

Out of habit, he went around to the front of the house to get his mail. The floods of color in his flower beds were the envy of his neighbors.

He went inside, moving straight through the living area he'd furnished sparsely, and dumped the mail on the kitchen counter, then pulled a large bottle of spring water from the fridge.

He glanced at his answering machine, saw he'd already accumulated four messages since he'd gone out for his run. Fearing at least one would be from the now-dreaded Caryn, he decided to make coffee and toast a couple of bagels before he played them back.

A guy needed fuel for certain tasks.

He tossed his sunglasses on top of his pile of mail and got down to the first order of business. While the coffee brewed, he switched on the portable TV, flipping through the morning talk shows to see if there was a topic of interest to him.

His bedroom VCR would have taped the *Today* show while he'd been out. He'd catch up with that later, see what was up in the world, skim through it for the news headlines. He'd brought the morning papers in before his run, and he'd get to them as well, spending at least an hour, if not two, absorbing the top stories, the metro reports, the crime.

You just never knew where the next book would come from.

He glanced again at the light blinking on his answering machine but decided his mail was a higher priority than his phone messages. Not that he was procrastinating, he thought as he sat at the counter with his single-man's breakfast and listened with half an ear to *Jerry Springer*.

He scooped back his hair, thought vaguely about a haircut and worked his way through the usual complement of bills and junk mail. There was a nice little packet of reader mail forwarded by his publisher that he decided to read and savor later, his monthly issue of *Prison Life* and a postcard from a friend vacationing in Maui.

Then he picked up a plain white envelope with his name and address carefully handwritten on it. The return address was San Quentin.

He received mail from prisoners routinely, but not, Noah thought with a frown, at his home address. Sometimes they wanted to kick his ass on general principles, but for the most part they were certain he'd want to write their story.

He hesitated over the letter, not sure if he should be annoyed or concerned that someone in one of those cages had his home address. But when he had opened it and skimmed the first lines, his heart gave a quick jerk that was both shock and fascination.

Dear Noah Brady,

My name is Sam Tanner. I think you'll know who I am. We are, in a way, connected. Your father was the primary investigating officer in my wife's murder, and the man who arrested me.

You may or may not be aware that he has attended all of my parole hearings since I began serving my sentence. You could say Frank and I have kept in touch.

I read with interest your book Hunt by Night. *Your clear-sighted and somewhat dispassionate look into the mind and methods of James Trolly made his systematic selection and mutilation of male prostitutes in West Hollywood more chilling and real than any of the stories in the media during his spree five years ago.*

As an actor I have a great appreciation for a strong, clearheaded writer.

It has been some years since I've bothered to speak to reporters, to the freelance journalists and writers who initially clamored to tell my story. I made mistakes in whom I trusted, and was paid back by having my words twisted to suit the public's thirst for scandal and gossip.

In reading your work, I've come to believe that you're interested in the truth, in the real people and events that took place. I find this interesting, given my connection to your father. Almost as if it's been fated. I've come to believe in fate over these last years.

I would like to tell you my story. I'd like you to write it. If you're interested, I think you know where to find me.

I'm not going anywhere for a few more months.

Sincerely,

Sam Tanner

'Well, well.' Noah scratched his chin and read over the high points of the letter again. When his phone rang, he ignored it. When Caryn's angry voice shot out accusing him of being an insensitive pig, cursing him and swearing revenge, he barely heard.

'Oh, I'm interested all right, Sam. I've been interested in you for twenty years.'

He had files stuffed full on Sam Tanner, Julie MacBride and the Beverly Hills murder his father had investigated. He'd kept them and had continued to accumulate data even after his painful visit to Olivia at college.

He'd put the book aside, but not his interest in the case. And not his determination to one day write the book that would tell the story from all angles.

But he'd put it aside for six years, he thought now, because every time he started to work on it again, he saw the way Olivia had looked at him when she'd stood by the desk in that little hotel room, with his papers gripped in her hands.

This time when that image tried to form, he blocked it out. He couldn't, and wouldn't, channel his work because of a blighted love affair.

An exclusive series of interviews with Sam Tanner. They'd have to be exclusive, Noah thought as he got to his feet to pace. He was going to make that a condition from the get-go.

He'd need a list of everyone involved, even peripherally. Family, friends, employees, associates. Excitement pumped through his blood as he began to outline his research strategy. Court transcripts. Maybe he could track down some of the members of the jury. Police reports.

The thought of that brought him up short. His father. He wasn't at all sure his father was going to be happy with the idea.

He headed to the shower to clean up. And to give himself time to think.

*

The Brady house hadn't changed a great deal over the years. It was still the same pale rose stucco, the lawn nicely mowed and the flowers on the edge of death. Since his father had retired from the force the year before, he'd piddled with a variety of hobbies including golf, photography, woodworking and cooking. He'd decided he hated golf after the first nine holes. He'd also decided that he had no eye for photography, no affinity for wood and no skill in the kitchen.

Six months after his retirement, Celia sat him down, told him she loved him more than she had the day they'd married. And if he didn't find something to do and get out of her house she was going to kill him in his sleep.

The local youth center saved his life and his marriage. Most afternoons he could be found there, coaching the kids on the basketball court as he'd once coached his son, listening to their complaints and triumphs and breaking up the inevitable fights and squabbles.

Mornings, after Celia had gone off to work, he spent puttering, doing crosswords or sitting in the backyard reading one of the paperback mystery novels he'd become addicted to since murder was no longer a part of his daily routine.

That's where Noah found him, his long legs stretched out in front of him as he relaxed in a lawn chair under a stingy patch of shade.

He wore jeans, ancient sneakers and a comfortably wrinkled cotton shirt. His hair had gone a shimmering pewter gray but remained full and thick.

'Do you know how hard it is to kill geraniums?' Noah glanced at the withered pink blooms struggling along the back deck. 'It almost has to be premeditated.'

'You'll never convict me.' Pleased to see his son, Frank set aside the latest John Sandford novel.

Merely shaking his head, Noah unwound the hose, switched it on and gave the desperate flowers another shot at life.

'Didn't expect to see you until Sunday.'

'Sunday?'

'Your mother's birthday.' Frank narrowed his eyes. 'You didn't forget?'

'No. I've already got her present. It's a wolf.' He turned his head to grin. 'Don't panic, she doesn't get to keep it here. She gets to adopt one in the wild, and they keep tabs on it for her. I figured she'd go for that – and the earrings I picked up.'

'Show-off,' Frank grumbled and crossed his feet at the ankles. 'You're still going out to dinner with us Sunday, though?'

'Wouldn't miss it.'

'You can bring that girl if you want, the one you've been seeing.'

'That would be Caryn, who just left me a message on my machine calling me a pig. I'm steering clear of her.'

'Good. Your mother didn't like her.'

'She only met her once.'

'Didn't like her. 'Shallow,' 'snooty,' 'stupid' I believe were the three words she used.'

'It's annoying how she's always right.' Satisfied the geraniums would live another day, Noah turned off the hose and began to wind it back on its wheel.

Frank said nothing for a moment, just watched while his son carefully aligned the hose. Carefully enough to make Frank's lips twitch. 'You know, I was a pretty good detective. I don't think you came here to water my flowers.'

When he couldn't use the hose to stall any longer, Noah slid his hands in the back pockets of his jeans. 'I got a letter this morning. Guy in San Quentin wants me to tell his story.'

'And?' Frank raised his eyebrows. 'You get fairly regular correspondence from criminals these days, don't you?'

'Yeah, most of it's useless. But I'm interested in this case. Been interested in it for a while.' He took off his sunglasses, met his father's eyes levelly. 'About twenty years now. It's Sam Tanner, Dad.'

There was a little hitch in Frank's heart rate. Beat, hesitation, beat. He didn't jolt. He'd been a cop too long to jump at shadows and ghosts, but he braced. 'I see. No, I don't see,' he said immediately and pushed out of his chair. 'I put that son of a bitch away and now he writes to you? He wants to talk to the son of the man who helped send him over, who's made goddamn sure he stayed over for twenty years? That's bullshit, Noah. Dangerous bullshit.'

'He mentioned the connection.' Noah kept his tone mild. He didn't want to argue, hated knowing he was going to upset his father, but his decision was already made. 'Why did you go to all his parole hearings?'

'Some things you don't forget. And because you don't, because you can't, you make sure the job stays done.' And he'd made a promise to a young girl with haunted eyes as they'd stood in the deep shadows of the forest. 'He hasn't forgotten either. What better way to pay me back than to use you?'

'He can't hurt me, Dad.'

'I imagine that's just what Julie MacBride thought the night she opened the door to him. Stay away from him, Noah. Put this one aside.'

'You haven't.' He held up a hand before Frank could speak. 'Just listen a minute. You did your job. It cost you. I remember how it was. You'd pace the floor at night, or come out here to sit in the dark. I know there were others that followed you home, but nothing ever like this one. So I never forgot it either. I guess you could say it's followed me, too. This one's part of us. All of us. I've wanted to write this book for years. I have to talk to Sam Tanner.'

'If you do that, Noah, and go on to write this book, drag out all that ugliness again, do you realize what it might do to Tanner's other victims? The parents, the sister. Her child?'

Olivia. No, Noah told himself, he was not going to cloud the issue with Olivia. Not now. 'I thought about what it might do to you. That's why I'm here. I wanted you to know what I'm going to do.'

'It's a mistake.'

'Maybe, but it's my life now, and my job.'

'You think he'd have contacted you if you weren't mine?' Fear and fury sprang out in equal measures, turning Frank's eyes hard, snapping into his voice like the crack of a bullet. 'The son of a bitch refuses to talk to anyone for years – and they've tried to get to him. Brokaw, Walters, Oprah. No comment, no interviews, no nothing. Now, just months before he's likely to get out, he contacts you, offers you the story on a plate. Damn it, Noah, it doesn't have to do with your work. It has to do with mine.'

'Maybe.' Noah's tone chilled as he slipped his sunglasses back on. 'And maybe it has to do with both. Whether or not you respect my work, it's what I do. And what I'm going to keep doing.'

'I never said I didn't respect your work.'

'No, but you never said otherwise either.' It was a bruise Noah just realized he'd been nursing. 'I'll take my breaks where I find them and make them work for me. I learned that from you. I'll see you Sunday.'

Frank stepped forward, started to speak. But Noah was already striding away. So he sat, feeling his age, and stared down at his own hands.

Noah's foul mood drove home with him, like a separate energy, an irritable passenger in the stone-gray BMW. He kept the top down, the radio up, trying to blow away the anger, drown out his thoughts.

He hated the sudden discovery that he was hurt because his father had never done a tap dance of joy over the success of his books.

It was stupid, he thought. He was old enough not to need the whistles and claps of parental approval. He wasn't eighteen and scoring the winning basket at the tail of the fourth quarter any longer. He was a grown man both happy and successful in his profession. He was well paid, and his ego got all the boosts it required from reviews and royalty checks, thank you very much.

But he knew, had known all along, that his father disapproved of the path he'd taken with his writing. Because neither had wanted to confront the other, little had been said.

Until today, Noah thought.

Sam Tanner had done more than offer a story to be told. He'd put the first visible crack in a relationship Noah had counted on all his life. It had been there before, hidden, from the first moment he'd decided to write about all the ripples on the river of murder.

Fiction would have been fine, Noah knew. Entertaining. But digging and exposing the realities, stripping down killers, victims, survivals for public consumption. That's what his father disliked – and couldn't understand.

And just now, because he didn't know how to explain it, Noah's mood teetered on the edge of vile.

Spotting Caryn's car parked in front of his house tripped it over the rest of the way.

He found her sitting on his back deck, her long, smooth legs clad in tiny pink shorts, a wide-brimmed straw hat protecting her face from the sun. When he opened the glass door, she looked up, her eyes brimming behind the amber lenses of her designer sunglasses. Her lips trembled.

'Oh, Noah. I'm so sorry. I don't know what came over me.'

He cocked his head. It would've been fascinating if it hadn't been so tedious. It was a pattern he recognized from their weeks together. Fight, curse, accuse, throw things, slam out. Then come back with tearful eyes and apologize.

Now, unless she'd decided to deviate from form, she would slither around him and offer sex.

When she rose, smiling tremulously as she crossed to him and slid her arms around him, he decided she just didn't have the imagination to improvise.

'I've been so unhappy without you these last few days.' She lifted her mouth to his. 'Let's go inside so I can show you how much I've missed you.'

It worried him a little that he wasn't tempted, not in the least.

'Caryn. It's not going to work. Why don't we just say it was fun while it lasted?'

'You don't mean it.'

'Yes.' He had to nudge her back so she'd stop rubbing against him. 'I do.'

'There's someone else, isn't there? All the time we were living together, you were cheating on me.'

'No, there's no one else. And we weren't living together. You just started staying here.'

'You bastard. You've already had another woman in our bed.' She rushed past him, into the house.

'It's not *our* bed. It's my bed. Goddamn it.' He was more weary than angry, until he walked into the bedroom and saw she was already ripping at his sheets. 'Hey! Cut it out.'

He made a grab for her, but she rolled onto the bed, leaped off the other side. Before he could stop her, she'd grabbed the bedside lamp and heaved it at him. The best he could do was block it so the base didn't rap him between the eyes.

The sound of the glass crashing on the floor snapped the already unsteady hold on his temper.

'Okay, that's it. Get out. Get the hell out of my house and stay away from me.'

'You never cared. You never thought about my feelings.'

'You're right, absolutely.' He went for her as she made a beeline for his prized basketball trophy. 'I didn't give a damn about you.' He panted it out as he struggled to get her out without losing any of his own skin to her long, lethal nails. 'I'm a pig, a creep, a son of a bitch.'

'I hate you!' She shrieked it, slapping and kicking as he dragged her to the front door. 'I wish you were dead!'

'Just pretend I am. And I'll do the same for you.' He shoved her outside, shut the door, then leaned back against it.

He let out a long breath, rolled his shoulders. Then because he hadn't heard her car start, glanced out the window. Just in time to see her rake her keys over the glossy finish of his BMW.

He roared like a wounded lion. By the time he had flung open the door and burst out, she was leaping into her own car, squealing away.

Hands clenched, he looked at the damage. Deep, nasty scratches formed letters on the hood. PI. At least she hadn't had the satisfaction of finishing the thought, he decided.

Okay, fine. He'd have the car repaired while he was out of town. It seemed like a very good time to head north to San Quentin.

Chapter Twelve

Noah's first distant glimpse of San Quentin made him think of an old fortress now serving as some sort of thematic resort complex. Disneyland for cons.

The building was the color of sand and stretched out over San Francisco Bay with its multilevels and towers and turrets with a faintly exotic air.

It didn't smack of prison unless you thought of the armed guards in those towers, the spread of security lights that would turn the air around it orange and eerie at night. And all the steel cages it held inside.

He'd opted to take the ferry from San Francisco to Marin County and now stood at the rail while it glided over water made choppy by the wind. He found the architecture of the prison odd and somehow very Californian, but doubted the inmates had much appreciation for the structure's aesthetics.

It had taken him only hours to clear through channels for permission to visit. It made Noah wonder if Tanner had connections on the inside that had helped smooth the way.

Didn't matter, Noah decided while the wind cut through his hair like jagged shards of glass. The results were what counted.

He'd taken a day to read through his files on the MacBride murder, to study, refresh his memory, to consider. He knew the man he would meet as well as anyone from the outside was able to, he imagined.

At least he knew the man Tanner had been.

A hardworking, talented actor with an impressive string of successful movies under his belt by the time he'd met Julie MacBride, his co-star in *Summer Thunder*. He'd also, by all accounts, had an impressive string of females associated with his name before he'd married. It had been a first marriage for both of them, though he'd been seriously involved with Lydia Loring, a very hot property during the seventies. The gossip columns had had a field day with their stormy and very public breakup once he'd set his sights on Julie.

He'd enjoyed his fame, his money and his women. And had continued to enjoy the first two after his marriage. There'd been no other women after Julie. Or, Noah mused, he'd been very, very discreet.

Insiders called him difficult, temperamental, then had begun to use terms like 'explosive temper,' 'unreasonable demands' when his two films after *Summer Thunder* had tanked at the box office.

He'd begun to show up late and unprepared for shooting, had fired his personal assistant, then his agent.

It became one of Hollywood's worst-kept secrets that he was using, and using heavy.

So he'd become obsessive about his wife, delusional about the people around him, focused on Lucas Manning as his nemesis and, in the end, violent.

In 1975, he'd been the top box-office actor in the country. By 1980, he'd become an inmate in San Quentin. It was a long way to fall in a short amount of time.

The careless spread of staggering wealth and fame, the easy access to the most beautiful women in the world, the scrambling of maître d's to provide the best tables, the A-list for parties, the cheers of fans. How would it feel to have that sliding through your fingers? Noah wondered. Add arrogance, ego, mix it with cocaine, a little freebasing, jealousy over an up-and-coming box-office rival and a shattered marriage, and you had a perfect formula for disaster.

It would be interesting to see what the last twenty years had added, or taken away, from Sam Tanner.

He was back in his rental car when the ferry docked, and anxious to get on with it. Though he hoped to be done with the initial interview in time to get back to the airport and catch the evening flight home, he'd tossed a few things in a bag just in case he decided to stay over.

He hadn't mentioned the trip to anyone.

As he waited his turn, he drummed his fingers on the wheel to the Spice Girls and inexplicably thought of Olivia MacBride.

Oddly, the image that came to his mind was of a tall, gangly girl with pale hair and tanned arms. Of sad eyes as they'd sat on a riverbank watching beavers splash. He had done his research, but had found nothing public on her since her childhood. A few speculations now and then in the press, a recap story, the reprint of that stunning photo of her grief when she'd been four – that was all the mass media could manage.

Her family had pulled the walls up, he thought, and she'd stayed behind them. Just as her father had stayed behind the thick sand-colored walls of his prison. It was an angle he intended to pursue.

When the time came, he'd do whatever it took to convince her to speak with him again, to cooperate with the book. He could only hope that after six years her bitterness toward him would have lost its edge. That the sensible – and wonderfully sweet – science student he'd spent such a lovely few days with would see the value and the purpose of what he meant to do.

Beyond that, he couldn't think of what it would be like to see her again. So he tucked her away in his mind and concentrated on today.

He drove his rental car down the road toward the prison, passed an old pier and a pumping station. He caught a glimpse of a paved trail which he assumed led down to the water, and what might have been a little park, though he wondered why anyone would want to loiter or picnic in the shadow of those forbidding walls.

The visitors' parking lot skirted a small, attractive beach, with the waters a dull iron gray beyond. He'd considered a tape recorder, or at least a notebook, but had decided to go in cold. Just impressions, this time. He didn't want to give Tanner the idea he was making a commitment.

The visitors' entrance was a long hall with a side door halfway down. The single window was covered with notices, preventing views from either side. There was a sign on the door that had a chill sliding down his spine even as his lips quirked in wry amusement:

PLEASE DO NOT KNOCK. WE KNOW YOU ARE OUT THERE. WE WILL GET TO YOU AS SOON AS POSSIBLE.

So he stood, alone in the empty hallway with the wind whistling stridently, waiting for those who knew he was there to get to him.

When they did, he relayed his business, gave his ID, filled out the required forms. There was no small talk, no polite smiles.

He'd been the route before – in New York, in Florida. He'd been on death row and felt the ice slick through his gut at the sound of doors sliding shut and footsteps echoing. He'd spoken to lifers, the condemned and already damned.

He'd smelled the hate, the fear and the calculation, as much a stink in the air as sweat and piss and hand-rolled cigarettes.

He was taken down a hallway, bypassing the main visitors' area, and shown into a small, cheerless room with a table and two chairs. The door was thick with a single window of reinforced glass.

And there, Noah had his first look at what had become of Sam Tanner.

Gone was the pampered screen idol with the million-dollar smile. This was a hard man, body and face. Noah wondered how much his mind had toughened as well. He sat, one hand chained, the bright orange prison jumpsuit baggy and stark. His hair was cut brutally short and had gone a nearly uniform ash gray.

The lines dug deep into his face gave him the look of a man well beyond his age of fifty-eight. And Noah remembered another inmate once telling him prison years were long dog years. Every one behind bars was the equal of seven out in the world.

The eyes were a sharp and cold blue that took their time studying Noah, barely flicked toward the guard when they were told they had thirty minutes.

'Glad you could make it, Mr. Brady.'

That hadn't changed, Noah realized. The voice was as smooth and rich and potent as it had been in his last movie. Noah sat as the door closed and the lock snicked into place at his back.

'How did you get my home address, Mr. Tanner?'

A ghost of a smile played around his mouth. 'I still have some connections. How's your father?'

Noah kept his eyes level and ignored the jolt in his gut. 'My father's fine. I can't say he sends his best.'

Sam's teeth bared in a fleeting grin. 'A straight-up cop, Frank Brady. I see him and Jamie . . . now and again. She's still a pretty woman, my former sister-in-law. I wonder just how close her and your old man are.'

'Did you get me all the way up here to annoy me, Tanner, with speculations on my father's personal life?'

The smile came back, small and sly. 'I haven't had much interesting conversation lately. Got any reals?'

Noah lifted a brow. He knew most of the basic prison terms. 'No, sorry. I don't smoke.'

'Fucking California.' With his free hand, Sam reached inside his jumpsuit, carefully removed the tape that affixed a single hand-rolled cigarette and wooden match to his chest. 'Making prisons nonsmoking facilities. Where do they come up with this shit?'

He lighted the match with his thumbnail, then puffed the cigarette to life. 'Used to be I had the resources for a full brick a day. A couple packs of reals is decent currency inside. Now I'm lucky to get a carton a month.'

'It's lousy the way they treat murderers these days.'

Those hard blue eyes only glimmered – amusement or disdain, Noah couldn't be sure. 'Are you interested in crime and punishment, Brady, or are you interested in the story?'

'One goes with the other.'

'Does it?' Sam blew out a stream of ugly-smelling smoke. 'I've had a long time to think about that. You know, I can't remember the taste of good scotch, or the smell of a beautiful woman. You can deal with the sex. There are plenty inside who'll bend over for you if that's what you want. Otherwise you've always got your hand. But sometimes you wake up in the middle of the night just aching for the smell of a woman.'

He jerked a shoulder. 'There ain't no substitute. Me, I read a lot to get through those times. I used to stick to novels, pick a part in one and imagine playing it when I got out. I loved acting.' He said it with the same cold look in his eyes. 'I loved everything about it. It took me a long time to accept that part of my life was over, too.'

Noah angled his head. 'Is it? What role are you playing here, Tanner?'

Abruptly, Sam leaned forward, and for the first time life sprang into his eyes, hot and real. 'This is all I've got. You think because you come in here and talk to cons you understand what it's like? You can get up and walk out anytime. You'll never understand.'

'There's not much stopping me from getting up and walking out now,' Noah said evenly. 'What do you want?'

'I want you to tell it, to put it all down. To say how it was then, how it is now. To say why things happened and why they didn't. Why two people who had everything lost it all.'

'And you're going to tell me all that?'

'Yeah, I'm going to tell you all of it.' Sam leaned back, drawing out the last stingy sliver of his smoke. 'And you're going to find out the rest.'

'Why? Why me, why now?'

'Why you?' Sam dropped the smoldering bit of paper and tobacco on the floor, absently crushed it out. 'I liked your book,' he said simply. 'And I couldn't resist the irony of the connection. Seemed almost like a sign. I'm not one of the pitiful who found God in here. God has nothing to do with places like this, and He doesn't come here. But there's fate, and there's timing.'

'You want to consider me fate, okay. What's the timing?'

'I'm dying.'

Noah skimmed his gaze coolly over Sam's face. 'You look healthy enough to me.'

'Brain tumor.' Sam tapped a finger on his head. 'Inoperable. The doctors say maybe a year, if I'm lucky – and if I'm lucky, I'll die in the world and not inside. We're working on that. It looks like the system's going to be satisfied with my twenty now that I'm dead anyway.'

He seemed to find that amusing and chuckled over it. It wasn't a sound that encouraged the listener to join in. 'You could say I've got a new sentence, short stretch with no possibility of parole. So, if you're interested, you'll have to work fast.'

'You've got something new to add to everything that's been said, printed, filmed over the last couple of decades?'

'Do you want to find out?'

Noah tapped a finger on the table. 'I'll think about it.' He rose. 'I'll get back to you.'

'Brady,' Sam said as Noah moved to the door. 'You didn't ask if I killed my wife.'

Noah glanced back, met his eyes dead on. 'Why would I?' he said and signaled for the guard.

Sam smiled a little. He thought the first meeting had gone well and never doubted Frank Brady's son would come back.

Noah sat in Prison Supervisor Diterman's office, surprised and a little flattered that his request for a meeting had been so quickly granted. Hollywood would never have cast George Diterman in the role of head of one of the country's most active prisons. With his thinning patch of hair, small build and round black-framed glasses, he looked like a man very low on the feeding chain of a midlevel accounting firm.

He greeted Noah with a brisk handshake and a surprisingly charming smile. 'I enjoyed your first book,' he began as he took his place behind his desk. 'And I'm already enjoying the second.'

'Thank you.'

'And should I assume you're here gathering information to write another?'

'I've just spoken with Sam Tanner.'

'Yes, I'm aware of that.' Diterman folded his small, neat hands on the edge of his desk. 'I cleared the request.'

'Because you admire my work or because of Tanner?'

'A little of both. I've been in this position in this facility for five years. During that period Tanner has been what you'd call a model prisoner. He stays out of trouble, he does his work in the prison library well. He follows the rules.'

'Rehabilitated?' Noah asked with just enough cynicism in his tone to make Diterman smile again.

'That depends on which definition you choose. Society's, the law's, this house's. But I can say that at some point, he decided to do his time clean.'

Diterman unlaced his fingers, pressed them together, laced them tidily again. 'Tanner's authorized me to give you access to his records and to speak to you frankly about him.'

He works fast, Noah mused. Fine. He'd been waiting a long time to begin this book, and he intended to work fast himself. 'Then why don't you, Supervisor, speak frankly to me about Inmate Tanner.'

'According to reports, he had a difficult time adjusting when he first came here. There were a number of incidents – altercations between him and the guards, between him and other prisoners. Inmate Tanner spent a large portion of 1980 in the infirmary being treated for a number of injuries.'

'He got into fights.'

'Consistently. He was violent and invited violence. He was transfered to solitary several times during his first five years. He also had an addiction to cocaine and found sources within the prison to feed that addiction. During the fall of 1982 he was treated for an overdose.'

'Deliberate or accidental?'

'That remains unclear, though the therapist leaned toward accidental. He's an actor, a good one.' Diterman's eyes remained bland, but Noah read sharp intelligence in them. 'My predecessor noted several times that Tanner was a difficult man to read. He played whatever role suited him.'

'Past tense.'

'I can only tell you that for the past several years he's settled in. His work in the library appears to satisfy him. He keeps to himself as much as it's possible to do so. He avoids confrontations.'

'He told me he has an inoperable brain tumor. Terminal.'

'Around the first of the year he complained of severe, recurring headaches, double vision. The tumor was discovered. Tests were run, and the consensus is he has perhaps a year. Most likely less than that.'

'How'd he take it?'

'Better than I think I would. There are details of his file and his counseling and treatment I can't share with you, as I'll require not only his permission, but other clearance.'

'If I decide to pursue this, to interview him, to listen, I'll need your co-operation as well as his. I'll need names, dates, events. Even opinions. Are you willing to give me those things?'

'I'll cooperate as much as I'm able. To be frank, Mr. Brady, I'd like to hear the entire story myself. I had a tremendous crush on Julie MacBride.'

'Who didn't?' Noah murmured.

He decided to stay the night in San Francisco, and after settling into a room with a view overlooking the bay, he ordered up a meal and set up his laptop. Once he'd plugged into the Internet, he did a search on Sam Tanner.

For a man who'd spent two decades behind bars without granting a single interview, there was a wealth of hits. A number of them dealt with movies, his roles, summaries and critiques. Those could wait.

He found references to a number of books on the case, including unauthorized biographies of both Sam and Julie. Noah had a number of them in his library and made a note to himself to read through them again. There were articles on the trial, mostly rehashes.

He found nothing particularly fresh.

When his meal arrived, Noah ate his burger and typed one-handed, book-marking any areas he might want to explore again.

He'd seen the photographs that popped before. The one of Sam, impossibly handsome, and a luminous Julie, both beaming beautifully into the camera. Another of Sam, shackled, being led out of the courthouse during the trial and looking ill and dazed.

And both of those men, Noah though, were inside the cool-eyed and calculating inmate. How many others would he find before his book was done?

That, Noah admitted, was the irresistible pull. Who lived behind those eyes? What was it that gripped a man and drove him to butcher the woman he claimed to love, the mother of his child? To destroy everything he swore mattered to him?

Drugs? Not enough, in Noah's opinion. And not in the court's opinion either, he recalled. The defense had fallen back on drugs during the sentencing phase, attempting to get the sentence reduced due to mitigating circumstances. It hadn't swayed the results.

The brutality of the crime had outweighed everything else. And, Noah thought now, the pathetic video testimony of the victim's four-year-old child. No jury could have turned their backs on that little girl, her tearful description of what she'd seen that night, and given Sam Tanner any pity.

Twenty to life, the first fifteen without possibility of parole.

Noah didn't intend to be judge or jury but to align facts. As far as he was concerned, drugs didn't matter. Drugs might blur the edges, remove inhibitions. They might bring out the beast, but the beast had to exist in order to act.

The hand that had plunged the scissors repeatedly into Julie MacBride had belonged to a monster. He didn't intend to forget that.

He could research the crime objectively, he could distance himself from the horror of it. that was his job. He could sit and listen to Sam Tanner, talk with him, become intimate with his mind and put it all down on paper. He could dissect the man, prowl around in his brain and note the changes that may or may not have taken place inside him over the last two decades.

But he wouldn't forget that one night in high summer, Sam Tanner hadn't been a man.

He started to begin a new search on Julie MacBride, then on impulse changed it to River's End Lodge and Campground. He sat back and sipped his coffee as their home page came up. Technology, he mused, was a wonderful thing.

There was an arty and appealing photo of the lodge, exactly as he remembered it. A couple of interior photos showed the lobby and one of the guest suites. There was a chatty little description, which touched on the history, the accommodations, the beauty of the national forest.

Another click took him to the recreational offerings – fishing, canoeing, hiking, a naturalist center . . .

He paused there and grinned. She'd done it, then. Built her center. Good for you, Liv.

They offered guided tours, a heated pool, health-club facilities.

He skimmed down, noting that weekend, full-week and special packages were offered. The proprietors were listed as Rob and Val MacBride.

Nowhere did he find Olivia's name.

'You still there, Liv?' he wondered. 'Yeah, you're still there. With the forest and the rivers. Do you ever think of me?'

Annoyed he'd had the thought, the question, he pushed away from the desk and stalked to the window. He looked out at the city, at lights, at traffic.

And wondered what had become of his ancient backpack.

Turning away, he flicked on the television, just for the noise. There were times when he couldn't think in silence. Because he was a man, and there was a remote at hand, he couldn't resist surfing the channels. He let out a short laugh when Julie MacBride, young, gorgeous and alive, filled the screen. Those striking amber eyes were glowing with love, with pleasure, with the sheen of tears as she raced down a long sweep of white stairs and into the arms of Sam Tanner.

Summer Thunder, Noah mused. Last scene. No dialogue. The music swells . . . He watched, hearing the flood of violins as the couple embraced, as Julie's warm flow of laughter joined it. As Sam lifted her off her feet, circling, circling in celebration of love found.

Fade-out.

Fate? Noah thought. Well, sometimes there was just no arguing with it.

He picked up a notebook, plopped down on the bed with it and began to make a list of names and questions.

Jamie Melbourne
David Melbourne
Roy and Val MacBride
Frank Brady
Charles Brighton Smith
Prosecution team? Who's still alive?
Lucas Manning
Lydia Loring
Agents, managers, publicists?
Rosa Sanchez (housekeeper)
Other domestic staff?

At the bottom of the list, he wrote 'Olivia MacBride.'

He wanted more from her than memories of one violent night. He wanted what she remembered of her parents together, what she remembered of them individually. The tone of their household, the undercurrents of marital distress.

There were always other angles to pursue. Had Julie been involved with Lucas Manning – giving credence to her husband's jealousy?

Would she have told her sister? Would the child have sensed it? The servants?

And wasn't it interesting, Noah decided, that his daughter hadn't been among the things Sam Tanner claimed to miss?

Oh yes, Olivia was key, Noah thought, and circled her name. This time, he couldn't allow himself to be distracted by feelings, by basic attraction, by even the connection of friendship.

They were both older now, and that was behind them. This time when they met, it would be the book first.

He wondered if she still wore her hair pulled back in a ponytail, if she still had that brief hesitation before she smiled.

'Give it a rest, Brady,' he muttered. 'That's history.'

He pushed himself up, then dug in his briefcase for the numbers he'd looked up and scribbled down before leaving L.A. Rain began to lash the windows as he made the call, and he adjusted his vague plans of going out and indulging in some San Francisco nightlife to a solo beer at the bar downstairs.

'Good afternoon, Constellations.'

'Noah Brady calling for Jamie Melbourne.'

'Ms. Melbourne is with a client. May I take a message?'

'Tell her I'm Frank Brady's son, and I'd like to speak with her. I'm out of town at the moment.' He glanced at the phone, then reeled off the number. 'I'll be in for another hour.'

That was a test, he mused as he hung up. Just to see how quickly the Brady name got a call back.

He stretched back out on the bed and had surfed through the channels twice when his phone rang. 'Brady.'

'Yes, this is Jamie Melbourne.'

'Thanks for getting back to me.' Within six minutes, Noah thought with a glance at his watch.

'Is this about your father? I hope he's well.'

'He's fine, thanks. This is about Sam Tanner.' He paused, waited, but there was no response. 'I'm in San Francisco. I spoke with him earlier today.'

'I see. I was under the impression he spoke to no one, particularly reporters or writers. You're a writer, aren't you, Noah?'

The first name, putting him in his place, he decided. Maintaining control. A good and subtle move. 'That's right. He spoke to me, and I'm hoping you will, too. I'd like to set up an appointment with you. I should be back in town by tomorrow evening. Do you have any time free Thursday or Friday?'

'Why?'

'Sam Tanner wants to tell his story. I'm going to write it, Ms. Melbourne, and I want to give you every opportunity to tell your part of it.'

'The man killed my sister and broke the hearts of every member of my family. What else do you need to know?'

'Everything you can tell me – unless you want the information I gather coming only from his point of view. That's not what I'm after here.'

'No, you're after another best-seller, aren't you? However you can get it.'

'If that were true, I wouldn't have called you. Just talk to me – off the record if you want. Then make up your mind.'

'Have you spoken with anyone else in my family?'

'No.'

'Don't. Come to see me Thursday at four. At my home. I'll give you an hour, no more.'

'I appreciate it. If I could have your address?'

'Get it from your father.' She snapped that out, her controlled voice finally breaking. 'He knows it.'

Noah winced as she broke the connection, though the click was quiet, almost discreet. Definitely stepping onto shaky ground there, he decided. She was predisposed not to cooperate, not to be objective about what he intended to accomplish.

He flipped through channels without interest as he considered. Sam hadn't told him about his death sentence in confidence. Perhaps he'd pass that information to Jamie, see if it made any difference to her. He could also use her reluctance to cooperate in his strategy with Sam.

Playing one against the other would result in more information from both of them – if he did it well.

And he'd just keep his own long-term and personal fascination with the case his little secret for now.

He drifted off with the rain pattering on the windows and the television blaring, and dreamed a dream he wouldn't remember of giant trees and green light, and a tall woman with golden eyes.

Chapter Thirteen

The same guard took Noah to the same room. This time he'd brought a notepad and a tape recorder. He set them both on the table. Sam glanced at them, said nothing, but Noah caught a quick glint in his eyes that might have been satisfaction. Or relief.

Noah took his seat, switched on the recorder. 'Let's go back, Sam. Nineteen seventy-three.'

'*Fever* was released in May, and was the biggest moneymaker of the summer. I got an Oscar nomination for it. I listened to "Desperado" every time I turned on the radio. The sixties were pretty well dead,' Sam said with what might have been amusement, 'and disco hadn't quite reared its ugly head. I was unofficially living with Lydia and having great sex and monumental fights. Pot was out, snow was in. There was always a party going on. And I met Julie MacBride.'

He paused, just a heartbeat of silence. 'Everything that had happened to me before that moment took second place.'

'You were married that same year.'

'Neither one of us was the cautious type, or the patient type.' His gaze drifted off, and Noah wondered what images he could see playing against the ugly bare walls. 'It didn't take us long to figure out what we wanted. What we wanted was each other. For a while, that was enough for both of us.'

'Tell me,' Noah said simply, and waited while Sam took out his contraband cigarette, lighted it.

'She'd been in Ireland with her sister, taking a couple weeks between projects. We met in Hank Midler, the director's, office. She came in – wearing jeans and a dark blue sweater. Her hair was pulled back. She looked maybe sixteen. She was the most beautiful thing I'd ever seen in my life.'

His gaze arrowed back, shot straight into Noah's eyes. 'That's not an exaggeration. It's the truth. I was used to women – to having them, enjoying them. One look at her, and she might have been the first. I think I knew, right then, she'd be the last. You may not understand that.'

'Yes, I do understand it.' He'd experienced that rush, that connection, when this man's daughter had opened her apartment door and given him a faintly annoyed frown.

'Been in love, have you, Brady?'

'I've been in something.'

Sam let out a short laugh, then looked past Noah again, seemed to dream. 'My belly clutched up,' he murmured. 'And my heart . . . I could actually feel it shaking inside me. When I took her hand it was like . . . yes. You. Finally. Later, she told me it had been exactly the same for her, as if we'd been moving through our lives to get to that moment. We talked about the script, went about the business as if both of us weren't reeling. Afterward, I asked her to dinner, and we agreed to meet at seven. When I got home, I told Lydia it was over.'

He paused, laughed a little, drew deep on the cigarette. 'Just over. I wasn't kind about it, wasn't cruel. The fact was, she'd simply ceased to exist for me. All I could think of was that at seven I'd see Julie again.'

'Was Julie involved with anyone at that time?'

'She'd been seeing Michael Ford. The press played it up, but it wasn't serious. Two weeks after we met, we moved in together. Quietly, or as quietly as we were able to.'

'You met her family?'

'Yes, that was important to her. It was a lot of work for me to bring Jamie around. She was very protective of Julie. She didn't trust me, thought Julie was just another fling. Hard to blame her,' he said with a jerk of his shoulders. 'I'd had plenty.'

'Did it bother you that Julie's name was linked to a number of men at that time? Ford was just the latest.'

'I didn't think of it then.' Sam pulled the stub of the cigarette out of his mouth, crushed it out with a restrained violence that had Noah's eyes narrowing. 'It was only later, when things got out of control. Then I thought about it. Sometimes it was all I could think about. The men who'd had her, the men who wanted her. The men she wanted. She was pulling away from me, and I wanted to know who was going to take my place. Who the hell was she turning to when she was turning away from me? Lucas Manning.'

Even after twenty years, saying the name scored his tongue. 'I knew there was something between them.'

'So you killed her to keep her.'

The muscles in Sam's jaws quivered once, and his eyes went blank. 'That's one theory.'

Noah gave him a pleasant smile. 'We'll talk about the rest of the theories some other time. What was it like working with her on the movie?'

'Julie?' Sam blinked, lifted a hand to rub it distractedly over his face.

'Yes.' Noah continued in the same mild tone. He'd thrown Sam off rhythm, exactly as he'd intended. He wasn't about to settle for well-rehearsed lines and perfect phrasing. 'You were getting to know each other on two levels during the shoot. As lovers, and as actors. Let's talk about what she was like as an actor.'

'She was good. Solid.' Sam dropped his hands into his lap, then lifted them onto the table as if he wasn't quite sure what to do with them. 'A natural. The term's overused, but it applied to her. She didn't have to work as hard as I did. She just felt it.'

'Did that bother you? That she was better than you?'

'I didn't say she was better.' His hands stilled, and his gaze whipped up, two hot blue points. 'We came at it from two different places, different schools. She had a phenomenal memory, and that helped her with lines. She never forgot a fucking line. But she tended to put herself into her director's hands, almost naively trusting him to make it all come together. She didn't know enough about the rest of the craft to risk input on angles, lighting, pacing.'

'But you did,' Noah interrupted before Sam could fall back into a rhythm.

'Yeah, I did. Midler and I went head-to-head plenty on that film, but we respected each other. I was sorry to hear he died a couple of years ago. He was a genius.'

'And Julie trusted him.'

'She practically worshiped him. The chance to work with him was the main reason she'd taken the part. And he knew how to showcase her, knew how to coax the best from her. She was like a sponge, soaking up the thoughts and feelings of her character, then pouring them out. I built the character, layer by layer. We made a good team.'

'Julie won the New York Film Critics' Award for her portrayal of Sarah in *Summer Thunder*. You were nominated but didn't win. Did that cause any friction between you?'

'I was thrilled for her. She was upset that I hadn't won. She'd wanted it more than I had. We'd been married less than a year at that time. We were as close to royalty as you can get in that town. We were completely in love, completely happy, and riding the wave. She shared everything with me then, understood me as no one ever had.'

'And the next year, when she was nominated for an Oscar for best actress for *Twilight's Edge*, and your movie got mixed reviews. How did that affect your relationship?'

A muscle twitched under Sam's left eye, but he continued to speak coolly. 'She was pregnant. We concentrated on that. She wanted a healthy baby a lot more than she wanted a statue.'

'And you? What did you want?'

Sam smiled thinly. 'I wanted everything. And for a while, that's just what I had. What do you want, Brady?'

'The story. From all the angles.' He leaned forward and switched off the tape recorder. 'I'm heading back to L.A.,' he continued as he began to pack his briefcase. 'I'll be talking to Jamie Melbourne tomorrow.'

He noted the way Sam's fingers jerked and curled on the table. 'Is there anything you want me to pass along to her?'

'She won't take anything from me but my death. She'll be getting that soon enough. She was jealous of Julie,' he said in a rush, and had Noah pausing. 'Julie could never see it, or never wanted to admit it, but Jamie had plenty of built-up jealousy over Julie's looks, her success, her style. She played the devoted sister, but if she'd had the chance, if she'd had the talent, she'd have knocked Julie aside, stepped over her and taken her place.'

'Her place with you?'

'She settled for Melbourne, music agent with no talent of his own. She played second lead to Julie all her life. When Julie was dead, Jamie finally got the spotlight.'

'Is that another theory?'

'If she hadn't tagged on to Julie, she'd still be running that lodge up in Washington. You think she'd have a big house, her business, her pussy-whipped husband if Julie hadn't cleared the way?'

Oh, there was resentment here, bitterness that had brewed for more than two decades. 'Why should that matter to you?'

'She's kept me in here, made damn sure I didn't get a decent shot at parole these last five years. Made it her goddamn mission to keep me inside. And all the while she's still sucking up what Julie left behind. You talk to her, Brady, you have a nice chat with her, and you ask her if she wasn't the one who talked Julie into filing for divorce. If she wasn't the one who pushed it all over the edge. And if she wasn't the one who built her whole fucking big-time business off her dead sister's back.'

The minute his plane took off, Noah ordered a beer and opened his lap-top. He wanted to get his thoughts and impressions into words while they were still fresh, and he wanted to get home, spread his notes out around him, start making calls, setting up interviews.

The rush of anticipation racing through his blood was a familiar sensation and told him he was committed now. There was no going back. The endless stream of research, digging, backtracking and puzzling didn't intimidate him. It energized him.

From now until it was done, Sam Tanner would be the focus of his life.

He wants to run the show, Noah wrote. *So do I. It's going to be an interesting tug-of-war. He's smart. I think people have underestimated him, seeing him purely as a spoiled and selfish pretty boy with a filthy temper. He's learned control, but the temper's still under it. And if his reaction to Jamie Melbourne is any indication, his temper can still be mean.*

I wonder how much of what he tells me will be the truth, what he sees as the truth, or outright lies.

One thing I'm sure of is that be wants the spotlight again. He wants to be recognized. He wants the attention that's been denied him since be walked into San Quentin. And he wants it on his terms. I don't think he's looking for sympathy. I don't think he gives a good goddamn about understanding. But this is his story. He's chosen the time to tell it, and he's chosen me to tell it to.

It's a good twist – the son of the cop who took him down writing the book. The press will play on it, and he knows it.

His comments on Jamie Melbourne are interesting. Truth, perception or lie? It'll be even more interesting to find out.

Most intriguing of all is the fact that he's yet to ask about Olivia, or to mention her by name.

He wondered if Jamie would.

Noah understood that Jamie Melbourne's publicity firm, Constellations, was one of the most prestigious in the entertainment business. It had branches in Los Angeles and New York and represented top names.

He also understood that prior to her sister's death, Jamie had represented only Julie, and had worked primarily out of her own home.

It was an unarguable fact that Jamie's star had risen after her sister's murder.

What that meant, Noah mused as he drove through the gates to the elaborate home in Holmby Hills, was yet to be seen.

According to his research, the Melbournes had moved into the estate in 1986, selling their more modest home and relocating here where they were known for their lavish parties.

The main house was three stories in sheer wedding-cake white with a long flowing front porch at the entrance flanked by columns. Rooms speared out from the central structure in two clean lines on opposite sides, with walls of glass winking out on richly blooming gardens and fussy ornamental trees.

Two gorgeous golden retrievers bounded across the lawn to greet him, tails slapping the air and each other in delight.

'Hey there.' He opened the car door and fell instantly in love. He was bending over, happily scratching ears and murmuring nonsense when Jamie walked over carrying a ratty tennis ball.

'They're Goodness and Mercy,' she said, but didn't smile as Noah looked up at her.

'Where's Shirley?'

A faint wisp of humor played around her mouth. 'She has a good home.' Jamie held up the ball. As one, both dogs quivered and sat, staring up with desperately eager eyes. Then she threw it, sending it sailing for the dogs to chase.

'Good arm,' Noah murmured.

'I keep in shape. It's too nice an afternoon to sit inside.' And she'd yet to decide if she wanted him in her home. 'We'll walk.'

She turned, heading away from where the dogs were wrestling deliriously over the ball.

Noah had to agree she kept in shape. She was fifty-two, and could have passed easily for forty – and was all the more attractive as she wasn't going for twenty.

There were a few lines, but they added strength to her face, and it was her eyes that drew the attention rather than the creases fanning out from them. They were dark, intelligent and unflinching. Her hair was a soft brown, cut in a just-above-chin-length wedge that set off the shape of her face and added to the image of a mature woman of style and no fuss.

She was small framed, slimly built and wore rust-colored slacks and a simple camp shirt with confidence and comfort. She walked like a woman who was used to being on her feet and knew how to get where she wanted to go.

'How is your father?' she asked at length.

'He's fine, thanks. I guess you know he retired last year.'

She smiled now, briefly. 'Yes. Does he miss his work?'

'I think he did, until he got involved with the neighborhood youth center. He loves working with kids.'

'Yes, Frank's good with children. I admire him very much.' She walked past a glossy bush that smelled delicately of jasmine. 'If I didn't, you wouldn't be here now.'

'I appreciate that, and your taking the time to see me, Ms. Melbourne.'

She didn't sigh out loud, but he saw the rise and fall of her shoulders. 'Jamie. He's spoken to me about you often enough that I think of you as Noah.'

'Has he? I didn't realize the two of you had had that much contact.'

'Frank was an integral part of the most difficult period of my life.'

'Most people tend to separate themselves from people who remind them of difficult periods.'

'I don't,' she said briefly and walked toward a large fan-shaped swimming pool bordered in white stone and cool pink flowers. 'Your father helped me through a tremendous loss, helped see that my family got justice. He's an exceptional man.'

Your father's a great man, Olivia had told him once. And later, *Beside him, you're very small.*

Noah turned off the ache of that and nodded. 'I think so.'

'I'm glad to hear it.'

As they skirted the pool, he could see the deep green of tennis courts in the distance. Tucked behind oleanders and roses was a scaled-down version of the main house.

'I don't like your work,' she said abruptly.

'All right.'

She stopped, turned to him. 'I don't understand it. Or why you do it. Your father dedicated his life to putting people who take the lives of others in prison. And you're dedicating yours to putting their names in print, to glorifying what they've done.'

'Have you read my work?'

'No.'

'If you had, you'd know I don't glorify the people I write about or what they've done.'

'Writing about them is glory enough.'

'Writing about them lays it out,' Noah corrected. 'The people, the acts, the history, the motives. The whys. My father was interested in the whys, too. How and when aren't always enough. Don't you want to know why your sister died, Jamie?'

'I know why she died. She died because Sam Tanner killed her. Because he was jealous and sick and vicious enough not to want her to live without him.'

'But they'd loved each other once, enough to marry and make a child. Enough, even when they were supposedly having serious marital difficulties, for her to open the door to him.'

'And for that last act of love, he killed her.' This time, Jamie's voice was hot and bitter. 'He used her feelings, her loyalty, her need to keep her family together. He used them against her just as surely as he used the scissors.'

'You could tell me about her the way no one else can. About what she thought, what she felt, about what happened to turn her life into a nightmare.'

'What about her privacy?'

'She's never had that, has she?' He said it gently. 'I can promise to give her the truth.'

She looked away again, wearily. 'There are a lot of degrees in the truth.'

'Give me yours.'

'Why is he letting you do this? Why is he talking to you, to anyone after all these years?'

'He's dying.' He said it straight and watched her face.

Something flickered across it, glinted in her eyes, then was gone. 'Good. How long is it going to take him?'

A hard woman, Noah thought, hard and honest. 'He has brain cancer. They diagnosed it in January and gave him under a year.'

'Well, justice wins. So he wants his brief time in the sun again before he goes to hell.'

'That may be what he wants,' Noah said evenly. 'What he'll get is a book written my way. Not his.'

'You'll write it with or without my cooperation.'

'Yes, but I'll write a better book with it.'

She believed he meant it. He had his father's clear, assessing eyes. 'I don't want to hate you for it,' she said almost to herself. 'I've centered all my hate on one place all these years. I don't want to diffuse it at this point – especially now that his time is nearly up.'

'But you have something to say, haven't you? Things you haven't said yet.'

'Maybe I do. I spoke with my husband about this yesterday. He surprised me.'

'How?'

'He thinks we should give you your interviews. To counter-balance what Sam tells you, David thinks, to make sure whatever ugliness he's formed in his mind doesn't stand on its own. We were there, part of their lives. We know what happened to it. So, yes, maybe I do have something to say.'

She ripped at a hibiscus, tore the fragile pink blossom to shreds. 'I'll talk to you, Noah, and so will David. Let's go inside so I can check my calendar.'

'Got any time now?' He smiled, a quick and charming flash. 'You said I could have an hour, and we've only used about half that.'

'That part must come from your mother,' Jamie mused. 'The fast dazzle. Frank's more subtle.'

'Whatever works.'

'All right. Come inside.'

'I need to get my things out of the car. Taping interviews protects both of us.'

'Just ring. Rosa will let you in.'

'Rosa? Would that be Rosa Sanchez?'

'Rosa Cruz now, and yes, the same Rosa who worked for Julie at one time. She's been with David and me for the past twenty years. Go get your tape recorder, Noah, you're still on the clock.'

He made it fast, though the dogs conned him into throwing the ball for them and made him wonder why he didn't get himself a dog of his own.

When he rang the bell, he noted that the long glass panes on either side of the grand white door were etched with calla lilies, and the marble urns that flanked them were spilling over with fuchsia in tones of deep reds and purples that were obviously well loved and well tended.

The woman who answered the door was very short and very wide, so that he thought of a barrel in a smartly pressed gray uniform. Her hair was the same color as the cloth and wound tidily, almost ruthlessly back into a nape bun. Her face was round and deep gold, her eyes a nut brown that snapped with disapproval.

All in all, Noah thought, she made a better guard than Goodness and Mercy, who were at that moment happily peeing on the tires of his rental car.

'Mr. Brady.' Her voice was richly Mexican and cold as February. 'Ms. Melbourne will see you in the solarium.'

'Thanks.' He stepped into a foyer wide as a ballroom and had to muffle a whistle of interest at the flood of crystal in the chandelier and what seemed like acres of white marble on the floor.

Rosa's heels clicked over it busily, giving him little time to study the art and furnishings of the living room. But what he did see told him the dogs weren't allowed to do any romping in that area.

The solarium was a towering glass dome snugged onto the south side of the house, crowded with flowers and plants and their exotic mix of scents. Water glistened its way down a stone wall and into a little pool where white water lilies floated.

Seats and benches were tucked here and there, and a pretty conversation area was arranged beside the tall glass. Jamie was already waiting on a generously sized rattan chair with cushions striped in cheery green and white.

On the rippled glass of a round table was a clear pitcher filled with amber iced tea, two tall glasses and a plate of what Noah thought of as girl cookies – tiny, frosted and shaped like hearts.

'Thank you, Rosa.'

'You have a cocktail party at seven.' Rosa relayed this with her eyebrows beetled into one straight line.

'Yes, I know. It's all right.'

She only sniffed, then muttered something in Spanish before she left them alone.

'She doesn't like me.'

'Rosa's very protective.' As he sat, Jamie leaned forward to pour the tea.

'It's a great house.' He glanced over her shoulder, through the glass to the flood of flowers beyond. 'Your dahlias are terrific, a nice match with the wild indigo and dusty miller.'

Jamie's brows rose. 'You surprise me, Noah. The horticultural limits of most young hunks stop at roses.' The grimace he didn't quite hide made her laugh and relax. 'And you can be embarrassed. Well, that's a relief. Was it the flower comment or the hunk reference?'

'Flowers are a hobby of mine.'

'Ah, the hunk then. Well, you're tall, built and have a very handsome face. So there you are.' She continued to smile, and indulged herself in a cookie.

'Your parents keep hoping you'll find the right woman and settle down.'

'What?'

Thoroughly amused now, she lifted the plate, offered it. 'Haven't they mentioned that to you?'

'No. Jesus.' He took a cookie, shaking his head as he set up his tape recorder. 'Women aren't high on my list right now. I just had a narrow escape.'

'Really?' Jamie tucked her legs up under her. 'Want to talk about it?'

His gaze shifted, met hers. 'Not while I'm on the clock. Tell me about growing up with Julie.'

'Growing up?' He'd broken her rhythm. 'Why? I thought you'd want to discuss that last year.'

'Eventually.' The cookies weren't half bad, so he had another. 'But right now I'd like to know what it was like being her sister. More, her twin sister. Tell me about that, about when you were kids.'

'It was a good childhood, for both of us. We were close, and we were happy. We had a great deal of freedom, I suppose, as children often do who grow up outside of the city. My parents believed in giving us responsibilities and freedom in equal measure. It's a good formula.'

'You grew up in a fairly isolated area. Did you have any other friends?'

'Hmm, a few, certainly. But we were always each other's best friend. We enjoyed each other's company, and liked most of the same things.'

'No squabbles, no sibling rivalry?'

'Nothing major. We had spats – I doubt anyone can fight like sisters or aim for the weak spots with more accuracy. Julie wasn't a pushover, and gave as good as she got.'

'She get a lot?'

Jamie nibbled on her cookie, smiled. 'Sure. I wasn't a pushover either. Noah, we were two strong-minded young girls growing up in each other's pockets. We had a lot of room, but we were . . . enclosed all the same. We sniped, we fought, we made up. We irritated each other, competed with each other. And we loved each other. Julie would take her licks, and she'd take her swipes. But she could never hold a grudge.'

'Could you?'

'Oh yes.' The smile again, slightly feline now. 'That was one thing I was always better at. With Julie, she'd go her round, aim her punches, then she'd forget it. One minute she'd be furious, stomp off with her nose in the air. And the next, she'd be laughing and telling me to hurry up and look at something, or it would be, "Oh come on, Jamie, get over it and let's go for a swim." And if I didn't get over it quickly enough, she'd keep poking at me until I did. She was irresistible.'

'You said holding grudges was the one thing you were better at. What was she better at?'

'Almost everything. She was prettier, sharper, quicker, stronger. Certainly more outgoing and ambitious.'

'Didn't you resent that?'

'Maybe I did.' She looked at him blandly. 'Then I got over it. Julie was born to be spectacular. I wasn't. Do you think I blamed her for that?'

'Did you?'

'Let's put this on another level,' Jamie said after a moment.

'Using an interest we both apparently share. Do you blame one rose for being a deeper color, a bigger bloom than the other? One isn't less than another, but different. Julie and I were different.'

'Then again, a lot of people overlook the smaller bloom and choose the more spectacular one.'

'But there's something to be said for slow bloomers, isn't there? She's gone.' Jamie picked up her glass and sipped, watching Noah over the rim. 'I'm still here.'

'And if she'd lived? What then?'

'She didn't.' Her gaze shifted away now, toward something he couldn't see. 'I'll never know what would have been in store for both of us if Sam Tanner hadn't come into our lives.'

Chapter Fourteen

'I was madly in love with Sam Tanner. And I spent many delightful hours devising ways in which he would die the most hideous and painful, and hopefully embarrassing, of deaths.'

Lydia Loring sipped her mineral water and lime from a tall, slim glass of Baccarat crystal and chuckled. Her eyes, a summery baby blue, flirted expertly with Noah and had him grinning back at her.

'Care to describe one of the methods for the record?'

'Hmmm. Well, let's see . . .' She trailed off, recrossing her very impressive legs. 'There was the one where he was found chained to the bed and wearing women's underwear. He'd starved to death. It took many horrible days.'

'So I take it the two of you didn't end your relationship in an amicable fashion.'

'Hell. We didn't do anything in an amicable fashion. We were animals from the first minute we laid hands on each other. I was crazy about him,' she added, running her finger around the rim of her glass. 'Literally. When they convicted him, I opened a bottle of Dom Perignon, seventy-five, and drank every single drop.'

'That was several years after your relationship ended.'

'Yes, and several years before my lovely vacation at Betty Ford's. I do, occasionally, still miss the marvelous zip of champagne.' She lifted a shoulder. 'I had problems, so did Sam. We drank hard, played hard, worked hard. We had outrageous sex, vicious fights. There was no moderation for either of us back then.'

'Drugs.'

'Rehabilitated,' she said, holding up a hand and flashing a killer smile. 'My body's a temple now, and a damn good one.'

'No arguing there,' Noah responded and made her purr. 'But there were drugs.'

'Honey, they were passed out like candy. Coke was our favorite party favor. Word was after Sam fell for Julie, she put a stop to that. But me, I just kept on flying. Wrecked my health, toppled my career, screwed up my personal life by marrying two money-grubbing creeps. When the eighties dawned, I was sick, broke, ruined. I got clean and clawed my way back. Sitcom guest shots, bit parts in bad movies. I took whatever I could get, and I was grateful. Then six years ago I got *Roxy*.'

She smiled over the situation comedy that had boosted her back to the top. 'A lot of people talk about reinventing themselves. I did it.'

'Not everyone would be so up-front about the mistakes they made along the way. You've always been brutally honest about what you did, where you were.'

'Part of my personal philosophy. I had fame once, and I handled it badly. I have it again, and I don't take any of it for granted.'

She glanced around the spacious dressing room with its plump sofa, fresh flowers. 'Some say *Roxy* saved my life, but they're wrong. *I* saved my life, and part of the process was putting my relationship with Sam Tanner in perspective. I loved him. He loved Julie. And look what that got her.'

She plucked a glossy green grape from a bowl, popped it in her mouth. 'Look what getting dumped by him got me.'

'How did you feel about her?'

'I hated her.' She said it cheerfully, without a hint of guilt. 'Not only did she have what I wanted, but she came off looking like the wholesome girl next door while I was the used-up former lover. I was thrilled when their marriage hit the rocks, when Sam started showing up at clubs and parties again. The old Sam. Looking for action, asking for trouble.'

'Did you give it to him? The action? The trouble?'

For the first time since the interview began, she hesitated. Stalling, she rose to refill her glass. 'I was different back then. Selfish, single-minded. Destructive. He'd come into a party, make some comment about Julie being tired or tied up. But I knew him, knew that edge in his eyes. He was unhappy and angry and restless. I was between marriages to Asshole Number One and Asshole Number Two. And I was still in love with Sam. Pitifully in love with him.'

She turned then, looking smart and sophisticated in the snazzy red suit she would wear to shoot the upcoming scene. 'This is painful. I didn't realize it would be painful. Well . . .' She lifted her glass in salute and offered him her signature self-mocking smile. 'Builds character. At one of those ubiquitous parties we indulged ourselves in during that regrettable era, Sam and I shared a couple of lines for old times' sake. I won't say who hosted the party, it doesn't really matter. It could have been anyone. We were in a bedroom, sitting at this ornate glass table. The mirror, the silver knife, the pretty little straws. I egged him on about Julie. I knew what buttons to push.'

Her gaze turned inward, and this time he thought he saw regret in them. 'He said he knew she was fucking Lucas – Lucas Manning. He was going to put a stop to that, by Christ, and she was going to pay for cheating on him. She was keeping his daughter away from him, turning the kid against him. He'd see them all in hell before she replaced him with that son of a bitch. They didn't know who they were dealing with, and he'd show them just who they were dealing with. He was ranting, and I pushed him along, telling him exactly what he wanted to hear. All I could think was, he'll leave her and come back to me. Where he belongs. Instead he turned on me, shoved me away. We ended up screaming at each other. Just before he slammed out he looked at me, sneered at me. He said I'd never have any class, never be anything but a second-rate whore pretending to be a star. That I'd never be Julie.

'Two days later, she was dead. He made her pay,' Lydia said with a sigh. 'If he'd killed her that night, the night he left me at that party, I don't think I'd have survived it. For purely selfish reasons I'm grateful he waited just long enough so I was sure he'd forgotten me again. You know, it took me years to realize how lucky I was he never loved me.'

'Did he ever hit you?'

'Sure.' The humor came back into her eyes. 'We hit each other. It was part of our sexual dance. We were violent, arrogant people.'

'But there weren't any reports of abuse or violence in his

marriage until the summer she died. What do you think about that?'

'I think she was able to change him, for a time. Or that he was able to change himself, for a time. Love can do that, or very great need. Noah . . .' She came back and sat. 'I believe he really, really wanted to be the person he was with her. And it was working. I don't know why it stopped working. But he was a weak man who wanted to be strong, a good actor who wanted to be a great one. Maybe, because of that, he was always doomed to fail.'

There was a brisk knock at the door. 'Ms. Loring? You're needed on the set.'

'Two minutes, honey.' She set her glass aside, grinned at Noah. 'Work, work, work.'

'I appreciate your squeezing some time into your schedule for me.'

When he rose, she eyed him up and down, with a sly cat smile on her face. 'I imagine I could . . . squeeze more if you're interested . . .'

'I'm bound to have some follow-up questions along the way.'

She stepped closer, tapped a finger to his cheek. 'You look like such a bright young man, Noah. I think you know I was talking about a more personal session.'

'Yeah. Ah, the thing is, Lydia, you scare me.'

She threw back her head and laughed in delight. 'Oh, what a lovely thing to say. What if I promise to be gentle?'

'I'd say you're a liar.' Relieved by her laugh, he grinned back at her.

'There, I said you were bright. Well . . .' She hooked her arm through his as they walked to the door. 'You know how to get in touch now if you change your mind. Older women are very creative, Noah.'

She turned, gave him a sharp, little nip on the bottom lip that had both heat and nerves swimming into his blood.

'Now you're really scaring me. One last thing?'

'*Mmmm.*' She turned again, leaned back against the door. 'Yes?'

'Was Julie having an affair with Lucas Manning?'

'All business, aren't you? I find that very sexy. But since I don't have time to attempt a worthwhile seduction, I'll tell you that I don't know the answer. At the time, there were two camps on that subject. The one that believed it – delighted in believing it – and the one that didn't, and wouldn't have if Julie and Lucas had been caught in bed naked at the Beverly Hills Hotel.'

'Which camp were you in?'

'Oh, the first, of course. I got off hearing anything negative or juicy about Julie in those days. But that was then, and this isn't. Later, years later, when Lucas and I had our obligatory affair—' She lifted her brows when his eyes narrowed. 'Oh, didn't dig that up, I see. Yes, Lucas and I had a few memorable months together. But he never told me if he'd slept with her. So I can only tell you I don't know. But Sam believed it, so it hardly matters.'

It mattered, Noah thought. Every piece mattered.

Like any self-respecting resident of Los Angeles, Noah conducted a great deal of business on the freeway. As he wound through traffic toward home, he used his cell phone to try to contact Charles Brighton Smith.

Sam Tanner's renowned defense attorney was seventy-eight, still practicing law when the mood struck him, on his fifth wife – this one a gorgeous twenty-seven-year-old paralegal – and currently enjoying the sun and surf at his island retreat on St. Bart's.

With tenacity, Noah managed to get as far as an administrative assistant who informed him in snippy tones that Mr. Smith was incommunicado, but the message and request for an interview would be related at the earliest convenience.

Interpreting that to mean anytime from tomorrow to never, Noah went to work on accessing a copy of the trial transcript.

He toyed with swinging off the exit to his parents' house, then decided he would treat his father professionally, try to keep their personal relationship separate. Somehow.

It was time, he thought, to sit down at his machine and begin working out an outline for the book. He'd already decided on the form. It wouldn't begin with the murder, as he'd once planned, but with all that had led up to it.

A section on Sam Tanner's rise through Hollywood, paralleled by a section on Julie MacBride's. The meeting that had changed them, the fast-forward love affair sliding, from all reports, into a blissful marriage that had produced a much-loved child.

Then the disintegration of that marriage, of love turning to obsession and obsession to violence.

And a section on the child. One who had seen the horrors of that violence. A section on the woman she'd become and how she lived with it.

Murder didn't stop with death. That, Noah thought as he turned toward home, was something he'd learned form his father. And what, most of all, he tried to illustrate in his work.

It hurt that the man he admired and respected most didn't understand that.

He parked, jingling his keys in his hand as he walked toward his front door. It annoyed him that he couldn't seem to shake that need for his father's approval. If I'd been a cop, he thought, scowling, that would've been just dandy. Then we'd sit around over a beer and talk shop, crime and punishment, and he'd brag about his son, the detective, at his weekly pinochle game.

But I write about murders instead of investigating them, so it's like some slightly embarrassing secret.

'Get over it, Brady,' he muttered, then started to jab the key in the lock.

He didn't need to. He didn't have to be a homicide detective to see the door was unlocked and not quite closed. The muscles of his stomach clutched into one tight, nasty ball as he gently nudged the door open.

He stood, staring in shock at the destruction of his house.

It looked as if a team of mad demons had danced over every surface, ripped and torn at every fabric, smashed every piece of glass.

He leaped inside, already swearing and felt only a quick flutter of relief when he saw his stereo equipment still in place.

Not a burglary then, he thought, hearing the buzz of blood in his head as he waded through the mess. Papers were strewn everywhere, glass and pottery crunched under his feet.

He found his bedroom in worse condition. The mattress had been shredded, the filling spilling out like guts from a belly wound. Drawers were upended and thrown against the wall to splinter the wood. When he found his favorite jeans sliced from the waist down to their frayed hems, the buzz turned to a roar.

'She's crazy. She's fucking insane.'

Then anger turned to sheer horror. 'No, no, no,' he hissed under his breath as he raced from the bedroom into his office. 'Oh God, oh shit.'

His basketball trophy was now stuck dead center in his computer monitor. The keyboard, ripped away from the unit, was covered with potting soil from the ornamental lemon tree that had thrived in the corner. His files were scattered, torn, covered with dirt.

Before it had been destroyed, his computer had been used to generate the single clean sheet of paper and message that was taped to the base of the trophy:

I WON'T STOP UNTIL YOU DO.

Rage washed through him like a tidal wave, in one vicious, screaming flood. Before he could think, he dug for his phone, then only cursed bitterly when he found the receiver smashed.

'Okay, Caryn, you want war, you got war. Lunatic bitch.'

He stormed back into the living room for the briefcase he'd dropped, tearing through it for his cell phone.

When he realized his hands were shaking, he walked outside, sucked in air, then just sat down and dropped his head into his hands.

He was sick, dizzy, with the fury still pumping through him in fast, hot beats. But under it was the baffled outrage of the victim. When he was able to use the phone, he didn't call Caryn, but his father.

'Dad. I've got a problem here. Can you come over?'

Twenty minutes later, Frank pulled up and Noah was sitting in exactly the same spot. He hadn't worked up the energy to go back inside but got to his feet now.

'Are you all right?' Moving fast, Frank came up the walk, took his son by the arm.

'Yeah, but ... well, take a look for yourself.' He gestured toward the door, then braced himself to step inside.

'God almighty, Noah.' This time Frank laid a hand on Noah's shoulder in support, even as he scanned the room, picking up details in the chaos. 'When did you find this?'

'About a half hour ago, I guess. I had an appointment in Burbank, just got back. I've been gone all day doing research.'

'Did you call the cops?'

'No, not yet.'

'That's the first step. I'll do it.' He took Noah's phone and made the call. 'The electronics are still here,' he began when he disconnected. 'You keep any cash in the house?'

'Yeah, some.' He stepped through the debris and into the office, kicking papers out of the way. He found his desk drawer in the corner, with a fifty-dollar bill under it. 'I probably had a couple of hundred,' he said, holding up the bill. 'I'd guess the rest is buried under here somewhere. Everything's still here, Dad. It's just trashed.'

'Yeah, I think we can rule out burglary.' He studied the monitor, felt a twinge of his own. He remembered when Noah had won that MVP trophy, the pride and excitement they'd shared. 'Got a beer?'

'I did, before I left this morning.'

'Let's see if you still do. And we'll go sit out on the deck.'

'It'll take me weeks to replace some of this data,' Noah said as he rose. 'Some I'll never be able to replace. I can buy a goddamn new computer, but not what was in it.'

'I know. I'm sorry, Noah. Let's go outside and sit down until the uniforms get here.'

'Sure, what the hell.' More sick than angry now, Noah found two beers in the refrigerator, popped tops on both and sat with Frank on the back deck.

'You got any idea who or why on this?'

Noah let out a short laugh, then tipped back the beer to drink deeply. 'Just a little bunny boiler I know.'

'Excuse me?'

'Caryn.' Noah dragged a hand through his hair, then sprang up to pace. 'A little clip from *Fatal Attraction*. She didn't take it well when I stopped seeing her. She'd been calling, leaving crazy messages. And the other day she was out here when I got home, all dewy-eyed and apologetic. When I didn't bite, she got nasty. Keyed my car on the way out.'

'You still have any of her messages on your machine?'

'No. My strategy was to ignore her so she'd go away.' He looked in through the deck door and the light of battle came back into his eyes. 'Didn't work. She's going to pay for this.'

'You know what she drives?'

'Sure.'

'We'll check with the neighbors, see if anyone saw her or her car in the area today. You give the cops her address and let them go have a talk with her.'

'Talk's not what I have in mind.'

'The best thing for you to do is stay clear. I know you're pissed, Noah,' he continued when Noah whirled around. 'And we can have her charged with breaking and entering, destruction of property, malicious mischief, and all manner of things if we can prove she did this.'

'Prove it, my ass. Who else? I knew she did it the minute I walked in.'

'Knowing and proving are different things. Could be she'll admit to it under a little pressure. But for now, you let the cops take the report, do their job, and you steer clear. Don't talk to her.' Worry clouded Frank's eyes at the battle light gleaming in his son's. 'Has she ever gotten physically violent with you?'

'Jesus, I outweigh her by sixty pounds.' He sat again, then looked up quickly. 'I never touched her that way. The last time she was here, she went at me and I hauled her out the door.'

Frank worked up a smile. 'You sure can pick 'em.'

'I'm giving celibacy a try for a while.' With a sigh, Noah picked up his beer again. 'Women are too much trouble. A couple of hours ago I got hit on by a TV star old enough to be my mother, and for a minute, it didn't seem like such a bad idea.'

'Your appointment in Burbank,' Frank said, primarily to keep Noah's mind off his problem for a little while.

'Yeah, Lydia Loring, she looks damn good.' He rubbed the bottle of beer between both hands. 'I'm interviewing people connected to Sam Tanner and Julie MacBride. I've been to San Quentin. I've talked to Tanner twice.'

Frank puffed out his cheeks. 'What do you want me to say?'

'Nothing.' Disappointment was just one more weight in his gut. 'But I'm hoping you'll cooperate, talk to me about the case, your investigation. I can't write the whole story, do justice to it, without your end. Sam Tanner has brain cancer. He has less than a year to live.'

Frank lowered his eyes to his beer. 'Some things come around,' he murmured. 'They take their own sweet time, but they come around.'

'Don't you want to know?' Noah waited until Frank looked up again. 'You never forgot this case, never really let go of it, or the people in it. He confessed, he recanted, then he shut up for twenty years. Only three people know what happened that night, and only two of them are still alive. One's dying.'

'And one was four years old, Noah. For pity's sake.'

'Yeah, and her testimony damned him. Tanner will talk to me. I'll convince Olivia MacBride to talk to me. But you're the one who strings them together. Are you going to talk to me?'

'He's still looking for glory. At the end, he's still looking for glory, and he'll twist what he tells you so that he gets it. The MacBride family deserves better.'

'I thought I deserved your respect. But I guess we don't always get what we deserve.' He got to his feet. 'The cops're here.'

'Noah.' Frank stood, touched a hand to his son's arm. 'Let's table this until we get what's going on here with you straightened out. Then we'll talk again.'

'Fine.'

'Noah.' Frank tightened his grip, accepted the look of anger in his son's eyes. 'Let's get through one problem at a time.' He nodded toward the living area. 'This is a pretty big one.'

'Sure.' Noah resisted the nasty urge to shrug the hand away. 'One problem at a time.'

It was one tedious routine followed by another. Telling his story to the police, answering their questions, watching them look over what was left of his things was only the first. He called his insurance company, reported the loss, dealt with the curiosity of the neighbors who wandered down.

Then he locked himself inside and wondered where to begin.

It seemed most practical to start in the bedroom, to see if he had any clothes worth salvaging or if he'd walk around naked until he could get more. He managed to pick through, find enough for one mixed load and dumped it all together in the washing machine.

He ordered a pizza, got out another beer and, sipping it, studied the living room. He wondered if it wouldn't be better all around to just hire a crew to come in with shovels and haul the entire mess away.

'Start from scratch, Brady,' he muttered. 'It could be liberating.'

He was still scoping it out when someone knocked on his door. Since it was too soon for the pizza, he considered ignoring it. But decided even another nosy neighbor was better than stewing in his own helpless disgust.

'Hey, Noah, don't you ever return phone calls? I've been . . . whoa, some party. Why wasn't I invited?'

Resigned, Noah closed the door behind his oldest friend. Mike Elmo had been part of his life since grade school. 'It was a surprise party.'

'I bet.' Mike hooked his thumbs in the pockets of the Dockers he'd bought because the commercials had convinced him women couldn't resist a guy wearing them and blinked out of eyes red rimmed from the contacts he couldn't quite adjust to. 'Man, this sucks.'

'Want a beer?'

'You bet. You get ripped off?'

'Just ripped.' Noah took the path he'd already kicked clear into the kitchen. 'Caryn's a little irritated that I dumped her.'

'Wow, she do this? Seriously twisted.' He shook his head, his chestnut-brown eyes soft and sad. 'I told you.'

Noah snorted and offered the beer. 'You told me she was your lifetime fantasy woman and tried to pump me for every sexual detail.'

'So my fantasy woman's twisted. What're you doing to do?'

'Drink this beer, eat some pizza and start cleaning it up.'

'What kind of pizza?'

'Pepperoni and mushroom.'

'Then I can give you a hand.' Mike plopped his chunky butt on a torn cushion. So do you think Caryn'd have sex with me now that you've split?'

'Jesus, Mike.' Noah enjoyed his first laugh in hours. 'Sure, I'll even put in a good word for you.'

'Cool. Rebound sex is very intense.' He stretched out his short legs, crossed his ankles. 'Oh yeah, I get a lot of rebound sex. Guys like you shake a woman off, they're prime for me.'

'I sure do appreciate your support and sympathy during this difficult time.'

'You can count on me.' He offered Noah his surprisingly sweet, puppy-dog smile out of his half-homely face. 'Hey, it's only stuff, and not really good stuff anyway. You go back to Ikea, or hit Pier I or something, and dump it all back in. Take you a few hours.'

Because he'd been thinking the same thing about the bulk of his furniture, Noah scowled. 'She broke my basketball trophy.'

Mike straightened, and a look of utter horror whitened his face.

'Not the MVP – not from the championship game of eighty-six?'

'Yeah.' And since that had gotten the kind of rise out of his friend that soothed the soul, he narrowed his eyes. 'She broke it by shoving it into my computer monitor.'

'That sick, evil bitch broke your computer? Christ, God.' He was up now, stumbling through the wreckage to Noah's office.

Computers were Mike's first love. Women could come and go – and for him it was usually the latter – but a good motherboard was always there for you. He actually yelped when he saw the damage, then leaped toward the once-sleek trophy.

'Jesus, she killed it dead. She mutilated it. Butchered it. What kind of a mind does this?' He turned back to Noah, his eyes wide and bright and blinking as his contacts haloed his vision. 'She should be hunted down like a dog.'

'I called the cops.'

'No, for this you need a vigilante like Dark Man, you need ruthlessness like the Terminator.'

'I'll give them a call next. Think you can salvage anything off the hard drive? She trashed every stinking one of my disks.'

'She's the Antichrist, Noah.' He shook his head sadly. 'I'll see what I can do, but don't hold out any hope. There's the pizza,' he said when he heard the knock. 'Let me fuel up, then I'll do what I can do. And you know what? I don't even want rebound sex with her now.'

Chapter Fifteen

It took Noah a week to get his house in order. The sorting, cleaning, dumping was purely a pain in the ass, but the demands of it kept him from feeling helpless.

A new computer was a priority, and with Mike egging him on, he bought a system that sent his friend into raptures of delight and envy.

He wouldn't have bought all the damn software games if Mike hadn't kept pushing them on him. And he sure as hell wouldn't have sat up half the night playing video pinball if he hadn't bought it in the first place.

But he told himself that was beside the point. He'd needed the distraction.

He outfitted his living room with cargo furniture, ordering straight out of an in-store catalog by pointing at a page and telling the salesman: 'Give me that.'

This delighted the salesman and saved Noah a headache.

Within two weeks, he could walk through his house without cursing and made serious inroads on reorganizing his office and regenerating lost data.

He had his car back, a new mattress, and a half-baked promise through Smith's admin for a meeting when the lawyer returned to California the following month.

And he managed to track down Lucas Manning.

Manning wasn't quite as cheerfully forthcoming as Lydia Loring had been, but he agreed to talk about Julie. Noah met him at Manning's Century City suite of offices. It always surprised and slightly disillusioned Noah that actors had big, plush executive offices.

They might as well be CEOs, he thought as he was cleared through several levels of security.

Manning greeted Noah with a professional smile and assessed him with eyes of storm gray. The years had turned his once burnished-gold-coin hair into the brilliance of polished pewter and filed down his face to the sharp points and angles of a scholar. According to the polls, women continued to find him one of the most appealing leading men in the business.

'I appreciate your taking the time to talk to me.'

'I might not have.' Manning gestured to a chair. 'But Lydia campaigned for you.'

'She's quite a woman.'

'Yes, she is. So was Julie, Mr. Brady, and even after all this time it's not easy for me to talk about what happened to her.'

No need for small talk, Noah thought, and following Manning's lead, he took out his recorder and pad. 'You worked together.'

'One of the happiest experiences of my life. She was a brilliant natural talent, an admirable woman and a good friend.'

'There are those who believed, and still believe, that you and Julie MacBride were more than friends.'

'We could have been.' Manning eased back, laid his hands on the ornately carved arms of his chair. 'If she hadn't been in love with her husband, we would have been. We were attracted to each other. Part of that was the intimacy of the roles we played, and part was simply a connection.'

'Sam Tanner believed you acted on that connection.'

'Sam Tanner didn't value what he had.' Manning's trained voice hardened at the edges and made Noah wonder if the delivery was emotion or simply skill. 'He made her unhappy. He was jealous, possessive, abusive. In my opinion, his addiction to drugs and alcohol didn't spark this abuse, it simply uncovered it.'

There was a bitterness still toward Tanner, Noah thought, every bit as ripe as Tanner's was toward him. 'Did she confide in you?'

'To an extent.' He lifted the fingers of one hand off the arm of the chair, then dropped them again, like a pianist hitting keys. 'She wasn't a whiner. I admit, I pressed her to talk to me, and we'd grown close during the filming, remained friends afterward. I knew she was troubled. At first she made excuses for him, then she stopped. Ultimately, she told me, in confidence, that she'd filed for divorce to snap him out of it, to force him to get help.'

'Did you and Tanner ever discuss it?'

Manning's lips twisted into a smile. Wry and experienced. 'He had a reputation for having a violent temper, for causing scenes. My career had just taken off, and I intended to be in it for the long haul. I avoided him. I'm not of the school that believes any press is good press, and I didn't want to see headlines splashed around gloating that Tanner and Manning had brawled over MacBride.'

'Instead they gloated that Manning and MacBride were an item.'

'There was nothing I could do about that. One of the reasons I agreed to this interview was to set the record straight about my relationship with Julie.'

'Then I have to ask, Why haven't you set the record straight before now? You've refused to discuss her in interviews since her death.'

'I set the record straight.' Manning angled his head slightly, lowered his chin. It was an aggressive stance with those storm-cloud eyes just narrowed. 'In court,' he continued. 'Under oath. But the media, the masses were never really satisfied. For some the idea of scandal, of illicit sex, was as much of a fascination as murder. I refused to play into it, to demean Julie that way.'

Maybe, Noah mused. Or maybe the mystery of it gave your rocketing career one more boost. 'And now?'

'Now you're going to write the book. Rumors around this town are that it'll be the definitive work on the Julie MacBride murder.' He smiled thinly. 'I'm sure you know that.'

'There are a lot of rumors around this town,' Noah said equably. 'I let my agent worry about that end of it. I just do the work.'

'Lydia said you were sharp. You're going to write the book,' he repeated. 'I'm part of the story. So I'll answer the questions I've refused to answer for the last twenty years. Julie and I were never lovers. Tanner and I never fought over her. The fact is, I'd have been delighted if both of those misconceptions had been true. The morning I heard what had happened to her remains the worst day of my life.'

'How did you hear?'

'David Melbourne called me. Julie's family wanted to block as much media as possible, and he knew the minute the press got wind of it, they'd start hammering me for comments, interviews, statements. Of course he was right,' Manning murmured. 'It was early. The call woke me. My private number. Julie had my private number.'

He closed his eyes and pain flickered over his face. 'He said, "Lucas, I have terrible, terrible news." I remember exactly how his voice broke, the grief in it. "Julie's dead. Oh God, God, Julie's dead. Sam killed her."'

He opened his eyes again, emotion rushing into them. 'I didn't believe it. Wouldn't. It was like a bad dream, or worse, worse, some scene I'd be forced to play over and over again. I'd just seen her the day before. She'd been beautiful and alive, excited about a script she'd just read. Then David told me she was dead.'

'Were you in love with her, Mr. Manning?'

'Completely.'

Manning gave him two full hours. Noah had miles of tape, reams of notes. He believed part of Manning's interview had been calculated, rehearsed. Timing, phrasing, pause and impact. But in it there was truth.

And with truth there was progress.

He decided to celebrate by meeting Mike at an off-the-strip bar called Rumors for a couple of drinks.

'She's giving me the eye.' Mike rolled his own watering eyes to the left and muttered into his pilsner.

'Which eye?'

'The *eye*, you know. The blonde in the short skirt.'

Noah considered his order of nachos. The energy from a good day's work bubbled under the surface of his skin and conversely helped him relax. 'There are one hundred and thirty-three blondes in short skirts in here. They all have eyes.'

'The one two tables over to the left. Don't look.'

Though he hadn't intended to, Noah shrugged. 'Okay. I'm going up to San Francisco again in a couple of days.'

'Why?'

'Work. The book. Remember?'

'Oh yeah, yeah. I'm telling you, she's definitely eyeing me. She just did the hair flip. Hair flipping's the second stage.'

'Go make a move, then.'

'I'm biding my time, scoping it out. What's it like inside San Quentin, anyway?' Mike tried a little eyebrow wiggle on the blonde to get her reaction.

'Depressing. You walk through a door, it locks behind you. Your hair stands on end when you hear that click.'

'So does he still look like a movie star? You never said.'

'No, he looks like a man who's spent twenty years in prison. Are you going to eat any of these?'

'After I talk to the blonde. I don't want nacho breath. Okay, that was five full seconds of eye contact. I'm going in.'

'My money's on you, pal.' Then Noah muttered as Mike swaggered away, 'She'll eat him alive.'

He amused himself watching the action. The dance floor was packed, bodies crammed against bodies in a shower of flashing colored lights and all bumping and twisting to the music.

It made him think of the night he'd taken Olivia dancing. And how he'd stopped hearing the music or anything but the beat of his own blood once his mouth tasted hers.

'Put it away, pal,' he muttered, and, scowling, picked up his beer. 'You blew that one.'

He sipped his beer and watched the show. He'd always enjoyed an occasional night in a club, getting blasted with music and voices, being pressed in with people and movement. Now he was sitting alone, while his oldest friend worked the blonde, and wishing he'd stayed home.

He pushed aside the nachos without interest, lifted his beer again and spotted Caryn crossing the floor toward his table.

'Of all the gin joints in all the towns,' he mumbled and took a longer, deeper drink.

'I thought you were playing hermit.' She'd decked herself out in a leather dress of electric blue that coated her like a tattoo and screamed to an abrupt halt just past her crotch. Her hair was in a thousand wild fuck-me curls, and her mouth was painted a hot, wet red.

It occurred to him that it was just that look that had made him think with his glands when he'd first seen her. He said nothing, lifted his glass again and did his best to stare through her.

'You set the cops on me.' She leaned down, planting her palms on the table and her impressive breasts directly at eye level. 'You got some nerve, Noah, getting your father to call out his gestapo friends to give me grief.'

He flicked his gaze up to hers, then over her shoulder where one of her friends was pulling desperately at her arm and muttering her name.

His lips curved in a viciously cold smile, and he pitched his voice just over the roar of music. 'Why don't you do us all a favor and get her out of here?'

'I'm talking to you.' Caryn jabbed a nail, painted the same wild blue as her dress, into his chest. 'You pay attention to me when I'm talking to you, you bastard.'

The control snapped in, even as he imagined squeezing his hands around her neck until her eyes popped. 'Back off.'

She jabbed him again, hard enough this time to break skin. Then let out a squeal of shock when he grabbed her wrist.

'Keep out of my way. You think you can trash my house, destroy my things and I'll do nothing? You keep the hell out of my way.'

'Or what?' She tossed her hair back, and to his disgust he saw it wasn't fear in her eyes, but excitement, edged with a glint of lust. 'Going to call Daddy again?' She raised her voice now, to just under a scream. Even in the din, it cut and had heads turning. 'I never touched your precious things. I wouldn't lower myself to go back in that house after the way you treated me, and you can't prove any different. If I'd been there I'd have burned it down – and I'd have made sure you were inside when I did.'

'You're sick.' He shoved her hand aside. 'And you're pitiful.' He was pushing his chair back when she slapped him. The ring on her finger nicked the corner of his mouth, and he tasted blood. His eyes went dark and flat as he got to his feet. 'You keep crossing that line, Caryn, and you're going to get run over.'

'We got a problem here?'

Noah merely glanced at security. The man's shoulders were wide as a canyon and his big, sharp smile didn't hold any humor. Before he could speak, Caryn had launched herself against the boulder of his chest, blinking until her eyes filled.

'He wouldn't leave me alone. He grabbed me.'

'Oh, for Christ's sake.'

'That's a damn lie.' This from Mike, who'd hopped to Noah's side. 'She started on him. She's a lunatic, wrecked his house last week.'

'I don't know what they're talking about.' Tears slid gracefully down her cheeks as she tipped her face back to the bouncer's. 'He hurt me.'

'I saw what happened.' A brunette with amused eyes and a slight Southern drawl strolled up. 'I was sitting right over there.' She gestured behind her, kept her voice low. 'This guy was having a beer at this table, minding his own business. She came up to him, got in his face, started poking at him and yelling abuse. Then she slugged him.'

The outrage had Caryn shrieking. She took a swipe at the brunette, missing by a mile as the bouncer nipped her around the waist. Her exit, kicking and screaming, caused quite a stir.

'Thanks.' Noah dabbed the back of his hand on his lip.

The brunette's smile was slow and friendly. 'Anytime.'

'I'm going to get you a fresh beer. Sit, relax.' Mike fussed around him like a mother. 'Man, that woman is over the edge and then some. I'll get the beer and some ice.'

'Your friend's very sweet.' She offered Noah a hand. 'I'm Dory.'

'Noah.'

'Yes, I got that from Mike already. He likes my friend.' She fluttered a hand toward the table where the blonde sat looking wide-eyed and prettily distressed. 'She likes him. Why don't you join us?'

She had a voice like cream, and skin to match, intelligent interest in her eyes and a sympathetic smile. And he was just too damn tired to start the dance. 'I appreciate it, but I'm going to take off. Go home, soak my head. I'm considering entering a monastery.'

She laughed, and because he looked as if he could use it, touched a light kiss to his cheek. 'Don't do anything rash. Ten, twenty years from now, you'll look back and smile at this little incident.'

'Yeah, that's about right. Thanks again, and tell Mike I'll catch him later.'

'Sure.' She watched him go with a little tug of regret.

He was lost in the forest, the lovely, deep woods with the low glow of light edged with green. There was silence, such silence he could swear he heard the air breathing. He couldn't find his way over the slick carpet of moss, through the tangle of dripping vines, beyond the great columns of trees that rose like an ancient wall.

He was looking for something . . . someone. He had to hurry, but whichever direction he took, he remained cupped there, in the ripe and green darkness. He heard the faint murmur of water from a stream, the sigh of the air and the drumming inside his head that was the frantic beat of his own blood.

Then, under it, like a whisper, came his name. *Noah . . . Noah . . .*

'Noah.'

He shot up in bed, fists raised, eyes still glazed and blinded by the dream, his heart cartwheeling madly in his chest.

'And you used to wake up with a smile on your face.'

'What? What?' He blinked his vision clear as the sharpest edge of the dream dulled and faded. 'Mom?' He stared at her, then flopped back, buried his face in his pillow. 'Jeez. Why don't you just bash me over the head with a tire iron next time?'

'Let's just say I didn't expect to find you still in bed at eleven o'clock in the morning.' She sat on the edge of the bed, then rattled the bakery box she carried. 'I brought pastries.'

His pulse had nearly leveled out, so he opened one eye – and it was full of suspicion. 'Not that carob crap?'

She sighed heavily. 'All my hard work for nothing. You still have your father's stomach. No, not carob. I brought my only son poisonous white sugar and fat.'

The suspicion remained, but around it was greedy interest. 'What do I have to do for them?'

She leaned over, kissed the top of his head. 'Get out of bed.'

'That's it?'

'Get out of bed,' she said again. 'I'll go make coffee.'

The idea of coffee and food thrilled him so much he was out of bed and pulling on his jeans before it struck him how weird it was to have his mother drop by with pastries on a Sunday morning.

He started out, rolled his eyes and went back for a T-shirt. She'd never let him chow down bare-chested. Since he'd gone that far, he brushed his teeth and splashed some water on his face.

Coffee was just scenting the air when he walked out.

'You know, you're a very creative young man,' Celia began. 'It baffles me that you didn't take a little more time, a little more care in furnishing your home.'

'I just live here.' He slid onto a stool at the counter. 'And this stuff suits the place.'

'Actually, it does.' She glanced back at the simple, straight lines and dark blue cushions. 'There's just not much of Noah around here.'

'I lost a lot of stuff.' He lifted his shoulder. 'I'll pick it up here and there, eventually.'

'Hmm.' She said nothing more, and turned away to get out mugs and plates until she could bank some of the fury. Every time she thought about what had been done to him, she wanted to march over to wherever that Caryn creature lived and wade in.

'So, what's Dad up to?'

'A basketball game, what else?' She poured the coffee, arranged the pastries on a plate. He'd already grabbed one when she turned and opened the fridge. 'You know, you'd be so much better off using your juicer than buying this processed stuff.'

His answer was muffled around Bavarian cream and only made her shake her head as she poured orange juice into a glass for him.

Leaning on the counter, she watched him eat. His eyes were heavy, she noted, his hair tousled and his T-shirt torn at the shoulder. Love, wonderfully warm, spurted through her.

He grinned a little, licking cream and chocolate off his thumb. She was so damn pretty, he thought, her hair bright as polished copper, her eyes an all-seeing blue. 'What?'

'I was just thinking how good-looking you are.'

The grin widened as he reached for another pastry. 'I was thinking the same thing about you. I get my good looks from my mom. She's a beaut. And right now, she's got something on her mind.'

'Yes, she does.' Taking her time, Celia moved around the counter, took a stool. She propped her feet on the stool between them, lifted her coffee and sipped. 'You know how I've made it a policy not to interfere in your life, Noah?'

His grin faded. 'Ah . . . yeah. I always appreciated that.'

'Good. Because with that foundation between us, I expect you to listen to what I have to say.'

'Uh-oh.'

She let that pass, tossed back the hair she still wore long enough to wrap into a fat braid. 'Mike called me this morning. He told me what happened last night.'

'Biggest mouth in the west,' Noah muttered.

'He was worried about you.'

'Nothing to worry about, and he shouldn't have bothered you with it.'

'Like he shouldn't have bothered me when you were twelve and that pimply-faced bully decided you'd make a nice punching bag every day after school?' She cocked an eyebrow. 'He was three years older and twice your size, but did you tell me he was pounding on you?'

Noah tried to sulk into his coffee, but his lips curved. 'Dick Mertz. You drove over to his house and went head-to-head with his Neanderthal father, told him to send his little Nazi out and you'd go a couple of rounds with him.'

'There are times,' Celia said primly, 'when it's difficult to remain a pacifist.'

'It was a proud moment in my life,' Noah told her, then sobered. 'I'm not twelve anymore, Mom, and I can handle my own bullies.'

'This Caryn isn't some playground misfit either, Noah. She's proven she's dangerous. She threatened you last night. For God's sake, she talked about burning your house down around you.'

Mike, you moron. 'It's just talk, Mom.'

'Is it? Are you sure?' When he opened his mouth, she merely stared until he shut it again. 'I want you to get a restraining order.'

'Mom—'

'It's basically all the police can do at this point, and it might very well intimidate her enough to make her stop, go away.'

'I'm not getting a restraining order.'

'Why?' A trickle of the genuine fear she felt broke through in the single word. 'Because it's not macho?'

He inclined his head. 'Okay.'

'Oh!' Frustrated, she slammed her coffee down and pushed off the stool. 'That's unbelievably stupid and shortsighted. What is your penis, your shield?'

'It's about as effective a shield as a piece of paper would be,' he pointed out as she stormed around the room. 'She'll lose interest quicker if I lie back a bit, then she'll latch onto some other poor bastard. The fact is, I'm going to be doing a lot of traveling over the next several months. I'm heading up to San Francisco in a few days.'

'Well, I hope you don't come back to a pile of ashes,' Celia snapped, then blew out a breath. 'I'm so *angry*, and I've got nowhere to put it.'

He smiled, opened his arms. 'Put it here, pal.'

She sighed again, hugely, then walked over to wrap her arms around him. 'I want to punch her, just once. Just one good shot.'

He had to laugh, and tightened his grip into a fierce squeeze. 'If you ever get the chance, I'll go your bail. Now stop worrying about me.'

'It's my job. I take my work very seriously.' She eased back, looked up. Despite the man's face, the man's stubble of beard, he was still her little boy. 'Now, I guess we move on to phase two. I know you and your father are tiptoeing around each other.'

'Let it go, Mom.'

'Not when it involves the two most important people in my life. The two of you were like a couple of polite strangers at my birthday dinner.'

'Would you rather we'd fought about it?'

'Maybe. Boy, I seem to have latent violent tendencies.' She smiled a little, smoothed a hand over his hair, wished she could smooth out his troubles as easily. 'I hate seeing both of you unhappy and distant.'

'This is *my* job,' he pointed out. 'And I take it very seriously.'

'I know you do.'

'He doesn't.'

'That's not true, Noah.' Her brow furrowed because she heard the unhappiness under the anger. 'He just doesn't completely understand what you do and why you do it. And this particular case was – is – very personal to him.'

'It's personal to me, too. I don't know why,' he said when she studied him. 'It just is, always has been. I have to follow through.'

'I know that, and I think you're right.'

The tension and resentment eased off his shoulders. 'Thanks.'

'I only want you to try to understand your father's feelings on it, and actually, I think you'll come to as you go deeper into the people and the events. Noah, he ached for that little girl. I don't think he's ever stopped aching for her. There've been other cases, other horrors, but that child stayed with him.'

She stayed with me, too, he thought. Right inside me. But he didn't say it. He hadn't wanted to think it. 'I'll be going up to Washington, to see if she's still there.'

Celia hesitated, suffered through the tug-of-war with loyalties. 'She's still there. She and your father have kept in touch.'

'Really?' Noah considered as he got up to pour more coffee. 'Well then, that should make things easier.'

'I'm not sure anything will make this easier.'

An hour later, when he was alone and slightly queasy from having inhaled four pastries, Noah decided it was as good a day as any to travel. This time he'd drive to San Francisco, he thought as he went to the bedroom to toss what few clothes he had in a bag. It would give him time to think, and he could make arrangements on the way for a few days at River's End.

It would give him time to prepare himself for seeing Olivia again.

Chapter Sixteen

Sam's nerves slithered under his skin like restless snakes. To keep them at bay he recited poetry – Sandburg, Yeats, Frost. It was a trick he'd learned during his early stage work, when he'd suffered horribly, and he had refined it in prison, where so much of the life was waiting, nerves and despair.

At one time he'd tried to calm himself, control himself, by running lines in his head. Bits and pieces of his movies in which he would draw the character up from his gut, become someone else. But that had led to a serious bout of depression during the first nickel of his time inside. When the lines were done, he was still Sam Tanner, he was still in San Quentin and there was no hope that tomorrow would change that.

But the poetry was soothing, helped stroke back that part of himself that was screaming.

When he'd come up for parole the first time, he'd actually believed they would let him go. They, the tangled mass of faces and figures of the justice system, would look at him and see a man who'd paid with the most precious years of his life.

He'd been nervous then, with sweat pooling in his armpits and his gut muscles twisted like thin rope. But beneath the fear had been a simple and steady hope. His time in hell was done, and life could begin again.

Then he'd seen Jamie, and he'd seen Frank Brady, and he'd known they'd come to make certain the doors of hell stayed locked.

She'd spoken of Julie, of her beauty and talent, her devotion to family. Of how one man had destroyed all that, out of jealousy and spite. How he had endangered and threatened his own child.

She'd wept while she'd addressed the panel, Sam recalled, quiet tears that had trickled down her cheeks as she spoke.

He'd wanted to leap to his feet when she'd finished, shouting, Cut! One-take wonder! A brilliant performance!

But he'd recited poetry in his head and remained still, his face blank, his hands resting on his thighs.

Then Frank had had his turn, the dedicated cop focused on justice. He'd described the scene of the murder, the condition of the body in the pitiless, formal detail of police-speak. Only when he'd talked of Olivia, of how he'd found her, did emotion slip into his voice.

It had been all the more effective.

Olivia had been nineteen then, Sam thought now. He'd tried to imagine her as a young woman – tall and slim with Julie's eyes and that quick smile. But he'd only seen a little girl with hair as golden as dandelion who'd always wanted a story at bedtime.

He'd known as Frank had looked at him, as their eyes had met and held, that parole wouldn't be granted. He'd known that this same scene would be repeated year after year, like a film clip.

The rage he'd felt wanted to spew from his mouth like vomit. In his head he'd found Robert Frost and gripped the lines like a weapon.

I have promises to keep, and miles to go before I sleep.

For the last five years he'd formed and refined those promises. Now, the son of the man who'd murdered his hope was going to help him keep them.

That was justice.

Over a month had passed since Noah had first come to see him. Sam had begun to worry that he wouldn't come back, that the seeds he'd so carefully planted hadn't taken root after all. Those plans, those hopes, those promises that had kept him alive and sane would shatter, leaving him only the sharp edges of failure.

But he'd come back, was even now being led to this miserable little room. Interior scene, day, Sam thought as he heard the locks slide open. Action.

Noah walked to the table, set down his briefcase. Sam could smell his shower on him, the hotel soap. He was dressed in jeans, a soft cotton shirt, black Converse high-tops. There was a small healing cut at the corner of his mouth.

Sam wondered if he knew how young he was, how enviably young and fit and free.

Noah took his tape recorder, a notebook and a pencil out of the briefcase. And when the door was shut and locked at his back, tossed a pack of Marlboros and a book of matches in front of Sam.

'Didn't know your brand.'

Sam tapped a fingertip on the pack, and his smile was sly and wry. 'One's the same as the other in here. They'll all kill you, but nobody lives forever.'

'Most of us don't know when or how it's going to end for us. How does it feel being someone who does?'

Sam continued to tap his finger on the pack. 'It's a kind of power, or would be if I were in the world. In here, one day's the same as the next anyway.'

'Regrets?'

'About being in here, or dying?'

'Either. Both.'

With a short laugh, Sam opened the cigarettes. 'Neither one of us has enough time for that list, Brady.'

'Just hit the high points.'

'I regret I won't have the same choices you do when this hour's up. I regret I can't decide: you know, I'd think I'd like a steak tonight, medium rare and a glass of good wine to go with it and strong black coffee after. Ever had prison coffee?

'Yeah.' It was a small thing to sympathize with. 'It's worse than cop coffee. What else do you regret?'

'I regret that when I'm finally able to make that choice again, have that steak, I'm not going to have much time to enjoy it.'

'That seems fairly simple.'

'No, there are those who have choices and those who don't. It's never simple to the ones who don't. What choice have you made?' He slid a cigarette out of the pack, angled it toward the recorder. 'With this. How far are you going to go with this?'

'All the way.'

Sam looked down at the cigarette, effectively shuttering his eyes and whatever was in them. He opened the book of matches, tore one off, struck it to flame. Now, with his eyes closed he drew in that first deep gulp of Virginia tobacco.

'I need money.' When Noah only lifted an eyebrow, Sam took a second drag. 'I'm getting out when my twenty's up, my lawyer's done that dance. I'm going to live on the outside for maybe six months. I want to live decently, with some dignity, and what I've got isn't going to run to that steak.'

He took another drag, a calming breath while Noah waited him out. 'It took everything I had to pay for my defense, and what you make in here isn't what you'd call a living wage. They'll pay you for the book. You'll get an advance, and with your second best-seller out there, it won't be chump change.'

'How much?'

The snakes began to stir under his skin again. He couldn't keep his promises without financial backing. 'Twenty thousand – that's one large one for every year I've been in. That'll buy me a decent room, clothes, food. It won't set me up at the BHH, but it'll keep me off the streets.'

It wasn't an unusual demand, nor did Noah consider it an unreasonable amount. 'I'll have my agent draw up an agreement. That suit you?'

The snakes coiled up and slept. 'Yeah, that suits me.'

'Do you plan to stay in San Francisco when you're released?'

'I think I've been in San Francisco long enough.' Sam's lips curved again. 'I want the sun. I'll go south.'

'L.A.?'

'Nothing much for me there. I don't think my old friends will be planning a welcome-home party. I want the sun,' he said again. 'And some privacy. Choices.'

'I spoke with Jamie Melbourne.'

Sam's hand jerked where it rested on the table. He lifted it, bringing the cigarette that smoldered between his fingers to his lips. 'And?'

'I'll be talking to her again,' Noah said. 'I'll be contacting the rest of Julie's family as well. I haven't been able to hook up with C.B. Smith yet, but I will.'

'I'm one of his few failures. We didn't part ways with great affection, but he had one of his young fresh faces spring the lock at twenty.'

'Affection isn't what you're going to get from the people I interview.'

'Have you talked to your father?'

'I'm doing background first.' Eyes sharp, Noah inclined his head. 'I won't agree to getting your approval on who I interview or what I use in the book. We go with this, you'll have to sign papers waiving those rights. Even if my publishers wouldn't insist on that, and they will, I would. Your story, Sam, but my book.'

'You wouldn't have a book without me.'

'Sure I would. It'd just be a different book.' Noah leaned back, his pose relaxed, his eyes hard as iron. 'You want choices? There's your first one. You sign the papers, you take the twenty thousand and I write the book my way. You don't sign, you don't get the money and I write it my way.'

There was more of his father in him than Sam had realized before. A toughness the beach-boy looks and casual style skimmed over. Better that way, Sam decided. Better that way in the end.

'I'm not going to live to see the book in print anyway. I'll sign the papers, Brady.' His eyes went cold, eyes that understood murder and had learned to live with it. 'Just don't fuck me up.'

Noah angled his head. 'Fine. But remember, you don't want to fuck me up either.'

He understood murder, too. He'd been studying it all his life.

Noah ordered a steak, medium rare, and a bottle of Côte d'or. As he ate, he watched the lights that swept over the bay glint and glow against the dark and listened to the replay of his latest interview with Sam Tanner.

But most of all he tried to imagine what it would be like to be eating that meal, drinking that wine, for the first time in over twenty years.

Would you savor it, he wondered, or feed like a wolf after a long winter's famine?

Sam, he thought, would savor it, bite by bite, sip by sip, absorbing the flavors, the texture, the deep red color of the wine in the glass. And if his senses threatened to overload from the sudden flood of stimuli, he'd slow down even more.

He had that kind of control now.

How much of the reckless, greedy-for-pleasure, out-of-control man he had been still strained for release inside him?

It was smarter to think of Sam as two men, the one he'd been, the one he was now, Noah decided. Pieces of both had always been there, he imagined, but this was very much a story of what had been and what was. So he could sit here, try to picture how the man he knew now would deal with a perfectly cooked steak and a glass of fine wine. And he could imagine the man who'd been able to command much, much more at the flick of a finger.

The man who'd taken Julie MacBride to bed the first time.

I want to tell you how it was when Julie and I became lovers.

It hadn't been an angle Noah had expected Sam to take, not so soon, and not so intimately. But none of his surprise came through in his voice as he'd told Sam to go ahead.

Listening now, Noah let himself slide into Sam's place, into the warm southern California night. Into a past that wasn't his. The words on the recording became images, and the images more of a memory than a dream.

There was a full moon. It sailed the sky and shot beams of light, like silver swords, over the dark glint of the ocean. The sound of the surf as it rose, crested, crashed on shore was like the constant beat of an eager heart.

They'd taken a drive down the coast, stopped for a ridiculous meal of fried shrimp served in red plastic baskets at a smudgy little diner where they'd hoped to go unnoticed.

She'd worn a long flowered dress and a foolish straw hat to hide that waterfall of rich blond hair. She hadn't bothered with makeup and her youth, her beauty, her outrageous freshness hadn't been any sort of disguise.

She'd laughed, licked cocktail sauce from her fingers. And heads had turned.

They wanted to keep their relationship private, though so far it consisted of drives like this one, a few more-elegant meals, conversations and their work. Shooting had begun the month before, drastically cutting into any personal time they could steal.

Tonight, they'd stolen a few hours to walk along that foaming surf, their fingers linked, their steps meandering.

'I love doing this.' Her voice was low and smooth, with just a hint of huskiness. She looked like an ingénue and sounded like a siren. It was part of the mystique that made her. 'Just walking, smelling the night.'

'So do I.' Though he never had before her. Before Julie he'd craved the lights, the noise, the crowds and the attention centered on him. Now, being with her filled all those needy corners. 'I love doing this even more.'

He turned her, and she circled fluidly into his arms. Her lips curved as his met them, and they parted, inviting him in. She flowed into him, with tastes both sweet and sharp, scents both innocent and aware. The quiet sound of pleasure she made echoed in his blood like the crash of the surf.

'You do it so well, too,' she murmured, and instead of easing away as she most often did, she pressed her cheek to his, let her body sway in tune to the sea. 'Sam.' His name sighed out of her. 'I want to be sensible, I want to listen to the people who tell me to be sensible.'

Desire for her was an ache in his belly, a burning in the blood. It took every ounce of control to keep his hands gentle. 'Who tells you to be sensible?'

'People who love me.' She leaned back, her deep amber eyes steady on his. 'I thought I could be, then I thought, Well, if I'm not, I'll enjoy myself. I'm not a child, why shouldn't I be one of Sam Tanner's women if I want?'

'Julie—'

'No, wait.' She stepped back, lifted a hand palm out to stop him. 'I'm not a child, Sam, and I can deal with reality. I only want you to be honest with me. Is that where we're heading? To me becoming one of Sam Tanner's women?'

She'd accept that. He could see it in her eyes, hear it in her voice. The knowledge both thrilled and terrified him. He had only to say yes, take her hand, and she would go with him.

She stood, her back to the dark sea with its white edges, the moonlight spearing down to cast their shadows on the sand. And waited.

For the truth, he thought, and realized the truth was what he wanted for both of them.

'Lydia and I aren't seeing each other anymore. Haven't been for weeks now.'

'I know.' Julie smiled a little. 'I read the gossip columns like anyone else. And I wouldn't be here with you tonight if you were still involved with someone else.'

'It's over between us,' he said carefully. 'It was over the first minute I saw you. Because the first minute I saw you, I stopped seeing anyone else, stopped wanting anyone else.

The first minute I saw you . . .' He stepped to her, slipped the straw hat away so that her hair tumbled down. 'I started falling in love with you. I still am. I don't think I'll ever stop.'

Her eyes filled so that the sheen of tears sparkled like diamonds against gold. 'What's the point of being in love if you're going to be sensible? Take me home with you tonight.'

She stepped back into his arms, and this time the kiss was dark and edged with urgency. Then she was laughing, a quick river of delight as she grabbed the hat from him and sent it sailing over the water.

Hands clasped again, they raced back to his car like children eager for a treat.

With another woman he might have rushed greedily into the oblivion of movement and mating, gulping it down, taking what his body craved and seeking the brutal pleasure of release.

With another woman he might have played the role of seducer, keeping part of himself separated, like a director orchestrating each step.

In both of those methods were power and satisfaction.

But with Julie he could do neither. The power was as much hers as his. Nerves hummed along his skin as they walked up the stairs in his house.

He closed the door of the bedroom behind them. He knew pieces of Lydia were still there, though she'd been viciously methodical in removing her things – and a number of his own – when she'd moved out. But a woman never shared a man's bed without leaving something of herself behind to force him to remember.

He had a moment to wish he'd tossed out the bed, bought a new one, then Julie was smiling at him.

'Yesterday doesn't matter, Sam. Only tonight matters.' She laid her hands on his cheeks. 'We're all that matters, all that's real. Touch me.' She whispered it as her mouth cruised over his. 'I don't want to wait any longer.'

It all slipped into place, the nerves fading away. When he swept her up, he understood this wasn't simply sex or need or gratification. It was romance. However many times he'd set the scene before, or had scenes set for him, he'd never believed in it.

He laid her on the bed, covering her mouth with his as this new feeling flowed through him. Love, finally, love. Her arms, soft, smooth, wrapped around him as the kiss went deep. For a moment, it seemed his world centered there. In that mating of lips.

He didn't tell himself to be gentle, to move slowly. He couldn't separate himself and direct the scene. He was lost in it, and her, the scent of her hair, the taste of her throat, the sound of her breath as it caught, released, caught again.

He slipped the thin straps of the dress from her shoulders, urged it down, down her body as he savored that lovely mouth. She shivered when he stroked her breast, gasped when he skimmed tongue and teeth over the nipple, then moaned when he drew her deep into his mouth.

She fit beneath him, slid against him, rose and fell with him. She said his name, only his name, and made his heart tremble.

He touched, and took, and gave more than he'd known he had to give to a woman. Her skin dewed, adding one more flavor, her muscles quivered, adding another layer of excitement.

He wanted to see all of her, to explore everything she had, everything she was. She was long and slender and lovely, so that even the ripple of ribs against her skin was a fascination.

When she opened for him, rose up to meet him, he slipped into her like a sigh and watched those eyes film with tears.

Slow, silky movement built to shudders. She cried out once, her nails biting into his hips, then again, like an echo as he poured himself into her.

Noah blinked his vision clear and heard only silence. The tape had run out, he realized. He started at the machine, more than a little stunned that the images had come quite so clear. And more than a little embarrassed to find himself hard and unquestionably aroused.

With Olivia's face in his mind.

'Jesus, Brady.' He picked up his wine with a hand not quite steady and took a long sip.

It was one of the side effects of crawling inside Sam Tanner, imagining what it was like to love and be loved by a woman like Julie MacBride. Remembering what it had been like to want the daughter that love had created.

But it was damned inconvenient when he didn't have any outlet for the sexual frustration now kicking gleefully in his gut.

He'd write it out, he decided. He'd finish his meal, turn on the tube for noise and write it out. Since the story had a core of possessive love and sexual obsession, he'd write in Sam's memory of the night he and Julie had become lovers.

Maybe it was idealized, he thought, and maybe there were times, moments, connections that produced the kinds of feelings Sam had spoken of.

For Noah, sex had always been a delightful part of life, a kind of sport that required some basic skills, a certain amount of protection and a healthy sense of team spirit.

But he was willing to believe that for some it could contain gilded emotions. He'd give Sam that night, and all the romantic swells that went with it. It was after all how the man remembered it – or wanted to. And the shimmering romance of it would only add impact to the murder itself.

He booted up his laptop, poured coffee from the room-service carafe that had kept it acceptably hot. But when he rose to turn on the television, he stopped by the phone, frowned at it.

What the hell, he thought, and going with impulse dug out the number for River's End. Within ten minutes, he'd made reservations for the beginning of the following week.

Sam Tanner had still not spoken of his daughter. Noah wanted to see if she would speak of him.

He worked until two, when he surfaced briefly to stare with no comprehension whatsoever at the television where a giant lizard was kicking the stuffing out of New York.

He watched a uniformed cop, who obviously had more balls than brains, take a few plugs at the lizard with his handgun, then get eaten alive.

It took Noah a moment to process that he was watching an old movie and not a news bulletin. That's when he decided his brain was fried for the night.

There was one more chore on his agenda, and though he knew it was just a little nasty to have waited until the middle of the night to deal with it, he picked up the phone and called Mike in L.A.

It took five rings, and the slur of sleep and bafflement in his friend's voice gave Noah considerable satisfaction.

'Hey. Did I wake you up?'

'What? Noah? Where are you?'

'San Francisco. Remember?'

'Huh? No . . . sort of. Jesus, Noah, it's two in the morning.'

'No kidding?' His brows drew together as he heard another voice, slightly muffled, definitely female. 'You got a woman there, Mike?'

'Maybe. Why?'

'Congratulations. The blonde from the club?'

'Ah . . . *hmmmm*.'

'Okay, okay, probably not the time to go into it. I'm going to be gone at least another week. I didn't want to call my parents and wake them up, and I'm going to be pretty busy in the morning.'

'Oh, but it's okay to call and wake me up?'

'Sure – besides, now that you're both awake, you might get another round going. Remember to thank me later.'

'Kiss my ass.'

'That's gratitude for you. Since you're so fond of calling my mother, give her a buzz tomorrow and let her know I'm on the road.'

There were some rustling sounds, making Noah imagine Mike was finally getting around to sitting up in bed. 'Listen, I just thought you needed a little . . .'

'Interference in my life. Stop pulling on your lip, Mike,' he said mildly, knowing his friend's nervous habits well. 'I'm not pissed off, particularly, but I figure you owe me. So give my mom a call and take care of my flowers while I'm gone.'

'I can do that. Look, give me a number where I can – whoa.'

The low smoke of female laughter had Noah raising an eyebrow. 'Later. I don't really want to have phone sex with you and the blonde. You let my flowers die, I'll kick your ass.'

The response was a sharp intake of breath, a great deal of

rustling and whispering. Rolling his eyes, Noah hung up on a wild burst of laughter.

Terrific, he thought and rubbed his hands over his face. Now he had two sexual adventures in his head. He decided to take a cold shower and go to bed.

The Forest

Enter these enchanted woods,
You who dare.

—George Meredith

Chapter Seventeen

He was surprised he remembered it so well, in such detail, with such clarity. As he drove, Noah caught himself bracing for the sensory rush as he came around a switchback, heartbeats before his field of vision changed from thick wood and sheer rock to stunning blue sky painted with the dazzling white peaks of mountains.

It was true that he'd driven this way once before, but he'd been only eighteen, it had been only one time. It shouldn't have been like coming home after a trip away, like waking up after a dream.

And it had been summer, he reminded himself, when the peaks were snowcapped, but the body of them green with the pines and firs that marched up their sides to give them the look of living, growing giants rather than the cold and still kings that reigned over the valleys.

He'd done his research, he'd studied photographs, the brochures, the travelogues, but somehow he knew they couldn't have prepared him for this sweep, for the contrasts of deep, silent forest and wildly regal peaks.

He continued the climb long after he passed the turnoff for River's End. He had time, hours if he chose, before he needed to wind his way down to the lowlands, the rain forest, the job.

Choices again. And his was to slip into a pull-off, get out of the car and stand. The air was cold and pure. His breath puffed out, and had little knives scoring his throat on the inhale. It seemed to him that the world was spread out before him, field and valley, hill and forest, the bright ribbon of river, the flash of lake.

Even as a car grinding into low gear passed behind him, he felt isolated. He couldn't decide if it was a feeling he enjoyed or one that troubled him, but he stood, letting the wind slap at his jacket and sneak under to chill his body, and studied the vast blue of the sky, with the white spears of mountains vivid against it like a design etched on glass.

He thought perhaps he'd stopped just here with his parents all those years ago, and remembered standing with his mother reading the guidebook.

The Olympic Range. And however vast and encompassing it seemed from this point, he knew that at lower elevations, in the forest where the grand trees ruled, it didn't exist. You would walk and walk in that dimness, or clatter up rocks on the tumbling hills and not see the stunning scope of them. Then you would take a turn, step out on a ridge, and there it would be. The vast sky-stealing stretch of it snatching your breath as if it had sneaked up on you instead of the other way around.

Noah took one last look, climbed back in his car and started down the switchback the way he'd come.

The trees took over. Became the world.

The detour took him a little more than an hour, but he still arrived at the lodge by three in the afternoon. He traveled up the same bumpy lane, catching glimpses of the stone and wood, the fairy-tale rooflines, the glint of glass that was the lodge.

He was about to tell himself it hadn't changed, when he spotted a structure nestled in the trees. It mirrored the style and materials of the lodge, but it was much smaller and not nearly as weathered.

The wooden sign over the double doorway read RIVER'S END NATURALIST CENTER. There was a walking path leading to it from the lane and another from the lodge. Wildflowers and ferns appeared to have been allowed to grow as they pleased around it, but his gardener's eye detected a human hand in the balance.

Olivia's hand, he thought, and felt a warm and unexpected spurt of pride.

It was undoubtedly manmade, but she had designed it to blend in so well it seemed to have grown there as naturally as the trees.

He parked his car, noted that the lot held a respectable number of vehicles. It was warmer here than it had been at the pull off. Warm enough, he noted, to keep the pansies and purple salvia happy in their long clay troughs near the entrance.

He swung on his backpack, took out his single suitcase and was just locking his car when a dog loped around the side of the lodge and grinned at him.

Noah couldn't think of another term for the expression. The dog's tongue lolled, the lips were peeled back and seemed to curve up, and the deep brown eyes danced with unmistakable delight.

'Hey there, fella.'

Obviously seeing this as an invitation, the big yellow lab pranced across the lot, plopped down at Noah's feet and lifted a paw.

'You the welcoming committee, boy?' Obligingly, Noah shook hands, then cocked his head. 'Or should I say girl. Your name wouldn't happen to be Shirley, would it?'

At the name, the dog let out one cheerful woof, then danced toward the entrance as if to tell Noah to come on, pal, get the lead out.

He was charmed enough to be vaguely disappointed when the dog didn't follow him inside.

He didn't see any dramatic changes in the lobby. Noah thought perhaps some of the furnishings had been replaced, and the paint was a soft, toasty yellow. But everything exuded such an aura of welcome and settled comfort that it might have been exactly so for a century.

The check-in was quick, efficient and friendly, and after having assured the clerk he could handle his baggage himself, he carried his bags, a package of information and his key up two squat sets of stairs in the main lobby and down a hallway to the right.

He'd requested a suite out of habit and because he preferred a separate area to set up his work. It was smaller than the rooms he remembered sharing with his parents, but certainly not cramped.

There was a nap-taking sofa, a small but sturdy desk, a table where guides and literature on the area were fanned. The art – running to watercolor prints of local flora – was better than decent, and the phone would support his modem.

He glanced at the view, pleased to have been given the side facing the back so it was untainted by cars. He dropped his suitcase on the chest at the foot of the sleigh bed of varnished golden wood and tossed the lid open. As his contribution to unpacking, he removed his shaving gear and dumped it on the narrow shelf over the white pedestal sink in the adjoining bath.

He considered the shower – he'd been in the car since six A.M. – and thought of the beer he might find in the lobby bar. After a mild debate he decided to take the first, then go hunt up the second.

He stripped, letting his clothes lie where they fell, then diddled with the controls of the shower until the water came out fast and hot. The minute he stepped under the spray, he groaned in pleasure.

Right decision, Brady, he thought as he let the water beat on his head. And after the beer, he'd wander around, scope out the place. He wanted to get a feel for the owners, to see if he could judge by how the staff and guests spoke of them which one of the MacBrides would be the best to approach.

He wanted to go over to the Center, find Olivia. Just look at her awhile.

He'd do that in the morning, he thought. After he got his bearings and a good night's sleep.

He toweled off, tugged on jeans. He gave some consideration to actually putting away the clothes in his bag. He opted instead to just dig out a shirt, when there was a hard rap on the door.

Noah quickly grabbed a shirt and carried it with him to the door.

He recognized her instantly. Later he would wonder why the recognition had been so immediate, and so intense. She'd certainly changed.

Her face was thinner, honed into sharp planes. Her mouth was firmer, still full and unpainted as it had been at nineteen, but it didn't strike him as innocent any longer.

And that gave him one hard tug of annoyance and regret.

He might have noted it wasn't smiling in welcome if he hadn't been dealing with the ridiculous and completely unexpected flash of pleasure.

Her hair had darkened to a color that reminded him of the caramels Mike's mother had always melted down at Hallowe'en and swirled onto apples. And she'd lopped it off. Lopped off all that gorgeous shiny hair. And yet it suited her better this way. On another woman he supposed the short, straight cut with the fringe of bang would have been called pixyish. But there was nothing fairylike about the woman in the doorway with her tall and leanly athletic build.

She smelled like the woods and carried a stoneware bowl filled with fresh fruit.

He felt the foolish grin break out on his face and could think of nothing to say but: 'Hi.'

'Compliments of River's End Lodge.' She thrust the bowl at him, straight into the gut and with enough force to earn a grunt from him.

'Ah, thanks.'

She was in the room in one long stride that had him backing up automatically. When she slammed the door at her back, he lifted his eyebrows. 'Do you come with the fruit? They hardly ever give you complimentary women in California.'

'You have a hell of a nerve, sneaking in here this way.'

Okay, he decided, all right, it wasn't going to be a friendly reunion. 'You're right, absolutely. I don't know what I was thinking of, calling ahead for reservations, registering at the desk that way.' He set the bowl down, gingerly rubbed his stomach. 'Look, why don't we take a minute to—'

'I'll give you a minute.' She rammed a finger into his chest. 'I'll give you a minute, then you can get your butt back to Los Angeles. You have no right coming here this way.'

'Of course I have a right. It's a goddamn hotel.' He lifted a hand. 'And don't poke at me again, okay?'

'I told you to stay away from me.'

'And I damn well did.' The flash in her eyes was a clear warning that had him narrowing his own. 'Don't hit me again, Liv. I mean it. I'm pretty well fed up with female abuse. Now we can sit down and discuss this like reasonable adults, or we can just stand here and snarl at each other.'

'I don't have anything to discuss with you. I'm *telling* you to go away and leave us alone.'

'That's not going to happen.' Deciding to play it another way, he sat, chose an apple from the bowl and stretched out his legs as he bit in. 'I'm not going anywhere, Olivia. You might as well talk to me.'

'I'm entitled to my privacy.'

'Sure you are. That's the beauty of it. You don't tell me anything you don't want to tell me.' He took another bite of the apple, then gestured with it. 'We can start with something simple, like what you've been doing with yourself the last half dozen years.'

Smug, smirky son of a bitch, she thought and spun away to pace. She hated that he looked the same, so much the same. The sun-streaked, wind-tossed hair, the full, firm mouth, the fascinating planes and angles of his face.

'If you were half the man your father is, you'd have some respect for my mother's memory.'

That edgy little barb winged home and hooked itself bloodily in his heart. Noah studied his apple, turning it around in his hand until he was certain he could speak calmly. 'You measured me by my father once before.' He lifted his gaze, and it was hard as granite. 'Don't do it again.'

Olivia jammed her hands in her pockets, shot a withering glance over her shoulder. 'You don't care what I think of you.'

'You don't know what I care about.'

'Money. They'll pay you big bucks for this book, won't they? Then you can bounce around on all the talk shows and spout off about yourself and the valuable insights you dug up on why my father butchered my mother.'

'Don't you want to know why?' He spoke quietly and watched those wonderful eyes reflect fury, misery, then snap back to fury.

'I know why, and it doesn't change anything. Go away, Noah. Go back and write about someone else's tragedy.'

'Liv.' He called out to her as she strode toward the door. 'I won't go away. Not this time.'

She didn't stop, didn't look back, but slammed the door smartly enough to have the pictures rattling on the walls. Noah tossed his apple in the air. 'Well, that was pleasant,' he muttered, and decided he'd more than earned that beer.

She went down the back stairs, avoiding the lobby and the people who would be milling around. She cut through the kitchen, only shaking her head when her name was called. She needed to get out, get out, get away until she could fight off the hideous pressure in her chest, the vicious roaring in her ears.

She had to force herself not to break out in a run, to try to outrace the panic that licked at her. She moved quickly into the forest, into the deep and the damp. Still, her breath wanted to come in pants, her knees wanted to shake. It wouldn't be permitted.

When she'd gone far enough, when the chances of anyone hiking down the path were slim, she sat down, there on the forest floor and rocked herself.

It was stupid. She'd been stupid, Olivia admitted as she pressed her forehead to her knees. She'd known he was coming. Jamie had told her he would, told her what he intended to do. Told her that she herself had decided to cooperate with him on the book.

That had generated the first genuine argument between them Olivia could remember.

Already, Noah Brady and his book were causing rifts in her family.

But she'd prepared herself to face him again. To deal with it. She wasn't the same naive, susceptible girl who'd fallen stupidly in love with him.

She hadn't expected that rush of feeling when he'd opened the door and smiled at her. So much the way he had six years before. She hadn't expected her heart to break again, not after she'd spent so much time and effort to heal it.

Temper was better than pain.

Still, she'd handled it – handled him – poorly.

She'd kept her eye out for his reservation. When it had come in, she'd promised herself she would go to his room after he'd checked in, so that she could talk to him, reason with him, in private. She would be calm, explain each one of her objections.

He was Frank Brady's son, after all. And Frank was one of the few people she trusted absolutely.

She arranged to take the fruit bowl up herself, had worked out exactly what she would say and how she would say it.

Welcome to River's End again, Noah. It's nice to see you. Can I come in for a minute?

Reasonable, calm, rational. But as she'd started toward his room the fear had crawled into her and she'd gripped her anger like a weapon to beat it back.

Then he'd opened the door, and smiled at her. Smiled, she thought now as she turned her head to rest her cheek on her updrawn knees, with absolute delight. As if there had never been betrayal, never been deceit.

And he'd looked so pleased and attractive – his hair dark and wet from the shower, his moss-green eyes lit with pleasure – that some ridiculous part of her had wanted to smile back.

So she'd attacked. What other choice had she had? she thought now. Instead of persuading him, or intimidating him, into backing away from the book, she was dead sure she'd convinced him to dig in his heels.

She wanted to be left alone. She wanted to protect her world and to be left alone inside it.

Why had Sam Tanner contacted Noah? No. Furious, she squeezed her eyes shut. She didn't want to think about that, about him. She didn't want to know. She'd put all that away, just as her grandmother had put her memories in the chest in the attic.

It had taken years to accomplish it. Years of secret visits to that attic, of nightmares, years of painful, guilty searches for any snippet of information about her parents.

And once she'd found all there was to find, she'd put it away, focused on the present and the future rather than the past. She found peace of mind, contentment in her work, a direction to her life.

All that was threatened now. Because Sam Tanner was getting out of prison, and Noah Brady was writing a book. Those were facts she couldn't ignore.

She glanced over as the lab raced down the path. The greeting took the form of a dancing leap and many sloppy kisses that had Olivia's tension breaking open so that a laugh could pour out.

'I can always count on you, can't I?' She nuzzled into Shirley's neck before she rose. 'Let's go home, girl. Let's just go home and worry about all this later.'

The food was great. Noah gave the MacBrides high marks on the lodge kitchen, particularly after indulging himself in two passes through the breakfast buffet. The service was right up there on a level with the food – warm, friendly, efficient without being obvious.

His bed had been comfortable, and if he'd been in the mood, he could have chosen from a very decent list of in-room movies.

He'd worked instead and now felt he deserved a morning to piddle.

Trouble was, he mused, looking out the window of the dining room at the steady, drumming rain, the weather wasn't quite as appealing as the rest of the fare.

Then again, the brochures had warned him to expect rainy

springs. And he couldn't say it wasn't picturesque in its way. A far cry from his own sunwashed California coast, but there was something compelling about the shadowy grays and greens and the liquid wall of rain. It didn't make him long to strap on his foul-weather gear and take a hike, but it was pleasant to study from inside the cozy warmth of the lodge.

He'd already made use of the health club and had found it expanded and nicely modernized since his last visit. They'd added an indoor pool, and even as he considered a swim he tossed the idea aside. He couldn't imagine he'd be the only one with the idea and the prospect of families splashing around and hooting at one another just didn't fit his plans.

He could get a massage, or make use of the lodge library, which he'd wandered into the evening before and found well stocked and welcoming.

Or he could do what he'd come for and start poking around.

He could hunt up Olivia and argue with her again.

The bark of male laughter had him glancing over, then narrowing his eyes in speculation. The man was dressed in a plaid flannel shirt and work trousers. His hair was thick, a Cary Grant silver that caught the overhead lights as he worked the dining room, stopping by tables of those who, like Noah, were lingering over that last cup of coffee.

His brows were defiantly dark, and though Noah couldn't catch the color of his eyes, he imagined they would be that odd and beautiful golden brown. He had the whipcord build and appearance of impossible fitness of an elderly outdoorsman.

Rob MacBride, Noah thought, and decided that lingering over coffee and rain watching had been the perfect way to spend his morning.

He sat back and waited for his turn.

It didn't take long for Rob to complete the circuit and pause by Noah's table with a quick grin. 'Pretty day, isn't it?'

'For ducks,' Noah said, since it seemed expected. He was rewarded with that deep, barking laugh.

'Rain's what makes us what we are here. I hope you're enjoying your stay.'

'Very much. It's a great place. You've made a few changes since I was here last, but you've kept the tone.'

'So, you've stayed with us before.'

'A long time ago.' Noah held out his hand. 'I'm Noah Brady, Mr. MacBride.'

'Welcome back.'

He watched for it, but saw no hint of recognition in Rob's eyes. 'Thanks. I came here with my parents, about twelve years ago. Frank and Celia Brady.'

'We're always pleased to have the next generation ...' The recognition came now, and along with it quiet grief. 'Frank Brady? Your father?'

'Yes.'

Rob stared out the window at the rain. 'That's a name I haven't thought of in a long time. A very long time.'

'If you'll sit down, Mr. MacBride, I'll tell you why I'm here.'

Rob shifted his gaze back, glanced at Noah's face. 'I guess that's the thing to do, isn't it? Hailey?' he called out to the waitress just clearing another station. 'Could you get us some coffee over here?'

He sat, laid his long, thin hands on the table. They showed the age, Noah noted; his face didn't. There was always some part of you, he mused, that was marked with time.

'Your father's well?'

'Yeah, he's good. Retired recently, drove my mother crazy for a while, then found something to keep himself busy and out of her hair.'

Rob nodded, grateful Noah had slipped into small talk. He found it kind. 'Man doesn't keep busy, he gets old fast. The lodge, the campground, the people who come and go here, that's what keeps me young. Got managers and such doing a lot of the day-to-day work now, but I still keep my hand in.'

'It's a place to be proud of. I've felt at home since I walked in the door.' Except for one small incident with your granddaughter, Noah thought, but decided it wouldn't be politic to mention it.

'I'll top that off, Mr. Brady.' Hailey said, then poured a cup for Rob.

'So did you go into police work like your dad?' he questioned.

'No. I'm a writer.'

'Really.' Rob's face brightened. 'Nothing like a good story. What sort of things do you write?'

'I write nonfiction. True crime.' He waited a beat as he could already see the awareness moving over Rob's face. 'I'm writing a book about what happened to your daughter.'

Rob lifted his cup, sipped slowly. When he spoke it wasn't anger in his voice, but weariness. 'Over twenty years now. Hasn't everything been said already?'

'I don't think so. I've had an interest in what happened since I was a kid. My father's connection, how it affected him made an impression on me.'

He paused, weighed his words, then decided to be as honest as he was able. 'I think, on some level, I'd always planned to write about it. I didn't know how I'd approach it, but I knew when the time came, I'd write it. The time came a few weeks ago when Sam Tanner contacted me.'

'Tanner. Why won't he let her rest?'

'He wants to tell his story.'

'And you think he'll tell you the truth?' Bitterness crackled in his voice like ice. 'You think the man who murdered my daughter, who sliced her to ribbons, is capable of telling the truth?'

'I can't say, but I can tell you I'm capable of separating truth from lies. I don't intend for this book to be Tanner's. I don't intend for what I write to be simply his view noted down on paper. I'm going to talk to everyone who was touched or involved. I've already begun to. That's why I'm here, Mr. MacBride, to understand and incorporate your view.'

'Julie was one of the brightest lights of my life, and he snuffed her out. He took her love, twisted it into a weapon and destroyed her with it. What other view could I possibly have?'

'You knew her in a way no one else could. You know them in a way no one else could. That's what matters.'

Rob lifted his hands, rubbed them over his face. 'Noah, do you have any idea how many times we were approached during the two years after Julie's death? To give interviews, to endorse books, movies, television features?'

'I can imagine, and I'm aware you refused them all.'

'All,' Rob agreed. 'They offered us obscene amounts of money, promises, threats. The answer was always no. Why do you think I would say yes now, after all these years, to you?'

'Because I'm not going to offer you money, or make any threats, and I'll only give you one promise. I'll tell the truth, and by telling it, I'll do right by your daughter.'

'Maybe you will,' Rob said after a moment. 'I believe you'll try to. But Julie's gone, Noah, and I have to think of the family I have left.'

'Would it be better for them for this book to be written without their input?'

'I don't know. The wound's not raw anymore, but it still aches from time to time. There have been moments I wanted to have my say, but they passed.' He let out a long sigh. 'A part of me, I admit, doesn't want her to be forgotten. Doesn't want what happened to her to be forgotten.'

'I haven't forgotten.' Noah waited while Rob's gaze jerked back to his face. 'Tell me what you want remembered.'

Chapter Eighteen

The Naturalist Center was Olivia's baby. It had been her concept, her design and in a very real sense her Holy Grail.

She'd insisted on using the money she'd inherited from her mother, and at twenty-one, degree fresh and crisp in her hand, she'd reached into her trust fund and built her dream.

She'd supervised every aspect of the center, from the laying of stone to the arrangement of seats in the small theater where visitors could watch a short documentary on the area's flora and fauna. She'd chosen every slide and each voice-over in the lobby area personally, had interviewed and hired the staff, commissioned the to-scale model of the Quinault Valley and rain forest and often worked as guide on the hikes the center offered.

In the year since she'd opened the doors to the public, she'd never been more content.

She wasn't going to allow Noah Brady to spoil that carefully structured contentment.

With her mind only half on the job, she continued to take her small group of visitors on their indoor tour of the local mammals.

'The Roosevelt, or Olympic, elk is the biggest of the wapiti. Large herds of Roosevelt elk make their home along the Olympic Peninsula. In a very real way, we owe the preservation of this area to this native animal, as it was to protect their breeding grounds and summer range that President Theodore Roosevelt, during the final days of his administration, issued the proclamation that created Mount Olympus National Monument.'

She glanced up as the main door opened and instantly felt her nerves fray.

Noah gave her a slight nod, a half grin, then began to wander around the main area, leaving a trail of wet behind him. As a matter of pride, Olivia continued her lecture, moving from elk to black-tailed deer, from deer to marten, but when she paused by the *Castor canadensis*, the beaver, and the memory of sitting on the riverbank with Noah flashed into her mind, she signaled to one of her staff to take over.

She wanted to turn around and go lock herself in her office. Paperwork was, always, a viable excuse. But she knew it would look cowardly. Worse, it would *feel* cowardly. So, instead, she walked over and stood beside him as he examined one of the enlarged slides with apparent fascination.

'So, that's a shrew.'

'A wandering shrew, *Sorex vagrans*, quite common in this region. We also have the Trowbridge, the masked and the dusky shrew. There are Pacific water shrews, northern water shrews and shrew moles, though the masked shrew is rare.'

'I guess I'm only acquainted with city shrews.'

'That's very lame humor.'

'Yeah, but you've gotta start somewhere. You did a great job here, Liv. I knew you would.'

'Really? I didn't realize you'd paid attention to any of my ramblings back then.'

'I paid attention to everything about you. Everything, Olivia.'

She shut down, shuttered over. 'I'm not going back there. Not now, not ever.'

'Fine, let's stay here then.' He wandered over and studied what he decided was a particularly ugly creature called a western big-eared bat. 'Want to show me around?'

'You don't give a damn about natural science, so why waste each other's time?'

'Pardon me, but you're talking to someone who was raised on whale song and the plight of the pelican. I'm a card-carrying member of Greenpeace, the Nature Conservancy and the World Wildlife Federation. I get calendars every year.'

Because she wanted to smile, she sighed. 'The documentary runs every hour on the half hour in the theater. You can catch it in ten minutes right through those doors to your left.'

'Where's the popcorn?'

Because she nearly did smile, she turned away. 'I'm busy.'

'No you're not.' He caught her arm, held it in what he hoped she'd consider a light, nonthreatening grip. 'You can make yourself busy, just as you can take a few minutes.'

'I don't intend to discuss my family with you.'

'Okay, let's talk about something else. How'd you come up with this? The design, I mean.' He used his free hand to gesture. 'It's no small deal, and looks a lot more entertaining than most of the nature places my mother dragged me into before I could fight back.'

'I'm a naturalist. I live here.'

'Come on, Liv, it takes more than that. Did you study design, too?'

'No, I didn't study design, I just saw it this way.'

'Well, it works. Nothing to scare the little kids away in here. It doesn't whisper educational in that dry, crackling voice or bounce out with chipper graphics that give the parents migraines. Nice colors, good space. What's through here?'

He moved past the reception counter, where books and post-cards of the area were neatly displayed for sale, and through a wide doorway.

'Hey, this is very cool.' Centered in a room where more displays of plant and animal life were on view was the model of the valley. 'Hawk's-eye view,' he said, leaning over it. 'And here we are. The lodge, the center.' He tapped his finger on the protective dome. 'There's the trail we took that day, isn't it, along the river? You even put in the beaver dam. Your grandparents have a house, though, don't they? I don't see it here.'

'Because it's private.'

He straightened, and his gaze seemed to drive straight into hers. 'Are you under this glass dome, Liv, tucked away where no one can get to you?'

'I'm exactly where I want to be.'

'My book isn't likely to change that, but what it might do is sweep out all the shadows that still hang over what happened that night. I've got a chance to bring the truth out, the whole of it. Sam Tanner's talking, for the first time since the trial, and a dying man often chooses to clear his conscience before it's over.'

'Dying?'

'The tumor,' Noah began, then watched with shocked alarm as her face went sheet white. 'I'm sorry. I thought you knew.'

All she felt was her throat, the burn of the words forcing their way out. 'Are you telling me he's dying?'

'He has brain cancer; he only has months left. Come on, you need to sit down.'

He took her arm, but she jerked herself free. 'Don't touch me.' She turned quickly and strode through the next doorway.

He would have let her go, told himself to let her go. But he could still see the shock glazing her eyes. Swearing under his breath, he went after her.

She had a long stride and the dead-ahead gait of a woman who would plow over obstacles on her way to the finish line. He told himself to remember that if he ever had to get in her way.

But he caught up just as she turned into an office past the theater area and nearly got flattened when she swung the door closed.

He managed to block it instead of walking face-first into it, then shut it behind him.

'This is an employees-only area.' Which was a stupid lie, she thought, but the best she had. 'Take a hike.'

'Sit down.' It appeared he was going to have to get in her way already, and so he took her arm once again, steered her around the desk and into the chair behind it. He had the impression of a small space, methodically organized, and crouching down, concentrated on her.

'I'm sorry.' He took her hand without either of them really being aware of the gesture. 'I wouldn't have dropped it on you that way. I thought Jamie would've told you.'

'She didn't. And it doesn't matter.'

'Of course it matters. Want some water or something?' He looked around hoping to spot a cooler, a jug, anything that would give him something to do.

'I don't need anything. I'm perfectly fine.' She looked down, saw her hand in his. With baffled shock she noted her fingers had linked with his and curled tight. Mortally embarrassed, she shook free.

'Stand up, for God's sake. All I need is someone coming in here and seeing you kneeling at my feet.'

'I wasn't kneeling.' But he straightened up, then opted to sit on the corner of the desk.

It was more than her hair she'd changed. This Olivia was a hell of a lot tougher, a hell of a lot edgier than the shy college student he'd tumbled for.

'You did speak with Jamie, didn't you, about my wanting to talk with you?'

'Yes.'

'Why didn't she tell you that Sam was dying?'

'We argued.' Olivia leaned back in her chair. Her head didn't feel light any longer. She just felt tired. 'We never argue, so that's one more thing I have to thank you and your book for. If she'd intended to tell me, I suppose it got lost in the fray.'

'He wants to tell his story before he dies. If he doesn't, it dies with him. Is that really what you want?'

The need she'd worked so hard to bury tried to claw its way free. 'It doesn't matter what I want, you'll do it anyway. You always planned to.'

'Yeah, I did. And I'm telling you straight out this time, up-front. The way I should have before.'

'I said I won't discuss that.' And just that coolly, she snapped the door shut. 'You want what you want. And as for him, he wants to purge himself before it's too late, and look for what? Forgiveness? Redemption?'

'Understanding, maybe. I think he's trying to understand himself how it all happened. I want your part of it, Liv. All the others I'll talk to are pieces of the whole, but you're the key. Your grandfather claims you have a photographic memory. Is that true?'

'Yes,' she said absently. 'I see words. It's just . . . my grandfather?' She leaped to her feet. 'You spoke to my grandfather.'

'Just after breakfast.'

'You stay away from him.'

'He came up to my table, which from what I observed, he's in the habit of doing with guests. I told him who I was and why I was here. If you have a problem with his agreeing to talk to me, you'll have to take it up with him.'

'He's over seventy. You have no business putting him through this.'

'I should be in such good shape at seventy. I didn't strap him on the rack and crank the wheel, for Christ's sake.' Damn it, would she forever make him feel guilty? 'We had a conversation over coffee. Then he agreed to a taped interview in my room. And when we finished the session, he didn't shuffle out bent and broken. He looked relieved. Sam isn't the only one with something to purge, Liv.'

It shook her enough to have her running a nervous hand through her hair. 'He agreed to it? He spoke with you about it? What did he say?'

'Oh, no.' Intrigued, Noah studied her. 'I don't prime the pump that way. I want what you tell me to come from you, not to be a reflection of what other people think and feel.'

'He never talks about it.'

What was that, under the surprise, Noah wondered. Hurt? 'He did today, and he agreed to at least one more interview before I leave.'

'What's going on? I don't understand what's going on around here.'

'Maybe it's just time. Why don't we try this? I'll talk to you, tell you about my wild and exciting life and all my fascinating opinions on the world in general. Once you see how charming and brilliant I am, you'll have an easier time talking to me.'

'You're not nearly as charming as you think you are.'

'Sure I am. Let's have dinner.'

Oh, they'd gone that route before. 'No.'

'Okay, that was knee-jerk, I could tell. Let's try again. Let's have dinner.'

This time she angled her head, took a steady five seconds. 'No.'

'All right, I'll just have to pay for you.'

Her eyes went molten, a deep, rich gold that made him think of old paintings executed by masters. 'You think I care about your money? That you can bribe me. You sleazy son of a—'

'Hold it, that's not what I meant. I meant I'd have to hire you – as in *ask for information on our day packages, including bikes guided by one of our professional naturalists*. The professional would be you. So which trail would you recommend for a nice, scenic hike tomorrow?'

'Forget it.'

'Oh no, you advertise, you follow through. I'm a paying customer. Now do you want to recommend a trail, or should I just pick one at random?'

'You want to hike?' Oh, she'd give him a hike, Olivia thought. She'd give him one for the books. 'That's fine, that's just what we're here for. Make the reservation out at the desk. Just give them my name and book it for seven tomorrow.'

'That would be A.M.?'

'Is that a problem, city boy?'

'No, just clarifying.' He eased off the desk and found himself a great deal closer to her than was comfortable for either of them. She smelled the same. For several dizzy minutes, it was all he could think about.

She smelled the same.

He felt the tug, the definite, unmistakable jerk in the gut of basic lust. And though he told himself not to do it, his gaze lowered to her mouth just long enough to make him remember.

'Well, *hmmm.*' He thought the reaction damn inconvenient all around and stepped aside. 'I'll see you in the morning, then.'

'Be sure to take one of our hiker's guides along with you, so you know how to dress for the trail.'

'I know how the hell to dress,' he muttered, and more annoyed with himself than he thought was fair, he strode out.

She made him feel guilty one minute, he thought, and angry the next. Protective, then aggressive. He damn well didn't want to be attracted to her again and add one more layer to cloud the issue.

He stopped by reception as instructed and booked the time. The clerk tapped out the information on her keyboard and offered him a cheery smile. 'If I could just have your name?'

'Just use my initials,' he heard himself saying. 'S.O.B.'

He had a feeling Olivia would get it.

Olivia knew her grandmother had been crying. She came in the back door out of habit, the wet dog prancing at her heels. It only took one look to have her heart squeezing.

Val insisted on preparing the evening meal. Every day, like clockwork, she could be found in the kitchen at six o'clock, stirring or slicing, with good homey scents puffing out of pots and Vanna White turning letters on the under-the-counter TV. Often, Val could be heard calling out advice or muttering pithy comments such as *Don't buy a vowel, you moron.* Or shaking her head because the contestant at the wheel couldn't guess A Stitch in Time Saves Nine to save his immortal soul.

It was a comforting routine, and one that rarely varied. Olivia would come in, pour a glass of wine – it had been a soft drink or juice in her youth – and set the table while the two of them just talked.

But tonight, she came in chilled to the bone, her rain gear slick with wet from the aimless walk she and Shirley had indulged in, and there was no incessant clapping or bright colors on the little TV screen. Pots simmered, Val stirred, but she kept her back to the room. There was no smile of greeting tossed over her shoulder.

'You keep that wet dog in the mudroom, Livvy.'

Because her voice was thick and a little rusty, Olivia recognized tears. 'Go on, Shirley, go lie down now.' Olivia shooed the dog back into the mudroom, where she curled up, a sulky look in her eyes, with her chew rope.

Olivia poured them both a glass of wine, and leaving the table unset, walked over to set her grandmother's on the counter by the stove. 'I know you're upset. I'm sorry this is happening.'

'It's nothing we need to talk about. We're having beef and barley stew tonight. I'm about ready to add the dumplings.'

Olivia's first instinct was to nod and get out the deep bowls. To let the subject bury itself again. But she wondered if Noah wasn't right about at least one thing. Maybe it was just time.

'Grandma, it's happening whether we talk about it or not.'

'Then there's no point in bringing it up.' She reached for the bowl where the dough was already mixed and ready. And, reaching blindly, knocked the glass off the counter. It shattered on the floor, a shower of glass and blood-red wine.

'Oh, what was that doing there? Don't you know better than to set a glass on the edge of the counter? Just look at my floor.'

'I'm sorry. I'll clean it up.' Olivia turned quickly to get the broom out of the closet and shushed the dog, who'd leaped up as if to defend the women-folk from invaders. 'Relax, Shirley, it's broken glass not a gunshot.'

But any amusement she felt vanished when she turned back and saw her grandmother standing, shoulders shaking, her face buried in a dish towel.

'Oh, I'm sorry, I'm sorry, I'm so sorry.' She dropped the broom and rushed over to grab Val close.

'I won't deal with it again. I can't. I told Rob to tell that young man to go. Just to pack his bags and go, but he won't do it. He says it's not right, and it won't change anything anyway.'

'I'll make him go.' Olivia pressed her lips to Val's hair. 'I'll send him away.'

'No, it won't matter. I knew that, even when I was fighting with Rob. It won't matter. It can't be stopped. We weren't able to stop any of the talk or the books twenty years ago; we won't stop it now. But I can't open my heart to that kind of grief again.'

She stepped back, wiping at her face. 'I can't and I won't. So you're to tell him not to come here asking me to talk. And I won't have it discussed in this house.'

'He won't come here, Grandma. I'll make sure of it.'

'I shouldn't have snapped at you about the glass. It's just a glass.' Val pressed her fingers to her left eye, then her temple. 'I've got a headache, that's all. Makes my temper short. You see to those dumplings for me, Livvy. I'll just go take some aspirin and lie down for a few minutes.'

'All right. Grandma—'

Val cut her off with a look. 'Just put the dumplings on, Livvy. Your grandfather gets cross if we eat much later than six-thirty.'

Just like that, Olivia thought as Val walked out of the kitchen. It was closed off, shut out. Not to be discussed. Another chest for the attic, she decided, and turned to pick up the broom.

But this time around, the lock wasn't going to hold.

Just after nine, about the time Noah was debating between a couple of hours' work or a movie break, Mike whistled his way up the walk of the beach house.

He'd meant to get there earlier, to give Noah's plants and flowers a good watering before full dark, but one thing had led to another. Namely one of his co-workers had challenged him to a marathon game of Mortal Kombat, which had led to dueling computers for two hours and eighteen minutes.

But victory was its own reward, Mike thought. And to sweeten the pot, he'd called his date and asked if she'd like to meet him at Noah's for a walk on the beach, a dip in his friend's hot tub and whatever else struck their fancy.

He didn't figure Noah would mind. And he'd pay off the usage by getting up early and seeing to the gardens.

He flipped the porch light on, then moseyed into the kitchen to see if good old Noah had any fancy wine suitable for hot tub seductions.

He studied labels, and trusting Noah's judgment on such details, chose one with a French-sounding name. He set it on the counter, wondering if it was supposed to breathe or not, then with a shrug, opened the refrigerator to see if Noah had any interesting food stocked.

He was still whistling, cheerfully debating between a package of brie and a plate of sad-looking fried chicken when he caught a flash of movement out of the corner of his eye.

He straightened fast, felt a brilliant burst of pain. He staggered back, reaching up thinking he'd bashed his head on the refrigerator.

His hand came away wet; he stared dumbly at the blood smearing his fingertips. 'Oh shit,' he managed, before the second blow buckled his knees and sent him down into the dark.

Chapter Nineteen

It was still raining when Noah's alarm buzzed at six. He slapped at it, opened his eyes to the gloom and considered doing what any sensible man did on a rainy morning. Sleeping through it.

But a few hours' cozy oblivion didn't seem worth the smirk and snippy comments Olivia would lay on him. Maybe it was pride, maybe he had something to prove to both of them, but either way, he rolled out of bed. He stumbled into the shower, which brought him up one level of consciousness, stumbled out again, then dressed for the day.

He decided anyone planning on tromping around in the trees in the rain had to be crazy. He figured out Olivia had known it was going to rain, had probably *arranged* for it to rain just to pay him back for being a jerk. He groused about it all the way down to the lobby, where he found several small groups of people suited up for the day and helping themselves to the complimentary coffee and doughnuts the inn provided for early hikers.

Most of them, Noah noted with complete bafflement, looked happy to be there.

At seven, riding on a caffeine-and-sugar high, he felt nearly human. He drummed up enough energy to flirt with the desk clerk, then snagged one last doughnut for the road and headed out.

He spotted Olivia immediately. She stood in the gloom, rain pattering on her bush-style hat, fog twisting around her boots and ankles as she spoke to a quartet of guests about their planned route for the morning. The dog milled around, charming head scratches and handshakes out of the early risers.

She acknowledged Noah with a nod, then watched the group head off.

'You set?'

Noah took another bite of his tractor wheel. 'Yeah.'

'Let's see.' She stood back, skimmed her measuring glance up, then down, then up again. 'How long have those boots been out of the box, ace?'

Less than an hour, Noah thought, as he'd bought them in San Francisco. 'So I haven't been hiking in a few years. Unless we're planning on climbing the Matterhorn, I'm up for it. I'm in shape.'

'Health-club shape.' She pressed a finger against his flat belly. 'Fancy health club, too. This won't be like your StairMaster. Where's your water bottle?'

Already irritated with her, he held out a hand, cupped it and let rain pool in his palm. Olivia only shook her head. 'Hold on a minute.' She turned on her heel and headed back into the lodge.

'Is it just me,' Noah asked Shirley, 'or does she browbeat everyone?' When the dog merely sat, shot the doughnut a hopeful look, Noah broke what was left in half, tossed it. Shirley caught it on the fly, gulped it whole, then belched cheerfully.

Noah was still grinning when Olivia jogged back out with a plastic water bottle and belt loop. 'You always take your own water,' Olivia began and to Noah's surprise began to nimbly hook the bottle to his belt.

'Thanks.'

'I had them charge it to your room.'

'No, I meant for the personal service. Mom.'

She nearly smiled. He caught the start of one in her eyes, then she shrugged and snapped her fingers for the dog, who went instantly to heel.

'Let's go.'

She intended to start him off on the basic nature trail, the mile loop recommended for inexperienced hikers and parents with small children. To lull him into complacency, she thought with an inner smirk.

Fog smoked along the ground, slid through the trees, tangled in the fronds of ferns. Rain pattered through it, a monotonous drum and plunk. The gloom thickened as they entered the forest, pressing down as if it had weight and turning the fog into a ghost river.

'God what a place.' He felt suddenly small, eerily defenseless. 'Can't you just see a clawed hand coming up out of the fog, grabbing your ankle and dragging you down? You'd have time for one short scream, then the only sound would be . . . slurping.'

'Oh, so you've heard about the Forest Feeder.'

'Come on.'

'We lose an average of fifteen hikers a year.' She lifted a shoulder in dismissal. 'We try to keep it quiet. Don't want to discourage tourists.'

'That's good,' Noah murmured, but gave the fog a cautious glance. 'That's very good.'

'That was easy,' she corrected. 'Very easy.' She took out a flashlight, shined it straight up. It had the effect of slicing a beam through the gloom and casting the rest into crawling shadows.

'The overstory here is comprised of Sitka spruce, western hemlock, Douglas fir and western red cedar. Each is distinctive in the length of its needles, the shape of its cones and, of course, the pattern of its bark.'

'Of course.'

She ignored him. 'The trees, and the profusion of epiphytes, screen out the sunlight and cause the distinctive green twilight.'

'What's an epiphyte?'

'Like a parasite. Ferns, mosses, lichen. In this cause they case no real harmful effect to their hosts. You can see how they drape, form a kind of canopy in the overstory. And here, below, they carpet the ground, cover the trunks. Life and death are constantly at work here. Even without the Forest Feeder.'

She switched off her light, pocketed it.

She continued the lecture as they walked. He listened with half an ear to her description of the trees. Her voice was attractive, just a shade husky. He had no doubt she kept her spiel in simple terms for the layman, but she didn't make him feel brainless.

It was enough, Noah realized, just to look. Enough just to be there with all those shapes and shadows and the oddly appealing scent of rot. To draw in air as thick as water. He'd thought he'd be bored or at the most resigned to using this route to draw her out. Instead, he was fascinated.

Despite the rain and fog there was a quiet green glow, an otherworldly pulse of it that highlighted thick tumbles of ferns and knotty hillocks coated with moss. Everything dripped and shimmered.

He heard a cracking sound from above and looked up in time to see a thick branch tumble down and crash to the forest floor. 'You wouldn't want to be under one of them, would you?'

'Widow maker,' she said with a dry smile.

He glanced at the branch again, decided it would have knocked him flat and out cold. 'Good thing for me we're not married.'

'Occasionally, the epiphytes absorb enough rain to weigh down the branch. Overburdened, it breaks. Down here, it'll become part of the cycle, providing a home for something else.' She stopped abruptly, held up a hand. 'Quiet,' she told him in a soft whisper and motioned for him to angle behind the wide column of a spruce.

'What?'

She only shook her head, pressed two fingers to his lips as if to seal them. She held them there, while he wondered how she'd react if he started to nibble. Then he heard whatever had alerted her and felt the dog quivering between them.

Without a clue as to what to expect, he laid a hand on her shoulder in a protective move and scanned through the trees and vines toward the sound of something large in motion.

They stepped out of the gloom, wading knee high through the river of fog. Twelve, no fifteen, he corrected, fifteen enormous elk, their racks like crowns.

'Where are the girls?' he muttered against Olivia's fingers and earned a quick glare.

One let out a bellow, a deep bugling call that seemed to shake the trees. Then they slipped through the shadows and the green, their passing a rumble on the springy ground. Noah thought he caught the scent of them, something wild, then they were moving away, slowly sliding into the shadows.

'The females,' Olivia said, 'travel in herds with the younger males. More mature males, such as what we just saw, travel in smaller herds, until late summer when all bets are off and they become hostile with one another in order to cull out or keep their harem.'

'Harem, huh?' He grinned. 'Sounds like fun. So, were those Roosevelt elk?' Noah asked. 'The kind you were talking about yesterday?'

If she was surprised he'd been paying attention, and had bothered to remember, she didn't show it. 'Yes. We often see them on this trail this time of year.'

'Then I'm glad we took it. They're huge, a long way from Bambi and family.'

'You can see Bambi and family, too. During rutting season there're some high times in the forest.'

'I'll just bet. Why didn't she bark? Or chase after them?' he asked, lowering a hand to Shirley's head.

'Training over instinct. You're a good girl, aren't you?' She crouched down to give Shirley a good, strong rub, then unwound the leash on her belt and hooked it to the dog's collar.

'What's that for?'

'We're moving off MacBride land. Dogs have to be leashed on government property. We don't like it much, do we?' she said to Shirley. 'But that's the rule. Or . . .' She straightened and looked Noah in the eye. 'We can circle back if you've had enough.'

'I thought we were just getting started.'

'It's your dime.'

They continued on. He saw she had a compass on her belt, but she didn't consult it. She seemed to know exactly where she was, and where she was going. She didn't hurry, but gave him time to look, to ask questions.

Rain sprinkled through the canopy, plopped onto the ground like the drip of a thousand leaky faucets. But the fog began to lift, thinning, tearing into swirls, creeping back into itself.

The trail she chose began to climb and climb steeply. The light changed subtly until it was a luminous green pearled by the weak sunlight that fell through small breaks in the canopy, and in the breaks he caught glimpses of color from wildflowers, the variance of shades and textures of the green.

'It reminds me of snorkeling.'

'What?'

'I've been snorkeling in Mexico,' he told her. 'You get good enough at it, you can go under for pretty decent periods and play around. The light's odd, not green like this really, but different, and the sun will cut through the surface, angle down. Everything's soft and full of shapes. Easy to get lost down there. Ever been snorkeling?'

'No.'

'You'd like it.'

'Why?'

'Well, you're stripped down to the most basic of gear and

you're taking on a world that isn't yours. You never know what you'll see next. You like surprises?'

'Not particularly.'

'Liar.' He grinned at her. 'Everybody likes surprises. Besides, you're a naturalist. The marine world might not be your forte, but you'd like it. My friend Mike and I spent two very memorable weeks in Cozumel a couple of years back.'

'Snorkeling?'

'Oh yeah. So what do you do for play these days?'

'I take irritating city boys through the forest.'

'I haven't irritated you for at least an hour. I clocked it. Wow! There it is.'

'What?' Thrown off, she spun around.

'You smiled. You didn't catch yourself that time and actually smiled at me.' He patted a hand to his heart. 'Now I'm in love. Let's get married and raise more labradors.'

She snorted out a laugh. 'There, you irritated me again. Mark your time.'

'No, I didn't.' He fell into step with her and thought how easy it was to slide back into a rhythm with her as well. 'You're starting to like me again, Liv. You're not going to be able to help yourself.'

'I may be edging toward tolerate, but that's a long way from like. Now here, if you watch the trail, you'll notice oxalis, liverwort—'

'I can never get enough liverwort. You ever get down to L.A.?'

'No.' She flicked a glance toward him, didn't quite meet his eyes. 'No.'

'I thought you might go visit your aunt now and then.'

'They come here, at least twice a year.'

'I got to tell you, it's tough to imagine Jamie tramping through the woods. That's one very impressive lady. Still, I guess that since this is where she grew up, she'd slide back in easily. What about her husband?'

'Uncle David? He loves her enough to come, to stay and to let my grandmother haul him off to fish on the lake. That's been the routine for years, even though everyone knows he hates fishing. If his luck's running bad, he actually catches some, then he has to clean them. Once we talked him into camping.'

'Only once?'

'I think that's how Aunt Jamie got her pearl-and-diamond necklace. It was his bribe that she never make him sleep in the woods again. No cell phones, no laptops, no room service.' She slid him a sidelong glance. 'You'd relate, I imagine.'

'Hey, I can give up my cell phone any time I want. It's not an addiction. And I've slept outside plenty.'

'In a tent pitched in your backyard.'

'And in Boy Scout camp.'

The laugh bubbled out without her realizing it. 'You were never a Boy Scout.'

'I was, too. For one brief, shining period of six and a half months. It was the uniforms that turned me away. I mean, come on, those hats are really lame.'

He was getting a little winded, but didn't want to break the flow now that he had her talking. 'You do the Girl Scout thing?'

'No, I was never interested in joining groups.'

'You just didn't want to wear that dumb beanie.'

'It was a factor. How're the boots holding up?'

'Fine. You can't miss with L. L. Bean.'

'You're starting to chug, ace. Want to stop?'

'I'm not chugging. That's Shirley. How come I'm supposed to use your name, but you don't use mine?'

'It keeps slipping my mind.' She tapped a finger on the water bottle dangling from his belt. 'Take a drink. Keep your muscles oiled. You'll note here that the vine maples are taller, more treelike than they are on the bottomland. You can see patches of soil through the mat. We've climbed about five hundred feet.'

The world opened up again, with smoky peaks and green valleys, with a sky that was like burnished steel. The rain had stopped, but the ground beneath his feet was still moldering with it and the air tasted as wet as the water he swallowed.

'What's this place?'

'We switched over to Three Lakes Trail.'

He could see how the river, the winding run of it, cut through forest and hill, the jagged islands of rock that pushed up through the stone-colored water like bunched fists. The wind flew into his face, roared through the tops of the trees at his back and was swallowed up by the forest.

'Nothing gentle about it, is there?'

'No. It's good to remember that. A lot of Sunday hikers don't, and they pay for it. Nature isn't kind. It's relentless.'

'Funny, I would have said you prefer it to people.'

'I do. Got your wind back?'

'I hadn't lost my wind.' Exactly.

'If we cross the bridge here, then follow the trail another three and a half miles, we'll come to the lake area. Or we can turn back.'

'I can do another three and a half miles.'

'All right, then.'

Big Creek Bridge spanned the water. He heard the rush of it as they crossed, felt the push and pull of the wind and adjusted his body to brace against it. Olivia hiked ahead as if they'd been strolling down Wilshire Boulevard.

He tried not to hate her for it.

In less than a mile, his feet were killing him and his quads were screaming. She hadn't bothered to mention the last leg was straight up. Noah gritted his teeth and kept pace.

He tried to keep his mind off his abused body by taking in the scenery, thinking about the massage he was going to book the minute he got back to the lodge, speculating on what Olivia had brought along for lunch.

He caught a flash out of the corner of his eye, glanced up in time to see something spring through the thinning trees. 'What was that?'

'Flying squirrel. That's a rare sighting during the day. They're nocturnal.'

'No shit? Like Rocky? Rocky and Bullwinkle,' he explained when she frowned at him. 'You know, the cartoon.'

'I don't watch a lot of TV.'

'You had to catch it when you were a kid.' He craned his neck, trying to get another glimpse. 'It's not just a cartoon; it's an institution. What else is up here, besides Rocky?'

'We provide a list of wildlife at the center.' She gestured to a tree where the bark had been stripped and the trunk scored with deep grooves. 'Bear. Those are bear scratchings.'

'Yeah?' Rather than being alarmed as she expected, he stepped closer, examining the scar with apparent fascination. 'Are they still hibernating now, or could we run into one?'

'Oh, they're up and about now. And hungry,' she added, just for the hell of it.

'Well.' He ran his fingers down one deep groove. 'As long as one doesn't come along for a midday snack and mistake me for a tree, it'd be interesting.'

He nearly forgot his aching muscles as they continued to climb. Chipmunks frolicked around the ground, up in the trees, chattering and scolding. A hawk sailed overhead with a regal spread of wings and a single wild cry that echoed forever. There was the glinting black passing of a raven and the first thin patch of snow.

'We can stop here.' Olivia shrugged off her pack and sent Noah a considering look as she crouched down to open it. 'I didn't think you'd make it, at least not without whining.'

'The whining was a close call a few times, but it was worth it.'

He looked out over the three lakes, each one the dull silver of an old mirror. Softly reflected in them, the mountains rippled on the surface, more shadow than image. The air was sharp with pine and cold and the soggy smell of the rain-soaked ground.

'As your prize for not whining, we have some of my grandmother's famous beef and barley stew.'

'I could eat an ocean of it.'

She pulled a small blanket out of her pack. 'Spread that out and sit down. You won't get an ocean, but you'll get enough to warm your belly and take your mind off how much your feet hurt.'

'I brought some of my complimentary fruit.' He smiled as he snapped the blanket. 'In case your plan was to starve me.'

'No, I thought about just ditching you in the forest and seeing if you ever found your way out. But I like your parents, and they would've been upset.'

He folded his legs and accepted the coffee she poured from a thermos into a cup. He wanted to slip off her hat so he could touch her hair. He loved the look of it, that sleek caramel cap with the sassy fringe. 'You could learn to like me, too.'

'I don't think so.'

He ruffled Shirley's head when she came over to sniff at his coffee. 'Your dog likes me.'

'She's Grandpop's dog. And she likes drinking out of toilets. Her taste is not to be trusted.'

'You're a hard woman, Liv. But you make great coffee. If we got married you could make it for me every morning and I'd treat you like a queen.'

'How about you make the coffee and I treat you like a serf?'

'Does that include tying me up and demanding sexual favors? Because I should tell you I've recently taken a vow of celibacy.'

She only laughed and got out a second thermos. 'Your virtue's safe with me.'

'Well, that's a load off my mind. Christ, that smells fabulous.'

'My grandmother's a hell of a cook.' She poured soup out of the wide-mouthed thermos into bowls.

'So, can I come to dinner?'

She kept her gaze focused on the thermos as she replaced the lid. 'When I got home last night, she'd been crying. My grandfather had told her you were here, what you wanted and that he'd talked to you. I don't know what they said to each other, but I know they haven't said much to each other since. And that she'd been crying.'

'I'm sorry for that.'

'Are you?' She looked up now. He'd expected her eyes to be damp, but they were burning dry and hot. 'You're sorry that you brought back an intolerable grief, caused a strain between two people who've loved each other for over fifty years and somehow shoved me straight into the middle of it?'

'Yes.' His eyes never wavered from hers. 'I am.'

'But you'll still write the book.'

'Yes.' He picked up his bowl. 'I will. It's already opened up, already gone too far to turn back. And here's a fact, Liv. If I back off this time, Tanner's still going to tell his story. He'll just tell it to someone else. That someone else might not be sorry, sorry enough to tread as carefully as possible, to make sure that whatever he writes is true. He wouldn't have the connection, however tenuous it is, to you and your family that makes it matter to him.'

'Now, you're a crusader?'

'No.' He let her bitterness roll off him, though there were a few sharp pricks on his skin. 'I'm just a writer. A good one. I don't have any illusions that what I write will change anything, but I hope it'll answer questions.'

Had he been this sure of himself before? She didn't think so. They'd both grown up quite a bit in the last six years. 'It's too late for the answers.'

'We disagree. I don't think it's ever too late for answers. Liv, hear me out.' He pulled off his hat, raked his fingers through his hair. 'There are things I never got to explain to you before.'

'I said—'

'Damn it, let me finish. I was ten when all this happened. My father was the biggest hero in my life; I guess he still is. Anyway, I knew about his job, and not just the ten-year-old's perception of him going after the bad guys. What he did mattered to me, made an impression on me. And I paid attention. When he came home after your mother's murder, there was grief on his face. I'd never seen it before, not from the job. Maybe there'd be anger, God knows sometimes he'd come home and look sick and tired, but I'd never seen him grieve. And I never forgot it.'

To give herself something to do, she picked up her bowl, stirred without interest at the stew. She heard more than frustration in his voice. She heard passion. And purpose. 'Isn't what you're doing now bringing back that grief?'

'You can't bring back what's never really gone away, and it hasn't, for any of you. I saw you on TV,' he continued. 'You were just a baby. They showed that clip dozens of times, when you ran out of the house, crying. Holding your hands over your ears. Screaming.'

She remembered the moment perfectly, could relive it if she chose – had relived it when she didn't. 'Are you offering me pity now?'

'So you can spit it back in my face.' He shook his head, studying her as he spooned up stew. She wasn't a defenseless and terrified little girl now. She'd toughened, and if she didn't take steps otherwise, she'd soon be hardened. 'I'm telling you I won't do that. I won't crowd and push. We'll take it at your pace.'

'I don't know if I'll agree or not,' she said after a moment. 'But I won't even consider talking to you unless you promise to leave my grandmother out of it. Leave her completely alone. She can't handle it. And I won't have you try to handle her.'

'All right.' He sighed at her suspicious frown. 'What? You want me to sign it in blood?'

'Maybe.' She ate only because she knew she'd need fuel for the hike back. 'Don't expect me to trust you.'

'You did once. You will again before we're finished.'

'You're annoyingly sure of yourself. There's a pair of harlequin ducks on the lake. You can just spot them, on the far side.'

He glanced over. He'd already figured out that she shifted over into the nature mode when she wanted to change the subject.

'I'll be here through the week,' he said. 'My home number's on file at the lodge. If you haven't decided by the time I leave, you can get in touch later. I'll come back.'

'I'll think about it.' She gave Shirley a biscuit out of the tin. 'Now be quiet. One of the best parts of being here is the quiet.'

Satisfied with the progress, Noah dug into his stew. He was toying with asking if there was more when the scream had him flipping the bowl in the air and leaping to his feet.

'Stay here,' he ordered. 'Stay right here.'

Olivia gaped at him for five seconds, then scrambled to her feet as he turned to run toward the sound. 'Stop, wait!' The breath hitched in her chest as she debated tackling him or just throwing herself in his path. She managed to grab his sleeve, yank, then nearly plowed into him after all as Shirley barreled into her, hoping a tussle was coming.

'Someone's in trouble.' The shriek stabbed the air again and had him pushing her back. 'I want you to stay here until I—'

'It's a marmot.' She fought back a laugh. 'Probably an Olympic marmot.'

'What the hell is that?'

She managed to compose her face. 'Also known as rockchuck, whistle-pig or whistler, though the warning call it makes isn't a whistle as it's made with the vocal cords. It isn't a damsel in distress, but a . . . there.'

With her hand still gripping his sleeve, she gestured. There were two of them with grizzled coats of gray-brown, their heavy bodies lumping along toward an outcrop of rocks. One of them stood up on its hind legs, sniffing the air, then eyeing dog and humans with a jaundiced eye.

'They're just out of hibernation, usually go into torpor in September and don't surface until May. Most likely their burrow is close by. The, ah, call is their early-warning system as they're slower than any of their predators.'

'Terrific.' He turned his head, eyed Olivia narrowly.

'Well, you were really brave. I felt completely protected from any terrifying marauding marmots.'

'Smartass.' He tapped his fist on her chin, then left it there. Her eyes were deep and gold with humor, her lips curved and soft.

Color glowed in her cheeks, and the wind ruffled her hair.

He saw the change in her eyes, the darkening of awareness as he'd seen it years before. He thought he heard her draw in one breath, sharply, as his fingers uncurled and turned up to skim her jaw.

He didn't calculate the move. He just made it. The minute his mouth closed over hers, his mind clicked in and shouted *mistake*! But his other hand was already sliding through her hair, his teeth were already nibbling on that full lower lip to enhance the taste.

She jerked once, as if that touch of mouth to mouth had shocked her, then went very still. In that stillness he felt the faintest of quivers, and her lips warmed under his.

The combination had him nudging her closer, had him deepening the kiss though some part of him knew he should never have turned down this road again.

She'd meant to shove him away, to stop him the instant she'd seen the thought come into his eyes, the instant she'd felt the answering trip of her own pulse.

He paralyzed her. The rush of feelings that geysered up inside her body stunned her, left her open to more, with her hand gripping his sleeve and the blood swirling dizzily in her head.

The way it had been between them before. Exactly as it had been.

The wind rushed by them, through them, sighing through the trees, and still she couldn't move. Not toward him or away, not to hold on or reject.

That drenching sensation of helplessness terrified her.

'Olivia.' He skimmed his hands over her face, fascinating by the angles of it, the texture.

Both of them had changed, and yet her flavor was the same, the shape of her mouth the same, the need swimming between them, exactly the same.

When he eased away, wanting to see it, needing to see it, he murmured again. Just 'Olivia.'

Now she pulled back, taking defense in temper. 'This isn't going to happen again.'

'Liv.' His voice was quiet and serious. 'It already is.'

No, she told herself. Absolutely not. 'Typical. That's just typical.' She spun around and strode back to the blanket to begin tossing everything back in her pack.

Typical? Noah couldn't think of anything typical about having the top of his head sheared off. He still couldn't pull all his thoughts back in, but he managed to walk over, turn her around.

'Listen—'

'Hands off.' She knocked them away. 'Do you think I don't know what this is about? If you can't convince me with your so-called logic and charm, add some physical stimuli. Just like before.'

'Oh no, you don't.' With a wiry strength she'd underestimated, he held her still when she would have shoved away. His eyes flashed with a temper she realized was much more potent than his lazy good looks indicated. 'You're not turning that around, not this way. You know damn well I didn't hike for four fucking hours just so I could cop a feel. If I'd wanted to move on you, I'd have done it in some nice, warm room before I had blisters.'

'You did move on me,' she corrected icily and only made him bare his teeth.

'I didn't plan it, it just happened. And you weren't fighting me off. You want to be pissed off about it, fine, but let's have it for the real reason.'

They glared at each other while Shirley whimpered and bumped her body between theirs. 'All right.' Olivia opted to retreat behind dignity. 'I'll be pissed off because you took advantage of a momentary weakness.'

'There's not a weak bone in your body,' he muttered and let her go. 'How long are you going to make me pay for a mistake I made six years ago? How many ways do you want me to apologize for it?'

'I don't want an apology. I want to forget it.'

'But you haven't. And neither have I. Do you want to know how many times I thought of you?'

'No.' She said it quickly, the single word a rush. 'No, I don't. If we want to find a way to deal with each other on this, Noah, then we concentrate on where we are now, not where we were then.'

'Is that the MacBride way? If it's tough to deal with, bury it?' He regretted it instantly, not only because it was out of line, but because of the unguarded flare of shock and misery in her eyes. 'Liv, I'm sorry.'

He reached for her, swearing under his breath as she jerked away. 'I'm sorry,' he said again, and very precisely. 'That was uncalled for. But you weren't the only one who was hurt. You sliced me in half that day. So maybe you're right. Maybe it's better to put it away and start now.'

They packed up in silence, taking scrupulous care not to touch in any way. When they were back in the forest, she became the impersonal guide, pointing out any plants of interest, identifying wildlife and blocking any personal conversation.

Noah decided she might as well have snugged that glass dome over herself. She was inside it now, and untouchable.

That would make it simpler all around, he told himself. He didn't want to touch her again. Couldn't, for his own survival, risk it.

He spent the last two hours of the hike dreaming about burning his boots and washing the lingering taste of her out of his mouth with a good, stiff drink.

Chapter Twenty

As the lodge came in sight, Noah's plan was simple. He was simple. He was going straight to the bar to buy a bottle, make that two bottles of beer. He was taking both up to his room where he would drink them during his hour-long hot shower.

If that didn't make him feel human again, well, he'd just order up some raw meat and gnaw at it.

The light was fading to a pearly gray with a few wild streaks of color in the western sky. But he wasn't in the mood to appreciate it.

For God's sake, he'd only kissed her. It wasn't as if he'd ripped her clothes off and dragged her to the ground for maniac sex. The fact that the image of doing just that held entirely too much appeal only made him grind his teeth as he pulled open the door to the lodge.

He turned to her, started to make some blisteringly polite comment on her ability as guide, when the desk clerk hurried over.

'Mr. Brady, you had a call from your mother. She said it was urgent.' Everything inside him froze, then started to churn sickly. 'My mother?'

'Yes, she called about an hour after you left this morning, and again at three. She asked that you call her at home as soon as you came in.'

He had a horrible and vivid image of cops coming to the door. Every family of those on the job knew what it meant when you opened the door and cops were standing there, their faces carefully blank.

His father was retired. It couldn't be. It couldn't.

'I—'

'You can call from in here.' Olivia took his arm gently, spoke with absolute calm. The blank fear on his face set off screams of alarm in her head, but her hand was steady as she led him past the desk and into a back office.

'You can dial direct from here. I'll just—' She started to step back, intending to give him privacy, but his hand clamped over hers.

He said nothing at all, just held on while he dialed the number. His grip on her anchored him as a dozen terrors spun through his head. His palm went sweaty on the receiver as it rang once, twice, then his mother's voice, rushed and breathless, had a spike of ice slicing into his gut.

'Mom?'

'Oh, Noah, thank goodness.'

'Dad?' He lived a thousand hells in the heartbeat it took her to answer.

'No, no, honey. It's not Frank. Your father's fine.' Before his knees could buckle with relief, she was rushing on. 'It's Mike, Noah.'

'Mike?' His fingers tightened on Olivia's, turning both their knuckles white. 'What's wrong? What happened?'

'Noah, I – God ... He's in the hospital. He's in a coma. We don't know how bad. They're running tests, they're doing everything they ...'

When she began to weep, Noah felt his guts slide into greasy knots. 'What happened? A car accident?'

'No, no. Someone hurt him. Someone hit him and hit him. From behind, they say. He was in your house last night.'

'At the beach house? He was at my place?' Denial and fear pounded through him. 'It happened last night?'

'Yes. I didn't hear about it until this morning, early this morning. Your father's at the hospital now. I'm going back. They'll only let one of us sit with him at a time, for just a few minutes. He's in Intensive Care.'

'I'll be there as soon as I can. I'll take the first flight out.'

'One of us will be at the hospital. Maggie and Jim—' Her voice broke again when she spoke of Mike's parents. 'They shouldn't be alone there.'

'I'm on my way. I'll come straight there. Mom ...' He could

think of nothing. Nothing. 'I'm on my way,' he said again. He hung up the phone, then just stared at it. 'My friend, he was attacked. He's in a coma. I have to go home.'

He still had her hand, but his grip was loose now. She could feel his fingers tremble. 'Go pack what you need. I'll call the airport, book you a flight.'

'What?'

Her heart broke for him. Looking at his pale face and stunned eyes, there was room for no other feeling but pity. 'It'll save time, Noah. Just go up and get what you need. I'll get you to the airport.'

'Yeah . . . God.' He snapped back, eyes clearing, face going hard and tight. 'Just get me a seat, whatever gets me to L.A. quickest. Standby if nothing else. I'll be ready in five minutes.'

He was as good as his word and was back at the office door before she'd completed the booking. He hadn't bothered to change, she noted, and carried only his backpack and laptop.

'You're set.' She rose quickly from behind the desk. 'It's a private airstrip about forty minutes from here, friends of my grandparents. They'll take off as soon as you get there.'

She snagged a set of keys off a board as she headed out of the office. She jogged to a Jeep in the side lot, unlocked it and climbed in as he tossed his pack in the back.

'I appreciate it.'

'It's all right. Don't worry about the rest of your things and your car. We'll deal with it.' She drove fast, her hands competent on the wheel, her eyes straight ahead. 'I'm sorry about your friend.'

The initial shakes had passed, but he laid his throbbing head back against the seat. 'I've known him forever. Second grade. He moved into the neighborhood. Pudgy kid, a complete dork. You were honor bound to beat the shit out of him. I was going to take my shot but just couldn't do it. He was so oblivious of his own dorkiness. Still is. He had this ridiculous crush on Marcia Brady.'

'Is she your cousin?'

'Huh? Oh, Brady. No, Marcia, Marcia, Marcia. *The Brady Bunch.*' He opened his eyes long enough to give her a look of astonishment, then sighed. 'Right, no TV. Doesn't matter. He's the sweetest person I know. Dead loyal and completely harmless. Son of a bitch!' He pounded his fist on the dash, then pressed his hands to his face. 'Son of a bitch. He's in a coma, a fucking coma. My mother was crying. She holds, she always holds. If she's breaking like that it has to be bad. Really bad.'

She wanted to pull over, for just a minute, to take him to her, hold on to him until he found some comfort. It was an urge she'd never felt with anyone other than family. So she tightened her hands on the wheel and punched the gas.

'It's my fault.' Noah dropped his hands on his lap, let them lie there limply.

'That's a ridiculous thing to say.' She kept her voice brisk, practical. Logic, she thought, was more productive than a comforting hug. 'You weren't even there.'

'I didn't take it seriously enough. I didn't take *her* seriously enough. I sent him over there. Water the goddamn plants. Water the plants, Mike. And I knew she was half crazy.'

'Who are you talking about?'

'I was seeing this woman for a while. It wasn't serious on my end, but I should have seen it. I just sort of drifted along with it – why the hell not? Good sex with a great body, a snappy-looking woman to hang out with. When it got complicated, I broke things off. Then it got nasty. There were some altercations, then the big one where she trashed my house while I was away.'

'Trashed your house?'

'Big time. I had to scoop up most of what was left with a shovel.'

'That's horrible. Really. Why didn't you have her arrested?'

'Couldn't prove it. Everybody knew she'd done it, just her style, but there wasn't much to be done about it. She tossed a few more threats in my face, made another scene. Then I go flying off, and tell Mike to water my flowers while I'm gone.'

'If this very bizarre woman is the one who hurt your friend, then it's her fault. It's her responsibility. It's her guilt.'

He said nothing to that. He was suffering, Olivia thought. She could feel the pain coming off him in shaky waves. And couldn't stand it. 'When . . . after my mother's death I went through a period where I blamed myself. I'd run away and I'd hidden in the closet. I didn't do anything to help her.'

'Jesus, Liv, you were four.'

'Doesn't matter. That doesn't matter, Noah. When you love someone and something terrible happens to them, it doesn't matter how old you are. After that,' she continued, 'I went through another stage when I blamed her. What the hell was she thinking? She let him in the house. She let the monster in,' she murmured and shuddered once. 'She let him in, and he took her away from me. She left me. I blamed her for that.'

She flinched when he lifted a hand to touch her cheek, then blew out a steadying breath. 'Maybe you have to go through those stages before you can get to the truth of it. Sam Tanner was to blame. He was the only one to blame. Not me, not my mother.'

'You're right. I owe you for this.'

'The lodge would have done the same for anyone.'

'No. I owe *you.*' He laid his head back again, closed his eyes and rode the rest of the way in silence.

Noah was running on nerves alone by the time he rushed off the elevator in ICU. During the flight he'd imagined Mike dead. Then jumped to giddy images of his friend popping up in bed and making a lame joke. When the cab had dropped him at the hospital, he was nearly ready to believe it had all been some weird dream.

Then he saw his mother sitting on a bench in the silent hallway, her arm around Maggie Elmo. Guilt and fear balled messily in his throat.

'Oh, Noah.' Celia got quickly to her feet to throw her arms around him. He felt her stomach quiver against his. 'I'm so glad you're here. There's no change,' she added in a whisper.

'I need to see him. Can I . . .' He shook his head, then forced himself to ease away and face Maggie. 'Mrs. Elmo.'

'Noah.' Tears began to trickle out of her already swollen eyes as she reached for him. He lowered to the bench, wrapped his arms tight around her. 'He'll want you here. He'll want to see you when he wakes up. He's going to wake up. Any minute now.'

He hung on to her faith as desperately as he held on to her. 'We've been taking turns going in.' Celia rubbed a hand over Noah's back. 'Frank and Jim are in there now. But Maggie has to lie down for a while.'

'No, I—'

'You said you'd lie down when Noah got here.' All but crooning the words, Celia drew Maggie to her feet. 'They've got a bed for you, remember? You just need to stretch out for a few minutes. We want to give Noah some time with Mike, don't we? I'll sit with you.' She sent Noah a quiet look, then still murmuring, led Maggie down the hall.

Swamped with grief, Noah lowered his head to his hands. He hadn't moved when Frank came through the double doors to the left and saw him. Saying nothing, Frank sat, laid an arm over Noah's shoulders.

'I don't know what to do,' Noah said when he could speak again.

'You're doing it. You're here.'

'I want to hurt her. I'm going to find a way to make her pay for this.'

'That's not what you need to focus on now.'

'You know she did this.' Noah straightened, stared at Frank with burning eyes. 'You know she did.'

'It's very possible. She'll be questioned as soon as they locate her, Noah.' He gripped Noah's shoulder, cutting off the vicious stream of oaths. 'She can't be charged without evidence.'

'She'll dance. Goddamn it, Dad, you know she'll dance around this. I'm not letting her get away with it.'

'I don't know that,' Frank said firmly. 'Neither do you. But I am telling you, as your father and as a cop, to stay away from her. If you follow through on what you're feeling right now, you'll only make matters worse. Let her box herself in, Noah, so we can put her away.'

If Mike died, Noah thought, they wouldn't be able to put her away deep enough.

He stayed at the hospital until dawn, then went to his parents' house, collapsed facedown on his childhood bed and dropped into oblivion for four hours.

When he'd showered off twenty-four hours of sweat and fatigue, he went into the kitchen.

His mother was there, dressed in an ancient terry-cloth robe and breaking eggs into a bowl. Because love for her burst through him, he went to her, wrapped his arms around her and hugged her back against him.

'Who are you and what have you done with my mother?'

She managed a quiet laugh, lifting a hand up and around to pat his face. 'I threw out the house rules this morning. Real eggs, real coffee all around. It's going to be another long day.'

'Yeah.' He looked over the top of her head, through the kitchen window into the yard beyond. 'Remember when Mike and I tried to build that fort out back? We got all this scrap wood together and these rusted nails. Of course, he stepped on one and had to get a tetanus shot.'

'Screamed bloody murder when he stepped on the nail. I thought he'd cut off an arm.' She let out a laughing sigh that ended perilously close to a sob. 'I love that boy. And I'm ashamed that after I heard what happened, my first thought was thank God it wasn't Noah. Oh, poor Maggie.'

She eased away, picked up the bowl again and began briskly beating eggs. 'We have to think positively. Think in healing white light. I've read a lot of books on it.'

He had to smile a little. 'I bet you have.'

'We're going to bring him out of this.' She got out a skillet, and the look she sent Noah was fierce and strong. 'Believe it.'

He wanted to, but every time he went into the tiny room in the hospital and saw Mike still and pale, his head swathed in bandages, his eyes sunk in shadowed bruises, his faith faltered.

As morning swam toward afternoon, he paced the corridor while rage built inside him. He couldn't let Caryn get away with what she'd done. He couldn't do anything but hope and pray and stand at his friend's bedside and talk nonsense just to block out the monotonous beep of machines.

She'd wanted a shot at him, he thought. By Christ, he'd give it to her. He turned toward the elevator, strode towards it, with hate blooming black in his heart.

'Noah?'

'What?' Fists already clenched, he glanced at the brunette. She wore a lab coat over shirt and trousers, with a stethoscope in her pocket. 'Are you one of Mike Elmo's doctors?'

'No. I—'

'I know you,' he interrupted. 'Don't I?'

'We met at the club – you and Mike, my friend and I. I'm Dory.'

'Right.' He rubbed his tired eyes. The pretty brunette with the Southern drawl who stood up for him the night Caryn had come in. 'You're a doctor?'

'Yes. Emergency medicine. I'm on my break and wanted to see how Mike was doing.'

'They just keep saying no change.'

'I'll check on that in a minute. You look like you could use some air. Let's take a walk.'

'I was just heading out.'

'Let's take a walk,' she repeated. She'd seen murder in a man's eye before. It wasn't a look you forgot. 'The last time I checked in, Mike's vitals were stable. His tests have been good.' She punched the elevator button. 'He's critical, but he's also young and healthy.'

'He's been in a coma for a day and a half.'

She nudged him into the elevator with her. 'Sometimes a coma is just the body's way of focusing in on healing. And he did come around once in the ambulance on the way here. It was brief, but I think he recognized me, and that's very positive sign.'

'You? You were with him?'

She stepped out on the main lobby, took his arm to lead him to the doors.

'We had a date. I was meeting him at your place. I was running late. We had a double suicide attempt come in. Lost one, saved the other. It was nearly ten by the time I got there.'

Outside she turned her face up to the sun, rolled her shoulders. 'God, it feels good out here. In any case, the door was open. Mike was on the kitchen floor, facedown. Glass all over the place. Wine bottle. It's probably what he was hit with. I went to work on him. I had my bag in the car. I called it in, did what I could on the scene. We had him in ER within thirty minutes.'

'Is he going to die?'

She didn't answer right away, but sat down on the curb, waited for Noah to join her. 'I don't know. Medically, he's got an even chance, maybe even a little better than even. There were no bone fragments in his brain, and that was a big one. Still, medicine has limits, and it's up to him now. I'm half crazy about him.'

'No kidding?'

'Yeah. I know he started off that night with this thing for Steph. And actually, I had the same kind of focus on you.' She tilted her face toward him and smiled. 'You were a little too distracted to notice, so I went back and sulked a little.'

'Yeah?'

She had to smile. 'Just a little. Mike and Steph went through the moves and motions. They sort of ran out of steam, and I felt sorry for Mike because he was worried about you and didn't know what to do about it. We started talking and had this big click happen. We started going out. Then we started staying in.'

'That was you the other night on the phone.'

'Yeah.'

'Mike Elmo and the sexy doctor.' Absurdly pleased, Noah shook his head. 'That's just terrific.' He grabbed her face in his hand and kissed her noisily. 'That's just great.'

She laughed and gave him a friendly pat on the knee. 'He thinks you walk on water. I didn't say that to make you sad,' she hurried on when the light went out of Noah's eyes. 'I said it because I think he's a pretty great guy, and he thinks you're pretty great guy. So, I figure he's right. And I figure that when I ran into you upstairs you'd had about enough and were going to go find that lunatic Caryn and . . . I was going to say do something you'd regret, but I don't think you'd regret it. Something that wouldn't help, that wouldn't solve anything, and that in the end would put you in the kind of jam Mike wouldn't like.'

'She wanted to hurt me. She didn't give a damn about Mike.'

'Noah, she did hurt you. She hurt you where it matters the most. Let's go back up. I only have a few more minutes left, and I want to see him.'

He nodded, got to his feet, then held down a hand for hers. 'I guess it's lucky I ran into you.'

'Why don't you buy me a beer after shift?' She grinned as they went back inside. 'You can tell me all kinds of embarrassing Mike stories.'

'What kind of friend would that make me?'

'He told me you got piss-faced the spring of your senior year in high school, and he dared you to run around the track bare-assed naked. And when you did, he took videos and showed them at your graduation party. He still has a copy, by the way.' Her smile brightened as they moved onto the elevator. 'You had very nice form at eighteen.'

'Oh yeah. Well, that's nothing. I've got much better stories on Mike. What time do you get off shift?'

'Seven, please God.'

'It's a date.' His mood almost light, he stepped off the elevator.

Then his heart crashed to his feet as he saw Maggie sobbing in his mother's arms.

'No.' The roar inside his head was so loud he couldn't hear his own voice as he repeated the denial over and over, as he raced down the corridor, yanking free of Dory's restraining hand.

'Noah, wait!' Celia shifted quickly to block his path before he could shove through the doors into ICU. 'Wait. Maggie, tell him. Tell Noah.'

'He opened his eyes.' She rocked back and forth on her heels, back and forth, then held out both hands to Noah. 'He opened his eyes. He said "Mom." He looked at me, and he said "Mom."'

'Stay here,' Dory ordered. 'Stay out here. Let me check.'

'The nurse came in, she called for the doctor.' Celia wiped at her own tears while Noah held Maggie. 'Frank and Jim are down in the cafeteria. Frank browbeat Jim into getting something to eat, then I was going to browbeat Maggie. He woke up, Noah.' She laid her head on the side of his shoulder. 'He woke up.'

Dory came back through the doors. Noah took one look at the brilliant smile on her face and buried his face in Maggie's hair.

Chapter Twenty-one

'So, when were you going to tell me about Doctor Delicious?'

Mike grinned, with most of his old twinkle. 'Is she a babe or what?'

'A prime babe, a brainy babe. So what's she doing hanging around with you?'

'She digs me. What can I say?' He still tended to tire easily, and the headaches came with tedious regularity. But they'd jumped him up to good condition after his stint in ICU and into a regular room.

His room was full of flowers, cards, balloons. He'd told Noah the nurses called it Party Central, a fact that pleased him enormously.

The day before Noah had brought in a brand-new laptop, loaded with every computer game it would hold. He'd called it occupational therapy, but knew it was part guilt, part unspeakable gratitude.

'I think I'm in, you know. With her,' Mike said, scrupulously staring at his fingers.

Noah gaped. 'You got a major bash on the head ten days ago. Ruined a damn fine bottle of wine, by the way. I think your brains are still scrambled.'

'I don't think this has a lot to do with brains.'

At a loss, Noah blew out a breath. '"You know" is a very big thing. You were only seeing her for a little while before you had your head broken. You've been stuck in a hospital bed ever since.'

'I have a really fond feeling for this hospital bed.' Mike gave the white sheets an affectionate pat. 'After last night.'

'Last night? *Here*? You had sex with her here?' It was fascinating.

'*Shh.* Tell the floor nurse, why don't you?' But Mike was still grinning. 'She came in to see me after her shift, one thing led to another. The another was really amazing, by the way.'

'Why the hell am I feeling sorry for you?' Noah wondered. 'You're getting all the action.'

He grabbed the can of Coke he'd brought in with him, chugged deeply.

'I asked her to marry me.'

And choked. 'Huh? What? Jesus, Mike.'

'She said yes.' Mike's grin turned into his puppy dog smile and turned his eyes soft. 'Can you beat that?'

'I think I'm having a stroke.' Noah pressed his fingers to his twitching eye. 'Call the nurse. No, better, call a doctor. Maybe I can get some action.'

'We're going to get married next spring, because she wants the works. You know, the church, the flowers, the white dress.'

'Wow.' It was the best he could do. Noah figured he'd better sit down, then realized he already was. 'Wow.'

'They're letting me out of here tomorrow. I want to buy her a ring right away. I need you to go with me. I don't know squat about buying an engagement ring.'

'What do I know about it?' Noah dragged his free hand through his hair and took a good, hard look. Mike's eyes were clear behind the thick lenses of his glasses. His smile was easy, almost lazily content. 'You really mean it, don't you?'

'I want to be with her. And when I am I keep thinking, this is right. This feels exactly right.' Vaguely embarrassed, he moved his shoulders. 'I don't know how to explain it.'

'I guess you just did. Nice going, Mike.'

'So, you'll give me a hand with the ring, right?'

'Sure. We'll get her a doozy.' With a sudden laugh, he surged to his feet. 'Goddamn. Married. And to a doctor. Damn good thing. She'll be able to stitch you up every time you walk into something or trip over your feet. Does she know you're a complete klutz?'

'Yeah, she loves that about me.'

'Go figure.' To show his affection, he punched Mike on the shoulder. 'I guess you won't be coming over and raiding my fridge every other night after . . .' He trailed off, remembering.

'It wasn't your fault. Look, we know each other well enough for me to see what's in your head.' To keep Noah from backing off, Mike grabbed his hand. 'You didn't know she was going to go postal.'

'I knew enough.'

'I knew as much as you did, and I didn't give a thought to going over there. For Christ's sake, Noah, Dory was coming.' Shaken by just the thought of it, Mike rubbed his hands over his face, his fingers sliding under his glasses to press against his eyes. 'Something could've happened to her, too. I'm the one who told her to meet me over there.'

'That's not—'

'It's the same thing,' Mike interrupted. 'I was there at the club that night. I heard what she said, saw how she was.' He turned to brood out his window at his view of palm trees. 'I wish I could remember, but I keep coming up against the blank. Nothing, not a fucking thing after the marathon after work. I remember kicking Pete Bester's ass at Mortal Kombat. Next thing I'm clear on is waking up and seeing Mom. All I know about the between is what people tell me. Maybe I saw her. If I could say I saw her, they'd lock her up.'

'They'd have to find her first. She skipped,' Noah added when Mike looked back at him. 'None of her friends know where she is, or they're not saying. She packed clothes, got a cash advance on her credit cards and split.'

'Can't they go after her for that, like *The Fugitive*.'

Even a half laugh felt good. 'Richard Kimble was innocent.'

'Yeah, but still.'

'She wasn't charged. I guess if they come up with some evidence they might take a look for her. Otherwise . . .' He lifted his shoulders, let them fall. 'Anyway, I don't think she'll be hassling either one of us, not for a while at least.'

'That's something. So, now that you know I'm going to live, and that crazy bitch is off somewhere, I guess you better get back to work.'

'Who says I haven't been working?'

'Your mother.'

'Man, what is it with you and my mother?'

'I'd always planned to marry her, but I thought your father

might shoot me. Dory knows she's my second choice, but she's so madly in love with me she doesn't care. But I digress,' he said with a grin. 'She said you've been letting the book coast, really only playing at it for the last week or so. I'd say it's time to get your lazy ass in gear.'

'I'll get to it.' Muttering, Noah wandered to the window.

'You don't have to worry about me anymore. I'm cool. Aside for the blank spot, I'm nearly back to normal.'

'You were never normal. I've been thinking about talking to Jamie Melbourne again, getting her husband to talk to me. Hassling that asshole admin of Smith's.'

'So do it.'

'I'm waiting for my car.' He knew it was stalling. 'The lodge arranged to have someone drive it down for me. Should be here tomorrow or the next day.'

'Then you can go home, make your calls and set up your interviews.'

Noah glanced back over his shoulder. 'You kicking me out?'

'What are friends for?'

What was she doing? What in God's name was she doing?

Olivia sat in the car, her fingers clamped on the steering wheel, and struggled to breathe. If she took slow, even breaths her heart would stop pounding. She could control it, control the frenzied jerk and throb of her pulse and beat back the panic attack.

She could do it, she could fight it off. She wouldn't let it take over.

But her hands wanted to tremble on the wheel, and the sheen of sweat had already pearled on her face as waves of heat then ice, heat then ice, surfed over her skin, through her belly, into her throat. She knew what she'd see if she looked in the rearview mirror. The wild, wide eyes, the glossy, translucent pallor.

The nausea rolled up, one long sick crest, from her feet to her stomach to her throat.

She gritted her teeth and fought it back, shoved it down even as the shudders shimmered over her in icy little bumps.

The scream wanted to rip out, it tore at her chest, clawing with sharpened demon claws. But all she released was a moan, a long keening sound drenched in despair, pressing her head back against the seat as she held on, held on.

Five seconds, then ten. Twenty. Until she willed herself, warred with her own mind, to snap clear.

Her breath came fast, as if she'd been running, but the sharpest edge of panic began to fade. Slowly, she ordered herself to relax, one muscle at a time. She opened her eyes, stared at her fingers, made them flex and release, flex and release.

Control. She had control. She was not a victim, would never, never be a victim. Not of circumstance or her own ill-buried fears.

With one last shuddering breath, she leaned back again. Better, that was better, she thought. It was just that it had come on so fast, had taken her completely by surprise. It had been more than two years since she'd had a full-blown panic attack.

Two years ago, she remembered, when she'd made plans to come to Los Angeles and visit her aunt and uncle. Then, she'd gotten as far as the airport when it had washed over her. The cold sweats, the shakes, the terrible need to get out, just get out and away from all the people.

She'd beaten it back, but she hadn't been able to face the plane, hadn't been able to face where it was going. The shame of that failure had drowned her in depression for weeks.

This time she'd gotten here, she reminded herself. She'd batted back the onslaught of the panic twice on the drive down and had been so certain she'd won completely.

She had won, she corrected. She was here, she was all right. She was back in control.

She'd been right to follow her impulse, to take the chore of returning Noah's car herself. Even though it had caused difficulties with her grandparents, she'd done the right thing. Concentrating on the drive had gotten her where she'd wanted to go. Where she hadn't been able to go for twenty years.

Or nearly gotten her there, she corrected, and, pushing the damp hair off her brow, she studied Noah's house.

It wasn't what she'd envisioned at all. It was pretty, almost feminine in the soft tones of the wood, the cheerful sweeps and spears of flowers.

His garden wasn't some haphazard bachelor attempt to brighten up his real estate, but a careful, clever arrangement by someone who not only knew flowers, but appreciated them.

She slipped out of the car, relieved that her legs were nearly steady. She intended to go straight to the door, knock, give him his keys and a polite smile. She'd ask him to call a cab, and get out and on her way to her aunt's as quickly as possible.

But she couldn't resist the flowers, the charm of verbena, the fresh chipper colors of Gerber daisies, the bright trumpets of the reliable petunias. He hadn't stuck with the ordinary, she noted, and had used the small space available on either side of the walk very well. Experimenting, she noted, crowding specimen to specimen so that it all tangled together in a natural burst rather than an obviously planned design.

It was clever and creative, and both the planting and maintaining must have involved a great deal of work. Still, he hadn't been quite as conscientious with the weeding as he might have been, and her gardener's heart had her crouching down to tug up the random invaders.

Within a minute she was humming and losing herself in a well-loved task.

Noah was so happy to see his car sitting in its usual spot that he overtipped the driver and bolted out of the cab.

'Oh baby, welcome home.' He murmured it, stroked a loving hand over the rear fender and had nearly executed a snappy dance of joy when he spotted Olivia.

The surprise came first, or he assumed the quick jerk in his stomach was surprise. Then came the warmth. She looked so damn pretty, kneeling by his flowers, a faded gray cap shading her eyes.

He started toward her, then hooked his thumbs in his front pockets because his hands wanted to touch. 'This is a surprise,' he said, and watched her head snap up, watched her body freeze. Like a doe in the crosshairs, Noah mused. 'I wasn't expecting to see you weeding my gummy snaps.'

'They needed it.' Furiously embarrassed, she got to her feet and brushed garden dirt off her hands. 'If you're going to plant flowers, you should tend to them.'

'I haven't had a lot of time just recently. What are you doing here, Liv?'

'Returning your car. You were told to expect it.'

'I was also expecting some burly guy named Bob behind the wheel. Not that I'm complaining. Come on in.'

'I just need you to call me a cab.'

'Come on in,' he repeated and moved past her to the door. 'At least I can give you a drink to pay for the weeding service.'

He unlocked the front door, glanced back to where she continued to stand. 'Don't be a nitwit. You might as well. Damn it!'

Liv's eyes widened as he leaped inside the door. She could hear him cursing. Curiosity won and had her following him inside.

He jabbed a code into a security panel just inside the door. 'Just had this installed. I keep forgetting it's here. If I set off the alarm again, my neighbors are going to lynch me. There.' He blew out a breath when the signal light blinked on green. 'Another small victory of man against machine. Have a seat.'

'I can't stay.'

'Uh-huh. I'll just get us a glass of wine while you think of the reason you can't sit down for fifteen minutes after driving all the way down the coast.'

'My aunt and uncle are expecting me.'

'This minute?' he asked from the kitchen.

'No but—'

'Well, then. You want some chips with this? I think I have some.'

'No. I'm fine.' But since she was here, what harm would it do to have one civil glass of wine?

She thought his living room was sparsely furnished, no-frills male, but not unattractive. Then she remembered he'd told her his home had been trashed. It certainly explained why everything looked showroom fresh and unused.

'I was glad to hear your friend's going to be okay.'

'It was touch-and-go the first couple of days.' And the thought of it could still give him a raw sensation in the gut. 'But yeah, he's going to be okay. In fact, he's going to be great. He got his skull fractured, fell in love and got engaged, not necessarily in that order – in just over a two-week period.'

'Good for him, on two out of three anyway.'

'We just bought her a ring this morning.'

'We?'

'He needed guidance. Let's drink to Mike.'

'Why not?' She touched the rim of her glass to his, then sipped. Then lifted her eyebrows. 'Pouilly-Fuissé on a weekday evening. Very classy.'

His grin flashed. 'You know your wine.'

'Must be the Italian from my grandmother's side.'

'And can the MacBride half build a Guinness?'

'I imagine.' It was just a little too comfortable, being here, being with him. It smacked of old patterns. 'Well, if you'd call—'

'Let's go out on the deck.' He took her hand, pulled her to the sliding door. He wasn't about to let her shake him off that quickly. 'Too early for sunset,' he continued, releasing her long enough to slide the door open. 'You'll have to come back. They can be pretty spectacular.'

'I've seen sunsets before.'

'Not from this spot.'

The breeze fluttered in off the ocean, whispered warm over her face. The water was bold and blue, chopping in against the shore, then rearing back for the next pass. The scent was of salt and heat, and the light undertone of sunscreen from the people sprinkled along the beach.

'Some backyard.'

'I thought the same thing about yours when I saw your forest.' He leaned against the rail, his back to the view, his eyes on her. 'Wanna come play in my backyard, Liv?'

'No, thanks. You've got a nice hand with flowers.' She flicked a finger over the soapwort, johnny-jump-ups and artesisa sharing space artistically in a stone tub.

'It shows my sensitive side.'

'It shows you know what looks good and how to keep it that way.'

'Actually, I learned out of compassion and annoyance. My mother was always planting something, then killing it. She'd go to the nursery, and the plants would scream and tremble. Once, I swear, I heard this coreopsis shrieking, 'No, no, not me! Take the Shasta daisies.' I couldn't stand it,' he continued when she laughed. 'I started having nightmares where all the plants she killed came back to life, brown, withered, broken, trailing dry dirt that crumbled from their roots as they formed an army of revenge.'

'Zombie zinnias.'

'Exactly.' He beamed, delighted with her, fascinated by the way her face warmed when she was amused and relaxed. 'Vampire violas, monster marigolds and gardenia ghouls. Let me tell you, it was pretty terrifying. In fact, I'm scaring myself just thinking about it.'

'As a naturalist, I can certify you're safe. As long as you keep them alive.'

'That's comforting.' He trailed a finger down her arm, from elbow to wrist, in the absentminded gesture of a man used to touching. She stepped back, the deliberate gesture of a woman who wasn't.

'I really have to go. I called Uncle David from Santa Barbara, so they're expecting me by now.'

'How long are you staying?'

'Just a few days.'

'Have dinner with me before you go.'

'I'm going to be busy.'

'Have dinner with me before you go.' As he repeated it, he touched her again, just an easy slide of fingertips along her jaw. 'I like seeing you. You wanted to start with a fresh slate. Give me a chance, Olivia.'

She could see it clearly, standing there with him while the sky exploded with sunset, music drifting out, something quiet with a throb to the bass. And while the sun turned red, while it melted into the sea, he would touch her as he had before. Cupping his hand on her face. He would kiss her as he had before. Slow and skilled and sexy.

And she'd forget why he was doing it. She'd forget to care why.

'You want a story.' She shifted away from his hand. 'I haven't decided if I'm giving it to you.'

'I want a story.' Temper simmered in his eyes, but his voice was cool.

'That's one level. I said I liked seeing you, and I meant it. That's another level entirely. I've thought about you, Olivia.'

He made a small move, a reangling of his body, and caged her between him and the rail. 'I've thought about you for years. Maybe I wish I hadn't, and you've made it clear you'd rather I didn't think of you at all.'

'It doesn't really matter what I'd rather.' He was crowding her, and along with the irritation from that was a sly lick of excitement.

'We can agree on that.' He set his wineglass on the rail. 'Do you know what went through my mind when I got home and saw you out front? This. Just this.'

'It wasn't slow this time. She could taste the bite of temper as his mouth crushed down on hers, the snaps of frustration as his hand fisted on the back of her shirt. Just as she could feel the hot surge of need that pumped from his body to slam against hers.

It was as primal as the world she lived in, as elemental as the sea that crashed behind them. As inevitable as the quest to mate. Want. Had she always wanted him? And had the wanting always been so savage?

She had to take. She had to feed.

She understood the feral, and threw herself into the edgy demand of the kiss. Her hands gripped fistfuls of all that thick sun-streaked hair, her tongue slashed against his. The vicious heat that burst in her blood told her she was alive and could seize whatever she wanted. As long as she wanted.

Power plunged into him, feeding off her reckless response. The taste of her was a rage through his system, shearing away everything else. He wanted to gorge himself on her in fast, greedy gulps until the frantic, clawing hunger was sated.

But the more he took, the more he craved.

He pulled back far enough to see her face, the wild wash of color, the sharp edge in her eyes. 'If you want me to believe you're pissed off about that, you're going to have to stop cooperating.'

She thought anger was probably the only sensation she wasn't feeling. 'Back off, Brady.'

'Look—'

'Just . . .' She blew out a breath, lifted a hand to his chest. 'Back off a minute.'

'Okay.' It was a surprise how much it cost him to step away, to break that contact of body to body. 'That far enough?'

'Yeah, that's fine. I'm not going to pretend I didn't expect that or wasn't looking for it on one of those levels you were talking about. I have some basic kind of attraction to you. I didn't intend to act on it.'

'Why?'

'Because it's not smart. But . . .' She picked up her glass again, or perhaps it was his, and sipped while she studied him. 'If I decide to be stupid, then we'll have sex. I'm not against sex, and I think you'd be pretty good at it.'

He opened his mouth, shut it again. Cleared his throat. 'Excuse me while I restart my heart. Let me get this clear in my head. You're considering being stupid and having sex with me.'

'That's right.' Good, she decided and sipped again. Damn good. Finally she'd thrown his rhythm off. 'Isn't that where you were heading?'

'In my own bumbling way, yeah, I suppose so.'

'There was nothing bumbling about that kiss.'

He rubbed a hand over the back of his neck. Had he actually thought he was getting to know her all over again? 'Why do I feel like I should thank you?'

She laughed, shrugged a shoulder. 'Look, Noah, why clutter up healthy animal instincts with emotions and excuses? I don't indulge in sex very often because, well, I'm busy and I'm picky. But when I do, I consider it a natural, sometimes entertaining act that shouldn't be tied up with a bunch of sticky pretenses. In other words, I approach it like a man.'

'Yeah, well. *Hmmm.*'

'If you're not interested on that level, no hard feelings.' She finished the wine, set it aside. 'And I do recall you mentioning a vow of chastity, so maybe this conversation is moot.'

'I wouldn't call it a vow, exactly. More like a . . . concept.'

'Then we both have something to think about. Now I really have to go.'

'I'll drive you.'

'A cab's fine.'

'No, I'll take you. A drive might clear my head. You're fascinating, Olivia. No wonder you've been stuck in my mind for years.' He took her hand again, a habit she was almost getting used to. 'Your stuff's still in the car, right?'

'Yes.'

'Let's go, then. Keys?'

She dug them out of her pocket, handed them over as they walked through the house. 'Aren't you going to set the alarm?'

'Shit. Right.' Conversation, he thought, after he'd punched in the code and locked up. Fresh conversation because he didn't think his system could handle any more on the subject they'd just discussed. 'So, did you have any trouble finding your way down here?'

'I had a map. I'm good at reading maps. And this is a great ride,' she added as she settled in the passenger seat. 'Handles like a dream.'

'You open her up?'

She gave him a wisp of a smile. 'Maybe.' Then she laughed, enjoying the rush of wind as the car picked up speed. 'It's a bullet. How many speeding tickets do you collect in the average year?'

He winced. 'I'm a cop's son. I have great respect for the law.'

'Okay, how many does your father have fixed for you during the average year?'

'Family doesn't keep track of small acts of love. You know he'd like to see you while you're here. My mother, too.'

'I don't know what plans my aunt may have made, if there'll be time.'

'I thought you didn't like pretenses.'

She picked up the sunglasses she'd left on his dash, slipped them on. 'All right. I don't know how I'll handle seeing him. I don't know how I'll handle being back here, even for a few days. I decided to come to find out.'

She balled her fists in her lap, then deliberately relaxed them. 'I don't remember Los Angeles. All I really remember is . . . Do you know where my mother's house is? Was?'

'Yeah.' He was working on the current owners to let him take a tour.

'Go there. I want to go there.'

'Liv, you can't get in.'

'I don't need to. I just need to see it.'

Panic was a whisper inside her head, an icy caress along her skin. But she made herself stand at the gate. The walls surrounding the estate were tall and thick and brilliantly white. Trees and distance screened the house, but she could catch glimpses of it, brilliantly white as well, with the soft red tile of the roof.

'There are gardens, I'm not sure I knew how many. Elaborate, wonderful gardens. One was tucked away under big, shady trees and had a little pool with goldfish and water lilies. It had a bridge over it. A white bridge, that my mother said was for the fairies.'

She crossed her arms over her chest, hugging her biceps and hunching over as if to fight off sudden cold. 'There was another with just roses. Dozens and dozens of rosebushes. He bought a white one when I was born and planted it himself. I remember him telling me that. He'd planted it himself because it was special, and when he had to go out of town, or whenever he came back, he'd leave a white rose on my pillow. I wonder if they kept the gardens the way they were.'

Noah said nothing, simply rubbed a hand over her back and listened.

'The house was so big. It seemed like a palace to me. Soaring ceilings and huge windows. Room after room after room, every one of them special somehow. I slept in a canopy bed.' She shuddered once, violently. 'I can't stand to have anything overhead while I sleep now. I hadn't realized why. Someone would tell me a story every night. My mother or him, or if they were going out, Rosa. But Rosa didn't tell the really good stories. Sometimes they'd have parties, and I could lie in bed and hear the music and people laughing. My mother loved having people around. They'd come all the time. Aunt Jamie, Uncle David. Her agent. Uncle Lou. He'd always bring me a peppermint stick. One of those thick, old-fashioned ones. I can't imagine where he got them.

'Lucas Manning came over a lot. It must've been around the time my – he left.' She couldn't say 'my father.' Simply couldn't bring herself to form the words. 'I just remember Lucas being there, in the house, out by the pool. He made my mother laugh. He was nice to me in an absent sort of way. Kids know that it's just show. I wanted to like him, because he made Mama laugh, but I just kept wishing Lucas would stop coming over, because if he did maybe my . . . maybe he'd come home.'

She rested her head against the bars of the gate. 'Then, of course, he came home. He came home and he killed her. And I can't do this. I can't do this. I can't.'

'It's all right.' Noah gathered her to him, holding her tight even though she stood stiffly with her fisted hands pressed to his chest to separate them. 'You don't have to. You don't need to be here now, Olivia.'

She made herself open her eyes again, stare over his shoulder at those flashes of white. 'I've been running away from and running toward this all my life. It's time I decided on a direction and stuck with it.'

Part of him wanted to scoop her up, cuddle her as he carried her back to the car and took her away. But someone had taken her away for most of her life. 'When you run away it comes after you, Liv. And it always catches up.'

Afraid he was right, feeling the monster nipping at her heels, she turned and walked back to the car.

Chapter Twenty-two

She had her color back by the time Noah swung up the drive toward the Melbourne mansion. It seemed to him she'd all but willed it back, just as she'd willed away that lost and grieving look from her eyes.

'Wow.' Her smile seemed natural, effortless as the house came into view. 'We have pictures of it, even videos, but they don't come up to the in-your-face.'

'One of those nice fixer-uppers priced for the young marrieds.'

She laughed, then swiveled in her seat as the dogs raced over the yard. 'There they are! Oh, I wish I could've brought Shirley.'

'Why didn't you?'

'I thought you might object to dog hair and slobber all over your pretty-boy car. And my grandfather would be lost without her.' She pushed out as soon as he'd stopped and all but dived into the dogs.

The vulnerable woman with haunted eyes who'd stood outside the gate of her childhood home might not have existed. It certainly wasn't the face she showed to her uncle as David Melbourne came out of the house.

She let out a whoop of delight and bounded toward him, half leaping into his arms for a fierce hug.

He'd aged well, Noah thought, comparing the man who held Olivia with the photos that dated back to the murder. He'd kept the weight off, and had either discovered the fountain of youth or had an excellent cosmetic surgeon.

The lines on his face were dashing rather than aging, as were the streaks of silver in his hair. He was dressed casually in buff-colored trousers and a Henley shirt the color of kiwis.

'Welcome, traveler.' He laughed, cupped her face. 'Let's look at you. Pretty as ever.'

'Missed you.'

'Goes double.' He kissed her, then hugging a protective arm around her shoulders, turned to Noah. The cooling of voice and eyes was subtle but unmistakable. 'It was nice of you to deliver my girl.'

'My pleasure.'

'Uncle David, this is Noah Brady.'

'Yes, I know.'

'I just need to get my things out of the trunk.'

'I'll get them.' Noah unlocked the trunk, took out the single suitcase.

'That's it?' David wanted to know.

'I'm only going to be here a couple of days.'

'How about giving Jamie some tips on packing light while you're here?'

'You pack as much as she does. Clotheshorse.'

He winced, took the case from Noah. 'Jamie got caught on the phone. She should be off by now. Why don't you run in, Livvy? Rosa's paced a rut in the foyer waiting for you to get here.'

'Aren't you coming?'

'Be right there.'

'All right. Thanks for the lift, Brady.'

'No problem, MacBride,' he said in the same tone. 'I'll be in touch.'

She said nothing to that, only jogged up the stairs and inside.

'I hope you'll forgive me for not asking you in,' David began. 'This reunion's a family affair.'

'Understood. You can say what you have to say to me out here.'

David inclined his head. 'You're perceptive, Noah. I imagine that's why you're good at your work.' He set Olivia's suitcase down, glanced toward the house. 'You seem to have established some kind of rapport with Livvy.'

'We're beginning to understand each other.' Again, he thought. Or maybe it was at last. 'Is that a problem for you?'

'I have no idea.' In what might have been a gesture of peace, David spread his hands. 'I don't know you.'

'Mr. Melbourne, I was under the impression you were supportive of the book I'm writing.'

'I was.' David sighed out a breath. 'I thought enough time had passed, enough healing had been done. And I believed that a writer of your caliber could do justice to the tragedy.'

'I appreciate that. What changed your mind?'

'I didn't realize how much this would upset Val.' Concern clouded his eyes, and he slipped his hands into his pockets. 'My mother-in-law. I feel partially responsible as I did support it, and that support certainly influenced Jamie into giving you her cooperation and then encouraged Livvy to do so. I lost my own mother when I was very young. Val's one of the most important people in my life. I don't want her hurt.'

Protection, Noah mused. The family was a puzzle made up of pieces of protection and defense. 'I've already given Liv my word that I won't contact her grandmother or ask her to talk to me. I'll keep her out of it as far as I'm able to.'

'The book itself pulls her into it.' He held up a hand before Noah could speak. 'I can't expect you to turn your back on your work because the ripple effect of that work will hurt people I love. But I want you to be aware of it. And I want you to consider that a man who murders would hardly flinch at lying. Sam Tanner isn't to be trusted, and my biggest regret is that he'll have time to die outside of prison rather than in it.'

'If you're worried he'll lie to me, if your feelings are that strong, you'd be smart to put them on record.'

David laughed, shook his head. 'Noah, personally, I'd love to sit down with you and tell you exactly what I feel, what I remember. I'm going to do my best to ease my mother-in-law's feelings over it, then, if I can, I'll talk to you. You'll have to excuse me now.' He picked up the suitcase. 'It's the first time Livvy's come to visit. I don't want to miss any time with her.'

Olivia loved the house and everything they'd done with it. She loved it for them – it was so obviously perfect for them with its elegance and pastels and soaring ceilings. But she preferred the rambling style and rooms soaked in colors of her grandparents' home.

She was glad she'd finally made herself come.

By the time she crawled into bed, she was worn to the bone by the drive, the emotion, the elaborate dinner her aunt had arranged and the nonstop conversation as they'd caught up with one another.

Still, her last thought before sleep sucked her under. It was of Noah standing on the deck of his pretty house, with his back to the sea.

Olivia came to the conclusion very quickly that while southern California suited Jamie down to her pedicure, it wasn't the town for Liv MacBride. She was sure of it halfway between the shopping expedition her aunt insisted on and the lunch at some trendy restaurant with a name she immediately forgot.

The lunch portions were stingy, the wait staff glossy enough to glow in the dark and the prices so remarkably outrageous she could do nothing but gasp.

'I had my stylist pencil in appointments later this afternoon,' Jamie began as she toyed with her field-green-and-wild-pepper salad. 'Marco is a genius and an event in himself. We can squeeze in a manicure, maybe a paraffin treatment.'

'Aunt Jamie.' Olivia sampled what had been billed as the nouveau-club and was in reality two pieces of bark bread cut into tiny triangles and filled with mysterious vegetables. She wondered if anyone ate real food in L.A. 'You're trying to make a girl out of me.'

'No, I'm not.' Jamie pouted. 'I'm just trying to give you a . . . well, just one girl day. You should have let me buy you that little black dress.'

'That little black dress was four thousand dollars and wouldn't hold up through one hike.'

'Every self-respecting female needs at least one killer black dress. I say we go back for it, and the lizard sandals, the Pradas. You put those together on that fabulous body of yours, men will start diving out of windows to fall at your feet.'

Olivia shook her head, laughed. 'I don't want to be responsible for that. And I don't need the dress, or the shoes, or the warehouse full of other things you tried to talk me into.'

'How can we be related?'

'Genetics are a tricky business.'

'I'm so glad you're here. I'm so glad you're not angry with me anymore.' Tears flooded her eyes, and she reached over and gripped Olivia's hand.

'I wasn't angry with you. Not you, not really. I'm sorry we argued.' She turned her hand over, gripped Jamie's tight. 'I was angry at Noah, which was just as useless. All those years ago, when you came up to visit and we went out into the forest that evening . . . you were honest with me. You let me be honest with you. Ever since, whenever I needed to talk about Mama, you listened. Whenever I had questions, you answered them.'

'Until you stopped asking,' Jamie murmured.

'I thought I should put it away. I thought I could. Someone who's smarter than I gave him credit for told me that whenever you run away from something it chases after you and it always catches up. I think I'm ready to change directions.'

'It won't be easy.'

'God, no. But I'll be honest with you again. I want to hear what he says about that night. I want to hear Sam Tanner's story.'

'So do I. We loved her,' Jamie said squeezing Olivia's hand. 'How could we not want to hear it for ourselves?'

'Grandma—'

'Has dealt with this in her own way, always. It doesn't make your way wrong or your needs wrong.'

'No, it doesn't. I guess I'm going to get in touch with Noah before I go back.'

'He's a nice man.' Jamie's smile changed texture, crept toward feline. 'And a very attractive one.'

'I noticed. I've just about decided to sleep with him.'

The little sound that popped out of Jamie's mouth was something between a grunt and a squeak. 'Well. Well then. Ah . . . Listen, why don't we blow this joint, go get a pizza and you can elaborate on that very interesting statement.'

'Great.' With relief, Olivia pushed her plate aside. 'I'm starved.'

Frank was sitting in his kitchen, enjoying the single predinner light beer his wife allowed him. On a notepad, he drew circles, squiggles, exes as he toyed with a new play for the basketball team he coached.

He'd have enjoyed some potato chips or Fritos with his beer, but Celia had come across his secret stash a few days before. He still couldn't figure out what the hell she'd been doing looking on the top shelf of the den closet, but he couldn't ask as he'd denied knowing the sour cream and onion chips were there.

He claimed Noah had probably left them. That was his story, Frank thought as he made do with a handful of salt-free pretzels. And he was sticking to it.

When the doorbell rang, he left his beer and his doodling on the table, thinking it might be one of his players. He didn't think it set the right tone for Coach to come to the door with a cold one in his hand.

It was a young woman, with the tall, rangy build he could have used on the court. A little too old to fit into his twelve-to-sixteen-year-old league, he thought; then images overlapped in his mind and had him grabbing for her hands.

'Liv. Livvy! My God, you're all grown up.'

'I didn't think you'd recognize me.' And the fact that he had, with such obvious delight, warmed her. 'I'd have known you anywhere. You look just the same.'

'Never lie to a cop, even a retired one. Come in, come in.' He pulled her inside. 'I wish Celia were here. She had a late-afternoon meeting. Sit down.' He fussed around the living room, picking up the newspaper, scooping a magazine off a chair. 'Let me get you something to drink.'

'I'm all right. I'm fine.' There was a pressure in her chest, heavy, tight. 'I told myself to call first. Then I didn't. I just came.'

He saw the battle for composure on her face. 'I'm glad you did. I knew you were grown-up, but every time I pictured you, even when I'd read your letters, I'd see a little girl.'

'I always see a hero.' She let herself go into his arms, let herself be held. And the jitters in her stomach quieted and eased. 'I knew I'd feel better. I knew it would be all right, if I could see you.'

'What's wrong, Livvy?'

'A lot of things. I'm figuring them out but—'

'Is this about Noah's book?'

'Part of it. About that, about him. He's your son.' She said it with a sigh and stepped back to stand on her own. 'And as much as I didn't want to, as much as I told myself I wouldn't, I trust him to do it right. It's going to be painful for me to talk to him, but I can do it. I will do it, in my own time. In my own way.'

'You can trust him. I don't understand his work, but I understand Noah.'

Puzzled, she shook her head. 'You don't understand his

work? How can you not understand his work? It's brilliant.'

It was Frank's turn for confusion. He sat on the arm of the sofa, staring at her. 'I have to say, I'm surprised to hear you say that. How you could feel that, as a survivor of a murder victim?'

'And the daughter of a murderer,' she finished. 'That's exactly why. I read his first book as soon as it came out. How could I resist it with his name on the cover?' And she'd hidden it in her room like a sin. 'I didn't expect to like it.' Hadn't wanted to, she thought. Had wanted to read it and condemn him. 'I still don't know if I can say I liked it, but I understood what he was doing. He takes the most wicked of crimes, the most horrid, the most unforgivable. And he keeps them that way.'

She waved a hand in annoyance at her own fumbling attempt to explain. 'When you hear about a murder on the news, or read about it in the paper, you say, oh, how awful, then you move on. He humanizes it, makes it real – so vividly real that you can't say, 'Oh, how awful,' then slide down the pillows and go to sleep. Everyone who was involved – he strips them down to their most desperate and agonized emotions.'

That, she realized, was what she feared about him the most. That he would strip her to the soul.

'He makes them matter,' she continued. 'So that what was done matters.'

She smiled a little, but her eyes were horribly sad. 'So that what his father did, every day, year in and year out, matters. You're his standard for everything that's right and strong.'

Just, she thought, as her father was her standard for everything evil and weak.

'Livvy.' Words clogged in Frank's throat. 'You make me ashamed that I never looked close enough.'

'You just see Noah. I'm nervous about talking to him.' She pressed her hand to her stomach. 'I don't want him to know that. I want us to try to do this on equal ground. Well, not quite equal,' she corrected, and her smile steadied. 'I'm going back home tomorrow, so he'll have to deal with me on my turf. I wondered, one of the things I wanted to ask, was if you and Mrs. Brady would like to come up sometime this summer, have a couple of free weeks at the lodge on the MacBrides. We've made a number of improvements, and I'd love you to see my Center and . . . Oh God. I'm sorry. God.'

She pressed both hands to her mouth, stunned that the words had tripped out, stumbling over one another in her rush to conceal the truth.

'Livvy—'

'No, I'm all right. Just give me a minute.' She walked to the front window, stared out through the pretty sheer curtains. 'I know he gets out in a few weeks. I thought, somehow I thought, if you were there, just for the first couple of days after . . . it would be all right. I haven't let myself really think about it, but the time's coming. Just a few weeks.'

She turned back, started to speak, to apologize again. But something in his face, the grim line of his mouth, the shadow in his eyes stopped her. 'What is it?'

'It's about him getting out, Liv. I was contacted this morning. I have some connections, and whenever there's something new about Tanner, I get a call. Due to his health, the hardship, overcrowded system, time served, his record in prison . . .' Frank lifted a hand, let it fall.

'They're letting him out sooner, aren't they? When?'

Her eyes were huge, locked on his. He thought of the child who'd stared at him from her hiding place. This time, he could do nothing to soften the blow.

'Two weeks ago,' he told her.

The phone shattered Noah's concentration into a thousand irretrievable shards. He swore at it, viciously, ignoring the second ring as he stared at the last line he'd written and tried to find the rhythm again.

On the third ring he snatched up the portable he'd brought in by mistake, squeezed it with both hands as if to strangle the caller, then flipped it on.

'What the hell do you want?'

'Just to say good-bye. 'Bye.'

'Wait. Liv. Wait, don't hang up, damn it. You don't return my calls for two days, and then you catch me at a bad moment.'

'I've been busy, which you obviously are, too. So—'

'Okay, okay. I'm sorry. That was rude. I'm a jerk. I've got the sackcloth right here. You got my messages?' All ten thousand of them, he thought.

'Yes, I haven't had time to return them until now. And

I only have a minute as it is. They're already boarding.'

'Boarding? What? You're at the airport? You're leaving already?'

'Yes, my plans changed.' Her father was out of prison. Was he already in L.A.? Is this where he would come first? She rubbed a hand over her mouth and schooled her voice to sound casual. 'I have to get back, and I thought I'd let you know. If you still want to talk to me, regarding your book, you can reach me at the lodge, the Center most likely.'

'Go back in the morning. One night can't make any difference. Olivia, I want to see you.'

'You know where to find me. We'll work out some sort of schedule that's convenient for the interviews.'

'I want . . .' You, he realized. How the hell had it gotten so mixed up a second time? 'The book isn't everything that's going on here, between us. Change your flight.' He hit keys rapidly to save data and close. 'I'll come pick you up.'

'I don't want to be here,' she said flatly. 'I'm going home.' To where it was safe. To where she could breathe. 'If you want interviews with me, you'll have to come to the lodge. It's final boarding. I'm leaving.'

'It's not just the damn interviews,' he began, but she'd already broken the connection.

Noah swung the phone over his shoulder, then halfway back to the desk before he managed to resist the urge to just beat it to bits of plastic.

The woman was making him nuts. She ran hot, cold, jumped up, down and sideways. How the hell was he supposed to keep up with her?

Now she was gone, leaping out of his reach before he had a real chance to grab hold. Now he was supposed to go chasing after her? Was that the game?

Disgusted, he kicked back in the chair, stared at the ceiling. No, she didn't work that way. It wasn't games with Olivia so much as it was a match. There was a big difference between the two.

There were details he needed to deal with, more data he needed to work through. And then, he thought, tossing the phone on the cluttered desk, then they'd just see about that match.

He was more than willing to go one-on-one.

*

Olivia didn't relax until the plane was in the air and she could nudge her seat back, close her eyes. Below, Los Angeles was falling away, out of reach and soon out of sight. There was nothing there for her now, no need to go back. The house that had once been her own personal castle was locked behind iron gates and belonged to someone else.

And the murder that had been done there, long since scrubbed away.

If and when Noah contacted her, she'd deal with it, and him. She'd proven to herself that she could get through that swarm of memories. Retelling them would only be words, words that couldn't hurt her now.

The monster was loose.

It seemed to whisper in her ear, a warning edged with a kind of jumping glee.

It didn't matter. She wouldn't let it matter. Whether or not they'd unlocked his cell, given him a suit of clothes and the money he'd earned over his years in a cage, he'd been dead to her for a long, long time.

She hoped she'd been dead to him as well. That he didn't think of her.

Or if he did, she prayed that every thought caused him pain.

She turned her head away from the window and willed herself to sleep.

Sleep didn't come easily to some. It was full of fear and sound and bloody images.

The monster was loose. And it cavorted in dreams, shambled on thick legs into the heart and poured out in bitter tears.

The monster was loose, and knew there would be no end, no finish without more death.

Livvy. The name was a silent sob, trembling in a desperate mind. The love for her was as real as it had been from the moment she'd been born. And the fear of her was as real as it had been on the night blood had been spilled.

She would be sacrificed only if there was no choice.

And the loss of her would be, forever, an open wound in the heart.

Chapter Twenty-three

'Out? What do you mean he's out?'

'He got out two weeks ago. His lawyer filed a hardship plea, and they bumped up his release date.' Frank settled down on a deck chair where his son had taken advantage of an overcast day and a quiet beach to work outside.

'Son of a bitch.' Noah pushed to his feet, paced from one end of the deck to the other. 'Son of a bitch. He must have known the last time I went to see him. He didn't tell me. I finally got a conference call scheduled with Smith this afternoon, and his assistant didn't mention it either. Well, where the hell did he go?'

'I don't have that information. Actually, I thought you might. I wouldn't mind keeping tabs on Tanner.' Frank thought of the shock and fear in Olivia's eyes. 'For old times' sake.'

'He hasn't bothered to give me his fucking forwarding address. The book's dead without him.' He stared down at his piles of papers, anchored with bottles, a conch shell, whatever came most handily. 'Without him and Liv, it stops. The rest fans out from them. Early release?' He looked back at Frank. 'Not parole, so he doesn't have to check in.'

'He served his time. The state of California considers him rehabilitated.'

'Do you?'

'Which part of you is asking the question? My son or the writer?'

Noah's face closed up immediately, went blank. 'Never mind.'

'I didn't mean I wouldn't answer, Noah. I was just curious.'

'You're the one who compartmentalizes what I am and what I do. For me, they're in the same drawer.'

'You're right. I've been giving that some thought recently.' Frank sighed, laid his hands on his knees. 'I thought you'd be a cop. I guess I had that idea in my head for a long time. I had this image of you coming on the job while I was still on it.'

'I know I disappointed you. But it's not what I am.'

The instinctive denial was on his tongue. Frank paused and gave his son the truth instead. 'I had no right to be disappointed. And I know it's not what you are, Noah, but some things die hard. You were always interested in what I did when you were a kid. You used to write up reports.' He laughed a little. 'You'd ask me all these questions about a case and write it all up. I didn't see that for what it was. When you went into journalism, I thought, well, he'll snap out of that. But you didn't and I was disappointed. That's my failure, not yours.'

'I never wanted to close cases, Dad. I wanted to study them.'

'I didn't want to hear that. Pride has two edges, Noah. When you started writing books, started digging into things that were over and done, I took it as a reflection on what I had done, as if you were saying that it wasn't enough to do the job, gather the evidence, make the arrest, get the conviction.'

'That's not it. That was never it.'

'No, but I let my pride get in the way of seeing what you were doing, why you were doing it and what it meant to you. I want you to know I'm sorry for that. More sorry that I never gave you the respect you deserved for doing work you were meant to do, and doing it well.'

'Well.' Emotion slid through him, carrying out the tension in his shoulders he hadn't been aware of. 'It's a day for surprises.'

'I've always been proud of who you are, Noah. You've never been anything but a joy to me, as a son and as a man.' Frank had to pause a moment before his tongue tangled.

'I wouldn't be what I am if you hadn't been there.'

'Noah.' Love was a swollen river in his throat. 'I hope one day you have a grown child say that to you. It's the only way to know how much it means.' He had to clear his throat before he embarrassed both of them. 'I'm going to give more consideration to what you do. Fair enough?'

'Yeah, that's fair enough.'

'I'll start by telling you I'll do that interview sort of thing, when you have the time for it.'

'I've got time now. How about you?'

'Now? Well, I . . .' He hadn't been prepared for it and found himself limping for an excuse.

'Just let me get a fresh tape.'

Noah knew when he had a fish on the line and made it fast. He came back out with a tape and two cans of Coke. 'It's not as hard as you think,' he said while he labeled the tape and snapped it into the recorder. 'You just talk to me, tell me about the case. Just the way you used to. You told me some about this one. I made notes on it even back then. Tanner made the nine-one-one call himself. I've got a transcript of it.'

Wanting accuracy rather than memory, Noah dug out the right file. 'He called it in at twelve forty-eight. *She's dead. My God, Julie. She's dead. The blood, it's everywhere. I can't stop the blood. Somebody help me.*' Noah set the paper aside. 'There's more, but that's the core of it. The nine-one-one operator asked him questions, kept getting the same response, but managed to get the address out of him.'

'The uniforms went in first,' Frank said. 'Standard procedure. They responded to the nine-eleven. The gate was open; so was the front door. They entered the premises and found the body and Tanner in the front parlor area. They secured the scene, reported a homicide and requested detectives. Tracy Harmon and I took the call.'

For Noah, it was as if he'd walked into the house that night with his father. He felt the warm rustle of air that stirred the palm fronds and danced through gardens silvered in moonlight. The house stood, white as a wish with windows blazing gold with lights.

Police cruisers were guard-dogging the front, one with its blue and red lights still spinning to shoot alarming color over the marble steps, the faces of cops, the crime scene van.

More light poured out of the open doorway.

A rookie, his uniform still academy fresh, vomited pitifully in the oleanders.

Inside, the grand chandelier dripped its waterfall of light on virgin white floors and highlighted the dark stain of the blood trail.

It smeared in all directions, across the foyer, down the wide hall, up the polished-oak stairway that swept regally to the left.

The smell of it was still ripe, the look of it still wet.

He was used to death, the violence of it. The waste of it. But his first glimpse of what had been done to Julie MacBride broke his heart. He remembered the sensations exactly, the sudden, almost audible snapping, the resulting churn of pity and horror in his gut. And the fast, overpowering flood of fury that burst into his head before he shut them away, locked them away, and did his job.

At first glance it appeared to have been a vicious struggle. The broken glass, the overturned furniture, the great spewing patterns of blood.

But there were patterns within patterns. The dead always left them. Her nails were unbroken and clean, the defensive wounds on her hands and arms shallow.

He'd come at her from behind. Later Frank would have this verified by the ME's findings, but as he crouched beside the body, he played the scene in his head.

The first blow had gone deep into her back, just below the shoulder blades. She'd probably screamed, stumbled, tried to turn. There would have been shock along with the pain. Had she seen his face? Seen what was in it?

He'd come at her again. Had she lifted an arm to block the blow? *Please, don't! God, don't!*

She'd tried to get away, knocking over the lamp, shattering glass, slicing her bare feet on it even as he sliced at her. She'd fallen, crawled, weeping. He'd driven the blades into her again and again, plunging with them, slashing with them even after she was still. Even after she was dead.

Two uniforms watched Sam in the adjoining room. As with his first glimpse of Julie, this image would implant itself on Frank's mind. He was pale and handsome. He smoked in quick jerks, his arm pistoning up and down, up and down as he brought the cigarette to his lips, drew in smoke, blew it out, drew it in again.

His eyes were off – glassy and wheeling in his head. Shock and drugs.

His wife's blood was all over him.

'Somebody killed her. Somebody killed Julie.' He said it again and again.

'Tell me what happened, Mr. Tanner.'

'She's dead. Julie's dead. I couldn't stop it.'

'Couldn't stop what?'

'The blood.' Sam stared down at his hands, then began to weep.

Sometime during that initial, disjointed interview, Frank remembered there was a child. And went to look for her.

In his office, Noah typed up his notes from the interview with his father. It helped to write it down, to see the words.

When his phone rang, he jolted, and realized that he had been lost, working for hours. The first streaks of sunset were now staining the sky through his window.

Noah pressed his fingers to his aching eyes and answered.

'It's Sam Tanner.'

Instinctively, Noah snatched up a pencil. 'Where are you?'

'I'm watching the sun go down. I'm outside, and I'm watching the sun go down over the water.'

'You didn't tell me they were letting you out early, Sam.'

'No.'

'Are you in San Francisco?'

'I was in San Francisco long enough. It's cold and it's damp. I wanted to come home.'

Noah's pulse picked up. 'You're in L.A.?'

'I got a room off of Sunset. It's not what it used to be, Brady.'

'Give me the address.'

'I'm not there now. Actually I'm down the road from you. Watching the sun set,' he said almost dreamily. 'Outside a place that serves tacos and beer and salsa that makes your eyes sting.'

'Tell me where you are. I'll meet you.'

Sam wore khakis and a short-sleeved chambray shirt, both so painfully new they'd yet to shake out the folding pleats. He sat at one of the little iron tables on the patio of the Mexican place and stared out over the water. Though business wasn't brisk, there was a sprinkling of people at other tables, kids with fresh faces who scooped up nachos and sipped at the beers they were barely old enough to order.

In contrast, Sam looked old, pale, and inexplicably more naive.

Noah ordered more tacos, another beer for each of them.

'What does it feel like?'

With a kind of wonder, Sam watched an in-line skater skim by. 'I spent a few days in San Francisco, to get my bearings. Then I took a bus down. Part of me kept expecting someone to stop me, take me back, say it had all been a mistake. Another part was waiting to be recognized, to hear someone call out, "Look, there's Sam Tanner", and run over for my autograph. There're two lives crossed over in the middle, and my mind keeps jumping back and forth between them.'

'Do you want to be recognized?'

'I was a star. An important actor. You need the attention, not just to feed the ego, but to stroke the child. If you weren't a child, how good an actor could you be? After a while, inside, I had to put that away. When I knew the appeals weren't going to work, the cage wasn't going to open, I had to put it away to survive. Then I got out and it all came flooding back. And as badly as I wanted someone to look at me, to *see* me and remember, it scared the shit out of me that someone would. Stage fright.' Sam gave a small, sick smile. 'There's something I haven't had to deal with in a long time.'

Noah said nothing while the waitress clunked their food and drinks down. Once she'd walked away, he leaned forward. 'Coming to L.A. was a risk, because someone's bound to recognize you sooner or later.'

'Where else would I go? It's changed. I got lost twice walking around. New faces everywhere, on the street, on the billboards. People driving around in big chunky Jeeps. And you can't smoke any fucking where.'

Noah had to laugh at the absolute bafflement in the statement. 'I imagine the food's some better than San Quentin's.'

'I forgot places like this existed.' Sam picked up a taco, studied it. 'I'd forgotten that before I went inside. If it wasn't the best, I wasn't interested. If I wasn't going to be seen, admired, envied, what was the point?'

He bit in, crunching the shell, ignoring the little bits of tomato and lettuce and sauce that plopped onto his plate. For a few moments he ate in concentrated silence, a kind of grim focus Noah imagined came from prison meals.

'I was an asshole.'

Noah lifted a brow. 'Can I quote you?'

'That's what this is about, isn't it? I had everything – success, adulation, power, wealth. I had the most beautiful woman in the world, who loved me. I thought I deserved it, all of it, so I didn't value what I had. I didn't value any of it or see it as any more than my due. So I lost it. All of it.'

Keeping his eyes on Sam's face, Noah sipped his beer. 'Did you kill your wife?'

He didn't answer at first, only watched the last sliver of sun sink red into the sea. 'Yes.' His gaze shifted, locked on Noah's. 'Did you expect me to deny it? What's the point? I served twenty years for what I did. Some will say it's not enough. Maybe they're right.'

'Why did you kill her?'

'Because I couldn't be what she asked me to be. Now ask me if I picked up the scissors that night and stabbed them into her back, her body, sliced them across her throat.'

'All right. Did you?'

'I don't know.' His eyes shifted to the water again, went dreamy again. 'I just don't know. I remember it two ways, and both seem absolutely real. I stopped thinking it mattered, then they told me I was going to die. I need to know, and you're going to figure out which of the two ways is real.'

'Which one are you going to tell me?'

'Neither, not yet. I need the money. I opened an account at this bank.' He brought out a scrap of paper. 'That's my account number. They do this electronic transfer. That'd be the best way.'

'All right.' Noah pocketed the paper. 'It'll be there tomorrow.'

'Then we'll talk tomorrow.'

Noah called Olivia the next morning, caught her at her desk at the Center. He was still damp from the shower after his run on the beach, just starting to pump up his system with coffee. The sound of her voice, brisk, businesslike, husky around the edges made him smile.

'Hello back, Ms. MacBride. Miss me?'

'Not particularly.'

'I don't believe it. You recognized my voice too easily.' He heard her sigh, certain she'd wanted it audible and full of exasperation.

'Why wouldn't I? You talk more than any three people I know put together.'

'And you don't talk enough, but I've got your voice in my head. I had a dream about you last night, all soft, watery colors and slow motion. We made love on the bank of the river, and the grass was cool and damp and wild with flowers. I woke up with the taste of you in my mouth.'

There was a moment of silence, a quiet catch of breath. 'That's very interesting.'

'Is someone in your office?'

'Momentarily. Thanks, Curtis, I'll take care of that.' There was another pause. 'That riverbank is a public area.'

He laughed so hard he had to slide onto a stool. 'I'm becoming seriously crazy about you, Liv. Did you like the flowers?'

'They're very nice and completely unnecessary.'

'Sure they were. They make you think of me. I want you to keep me right in the front of your mind, Liv, so we can pick things up when I get there.'

'When do you plan to make the trip?'

'One or two weeks – sooner, if I can manage it.'

'The lodge is booked well in advance this time of year.'

'I'll think of something. Liv, I need to tell you I've seen Tanner, spoken with him. He's here in Los Angeles.'

'I see.'

'I thought you'd feel better knowing where he is.'

'Yes, I suppose I do. I have to go—'

'Liv, you can tell me how you feel. Aside from the book, just as someone who cares about you. You can talk to me.'

'I don't know how I feel. I only know I can't let where he is or what he's doing change my life. I'm not going to let anything or anyone do that.'

'You may find out some changes don't have to hurt. I'll let you know when I plan to come in. Keep thinking about me, Olivia.'

She hung up, let out a long breath. 'Keep dreaming,' she murmured and skimmed a finger over the petals of a sunny daisy.

She hadn't been able to resist keeping them in her office where she could see them when she was stuck at her desk and itching to get outside.

She'd recognized what he'd done as well, and found it incredibly sweet and very clever. The flowers he ordered were all from the varieties he had in his own garden. The garden she hadn't been able to resist. He had to know that looking at them would make her think of him.

She'd have thought of him anyway.

And she'd lied when she'd told him she didn't miss him. It

surprised her how much she did and worried her just a little to realize she wished they were different people in a different situation. Then they could be lovers, maybe even friends, without the shadows clinging to the corner of their relationship.

She'd never been friends with a lover, she thought. Had never really had a lover, as that term added dimension and intimacy to simple sex.

But she thought Noah would insist on being both. If she wanted him, she would have to give more than she'd been willing, or able, to give to anyone before.

One more thing to think about, she decided, and rubbing the tension from her neck, swiveled back to her keyboard and began to input her ideas for the fall programs with an eye to the elementary school field trips she hoped to implement.

She answered the knock on her door with a grunt.

'Was that a come in or go to hell?' Rob wanted to know as he gently shook the package he carried.

'It's come in to you, and go to hell for anyone else. I'm just working out some fall programs.' She angled her head as she swiveled her chair around. 'What's in the box?'

'Don't know. It came to the lodge, looks like an overnight from Los Angeles, to you.'

'Me?'

'I'd guess it's from the same young man who sent you the flowers.' He set the package on the desk. 'And I say he has fine taste in women.'

'Which you say with complete objectivity.'

'Of course.' Rob sat on the corner of the desk, reached for her hands. 'How's my girl?'

'I'm fine.' She gave his hand a reassuring squeeze. 'Don't worry about me, Grandpop.'

'I'm allowed to worry. It's part of the job description.' And she'd been so tense, so pale when she'd come back from California. 'It doesn't matter that he's out, Livvy. I've made my peace with that. I hope you will.'

'I'm working on it.' She rose, moved away to tidy files that didn't need tidying. 'Noah just called. He wanted to let me know he'd seen him, spoken to him.'

'It's best you know.'

'Yes, it is. I appreciate that he understands that, respects that.

That he doesn't treat me as if I were so fragile I'd break, that I needed to be protected from . . .' She trailed off, felt a wave of heat wash into her face. 'I didn't mean—'

'It's all right. I don't know if we did the right thing, Livvy, bringing you here, closing everything else out. We meant it for the best.'

'Bringing me here was exactly the right thing.' She dropped the files and stepped over to hug him tight. 'No one could have given me more love or a better home than you and Grandma. We won't let thoughts of him come in here and make us question it.' Her eyes stormed with emotion when she drew back. 'We won't.'

'I still want what's best for you. I'm just not as sure as I once was that it is. This young man . . .' He nodded towards the flowers. 'He's bringing you an awful lot to face at one time. But he's got a straight look in his eyes, makes me want to trust him with you.'

'Grandpop.' She bent, kissed his cheek. 'I'm old enough, and smart enough, to decide that for myself.'

'You're still my baby. Aren't you going to open the package?'

'No, it'll only encourage him.' She grinned. 'He's trying to charm me.'

'Is he?'

'I suppose he is, a little. He's planning on coming back soon. I'll decide just how charmed I am when I see him again. Now, go to work, and let me do the same.'

'He comes back around, I'm keeping an eye on him.' Rob winked as he got up and headed for the door. Then he stopped, one hand on the knob, and glanced back. 'Did we keep you too close, Livvy? Hold you too tight?' He shook his head before she could answer. 'Yes or no, you grew your own way. Your mother'd be proud of you.'

When the door closed behind him, she sat down, struggled with the tears that were a hot mix of grief and joy. She hoped he was right, that her mother would be proud, and not see her daughter as a woman who was too aloof, too hard, too afraid to open herself to anyone but the family who'd always been there.

Would Julie, bright, beautiful Julie, ask her daughter, Where are your friends? Where are the boys you pined for, the men you loved? Where are the people you've touched or made part of your life?

What would the answer be? Olivia wondered. There's no one. No one.

It made her so suddenly, so unbearably sad the tears threatened again. Blinking them away, she stared at the package on her desk.

Noah, she thought. He was truing to reach her. Wasn't it time she let him?

She dug out the Leatherman knife from her pocket, used the slim blade to break the sealing tape. Then she paused, let herself feel the anticipation the pleasure. Let herself think of him as she lifted the lid.

Hurrying now, she probed through the protective blizzard of Styrofoam chips, spilling them out onto the desk as she worked the content out. Glass or china, she thought, some sort of figurine. She wondered if he'd actually tracked down a statue of a marmot, was already laughing at the idea when she freed the figure.

The laugh died in her throat, tumbled with the avalanche of icy panic that roared through her chest. Her own rapid breathing became a crashing scream in her head. She dropped the figurine as if it were a live snake, poised to strike.

And stared, trembling and swaying, at the benevolent and beautiful face of the Blue Fairy poised atop the music box.

Chapter Twenty-four

'I never wanted to be alone.' Sam held the coffee Noah had given him and squinted against the sun. 'Being alone was like a punishment to me. A failure. Julie was good at it, often preferred it. She didn't need the spotlight the way I did.'

'Did or do?' Noah asked, and watched Sam smile.

'I've learned there are advantages to solitude. Julie always knew that. When we separated, when I bought the place in Malibu, the prospects of living there alone was nearly as terrifying as living without her. I don't remember much about the Malibu house. I guess it was similar to this.'

He glanced back at the house, the creamy wood, clear streams of glass, the splashes of flowers in stone tubs. Then out to the ocean. 'The view wouldn't have been much different. You like it here, being alone?'

'My kind of work requires big chunks of solitude.'

Sam only nodded and fell silent.

Noah had debated the wisdom of conducting the interviews at his own place. In the end, it had seemed most practical. They'd have the privacy he required and, by setting up on the deck, give Sam his wish to be outside. He hadn't been able to come up with a good argument against it, as Sam already had his address.

He waited while Sam lit another cigarette. 'Tell me about the night of August twenty-eighth.'

'I didn't want to be alone,' Sam said again. 'I wasn't working, had just fired my agent. I was pissed off at Julie. Who the hell did she think she was, kicking me out of the house when she was the one fucking around? I called Lydia. I wanted company, I wanted sympathy. She hated Julie, so I knew she'd say what I wanted to hear. I figured we'd get high and have sex – like old times. That'd teach Julie a lesson.'

His hand bunched into a fist on his knee, and he began to tap it there, rhythmically. 'She wasn't home. Her maid said she was out for the evening. So I was pissed off about that, too. Couldn't depend on anyone, no one was there when you needed them. Worked myself up pretty good. There were others I could have called, but I thought fuck them. I did a line to prime myself up, then got in the car and headed into L.A.'

He paused, rubbing lightly at his temple as if he had a headache brewing, then went back to tapping his fist on his knee. 'I don't know how many clubs I hit. It came out in the trial, different people seeing me at different places that night. Saying I was belligerent, looking for trouble. How did they know what I was looking for when I didn't?'

'Witnesses stated you were looking for Lucas Manning, got into a shoving match with security at one of the clubs, knocked over a tray of drinks at another.'

'Must have.' Sam moved his shoulder casually, but his hand continued its hard, steady rhythm. 'It's blur. Bright lights, bright colors, faces, bodies. I did another line in the car. Maybe two before I drove to our house. I'd been drinking, too. I had all this energy and anger and all I could think of was Julie. We'd settle this, goddamn it. Once and for all.'

He sat back, closed his eyes. His hand stilled, then began to claw at his knee. 'I remember the way the trees stood out against the sky, like a painting. And the headlights of other cars were like suns, burning against my eyes. I could hear the sound of my heartbeat in my head. Then it goes two ways.'

He opened his eyes, blue and intense, and stared into Noah's. 'The gate's locked. I know he's in there with her. The son of a bitch. When she comes on the intercom I tell her to open the gate, I need to talk to her. I'm careful, really careful, to keep my tone calm. I know she won't let me in if she knows I've been using. She won't let me in if she knows I'm primed. She tells me it's late, but I persist, I persuade. She gives in. I drive back to the house. The moonlight's so bright it hurts my eyes. And she's standing in the door, the light behind her. She's wearing the white silk nightgown I'd bought her for our last anniversary. Her hair's down around her shoulders, her feet are bare. She's so beautiful. And cold, her face is cold, like something carved out of marble. She tells me to make it quick, she's tired, and walks into the parlor.

'There's a glass of wine on the table, and the magazines. The scissors. They're silver and long-bladed sitting on the glass top. She picks up her wine. She knows I'm high now, so she's angry. "Why are you doing this to yourself?" she asks me. "Why are you doing this to me, to Livvy?"'

Sam lifted a hand to his lips, rubbed them, back and forth, back and forth. 'I tell her it's her fault, hers because she let Manning put his hands on her, because she put her career ahead of our marriage. It's an old argument, old ground, but this time it takes a different turn. She says she's through with me, there's no chance for us, and she wants me out of her life. I make her sick, I disgust her.'

Still the actor, he punched the words, used pauses and passion. 'She doesn't raise her voice, but I can see the words coming out of her mouth. I see them as dark red smoke, and they choke me. She tells me she's never been happier since she kicked me out and has no intention of weighing herself down with a has-been with a drug problem. Manning isn't just a better actor, he's a better lover. And I was right all along, she's tired of denying it. He gives her everything I can't.'

Noah watched Sam's eyes go glassy and narrowed his own.

'She turned away from me as if I was nothing,' Sam muttered, then lifted his voice to a half shout. 'As if everything we'd had together was nothing. The red smoke from her words is covering my face, it's burning in my throat. The scissors with the long silver blades are in my hands. I want to stab them through her, deep inside her. She screams, the glass flies out of her hand, shatters. Blood pours out of her back. Like I'd pulled a cork out of a bottle of perfect red wine. She stumbles, there's a crash. I can't see through the smoke, just keep hacking with the scissors. The blood's hot on my hands, on my face. We're on the floor, she's crawling, the scissors are like part of my hand. I can't stop them. I can't stop.'

His eyelids shuttered closed now, and the hands on his knees were bone-white fists. 'I see Livvy in the doorway, staring at me with her mother's eyes.'

His hand shook as he picked up his coffee. He sipped, long and deep like a man gulping for liquid after wandering the desert.

'That's one way I remember it. Can I have something cold now? Some water?'

'All right.' Noah switched off the recorder, rose, went inside to the kitchen. Then he laid his palms on the counter. Icy sweat shivered over his skin. The images of the murder were bad enough. He'd read the transcripts, studied the reports. He'd known what to expect. But it had been the perfect artistry of Sam's narrative that knotted his stomach. That, and the thought of Olivia crawling out of her child's bed and into a nightmare.

How many times had she relived it? he wondered.

He poured two glass of mineral water over ice, braced himself to go back out and continue.

'You're wondering if you can still be objective,' Sam said when Noah stepped out again. 'You're wondering how you can stand to sit here with me and breathe the same air.'

'No.' Noah passed him the water, sat. 'That's part of my job. I'm wondering how you live with yourself. What you see when you look in the mirror every morning.'

'They kept me on suicide watch for two years. They were right. But after a while, you learn to go from one day to the next. I loved Julie, and that love was the best part of my life. It still wasn't enough to make me a man.'

'And twenty years in prison did?'

'Twenty years in prison made me sorry I'd destroyed everything I'd been given. Cancer made me decide to take what was left.'

'What's left, Sam?'

'The truth, and facing it.' He took another sip of water. 'I remember that night another way, too. It starts off the same, toking up, cruising, letting the drug feed the rage. But this time the gates are open when I get there. Boy, that pisses me off. What the hell is she thinking? We're going to have a little talk about that. If Manning's inside . . . I know damn well he's in there. I can see him pumping himself into my wife. I think about killing him, with my bare hands, while she watches. The door of the house is wide open. Light's spilling out. This really gets me. I walk in, looking for a fight. I start to go upstairs, sure I'll catch them in bed, but I hear the music from the parlor. They must be fucking in there, with the music on, the door open and my daughter upstairs. Then I . . .'

He stopped, took a long drink, then set the glass aside. 'There's blood everywhere. I didn't even recognize it for what it was at first. It's too much to be real. There's broken glass, smashed. The lamp we'd bought on our honeymoon is shattered on the floor. My head's buzzed from coke and vodka, but I'm thinking Jesus, Jesus, there's been a break-in. And I see her. Oh God, I see her on the floor.'

His voice broke, wavered, quavered, just as perfectly delivered as the stream of violence in his first version. 'I'm kneeling beside her, saying her name, trying to pick her up. Blood, there's blood all over her. I know she's dead, but I tell her to wake up, she has to wake up. I pulled the scissors out of her back. If I took them out, they couldn't hurt her. And there was Livvy, staring at me.'

He took a cigarette from the pack on the table and struck a match, and the flame shivered as if in a brisk wind. 'The police didn't buy that one.' He blew out smoke. 'Neither did the jury. After a while, I stopped buying it, too.'

'I'm not here to buy anything, Sam.'

'No.' He nodded but it was a sly look, a con's look. 'But you'll wonder, won't you?'

'According to Manning, he and Julie never had an affair. Not for lack of trying on his part, he was up-front about that.' Noah stood with his father outside the youth center while a group of kids fought through a pickup game on the newly blacktopped basketball court. 'He was in love with her – or infatuated, spent a lot of time with her – but she considered him a friend.'

'That's the way he played it during the investigation.'

'Did you believe him?'

Frank sighed, shook his head as he watched one of his boys bobble a pass. 'He was convincing. The housekeeper's testimony backed him up. She swore no man had ever spent the night in that house but the man her mistress had been married to. She was fiercely loyal to Julie and could have been covering. But we never shook her on it. The only evidence to the contrary was Sam Tanner's belief and the usual gossip. As far as the case went, it didn't matter one way or the other. Tanner believed in the affair, so to him it was real and part of the motive.'

'Don't you find it odd that Manning and Lydia Loring ended up as lovers even for only a few months?'

'That's why they call it Holly-Weird, pal.'

'Just hypothetically, if you hadn't had Tanner cold, where else would you have looked?'

'We had him cold, and we still looked. We interviewed Manning, Lydia, the housekeeper, the agent, the family. Particularly the Melbournes, as they both worked for Julie. Actually, we took a long look at Jamie Melborne. She inherited a considerable sum upon her sister's death. We went through Julie's fan mail, culled out the loonies and took a look at them in case an obsessed fan had managed to get in through the security. The fact is, Tanner was there. His prints were all over the murder weapon. He had motive, means and opportunity. And his own daughter saw him.'

Frank shifted. 'I had some trouble with the case during the first few days. It didn't hold as solid as I wanted it to.'

'What do you mean, it didn't hold?'

'Just that the way Tanner behaved, the way he mixed up two different nights – two different altercations with Julie in his head – or pretended to . . . It didn't sit at first. Then he lawyered and went hard. I realized he'd been playing me. Don't let him play you, Noah.'

'I'm not.' But he jammed his hands into his pockets, paced away, paced back. 'Just hear me out. A few days ago he told me two versions of that night. The first jibes with your findings, almost a perfect match. He's into the part when he's describing it. He could've been replaying a murder scene in a brutal movie. Then he tells me the other way, the way he got there and found her. His hands shake, and he goes pale. His voice races up and down like a roller coaster.'

'Which did you believe?'

'Both.'

Frank nodded. 'And he told you last the way that makes him innocent. Let that impression dig the deepest.'

Noah hissed out a breath. 'Yeah, I thought of that.'

'Maybe he still wishes it was the second way. One thing I believed, Noah, is that after, he wished she hadn't opened the door that night. And you can't ever forget that one vital point,' Frank added. 'He's an actor and knows how to sell himself.'

'I'm not forgetting,' Noah murmured. But he was wondering.

*

He decided to swing by and see his mother. He planned on heading to Washington the following day. This time he'd fly up, then rent a car. He didn't want to waste time on the road.

Celia was sitting on their little side deck, going through the mail and sipping a tall glass of herbal sun tea. She lifted her cheek for Noah to kiss, then wagged a form letter at him. 'Have you seen this? They're threatening to cut the funding for the preservation of the northern elephant seal.'

'Must've missed that one.'

'It's disgraceful. Congress votes itself a raise, spends millions of taxpayer dollars on studies to study studies of studies, but they'll sit back and let another of the species on our planet become extinct.'

'Go get 'em, Mom.'

She huffed, put the letter aside and opened another. 'Your father's at the youth center.'

'I know, I was just there. I thought I'd come by and see you before I headed to Washington tomorrow.'

'I'm glad you did. Why don't you stay for dinner? I've got a new recipe for artichoke bottoms I want to try out.'

'Gee, that sounds . . . tempting, but I have to pack.'

'Liar,' she said with a laugh. 'How long will you be gone?'

'Depends.'

'Is the book giving you trouble?'

'Some, nothing major.'

'What then?'

'I've got a little hang-up going.' He picked up her tea, sipped. Winced. She refused to add even a grain of sugar. 'A personal-level hang-up. On Olivia MacBride.'

'Really?' Celia drew out the word, giving it several syllables, and grinned like a contented cat. 'Isn't that nice?'

'I don't know how nice it is or why you'd be so pleased about it. You haven't seen her since she was a kid.'

'I've read her letters to your father. She appears to me a smart, sensible young woman, which is a far cry from your usual choice, particularly that creature Caryn. She still hasn't turned up, by the way.'

'Fine. Let her stay in whatever hole she dug for herself.'

'I suppose I have to agree. And to backtrack, I like hearing you say you're interested in someone. You never tell me you're interested in a woman. Just that you're seeing one.'

'I've been interested in Liv for years.'

'Really? How? She was, what, twelve, when you last saw her.'

'Eighteen. I went up to see her six years ago, when she was in college.'

Surprised, Celia stopped opening mail. 'You went to see her? You never mentioned it.'

'No, mostly because I wasn't too happy with the way it worked out.' He blew out a breath. 'Okay, condensed version. I wanted to write the book, even then. I went to see her to talk her into cooperating. Then I saw her, and . . . Man, it just blasted through me. I couldn't think, with all the stuff going on inside me just looking at her, I didn't think.'

'Noah.' Celia closed a hand over his. 'I had no idea you'd ever felt that way, with anyone.'

'I've felt that way with her, and I ruined it. When she found out why I was there, it hurt her. She wouldn't listen to apologies or explanations. She just closed the door.'

'Has she opened it again?'

'I think she's pulled back a couple of the locks.'

'You weren't honest with her before, and it ended badly. That should tell you something.'

'It does. But first I have to wear her down.' Because he felt better having just said it all out loud, he smiled. 'She's a hell of a lot tougher than she was at eighteen.'

'You'll think more of her if she makes you work.' She patted his hand, then went back to the mail. 'I know you, Noah. When you want something, you go after it. Maybe not all at once, but you keep at it until you have it.'

'Well, it feels like I've been going after Olivia MacBride most of my life. Meanwhile . . . Mom? What is it?' She'd gone deadly pale, had him leaping up fearing a heart attack.

'Noah. Oh God.' She gripped the hand he'd pressed to her face. 'Look. Look.'

He pulled the paper out of her hand, ignoring it while he struggled to keep them both calm. 'Take it easy. Just sit still. Catch your breath. I'll call the doctor.'

'No, for God's sake, look!' She took his wrist, yanked the paper he held back down.

He saw it then. The photocopy was fuzzy, poorly reproduced,

but he recognized the work of the police photographer documenting the body of Julie MacBride at the scene of the murder.

He had a copy of the picture in his own files, and though he'd looked at it countless times, the stark black and white was freshly appalling.

No, not a photocopy, he realized. Computer-scanned, just as the bold letters beneath the picture were computer-generated.

IT CAN HAPPEN AGAIN.
IT CAN HAPPEN TO YOU.

Rage, cold and controlled, coated him as he looked into his mother's horrified, baffled eyes. 'He flicked the wrong switch this time,' Noah murmured.

He waited until his father came racing home. But no amount of arguing or pleading could make him wait until the police arrived.

The son of a bitch had played him all right and had nearly sucked him in. Now he'd threatened his family. Revenge, Noah supposed as he slammed out of his car and strode down Sunset. Revenge against the cop who'd helped lock him away. Go after the family. Lure the son in, dangle the story, take the money, then terrorize the wife.

Noah pushed through the front entrance of the apartment unit, flicked a glance at the elevator and chose the stairs. The mighty had fallen here, he thought. The paint was peeling, the treads grimy, and he caught the sweet whiff of pot still clinging to the air.

But he hadn't fallen far enough.

The bastard liked women as his victims. Noah pounded a fist on the door of the second-floor apartment. Women and little girls. They'd just see how well he handled it when he had a man to deal with.

He pounded again and seriously considered kicking the door in. The cold edge of his rage had flashed to a burn.

'If you're looking for the old man, he split.'

Noah glanced around, saw the woman – hell, the hooker, he corrected.

'Split where?'

'Hey, I don't keep tabs on the neighbors, honey. You a cop?'

'No, I've got business with him, that's all.'

'Look a little like a cop,' she decided after an expert up-and-down survey. 'Parole officer?'

'What makes you think he needs one?'

'Shit, you think I can't spot a con? He did some long time. What he do, kill somebody?'

'I just want to talk to him.'

'Well, he ain't here.' She kept moving, giving Noah a unattractive whiff of cheap perfume and stale sex. 'Packed up his little bag and moved out yesterday.'

Long after the Center had closed for the day, Olivia worked in her office. The paperwork had a nasty habit of building up on her during late spring and summer. She much preferred taking groups on the trail, giving lectures or heading a tour of the backcountry for a few days.

She caught herself staring at the phone, again, and muttered curses under her breath. It was humiliating, absolutely mortifying, to realize that part of the reason she was working late again was the hope that Noah would call.

Which he hadn't done in two days, she reminded herself. Not that he was under any obligation to call her, of course. Not that she couldn't, if she wanted to, call him. Which she wouldn't do because, damn it, it would look at if she was hoping he'd call.

She was acting like a high-school girl with a crush. At least she thought she was. She'd never been a high-school girl with a crush. Apparently she'd had more sense at sixteen than she had now.

Now she daydreamed over the flowers he'd sent. She remembered the exact tone of his voice when he'd said her name. After he'd kissed her. The texture of his hands against her face. The little lurch of shock and pleasure in her own stomach.

The way he talked and talked, she thought now, poking and prodding at her until she gave up and laughed. He'd been the first man she'd ever been attracted to who could make her laugh.

He was certainly the only man she'd ever thought about after he was out of sight.

No, maybe she should say the second man, as the younger version of Noah had attracted her, charmed her, confused her. They were both just different enough now for this . . . whatever it was between them, to be somehow new. And very compelling.

Which, she supposed, said as much about her as it did about him.

She hadn't wanted anything but surface involvements, and she hadn't wanted many of those.

Why in the world was she sitting here analyzing her feelings when she didn't want to have any feelings in the first place? She had enough to worry about without adding Noah Brady to the mix.

She glanced toward her little storage closet. She'd buried the music box under the packing, stuffed it in the closet. Why had he sent it? Was it a peace offering or a threat? She didn't want the first and refused to be intimidated by the second.

But she hadn't been able to throw it away.

When the phone rang, she jumped foolishly, then rolled her eyes in annoyance. It had to be Noah, she thought. Who else would call so late? She caught herself before she could snatch eagerly at the receiver, deliberately let it ring three full times while she took careful breaths.

When she picked it up, her voice was cool and brisk. 'River's End Naturalist Center.'

She heard the music, just the faint drift of it, and imagined Noah setting a scene for a romantic phone call. She started to laugh, to open her mouth to make some pithy comment, then found herself unable to speak at all.

She recognized it now, Tchaikovsky's *Sleeping Beauty.*

The soaring, liquid, heartbreaking notes of it that took her back to a warm summer night and the metallic scent of blood.

Her hand tightened on the receiver while the panic-trip of her heart filled her head. 'What do you want?' Her free hand pressed and rubbed between her breasts as if to shove back the rising pressure. 'I know who you are. I know what you are.'

The monster was free.

'I'm not afraid of you.'

It was a lie. Terror, hot, greasy flows of it swam into her belly and slicked over her skin. She wanted to crawl under her desk, roll up into a ball. Hide. Just hide.

'Stay away from me.' Fear broke through, spiking her voice. 'Just stay away!'

She slammed the receiver down and, with panic bubbling madly in her throat, ran.

The doorknob slipped out of her hand, making her whimper

with frustration until she could cement her grip. The Center was dark, silent. She nearly cowered back, but the phone rang again. Her own screams shocked her, sent her skidding wildly across the floor. Her breath tore out of her lungs, sobbed through the silence. She had to get out. To run. To be safe.

And as she reached for the door, the knob turned sharply. The door opened wide, and in its center was the shadow of a man.

Her vision went gray and hazy. Dimly she heard someone call her name. Hands closed over her arms. She felt herself sway, then slide through them into the black.

'Hey, hey, hey. Come on. Come back.'

Her head reeled. She felt little pats on her face, the brush of lips over hers. It took her a moment to realize she was on the floor, being rocked like a baby in Noah's lap.

'Stop slapping me, you moron.' She lay still, weak from embarrassment and the dregs of panic.

'Oh yeah, that's better. Good.' He covered her mouth with his, poured an ocean of relief into the kiss. 'That's the first time I ever had a woman faint at my feet. Can't say I like it one damn bit.'

'I didn't faint.'

'You did a mighty fine imitation, then.' She'd only been out for seconds, he realized, though it had seemed to take a lifetime for her to melt in his grip. 'I'm sorry I scared you, coming in that way. I saw your office light.'

'Let me up.'

'Let's just sit here a minute. I don't think my legs are ready to try standing yet.' He rested his cheek on hers. 'So, how've you been otherwise?'

She wanted to laugh, and to weep. 'Oh, just fine thanks. You?'

He shifted her so he could grin into her face. Then just the look of her, clear amber eyes, pale skin, had something moving inside him. 'I really missed you.' His hand roamed through her hair now, stroking. 'It's so weird. Do you know how much time we've actually spent together?'

'No.'

'Not enough,' he murmured, and lowered his mouth to hers again. This time her lips were soft and welcomed him. Her arms lifted and enfolded him. He felt himself sink, then settle so that even the wonder of it seemed as natural as breathing.

She had no defenses now. He drew her in, soft, slow, sure until there was nothing but that stirring mating of lips.

'Liv.' He traced kisses along her jaw, up to her temple. 'Let me close the door.'

'Hmm?'

Her sleepy answer had sparks of heat simmering inside the warmth. 'The door.' His hand brushed over her breast, his fingers spreading as she arched toward him. 'I don't want to make love with you in an open doorway.'

She made another humming sound, scraping her teeth over his bottom lip as she slapped at the door in an attempt to close it herself.

Then the phone rang, and she was clawing to get free.

'It's just the phone. Christ.' To defend himself, he clamped his arms over hers.

'It's him. Let me go! It's him.'

He didn't ask whom she meant. She only used that tone when she spoke of her father. 'How do you know?'

Her eyes wheeled white with panic. 'He called before – just before.'

'What did he say to you?'

'Nothing.' Overwhelmed, she curled up, clamped her hands over her ears. 'Nothing, nothing.'

'It's okay, it's all right. Stay right here.' He nudged her aside and with blood in his eye strode into the office. Even as he reached for the receiver, the ringing stopped.

'It was him.' She'd managed to get up, managed to walk to the door. But she was shaking. 'He didn't say anything. He just played the music. The music my mother had on the stereo the night he killed her. He wants me to know he hasn't forgotten.'

Chapter Twenty-five

He'd managed to book a room, but had been warned it was only available for one night. For the remainder of the month, the lodge was fully booked. There were a couple of campsites still available, but he couldn't work up any enthusiasm in that area.

Still, he was going to have to snag one, and buy himself some camping equipment if he meant to stay.

And he meant to stay.

His original plan had been to rent a snazzy suite in some hotel within reasonable driving distance where he could work in comfort and seduce Olivia in style. After what he'd learned the night before, he wasn't willing to stay that far away.

He intended to keep an eye on her. The only way to accomplish that was to stay put and to be more stubborn than she was.

There'd been a test of that the night before as well. She'd told him about the phone call, the music box, and her fear had been alive in the room with them. But the moment she'd gotten it out, she'd toughened up again, stepped back from him.

He thought part of it had been an incredibly misplaced sense of embarrassment at showing a weakness. But on another level, he decided this was the way she'd shored up any holes in her defenses for years. She set it aside, closed it off and refused to talk about it.

She'd fired up when he'd said he was taking her home. She knew the way, he'd get lost on the way back, she didn't need a bodyguard. And wouldn't be *taken* anywhere by anyone.

Noah stepped out on his tiny first-floor patio and scanned the deep green of the summer forest.

He'd never actually dragged a woman to his car before, he

thought now. Never seriously wrestled with one in a personal match that didn't have the end goal of sex on the minds of both participants. And he'd never come quite so close to losing to a girl.

He rubbed his bruised ribs absently.

He wondered if he should be ashamed of having enjoyed it quite so much, then decided against it. He'd gotten her home safely, had managed to block her last punch long enough to punctuate his victory with a very satisfying kiss.

Until she'd bitten him.

God, he was crazy about her.

And concerned enough to make him determined to deal with Sam Tanner. To keep Olivia safe and to give her some peace of mind.

He went back inside and called his father. 'How's Mom?'

'She's fine. I drove her in to work today and browbeat a promise out of her that she wouldn't go anywhere alone. I'll be driving her to and from until . . . until.'

'No word on Tanner?'

'No. He withdrew two thousand in cash from his bank account. He rented his room by the week and had paid up. We're – the police are interested in questioning him about the picture, but there's not a lot they can do. I tugged some strings and had a couple of my buddies check the airports and train stations for reservations in his name. Nothing.'

'He needs to be found. Hire a detective. The best you know. I can afford it.'

'Noah—'

'This is my party, I foot the bill. I'll arrange for you to leave messages for me here at the lodge. I'm going to be doing the tent thing for a while and I might not have my cell phone on me, so I won't always be reachable. I'll be checking in as often as I can.'

'Noah, if he's decided it's payback, you're a target. He's dying, he's got nothing to lose.'

'I grew up with a cop. I know how to handle myself. Take care of Mom.'

Frank waited a beat. 'I know how to take care of what's mine. Watch yourself, Noah.'

'Same goes.' He hung up, then paced the little room while he tried to juggle an idea out of his mind. When it came, it was so simple, so perfect, he grinned. 'I know how to take care of what's mine, too,' he murmured. And hoping she'd cooled off, he went to find Olivia.

She hadn't cooled off. In fact, she was nursing her temper as a devoted mother would a fretful baby. She'd take spit-in-his-eye temper over the sick, shaky panic she felt every time her office phone rang.

So she nurtured it, she used it, she all but wallowed in it.

When Noah walked into her office, she got to her feet, slowly, her eyes cold, steady. Like a gunfighter, she shot fast and from the hip.

'Get your sorry ass out of my office. And off MacBride property. If you're not checked out and gone inside of ten minutes, I'm calling the cops and having you charged with assault.'

'You'll never make it stick,' he said with a cheer he knew would infuriate her. 'I'm the one with the bruises. Don't swear,' he added quickly and shut the door at his back. 'There're young, impressionable children out there. Now, I've got a deal for you.'

'A deal for me?' She bared her teeth in a snarl, then jerked back when the phone rang.

Before she could move, Noah snatched it off the hook himself. 'River's End Naturalist Center. Ms. MacBride's office. This is Raoul, her personal assistant. I'm sorry, she's in a meeting. Would you like—'

'Idiot.' She hissed at him and wrestled the phone out of his hand. 'This is Olivia MacBride.'

Noah shrugged, then wandered around the room as she dealt with business. When she ended the conversation, then said nothing, he checked the soil of a nicely blooming African violet. 'I've been thinking about taking a few days to get away from technology,' he decided. 'To test myself. Man against nature, you know.' He looked back.

She was still standing, but she had her hands linked together now. The fire had gone out of her eyes, leaving them carefully blank.

'I'd think less of you if you weren't afraid, because then I'd think you were stupid.' He said it quietly, with just the slightest edge of annoyance. How could he see so much, she wondered, without even seeming to look?

'I'm not a damsel in distress. I can take care of myself.'

'Good, because I'm hoping you'll be looking after me the next few days. I want to do some hiking and camping in the backcountry.'

Her laugh came fast and was none too flattering. 'The hell you do.'

'Three days. You and me.' He held up a finger before she could laugh again. 'We get away for a while. You do what you do best. And so do I. You'd agreed to interviews, so we'll talk. This place is something you love, and I want you to show it to me. I want to see what you see when you look at it.'

'For the book.'

'No, for me. I want to be alone with you.'

She could feel her resolve, and her temper, melting. 'I've rethought that situation, and I'm not interested.'

'Yes, you are.' Unoffended, he took her hand, skimming his thumb over her knuckles. 'You're just mad at me because I outmuscled you last night. Actually, it wasn't— ' He broke off as he glanced down at her hand and saw the faint trail of bruises just above her wrist. 'I guess I'm not the only one with bruises.' He lifted her wrist, kissed it. 'Sorry.'

'Cut it out.' She slapped his hand away. 'All right, I'm mad because you saw me at my worst, my weakest, and I let you see it. I'm mad because you wouldn't leave me alone, and I'm mad because I like being with you even when you irritate me.'

'You can count on staying mad for a while, then. I'm not going anywhere until we figure everything out. Let's go play in the forest, Livvy.'

'I have work.'

'I'm a paying client. And as part of the deal, you can give me a list of what I need and I'll buy what's available at the lodge. Between the guide fee and the equipment, you're going to take in a couple of grand easy. Delegate, Liv. You know you can.'

'You also need backcountry permits.'

'What'll they think of next?'

'Twenty-four hours, you'll be crying for your laptop.'

'Bet?'

'Hundred bucks.'

'Deal.' He gave her hand a squeeze.

*

He hadn't expected her to send over a list that included wardrobe, detailing down to how many pairs of socks and underwear she recommended he take for the trip. It was like being twelve again and getting a to-do list from his mother.

He bought the gear, including a new backpack, as she'd pointed out on her list that his was too small and had a number of holes in it. And though they were going to weigh him down, he bought two bottles of wine and nested them inside spare socks.

Camping was one thing. Going primitive was another.

By the time he was done, he figured he'd be carrying thirty-five pounds on his back. And imagined after five miles or so it would weigh like a hundred.

With some regret he locked his cell phone and laptop in the trunk of the rental car. 'I'll be back, boys,' he murmured.

'Looks like I'm going to win that hundred bucks before we leave.'

'That wasn't whining. It was a fond farewell.'

He turned and studied her. She wore jeans, roomy and faded, a River's End T-shirt and a light jacket tied around her waist. Sturdy boots, he noted, with a number of impressive nicks and scars on the leather. She carried her pack as though it were weightless.

The smirk suited her. 'You sure you're up for this?'

'I'm raring.'

She adjusted the cap that shaded her eyes, then jerked her thumb. 'Let's get started.'

He found the forest more appealing if no less primitive without the rain they'd hiked through the last time. Little slivers of sunlight fought their way through gaps in the overstory, shimmering unexpectedly on the now-lush green leaves of the maples and the fragile blades of ferns.

The air cooled. Ripened.

He remembered and recognized much of the life around him now. The varied patterns of bark on the giant trees, the shape of leaves of the shrub layer. The vast, nubby carpets of moss didn't seem quite so foreign, nor did the knobs and scallops of lichen.

He gave her silence as his muscles warmed to the pace and tuned his ears to the rustles and calls that brought music to the forest.

She waited for him to speak, to ask questions or fall into one of those casual monologues he was so skilled at. But he said nothing, and the vague tension she'd strapped on with her pack slid away.

They crossed a narrow stream that bubbled placidly, skirted a leafy bed of ferns, then began to climb the long, switchbacking trail that would take them into backcountry.

Vine maple grew thick, an elastic tangle of inconvenience along the trail. Olivia avoided it when she could, worked through it when she couldn't and once grabbed at it quickly before it would swing back and thwack Noah in the face.

'Thanks.'

'I thought you'd lost your voice.'

'You wanted quiet.' He reached over to rub his hand over the back of her neck. 'Had enough?'

'I just tune you out when you talk too much.'

Noah chuckled then went on.

'I really like being with you, Liv.' He took her hand, sliding his fingers through hers. 'I always did.'

'You'll throw off your pace.'

'What's the hurry?' He brought her hand to his lips in an absent gesture.

'I thought you'd bring Shirley.'

'She sticks with Grandpop most days, and dogs aren't allowed in the backcountry. Here, look.' She stopped abruptly and crouched, tapping a finger beside faint imprints on the trail.

'Are those—'

'Bear tracks,' she said. 'Pretty fresh, too.'

'How do you know that? They always say that in the movies. The tracks are fresh,' he said in a grunting voice. 'He passed through here no more than an hour ago wearing a black hat, eating a banana and whistling "Sweet Rosie from Pike".'

He made her laugh. 'All the bears I know whistle show tunes.'

'You made a joke, Liv.' He ducked his head and gave her a loud kiss. 'Congratulations.'

She scowled at him and rose. 'No kissing on the trail.'

'I didn't read that in my camper's guide.' He got to his feet and started after her. 'How about eating? Is there eating on the trail?'

She'd anticipated his stomach. Digging into her pocket, she pulled out a bag of trail mix, passed it to him.

'Yum-yum, bark and twigs, my favorite.' But he opened the bag and offered her a share.

He would have taken her hand again, but the trail narrowed and she bumped him back. Still, he thought she'd smiled more in the last ten minutes than she usually did in a full day. Some time alone together in the world she loved best was working for both of them.

'You have a great butt, Liv.'

This time she didn't bother to hold on to the vine maple and smiled again when she heard the slap and his muffled curse. Olivia took a swig from her canteen as they climbed. The light sweat she'd worked up felt good; it felt healthy. Her muscles were limber, her mind clear. And, she admitted, she was enjoying the company.

She'd chosen this trail, one that skirted up the canyon, because other hikers rarely chose to negotiate it. Long switchbacks leading to steep terrain discouraged many. But she considered it one of the most beautiful and appreciated the solitude.

They moved through the lush forest, thick with green, climbing up and down ridges, along a bluff that afforded views of the river that ran silver and smooth. Wildlife was plentiful here where the majestic elk wandered and raccoon waddled to wash.

'I have dreams about this.' Noah spoke half to himself as he stopped, just to look.

'About hiking?'

'No, about being here.' He tried to catch hold of them, the fragments and slippery pieces of subconscious. 'Green and thick, with the sound of water running by. And . . . I'm looking for you.' His gaze snapped to hers, held with that sudden intensity that always rocked her. 'Olivia. I've been looking for you for a long time.'

When he stepped forward, she felt her heart flutter wildly. 'We have a long way to go.'

'I don't think so.' Gently, he laid his hands on her shoulders, slid them down to cuff her wrists. 'Come here a minute.'

'I don't—'

'Want kissing on the trail,' he finished. 'Too bad.' He dipped his head, brushed his lips over hers once. Then again. 'You're shaking.'

'I am not.' Her bones had gone too soft to tremble.

'Maybe it's me. Either way, it looks like this time I finally found you.'

She was afraid he was right.

She drew away and, too unsteady to speak, continued up the trail.

The first wet crossing was over a wide stream where the water ran clear and fast. A log bridge spanned it, and dotting the banks were clumps of wild foxglove with deep pink bells and a scatter of columbine with its bicolored trumpets. The scenery took a dramatic turn, from the deep, dank green of the river basin to the stunning old-growth forest where light speared down in shafts and pools.

And the ancient trees grew straight as soldiers, tall as giants, their tops whispering sealike in the wind that couldn't reach the forest floor.

Through their branches he could see the dark wings of an eagle picked out against the vivid blue of the summer sky.

Here among the ferns and mosses were bits and splashes of white, the frilly tips of fringecups, the blood-red veins of wood sorrel against its snowy petals, the tiny cups of tiarella.

Fairy flowers, Noah thought, hiding in the shade or dancing near the fitful stream.

Saying nothing, he dragged off his pack.

'I take that to mean you want a break.'

'I just want to be here for a while. It's a great spot.'

'Then you don't want a sandwich.'

His brows went up. 'Who says?'

Even as she reached up to release her pack, he was behind her, lifting it off. She figured it was fifty percent courtesy, fifty percent greed for the food she had packed inside. Since she could appreciate both, she unzipped the compartment that held sandwiches and vegetable sticks.

He was right about the spot. It was a great one in which to sit and relax, to let the body rest and recharge. Water in the thin stream chugged over rocks and sparkled in the narrow beams of sunlight filtering through the canopy. The scent of pine sharpened the air. Ferns fanned over the bank, lushly green. A duet of wood thrush darted by with barely a sound, and deeper in the woods came the cackling call of a raven.

'How often do you get out here?' Noah asked her when only crumbs remained.

'I take groups out four or five times a year anyway.'

'I didn't mean a working deal. How often do you get out here like this, to sit and do nothing for a while?'

'Not in a while.' She breathed deep, leaning back on her elbows and closing her eyes. 'Not in too long a while.'

She looked relaxed, he noted. As if at last her thoughts were quiet. He had only to shift to lay his hand over hers, to lay his lips over hers.

Gently, so sweetly her heart sighed even as she opened her eyes to study him. 'You're starting to worry me a little, Noah. Tell me, what are you after?'

'I think I've been pretty up-front about that. And I wonder why it surprises both of us that through all this, maybe right from the beginning of all this, I've had feelings for you. I want some time to figure out what those feelings are. Most of all, Liv, right now, I want you.'

'How healthy is it, Noah, that this connection you believe in has its roots in murder? Don't you ever ask yourself that?'

'No. But I guess you do.'

'I didn't before six years ago. But yes, I do now. It's an intricate part of my life and who I am. An intimate part of it. Monster and victim, they're both inside of me.' She drew her knees up, wrapped her arms around them. It disturbed her to realize she'd never spoken like that to anyone before, not even family. 'You need to think about that before any of this goes . . . anywhere.'

'Liv.' He waited until she turned her head toward him, then his hands caught her face firmly, his mouth crushed down hard and hot and heady on hers. 'You need to think about that,' he told her. 'Because this is already going everywhere, and for me at least, it's going there pretty damn fast.'

More disturbed than she wanted to admit, she got to her feet. 'Sex is easy, it's just a basic human function.'

He kept his eyes on hers as he rose, the deep green diving in and absorbing her. 'I'm going to enjoy, really enjoy proving you wrong.' Then in an abrupt change of mood she couldn't keep up with, he hauled up his pack, and shot her a blatantly arrogant grin. 'When I'm inside you, Olivia, the one thing I promise you won't feel is easy.'

She decided it was wiser not to discuss it. He couldn't understand her, the limitations of her emotions, the boundaries she'd had to erect for self-preservation. And he, she admitted as they headed up the trail again, was the first man who had made her feel even a twinge of regret for the necessity.

She liked being with him. That alone was worrying. He made her forget he'd once broken her heart, made her forget she didn't want to risk it again. Other men she'd dealt with had bored or irritated her within weeks. Olivia had never considered that a problem, but more a benefit. If she didn't care enough to get involved, there was no danger of losing her way, losing her head or her heart.

And ending up a victim.

The sunlight grew stronger as they climbed, the light richer. White beams of it shot down in streams and bands and teased the first real spots of color out of the ground.

There were the deep scarlet bells of wild penstemon, the crisp yellow of paintbrush. New vistas flashed as they hiked along a ridge with the long, long vees of valleys below, the sharp rise of forested hills rising around them.

At the next wet crossing, the river was fast and rocky with a thundering waterfall tumbling down the face of the cliff.

'There. Over there.' Olivia gestured, then dug for her binoculars. 'He's fishing.'

'Who?' Noah narrowed his eyes and followed the direction of her hand. He saw a dark shape hunched on an island of rock in the churning river. 'Is that – Christ! It's a bear.' He snatched the binoculars Olivia offered and stared through them.

The bear slammed into his field of vision, nearly made him jolt. He leaned forward on the rustic bridge and studied the bear as the bear studied the water. In a lightning move, one huge black paw swept into the stream, spewing up drops. And came out again locked around a wriggling fish that flashed silver in the sun.

'Got one! Man, did you see that? Snagged it out of the water, first try.'

She hadn't seen. She'd been watching Noah – the surprise and excitement on his face, the utter fascination in it.

Noah shook his head as the bear devoured his snack. 'Great fishing skills, lousy table manners.' He lowered the binoculars, started to hand them back and caught Olivia staring at him.

'Something wrong?'

'No.' Maybe everything, she thought, is either very wrong or very right. 'Nothing. We'd better go if we want to make camp before we lose the light.'

'Got a specific place in mind?'

'Yes. You'll like it. We'll follow the river now. About another hour.'

Another hour.' He shifted his pack on his shoulders. 'Are we heading to Canada?'

'You wanted backcountry,' she reminded him. 'You get backcountry.'

She was right about one thing, Noah decided when they reached the site. He liked it. They were tucked among the giant trees with the river spilling over tumbled rocks. The light was gilded, the wind a whisk of air that smelled of pine and water.

'I'm going upstream to catch dinner.' As she spoke she took a retractable rod out of her pack.

'Very cool.'

'If I get lucky, we eat like bears tonight. If I don't, we have some dehydrated food packs.'

'Get lucky, Liv.'

'Can you set up the tent while I'm fishing?'

'Sure, you go hunt up food, I'll make the nest. I have no problem with role reversal whatsoever.'

'Ha. If you want to wander, just stay in sight of the river, check your compass. If you get lost—'

'I won't. I'm not a moron.'

'If you get lost,' she repeated. 'Sit down and wait for me to find you.' He looked so insulted, she patted his cheek. 'You've done just fine so far, city boy.'

He watched her go and promised himself he would do a whole lot better.

Chapter Twenty-six

The tent didn't come with instructions, which Noah thought was a definite flaw in the system. By his calculation, setting up camp took him about triple the amount of time and energy it would have taken Olivia. But he decided he'd keep that little bit of information to himself.

She'd been gone more than an hour by the time he was reasonably sure the tent would stay in an upright position. Assuming she wasn't having the same luck the bear had had with fishing, he explored their other menu choices. Dry packs of fruit, dehydrated soup and powdered eggs assured him that while they might not eat like kings, they wouldn't starve.

With nothing left on his chore list and no desire to explore after a full day of hiking, he settled down to write in longhand.

It was Olivia he concentrated on, what she had done with her life, the goals she'd focused on, what, in his mind, she'd accomplished and the ways he calculated she'd limited herself. The roots of her childhood had caused her to grow in certain directions, even while stunting her in others.

Would she have been more open, more sociably inclined if her mother had lived? Would she have been less driven to stand on her own if she'd grown up the pampered, indulged child of a Hollywood star?

How many men would have walked in and out of her life? Did she ever wonder? Would all that energy and intelligence have been channeled into the entertainment field, or would she still have gone back to her mother's roots and chosen the isolation?

Considering it, considering her, he let his notebook rest on his knee and just looked. The stream gurgled by. The trees towered, their topmost branches spearing through sky and dancing to the wind. The stillness was broken by the music of the water, the call of birds that nested and fed in the forest around him. He saw a lone elk, its rack crown-regal, slip out of the trees and pause to drink downstream.

He wished he had the skill to draw, but contented himself with etching the memory on his mind as the elk strode without hurry into the deepening shadows of the great firs.

She would have come back, Noah decided. Perhaps her life wouldn't have been centered here, but she would have been pulled back to this, time and again. As her mother had been.

Sense memory, he thought, or the roots that dig themselves into the heart before we're old enough to know it. She would have needed this place, the smells and the sounds of it. She needed it now, not only for her work and her peace of mind. It was here she could find her mother.

The cry of an eagle had him looking up, watching the flight. She spread her wings here, too, Noah decided. But did she realize that for every time she soared, she offset it by running back to the closet and closing herself into the dark?

He wrote down his thoughts, his impressions, listened to the life ebb and swell around him. When his mind drifted, he stretched out on the bank and slipped into dreams.

She had three fine trout. She'd caught the first two within an hour, but knowing his appetite, she'd taken the time to wait for the third to take the hook. She'd found a nice bramble of huckleberries. Her hat was full of them, and their sweet taste sat nicely on her tongue as she wandered back to camp.

The time alone had quieted her mind, and soothed away the edge of nerves being too close and too long in Noah's company seemed to produce. Her problem, she reminded herself. She just wasn't used to being with a man on the level Noah Brady insisted on. She was no more ready for him now than she'd been at eighteen.

Sexually it should have been simple enough. But he kept tangling intimacy and friendship so casually she found herself responding in kind before she'd thought it through.

Thinking it through was vital.

She liked him well enough, she thought now. He was a likable man. So much so she tended to forget how close he could get, how much he could see. Until his eyes went dark and quiet and simply stripped her down to her deepest secrets.

She didn't want a man who could see inside her that way. She preferred the type that skimmed the surface, accepted it and moved on.

If admitting that caused an ache around her heart, she'd live with it. Better an ache than pain.

Better alone than consumed.

She thought they'd deal with each other well enough now. This was her turf, after all, and she had the home advantage. She'd made the decision to talk to him about her childhood, what she remembered, what she'd experienced. It wouldn't be without difficulty, but she'd made the choice.

A choice, she understood, she couldn't have made when he'd come to her at college. She'd been too soft yet, too unsteady. He might have talked her into it, because she'd been so in love with him, but it would have been a disaster for her.

In some part of her heart she'd always wanted to say it all, to get it out and remember her mother in some tangible way. Now she was ready for it. This was her opportunity, and she was grateful she could speak of it to someone she respected.

To someone, she realized, who understood well enough to make it all matter.

She saw him sleeping by the stream and smiled. She'd pushed him hard, she thought, and he'd held together. A glance around camp showed her he'd done well enough there, too. She secured her line and placed the fish into the running water to keep them fresh, then settled down beside him to watch the water.

He sensed her, and she became part of the dream where he walked through the forest in the soft green light. He shifted toward her, reached out to touch. Reached out to take.

She pulled away, an automatic denial. But the half-formed protest she'd begun to make slipped back down her throat as his eyes opened, green and intense. Her breath caught at what she saw in them, in the way they stayed locked on hers as he sat up and took her face in his hands. Held it as if he had the right. As if he'd always had the right.

'Look, I don't—'

He only shook his head to stop the words, and his eyes never left hers as he drew her closer, as his mouth covered hers. And the taste was ripe and hot and ready.

She trembled, maybe in protest, maybe in fear. He wouldn't accept either. This time she would take what he had to give her, what he'd just come to realize he'd held inside for years to give her, only.

His hands moved from her face, through her hair, over her shoulders as the kiss roughened, and he pushed her back on the ground and covered her.

Panic scrambled inside her to race with desire that had sprung up fast and feral. She pushed at his shoulders as if to hold him off even as she arched up to grind need against need.

'I can't give you what you want. I don't have it in me.'

How could she not see what he saw? Not feel what he felt? He took his mouth on a journey of her face while she quivered under him. 'Then take what you want.' His lips brushed hers, teasing, testing. 'Let me touch you.' He skimmed his hand up her ribs, felt the ripple of reaction as his fingers closed lightly over her breast. 'Let me have you. Here, in the sunlight.'

He lowered his mouth to within a whisper of hers, then shifted it to her jaw and heard her moan. The taste of her there, just there along that soft, vulnerable spot where her pulse beat thick and fast, flooded into him.

He said her name, only her name, and she was lost.

Her fingers dug into his shoulders, then dragged through his hair to fist hard, to bring his mouth back to hers so she could pull him under with her.

A savage rush of delight, a raw edge of desire. She felt them both as his mouth warred with hers, knew the reckless greed as he yanked her shirt up, tore it away and filled his hands with her.

Strong and possessive, flesh molding flesh with the rocky ground under her back and the primitive beat of blood in her veins. For the first time when a man's body pressed down on hers, she yielded. To him, to herself. As something inside her went silky, her mind went blissfully blank, then filled with him.

He felt the change, not just in the giving of her body, the deepening of her breath. Surrender came sweet and unexpected.

She was still the woman he'd fallen headlong in love with.

His hands slowed, gentled, soothing trembles, inciting more.

With a kind of lazy deliberation that sent her head reeling, he began a long, savoring journey.

Pleasure shimmered over her skin, warmed it, sensitized it. She rose fluidly when he lifted her, cradled her. With a murmur of approval, she stripped his shirt away and reveled in the slick slide of flesh against flesh, of the surprising bunch of muscles under her hands, the comforting beat of his heart against hers.

'More.' In that dreamy altered state, she heard her own breathless demand and arched back to offer. 'Take more.'

She was willow slim and water soft. The lovely line of her throat drew his lips over and down. The curve of her breast a fascination, the taste of it fresh and his. Her breath hitched and released as he closed his mouth over her.

Need leaped in his belly.

There was more. More to taste, more to take. As her skin and muscles quivered, his mouth grew more urgent. Every demand was answered, a moan, a movement, a murmur.

He unhooked her jeans and when he skimmed his tongue under denim, her shocked jerk of response had dark and dangerous images swirling in his mind. He dragged them over her hips, and even as she reared up, took what he wanted.

It was a hot, smothering swell of sensation, air too thick to breathe, blood roaring to a scream in her ears. With mouth and teeth and tongue he drove her toward a peak she wasn't prepared to face. She choked out his name, fighting against a panicked excitement that threatened to swallow her whole.

Then her hands were gripped in his, held fast. Heat pumped through her, dewing her skin, scorching through her system until pain and pleasure fused into one vicious fist. The pressure of it had her strangling for air, straining for freedom even as her hips arched.

Then everything inside her broke apart, shattered into pieces that left her limp and defenseless.

Her cry of release shuddered through him. Her hands went lax in his. Everything he wanted whittled down to her, this place, this moment. So he watched her face as he drove her up again. Again.

Her eyes flew open, wide with shock, blind with pleasure. Her lips trembled as her breath tore through them. Sunlight scattered over her skin as she poured into his hand.

Blood screaming, muscles quivering, he held himself over her.

'Olivia.' Her name was raw in his throat and full of need. 'Look at me when I take you.' His eyes were as green and deep as the shadows behind them. 'Look at me when we take each other. Because it matters.'

He drove himself deep, buried himself inside her. Even as his vision dimmed at the edges he held on. The woman, the moment, and his certainty of each. Clinging to that clarity for another instant, he lowered his brow to hers. 'It's you,' he managed. 'It's always been you.'

Then his mouth took hers in a kiss as fierce as the sudden plunging of his body.

She couldn't move. Not only because he pinned her to the ground with the good, solid weight of a satisfied man, but because her own body was weak and her system still rocking from the sensory onslaught.

And because her mind, no matter how she fought to clear it, remained dazzled and dim.

She told herself it was just sex. It was important to believe it. But it had been beyond anything she'd ever experienced, and beneath the drugged pleasure was a growing unease.

She'd always considered sex a handy release valve, a necessary human function that was often an enjoyable exercise. Orgasms ranged from a surprising burst of pleasure to a slight ping of sensation, and she'd always considered herself responsible either way.

With Noah she didn't feel she'd had a chance to be responsible. He'd simply swept her up and along. She'd lost control, not only of her body but also of her will. And because of it she'd given him a part of herself she hadn't known existed. A part she hadn't wanted to exist.

She needed to get it back and lock it away again.

But when she started to shift, to push him aside, he simply tucked her up, rolled over and trapped her in a sprawl over him.

She wanted to lay her head over his heart, close her eyes and stay just as they were forever.

It scared her to death.

'It'll be dark soon. I have to get the cook camp set up, a fire started.'

He stroked a hand over her hair, enjoying the way it flowed to a stop at the nape of her neck. 'There's time.'

She pushed off, he pulled her back. It infuriated her that she was continually underestimating his strength – and his stubbornness. 'Look, pal, unless you want to go cold and hungry, we need wood.'

'I'll get it in a minute.' To make sure she stayed where he wanted her to, he reversed positions again, studied her face.

'You want to pull away, Liv. I won't let you. Not again.' He tried to disguise his hurt. 'You want to pretend that this was just a nice, hot bout of sex in the woods, no connection to what we started before, years ago.' He fisted a hand in her hair. 'But you can't. Can you?'

'Let me up, Noah.'

'And you're telling yourself it won't happen that way again,' Noah said angrily. 'That you won't feel what you felt with me again. But you're wrong.'

'Don't tell me what I think, what I feel.'

'I'm telling you what I see. It's right there, in you eyes. You have a hard time lying with them. So look at me.' He lifted her hips and slipped inside her again. 'Look at me and tell me what you think now. What you feel.'

'I don't—' He thrust hard and deep, hammering the orgasm through her. 'Oh, God.' She sobbed it out, arms and legs wrapping around him.

Driven as much by triumph as frustration he took her in a wild fury until he emptied.

When she was still shuddering, he rolled aside and, saying nothing, rose, dressed, then went to gather firewood.

She wondered why she'd ever believed she could handle him or herself around him. No one else had ever managed to befuddle her quite so much or so often.

He'd convinced her to be with him alone when she knew it was best if she conducted business with him in more traditional surroundings. He made her laugh when she didn't want to find him amusing. He made her think about things, about pain she'd so carefully tucked away.

Now he'd lured her into sex on the bank of a stream in daylight, along a route that, while not well traveled, was public land. If it had gone according to her own plans, they would have had their evening meal, perhaps some conversation, then some civilized, uncomplicated sex in the dark privacy of the tent.

Once that was out of the way, it would have been back to business.

Instead, everything was tangled up again. He was angry with her for something she couldn't, and wouldn't, change. And yes, something she hadn't quite forgiven him for. She was left feeling unsteady, inadequate and uneasy.

To compensate, she ignored him and went about the business of setting up the cook camp several safe feet from the sleeping area. She hung the food high, then gathered her tools and got down to the business of cleaning the fish for their dinner.

He was just like every other man, she told herself. Insulted because a woman isn't tongue-tied with delight at his sexual prowess. Miffed because she wasn't moony-eyed in infatuation, which he'd use up then discard anyway the minute it started to cramp his style.

It was a hell of a lot smarter to think like a man yourself, she decided, and avoid the pitfalls.

Let him sulk, she thought as she carefully buried the fish waste. When she heard him approach, she sniffed in derision and had no clue just how sulky her own face was when she lifted it to look up at him.

'What do you want?'

He decided, wisely, that she'd kick him in the ass if she had any idea just how easily he could read her. So he just held out the wine he'd poured. 'I brought some along. It's been cooling in the stream. Figured you'd be up for a glass about now.'

'I need to cook this fish.' She ignored the wine and strode back toward the fire.

'Tell you what.' Tongue tucked in his cheek, he strolled after her. 'Since you caught it and cleaned it – neither of which I have any experience in – I'll cook it.'

'This isn't your pretty kitchen. I don't want my catch going to waste.'

'Ah, a direct challenge.' He pushed the wine at her and snatched the skillet. 'Sit down, drink your wine and watch the master.'

She shrugged her shoulders and plucked a berry out of her hat. 'You screw it up, I'm not catching more.'

'Trust me.' His eyes met hers, held. 'I won't disappoint you, Liv.'

'You don't risk disappointment if you handle things yourself.'

'True enough, but you miss some interesting adventures. I had to learn to cook,' he continued, and changed the tone to light as he dribbled oil in the skillet. 'Out of self-defense. My mother believes tofu is all four of the major food groups. You have no idea what it's like to be a growing boy and be faced with a meal of tofu surprise after a hard day of school.'

Despite herself, her interest was caught. He'd unearthed the bag of herded flour she'd packed and was expertly coating the fish. Without thinking, she sipped the wine and found the light Italian white perfect.

She barely managed to muffle a sigh. 'I don't understand you.'

'Good, that's progress. You've spent most of our time together this round being sure you did and getting it dead wrong.' Satisfied, he slipped the fish into the hot oil to sizzle.

'An hour ago you were furious with me.'

'You got that right.'

'And now you're pouring wine, frying fish and sitting there as if nothing happened.'

'Not as if nothing happened.' For him everything had happened. He just had to wait for her to catch up. 'But I figure you're pissed off enough for both of us, so why waste the energy?'

'I don't like to be handled.'

His gaze flashed back to her. 'Neither do I.'

'We both know you wanted to come up here so I'd talk to you about your book without distractions or interruptions. But you haven't said anything about it.'

'I wanted to give you a day, to give us both a day. I wanted you.' He ran a finger down her arm. 'I still want you. I'd like it better if you were more comfortable with that.'

'I'd like it better if you'd keep it simple.'

'Well.' He poked at the fish. 'One of us isn't going to get what he or she wants. Better get the plates, partner. These boys are nearly ready.'

'Noah.'

'Hmm?' He glanced up, a tender look on his face, and her heart wanted to melt. So she shook her head. 'Nothing,' she said and reached for the plates.

*

Later, when the meal was finished and the forest dark and full of sound, it was she who turned to him. She who needed arms around her to chase away the dreams that haunted her and the fear that stalked with them.

And he was there, to hold her in the night, to move with her in a sweet and easy rhythm.

So when she slept, she slept curled against him, her hand fisted over his heart, her head in the curve of his shoulder. Noah lay awake, watching the play of moonlight over the tent, listening to the call of a coyote, the hoot of an owl and the short scream of its prey.

He wondered how it was possible that he'd never stopped loving her and what either of them, both of them, were going to do about it.

The monster

Deep into that darkness peering, long
I stood there wondering, fearing,
Doubting, dreaming dreams no mortal
ever dared to dream before.

—Edgar Allan Poe

Chapter Twenty-seven

Groggy, achy, Noah woke to birdsong. He sat up, tugged his jeans on and thought vaguely of breakfast. Through the sharp scent of pine and earth, he caught the wonderfully civilized aroma of coffee. And could have wept with gratitude for Olivia's consistent efficiency.

She'd built the morning campfire and had the coffeepot heating nicely. He burned his fingers on the handle, hissed a mild curse, then snatched up the cloth she'd left folded nearby to protect his hand.

One long sip had his eyes clearing and his system revving up. God bless a woman who appreciated strong black coffee, he thought, then stepped closer to the river to look for her.

Mists climbed up from the water to twine with sunbeams into silver and gold ribbons. A herd of deer drank lazily at the point where the stream curved like a bent finger and vanished into the trees.

And he saw her, hair wet and gleaming as she floated through the gilt-edged mists upstream, watching him with eyes as tawny as a cat's and just as wary.

She looked as though she belonged there, in the wild, in that unearthly, shimmering light.

The water rippled as she moved her arms, her shoulders rising over the surface. The mists seemed to open for her, then close again.

'I didn't expect you up so soon.' Her voice was quiet, but her eyes seemed full of storms.

'I'm an early riser. How's the water?'

'Wet.'

And freezing, he imagined. Still, he drank down the last of his coffee, then set the cup aside to pull off his jeans. He saw her eyes waver, then steady. What worries you, Olivia? he wondered. That it won't be the way it was between us last night? Or the possibility it will be?

The water was dazzlingly cold on his bare skin, and he saw her lips twitch when he winced. For no other reason than that, he bit back a yelp as he let himself slide in. He imagined his body going blue from the neck down.

'You're right,' he said when he was reasonably sure his teeth wouldn't chatter. 'It's wet, all right.'

It surprised her that he kept two arm spans' distance between them. She'd expected him to move toward her, move in. He never seemed to do exactly what she expected. That, she could have told him, was what worried her most.

He was never precisely what she anticipated.

And her feelings for him were anything but what she'd planned.

When he closed the distance between them, she was almost relieved. This followed logic. Morning sex, basic human need. Then they would get along with the business of the day on equal footing.

But he only curled his fingertips around hers and watched her face. 'You make great coffee, Liv.'

'If you can't dance on it, it isn't coffee.'

'Where are we going today?'

She frowned at him. 'I assumed you'd want to get started on the interview.'

'We'll get to it. Which trail do you like from here?'

It was his party, she reminded herself, and shrugged. 'There's a nice route up into the mountains from here. Wonderful views, some good alpine meadows.'

'Sounds like a plan. Do you want me to touch you?'

Her gaze jerked back to his. 'What?'

'Do you want me to touch you, or would you rather I didn't?'

'We've had sex,' she said carefully. 'I liked it well enough.'

He let out a short laugh. 'No need to pump up my ego,' he said and brushed a wet strand of hair from her cheek. 'Besides, that's not what I asked you. I asked if you wanted me to touch you now.' With his eyes locked on hers, he skimmed his finger down her throat, over her shoulder. 'To make love with you *now*.'

'You're already touching me.'

Her skin shivered as he traced his finger down the center of her body, slicked it into her. 'Yes or no,' he murmured when her breath snagged.

The liquid weight settled low in her stomach, urging her hips to move, setting a pace for her own pleasure. Heat ran up her body in one long, shuddering roll. Giving in to it, to him, she gripped his hair, dragged him to her.

'Yes,' she said against his mouth.

She opened to him, clamping her legs around his waist, prepared for that fast, hard race to climax. Craving it. But he used his hands on her, drove her up and over, up and over until she was gasping out his name.

He wondered that the water didn't simply churn red and burst into flame from his need for her. He wondered how he could have lived all his life not having her wrapped around him just like this. Long limbs, slim and strong, soft, slippery skin that sparkled with wet in the sun. He drew her head back so that the kiss could go deep and deep, spin out endlessly while the sun broke through the mist with a burst of light, turned the water to a clear moving mirror around them.

He found purchase on the rough riverbed, braced, then slid into her in one long, slow stroke. 'Hold on to me, Liv.' His breathing was ragged, and he buried his face in the curve of her throat, nipped there to hear her moan. 'Come around me,' he murmured, and felt her muscles clamp him like a hot vise as the climax shot through her.

Through the drumbeat of her heart, in her head, she heard him murmur to her, but could no longer separate promises from demand. His voice was only one more velvet layer, one more source of fogged pleasure. But when she felt his body tighten, she curled herself around him, holding fast so they could tumble off the last edge together.

He didn't let her go. She waited for him to release her, to drift back, aim a quick, triumphant grin and climb out of the water for a second shot of coffee.

But he held her fast, held her close, his lips rubbing lightly from her temple to her jaw in a sweet and soothing motion that left her more shaken than sex.

She had to get away, she thought, ease back before she let herself slip into intimacy. 'The water's cold.'

'Cold, hell It's freezing.' He nibbled his way to her ear, enjoying the way her heart continued to riot against his. 'You know, the minute your mind clears, your body tenses up. Why do you do that?'

'I don't know what you mean. We have to get out. We need to get started if— '

He turned his head, crushed his mouth against hers. 'We've already started, Liv. We started a long time ago.' He cupped her chin in his hand, then released her to turn to the bank. 'We have to figure out where we want to finish.'

She fixed powdered eggs, and they polished off the pot of coffee. He agreed with her plan to keep camp where they were and consider the hike she outlined a day trip that could be managed round trip in an easy five hours.

Carrying light packs, they started the climb on a rough track that led to rougher ridges. The valley fell away to their right, the forest marched toward the sky to the left. With the river winding below, they moved up into cool, crisp air where eagles soared and no sign of man could be seen.

He thought she maneuvered the dizzying switchbacks as other women would a ballroom floor, with a kind of casual feminine grace that spoke of supreme confidence.

She was patient when he stopped to take pictures, and he stopped often. She answered his questions – and he had more than she'd expected – in clear and simple terms. And she stood by, silently amused, when he drew to a halt and stared as the trail curved and the sky was swept by mountains.

'If you planted a house here, you'd never get anything done. How could you stop looking?'

Why couldn't he be shallow and simple as she'd wanted him to be? 'It's public land.'

He only shook his head, taking her hand to link fingers. 'Just think of it for a minute. We're the only two people in the world, and we've landed here. We could spend our whole life right here, with our brains dazzled.'

Blue, white, green and silver. The world was made up of

those strong colors and just the blurred smudges of more. Peaks and valleys and the rush of water. The feel of his hand warm in hers, as if it was meant to be.

And nothing else, no one else existed. No fear, no pain, no memories, no tomorrows.

Because she discovered she could yearn for that, she drew away. 'You wouldn't be so happy with it in the dead of winter when you'd freeze your ass off and couldn't get a pizza delivery.'

He looked at her, quiet, patient and made her ashamed. 'What would you miss most if you could never go back?'

'My family.'

'No, not people. What thing would you miss most?'

'The green,' she said instantly and without thought. 'The green light, and the green smell of the forest. It's different up here,' she continued as they began to walk again. 'Open, cool, with the forest well past peak.'

'Not as many places to hide.'

'I'm not hiding. This is iceland-moss,' she told him, gesturing to a curly clump of yellow-green. 'It's the best-known lichen in human consumption. In Sweden it's sold as an herbal medicine.' She caught his look and lifted her eyebrows. 'What?'

'I just like that snippy tone you get when you're annoyed and start a nature lecture.'

'If you don't want to know what you're looking at, fine.'

'No, I do. Besides, when you start talking about lichens and fungi, I get this urge to make wild animal love with you.'

'Then I'll have to switch to wildflowers.'

'It won't help. I'll still want to jump you.' A flash of pink caught his eye. 'Hey, are those bleeding hearts? Growing wild.'

'That's right.' Her annoyance didn't have a chance against his honest enthusiasm as he scrambled over some rocks to get a closer look. 'Very much like your garden variety in appearance. Don't touch,' she warned. 'We maintain low impact here.'

'I don't have the right shade or soil to grow these at home. Tried them at Mom's, but that was the next thing to murder. I've always liked the look of them.'

'We have some nice specimens in the garden at my grandparents'. We'll go this way.' She climbed over the rocks and chose a new heading. 'I think I know a spot you'll like.'

The track moved inside the edge of the forest, a steep incline with tumbles of rocks to one side where flowers forced their way through cracks and rooted ruthlessly in thin soil.

He heard the sound of drumming and grinned like a boy when they passed a cliff face sheared with a roaring fall of water. A dozen times he had to resist the urge to stop and pluck up handfuls of the hardy wildflowers.

His muscles began to burn, his feet to beg for rest. He was about to give in to both when she clattered over a hunched fist of rocks and turned to give him a hand up.

'That five hours was round trip, right, bwana?' Puffing a little, he gripped her hand and hauled himself up. 'Because otherwise I'm just going to – Oh, Jesus.'

He forgot his aches and pains and fatigue and filled himself on the view.

It was an ocean of flowers, rivers of color flowing through green and washing up toward a slope of forested peak that shot into the blue like the turret of a castle. At the highest points, curving pools of snow shimmered through the rock and trees and made the flowers only more of a miracle to him.

Butterflies danced, white, yellow, blue, flirting with the blooms, or settled delicately onto them with a quiet swish of wings.

'Amazing. Incredible. This is where we put the house.'

This time she laughed.

'What are those, lupines?'

'You have a good eye. Broadleaf lupines – the common western blue butterfly prefers them. Those are mountain daisies mixed with them. Those there, the white with the yellow center, are avalanche lilies.'

'And yarrow.' He studied the fernlike leaves and flat white blossoms.

'You know your flowers. You don't need me up here.'

'Yes.' He took her hand again. 'I do. It was worth every step.' He turned and caught her unprepared with a soft and stirring kiss. 'Thanks.'

'At River's End you get what you pay for.' She started to turn away, but he had her arms, eased her back around. 'Don't.' She closed her eyes before his mouth could capture hers again.

'Why?'

'I— ' She opened her eyes again and could do nothing about the emotions that swirled into them. 'Just don't.'

'All right.' Instead he lifted her hand to his lips, pressed them lightly to the knuckle of each finger and watched confusion join the clouds in her eyes.

'What are you looking for, Noah?'

He kept his eyes on hers, opened her fisted hand to press his lips to the center of her palm. 'I've already found it. You just have to catch up.'

He was afraid there was only one way for that to begin. 'Let's sit down, Liv. This is a good spot. It's a good time.' He shrugged off his pack, sat on a rock and opened it to find his tape recorder.

Seeing it in his hand, she felt her breath go thick and hot in her lungs. 'I don't know how to do this.'

'I do. I want to tell you something first.' He set the recorder beside him, then hunted out his notepad. 'I considered giving up the idea of this book. Setting it aside, as I did when I hurt you before.' He opened the notebook, then looked at her. 'It wouldn't have done any good, this time around. It would've been in the back of my mind. Always. Just as it would be in the back of yours. I can't quite figure out, Liv, if that's standing between us or if it's why we're here together. Why we've come back together after all this time. Why we're lovers now. But I do know that if we don't finish it, we'll keep running in place. I need to go forward. So do you.'

'I said I'd do it. I keep my word.'

'And hate me for it? Blame me for being the one who brought it to the surface? Just the way you hated me that day in the hotel?'

'You lied to me.'

'I know I did. I've never been sorrier for anything in my life.'

She'd expected him to deny it, to make excuses, rationalize. And she should have known better. He was a man with honor, one who'd been raised with it and with compassion. It was why what he did mattered, she thought now. Why he mattered.

'I don't hate you, Noah, and I won't hate you for being honest about doing what you feel you need to do. But what I do feel is my own business.'

'Not anymore it isn't.' He said it lightly, but she heard the undercoating of steel in the tone. 'But we can talk about that – about us – later.'

'There is no us.'

'Think again.' This time the steel was in his eyes. 'But for now, why don't you sit down?'

'I don't need to sit.' But she dragged off her pack, uncapped her water bottle.

'Fine. Tell me about your mother.'

'I was four when she died. You'd learn more about her from other sources.'

'When you remember her, what do you think of first?'

'Her scent. The scent she kept in one of her bottles on her vanity. I thought they were magic. There was one in cobalt with a silver band winding around it. It was something unique to her, warm, lightly sweet with a faint hint of jasmine. Her skin always carried that scent, and when she'd hug me or pick me up, it was strongest just . . .' Olivia touched her fingers to her own throat just under the jaw. 'I liked to sniff her there, and she'd laugh.

'She was so beautiful.' Her voice thickened as she turned away to stare out over the sea of flowers. 'You can't know, really. I've seen her movies now, all of them. Countless times. But she was so much more beautiful than they could capture. She moved like a dancer, as if gravity were simply something she tolerated. I know she was a brilliant actress. But she was a wonderful mother. Patient and fun and . . . careful. Careful to be there, to pay attention, to let me know that whatever else there was, I was the center of the world. Do you understand that?'

'Yes. I was lucky in that area, too.'

She gave in and sat beside him. 'I suppose I was spoiled. I had time and attention and a houseful of toys and indulgences.'

'To me the only spoiled children are the ones who have no appreciation or respect for those things. I'd say you were just loved.'

'She loved me very much. I never had any cause to doubt that, even when she scolded me about something. And I adored her. I wanted to be exactly like her. I used to look at myself in the mirror and imagine how I would grow up to be just like Mama.'

'You look very much like her.'

'I don't.' She pushed off the rock in one sharp movement. 'I'm not beautiful. I don't want to be. And I'll never be judged on my looks as she was, too often was. That's what killed her. In this fairy tale, the beast killed beauty.'

'Because she was beautiful?'

'Yes. Because she was desirable. Because men wanted her and he couldn't stand that. He couldn't tolerate the very thing that had drawn him to her in the first place. Her face, her body, her manner. If it appealed to him, it appealed to other men, and there would be no other men. The one way he could keep her only to himself was to destroy her. No matter how much she loved him, it wasn't enough.'

'Did she love him?'

'She cried for him. She didn't think I knew, but I did. I heard her one night with Aunt Jamie after I was supposed to be in bed. Earlier that summer when it stayed light until late. They were in Mama's room, and I could see from where I stood beside the door, in the mirror, the reflection of them as they sat on the bed. My mother crying and Aunt Jamie with her arms around her.'

And just like that, she took both of them back.

'What will I do? Jamie, what will I do without him?'

'You'll be fine, Julie. You'll get through this.'

'It hurts.' Julie turned her face into Jamie's shoulder, felt the sturdiness, longed for it. 'I don't want to lose him, to lose everything we have together. But I just don't know how to keep it.'

'You know you can't keep going on the way you have been these last few months. Jule.' Jamie eased back to brush the deep gold hair from her sister's face. 'He's hurt you, not just your heart, but you. I can't sit by when I see bruises on you that he put there.'

'He doesn't mean it.' Julie rubbed her hands over her face, drying the tears as she rose. 'It's the drugs. They change him. I don't understand why he started them again. I don't know what he finds in them that I haven't given him.'

'Listen to yourself.' A whip of anger in her voice, Jamie pushed to her feet. 'Are you taking the blame for this? For him finding his kicks and his ego in cocaine and pills and alcohol?'

'No, no, but if I could just understand what's missing, what he's looking for that isn't there ... Oh God.' She squeezed her eyes tight and raked back her hair. 'We were so happy. Jamie, you know we were happy. We were everything to each other, and when Livvy came it was like ... like

a circle completed. Why didn't I notice when he started to crack – that circle? How wide was the gap before I saw what was happening? I want to go back. I want my husband back, Jamie.' She turned around, one hand pressed to her belly. 'I want another child.'

'Oh God. Oh, Julie.' She was across the room, wrapped around her sister in two strides. 'Don't you see what a mistake that would be now? Just now?'

'Maybe it is, but maybe it's the answer. I told him tonight. I had Rosa fix us this wonderful dinner. Candles and music and champagne. And I told him I wanted us to have another child. He was so happy at first. So much like Sam. We laughed and held each other and started thinking up names, just as we did for Livvy. Then all at once, all of a sudden, he got moody and distant and he said . . .' The tears began to stream again. 'He said how did he know it would be his? How did he know I wasn't already carrying Lucas's bastard?'

'That son of a bitch. How dare he say such a thing to you.'

'I hit him. I didn't think, I just struck out and shouted at him to get out, get the hell out. And he did. He stared right through me, and he left. I don't know what to do.'

She sat on the bed again, covered her face with her hands and wept. 'I don't know what to do.'

Noah said nothing as Olivia stood as she was, one hand still covering her stomach as her mother's had. She'd taken him back, taken him there into the intimacy of that bedroom, into the female misery and despair. The words, the voices, the movements flowing out of her.

Now, without looking at him, she dropped her hand. 'I went back to my room, and I told myself Mama was rehearsing. She did that a lot. So I told myself Mama was being a movie, that she wasn't talking about my father. I went to sleep. And later that night I woke up and he was in my room. He'd turned on my music box and I was so happy. I asked him to tell me a story.'

Her eyes cleared when she focused on Noah again. 'He was high. I didn't know it then. I only knew he was angry when he shouted and he broke my music box. I only knew he wasn't the way Daddy was when my mother came rushing in and he hurt her. I hid in the closet. I hid while she cried and fought with him and locked him out of the room. Then she came and sat with me and told me everything would be all right. She called the police on my little phone, and she filed for divorce.

'It took him less than four months to come back and kill her.'

Noah turned off his recorder, slid off the rock and walked to her.

In automatic defense she stepped back. 'No. I don't want to be held. I don't want to be comforted.'

'Tough luck, then.' He wrapped his arms around her, holding firm when she struggled. 'Lean a little,' he murmured. 'It won't hurt.'

'I don't need you.' She said it fiercely.

'Lean anyway.'

She held herself stiff another moment, then went limp. Her head rested on his shoulders, and her arms came up to wrap loosely around his waist.

She leaned a little, but she kept her eyes open. And she didn't weep.

Chapter Twenty-eight

Noah asked questions on the hike back to camp, dozens of them. But he didn't mention her parents. He asked about her work, her routines, the Center and the lodge. She recognized what he was doing and couldn't decide if she resented or appreciated his deliberate attempt to put her at ease again.

Couldn't quite fathom why it worked so well.

Every time she put up a barrier, he wiggled around it and made her comfortable again. It was a skill she had to admire. And when they stopped again, to look again, she found herself sitting shoulder to shoulder with him as if she'd known him all her life.

She supposed, in some odd way, she had.

'Okay, so we build the house right up there.' He gestured behind him to a rocky incline.

'I told you, this is public land.'

'Work with me here, Liv. We put it up there, with big windows looking out this way so we catch the sunset at night.'

'That'd be tough, since that's south.'

'Oh. You sure?'

She gave him a bland look with humor ghosting around her mouth. 'West,' she said and pointed.

'Fine. So the living room faces that way. We need a big stone fireplace in there. I think we should keep it open, really high ceilings with like a balcony deal. No closed spaces. Four bedrooms.'

'Four?'

'Sure. You want the kids to have their own rooms, don't you? Five bedrooms,' he corrected, enjoying the way her eyes widened.

'One for a guest room. Then I need office space, good-sized room, lots of shelves and windows. That should face east. Where do you want your office?'

'I have an office.'

'You need a home office, too. You're a professional woman. I think it should be next to mine, but we'll have to have rules about respecting each other's space. We'll put them on the third floor.' His fingers linked with hers. 'That'll be our territory. Kids' play area should be on the main level, with windows looking into the forest so they never feel closed in. What do you think about an indoor pool?'

'I wouldn't consider a home without one.'

He grinned, then caught her off balance by leaning in, capturing her mouth in a long, hard kiss. 'Good. The house should be stone and wood, don't you think?'

His hand was in her hair, just toying with the ends. 'This is hardly the spot for vinyl siding.'

'We'll plant the garden together.' His teeth scraped lightly over her bottom lip. 'Kiss me back, Olivia. Slide in. Just once.'

She already was, couldn't do otherwise. The picture he painted was so soft, so dreamy she glided inside it. And found him. Found him surprisingly solid and real. And there. The sound she made was equal parts despair and delight as her arms locked tight around him.

How could it be he who snapped it all into place? Who made it all fit? All the misty wishes of childhood, all the half-formed fantasies of a young girl, all the darker needs of a woman swirled together inside her and re-formed into just one question.

He was the answer.

Rocked by the tumble of her own heart, she jerked back. She couldn't let it happen, not with him. Not with anyone. 'We have to get started.'

There was fear in her eyes. He wasn't quite sure how he felt about being the one to cause it. 'Why are you so sure I'll hurt you again?'

'I'm not sure of anything when it comes to you, and I don't like it. We need to go. There's more than an hour left to hike before we hit camp.'

'Time's not the problem here. So why don't we— ' He broke off as a movement behind her caught his eye. He shifted his gaze, focused and felt the blood drain out of his head. 'Jesus Christ. Don't move.'

She smelled it now – the wild and dangerous scent. Her heart slammed once against her ribs, and before she could get to her feet, Noah was springing up to put himself between her and the cougar.

It was a full-grown male, perched on the rocks just above with his eyes glinting in the sunlight. Now he shifted, let out a low, guttural growl and flashed teeth.

'Keep your eyes on his,' Olivia instructed as she rose. 'Don't run.'

Noah already had his hand on the hilt of his knife. He had no intention of running. 'Go.' He bared his own teeth and shifted when Olivia tried to step out from behind him. 'Start moving back down the trail.'

'That's exactly right.' She kept her voice clam. 'No sudden moves, no fleeing motions. We just ease back, give him room. He's got the advantage. Higher ground. And he's showing aggressive behavior. Don't take your eyes off him, don't turn your back.'

'I said, 'Go.' It took every ounce of willpower not to turn around and shove her down the trail. One thin stream of sweat trickled down his back.

'He must have a kill near here. He's just trying to protect it.' She bent, keeping her eyes on the cat's, and scooped up two rocks. 'Back away, we just back away.'

The cat hissed again, and his ears went back flat. 'Yell!' Olivia ordered, continuing the backward motion even as she winged the first rock. It struck the cougar sharply on the side.

She continued to shout, heaved the second rock. The cat spat furiously, swiped at the air. And as Noah drew the knife from his belt, the cat slunk away.

Noah continued to move slowly, kept Olivia behind him, scanning rock and brush. 'Are you all right?'

'Stupid! Just plain stupid!' She tore her cap off, kicked at a rock. 'Sitting there necking as if we were in the backseat of a Buick. I wasn't paying attention. What the hell is wrong with me?'

Furious with herself, she pulled the cap back on, wiped her sweaty palms on her things. 'I know better than that. Sightings of cougar are rare, but they happen. So do attacks, especially if you're just an idiot.' She pressed her hands to her eyes, rubbed hard. 'I wasn't looking for signs, I wasn't even looking. And then sitting there that way, without keeping alert. I'd fire any one of my guides for that kind of careless behavior.'

'Okay, you're fired.' He'd yet to sheathe his knife and remained braced. 'Let's just keep moving.'

'He's not bothered with us now.' She blew out a breath. 'He was protecting a kill, doing what he's meant to do. We're the intruders here.'

'Fine. I guess we'll build the house somewhere else.'

She opened her mouth, shut it, then shocked herself by laughing. 'You're a moron, Noah. I almost got you killed or certainly maimed. What the hell were you going to do with that, city boy?' She swiped a hand over her face and tried to choke back a giggle as she eyed his knife.

He turned the knife in his hand, considering the blade. 'Protect the womenfolk.'

She snorted out another laugh, shook her head. 'I'm sorry. I'm sorry. It's not funny. This must be a reaction to gross stupidity. I've seen cougar a few times, but never that close up, and I've always been on higher ground.'

She blew out another breath, relieved that her stomach was settling down from its active jumping. And that's when she noticed his hands were rock steady.

He hadn't so much as flinched, she realized. Wasn't that amazing? 'You handled yourself.'

'Gee, thanks, Coach.' He slid the knife away.

'No.' Calm again, she laid a hand on his arm. 'You really handled yourself. I wouldn't have expected it. I keep underestimating you, Noah. I keep trying to fit you into a slot, and you won't go.'

'Maybe you just haven't found the right slot yet.'

'Maybe, but I don't think you fit into anything unless you want to.'

'And what about you? Where do you want to fit. Liv?'

'I'm where I want to be.'

'Not the place, Liv. We're not talking about forest or ocean here.'

'I'm where I want to be,' she repeated. Or where, she admitted, she'd thought she wanted to be.

'I have work that matters and a life that suits me.'

'And how much room is there, in your slot?'

She looked at him, then away again. 'I don't know. I haven't had to make any.'

'Get ready to,' was all he said.

Neither of them was sure if it was a command or a suggestion.

He offered to try his hand at fishing, but she pointed out he didn't have a license and shot that down. Accepting that, he insisted on making soup instead, and entertained her with stories of childhood adventures with Mike.

'He decides in-line skating is the way to get chicks.'

Noah sampled the soup, decided it could have been worse. 'Coordination isn't Mike's strong point, but at sixteen a guy's brain is really just one big throbbing gland, so he blows most of his savings on the blades. I figure, what the hell, maybe he's on to something and get myself a pair, too. We head to Venice to try out his theory.'

He paused, poured them both more wine. The light was still strong, the air wonderfully cool. 'The place is lousy with girls. Tall ones, short ones, wearing tiny little shorts. You gotta cruise first, scope things out. I home in on this little blonde in one of the girl packs.'

Olivia choked. 'Girl packs?'

'Come on, your species always travels in packs. Law of the land. I'm working out how to cull her out of the herd while we strap on the blades. Then Mike gets up on his feet for about three seconds before his feet go out from under him. He pinwheels his arms, knocks this guy skating by in the face, they both go down like redwoods. Mike smacks his head on the bench and knocks himself out cold. By the time he comes to, I've lost the blonde, and end up taking Mike to the ER, where he had a standing appointment.'

'A little accident-prone?'

'He could hurt himself in his sleep.'

'You love him.'

'I guess I do.' And because there'd been something wistful in his statement, he studied her face. 'Who'd you hang with when you were a kid?'

'No one. There were a few when – before I moved up here, but after . . . Sometimes I'd play with kids at the lodge or campground, but they came and went. I don't have any lasting attachments like your Mike. He's doing all right now?'

'Yeah. He bounces.'

'Did they ever find the person who broke into your house and hurt him?'

'No. Maybe it's better that way. I'm not sure what I'd do if I got my hands on her. She could've killed him. Anything I could do to her wouldn't be enough.'

There was a dark side here, a latent violence she could see in his eyes. She'd had glimpses of it once or twice before. Oddly enough it didn't make her uneasy, as hints of violence always did. It made her feel . . . safe, she supposed. And she wondered why.

'Anything you could do wouldn't change what already happened.'

'No.' He relaxed again. 'But I'd like to know why. Knowing why matters. Don't you need to know why, Olivia?'

She took his empty bowl, and hers, then rose. 'I'll wash these.' She started toward the stream, hesitated. 'Yes. Yes, I need to know why.'

While she washed the bowls, Noah took out his tape recorder, snapped in a fresh tape. He had his notepad and pencil ready when she came back.

He saw the stress. It showed in the way her color faded to a delicate ivory. 'Sit down.' He said it gently. 'And tell me about your father.'

'I don't remember that much about him. I haven't seen him for twenty years.'

Noah said nothing. He could have pointed out that she remembered her mother very clearly.

'He was very handsome,' Olivia said at length. 'They looked beautiful together. I remember how they'd dress up for parties, and how I thought everyone's parents were beautiful and had beautiful clothes and went out to parties, had their pictures in magazines and on TV. It just seemed so natural, so normal. They seemed so natural together.

'They loved each other. I know that.' She spoke slowly now, a line of concentration between her elegant, dark brows. 'They loved me. I can't be wrong about that. In their movie together, they just . . . shimmered with what they felt for each other. It radiates from them. I remember how it did that, how they did that whenever they were in the same room. Until it started to change.'

'How did it change?'

'Anger, mistrust, jealousy. I wouldn't have had words for it then. But that shimmer was smudged, somehow. They fought. Late at night at first. I'd hear not the words so much but the voices, the tone of them. And it made me feel sick.'

She lifted her glass, steadied herself. 'Sometimes I could hear him pacing the hall outside, saying lines or reciting poetry. Later I read some article on him where he said he often recited poetry to help him calm down before an important scene. He suffered from stage fright.

'Funny, isn't it? He always seemed so confident. I think he must have used the same sort of method to calm himself down when they were fighting. Pacing the hall, reciting poetry. "For man, to man so oft unjust, is always so to women; one sole bond awaits them, treachery is all their trust."' She sighed once. 'That's Byron.'

'Yes, I know.'

She smiled again, but her eyes were so horribly sad. 'You read poetry, Brady?'

'I was a journalism major. I read everything.' He feathered his fingers along her cheek. '"Give sorrow words; the grief that does not speak whispers the o'er-fraught heart and bids it break."'

It touched her. 'With or without words, my heart's survived. It's my mother's heart that was broken, and she who didn't survive what he wanted from her, or needed. And I haven't spoken of it to anyone except Aunt Jamie, and then only rarely. I don't know what to say now. He'd pick me up.'

Her voice cracked, but she tried to control herself. 'In one fast swoop so that my stomach would stay on my feet for a minute. It's delicious feeling when you're a child. "Livvy, my love," he'd call me, and dance with me around the living room. The room where he killed her. And when he'd hold me, I'd feel so safe. When he'd come in to tell me a story – he told such wonderful stories – I'd feel so happy. I was his princess, he'd say. And whenever he had to go away to a shoot, I'd miss him so much my heart would hurt.'

She pressed a hand to her mouth, as if to hold in the words and the pain. Then made herself drop it. 'That night when he came into my room and broke the music box, and shouted at me, it was as if someone had stolen my father, taken him away. It was never, never the same after that night. That whole summer I waited for him to come back, for everything to be the way it was. But he never did. Never. The monster came.'

Her breath caught, two quick inward gasps. And her hand shook, spilling wine. Instinctively, Noah snagged the glass before it slipped out of her fingers. Even as he said her name she pressed both fists to her rampaging heart.

'I can't.' She barely managed to get the words out. Her eyes were huge with pain and shock and staring blindly into his. 'I can't.'

'It's all right. Okay.' He dropped his pad, the glass, everything and wrapped his arms around her. Her hands were trapped between them, but he could feel her heart race, he could feel the sharp, whiplash shudders that racked her. 'Don't do this to yourself. Don't. Let go. If you don't let go, you'll break to pieces.'

'I can still see it. I can still see it. Him kneeling beside her, the blood and broken glass. The scissors in his hand. He said my name, he said my name in my father's voice. I'd heard her scream, I'd heard it. Her scream, breaking glass. That's what woke me up. But I went into her room and played with her bottles. I was playing in her room when he was killing her. Then I ran away and never saw her again. They never let me see her again.'

There was nothing he could say; there was no comfort in words. He held her, stroking her hair while the sun left the sky and sent the light to gloaming.

'I never saw either of them again. We never talked of them in our house. My grandmother locked them in a chest in the attic to save her heart. And I spoke of her secretly to Aunt Jamie and felt like a thief for stealing the pieces of my mother she could give me. I hated him for that, for making me have to steal my mother back in secret whispers. I wanted him to die in prison, alone and forgotten. But he's still alive. And I still remember.'

He pressed his lips to her hair, rocking her as she wept. The hot tears dampening his shirt relieved him. However much they cost her to shed, she'd be better for them. He swung her legs over, drawing her into his lap to cradle her there like a child until she went lax and silent.

Her head ached like a fresh wound, and her eyes burned. The fatigue was suddenly so great she would have stumbled into sleep if she hadn't held herself back. But the raw churning in her stomach had ceased, and the agonizing pressure in her chest was gone.

Tired and embarrassed, she pulled back from him. 'I need some water.'

'I'll get it.' He shifted her aside to get up and fetch a bottle. When he came back, he crouched in front of her, then brushed a tear from her cheek with his thumb. 'You look worn out.'

'I never cry. It's useless.' She uncapped the bottle, drank deep to ease her dry throat. 'The last time I cried was because of you.'

'I'm sorry.'

'I was so hurt and angry when I found out why you'd really come. After I made you leave, I cried for the first time since I was a child. You had no idea what I'd let myself feel about you in those two days.'

'Yes, I did,' he murmured. 'It scared me. Nearly as much as what I felt for you scared me.'

When she started to get up, he simply planted his hands on her thighs, locked his gaze to hers and held her in place. 'What? You don't want to hear about it?'

'It was a long time ago.'

'Not so long, but maybe just long enough. It's a good thing you booted me out, Liv. We were both too young for what I wanted from you then. Both parts of what I wanted.'

'You're getting your book now,' she said evenly. 'And we're acting on the attraction. So I guess we're both finally grown-up.'

He moved fast, stunning her when he dragged her to her feet, nearly lifted her off them. His eyes had gone sharp, like the keen edge of a blade. 'You think all I want from you is the book and sex? Goddamn it, is that what you think or is that what you choose to think? That way, you don't have to give too much back or take any real risks.'

'You think baring my soul to you about my parents isn't a risk?' She shoved him back, hard. 'You think knowing anyone with the price and the interest will buy my memories and feelings isn't a risk?'

'Then why are you doing it?'

'Because it's time.' She pushed her hair back from her damp cheeks. 'You were right about that. Does that satisfy you? You were right. I need to say it, to get it out, and maybe somewhere in your damn book I'll see why it had to happen. Then I can bury them both.'

'Okay.' He nodded. 'That covers that part. What about the rest? What about you and me?'

'What about it?' she shot back. 'We had a few sparks some years ago and decided to act on them now.'

'And that's it for you? A few sparks?'

She stepped back as he moved in. 'Don't crowd me.'

'I haven't even started crowding you. That's your problem, Liv, never letting anyone get quite close enough to share your space. I want your body, fine if you're in the mood, but everything else is off-limits. That doesn't work for me. Not with you.'

'That's your problem.'

'Damn right.' He grabbed her arm, spinning her back when she turned. 'And it's yours, too. I have feelings for you.'

He released her abruptly to pace away, to stand all but vibrating with frustration on the bank of the stream. The light was gone now, so the low fire flickered gold and the first shimmer of the rising moon sifted through the trees.

'Do you think this is a snap for me?' he said wearily. 'Because I've had other women in my life, it's a breeze for me to deal with the only one who's ever mattered?'

He turned back. She stood where he'd left her, but had lifted her arms to cross them defensively around her. Those delicate fingers of moonlight shivered over her, pale silver.

'Olivia, the first time I saw you, you were a baby. Something about you reached right out, so much more than that sad image on the television screen, and grabbed me. It's never let go. I didn't see you again until you were twelve, gangly and brave and all haunted eyes. There was a connection. There was nothing sexual about it.'

He started back toward her, watched her shift slightly, as if to brace. 'I never forgot you. You were in and out of my head. Then you were eighteen. You opened the door of your apartment, and there you were, tall and slender and lovely. A little distracted, a little impatient. Then your eyes cleared. God, I've had your eyes in my head as long as I can remember. And you smiled at me and cut me off at the knees. I've never been the same.' He stopped a foot away from her and saw she was trembling.

'I've *never* been the same.'

Her skin was shivering, her heart beating too fast. 'You're fantasizing, Noah. You're letting your imagination run wild.'

'I did plenty of fantasizing about you.' He was calm now, certain because he could see her nerves. 'But it didn't come close. I did some compensating, too. But there was never a woman who pulled at me the way you do. Straight from the gut. I know I hurt you. I didn't understand you or myself well enough then. Even when I came here and saw you again, I didn't understand it. I just knew seeing you thrilled me. I've never gotten over you. Do you know what it was like to realize I'd never gotten over you?'

Panic wanted to rise, taunted her to run. Pride had her standing her ground. 'You're mixing things up, Noah.'

'No, I'm not.' He reached up, touched her face, then framed it in his hands. 'Look at me, Liv. Look. There's one thing I'm absolutely clear on. I'm so completely in love with you.'

A messy mix of joy and terror clogged her throat. 'I don't want you to be.'

'I know.' He touched his lips gently to hers. 'It scares you.'

'I don't want this.' She gripped his wrists. 'I won't give you what you're looking for.'

'You are what I'm looking for, and I've already found you. Next step is to figure out what you want, and what you're looking for.'

'I told you I already have everything I want in my life.'

'If that were true, I wouldn't scare you. I'm going to build a life with you, Olivia. I've been waiting to start and didn't even know it. It's only fair I give you time to catch up.'

'I'm not interested in marriage.'

'I haven't asked you yet,' he pointed out and his lips parted as they covered hers again. 'But I'll get to that. Meanwhile, just tell me one thing.' He cruised into the kiss so that they could both float on it. 'Is what you're feeling for me just a few sparks?'

It was warmth she felt, a steady stream of it, and a longing so deep, so aching, it beat like a heart. 'I don't know what I feel.'

'Good answer. Let me love you.' He walked her backward toward the tent, muddling her brain with hands and lips. 'And we'll see if the answer changes.'

He was patient and thorough and showed her what it was to be touched by a man who loved her. Each time she tried to hold back, he would simply find a new way to slide through her defenses. To fill a heart reluctant to be filled. To steal a heart determined not to be taken.

When he moved inside her, slow and smooth and deep, he saw the answer he wanted in her eyes. 'I love you, Olivia.'

He closed his mouth over hers, drew in her ragged breath and wondered how long he would wait to hear her say it.

Chapter Twenty-nine

The man was so carelessly cheerful, Olivia thought, it was all but impossible not to respond in kind. It didn't matter that the morning had dawned with a thin, drizzling rain that would undoubtedly have them soaked within an hour of the hike back.

He woke up happy, listened to the drumming and said it was a sign from God that they should stay in the tent and make crazy love.

Since he rolled on top of her and initiated a sexy little wrestling match, she couldn't come up with a logical argument against the plan. And for the first time in her life laughed during sex.

Then just when she'd convinced herself that good sex shouldn't be a barometer of her emotions, he nuzzled her neck, told her to stay put and that he'd see to the coffee.

She snuggled into the warm cocoon of the tent and wallowed in the afterglow of lovemaking. She hadn't let herself be pampered since childhood. She had taught herself to believe that if she didn't take care of herself, see to details personally and move consistently forward in the direction she'd mapped out, she would be handing control of her life over to someone else.

As her mother had done. And yes, she thought closing her eyes, perhaps even as her father had done. Love was a weakness, or a weapon, and she'd convinced herself that she'd never permit herself to feel it for anyone beyond family.

Didn't she have both potentials inside her? The one to surrender to it completely, and the one to use it violently? How could she risk turning that last key in that last lock and open herself to what she already knew she had inside her for Noah?

Then he nudged his way back into the tent, two steaming cups in his hand. His sun-streaked hair was damp with rain, his feet bare and the jeans he'd tugged on unbuttoned. The wave of love swamped her, closed over heart and head.

'I think I saw a shrew.' He passed her the coffee and settled down with his own. 'Don't know if it was a wandering or a dusky, but I'm pretty sure it was a shrew.'

'The wandering's found more often in the lowlands,' she heard herself say. 'At this altitude it was probably a dusky.'

'Whichever, it looked mostly like a mouse and was rooting around, for breakfast, I guess.'

'They eat constantly, rarely go over three hours without a meal. Very like some city boys I know.'

'I haven't even mentioned breakfast.' He fortified himself with coffee. 'I thought about it, but I haven't mentioned it. The weather's going to get better.' She merely lifted an eyebrow and glanced up toward the roof of the tent and the steady tapping of rain. 'An hour, tops. And it'll clear,' he insisted. 'If I'm right, you cook breakfast in the sunshine. If I'm wrong, I do it in the rain.'

'Deal.'

'So, how about a date when we get back?'

'Excuse me?'

'A date, you know. Dinner, a movie, making out in my rental car.'

'I thought you'd be heading back to L.A. soon.'

'I can work anywhere. You're here.'

It was so simple for him, she realized. 'I keep trying to take a step back from you. You keep moving forward.'

He smoothed her tousled hair with his fingers. 'Is that a problem for you?'

'Yes, but not as much as I thought it would be. Not as much as it should be.' She took a breath, braced herself. 'I care about you. It's not easy for me. I'm no good at this.'

He leaned forward, pressed his lips to her forehead and said, 'Practice.'

While Noah and Olivia were inside the tent in the rain-splattered forest, Sam Tanner looked out the window of the rented cabin and into the gloom.

He'd never understood what had drawn Julie to this place, with its rains and chill, its thick forests and solitude. She'd been made for the light, he thought. Spotlights, the elegant shimmer of chandeliers, the hot white flash of exotic beaches.

But she'd always been pulled back here by some invisible tie. He realized now that he'd done his best to break that tie. He'd made excuses not to go with her, or he'd juggled their demands to prevent her from going alone. They'd only made the trip twice after Olivia was born.

He'd ignored Julie's need for home because he hadn't wanted anyone or anything to be more important to her than he was.

Before they could slide away from him, he picked up the mini-recorder he'd bought and put those thoughts on tape. He intended to speak with Noah again, but wasn't sure how much more time he had. The headaches were raging down on him like a freight train and with terrifying regularity now.

He suspected the doctors had overestimated his time, and the tapes were his backup.

Whatever happened, whenever it happened, he was going to be sure the book found its way.

He had everything he needed. He'd stocked the kitchen with food from the resort's grocery store. There were times he didn't have the energy for the dining room. He had plenty of tapes and batteries to continue his story until he was able to reach Noah again.

Where the hell is he? Sam thought with a flush of anger. Time was running out, and he needed that connection. He needed not to be alone.

The headache began to build in the center of his skull. He shook pills out of bottles – some prescription, some he'd risked buying on the street. He had to beat the pain. He couldn't think, couldn't function if he let the pain take over.

And he had so much to do yet. So much to do.

Olivia, he thought grimly. There was a debt to pay.

He set the bottles back on the table, beside the long gleaming knife and the Smith & Wesson .38.

Noah might have felt smug about being right about the rain, but he felt even better when they reached the lowland forest. He could start dreaming of a hot shower now, a quiet room and several hours alone with his computer and a phone.

'You've lost two bets to me now,' he reminded her. 'It stopped raining, and I never whined for my laptop.'

'Yes, you did. You just did it in your head.'

'That doesn't count. Pay up. No, forget I said that. I'll take it in trade. We'll call it even if you find me a room where I can work for a few hours.'

'I can probably come up with something.'

'And a place I can shower and change?' He smiled when she slanted him a look. 'I'm on line for a room at the lodge if you get any cancellations, but meanwhile I'm relegated to a campsite and public showers. I'm very shy.'

Delighted with her giggle, he grabbed her hand. 'Except around you. You can shower with me. We take conservation very seriously in my family.'

She scowled, but only for form's sake. 'We can swing by the house,' she said after checking her watch. 'My grandmother should be out with one of the children's groups for a while yet, then she generally goes marketing. You've got an hour, Brady, to get yourself cleaned up and out. I don't want her upset.'

'That's not a problem.' He told himself he wouldn't let it be. 'But she's going to have to meet me eventually, Liv. At the wedding, anyway.'

'Ha ha.' She tugged her hand free.

'We can make another bet. I say I can charm her inside of an hour.'

'No deal.'

'You're just afraid because you know she'll come over to my side and tell you what a blind fool you are for not throwing yourself at my feet.'

'You really need to get a grip.'

'Oh, I've got one.' And I've got you, he thought. We're both just figuring that out.

He saw the flickers of color first, through the trees and the green wash of light. Dabs and dapples of red and blue and yellow, then the glint that was stronger sunlight shooting off glass.

When he stepped into the clearing, he stopped, pulling Olivia to a halt beside him.

When he'd driven her home, it had been dark, deep and dark, and he'd only seen the shape of shadow against night, and the flickers of light in a window.

Now, he thought the house looked like a fairy tale with its

varied rooflines and sturdy old wood and stone, flowers flowing at its base and sprinkling into sweeps of pretty colors and shapes.

There were two rockers on the porch, pots filled with more brilliant flowers and generous windows on all sides that would have opened the inside world up to the forest.

'It's perfect.'

She watched his face as he said it, as surprised to see he meant just that as by the rush of pleasure it gave her.

'It's been the MacBrides' home for generations,' she told him.

'No wonder.'

'No wonder what?'

'No wonder it's your place. It's exactly right for you. This, not the house in Beverly Hills. That would never have been you.'

'I'll never know that.'

He turned from the house to look into her eyes. 'Yes, you do.'

With someone else she might have shrugged it off. With anyone else, she wouldn't have spoken of it. 'Yes, I do know that. How do you?'

'You've been inside me for twenty years.'

'That doesn't make sense.'

'It doesn't have to. What I know is that when I try to project twenty years from now, you're still there.'

Her heart did one long, slow roll. She had to look away to steady it. 'God, you get to me.' She shook her head when his hands came to her shoulders, when he shifted her back to him. 'No, not now.'

'Always,' he said quietly, and settled his lips softly, dreamily on hers.

Without a sound, without a struggle, her arms came up and around him, her body leaned in. Not surrender, not this time. This time acceptance.

Emotions stormed through him, fast and hot and needy. And his mouth grew rough on hers. 'Tell me,' he demanded. He was wild to hear the words, to hear from her lips what he could taste on them.

She wanted to, wanted to fling herself off the edge and trust him to fall with her. The fear and the joy of it roared in her head. She teetered there, pulled in both directions, and only jerked away when she heard the sound of an engine laboring up the lane.

'Someone's coming.'

He kept his hands on her shoulders, his eyes on hers. 'You're in love with me. Just say it.'

'I – it's the truck. It's my grandmother.' She pressed a hand to her mouth. 'God, what have I done?'

The truck was already rounding the turn. Too late to ask him to go, Olivia realized. Too late even if the glint in his eye told her he wouldn't have quietly slipped into the trees.

She turned away, braced herself as the truck pulled up. 'I'll handle this.'

'No.' He took her hand in a firm grip. 'We'll handle it.'

Val sat where she was as they walked to the truck. Her fingers were tight on the wheel. She saw the distress and apology on Olivia's face and looked away from it.

'Grandma.' Olivia stopped at the driver's side, rested her free hand on the base of the open window.

'So, you're back.'

'Yes, just now. I thought you'd be with the children's group.'

'Janine took it.' Rage had her by the throat, whipping the words out before she could stop them. 'Did you think to sneak in and out before I got home?'

Stunned, Olivia blinked, stood numbly as Noah shifted in front of her, much as he had to shield her from the cougar. 'I asked Olivia if I could shower and change, since the lodge is booked. I'm Noah Brady, Mrs. MacBride.'

'I know who you are. This is Livvy's home,' she said shortly. 'If she's told you that you can use it to clean up, that's her right. But I have nothing to say to you. Move aside,' she ordered. 'I have groceries to put away.'

She dragged at the wheel and, without another glance at either of them, drove around the back of the house.

'I broke my word to her,' Olivia murmured.

'No, you didn't.'

She let out a shuddering breath that caught in her throat as he started after the truck. 'What are you doing? Where are you going?'

'To help your grandmother carry in the groceries.'

'Oh, for Christ's sake.' She caught up, dragged at his arm. 'Just go! Can't you see how I hurt her?'

'Yeah, I can see it. And I can damn well see how she's hurt you.' The steel was back in his voice as he took her wrist, pulled her hand away. 'I'm not backing off. You're both going to have to deal with that.'

He strode to the back of the house and, before Val could protest, plucked a bag out of her hand. Reaching into the bed of the truck, he hauled out another. 'I'll take these in.'

He carted them onto the back porch and let himself in through the kitchen door.

'I'm sorry.' Olivia rushed to Val. 'Grandma, I'm so sorry. I wouldn't have – I'll make him go.'

'You've already made your choices.' Back stiff, Val reached in for another bag.

'I wasn't thinking clearly. I'm sorry.' She could taste hysteria bubbling in her own throat. 'I'm so sorry. I'll make him go.'

'No, you won't.' Struggling to hold his temper, Noah came back out. He walked to the truck, took the last two bags. 'Any more than I'll make you do anything. If you want to take it out on someone, Mrs. MacBride, take it out on me.'

'Noah, would you just *go*?'

'And leave you here feeling guilty and unhappy?' He gave her a long, quiet look that had Val's eyes narrowing. 'You know better. I'm sorry we disagree about the book,' he continued, turning back to Val. 'I'm sorry that my being here upsets you. But the fact is, I'm going to write the book, and I'm going to be a part of Olivia's life. I hope we can come to terms about both, because she loves you. She loves you enough, and is grateful enough for everything you've done for her and been to her, that if it comes down to a choice between your peace of mind and her own happiness, she'll choose you.'

'That's not fair,' Olivia began, and Val cut her off with a lifted hand.

The wound inside her might have broken open again, might have been raw and viciously painful. But her eyes were still clear, they were still sharp. She wanted to dislike his face, to find it cold and hard and ruthless. She wanted to see self-interest, perhaps coated with a thin sheen of polish.

Instead she saw the glint of anger that hadn't faded since it had flashed into his eyes when she'd snapped at Olivia. And she saw the strength she'd once seen in his father's face.

'That book will not be discussed in this house.'

Noah nodded. 'Understood.'

'There're perishables in those bags,' Val said as she turned away. 'I have to get them put away.'

'Just give them to me,' Olivia began, then hissed in frustration when he simply walked past her and into the house behind her grandmother.

Left with no choice, Olivia dragged off her pack, dumped it on the porch and hurried in after them.

Already unloading bags, Val glanced toward the door as Olivia came in. She saw nerves, ripe and jittery, in her granddaughter's eyes. It made her feel ashamed.

'You might as well take that pack off,' she said to Noah. 'I imagine you're sick of carrying it by now.'

'If I admitted that, Liv would smirk at me. She wants me to think she thinks I'm a shallow urbanite who can't tell east from west.'

'You can't,' Olivia murmured and had Noah grinning at her.

'I was just testing you.'

'And are you?' Val asked. If she'd been blind, she would have seen the bond in the look that passed between them. 'A shallow urbanite.'

'No, ma'am, I'm not. The fact is I've fallen in love, not just with Liv – though that came as a jolt to both of us – but with Washington. At least your part of it. I've already picked some spots where we could build our house, but Liv says we'd run into trouble because it's a national park.'

'He's just babbling,' Olivia managed when she had untangled her tongue. 'There isn't—'

'Spending a few days at the lodge or camping isn't like living here,' Val interrupted.

'I don't guess it is.' Noah leaned back comfortably against the counter. 'But I'm a pretty flexible guy about some things. And this is where she's happy. This is home for her. As soon as I saw this place, I thought she'd like to get married right here in the yard, between the flowers and the forest. That would suit her, wouldn't it?'

'Oh, stop it!' Olivia burst out. 'There isn't—'

'I wasn't talking to you,' Noah said mildly, then offered Val an easy smile. 'She's crazy about me, but she's having a little trouble, you know, settling into it.'

Val nearly smiled. It broke her heart, then filled it again to see the amused exasperation on her little girl's face. 'You're a clever young man, aren't you?'

'I like to think so.'

She sighed a little as she neatly folded the last brown bag. 'You might as well go get the rest of your things. You can stay in the guest room.'

'Thanks. I'll just leave the pack here.' He turned, caught Olivia by the chin while she was still trying to catch up and kissed her, warmly, deeply. 'I won't be long.'

'I—' The screen door slapped smartly behind him, and Olivia threw up her hands. 'You didn't have to do that. He'll be fine at the campground. You'll just be uncomfortable if he stays here.'

Val walked over to tuck the bags away in the broom closet. 'Are you in love with him?'

'I – it's just . . .' She trailed off helplessly as Val turned back to look at her.

'Are you in love with him, Livvy?'

She could only nod as tears swam into her eyes.

'And if I said I don't want him around here, I don't want you to have anything to do with him? That you owe me the loyalty to respect my feelings on this?'

'But—'

'I'll never have peace if you let that man into your life.'

She went white, white and rigid with the lance of pain. This was the woman who had given her everything, who had opened her arms, her heart, her home. She had to grip the edge of the counter to steady herself. 'I'll go . . . I'll go tell him he has to leave.'

'Oh. Oh, Livvy.' Val dropped into a chair, covering her face as she burst into tears.

'Don't! Don't cry. I'll send him away. He won't come back.' Already on her knees, Olivia wrapped her arms around Val's waist. 'I won't see him again.'

'He was right.' Eyes drenched, Val framed Olivia's pale face. 'I wanted to throw it back in his face, but he was right. You'd turn away from him, from your own heart if you thought it was what I needed. I wanted him to be the selfish one, but I'm the one who's been selfish.'

'No. Never.'

'I've hoarded you, Livvy.' With an unsteady hand, Val brushed at Olivia's hair. 'As much for your sake as mine in the beginning, but . . . As time passed, just for me. I lost my Julie, and I promised myself nothing would ever happen to you.'

'You took care of me.'

'Yes, I took care of you.' Tears streaming still, Val pressed a kiss to Olivia's forehead. 'I loved you, and, Livvy, I needed you. I needed you so desperately. So I never let you go, not really.'

'Don't cry, Gran.' It ripped her to shreds to see the tears.

'I have to face it. We both do. I never let either of us face it, Livvy. Every time your grandfather would try to talk to me about it, to make me see, I closed off. Even just a few days ago, I wouldn't listen to him. I knew he was right, but I wouldn't listen. Now it's taken an outsider to make me face it.'

'Everything I have, everything I am, I owe to you.'

'It's not a debt.' Anger with herself made Val's voice sharp. 'I'm ashamed to know I let you think it was or should be. I'm ashamed that I pulled back from you when you chose to cooperate with this book. I could see it was something you needed, but I pulled back, deliberately, and made you suffer for it. I put a wedge between us, and I was too proud, too afraid to pull it out again.'

'I have to know why it happened.'

'And I've never let you. I've never let any of us.' Val drew Olivia closer, rested her cheek on the soft cap of hair. 'I still don't know if I can face it all. But I do know I want you to be happy. Not just safe. Being safe isn't enough to live on.'

Steadier, Val eased back, rubbed the tears away. 'It's best if your young man stays here.'

'I don't want him to upset you.'

Val took what she hoped was the next step and managed a smile. 'I'd rather he stay here where I can keep an eye on him and see if he's good enough for you. If I decide he's not, I'll see that your grandfather whips him into shape.'

Olivia turned her cheek into Val's hand. 'He claims he can charm you in less than an hour.'

'Well, we'll just see about that.' Rising, Val plucked out a tissue, blew her nose. 'It takes more than a pretty face to charm me. I'll make up my own mind in my own time.' Her head felt a little hollow from the emotional ride.

'I suppose I'd better go up and see that the guest room's in order.'

'I'll do it. I'll just take my pack up.' She hefted it. 'I should run over to the Center, check on things. It won't take me long.'

'Take your time. It'll give me a chance to interrogate your young man. You never brought one home with you before for me to make squirm.'

'He's slippery.'

'I'm quick.'

'Gran, I love you so much.'

'Yes, I know you do. Go on. I need to make myself presentable. We'll talk more, Livvy,' she murmured after Olivia started up the stairs. 'It's long past time we talked.'

Her step was light as she crossed the upstairs hall to her room. She was in love, and it didn't hurt a bit. The gaps that had widened between her and her grandmother over the past months were closing.

The future was a wide, wonderful space overflowing with possibilities. Wanting to hurry, she flung open the door of her room. And the joy that had just begun to fill her soul fell away.

There, on the pillow of her bed, bathed in a quiet stream of sunlight, lay a single white rose.

Chapter Thirty

She couldn't breathe. Her head rang, wild, frantic bells that vibrated down from her skull, pealed down her spine, beat along her numbed legs until she simply collapsed forward on her hands and knees and began to suck for air like a woman drowning.

There was a terrible urge to crawl away.

Into the closet, into the dark.

She fought it and the ice-pick jabs of panic in her chest. She pressed her hand to her shirt, then stared down it, surprised it wasn't covered with blood.

The monster was here.

In the house. He'd been in the house. With the thought of that chuckling hideously in her ear, she lunged to her feet, stumbled over the pack she'd dropped. Momentum carried her forward so that she fell on the bed, her fingers inches away from the stem of that perfect white rose.

She snatched her hand away as if the flower were a snake, filled with venom and ready to strike.

She reared back, her eyes wide and round, the scream tearing at her throat for release.

In the house, she thought again. He'd come into the house. And her grandmother was down in the kitchen, alone. Her hand might have shaken, but she reached for the knife at her belt, unsheathed it so that blade hissed against leather. And she moved quietly toward the door.

She wasn't helpless child now, and she would protect what she loved.

He wouldn't still be inside. She tried to reason with herself, to follow logic, but she could still taste the fear.

She slipped out into the hall, keeping her back against the wall. Her ears were cocked for any sound, and the hilt of the knife was hot in her hand.

She moved quietly from room to room, carefully as she would when tracking a deer. She searched each one for a sign, for a scent, a change in the air. Her knees trembled as she crossed to the attic door.

Would he hide there where the memories were locked away? Would he know somehow that everything precious of her mother was neatly stored up those narrow stairs?

She imagined herself going up, climbing those steps, hearing the faint creak of her weight against the old wood. Then seeing him, standing there with the chest lid flung open, and her mother's scent struggling to life in the musty air.

The bloody scissors in his hand, and the deranged eyes of the monster looking out from her father's face.

She all but willed it to be so as her fingers trembled against the knob. She would raise her knife and drive it into him, as he'd once driven the blades into her mother. And she would end it.

But her hand lay limply on the knob, and her brow pressed against the wood of the door. For the first time in two decades, she wanted desperately to weep and couldn't.

At the sound of a car rounding the lane, she slid the bolt home under the knob and ran on jellied legs to a window.

The first fresh spurt of fear when she didn't recognize the car shimmered into relief when she saw Noah climb out. Her hands curled on the sill as she scanned the trees, the lengthening shadows.

Was he out there? Was he watching?

She spun around, desperate to run downstairs now, to let the terror spill out so someone else could take it away.

And thought of her grandmother.

No, no, she couldn't frighten her that way. She would handle it herself. Cautious, she slid the knife back in its sheath, but left the safety unsnapped.

She leaned against the wall again, taking slow, even breaths. When she heard Noah's step on the stairs, she moved back into the hall.

'She's starting to warm up to me. Asked if I liked grilled pork chops.'

'Let me give you a hand with that.' How steady her voice was, she thought. How cool. She reached out to take his laptop case and left him with his bag and gear. 'The guest room's in here. It has its own bath.'

'Thanks.' He followed her inside, glancing around as he dropped his bags on the bed. 'This is a hell of a lot more appealing than a pup tent on a campsite. And guess who's here?'

'Here?'

His eyes narrowed on her face at the thready ring to her voice. 'What's the matter, Liv?'

She shook her head, lowered to the edge of the bed. She needed a minute, just another minute. 'Who's here?'

'My parents.' He took a good look at her now and, sitting beside her, took her hand. It was clammy and cold.

'Frank? Frank's here?' Her hand turned over in his, gripped like a vise.

'At the lodge,' Noah said slowly. 'They'd booked a room a while back. I want you to tell me what's wrong.'

'I will. Frank's here.' She let her head drop weakly on Noah's shoulder. 'I asked him to come. When I was in L.A. I went to his house and asked him if he could. And he did.'

'You matter to him. You always did.'

'I know. It's like a circle, and it keeps going. All of us around and around. We can't stop, just can't stop going around until it's all finished. He's been in the house, Noah.'

'Who?'

She straightened up, and though her cheeks were still pale, her eyes were level. 'My father. He's been in the house.'

'How do you know?'

'There's a rose on my bed. A white rose. He wants me to know he's come back.'

The only change was a hardness that came into his eyes and a coldness that glinted into the green. 'Stay here.'

'I've looked.' She tightened her grip on his hand. 'I've already looked through the house. Except for the attic. I couldn't go into the attic because . . .'

'Damn right you couldn't go into the attic.' The idea of it made his stomach churn. 'You stay in here or go downstairs with your grandmother.'

'No, you don't understand. I couldn't go up because I wanted him to be there. I wanted it because I wanted to go up and kill him. Kill my father. God help me, I could see it, the way I'd ram the knife into him. The way his blood would run over my hands. I wanted it. I wanted it. What does that make me?'

'Human.' He snapped it out, the word as effective as a slap. She jerked back, shuddered once.

'No. It would have made me what he is.'

'Did you go up, Olivia?'

'No. I locked the door from the outside.'

'Lock this one from the inside, and wait for me.'

'Don't go.'

'He's not here.' He got to his feet. 'But you'll feel better if we make sure. Lock the door,' he ordered. 'And wait.'

Despising herself, she did just that. Hid, as she had hidden before. When he came back, she opened the door and looked at him with empty eyes.

'There's no one there. I didn't see any indication there had been. We need to tell your grandparents.'

'It'll frighten my grandmother.'

'She has to know. See if you can track down your grandfather. Call the lodge. I'll call my parents.' He skimmed his knuckles over her cheek. 'You'll feel better if you have your cop.'

'Yes. Noah.' She laid a hand on his arm. 'When I saw you get out of the car just now, I knew I could lean on you. I wanted to.'

'Liv. If I told you I'd take care of you, it'd just piss you off, wouldn't it?'

She gave a watery laugh and sat back on the bed again. 'Yeah, not now because I'm shaky, but later.'

'Well, since you're shaky, I'll risk it. I'm going to take care of you.' He took her face in his hands and kissed her. 'Believe it. Now call your grandfather.'

He'd taken such a risk. Such a foolish and satisfying risk. How easily he could have been caught.

And then what?

He wasn't ready to face that yet. Not quite yet. As he sat in his room, he lifted a glass of bourbon to his lips with a hand that still shook slightly.

But not with fear. With excitement. With life.

For twenty years, he'd had no choice but to follow the rules. To do what was expected. To play the game. He couldn't have known, could never have anticipated what it was like to be free of that.

It was terrifying. It was liberating.

She would know what the rose meant. She wouldn't have forgotten the symbolism of it.

Daddy's home.

He drank again, felt such power after so many years of powerlessness.

He'd nearly been caught. What incredible timing. He'd barely left the house by the back door – wasn't it wonderful that such people trusted the fates and left their doors unlocked – when he'd seen them step out of the trees.

Livvy, little Livvy and the son of the cop. That was irony enough for any script. The cycle, the circle, the whims of fortune that would have the daughter of the woman he loved connect with the son of the cop who'd investigated her murder.

Julie, his beautiful Julie.

He'd thought it would be enough just to frighten Livvy, enough to make her think of that bloody night so many years ago, to remember what she'd seen and run from.

How could he have known, after all these years, that he would look at her as she turned to another man and see Julie? Julie pressing that long, slim body against someone else?

How could he have known he'd remember, in a kind of nightmare frenzy, what it was to destroy what you loved? And need so desperately to do it all again?

And when it was done . . . He picked up the knife and turned it under the lamplight . . . It would be over. The circle finally closed.

There would be nothing left of the woman who'd turned him away.

'You'll need to take basic precautions.' Frank sat in the MacBride living room, his blood humming. Back on the job, he thought. To finish one that had never felt closed.

'For how long?' Olivia asked. It was her grandmother who concerned her most. But the crisis appeared to have steadied Val. She sat, shoulders straight, eyes alert, mouth hard.

'As long as it takes. You're going to want to avoid going out alone, staying in groups as much as possible. And start locking the doors.'

Olivia had had time to settle, time to think. So she nodded. 'There really isn't anything we can do, is there?'

He remembered the little girl hiding in the closet, and the way she'd reached out to him. She was a woman now, and this time he couldn't just pick her up and take her to safety. 'I'm going to be as honest with you as I can, Livvy. So far, he hasn't done anything we can push him on.'

'Stalking,' Noah snapped out. 'Trespassing. Breaking and entering.'

'First you have to prove it.' Frank held up a hand. 'If we manage to do that, the police might be able to hassle him, but not much more. A phone call with no specific threat, a gift and a flower put into an unlocked house. He could argue that he just wanted to make contact with the daughter he hasn't seen in twenty years. There's no law against it.'

'He's a murderer.' Rob stopped his restless pacing and laid a hand on Olivia's shoulder.

'Who's served his time. And the fact is . . .' Frank scanned the faces in the room. 'The contact may be all he wants.'

'Then why didn't he speak to me, over the phone?'

Frank focused on Olivia. She was a little pale, but holding up well. Underneath the composure, he imagined her nerves were screaming. 'I can't get into his head. I never could. Maybe that's why I could never put this one aside.'

You're what's left of Julie, Frank thought. All he has left of her. And you're what helped put him away. And she knew it. he could see the knowledge of it burning in her eyes.

'What we can do is ask the local police to do some checking,' he continued. 'Do what they can to find out if Tanner's in the area.'

Olivia nodded again, kept her hands still in her lap. 'And if he is?'

'They'll talk to him.' And so will I, Frank thought. 'If he contacts you, let me know about it right away. If there's more, we may be able to push on the stalking.' He hesitated, then got to his feet. 'Remember one thing, Livvy. He's on your ground. Out of his element. And he's alone. You're not.'

It bolstered her, as it was meant to. She rose as well. 'I'm glad you're here.' She smiled at Celia. 'Both of you.'

'We all are.' Val stepped forward. 'I hope you'll stay for dinner.'

'You have so much on your mind,' Celia began.

'We'd like you to stay.' Val laid a hand on Celia's arm, and there was a plea in her eye, woman to woman.

'Then why don't I give you a hand? I haven't had a chance to tell you how much I like your home.' As they started out, with Celia's arm draped over Val's shoulders, Olivia wondered who was leading whom.

'I haven't even offered you a drink.' Rob struggled to slip into the role of host. 'What can I get you?'

Coffee, Frank started to say. He always drank coffee when he was working. But Olivia moved to Rob, slid her arm through his. 'We have a really lovely Fumé Blanc. Noah's fond of good wine. Why don't you make yourselves comfortable while we open a bottle?'

'That would be nice. Wouldn't mind stretching my legs a bit first. Noah, why don't we take a walk?'

He wanted to object, to keep Olivia in sight. But it had been more order than request, and he knew there was a reason for it. 'Sure. We'll take a look at Mr. MacBride's garden so you can mourn your own failure.' As much for himself as to make a point, he turned to Olivia, brushed a kiss over her mouth. 'Be right back.'

Frank waited until they were outside. Even as they stepped off the porch, his eyes were scanning. 'I take it there's more between you and Livvy than the book.'

'I'm in love with her. I'm going to marry her.'

The sudden hitch in his step had Frank coming up short, blowing out a breath. 'Next time, son, remember my age and tell me to sit down first.'

Noah was braced for a fight, craved one. 'You have a problem with that?'

'No, anything but.' Calmly, Frank studied his son's face. 'But it sounds like you do.'

'I brought this on her.'

'No. No, you didn't.' Deliberately he moved away from the house, wanting to be certain their voices didn't carry through open windows. 'If Tanner wanted to get to her, he'd have found a way. You didn't lead him here, Noah.'

'The fucking book.'

'Maybe he looked at it as a tool, maybe he just wanted the

spotlight again.' Frank shook his head. 'Or maybe he started out wanting to tell his story, just as he told you. I've never been able to get a handle on him. I'll tell you this, if you don't keep your head clear, you never will either. And you won't help her.'

'My head's clear.' And his rage was cold. 'Clear enough to know if I find him before the cops do, I'll do more than talk. He's terrorizing her, and he brought Mom into it. He's used me for part of it.'

He strode around the edge of the garden, where the last soft light lay like silk over the celebration of flowers. 'Goddamn it. I sat with him. I looked him in the eye. I listened to him. I'm supposed to know what's inside people, when they're stringing me along. And I'd started to believe he'd been innocent.'

'So had I at one point. Why did you?'

Noah jammed his hands into his pockets, started into the trees. 'He loved her. However fucked-up he was, he loved her. He still does. You can see it when he talks about her. She was it for him. I know what that feels like now. When you have that inside you, how can you get past it to kill?'

He shook his head before Frank could speak. 'And that's stupid because it happens all the time. Drugs, alcohol, obsession, jealousy. But a part of me bought into it, wanted to buy into it.'

'You love her. He's her father. There's something else, Noah. They found Caryn.'

'What?' For a minute the name meant nothing. 'Doesn't matter now.'

'It might. She turned up in New York. Hooked up with a photographer she met at a party. A rich photographer.'

'Good for her. Hope she stays there. A whole continent between us ought to be enough.' Then he thought of Mike. 'Did they pull her in?'

'She was questioned. Denied it. Word is she got pretty violent in denying it.'

'Typical.'

'She also has an alibi for the night Mike was hurt. The party. A couple of dozen people saw her at this deal up in the hills.'

'So she slipped out for a while.'

'It doesn't look like it. The alibi's holding. We have the time of the attack narrowed to thirty minutes between when Mike got to the house and Dory found him. During that half-hour period,

Caryn was snuggled up to the photographer in front of twenty witnesses.'

'That doesn't . . .' He trailed off, felt his insides lurch. 'Tanner? God.' He dragged his hands free, pressed his fingers to his eyes. 'He knew where I lived. He was out by then, and he knew where to find me. The son of a bitch, what was the point?'

'Did you let him see any of your work?'

'No, of course not.'

'Could be as simple as that. He wanted to see where you were heading with it. Top billing was important to him, probably still is. And you'd have names, addresses in your files. Notes, tapes.'

'Revenge? Does it come down to that? Getting back at the people who testified against him?'

'I don't know. But he's dying, Noah. What does he have to lose?'

He had nothing to lose. So he sat, sipping his drink and watching night fall. The pain was nicely tucked under the cushion of drugs, and the drugs were dancing with alcohol.

Just like old times.

It made him want to laugh. It made him want to weep.

Time was running out, he thought. Wasn't it funny, wasn't it wonderfully funny how it had crawled for twenty years, only to sprint like a runner at the starting block now that he was free?

Free to do what? To die of cancer?

Sam studied the gun, lifted it, stroked it. No, he didn't think he'd let the cancer kill him. All he needed was the guts.

Experimentally he turned the gun, looked keenly into the barrel, then slipped it like a kiss between his lips.

It would be fast. And if there was pain, it would be over before it really began. His finger flirted with the trigger.

He could do it. It was just another kind of survival, wasn't it? He'd learned all about survival in prison.

But not yet. First there was Livvy.

Most of all, there was Livvy.

Through the meal, no one spoke of it. conversation ran smoothly, gliding over underlying tensions. After the first ten minutes, Noah gazed at his mother with admiration. She drew Olivia out, chattering on about the Center, asking her opinion about everything from the plight of the northern pocket gopher – where did she get this stuff – to the mating habits of osprey.

He decided either Olivia was as skilled an actress as her mother had been, or she was enjoying herself.

Val lifted a bowl of herbed potatoes and passed them to Frank. 'Have some more.'

'I'm going to have to make serious use of your health club tomorrow.' But he accepted the bowl and helped himself to another serving. 'This is a fantastic meal, Val.'

'Frank tolerates my cooking,' Celia put in.

'Cooking?' Frank winked at Noah and handed off the bowl. 'When did you start cooking?'

'Listen to that,' she said as she gave him a playful punch. 'All the years I've slaved over a hot stove for my men.'

'All the tofu that gave their lives,' Noah murmured, and earned a punch of his own. 'But you sure are pretty, Mom. Isn't she pretty?' He grabbed her hand and kissed it.

'You think that gets around me?'

He scooped up potatoes. 'Yeah.'

And that's what did it for Val. How could she hold back against a boy who so clearly loved his mother? She lifted a basket, offered it. 'Have another roll, Noah.'

'Thanks.' This time when he smiled at her, she smiled back.

They lingered over coffee. Under different circumstances, Noah mused, the MacBrides and the Bradys would have slipped into an easy friendship, without complications, with no shadows.

But the shadows were flickering back. He could see them in the way Olivia would glance at the windows, quick glimpses at the dark. The way his father studied the house, a cop's assessment of security.

And he saw the strain on Val MacBride's face when his parents got ready to leave.

'I'll be at your naturalist talk at the Center tomorrow.' Celia slipped on a light jacket on. 'And I'm hoping there's still room for one more on your guided hike.'

'We'll make room.'

Celia ignored Olivia's extended hand and caught her up in a hard hug. 'I'll see you in the morning, then. Val, Rob, thanks for a wonderful meal.' And when she embraced Val, she murmured in her ear. 'Stay strong. We're right here.'

She gave Val's back a bolstering pat, then took Noah's arm. 'Walk your mother to the car.' It would, they both knew, give Frank a chance to reassure the MacBrides.

Celia breathed deep of the night and wondered how Frank would feel about buying a little holiday cabin in the area. They were used to having their chick close by, after all.

It was a good place for roots, she thought, drawing in the scent of growing things. A good place for her son.

She turned to him, took his face in her hands. 'You're smart and you're clever and you've always been a joy to me. If you let that girl get away, I'll kick your butt.'

He lifted an eyebrow. 'Do you know everything?'

'About you, I do. Have you asked her to marry you?'

'Sort of. She's work. Yeah, just as you said she would be,' he added when Celia rolled her eyes. 'But she's not going to get away from me. And I'm not going to let anything happen to her.'

'I always wondered who you'd fall in love with and bring into our lives. And I always promised myself that whoever it was, no matter how irritated I might be by her, I'd be a quiet, noninterfering mother-in-law. And you can wipe that smirk off your face right now, young man.'

'Sorry. I thought I heard you say something about you being quiet.'

'I'll ignore that, and tell you how much I appreciate you choosing a woman I can admire, respect and love.'

'I didn't choose her. I think I ran out of choices the minute I saw her.'

'Oh.' Celia stepped back, sniffling. 'That's going to make me cry. I want grandbabies, Noah.'

'Is that from the quiet, noninterfering part of you?'

'Shut up.' Then she hugged him, held on fierce and tight. 'Be careful. Please, be very careful.'

'I will. With her. With all of it.' He stared over his mother's shoulder, into the shadows. 'He's not going to harm us.'

Chapter Thirty-one

He waited until the house was quiet to go to her. He knocked softly but didn't wait for her answer. And saw the moment she turned from the window that she hadn't expected him.

'Did you really think I'd leave you alone tonight?'

'I don't think it's appropriate that we sleep together in my grandparents' house.'

He had to give himself a minute. 'Are you saying that to make me mad or because you actually believe the only reason I'm here is to sleep with you?'

She shrugged, then turned away again. The wind had risen to sing through the treetops. That, and the sound of the night birds, was a music that always soothed her.

But not tonight.

She'd tried a hot bath, the herbal tea her grandmother enjoyed before bed-time. They'd added yet another layer of fatigue to her body and did nothing to soothe her mind.

'I don't have any objections to sex,' she said coolly, willing him to leave before she pulled him in any deeper. 'But I'm tired, and my grandparents are sleeping at the end of the hallway.'

'Fine, go to bed.' He walked to her shelves, scanned the titles of books and plucked one at random. 'I'll just sit here and read awhile.'

She closed her eyes while her back was to him, then composing her features carefully, faced him. 'Maybe we should straighten this out before it goes any farther. The few days in the backcountry was fun. More fun than I'd expected. I like you, more than I anticipated. Because I do, I don't want to hurt you.'

'Yes, you do.' He set the book aside, sat down. 'The question is why.'

'I don't want to hurt you, Noah.' Some of the emotion pumping inside her leaked into her voice. 'We had an interesting time together, we had great sex. Now I've got a lot more on my mind. And the simple fact is I don't want what you seem to believe you want from us. I'm not built for it.'

'You're in love with me, Olivia.'

'You're deluding yourself.' She shoved open the French doors and stepped out onto the narrow terrace.

'The hell I am.'

She hadn't expected him to move that quickly, certainly not that quietly, but he was beside her, spinning her around, and the temper in his eyes was ripe and hot. 'Do I have to make you say it?' He yanked her against him. 'Is that the only way? You can't even give me the words freely?'

'What if I am in love with you? What if I am?' She fought her way free, stood back with the wind whipping at her thin robe. 'It won't work. I won't let it.' Her voice rose. With an effort, she controlled it before she gave in to the urge to shout. 'Maybe if I didn't care, I'd let it happen.'

'That makes sense, that explains everything. If you didn't love me, we could be together.'

'Because it wouldn't matter. I'm afraid, and you'd see to it I wasn't alone. I'd let you do what you seem so hell-bent on doing and take care of me, at least until this is over.'

A little calmer, he reached out to touch the ends of her hair. 'I knew it was a mistake to say that. Taking care of you isn't taking you over, Liv.'

'You've got this nurturing streak. You can't help yourself.'

The idea so completely baffled him, he could only stare. 'No, I don't.'

'Oh, for God's sake.' She stormed past him, back into the room. 'You want to look after everyone you care about. Listen to yourself sometime when you talk about Mike. You're always coming to his rescue. You don't even realize it. It's second nature. It's the same with your parents.'

'I don't rescue my parents.'

'You tend to them, Noah. It's lovely, really lovely. Just tonight, I'm listening to your mother talk about how you come by their house and try to save her flowers. Or how you go hang out with your father at the youth center, take him pizza.'

'He might starve otherwise. It's not tending.' It was a word that made him want to squirm. 'It's just family.'

'No, it's just you.' And she could have drowned in love with him for no other reason. He was beautiful – inside and out.

'You focus,' she continued. 'You listen, and you make things matter. All the things I wanted to believe about you, all the ways I tried to tell myself you were shallow or careless were just ways to stop myself from feeling. Because I can't.'

'Won't,' he corrected. 'I sound like a pretty good catch.' He started toward her. 'Why are you trying to shake me off the hook?'

'I don't come from the kind of people you come from. My mother was a victim, my father a murderer. That's what I have inside me.'

'So everyone who comes from a difficult or violent background isn't capable of love?'

'This isn't a debate. I'm telling you the way it is. I'm telling you I don't want to be involved with you.'

'How are you going to stop it?'

'I already have.' Her voice went flat and cool now as she turned toward the door. 'We're done. I've given you all I can give you on the book. There's no need for you to stay past morning.'

He walked toward the door she opened. Her heart was bleeding as she shifted aside. Later she would tell herself she should have seen it coming, should have recognized the cool, reckless light in his eye.

He gripped her wrist to move it away from the knob. Closed the door. Turned the lock. 'If we play it your way and I go along with the idea that you can turn your feelings on and off as easily as I turned that lock, then all we really had between us was business – which is concluded – and sex. Would that be an accurate statement?'

He had her backed against the door, trapped there. When the first shock passed, she realized he frightened her. And along with the fear rode a terrible excitement. 'Close enough. It's better that way, for both of us.'

'Sure, let's keep it simple. If it's just about sex—' He yanked the tie of her robe away. 'Then let's take it.'

She jerked her chin up, forced herself to meet his eyes. 'Fine.'

But his mouth was already crushed to hers, tasting of fury and violence. His fingers plunged into her, ripping her over a brutal peak before her mind could keep pace with her body. She cried out, shock, denial, delight, and the sound was muffled against his ruthless mouth.

He tore her robe aside even as he drove her deeper, faster, into the pumping heat.

'It doesn't matter. It's just sex.' Hurt and anger speared through him, and he let the keener edge of desire rule.

His hands were rough when he dragged her to the bed, his body hard and demanding when he pressed down on hers. He gave her no time, no choice. But he gave her pleasure.

Her nails dug into his shoulders, but not in protest. Beneath his, her body shuddered and writhed, and the sounds in her throat were the low animal moans of mating.

This was not the playful tumble he'd shown her or the gentle thoroughness of seduction. Heat instead of warmth, greed unbalanced by generosity.

She tore at his clothes, and raked her nails down his sweat-slicked back. With oaths instead of promises, he jerked up her hips and slammed himself into her. She was hot and wet and fisted around him urgently as her body bowed up, a quaking bridge.

Her skin glinted with damp in the lamplight, her eyes stared, dark with shock, into his. She couldn't survive it. It was one terrified thought that raced through her spinning brain. No one could survive this brutal heat, these battering fists of sensation.

She fought to swallow air and breathed out his name.

The orgasm sliced through her, twin edges of pleasure and pain. It opened her, left her helpless and exposed.

He hung on, like a man clinging to a ledge by his fingertips as the blood beat like thunder in his head, his heart, his loins. 'Say it.' He panted it out, gripping her hips so that she had no choice but to take more of him. 'Give me the words. Damn it, Liv, tell me now.'

His face filled her vision. There was nothing else. 'I love you. Oh God.' Her hand slid away from him to lie limply on the bed. 'Noah.'

He let go of the ledge, and when the last desperate thrust emptied him, he collapsed on her.

He could feel her trembling, and the staccato beat of her heart against his. Who won? he wondered and rolled away from her.

'I'm trying to be sorry for treating you that way,' he said. 'But I'm not.'

'There wouldn't be any point in it.' She was cold, she realized, growing cold because he was moving away.

'I won't leave in the morning. I won't leave until this is resolved. You'll have to find a way to deal with that.'

'Noah.' She sat up, then began to shiver. 'The lack's in me. It's not you.'

'That makes it just fine, then.' He rolled off the bed, scooped up his jeans. 'I told my mother you were work. That's not the half of it. You're a battle, Liv. You're a fucking combat zone, and I never know if you're going to wave the white flag, attack, or just turn tail and retreat. And maybe you're right.' He jammed his legs into the pants and dragged them up. 'Maybe it's just not worth it.'

It was the first time in six years he'd hurt her, really hurt her. She stared, speechless as the shock wave of it shook through her. The words were lethal enough, but he'd said them with such steely finality, with such a wintry indifference that she wrapped her arms tight to ward off the vicious chill.

'You're cold.' He reached down for her robe, tossed it onto the tangled sheets. 'Go to bed.'

'You think you can speak to me like that, then walk away?'

'Yeah, I do.' He found what was left of his shirt and stuffed it in his pocket.

'You son of a bitch.' He only lifted a brow when she scrambled off the bed, punched her arms through the sleeves of her robe. 'I'm a combat zone? Well, who the hell asked you to sign up for the fight?'

'I guess we can say I was drafted. Lock those outside doors,' he instructed and turned to leave.

'Don't you dare walk out. You started this. You can't possibly understand. You have no idea what it's like for me. You pop into my life whenever you damn well please, and I'm just supposed to go along?'

'You kick me out of your life whenever you damn well please,' he retorted. 'And I'm just supposed to go along.'

'You want to talk about love and marriage, building houses, having children, and I don't know what's going to happen tomorrow.'

'Is that all? Well, just let me consult my crystal ball.'

Ordinarily, the killing look she shot him would have made him want to grin. Now he simply studied her with mild interest as she swore at him and spun away to pace. 'Always a slick answer, always a joke. I just want to slap you.'

'Go ahead. I don't hit girls.'

He knew that would do it. She stopped on a dime, swung around all balled fists, quivering muscles and fiery eyes. Her breath heaved as she fought for control, and her cheeks flushed with furious color.

Under the wall of temper he'd built leaked a stream of sheer admiration for her willpower. She wanted to wale into him but wouldn't give him the satisfaction. God, what a woman.

'I prefer being civilized,' she told him.

'No, you don't. But you're probably smart enough to know if you take a swipe at me we'll just end up in bed again. You lose control there, when I'm touching you, when I'm inside you. You forget to pick up all the emotional baggage you've carted around all your life, and it's just you and me.'

'Maybe you're right. Maybe you're exactly right. But I can't spend my life in bed with you, and the baggage is right there waiting when I get up.'

'So throw some of it out, Liv, and travel light.'

'You're so smug, aren't you?' She detested the bitter taste of the words. 'With your nice, cozy suburban childhood? Mom and Dad puttering around the house on weekends and you and all your pals ready to ride your bikes to the park after school.'

Progress, he thought, and settled into the fight. Finally, she was cutting through the shield. 'I'd say it wasn't quite like Beaver Cleaver, but you wouldn't know who the hell I was talking about since you didn't watch TV.'

'That's right, I didn't. Because my grandmother was afraid they'd run a story on my mother, or I'd turn it on and see one of her movies or one of the movies made about her. I didn't go to school because someone might have recognized me, and there'd be talk. Or there'd be an accident. Or God knows. I didn't have my parents lazing around the house on a Sunday afternoon because one was dead and the other in prison.'

'So how can you have a normal life now? That's a pitiful excuse for being afraid to trust your own feelings.'

'And what if it is?' Shame tried to wash through her temper, but she dammed it up. 'Who are you to judge me? Who have you lost? You can't know what it's like to lose one of the most vital people in your life to violence. To see it. To be part of it.'

'For Christ's sake, my father was a cop. Every time he strapped on his weapon and left the house, I knew he might not come back. Some nights when he was late, I'd sit by the window in the dark and wait for his car.' He'd never told anyone that, not even his mother. 'I lost him a thousand different ways over a thousand different nights in my head. Don't tell me I don't understand. My heart breaks for you, for what you lost, but goddamn it, don't tell me I don't understand.'

Because it ripped at him, he swung around toward the door. 'The hell with this.'

'Wait.' She would have rushed to the door to stop him, but her knees were shaking. 'Please. I didn't think. I didn't think of it.' Her eyes were damp and bleak. 'I'm sorry. Don't go. Please, don't go. I need air.'

She made it through the terrace doors, reached out for the banister and held on to it. When she heard him step out behind her, she closed her eyes. Relief, shame, love ran through her in a twisting river.

'I'm a mess, Noah. I've always set goals and marched right toward them. It was the only way I could get through everything. I could put what happened out of my head for long periods of time and just focus on what I was going to do, what I would accomplish. I didn't make friends. I didn't put any effort into it. People were just a distraction. No, don't.' She said it quietly and shifted aside when he brushed a hand over her hair. 'I don't think I can tell you if you're touching me.'

'You're shivering. Come inside and we'll talk.'

'I'm better outside. I'm always better outside.' She drew a deep breath. 'I took my first lover two weeks after you came to see me at college. I let myself think I was a little in love with him, but I wasn't. I was in love with you. I fell in love with you when you sat down beside me on the riverbank, near the beaver dam, and you listened to me. It wasn't a crush.'

She gathered the courage to turn then, to face him. 'I was only twelve, but I fell in love with you. When I saw you again, it was as if everything inside me had just been waiting. Just waiting,

Noah. After you left, I closed all that off again. You were right, what you said about my turning my feelings on and off. I could. I did. I went to bed with someone else just to prove it. It was cold, calculated.'

'I'd hurt you.'

'Yes. And I made sure I remembered that. I made sure I could pull that out so you couldn't do it again. Even after all this time, I didn't want to believe you could understand what I felt. About what happened to my mother, to me, to my family. But I think a part of me always knew you were the only one who really could. The book isn't just for you.'

'No, it isn't.'

'I don't know if – I'm not sure—' She broke off again, shook her head in frustration. 'I wanted to make you go. I wanted to make you mad enough to go because no one's ever mattered to me the way you do. It terrifies me.'

'I won't hurt you again, Liv.'

'Noah, it's not that.' Her eyes glowed against the dark. 'It's the other way around this time. What's inside of me, what could be in there and could leap out one day and–'

'Stop it.' The order cut her off like a slap. 'You're not your father any more than I'm mine.'

'But you know yours, Noah.' Still, for the first time she reached out to touch him, laid a hand on his cheek. 'Everything I feel for you . . . it fills me up inside. All the places I didn't know were empty, they're just full of you.'

'Christ, Liv.' His voice went rough and thick. 'Can't you see it's the same for me?'

'Yes. Yes, I can. I've been happier with you than I thought I could be. More with you than I thought I wanted to be. But even with that, I'm afraid of the things that you want. The things you have a right to expect. I don't know if I can give them to you or how long it'll take me. But I do know I love you.'

She remembered the words he'd used to tell her and gave them back to him. 'I'm so completely in love with you. Can that be enough for now?'

He reached up to take the hand that rested on his cheek, to press his lips to the center of her palm like a promise. 'That's exactly enough for now.'

Later, he dreamed of running through the forest, with the chill damp soaking through the fear sweat on his skin and his heart galloping in wild hoofbeats in his chest. Because he couldn't find her, and the sound of her scream was like a sword slicing through his gut.

He woke with a jerk to the pale silver of oncoming dawn with the last fierce call of an owl dying in the air. And Olivia curled warm against him.

The rain was holding off. But it would come before nightfall. Olivia could just smell the testing edge of it in the air as she guided her group into the trees. She'd done a head count of fifteen and had been foolishly grateful to see Celia among them.

The fact that she was there had been enough to help Olivia convince Noah to take some time in his quiet room to work.

She explained the cycle of survival, succession, tolerance of the rain forest. The give and take, the nurturing of life by the dead.

It was the trees that always caught the attention first, the sheer height of them. Out of habit, Olivia took the time to let her audience crane their necks, murmur in awe, snap their pictures while she talked of the significance and purpose of the overstory. It always took awhile before people began to notice the smaller things.

Her talks were never carved in stone. She was good at gauging the pace and rhythm of her group and gearing a talk to suit it. She moved along to point out the deep grooves that identified the bark of the Douglas fir, the faint purple cast of the cones of the western hemlock.

Every tree had a purpose, even if it was to die and become a breeding ground for saplings, for fungi, for lichen. If it was to fall, striking others down, it would leave a tear in the overstory so that busy annuals could thrive in the swath of sunlight.

It always amused her when they moved deeper and the light became dimmer, greener, that her groups would become hushed. As if they'd just stepped into a church.

As she lectured, she followed the familiar pattern, scanning faces to see who was listening, who was simply there because their parents or spouse had nagged them into it. She liked to play to those especially, to find something to intrigue them so that when they stepped out into the light again, they took something of her world with them.

A man caught her eye. He was tall, broad at the shoulders, with a fresh sunburn on his face that indicated someone unused to or unwise in the sun. He wore a hat and a long-sleeved shirt with jeans so obviously new they could have stood on their own. Despite the soft light he kept his sunglasses in place. She couldn't see his eyes through the black lenses but sensed they were on her face. That he was listening.

She smiled at him, an automatic response to his attentiveness. And her gaze had already moved on when his body jerked in reaction.

She had an avid amateur photographer in the group who was crouched by a nurse log, lens to fungi. She used his interest as a segue, identifying the oyster mushroom he was trying to capture on film.

She shifted over, pointed out a ring of lovely pure white caps. 'These are called Destroying Angels and while rare here are deadly.'

'They're so beautiful,' someone commented.

'Yes. Beauty is often deadly.'

Her gaze was drawn back to the man in the sunglasses. He'd moved closer, and while most of the others were hunting up other groups of mushroom and chattering, he stood still and silent. As if waiting.

'Any of you who go on unguided hikes or camp in the area, please exercise caution. However appealing nature may be, however lovely, it has its own defenses. Don't think that if you see an animal has nibbled on a mushroom or a berry patch, that makes it safe. It's wiser, and your experience in the forest will be more enjoyable, if you simply look.'

There was a peculiar tightness in her chest, a sensation that made her want to rub the heel of her hand between her breasts to loosen it. She recognized it – an early warning of a panic attack.

Stupid, she told herself, taking steady breaths as she took the group on a winding trail around nurse logs and ferns. She was perfectly safe. There was nothing here but the forest she knew and a handful of tourists.

The man had moved closer yet, close enough so that she could see a light sheen of sweat on his face. She felt cold and vaguely queasy.

'The cool dampness—' Why was he sweating? she wondered.

'The cool dampness,' she began again, 'in the Olympic rain forest provides the perfect environment for the exuberant growth you see around you. It supports the greatest weight of living matter, per acre, in the world. All the ferns, mosses and lichens you see live here epiphytically. Meaning they make their life on another plant, whether in the overstory of the forest, on the trunks of living trees or in the corpse of a dead one.'

The image of her mother's body flashed into her mind. 'While many of the plants we see here grow elsewhere, it's only in this area that many of the species reach true perfection. Here on the west side of the Olympic Mountains, in the valleys of Ho, Quinault and Queets, there is the ideal blend of saturation, mild temperatures and topography in perfect proportions to support this prime-temperate rain forest.'

The routine of lecture steadied her. The smattering of comments and questions engaged her mind.

The call of an eagle had everyone looking up. Though this thick canopy barred the sky, Olivia used the moment to shift into an explanation of some of the birds and mammals found in the forest.

The man in the sunglasses bumped against her, gripped her arm. She jolted and had nearly shoved him away when she saw he'd tripped in a tangle of vine maple.

'I'm sorry.' His voice was barely a whisper, but his hand stayed on her arm. 'I didn't mean to hurt you.'

'You didn't. The vine maple's been tripping up hikers for centuries. Are you all right? You look a little shaky.'

'I'm ... You're so ...' His fingers trembled on her arm. 'You're very good at your job. I'm glad I came today.'

'Thank you. We want you to enjoy yourself. Do I know you?'

'No.' His hand slid down her arm, brushed lightly over the back of hers, then dropped away. 'No, you don't know me.'

'You look like someone. I can't quite place it. Have you—'

'Miss! Oh, Miss MacBride, can you tell us what these are?'

'Yes, of course. Excuse me a minute.' She skirted over to a trio of women who huddled around a large sheet of dark red lichen. 'It's commonly called dog lichen. You can see – if you use your imagination – the illusion of dog's teeth in the rows.'

The pressure was back, like a vise around her ribs. She caught herself rubbing her hand where the man's fingers had brushed.

She knew him, she told herself. There was something . . . She turned around to look at him again. He was gone.

Heart pumping, she counted heads. Fifteen. She'd signed on for fifteen, and she had fifteen. But he'd been there, first at the edges of the group, then close in.

She walked over to Celia. 'You're wonderful,' Celia told her and gave her a brilliant smile. 'I want to live right here, with dog lichen and Destroying Angels and licorice ferns. I can't believe how much you know.'

'Sometimes I forget I'm supposed to entertain as well as educate and get too technical.'

Celia skimmed her gaze over the group. 'Looks to me like everyone is well entertained.'

'I hope so. Did you happen to notice a tall man, short gray hair, sunglasses. Sunburned, good build. Mid-sixties, I guess.'

'Actually, I haven't paid much attention to the people. I got caught up. Lose someone?'

'No, I . . . No,' she said more firmly. 'He must have been out on his own and just joined in for a bit. It's nothing.' But she rubbed the back of her hand again. 'Nothing.'

When she got back to the Center, Olivia was pleased to see several members of her group had been interested enough to head to the book area. A good guided hike could generate nice sales of books.

'Why don't I buy you lunch?' Celia asked.

'Thanks, but I really have work.' She caught the look, sighed a little. 'You don't have to worry. I'm going to be chained to my desk for quite a while. Then I have an interior lecture scheduled and another guided hike, then another lecture. The only place I'll be alone until six o'clock is in my office.'

'What time's the first lecture?'

'Three o'clock.'

'I'll be here.'

'At this rate, I'll have to offer you a job.'

Celia laughed, then gave Olivia's shoulder a little squeeze. 'It's annoying, isn't it, having people hovering.'

'Yes.' The minute she said it, she winced. 'I'm sorry. That was rude. I didn't mean—'

'I'd hate it, too,' Celia interrupted, then surprised Olivia by kissing her cheek. 'We'll get along very well, Liv. I promise. I'll see you at three.'

Oddly amused, Olivia walked through the Center to the concession area and picked up a Coke and a box of raisins to fortify her through the paperwork on her desk.

She detoured, winding through each area on the way to her office. When she realized she was looking for the man with the sunburned face, she ordered herself to stop being an idiot.

She pulled off her cap, stuck it in her back pocket, then carried her snack to her office. As she stepped inside, she checked her watch to gauge her time.

Two paces from her desk, she froze. And stared at the single white rose lying across the blotter. The can of Coke slipped out of her hand and landed with a thud at her feet.

His face had changed. Twenty years – twenty years in prison had changed it. Somehow she'd known, but she hadn't been prepared. Breathing shallowly she rubbed the hand he'd touched.

'Daddy. Oh God.'

He'd been so close. He'd touched her. He'd put his hand on her, and she hadn't known who he was. She'd looked into his face and hadn't known him.

All those years ago, with the security glass between them, Jamie had told him Olivia would never know him.

His daughter, and she'd given him the absent smile of one stranger to another.

He sat on a bench in deep shade, washed down pills with bottled water. Wiped the clammy sweat from his face with a handkerchief.

She *would* know him, he promised himself. Before another day passed, she would look at him and know him. Then it would be finished.

Chapter Thirty-two

It irritated Noah that he couldn't connect with Lucas Manning. Unavailable. Out of town. Incommunicado. He wanted a follow-up interview, and he wanted it soon.

Then there was Tanner himself.

Oh, they'd talk again all right, Noah thought as he pushed himself away from his laptop and paced to the window. He had a great deal to say to Sam Tanner. Maybe the son of a bitch thought the book would be a tool, perhaps even a weapon. But it was going to be neither.

When it was done, it would be the truth. And when it was done, if he had any skill, it would be a closing for Olivia.

The closing of that hideous part of her life and the opening of their life together.

She would be finished with her guided hike by now, he decided. And he could use a break from the book. So what was stopping him from going over to the Center? She might be a little annoyed, accuse him of checking up on her.

Well, that was something she'd have to get used to. He intended to spend the next sixty years, give or take, making sure she was safe and happy.

He shut down his machine and walked downstairs through the empty house. The MacBrides were at the lodge, and he imagined his mother had nudged them into having a meal with her. Bless her heart.

He checked the doors before he left, making sure they were secured. And, as a cop's son, just shook his head at the locks. Anyone who wanted in, he thought, would get in.

He'd learned that the hard way.

Following instinct, he detoured toward the garden, and casting one guilty look over his shoulder, plucked a handful of flowers to take to Olivia.

They'd make her smile, he thought, even as she pretended to be peeved that he'd stolen them from her grandfather.

He straightened quickly at the sound of a car and remembered he hadn't thought to hook his knife onto his belt. The wavering sun glinted off chrome and glass, then cleared so that he recognized Jamie Melbourne at the wheel.

By the time he'd walked to the car, she'd shoved the door open and jumped out. 'Are they all right? Is everyone all right?'

'Everyone's fine.'

'Oh God.' She leaned weakly against the fender, dragged a hand through her hair. She wasn't quite as polished as usual, he noted. Her makeup was sketchy, her eyes shadowed and her simple slacks and blouse travel-crushed.

'I – all the way up here, I imagined all sorts of things.' She dropped her hand, closed her eyes a moment. 'My mother called me last night, told me. She said he'd been here. Inside the house.'

'It looks that way. Why don't you sit down?'

'No, no, I've been sitting. On the plane, in the car. I couldn't get here any sooner. She didn't want me to come, but I had to. I had to be here.'

'No one's seen him, at least not that I've heard. Liv's at the Center, and your parents are at the lodge with mine.'

'Good. Okay.' She heaved out a long breath. 'I'm not a hysterical person. I think once you've faced the worst and survived it, you cope with anything. But I came very, very close to losing it last night. David was in Chicago, and I couldn't reach him for what seemed like hours. It probably wasn't more than twenty minutes until my brain clicked back and I thought of his cell phone.'

Because she looked as if she needed it, Noah gave her a smile. 'I love technology.'

'I sure had good thoughts about it last night. Nothing's ever sounded so good as his voice. He's on his way. Canceled the rest of his meetings. We all need to be together until . . .' Her eyes went dark. 'Until what, Noah?'

'Until it's over,' was all he said.

'Well, I'd better get my bag inside – and have a good, stiff drink.'

'I'll get it for you.'

'No, it's just a carry-on. God knows what I threw in it this morning. I probably have a cocktail dress and hiking boots in there. And, to be honest, I could use a few minutes on my own to pull it together.'

'I just locked up.' He pulled the key Rob had unearthed for him out of his pocket.

'I bet they haven't done that more than half a dozen times since I was born.' She took the key, studied it. 'How's my mother holding up?'

'She's tougher than you think. Maybe than she thought.'

'I hope you're right,' Jamie murmured as she opened the trunk and pulled out a tote. 'Well, I've got about six thousand calls to make to finish shifting my schedule around.' She slung the tote strap over her shoulder, then glanced at the flowers in Noah's hand. 'Going to see your girl.'

'That was the plan.'

'I like your plan. I think you're good for her.' She studied his face. 'You're a sturdy one under it all, aren't you, Noah Brady?'

'She'll never have to worry if I'll be there, never have to wonder if I love her.'

'That's nice.' The fatigue seemed to lift from her eyes. 'I know just how important that is. It's funny, Julie wanted that – no, more than that – and I found it. I'm glad her daughter has, too.'

He waited until she was in the house, until she'd locked the door behind her. With his senses alert, he walked into the trees to follow the trail to the Center.

From the shadows he watched, turning the weapon in his hand. And weeping.

Olivia was dead calm, and she was damn well going to stay that way. For ten minutes after seeing the rose, she'd sat on the floor, shaking. But she hadn't run. She'd fought back the panic, pulled herself to her feet.

She'd ordered herself to be calm and to act. As quietly as possible, she asked every member of the staff she could find if they'd noticed anyone going into her office. Each time the answer was no, and each time she followed it up by giving a description of her father, as she'd seen him that morning.

When she had all the answers she could gather, she walked outside and started toward the lodge.

'Hey!'

Her body wanted to jerk, and she forced it still. Then absorbed the flow of relief when she saw Noah coming across the parking lot toward her.

Normal, she promised herself. She would be normal.

'My grandfather's going to scalp you for picking his prize lilies.'

'No, he won't, because he'll know I was swept away by romance.'

'You're an idiot. Thank you.'

She gave him the smile he'd expected, but there was strain at the edges. 'You need a break. Why don't you get someone to fill in for you the rest of the day?'

'I need to do my job. It's important to me. I was just about to go over and find Frank.' She glanced around. People were coming and going. In and out of the lodge, the Center, the forest. 'Let's sit down a minute.'

She led him around the side and to a bench in the deep shade where her father had sat a short time before.

'There's another white rose. It was on my desk in my office.'

'Go inside the lodge.' Noah's voice was cool. 'I'll look around.'

'No, wait. I questioned the staff. No one noticed anyone going into my office. But a couple of them did notice someone this morning when I was setting up the group out here. A tall man, short gray hair, sunburned. He wore dark glasses and a fielder's cap, stiff new jeans and a blue long-sleeved shirt.' She pressed her lips together. 'I noticed him, too, during the hike. He slipped into the group. I kept getting this feeling, this uneasiness, but I couldn't pin it down. He spoke to me. He touched my hand. I didn't recognize him. He's changed, he looks old – years older than he should and . . . hard. But part of me knew. And when I saw the rose, his face was right there. My father.'

'What did he say to you, Liv?'

'It wasn't anything important, just that I was good at my job, that he was glad he'd come. Funny, isn't it, twenty years down the road and he compliments me on my work. I'm all right,' she said when Noah put his arm around her. 'I'm okay. I always wondered what it would be like if I saw him again. It was nothing like I imagined. Noah, he didn't look like a monster. He looked ill, and tired. How could he have done what he did, how could he be doing this now, and just look tired?'

'I doubt he knows the answer to that himself. Maybe he's just caught up, Liv, in the then and the now. And he just can't stop.'

He caught a movement, a bit of color, shifted his gaze. And watched Sam Tanner step out of the forest. Noah got to his feet, gripped a hand on Olivia's arm to pull her up beside him.

'Go into the lodge, find my father. Then stay there.'

She saw him, too, just at the moment when he spotted them, when he stopped short on the far edge of the parking lot. They stared at each other in the windy silence, as they had once stared at each other across a bloody floor.

Then he turned and walked quickly toward the trees.

'Go find my father,' Noah repeated and in a quick movement, unsnapped her knife sheath from her belt. 'Tell him what happened here. Then stay.' He turned, took her hard by the shoulders. 'Do you hear me, Liv? You stay inside. With my mother. Call your aunt at the house. Tell her to stay put, with the doors locked.'

'What? Aunt Jamie?'

'She got here just as I was leaving. Do it now.'

She shook herself to break out of the fog, then watched in dull horror as Noah strapped her knife to his own belt. 'No, you're not going after him.'

He simply gave her one steel-edged look, then turned her in the direction of the lodge. 'Go inside now.'

'You won't find him.' She shouted it, snatching at Noah's arm as he strode away. 'You don't know what he's capable of if you do.'

'He doesn't know what I'm capable of either. Goddamn it.' He whirled on her, fury hardening his face. 'Love isn't enough. You have to trust me. Go get your cop, and let's deal with this.'

With no choice, Olivia watched him sprint to the trees and vanish.

Noah had to rely on his senses. His hearing, straining to catch the rustling of brush. To the left? The right? Straight ahead. As he moved deeper, the false green twilight fell so that he strained his eyes, waiting to see a movement, the subtle sway of a low branch, the vibration of a thickly tangled vine.

He was younger, faster, but the forest itself could cloak prey as well as hunter.

He moved deeper, keeping his breathing slow and even so the soft sound of it wouldn't distract him. As he walked, his boots treading silently on the cushion of moss, he could hear the low rumble of thunder.

A storm was brewing.

'There's no point in running, Tanner.' He called out as he closed his hand over the hilt of Olivia's knife. It never occurred to him to wonder if he could use it. 'It's already over. You'll never get to her. You'll never touch her.'

His own voice echoed back to him, cold and still, and was followed by the strident call of a bird and the rush of wind through high branches.

Instinct had him winding in the direction of the house, into the thick beauty of the ripe summer forest, past the gleaming white river of deadly mushrooms, around the delicate sea of fanning ferns.

Rain began to hiss through the canopy and slither in thin trickles to the greedy green ground.

'She's your own daughter. What good will it do you? What point is there in hurting her now?'

'None.' Sam stepped out from the bulk of a fir. The gun in his trembling hand gleamed dull silver. 'There was never a point. Never a reason. I thought you knew.'

Olivia hit the doors of the lobby and burst inside. She looked frantically right and left. Guests were milling around or parked on the sofas and chairs. The hum of conversation roared in her ears.

She didn't know where to find Frank. The dining room, the library, his own suite, one of the terraces. The lodge was a honeycomb of rooms and carefully arranged spaces where guests could loiter at their leisure.

Noah was already in the forest. She couldn't take the time.

She spun on her heel, raced to the front desk. 'Mark.'

She grabbed the young desk clerk, dragged him toward the door leading to the back rooms. 'My grandparents, have you seen them?'

'An hour or so ago. They came through with some people. What's the matter? What's the problem?'

'Listen to me.' Panic was trying to claw through control. 'Listen carefully, it's important. I need you to find Frank Brady. He's a guest here. I need you to find him as quickly as you can. You tell him . . . Are you listening to me?'

'Yeah.' His Adam's apple bobbed. 'Sure. Frank Brady.'

'You find him, and you find him fast. You tell him that Sam Tanner went into the forest. The east side, Lowland Trail. Have you got that.'

'East side, Lowland Trail.'

'Tell him Noah went after him. Tell him that. Get one of the staff to call my house. My aunt's there. She's to stay inside. It's vital that she stay inside and wait to hear from me. No one's to go into the forest. Make an announcement. No one's to go in there until I clear it. Do whatever you can to keep guests in or around the lodge. Whatever it takes.'

'Inside? But why—'

'Just do it,' she snapped. 'Do it now.' And shoving him aside, she sprinted into the rear office.

She needed something, anything. Some kind of weapon. A defense. Frantic, she swept her hands over the desk, yanked open drawers.

She saw the scissors, the long silver blades, and snatched at them. Was it justice? she wondered as they trembled in her hand. Or was it just fate?

She slid the blades under her belt, secured the eyes of the handles and bolted.

The rain began to fall as she raced out of the clearing and into the trees.

Noah's mind was clear as glass, detached from the physical jeopardy of the gun and focused on the man. A part of him knew he could die here, in the verdant darkness, but he moved past it and faced whatever hand fate had begun to deal him twenty years before.

'No point, Sam? All of it, all those years you spent away come down to you and me standing in the rain?'

'You're just a bonus. I didn't expect to talk to you again. I've got some tapes for you. For the book.'

'Still looking to be the star? I won't make you one. Do you think I'll let you walk out of here, give her one more moment's pain? You'll never touch her.'

'I did.' Sam lifted free hand, rubbed his thumb and fingertips together. 'I was so close. I could smell her. Just soap. She grew up so pretty. She has a stronger face than Julie's. Not as beautiful, but stronger. She looked at me. She looked right at me and didn't know me. Why would she?' he murmured. 'Why would she know me? I've been as dead to her as her mother for twenty years.'

'Is that why you arranged all this? To come alive for her? Start me on the book so I'd dig up old memories. Put you back in her head, so when you got out you could start on her.'

'I wanted her to remember me. Goddamn it, I'm her father, I wanted her to remember me.' He lifted his hand again, drilled his fingertips into his temple where pain began to hammer. 'I've got a right. A right to at least that.'

'You lost your rights to her.' Noah edged closer. 'You're not part of her anymore.'

'Maybe not, but she's part of me. I've waited nearly a third of my life just to tell her that.'

'And to terrify her because she knows what you are, she saw what you were. She was a baby, innocent, and taking that innocence wasn't enough? You sent the music box to remind her that you weren't done. And the phone calls, the white roses.'

'Roses.' A dreamy smile came to his lips. 'I used to put a white rose on her pillow. My little princess.' He pressed his hand to the side of his head again, dragging it back, knocking his cap aside. 'They don't make drugs like they used to. The kind I remember, you'd never feel the pain.'

He blinked, his eyes narrowing abruptly. 'Music box?' He gestured with the gun, an absent gesture that had Noah halting. 'What music box?'

'The Blue Fairy. The one you broke the night you knocked your wife around in Olivia's room.'

'I don't remember. I was coked to my eyeballs.' Then his eyes cleared. 'The Blue Fairy. I knocked it off her dresser. I remember. She cried, and I told her I'd buy her another one. I never did.'

'You sent her one a few days ago.'

'No. I'd forgotten. I should have made that up to her. I shouldn't have made her cry. She was such a good little girl. She loved me.'

Despite the cold wall of rage, pity began to eke through. 'You're sick and you're tired. Put the gun down and I'll take you back.'

'For what? More doctors, more drugs? I'm already dead, Brady. I've been dead for years. I just wanted to see her again. Just once. And just once, I wanted her to see me. She's all I have left.'

'Put the gun down.'

With a puzzled expression, Sam glanced down at the gun in his hand. Then he began to laugh. 'You think this is for you? It's for me. I didn't have the guts to use it. I've been gutless all my fucking life. And you know what, Brady, you know what I figured out when I stuck the barrel in my mouth? When I had my finger on the trigger and couldn't pull it?'

His voice became confident and clear. 'I didn't kill Julie. I wouldn't have had the guts.'

'Let's go talk about it.' As Noah stepped forward, reaching out with one hand for the gun, there was a crash in the brush, a blur of movement.

He felt pain rip along his shoulder as he turned, heard a scream that wasn't his own. He saw David Melbourne's contorted face as the force of the attack sent him ramming against Sam, tumbling them both to the ground.

Noah rolled aside, agony spearing through his wounded shoulder as he thrust his hands up, caught the wrist of David's knife hand. Noah's lips peeled back in a snarl of effort as his bloody hands began to slip.

The blade stabbed into the rain-slimed moss, a breath from his face. Rearing up, Noah bucked him aside, then rolled for the gun that lay on the ground.

As he snatched it up, David fled into the trees.

'I never thought of him.' With the side of his face scratched and oozing blood, Sam crawled over. His eyes were glassy from the pain rolling inside his head. 'I should have known, because I never thought of him. A dozen other men, I thought of them. She would never have looked at them, that was my delusion, but I thought of them. Never him.'

As he spoke, he fumbled to tie his handkerchief around the gash in Noah's shoulder. 'He should've just waited for me to die instead of trying to kill me.'

Wincing against the pain, Noah gripped Sam's shirtfront. 'Not you. It's Olivia he wants now.'

'No.' Fear coated over the agony in his eyes. 'No, not Livvy. We have to find him. Stop him.'

There wasn't time to debate. 'He's heading deeper in, but he may circle around, head toward the house.' Noah hesitated only a moment. 'Take this.' He unsnapped Olivia's sheath. 'They're looking for you by now. If my father comes across you with a gun—'

'Frank's here?'

'That's right. Melbourne won't get far. You head toward the house. I'll do what I can to pick up his trail.'

'Don't let him hurt Livvy.'

Noah checked the gun and raced into the green.

Olivia wanted to rush headlong into the trees, run blindly through the shadows, shout for Noah. It took every ounce of control to move slowly, to look for signs.

Her turf, she reminded herself.

But there'd been dozens of people in that edge of the forest, leaving crisscrossing prints. The ground was percolating with rain now, and she would lose even these prints if she didn't choose soon. He'd come in at a sprint, she remembered, and judged the length between strides.

Noah had long legs.

So did her father.

She headed due south and into the gloom.

The rain was alive, murmuring as it forced its way through the tangle of vines and drapery overhead. The air was thick with it and the pervasive scent of rot. Small creatures scurried away, sly rustles in the dripping brush. And as the wind cooled the treetops, a thin fog skinned over the ground and smoked over her boots.

She moved more quickly now, trying to outpace the fear. Every shadow was a terror, every shape a threat. Ferns, slick with rain, slithered around her legs as she hurried deeper into the forest and father away from safety.

She lost the trail, backtracked, could have wept with frustration. The quiet chuckle of panic began to dance in her chest. She focused on the forest floor, searching for a sign. And caught her breath with relief, with something almost like triumph, when she picked up the tracks again.

Nerves skipped and skidded over her skin as she followed the trail of the man she loved. And of the man who'd shattered her life.

When she heard the scream, fear plunged into her heart like a killing blade.

She forgot logic, she forgot caution and she ran as though her life depended on it.

Her feet slipped, sliding wild over the moldering ground. Fallen logs seemed to throw themselves into her path, forcing her to leap and stumble. Fungi, slimy with rain, burst wetly under her boots. She went down hard, tearing moss with the heels of her hands, sending shock waves stinging into her knees.

She lunged to her feet, breathless, pushed herself off the rough bark of a hemlock and pushed blindly through vines that snaked out to snatch at her arms and legs. She beat and ripped at them, fought her way clear.

Rain soaked her hair, dripped into her eyes. She blinked it away and saw the blood.

It was soaking into the ground, going pale with wet. Shaking, she dropped to her knees, touched her fingertips to the stain, and brought them back, red and wet.

'Not again. No, not again.' She rocked herself, mourning in the sizzle of rain, cringing into a ball as the fear hammered at her, screamed into her mind, burst through her body like a storm of ice.

'Noah!' She shouted it once, listened to the grieving echo of it. Shoving to her feet, she ran her smeared fingers over her face, then screamed it.

With her only thought to find him, she began to run.

He'd lost his direction, but he thought he still had the scent of his quarry. The gun was familiar in his hand now, as if it had always been there. He never doubted he could use it. It was part of him now. Everything that was primitive about the world he was in was inside him now.

Life and death and the cold-blooded will to survive.

Twenty years, the man had hidden what he was, what he'd done. He'd let another grow old in a cage, had played the devoted husband to his victim's sister, the indulgent uncle to her daughter.

Murder, bloody murder had been locked inside him, while he prospered, while he posed. And when the key had started to turn in the door to Sam Tanner's cage, it had set murder free again.

The break-ins, the attack on Mike. An attempt to stop the book, Noah thought as he moved with deliberate strides through the teeming woods. to beat back the guilt, the fear of exposure that must have tried to claw out of him hundreds of times over twenty long years.

And once again, he'd turned the focus on Sam, once again structured his acts to point the accusations at an innocent man.

But this time it was Olivia he'd hunted. Fear that she'd seen him that night, would remember some small detail that had been tucked in a corner of her mind all this time. A detail that might jibe with the story Sam wanted to tell.

Yes, it was logical, the cold-blooded logic that would fit a man who could murder his wife's sister, then live cozily with her family for another generation.

Then the balance had shifted on him, with the possibility of a book, another in-depth look at the case, the interviews with Olivia urging her to talk about the night her family had conveniently buried along with Julie.

But she couldn't talk, couldn't think, couldn't remember if she was too afraid. Or if she was dead.

Then he heard her scream his name.

Chapter Thirty-three

The monster was back. The smell of him was blood. The sound of him was terror.

She had no choice but to run, and this time to run toward him.

The lush wonder of forest that had once been her haven, that had always been her sanctuary, spun into a nightmare. The towering majesty of the trees was no longer a grand testament to nature's vigor, but a living cage that could trap her, conceal him. The luminous carpet of moss was a bubbling bog that sucked at her boots. She ripped through ferns, rending their sodden fans to slimy tatters, skidded over a rotted log and destroyed the burgeoning life it nursed.

Green shadows slipped in front of her, beside her, behind her, seemed to whisper her name.

Livvy, my love. Let me tell you a story.

Breath sobbed out of her lungs, set to grieving by fear and loss. The blood that still stained her fingertips had gone ice-cold.

Rain fell, a steady drumming against the windswept canopy, a sly trickle over lichen-draped bark. It soaked into the greedy ground until the whole world was wet and ripe and somehow hungry.

She forgot if she was hunter or hunted, only knew in some deep primal instinct that movement was survival.

She would find him, or he would find her. And somehow it would be finished. She would not end as a coward. And if there was any light in the world, she would find the man she loved. Alive.

She curled the blood she knew was his into the palm of her hand and held it like hope.

Fog snaked around her boots, broke apart at her long, reckless strides. Her heartbeat battered her ribs, her temples, her fingertips in a feral, pulsing rhythm.

She heard the crack overhead, the thunder snap of it, and leaped aside as a branch, weighed down by water and wind and time, crashed to the forest floor.

A little death meant fresh life.

She closed her hand over the only weapon she had and knew she would kill to live.

And through the deep green light haunted by darker shadows, she saw the monster as she remembered him in her nightmares.

Covered with blood, and watching her.

Fury that was as much hate as fear spurted through her in a bitter kind of power. 'Where's Noah? What have you done to him?'

He was on his knees, his hand pressed to his side where blood spilled out of him. The pain was so huge it reached to the bone, to the bowels.

'Livvy.' He whispered it, both prayer and plea. 'Run.'

'I've been running from you all my life.' She stepped closer, driven forward by a need that had slept inside her since childhood. 'Where's Noah?' she repeated. 'I swear I'll kill you if you've taken someone else I love.'

'Not me. Not then, not now.' His vision wavered. She seemed to sway in front of him, tall and slim with her mother's eyes. 'He's still close. For God's sake, run.'

They heard it at the same moment, the thrashing through the brush. She spun around, her heart leaping with hope. At her feet, Sam's heart tripped with terror.

'Stay away from her.' Sheer will pushed him to stand. He tried to shove Olivia behind him, but only collapsed against her.

'You should have died in prison.' David's face was wet with rain and blood. The knife in his hand ran with both. 'None of this would have happened if you'd just died.'

'Uncle David.' The shock of seeing him, his eyes wild, his clothes splattered, had her stepping forward. With a strength born of desperation, Sam jerked her back, held her hard against him.

'He killed her. Listen to me. He killed her. He wanted her and couldn't have her. Don't go near him.'

'Step away from him, Livvy. Come here to me.'

‘I want you to run,’ Sam said urgently. ‘Run the way you did that night and find a place to hide. Find Noah.’

‘You know better than to listen to him.’ David’s smile made her blood go cold. ‘You saw what he did to her that night. He was never good enough for her. Never right. I’ve always been there for you, haven’t I, Livvy?’

‘She never wanted you.’ Sam’s voice was slurred and slow as he fought to stay conscious. ‘She never loved anyone but me.’

‘Shut up!’ The parody of a smile became a snarl. His face flushed dark and ugly. ‘It should have been me. She would have come to me if you hadn’t gotten in the way.’

‘Oh God. Oh, my God.’ Olivia stared at David and braced to take her father’s weight. ‘You. It was you.’

‘She should have listened to me! I *loved* her. I always loved her. She was so beautiful, so perfect. I would have treated her like an angel. What did he do for her? He dragged her down, made her miserable, only thought of himself.’

‘You’re right. I treated her badly.’ Sam slumped against Olivia, murmured, ‘Run.’ But she only shook her head and held on to him. ‘I didn’t deserve her.’

‘I would have given her everything.’ Tears slipped out of David’s eyes now, and his knife hand dropped to his side. ‘She would never have been unhappy with me. I settled for second best and gave Jamie everything I would have given Julie. Why should I have settled when she was finally going to divorce you? When she finally saw you for what you were. She was meant to come to me then. It was meant.’

‘You went to the house that night.’ Sam’s side was numb. He levered himself straight, caught his breath and prayed for the strength to step away from his daughter.

‘Do you know how much courage it took for me to go to her, to give her everything that was in my heart? She let me in and smiled at me. She was doing her clippings and having a glass of wine. The music was on, her favorite Tchaikovsky. She said it was nice to have company.’

‘She trusted you.’

‘I poured my soul out to her. I told her I loved her, always had. That I wanted her. That I was leaving Jamie and we could be together. She looked at me as if I were insane. Pushed me away when I tried to hold her. She told me to leave and we'd forget I'd ever spoken of it. Forget.' He spat the word out.

'She loved my father,' Olivia murmured. 'She loved my father.'

'She was *wrong!* I only tried to convince her she was wrong, I only wanted to make her see. If she hadn't struggled against me, I wouldn't have ripped her robe. Then she turned on me, shouted at me to get out of her house. She said she would tell Jamie everything. She said I was scum. Scum! That she would never see me again, never speak to me. I – I couldn't hear what she was saying, it was so vile. She turned her back on me, turned away as if I were nothing. And the scissors were in my hand. Then they were in her. I think she screamed,' he said softly. 'I'm not sure. I don't know. I only remember the blood.'

His eyes focused again, fixed on Olivia. 'It was an accident, really. One moment, one terrible mistake. But I couldn't take it back, could I? I couldn't change it.'

She had to be calm, Olivia ordered herself. Her father was bleeding badly. She had no doubt that she could outdistance and lose her uncle in the forest. But how could she leave her father? How could she run away and hide again?

She would stand, protect. And pray for help to come. 'You held me while I cried for her.'

'I cried, too!' It enraged David that she didn't understand. Just like her mother. Just like Julie. 'If she'd only listened, it would never have happened. Why should I have paid for that? He's the one who hurt her; he's the one who deserved to pay. I had to protect myself, my life. I had to get out. There was so much blood, I was nearly sick.'

'How did you get out of the house and back home?' Olivia asked and strained her ears for a sound – heard only the thrashing of rain. 'Aunt Jamie would have seen the blood.'

'I stripped off my clothes, bundled them up. I went outside, to the pool, and washed the blood off. I washed it all away. There were always spare clothes in the changing house, no one would ever notice. I could get rid of my own later, a dumpster in the city. I went back in the house because I thought it might be a dream. But it wasn't. I thought I heard you upstairs. I thought I heard you, but I couldn't be sure.'

'I woke up. I heard Mama scream.'

'Yes, I found out later. I had to get home in case Jamie woke up and realized I'd slipped out. It wasn't until they brought you to us that I wondered if you'd seen me. I wondered if you'd heard. Twenty years, I've wondered. I've waited.'

'No, I didn't see you. I never knew.'

'It would have stayed that way. Everyone put it aside, everyone closed the door, until the book. How could I be sure? How could I know for sure that you hadn't heard my voice, that you hadn't looked out the window, seen my car? It ruined my life, don't you see? I'd done everything to make it work, everything to make up for that one single night.'

'You let my father go to prison.'

'I was in prison, too.' Tears leaked out of his eyes. 'I was paying, too. I knew you'd be just like her. I knew when it came down to a choice, you'd choose him. I always loved you, Livvy. You should have been ours. Mine and Julie's. But that's over now. I have to protect myself. I have to end it.'

He lunged toward her, leading with the knife.

It was like his dream, the dark, the trees, the murmur of rain and wind. He could run until his heart burst out of his chest and he couldn't find her. Every rustle had him turning in a new direction, every call of a night bird was the sound of her voice.

The bone-numbing terror that he would be too late, that he would never wake up from this nightmare and find her curled against him, drove him harder.

She was somewhere in the vast, twisting maze of the forest. Somewhere just beyond his reach.

He stopped, leaning against the bulk of a hemlock to clear the tumble of his mind. The air was so thick, every breath he took was like gulping in water. His shoulder was on fire, the white handkerchief tied over the wound long since gone red.

He stood very still for a moment and listened. Was that the murmur of voices, or just the rain? Sound seemed to shoot at a dozen different angles, then swallow itself. The only compass he had now was his gut. Trusting it, he turned west.

This time, when she screamed, he was close.

Sam shoved her clear and, with the little strength he had left, drove his body into David's. When the knife sliced through him again, he felt nothing but despair. As he staggered and fell, Olivia leaped to her feet and tried to catch him.

It happened quickly, her father slipping out of her hands, the sound of running feet slapping against the saturated ground. And the quick prick of a knife at her throat.

'Let her go.' Noah braced his feet, held the gun in the classic police grip. Fear was a hot river in his blood.

'I'll kill her. You know I will. Drop the gun, or I'll slice her throat and be done with it.'

'And lose your shield? I don't think so.' Oh God, Liv, oh God, don't move. He gazed quickly at her face, saw the blank shock in her eyes, the thin trickle of red sliding down the slim column of her throat. 'Step away from her, step back.'

'Put the gun down!' He jerked Olivia's head up with the flat of the blade. 'She's dead, do you hear me. She's dead if you don't do it now!'

'He'll kill me anyway.'

'Shut up! Shut the hell up!' He nicked her again, and she saw Noah's hands jerk, then start to lower.

'Don't do it. Don't hurt her.'

'Put it down!'

She heard the roar of their voices in her head, saw the decision in Noah's eyes. 'He'll kill me no matter what you do. Then he'll kill you. Don't let him take someone else I love. Don't let him win.'

Her hand closed over the cold metal eyes of the scissors, drew them out in one quick, smooth motion, then plunged them viciously into his thigh.

He screamed, high and bright, his knife hand jerking up, then dropping. She shoved her body away from his, yanking the scissors clear. Then held them out as he leaped toward her.

She heard the bullet ring out, one sharp snap. Saw the bright blossom of blood bloom high on his chest and the puzzled shock in his eyes as he fell toward her.

She didn't step back. And she would never ask herself if she'd had time to do so. The killing point of the scissors slid silently into his belly.

The weight of him bore her to the ground. Before she could roll clear, Noah pulled her up and against him. His arms that had been so steady began to quiver.

'You're all right. You're okay.' He said it again, then once again as his hands ran shakily over her. 'He cut you.' His fingers brushed gently at her throat. 'Oh God, Liv.'

She was crushed against him again, burrowed into him. Her head went light, seemed to circle somewhere just beyond her shoulders. 'I thought he might have killed you. I saw the blood and I thought . . . No!' She jerked back, her hands vising on Noah's face. 'Daddy.'

She pulled away and stumbled to the ground beside her father. 'Oh no, no, no. Don't. Please. I'm so sorry. I'm sorry, Daddy.' She had nothing but her hands to press against his wound to try to stem the bleeding.

'Don't cry, Livvy.' He reached up to touch her face. 'This is the best way for me. My time's running out, anyway. I needed to see you again. It was the last thing I had to do. You've got your mother's eyes.' He smiled a little. 'You always did. I let her down in so many ways.'

'Don't, please don't.' She pressed her face to his neck. 'Noah, help me.'

'If I'd been what I should have been, what she believed I could be, she'd still be alive.'

'Don't talk now. We have to stop the bleeding. They'll find us soon.' Her hands fumbled with the scraps of cloth Noah gave her. 'They're looking, and we'll get you to the hospital.'

'You're a smart girl, you know better.' His eyes were clouding over, but they shifted to Noah. 'She's a smart one, isn't she, Brady?'

'That's right.' He pressed another scrap of his shirt to the wound in Sam's side. 'So listen to her.'

'I'd rather die a hero.' His short laugh ended in a racking cough. 'There's enough of the old me in here to rather enjoy that. Is that son of a bitch dead?'

'As Moses,' Noah told him.

'Thank Christ for that.' The pain was floating away. 'Livvy.' He gripped her hand. 'When I was looking for you that night, when you saw me, I wasn't going to hurt you.'

'I know that. I know. Don't leave me now that I've just gotten you back.'

'I'm sorry, Livvy. I wanted you to look at me once, just once, and know who I was. In the end I kept you safe. Maybe that makes up for all the years I didn't.' His vision wavered and dimmed. 'Write the book, Brady. Tell the truth.'

'Count on it.'

'Take care of my little girl. Kiss me good-bye, Livvy love.'

With tears flooding her throat, she pressed her lips to his cheek. And felt his hand go lax in hers. Her grief was one long, low moan.

Noah sat with her while she cradled her father's body and wept in the rain.

She slept because Noah poured a sedative down her throat. When she woke, logy with drugs and grief and shock, it was midday.

She heard the birdsong, felt the sun on her face. And, opening her eyes, saw him sitting beside her.

'You didn't sleep.'

He was already holding her hand. He couldn't seem to let go. 'I did for a bit.'

'Everything that happened, it's all in my head, but it feels as if it's wrapped in cotton.'

'Just leave it that way for now.'

He looked so wonderful, she thought. So hers, with his exhausted eyes and stubble of beard. 'You saved my life.'

'Just part of the service.' He leaned down to kiss her. 'Don't make me do it again.'

'That's a deal. How's your shoulder?'

'Well, I could say it's nothing, but why lie? It hurts like a bitch.'

She sat up, tugged up the sleeve of his T-shirt and pressed her lips to the bandage.

'Thanks. Why don't you try to get some more sleep?'

'No, I really need to get out.' She looked into his eyes. 'I need to walk. Walk in the forest with me, Noah.'

When she was dressed, she held out a hand for his. 'My family?'

'They're still asleep. Your grandparents were up with Jamie until almost dawn.'

She nodded, started out quietly. 'Your parents?'

'In the spare room.'

'They'll need us, all of them. I need this first.'

They went down the back stairs and left through the kitchen door.

'Your father,' she began. 'When they found us, I don't think he knew whether he was proud of you or horrified.' She let out a breath, drew another in. 'I think he was both.'

'He taught me how to handle guns, to respect them. I know he hoped I'd never have to use one.'

'I don't know how to feel, Noah. All these years I thought my father was a murderer, the worst kind of murderer. I lost him when I was four, and now I have him back. I have him back in a way that changes everything. And I can never tell him.'

'He knew.'

'It helps to have that, to hold on to that.' She tightened her hand on his as they moved into the trees. 'I didn't run. I didn't leave him. This time I didn't run and hide. I can live with all the rest becausc this time, I didn't run.'

'Liv, you gave him exactly what he wanted at the end of his life. You looked at him, and you knew him. He told me that was the last thing he needed.'

She nodded, absorbing that into the grief. 'All my life, I loved my uncle. I shifted him into my father figure, admired him, trusted him. He wasn't what I thought he was, any more than my father was what I thought he was. Oh God. God, Noah, how is Aunt Jamie going to cope with this? How is she going to live with it?'

'She has you, your family. She'll get through it.'

'I hope she'll stay here, for a while at least. Stay here and heal.'

'I think she needs to hear you say just that.'

She nodded again and leaned against him a little. 'You're good at knowing what people need to hear.' She let out a sigh. 'I was afraid I wouldn't be able to come in here again and feel what I've always felt. But I can. It's so beautiful. So alive. No monsters here.'

'Not ever again.'

'I love this place.' It had sheltered her, given her life. Now, she had a choice. To stay with the old, or to start the new.

She let go of Noah's hand, turned in a circle. 'But there's this other spot, along the coast. Heavily wooded, excellent old forest with a view of the Pacific raging up against the cliffs.' She stopped, met his eyes soberly. 'That's where we should build the house.'

He stared at her while a rage of emotions gushed into him, then settled in quiet joy. 'How many bedrooms?'

'Five, as previously discussed.'

'Okay. Stone or wood?'

'Both.' Her lips twitched, her eyes glowed now, as he nodded and stepped toward her.

'When?'

'As soon as you ask me to marry you, which you've neglected to do so far.'

'I knew I'd forgotten something.' She laughed when he hauled her into his arms. 'I've waited a long time for you.' He brushed his lips over hers, then lingered, deepened the kiss. 'Don't make me wait anymore. Marry me.'

'Yes.' She framed his face with her hands. 'Between the forest and the flowers. And soon.' She smiled at him, drawing him close to touch her lips to his cheek. 'I love you, Noah. I want to start a life with you. Now. We've both waited long enough.'

THE REEF

Nora Roberts

The *New York Times* bestseller

Tate Beaumont, a beautiful student of marine archaeology, and Matthew Lassiter, a sea-scarred young man, share a dream of finding Angelique's Curse, the jewelled amulet surrounded by legend and said to be long lost at the bottom of the Caribbean.

Forced into a reluctant partnership with Matthew and his uncle, Tate soon learns that her arrogant but attractive fellow diver holds as many secrets as the sea itself. And when the truth emerges about the mysterious death of Matthew's father eight years earlier, desire – and danger – begin to rise to the surface.

'Nora Roberts is at the top of her game'
People

'A consistently entertaining writer'
USA Today

'The publishing world might be hard-pressed to find an author with a more diverse style or fertile imagination than Roberts'
Publishers Weekly

978-0-7499-3159-9

HIGH NOON

Nora Roberts

Those closest to you can do the most harm

Phoebe MacNamara first comes face to face with Duncan Swift high up on a rooftop, as she tries to stop one of his ex-employees from jumping. As Savannah's chief hostage negotiator, Phoebe is talented, courageous and willing to risk her life to save others – and Duncan is determined to keep this intriguing woman in his life.

But Phoebe has made enemies too. When she is viciously assaulted and sent threatening messages, she realises that someone is out to destroy her – both professionally and personally. With Duncan by her side, Phoebe must discover just who is pursuing her, before it's too late . . .

'Women are addicted to her contemporary novels as chocoholics are to Godiva . . . Roberts is a superstar'
New York Times

978-0-7499-3898-7

Other bestselling titles available by mail:

☐	Divine Evil	Nora Roberts	£6.99
☐	The Reef	Nora Roberts	£6.99
☐	Blue Smoke	Nora Roberts	£6.99
☐	High Noon	Nora Roberts	£6.99
☐	Sanctuary	Nora Roberts	£6.99
☐	Montana Sky	Nora Roberts	£6.99
☐	Northern Lights	Nora Roberts	£6.99
☐	Tribute	Nora Roberts	£11.99

The prices shown above are correct at time of going to press. However, the publishers reserve the right to increase prices on covers from those previously advertised, without further notice.

PIATKUS

Please allow for postage and packing: **Free UK delivery.**
Europe; add 25% of retail price; Rest of World; 45% of retail price.

To order any of the above or any other Piatkus titles, please call our credit card orderline or fill in this coupon and send/fax it to:

Piatkus Books, P.O. Box 121, Kettering, Northants NN14 4ZQ
Fax: 01832 733076 Tel: 01832 737526
Email: aspenhouse@FSBDial.co.uk

☐ I enclose a UK bank cheque made payable to Piatkus for £ ....
☐ Please charge £ ...... to my Visa, Delta, Maestro.

☐☐☐☐☐☐☐☐☐☐☐☐☐☐☐☐

Expiry Date ☐☐☐☐ Maestro Issue No. ☐☐

NAME (BLOCK LETTERS please) ....

ADDRESS ....

....

....

Postcode .... Telephone ....

Signature ....

Please allow 28 days for delivery within the UK. Offer subject to price and availability.

Nora Roberts is the *New York Times* bestselling author of more than 190 novels. Under the pen name J. D. Robb, she is the author of the *New York Times* bestselling futuristic suspense series, which features Lieutenant Eve Dallas and Roarke. There are more than 300 million copies of her books in print, and she has had more than 150 *New York Times* bestsellers.

Visit her website at www.nora-roberts.co.uk

By Nora Roberts

Homeport
The Reef
River's End
Carolina Moon
The Villa
Midnight Bayou
Three Fates
Birthright
Northern Lights
Blue Smoke
Montana Sky
Angels Fall
High Noon
Divine Evil
Tribute
Sanctuary

Three Sisters Island Trilogy:
Dance Upon the Air
Heaven and Earth
Face the Fire

Chesapeake Bay Quartet:
Sea Swept
Rising Tides
Inner Harbour
Chesapeake Blue

The Key Trilogy:
Key of Light
Key of Knowledge
Key of Valour

In the Garden Trilogy:
Blue Dahlia
Black Rose
Red Lily

The Irish Trilogy:
Jewels of the Sun
Tears of the Moon
Heart of the Sea

The Circle Trilogy:
Morrigan's Cross
Dance of the Gods
Valley of Silence

The Dream Trilogy:
Daring to Dream
Holding the Dream
Finding the Dream

The Sign of Seven Trilogy:
Blood Brothers
The Hollow
The Pagan Stone

As J. D. Robb:

Naked in Death
Glory in Death
Immortal in Death
Rapture in Death
Ceremony in Death
Vengeance in Death
Holiday in Death
Conspiracy in Death
Loyalty in Death
Witness in Death
Judgement in Death
Betrayal in Death
Seduction in Death
Reunion in Death
Purity in Death
Portrait in Death
Imitation in Death
Divided in Death
Visions in Death
Survivor in Death
Origin in Death
Memory in Death
Born in Death
Innocent in Death
Creation in Death
Strangers in Death

By Nora Roberts and J. D. Robb

Remember When

SEA SWEPT

NORA ROBERTS

PIATKUS

PIATKUS

First published in the United States in 1998 by
G. P. Putnam's Sons
First published in Great Britain in 2002 by
Judy Piatkus (Publishers) Ltd
Reprinted 2002 (twice), 2003, 2004 (twice), 2005, 2006, 2007 (twice), 2008, 2009

A CIP catalogue record for this book
is available from the British Library

ISBN 978-0-7499-3332-6

Typeset by Phoenix Photosetting, Chatham, Kent
Printed and bound in the UK by
CPI Mackays, Chatham, ME5 8TD

Papers used by Piatkus Books are natural, renewable and recyclable products made from wood grown in sustainable forests and certified in accordance with the rules of the Forest Stewardship Council.

Mixed Sources
Product group from well-managed
forests and other controlled sources
www.fsc.org Cert no. SGS-COC-004081
© 1996 Forest Stewardship Council

Piatkus Books
An imprint of
Little, Brown Book Group
100 Victoria Embankment
London EC4Y 0DY

An Hachette Livre UK Company
www.hachettelivre.co.uk

www.piatkus.co.uk

For Mary Blayney
of the warm and generous heart

PROLOGUE

CAMERON QUINN WASN'T quite drunk. He could get there if he put his mind to it, but at the moment he preferred the nice comfortable buzz of the nearly there. He liked to think it was just the two-steps-short-of-sloppy state that was holding his luck steady.

He believed absolutely in the ebb and flow of luck, and right now his was flowing fast and hot. Just the day before, he'd raced his hydrofoil to victory in the world championship, edging out the competition by the point of the bow and breaking the standing record for time and speed.

He had the glory, and the hefty purse, and he'd taken both over to Monte Carlo to see how they held up.

They held up just dandy.

A few hands of baccarat, a couple of rolls of the dice, the turn of a card, and his wallet weighed heavier. Between the paparazzi and a reporter from *Sports Illustrated*, the glory showed no signs of dimming either.

Fortune continued to smile—no, make that leer, Cameron thought—by turning him toward that little jewel in the Med at the same time that popular magazine was wrapping its swimsuit-edition shoot.

And the leggiest of those long-stemmed gifts from God had turned her high-summer blue eyes on him, tipped her full, pouty lips up in an invitational smile a blind man could have spotted, and opted to stay on a few days longer.

And she'd made it clear that with very little effort, he could get a whole lot luckier.

Champagne, generous casinos, mindless, no-strings sex. Yes indeed, Cameron mused, luck was definitely being his kind of lady.

When they stepped out of the casino into the balmy March night, one of the ubiquitous paparazzi leaped out, snapping frantically. The woman pouted—it was, after all, her trademark look—but gave her endless mane of ribbon-straight silvery-blond hair an artful toss and shifted her killer body expertly. Her red-is-the-color-of-sin dress, barely thicker than a coat of paint, made an abrupt halt just south of the Gates of Paradise.

Cameron just grinned.

"They're such pests," she said with a hint of a lisp or a French accent. Cameron was never sure which. She sighed, testing the strength of that thin silk, and let Cameron guide her down the moon-dappled street. "Every place I look is a camera. I'm so weary of being viewed as an object for the pleasure of men."

Oh, yeah, right, he mused. And because he figured the pair of them were as shallow as a dry creek after a drought, he laughed and turned her into his arms. "Why don't we give him something to splash on page one, sugar?"

He brought his mouth down to hers. The taste of her tickled his hormones, engaged his imagination, and made him grateful their hotel was only two blocks away.

She skimmed her fingers up into his hair. She liked a man with plenty of hair, and his was full and thick and as dark as the night around them. His body was hard, all tough muscle and lean, disciplined lines. She was very choosy about the body of a potential lover, and his more than met her strict requirements.

His hands were just a bit rougher than she liked. Not

the pressure or movement of them—that was lovely—but the texture. They were a working man's hands, but she was willing to overlook their lack of class because of their skill.

His face was intriguing. Not pretty. She would never be coupled, much less allow herself to be photographed, with a man prettier than she. There was a toughness about his face, a hardness that had to do with more than tanned skin tight over bones. It was in the eyes, she thought as she laughed lightly and wiggled free. They were gray, more the color of flint than smoke, and they held secrets.

She enjoyed a man with secrets, as none of them were able to keep them from her for long.

"You're a bad boy, Cameron." The accent was on the last syllable. She tapped a finger against his mouth, a mouth that held no softness whatsoever.

"So I've always been told—" He had to think for a moment as her name skimmed along the edges of his memory. "Martine."

"Maybe, tonight, I'll let you be bad."

"I'm counting on it, sweetie." He turned toward the hotel, slanted a glance over. At six feet, she was nearly eye to eye with him. "My suite or yours?"

"Yours." She all but purred it. "Perhaps if you order up another bottle of champagne, I'll let you try to seduce me."

Cameron cocked an eyebrow, asked for his key at the desk. "I'll need a bottle of Cristal, two glasses, and one red rose," he told the clerk while keeping his eyes on Martine. "Right away."

"Yes, Monsieur Quinn, I'll take care of it."

"A rose." She fluttered at him as they walked to the elevator. "How romantic."

"Oh, did you want one too?" Her puzzled smile warned him humor wasn't going to be her strong point. So they'd forget the laughs and conversation, he decided, and shoot straight for the bottom line.

The minute the elevator doors closed them in, he pulled

her against him and met that sulky mouth with his own. He was hungry. He'd been too busy, too focused on his boat, too angled in on the race to take any time for recreation. He wanted soft skin, fragrant skin, curves, generous curves. A woman, any woman, as long as she was willing, experienced, and knew the boundary lines.

That made Martine perfect.

She let out a moan that wasn't altogether feigned for his benefit, then arched her throat for his nipping teeth. "You go fast."

He slid his hand down the silk, up again. "That's how I make my living. Going fast. Every time. Every way."

Still holding her, he circled out of the elevator, down the corridor to his rooms. Her heart was rapping hard against his, her breath catching, and her hands . . . well, he figured she knew just what she was doing with them.

So much for seduction.

He unlocked the door, shoved it open, then closed it by bracing Martine against it. He pushed the two string-width straps off her shoulders and with his eyes on hers helped himself to those magnificent breasts.

He decided her plastic surgeon deserved a medal.

"You want slow?"

Yes, the texture of his hands was rough, but God, exciting. She brought one mile-long leg up, wrapped it around his waist. He had to give her full marks for a sense of balance. "I want now."

"Good. Me too." He reached up under her excuse for a skirt and ripped away the whisper of lace beneath. Her eyes went wide, her breath thickened.

"Animal. Beast." And she fastened her teeth in his throat.

Even as he reached for his fly, the knock sounded discreetly on the door behind her head. Every ounce of blood had drained out of his head to below his belt. "Christ, service can't be that good here. Leave it outside," he demanded and prepared to take the magnificent Martine against the door.

"Monsieur Quinn, I beg your pardon. A fax just came for you. It was marked urgent."

"Tell him to go away." Martine wrapped a hand around him like a clamp. "Tell him to go to hell and fuck me."

"Hold on. I mean," he continued, unwrapping her fingers before his eyes could cross. "Wait just a minute." He shifted her behind the door, took a second to be sure he was zipped, then opened it.

"I'm sorry to disturb—"

"No problem. Thanks." Cameron dug in his pocket for a bill, didn't bother to check the denomination, and traded it for the envelope. Before the clerk could babble over the amount of the tip, Cameron shut the door in his face.

Martine gave that famous head toss again. "You're more interested in a silly fax than me. Than this." With an expert hand, she tugged the dress down, wiggling free of it like a snake shedding skin.

Cameron decided whatever she'd paid for that body, it had been worth every penny. "No, believe me, baby, I'm not. This'll just take a second." He ripped the envelope open before he could give in to the urge to ball it up, toss it over his shoulder, and dive headlong into all that female glory.

Then he read the message and his world, his life, his heart stopped.

"Oh, Jesus. Goddamn." All the wine cheerfully consumed throughout the evening swam giddily in his head, churned in his stomach, turned his knees to water. He had to lean back against the door to steady himself before reading it again.

Cam, damn it, why haven't you returned a call? We've been trying to reach you for hours. Dad's in the hospital. It's bad, as bad as it gets. No time for details. We're losing him fast. Hurry. Phillip.

Cameron lifted a hand—one that had held the wheel of dozens of boats, planes, cars that raced, one that could show a woman shuddery glimpses of heaven. And the hand shook as he dragged it through his hair.

"I have to go home."

"You are home." Martine decided to give him another chance and stepped forward to rub her body over his.

"No, I have to go." He nudged her aside and headed for the phone. "You have to go. I need to make some calls."

"You think you can tell me to go?"

"Sorry. Rain check." His mind just wouldn't engage. Absently he pulled bills out of his pocket with one hand, picked up the phone with the other. "Cab fare," he said, forgetting she was booked in the same hotel.

"Pig!" Naked and furious, she launched herself at him. If he had been steady, he'd have dodged the blow. But the slap connected, and the quick swipe. His ears rang, his cheek stung, and his patience snapped.

Cameron simply locked his arms around her, revolted when she took that as a sexual overture, and carted her to the door. He took the time to scoop up her dress, then tossed both the woman and the silk into the hall.

Her shriek rattled the teeth in his head as he threw the bolt. "I'll kill you. You pig! You bastard! I'll kill you for this. Who do you think you are? You're nothing! Nothing!"

He left Martine screaming and pounding at the door and went into the bedroom to throw a few necessities into a bag.

It looked like luck had just taken the nastiest of turns.

One

Cam called in markers, pulled strings, begged favors, and threw money in a dozen directions. Hooking transportation from Monaco to Maryland's Eastern Shore at one o'clock in the morning wasn't an easy matter.

He drove to Nice, bulleting down the winding coastal highway to a small airstrip where a friend had agreed to fly him to Paris—for the nominal fee of a thousand American dollars. In Paris he chartered a plane, for half again the going rate, and spent the hours over the Atlantic in a blur of fatigue and gnawing fear.

He arrived at Washington Dulles Airport in Virginia at just after six A.M. eastern standard time. The rental car was waiting, so he began the drive to the Chesapeake Bay in the dark chill of predawn.

By the time he hit the bridge crossing the bay, the sun was up and bright, sparkling off the water, glinting off boats already out for the day's catch. Cam had spent a good part of his life sailing on the bay, on the rivers and inlets of this part of the world. The man he was racing to see had shown him much more than port and starboard.

Whatever he had, whatever he'd done that he could take pride in, he owed to Raymond Quinn.

He'd been thirteen and racing toward hell when Ray and Stella Quinn had plucked him out of the system. His juvenile record was already a textbook study of the roots of the career criminal.

Robbery, breaking and entering, underage drinking, truancy, assault, vandalism, malicious mischief. He'd done as he'd pleased and even then had often enjoyed long runs of luck where he hadn't been caught. But the luckiest moment of his life had been being caught.

Thirteen years old, skinny as a rail and still wearing the bruises from the last beating his father had administered. They'd been out of beer. What was a father to do?

On that hot summer night with the blood still drying on his face, Cam had promised himself he was never going back to that run-down trailer, to that life, to the man the system kept tossing him back to. He was going somewhere, anywhere. Maybe California, maybe Mexico.

His dreams had been big even if his vision, courtesy of a blackened eye, was blurry. He had fifty-six dollars and some loose change, the clothes on his back, and a piss-poor attitude. What he needed, he decided, was transportation.

He copped a ride in the cargo car of a train heading out of Baltimore. He didn't know where it was going and didn't care as long as it was away. Huddled in the dark, his body weeping at every bump, he promised himself he'd kill or he'd die before he went back.

When he crept off the train, he smelled water and fish, and he wished to God he'd thought to grab some food somewhere. His stomach was screamingly empty. Dizzy and disoriented, he began to walk.

There wasn't much there. A two-bit little town that had rolled up its streets for the night. Boats bumping at sagging docks. If his mind had been clear, he might have considered breaking into one of the shops that lined the waterfront, but it didn't occur to him until he had passed through town and found himself skirting a marsh.

The marsh's shadows and sounds gave him the willies. The sun was beginning to break through the eastern sky, turning those muddy flats and that high, wet grass gold. A huge white bird rose up, making Cam's heart skip. He'd never seen a heron before, and he thought it looked like something out of a book, a made-up one.

But the wings flashed, and the bird soared. For reasons he couldn't name, he followed it along the edge of the marsh until it disappeared into thick trees.

He lost track of how far and what direction, but instinct told him to keep to a narrow country road where he could easily tuck himself into the high grass or behind a tree if a black-and-white cruised by.

He badly wanted to find shelter, somewhere he could curl up and sleep, sleep away the pangs of hunger and the greasy nausea. As the sun rose higher, the air grew thick with heat. His shirt stuck to his back; his feet began to weep.

He saw the car first, a glossy white 'Vette, all power and grace, sitting like a grand prize in the misty light of dawn. There was a pickup beside it, rusted, rugged and ridiculously rural beside the arrogant sophistication of the car.

Cam crouched down behind a lushly blooming hydrangea and studied it. Lusted after it.

The son of a bitch would get him to Mexico, all right, and anywhere else he wanted to go. Shit, the way a machine like that would move, he'd be halfway there before anybody knew it was gone.

He shifted, blinked hard to clear his wavering vision, and stared at the house. It always amazed him that people lived so neatly. In tidy houses with painted shutters, flowers and trimmed bushes in the yard. Rockers on the front porch, screens on the windows. The house seemed huge to him, a modern white palace with soft blue trim.

They'd be rich, he decided, as resentment ground in his

stomach along with hunger. They could afford fancy houses and fancy cars and fancy lives. And a part of him, a part nurtured by a man who lived on hate and Budweiser, wanted to destroy, to beat all the bushes flat, to break all the shiny windows and gouge the pretty painted wood to splinters.

He wanted to hurt them somehow for having everything while he had nothing. But as he rose, the bitter fury wavered into sick dizziness. He clamped down on it, clenching his teeth until they, too, ached, but his head cleared.

Let the rich bastards sleep, he thought. He'd just relieve them of the hot car. Wasn't even locked, he noted and snorted at their ignorance as he eased the door open. One of the more useful skills his father had passed on to him was how to hot-wire a car quickly and quietly. Such a skill came in very handy when a man made the best part of his living selling stolen cars to chop shops.

Cam leaned in, shimmied under the wheel, and got to work.

"It takes balls to steal a man's car right out of his own driveway."

Before Cam could react, even so much as swear, a hand hooked into the back of his jeans and hauled him up and out. He swung out, and his bunched fist seemed to bounce off rock.

He got his first look at the Mighty Quinn. The man was huge, at least six-five and built like the offensive line of the Baltimore Colts. His face was weathered and wide, with a thick shock of blond hair that glinted with silver surrounding it. His eyes were piercingly blue and hotly annoyed.

Then they narrowed.

It didn't take much to hold the boy in place. He couldn't have weighed a hundred pounds, Quinn thought, if he'd fished the kid out of the bay. His face was filthy and badly battered. One eye was nearly swollen shut, while the other, dark slate gray, held a bitterness no child should feel.

There was blood dried on the mouth that managed to sneer despite it.

Pity and anger stirred in him, but he kept his grip firm. This rabbit, he knew, would run.

"Looks like you came out on the wrong end of the tussle, son."

"Get your fucking hands off me. I wasn't doing nothing."

Ray merely lifted a brow. "You were in my wife's new car at just past seven on a Saturday morning."

"I was just looking for some loose change. What's the big fucking deal?"

"You don't want to get in the habit of overusing the word 'fuck' as an adjective. You'll miss the vast variety of its uses."

The mildly tutorial tone was well over Cam's head. "Look, Jack, I was just hoping for a couple bucks in quarters. You wouldn't miss it."

"No, but Stella would have dearly missed this car if you'd finished hot-wiring it. And my name isn't Jack. It's Ray. Now, the way I figure it you've got a couple of choices. Let's outline number one: I haul your sorry butt into the house and call the cops. How do you feel about doing the next few years in a juvenile facility for badasses?"

Whatever color Cam had left in his face drained away. His empty stomach heaved, his palms suddenly covered in sweat. He couldn't stand a cage. Was sure he would die in a cage. "I said I wasn't stealing the goddamn car. It's a four-speed. How the hell am I supposed to drive a four-speed?"

"Oh, I have a feeling you'd manage just fine." Ray puffed out his cheeks, considered, blew out air. "Now, choice number two—"

"Ray! What are you doing out there with that boy?"

Ray glanced toward the porch, where a woman with wild red hair and a ratty blue robe stood with her hands on her hips.

"Just discussing some life choices. He was stealing your car."

"Well, for heaven's sake!"

"Somebody beat the crap out of him. Recently, I'd say."

"Well." Stella Quinn's sigh could be heard clearly across the dewy green lawn. "Bring him in and I'll take a look at him. Hell of a way to start the morning. Hell of a way. No, you get inside there, idiot dog. Fine one you are, never one bark when my car's being stolen."

"My wife, Stella." Ray's smile spread and glowed. "She just gave you choice number two. Hungry?"

The voice was buzzing in Cam's head. A dog was barking in high, delighted yips from miles and miles away. Birds sang shrilly and much too close by. His skin went brutally hot, then brutally cold. And he went blind.

"Steady there, son. I'll get you."

He fell into the oily black and never heard Ray's quiet oath.

When he woke, he was lying on a firm mattress in a room where the breeze ruffled the sheer curtains and carried in the scent of flowers and water. Humiliation and panic rose up in him. Even as he tried to sit up, hands held him down.

"Just lie still a minute."

He saw the long, thin face of the woman who leaned over him, poking, prodding. There were thousands of gold freckles over it, which for some reason he found fascinating. Her eyes were dark green and frowning. Her mouth was set in a thin, serious line. She'd scraped back her hair, and she smelled faintly of dusting powder.

Cam realized abruptly that he'd been stripped down to his tattered Jockeys. The humiliation and panic exploded.

"Get the hell away from me." His voice came out in a croak of terror, infuriating him.

"Relax now. Relax. I'm a doctor. Look at me." Stella leaned her face closer. "Look at me now. Tell me your name."

His heart thundered in his chest. "John."

"Smith, I imagine," she said dryly. "Well, if you have the presence of mind to lie, you're not doing too badly." She shined a light in his eyes, grunted. "I'd say you've got yourself a mild concussion. How many times have you passed out since you were beat up?"

"That was the first." He felt himself coloring under her unblinking stare and struggled not to squirm. "I think. I'm not sure. I have to go."

"Yes, you do. To the hospital."

"No." Terror gave him the strength to grab her arm before she could rise. If he ended up in the hospital, there would be questions. With questions came cops. With cops came the social workers. And somehow, before it was over, he'd end up back in that trailer that stank of stale beer and piss with a man who found his greatest relief in pounding on a boy half his size.

"I'm not going to any hospital. I'm not. Just give me my clothes. I've got some money. I'll pay you for the trouble. I have to go."

She sighed again. "Tell me your name. Your real one."

"Cam. Cameron."

"Cam, who did this to you?"

"I don't—"

"Don't lie to me," she snapped.

And he couldn't. His fear was too huge, and his head was starting to throb so fiercely he could barely stop the whimper. "My father."

"Why?"

"Because he likes to."

Stella pressed her fingers against her eyes, then lowered her hands and looked out of the window. She could see the water, blue as summer, the trees, thick with leaves, and the sky, cloudless and lovely. And in such a fine world, she thought, there were parents who beat their children because they liked to. Because they could. Because they were there.

"All right, we'll take this one step at a time. You've been dizzy, experienced blurred vision."

Cautious, Cam nodded. "Maybe some. But I haven't eaten in a while."

"Ray's down taking care of that. Better in the kitchen than me. Your ribs are bruised, but they're not broken. The eye's the worst of it," she murmured, touching a gentle finger to the swelling. "We can treat that here. We'll clean you up and doctor you and see how you do. I am a doctor," she told him again, and smiled as her hand, blissfully cool, smoothed his hair back. "A pediatrician."

"That's a kid doctor."

"You still qualify, tough guy. If I don't like how you do, you're going in for X-rays." She reached into her bag for antiseptic. "This is going to sting a little."

He winced, sucked in his breath as she began to treat his face. "Why are you doing this?"

She couldn't stop herself. With her free hand she brushed back a messy shock of his dark hair. "Because I like to."

THEY'D KEPT HIM. IT HAD been as simple as that, Cam thought now. Or so it had seemed to him at the time. He hadn't realized until years later how much work, effort, and money they'd invested in first fostering, then adopting him. They'd given him their home, their name, and everything worthwhile in his life.

They'd lost Stella nearly eight years ago to a cancer that had snuck into her body and eaten away at it. Some of the light had gone out of that house on the outskirts of the little water town of St. Christopher's, and out of Ray, out of Cam, and out of the two other lost boys they'd made their own.

Cam had gone racing—anything, anywhere. Now he

was racing home to the only man he'd ever considered his father.

He'd been to this hospital countless times. When his mother had been on staff, and then when she'd been in treatment for the thing that killed her.

He walked in now, punchy and panicked, and asked for Raymond Quinn at the admission's desk.

"He's in Intensive Care. Family only."

"I'm his son." Cameron turned away and headed for the elevator. He didn't have to be told what floor. He knew too well.

He saw Phillip the moment the doors opened onto ICU. "How bad?"

Phillip handed over one of the two cups of coffee he held. His face was pale with fatigue, his normally well-groomed tawny hair tousled by his hands. His long, somewhat angelic face was roughened by stubble, and his eyes, a pale golden brown, shadowed with exhaustion.

"I wasn't sure you'd make it. It's bad, Cam. Christ, I've got to sit down a minute."

He stepped into a small waiting area, and dropped into a chair. The can of Coke in the pocket of his tailored suit clunked. For a moment he stared blindly at the morning show running brightly on the TV screen.

"What happened?" Cam demanded. "Where is he? What do the doctors say?"

"He was heading home from Baltimore. At least Ethan thinks he'd gone to Baltimore. For something. He hit a telephone pole. Dead on." He pressed the heel of his hand to his heart because it ached every time he pictured it. "They say maybe he had a heart attack or a stroke and lost control, but they're not sure yet. He was driving fast. Too fast."

He had to close his eyes because his stomach kept trying to jump into his throat. "Too fast," he repeated. "It took them nearly an hour to cut him out of the wreck. Nearly an hour. The paramedics said he was conscious on and off. It was just a couple miles from here."

He remembered the Coke in his pocket, opened the can, and drank. He kept trying to block the image out of his head, to concentrate on the now, and the what happened next. "They got ahold of Ethan pretty quick," Phillip continued. "When he got here Dad was in surgery. He's in a coma now." He looked up, met his brother's eyes. "They don't expect him to come out of it."

"That's bullshit. He's strong as an ox."

"They said . . ." Phillip closed his eyes again. His head felt empty, and he had to search for every thought. "Massive trauma. Brain damage. Internal injuries. He's on life support. The surgeon . . . he . . . Dad's a registered organ donor."

"Fuck that." Cam's voice was low and furious.

"Do you think I want to consider it?" Phillip rose now, a tall, rangy man in a wrinkled thousand-dollar suit. "They said it's a matter of hours at most. The machines are keeping him breathing. Goddamn it, Cam, you know how Mom and Dad talked about this when she got sick. No extreme measures. They made living wills, and we're ignoring his because . . . because we can't stand not to."

"You want to pull the plug?" Cam reached out, grabbed Phillip by the lapels. "You want to pull the goddamn plug on him?"

Weary and sick at heart, Phillip shook his head. "I'd rather cut my hand off. I don't want to lose him any more than you do. You'd better see for yourself."

He turned, led the way down the corridor, where the scent was hopelessness not quite masked by antiseptics. They moved through double doors, past a nurse's station, past small glass-fronted rooms where machines beeped and hope hung stubbornly on.

Ethan was sitting in a chair by the bed when they walked in. His big, calloused hand was through the guard and covering Ray's. His tall, wiry body was bent over, as if he'd been talking to the unconscious man in the bed beside him. He stood up slowly and, with eyes bruised from lack of sleep, studied Cam.

"So, you decided to put in an appearance. Strike up the band."

"I got here as soon as I could." He didn't want to admit it, didn't want to believe it. The man, the old, terrifyingly frail man, lying in the narrow bed, was his father. Ray Quinn was huge, strong, invincible. But the man with his father's face was shrunken, pale and still as death.

"Dad." He moved to the side of the bed, leaned down close. "It's Cam. I'm here." He waited, somehow sure it would take only that for his father's eyes to open, to wink slyly.

But there was no movement, and no sound except the monotonous beep of the machines.

"I want to talk to his doctor."

"Garcia." Ethan scrubbed his hands over his face, back into his sun-bleached hair. "The brain cutter Mom used to call Magic Hands. The nurse'll page him."

Cam straightened, and for the first time he noticed the boy curled up asleep in a chair in the corner. "Who's the kid?"

"The latest of Ray Quinn's lost boys." Ethan managed a small smile. Normally it would have softened his serious face, warmed the patient blue eyes. "He told you about him. Seth. Dad took him on about three months ago." He started to say more but caught Phillip's warning look and shrugged. "We'll get into that later."

Phillip stood at the foot of the bed, rocking back and forth on his heels. "So how was Monte Carlo?" At Cam's blank stare, he shrugged his shoulder. It was a gesture all three of them used in lieu of words. "The nurse said that we should talk to him, to each other. That maybe he can . . . They don't know for sure."

"It was fine." Cam sat and mirrored Ethan by reaching for Ray's hand through the bed guard. Because the hand was limp and lifeless, he held it gently and willed it to squeeze his own. "I won a bundle in the casinos and had a very hot French model in my suite when your fax came through." He shifted, spoke directly to Ray. "You should have seen her. She was incredible. Legs up to her ears, gorgeous man-made breasts."

"Did she have a face?" Ethan asked dryly.

"One that went just fine with the body. I tell you, she was a killer. And when I said I had to leave, she got just a little bitchy." He tapped his face where the scratches scored his cheek. "I had to toss her out of the room into the hall before she tore me to ribbons. But I did remember to toss her dress out after her."

"She was naked?" Phillip wanted to know.

"As a jay."

Phillip grinned, then had his first laugh in nearly twenty hours. "God, leave it to you." He laid his hand over Ray's foot, needing the connection. "He'll love that story."

IN THE CORNER, SETH pretended to be asleep. He'd heard Cam come in. He knew who he was. Ray had talked about Cameron a lot. He had two thick scrapbooks filled to busting with clippings and articles and photos of his races and exploits.

He didn't look so tough and important now, Seth decided. The guy looked sick and pale and hollow-eyed. He'd make up his own mind about what he thought of Cameron Quinn.

He liked Ethan well enough. Though the man'd work your butt raw if you went out oystering or clamming with him. He didn't preach all the time, and he'd never once delivered a blow or a backhand even when Seth had made mistakes. And he fit Seth's ten-year-old view of a sailor pretty well.

Rugged, tanned, thick curling hair with streaks of blond in the brown, hard muscles, salty talk. Yeah, Seth liked him well enough.

He didn't mind Phillip. He was usually all pressed and polished. Seth figured the guy must have six million ties, though he couldn't imagine why a man would want even one. But Phillip had some sort of fancy job in a fancy office in Baltimore. Advertising. Coming up with slick ideas to sell things to people who probably didn't need them anyway.

Seth figured it was a pretty cool way to run a con.

Now Cam. He was the one who went for the flash, who lived on the edge and took the risks. No, he didn't look so tough, he didn't look like such a badass.

Then Cam turned his head, and his eyes locked onto Seth's. Held there, unblinking and direct until Seth felt his stomach quiver. To escape, he simply closed his eyes and imagined himself back at the house by the water, throwing sticks for the clumsy puppy Ray called Foolish.

Knowing the boy was awake and aware of his gaze, Cam continued to study him. Good-looking kid, he decided, with a mop of sandy hair and a body that was just starting to go gangly. If he grew into his feet, he'd be a tall one before he was finished sprouting. He had a kiss-my-ass chin, Cam observed, and a sulky mouth. In the pretense of sleep, he managed to look harmless as a puppy and just about as cute.

But the eyes . . . Cam had recognized that edge in them, that animal wariness. He'd seen it often enough in the mirror. He hadn't been able to make out the color, but they'd been dark. Blue or brown, he imagined.

"Shouldn't we park the kid somewhere else?"

Ethan glanced over. "He's fine here. Nobody to leave him with anyhow. On his own he'd just look for trouble."

Cam shrugged, looked away, and forgot him. "I want to talk to Garcia. They've got to have test results, or something. He drives like a pro, so if he had a heart attack or a stroke . . ." His voice trailed off—it was simply too much to contemplate. "We need to know. Standing around here isn't helping."

"You need to do something," Ethan said, his soft voice a sign of suppressed temper, "you go on and do it. Being here counts." He stared at his brother across Ray's unconscious form. "It's always what counted."

"Some of us didn't want to dredge for oysters or spend our lives checking crab pots," Cam shot back. "They gave us a life and expected us to do what we wanted with it."

"So you did what you wanted."

"We all did," Phillip put in. "If something was wrong with Dad the last few months, Ethan, you should have told us."

"How the hell was I supposed to know?" But he had known something, just hadn't been able to put his finger on it. And had let it slide. That ate at him now as he sat listening to the machines that kept his father breathing.

"Because you were there," Cam told him.

"Yeah, I was there. And you weren't—not for years."

"And if I'd stayed on St. Chris he wouldn't have run into a damn telephone pole? Christ." Cam dragged his hands through his hair. "That makes sense."

"If you'd been around. If either of you had, he wouldn't have tried to do so much on his own. Every time I turned around he was up on a damn ladder, or pushing a wheelbarrow, or painting his boat. And he's still teaching three days a week at the college, tutoring, grading papers. He's almost seventy, for Christ's sake."

"He's only sixty-seven." Phillip felt a hard, ice-edged chill claw through him. "And he's always been healthy as a team of horses."

"Not lately he hasn't. He's been losing weight and looking tired and worn-out. You saw it for yourself."

"All right, all right." Phillip scrubbed his hands over his face, felt the scrape of a day's growth of beard. "So maybe he should have been slowing down a little. Taking on the kid was probably too much, but there wasn't any talking him out of it."

"Always squabbling."

The voice, weak and slurred, caused all three men to jolt to attention.

"Dad." Ethan leaned forward first, his heart fluttering in his chest.

"I'll get the doctor."

"No. Stay," Ray mumbled before Phillip could rush out of the room. It was a hideous effort, this coming back, even for a moment. And Ray understood he had moments only. Already his mind and body seemed separate things, though he could feel the pressure of hands on his hands, hear the sound of his sons' voices, and the fear and anger in them.

He was tired, oh, God, so tired. And he wanted Stella. But before he left, he had one last duty.

"Here." The lids seemed to weigh several pounds apiece, but he forced his eyes to open, struggled to focus. His sons, he thought, three wonderful gifts of fate. He'd done his best by them, tried to show them how to become men. Now he needed them for one more. Needed them to stay a unit without him and tend the child.

"The boy." Even the words had weight. It made him wince to push them from mind to lips. "The boy's mine. Yours now. Keep the boy, whatever happens, you see to him. Cam. You'll understand him best." The big hand, once so strong and vital, tried desperately to squeeze. "Your word on it."

"We'll take care of him." At that moment, Cam would have promised to drag down the moon and stars. "We'll take care of him until you're on your feet again."

"Ethan." Ray sucked in another breath that wheezed through the respirator. "He'll need your patience, your heart. You're a fine waterman because of them."

"Don't worry about Seth. We'll look after him."

"Phillip."

"Right here." He moved closer, bending low. "We're all right here."

"Such good brains. You'll figure how to make it all work. Don't let the boy go. You're brothers. Remember you're brothers. So proud of you. All of you. Quinns." He smiled a little, and stopped fighting. "You have to let me go now."

"I'm getting the doctor." Panicked, Phillip rushed out

of the room while Cam and Ethan tried to will their father back to consciousness.

No one noticed the boy who stayed curled in the chair, his eyes squeezed tightly shut against hot tears.

TWO

THEY CAME ALONE AND in crowds to wake and to bury Ray Quinn. He'd been more than a resident of the dot on the map known as St. Christopher's. He'd been teacher and friend and confidant. In years when the oyster crop was lean, he'd helped organize fund-raisers or had suddenly found dozens of odd jobs that needed to be done to tide the watermen over a hard winter.

If a student was struggling, Ray found a way to carve out an extra hour for a one-on-one. His literature classes at the university had always been filled, and it was rare for one to forget Professor Quinn.

He'd believed in community, and that belief had been both strong and supple in deed. He had realized that most vital of humanities. He had touched lives.

And he had raised three boys that no one had wanted into men.

They had left his gravesite buried in flowers and tears. So when the whispering and wondering began, it was most often hushed quickly. Few wanted to hear any gossip that reflected poorly on Ray Quinn. Or so they said, even as their ears twitched to catch the murmurs.

Sexual scandals, adultery, illegitimate child. Suicide.

Ridiculous. Impossible. Most said so and meant it. But others leaned a bit closer to catch every whisper, knit their brows, and passed the rumor from lip to ear.

Cam heard none of the whispers. His grief was so huge, so monstrous, he could barely hear his own black thoughts. When his mother had died, he'd handled it. He'd been prepared for it, had watched her suffer and had prayed for it to end. But this loss had been too quick, too arbitrary, and there was no cancer to blame for it.

There were too many people in the house, people who wanted to offer sympathy or share memories. He didn't want their memories, couldn't face them until he'd dealt with his own.

He sat alone on the dock that he'd helped Ray repair a dozen times over the years. Beside him was the pretty twenty-four-foot sloop they'd all sailed in countless times. Cam remembered the rig Ray had had that first summer—a little Sunfish, an aluminum catboat that had looked about as big as a cork to Cam.

And how patiently Ray had taught him how to sail, how to handle the rigging, how to tack. The thrill, Cam thought now, of the first time Ray had let him handle the tiller.

It had been a life-altering experience for a boy who'd grown up on hard streets—salty air in his face, wind snapping the white canvas, the speed and freedom of gliding over water. But most of all, it had been the trust. Here, Ray had said, see what you can do with her.

Maybe it had been that one moment, on that hazy afternoon when the leaves were so full and green and the sun already a white-hot ball behind the mist, that had turned the boy toward the man he was now.

And Ray had done it with a grin.

He heard the footsteps on the dock but didn't turn. He continued to look out over the water as Phillip stood beside him.

"Most everybody's gone."

"Good."

Phillip slipped his hands into his pockets. "They came for Dad. He'd have appreciated it."

"Yeah." Tired, Cam pressed his fingers to his eyes, let them drop. "He would have. I ran out of things to say and ways to say them."

"Yeah." Though he made his living with clever words, Phillip understood exactly. He took a moment to enjoy the silence. The breeze off the water had a bit of a bite, and that was a relief after the crowded house, overheated with bodies. "Grace is cleaning up in the kitchen. Seth's giving her a hand. I think he's got a case on her."

"She looks good." Cam struggled to shift his mind to someone else. Anything else. "Hard to imagine her with a kid of her own. She's divorced, right?"

"A year or two ago. He took off right before little Aubrey was born." Phillip blew out a breath between his teeth. "We've got some things to deal with, Cam."

Cam recognized the tone, and the tone meant it was time for business. Resentment bubbled up instantly. "I was thinking of taking a sail. There's a good wind today."

"You can sail later."

Cam turned his head, face bland. "I can sail now."

"There's a rumor going around that Dad committed suicide."

Cam's face went blank, then filled with red-hot rage. "What the fuck is this?" he demanded as he shot to his feet.

There, Phillip thought with dark satisfaction, that got your attention. "There's some speculation that he aimed for the pole."

"That's just pure bullshit. Who the hell's saying that?"

"It's going around—and some of it's rooting. It has to do with Seth."

"What has to do with Seth?" Cam began to pace, long, furious strides up and down the narrow dock. "What, do they think he was crazy for taking the kid on? Hell, he was crazy for taking any of us on, but what does that have to do with an accident?"

"There's some talk brewing that Seth is his son. By blood."

That stopped Cam dead in his tracks. "Mom couldn't have kids."

"I know that."

Fury pounded in his chest, a hammer on steel. "You're saying that he cheated on her? That he went off with some other woman and got a kid? Jesus Christ, Phil."

"I'm not saying it."

Cam stepped closer until they were face to face. "What the hell are you saying?"

"I'm telling you what I heard," Phillip said evenly, "so we can deal with it."

"If you had any balls you'd have decked whoever said it in their lying mouth."

"Like you want to deck me now. Is that your way of handling it? Just beat on it until it goes away?" With his own temper bubbling, Phillip shoved Cam back an inch. "He was my father too, goddamn it. You were the first, but you weren't the only."

"Then why the hell weren't you standing up for him instead of listening to that garbage? Afraid to get your hands dirty? Ruin your manicure? If you weren't such a damn pussy, you'd have—"

Phillip's fist shot out, caught Cam neatly on the jaw. There was enough force behind the punch to snap Cam's head back, send him staggering for a foot or two. But he regained his balance quickly enough. With eyes dark and eager, he nodded. "Well, then, come on."

Hot blood roaring in his head, Phillip started to strip off his jacket. Attack came swiftly, quietly and from behind. He barely had time to curse before he was sailing off the dock and into the water.

Phillip surfaced, spat, and shoved the wet hair out of his eyes. "Son of a bitch. You son of a bitch."

Ethan had his thumbs tucked in his front pockets now and studied his brother as Phillip treaded water. "Cool off," he suggested mildly.

"This suit is Hugo Boss," Phillip managed as he kicked toward the dock.

"That don't mean shit to me." Ethan glanced over at Cam. "Mean anything to you?"

"Means he's going to have a hell of a dry-cleaning bill."

"You, too," Ethan said and shoved Cam off the dock. "This isn't the time or place to go punching each other. So when the pair of you haul your butts out and dry off, we'll talk this through. I sent Seth on with Grace for a while."

Eyes narrowed, Cam skimmed his hair back with his fingers. "So you're in charge all of a sudden."

"Looks to me like I'm the only one who kept his head above water." With this, Ethan turned and sauntered back toward the house.

Together Cam and Phillip gripped the edge of the dock. They exchanged one long, hard look before Cam sighed. "We'll throw him in later," he said.

Accepting the apology, Phillip nodded. He pulled himself up on the dock and sat, dragging off his ruined silk tie. "I loved him too. As much as you did. As much as anyone could."

"Yeah." Cam yanked off his shoes. "I can't stand it." It was a hard admission from a man who'd chosen to live on the edge. "I didn't want to be there today. I didn't want to stand there and watch them put him in the ground."

"You were there. That's all that would have mattered to him."

Cam peeled off his socks, his tie, his jacket, felt the chill of early spring. "Who told you about—who said those things about Dad?"

"Grace. She's been hearing talk and thought it best that we knew what was being said. She told Ethan and me this morning. And she cried." Phillip lifted a brow. "Still think I should have decked her?"

Cam heaved his ruined shoes onto the lawn. "I want to know who started this, and why."

"Have you looked at Seth, Cam?"

The wind was getting into his bones. That was why he suddenly wanted to shudder. "Sure I looked at him." Cam turned, headed for the house.

"Take a closer look," Phillip murmured.

WHEN CAM WALKED INTO the kitchen twenty minutes later, warm and dry in a sweater and jeans, Ethan had coffee hot and whiskey ready.

It was a big, family-style kitchen with a long wooden table in the center. The white countertops showed a bit of age, the wear and tear of use. There'd been talk a few years back of replacing the aging stove. Then Stella had gotten sick, and that had been the end of that.

There was a big, shallow bowl on the table that Ethan had made in his junior year in high school wood shop. It had sat there since the day he'd brought it home, and was often filled with letters and notes and household flotsam rather than the fruit it had been designed for. Three wide, curtainless windows ranged along the back wall, opening the room up to the yard and the water beyond it.

The cabinet doors were glass-fronted, and the dishes inside plain white stoneware, meticulously arranged. As would be, Cam thought, the contents of all the drawers. Stella had insisted on that. When she wanted a spoon, by God, she didn't want to search for one.

But the refrigerator was covered with photos and newspaper clippings, notes, postcards, children's drawings, all haphazardly affixed with multicolored magnets.

It gave his heart a hitch to step into that room and know his parents wouldn't ever again be there.

"Coffee's strong," Ethan commented. "So's the whiskey. Take your choice."

"I'll have both." Cam poured a mug, added a shot of

Johnnie Walker to the coffee, then sat. "You want to take a swing at me, too?"

"I did. May again." Ethan decided he wanted his whiskey alone and neat. And poured a double. "Don't much feel like it now." He stood by the window, looking out, the untouched whiskey in his hand. "Maybe I still think you should have been here more the last few years. Maybe you couldn't be. It doesn't seem to matter now."

"I'm not a waterman, Ethan. I do what I'm good at. That's what they expected."

"Yeah." He couldn't imagine the need to run from the place that was home, and sanctuary. And love. But there was no point in questioning it, or in holding on to resentments. Or, he admitted, casting blame. "The place needs some work."

"I noticed."

"I should have made more time to come around and see to things. You always figure there's going to be plenty of time to go around, then there's not. The back steps are rotting out, need replacing. I kept meaning to." He turned as Phillip came into the room. "Grace has to work tonight, so she can't keep Seth occupied for more than a couple hours. You lay it out, Phil. It'll take me too long."

"All right." Phillip poured coffee, left the whiskey alone. Rather than sit, he leaned back against the counter. "It seems a woman came to see Dad a few months back. She went to the college, caused a little trouble that nobody paid much attention to at the time."

"What kind of trouble?"

"Caused a scene in his office, a lot of shouting and crying on her part. Then she went to see the dean and tried to file sexual molestation charges against Dad."

"That's a crock."

"The dean apparently thought so, too." Phillip poured a second cup of coffee and this time brought it to the table. "She claimed Dad had harassed and molested her while she was a student. But there was no record of her ever being a student at the college. Then she said she'd just been auditing his class because she couldn't afford full tuition. But nobody could verify that either. Dad's rep stood up to it, and it seemed to go away."

"He was pretty shaken," Ethan put in. "He wouldn't talk to me about it. Wouldn't talk to anybody. Then he went away for about a week. Told me he was going down to Florida to do some fishing. He came back with Seth."

"You're trying to tell me people think the kid's his? For Christ's sake, that he had something going on with this bimbo who waits, what, ten, twelve years to complain about it?"

"Nobody thought too much of it then," Phillip put in. "He had a history of bringing strays home. But then there was the money."

"What money?"

"He wrote checks, one for ten thousand dollars, another for five, and another for ten over the last three months. All to Gloria DeLauter. Somebody at the bank noticed and mumbled to somebody else, because Gloria DeLauter was the name of the woman who'd tried to hang him up on the sexual misconduct charges."

"Why the hell didn't somebody tell me what was going on around here?"

"I didn't find out about the money until a few weeks ago." Ethan stared down into his whiskey, then decided it would do him more good inside than out. He downed it, hissed once. "When I asked him about it, he just told me the boy was what was important. Not to worry. As soon as everything was settled he'd explain. He asked me for some time, and he looked so . . . defenseless. You don't know what it was like, seeing him scared and old and fragile. You didn't see him, you weren't here to see him. So I waited." Whiskey and guilt paired with resentment and grief to burn a hole inside him. "And I was wrong."

Shaken, Cam pushed back from the table. "You think he was paying blackmail. That he diddled some student a dozen years ago and knocked her up? And now he was paying so she'd keep quiet. So she'd hand over the kid for him to raise?''

''I'm telling you what was, and what I know.'' Ethan's voice was even, his eyes steady. ''Not what I think.''

''I don't know what I think,'' Phillip said quietly. ''But I know Seth's got his eyes. You only have to look at him, Cam.''

''No way he fucked with a student. And no way he cheated on Mom.''

''I don't want to believe it.'' Phillip set down his mug. ''But he was human. He could have made a mistake.'' One of them had to be realistic, and he decided he was elected. ''If he did, I'm not going to condemn him for it. What we have to do is figure out how to do what he asked. We have to find a way to keep Seth. I can find out if he started adoption proceedings. They couldn't be final yet. We're going to need a lawyer.''

''I want to find out more about this Gloria DeLauter.'' Deliberately, Cam unclenched his fists before he could use them on something, or someone. ''I want to know who the hell she is. Where the hell she is.''

''Up to you.'' Phillip shrugged his shoulders. ''Personally, I don't want to get near her.''

''What's this suicide crap?''

Phillip and Ethan exchanged a look, then Ethan rose and walked to a kitchen drawer. He pulled it open, took out a large sealed bag. It hurt him to hold it, and he saw by the way Cam's eyes darkened that Cam recognized the worn green enameled shamrock key ring as their father's.

''This is what was inside the car after the accident.'' He opened it, took out an envelope. The white paper was stained with dried blood. ''I guess somebody—one of the cops, the tow truck operator, maybe one of the paramedics—looked inside and read the letter, and they didn't trouble to keep it to themselves. It's from her.'' Ethan tapped out the letter, held it out to Cam. ''DeLauter. The postmark's Baltimore.''

''He was coming back from Baltimore.'' With dread,

Cam unfolded the letter. The handwriting was a large, loopy scrawl.

Quinn, I'm tired of playing nickel and dime. You want the kid so bad, then it's time to pay for him. Meet me where you picked him up. We'll make it Monday morning. The block's pretty quiet then. Eleven o'clock. Bring a hundred and fifty thousand, in cash. Cash money, Quinn, and no discounts. You don't come through with every penny, I'm taking the kid back. Remember, I can pull the plug on the adoption any time I want. A hundred and fifty grand's a pretty good bargain for a good-looking boy like Seth. Bring the money and I'm gone. You've got my word on it. Gloria

"She was selling him," Cam murmured. "Like he was a—" He stopped himself, looked up sharply at Ethan as he remembered. Ethan had once been sold as well, by his own mother, to men who preferred young boys. "I'm sorry, Ethan."

"I live with it," he said simply. "Mom and Dad made sure I could. She's not going to get Seth back. Whatever it takes, she won't get her hands on him."

"We don't know if he paid her?"

"He emptied his bank account here," Phillip put in. "From what I can tell—and I haven't gone over his papers in detail yet—he closed out his regular savings, cashed in his CDs. He only had a day to get the cash. That would have come to about a hundred thousand. I don't know if he had fifty more—if he had time to liquidate it if he did."

"She wouldn't have gone away. He'd have known that." Cam put the letter down, wiped his hands on his jeans as if to clean them. "So people are whispering that he killed himself in what—shame, panic, despair? He wouldn't have left the kid alone."

"He didn't." Ethan moved to the coffeepot. "He left him with us."

"How the hell are we supposed to keep him?" Cam sat again. "Who's going to let us adopt anybody?"

"We'll find a way." Ethan poured coffee, added enough

sugar to make Phillip wince in reaction. "He's ours now."

"What the hell are we going to do with him?"

"Put him in school, put a roof over his head, food in his belly, and try to give him something of what we were given." He brought the pot over, topped off Cam's coffee. "You got an argument?"

"Couple dozen, but none of them get past the fact that we gave our word."

"We agree on that, anyway." Frowning, Phillip drummed his fingers on the table. "But we've left out one pretty vital point. None of us knows what Seth's going to have to say about it. He might not want to stay here. He might not want to stay with us."

"You're just looking to complicate things, as usual," Cam complained. "Why wouldn't he?"

"Because he doesn't know you, he barely knows me." Phillip lifted his cup and gestured. "The only one he's spent any time with is Ethan."

"Didn't spend all that much with me," Ethan admitted. "I took him out on the boat a few times. He's got a quick mind, good hands. Doesn't have much to say for himself, but when he does, he's got a mouth on him. He's spent some time with Grace. She doesn't seem to mind him."

"Dad wanted him to stay," Cam stated with a shrug. "He stays." He glanced over at the sound of a horn tooting three quick beeps.

"That'll be Grace dropping him back off on her way to Shiney's Pub."

"Shiney's?" Cam's brows shot up. "What's she doing down at Shiney's?"

"Making a living, I expect," Ethan returned.

"Oh, yeah." A slow grin spread. "Does he still have his waitresses dress in those little skirts with the bows on the butt and the black fishnet stockings?"

"He does," Phillip said with a long, wistful sigh. "He does indeed."

"Grace would fill out one of those outfits pretty well, I'd imagine."

"She does." Phillip smiled. "She does indeed."

"Maybe I'll just mosey down to Shiney's later."

"Grace isn't one of your French models." Ethan pushed back from the table, took his mug and his annoyance to the sink. "Back off."

"Whoa." Behind Ethan's back, Cam wiggled his brows at Phillip. "Backing off, bro. Didn't know you had your eye aimed in that particular direction."

"I don't. She's a mother, for Christ's sake."

"I had a really fine time with the mother of two in Cancun last winter," Cam remembered. "Her ex was swimming in oil—olive oil—and all she got in the divorce settlement was a Mexican villa, a couple of cars, some trinkets, art, and two million. I spent a memorable week consoling her. And the kids were cute—from a distance. With their nanny."

"You're such a humanitarian, Cam," Phillip told him.

"Don't I know it."

They heard the front door slam and looked at each other. "Well, who talks to him?" Phillip wanted to know.

"I'm no good at that kind of stuff." Ethan was already edging toward the back door. "And I've got to go feed my dog."

"Coward," Cam muttered as the door shut at Ethan's back.

"You bet. Me, too." Phillip was up and moving. "You get first crack. I've got those papers to go through."

"Wait just a damn minute—"

But Phillip was gone, and cheerfully telling Seth that Cameron wanted to talk to him. When Seth came to the kitchen door, the puppy scrambling at his heels, he saw Cam scowling as he poured more whiskey in his coffee.

Seth stuck his hands in his pockets and lifted his chin. He didn't want to be there, didn't want to talk to anybody. At Grace's he'd been able to just sit on her little stoop, be alone with his thoughts. Even when she'd come out for a little while and sat beside him with Aubrey on her knee, she'd let him be.

Because she understood he'd wanted to be quiet.

Now he had to deal with the man. He wasn't afraid of big hands and hard eyes. Wouldn't—couldn't—let himself be afraid. He wouldn't care that they were going to kick him loose, toss him back like one of the runt fish Ethan pulled out of the bay.

He could take care of himself. He wasn't worried.

His heart scrambled in his chest like a mouse in a cage.

"What?" The single word was ripe with defiance and challenge. Seth stood, his legs locked, and waited for a reaction.

Cam only continued to frown and sip his doctored coffee. With one hand, he absently stroked the puppy, who was trying valiantly to climb into his lap. He saw a scrawny boy wearing jeans still stiff and obviously new, a screw-you sneer, and Ray Quinn's eyes. "Sit down."

"I can stand."

"I didn't ask you what you could do, I told you to sit down."

On cue, Foolish obediently plopped his fat butt on the floor and grinned. But boy and man stared at each other. The boy gave way first. It was the quick jerk of the shoulders that had Cam setting his mug down with a click. It was a Quinn gesture, through and through. Cam took a moment to settle, tried to gather his thoughts. But they remained scattered and elusive. What the hell was he supposed to say to the boy?

"You get anything to eat?"

Seth watched him warily from under girlishly thick lashes. "Yeah, there was stuff."

"Ah, Ray, did he talk to you about . . . things. Plans for you?"

The shoulders jerked again. "I don't know."

"He was working on adopting you, making it legal. You knew about that."

"He's dead."

"Yeah." Cam picked up his coffee again, let the pain roll through. "He's dead."

"I'm going to Florida," Seth burst out as the idea slammed into his mind.

Cam sipped coffee, angled his head as if mildly interested. "Oh, yeah?"

"I got some money. I figured I'd leave in the morning, catch a bus south. You can't stop me."

"Sure I can." More comfortable now, Cam leaned back in his chair. "I'm bigger than you. What do you plan to do in Florida?"

"I can get work. I can do lots of things."

"Pick some pockets, sleep on the beach."

"Maybe."

Cam nodded. That had been his plan when his destination had been Mexico. For the first time he thought he might be able to connect with the boy after all. "I guess you can't drive yet."

"I could if I had to."

"Harder to boost a car these days unless you've got some experience. And you need to be mobile to keep ahead of the cops. Florida's a bad idea."

"That's where I'm going." Seth set his jaw.

"No, it isn't."

"You're not sending me back." Seth lurched up from the chair, his thin frame vibrating with fear and rage. The sudden move and shout sent the puppy racing fearfully from the room. "You got no hold over me, you can't make me go back."

"Back where?"

"To her. I'll go right now. I'll get my stuff and I'm gone. And if you think you can stop me, you're full of shit."

Cam recognized the stance—braced for a blow but ready to fight back. "She knock you around?"

"That's none of your fucking business."

"Ray made it my fucking business. You head for the door," he added as Seth shifted to the balls of his feet, "I'll just haul you back." Cam only sighed when Seth made his dash.

Even as he caught him three feet before the front door, he had to give Seth credit for speed. And when he caught the boy around the waist, took the backhanded fist on his already tender jaw, he gave him credit for strength.

"Get your goddamn hands off me, you son of a bitch. I'll kill you if you touch me."

Grimly, Cam dragged Seth into the living room, pushed him into a chair, and held him there with their faces close. If it had just been anger he saw in the boy's eyes, or defiance, he wouldn't have cared. But what he saw was raw terror.

"You got balls, kid. Now try to develop some brains to go with them. If I want sex, I want a woman. Understand me?"

He couldn't speak. All he'd known when that hard, muscled arm had wrapped around him was that this time he wouldn't be able to escape. This time he wouldn't be able to fight free and run.

"There's nobody here who's going to touch you like that. Ever." Without realizing it, Cam had gentled his voice. His eyes remained dark, but the hardness was gone. "If I lay hands on you, the worst it means is I might try to knock some sense into you. You got that?"

"I don't want you to touch me," Seth managed. His breath was gone. Panic sweat slicked his skin like oil. "I don't like being touched."

"Okay, fine. You sit where I put you." Cam eased back, then pulled over a footstool and sat. Since Foolish was now shivering in terror, Cam plucked him up and dumped him in Seth's lap. "We got a problem," Cam began, and prayed for inspiration on how to handle it. "I can't watch you twenty-four hours a day. And if I could, I'm damned if I would. You take off for Florida, I'm going to have to go find you and haul you back. That's really going to piss me off."

Because the dog was there, Seth stroked him, gaining comfort while giving it. "What do you care where I go?"

"I can't say I do. But Ray did. So you're going to have to stay."

"Stay?" It was an option Seth had never considered. Certainly hadn't allowed himself to believe. "Here? When you sell the house—"

"Who's selling the house?"

"I—" Seth broke off, decided he was saying too much. "People figured you would."

"People figured wrong. Nobody's selling this house." It surprised Cam just how firm his feelings were on that particular point. "I don't know how we're going to manage it yet. I'm still working on that. But in the meantime, you'd better get this into your head. You're staying put." Which meant, Cam realized with a jolt, so was he.

It appeared his luck was still running bad.

"We're stuck with each other, kid, for the next little while."

THREE

CAM FIGURED THIS HAD to be the weirdest week of his life. He should have been in Italy, prepping for the motocross he'd planned to treat himself to. Most of his clothes and his boat were in Monte Carlo, his car was in Nice, his motorcycle in Rome.

And he was in St. Chris, baby-sitting a ten-year-old with a bad attitude. He hoped to Christ the kid was in school where he belonged. They'd had a battle royal over that little item that morning. But then, they were at war over most everything.

Kitchen duty, curfews, laundry, television picks. Cam shook his head as he pried off the rotting treads on the back steps. He'd swear the boy would square up for a bout if you said good morning.

And maybe he wasn't doing a fabulous job as guardian, but damn it, he was doing his best. He had the tension headache to prove it. And mostly, he was on his own. Phillip had promised weekends, and that was something. But it also left five hideous days between. Ethan made a point of coming by and staying a few hours every evening after he pulled in the day's catch.

But that left the days.

Cam would have traded his immortal soul for a week in Martinique. Hot sand and hotter women. Cold beer and no hassles. Instead he was doing laundry, learning the mysteries of microwave cooking, and trying to keep tabs on a boy who seemed hell-bent on making life miserable.

"You were the same way."

"Hell I was. I wouldn't have lived to see twelve if I'd been that big an idiot."

"Most of that first year Stella and I used to lie in bed at night and wonder if you'd still be here in the morning."

"At least there were two of you. And . . ."

Cam's hand went limp on the hammer. His fingers simply gave way until it thudded on the ground beside him. There in the old, creaking rocker on the back porch sat Ray Quinn. His face was wide and smiling, his hair a tousled white mane that grew long and full. He wore his favored gray fishing pants, a faded gray T-shirt with a red crab across the chest. His feet were bare.

"Dad?" Cam's head spun once, sickly, then his heart burst with joy. He leaped to his feet.

"You didn't think I'd leave you fumbling through this alone, did you?"

"But—" Cam shut his eyes. He was hallucinating, he realized. It was stress and fatigue, grief tossed in.

"I always tried to teach you that life's full of surprises and miracles. I wanted you to open your mind not just to possibilities, Cam, but to impossibilities."

"Ghosts? God!"

"Why not?" The idea seemed to cheer Ray immensely as he let loose with one of his deep, rumbling laughs. "Read your literature, son. It's full of them."

"Can't be," Cam mumbled to himself.

"I'm sitting right here, so it looks like it can. I left too many things unfinished around here. It's up to you and your brothers now, but who says I can't give you a little help now and again?"

"Help. Yeah, I'm going to need some serious help. Starting with a psychiatrist." Before his legs gave out on him, Cam picked his way through the broken stairs and sat down on the edge of the porch.

"You're not crazy, Cam, just confused."

Cam took a steadying breath and turned his head to study the man who lazily rocked in the old wooden chair. The Mighty Quinn, he thought while the air whooshed out of his lungs. He looked solid and real. He looked, Cam decided, there.

"If you're really here, tell me about the boy. Is he yours?"

"He's yours now. Yours and Ethan's and Phillip's."

"That's not enough."

"Of course it is. I'm counting on each of you. Ethan takes things as they come and makes the best of them. Phillip wraps his mind around details and ties them up. You push at everything until it works your way. The boy needs all three of you. Seth's what's important. You're all what's important."

"I don't know what to do with him," Cam said impatiently. "I don't know what to do with myself."

"Figure out one, you'll figure out the other."

"Damn it, tell me what happened. Tell me what's going on."

"That's not why I'm here. I can't tell you if I've seen Elvis either." Ray grinned when Cam let out a short, helpless laugh. "I believe in you, Cam. Don't give up on Seth. Don't give up on yourself."

"I don't know how to do this."

"Fix the steps," Ray said with a wink. "It's a start."

"The hell with the steps," Cam began, but he was alone again with the sound of singing birds and gently lapping water. "Losing my mind," he murmured, rubbing an unsteady hand over his face. "Losing my goddamn mind."

And rising, he went back to fix the steps.

• • •

ANNA SPINELLI HAD THE radio blasting. Aretha Franklin was wailing out of her million-dollar pipes, demanding respect. Anna was wailing along with her, deliriously thrilled with her spanking-new car.

She'd worked her butt off, budgeted and juggled funds to afford the down payment and the monthly installments. And as far as she was concerned it would be worth every carton of yogurt she ate rather than a real meal.

Despite the chilly spring air, she'd have preferred to have the top down as she sped along the country roads. But it wouldn't have looked professional to arrive windblown. Above all else, it was essential to appear and behave in a professional manner.

She'd chosen a plain and proper navy suit and white blouse for this home visit. What she wore under it was nobody's business but her own. Her affection for silk strained her ever beleaguered budget, but life was for living, after all.

She'd fought her long, curling black hair into a tidy bun at the nape of her neck. She thought it made her look a bit more mature and dignified. Too often when she wore her hair down she was dismissed as a hot number rather than a serious-minded social worker.

Her skin was pale gold, thanks to her Italian heritage. Her eyes, big and dark and almond-shaped. Her mouth was full, with a ripe bottom lip. The bones in her face were strong and prominent, her nose long and straight. She wore little makeup during business hours, wary of drawing the wrong kind of attention.

She was twenty-eight years old, devoted to her work, satisfied with the single life, and pleased that she'd been able to settle in the pretty town of Princess Anne.

She'd had enough of the city.

As she drove between long, flat fields of row crops with the scent of water a hint on the breeze through her window, she dreamed of one day moving to such a place. Country lanes and tractors. A view of the bay and boats.

She'd need to save up, to plan, but one day she hoped to manage to buy a little house outside of town. The commute wouldn't be so hard, not when driving was one of her greatest personal pleasures.

The CD player shifted, the Queen of Soul to Beethoven. Anna began to hum the "Ode to Joy."

She was glad the Quinn case had been assigned to her. It was so interesting. She only wished she'd had the chance to meet Raymond and Stella Quinn. It would take very special people to adopt three half-grown and troubled boys and make it work.

But they were gone, and now Seth DeLauter was her concern. Obviously the adoption proceedings couldn't go forward. Three single men—one living in Baltimore, one in St. Chris, and the other wherever he chose to at the moment. Well, Anna mused, it didn't appear to be the best environment for the child. In any case, it was doubtful they would want guardianship.

So Seth DeLauter would be absorbed back into the system. Anna intended to do her best by him.

When she spotted the house through the greening leaves, she stopped the car. Deliberately she turned the radio down to a dignified volume, then checked her face and hair in the rearview mirror. Shifting back into first, she drove the last few yards at a leisurely pace and turned slowly into the drive.

Her first thought was that it was a pretty house in a lovely setting. So quiet and peaceful, she mused. It could have used a fresh coat of paint, and the yard needed tending, but the slight air of disrepair only added to the hominess.

A boy would be happy here, she thought. Anyone would. It was a shame he'd have to be taken away from it. She sighed a little, knowing too well that fate had its whims. Taking her briefcase, she got out of the car.

She hitched her jacket to make certain it fell in line. She wore it a bit loose, so it wouldn't showcase distracting curves. She started toward the front door, noting that the perennial beds flanking the steps were beginning to pop.

She really needed to learn more about flowers; she made a mental note to check out a few gardening books from the library.

She heard the hammering and hesitated, then in her practical low heels cut across the lawn toward the back of the house.

He was kneeling on the ground when she caught sight of him. A black T-shirt tucked into snug and faded denim. From a purely female outlook, it was impossible not to react and approve of him. Muscles—the long and lean sort—rippled as he pounded a nail into wood with enough anger, Anna mused, enough force, to send vibrations of both into the air to simmer.

Phillip Quinn? she wondered. The advertising executive. Highly doubtful.

Cameron Quinn, the globe-trotting risk-taker? Hardly.

So.this must be Ethan, the waterman. She fixed a polite smile on her face and started forward. "Mr. Quinn."

His head came up. With the hammer still gripped in his hand, he turned until she saw his face. Oh, yes, the anger was there, she realized, full-blown and lethal. And the face itself was more compelling and certainly tougher than she'd been prepared for.

Some Native American blood, perhaps, she decided, would account for those sharp bones and bronzed skin. His hair was a true black, untidy and long enough to fall over his collar. His eyes were anything but friendly, the color of bitter storms.

On a personal level, she found the package outrageously sexy. On a professional one, she knew the look of an alley brawler when she saw one, and decided on the spot that whichever Quinn this was, he was a man to be careful with.

He took his time studying her. His first thought was that legs like that deserved a better showcase than a drab navy skirt and ugly black shoes. His second was that when a woman had eyes that big, that brown, that beautiful, she probably got whatever she wanted without saying a word.

He set the hammer down and rose. "I'm Quinn."

"I'm Anna Spinelli." She kept the smile in place as she walked forward, hand extended. "Which Quinn are you?"

"Cameron." He'd expected a soft hand because of the eyes, because of the husky purr of her voice, but it was firm. "What can I do for you?"

"I'm Seth DeLauter's caseworker."

His interest evaporated, and his spine stiffened. "Seth's in school."

"I'd hope so. I'd like to speak with you about the situation, Mr. Quinn."

"My brother Phillip's handling the legal details."

She arched a brow, determined to keep the small polite smile in place. "Is he here?"

"No."

"Well, then, if I could have a few moments of your time. I assume you're living here, at least temporarily."

"So what?"

She didn't bother to sigh. Too many people saw a social worker as the enemy. She'd done so once herself. "My concern is Seth, Mr. Quinn. Now we can discuss this, or I can simply move forward with the procedure for his removal from this home and into approved foster care."

"It'd be a mistake to try that, Miz Spinelli. Seth isn't going anywhere."

Her back went up at the way he drawled out her name. "Seth DeLauter is a minor. The private adoption your father was implementing wasn't finalized, and there is some question about its validity. At this point, Mr. Quinn, you have no legal connection to him."

"You don't want me to tell you what you can do with your legal connection, do you, Miz Spinelli?" With some satisfaction he watched those big, dark eyes flash. "I didn't think so. I can resist. Seth's my brother." The saying of it left him shaken. With a jerk of his shoulder, he turned. "I need a beer."

She stood for a moment after the screen door slammed.

When it came to her work, she simply didn't permit herself to lose her temper. She breathed in, breathed out three times before climbing the half-repaired steps and going into the house.

"Mr. Quinn—"

"Still here?" He twisted the top off a Harp. "Want a beer?"

"No. Mr. Quinn—"

"I don't like social workers."

"You're joking." She allowed herself to flutter her lashes at him. "I never would have guessed."

His lips twitched before he lifted the bottle to them. "Nothing personal."

"Of course not. I don't like rude, arrogant men. That's nothing personal either. Now, are you ready to discuss Seth's welfare, or should I simply come back with the proper paperwork and the cops?"

She would, Cam decided after another study. She might have been given a face suitable for painting, but she wasn't a pushover. "You try that, and the kid's going to bolt. You'd pick him up sooner or later, and he'd end up in juvie—then he'd end up in a cell. Your system isn't going to help him, Miz Spinelli."

"But you can?"

"Maybe." He frowned into his beer. "My father would have." When he looked up again, there were emotions storming in his eyes that pulled at her. "Do you believe in the sanctity of a deathbed promise?"

"Yes," she said before she could stop herself.

"The day my father died I promised him—we promised him—that we'd keep Seth with us. Nothing and no one is going to make me break my word. Not you, not your system, not a dozen cops."

The situation here wasn't what she'd expected to find. So she would reevaluate. "I'd like to sit down," Anna said after a moment.

"Go ahead."

She pulled out a chair at the table. There were dishes in

the sink, she noted, and the faint smell of whatever had been burnt for dinner the night before. But to her that only meant someone was trying to feed a young boy. "Do you intend to apply for legal guardianship?"

"We—"

"You, Mr. Quinn," she interrupted. "I'm asking you if that is your intention." She waited, watching the doubts and resistance sweep over his face.

"Then I guess it is. Yeah." God help them all, he thought. "If that's what it takes."

"Do you intend to live in this house, with Seth, on a permanent basis?"

"Permanent?" It was perhaps the only truly frightening word in his life. "Now I have to sit down." He did so, then pinched the bridge of his nose between his thumb and forefinger to relieve some of the pressure. "Christ. How about we use 'for the foreseeable future' instead of 'permanent'?"

She folded her hands on the edge of the table. She didn't doubt his sincerity, would have applauded him for his intentions. But . . . "You have no idea what you're thinking of taking on."

"You're wrong. I do, and it scares the hell out of me."

She nodded, considering the answer a point in his favor. "What makes you think you would be a better guardian for a ten-year-old boy, a boy I believe you've known for less than two weeks, than a screened and approved foster home?"

"Because I understand him. I've been him—or part of him. And because this is where he belongs."

"Let me lay out some of the bigger obstacles to what you're planning. You're a single man with no permanent address and without a steady income."

"I've got a house right here. I've got money."

"Whose name is the house in, Mr. Quinn?" She only nodded when his brows knit. "I imagine you have no idea."

"Phillip will."

"Good for Phillip. And I'm sure you have some money, Mr. Quinn, but I'm speaking of steady employment. Going around the world racing various forms of transportation isn't stable employment."

"It pays just fine."

"Have you considered the risk to life and limb of your chosen lifestyle when you propose to take on a responsibility like this? Believe me, the court will. What if something happens to you when you're trying to break land and speed records?"

"I know what I'm doing. Besides, there are three of us."

"Only one of you lives in this house where Seth will live."

"So?"

"And the one who does isn't a respected college professor with the experience of raising three sons."

"That doesn't mean I can't handle it."

"No, Mr. Quinn," she said patiently, "but it is a major obstacle to legal guardianship."

"What if we all did?"

"Excuse me?"

"What if we all lived here? What if my brothers moved in?" What a damn mess, Cam thought, but he kept going. "What if I got a . . ." Now he had to take a deep swallow of beer, knowing the word would stick in his throat. "A job," he managed.

She stared at him. "You'd be willing to change your life so dramatically?"

"Ray and Stella Quinn changed my life."

Her face softened, making Cam blink in surprise as her generous mouth curved in a smile, as her eyes seemed to go darker and deeper. When her hand reached out, closed lightly over his, he stared down at it, surprised by a quick jolt of what was surely pure lust.

"When I was driving here, I was wishing I could have met them. I thought they must have been remarkable people. Now I'm sure of it." Then she drew back. "I'll need to speak with Seth, and with your brothers. What time does Seth get home from school?''

''What time?'' Cam glanced at the kitchen clock without a clue. ''It's sort of . . . flexible.''

''You'll want to do better than that if this gets as far as a formal home study. I'll go by the school and see him. Your brother Ethan.'' She rose. ''Would I find him at home?''

''Not at this time of day. He'll be bringing in his catch before five.''

She glanced at her watch, gauged her time. ''All right, and I'll contact your other brother in Baltimore.'' From her briefcase she took a neat leather notebook. ''Now, can you give me names and addresses of some neighbors. People who know you and Seth and who would stand for your character. The good side of your character, that is.''

''I could probably come up with a few.''

''That's a start. I'll do some research here, Mr. Quinn. If it's in Seth's best interest to remain in your home, under your care, I'll do everything I can to help you.'' She angled her head. ''If I reach the opinion that it's in his best interest to be taken out of your home, and out of your care, then I'll fight you tooth and nail to make that happen.''

Cam rose as well. ''Then I guess we understand each other.''

''Not by a long shot. But you've got to start somewhere.''

THE MINUTE SHE WAS out of the house, Cam was on the phone. By the time he'd been passed through a secretary and an assistant and reached Phillip, his temper had spilled over.

''There was a goddamn social worker here.''

''I told you to expect that.''

''No, you didn't.''

"Yes, I did. You don't listen. I've got a friend of mine—a lawyer—working on the guardianship. Seth's mother took a hike; as far as we can tell, she's not in Baltimore."

"I don't give a damn where the mother is. The social worker was making noises about taking Seth."

"The lawyer's putting through a temporary guardianship. It takes time, Cam."

"We may not have time." He shut his eyes, tried to think past the anger. "Or maybe I bought us some. Who owns the house now?"

"We do. Dad left it—well, everything—to the three of us."

"Fine, good. Because you're about to change locations. You're going to need to pack up those designer suits of yours, pal, and get your butt down here. We're going to be living together again."

"Like hell."

"And I've got to get a goddamn job. I'm going to expect you by seven tonight. Bring dinner. I'm sick to death of cooking."

It gave him some satisfaction to hang up on Phillip's vigorous cursing.

ANNA FOUND SETH SULLEN and smart-mouthed and snotty. And liked him immediately. The principal had given her permission to take him out of class and use a corner of the empty cafeteria as a makeshift office.

"It would be easier if you'd tell me what you think and feel, and what you want."

"Why should you give a damn?"

"They pay me to."

Seth shrugged and continued to draw patterns on the table with his finger. "I think you should mind your own business, I feel bored, and I want you to go away."

"Well, that's enough about me," Anna said and had the pleasure of seeing Seth struggle to suppress a smile. "Let's talk about you. Are you happy living with Mr. Quinn?"

"It's a cool house."

"Yes, I liked it. What about Mr. Quinn?"

"He thinks he knows everything. Thinks he's a BFD because he's been all over the world. He sure as hell can't cook, let me tell you."

She left her pen on the table and folded her hands over her notebook. He was much too thin, she thought. "Do you go hungry?"

"He ends up going to get pizza or burgers. Pitiful. I mean what's it take to work a microwave?"

"Maybe you should do the cooking."

"Like he'd ask me. The other night he blows up the potatoes. Forgets to poke holes in them, you know, and bam!" Seth forgot to sneer, laughing out loud instead. "What a mess! He swore a streak then, man, oh, man."

"So the kitchen isn't his area of expertise." But, Anna decided, he was trying.

"You're telling me. He's better off when he's going around hammering things or fiddling with that cool-ass car. Did you see that 'Vette? Cam said it was his mom's and she had it for like ever. Drives like a rocket, too. Ray kept it in the garage. Guess he didn't want to get it out."

"Do you miss him? Ray?"

The shoulder shrugged again, and Seth's gaze dropped. "He was cool. But he was old and when you get old you die. That's the way it is."

"What about Ethan and Phillip?"

"They're okay. I like going out on the boats. If I didn't have school, I could work for Ethan. He said I pulled my weight."

"Do you want to stay with them, Seth?"

"I got no place to go, do I?"

"There's always a choice, and I'm here to help you find the one that works best for you. If you know where your mother is—"

"I don't know." His voice rose, his head snapped up. His eyes darkened to nearly navy against a pale face. "And I don't want to know. You try to send me back there, you'll never find me."

"Did she hurt you?" Anna waited a beat, then nodded when he only stared at her. "All right, we'll leave that alone for now. There are couples and families who are willing and able to take children into their home, to care for them, to give them a good life."

"They don't want me, do they?" The tears wanted to come. He'd be damned if he'd let them. Instead his eyes went hot and burning dry. "He said I could stay, but it was a lie. Just another fucking lie."

"No." She grabbed Seth's hand before he could leap up. "No, they do want you. As a matter of fact, Mr. Quinn—Cameron—was very angry with me for suggesting you should go into another home. I'm only trying to find out what you want. And I think you just told me. If living with the Quinns is what you want, and what's best for you, I want to help you to get that."

"Ray said I could stay. He said I'd never have to go back. He promised."

"If I can, I'll try to help him keep that promise."

FOUR

SINCE THERE SEEMED TO be nothing cold to drink in the house but beer, carbonated soft drinks, and some suspicious-looking milk, Ethan put the kettle on to boil. He'd brew up some tea, ice it, and enjoy a tall glass out on the porch while evening moseyed in.

He was in hour fourteen of his day and ready to relax.

Which wasn't going to be easy, he decided while he hunted up tea bags and overheard Cam and Seth holding some new pissing match in the living room. He figured they must enjoy sniping at each other or they wouldn't spend so much time at it.

For himself, he wanted a quiet hour, a decent meal, then one of the two cigars he allowed himself per day. The way things sounded, he didn't think the quiet hour was going to make the agenda.

As he dumped tea bags in the boiling water, he heard feet stomping up the stairs, followed by the bullet-sharp sound of a slamming door.

"The kid's driving me bat-shit," Cam complained as he stalked into the kitchen. "You can't say boo to him without him squaring up for a fight."

"Mm-hmm."

"Argumentative, smart-mouthed, troublemaker." Feeling grossly put upon, Cam snagged a beer from the fridge.

"Must be like looking in a mirror."

"Like hell."

"Don't know what I was thinking of. You're such a peaceable soul." Moving at his own relaxed pace, Ethan bent down to search out an old glass pitcher. "Let's see, you were just about fourteen when I came along. First thing you did was pick a fight so you'd have the excuse to bloody my nose."

For the first time in hours, Cam felt a grin spread. "That was just a welcome-to-the-family tap. Besides, you gave me a hell of a black eye as a thank-you."

"There was that. Kid's too smart to try to punch you," Ethan continued and began to dump generous scoops of sugar into the pitcher. "So he razzes you instead. He sure as hell's got your attention, doesn't he?"

It was irritating because it was true. "You got him pegged so neatly, why don't you take him on?"

"Because I'm on the water every morning at dawn. Kid like that needs supervision." That, Ethan thought, was his story and he'd stick to it through all the tortures of hell. "Of the three of us, you're the only one not working."

"I'm going to have to fix that," Cam muttered.

"Oh, yeah?" With a mild snort, Ethan finished making the tea. "That'll be the day."

"The day's coming up fast. Social worker was here today."

Ethan grunted, let the implications turn over in his mind. "What'd she want?"

"To check us out. She's going to be talking to you, too. And Phillip. Already talked to Seth—which is what I was trying to diplomatically ask him about when he started foaming at the mouth again."

Cam frowned now, thinking more of Anna Spinelli of the great legs and tidy briefcase than of Seth. "If we don't pass, she's going to work on pulling him."

"He isn't going anywhere."

"That's what I said." He dragged his hand through his hair again, which for some reason reminded him he'd meant to get a haircut. In Rome. Seth wasn't the only one not going anywhere. "But, bro, we're about to make some serious adjustments around here."

"Things are fine as they are." Ethan filled a glass with ice and poured tea over it so that it crackled.

"Easy for you to say." Cam stepped out on the porch, let the screen door slap shut behind him. He walked to the rail, watched Ethan's sleek Chesapeake Bay retriever, Simon, play tag and tumble with the fat puppy. Upstairs, Seth had obviously decided to seek revenge by turning his radio up to earsplitting. Screaming headbanger rock blasted through the windows.

Cam's jaw twitched. He'd be damned if he'd tell the kid to turn it down. Too clichéd, too terrifyingly adult a response. He sipped his beer, struggled to loosen the knots in his shoulders, and concentrated on the way the lowering sun tossed white diamonds onto the water.

The wind was coming up so that the marsh grass waved like a field of Kansas wheat. The drake of a pair of ducks that had set up house where the water bent at the edge of the trees flew by quacking.

Lucy, I'm home, was all Cam could think, and it nearly made him smile again.

Under the roar of music he heard the gentle rhythmic creak of the rocker. Beer fountained from the lip of the bottle when he whirled. Ethan stopped rocking and stared at him.

"What?" he demanded. "Christ, Cam, you look like you've seen a ghost."

"Nothing." Cam swiped a hand over his face, then carefully lowered himself to the porch so he could lean back against the post. "Nothing," he repeated, but set the beer aside. "I'm a little edgy."

"Usually are if you stay in one place more than a week."

"Don't climb up my back, Ethan."

"Just a comment." And because Cam looked exhausted and pale, Ethan reached in the breast pocket of his shirt, took out two cigars. It wouldn't hurt to change his smoke-after-dinner routine. "Cigar?"

Cam sighed. "Yeah, why not?" Rather than move, he let Ethan light the first and pass it to him. Leaning back again, he blew a few lazy smoke rings. When the music shut off abruptly, he felt he'd achieved a small personal victory.

For the next ten minutes, there wasn't a sound but the lap of water, the call of birds, and the talk of the breeze. The sun dropped lower, turning the western sky into a soft, rosy haze that bled into the water and blurred the horizon. Shadows deepened.

It was like Ethan, Cam mused, to ask no questions. To sit in silence and wait. To understand the need for quiet. He'd nearly forgotten that admirable trait of his brother's. And maybe, Cam admitted, he'd nearly forgotten how much he loved the brother Ray and Stella had given him.

But even remembering, he wasn't sure what to do about it.

"See you fixed the steps," Ethan commented when he judged Cam was relaxing again.

"Yeah. The place could use a coat of paint, too."

"We'll have to get to that."

They were going to have to get to a lot of things, Cam thought. But the quiet creak of the rocker kept taking his mind back to that afternoon. "Have you ever had a dream while you were wide awake?" He could ask because it was Ethan, and Ethan would think and consider.

After setting the nearly empty glass on the porch beside the rocker, Ethan studied his cigar. "Well . . . I guess I have. The mind likes to wander when you let it."

It could have been that, Cam told himself. His mind had wandered—maybe even gotten lost for a bit. That could have been why he'd thought he saw his father rocking on the porch. The conversation? Wishful thinking, he decided. That was all.

"Remember how Dad used to bring his fiddle out here? Hot summer nights he'd sit where you're sitting and play for hours. He had such big hands."

"He could sure make that fiddle sing."

"You picked it up pretty well."

Ethan shrugged, puffed lazily on his cigar. "Some."

"You ought to take it. He'd have wanted you to have it."

Ethan shifted his quiet eyes, locked them on Cam's. Neither spoke for a moment, nor had to. "I guess I will, but not right yet. I'm not ready."

"Yeah." Cam blew out smoke again.

"You still got the guitar they gave you that Christmas?"

"I left it here. Didn't want it banging around with me." Cam looked at his fingers, flexed them as though he were about to lay them on the strings. "Guess I haven't played in more than a year."

"Maybe we should try Seth on some instrument. Mom used to swear playing a tune pumped out the aggression." He turned his head as the dogs began to bark and race around the side of the house. "Expecting somebody?"

"Phillip."

Ethan's brows lifted. "Thought he wasn't coming down till Friday."

"Let's just call this a family emergency." Cam tapped out the stub of the cigar before he rose. "I hope to Christ he brought some decent food and none of that fancy pea pod crap he likes to eat."

Phillip strode into the kitchen balancing a large bag on top of a jumbo bucket of chicken and shooting out waves of irritation. He dumped the food on the table, skimmed a hand through his hair, and scowled at his brothers.

"I'm here," he snapped as they came through the back door. "What's the damn problem?"

"We're hungry," Cam said easily, and peeling the top from the bucket, he grabbed a drumstick. "You got dirt on your 'I'm an executive' pants there, Phil."

"Goddamn it." Furious now, Phillip brushed impatiently at the pawprints on his slacks. "When are you going to teach that idiot dog not to jump on people?"

"You cart around fried chicken, dog's going to see if he can get a piece. Makes him smart if you ask me." Unoffended, Ethan went to a cupboard for plates.

"You get fries?" Cam poked in the bag, snagged one. "Cold. Somebody better nuke these. If I do it they'll blow up or disintegrate."

"I'll do it. Get something to dish up that cole slaw."

Phillip took a breath, then one more. The drive down from Baltimore was long, and the traffic had been ugly. "When you two girls have finished playing house, maybe you'll tell me why I broke a date with a very hot-looking CPA—the third date by the way, which was dinner at her place with the definite possibility of sex afterward—and instead just spent a couple hours in miserable traffic to deliver a fucking bucket of chicken to a couple of boobs."

"First off, I'm tired of cooking." Cam heaped cole slaw on his plate and took a biscuit. "And even more tired of tossing out what I've cooked because even the pup—who drinks out of the toilet with regularity—won't touch it. But that's only the surface."

He took another hefty bite of chicken as he walked to the doorway and shouted for Seth. "The kid needs to be here. We're all in this."

"Fine. Great." Phillip dropped into a chair, tugged at his tie.

"No use sulking because your accountant isn't going to be running your figures tonight, pal." Ethan offered him a friendly smile and a plate.

"Tax season's heating up." With a sigh, Phillip scooped out slaw. "I'll be lucky to get a warm look from her until after April fifteenth. And I was so close."

"None of us is likely to be getting much action for the next little while." Cam jerked a head as Seth's feet pounded down the stairs. "The patter of little feet plays hell with the sex life."

Cam tucked away the urge for another beer and settled on iced tea as Seth stepped into the kitchen. The boy scanned the room, his nose twitching at the scent of spicy chicken, but he didn't dive into the bucket as he would have liked to.

"What's the deal?" he demanded and tucked his hands in his pockets while his stomach yearned.

"Family meeting," Cam announced. "With food. Sit." He took a chair himself as Ethan put the freshly buzzed fries on the table. "Sit," Cam repeated when Seth stayed where he was. "If you're not hungry you can just listen."

"I could eat." Seth sauntered over to the table, slid into a chair. "It's got to be better than the crud you've been trying to pass off as food."

"You know," Ethan said in his mild drawl before Cam could snarl, "seems to me I'd be grateful if somebody tried to put together a hot meal for me from time to time. Even if it was crud." With his eyes on Seth, Ethan tipped down the bucket, contemplated his choices. "Especially if that somebody was doing the best he could."

Because it was Ethan, Seth flushed, squirmed, then shrugged as he plucked out a fat breast. "Nobody asked him to cook."

"All the more reason. Might work better if you took turns."

"He doesn't think I can do anything." Seth sneered over at Cam. "So I don't."

"You know, it's tempting to toss this little fish back into the pond." Cam dumped salt on his fries and struggled to hold onto a simmering temper. "I could be in Aruba this time tomorrow."

"So go." Seth's eyes flashed up, full of anger and defiance. "Go wherever the hell you want as long as it's out of my face. I don't need you."

"Smart-mouthed little brat. I've had it." Cam had a long reach and used it now to shoot a hand across the table and pluck Seth out of his chair. Even as Phillip opened his mouth to protest, Ethan shook his head.

"You think I've enjoyed spending the last two weeks baby-sitting some snot-nosed monster with a piss-poor attitude? I've put my life on hold to deal with you."

"Big deal." Seth had turned sheet-white and was ready for the blow he was sure would come. But he wouldn't back down. "All you do is run around collecting trophies and screwing women. Go back where you came from and keep doing it. I don't give a shit."

Cam watched the edges of his own vision turn red. Fury and frustration hissed in his blood like a snake primed to strike.

He saw his father's hands at the end of his arms. Not Ray's, but the man who had used those hands on him with such casual violence throughout his childhood. Before he did something unforgivable, he dropped Seth back into his chair. His voice was quiet now, and the room vibrated with his control.

"If you think I'm staying for you, you're wrong. I'm staying for Ray. Have you got any idea where the system will toss you if one of us decides you're not worth the trouble?"

Foster homes, Seth thought. Strangers. Or worse, *her*. Because his legs were trembling badly, he locked his feet around the legs of his chair. "You don't care what they do with me."

"That's just one more thing you're wrong about," Cam said evenly. "You don't want to be grateful, fine. I don't want your goddamn gratitude. But you'll start showing some respect, and you'll start showing it now. It's not just me who's going to be hounding your sorry ass, pal. It's the three of us."

Cam sat down again, waited for his composure to solidify. "The social worker who was here today—Spinelli, Anna Spinelli—has some concerns about the environment."

"What's wrong with the environment?" Ethan wanted

to know. The nasty little altercation had cleared the air, he decided. Now they could get to the details. "It's a good, solid house, a nice area. School's good, crime's low."

"I got the impression *I'm* the environment. At the moment, I'm the only one here, supervising things."

"The three of us will go down as guardians," Phillip pointed out. He poured a glass of iced tea and set it casually next to the hand Seth had fisted on the table. He imagined the boy's throat would be burning dry right about now. "I checked with the lawyer after you called. The preliminary paperwork should go through by the end of the week. There'll be a probationary period—regular home studies and meetings, evaluations. But unless there's a serious objection, it doesn't look like a problem."

"Spinelli's a problem." Cam refused to let the altercation spoil his appetite and reached for more chicken. "Classic do-gooder. Great legs, serious mind. I know she talked to the kid, but he's not inclined to share their conversation, so I'll share mine. She had doubts about my qualifications as guardian. Single man, no steady means of employment, no permanent residence."

"There are three of us." Phillip frowned and poked at his slaw. A trickle of guilt was working through, and he didn't care for it.

"Which I pointed out. Miz Spinelli of the gorgeous Italian eyes countered with the sad fact that I happen to be the only one of the three of us actually living here with the kid. And it was tactfully implied that of the three of us I'm the least likely candidate for guardian. So I tossed out the idea of all of us living here."

"What do you mean living here?" Phillip dropped his fork. "I work in Baltimore. I've got a condo. How the hell am I supposed to live here and work there?"

"That'll be a problem," Cam agreed. "Bigger one will be how you'll fit all your clothes into that closet in your old room."

While Phillip tried to choke out a response, Ethan tapped a finger on the edge of the table. He thought of his small, and to him perfect, house. The quiet and solitude of it. And he saw the way Seth stared down at his plate with dark, baffled eyes. "How long you figure it would take?"

"I don't know." Cam dragged both hands back through his hair. "Six months, maybe a year."

"A year." All Phillip could do was close his eyes. "Jesus."

"You talk to the lawyer about it," Cam suggested. "See what's what. But we present a united front to Social Services or they're going to pull him. And I've got to find work."

"Work." Phillip's misery dissolved in a grin. "You? Doing what? There aren't any racetracks in St. Chris. And the Chesapeake, God bless her, sure ain't the Med."

"I'll find something. Steady doesn't mean fancy. I'm not looking at something I'll need an Armani suit for."

He was wrong, Cam realized. This damn business *was* going to spoil his appetite. "The way I figure it, Spinelli's going to be back tomorrow, the next day at the latest. We have to hammer this out, and it has to look like we know what the hell we're doing."

"I'll take my vacation time early." Phillip bid farewell to the two weeks he'd planned to spend in the Caribbean. "That buys us a couple of weeks. I can work with the lawyer, deal with the social worker."

"I'll deal with her." Cam smiled a little. "I liked the looks of her, and I ought to get some perks out of this. Of course, all this depends on what the kid said to her today."

"I told her I wanted to stay," Seth mumbled. Tears were raw in his stomach. The food sat untouched on his plate. "Ray said I could. He said I could stay here. He said he'd fix it so I could."

"And we're what's left of him." Cam waited until Seth lifted his gaze. "So we'll fix it."

• • •

LATER, WHEN THE MOON was up and the dark water was slashed by its luminous white beam, Phillip stood on the dock. The air was cold now, the damp wind carrying the raw edge of the winter that fought not to yield to spring.

It suited his mood.

There was a war raging inside him between conscience and ambition. In two short weeks, the life he had planned out, plotted meticulously, and implemented with deliberation and simple hard work had shattered.

Now, still numb with grief for his father, he was being asked to transplant himself, to compromise those careful plans.

He'd been thirteen when Ray and Stella Quinn took him in. Most of those years he'd spent on the street, dodging the system. He was an accomplished thief, an enthusiastic brawler who used drugs and liquor to dull the ugliness. The projects of Baltimore were his turf, and when a drive-by shooting left him bleeding on those streets, he was prepared to die. To simply end it.

Indeed, the life he'd led up to the point when he wound up in a gutter choked with garbage ended that night. He lived, and for reasons he never understood, the Quinns wanted him. They opened a thousand fascinating doors for him. And no matter how often, how defiantly he tried to slam them shut again, they didn't allow it.

They gave him choices, and hope, and a family. They offered him a chance for an education that had saved his soul. He used what they'd given him to make himself into the man he was. He studied and worked, and he buried that miserable boy deep.

His position at Innovations, the top advertising firm in the metropolitan area, was solid. No one doubted that Phillip Quinn was on the fast track to the top. And no one who knew the man who wore the elegant tailored suits, who could order a meal in perfect French and always knew the proper wine, would have believed he had once bartered his body for the price of a dime bag.

He had pride in that, perhaps too much pride, but he considered it his testament to the Quinns.

There was enough of that selfish, self-serving boy still inside him to rebel at the thought of giving up one inch of it. But there was too much of the man Ray and Stella had molded to consider doing otherwise.

Somehow he had to find the compromise.

He turned, looked back at the house. The upstairs was dark. Seth was in bed by now, Phillip mused. He didn't have a clue how he felt about the boy. He recognized him, understood him, and he supposed resented just a bit those parts of himself he saw in young Seth DeLauter.

Was he Ray Quinn's son?

There, Phillip thought as his teeth clenched—more resentment at even the possibility of it. Had the man he'd all but worshiped for more than half his life really fallen off his pedestal, succumbed to temptation, betrayed wife and family?

And if he had, how could he have turned his back on his own blood? How could this man who had made strangers his own ignore for more than a decade a son who'd come from his own body?

We've got enough problems, Phillip reminded himself. The first was to keep a promise. To keep the boy.

He walked back, using the back porch light to guide him. Cam sat on the steps, Ethan in the rocker.

"I'll go back into Baltimore in the morning," Phillip announced. "I'll see what the lawyer can firm up. You said the social worker was named Spinelli?"

"Yeah." Cam nursed a cup of black coffee. "Anna Spinelli."

"She'd be county, probably out of Princess Anne. I'll pass that on." Details, he thought. He'd concentrate on the facts. "The way I see it, we're going to have to come off as three model citizens. I already pass." Phillip smiled thinly. "The two of you are going to have to work on your act."

"I told Spinelli I'd get a job." Even the thought of it disgusted Cam.

"I'd hold off on that a while." This came from Ethan, who rocked quietly in the shadows. "I got an idea. I want to think on it a while more. Seems to me," he went on, "that with Phil and me around, both of us working, you could be running the house."

"Oh, Jesus" was all Cam could manage.

"It goes like this." Ethan paused, rocked, continued. "You'd be what they'd call primary caregiver. You're available if the school calls with a problem, if Seth gets sick or whatever."

"Makes sense," Phillip agreed and, feeling better, he grinned at Cam. "You're Mommy."

"Fuck you."

"That's no way for Mommy to talk."

"If you think I'm going to be stuck washing your dirty socks and swabbing the toilet, you wasted that fine education you're so proud of."

"Just temporarily," Ethan said, though he enjoyed the image of his brother wearing an apron and hunting up cobwebs with a feather duster. "We'll work out shifts. Seth ought to have some regular chores too. We always did. But it's going to fall to you for the next few days anyway, while Phillip figures out how we handle the legal end and I see how I can juggle my time."

"I've got business of my own to deal with." The coffee was beginning to burn a hole in his gut, but Cam drank it down anyway. "My stuff's scattered all over Europe."

"Well, Seth's in school all day, isn't he?" Absently Ethan reached down to stroke the dog snoring beside his chair.

"Fine. Great." Cam gave up. "You," he said, pointing at Phillip, "bring some groceries back with you. We're out of damn near everything. And Ethan can throw whatever you bring in together into a meal. Everybody makes their own bed, goddamn it. I'm not a maid."

"What about breakfast?" Phillip said dryly. "You're

not going to send your men off in the morning without a hot meal, are you?''

Cam eyed him balefully. ''You're enjoying this, aren't you?''

''Might as well.'' He sat on the steps beside Cam, leaned back on his elbows. ''Somebody ought to talk to Seth about cleaning up his language.''

''Oh, yeah.'' Cam merely snorted. ''That'll work.''

''He swears that way in front of the neighbors, the social worker, his teachers, it's going to give a bad impression. How's his schoolwork anyway?''

''How the hell should I know?''

''Now, Mother—'' Phillip grunted, then laughed when Cam's elbow jabbed his ribs.

''Keep it up and you're going to end up with another ruined suit, ace.''

''Let me change and we can go a couple rounds. Or better yet . . .'' Phillip arched a brow, slid his gaze over toward Ethan, then back to Cam.

Approving the plan, Cam scratched his chin, set down his empty cup. They shot off the steps in tandem, so fast that Ethan barely had a chance to blink.

His fist shot out, was blocked, and he was hauled out of the chair by armpits and ankles, cursing all the way. Simon leaped up to bark delightedly and raced circles around the men who hauled his struggling master off the porch.

Inside the kitchen, the pup wiggled madly and yipped in answer. To keep him close, Seth pulled off a chunk of the chicken he'd come down to forage and dropped it on the floor. While Foolish gobbled, Seth watched in puzzled amazement as the silhouettes headed for the dock.

He'd come down to fill his empty belly. He was used to moving quietly. He'd stuffed his mouth with chicken and listened to the men talk.

They acted like they were going to let him stay. Even when they didn't know he was there to hear, they talked as if it was a simple fact. At least for now, he decided, until they forgot they'd made a promise, or no longer cared.

He knew promises didn't mean squat.

Except Ray's. He'd believed Ray. But then he'd gone and died and ruined everything. Still, every night he spent in this house, between clean sheets with the puppy curled beside him, was an escape. Whenever they decided to ditch him, he'd be ready to run.

Because he'd die before he went back to where he'd been before Ray Quinn.

The pup was nosing at the door, drawn by the sound of laughter and barking and the shouts. Seth fed him more chicken to distract him.

He wanted to go out too, to run across the lawn and join in that laughter, that fun . . . that family. But he knew he wouldn't be welcome. They'd stop and they'd stare at him as if they wondered where the hell he'd come from and what the hell they were supposed to do about it.

Then they'd tell him to get back to bed.

Oh, God, he wanted to stay. He just wanted to be here. Seth pressed his face against the screen, yearning with all his heart to belong.

When he heard Ethan's long, laughing oath, the loud splash that followed it, and the roars of male satisfaction that came next, he grinned.

And he stayed there, grinning even as a tear escaped and trickled unnoticed down his cheek.

Five

Anna got in to work early. Odds were her supervisor would already be at her desk. You could always count on Marilou Johnston to be at her desk or within hailing distance.

Marilou was a woman Anna both admired and respected. When she needed advice, there was no one whose opinion she valued more.

When she poked her head around the open office door, Anna smiled a little. As expected, Marilou was there, buried behind the files and paperwork on her cluttered desk. She was a small woman, barely topping five feet. She wore her hair close-cropped for convenience as much as style. Her face was smooth, like polished ebony, and the expression on it could remain composed even during the worst crises.

A calm center was how Anna often thought of Marilou. Though how she could be calm when her life was filled with a demanding career, two teenage boys, and a house that Anna had seen for herself was constantly crowded with people was beyond her.

Anna often thought she wanted to be Marilou Johnston when she grew up.

"Got a minute?"

"Sure do." Marilou's voice was quick and lively, ripe with that Southern Shore accent that caught words between a drawl and a twang. She waved Anna to a chair with one hand and fiddled with the round gold ball in her left ear. "The Quinn-DeLauter case?"

"Right the first time. There were a couple of faxes waiting for me yesterday from the Quinns' lawyer. A Baltimore firm."

"What did our Baltimore lawyer have to say?"

"The gist of it is they're pursuing guardianship. He'll be pushing through a petition to the court. They're very serious about keeping Seth DeLauter in their home and under their care."

"And?"

"It's an unusual situation, Marilou. Up 'til now I've only spoken with one of the brothers. The one who lived in Europe until recently."

"Cameron? Impressions?"

"He certainly makes one." And because Marilou was also a friend, Anna allowed herself a grin and a roll of her eyes. "A treat to look at. I came across him when he was repairing the back porch steps. I can't say he looked like a happy man, but he was certainly a determined one. There's a lot of anger there, and a lot of grief. What impressed me the most—"

"Other than his looks?"

"Other than his looks," Anna agreed with a chuckle, "was the fact that he never questioned keeping Seth. It was simply fact. He called Seth his brother. He meant it. I'm not sure he knows exactly how he feels about it, but he meant it."

She went on, while Marilou listened without comment, detailing the conversation, Cam's willingness to change his life, and his lifestyle, his concerns that Seth would bolt if he were taken out of the home.

"And," she continued, "after speaking with Seth, I tend to agree with him."

"You think the boy's a runner?"

"When I suggested foster care, he became angry, resentful. And afraid. If he feels threatened, he'll run." She thought of all the children who ended up on the mean streets of inner cities, homeless, desperate. She thought of what they did to survive. And she thought of how many didn't survive at all.

It was her job to keep this one child, this one boy, safe.

"He wants to stay there, Marilou. Maybe he needs to. His feelings about his mother are very strong, and very negative. I suspect abuse, but he's not ready to discuss it. At least not with me."

"Is there any word on the mother's whereabouts?"

"No. We have no idea where she is, or what she'll do. She signed papers allowing Ray Quinn to begin adoption proceedings, but he died before they were finalized. If she comes back and wants her son . . ." Anna shook her head. "The Quinns would have a fight on their hands."

"You sound as though you'd be in their corner."

"I'm in Seth's," Anna said firmly. "And I'm going to stay there. I spoke with his teachers." She pulled out a file as she spoke. "I have my report on that. I'm going back today to speak with some of the neighbors, and hopefully to meet with all three of the Quinns. It may be possible to stop the temporary guardianship until I complete the initial study, but I'm inclined against it. That boy needs stability. He needs to feel wanted. And even if the Quinns only want him because of a promise, it's more than he's had before, I believe."

Marilou took the file, set it aside. "I assigned this case to you because you don't look just at the surface. And I sent you in cold because I wanted your take. Now I'll tell you what I know about the Quinns."

"You know them?"

"Anna, I was born and raised on the Shore." She smiled, beautifully. It was a simple fact, but one she had great pride in. "Ray Quinn was one of my professors at college. I admired him tremendously. When I had my two boys, Stella Quinn was their pediatrician until we moved to Princess Anne. We adored her."

"When I was driving out there yesterday I kept wishing I'd had the chance to meet them."

"They were exceptional people," Marilou said simply. "Ordinary, even simple in some ways. And exceptional. Here's a case in point," she added, leaning back in her chair. "I graduated from college sixteen years ago. The three Quinns were teenagers. You heard stories now and again. Maybe they were a little wild, and people wondered why Ray and Stella had taken on half-grown men with bad tendencies. I was pregnant with Johnny, my first, working my butt off to get my degree, and help my husband, Ben, pay the rent. He was working two jobs. We wanted a better life for ourselves, and we sure as hell wanted one for the baby I was carrying."

She paused, turned the double picture frame on her desk to a closer angle so that she could see her two young men smile out at her. "I wondered too. Figured they were crazy, or just playing at being Samaritans. Professor Quinn called me into his office one day. I'd missed a couple of classes. Had the worst case of morning sickness known to woman."

It still made her grimace. "I swear I don't understand how some women reminisce over that kind of thing. In any case, I thought he was going to recommend me dropping his class, which meant losing the credits toward my degree. With me an inch away—an inch away and I would be the first in my family with a college degree. I was ready to fight. Instead, he wanted to know what he could do to help. I was speechless."

She smiled, remembering, then beamed over at Anna. "You know how impersonal college can be—the huge lectures where a student is just one more face in the crowd. But he'd noticed me. And he'd taken the time to find out something about my situation. I burst into tears. Hormones," she said with a wry grin. "Well, he patted my hand, gave me some tissues, and let me cry it out. I was on a scholarship, and if my grades dropped or I blew a class, I could lose it. I only had one more semester. He said for me not to worry, we'd work it all out, and I was going to get my degree. He started talking, about this and that, to calm me down. He was telling me some story about teaching his son to drive. Made me laugh. It wasn't until later, I realized he hadn't been talking about one of the boys he'd taken in. Because that's not what they were to him. They were his."

A sucker for a happy ending, Anna sighed. "And you got your degree."

"He made sure I did. I owe him for that. Which is why I didn't tell you about this until you'd formed some impressions of your own. As for the three Quinns, I don't really know them. I've seen them at two funerals. Saw Seth DeLauter with them at Professor Quinn's. For personal reasons I'd like to see them have a chance to be a family. But . . ." She laid her hands palm to palm. "The best interest of the boy comes before that—and the structure of the system. You're thorough, Anna, and you believe in structure and in the system. Professor Quinn would have wanted what's best for Seth, and to repay an old debt, I gave him you."

Anna blew out a long breath. "No pressure, huh?"

"Pressure's all we've got around here." As if on cue, her phone began to ring. "And the clock's running."

Anna rose. "I'd better get to work, then. Looks like I'll be in the field most of today."

IT WAS NEARLY ONE P.M. when Anna pulled up in the Quinns' drive. She'd managed to conduct interviews with three of the five names Cam had given her the day before, and she hoped to expand on that before too much more time passed.

Her call to Phillip Quinn's office in Baltimore had given her the information that he was on leave for the next two weeks. She was hoping she would find him here and be able to file an impression of another Quinn.

But it was the pup who greeted her. He barked ferociously even as he backed rapidly away from her. Anna watched with amusement as he peed on himself in terror. With a laugh, she crouched down, held out a hand.

"Come on, cutie, I won't hurt you. Aren't you sweet, aren't you pretty?" She kept murmuring to him until he bellied over to sniff her hand, then rolled over in ecstasy as she scratched him.

"For all you know, he's got fleas and rabies."

Anna glanced up and saw Cam in the front doorway. "For all I know, so do you."

With a snort of a laugh and his hands tucked in his pockets, he came out on the porch. It was a brown suit today, he noted. For the life of him he couldn't figure why she'd pick such a dull color. "I guess you're willing to risk it, since you're back. Didn't expect you so soon."

"A boy's welfare is at stake, Mr. Quinn. I don't believe in taking my time under the circumstances."

Obviously charmed by her voice, the puppy leaped up and bathed her face. The giggle escaped before she could stop it—a sound that made Cam raise his eyebrows—and defending herself from the puppy's eager tongue, she rose. Tugged down her jacket. And her dignity.

"May I come in?"

"Why not?" This time he waited for her, even opened the door and let her go in ahead of him.

She saw a large and fairly tidy living area. The furniture showed some wear but appeared comfortable and colorful. The spinet in the corner caught her eye. "Do you play?"

"Not really." Without realizing it, Cam ran a hand over the wood. He didn't notice that his fingers left streaks in the dust. "My mother did, and Phillip's got an ear for it."

"I tried to reach your brother Phillip at his office this morning."

"He's out buying groceries." Because he was pleased to have won that battle, Cam smiled a little. "He's going to be living here . . . for the foreseeable future. Ethan, too."

"You work fast."

"A boy's welfare is at stake," he said, echoing her.

Anna nodded. At a distant rumble of thunder, she glanced outside, frowned. The light was dimming, and the wind beginning to kick. "I'd like to discuss Seth with you." She shifted her briefcase, glanced at a chair.

"Is this going to take long?"

"I couldn't say."

"Then let's do it in the kitchen. I want coffee."

"Fine."

She followed him, using the time to study the house. It was just neat enough to make her wonder if Cam had been expecting her. They passed a den where the dust was layered over tables, the couch was covered with newspapers, and shoes littered the floor.

Missed that, didn't you? she thought with a smirk. But she found it endearing.

Then she heard his quick and vicious oath and nearly jumped out of her practical shoes.

"Goddamn it. Shit. What the hell is this? What next? Jesus Christ." He was already sloshing through the water and suds flowing over the kitchen floor to slap at the dishwasher.

Anna stepped back to avoid the flood. "I'd turn that off if I were you."

"Yeah, yeah, yeah. Now I've got to take the bitch apart." He dragged the door open. An ocean of snowy-white suds spewed out.

Anna bit the inside of her cheek, cleared her throat. "Ah, what kind of soap did you use?"

"Dish soap." Vibrating with frustration, he yanked a bucket out from under the sink.

"Dish*washer* soap or dish-washing soap?"

"What the hell's the difference?" Furious, he started to bail. Outside, the rain began to fall in hard, driving sheets.

"This." Keeping her face admirably sober, she gestured

to the river running over the floor. "This is the difference. If you use the liquid for hand-washing dishes in a dishwasher, this is the inevitable result."

He straightened, the bucket in his hand, and a look of such pained irritation on his face, she couldn't hold back the laugh. "Sorry, sorry. Look, turn around."

"Why?"

"Because I'm not willing to ruin my shoes or my hose. So turn around while I take them off and I'll give you a hand."

"Yeah." Pathetically grateful, he turned his back, and even did his best not to imagine her peeling off her stockings. His best wasn't quite good enough, but it was the effort that counted. "Ethan handled most of the kitchen chores when we were growing up. I did my share, but it doesn't seem to have stuck with me."

"You seem to be out of your element." She tucked her hose neatly in her shoes, set them aside. "Get me a mop. I'll swab, you get the coffee."

He opened a long, narrow closet and handed her a string mop. "I appreciate it."

Her legs, he noted as he sloshed over for mugs, didn't need hose. They were a pale and fascinating gold in color, and smooth as silk. When she bent over, he ran his tongue over his teeth. He'd had no idea a woman with a mop would be quite so . . . attractive.

It's so amazingly pleasant, he realized, to be here, with the rain drumming, the wind howling, and a pretty, barefoot woman keeping him kitchen company. "You seem to be in your element," he commented, then grinned when she turned her head and eyed him balefully. "I'm not saying it's woman's work. My mother would have skinned me for the thought. I'm just saying you seem to know what you're doing."

As she'd worked her way through college cleaning houses, she knew very well. "I can handle a mop, Mr. Quinn."

"Since you're mopping my kitchen floor, you ought to make it Cam."

"About Seth—"

"Yeah, about Seth. Do you mind if I sit down?"

"Go ahead." She caught herself before she began to hum. The mindless chore, the rain, the isolation were just a tad too relaxing. "I'm sure you know I spoke with him yesterday."

"Yeah, and I know he told you he wanted to stay here."

"He did, and it's in my report. I also spoke with his teachers. How much do you know about his schoolwork?"

Cam shifted. "I haven't had a lot of time to get into that yet."

"Mmm-hmm. When he was first enrolled, he had some trouble with the other students. Fistfights. He broke one boy's nose."

Good for him, Cam thought with a surprising tug of pride, but he did his best to look disapproving. "Who started it?"

"That's not the point. However, your father handled the situation. At this point I'm told that Seth keeps mostly to himself. He doesn't participate in class, which is another problem. He rarely turns in his homework assignments, and those he does bother to turn in are most often sloppily done."

Cam felt a new headache begin to brew. "So the kid's not a scholar—"

"On the contrary." Anna straightened up, leaned on the mop. "If he participated even marginally in class, and if his assignments were done and turned in on time, he would be a straight A student. He's a solid B student as it is."

"So what's the problem?"

Anna closed her eyes a moment. "The problem is that Seth's IQ and evaluation tests are incredibly high. The child is brilliant."

Though he had his doubts about that, Cam nodded. "So, that's a good thing. And he's getting decent grades and staying out of trouble."

"Okay." She would try this a different way. "Suppose you were in a Formula One race—"

"Been there," he said with wistful reminiscence. "Done that."

"Right, and you had the finest, fastest, hottest car in the field."

"Yeah." He sighed. "I did."

"But you never tested its full capabilities, you never went full-out, you never punched it on the turns or popped it into fifth and poured down the straights."

His brow lifted. "You follow racing?"

"No, but I drive a car."

"Nice car, too. What have you had it up to?"

Eighty-eight, she thought with secret glee, but she would never admit it. "I consider a car transportation," she said, lying primly. "Not a toy."

"No reason it can't be both. Why don't I take you out in the 'Vette? Now that's a fine mode of entertaining transportation."

While she would have loved to indulge in the fantasy of sliding behind the wheel of that sleek white bullet, she had a point to make. "Try to stick with the analogy here. You're racing a superior machine. If you didn't drive that car the way it was meant to be driven, you'd be wasting its potential, and maybe you'd still finish in the money, but you wouldn't win."

He got her point, but couldn't help grinning. "I usually won."

Anna shook her head. "Seth," she said with admirable patience. "We're talking about Seth. He's socially stunted, and he defies authority consistently. He's regularly given in-school suspension. He needs supervision here at home when it comes to this area of his life. You're going to have to take an active roll in his schoolwork and his behavior."

"Seems to me a kid gets B's he ought to be left the hell alone." But he held up a hand before she could speak. "Potential. I had potential drummed into my head by the best. We'll work on it."

"Good." She went back to mopping. "I had communications from your lawyer in regard to the guardianship. It's likely you'll be granted that, at least temporarily. But you can expect regular spot checks from Social Services."

"Meaning you."

"Meaning me."

Cam paused a moment. "Do you do windows?"

She couldn't help it, she laughed as she dumped sudsy water into the sink. "I've also talked to some of your neighbors and will talk to more." She turned back. "From this point on, your life's an open book for me."

He rose, took the mop, and to please himself stood just an inch closer than was polite. "You let me know when you get to a chapter that interests you, on a personal level."

Her heart gave two hard knocks against her ribs. A dangerous man, she thought, on a personal level. "I don't have time for much fiction."

She started to step back, but he took her hand. "I like you, Miz Spinelli. I haven't figured out why, but I do."

"That should make our association simpler."

"Wrong." He skimmed his thumb over the back of her hand. "It's going to make it complicated. But I don't mind complications. And it's about time my luck started back on an upswing. You like Italian food?"

"With a name like Spinelli?"

He grinned. "Right. I could use a quiet meal in a decent restaurant with a pretty woman. How about tonight?"

"I don't see any reason why you shouldn't have a quiet meal in a decent restaurant with a pretty woman tonight." Deliberately, she eased her hand free. "But if you're asking me for a date, the answer's no. First, it wouldn't be smart; second, I'm booked."

"Damn it, Cam, didn't you hear me honking?"

Anna turned and saw a soaking wet and bitterly angry man cart two heaping bags of groceries into the room. He was tall, bronzed, and very nearly beautiful. And spitting mad.

Phillip shook the hair out of his eyes and focused on Anna. The shift of expression was quick and smooth—from snarling to charming in the space of a single heartbeat.

"Hello. Sorry." He dumped the bags on the table and smiled at her. "Didn't know Cam had company." He spied the bucket, the mop held between them, and leaped to the wrong conclusion. "I didn't know he was going to hire domestic help. But thank God." Phillip grabbed her hand, kissed it. "I already adore you."

"My brother Phillip," Cam said dryly. "This is Anna Spinelli, with Social Services. You can take your Ferragamo out of your mouth now, Phil."

The charm didn't shift or fade. "Ms. Spinelli. It's nice to meet you. Our lawyer's been in touch, I believe."

"Yes, he has. Mr. Quinn tells me you'll be living here now."

"I told you to call me Cam." He walked to the stove to top off his coffee. "It's going to be confusing if you're calling all of us Mr. Quinn." Cam heard the rattle at the back door and got out another mug. "Especially now," he said as the door burst open and let in a dripping dog and man.

"Christ, this bitch blew in fast." Even as Ethan dragged off his slicker, the dog set his feet and shook furiously. Anna only winced as water sprayed her suit. "Barely smelled her before—"

He spotted Anna and automatically pulled off his soaked cap, then scooped a hand through his damp, curling hair. Seeing woman, bucket, mop, he thought guiltily about his muddy boots. "Ma'am."

"My other brother, Ethan." Cam handed Ethan a steaming cup of coffee. "This is the social worker your dog's just sprayed water and dog hair all over."

"Sorry. Simon, go sit."

"It's all right," Cam went on. "Foolish already slobbered all over her, and Phillip just got finished hitting on her."

Anna smiled blandly. "I thought you were hitting on me."

"I asked you to dinner," Cam corrected. "If I'd been hitting on you, I wouldn't have been subtle." Cam sipped his coffee. "Well, now you know all the players."

She felt outnumbered, and more than a little unprofessional standing there in the dimly lit kitchen in her bare feet, facing three big and outrageously handsome men. In defense, she pulled out every scrap of dignity and reached for a chair.

"Gentlemen, shall we sit down? This seems to be an ideal time to discuss how you plan to care for Seth." She angled her head at Cam. "For the foreseeable future."

"WELL," PHILLIP SAID AN hour later. "I think we pulled that off."

Cam stood at the front door, watching the neat little sports car drive away in the thinning rain. "She's got our number," Cam muttered. "She doesn't miss a trick."

"I liked her." Ethan stretched out in the big wing chair and let the puppy climb into his lap. "Get your mind out of the sewer, Cam," he suggested when Cam snickered. "I mean I liked her. She's smart, and she's professional, but she's not cold. Seems like a woman who cares."

"And she's got great legs," Phillip added. "But regardless of all that, she's going to note down every time we screw up. Right now, I figure we've got the upper hand. We've got the kid, and he wants to stay. His mother's run off to God knows where and isn't making any noises—at the moment. But if pretty Anna Spinelli talks to too many people around St. Chris, she's going to start hearing the rumors."

He dipped his hands in his pockets and started to pace. "I don't know if they're going to count against us or not."

"They're just rumors," Ethan said.

"Yeah, but they're ugly. We've got a good shot at keeping Seth because of Dad's reputation. That reputation gets smeared, and we'll have battles to fight on several fronts."

"Anyone tries to smear Dad's rep, they're going to get more than a fight."

Phillip turned to Cam. "That's just what we have to avoid. If we start going around kicking ass, it's only going to make things worse."

"So you be the diplomat." Cam shrugged and sat on the arm of the sofa. "I'll kick ass."

"I'd say we're better off dealing with what is than what might be." Thoughtfully, Ethan stroked the puppy. "I've been thinking about the situation. It's going to be rough for Phillip to live here and commute back and forth to Baltimore. Sooner rather than later, Cam's going to get fed up with playing house."

"Sooner's already here."

"I was thinking we could pay Grace to do some of the housework. Maybe a couple days a week."

"Now that's an idea I can get behind one hundred percent." Cam dropped onto the sofa.

"Trouble with that is it leaves you with nothing much to do. The idea is for the three of us to be here, share responsibility for Seth. That's what the lawyer says, that's what the social worker says."

"I said I'd find work."

"What are you going to do?" Phillip asked. "Pump gas? Shuck oysters? You'd put up with that for a couple of days."

Cam leaned forward. "I can stick. Can you? Odds are, after the first week of commuting, you'll be calling from Baltimore with excuses about why you can't make it back. Why don't you stay here and try pumping gas or shucking oysters for a while?"

The argument was inevitable. In minutes they were both up and nose to nose. It took several attempts before Ethan's voice got through. Cam stepped back and with a puzzled frown turned. "What?"

"I said I think we ought to try building boats."

"Building boats?" Cam shook his head. "For what?"

"For business." Ethan took out a cigar, but ran it through his fingers rather than lighting it. His mother hadn't allowed smoking in the house. "We got a lot of tourists coming down this way in the last few years. And a lot more people moving down to get out of the city. They like to rent boats. They like to own boats. Last year I built one in my spare time for this guy out of D.C. Little fourteen-foot skiff. Called me a couple months ago to see if I'd be interested in building him another one. Wants a bigger boat, with a sleep cabin and galley."

Ethan tucked the cigar back in his pocket. "I've been thinking on it. It'd take me months to do it alone, in my spare time."

"You want us to help you build a boat?" Phillip pressed his fingers to his eyes.

"Not one boat. I'm talking about going into business."

"I'm in business," Phillip muttered. "I'm in advertising."

"And we'd be needing somebody who knew about that kind of thing if we were starting a business. Boat building's got a history in this area, but nobody's doing it anymore on St. Chris."

Phillip sat. "Did it occur to you that there might be a reason for that?"

"Yeah, it occurred to me. And I thought about it, and I figure it's because nobody's taking the chance. I'm talking wooden boats. Sailing vessels. A specialty. And we already got one client."

Cam rubbed his chin. "Hell, Ethan, I haven't done that kind of work seriously since we built your skipjack. That's been—Jesus—almost ten years."

"And she's holding, isn't she? So we did a good job with her. It's a gamble," he added, knowing that single word was the way to Cam's heart.

"We've got money for start-up costs," Cam murmured, warming up to the idea.

"How do you know?" Phillip demanded. "You don't

have a clue how much money you need for start-up costs.''

''You'll figure it out.'' A roll of the dice, Cam thought. He liked nothing better. ''Christ knows, I'd rather be swinging a hammer than a damn vacuum hose. I'm in.''

''Just like that?'' Phillip threw up his hands. ''Without a thought to overhead, profit and loss, licenses, taxes, insurance. Where the hell are you going to set up shop? How're you going to run the business end?''

''That's not my problem,'' Cam said with a grin. ''That would be yours.''

''I have a job. In Baltimore.''

''I had a life,'' Cam said simply, ''in Europe.''

Phillip paced away, back, away again. Trapped, was all he could think. ''I'll do what I can to get things started. This could be a huge mistake, and it's going to cost a lot of money. And you'd both better consider that the social worker might take a dim view of us starting a risky business at this point. I'm not giving up my job. At least that's one steady income.''

''I'll talk to her about it,'' Cam decided on impulse. ''See how she reacts. You'll talk to Grace about pitching in around the house?'' he asked Ethan.

''Yeah, I'll go down to the pub and run it by her.''

''Fine. That leaves you to deal with Seth tonight.'' He smiled thinly at Phillip. ''Make sure he does his homework.''

''Oh, God.''

''Now that that's settled,'' Cam eased back, ''who's cooking dinner?''

SIX

TRACKING DOWN ANNA Spinelli was the perfect excuse to escape the post-dinner chaos at home. It meant the dishes were someone else's problem—and that he couldn't be pulled into the homework argument that had just begun to heat up between Phillip and Seth.

In fact, as far as Cam was concerned, a rainy evening drive to Princess Anne was high entertainment. And that was pretty pitiful for a man who'd grown accustomed to jetting from Paris to Rome.

He tried not to think about it.

He'd arranged to have his hydrofoil stored, his clothes packed up and sent. He had yet to have his car shipped over, though. It was just a bit too permanent a commitment. But between the time spent repairing steps and doing laundry, he'd entertained himself by tuning up and tinkering with his mother's prized 'Vette.

It gave him a great deal of pleasure to drive it—so much that he accepted the speeding ticket he collected just outside of Princess Anne without complaint.

The town wasn't the hive of activity it had been during the eighteenth and nineteenth centuries when tobacco had been king and wealth poured into the area. But it was pretty enough, Cam supposed, with the old homes restored and preserved, the streets clean and quiet. Now that tourism was becoming the newest deity for the Shore, the charm and grace of historic towns were a huge economic draw.

Anna's apartment was less than half a mile from the offices of Social Services. Easy walking distance to work, to the courts. Shopping was convenient. He imagined she'd chosen the old Victorian house for those reasons as well as for the ambience.

The building was tucked behind big trees, their branches now hazed with new leaves. The walkway was cracked but flanked by daffodils that were ready to pop out with sunny yellow. Steps led to a covered veranda. The plaque beside the door stated that the house was on the historic register.

The door itself was unlocked and led Cam into a hallway. The wood floor was a bit worn, but someone had troubled to polish it to a dull gleam. The mail slots on the wall were brass, again polished, and indicated that the building had been converted to four apartments. A. Spinelli occupied 2B.

Cam trooped up the creaking stairs to the second floor. The hallway was more narrow here, the lights dimmer. The only sound he heard was the muffled echo of what sounded like a riotous sitcom from the television of 2A.

He knocked on Anna's door and waited. Then he knocked again, tucked his hands in his pockets, and scowled. He'd expected her to be home. He'd never considered otherwise. It was nearly nine o'clock, a weeknight, and she was a civil servant.

She should have been quietly at home, reading a book or filling out forms and reports. That was how practical career women spent their evenings—though he hoped eventually to show her a more entertaining way to pass the time.

Probably at some women's club meeting, he decided, annoyed with her. He searched the pockets of his black leather bomber jacket for a scrap of paper and was about to disturb 2A in hopes of borrowing something to write on and with when he heard the quick, rhythmic click that an experienced man recognized as a woman's high heels against wood.

He glanced down the hall, pleased that his luck had changed.

He barely noticed that his jaw dropped.

The woman who walked toward him was built like a man's darkest fantasy. And she was generous enough to showcase that killer body in a snug electric-blue dress scooped low at the breasts and cut high on the thighs. It left nothing—and everything to a male's imagination.

The click of heels on wood was courtesy of ice pick heels in the same shocking color, which turned her legs into endless fascination.

Her hair, dewy with rain, curled madly to her shoulders, a thick ebony mane that brought images of gypsies and campfire sex to mind. Her mouth was red and wet, her eyes huge and dark. The scent of her reached him ten seconds before she did and delivered a breathtaking punch straight to the loins.

She said nothing, only narrowed those amazing eyes, cocked one glorious hip, and waited.

"Well." He had to work on getting his breath back. "I guess you've never heard the one about hiding your light under a bushel."

"I've heard it." She was furious to find him on her doorstep, furious that she was without her professional armor. And even more furious that he'd been on her mind throughout the evening a great deal more than her date. "What do you want, Mr. Quinn?"

Now he grinned, fast and sharp as a wolf baring fangs. "That's a loaded question at the moment, Miz Spinelli."

"Don't be ordinary, Quinn. You've avoided that so far."

"I promise you, I don't have a single ordinary thought in my mind." Unable to resist, he reached out to toy with the ends of her hair. "Where ya been, Anna?"

"Look, it's well after business hours, and my personal life isn't—" She broke off, struggled not to curse or moan as the door across the hall opened.

"You're back from your date, Anna."

"Yes, Mrs. Hardelman."

The woman of about seventy was wrapped in a pink chenille robe and peered over the glasses perched on her nose. Heat and canned laughter poured out into the hall. She beamed at Cam, the smile lighting her pleasant face. "Oh, he's much better-looking than the last one."

"Thanks." Cam stepped over and smiled back. "Does she have a lot of them?"

"Oh, they come and they go." Mrs. Hardelman chuckled and fluffed at her thin white hair. "She never keeps them."

Cam leaned companionably on the doorjamb, enjoying the sounds of frustration Anna made behind him. "Guess she hasn't found one worth keeping yet. She sure is pretty."

"And such a nice girl. She picks up things at the market for us if Sister and I aren't feeling up to going out. Always offers to drive us to church on Sunday. And when my Petie died, Anna took care of the burial herself."

Mrs. Hardelman looked over at Anna with such affection and sweetness, Anna could only sigh. "You're missing your show, Mrs. Hardelman."

"Oh, yes." She glanced back into the apartment, where the television blasted. "I do love my comedies. You come back now," she told Cam and gently closed the door.

And because Anna was perfectly aware that her neighbor wouldn't be able to resist peeping through the security hole hoping to catch a romantic good-night kiss, she dug out her keys.

"You might as well come in since you're here."

"Thanks." He crossed the hall, waiting while she unlocked her door. "You buried your neighbor's husband."

"Her parakeet," Anna corrected. "Petie was a bird. She

and her sister have both been widows for about twenty years. And all I did was get a shoe box and dig a hole out back next to a rosebush.''

He brushed a hand over her hair again as she pushed the door open. ''It meant something to her.''

''Watch your hands, Quinn,'' she warned and flicked on the lights.

To indicate that he was willing to oblige, he held them out, then tucked them into his pockets while he studied the room. Soft, deep cushions, bright, bold colors. He decided the choices meant she had a deep-rooted sensual side.

He liked to think that.

The room was spacious, and she'd furnished it sparingly. The sofa was big and plush enough for sleeping, but there was only a wide upholstered chair and two tables to keep it company.

Yet she'd covered the walls with art. Prints, posters, pen-and-ink sketches. They were of places rather than people, and many of the scenes he recognized. The narrow streets of Rome, the wild cliffs of western Ireland, the classy little cafes of Paris.

''I've been here.'' He tapped the frame of the Paris cafe.

''How nice for you.'' She said it dryly, trying not to resent the fact that her pictures were the only way she could afford to travel. For now. ''Now, what are you doing here?''

''I wanted to talk to you about—'' He made the mistake of turning, looking at her again. She was obviously a very annoyed woman, but it only added to her appeal. Her eyes and mouth were sulky, her body braced in challenge. ''Christ, you're a looker, Anna. I was attracted to you before—I imagine you caught that—but . . . who knew?''

She didn't want to be flattered. She certainly didn't want her heartbeat to pick up speed and lose its steady rhythm. But it was difficult to control either reaction when a man like Cameron Quinn was standing there looking at her as if he'd like to start nibbling at any single part of her body and keep going till he'd devoured it all.

She took a careful breath. "You wanted to talk to me about . . . ?" she prompted.

"The kid, stuff. How about some coffee? That's civilized, right?" He decided to test them both by walking to her. "I figure you expect me to act civilized. I'm willing to give it a shot."

She brooded a moment, then pivoted on those sexy blue heels. Cam appreciated the rear view, rolled his eyes toward heaven, then followed her to the spotless counter that separated living room and kitchen. He leaned on it, pleased that the location gave him a perfect view of her legs.

Then he heard the electric rumble and caught the amazing scent of fresh coffee. "You grind your own beans?"

"If you're going to make coffee, you might as well make good coffee."

"Yeah." He closed his eyes to better appreciate the aroma. "Oh, yeah. Do I have to marry you to get you to make my coffee every day, or can we just live together?"

She looked over her shoulder, lifted her brows at his wide, winning grin, then got back to the task at hand.

"I bet you've used that look to shut men down with enormous success. But me, I like it. So where were you tonight?"

"I had a date."

He moved around the counter. The kitchen area was small, no more than a narrow passageway. He liked being close enough so that her scent mixed with the smell of coffee. "Early evening," he commented.

"It was going to be." She felt the hair on the back of her neck prickle. He was too damn close. Instinctively she employed her usual method with men who crowded her space. She rammed her elbow into his gut.

"Practiced move," he murmured and, rubbing his stomach, backed off an inch. "Do you ever have to use it in your social worker mode?"

"Rarely. How do you want your coffee?"

"Strong and black."

She set it to brew, turned around, and bumped solidly into him. Her radar, she decided as his hands came up to take her arms, had definitely been off. Or, she was forced to admit, she'd ignored it because she'd wondered how they might fit.

Well, now she knew.

He deliberately kept his eyes on her face, didn't let them dip down to the small gold cross nestled between her breasts. He wasn't particularly devout, but he was afraid he would go to hell for having lascivious thoughts about the framework for a religious symbol.

Besides, he liked her face.

"Quinn," she said with a long, irritated sigh. "Back off."

"You dropped the *Mister* Quinn. Does that mean we're pals?"

Because he smiled when he said it, and because he did step back, she found herself chuckling. "Jury's still out."

"I like the way you smell, Anna. Lusty, provocative. Challenging. Of course, I like the way Miz Spinelli smells, too. Quiet and practical and subtle."

"All right . . . Cam." She turned, took out two pretty, deep cups from the cupboard. "Let's stop dancing and agree that we're attracted to each other."

"I was hoping once we agreed to that we'd start dancing."

"Wrong." She tossed her hair back and poured coffee. "I'm Seth's caseworker. You're proposing to be his guardian. It would be incredibly unwise for either of us to act on a physical attraction."

He picked up the cup, leaned back against the counter. "I don't know about you, but I love doing stuff that's unwise. Especially if it feels good." He brought the cup to his lips, then smiled slowly. "And I bet acting on that physical attraction would feel damn good."

"It's fortunate that I happen to be very wise." With a mirroring smile, she leaned back on the opposite counter.

"Now, you wanted to discuss Seth—and stuff, as I believe you put it."

Seth, the rest of his brothers, and the situation had gone completely out of his mind. He supposed he'd used it as an excuse to see her. That was something to consider later. "I have to admit, coming into Princess Anne to talk to you was a great reason to escape. I was about to get stuck with dish duty, and Phil and the kid were already into round one on the homework issue."

"I'm glad someone's dealing with his schoolwork. And why don't you ever refer to Seth by his name?"

"I do. Sure I do."

"No, not as a rule." She cocked her head. "Is that a habit of yours, Cameron, to avoid the personal contact of names with people you don't intend to have an important or permanent relationship with?"

Her point, he was forced to admit, but he lifted a brow. "I use your name."

He saw her blink, heard her sigh, then she waved the issue away. "What about Seth?"

"It's not about him, directly. Except I figure we're starting to divvy things up more evenhandedly. Phil's the best to keep on him—keep on Seth," he corrected with emphasis, "about school because for some reason Phil actually liked school. And we decided to get somebody to come in and deal with most of the housework a couple of days a week."

She still had a picture of him standing in a puddle of suds with a look of baffled fury on his face. Her lips wanted badly to twitch into a smile. "You'll be happier."

"I hope never to see another vacuum cleaner bag. Ever had one rip on you?" He shuddered deliberately and made her laugh. "Anyhow, Ethan had this brainstorm. I'm at loose ends, Phillip needs something to occupy him if he's going to be staying here—though he figures on commuting to Baltimore for now. So we're going into business."

"Into business? What kind of business?"

"Boat building."

She lowered her cup. "You're going to build boats?"

"I've built plenty—so has Ethan. And actually, though Phil went over to the suit-and-tie life, he's done some himself. The three of us worked on the skipjack that Ethan still sails."

"That's fine for recreation, for personal use, for a hobby. But to consider starting a business, a risky one, at the very time when you're trying to take on a minor dependent . . ."

"He won't go hungry. For Christ's sake, Ethan holds his own on the bay, and Phil's got that desk job in Baltimore. I could get busywork, but what's the point?"

"I'm only pointing out that a venture of this nature would consume a great deal of money and time, particularly during the first months. Stability—"

"Isn't every damn thing." Annoyed, he set his coffee down and began to pace. "Shouldn't the kid learn there's more to life than nine-to-fiving it? That there can be choices, that you can take a chance? How good is it for him if I'm stuck in that house dusting furniture and hating every goddamn minute of it? Ethan's already got one client, and if Ethan brought this up you can believe he's weighed it from every angle. Nobody thinks things through as much as he does."

"And since you felt you wanted to discuss this with me, I'm simply trying to do the same. Weigh it from every angle."

"And you think it would be better if I went out and got some nice, stable, time-clock job that brings in a nice, stable, time-clock paycheck every week." He stopped in front of her. "Is that the kind of man who appeals to you? The kind who reports in at nine five days a week, who takes you out to dinner on a rainy night and lets you get away at a reasonable hour without even trying to convince you to take off what there is of that dress?"

She took a minute, reminding herself it wouldn't solve anything if both of them lost the battle with temper. "What appeals to me, what I wear, and how I choose to spend my evenings aren't the issues here. As Seth's caseworker, I'm concerned that his home life be as stable and happy as possible."

"Why should me building boats make him unhappy?"

"My question regarding this idea of yours is whether your attention will be taken away from him and turned toward this new business. A business that you would, I imagine, find exciting, challenging, and interesting, at least for a time."

His eyes narrowed. "You just don't think I can stick, do you?"

"That's yet to be proved. But I do think you'll try. What worries me is that you're not trying for Seth, you're trying for your father. For your parents. I don't think that's a count against you, Cam," she said more gently. "But it's not a point in Seth's favor."

How the hell did you argue with a woman who insisted on dotting every *i*? he wondered. "So you think he's better off with strangers?"

"No, I think he's better off with you and your brothers." She smiled, satisfied that she had shut him up for the moment. "And that's what went into my report. This idea of starting a boat-building business is something new to think about, and I hope none of you intends to rush into it."

"Do you sail?"

"No, I've never tried it. Why?"

"I'd never been on a boat in my life until Ray Quinn took me out."

Because he remembered how those eyes of hers could warm with compassion, he decided to tell her how it had been for him. "I was scared to death, but too tough to admit it. I'd only been with them a few days, never figured I'd stay. He took me out on this little Sunfish he had back then. Told me the air would do me good."

All he had to do was think, and the image of that morning came clear as sunlight in his head. "My father was a big man. The Mighty Quinn. Built like a bull. I knew that little boat was going to tip over, and I'd probably drown, but he had a way of getting you to do things.''

Love, Anna thought. It was pure and simple love in his voice. It attracted her, she admitted, every bit as much as that toughly handsome face. ''Could you swim?''

''No—but I still hated it that he made me wear a PFD. Personal flotation device,'' he explained. ''Life jacket. Figured it was for sissies.''

''You'd rather have drowned?''

''Hell, no, but I had to make him think so. Anyway, I sat in the stern, my stomach clutched. I was wearing these sunglasses my mother—Stella,'' he corrected, for she'd been Stella then—''had dug up somewhere because my eye was pretty banged up and the sunlight hurt.''

He'd been beaten, abused, neglected, she remembered, when the Quinns had found him. Her heart went out to the little boy. ''You must have been terrified.''

''Down to the bone, but I'd have choked on my tongue before I'd have admitted it. He must have known that,'' Cam said quietly. ''He always knew what was in my head. It was hot, and the humidity was up so that every time you took a breath it was like swallowing water. He said it would be cooler when we moved out of the gut and onto the river, but I didn't believe him. I figured we'd just sit there and fry. The boat didn't even have a motor. Christ, he laughed when I said that. He told me we had something better than a motor.''

He'd forgotten his coffee, and even the point of the story drifted away in the memory. ''We headed out across the water, slow and easy at first, the boat rocked when we turned into the bend, and I figured that was it. Game over. This heron came out of the trees. I'd seen it once before. At least I like to think it was the same one. It winged right over the boat, wings spread to trap the air. And then we caught the wind and that little sail filled. We started to fly. He turned around and grinned at me. I didn't even know I was grinning back until I split my lip open again. I'd never felt like that before in my life. Not once.''

Without thinking, he lifted his hand and tucked her hair behind her ear. ''Not once in my life.''

''It changed you.'' She knew that single moments, both simple and dramatic, could alter courses forever.

''It started to. A boat on the water, and people who were giving me a chance. It wasn't much more complicated than that. It doesn't have to be that much more complicated here. We'll have the kid swing the hammer, put some sweat and effort into building a boat. If it's going to be a Quinn operation, that includes him.''

Her smile came quickly, fully, and to his surprise, she patted him on the cheek. ''That last part said it all. It's a gamble. I'm not sure if it's the time or the place for one, but . . . it should be interesting to watch.''

''Is that what you're going to do?'' He eased forward, nudging her back against the counter. ''Watch me?''

''I don't intend to take my eyes off you—on a professional level—until I'm assured that you and your brothers provide Seth with the proper home and guardianship.''

''Fair enough.'' He moved in just a little closer, just a fraction till two well-toned bodies brushed. ''And how about on a personal level?''

She weakened enough to let her gaze skim down, linger. His mouth was definitely tempting—dangerous and very close. ''Keeping my eyes on you on a personal level isn't a hardship. A mistake, maybe—but not a hardship.''

''I always figure if you're going to make a mistake . . .'' He put his hands on the counter, caging her. ''Make it a big one. What do you say, Anna?'' He dipped his head a little lower, hovered.

She tried to think, to consider the consequences. But there were times when needs, desire, and lust simply overpowered logic. ''Hell,'' she muttered and, cupping her hand at the back of his neck, dragged his mouth down on hers.

It was exactly as she wanted. Hungry and fierce and mindless. His mouth was hot, and it was hard, and it was almost heathen as he crushed down to devour hers. She gave in to it, gave all to it, a moment's madness where body ruled mind and blood roared over reason.

And the thrill snapped through her like a whip, sharp, painful, and with a quick, shocking burn.

"Christ." His breath was gone, his mind was reeling. Reflexively, his hands dug into the counter before he jerked them away and filled them with her.

Whatever he'd expected, whatever he'd imagined didn't come close to the volcano that had so suddenly erupted in his arms. He dragged a hand through her hair, the wild, curling mass of it, fisted it there, then plundered as if his life depended on it.

"Can't," she managed, but her arms wound around him, banded around him until it seemed his heart wasn't merely thundering against hers but inside hers. Her moan was a rumble of desperate, delirious pleasure that sounded in her throat exactly where his teeth nipped, then scraped, then dug greedily into flesh.

The counter bit into her back, her fingers bit into his hips as she dragged him closer. Oh, God, she wanted contact, friction, more. She found his mouth with hers again, plunged blindly into the next kiss.

Just one more, she promised herself, meeting, matching his reckless demand.

Her scent seduced his senses. Her name was a murmur on his lips, a whisper in his mind. Her body was a glorious banquet melded to his. No woman had ever filled him so quickly, so completely, so utterly to the exclusion of all else.

"Let me." It was a plea, and he'd never in his life begged for a woman. "For God's sake, Anna, let me have you." His hands ran up her legs, those endless thighs. "Now."

She wanted. It would be so easy to take, and be taken. But easy, she knew, was rarely right.

"No. Not now." Regret smothered her even as she lifted her hands to frame his face. For a moment longer, her mouth stayed on his. "Not yet. Not like this."

Her eyes were dark, clouded. He knew enough of a woman's pleasures and his own skills to believe he could make them go blind. "It's perfect like this."

"The timing's wrong, the circumstances. Wait." Someone had to move, she decided. To break that contact. She sidestepped, let out a shaky breath. She closed her eyes, lifted a hand to hold him off. "Well," she managed after another moment, "that was insane."

He took the hand she'd raised, brought it to his lips and nipped his teeth into her forefinger. "Who needs sanity?"

"I do." She nearly managed a genuine smile as she tugged her hand free. "Not that I don't regret that deeply at this moment, but I do need it. Wow." She drew in another long breath, pushed her hands up through her hair. "Cameron. You're every bit as potent as I expected."

"I haven't even started."

The smile widened. "I bet. I just bet." She eased back a little more, picked up her rapidly cooling coffee. "I don't know as that episode's going to make either one of us sleep easier tonight, but it was bound to happen." She angled her head when his eyes narrowed. "What?"

"Most women, especially in your position, would make excuses."

"For what?" She lifted a shoulder and promised herself her system would level again eventually. "That was as much my doing as yours. I wondered what it might be like to get my hands on you from the first time I saw you."

Cam decided he might never be the same again. "I think I'm crazy about you."

"No, you're not." She laughed and handed him his coffee. "You're intrigued, you're attracted, you've got a good healthy case of lust, but those are entirely different matters. And you don't even know me."

"I want to." He let out a short laugh. "And that's a big surprise to me. I don't usually care one way or the other."

"I'm flattered. I'm not sure if that's a tribute to your charm or my own stupidity, but I'm flattered. But—"

"Damn, I knew that was coming."

"But," she repeated and set her cup in the sink. "Seth is my priority. He has to be." The warmth that was both compassion and understanding came into her eyes, and it touched something in him that was buried under that healthy lust. "And he should be yours. I hope I'm around if and when that happens."

"I'm doing everything I can think of."

"I know you are. And you're doing more than most would." She touched his arm briefly, then moved away. "I have a feeling you've got more inside you yet. But . . ."

"There it is again."

"You'd better go now."

He wanted to stay, even if it was just to stand there and talk to her, to be. "I haven't finished my coffee."

"It's cold. And it's getting late." She glanced toward the window where raindrops ran like tears. "And the rain makes me wonder about things I shouldn't be wondering about."

He winced. "I don't suppose you said that to make me suffer."

"Sure I did." She laughed again and moved to the door, opened it wide to make her point. "If I'm going to, why shouldn't you?"

"Oh, I like you, Anna Spinelli. You're a woman after my own heart."

"You're not interested in a woman going for your heart," she said as he crossed the room. "You want one who's after your body."

"See, we're getting to know each other already."

"Good night." She didn't evade when he pulled her in for another kiss as he walked out the door. Evading would have been a pretense, and she wasn't one to delude herself.

So she met the kiss with teasing heat and honest enthusiasm. Then she shut the door in his face.

And then she leaned back against it weakly.

Potent? That wasn't the half of it. Her pulse was likely to stay on overdrive for hours. Maybe days.

She wished she didn't feel so damn happy about it.

SEVEN

CAM WAS SCOWLING AT a basket full of pink socks and Jockey shorts when the phone rang. He knew damn well the socks and underwear had been white—or close to it—when he'd dumped them in the machine. Now they were Easter-egg pink.

Maybe they just looked that way because they were wet.

He pulled them out to stuff them in the dryer, saw the red sock hiding among the pink. And bared his teeth.

Phillip, he vowed, was a dead man.

"Fuck it." He dumped them inside, slapped the dryer on what he hoped was broil and went to answer the phone.

He remembered, just in time, to turn down the little portable TV tucked in the corner of the counter. It wasn't as if he was actually watching it, it certainly wasn't that he was paying any attention at all to the passion and betrayals of the late-morning soap opera.

He'd just switched it on for the noise.

"Quinn. What?"

"Hey, Cam. Took some doing to track you down, hoss. Tod Bardette here."

Cam reached into an open bag of Oreos on the counter and took out a handful. "How's it going, Tod?"

"Well, I have to tell you it's going pretty damn good. I've been spending some time anchored off the Great Barrier Reef."

"Nice spot," Cam muttered over a cookie. Then his brows shot up as an impossibly gorgeous woman tumbled into bed with a ridiculously handsome man on the tiny screen across the kitchen.

Maybe there was something to this daytime TV after all.

"It'll do. Heard you kicked ass in the Med a few weeks ago."

A few weeks? Cam thought while he munched on a second cookie. Surely it had been a few years ago that he'd flown across the finish line in his hydrofoil. Blue water, speed, cheering crowds, and money to burn.

Now he was lucky if he found enough milk in the fridge to wash down a stale Oreo.

"Yeah, that's what I heard too."

Tod gave a rich chuckle. "Well, the offer to buy that toy from you still holds. But I got another proposition coming at you."

Tod Bardette always had another proposition coming at you. He was the rich son of a rich father from East Texas who used the world as his playground. And he was boat happy. He raced them, sponsored races, bought and sold them. And collected wives, trophies, and his share of the purse with smooth regularity.

Cam had always felt Tod's luck had run hot since conception. Since it never hurt to listen—and the bedroom scene had just been displaced by a commercial featuring a giant toilet brush, he switched off the set.

"I'm always ready to hear one."

"I'm setting up a crew for La Coupe Internationale."

"The One-Ton Cup?" Cam felt his juices begin to flow, and he lost all interest in cookies and milk. The international race was a giant in the sailing world. Five legs, he thought, the final one an ocean race of three hundred grueling miles.

"You got it. You know the Aussies took the cup last

year, so it's being held down here in Australia. I want to whip their butts, and I've got a honey of a boat. She's fast, hoss. With the right crew she'll bring the cup back to the U S of A. I need a skipper. I want the best. I want you. How soon can you get Down Under?''

Give me five minutes. That's what he wanted to say. He could have a bag packed in one, hop a plane and be on his way. For men who raced, it was one of life's golden opportunities. Even as he opened his mouth, his gaze landed on the rocker outside the kitchen window.

So he closed his eyes, listened resentfully to the hum of the pink socks drying in the utility room behind him.

''I have to pass, Tod. I can't get away now.''

''Lookie here, I'm willing to give you some time to put your affairs—pun intended,'' he said with a snorting laugh, ''in order. Take a couple weeks. If you've got another offer, I'll beat it.''

''I can't do it. I've got—'' Laundry to do? A kid to raise? Damn if he was going to humiliate himself with that piece of information. ''My brothers and I started a business,'' he said on impulse. ''I've got a commitment here.''

''A business.'' This time Tod's laugh was long and delighted. ''You? Don't pull my leg so hard, it hurts.''

Now Cam's eyes narrowed. He didn't doubt Tod Bardette of East Texas would be joined by others of his friends and acquaintances in laughing at the idea of Cameron Quinn, businessman.

''We're building boats,'' he said between his teeth. ''Here on the Eastern Shore. Wooden boats. Custom jobs,'' he added, determined to play it to the hilt. ''One of a kinds. In six months, you'll be paying me top dollar to design and build you a boat by Quinn. Since we're old friends, I'll try to squeeze you in.''

''Boats.'' The interest in Tod's voice picked up. ''Well now, you know how to sail them, guess maybe you'd know how to build them.''

''There's no maybe about it.''

''That's an interesting enterprise, but come on, Cam,

you're not a businessman. You're not going to stay stuck on some pretty little bay in Maryland eating crabs and nailing planks. You know I'll make this race worth your while. Money, fame and fortune." And he chuckled. "After we win, you can go back and put a couple of little sloops together."

He could handle it, Cam promised himself. He could handle the insults, the frustration of not being able to pack and go as he chose. What he wouldn't do was give Bardette the satisfaction of knowing he was ruffled. "You're going to have to find another skipper. But if you want to buy a boat, give me a call."

"If you actually get one finished, give me a call." A sigh came through the receiver. "You're missing the chance of a lifetime here. You change your mind in the next couple hours, get in touch. But I need to nail down my crew this week. Talk to you."

And Cam was listening to a dial tone.

He didn't hurl the receiver through the window. He wanted to, considered it, then figured he'd be the one sweeping up the glass, so what would be the point?

So he hung up the phone, with careful deliberation. He even took a deep breath. And if whatever he'd put in the washing machine hadn't chosen that moment to spin out of balance and send the machine hopping, he wouldn't have slammed his fist into the wall.

"I thought for a minute there you were going to pull it off."

He whirled, and saw his father sitting at the kitchen table, chuckling. "Oh, God, this caps it."

"Why don't you get some ice for your knuckles?"

"It's all right." Cam glanced down at them. A couple of scrapes. And the sharp pain was a good hold on reality. "I thought about this, Dad. Really thought about it. I just don't believe you're here."

Ray continued to smile. "You're here, Cam. That's what matters. It was tough turning down a race like that. I'm grateful to you. I'm proud of you."

"Bardette said he had a honey of a boat. With his money behind it . . ." Cam pressed his hands on the counter and stared out the window toward the quiet water. "I could win that bastard. I captained a crew to second in the Little America's Cup five years ago, and I took the Chicago-Mackinac last year."

"You're a fine sailor, Cam."

"Yeah." He curled his fingers into fists. "What the hell am I doing here? If this keeps up I'm going to get hooked on soap operas. I'll start thinking Lilac and Lance are not only real people but close personal friends. I'll start obsessing that my whites aren't white enough. I'll clip coupons and collect recipes and go the rest of the way out of my fucking mind."

"I'm surprised at you, thinking of tending a home in those terms." Ray's voice was sharp now, with disappointment around the edges. "Making a home, caring for family is important work. The most important work there is."

"It's not my work."

"It seems it is now. I'm sorry for that."

Cam turned back. If you were going to have a conversation with a hallucination, you might as well look at it. "For what? For dying on me?"

"Well, that was pretty inconvenient all around."

He would have laughed, the comment and the ironic tone were so typically Ray Quinn. But he had to get out what was nibbling at his mind. "Some people are saying you aimed for the pole."

Ray's smile faded, and his eyes turned sober and sad. "Do you believe that?"

"No." Cam let out a breath. "No, I don't believe that."

"Life's a gift. It doesn't always fit comfortably, but it's precious. I wouldn't have hurt you and your brothers by throwing mine away."

"I know that," Cam murmured. "It helps to hear you say it, but I know that."

"Maybe I could have stopped things. Maybe I could have done things differently." He sighed and turned the gold wedding band around and around on his finger. "But I didn't. It's up to you now, you and Ethan and Phillip. There was a reason the three of you came to me and Stella. A reason the three of you came together. I always believed that. Now I know it."

"And what about the kid?"

"Seth's place is here. He needs you. He's in trouble right now, and he needs you to remember what it was like to be where he is."

"What do you mean, he's in trouble?"

Ray smiled a little. "Answer the phone," he suggested seconds before it rang.

And then he was gone.

"I've got to start getting more sleep," Cam decided, then yanked the receiver off the hook. "Yeah, yeah."

"Hello? Mr. Quinn?"

"Right. This is Cameron Quinn."

"Mr. Quinn, this is Abigail Moorefield, vice principal of St. Christopher Middle School."

Cam felt his stomach sink to his toes. "Uh-huh."

"I'm afraid there's been some trouble here. I have Seth DeLauter in my office."

"What kind of trouble?"

"Seth was in a fight with another student. He's being suspended. Mr. Quinn, I'd appreciate it if you could come to my office so matters can be explained to you and you can take Seth home."

"Great. Wonderful." At his wits' end, Cam dragged a hand through his hair. "On my way."

The school hadn't changed much, Cam noted, since he'd done time there. The first morning he'd passed through those heavy front doors, Stella Quinn had all but dragged him.

He was nearly eighteen years older now, and no more enthusiastic.

The floors were faded linoleum, the light bright from wide windows. And the smell was of contraband candy and kid sweat.

Cam jammed his hands in his pockets and headed for the administration offices. He knew the way. After all he'd beaten a path to those offices countless times during his stay at St. Chris Middle.

It wasn't the same old eagle-eyed secretary manning the desk in the outer room. This one was younger, perkier, and beamed smiles all over him. "May I help you?" she asked in a bouncing voice.

"I'm here to post bail for Seth DeLauter."

She blinked at that, and her smile turned puzzled. "I beg your pardon?"

"Cameron Quinn to see the VP."

"Oh, you mean Mrs. Moorefield. Yes, she's expecting you. Second door down the little hallway there. On the right." Her phone rang and she plucked it up. "Good morning," she sang, "St. Christopher's Middle School. This is Kathy speaking."

Cam decided he preferred the battle-ax who had guarded the offices in his day to this terminally pert newcomer. Even as he started toward the door, his back went up, his jaw set—and his palms went damp.

Some things, he supposed, never changed.

Mrs. Moorefield was sitting behind her desk, calmly entering data into a computer. Cam thought her fingers moved efficiently. And the movement suited her. She was neat and trim, probably early fifties. Her hair was short and sleek and light brown, her face composed and quietly attractive.

Her gold wedding band caught the light as her fingers moved over the keys. The only other jewelry she wore were simple gold shells at her ears.

Across the room, Seth was slumped in a chair, staring up at the ceiling. Trying to look bored, Cam assumed, but coming off as sulky. Kid needed a haircut, he realized and wondered who was supposed to deal with that. He was wearing jeans frayed to strings at the cuffs, a jersey two sizes too big, and incredibly dirty high-tops.

It looked perfectly normal to Cam.

He rapped on the doorjamb. Both the vice principal and Seth glanced over, with two dramatically different expressions. Mrs. Moorefield smiled in polite welcome. Seth sneered.

"Mr. Quinn."

"Yeah." Then he remembered he was supposed to be here as a responsible guardian. "I hope we can straighten this out, Mrs. Moorefield." He stuck his own polite smile into place as he stepped to her desk and offered a hand.

"I appreciate your coming in so quickly. When we have to take regrettable disciplinary action such as this against a student, we want the parents or responsible parties to have the opportunity to understand the situation. Please, Mr. Quinn, sit down."

"What is the situation?" Cam took his seat and found he didn't like it any more than he used to.

"I'm afraid Seth physically attacked another student this morning between classes. The other boy is being treated by the school nurse, and his parents have been informed."

Cam lifted a brow. "So where are they?"

"Both of Robert's parents are at work at the moment. But in any case—"

"Why?"

Her smile returned, small, attentive, questioning. "Why, Mr. Quinn?"

"Why did Seth slug Robert?"

Mrs. Moorefield sighed. "I understand you've only recently taken over as Seth's guardian, so you may not be aware that this isn't the first time he's fought with other students."

"I know about it. I'm asking about this incident."

"Very well." She folded her hands. "According to Robert, Seth demanded that Robert give him a dollar, and when Robert refused to pay him, Seth attacked him. At this point," she added, shifting her gaze to Seth, "Seth has neither confirmed nor denied. School policy requires that students be suspended for three days as a disciplinary action when involved in a fight on school premises."

"Okay." Cam rose, but when Seth started to get up, he pointed a finger. "Stay," he ordered, then crouched until they were eye to eye. "You try to shake this kid down?"

Seth jerked a shoulder. "That's what he says."

"You slugged him."

"Yeah, I slugged him. Went for the nose," he added with a thin smile, and shoved at the straw-colored hair that flopped into his eyes. "It hurts more."

"Why'd you do it?"

"Maybe I didn't like his fat face."

With his patience as frayed as Seth's jeans, Cam gripped Seth by the shoulders. When Seth winced and hissed in a breath, alarm bells went off. Before Seth could evade him, Cam tugged the arm of the oversized jersey down. Nasty little bruises—knuckle rappers, Cam would have called them—ran from Seth's shoulder to his elbow.

"Get off me." His face heated with shame, Seth squirmed, but Cam merely shifted him. Scrapes were scored high on Seth's back, red and raw.

"Hold still." Cam moved his grip and laid his hands on the arms of the chair. His eyes stayed on Seth. "You tell me what went down. And don't even think about lying to me."

"I don't want to talk about it."

"I didn't ask you what you wanted. I'm telling you to spill it. Or," he said, lowering his voice so only Seth could hear, "are you going to let that punk get away clean?"

Seth opened his mouth, closed it again. He had to set his jaw so it wouldn't wobble. "He was pissed off. We had this history test the other day and I aced it. An idiot could've gotten an ace, but he's less than an idiot and he flunked. So he kept hassling me, dogged me down the hall, jabbing at me. I walked away because I'm sick to death of ISS."

"Of what?"

Seth rolled his eyes. "In-School Suspension. It's boring. I didn't want to do more time, so I walked. But he kept jabbing and calling me names. Egghead, teacher's pet, and all that shit. Didn't let it bother me. But then he shoved me back against the lockers and he said I was just a son of a whore and everybody knew it, so I decked him."

Shamed and sick, he jerked a defiant shoulder. "So I get a three-day vacation. Big deal."

Cam nodded and rose. When he turned around his eyes were nearly black with fury. "You're not suspending this kid for defending himself against an ignorant bully. And if you try, I'll go over your head to the Board of Education."

Shocked to the core, Seth stared up at Cam. Nobody had ever stood up for him. He'd never expected anyone to stand up for him.

"Mr. Quinn—"

"Nobody calls my brother a son of a whore, Mrs. Moorefield. And if you don't have a school policy against vicious name-calling and harassment, you damn well should. So I'm telling you, you better take another look at this situation. And you better rethink just who gets suspended here. *And* you can tell little Robert's parents that if they don't want their kid crying over a bloody nose, they better teach him some manners."

She took a moment before speaking. She'd been teaching and counseling children for nearly thirty years. What she saw on Seth's face at that moment was hope, stunned and wary, but hope nonetheless. It was a look she didn't want to extinguish.

"Mr. Quinn, you can be certain that I will investigate this matter further. I wasn't aware that Seth had been injured. If you'd like to take him down to the nurse while I speak with Robert and . . . others—"

"I can take care of him."

"As you wish. I'll hold the suspension in abeyance until I've satisfied myself with the facts."

"You do that, Mrs. Moorefield. But I'm satisfied with the facts. Now I'm taking Seth home for the rest of the day. He's had enough."

"I agree with you."

The child hadn't looked shaken when he'd come into her office, she thought. He'd looked cocky. He hadn't looked shaken when she'd told him to sit down and called his home. He'd looked belligerent.

But he looked shaken now, finally, with his eyes wide and stunned and his hands gripping the arms of the chair. The thin, hard shield he'd kept tight around him, a shield neither she nor any of his teachers had been able to so much as scratch, appeared to be deeply dented.

Now, she decided, they would see what they could do for him.

"If you will bring Seth into school in the morning and meet with me here, we'll resolve the matter."

"We'll be here. Let's go," he said to Seth and headed out.

As they walked down the hall toward the front doors, their footsteps echoed hollowly. Cam glanced down, noted that Seth was staring at his shoes.

"Still gives me the creeps," he said.

Seth shoved at the door. "What?"

"The way it sounds when you take the long walk to the VP's office."

Seth snorted, hunched his shoulders and kept walking. His stomach felt as if a thousand butterflies had gone to war inside it.

The American flag on the pole near the parking lot snapped in the wind. From an open window behind them, the pathetically off-key sounds of a mid-morning music class clamored. The elementary school was separated from the middle by a narrow swatch of grass and a few sad-looking evergreen bushes.

Across the small outdoor track stood the brown brick of the high school. It seemed smaller now, Cam noted, almost quaint, and not at all like the prison he'd once imagined it to be.

He remembered leaning lazily against the hood of his first secondhand car in the parking lot and watching girls. Walking through those noisy hallways from class to class, and watching girls. Sitting in the butt-numbing chairs during brain-numbing classes. And watching girls.

The fact that his high school experience came back to him in a parade of varying female forms made him almost sentimental.

Then a bell rang shrilly, and the noise level through the open windows behind him erupted. Sentiment dried up quickly. Thank God, was all he could think, that chapter of his life was over.

But it wasn't over for the kid, he remembered. And since he was here, he could try to help him through it. They opened opposite doors of the 'Vette, and Cam paused, waited for their eyes to meet. "So, do you figure you broke the asshole's nose?"

A glimmer of a smile worked around Seth's mouth. "Maybe."

"Good." Cam got in, slammed the door. "Going for the nose is fine, but if you don't want a lot of blood messing things up, go for the belly. A good, solid short arm punch to the gut won't leave as much evidence."

Seth considered the advice. "I wanted to see him bleed."

"Well, you make your choices in life. Pretty good day for a sail," he decided as he started the engine. "Might as well."

"I guess." Seth picked at the knee of his jeans. Someone had stood up for him, was all his confused mind could think. Had believed him, defended him and taken his part. His arm hurt, his shoulders ached, but someone had taken his part. "Thanks," he muttered.

"No problem. You mess with one Quinn, you mess with them all." He glanced over as he drove out of the lot and saw Seth staring at him. "That's how it shakes down. Anyway, let's get some burgers or something to take on the boat."

"Yeah, I could eat." Seth swiped a hand under his nose. "Got a dollar?"

When Cam laughed and punched the accelerator it was one of the best moments of Seth's life.

THE WIND WAS OUT OF the southwest and steady so that the marsh grasses waved lazily. The sky was clear and cheerfully blue, the perfect frame for the heron that rose up, out of the waving grass over the glinting water, then down like a flashing white kite to catch an early lunch.

On impulse, Cam had tossed some fishing gear into the boat. With any luck they'd have fried fish for dinner.

Seth already knew more about sailing than Cam had expected. He shouldn't have been surprised by it, he realized. Anna had said the boy had a quick mind, and Ethan would have taught him well, and patiently.

When he saw how easily Seth handled the lines, he trusted him to trim the jib. The sails caught the wind, and Cam found speed.

God, he had missed it. The rush, the power, the control. It poured through him, clearing his mind of worries, obligations, disappointments, even grief. Water below and sky above, and his hands on the helm coaxing the wind, daring it, tricking it into giving more.

Behind him, Seth grinned and caught himself just before he yelled out in delight. He'd never gone so fast. With Ray it had been slow and steady, with Ethan work and wonder. But this was a wild, free ride, rising and falling with the waves, shooting like a long white bullet to anywhere.

The wind nearly took his cap, so he turned the bill backward so the breeze wouldn't catch it and flip it away.

They skimmed across the shoreline, passed the waterfront docks that were the hub of St. Chris before they finally slowed. An old skipjack no longer in use was docked there, a symbol to the waterman's way of life.

The men and women who harvested the bay brought

their day's catch there. Flounder and sea trout and rockfish at this time of year, and . . .

"What's the date?" Cam demanded as he glanced over his shoulder.

"Like the thirty-first." Seth shoved up his wraparound sunglasses and stared at the dock. He was hoping for a glimpse of Grace. He wanted to wave to someone he knew.

"Crab season starts tomorrow. Hot damn. Guarantee you tomorrow Ethan brings home a bushel of beauties. We'll eat like kings. You like crabs, right?"

"I dunno."

"What do you mean you don't know?" Cam popped the top of a Coke and guzzled. "Haven't you had crab before?"

"No."

"You'd better prepare your mouth for a treat, then, kid, because you'll have it tomorrow."

Mirroring Cam's move, Seth reached for a soft drink himself. "Nothing you cook's a treat."

It was said with a grin and received with one. "I can do crab just fine. Nothing to it. Boiling water, lots of spices, then you pop those snapping bastards into the pot—"

"Alive?"

"It's the only way."

"That's sick."

Cam merely shifted his stance. "They aren't alive for long. Then they're dinner. Add a six-pack of beer and you got a feast. Another few weeks, and we're talking soft-shell blues. You plop 'em between a couple pieces of bread and bite in."

This time Seth actually felt his stomach roll. "Not me."

"Too squeamish?"

"Too civilized."

"Shit. Sometimes on Saturday in the summer Mom and Dad used to bring us down to the docks. We'd get us some soft-shell crab sandwiches, a tub of peanut oil fries, and watch the tourists try to figure out what to eat. Laughed our asses off.''

The memory made him suddenly sad, and he tried to shake off the mood. ''Sometimes we sailed down like this. Or we'd cruise down to the river and fish. Mom wasn't much on fishing, so she'd swim, then she'd head to shore and sit on the bank and read.''

''Why didn't she just stay home?''

''She liked to sail,'' Cam said softly. ''And she liked being there.''

''Ray said she got sick.''

''Yeah, she got sick.'' Cam blew out a breath. She had been the only woman he'd ever loved, the only woman he'd ever lost. The missing of her could still creep up and cut him off at the knees.

''Come about,'' he ordered. ''Let's head down the Annemessex and see if anything's biting.''

It didn't occur to either of them that the three hours they spent on the water was the most peaceful interlude either had experienced in weeks.

And when they returned home with six fat striped bass in the cooler, they were for the first time in total harmony.

''Know how to clean them?'' Cam asked.

''Maybe.'' Ray had taught him, but Seth was no fool. ''I caught four of the six, that ought to mean you clean them.''

''That's the beauty of being boss,'' Cam began, then stopped dead when he saw sheets snapping on the ancient clothesline. He hadn't seen anything hanging out on the line since his mother had gotten sick. For a moment he was afraid he was having another hallucination, and his mouth went dry.

Then the back door opened, and Grace Monroe stepped out on the porch.

''Hey, Grace!''

It was the first time Cam had heard Seth's voice raised in happiness and pure boyish pleasure. It surprised him enough to make him look over sharply, then nearly drop the cooler on his foot as Seth let go of his end and dashed forward.

"Hey, there." She had a warm voice that contrasted with cool looks. She was tall and slim, with long limbs she'd once dreamed of using as a dancer.

But Grace had learned to put most of her dreams aside.

Her hair was boyishly short, and that was for convenience. She didn't have the time or energy to worry about style. It was a dark, honey blond that was often streaked with paler color during the summer. Her eyes were a quiet green and all too often had shadows dogging them.

But her smile was pure and sunny and never failed to light up her face, or to set the dimple just beside her mouth winking.

A pretty woman, Cam thought, with the face of a pixie and the voice of a siren. It amazed him that men weren't throwing themselves at her feet.

The boy all but did, Cam noted, surprised when Seth just about ran into her open arms. He hugged and was hugged—this prickly kid who didn't like to be touched. Then he flushed and stepped back and began to play with the puppy, who'd followed Grace out of the house.

"Afternoon, Cam." Grace shielded her eyes from the sun with the flat of her hand. "Ethan came by the pub last night and said y'all could use a hand around here."

"You're taking over the housework."

"Well, I can give you three hours two days a week until—"

She got no farther, for Cam dumped the cooler, took the steps three at a time, and grabbed her into a loud, enthusiastic kiss. It set Seth's teeth on edge to see it, even as Grace stuttered and laughed.

"That's nice," she managed, "but you're still going to have to pay me."

"Name your price. I adore you." He snatched her hands and planted more kisses there. "My life for you."

"I can see I'm going to be appreciated around here—

and needed. I've got those pink socks soaking in some diluted bleach. Might do the trick."

"The red sock was Phil's. He's responsible. I mean, what reasonable guy even owns a pair of red socks?"

"We'll talk more about sorting laundry—and checking pockets. Someone's little black book went through the last cycle."

"Shit." He caught her arched-brow look down at the boy and cleared his throat. "Sorry. I guess it was mine."

"I made some lemonade, and I was going to put a casserole together, but it looks like you may have caught your supper."

"Tonight's, but we could do with a casserole too."

"Okay. Ethan wasn't really clear about what you'd need or want done. Maybe we should go over things."

"Darling, you do whatever you think we need, and it'll be more than we can ever repay."

She'd already seen that for herself. Pink underwear, she mused, dust an inch thick on one table and unidentified substances sticking to another. And the stove? God only knew when it had last been cleaned.

It was good to be needed, she thought. Good to know just what had to be done. "We'll take it as it goes, then. I may have to bring the baby along sometimes. Julie minds her at night when I'm working at the pub, but I can't always find somebody to take her otherwise. She's a good girl."

"I can help you watch her," Seth offered. "I get home from school at three-thirty."

"Since when?" Cam wanted to know, and Seth shrugged.

"When I don't have ISS."

"Aubrey loves playing with you. I've got another hour here today," she said because she was a woman constantly forced to budget time. "So I'll make up that casserole and put it in the freezer. All you have to do is heat it up when you want it. I'll leave you a list of cleaning supplies you're low on, or I can pick them up for you if you like."

"Pick them up for us?" Cam could have knelt at her feet. "Want a raise?"

She laughed and started back inside. "Seth, you see that that pup stays out of the fish guts. He'll smell for a week otherwise."

"Okay, sure. I'll be finished in a few minutes and I'll be in." He stood up, then stepped off the porch so Grace wouldn't hear him through the door. Manfully, he sized up Cam. "You're not going to start poking at her, are you?"

"Poking at her?" He was blank for a moment, then shook his head. "For God's sake." Hefting the ice chest, he started around the side of the house to the fish-cleaning table. "I've known Grace half my life, and I don't poke at every woman I see."

"Okay, then."

It was the boy's tone that made Cam run his tongue around his teeth as he set the cooler down. Possessive, proprietary, and satisfied. "So . . . you got your eye on her yourself, huh?"

Seth colored a little, opened the drawer for the fish scaler. "I just look out for her, that's all."

"She sure is pretty," Cam said lightly and had the pleasure of seeing Seth's eyes flash with jealousy. "But as it happens I'm poking at another woman right now, and it gets sticky if you try that with more than one at a time. And this particular female is going to take a lot of convincing."

EIGHT

HE DECIDED TO GET started on poking at Anna. Since she was on his mind, Cam left Seth to deal with the last couple of fish on his own and wandered inside. He made appreciative noises at whatever Grace was putting together over at the stove, then wandered upstairs.

He'd have a little more privacy on the phone in his room. And Anna's business card was in his pocket.

At the door to his room, he stopped and could have wept with gratitude. Since his bed was freshly made, the plain green spread professionally smoothed, the pillows plumped, he knew some of the sheets hanging out on the line were his.

Tonight he would sleep on fresh, clean sheets he hadn't even had to launder. It made the prospect of sleeping alone a little more tolerable.

The surface of his old oak dresser wasn't just dust-free. It gleamed. The bookshelves that still held most of his trophies and some of his favorite novels had been tidied, and the overstuffed chair he'd taken to using as a catchall was now empty. He hadn't a clue where she'd put his things, but he imagined he'd find them in their logical place.

He supposed he'd gotten spoiled living in hotels over the last few years, but it did his heart good to walk into his bedroom and not see a half a dozen testy little chores waiting for attention.

Things were looking up, so he plopped down on the bed, stretched out, and reached for the phone.

"Anna Spinelli." Her voice was low, professionally neutral. He closed his eyes to better fantasize how she looked. He liked the idea of imagining her behind some bureaucratic desk wearing that tight little blue number she'd had on the night before.

"Miz Spinelli. How do you feel about crabs?"

"Ah . . ."

"Let me rephrase that." He scooted down until he was nearly flat and realized he could be asleep in five minutes without really trying. "How do you feel about eating steamed crabs?"

"I feel favorable."

"Good. How about tomorrow night?"

"Cameron—"

"Here," he specified. "At the house. The house that's never empty. Tomorrow's the first day of crab season. Ethan'll bring home a bushel. We'll cook them up. You can see how the Quinns—what would you call it?—relate, interact. See how Seth's getting along—acclimating to this particular home environment."

"That's very good."

"Hey, I've dealt with social workers before. Of course, never one who wore blue high heels, but . . ."

"I was off the clock," she reminded him. "However, I think dinner might be a workable idea. What time?"

"Six-thirty or thereabouts." He heard the flap of papers and found himself slightly annoyed that she was checking her calendar.

"All right, I can do that. Six-thirty."

She sounded entirely too much like a social worker

making an appointment to suit him. "You alone in there?"

"In my office? Yes, at the moment. Why?"

"Just wondering. I've been wondering about you on and off all day. Why don't you let me come into town and get you tomorrow, then I could drive you home. We could stop and—I'd say climb into the backseat, but the 'Vette doesn't have one. Still, I think we could manage."

"I'm sure we could. Which is why I'll drive myself down."

"I'm going to have to get my hands on you again."

"I don't doubt that's going to happen. Eventually. In the meantime—"

"I want you."

"I know."

Because her voice had thickened and didn't sound quite so prim, he smiled. "Why don't I tell you just what I'd like to do to you? I can go step by step. You can even take notes in your little book for future reference."

"I . . . think we'd better postpone that. Though I may be interested in discussing it at another time. I'm afraid I have an appointment in a few minutes. I'll see you and your family tomorrow evening."

"Give me ten minutes alone with you, Anna." He whispered it. "Ten minutes to touch you."

"I—we can try for that time frame tomorrow. I have to go. Good-bye."

" 'Bye." Pleased that he'd rattled her, he slid the phone back on the hook and let himself drift off into a well-deserved nap.

HE WAS AWAKENED JUST over an hour later by the slamming of the front door and Phillip's raised and furious voice.

"Home, sweet home," Cam muttered and rolled out of bed. He stumbled to the door and down the hall to the steps. He was a lousy napper, and whenever he indulged he woke up groggy, irritable, and in desperate need of coffee.

By the time he got downstairs, Phillip was in the kitchen uncorking a bottle of wine. ''Where the hell is everybody?'' Phillip demanded.

''I dunno. Get out of my way.'' Rubbing one hand over his face, Cam poured the dregs of the pot into a mug, stuck the mug in the microwave, and punched numbers at random.

''I've been informed by the insurance company that they're holding the claim until such time as an investigation is complete.''

Cam stared at the microwave, willing those endless two minutes to pass so he could gulp caffeine. His bleary brain took in insurance, claim, investigation, and couldn't correlate the terms. ''Huh?''

''Pull yourself together, damn it.'' Phillip gave him an impatient shove. ''They won't process Dad's policy because they suspect suicide.''

''That's bullshit. He told me he didn't kill himself.''

''Oh, really?'' Sick and furious, Phillip still managed to raise an ironic eyebrow. ''Did you have this conversation with him before or after he died?''

Cam caught himself, but very nearly flushed. Instead he cursed again and yanked open the microwave door. ''I mean, there's no way he would have, and they're just stalling because they don't want to pay off.''

''The point is, they're not paying off at this time. Their investigator's been talking to people, and some of those people were apparently delighted to tell him the seamier details of the situation. And they know about the letter from Seth's mother—the payments Dad made to her.''

''So.'' He sipped coffee, scalded the roof of his mouth, and swore. ''Hell with it. Let them keep their fucking blood money.''

''It's not as simple as that. Number one is if they don't pay, it goes down that Dad committed suicide. Is that what you want?''

"No." Cam pinched the bridge of his nose to try to relieve some of the pressure that was building. He'd lived most of his life without headaches, and now it seemed he was plagued with them.

"Which means we'd have to accept their conclusions, or we'd have to take them to court to prove he didn't, and it'd be one hell of a public mess." Struggling to calm himself, Phillip sipped his wine. "Either way it smears his name. I think we're going to have to find this woman—Gloria DeLauter—after all. We have to clear this up."

"What makes you think finding her and talking to her is going to clear this up?"

"We have to get the truth out of her."

"How, through torture?" Not that it didn't have its appeal. "Besides, the kid's scared of her," Cam added. "She comes around, she could screw up the guardianship."

"And if she doesn't come around we might never know the truth, all of the truth." He needed to know it, Phillip thought, so he could begin to accept it.

"Here's the truth as I see it." Cam slammed his mug down. "This woman was looking for an easy mark and figured she'd found one. Dad fell for the kid, wanted to help him. So he went to bat for him, just the way he did for us, and she kept hitting him up for more. I figure he was upset coming home that day, worried, distracted. He was driving too fast, misjudged, lost control, whatever. That's all there is to it."

"Life's not as simple as you live it, Cam. You don't just start in one spot, then finish in the other as fast as you can. Curves and detours and roadblocks. You better start thinking about them."

"Why? That's all you ever think about, and it seems to me we've ended up in exactly the same place."

Phillip let out a sigh. It was hard to argue with that, so he decided a second glass of wine was in order. "Whatever you think, we've got a mess on our hands and we're going to have to deal with it. Where's Seth?"

"I don't know where he is. Around."

"Christ, Cam, around where? You're supposed to keep an eye on him."

"I've had my eye on him all damn day. He's around." He walked to the back door, scanned the yard, scowled when he didn't see Seth. "Probably around front, or taking a walk or something. I'm not keeping the kid on a leash."

"This time of day he should be doing his homework. You've only got to watch out for him on your own a couple of hours after school."

"It didn't work out that way today. There was a little holiday from school."

"He hooked? You let him hook when we've got Social Services sniffing around?"

"No, he didn't hook." Disgusted, Cam turned back. "Some little jerk at school kept razzing him, poked bruises all over him and called him a son of a whore."

Phillip's stance shifted immediately, from mild annoyance to righteous fury. His gilt eyes glittered, his mouth thinned. "What little jerk? Who the hell is he?"

"Some fat-faced kid named Robert. Seth slugged him, and they said they were going to suspend him for it."

"Hell they are. Who the hell's principal now, some Nazi?"

Cam had to smile. When push came to shove, you could always count on Phillip. "She didn't seem to be. After I went down and we got the whole story out of Seth, she shifted ground some. I'm taking him back in tomorrow for another little conference."

Now Phillip grinned, wide and wicked. "You? Cameron Kick-Ass Quinn is going in for a parent conference at the middle school. Oh, to be a fly on the wall!"

"You won't have to be, because you're coming too."

Phillip swallowed wine hastily before he choked. "What do you mean, I'm coming?"

"And so's Ethan," Cam decided on the spot. "We're all going. United front. Yeah, that's just the way it's going to be."

"I've got an appointment—"

"Break it. There's the kid." He spotted Seth coming out of the woods with Foolish beside him. "He's just been fooling around with the dog. Ethan ought to be along any minute, and I'm tagging him for this deal."

Phillip scowled into his wine. "I hate it when you're right. We all go."

"It should be a fun morning." Satisfied, Cam gave Phillip a friendly punch on the arm. "We're the big guys this time. And when we win this little battle with authority, we can celebrate tomorrow night—with a bushel of crabs."

Phillip's mood lightened. "April Fool's Day. Crab season opens. Oh, yeah."

"We got fresh fish tonight—I caught it, you cook it. I want a shower." Cam rolled his shoulders. "Miz Spinelli's coming to dinner tomorrow."

"Uh-huh, well, you—what?" Phillip whirled as Cam started out of the room. "You asked the social worker to dinner? Here?"

"That's right. Told you I like her looks."

Phillip could only close his eyes. "For God's sake, you're hitting on the social worker."

"She's hitting on me, too." Cam flashed a grin. "I like it."

"Cam, not to put down your warped idea of romance, but use your head. We've got this problem with the insurance company. And we've got a problem with Seth at school. How's that's going to play to Social Services?"

"We don't tell them about the first, and we give them the straight story on the second. I think that's going to go over just fine with Miz Spinelli. She's going to love it that the three of us went in to stand for Seth."

Phillip opened his mouth, reconsidered, and nodded. "You're right. That's good." Then as new thoughts began to play, he angled his head. "Maybe you could use your . . . influence on her to get her to move this case study along, get the system out of our hair."

Cam said nothing for a moment, surprised at how angry even the suggestion of it made him. So his voice was quiet.

"I'm not using anything on her, and it's going to stay that way. One situation has nothing to do with the other. That's staying that way too."

When Cam strode off, Phillip pursed his lips. Well, he thought, wasn't that interesting?

AS ETHAN GUIDED HIS boat toward the dock, he spotted Seth in the yard. Beside Ethan, Simon gave a high, happy bark. Ethan ruffled his fur. "Yeah, fella, almost home now."

While he worked the sails, Ethan watched the boy toss sticks for the pup. There had always been a dog in this yard to chase sticks or balls, to wrestle in the grass with. He remembered Dumbo, the sweet-faced retriever he'd fallen madly in love with when he'd come to the Quinns.

He'd been the first dog to play with, to be comforted by, in Ethan's life. From Dumbo he'd learned the meaning of unconditional love, had certainly trusted the dog long before he'd trusted Ray and Stella Quinn or the boys who would become his brothers.

He imagined Seth felt much the same. You could always depend on your dog.

When he'd come here all those years ago, damaged in body and soul, he had no hope that his life would really change. Promises, reassurances, decent meals and decent people meant nothing to him. So he'd considered ending that life.

The water had drawn him even then. He imagined himself walking out into it, drifting out until it was over his head. He didn't know how to swim then, so it would have been simple. Just sinking down and down and down until there was nothing.

But the night he'd slipped out to do it, the dog had come with him. Licking his hand, pressing that warm, furry body against his legs. And Dumbo had brought him a stick, tail wagging, big brown eyes hopeful. The first time, Ethan threw the stick high and far and in fury. But Dumbo chased it happily and brought it back. Tail wagging.

He threw it again, then again, then dozens of times. Then he simply sat down on the grass, and in the moonlight cried his heart out, clutching the dog like a lifeline.

The need to end it had passed.

A dog, Ethan thought now as he rubbed a hand over Simon's head, could be a glorious thing.

He saw Seth turn, catch sight of the boat. There was the briefest of hesitations, then the boy lifted a hand in greeting and with the pup raced to the dock.

"Secure the lines, mate."

"Aye, aye." Seth handled the lines Ethan tossed out competently enough, slipping the loop over the post. "Cam said how you'd be bringing crabs tomorrow."

"Did he?" Ethan smiled a little, pushed back his fielder's cap. Thick brown hair tickled the collar of his work-stained shirt. "Go on, boy," he murmured to the dog, who was sitting, vibrating in place as he waited for the command to abandon ship. With a celebrational bark, Simon leaped into the water and swam to shore. "As it turns out, he's right. Winter wasn't too hard and the water's warming up. We'll pull in plenty. Should be a good day."

Leaning over the side, he pulled up a crab pot that dangled from the dock. "No winter hair."

"Hair, why would there be hair in an old chicken wire box?"

"Pot. It's a crab pot. If I pulled this up and it was hairy—full of blond seaweed—it'd mean the water was too cold yet for crabs. Seen them that way, nearly into May, if there's been a bad winter. That kind of spring, it's hard to make a living on the water."

"But not this spring, because the water's warm enough for crabs."

"Seems to be. You can bait this pot later—chicken necks or fish parts do the job fine—and in the morning we may just find us a couple of crabs sulking inside. They fall for it every time.''

Seth knelt down, wanting a closer look. ''That's pretty stupid. They look like big ugly bugs, so I guess they're bug-dumb.''

''Just more hungry than smart, I'd say.''

''And Cam says you boil them alive. No way I'm eating those.''

''Suit yourself. Me, I figure on going through about two dozen come tomorrow night.'' He let the pot slip back into the water, then leaped expertly from boat to dock.

''Grace was here. She cleaned the house and stuff.''

''Yeah?'' He imagined the house would smell lightly of lemon. Grace's house always did.

''Cam kissed her, right on the mouth.''

Ethan stopped walking, looked down at Seth's face. ''What?''

''Smackaroo. It made her laugh. It was like a joke, I guess.''

''Like a joke, sure.'' He shrugged and ignored the hard, sick ball in his gut. None of his business who Grace kissed. Nothing to do with him. But he found his jaw clenched when Cam, hair dripping, stepped out on the back porch.

''How's the crab business looking?''

''It'll do,'' Ethan said shortly.

Cam lifted his brows at the tone. ''What, did one crawl out of the pot early and up your butt?''

''I want a shower and a beer.'' Ethan moved past him and into the house.

''Woman's coming for dinner tomorrow.''

That stopped Ethan again, and he turned, keeping the screen door between them. ''Who?''

''Anna Spinelli.''

''Shit,'' was Ethan's only comment as he walked away.

''Why's she coming? What does she want?'' Panic rose up inside Seth like a fountain and spewed out in his voice before he could stop it.

''She's coming because I asked her, and she wants a

crab dinner.'' Cam tucked his thumbs in his pockets, rocked back on his heels. Why the hell was he the one who always had to handle this white-faced fear? ''I figure she wants to see if all we do around here is fart and scratch and spit. We can probably hold off on that for one evening. You gotta remember to put the toilet seat down, though. Women really hate when you don't. They make it a social and political statement if you leave it up. Go figure.''

Some of the tension eased out of Seth's face. ''So, she's just, like, coming to see if we're slobs. And Grace cleaned everything up and you're not cooking, so it's mostly okay.''

''It'll be more than mostly if you watch that foul mouth of yours.''

''Yours is just as foul.''

''Yeah, but you're shorter than I am. And I don't intend to ask you to pass the fucking potatoes in front of her.''

Seth snorted at that, and his rock-hard shoulders relaxed. ''Are you going to tell her about that shit in school today?''

Cam blew out a breath. ''Practice finding an alternate word for 'shit,' just for tomorrow night. Yeah, I'm going to tell her what happened in school. And I'm telling her that Phil and Ethan and I went in with you tomorrow to deal with it.''

This time all Seth could do was blink. ''All of you? You're all going?''

''That's right. Like I said, you mess with one Quinn, you mess with them all.''

It shocked and appalled and terrified them both when tears sprang to Seth's eyes. They swam there for a moment, blurring that deep, bright blue. Instantly both of them stuck their hands in their pockets and turned away.

''I have to do . . . something,'' Cam said, groping. ''You go . . . wash your hands or whatever. We'll be eating pretty soon.''

Just as he worked up the nerve to turn, intending to lay a hand on Seth's shoulder, to say something that would undoubtedly make them both feel like idiots, the boy darted inside and rushed through the kitchen.

Cam pressed his fingers to his eyes, massaged his temples, dropped his arms. "Jesus, I've got to get back to a race where I know what I'm doing." He took a step toward the door, then shook his head and walked quickly away from it. He didn't want to go inside with all that emotion, all that need, swirling in the air.

God, what he wanted was his freedom back, to wake up and find it had all been a dream. Better, to wake up in some huge, anonymous hotel bed in some exotic city with a hot, naked woman beside him.

But when he tried to picture it, the bed was the same one he slept in now, and the woman was Anna.

As a substitute it wasn't such a bad deal, but . . . it didn't make the rest of it go away. He glanced up at the windows of the second floor as he walked around the house. The kid was up there, pulling himself together. And he was out here, trying to do the same thing.

The look the kid had shot him, Cam thought, just before things got sloppy. It had stirred up his gut. He'd have sworn he'd seen trust there, and a pathetic, almost desperate gratitude that both humbled and terrified him.

What the hell was he going to do with it? And when things settled down and he could pick up his own life again . . . That had to happen, he assured himself. Had to. He couldn't stay in charge like this. Couldn't be expected to live like this forever. He had places to go, races to run, risks to take.

Once they had everything under control, once they did what needed to be done for the kid and got this business Ethan wanted established, he'd be free to come and go as he pleased again.

A few more months, he decided, maybe a year, then he was out of here. No one could possibly expect more from him.

Not even himself.

Nine

Vice principal Moorefield studied the three men who stood like a well-mortared wall in her office. The outward appearance would never indicate they were brothers. One wore a trim gray suit and perfectly knotted tie, another a black shirt and jeans, and the third faded khakis and a wrinkled denim work shirt.

But she could see that at the moment they were as united as triplets in the womb.

"I realize you have busy schedules. I appreciate all of you coming in this morning."

"We want to get this straightened out, Mrs. Moorefield." Phillip kept a mild, negotiating smile on his face. "Seth needs to be in school."

"I agree. After Seth's statement yesterday, I did some checking. It does appear as though Robert instigated the incident. There does seem to be some question over the motivation. The matter of the petty extortion—"

Cam held up a hand. "Seth, did you tell this Robert character to give you a dollar?"

"Nah." Seth tucked his thumbs in his front pockets, as he'd seen Cam do. "I don't need his money. I don't even talk to him unless he gets in my face."

Cam looked back at Mrs. Moorefield. ''Seth says he aced that test and Robert flunked. Is that right?''

The vice principal folded her hands on her desk. ''Yes. The test papers were handed back yesterday just before the end of class, and Seth received the highest grade. Now—''

''Seems to me,'' Ethan interrupted in a quiet voice, ''that Seth told you straight, then. Excuse me, ma'am, but if the other boy lied about some of it, could be he's lying about all of it. Seth says the boy came after him, and he did. He said it was about this test, so I figure it is.''

''I've considered that, and I tend to agree with you, Mr. Quinn. I've spoken with Robert's mother. She's no happier than you are about this incident, or about the fact that both boys are to be suspended.''

''You're not suspending Seth.'' Cam planted his feet. ''Not over this—not without a fight.''

''I understand how you feel. However, blows were exchanged. Physical violence can't be permitted here.''

''I'd agree with you, Mrs. Moorefield, under most circumstances.'' Phillip laid a hand on Cam's arm to prevent him from stepping forward. ''However, Seth was being physically and verbally attacked. He defended himself. There should have been a teacher monitoring the hallway during the change of classes. He should have been able to depend on an adult, on the system to protect him. Why didn't one come forward to do so?''

Moorefield puffed out her cheeks, blew out a breath. ''That's a reasonable question, Mr. Quinn. I won't start weeping to you about budget cuts, but it's impossible, with a staff of our size, to monitor all the children at all times.''

''I sympathize with your problem, but Seth shouldn't have to pay for it.''

''There's been a rough time recently,'' Ethan put in. ''I don't figure that kicking the boy out of school for a couple days is going to help him any. Education's supposed to be more than learning—leastways that's how we were taught. It's supposed to help build your character and help teach you how to get on in the world. If it tells you that you get booted for doing what you had to, for standing up for yourself, then something's wrong with the system."

"You punish him the same way you punish the boy who started it," Cam said, "you're telling him there's not much difference between right and wrong. That's not the kind of school I want my brother in."

Moorefield steepled her hands, looked over the tips of her fingers at the three men, then down at Seth. "Your evaluation tests were excellent, and your grades are well above average. However, your teachers say you rarely turn in homework assignments and even more rarely participate in class discussion."

"We're dealing with the homework." Cam gave Seth a subtle nudge. "Right?"

"Yeah, I guess. I don't see why—"

"You don't have to see." Cam cut him off with one lowering glance. "You just have to do it. We can't sit in the classroom with him and make him open his mouth, but he'll turn in his homework."

"I imagine he will," she murmured. "This is what I'll agree to do. Seth, because I believe you, you won't be suspended. But you will go on a thirty-day probation. If there are no more disruptive incidents, and your teachers report that you have improved your at-home-assignment record—we'll put this matter aside. However, your first homework assignment comes now and from me. You have one week to write a five-hundred-word essay on the violence in our society and the need for peaceful resolutions to problems."

"Oh, man—"

"Shut up," Cam ordered mildly. "That's fair," he said to Mrs. Moorefield. "We appreciate it."

"THAT WASN'T SO BAD." Phillip stepped back into the sunlight and rolled his shoulders.

"Speak for yourself." Ethan snugged his cap back on his head. "I was sweating bullets. I don't want to have to do that again in this lifetime. Drop me off at the waterfront. I can get a ride out to the boat. Jim's working her, and he ought to have pulled in a nice mess of crabs by now."

"Just make sure you bring us home our share." Cam piled into Phillip's shiny navy blue Land Rover. "And don't forget we've got company coming."

"Not going to forget," Ethan mumbled. "Principals in the morning, social workers in the evening. Christ Jesus. Every time you turn around, you have to talk to somebody."

"I intend to keep Miz Spinelli occupied."

Ethan turned around to look at Cam. "You just can't leave females alone, can you?"

"What would be the point? They're here."

Ethan only sighed. "Somebody better pick up more beer."

CAM VOLUNTEERED TO get the beer late that afternoon. It wasn't altruism. He didn't think he could stand listening to Phillip another five minutes. Going to the market was the best way to get out of the house and away from the tension while Phillip drafted and perfected a letter to the insurance company on his snazzy little laptop computer.

"Get some salad stuff while you're out," Phillip shouted, causing Cam to turn back and poke his head in the kitchen where Phillip was typing away at the table.

"What do you mean, salad stuff?"

"Field greens—for God's sake, don't come back here with a head of iceberg and a couple of tasteless hothouse tomatoes. I made up a nice vinaigrette the other day, but there's not a damn thing around here to put it on. Get some plum tomatoes if they look decent."

"What the hell do we need all that for?"

Phillip sighed and stopped typing. "First, because we want to live long and healthy lives, and second because you invited a woman to dinner—a woman who's going to look at how we deal with Seth's nutritional needs."

"Then you go to the goddamn store."

"Fine. You write this goddamn letter."

He'd rather be burned alive. "Field greens, for sweet Christ's sake."

"And get some sourdough bread. And we're nearly out of milk. Since I'm going to be bringing my juicer the next time I get back to Baltimore, pick up some fresh fruit, some carrots, zucchini. I'll just make a list."

"Hold it, hold it." Cam felt the controls slipping out of his hands and struggled to shift his grip. "I'm just going for beer."

"Whole wheat bagels," Phillip muttered, busily writing.

THIRTY MINUTES LATER, Cam found himself pondering the produce section of the grocery store. What the hell was the difference between green leaf and romaine lettuce, and why should he care? In defense, he began loading the cart at random.

Since that worked for him, he did the same thing through the aisles. By the time he reached checkout, he had two carts, overflowing with cans, boxes, bottles, and bags.

"My goodness, you must be having a party."

"Big appetites," he told the checkout clerk, and after a quick search of his brain pegged her. "How's it going, Mrs. Wilson?"

"Oh, fair enough." She ran items expertly over the belt and scanner and into bags, her quick, red-tipped fingers moving like lightning. "Too pretty a day to be stuck inside here, I can tell you that. I get off in an hour and I'm going out chicken-necking with my grandson."

"We're counting on having crab for dinner ourselves.

Probably should have bought some chicken necks for the pot off our dock.''

''Ethan'll keep you supplied, I imagine. I'm awful sorry about Ray,'' she added. ''Didn't really get to tell you so after the funeral. We're sure going to miss him. He used to come in here once or twice a week after Stella passed, buy himself a pile of those microwave meals. I'd tell him, 'Ray, you got to do better for yourself than that. A man needs a good slab of meat now and then.' But it's a hard thing cooking for one when you're used to family.''

''Yeah.'' It was all Cam could say. He'd been family, and he hadn't been there.

''Always had some story to tell about one of you boys. Showed me pictures and things from foreign newspapers on you. Racing here, racing there. And I'd say, 'Ray, how do you know if the boy won or not when it's written in I-talian or Fran-say?' We'd just laugh.''

She checked the weight on a bag of apples, keyed them in. ''How's that young boy? What's his name, now? Sam?''

''Seth,'' Cam murmured. ''He's fine.''

''Good-looking boy. I said to Mr. Wilson when Ray brought him home, 'That's Ray Quinn for you, always keeping his door open.' Don't know how a man of his age expected to handle a boy like that, but if anybody could, Ray Quinn could. He and Stella handled the three of you.''

Because she smiled and winked, he smiled back. ''They did. We tried to give them plenty to handle.''

''I expect they loved every minute of it. And I expect the boy, Seth, was company for Ray after y'all grew up and lit out. I want you to know I don't hold with what some people are saying. No, I don't.''

Her mouth thinned as she rang up three jumbo boxes of cold cereal. With a cluck of her tongue and a shake of her head, she continued. ''I tell them straight to their face if they do that nasty gossiping in my hearing that if they had a Christian bone in their body, they'd mind their tongues.''

Her eyes glittered with fury and loyalty. ''Don't you pay

any mind to that talk, Cameron, no mind at all. Why the idea that Ray would have had truck with that woman, that the boy was his by blood. Not one decent mind's going to believe that, or that he'd run into that pole on purpose. Makes me just sick to hear it."

It was making Cam sick now. He wished to God he'd never come in the store. "Some people believe lies, Mrs. Wilson. Some people would rather believe them."

"That they do." She nodded her head twice, sharply. "And even if they don't, they like to spread them around. I want you to know that Mr. Wilson and me considered Ray and Stella good friends and good people. Anybody says something I don't like about them around me's going to get their ears boxed."

He had to smile. "As I remember, you were good at that."

She laughed now, a kind of happy hoot. "Boxed yours that time you came sniffing too close to my Caroline. Don't think I didn't know what you were after, boy."

"Caroline was the prettiest girl in tenth grade."

"She's still a picture. It's her boy I'm going chicken-necking with. He'll be four this summer. And she's carrying her second into the sixth month now. Time does go right by."

It seemed it did, Cam thought when he was back at home and hauling bags of groceries into the house. He knew Mrs. Wilson had meant everything she'd said for the best, but she had certainly managed to depress him.

If someone who'd been a staunch friend of his parents was being told such filthy lies, they were spreading more quickly, and more thickly, than he'd imagined. How long could they be ignored before denials had to be given and a stand taken?

Now he was afraid they would have no choice but to take Phillip's advice and find Seth's mother.

The kid was going to hate that, Cam knew. And what would happen to the trust he'd seen swimming in Seth's eyes?

"Guess you want a hand with that stuff." Phillip stepped into the kitchen. "I was on the phone. The lawyer. Temporary guardianship's a lock. There's step one anyway."

"Great." He started to relay the conversation in the grocery store, then decided to let it ride for the night. Goddamn it, they'd won two battles that day. He wasn't going to see the rest of the evening spoiled by wagging tongues.

"More out in the car," he told Phillip.

"More what?"

"Bags."

"More?" Phillip stared at the half dozen loaded brown bags. "Jesus, Cam, I didn't have more than twenty items on that list."

"So I added to it." He pulled a box out, tossed it on the counter. "Nobody's going to go hungry around here for a while."

"You bought Twinkies? *Twinkies?* Are you one of the people who believe that white stuff inside them is one of the four major food groups?"

"The kid'll probably go for them."

"Sure he will. You can pay his next dentist bill."

His temper dangerously close to the edge, Cam whirled around. "Look, pal, he who goes to the store buys what he damn well pleases. That's a new rule around here. Now do you want to get that stuff out of the car or let it fucking rot?"

Phillip only lifted a brow. "Since shopping for food puts you in such a cheery mood, I'll take that little chore from now on. And we'd better start a household fund to draw from for day-to-day incidentals."

"Fine." Cam waved him away. "You do that."

When Phillip walked out, Cam began to stuff boxes and cans wherever they fit. He would let somebody else worry about organizing. In fact, he'd let anybody else worry about it. He was done for a while.

He started out, and when he hit the front door saw that Seth had arrived home. Phillip was passing him bags, and the two of them were talking as if they hadn't a care in the world.

So, he'd go out the back, he decided, let the two of them handle things for a couple of hours. As he turned, the puppy yipped at him, then squatted and peed on the rug.

"I suppose you expect me to clean that up." When Foolish wagged his tail and let his tongue loll, all Cam could do was close his eyes.

"I still say the essay's a raw deal," Seth complained as he walked into the house. "That kind of stuff's crap. And I don't see why—"

"You'll do it." Cam pulled the bag out of Seth's arms. "And I don't want to hear any bitching about it. You can get started right after you clean up the mess your dog just made on the rug."

"My dog? He's not mine."

"He is now, and you better make sure he's housebroken all the way or he stays outside."

He stalked off toward the kitchen, with Phillip, who was trying desperately not to laugh, following.

Seth stood where he was, staring down at Foolish. "Dumb dog," he murmured, and when he crouched down, the puppy launched himself into Seth's arms, where he was welcomed with a fierce hug. "You're my dog now."

ANNA TOLD HERSELF SHE would and could be perfectly professional for the evening. She'd cleared the informal visit with Marilou, just to keep it official. And the truth was, she wanted to see Seth again. Every bit as much as she wanted to see Cam.

Different reasons, certainly, and perhaps different parts of her, but she wanted to see them both. She could handle both sides of her heart, and her mind. She'd always been able to separate areas of her life and conduct them all in a satisfactory manner.

This situation wouldn't be any different.

Verdi soared out of her speakers, wild and passionate. She rolled her window up just enough that the breeze didn't disturb her hair. She hoped the Quinns would allow her a few moments alone with Seth, so she could judge for herself, without influence, how he was feeling.

She hoped she could steal a few moments alone with Cam, so she could judge for herself how she was feeling.

Itchy, she admitted. Needy.

But it wasn't always necessary, or possible to act on feelings, however strong they might be. If, after seeing him again, she felt it best for all concerned to take a large step back, she would do so.

She had no doubt the man had an iron will. But so did Anna Spinelli. She would match herself against Cameron Quinn in that respect any day. And she could win.

Even as she reassured herself of that one single fact, Anna pulled her spiffy little car into the drive.

And Cam walked out onto the porch.

They stayed where they were for just a moment, eyeing each other. When he came off the porch and onto the walk, that hard body tucked into snug black, that dark hair unruly, those smoky eyes unreadable, her heart took one helpless spin and landed with a thud.

She wanted that tough-looking mouth on her, those rough-palmed hands on her. She wanted that all-male body pinning hers to a mattress, moving with the speed that was so much a part of his life. It was idiotic to deny it.

But she'd handle him, Anna promised herself. She only hoped she could handle herself.

She stepped out, wearing a prim, boxy suit the color of a bird's nest. Her hair was pulled up and back and ruthlessly controlled. Her unpainted lips curved in a polite, somewhat distant smile, and she carried her briefcase.

For reasons that baffled him, Cam had precisely the same reaction he'd had when she'd clipped down her hallway on stiletto heels that rainy night. Instant and raging lust.

When he started toward her, she angled her head, just a

little, just enough to send the warning signal. The hands-off sign was clear as a shout.

But he leaned forward a bit when he reached her, sniffed at her hair. "You did that on purpose."

"Did what on purpose?"

"Wore the don't-touch suit and the sex goddess perfume at the same time just to drive me crazy."

"Listen to the suit, Quinn. Dream about the perfume." She started past him, then looked down coolly when his hand clamped over her arm. "You're not listening."

"I like to play games as much as the next guy, Anna." He tugged until she turned and they were again face to face. "But you may have picked a bad time for this one."

There was something in his eyes, she realized, something along with desire, annoyance. And because she recognized it as unhappiness, she softened. "Has something happened? What's wrong?"

"What's right?" he tossed back.

She put a hand over the one still clamped to her arm and squeezed lightly. "Rough day?"

"Yes. No. Hell." Giving up, he let her go and leaned back on the hood of her car. It was a testimony to her compassion that she was able to stifle a wince. She'd just had it washed and waxed. "There was this thing at school this morning."

"Thing?"

"You'll probably get some official report or something about it, so I want to give you our side personally."

"Uh-oh, sides. Well, let's hear it."

So he told her, found himself heating up again when he got to the point where he'd seen the bruises on Seth's arm, and ended up pushing himself off the car and stalking around it as he finished the story of how it had been resolved.

"You did very well," Anna murmured, nearly laughing when he stopped and stared at her suspiciously. "Of course hitting the other boy wasn't the answer, but—"

"I think it was a damn good answer."

"I realize that, and we'll just let it go for now. My point is, you did the responsible and the supportive thing. You went down, you listened, you convinced Seth to tell you the truth, and then you stood up for him. I doubt he was expecting you to."

"Why shouldn't I—why wouldn't I? He was right."

"Believe me, not everyone goes to bat for their children."

"He's not my kid. He's my brother."

"Not everyone goes to bat for his brother," she corrected. "The three of you going in this morning was exactly right, and again unfortunately more than everyone would do. It's a corner turned for all of you, and I suspect you understand that. Is that what's upset you?"

"No, that's piddly. Other things, doesn't matter." He could hardly tell her about the investigation into his father's death or the village gossip over it at this precarious point. Nor did he think it would count in their favor if he confessed he was feeling trapped and dreaming of escape.

"How's Seth taking it?"

"He's cool with it." Cam shrugged a shoulder. "We went sailing yesterday, did some fishing. Blew off the day."

She smiled again, and this time her heart was in it. "I'd hoped I'd be around to see it happening. You're starting to fall for him."

"What are you talking about?"

"You're starting to care about him. Personally. He's beginning to be more than an obligation, a promise to be kept. He matters to you."

"I said I'd take care of him. That's what I'm doing."

"He matters to you," she repeated. "That's what's worrying you, Cam. What happens if you start caring too much. And how do you stop it from happening."

He looked at her, the way the sun dropped down in the sky at her back, the way her eyes stayed warm and dark on his. Maybe he was worrying, he admitted, and not just about his shifting feelings for Seth. "I finish what I start,

Anna. And I don't walk away from my family. Looks like the kid qualifies there. But I'm a selfish son of a bitch. Ask anybody."

"Some things I prefer to find out for myself. Now am I getting a crab dinner or not?"

"Ethan ought to have the pot going by now." He moved forward as if to lead her inside. Then, judging the moment when she relaxed, he yanked her into his arms and caught her up in a hot, heart-hammering kiss.

"See, that was for me," he murmured when they were both breathless and quivering. "Want it, take it. I warned you I was selfish."

Anna eased back, calmly adjusted her now rumpled jacket, ran a hand over her hair to assure herself it was in place. "Sorry, but I'm afraid I enjoyed that every bit as much as you did. So it doesn't qualify as a selfish act."

He laughed even as his pulse scrambled. "Let me try it again. I can pull it off this time."

"I'll take a rain check. I want my dinner." With that, she sauntered up the steps, knocked briefly, and slipped into the house.

Cam just stood where he was, grinning. This was a woman, he thought, who was going to make this episode of his life a memorable one.

By the time Cam made his way inside and to the kitchen, Anna was already chatting with Phillip and accepting a glass of wine.

"You drink beer with crabs," Cam told her and got one out of the fridge for himself.

"I don't seem to be eating any at the moment. And Phillip assures me this is a very nice wine." She sipped, considered, and smiled. "He's absolutely right."

"It's one of my favorite whites." Since she'd approved, Phillip topped off her glass. "Smooth, buttery, and not overpowering."

"Phil's a wine snob." Cam twisted off the top and lifted the bottle of Harp to his lips. "But we let him live here anyway."

"And how is that working out?" She wondered if they realized how male the house seemed. Tidy as a pin, yes, but without even a whiff of female. "It must be odd adjusting to the three of you in the same household again."

"Well, we haven't killed each other." Cam bared his teeth in a smile at his brother. "Yet."

With a laugh she walked to the window. "And where is Seth?"

"He's with Ethan," Phillip told her. "They're doing the crabs around at the pit."

"The pit?"

"Around the side." Cam took her hand and tugged her toward the door. "Mom wouldn't let us cook crab in the house. She might have been a doctor, but she could be squeamish. Didn't like to watch." He drew her off the porch and down the steps as he spoke. "Dad had this brick pit around the side of the house. Fell down my first summer. He didn't know much about laying bricks. But we rebuilt it."

When they stepped around the corner, she saw Ethan and Seth standing by a huge kettle over an open fire in a lopsided brick-sided pit. Smoke billowed, and from a big steel barrel on the ground came the scraping and clattering of claws.

Anna looked from barrel to kettle and back again. "You know what, I think I can be a bit squeamish myself."

She stepped back, turned to the view of the water. She didn't even mind that Cam laughed at her, especially when she heard Seth's voice raised in desperate excitement.

"Are you dumping them in now? Oh, man, shit, that is so *gross*."

"I told him to watch his mouth tonight, but he doesn't know you're here yet."

She only shook her head. "He sounds very normal." She winced a little when she heard a clatter and Seth's wild exclamation of delight and disgust. "And I'd think what's happening around the corner is just barbaric enough to thrill him.'' Her hand lifted quickly, protectively, to her hair when she felt a tug.

''I like it down.'' Cam tossed the pin he'd pulled out aside.

''I want it up,'' she said mildly and began to walk toward the water.

''I bet we're going to knock heads about all kinds of things.'' He sipped his beer and sent her a sidelong look as they walked. ''Ought to keep it all interesting.''

''I doubt either of us will be bored. Seth comes first, Cam. I mean that.'' She paused, listened to the musical lap of water against the hull of the boats, the sloping shoreline. Topping one of the markers was a huge nest. Buoys bobbed in the tide.

''I can help him, and it's unlikely we'll always agree on what's right for him. It'll be essential to keep that issue completely separate when we end up in bed.''

He was grateful he hadn't taken another sip from the bottle. No doubt in his mind he'd have choked on it. ''I can do that.''

She lifted her head as an egret soared by, and wondered if the nest belonged to her. ''When I'm certain I can, we'll use my bed. My apartment's more private than your house.''

He rubbed a hand over his stomach in a futile attempt to calm himself. ''Lady, you're right up front, aren't you?''

''What's the point in being otherwise? We're grown-ups, unattached.'' She shot him a look—a flick of the lashes, an arch of a brow. ''But if you're the type who'd prefer me to pretend reluctance until seduction, sorry.''

''No, I'm all right with it this way.'' If he didn't overheat and explode in the meantime. ''No games, no pretenses, no promises. . . . Where the hell do you come from?'' he finished, fascinated.

''Pittsburgh,'' she said easily and started back toward the house.

''That's not what I meant.''

"I know. But if you intend to sleep with me, you should have some interest in the basic facts. No games, no pretenses, no promises. That's fine. But I don't have sex with strangers."

He put a hand on her arm before she wandered too close to the house. He wanted another moment alone. "Okay, what are the basic facts?"

"I'm twenty-eight, single, of Italian descent. My mother . . . died when I was twelve and I was raised primarily by my grandparents."

"In Pittsburgh."

"That's right. They're wonderful—old-fashioned, energetic, loving. I can make a terrific red sauce from scratch—the recipe's been passed down in my family for generations. I moved to D.C. right after college, worked there and did some graduate studies. But Washington didn't suit me."

"Too political?"

"Yes, and too urban. I was looking for something a little different, so I ended up down here."

Cam glanced around the quiet yard, the quiet water. "It's different from D.C., all right."

"I like it. I also like horror novels, sappy movies, and any kind of music except jazz. I read magazines from back to front and don't know why, and though I'm comfortable with all sorts of people, I don't particularly like large social functions."

She stopped, considered. They would see, she decided, how much more he'd want to find out. "I think that's enough for now, and my glass is nearly empty."

"You're nothing like my first impression of you."

"No? I think you're exactly like mine of you."

"Do you speak Italian?"

"Fluently."

He leaned forward and murmured a highly charged and sexually explicit suggestion in her ear. Some women might have slapped his face, others might have giggled, some certainly would have blushed. Anna merely made a humming sound in her throat.

"Your accent's mediocre, but your imagination is exceptional." She gave his arm a light pat. "Be sure to ask me again—some other time."

"Damn right I will," Cam muttered, and watched her smile in an easy, open manner at Seth as he came barreling around the corner of the house.

"Hello, Seth."

He skidded to a halt. That wary and distant look came into his eyes. His shoulders hunched. "Yeah, hi. Ethan says we can eat anytime."

"Good, I'm starved." Though she knew he was braced against her, she kept walking toward him. "I hear you went sailing yesterday."

Seth's gaze slid by her, locked accusingly on Cam's. "Yeah. So?"

"I've never been." She said it quickly, sensing that Cam's indrawn breath was the signal for a sharp reminder of manners. "Cam offered to let me tag along with you sometime."

"It's his boat." Then catching the dark scowl on Cam's face, Seth shrugged. "Sure, that'd be cool. I'm supposed to go get a ton of newspaper to spread on the porch. That's the way you eat crabs."

"Right." Before he could dash off, she bent down and whispered in his ear. "Good thing for us Cam didn't cook them."

That got a snicker out of him and a quick, fleeting grin before he turned and ran inside.

TEN

SHE WASN'T SO BAD. FOR a social worker. Seth came to this thoughtful conclusion about Anna after he'd retreated to his room, ostensibly to work on his anti-violence essay. He was drawing pictures instead, quick little sketches of faces. He had a stupid week to write the stupid thing, didn't he? Wouldn't take more than a couple of hours once he got down to doing it. Which was a raw deal all around, but better than letting fat-faced Robert get him suspended.

He could still close his eyes and bring up the image of all three of the Quinns standing in the principal's office. All three of them standing beside him and facing down the all-powerful Moorefield. It was so . . . cool, he decided and began to doodle the moment in his notebook.

There . . . there was Phillip in his fancy suit with his hair just right and his kind of narrow face. He looked like one of the magazine ads, Seth thought, the ones that sold stuff only rich guys could buy.

Next he sketched in Ethan, all serious-faced, Seth mused, his hair a little shaggy even though Seth remembered how he'd combed it just before they'd gone into the school. He looked exactly like what he was. The kind of guy who made his living and lived his life outdoors.

And there was Cam, rough and tough with that light of mean in his eyes. Thumbs hooked in the front pockets of his jeans. Yeah, that was it, Seth decided. He most always stood like that when he was ticked off. Even in the rough sketch he came across as someone who'd done most everything and planned to do a whole lot more.

Last he sketched in himself, trying to see what others would see. His shoulders were too thin and bony, he thought with some disappointment. But they wouldn't always be. His face was too thin for his eyes, but it would fill out too. One day he'd be taller, and stronger, and he wouldn't look like such a puny kid.

But he'd kept his head up, hadn't he? He hadn't been afraid of anything. And he didn't look like he'd just wandered into the picture. He looked—almost—like he belonged there.

Mess with one Quinn, mess with them all. That's what Cam had said—and he must have meant it. But he wasn't a Quinn, Seth thought, frowning as he held up the sketch to study details. Or maybe he was, he just didn't know. It hadn't mattered to him if Ray Quinn had been his father like some people said. All that had mattered was that he was away from *her*.

It hadn't mattered who his father was. Still didn't, he assured himself. He just didn't give a rat's ass. All he wanted was to stay here, right here.

Nobody had used the back of their hand or their fists on him for months now. Nobody got blitzed out on drugs and laid around so long and so still he thought they were dead. Secretly hoped they were. No flabby guys with sweaty hands tried to grope him.

He wasn't even going to think about that.

Eating crabs had been pretty cool, too. Good and messy, he remembered with a grin. You got to eat them with your hands. The social worker didn't act all prim and girly about it either. She just took off her jacket and rolled up her sleeves. It didn't seem like she was watching to see if he burped or scratched his butt or anything.

She'd laughed a lot, he remembered. He wasn't used to women laughing a lot when they weren't coked up. And that was a different kind of laughing, Seth knew. Miss Spinelli's wasn't wild and hard and desperate. It was low and, well, smooth, he supposed.

Nobody'd told him he couldn't have more, either. Man, he'd bet he ate a hundred of those ugly suckers. He didn't even mind eating the salad, though he pretended he did.

He hadn't had that gnawing, sick feeling in his stomach that was desperate hunger for a long time now, so long he might have forgotten the sensation. But he hadn't forgotten. He hadn't forgotten anything.

He'd worried some that the social worker would want to pull him back in, but she seemed pretty okay to him. And he saw her sneaking little bits of crab and bread to Foolish, so she couldn't be all bad.

But he'd have liked her better if she was a waitress or something like Grace.

When the light knock sounded on his door, Seth slapped the notebook closed on his sketches and quickly opened another, where the first dozen words of his five-hundred-word essay were scrawled.

"Yeah?"

Anna poked her head in. "Hi. Can I come in a minute?"

It was weird being asked, and he wondered if she would just turn around and go if he said no. But he shrugged. "I guess."

"I have to leave soon," she began, taking a quick survey of the room. A twin bed, inexpertly made, a sturdy dresser and desk, a wall of shelves that held a few books, a portable stereo that looked very new, and a pair of binoculars that didn't. There were white miniblinds at the windows and a pale-green paint on the walls.

It needed junk, she thought. A boy's junk. Ancient broken toys, posters tacked to the walls. But the puppy snoring in the corner was a very good start.

"This is nice." She wandered to the window. "You've got a good view, water and trees. You get to watch the birds. I bought a book on local waterfowl when I moved here from D.C. so I could figure out what was what. It must be nice to see egrets every day."

"I guess."

"I like it here. It's hard not to, huh?"

He shrugged his shoulders, took the cautious route. "It's okay. I got no problems with it."

She turned, glanced down at his notebook. "The dreaded essay?"

"I started it." Defensively, he pulled the notebook closer—and knocked the other one to the floor. Before he could snatch it up, Anna crouched to pick it up herself.

"Oh, look at this!" It had fallen open to a sketch of the puppy, just his face, straight on, and she thought the artist had captured that sweet and silly expression perfectly. "Did you sketch this?"

"It's no big deal. I'm working on the damn essay, aren't I?"

She might have sighed over his response, but she was too charmed by the sketch. "It's wonderful. It looks just like him." Her fingers itched to turn the pages, to see who else Seth might have drawn. But she resisted and set the notebook down. "I can't draw a decent stick man."

"It's nothing. Just fooling around."

"Well, if you don't want it, maybe I could have it?"

He thought it might be a trick. After all, she had her jacket back on, was carrying her briefcase. She looked like Social Services again rather than the woman who'd rolled up her sleeves and laughed over steamed crabs. "What for?"

"I can't have pets in my apartment. Just as well," she added. "It wouldn't be fair to keep one closed in all day while I'm at work, but . . ." Then she smiled and glanced over at the sleeping puppy. "I really like dogs. When I can afford a house and a yard, I'm going to have a couple of them. But until then, I have to play with other people's pets."

It seemed odd to him. In Seth's mind adults ruled—often with an iron hand. Did what they wanted when they wanted. "Why don't you just move someplace else?"

"The place I've got is close to work, the rent's reasonable." She looked toward the window again, to the stretch of land and water. Both were deep with shadows as night moved in. "It has to do until I can manage to get the house and yard." She wandered to the window, drawn to that quiet view. The first star winked to life in the eastern sky. She nearly made a wish. "Somewhere near the water. Like this. Anyway . . ."

She turned back and sat on the side of the bed facing him. "I just wanted to come up before I left, see if there's anything you wanted to talk about, or any questions you wanted to ask me."

"No. Nothing."

"Okay." She hadn't really expected him to talk to her freely. Yet. "Maybe you'd like to know what I see here, what I think." She took his shoulder jerk as assent. "I see a houseful of guys who are trying to figure out how to live with each other and make it work. Four very different men who are bumping up against each other. And I think they're going to make some mistakes, and most certainly irritate each other and disagree. But I also think they'll work it out—eventually. Because they all want to," she added with an easy smile. "In their own ways they all want the same thing."

She rose and took a card out of her briefcase. "You can call me whenever you want. I put my home number on the back. I don't see any reason for me to come back—in an official capacity—for a while. But I may come back for a puppy fix. Good luck with the essay."

When she started for the door, Seth went with impulse and tore the sketch of Foolish out of his notebook. "You can have this if you want."

"Really?" She took the page, beamed at it. "God, he's

cute. Thanks.'' He jerked back when she bent to kiss his cheek, but she brushed her lips across it lightly, then straightened. She stepped back, ordering herself to keep an emotional distance. ''Say good night to Foolish for me.''

Anna slipped the sketch in her briefcase as she walked downstairs. Phillip was noodling at the piano, his fingers carelessly picking out some bluesy number. It was another skill she envied. It was a constant disappointment to her that she had no talent.

Ethan was nowhere to be seen, and Cam was restlessly pacing the living room.

She thought that might be a very typical overview of all three men. Phillip elegantly whiling away the time, Ethan off on some solitary pursuit. And Cam working off excess energy.

With the boy up in his room, drawing his pictures and thinking his thoughts.

Cam glanced up, and when their eyes locked, the ball of heat slammed into her gut.

''Gentlemen, thank you for a wonderful meal.''

Phillip rose and held out a hand to take hers. ''We have to thank you. It's been too long since we had a beautiful woman to dinner. I hope you'll come back.''

Oh, he's a smooth one, she decided. ''I'd like that. Tell Ethan he's a genius with a crab. Good night, Cam.''

''I'll walk you out.''

She'd counted on it. ''First thing,'' she said when they stepped outside. ''From what I can see, Seth's welfare is being seen to. He has proper supervision, a good home, support with his school life. He could certainly use some new shoes, but I don't imagine there's a boy of ten who couldn't.''

''Shoes? What's wrong with his shoes?''

''Regardless,'' she said, turning to him when they reached her car. ''All of you still have adjustments to make, and there's no doubt he's a very troubled child. I suspect he was abused, physically and perhaps sexually.''

"I figured that out for myself," Cam said shortly. "It won't happen here."

"I know that." She laid a hand on his arm. "If I had a single doubt in that area he wouldn't be here. Cam, he needs professional counseling. You all do."

"Counseling? That's crap. We don't need to pour our guts out to some underpaid county shrink."

"Many underpaid county shrinks are very good at their job," she said dryly. "Since I have a degree in psychology myself, I could be considered an underpaid county shrink, and I'm good at mine."

"Fine. You're talking to him, you're talking to me. We've been counseled."

"Don't be difficult." Her voice was deliberately mild because she knew it would spark a flash of annoyance in his eyes. It was only fair, she thought, as he'd annoyed her.

"I'm not being difficult. I've cooperated with you from the get-go."

More or less, she mused, and continuing to be fair, admitted it was more than she'd expected. "You've made a solid start here, but a professional counselor will help all of you get beneath the surface and deal with the root of the problems."

"We don't have any problems."

She hadn't expected such hard-line resistance to such a basic step, but realized she should have. "Of course you do. Seth's afraid to be touched."

"He's not afraid to let Grace touch him."

"Grace?" Anna pursed her lips in thought. "Grace Monroe, from the list you gave me?"

"Yeah, she's doing the housework now, and the kid's nuts about her. Might even have a little crush."

"That's good, that's healthy. But it's only a start. When a child's been abused, it leaves scars."

What the hell were they talking about this for? he thought impatiently. Why were they talking about shrinks and digging at old wounds when all he'd wanted was a few minutes of easy flirtation with a pretty woman?

"My old man beat the hell out of me. So what? I survived." He hated remembering it, hated standing in the shadow of the house that had been his sanctuary and remembering. "The kid's mother knocked him around. Well, she's not going to get the chance to do it again. That chapter's closed."

"It's never closed," Anna said patiently. "Whatever new chapter you start always has some basis in the one that came before. I'm recommending counseling to you now, and I'm going to recommend it in my report."

"Go ahead." He couldn't explain why it infuriated him even to think about it. He only knew he'd be damned if he would ask himself or any of his brothers to open those long-locked doors again. "You recommend whatever you want. Doesn't mean we have to do it."

"You have to do what's best for Seth."

"How the hell do you know what's best?"

"It's my job," she said coolly now, because her blood was starting to boil.

"Your job? You got a college degree and a bunch of forms. We're the ones who lived it, who are living it. You haven't been there. You don't know anything about it, what it's like to get your face smashed in and not be able to stop it. To have some bureaucratic jerk from the county who doesn't know dick decide what happens to your life."

Didn't know? She thought of the dark, deserted road, the terror. The pain and the screams. Can't be personal, she reminded herself, though her stomach clutched and fluttered. "Your opinion of my profession has been crystal-clear since our first meeting."

"That's right, but I cooperated. I filled you in, and all of us took steps to make this work." His thumbs went into his front pockets in a gesture Seth would have recognized. "It's never quite enough, though. There's always something else."

"If there weren't something else," she returned, "you wouldn't be so angry."

"Of course I'm angry. We've been working our butts off here. I just turned down the biggest race of my career. I've got a kid on my hands who looks at me one minute as if I'm the enemy and the next as if I'm his salvation. Jesus Christ."

"And it's harder to be his salvation than his enemy."

Bull's-eye, he thought with growing resentment. How the hell did she know so much? "I'm telling you, the best thing for the kid, for all of us, is to be left alone. He needs shoes, I'll get him goddamn shoes."

"And what are you going to do about the fact that he's afraid to be touched, even in the most casual way, by you or your brothers? Are you going to buy his fear away?"

"He'll get over it." Cam was dug in now and refused to allow her to pry him out.

"Get over it?" A sudden fury had her almost stuttering out the words. Then they poured out in a hot stream that made the flash of pain in her eyes all the more poignant. "Because you want him to? Because you tell him to? Do you know what it's like to live with that kind of terror? That kind of shame? To have it bottled up inside you and have little drops of that poison spill out even when someone you love wants to hold you?"

She ripped open her car door, tossed her briefcase in. "I do. I know exactly." He grabbed her arm before she could get into the car. "Get your hand off me."

"Wait a minute."

"I said get your hand off me."

Because she was trembling, he did. Somewhere during the argument she'd gone from being professionally irritated to being personally enraged. He hadn't seen the shift.

"Anna, I'm not going to let you get behind the wheel of this car when you're this churned up. I lost someone I cared about recently, and I'm not going to let it happen again."

"I'm fine." Though she bit off the words, she followed them up by a long, steadying breath. "I'm perfectly capable of driving home. If you want to discuss the possibility of counseling rationally, you can call my office for an appointment.''

''Why don't we take a walk? Both of us can cool off.''

''I'm perfectly cool.'' She slipped into her car, nearly slammed the door on his fingers. ''You might take one, though, right off the dock.''

He cursed when she drove away. Briefly considered chasing her down, pulling her out of the car and demanding that they finish the damn stupid argument. His next thought was to stalk back into the house and forget it. Forget her.

But he remembered the wounded look that had come into her eyes, the way her voice had sounded when she'd said she knew what it was like to be afraid, to be ashamed.

Someone had hurt her, he realized. And at that moment everything else faded to the background.

ANNA SLAMMED THE door of her apartment, yanked off her shoes, and heaved them across the room. Her temper was not the type that flashed and boiled, then cooled. It was a simmering thing that bubbled and brewed, then spewed over.

The drive home hadn't calmed her down at all; it had merely given her rising emotions enough time to reach a peak.

She tossed her briefcase on the sofa, stripped off her suit jacket, and threw it on top. Ignorant, hardheaded, narrow-minded man. She fisted her hands and rapped them against her own temples. What had made her think she could get through to him? What had made her think she wanted to?

When she heard the knock on her door, she bared her teeth. She expected her across-the-hall neighbor wanted to exchange some little bit of news or gossip.

She wasn't in the mood.

Determined to ignore it until she could be civilized, she began yanking pins out of her hair.

The knock came again, louder now. "Come on, Anna. Open the damn door."

Now she could only stare as shock and fury made her ears ring. The man had followed her home? He'd had the *nerve* to come all the way to her door and expect to be welcomed inside?

He probably thought she'd be so consumed with lust that she'd jump him and have wild sex on the living room floor. Well, he was in for a surprise of his own.

She strode to the door, yanked it open. "You son of a bitch."

Cam took one look at her flushed and furious face, the wild, tumbling hair, the eyes that sparkled with vengeance, and decided it was undoubtedly perverse to find that arousing.

But what could he do about it?

He glanced down at her clenched fist. "Go ahead," he invited. "But if you belt me you'll have to write a five-hundred-word essay on violence in our society."

She made a low, threatening sound in her throat and tried to slam the door in his face. He was quick enough to slap a hand on it, strong enough to put his weight against it and hold it open. "I wanted to make sure you got home all right," he began as they struggled with the door. "And since I was in the neighborhood, I thought I should come up."

"I want you to go away. Very far away. In fact, I want you to go all the way to hell."

"I get that, but before I take the trip, give me five minutes."

"I've already given you what I now consider entirely too much of my time."

"So what's five more minutes?" To settle it, he braced the door open with one hand—which she found infuriating—and stepped inside.

"If it wasn't for Seth, I'd call the cops right now and have your butt tossed in jail."

He nodded. He'd dealt with his share of furious women and knew there was a time to be careful. "Yeah, I get that too. Listen—"

"I don't have to listen to you." Using the flat of her hand, she shoved him hard in the chest. "You're insulting and you're hardheaded and you're *wrong*, so I don't have to listen to you."

"I'm not wrong," he tossed back. "*You're* wrong. I know—"

"Every damn thing," she interrupted. "You drop in from bouncing around all over the world playing hotshot daredevil, and suddenly you know everything about what's best for a ten-year-old boy you've known barely a month."

"I was not playing at being a hotshot daredevil. I was making a career out of it!" He erupted, his purpose of conciliation and peacemaking shattering to bits. "A goddamn good one. And I do know what's best for the kid. I'm the one who's been there day and night. You spend a couple of hours with him and figure you got a better handle on it. That's just bullshit."

"It's my job to have a handle on it."

"Then you should know that every situation is different. Maybe it works for some people to spill their guts to a stranger and have their dreams analyzed." He'd worked it out carefully, logically on the way over. He was determined to be absolutely reasonable. "Nothing wrong with that, if it's what does it for you. But you can't rubber-stamp this. You have to look at the circumstances and the personalities here and, you know, make adjustments."

She couldn't get her breathing under control, so she finally stopped trying. "I don't rubber-stamp the people I'm chosen to help. I study and I evaluate, and goddamn you, I care. I am not some bureaucratic jerk who doesn't know dick. I'm a trained caseworker with over six years' experience, and I got that training and that experience because I know exactly what it's like to be on the other side, to be hurt and scared and alone and helpless. And no one whose case is assigned to me is just a name on a form.''

Her voice broke, shocking her to silence. Quickly she stepped back, pressing one hand to her mouth, holding the other up to signal him away. She felt it rising inside her, knew she wouldn't be able to stop it. ''Get out,'' she managed. ''Get out of here now.''

''Don't do that.'' Panic closed his throat as the first hot tears spilled down her cheeks. Furious women he understood and could deal with. The ones who wept destroyed him. ''Time out. Foul. Jesus, don't do that.''

''Just leave me alone.'' She turned away, thinking only of escape, but he wrapped his arms around her, buried his face in her hair.

''I'm sorry, I'm sorry, I'm sorry.'' He'd have apologized for anything, everything, if only to put them back on even ground. ''I was wrong. I was out of line, whatever you said. Don't cry, baby.'' He turned her around, holding her close. He pressed his lips to her forehead, her temple. His hands stroked her hair, her back.

Then his mouth was on hers, gently at first, to comfort and soothe while he continued to murmur mindless pleas and promises. But her arms lifted, wrapped around his neck, her body pressed into his, and her lips parted, heated.

The change happened quickly and he was lost in her, drowning in her. The hand that had stroked gently through her hair now tangled in it, fisted as the kiss rushed toward searing.

Take me away, was all she could think. Don't let me reason, don't let me think. Just take me. She wanted his hands on her, his mouth on her, she wanted to feel her muscles quiver with need under his fingers. With that strong, half-wild taste of his filling her, she could let everything go.

She trembled against him, shuddered in his arms, and the sound she made against his desperate mouth might have been a whimper. He jerked back as if he'd been stung, and though his hands weren't completely steady he kept them on her arms, and kept her at arm's length.

"That wasn't—" He had to stop, give himself a minute. His mind was mush and was unlikely to clear if she continued to look at him with those dark, damp eyes that were clouded with passion. "I don't believe I'm going to say this, but this isn't a good idea." He ran his hands up and down her arms as he struggled to hold on to control. "You're upset, probably not thinking . . ." He could still taste her, and the flavor on his tongue had outrageous hunger stirring in his belly. "Christ, I need a drink."

Annoyed with both of them, she swiped the back of her hand over her cheek to dry it. "I'll make coffee."

"I wasn't talking about coffee."

"I know, but if we're going to be sensible, let's stick with coffee."

She stepped into the kitchen area and kept herself busy with the homey process of grinding beans and brewing. Every nerve in her body was on edge. Every need she'd ever had or imagined having was brutally aroused.

"If we'd finished that, Anna, you might have thought I used the situation."

She nodded, continued to fix coffee. "Or I would have wondered if I had. Either way, bad idea. It's important to me never to mix sex and guilt." She looked at him then, quietly, levelly. "It's vital to me."

And he knew. Knowing, he suffered both helpless rage and helpless pity. "Christ, Anna. When?"

"When I was twelve."

"I'm sorry." It made him sick, in his gut, in his heart. "I'm sorry," he said again, inadequately. "You don't have to talk about it."

"That's where we disagree. Talking about it is finally what saved me." And he would listen, she thought. And he would know her. "My mother and I had gone to Philadelphia for the day. I wanted to see the Liberty Bell because we were studying about the Revolutionary War in school. We had this clunker of a car. We drove over, saw the sights. We ate ice cream and bought souvenirs."

"Anna—"

Her head whipped up, a direct challenge. "Are you afraid to hear it?"

"Maybe." He raked a hand through his hair. Maybe he was afraid to hear it, afraid of what it would change between them. Another roll of the dice, he thought, then looked at her, waiting patiently. And he understood he needed to know. "Go ahead."

Turning, she chose cups from the cabinet. "It was just the two of us. It always had been. She'd gotten pregnant when she was sixteen and would never say who the father was. Having me complicated her life enormously and must have brought her a great deal of shame and hardship. My grandparents were very religious, very old school." Anna laughed a little. "Very Italian. They didn't cut my mother out of their lives, but my sense was that it made her uncomfortable to have more than a peripheral part in them. So we had an apartment about a quarter the size of this one."

She brought the pot to the counter, poured the rich, dark coffee. "It was in April, on a Saturday. She'd taken off work so we could go. We had the best day, and we stayed later than we'd planned because we were having fun. I was half asleep on the ride back, and she must have made a wrong turn. I know we got lost, but she just joked about it. The car broke down. Smoke started pouring out from under the hood. She pulled over to the side and we got out. Just started giggling. What a mess, what a fix."

He knew what was coming, and it sickened him. "Maybe you should sit down."

"No, I'm all right. She thought it was the radiator needing water," Anna continued. Her eyes unfocused as she looked back. She could remember how warm it had been, how quiet, and how the moon had drifted in and out of smoky-looking clouds. "We were going to hike back to the closest house and see if we could get some help. A car came along, stopped. There were two men inside, and one of them leaned out and asked us if we had a problem."

She lifted her coffee, sipped. Her hands were steady now. She could say it all again and live through it all again. "I remember the way her hand squeezed mine, clamped down so hard it hurt. I realized later that she was afraid. They were drunk. She said something about just walking down to her brother's house, that we were fine, but they got out of the car. She pushed me behind her. When the first one grabbed her, she yelled at me to run. But I couldn't. I couldn't move. He was laughing and pawing at her, and she was fighting him. And when he dragged her off the road and pushed her down, I ran up and tried to pull him off. But of course I couldn't, and the other man yanked me off and tore my shirt."

A defenseless woman and a helpless child. Cam's hands fisted at his sides as both rage and impotence coursed through him. He wanted to go back to that night, that deserted road, and use them viciously.

"He kept laughing," Anna said quietly. "I saw his face very clearly for a moment or two. Like it was frozen in front of my eyes. I kept hearing my mother screaming, begging them not to hurt me. He was raping her, I could hear him raping her, but she kept begging them to leave me alone. And she must have seen that that wasn't going to happen, and she fought harder. I could hear the man hitting her, yelling at her to shut up. It didn't seem real, even when he was raping me it didn't seem like it could be real. Just an awful dream that went on and on and on.

"When they were finished, they stumbled back to their car and drove away. They just left us there. My mother was unconscious. He'd beaten her badly. I didn't know what to do. They said I went into shock, but I don't remember anything until I was in the hospital. My mother never regained consciousness. She was in a coma for two days, then she died."

"Anna, I don't know what to say to you. What can be said to you."

"I didn't tell you for your sympathy," she said. "She was twenty-seven, a year younger than I am now. It was a long time ago, but you don't forget. It never goes away completely. And I remember everything that happened that night, everything I did afterward—after I went to live with my grandparents. I did everything I could to hurt them, to hurt myself. That was my way of dealing with what had happened to me. I refused counseling,'' she told him coolly. ''I wasn't going to talk to some thin-faced, dried-up shrink. Instead I picked fights, looked for trouble, found it. I had indiscriminate sex, used drugs, ran away from home, and butted up against the social workers and the system.''

She picked up the jacket she'd stripped off earlier and folded it neatly now. ''I hated everyone, myself most of all. I was the one who had wanted to go to Philadelphia. I was the reason we were there. If I hadn't been with her, she would have gotten away.''

''No.'' He wanted to touch her but was afraid to. Not because she seemed fragile—she didn't. She seemed impossibly strong. ''No, you weren't to blame for any of it.''

''I felt the blame. And the more I felt it, the more I struck out at everyone and everything around me.''

''Sometimes it's all you can do,'' he murmured. ''Fight back, run wild, until you get it all out.''

''Sometimes there's nothing to fight, and nowhere to run. For three years I used what had happened that night to do whatever I chose.'' She looked at Cam again with a quick, ironic lift and fall of brow. ''I didn't choose well. I thought I was a pretty tough cookie when I ended up in juvie. But my caseworker was tougher. She pushed and she prodded and she hounded me. Because she refused to give up on me, she got through. And because my grandparents refused to give up on me, I got through.''

Carefully, she laid the jacket back over the arm of the sofa. ''It could have been different. I could have stayed just one more failed statistic in the system. But I didn't.''

He thought it was amazing that she had turned a horror into such strength. She was amazing for choosing work that would have to remind her daily of what had ripped her life apart. ''And you decided to pay it back. To go into the kind of work that had turned you around.''

''I knew I could help. And yes, I owed a debt, the same way you feel you owe one. I survived,'' she said, looking him dead in the eyes again, ''but survival isn't enough. It wasn't enough for me, or for you. And it won't be enough for Seth.''

''One thing at a time,'' he murmured. ''I want to know if they caught the bastards.''

''No.'' She'd long ago learned to accept and to live with that. ''It was weeks before I was coherent enough to make a statement. They never caught them. The system doesn't always work, but I've learned, and I believe, it does its best.''

''I've never thought so, and this doesn't change my mind.'' He started to reach out, hesitated, then tucked his hand into his pocket. ''I'm sorry I hurt you. That I said things that made you remember.''

''It's always there,'' she told him. ''You cope and you put it aside for long periods of time. It comes back now and again, because it never really goes away.''

''Did you have counseling?''

''Eventually, yes. I—'' She broke off, sighed. ''All right, I'm not saying counseling works miracles, Cam. I'm telling you it can be helpful, it can be healing. I needed it, and when I was finally ready to use that help, I was better.''

''Let's do this.'' He did touch her now, just laid a hand over hers on the counter. ''We'll leave it as an option. Let's see how things go . . . all around.''

''See how things go.'' She sighed, too tired to argue. Her head ached, and her body felt hollowed out and fragile. ''I agree with that, but I'll still recommend counseling in my report.''

''Don't forget the shoes,'' he said dryly and was vastly relieved when she laughed.

''I won't have to mention them, because I know you'll have him at the store by the weekend.''

"We could call it a compromise. I seem to be getting better at them lately."

"Then you must have been incredibly obstinate before."

"I think the word my parents used was 'bullheaded.' "

"It's comforting to be understood." She looked down at the hand covering hers. "If you asked to stay, I couldn't say no."

"I want to stay. I want you. But I can't ask tonight. Bad timing all around."

She understood how some men felt about a woman who'd been sexually attacked. Her stomach seized into hard knots. But it was best to know. "Is it because I was raped?"

He wouldn't let it be. He refused to allow what had happened to her affect what would happen between them. "It's because you couldn't say no tonight and tomorrow you might be sorry you didn't."

Surprised, she looked up at him again. "You're never quite what I expect you to be."

He wasn't quite what he expected either, not lately. "This thing here. Whatever it is, isn't quite what I expected it to be. How about a Saturday night date?"

"I have a date Saturday." Her lips curved slowly. The knots in her stomach had loosened. She hadn't even been aware of it. "But I'll break it."

"Seven o'clock." He leaned across the counter, kissed her, lingered over it, kissed her again. "I'm going to want to finish this."

"So am I."

"Well." He heaved a sigh and started for the door while he was sure he could. "That's going to make the drive home easier."

He paused, turned around to look at her. "You said you survived, Anna, but you didn't. You triumphed. Everything about you is a testament to courage and strength." When she stared at him, obviously stunned, he smiled a little. "You didn't get either from a social worker or a counselor. They just helped you figure out how to use it. I figure you got it from your mother. She must have been a hell of a woman."

"She was," Anna murmured, near tears again.

"So are you." Cam closed the door quietly behind him.

He decided he would take his time driving home. He had a lot to think about.

ELEVEN

PRETTY SATURDAY MORNINGS in the spring were not meant to be spent indoors or on crowded streets. To Ethan they were meant to be spent on the water. The idea of shopping—actually shopping—was very close to terrifying.

"Don't see why we all have to do this."

Because he'd gotten to the Jeep first, Cam rode in front. He turned his head to spare Ethan a glance. "Because we're all in this. The old Claremont barn's for rent, right? We need a place if we're going to build boats. We have to make the deal."

"Insanity," was all Phillip had to say as he turned down Market Street in St. Chris.

"Can't go into business if you don't have a place of business," Cam returned. He found that single fact inarguably logical. "So we take a look at it, make the deal with Claremont, and get started."

"Licenses, taxes, materials. Orders, for God's sake," Phillip began. "Tools, advertising, phone lines, fax lines, bookkeeping."

"So take care of it." Cam shrugged carelessly. "Soon

as we sign the lease and get the kid his shoes, you can do whatever comes next."

"*I* can do it?" Phillip complained at the same time Seth muttered he didn't need any damn shoes.

"Ethan got our first order, I found out about the building. You take care of the paperwork. And you're getting the damn shoes," he told Seth.

"I don't know how come you're the boss of everybody."

Cam could only manage a short, grim laugh. "Me either."

The Claremont building wasn't really a barn, but it was as big as one. In the mid-1700s it had been a tobacco warehouse. After the Revolutionary War, the British ships no longer sailed to St. Chris carrying their wide variety of goods. Businesses that had boomed went bankrupt.

The revival in the late 1800s grew directly from the bay. With improved methods of canning and packing the national market for oysters opened up and St. Chris once again prospered. And the old tobacco warehouse was refitted as a packinghouse.

Then the oyster beds played out, and the building became a glorified storage shed. Over the last fifty years it had been empty as often as it was filled.

From the outside it was unpretentious. Sun- and weather-faded brick, thumb-size holes in the mortar. A sagging old roof that was desperately in need of reshingling. What windows it could boast were small and stingy. Most were broken, all were filthy.

"Oh, yeah, this looks promising." Already disgusted, Phillip parked in the pitted lot at the side of the building.

"We need space," Cam reminded him. "It doesn't have to be pretty."

"Good thing, because this doesn't come close to pretty."

A bit more interested now, Ethan climbed out. He walked up to the closest window, used the bandanna from his back pocket to rub off most of the grime so he could peer through. "It's a good space. Got cargo doors at the back, a dock. Needs a little work."

"A little?" Phillip stared in over Ethan's shoulder. "Floor's rotting out. It's got to be infested with vermin. Probably termites and rodents."

"Probably be a good idea to mention that to Claremont," Ethan decided. "Keep the rent down." Hearing the tinkle of glass breaking, he saw that Cam had just put his elbow through an already cracked window. "Guess we're going inside."

"Breaking and entering." Phillip only shook his head. "That's a good start."

Cam flipped the pathetic lock on the window and shoved it up. "It was already broken. Give me a minute." He boosted himself inside, disappeared.

"Cool," Seth decided, and before a word could be spoken he climbed inside too.

"Nice example we're setting for him." Phillip ran a hand over his face and wished fervently he'd never given up smoking.

"Well, think of it this way. You could have picked the locks. But you didn't."

"Right. Listen, Ethan, we've got to think about this. There's no reason why you can't—we can't—build that first boat at your place. Once we start renting buildings, filing for tax numbers, we're committed."

"What's the worst that can happen? We waste some time and some money. I figure I've got enough of both." He heard the mix of Cam's and Seth's laughter echoing inside. "And maybe we'll have some fun while we're at it."

He started around to the front door, knowing Phillip would grumble but follow.

"I saw a rat," Seth said in pure delight when Cam shoved the front door open. "It was awesome."

"Rats." Phillip studied the dim space grimly before stepping inside. "Lovely."

"We'll have to get us a couple of she-cats," Ethan decided. "They're meaner than toms."

He looked up, scanning the high ceiling. Water damage showed clearly in the open rafters. There was a loft, but the steps leading up to it were broken. Rot, and very likely rats, had eaten at the scarred wood floor.

It would require a great deal of cleaning out and repair, but the space was generous. He began to allow himself to dream.

The smell of wood under the saw, the tang of tongue oil, the slap of hammer on nail, the glint of brass, the squeak of rigging. He could already see the way the sun would slant in through new, clean windows onto the skeleton of a sloop.

"Throw up some walls, I guess, for an office," Cam was saying. Seth dashed here and there, exploring and exclaiming. "We'll have to draw up plans or something."

"This place is a heap," Phillip pointed out.

"Yeah, so it'll come cheap. We put a couple thousand into fixing it up—"

"Better to have it bulldozed and start over."

"Phil, try to control that wild optimism." Cam turned to Ethan. "What do you think?"

"It'll do."

"It'll do what?" Phillip threw up his hands. "Fall down around our ears?" At that moment a spider—which Phillip estimated to be about the size of a Chihuahua—crawled over the toe of his shoe. "Get me a gun," he muttered.

Cam only laughed and slapped him on the back. "Let's go see Claremont."

STUART CLAREMONT WAS a little man with hard eyes and a dissatisfied mouth. The little chunks of St. Christopher that he owned were most often left to fall into disrepair. If his tenants complained loudly enough, he occasionally, and grudgingly, tinkered with plumbing or heat or patched a roof.

But he believed in saving his pennies for a rainy day. In Claremont's mind, it never rained quite hard enough to part with a cent.

Still, his house on Oyster Shell Lane was a showplace. As anyone in St. Chris could tell you, his wife, Nancy, could nag the ears off a turnip. And she ruled that roost.

The wall-to-wall carpet was thick and soft, the walls prettily papered. Fussy curtains were ruthlessly coordinated with fussy upholstery. Magazines lay in military lines over a gleaming cherry wood coffee table that matched gleaming cherry wood end tables that matched gleaming cherry wood occasional tables.

Nothing was out of place in the Claremont house. Each room looked like a picture from a magazine. Like the picture, Cam mused, and not at all like life.

"So, you're interested in the barn." With a stretched-out grin that hid his teeth, Claremont ushered them all into his den. It was decorated in English baronial style. The dark paneling was accented with hunting prints. There were deep-cushioned leather chairs in a port wine shade, a desk with brass fittings, and a brick fireplace converted to gas.

The big-screen television seemed both out of place and typical.

"Mildly," Phillip told him. It had been agreed on the drive over that Phillip would handle the negotiations. "We've just started to look around for space."

"Terrific old place." Claremont sat down behind his desk and gestured them to chairs. "Lots of history."

"I'm sure, but we're not interested in history in this case. There seems to be a lot of rot."

"A bit." Claremont waved that away with one short-fingered hand. "You live round here, what can you expect? You boys thinking of starting some business or other?"

"We're considering it. We're in the talking-about-it stages."

"Uh-huh." Claremont didn't think so, or the three of them wouldn't be sitting on the other side of his desk. As he considered just how much rent he could pry out of them for what he considered an irritating weight around his neck, he looked at Seth. "Well, we'll talk about it, then. Maybe the boy here wants to go outside."

"No, he doesn't," Cam said without a smile. "We're all talking about it."

"If that's the way you want it." So, Claremont thought, that's the way it was. He could hardly wait to tell Nancy. Why, he'd had a good, close-up look at the kid now, and a half-blind idiot could see Ray Quinn in those eyes. Saint Ray, he thought sourly. It looked like the mighty had fallen, yes sir. And he was going to enjoy letting people know what was what.

"I'm looking for a five-year lease," he told Phillip, correctly judging who would be handling the business end.

"We're looking for one year at this point, with an option for seven. Of course, we'd expect certain repairs to be completed before we took occupancy."

"Repairs." Claremont leaned back in his chair. "Hah. That place is solid as a rock."

"And we'd require termite inspection and treatment. Regular maintenance would, of course, be our responsibility."

"Ain't no damn bugs in that place."

"Well, then." Phillip smiled easily. "You'd only have to arrange for the inspection. What are you asking for in rent?"

Because he was annoyed, and because he'd always despised Ray Quinn, Claremont bumped up his figure. "Two thousand a month."

"Two—" Before Cam could choke out his pithy opinion, Phillip rose.

"No point in wasting your time, then. We appreciate you seeing us."

"Hold it, hold it." Claremont chuckled, fought off the little tug of panic at having a deal slip through his grasping fingers so quickly. "Didn't say that wasn't negotiable. After all, I knew your daddy . . ." He aimed that tight-lipped smile directly at Seth. "Knew him more than twenty-five years. I wouldn't feel right if I didn't give his . . . boys a little break."

"Fine." Phillip settled down again, resisted rubbing his hands together. He forgot all his objections to the overall plan in his delight in the art of the deal. "Let's negotiate."

"WHAT THE HELL HAVE I done?" Thirty minutes later, Phillip sat in his Jeep, methodically rapping his head against the steering wheel.

"A damn good job, I'd say." Ethan patted him on the shoulder. He'd reached the Jeep ahead of Cam this time and had taken winner's point in the front seat. "Cut his opening price in half, got him to agree to paying for most of the repairs if we do them ourselves, and confused him enough to have him go for the what-was-it—rent control clause if we take the seven-year option."

"The place is a dump. We're going to pay twelve thousand dollars a year—not including utilities and maintenance—for a pit."

"Yeah, but now it's our pit." Pleased, Cam stretched out his legs—or tried. "Pull that seat up some, Ethan, I'm jammed back here."

"Nope. Maybe you should drop me back by the place. I can start figuring things, and I can get a lift home later."

"We're going shopping," Cam reminded him.

"I don't need any damn shoes," Seth said again, but in reflex rather than annoyance.

"You're getting damn shoes, and you're getting a damn haircut while we're at it, and we're all going to the damn mall."

"I'd rather get hit with a brick than go to the mall on

a Saturday.'' Ethan hunched down in his seat, pulled the brim of his cap low over his eyes. He couldn't bear to think about it.

''When you start working in that death trap,'' Phillip told him, ''you'll likely be hit with a ton of them.''

''If I have to get a haircut, everybody's getting one.''

Cam glanced briefly at Seth's mutinous face. ''You think this is a democracy? Shit. Grab some reality, kid. You're ten.''

''You could use one.'' Phillip met Cam's eyes in the rearview mirror as he drove north out of St. Chris. ''Your hair's longer than his.''

''Shut up, Phil. Ethan, goddamn it, pull your seat up.''

''I hate the mall.'' In defiance, Ethan stretched his own legs out and tipped the back of his seat down a notch. ''It's full of people. Pete the barber's still got his place on Market Street.''

''Yeah, and everybody who walks out of it looks like Beaver Cleaver.'' Frustrated, Cam gave the back of Ethan's seat a solid kick.

''Keep your feet off my upholstery,'' Phillip warned. ''Or you'll walk to the damn mall.''

''Tell him to give me some room.''

''If I have to get shoes, I get to pick them out. You don't have any say in it.''

''If I'm paying for the shoes, you'll wear what I tell you and like it.''

''I'll buy the stinking shoes myself. I got twenty dollars.''

Cam snorted out a laugh. ''Try to get a grip on that reality again, pal. You can't buy decent socks for twenty these days.''

''You can if you don't have to have some fancy designer label on them,'' Ethan tossed in. ''This ain't Paris.''

''You haven't bought decent shoes in ten years,'' Cam threw back. ''And if you don't pull up that frigging seat, I'm going to—''

''Cut it out!'' Phillip exploded. ''Cut it out right now

or I swear I'm going to pull over and knock your heads together. Oh, my God." He took one hand off the wheel to drag it down his face. "I sound like Mom. Forget it. Just forget it. Kill each other. I'll dump the bodies in the mall parking lot and drive to Mexico. I'll learn how to weave mats and sell them on the beach at Cozumel. It'll be quiet, it'll be peaceful. I'll change my name to Raoul, and no one will know I was ever related to a bunch of fools."

Seth scratched his belly and turned to Cam. "Does he always talk like that?"

"Yeah, mostly. Sometimes he's going to be Pierre and live in a garret in Paris, but it's the same thing."

"Weird," was Seth's only comment. He pulled a piece of bubble gum out of his pocket, unwrapped it, and popped it into his mouth. Getting new shoes was turning into an adventure.

IT WOULD HAVE STOPPED at shoes if Cam hadn't noticed that the seat of Seth's jeans was nearly worn through. Not that he thought that was a big deal, he assured himself. But it was probably best, since they were there anyway, to pick up a couple of pairs of jeans.

He had no doubt that if Seth hadn't bitched so much about trying on jeans, he himself wouldn't have felt compelled to push on to shirts, to shorts, to a windbreaker. And somehow they'd ended up with three ball caps, an Orioles sweatshirt, and a glow-in-the-dark Frisbee.

When he tried to think back to exactly where he'd taken that first wrong turn, it all became a blur of clothes racks, complaining voices, and cash registers churning.

The dogs greeted them with wild and desperate enthusiasm the minute they pulled into the drive. This would have been endearing but for the fact that the pair of them reeked of dead fish.

With much cursing and shoving and threats, the humans escaped into the house, shutting the dogs with their hurt feelings outside. The phone was ringing.

"Somebody get that," Cam pleaded. "Seth, take this junk upstairs, then go give those stinking dogs a bath."

"Both of them?" The thought thrilled him, but he thought it best to complain. "How come I have to do it?"

"Because I said so." Oh, he hated falling back on something that lame, and that adult. "The hose is around back. God, I want a beer."

But because he lacked the energy even for that, he dropped into the closest chair and stared glassy-eyed at nothing. If he had to face that mall again in this life, he promised himself, he would just shoot himself in the head and be done with it.

"That was Anna," Phillip told him as he wandered back into the living room.

"Anna? Saturday night." He couldn't stop the groan. "I need a transfusion."

"She said to tell you she'd take care of dinner."

"Good, fine. I've got to pull myself together. The kid's yours and Ethan's for tonight."

"He's Ethan's," Phillip corrected. "I've got a date myself." But he sank into a chair and closed his eyes. "It's not even five o'clock and all I want to do is crawl into bed and oblivion. How do people do this?"

"He's got enough clothes to last him a year. If we only have to do it once a year, how bad can it be?"

Phillip opened one eye. "He's got spring and summer clothes. What happens when fall gets here? Sweaters, coats, boots. And he's bound to outgrow every damn thing we bought today."

"We can't allow that to happen. There must be a pill or something we can give him. And maybe he's got a coat already."

"He came pretty much with the clothes on his back. Dad didn't get a package deal this time either."

"Okay, we'll think about that later. Lots later." Cam

pressed his fingers to his eyes. "You saw the way Claremont looked at him, didn't you? That nasty little gleam in his beady little eyes."

"I saw it. He'll talk, and he'll say what he wants to say. Nothing we can do about it."

"You think the kid knows anything, one way or the other?"

"I don't know what Seth knows. I can't get a handle on him. But I'm going to look into investigators on Monday. Check on tracking down the mother."

"Asking for trouble."

"We've already got trouble. The only way to deal with it is to gather information. If it turns out that Seth's a Quinn by blood, then we deal with that."

"Dad wouldn't have hurt Mom that way. Marriage wasn't just a thing to them. It was *the* thing. And they were solid."

"If he'd slipped, he'd have told her." That Phillip firmly believed. "And they'd have worked it out. That part of their lives wasn't our business, and it wouldn't be our business now but for Seth."

"He wouldn't have slipped," Cam murmured, determined to believe it. "I'll tell you one thing I got from them. You get married, you make that promise, that's it. I figure that's why the three of us are still on the single side of life."

"Maybe. But we can't ignore the talk, the suspicions. And if the insurance company balks on paying off Dad's policy, it's going to put all four of us in a bind. Especially since we just signed a lease for that hellhole."

"We'll be okay. Luck's starting to move in our direction."

"Oh?" Phil asked as Cam rose. "How do you figure that?"

"Because I'm about to spend the evening with one of the sexiest women on the planet. And I intend to get very lucky." He glanced back as he started up the stairs. "Don't wait up, bro."

When he stepped into his bedroom, Cam heard the commotion from the backyard. He walked to the window and looked down on Seth and the dogs. Simon was sitting stoically while Seth soaped him down. Foolish raced in mad circles, barking in excitement and terror at the hose that was pouring out water where it had been carelessly tossed on the grass.

Of course, the kid was wearing his brand-new shoes, which were now soaking wet and muddy. He was laughing like a loon.

He hadn't known the boy could laugh like that, Cam realized as he kept watching. He hadn't known he could look like that, unreservedly happy and young and silly.

Simon stood up, gave a long, violent shake that sent water and soap flying. Backing up, Seth slipped in the wet grass and tumbled onto his back. He continued to howl with laughter as both dogs pounced on him. They wrestled over the water and mud and soap until the three of them were soaked and filthy.

Upstairs Cam just stood watching with a mile-wide grin on his face.

THE IMAGE POPPED IN his head when he headed down the hallway to Anna's apartment. He wanted to be able to tell her about it over dinner. He wanted to share it—and he thought it would certainly soften her every bit as much as a quiet meal in a candlelit restaurant.

The roses he'd picked up on the way weren't going to hurt either. He sniffed them himself. If he was any judge of the female mind and heart, he'd bet his full stake that Anna Spinelli had a weak spot for yellow roses.

Before he could knock on Anna's door, the door across the hall swung open. "Hello, there, you must be the new boyfriend."

"Hi, Mrs. Hardelman. We met a few days ago."

"No, we didn't. You met Sister."

"Oh." He smiled cautiously. She looked exactly like the woman who had popped out of that door before, even down to the pink chenille robe. "Well . . . how's it going?"

"You brought her flowers. She'll like that. My beaux used to bring me flowers, and my Henry, God rest his soul, brought me lilacs every May. You think lilacs next month, young man, if Anna lets you keep coming around. Most of them she scoots along, but maybe she'll keep you."

"Yeah." He managed to smile even as his heart stopped at the words "keep you." "Maybe." On impulse he pulled one of the roses out and gave it to her with a neat little flourish.

"Oh!" A girlish blush rose pink on her wrinkled face. "Oh, my goodness." Her eyes gleamed with pleasure as she sniffed it. "How lovely. How sweet. Why, if I were forty years younger, I'd fight Anna for you." She winked flirtatiously. "And I'd win."

"No contest." He flashed her a return wink and a grin. "Ah, say hi to . . . Sister."

"You have a nice time tonight. You go dancing," she added as she shut the door.

"Good idea." And chuckling to himself, Cam knocked.

When she answered, looking sexy enough to gobble up in three quick bites, he decided the dance should begin immediately. He snatched her up, whirled her around to the throbbing, elemental beat of classic Bruce Springsteen and the E Street Band. Then he dipped her as she laughed and stumbled.

"Well, hello." Enjoying the quick dizziness, she chuckled. "Let me up. You've got me off balance."

"That's just where I want you. Off balance." He lowered his mouth to hers in a molten kiss that melted every bone in her body. With her head spinning, she clutched at his shoulders.

"Door's still open," she managed and flailed out with a hand to slam it shut.

"Good thinking." He brought her up slowly, inch by inch, his mouth still nibbling busily on hers. "Your neighbor said I should take you dancing."

"Oh." She was surprised steam wasn't pumping out of her pores. "Is that what that was?"

"That was just a sample." He caught her bottom lip between his teeth, tugged, released. "Wanna tango, Anna?"

"I think we'd better sit this one out." But she pressed a hand to her heart to hold it in place as she eased out of his arms. "You brought me flowers." She buried her face in them as she took them from him. "Figured I was a sucker for rosebuds, did you?"

"Yeah."

"You're right." She laughed over the blooms. "I'll put them in water. You can pour us some wine. I've got it breathing on the counter. Glasses are right there."

"Okay. I—" He looked over, saw a shiny pot steaming on the stove, a platter of antipasto on the counter. "What's all this?"

"Dinner." She crouched down at a kitchen cupboard to locate a vase. "Didn't Phillip give you my message?"

"I thought when you told him you'd take care of it, you meant you had someplace you wanted to go and you'd make the reservations." He plucked a stuffed mushroom off the platter, sampled it, and sighed in pure sensory delight. "I didn't think you'd be cooking for me."

"I like to cook," she said easily as she filled a pale pink vase with water. "And I wanted to be alone with you."

He swallowed quickly. "Hard to argue with that. What are we having?"

"Linguini, with the famous Spinelli family red sauce."

She turned to take the glass of Merlot he'd poured for her. Her face was just a little flushed from the kitchen heat. The dress she'd chosen was the color of ripe peaches and molded her curves like a lover's hands. Her hair was down and curling madly, and her lips were painted nearly the same color as the wine she sipped.

Cam decided if they were to have more than a three-second conversation before he grabbed her again, he'd better stay on the opposite side of the counter.

"It smells incredible."

"It tastes better."

Her pulse was hammering everywhere at once. The way he'd looked at her, just that one long, intense, and measuring stare before he smiled, had brought out her need, a low and nagging ache of need, throbbing incessantly. On an impulse she reached back and turned the flame under the pot off. Keeping her eyes on Cam's, she walked around the counter.

"So do I," she told him. She set her glass aside, then took his, placed it on the counter. She shook her hair back, tipped her face up to his, smiled slowly. "Try me."

TWELVE

HIS BLOOD WAS ALREADY pounding, a hard, primal beat, as he took a step forward. He looked into her eyes, wanting to see every shift and flicker of emotion. "I'm going to want to do more than try. So be sure."

Sometimes, she thought, you had to go with your instincts, with your cravings. At that moment hers, all of hers, centered on him. "You wouldn't be here tonight if I wasn't."

With a slow curving of lips, she reached up and twined his hair around her finger. She could handle him. She was sure of it.

He put his hands on her hips. This was no pencil-slim model with a body like a boy, but a woman. And he wanted her. He smiled back. He could handle her. He was sure of it. "You like to gamble, Anna?"

"Now and then."

"Let's roll the dice."

He brought her against him in one hard jerk, one that made her breath catch and release an instant before his mouth was on hers. The kiss was quickly desperate, quickly ravenous, tongues tangling, teeth nipping. The little feral purrs that sounded in her throat went straight to his head like hot whiskey.

She tugged his shirt free of his waistband, then her hands shot under. Flesh and muscle, she needed to feel it. With a hum of pleasure she kneaded and scraped and stroked until that flesh seemed to burn under her fingers, and those muscles hardened like iron.

She wanted those muscles, that strength pitted against her own.

He fumbled at the back of her dress, searching for a zipper, and she laughed breathlessly with her mouth at his throat. "It doesn't have a zipper." She closed her teeth over his jaw and didn't bother to be gentle. "You have to . . . peel it off."

"Jesus." He tugged the snug, stretchy material off her shoulder and replaced it with teeth as the craving for the taste of flesh, her flesh, overwhelmed him.

They circled like dancers, though their pace outdistanced the dreamy strains of the Chopin prelude that had replaced the Boss. He toed off his shoes. She rushed open the buttons of his shirt. His head was swimming as they bumped into the bedroom door. She laughed again, but the sound slipped toward a moan when he yanked the dress down to her waist, when those eyes of smoked steel streaked down, when he lowered his head and began to devour the flesh above the black lace edge of her bra.

His tongue slid under, teasing and tasting until her knees were loose and her head full of flashing lights and colors. She'd known he could do this to her, take her to that teetering edge of reason and insanity. She'd wanted him to. More, she'd wanted to take him there with her.

The wanting was huge, ruthlessly keen, recklessly primitive. And for now, for both of them, it was all that mattered.

Murmuring mindlessly, she dragged off his shirt and dug her nails into the hard ridge of his shoulders. His chest was broad and firm, the flesh hot and smooth under her roaming hands. There were scars, under the shoulder, along the ribs. The body, she thought, of a risk-taker, of a man who played to win.

With a quick and expert flick of his fingers, he opened the front hook and let her breasts fill his greedy hands. She was magnificent. Golden skin and lush curves. He thought her body almost impossibly perfect. Yet it was erotically real, soft and firm and smooth and fragrant. He wanted to bury himself in her, but when she tugged at the button of his slacks, he shook his head.

"Uh-uh. I want you in bed." He brought her hands up until they circled his neck, brought his mouth down until the kiss was savage and stunning. "I want you under me, over me, wrapped around me."

She kicked off one shoe, balancing herself as they swayed toward the bed. "I want you inside me." Kicked off the other as they tumbled to the mattress.

She rolled over him first, straddling him. The light was nearly gone. Only a pale wash from the setting sun slipped through the windows. Shadows shifted. Her lips were hungry, restless, racing over his face, his throat. Though she had wanted men before, now there was a ferocious and primal greed sweeping through her that she'd never experienced. She would take him, was all she could think, take what she wanted and ease this almost unbearable need.

When she arched back and her upper body was silhouetted in that fragile light, the breath clogged in his lungs. He wanted with an urgency he couldn't remember feeling for anything or anyone else. The desire to take, to possess, to own, surged violently in his already raging blood.

He reared up, gripping her hair in one hand, yanking her head back to expose that long column of throat to his mouth. He could have anything with her. Would have everything.

He was rougher than he meant to be as he pushed her back on the bed. His breath was already heaving as he locked his hands with hers. Her eyes were dark and gleaming—the kind of eyes, he thought, for a man to drown in.

Her hair a tangled mass of black silk against the deep bronze of the spread. The scent of her was more than a provocative invitation. It was a smoldering demand.

Take me, it seemed to say. If you dare.

"I could eat you alive," he murmured and once more crushed his mouth to hers.

He held her down, knowing that if she wrestled free it would be over too soon. Fast, God, yes, he wanted fast, but he didn't want it to end. He thought he could live his life right here in this bed with Anna's quivering body under his.

Her hands flexed under his, her body arched when he drew the tip of her breast into his mouth. He could feel her heartbeat stumble as he used teeth, tongue, lips to taste, to pleasure them both.

When he'd filled himself on her, fed himself on her, he released her hands to touch, and be touched.

They rolled over the bed, groping, tugging at the clothes that remained between them. Their breath was quick and labored, punctuated by half gasps and low moans that spoke of turbulent thrills and dark delights. Sensation slid over sensation, building trembling layers toward delirium. She shuddered under his hands, nearly wept, as each new lash of pleasure whipped through her, each sharp and separate.

She fought to bring him the same barbed and edgy ache.

His hand closed over her, and she was hot and wet and ready. Her body arched, her nails bit into his back as her system exploded to peak.

Then they went mad.

She would remember only a battle for more. And more. Still more. Wild animal sex, a craving to mate. Seeking hands slid off damp flesh, hungry mouth sought hungry mouth. She came again, and her cry of release was a half sob of both triumph and helplessness.

The light was gone, but he could still see her. The glint of those dark eyes, the generous shape of that beautiful mouth. The blood roared in his head, in his heart, in his loins. He could think only *now* and drove himself hard and deep inside her.

His vision grayed, his mind reeled. They remained poised for a shivering moment, joined, mated. He wasn't even aware that his hands sought hers, that their fingers locked into fists.

Then they began to move, a race now full of speed and urgency. There was the good, healthy sound of damp flesh slapping against damp flesh. Their gazes met and held. He watched her eyes go blind and opaque as she crested, he heard the moan tear from her lips an instant before he closed his over hers to swallow the sound.

Her hips pumped like pistons, urging him on, driving him closer to his own jagged brink. He hammered himself into her, holding onto the edge by his fingertips. Watching her, watching her while the need for release clawed viciously at his gut. Then her body went taut, a drawn bow of shock and pleasure.

It was her scream he swallowed as he let himself fall.

HE COULDN'T POSSIBLY move. Cam was certain that if someone held a gun to his head at that moment, he would simply lie there and take the bullet. At least he'd die a satisfied man.

He couldn't think of a better place to be than stretched out over Anna's curvy body, with his face buried in her hair. And if he stayed there long enough, he might get his second wind.

The music had changed again. When his mind cleared enough for him to tune in to it, he recognized Paul Simon's clever twists of lyrics and melody. He nearly drifted off as he was invited to call the singer Al.

"If you fall asleep on top of me, I'm going to have to hurt you."

He drummed up the energy to smile. "I'm not going to sleep. I'm thinking about making love to you again."

"Oh." She stroked her hands down his back to his hips. "Are you?"

"Yeah. Just give me a couple of minutes."

"I'd be glad to. If I could breathe."

"Oh." Lazily he propped himself on his elbows and looked down at her. "Sorry."

She only grinned. "No, you're not. You're smug. But so am I, so that's okay."

"It was great sex."

"It was great sex," she agreed. "Now I'm going to finish dinner. We'll need fuel if we're going to try that again."

Both delighted and baffled, he shook his head. "You're a fascinating woman, Anna. No games, no pretenses. Looking the way you do, you could have men jumping through hoops."

She gave him a little shove so she could wiggle free. "What makes you think I haven't? You're exactly where I wanted you, aren't you?" Smiling, she rose and walked naked to the closet.

"That's a hell of a body you've got there, Miz Spinelli."

She glanced over her shoulder as she wrapped herself in a short red robe. "Same to you, Quinn."

She headed out to the kitchen, humming to herself as she turned the heat back on under the sauce, filled a pot with water for the pasta. Lord, it was lovely, she thought, to feel so loose, so limber, so liberated. However reckless it might be for her to take Cameron Quinn as a lover, the results were worth every risk.

He'd made her aware of every inch of her body, and every inch of his. He made her feel painfully alive. And best of all, she mused as she took out the bread she wanted to toast lightly, he seemed to understand her.

It was one thing to be wanted by a man, to be satisfied by a man. But it warmed her heart to be liked by the man who desired her.

She turned and picked up her wine just as Cam came

out of the bedroom. He'd pulled on his slacks but hadn't bothered to hook them. Anna sipped slowly while she studied him over the rim of her glass. Broad shoulders, hard chest, the waist that tapered to narrow hips and long legs. Oh, yes, he had a terrific body.

And for now it was all hers.

She lifted a pepper from the tray and held it up to his lips.

"It's got bite," Cam said as the heat filled his mouth.

"Um-hmm. I like . . . bite." She picked up his wine and handed it to him. "Hungry?"

"As a matter of fact."

"It won't be long." And because she recognized the look in his eye, she slipped around the counter to stir her sauce. "The water's nearly on the boil."

"You know what they say about a watched pot," he began and started around the counter after her. It was the sketch on the refrigerator that distracted him from his half-formed plan to wrestle her to the kitchen floor. "Hey, that looks just like Foolish."

"It is Foolish. Seth drew it."

"Get out!" He hooked a thumb in his pocket as he took a closer study. "Really? It's damn good, isn't it? I didn't know the kid could draw."

"You would, if you spent more time with him."

"I spend time with him every day," Cam muttered. "He doesn't tell me dick." Cam didn't know where the vague annoyance had come from, but he didn't care for it. "How'd you get this out of him?"

"I asked," she said simply, and slid linguini into the boiling water.

Cam shifted on his feet. "Look, I'm doing the best I can with the kid."

"I didn't say you weren't. I just think you'll do better—with a little more practice and a little more effort."

She pushed her hair back. She hadn't meant to get into this. Her relationship with Cam was supposed to have two separate compartments, without their contents getting mixed up together. ''You're doing a good job. I mean that. But you've got a long way to go, Cam, in gaining his trust, his affection. Giving your own. He's an obligation you're fulfilling, and that's admirable. But he's also a young boy. He needs love. You have feelings for him. I've seen them.'' She smiled over at him. ''You just don't know what to do with them yet.''

Cam scowled at the sketch. ''So now I'm supposed to talk to him about drawing dogs?''

Anna sighed, then turned to frame Cam's face in her hands. ''Just talk to him. You're a good man with a good heart. The rest will come.''

Annoyed again, he gripped her wrists. He couldn't have said why the quiet understanding in her voice, the amused compassion in her eyes made him nervous. ''I'm not a good man.'' His grip tightened just enough to make her eyes narrow. ''I'm selfish, impatient. I go for the thrills because that's what suits me. Paying your debts doesn't have anything to do with having a good heart. I'm a son of a bitch, and I like it that way.''

She merely arched a brow. ''It's always wise to know yourself.''

He felt a little flutter of panic in his throat and ignored it. ''I'll probably hurt you before we're done.''

Anna tilted her head. ''Maybe I'll hurt you first. Willing to risk it?''

He didn't know whether to laugh or swear and ended up pulling her into his arms for a smoldering kiss. ''Let's eat in bed.''

''That was the plan,'' she told him.

THE PASTA WAS COLD BY the time they got to it, but that didn't stop them from eating ravenously.

They sat cross-legged on her bed, knees bumping, and ate in the glow of the half dozen candles she'd lighted.

Cam shoveled in linguini and closed his eyes in pure sensory pleasure. "Goddamn, this is good."

Anna wound pasta expertly around her fork and bit. "You should taste my lasagna."

"I'm counting on it." Relaxed and lazy, he broke a piece of the crusty bread she'd put into a wicker basket and handed half to her.

Her bedroom, he'd noted, was different from the rest of the apartment. Here she hadn't gone for the practical, for the streamlined. The bed itself was a wide pool covered in soft rose sheets and a slick satin duvet in rich bronze. The headboard was a romantic arch of wrought iron, curvy and frivolous and plumped now with a dozen fat, colorful pillows.

The dresser he pegged as an antique, a heavy old piece of mahogany refinished to a rosy gleam. It was covered with pretty little bottles and bowls and a silver-backed brush. The mirror over it was a long oval.

There was a mahogany lady's vanity with a skirted stool and glinting brass handles. For some reason he'd always found that particular type of furniture incredibly sexy.

A copper urn was filled with tall, fussy flowers, the walls were crowded with art, and the windows framed in the same rich bronze as the spread.

This, he thought idly, was Anna's room. The rest of the apartment was still Miz Spinelli's. The practical and the sensual. Both suited her.

He reached over the side of the bed to the floor, where he'd put the bottle of wine. He topped off her glass.

"Trying to get me drunk?"

He flashed a grin at her. Her hair was tangled, the robe loose enough to have one shoulder curving free. Her big dark eyes seemed to laugh at both of them. "Don't have to—but it might be interesting anyway."

She smiled, shrugged and drank. "Why don't you tell me about your day?"

"Today?" He gave a mock shudder. "Nightmare time."

"Really." She twirled more pasta, fed it to him. "Details."

"Shopping. Shoes. Hideous." When she laughed, he felt the smile split his face. God, she had a great laugh. "I made Ethan and Phillip go with me. No way I was facing that alone. We had to practically handcuff the kid to get him to go. You'd think I was fitting him for a straitjacket instead of new high-tops."

"Too many men don't appreciate the joys, challenges, and nuances of shopping."

"Next time, you go. Anyway, I had my eye on this building on the waterfront. We checked it out before we headed to the mall. It'll do the job."

"What job?"

"The business. Boat building."

Anna set her fork down. "You're serious about that."

"Dead serious. The place'll do. It needs some work, but the rent's in line—especially since we're strong-arming the landlord into paying for most of the basic repairs."

"You want to build boats."

"It'll get me out of the house, keep me off the streets." When she didn't smile back, he shrugged his shoulder. "Yeah, I think I could get into it. For now, anyway. We'll do this one for the client Ethan's already got lined up, see how it goes from there."

"I take it you signed a lease."

"That's right. Why putz around?"

"Some might say caution, consideration, details."

"I leave the caution and consideration to Ethan, the details to Phillip. If it doesn't work, all we've lost is a few bucks and a little time."

Odd how that prickly temper suited him, she mused. It went so well with those dark, damn-it-all looks. "And if it does work," she added. "Have you thought of that?"

"What do you mean?"

"If it works, you'll have taken on another commitment. It's getting to be a habit." She laughed now, at the expression of annoyance and surprise on his face. "It's going to be fun to ask you how you feel about all this in six months or so.'' She leaned forward and kissed him lightly. ''How about some dessert?''

The nagging worry the word ''commitment'' had brought on faded back as her lips rubbed over his. ''Whatcha got?''

''Cannoli,'' she told him as she set their plates on the floor.

''Sounds good.''

''Or—'' Watching him, she unbelted her robe, let it slide off her shoulders. ''Me.''

''Sounds better,'' he said and let her pull him to her.

IT WAS JUST AFTER THREE when Seth heard the car pull into the drive. He'd been asleep but having dreams. Bad ones, where he was back in one of those smelly rooms where the walls were stained and thinner than his drawing paper, and every sound carried through them.

Sex noises—grunts and groans and creaking mattresses—his mother's nasty laugh when she was coked up. It made him sweat, having those dreams. Sometimes she would come in to where he was trying to find comfort and sleep on the musty sofa. If her mood was good, she would laugh and give him smothering hugs, waking him out of a fitful sleep into the smells and sounds of the world she'd dragged him into.

If her mood was bad, she would curse and slap and often end up sitting on the floor crying wildly.

Either way made for one more miserable night.

But worse, hundreds of times worse, was when one of the men she'd taken to bed slipped out, crept across the cramped room, and touched him.

It hadn't happened often, and waking up screaming and swinging drove them off. But the fear lived inside him like a red-hot demon. He'd learned to sleep on the floor behind the sofa whenever she had a man around.

But this time Seth hadn't waked from nightmare to worse. He fought his way out of the sweaty dream and found himself on clean sheets, with a snoring puppy curled beside him.

He cried a little, because he was alone and there was no one to see. Then he snuggled closer to Foolish, comforted by the soft fur and steady heartbeat. The sound of the car coming in stopped him from drifting back to sleep.

His first thought was *cops!* They'd come to get him, to haul him away. Then he told himself, even as his heart jumped up to pound in his throat, that he was being a baby. Still, he crept out of bed, padded silently to the window to look.

He had a hiding place picked out if one was needed.

It was the 'Vette. Seth told himself he'd have recognized the sound of its engine if he hadn't been half asleep. He saw Cam get out, heard the soft, cheerful whistling.

Been out poking at some woman, Seth decided with a sneer. Grown-ups were so predictable. When he remembered that Cam was supposed to have dinner with the social worker that night, his eyes went wide, his jaw dropped.

Man, oh, man, he thought. Cam was bouncing on Miss Spinelli. That was so . . . weird. So weird, he realized he didn't know how he felt about it. One thing for sure, he realized as Cam whistled his way to the door—Cam felt just fine and dandy about it.

When he heard the front door close, he snuck to his own bedroom door. He wanted to get a quick peek, but at the sound of feet coming up the stairs he dived back into bed. Just in case.

The puppy whimpered, began to stir, and Seth slammed his eyes shut as the door opened.

When the footsteps came slowly, quietly toward the bed, his heart began to pound in his chest. What would he do? he thought in a sick panic. God, what could he do? Foolish's tail began to thump on the bed as Seth cringed and waited for the worst.

"Guess you think this is a pretty good deal, lazing around half the day, getting your belly filled, having a nice soft bed at night," Cam murmured.

His voice was slightly slurred from lack of sleep, but to Seth it sounded like drugs or liquor. He struggled to keep his breathing slow and steady while his heartbeat pounded like a jackhammer against his ribs, in his head.

"Yeah, you fell into roses, didn't you? And didn't have to do a thing to earn it. Goofy-looking dog." Seth nearly blinked, realizing Cam was speaking to Foolish and not him. "It'll be his problem, won't it, when you're grown and take up more of the bed than he does."

Cautious, Seth slitted his eyes open just enough so he could see through his lashes. He saw Cam's hand come down, give Foolish a quick, careless stroke. Then the tangled sheets and blanket came up, smoothed over his shoulders. That same hand gave Seth's head a quick and careless stroke.

When the door closed again, Seth waited thirty full seconds before daring to open his eyes. He looked straight into Foolish's face. The pup seemed to be grinning at him as though they'd gotten away with something. Grinning back, Seth draped an arm around the pup's pudgy body.

"I guess it is a pretty good deal, huh, boy?" he whispered.

In agreement, Foolish licked Seth's face, then yawning hugely, settled down to sleep again.

This time, when Seth dropped off to sleep, there were no sweaty dreams to haunt him.

THIRTEEN

"YOU'RE AWFULLY DAMN happy these days."

Cam acknowledged Phillip's pithy comment with a shrug and kept on whistling while he worked. They were making decent progress on what Cam jokingly thought of as their shipyard. It was hard, sweaty, filthy work.

And every time Cam compared it to laundry detail, he praised God.

Though what windows weren't broken were open wide, the air still carried a vague chemical scent. At Phillip's insistence they'd bought a batch of insect bombs and blasted the place with killing fog. When it cleared, the death toll was heavy. It took nearly a half a day just to clear out the corpses.

Replacement windows were slated to be delivered that day. Claremont had bitched bitterly about the expense—despite the deal he got on them because his brother-in-law managed the lumber company in Cambridge and had sold them to him at cost. He'd been only slightly mollified that the Quinns would rip out the old windows and install the new ones, saving him from hiring laborers.

If the fact that the improvements to the building would

spike the potential resale value pleased him, he kept that small delight to himself.

They'd pried or punched out rotted boards and hauled them outside to a steadily growing pile of discards. The metal banister of the stairs leading up to the overhead loft was rusted through, so they yanked it out. Claremont was able to finesse the proper permits, so they were tossing up a couple of walls to close in what would be a bathroom.

Because Cam considered this kind of work a hobby, one he enjoyed, and he came home most nights to a clean house and had a pretty woman willing to tango with him whenever time and circumstances permitted, he figured he had a right to be happy.

Hell, the kid had even been doing his homework—most of the time. He had turned in the much-despised essay and was halfway through his probation without incident.

Cam figured his luck had been running hot and strong for the past couple of weeks.

As far as Phillip was concerned, it had been the worst two weeks of his life. He had barely spent any time in his apartment, had lost his favorite pair of Magli loafers to the gnawing puppy teeth of Foolish, hadn't seen the inside of a single four-star restaurant, and hadn't so much as sniffed a woman.

Unless he counted Mrs. Wilson at the supermarket, and he damn well didn't.

Instead, he was handling and juggling and bouncing details that no one else so much as thought about, getting blisters on his hands swinging a hammer, and spending his evenings wondering what had happened to life as he'd known it.

The fact that he knew Cam was getting regular sex fried the hell out of him.

When the board he lifted gifted him with a fat splinter in the thumb, he swore ripely. "Why the hell didn't we hire carpenters?"

"Because, as keeper of our magic funds, you pointed out it's cheaper this way. And Claremont gave us the first month's rent free if we did it ourselves.'' Cam took the board himself, placed it, and began to hammer in the next stud. ''You said it was a good deal.''

Gritting his teeth, he yanked out the splinter, sucked on his aching thumb. ''I was insane at the time.''

Phillip stepped back, hands on his hips above his tool belt, and surveyed the area. It was filthy. Dirt, sawdust, piles of refuse, stacks of lumber, sheets of plastic. This was not his life, he thought again, as the sound of Cam's hammer thudded in time with the gritty rock beat of Bob Seger that pumped out of the radio.

''I must have been insane. This place is a dump.''

''Yep.''

''Setting up this idiotic business is going to devour our capital.''

''No doubt about it.''

''We'll go under in six months.''

''Could be.''

Phillip scowled and reached down for the jug of iced tea. ''You don't give a good damn.''

''If it bombs, it bombs.'' Cam tucked his hammer back in his belt, took out his measuring tape. ''We're no worse off. But if it makes it, if it just bumps along for a while, we'll have what we need.''

''Which is?''

Cam picked up the next board, eyeballed it along its length, then set it over the sawhorses. ''A business—which Ethan can run after the dust settles. He gets himself a couple of part-timers—off-season watermen—he builds three or four boats a year to keep it afloat.''

He paused long enough to mark the board, run the saw. Dust flew and the noise was awesome. Cam set the power saw aside, hefted the board into place. ''I'll give him a hand now and then, you'll keep track of the money end. But it ought to give us room to move some. I can get in a few races a year, you can get back to bilking the consumer with jazzy ads.'' He pulled out his hammer. ''Everybody's happy.''

Phillip cocked his head, scratched his chin. "You've been thinking."

"That's right."

"When do you figure this slide back to normality's going to happen?"

Cam swiped at the sweat on his forehead with the back of his hand. "The faster we get this place up and running, the faster we get the first boat done."

"Which explains why you've been busting your ass, and mine. Then what?"

"I've got enough contacts to line up a second job, even a third." He thought of Tod Bardette—the bastard—even now priming a crew for the One-Ton Cup. Yeah, he could finesse Bardette into a boat by Quinn. And there were others, plenty of others, who would pay and pay well. "I figure my main contribution to this enterprise is contacts. Six months," he said. "We can handle six months."

"I'm going back to work Monday," Phillip told him, braced for a fight. "I've got to. I'm flexing time so I'll only be in Baltimore Monday through Thursday. It's the best I can do."

Cam considered. "Okay. I don't have a problem with that. But you'll be busting ass on weekends."

For six months, Phillip thought. More or less. Then he hissed out a breath. "One factor you haven't worked into your plan. Seth."

"What about him? He'll be here. He's got a place to live. I'm going to use the house as a base."

"And when you're off breaking records and female hearts in Monte Carlo?"

Cam scowled and rapped the hammer harder than necessary on the head of the nail. "He doesn't want to be in my damn pocket all the time. You guys'll be around when I'm not. The kid's going to be taken care of."

"And if the mother comes back? They haven't been able to find her. Nothing. I'd feel better if we knew where she is and what she's up to."

"I'm not thinking about her. She's out of the picture."

Has to be, Cam insisted, remembering the look of pasty-faced terror on Seth's face. "She's not going to mess with us."

"I'd like to know where she is," Phillip said again. "And what the hell she was to Dad."

CAM PUT IT OUT OF HIS mind. His way of handling loose ends was to knot them up together and forget about them. The immediate problem, as he saw it, was getting the building in shape, ordering equipment, tools, supplies. If the business was a means to an end, it had to begin.

Every day he worked on the building was one day closer to escape. Every dollar he poured into supplies and equipment was an investment in the future. His future.

He was keeping his promise, he told himself. His way.

With the sun beating down on his back and a faded blue bandanna tied around his head, he ripped broken shingles off the roof. Ethan and Phillip were working behind him, replacing shingles. Seth appeared to be having a fine time winging the discarded ones from roof to ground, and a satisfying pile was forming below.

It was a cool place to be as far as Seth was concerned. Up on the roof with the sun beating down and the occasional gull flying by. You could see just about everything from up here. The town, with its straight streets and square yards. The old trees popping up out of the grass. The flowers were okay, too. From up here they were just blobs and dots of color. Someone was mowing, and the sound carried up to him like a distant hum.

He could see the waterfront, with the boats at dock or cruising along the water. A couple of kids were sailing a little skiff with blue sails, and because he envied them, he looked away toward the docks.

There were people, shopping or strolling or eating lunch at one of the outdoor tables with umbrellas. Tourists were watching the show the crab pickers put on. He liked to sneer at the tourists; when he did, he didn't envy the boys in their neat little boat quite so much.

He wished he had the binoculars Ray had given him so he could see even farther. He wished he could sit up here sometime with his sketchbook.

Everything looked so . . . clean from up here. The sky and water both so blue, the grass and leaves so green. You could smell the water if you took a good sniff—and maybe that was hot dogs grilling.

The scent made his stomach growl with hunger. He shifted a little and looked at Cam out of the corner of his eye. Man, he wished he had muscles like that. With muscles like that you could do anything and nobody could stop you. If a guy had muscles like that he would never have to be afraid of anything, anyone, ever in his whole life.

Testing his own biceps with his finger, he was far from satisfied. He thought maybe if he got to use tools, he could harden them up.

"You said I could pull some of them off," Seth reminded him.

"Later."

"You said later before."

"I'm saying it again." It was hot, nasty, tedious work, and Cam wanted it over as much as he wanted to breathe. He'd already sweated through his T-shirt and pulled it off. His back gleamed damp and his throat was desert-dry. He pried off another square and watched Seth send it soaring. "You throwing them in the same place?"

"That's what you said to do."

He eyed the boy. Seth's hair stuck out from under an Orioles fielder's cap that Cam had ended up buying him when they went to a game the week before. Now that he thought of it, Cam didn't think he'd seen the kid without the cap since he got it.

The ball game had been an impulse, he thought now, just one of those things. But it had given him a sharp tug to see the way Seth's eyes had gone huge at the sight of

Camden Yards. How he'd sat there, a hot dog clutched and forgotten in his hand as he watched every movement on the field.

And it had made Cam laugh when Seth's serious and firm opinion had been "it looks like shit on TV compared to this."

He watched Seth send another shingle flying and wondered if he should teach the kid how to field a ball. Instantly, the fact that he had had the thought irritated him. "You're not looking where you're throwing them."

"I know where they're going. If you don't like how I do it, you can throw them down yourself. You said I could pull some off."

Not worth it, Cam told himself. Not worth the effort to argue. "Fine, you want to rip shingles off the damn roof. Here, look, see how I'm doing this? You use the claw of the hammer and—"

"I've been watching you for an hour. It doesn't take brains to rip off shingles."

"Fine," Cam said between his teeth. "You do it." He shoved the hammer into Seth's eager hand. "I'm going down. I need a drink."

Cam went nimbly down the ladder, trying to assure himself that all ten-year-old boys were snotty assholes. And the more shingles the kid ripped free, the fewer there would be for him to do himself. If he survived the day, he had another Saturday night date with Anna. He wanted to make the most of it.

Now there was a woman, he thought as he grabbed the jug of ice water and glugged some down. Damn near the perfect woman. Though it occasionally gave him an uneasy feeling in the gut to think of her that way, it was tough to find the flaws.

Beautiful, smart, sexy. That great laugh she let loose so often. Those gorgeous, warm, understanding eyes. The wild spirit of adventure tucked into the practical public servant suits.

And she could cook.

He chuckled to himself and pulled out another bandanna to mop his face.

Why, if he was the settling-down type, he would snatch her right up. Get a ring on her finger, say the I-do's, and tuck her into his house—his bed—on a permanent basis.

Hot meals, hot sex.

Conversation. Laughter. Slow smiles to wake you up in the morning. Shared looks that said more than dozens of words.

When he caught himself staring into space, the jug dangling from his fingers and a stupid grin on his face, he shook himself hard. Let out a long breath.

The sun had baked his brain, he decided. Permanent wasn't his style. Never had been. And marriage—the word made him shudder—was for other people.

Thank God Anna wasn't looking for any more than he was. A nice, easy, no strings, no frills relationship suited them both.

To ensure that his mind didn't go hot again, he dumped frigid water over his head. Six months, he promised himself as he started back outside. Six months and he would start easing himself back into his own world. Competition, speed, glittery parties, and women who were only looking for a fast ride.

When the thought of it fell flat, when the image of it all left him hollow inside, he swore. It was what he wanted, goddamn it. What he knew. Where he belonged. He wasn't cut out to spend his life building boats for other people to sail, raising a kid and worrying about matching socks.

Sure, maybe he'd teach the kid how to field a grounder or a pop fly, but that was no big deal. Maybe Anna Spinelli was firmly hooked in his brain, but that didn't have to be a big deal either.

He needed room, he needed freedom.

He needed to race.

His thoughts were boiling as he stepped outside. The aluminum extension ladder nearly crashed on top of him.

His hot oath and the muffled scream overhead sounded as one.

When he looked up, his heart simply stopped beating.

Seth dangled from his fingertips from the broken frame of a window twenty feet above. In the space of a trio of heartbeats, Cam saw the pattern on the bottom of the new high-tops, the dangling laces, the droopy socks. Before he could draw the first breath, both Ethan and Phillip were leaning over the roof and struggling to reach Seth.

"You hold on," Ethan shouted. "Hear me?"

"Can't." Panic made Seth's voice thin, and very, very young. "Slipping."

"We can't reach him from here." Phillip's voice was deadly calm, but his eyes as they stared down at Cam's were bright with fear. "Put the ladder up. Quick."

He made the decision in seconds, though it seemed like the rest of his life. Cam gauged the time it would take to haul the ladder into place, to climb up or climb down to where Seth hung. Too long, was all he could think, and he moved to stand directly under Seth.

"You let go, Seth. Just let go. I'll catch you."

"No. I can't." His fingers were raw and bleeding and nearly gave way as he shook his head fiercely. Panic skittered up his spine like hungry mice. "You won't."

"Yes, you can. I will. Close your eyes and just let go. I'm here." Cam planted his legs apart and ignored his own trembling heart. "I'm right here."

"I'm scared."

"Me, too. Let go. Do it!" he said so sharply that Seth's fingers released on instinct.

It seemed as though he fell forever, endlessly. Sweat poured down Cam's face. Air refused to come into Seth's lungs. Though his eyes stung from sun and salt, Cam never took them off the boy. His arms were there, braced and ready as Seth tumbled into them.

Cam heard the explosion of breath, his, Seth's, he didn't know which as they both fell heavily. Cam used his body to cushion the boy, took the hard ground on his bare back.

But in an instant, he was up on his knees. He spun Seth around and plastered the boy against him.

"Christ! Oh, Christ!"

"Is he all right?" Ethan shouted from above.

"Yeah. I don't know. Are you okay?"

"I think. Yeah." He was shaking badly, his teeth chattering, and when Cam loosened his hold enough to look into his face he saw deathly pale skin and huge, glassy eyes. He sat down on the ground, pulled Seth into his lap, and pushed the boy's head between his knees.

"Just shaken up," he called to his brothers.

"Nice catch." Phillip sat back on the roof, rubbed his hands over his clammy face, and figured his heart rate would get back to normal in another year or two. "Jesus, Ethan, what was I thinking of, sending that kid down for water?"

"Not your fault." Hoping to steady both of them, Ethan squeezed Phillip's shoulder. "Nobody's fault. He's okay. We're okay." He looked down again, intended to tell Cam to get the ladder. But what he saw was the man holding on to the boy, his cheek pressed to the top of the boy's hair.

The ladder could wait.

"Just breathe," Cam ordered. "Just take it slow. You got the wind knocked out of you, that's all."

"I'm okay." But he kept his eyes closed, terrified that he would throw up now and totally humiliate himself. His fingers were burning, but he was afraid to look. When it finally sank in that he was being held, and held close, it wasn't sick panic, it wasn't shuddering disgust that raced through him.

It was gratitude, and a sweet, almost desperate relief.

Cam closed his eyes as well. And it was a mistake. He saw Seth falling again, falling and falling, but this time he wasn't quick enough, or strong enough. He wasn't there at all.

Fear bent under fury. He whirled Seth around until their faces were close and shook him. "What the hell were you doing? What were you thinking of? You idiot, you could have broken your neck."

"I was just—" His voice hitched, mortifying him. "I was only—I didn't know. My shoe was untied. I must've stepped wrong. I only . . ."

But the rest of the words were muffled against Cam's hard, sweaty chest as he was pulled close again. He could feel the rapid beat of Cam's heart, hear it thunder under his ear. And he closed his eyes again. And slowly, testingly, his arms crept around to hold.

"It's all right," Cam murmured, ordering himself to calm down. "Wasn't your fault. You scared the shit out of me."

His hands were trembling, Cam realized. He was making a fool of himself. Deliberately, he pulled Seth back and grinned. "So, how was the ride?"

Seth managed a weak smile. "I guess it was pretty cool."

"Death-defying." Because they were both feeling awkward, they eased back slowly, warily. "Good thing you're puny yet. You had any weight on you, you might have knocked me out cold."

"Shit," Seth said, because he couldn't think of anything else.

"Messed up your hands some." Cam frowned consideringly at the bloody, torn fingertips. "Guess we better get the rest of the crew down and fix you up."

"It's nothing." It hurt like fire.

"No use having you bleed to death." Because his hands still weren't quite steady, Cam made quick work of lifting the ladder into place. "Go on in and get the first aid kit," he ordered. "Looks like Phil was on the mark when he made us buy the damn thing. We might as well use it on you."

After he watched Seth go inside, out of sight, Cam simply lowered his brow to the side of the ladder. His stomach continued to jump, and a headache he hadn't been aware of until that instant roared through his temples like a freight train.

"You okay?" Ethan put a hand on Cam's shoulder the minute he was on the ground.

"I've got no spit. My spit's dried clean up. Never been so fucking scared."

"That makes three of us." Phillip glanced around. Because his knees were still wobbly, he sat on one of the rungs of the ladder. "How bad are his hands? Does he need a doctor?"

"Fingers are ripped up some. It's not too bad." At the sound of a car pulling into the loose-gravel lot, he turned to see who it was. And his jittery stomach sank. "Oh, perfect. Sexy social worker at three o'clock."

"What's she doing here?" Ethan pulled his cap down lower on his head. He hated having women around when he was sweaty.

"I don't know. We have a date tonight, but not until seven. She's going to have some damn female thing to say about us having the kid up there in the first place."

"So we won't tell her," Phillip murmured even as he shot Anna a charming, welcoming smile. "Well, this brightens the day. Nothing better than to see a beautiful woman after a tough morning's work."

"Gentlemen." She only smiled when Phillip took her hand and brought it to his lips. Amusement rippled through her. Three men, three brothers, three reactions. Phillip's polished welcome, Ethan's vaguely embarrassed nod, and Cam's irritated scowl.

And there was no doubt each and every one of them looked outrageously male and appealing in sweat and tool belts.

"I hope you don't mind. I wanted to see the building, and I did come bearing gifts. There's a picnic hamper in my car—men food," she added. "For anyone who'd like a lunch break."

"That was nice of you. Appreciate it." Ethan shifted his feet. "I'll go fetch it out of your car."

"Thanks." She surveyed the building, tipped down her round-lensed wire-rimmed sunglasses, studied it again. All she could think was that she was glad she'd dressed casually for this impromptu visit, in roomy jeans and a T-shirt. There was no way to go in there, she imagined, and come out clean. "So this is it."

"The start of our empire," Phillip began, having just figured out that he could take her on a tour around the outside and give Cam enough time to clean Seth up—and shut him up—when the boy came out.

The color was back in his face—which was filthy with sweat, dirt, and the blood that he'd smeared on his cheeks from his fingers. His white Just Do It T-shirt was in the same condition. He carried the first aid kit like a banner.

Alarm shot into Anna's eyes. She was rushing toward Seth, taking him gently by the shoulders before either Cam or Phillip could think of a reasonable story. "Oh, honey, you're hurt. What happened?"

"Nothing," Cam began. "He just—"

"I fell off the roof," Seth piped up. He'd calmed down while he was inside and had gone from being weak-kneed to wildly proud.

"Fell off the—" Shocked to numbness, Anna instinctively began to check for broken bones. Seth stiffened, then squirmed, but she continued grimly until she was satisfied. "My God. What are you doing walking around?" She turned her head long enough to aim a furious glare at Cam. "Have you called an ambulance?"

"He doesn't need a damn ambulance. It's just like a woman to fall to pieces."

"Fall to pieces." Keeping a protective hand on Seth's shoulder, she whirled on them. "Fall to pieces! The three of you are standing around here like a herd of baboons. The child could have internal injuries. He's bleeding."

"Just my fingers." Seth held them out, admiring them. Man, was he going to be the hot topic in school come Monday! "I slipped off the ladder coming down, but I caught myself on the window frame up there." He pointed it out helpfully, while Anna's head spun from the height. "And Cam told me to let go and he'd catch me, and I did and he did."

"Damn kid won't say two words half the time," Cam muttered to Phillip. "The other half he won't shut the hell up. He's fine," he said, lifting his voice. "Just knocked the wind out of him."

She didn't bother to respond, only sent him one long, fulminating look before turning back to smile at Seth. "Why don't I take a look at your hands, honey? We'll clean them up and see if you need stitches." She lifted her chin, but the shaded glasses didn't quite conceal the heat in her eyes. "Then I'd like to speak with you, Cameron."

"I bet you would," he mumbled as she led Seth toward her car.

Seth found he didn't mind being babied a bit. It was a new experience to have a woman fuss over a little blood. Her hands were gentle, her voice soothing. And if his fingers throbbed and stung, it was a small price to pay for what now seemed a glorious adventure.

"It was a long way down," he told her.

"Yes, I know." Thinking of it only made the ball of anger in her stomach harden. "You must have been terrified."

"I was only scared for a minute." He bit the inside of his cheek so he wouldn't whimper as she carefully bandaged his wounds. "Some kids would've screamed like a girl and wet their pants."

He wasn't sure if he'd screamed or not—that part was a blur—but he'd checked his jeans and knew he was okay there. "And Cam, he was pissed off. You'd think I kicked the damn ladder out from under me on purpose."

Her head came up. "He yelled at you?"

He started to expand on that, but there was something about her eyes that made it hard to tell an out-and-out lie. "For a minute. Mostly he just got goofy about it. You'd think I'd had my arm whacked off the way he was carrying on, patting on me and stuff."

He shrugged, but remembered the warm glow in his gut at being held close, safe, tight. "Some guys, you know? They can't take a little blood."

Her smile softened, and she reached up to brush his hair back. "Yeah, I know. Well, you're in pretty good shape for a guy who likes to dive off roofs. Don't do it again, okay?"

"Once was enough."

"Glad to hear it. There's fried chicken in the hamper—unless they've eaten it all."

"Yeah. Man, I could eat a dozen pieces." He started to race off, then felt a tug on his conscience. It was another rare sensation, and it caused him to turn back and meet her eyes. "Cam said he'd catch me, and he did. He was cool."

Then he ran toward the building, shouting for Ethan to save him some damn chicken.

Anna only sighed. She sat there on the side of the passenger seat while she put the first aid kit back in order. When the shadow fell across her, she continued to tidy up. She could smell him, sweat, man, the faint undertones of the soap from his morning shower. She knew his scent so well now—and the way it would mix with her own—that she could have picked him out of a roomful of men had she been handcuffed and blindfolded.

And though it was certainly true that she'd been curious about the building, it was really only a handy excuse to drive over from Princess Anne to see him.

"I don't suppose there's any point in me telling you that boys Seth's age shouldn't be going up and down extension ladders unsupervised."

"I don't suppose there is."

"Or that boys his age are careless, often awkward, and clumsy."

"He's not clumsy," Cam said with some heat. "He's agile as a monkey. Of course," he added with a sneer in his voice, "the rest of us are baboons, so that fits."

She closed the first aid kit, rose, and handed it to him.

"Apparently," she agreed. "However, accidents happen, no matter how careful you are, no matter how hard you try to prevent them. That's why they're accidents."

She looked at his face. The irritation was still there, she noted—with her, with circumstances. And oh, that underlying anger that never seemed to fade completely away was very, very close to the surface.

"So," she said softly, "how many years of your life did that little event shave off?"

He let out a breath. "A couple of decades. But the kid handled himself."

He turned a little, to look back toward the building. It was then that Anna saw the smears of blood on his back. Smears, she realized after her heart's first leap, that had come from Seth's hands. The boy had been held, she thought. And the boy had held on.

Cam turned back, caught her smiling. "What?"

"Nothing. Well, since I'm here, and you're all eating my food, I think I'm entitled to a tour."

"How much of this business are you going to have to put in one of your reports?"

"I'm not on the clock," she told him, more sharply than she intended. "I thought I was coming to pay a visit to friends."

"I didn't mean it that way, Anna."

"Really?" She stepped around the car door and slammed it shut at her back. Damn it, she had come to see him, to be with him, not to fit in an unannounced home visit. "What I will put in my next report, unless I see something to the contrary, is that it's my opinion that Seth is bonding with his guardians and they with him. I'll make sure you get a copy. I'll take a rain check on the tour. You can get the hamper back to me at your convenience."

She thought it was a great exit as exits went, striding around the car while she tossed off her lines. Her temper was flaring but just under control. Then he grabbed her as she reached for the car door and spoiled it.

She whirled around swinging, but her fist slid off his

damp chest and ruined the impact. "Hands off."

"Where are you going? Just hold it a minute."

"I don't have to hold anything, and I don't want you holding me." She shoved at him with both hands. "God, you're filthy!"

"If you'd just be still and listen—"

"To what? You don't think I get it? You don't think I've clued in to what you saw, what you thought when I pulled up. 'Oh, hell, here comes the social worker? Close ranks, boys.' " She jerked back. "Well, fuck you."

He could have denied it, could have taken the I-don't-know-what-you're-talking-about approach and done an expert job of it. But her eyes had the same effect on him as they'd had on Seth. They wouldn't let his tongue wrap itself around a decent lie.

"Okay, you're right. It was knee-jerk."

"At least you have the decency to be honest." The depth of the hurt infuriated her as much as it surprised her.

"I don't know what you're so frosted about."

"Don't you?" She tossed back her hair. "Then I'll tell you. I looked at you and saw a man who also happens to be my lover. You looked at me and saw a symbol of a system you don't trust or respect. Now that that's cleared up, get out of my way."

"I'm sorry." He dragged the bandanna off because his head was splitting. "You're right again, and I'm sorry."

"So am I." She started to open the car door.

"Will you give me a damn minute here?" Instead of reaching for her again, he dragged his hands through his hair. It wasn't the impatient tone that stopped her, but the weariness of the gesture.

"All right." She let go of the door handle. "You've got a minute."

He didn't think there was another woman on the planet he'd explained himself to more than the one watching him now with a faint frown. "We were all a little shaken up right then. The timing couldn't have been worse. Goddamn it, my hands were still shaking."

He hated to admit that—hated it. To gather some control, he turned away, paced off, paced back. "I was in a wreck once. About three years ago. Grand Prix. Hit the chute, misjudged, went into a hell of a spin. The car was breaking apart around me. The worst fear is invisible fire. Vapors catching hold. I had this flash of myself burned to a crisp. Just for an instant, but it was vivid."

He balled the bandanna up in his hand, then pulled it out smooth. "I'm telling you, Anna, I swear to you, standing under that kid and watching his shoelaces dangle was worse. Hell of a lot worse."

How could she hold on to her anger? And why couldn't he see that he had such a huge well of love to give if he would only let himself dip into it freely? He'd said that he would probably hurt her, but she hadn't known it would come so soon, or from this direction.

She hadn't been looking in the right direction. She hadn't known she was falling in love with him.

"I can't do this," she said, half to herself, and wrapped her hands around her arms to warm them. The chill penetrated, even though she stood in streaming sun. How many steps had she taken toward love, she wondered, and how many could she take back to save herself? "I don't know what I was thinking of. Being involved with you on a personal level only complicates our mutual interest in the child."

"Don't back off from me, Anna." He experienced another level of fear now, one he'd never felt before. "So we take a few wrong steps. We get the balance back. We're good together."

"We're good in bed," she said and blinked when she saw what might have been hurt flash in his eyes.

"Only?"

"No," she said slowly as he stepped toward her, "not only. But—"

"I've got something for you inside me, Anna." He forgot his hands were grimy and laid them on her shoulders. "I haven't used it up yet. This thing with you, it's one of the first times I haven't wanted to rush to the finish line.''

They would still get there, she realized. She would have to be prepared for him to reach that line, and cross it, ahead of her. ''Don't mix up who I am and what I am,'' she told him quietly. ''You have to be honest with me, or the rest of it means nothing.''

''I've been more up front with you than I've ever been with a woman before. And I know who you are.''

''All right.'' She laid a hand on his cheek when he bent to kiss her. ''We'll see what happens next.''

FOURTEEN

IT WAS A GOOD SPRING afternoon. Balmy air, fine wind, and just enough cloud cover to filter the sun and keep it from baking your flesh down to your bones. When Ethan guided his workboat into dock, the waterfront was busy with tourists who'd come to see the watermen work and the busy fingers of the crab pickers fly.

He had reached his quota early, which suited him fine. The water tanks under the faded striped awning of his boat were crawling with annoyed crabs that would find their way into the pot by nightfall. He would turn in his catch and leave his mate to diddle with the engine. It was running just a tad rough. He planned to take himself over to the building to see how the plumbing was coming.

He was itching to have it done, and Ethan Quinn wasn't a man who itched for much—at least, he didn't allow himself to think he did. But the boat building enterprise was a little private dream that he'd nurtured for some time now. He thought it was about ripe.

Simon let out one sharp, happy woof as the boat bumped the pilings. Even as Ethan prepared to secure the lines, there were hands reaching for them. Hands he recognized before he lifted his gaze to the face. Long, pretty hands that wore no rings or polish.

"I've got it, Ethan."

He looked up and smiled at Grace. "Appreciate it. What're you doing on the docks midday?"

"Picking crabs. Betsy was feeling off this morning, so they were short a pair of hands. My mother wanted Aubrey for a couple of hours anyway."

"You ought to take some time for yourself, Grace."

"Oh . . ." She secured the lines expertly, then straightened to run a hand through her short cap of hair. "One of these days. Did y'all finish up that ham casserole I made the other day?"

"Fought over the last bite. It was great. Thanks." Now that he'd about run out of easy conversation and was standing on the dock beside her, he didn't know what to do with his hands. To compensate, he scratched Simon's head. "We pulled in a nice catch today."

"So I see." But her smile didn't reach her eyes, and she was gnawing on her lip. A sure sign, Ethan thought, that what was on Grace's mind was trouble.

"Is there a problem?"

"I hate to take up your time when you're busy, Ethan." Her eyes scanned the docks. "Could you walk with me a minute?"

"Sure. I could use something cold. Jim, you handle things from here all right?"

"You got it, Cap'n."

With the dog trotting between them, Ethan tucked his hands in his pockets. He nodded when a familiar voice called out a greeting, barely noticed the quick fingers of the crab pickers, who put on quite a show while they worked. He noticed the smells because he was so fond of them—water, fish, salt in the air. And the subtle notes of Grace's soap and shampoo.

"Ethan, I don't want to cause you or your family any grief."

"You couldn't, Grace."

"You may already know. It just bothers me so much. I just hate it so much." Her voice lowered, sizzling with a temper that Ethan knew was rare. He saw that her face was set, her mouth grim, and he decided to forgo that cold drink and lead her farther away from the docks.

"You better tell me, get it off your mind."

"And put it on yours," she said with a sigh. She hated to do it. Ethan was always there if you had trouble or needed a shoulder. Once she'd wished he would offer her more than a shoulder . . . but she'd learned to accept the way things were.

"It's best that you know," she said, half to herself. "You can't deal with things unless you know. There's an investigator for the insurance company talking to people, asking questions about your father, about Seth too."

Ethan laid a hand on her arm briefly. They were far enough away from the docks, from the storefronts and the jangle of traffic. He'd thought they were done with that. "What kind of questions?"

"About your daddy's state of mind the last few weeks before his accident. About him bringing Seth home. He came to see me this morning, first thing. I thought it was better to talk to him than not." She looked at Ethan, relieved when he nodded. "I told him Ray Quinn was one of the finest men I've ever known—and gave him a piece of my mind about going around trying to pick up nasty gossip."

Because Ethan smiled at that, her lips curved. "Well, he made me so mad. Claims he's only doing his job, and his manner's mild as skim milk. But it bothered me, especially when he asked if I knew anything about Seth's mother or where he'd come from. I told him I didn't and that it didn't matter. Seth was where he was supposed to be, and that was that. I hope I did the right thing."

"You did just fine."

Her eyes were the color of stormy seas now, as emotions churned through her. "Ethan, I know it'll hurt if some people talk, if some of them say things they've got no business saying. It doesn't mean anything," she continued and took his hands in hers. "Not to anyone who knows your family."

"We'll get through it." He gave her hands a quick squeeze, then didn't know if he should hold on to them or let go. "I'm glad you told me." He let go. But he kept looking at her face, looked so long that the color began to rise in her cheeks. "You're not getting enough sleep," he said. "Your eyes are tired."

"Oh." Embarrassed, annoyed, she brushed her fingertips under them. Why was it the man only seemed to notice if something was wrong with her? "Aubrey was a little fussy last night. I've got to get back," she said quickly and gave the patient Simon a quick rub. "I'll be by the house tomorrow to clean."

She hurried off, thinking hopelessly that a man who only noticed when you looked tired or troubled would never pay you any mind as a woman.

But Ethan watched her walk away and thought she was too damn pretty to work herself like a mule.

THE INSPECTOR'S NAME was Mackensie, and he was making the rounds. So far, his notes contained descriptions of a man who was a saint with a halo as wide and bright as the sun. A selfless Samaritan of a man who not only loved his neighbors but cheerfully bore their burdens, who had with his faithful wife beside him saved large chunks of humanity and kept the world safe for democracy.

His other notations termed Raymond Quinn a pompous, interfering, holier-than-thou despot, who collected bad young boys like other men collected stamps and used them to provide him with slave labor, an ego balm, and possibly prurient sexual favors.

Though Mackensie had to admit the latter was more interesting, that view had come from only a scattered few.

Being a man of details and caution, he realized that the truth probably lay somewhere in between the saint and the sinner.

His purpose wasn't to canonize or condemn one Raymond Quinn, policy number 005-678-LQ2. It was simply to gather facts, and those facts would determine whether the claim against that policy would be paid or disputed.

Either way, Mackensie got paid for his time and his efforts.

He'd stopped off and grabbed a sandwich at a little grease spot called Bay Side Eats. He had a weakness for grease, bad coffee, and waitresses with names like Lulubelle.

It was why, at age fifty-eight, he was twenty pounds overweight—twenty-five if he didn't tip the scale a few notches back from zero before he stepped on it—had a chronic case of indigestion, and was twice divorced.

He was also balding and had bunions, and an eyetooth that ached like a bitch in heat. Mackensie knew he was no physical prize, but he knew his job, had thirty-two years with True Life Insurance, and kept records as clean as a nun's heart.

He pulled his Ford Taurus into the pitted gravel lot beside the building. His last contact, a little worm named Claremont, had given him directions. He would find Cameron Quinn there, Claremont had told him with a tight-lipped smile.

Mackensie had disliked the man after five minutes in his company. The inspector had worked with people long enough to recognize greed, envy, and simple malice even when they were layered over with charm. Claremont didn't have any layers that Mackensie had noticed. He was all smarm.

He belched up a memory of the dill pickle relish he'd indulged in at lunch, shook his head, and thumbed out his hourly dose of Zantac. There was a pickup truck in the lot, an aging sedan, and a spiffy classic Corvette.

Mackensie liked the looks of the 'Vette, though he

wouldn't have gotten behind the wheel of one of those death traps for love or money. No, indeed. But he admired it anyway as he hauled himself out of his car.

He could admire the looks of the man as well, he mused, when a pair of them stepped out of the building. Not the older one with the red-checked shirt and clip-on tie. Paper pusher, he decided—he was good at recognizing types.

The younger one was too lean, too hungry, too sharp-eyed to spend much time pushing papers. If he didn't work with his hands, Mackensie thought, he could. And he looked like a man who knew what he wanted—and found a way to make it so.

If this was Cameron Quinn, Mackensie decided that Ray Quinn had had his hands full while he was alive.

Cam spotted Mackensie when he walked the plumbing inspector out. He was feeling pretty good about the progress. He figured it would take another week to complete the bathroom, but he and Ethan could do without that little convenience that much longer.

He wanted to get started, and since the wiring was done and that, too, had passed inspection, there was no need to wait.

He tagged Mackensie as some sort of paper jockey. Jiggling his memory, he tried to recall if he had another appointment set up, but he didn't think so. Selling something, he imagined, as Mackensie and the inspector passed each other.

The man had a briefcase, Cam noted wearily. When people carried a briefcase it meant there was something inside they wanted to take out.

"You'd be Mr. Quinn," Mackensie said, his voice affable, his eyes measuring.

"I would."

"I'm Mackensie, True Life Insurance."

"We've got insurance." Or he was nearly sure they did. "My brother Phillip handles those kinds of details." Then it clicked, and Cam's stance shifted from relaxed to on guard. "True Life?"

"That's the one. I'm an investigator for the company. We need to clear up some questions before your claim on your father's policy can be settled."

"He's dead," Cam said flatly. "Isn't that the question, Mackensie?"

"I'm sorry for your loss."

"I imagine the insurance company's sorry it has to shell out. As far as I'm concerned, my father paid in to that policy in good faith. The trick is you have to die to win. He died."

It was warm in the sun, and the pastrami on rye with spicy mustard wasn't settling well. Mackensie blew out a breath. "There's some question about the accident."

"Car meets telephone pole. Telephone pole wins. Trust me, I do a lot of driving."

Mackensie nodded. Under other circumstances he might have appreciated Cam's no-bullshit tone. "You'd be aware that the policy has a suicide clause."

"My father didn't commit suicide, Mackensie. And since you weren't in the car with him at the time, it's going to be tough for you to prove otherwise."

"Your father was under a great deal of stress, emotional upheaval."

Cam snorted. "My father raised three badasses and taught a bunch of snot-nosed college kids. He had a great deal of stress and emotional upheaval all his life."

"And he'd taken on a fourth."

"That's right." Cam tucked his thumbs in his front pockets, and his stance became a silent challenge. "That doesn't have anything to do with you or your company."

"As it bears on the circumstances of your father's accident. There's a question of possible blackmail, and certainly a threat to his reputation. I have a copy of the letter found in his car at the scene."

When Mackensie opened his briefcase, Cam took a step forward. "I've seen the letter. All it means is there's a woman out there with the maternal instincts of a rabid alley cat. You try to say that Ray Quinn smashed into that pole because he was afraid of some two-bit bitch, I'll bury your insurance company."

Fury he thought he'd already passed through sprang back, full-blown and fang-sharp. "I don't give a good goddamn about the money. We can make our own money. True Life wants to welsh on the deal, that's my brother's area—and the lawyer's. But you or anybody else messes with my father's rep, you'll deal with me."

The man was a good twenty-five years younger, Mackensie calculated, tough as a brick and mad as a starving wolf. He decided it would be best all round if he changed tactics. "Mr. Quinn, I have no interest or desire to smear your father's reputation. True Life's a good company, I've worked for them most of my life." He tried a winning smile. "This is just routine."

"I don't like your routine."

"I can understand that. The gray area here is the accident itself. The medical reports confirm that your father was in good physical shape. There's no evidence of a heart attack, a stroke, any physical reason that would have caused him to lose control of his car. A single-car accident, an empty stretch of road on a dry, clear day. The accident-reconstruction expert's findings were inconclusive."

"That's your problem." Cam spotted Seth walking down the road from the direction of school. And there, he thought, is mine. "I can't help you with it. But I can tell you that my father faced his problems, square on. He never took the easy way. I've got work to do." Leaving it at that, Cam turned away and walked toward Seth.

Mackensie rubbed eyes that were tearing up from the sunlight. Quinn might have thought he'd added nothing to the report, but he was wrong. If nothing else, Mackensie could be sure the Quinns would fight for their claim to the bitter end. If not for the money, for the memory.

"Who's that guy?" Seth asked as he watched Mackensie head back to his car.

"Some insurance quack." Cam nodded down the street

where two boys loitered a half a block away. "Who're those guys?"

Seth gave a careless glance over his shoulder, followed it with a shrug. "I don't know. Just kids from school. They're nobody."

"They hassling you?"

"Nah. Are we going up on the roof?"

"Roof's done," Cam murmured and watched with some amusement as the two boys wandered closer, trying and failing to look disinterested. "Hey, you kids."

"What're you doing?" Seth hissed, mortified.

"Relax. Come on over here," Cam ordered as both boys froze like statues.

"What the hell are you calling them over for? They're just jerks from school."

"I could use some jerk labor," Cam said mildly. It had also occurred to him that Seth could use some companions of his own age. He waited while Seth squirmed and the two boys held a fast, whispering consultation. It ended with the taller of the two squaring his shoulders and swaggering down the road on his battered Nikes.

"We weren't doing anything," the boy said, his tone of defiance slightly spoiled by a lisp from a missing tooth.

"I could see that. You want to do something?"

The boy slid his eyes to the younger kid, then over to Seth, then cautiously up to Cam's face. "Maybe."

"You got a name?"

"Sure. I'm Danny. This is my kid brother, Will. I turned eleven last week. He's only nine."

"I'll be ten in ten months," Will stated and rapped his brother in the ribs with his elbow.

"He still goes to elementary," Danny put in with a sneer, which he generously shared with Seth. "Baby school."

"I'm not a baby."

As Will's fist was already clenched and lifted, Cam took hold of it, then lightly squeezed his upper arm. "Seems strong enough to me."

"I'm plenty strong," Will told him, then grinned with the charm of an angelic host.

"We'll see about that. See all this crap piled up around here? Old shingles, tar paper, trash?" Cam surveyed the area himself. "You see that Dumpster over there? The crap goes in the Dumpster, you get five bucks."

"Each?" Danny piped up, his hazel eyes glinting in a freckled face.

"Don't make me laugh, kid. But you'll get a two-dollar bonus if you do it without me having to come out and break up any fights." He jerked a thumb at Seth. "He's in charge."

The minute Cam left them alone, Danny turned to Seth. They sized each other up in narrow-eyed silence. "I saw you punch Robert."

Seth shifted his balance evenly. It would be two against one, he calculated, but he was prepared to fight. "So what?"

"It was cool," was all Danny said and began to pick up torn shingles.

Will grinned happily up into Seth's face. "Robert is a big, fat fart, and Danny said when you socked him he bled and bled."

Seth found himself grinning back. "Like a stuck pig."

"Oink, oink," Will said, delighted. "We can buy ice cream with the money up at Crawford's."

"Yeah . . . maybe." Seth started to gather up trash, with Will cheerfully dogging his heels.

ANNA WASN'T HAVING A good day. She'd started out the morning running her last pair of hose before she even got out her front door. She was out of bagels, and yogurt, and, she admitted, almost every damn thing, because she'd been spending too much time with Cam or thinking about Cam to keep to her usual marketing routine.

When she stopped off to mail a letter to her grandparents, she chipped a nail on the mailbox. Her phone was already ringing when she walked into her office at eight-thirty, and the hysterical woman on the other end was demanding to know why she had yet to receive her medical card.

She calmed the woman down, assured her she would see to the matter personally. Then, simply because she was there, the switchboard passed through a whining old man who insisted his neighbors were child abusers because they allowed their offspring to watch television every night of the week.

"Television," he told her, "is the tool of the Communist left. Nothing but sex and murder, sex and murder, and subliminal messages. I read all about them."

"I'm going to look into this, Mr. Bigby," she promised and opened her top drawer, where she kept her aspirin.

"You'd better. I tried the cops, but they don't do nothing. Those kids're doomed. Going to need to deprogram them."

"Thank you for bringing this to our attention."

"My duty as an American."

"You bet," Anna muttered after he'd hung up.

Knowing that she was due in family court at two that afternoon, she booted up her computer, intending to call up the file to review her reports and notes. When the message flashed across her screen that her program had committed an illegal act, she didn't bother to scream. She simply sat back, closed her eyes, and accepted that it was going to be a lousy day.

It got worse.

She knew her testimony in court was key. The Higgins case file had come across her desk nearly a year ago. The three children, ages eight, six, and four, had all been physically and emotionally abused. The wife, barely twenty-five, was a textbook case of the battered spouse. She'd left her husband countless times over the years, but she always went back.

Six months before, Anna had worked hard and long to get her and her children into a shelter. The woman had stayed less than thirty-six hours before changing her mind. Though Anna's heart ached for her, it had come down to the welfare of the children.

Their pinched faces, the bruises, the fear—and worse, the dull acceptance in their eyes—tormented her. They were in foster care with a couple who was generous enough and strong enough to take all of them. And seeing those foster parents flanking the three damaged boys, she vowed she would do everything in her power to keep them there.

"Counseling was recommended in January of last year when this case first came to my attention," Anna stated from the witness stand. "Both family and individual. The recommendation was not taken. Nor was it taken in May of that same year when Mrs. Higgins was hospitalized with a dislocated jaw and other injuries, or in September when Michael Higgins, the eldest boy, suffered a broken hand. In November of that year Mrs. Higgins and her two oldest sons were all treated in ER for various injuries. I was notified and assisted Mrs. Higgins and her children in securing a place in a women's shelter. She did not remain there two full days."

"You've been caseworker of record on this matter for more than a year." The lawyer stood in front of her, knowing from experience it wasn't necessary to guide her testimony.

"Yes, more than a year." And she felt the failure keenly.

"What is the current status?"

"On February sixth of this year, a police unit responding to the call from a neighbor found Mr. Higgins under the influence of alcohol. Mrs. Higgins was reported as hysterical and required medical treatment for facial bruises and lacerations. Curtis, the youngest child, had a broken arm. Mr. Higgins was taken into custody. At that time, as I was the caseworker of record, I was notified."

"Did you see Mrs. Higgins and the children on that day?" the lawyer asked her.

"Yes. I drove to the hospital. I spoke with Mrs. Higgins. She claimed that Curtis had fallen down the stairs. Due to the nature of his injuries, and the history of the case, I didn't believe her. The attending physician in ER shared my opinion. The children were taken into foster care, where they have remained since that date."

She continued to answer questions about the status of the case file and the children themselves. Once, she drew a smile out of the middle boy when she spoke of the T-ball team he'd been able to join.

Then Anna prepared herself for the irritation and tedium of cross-examination.

"Are you aware that Mr. Higgins has voluntarily entered an alcohol rehabilitation program?"

Anna spared one glance at the Higginses' pro bono lawyer, then looked directly into the father's eyes. "I'm aware that over the past year, Mr. Higgins has claimed to have entered a rehabilitation program no less than three times."

She saw the hate and fury darken his face. *Let him hate me*, she thought. She'd be damned if he would lay hands on those children again. "I'm aware that he's never completed a program."

"Alcoholism is a disease, Ms. Spinelli. Mr. Higgins is now seeking treatment for his illness. You would agree that Mrs. Higgins has been a victim of her husband's illness?"

"I would agree that she has suffered both physically and emotionally at his hands."

"And can you possibly believe that she should suffer further, lose her children and they her? Can you possibly believe that the court should take these three little boys away from their mother?"

The choice, Anna thought, was hers. The man who beat her and terrorized their children, or the health and safety of those children. "I believe she will suffer further, until she makes the decision to change her circumstances. And it's my professional opinion that Mrs. Higgins is incapable of caring for herself, much less her children, at this time."

"Both Mr. and Mrs. Higgins now have steady employment," the lawyer continued. "Mrs. Higgins has stated, under oath, that she and her husband are reconciled and continuing to work on their marital difficulties. Separating the family will, as she stated, only cause emotional pain for all involved."

"I know she believes that." Her steady look at Mrs. Higgins was compassionate, but her voice was firm. "I believe that there are three children whose welfare and safety are at stake. I'm aware of the medical reports, the psychiatric reports, the police reports. In the past fifteen months, these three children have been treated in the emergency room a combined total of eleven times."

She looked at the lawyer now, wondering how he could stand in a court of law and fight for what was surely the destruction of three young boys. "I'm aware that a four-year-old boy's arm was snapped like a twig. I strongly recommend that these children remain in licensed and supervised foster care to ensure their physical and emotional safety."

"No charges have been filed against Mr. Higgins."

"No, no charges have been filed." Anna shifted her gaze to the mother, let it rest on that tired face. "That's just another crime," she murmured.

When she was finished, Anna passed by the Higginses without a glance. But behind the rail, little Curtis reached out for her hand. "Do you have a lollipop?" he whispered, making her smile.

She made a habit of carrying them for him. He had a weakness for cherry Tootsie Roll Pops. "Maybe I do. Let's see."

She was reaching into her purse when the explosion came from behind her. "Get your hands off what's mine, you bitch."

As she started to turn, Higgins hit her full force, knocking her sprawling and sending Curtis to the floor with her in a heap of screams and wails. Her head rang like church bells and stars dazzled her eyes. She could hear screams and curses as she managed to push herself up to her hands and knees.

Her cheek ached fiercely where it had connected with the seat of a wooden chair. Her palms sang from skidding on the tile floor. And damn it, the new hose she had bought to replace the ones she'd run were torn at the knees.

"HOLD STILL," MARILOU ordered. She was crouched in Anna's office, grimly doctoring the scrapes.

"I'm all right." Indeed, the injuries were minor. "It was worth it. That little demonstration in open court ensures that he won't get near those kids for quite a while."

"You worry me, Anna." Marilou looked up with those dark, gleaming eyes. "I'd almost think you enjoyed being tackled by that two-hundred-pound putz."

"I enjoyed the results. Ouch, Marilou." She blew out a breath as her supervisor rose to examine the bruise on Anna's cheek. "I enjoyed filing charges for assault, and most of all I enjoyed seeing those kids go home with their foster family."

"A good day's work?" With a shake of her head, Marilou stepped back. "It worries me, too, that you let yourself get too close."

"You can't help from a distance. So much of what we do is just paperwork, Marilou. Forms and procedures. But every now and again you get to do something—even if it's only getting tackled by a two-hundred-pound putz. And it's worth it."

"If you care too much, you end up with more than a couple of bruises and a skinned knee."

"If you don't care enough, you should find another line of work."

Marilou blew out a breath. It was difficult to argue when she felt exactly the same way. "Go home, Anna."

"I've got another hour on the clock."

"Go home. Consider it combat pay."

"Since you put it that way. I could use the hour. I don't have anything in the house to eat. If you hear any more on—" She broke off and looked up at the knock on her doorjamb. Her eyes widened. "Cameron."

"Miz Spinelli, I wonder if you have a minute to—" His smile of greeting transformed into a snarl. The light in his eyes turned hot and sharp as a flaming sword. "What the hell happened to you?" He was in the room like a shot, filling it, nearly barreling over Marilou to get to Anna. "Who the hell hit you?"

"No one, exactly, I was—"

Instead of giving her a chance to finish, he whirled on Marilou. Torn between fascination and amusement, Marilou backed up a step and held her hands up, palms out. "Not me, champ. I only browbeat my staff. Never lay a finger on them."

"There was a ruckus in court, that's all." Struggling to be brisk and professional despite her bare legs and feet, Anna rose. "Marilou, this is Cameron Quinn. Cameron, Marilou Johnston, my supervisor."

"It's a pleasure to meet you, even under the circumstances." Marilou held out a hand. "I was a student of your father's a million years ago. I quite simply adored him."

"Yeah, thanks. Who hit you?" he demanded again of Anna.

"Someone who is even now on the wrong side of a locked cell." Quickly, Anna worked her bare feet back into her low-heeled pumps. "Marilou, I'm going to take you up on the hour off." Her only thought now was to get Cam out, away from Marilou's curious and all-too-observant eyes. "Cameron, if you need to speak with me about Seth, you could give me a ride home." She slipped on her dove-gray jacket, smoothed it into place. ‘‘It’s not far. I’ll buy you a cup of coffee.’’

‘‘Fine. Sure.’’ When he caught her chin in his hand, a tug-of-war of pleasure and alarm raged inside her. ‘‘We’ll talk.’’

‘‘I’ll see you tomorrow, Marilou.’’

‘‘Oh, yes.’’ Marilou smiled easily while Anna hurriedly gathered her briefcase. ‘‘We’ll talk, too.’’

FIFTEEN

ANNA KEPT HER MOUTH firmly shut until they were out of the building and safely alone in the parking lot. "Cam, for God's sake."

"For God's sake, what?"

"This is where I work." She stopped at his car, turned to face him. "Where I work, remember? You can't come storming into my office like an outraged lover."

He took her chin in hand again, leaned his face close. "I *am* an outraged lover, and I want the name of the son of a bitch who put his hands on you."

She wouldn't allow herself to be thrilled by the violence sparking around him. It would be, she reminded herself as her stomach gave a delicious little hop, completely unprofessional.

"The person in question is being dealt with by the proper authorities. And you're not allowed to be a lover, outraged or otherwise, during business hours."

"Yeah? Try and stop me," he challenged and leading with his temper, crushed his mouth to hers.

She wiggled for a moment. Anyone could peek out an office window and see. The kiss was too hot, too heady for a daylight embrace in an office parking lot.

The kiss was also too hot, too heady to resist. She gave in to it, to him, to herself, and wrapped her arms around him. "Will you cut it out?" she said against his mouth.

"No."

"Okay, then, let's take this indoors."

"Good idea." With his mouth still on hers, he reached back to open the car door.

"I can't get in until you let me go."

"Good point." He released her, then surprised her by gently, tenderly brushing his lips over the bruise on her cheek. "Does it hurt?"

Her heart was still flopping. "Maybe a little." She got inside, deliberately reaching for her seat belt, keeping her moves efficient and casual.

"What happened?" he asked as he slid in beside her.

"Abusive father of three, wife beater, didn't care for my testimony in family court today. He shoved me. I had my back turned or he'd have gotten a hard knee to the groin, but as it was I was off balance. Did a nosedive—which would have been embarrassing but for the fact that he's now in lockup and the kids are with their foster family."

"And the wife?"

"I can't help her." Anna let her aching head fall back. "You have to pick your battles."

He said nothing to that. He'd been thinking the same thing. It was why he'd decided to dump three kids on Ethan and come to see her. He'd made up his mind to tell her about the insurance investigation, the speculations about Seth's connection to his father, the search that Phillip had instigated for Seth's mother.

He'd decided to tell her everything, to ask her advice, to get her take. Now he found himself wondering if that was the wisest course—for her, for him, for Seth.

It would wait, he told himself, and rationalized his postponement: she'd had a rough time, needed a little attention.

"So, do you get knocked around much in your line of work?"

"Hmm? No." She laughed a little as he pulled up in

front of her building. "Now and again somebody takes a swing or throws something at you, but mostly it's just verbal abuse."

"Fun job."

"It has its moments." She took his hand, walked alongside him. "Did you know that television is the tool of the Communist left?"

"I hadn't heard that."

"I'm here to tell you." She used her key to check her mail slot, gathered letters and bills and a fashion magazine. "*Sesame Street* is just a front."

"I always suspected that big yellow bird."

"Nah, he's just a shill. The frog's the mastermind." She put her finger to her lips as they approached her door. They snuck in together like kids hooking school. "I just didn't want to have the sisters fussing over me."

"Mind if I do?"

"That depends on your definition of fussing."

"We'll start here." He slipped his arms around her waist, touched his lips to hers.

"I suppose I could tolerate that." She helped him deepen the kiss. "What are you doing here, Cam?"

"I had a lot on my mind." His lips brushed over the bruise again, then lower, to her jawline. "You, mostly. I wanted to see you, be with you, talk to you. Make love to you."

Her lips curved against his. "All at the same time."

"Why not? I did have this thought about taking you out to dinner . . . but now I'm thinking maybe we could order pizza."

"Perfect." She said it with a sigh. "Why don't you pour us some wine, and I'll change?"

"There's this other thing." He worked his way over to her ear. "Something I've been wanting to do. I've been wondering what it would be like to get Miz Spinelli out of one of her dedicated-public-servant suits."

"Have you?"

"Since the first time I saw you."

She smiled wickedly. "Now's your chance."

"I was hoping you'd say that." He brought his mouth back to hers, hungrier now, more possessive. This time her sigh caught on a trembling gasp as he jerked her jacket off her shoulders and trapped her arms. "I'm wanting the hell out of you. Day and night."

Her voice was throaty now, dark with need. "I guess that makes it handy, since I want the hell out of you too."

"It doesn't scare you?"

"Nothing about you and me scares me."

"And what if I said I want you to let me do anything I want to you? Everything?"

Her heart fluttered to her throat, but her eyes stayed steady. "I'd say who's stopping you?"

With desire dark and dangerous in his eyes, he skimmed his gaze down, then back to her face. "I wonder what Miz Spinelli wears under these prim little blouses."

"I don't think a man like you is going to let a few buttons keep him from finding out."

"You're right." He shifted his hands from her jacket to the crisply pressed cotton of her blouse. And ripped. He watched her eyes go wide and shocked. And aroused. "If you want me to stop, I will. I won't do anything you don't want."

He'd torn her blouse. And it had thrilled her. He waited, watching, for her to say stop or go. And it thrilled her even more. She understood she hadn't been completely truthful when she'd told him nothing about them scared her. She was afraid of what might be happening to her heart.

But here, in physical love, she knew she could match him.

"I want everything. All."

His blood leaped. Still, he kept his touch light, teasing, running the back of his hand above the slick white material of her demi-cut bra. "Miz Spinelli." He drawled it while his fingers slipped beneath the polished satin to rub against her stiffened nipple. "How much can you take?"

His light tugs had heat spiraling through her system.

Already the air was thick. "I think we're about to find out."

Slowly, his eyes on her face, he backed her against the wall. "Let's start here. Brace yourself," he murmured, and his hand shot under her skirt and tore aside the lacy swatch she wore beneath. Her breath exploded out, and she nearly laughed. Then he plunged his fingers into her, lancing that hard, rough shock of pleasure through her unprepared system. The orgasm ripped through her, emptying her mind, stealing her breath. When her knees gave way, he simply held her against the wall.

"Take more." He was desperate to watch her take more, to see the shocked excitement capture her face, to see those gorgeous eyes go wild and blind.

She gripped his shoulders for balance. With her head tipped back he could see the pulse in her throat beat madly and was compelled to taste just there. She moaned against him, moved against him, her breath hitching when he yanked the jacket and what was left of her blouse away.

She was helpless, staggered. The assault on her senses left her limbs shuddering and her heart hammering. She said his name, tried to, but it caught on a gasp as he spun her around. Her damp palms pressed to the wall.

He tore at the button of her skirt. She felt it give way, shivering as the material slid over her hips and pooled at her feet. His hands were on her breasts, molding, sliding from satin to flesh and back again. Then he tore that as well, and she gloried in the sound of the delicate material rending.

His teeth nipped into her shoulder. And his hands—oh, his hands were everywhere, driving her toward madness, then beyond. Rough palms against smooth skin, clever fingers pressing, sliding.

The breath that had torn ragged through her lips began to slow. Pleasure was thick, and midnight dark. She felt herself slipping into some erotic half-world where there was only sensation.

Slick, stunning, and sinful.

The wall was smooth and cool; his hands were not. The contrasts were unbearably arousing.

When he spun her around again, her eyes were dazzled by the sunlight. He was still fully dressed and she was naked. She found it exquisitely erotic, and could say nothing as he slowly lifted her arms above her head, bracketed her wrists with one hand.

Watching her, he combed his hand roughly through her hair to scatter pins. "I want more." He could barely speak. "Tell me you want more."

"Yes, I want more."

He pressed his body to hers, soft cotton, rough denim against damp flesh. And the kiss he took from her left her mind spinning.

Then his mouth went to work on her quivering body.

He wanted all the tastes of her, the dark honey of her mouth, the damp silk of her breasts. There was the creamy taste of her belly, the polished satin of her thighs.

Then the heat, the furnace flood of it as he licked his way between them.

Everything. All, was all he could think. Then more.

Her hands gripped his hair, pressing his face closer as she climbed to peak. It was her cry, the half scream, that broke the final link on his control. It had to be now.

He freed himself, then pressed against her. "I need to fill you." He panted the words out. "I want you to watch me when I do."

He drove into her where they stood, and their twin groans tangled in the air.

Afterward, he carried her to bed, lay down beside her. She curled up against him like a child, a gesture he found surprisingly sweet. He watched her sleep, thirty minutes, then a hour. He couldn't stop touching her—a hand through her hair, fingertips over the bruise on her face, a stroke over the curve of her shoulder.

Had he said he had something inside of him for her? He began to worry just what that something might be. He'd never felt compelled to stay with a woman after sex.

Had never felt the need to just look at her while she slept, or to touch only for the sake of touching and not to arouse.

He wondered what odd and slippery level they'd reached.

Then she stirred, sighed, and her eyes fluttered open and focused on him. When she smiled, his heart quite simply turned over in his chest.

"Hi. Did I fall asleep?"

"Looked like it to me." He searched for some glib remark, something light and frivolous, but all he could find to say was her name. "Anna." And he lowered his mouth to hers. Tenderly, softly, lovingly.

The sleep had cleared from her eyes when he drew away, but he couldn't read them. She breathed in once, slowly, then out again. "What was that?"

"Damned if I know." Both of them eased back cautiously. "I think we'd better order that pizza."

Relief and disappointment warred inside her. Anna put all her effort into supporting the relief. "Good idea. The number's right next to the kitchen phone. If you don't mind calling it in, I'd like to grab a quick shower, get some clothes on."

"All right." With casual intimacy he stroked a hand over her hip. "What do you want on it?"

"All I can get." She waited while he laughed and was pleased that he rolled out of bed first. She needed another minute.

"I'll pour the wine."

"Terrific." The minute she was alone, she turned her face into the pillow and let out a muffled scream of frustration. Steps back? she thought, furious with herself. Where did she get the idiotic idea she could take a few steps back? She was over her head in love with him.

My fault, she reminded herself, my problem. Sitting up, she pressed a hand to her traitorous heart. And my little secret, she decided.

• • •

SHE FELT BETTER WHEN she was dressed and had a light shield of makeup in place. She'd given herself a good talking-to in the shower. Maybe she was in love with him. It didn't have to be a bad thing. People fell in and out of love all the time, and the wise ones, the steady ones, enjoyed the ride.

She could be wise and steady.

She certainly wasn't looking for happily ever after, a white knight, a Prince Charming. Anna had outgrown fairy tales long ago, and all of her innocence had cemented into reality on the side of a deserted road at the age of twelve. She'd learned to make herself happy because for too many years following the rape it had seemed she was helpless to do anything but make herself and everyone near her miserable.

She'd survived the worst. There was no doubt she could survive a slightly dented heart.

In any case, she'd never been in love before—she had skirted around it, breezed over it, wriggled under it, but had never before run headlong into it. It could be a marvelous adventure, certainly a learning experience.

And any woman who found herself a lover like Cameron Quinn had plenty of blessings to count.

So she was smiling when she came into the living room and found Cam, sipping wine, staring at the cover of her latest fashion magazine. He'd put music on. Eric Clapton was pleading with Laylah.

When she came up behind him and pecked a kiss on the back of his neck, she didn't expect his jolt of surprise.

It was guilt, plain and simple, and he hated it. He nearly bobbled the wine and had to fight to keep his face composed.

The pouty face on the cover of the magazine in his hand was a certain long-stemmed French model named Martine.

"Didn't mean to startle you." She raised an eyebrow as she looked at the magazine in his hands. "Absorbed with this summer's new pastels, were you?"

"Just passing the time. Pizza should be along in a minute.'' He started to set the magazine down, wanted sincerely to bury it under the sofa cushions, but she was nipping it out of his hand.

''I used to hate her.''

His throat was uncomfortably dry. ''Huh?''

''Well, not Martine the Magnificent exactly. Models like her. Slim and blond and perfect. I was always too round and too brunette. This,'' she added, giving her wet, curling hair a tug, ''made me insane as a teenager. I tried everything imaginable to straighten it.''

''I love your hair.'' He wished she'd turn the damn magazine facedown. ''You're twice as beautiful as she is. There's no comparison.''

Her smile came quick and warm around the edges. ''That's very sweet.''

''I mean it.'' He said it almost desperately—but thought it best not to add that he'd seen both of them naked and knew what he was talking about.

''Very sweet. Still, I wanted so badly to be slim and blond and hipless.''

''You're real.'' He couldn't stop himself. He took the magazine and tossed it over his shoulder. ''She's not.''

''That's one way to put it.'' Enjoying herself, she cocked her head. ''Seems to me you race-around-the-world types usually go for the supermodels—they look so good draped over a man's arm.''

''I barely know her.''

''Who?''

Jesus, he was losing it. ''Anybody. There's the pizza,'' he said with great relief. ''Your wine's on the counter. I'll get the food.''

''Fine.'' Without a clue as to what was suddenly making him so edgy, she wandered to the kitchen for her drink.

Cam saw that the magazine had fallen faceup so it appeared that Martine was aiming those killer blue eyes right at him. It brought back the memory of a scored cheek and a spitting female. He cast a wary glance at Anna. It wasn't an experience he cared to repeat.

As he paid the delivery boy, Anna took the wine out to her tiny balcony. "It's a nice evening. Let's eat out here."

She had a couple of chairs and a small folding table set out. Pink geraniums and white impatiens sprang cheerfully out of clay pots.

"If I ever manage to save enough for a house, I want a porch. A big one. Like you have." She went back in for plates and napkins. "And a garden. One of these days I'm going to learn something about flowers."

"A house, garden, porches." More comfortable out in the air, he settled down. "I pictured you as a town girl."

"I always have been. I'm not sure suburbia would suit me. Fences with neighbors just over them. Too much like apartment living, I'd think, without the privacy and convenience." She slid a loaded slice of pizza onto her plate. "But I'd like to give home owning a shot—somewhere in the country. Eventually. The problem is, I can't seem to stick to a budget."

"You?" He helped himself. "Miz Spinelli seems so practical."

"She tries. My grandparents were very frugal, had to be. I was raised to watch my pennies." She took a bite and drew in a deep, appreciative breath before speaking over a mouthful of cheese and sauce. "Mostly I watch them roll away."

"What's your weakness?"

"Primarily?" She sighed. "Clothes."

He looked over his shoulder, through the door to her clothes, heaped in a tattered pile on the floor. "I think I owe you a blouse . . . and a skirt, not to mention the underwear."

She laughed lustily. "I suppose you do." She stretched out, comfortable in pale-blue leggings and an oversized white T-shirt. "This was such a hideous day. I'm glad you came by and changed it."

"Why don't you come home with me?"

"What?"

Where the hell had that come from? he wondered. The

thought hadn't even been in his mind when the words popped out of his mouth. But it must have been, somewhere. "For the weekend," he added. "Spend this weekend at the house."

She brought her pizza back to her lips, bit in carefully. "I don't think that would be wise. There's an impressionable young boy in your home."

"He knows what the hell's going on," he began, then caught the look—the Miz Spinelli look—in her eye. "Okay, I'll sleep on the sofa downstairs. You can lock the bedroom door."

Her lips quirked. "Where do you keep the key?"

"This weekend I'll be keeping it in my pocket. But my point is," he continued when she laughed, "you can have the bedroom. On a professional level it'll give you some time with the kid. He's coming along, Anna. And I want to take you sailing."

"I'll come over Saturday and we can go sailing."

"Come Friday night." He took her hand, brought her knuckles to his lips. "Stay till Sunday."

"I'll think about it," she murmured and drew her hand away. Romantic gestures were going to undo her. "And I think if you're going to have a houseguest, you should check with your brothers. They might not care to have a woman underfoot for a weekend."

"They love women. Especially women who cook."

"Ah, so now I'm supposed to cook."

"Maybe just one little pot of linguini. Or a dish of lasagna."

She smiled and took another slice of pizza. "I'll think about it," she said again. "Now tell me about Seth."

"He made a couple of buddies today."

"Really? Terrific."

Her eyes lit with such pleasure and interest, he couldn't help himself. "Yeah, I had them all up on the roof, practiced catching them as they fell off."

Her mouth fell open, then shut again on a scowl. "Very funny, Quinn."

"Gotcha. A kid from Seth's class and his kid brother. I bought them for five bucks as slave labor. Then they wheedled an invite out to the house for dinner, so I stuck Ethan with them."

She rolled her eyes. "You left Ethan alone with three young boys?"

"He can handle it. I did for a couple of hours this afternoon." And, he recalled, it hadn't been so bad. "All he has to do is feed them and make sure they don't kill each other. Their mother's picking them up at seven-thirty. Sandy McLean—well, Sandy Miller now. I went to school with her."

He shook his head, amazed and baffled. "Two kids and a minivan. Never would've figured that for Sandy."

"People change," she murmured, surprised at how much she envied Sandy Miller and her minivan. "Or they weren't precisely what we imagined them to be in the first place."

"I guess. Her kids are pistols."

Because he said it with such easy good humor, she smiled again. "Well, now I see why you popped up at my office. You wanted to escape the madness."

"Yeah, but mostly I just wanted to rip your clothes off." He took another slice himself. "I did both."

And, he thought, as he sipped his wine and watched the sun go down with Anna beside him, he felt damn good about it.

SIXTEEN

DRAWING WASN'T ETHan's strong point. With the other boats he'd built, he'd worked off very rough sketches and detailed measurements. For the first boat for this client, he'd fashioned a lofting platform and had found working from it was easier and more precise.

The skiff he'd built and sold had been a basic model, with a few tweaks of his own added. He'd been able to see the completed project in his mind easily enough and had no trouble envisioning side or interior views.

But he understood that the beginnings of a business required all the forms Phillip had told him to sign and needed something more formal, more professional. They would want to develop a reputation for skill and quality quickly if they expected to stay afloat.

So he'd spent countless hours in the evenings at his desk struggling over the blueprints and drawings of their first job.

When he unrolled his completed sketches on the kitchen table, he was both pleased and proud of his work. "This," he said, holding down the top corners, "is what I had in mind."

Cam looked over Ethan's shoulder, sipped the beer he'd just opened, grunted. "I guess that's supposed to be a boat."

Insulted but not particularly surprised by the comment, Ethan scowled. "I'd like to see you do better, Rembrandt."

Cam shrugged, sat. Upon closer, more neutral study, he admitted he couldn't. But that didn't make the drawing of the sloop look any more like a boat. "I guess it doesn't matter much, as long as we don't show your art project to the client." He pushed the sketch aside and got down to the blueprints. Here, Ethan's thoughtful precision and patience showed through. "Okay, now we're talking. You want to go with smooth-lap construction."

"It's expensive," Ethan began, "but it's got advantages. He'll have a strong, fast boat when we're finished."

"I've been in on a few," Cam murmured. "You've got to be good at it."

"We'll be good at it."

Cam had to grin. "Yeah."

"The thing is . . ." As a matter of pride, Ethan nudged the sketch of the completed boat back over. "It takes skill and precision to smooth-lap a boat. Anybody who knows boats recognizes that. This guy, he's a Sunday sailor, doesn't know more than basic port and starboard—he's just got money. But he hangs with people who know boats."

"And so we use him to build a rep," Cam finished. "Good thinking." He studied the figures, the drawings, the views. It would be a honey, he mused. All they had to do was build it. "We could build a lift model."

"We could."

Building a lift model was an old and respected stage of boat building. Boards of equal thickness would be pegged together and shaped to the desired hull form. Then the model could be taken apart so that the shape of the mold frames could be determined. Then the builders would trace the shape of the planks, or lifts, in their proper relation to one another.

"We could start the lofting," Cam mused.

"I figured we could start work on that tonight and continue tomorrow."

That meant drawing the full-sized shape of the hull on a platform in the shop. It would be detailed, showing the mold sections—and those sections would be tested by drawing in the longitudinal curves, waterlines.

"Yeah, why wait?" Cam glanced up as Seth wandered in to raid the refrigerator. "Though it would be better if we had somebody who could draw worth diddly," he said casually and pretended not to notice Seth's sudden interest.

"As long as we have the measurements, and the work's first class, it doesn't matter." Defending his work, Ethan smoothed a hand over his rendition of the boat.

"Just be nicer if we could show the client something jazzy." Cam lifted a shoulder. "Phillip would call it marketing."

"I don't care what Phillip would call it." The stubborn line began to form between Ethan's eyebrows, a sure sign that he was about to dig in his heels. "The client's satisfied with my other work, and he's not going to be critiquing a drawing. He wants a damn boat, not a picture for his wall."

"I was just thinking . . ." Cam let it hang as Ethan, obviously irritated, rose to get his own beer. "Lots of times in the boatyards I've known, people come around, hang out. They like to watch boats being built—especially the people who don't know squat about boat building but think they do. You could pick up customers that way."

"So?" Ethan popped the top and drank. "I don't care if people want to watch us rabbeting laps." He did, of course, but he didn't expect it would come to that.

"It'd be interesting, I was thinking, if we had good framed sketches on the walls. Boats we've built."

"We haven't built any damn boats yet."

"Your skipjack," Cam pointed out. "The workboat.

The one you already did for our first client. And I put in a lot of time on a two-masted schooner up in Maine a few years ago, and a snazzy little skiff in Bristol.''

Ethan sipped again, considering. ''Maybe it would look good, but I'm not voting to hire some artist to paint pictures. We've got an equipment list to work out, and Phil's got to finish fiddling with the contract for *this* boat.''

''Just a thought.'' Cam turned. Seth was still standing in front of the wide-open refrigerator. ''Want a menu, kid?''

Seth jolted, then grabbed the first thing that came to hand. The carton of blueberry yogurt wasn't what he'd had in mind for a snack, but he was too embarrassed to put it back. Stuck with what he considered Phillip's health crap, he got out a spoon.

''I got stuff to do,'' he muttered and hurried out.

''Ten bucks says he feeds that to the dog,'' Cam said lightly and wondered how long it would take Seth to start drawing boats.

HE HAD A DETAILED AND somewhat romantic sketch of Ethan's skipjack done by morning. He didn't need Phillip's presence in the kitchen to remind him it was Friday. The day before freedom. Ethan was already gone, sailing out to check crab pots and rebait. Though Seth had tried to plot how to catch all three of them together, he simply hadn't been able to figure out how to delay Ethan's dawn departure. But two out of three, he thought as he passed the table where Cam was brooding silently over his morning coffee, wasn't bad.

It took at least two cups of coffee before any man in the Quinn household communicated with more than grunts. Seth was already used to that, so he said nothing as he set down his backpack. He had his sketchbook, with his finger wedged between the pages. He dropped it on the table as if it didn't matter to him in the least, then, with his heart skipping, rummaged through the cupboards for cereal.

Cam saw the sketch immediately. Smiling into his coffee, he said nothing. He was considering the toast he'd managed to burn when Seth came to the table with a box and a bowl. "That damn toaster's defective."

"You turned it up to high again," Phillip told him and finished beating his egg-white-and-chive omelette.

"I don't think so. How many eggs are you scrambling there?"

"I'm not scrambling any." Phillip slid the eggs into the omelette pan he'd brought from his own kitchen. "Make your own."

Jeez, was the guy blind or what? Seth wondered. He poured milk on his cereal and gently nudged the sketchbook an inch closer to Cam.

"It wouldn't kill you to add a couple more while you're doing it." Cam broke off a piece of the charcoaled toast. He had almost learned to like it that way. "I made the coffee."

"The sludge," Phillip corrected. "Let's not get delusions of grandeur."

Cam sighed lustily, then rose to get a bowl. He picked up the cereal box that sat beside Seth's open sketchbook. He could all but hear the boy grind his teeth as he sat back down and poured. "Probably going to have company this weekend."

Phillip concentrated on browning the omelette to perfection. "Who?"

"Anna." Cam slopped milk into his bowl. "I'm going to take her sailing, and I think I've got her talked into cooking dinner."

All the guy could think about was girls and filling his gut, Seth decided in disgust. He used his elbow to shove the sketch pad closer. Cam never glanced up from his cereal bowl.

When he saw Phillip slide the omelette from pan to plate, he judged it time to make his move. Seth's face was a study in agonized fury. "What's this?" Cam said absently, cocking his head to view the sketch that was by now all but under his nose.

Seth nearly rolled his eyes. It was about damn time. "Nothing," he muttered, and gleefully kept eating.

"Looks like Ethan's boat." Cam picked up his coffee, glanced at Phillip. "Doesn't it?"

Phillip stood, sampling the first bite of his breakfast, approving it. "Yeah. It's a good drawing." Curious, he looked at Seth. "You do it?"

"I was just fooling around." The flush of pride was creeping up his neck and leaving his stomach jittery.

"I work with guys who can't draw this well." Phillip gave Seth an absent pat on the shoulder. "Nice work."

"No big deal," Seth said with a shrug as the thrill burst through him.

"Funny, Ethan and I were just talking about using sketches of boats in the boatyard. You know, Phil, like advertising our work."

Phillip settled down to his eggs, but lifted a brow in both surprise and approval. "You thought of that? Color me amazed. Good idea." He studied the sketch more closely as he worked it through. "Frame it rough, keep the edges of the sketch raw. It should look working-man, not fancy."

Cam made a sound in his throat, as if he were mulling it over. "One sketch won't make much of a statement." He frowned at Seth. "I guess you couldn't do a few more, like of Ethan's workboat? Or if I got some pictures of a couple of the boats I've worked on?"

"I dunno." Seth fought to keep the excitement out of his voice. He nearly succeeded in keeping his eyes bored when they met Cam's, but little lights of pleasure danced in them. "Maybe."

It didn't take Phillip long to clue in. Catching the drift, he reached for his coffee and nodded. "Could make a nice statement. Clients who came in would see different boats we've done. It'd be good to have a drawing of the one you're starting on."

Cam snorted. "Ethan's got a pathetic sketch. Looks like a kindergarten project. Don't know what can be done about it." Then he looked at Seth, narrowed his eyes. "Maybe you can take a look at it."

Seth felt laughter bubble up in his throat and gamely swallowed it. "I suppose."

"Great. You got about ninety seconds to make the bus, kid, or you're walking to school."

"Shit." Seth scrambled up, grabbed his backpack, and took off in a flurry of pounding sneakers.

When the front door slammed, Phillip sat back. "Nice work, Cam."

"I have my moments."

"Every now and again. How'd you know the kid could draw?"

"He gave Anna a picture he'd done of the pup."

"Hmm. So what's the deal with her?"

"Deal?" Cam went back to his pitiful toast and tried not to envy Phillip his eggs.

"Spending the weekend, sailing, cooking dinner. Haven't seen you sniffing around any other woman since she came on the scene." Phillip grinned into his coffee. "Sounds serious. Almost . . . domestic."

"Get a grip." Cam's stomach took an uncomfortable little lurch. "We're just enjoying each other."

"I don't know. She looks like the picket-fence type to me."

Cam snorted. "Career woman. She's smart, she's ambitious, and she's not looking for complications." She wanted a house in the country, Cam remembered, near the water, with a yard where she could plant flowers.

"Women always look for complications," Phillip said positively. "Better watch your step."

"I know where I'm going, and how to get there."

"That's what they all say."

• • •

ANNA WAS DOING HER best not to look for, or find, complications. It was one of the reasons she'd decided against seeing Cameron on Friday night. She made work her excuse and compromised by telling him she'd be at his house bright and early Saturday morning for a sail. When he wheedled, she weakened and promised to make lasagna.

The part of her that gained so much pleasure from watching others eat what she'd prepared herself came from her grandmother. Anna believed that was something to be proud of.

Though she didn't commit to spending the night, they both realized it was understood.

She took the evening for herself, changing out of her suit and into baggy sweats. She put some of her favorite music on, nestling Billie Holiday between Verdi and Cream. She poured a glass of good red wine and watched the sun set.

It was time, she knew, long past time, to do some clear thinking, some objective analyzing. She'd known Cameron Quinn only a matter of weeks, yet she'd allowed herself to become more involved with him than with any other man who'd touched her life.

This level of involvement hadn't been in her plans. She usually planned so well. Steps she took, both professionally and personally, were always carefully thought out. She knew that was a protective action, one she had decided upon coolly and at an early age. If she thought about where each step was leading or could lead, held back on impulse, and depended on intellect, it was much harder to make a mistake.

She felt she'd made too many mistakes years before. If she had continued along the path she blindly raced down after losing her innocence and her mother, she would have been doomed.

She'd had to learn not to blame herself for the things she had done during that dark part of her life, not to wallow in guilt for the hurt she'd caused the people who loved her. Guilt was a negative emotion. Anna preferred positive actions, results, direction.

What she had chosen and accomplished had been for her grandparents, for her mother, and for that terrified child curled on the side of a dark road.

It had taken time, a long healing time, before it came to her that while she'd lost her mother, her grandparents had lost their only child. A daughter they loved. Despite their grief, they opened their home to Anna; despite her destructive actions, their hearts never faltered.

Eventually she learned to accept the loss, the horrors she'd experienced. More, she learned to accept that everything she had done for the two years following that night was the result of a wounded soul. She was fortunate to have people love her enough to help her heal.

When she found her way again, she promised herself that she would never be reckless again.

Impulse was saved for foolish things. Spending sprees, long, fast drives to nowhere. It had become so important to her that she remain basically practical, motivated, and rational that she had buried that reckless bent of her heart. Now, she thought, it was that same heart that had led her to this.

Loving Cameron Quinn was ridiculously reckless. And she knew it was going to cost her.

But her emotions were her own responsibility, she decided. That was something she had learned the hard way. She would handle them, and she would survive them.

But it was just so odd, she admitted, and leaned against the open patio door to catch the early-evening breeze. She'd always believed that if she ever experienced love, she would be aware of every stage of it. She'd hoped to enjoy it—the gradual slide she'd imagined, the mutual awareness of deepening feelings.

But there had been no gradual slide, no gentle fall with Cam. It was one fast, hard tumble. One moment, she felt attraction, interest, enjoyment. Then it seemed she no more than blinked before she was headlong in love.

She imagined it would scare him to death—as he was racing for the hills. The image made her laugh a little. They were well matched there, she decided. She would like to do some fast running in the opposite direction herself. She'd been prepared for an affair but far from ready for a love affair.

So analyze, she ordered herself. What was it about him that made the difference? His looks? On a little hum of pleasure, she closed her eyes. There was little doubt that's what had gained her attention initially. What woman wouldn't look twice, then look again at those dangerous, dark looks? The restless steel-colored eyes, the firm mouth that was equally appealing in a grin or a snarl. His body was the perfect female fantasy of tough muscle, rough hands, and lean lines.

Naturally she'd been attracted. And his quick mind had intrigued her. So had his arrogance, she admitted—though it was a lowering thought. But it was his heart that had changed everything. Oh, she hadn't expected that generous heart—recklessly generous. He had so much to give and was so unaware of it.

He thought himself selfish, hard-bitten, even cold. And she imagined he could be. But where it counted most, he was warm and giving. She didn't think he was fully aware of how much he was offering Seth or how their relationship was changing.

She sincerely doubted he fully understood that he loved the boy. And Anna realized it was that blind spot in Cam to his own goodness that had undone her.

She supposed, when it came down to it, falling in love with him had actually been sensible.

Staying in love with him would be disastrous. She would have to work on that.

The phone rang, distracting her. Carrying her wine, she walked back in and picked up the portable on the coffee table. "Hello."

"Miz Spinelli. Working?"

She couldn't stop the smile. "Working something out,

yes.'' An aria soared out of her stereo as she sat down, propped her feet on the coffee table. ''You?''

''Ethan and I have a little something we'll fiddle with tonight yet. Then I'm not even going to think about work until Monday.''

He had a portable phone himself and had wandered outside, where he might find some privacy. It was Seth's turn to do the dinner dishes, and he heard another plate hit the floor with a crash. ''They're calling for fair weather tomorrow.''

''Are they? That's handy.''

''You could still drive up tonight.''

It was tempting, but she'd already given in to too many impulses where he was concerned. ''I'll be there early enough in the morning.''

''I don't suppose you have a bikini. A red one.''

She tucked her tongue in her cheek. ''No, I don't . . . mine's blue.''

He waited a beat. ''Don't forget to pack.''

''If I pack—if I stay—I keep the key to the bedroom door.''

''You're so strict.'' He watched an egret sail over the water and into a nest atop a marker. Making for home, he thought, settling in.

''Just cautious, Quinn. And very smart. How's the building coming?''

''Along,'' he murmured. He liked hearing her voice, feeling the moist air move, watching the evening slide gentle as a kiss over water and trees. ''I'll show you when you're here.''

He wanted to show her Seth's sketch. He'd framed it himself that afternoon and wanted to share it with . . . someone who mattered. ''We'll probably get started on the first boat next week.''

''Really? That quick?''

''Why wait? It's time to put our money down and see how the dice fall. I've been feeling lucky lately.'' From the house behind him he heard the puppy bark madly, followed by Simon's deeper tones. Then Phillip's voice, raised in a half shout, half laugh and echoed by the rarely heard sound of Seth's giggle.

It made him turn, stare at the house. The back door opened, and the two canine forms bulleted out, tumbling over each other as they reached the steps. And there, framed in the doorway with the kitchen light washing through, was the boy, grinning.

Whatever pulled at Cam's heart pulled hard. For a moment, just one wild moment, he thought he heard the creak of the porch rocker and his father's low chuckle.

"Jesus, it's weird," he murmured.

The connection began to waver and crackle as he walked. "What?"

"Everything." He found himself gripping the phone tighter, yearning for her with a wild, almost desperate desire. "You should be here. I miss you."

"I can't hear you."

He realized he'd been stepping away from the house, a kind of knee-jerk denial of the sensation of being drawn in.

Coming home. Settling in.

With a shake of his head, he walked back until the connection cleared, and thanked God for the vagaries of technology. "I said . . . what are you wearing?"

She laughed softly, looked down at her baggy, practical sweats. "Why, nothing much," she purred, and both of them fell into the ease of phone flirting with various sensations of relief.

A SHORT TIME LATER, Cam set the phone on the porch steps and wandered down to the dock. Water lapped gently against the hull of the boat. Night birds were stirring, and the deep two-toned call of an owl in the woods beyond led the chorus. The sea was ink-dark under the fragile light of a thumbnail moon.

There was work to do. He knew Ethan would be waiting for him. But he needed to sit there by the water for a moment. To sit in the quiet while stars winked on and the owl called endlessly, patiently, for its mate.

He didn't jump when he saw the movement beside him. He was getting used to it. He couldn't count the times he'd sat on this same dock under this same sky with his father. It occurred to him that it was probably a little different to sit here with his father's ghost, but what the hell. Nothing about his life was the same as it once had been.

"I knew you were here," Cam said quietly.

"I like to keep an eye on things." Ray, dressed in fisherman's pants and a short-sleeved sweatshirt that Cam remembered had once been bright blue, dangled a line in the water. "Been a while since I did any night fishing."

Cameron decided that if Ray pulled up a wriggling catfish, it would most likely send him over the thin edge of sanity. "How close an eye?" he asked, thinking of Anna and just what the two of them did in the dark.

Ray chuckled. "I always respected my boys' privacy, Cam. Don't you worry about that. She sure is a looker," he said lightly. "She tries to cover it up when she's working, but a man with a good eye can see through it. You always had a good eye for the ladies."

"How about you?" Cam hated himself for asking. It was such a peaceful night, such a perfect one. But he never knew how long these visitations—hallucinations, whatever they were—would last. He had to ask. "How was your eye for the ladies, Dad?"

"Sharp enough—landed on your mother, didn't it?" And Ray sighed. "I never touched another woman after I made my vows to Stella, Cam. I looked, I appreciated, I enjoyed, but I never touched."

"You have to tell me about Seth."

"I can't. It's not the way it has to be. You did a good thing by the boy, making him a part of the business you're starting by using his drawings. He needs to feel that he's a part of things. I wish I'd had more time with him, with all of you. But that's not the way it has to be either.''

''Dad—''

''You know what I miss, Cam? The silliest things. Watching the three of you argue over something. There were times when your mother and I thought you'd bicker us crazy, but I miss that now. And early-morning fishing when the sun just starts to burn off the mist over the water. I miss teaching. I miss seeing that look on a student's face when something you say, just one thing, clicks and opens the mind. I miss pretty girls in summer dresses and lying in bed at three o'clock in the morning listening to rain on the roof.''

Then he turned his head and smiled. His eyes were as bright and brilliantly blue as the sweatshirt had once been. ''You should appreciate those things while you have them, but you never do. Not all the way. Too busy living. Now and again, you should try to stop to appreciate the little things. They'll build up if you do.''

''I've got a little more on my mind than rain on the roof right now.''

''I know. You've got a mess on your hands, but you're sorting it. You've still got to figure out what you want, and what you need, and what's inside you. You've got more in there than you think.''

''I want answers. I need answers.''

''You'll find them,'' Ray said complacently. ''When you slow down.''

''Tell me this. Do Ethan and Phillip know you're . . . here?''

''They will.'' Ray smiled again. ''When it's time for it. It should be a nice day for sailing tomorrow. Enjoy the little things,'' he said and faded away.

SEVENTEEN

HE WAS WATCHING FOR her. Cam figured it was just one more first in his life. He'd never watched and waited for a woman that he could recall. Even as a teenager, they had come to him. Calling on the phone, wandering by the house, loitering near his locker at school. He supposed he'd gotten used to it. Spoiled by it.

He had never faced the typical male terror of asking for that first date. He'd been asked out when he was fifteen by the luscious Allyson Brentt. An older woman of sixteen. She even picked him up at his front door in her daddy's '72 Chevy Impala. He wasn't sure how he felt about being driven around by a girl. Until Allyson had parked on Blue Crab Drive and suggested they make use of the backseat.

He didn't mind that a bit.

Losing his virginity to pretty, fast-handed Allyson at fifteen was a sweaty and delightful experience. And Cam had never looked back.

He liked women, liked everything about them—even the annoying parts. It was what made them female, and he figured men got the best part of the deal. They got to look, they got to touch and smell. And unless they were complete morons, they could usually wriggle out of those soft arms and move on to the next ones without too much trouble.

He'd never been a moron.

But he watched for Anna, and waited for her. And wondered what it was about her that made him not quite so anxious to wriggle.

Maybe it was the lack of pressure, he mused as he wandered away from the dock toward the side of the house to listen for her car. Again. It could be the very lack of any expectations. She was joyfully sexual, and she didn't seem to expect a lot of romantic trappings. She'd come from a painful childhood, yet she'd gotten past the damage and made herself into something strong and whole.

He admired that.

The way she could, and did, play up or play down her looks fascinated him. That duality kept him wondering who she would be. And yet both parts of her fit so smoothly together, a man could barely see the seam.

The more he thought about her, the more he wanted her.

"What're you doing?"

He nearly jumped out of his skin when Seth came up behind him. He'd been staring at the road, all but willing Anna to pull into the drive. Now he jammed his hands in his pockets, mortified.

"Nothing, just walking around."

"You weren't walking," Seth pointed out.

"Because I'd stopped. Now I'm walking again. See?"

Seth rolled his eyes at Cam's back, then caught up with him. "What am I supposed to do?"

Cam feigned intense interest in the candy-red tulips sunning themselves along the edge of the house. "About what?"

"Stuff. Ethan's out on the workboat and Phillip's closed up in the office doing computer stuff."

"So?" He leaned down to tug up a weed—at least he

thought it was a weed. Where the hell was she? "Where are those kids you've been hanging with?"

"They had to go to the store and have lunch with their grandmother." Seth sneered on principle. "I don't have anything to do. It's boring."

"Well, go . . . clean your room or something."

"Come on."

"Jesus, what am I, your social director? Is the TV broken?"

"Nothing on Saturday mornings but kid shit."

"You *are* a kid," Cam pointed out and heard the sound of an approaching car with vast relief. "Teach that brain-dead dog of yours some tricks."

"He's not brain-dead." Instantly insulted, Seth turned and whistled for the pup. "Watch." Foolish raced up, carrying what appeared to be a can of beer in his mouth.

"Yeah, chewing on aluminum. That's brilliant. Look, I don't—" But Cam broke off when Seth snapped a finger, pointed, and Foolish plopped his butt on the ground.

"He does it on voice command, too," Seth said matter-of-factly as he rubbed Foolish's head in reward. "But I've got him responding to hand signals." He held a hand out, and Foolish gamely lifted a paw.

"That's pretty good." Pride and surprise mixed in his voice. "How long did it take you to teach him that?"

"Just a couple hours here and there."

All three watched as Anna pulled into the drive. Foolish was the first to rush to greet her.

"He doesn't do real good with Stay yet," Seth confided. "But we haven't worked on it long."

He didn't do real good with Down, either. The minute Anna stepped out of the car Foolish was leaping and yipping, his tongue lashing out joyfully to lick everywhere.

Cam figured the dog had the right idea. He'd have liked to jump on her and start licking himself. She wore jeans that were faded to a soft, pale blue and a lipstick-red top tucked into the waistband. It was a simple outfit that borrowed from the practical and the siren.

And made Cam's mouth water.

"She looks different with her hair down," Seth commented.

"Yeah." He wanted his hands on it, on her. And that was that.

She was crouched down, purring at the puppy, who had flopped adoringly on his back to have his belly rubbed. Her head came up, and even with the shaded glasses, Cam could see her eyes widen in awareness, then shift warningly to the child who walked behind him.

Ignoring the signal, he hauled her to her feet, gave her one good yank that made her stumble over the pup and against him, and closed his mouth over her sputtering protest.

It was like being swallowed by the sun, was all she could think. The heat was huge and had reached flash point before she could draw the first breath. Need, restless and greedy, pumped out of him and slammed into her at alarming speed. The wild drumming of a woodpecker hunting breakfast echoed through the still air and matched the frantic beat of her heart. All she could do was hold on until he'd devoured enough of what he wanted from her to satisfy him.

When he eased her back, those clever lips curved—a smug look she was sure she would resent when her head settled back on her shoulders again. "Morning, Anna."

"Good morning." She cleared her throat, stepped back, and made herself look over at Seth. He appeared to be more bored than shocked, so she worked up a smile for him. "Good morning, Seth."

"Yeah, hi."

"Your dog's growing into his feet." Because she needed the distraction, she looked down at Foolish and held out a hand. He planted his rump and lifted a paw, charming her. "Oh, aren't you smart?" She crouched again, shook his paw, tugged his ears. "What else can you do?"

"We're working on a couple of things." Foolish had

just run through his entire repertoire, but Seth didn't want to say so.

"You make a good team. I've got some groceries in the car," she said casually. "Makings for dinner. Give me a hand?"

"Yeah, all right." He shot a resentful look at Cam. "I've got nothing else to do."

"We're going sailing, aren't we?" She said it brightly, amused when she saw Cam's mouth fall open and Seth look at her with sharp, interested eyes.

"Am I going?"

"Of course." She turned, opened the car door, then handed him a bag. "As soon as we put this stuff away. I hope I'm a quick learner. I know next to nothing about boats."

Cheered, Seth settled bags on each hip. "Nothing to it. But you should have a hat." With this, he carted his bags toward the house.

"I was figuring on it being just you and me," Cam told her. And he'd had a nice fantasy going about slipping into some quiet bend of the river and making rocky love to her in the bottom of the boat.

"Were you?" She took out a small overnight bag, pushed it into his hands. "I'm sure it'll be great fun with the three of us."

She closed her car door, patted Cam's cheek, then sauntered into the house behind Seth.

IT TURNED OUT TO BE the four of them. Seth insisted on taking Foolish, and with Anna backing him all the way, they outvoted Cam.

It was tough to stay annoyed when his crew was so damn cheerful. Foolish sat on a bench, wearing an ancient doggie life jacket that had belonged to one of Ray and Stella's numerous dogs, and barked happily at waves and birds.

Seth, already munching on one of the sandwiches from the cooler, dutifully explained to Anna the mystery of the rigging.

She looked so damned cute, Cam thought, with one of his old and battered Orioles caps on her head, watching studiously as Seth identified each line.

He maneuvered through the channels, motoring between markers at an easy speed, working through what the locals called Little Neck River into Tangier Sound and toward the bay.

There was a light chop, and Cam glanced back to see how Anna would weather it. She was kneeling in the stern, leaning over the rail, but he saw with a grin that it wasn't because of a queasy stomach. Her smile was huge, her finger pointing eagerly as she caught sight of the clumps of trees and spreading marshes of Smith Island.

He called for Seth to hoist sail.

It was a moment Anna would never forget. City life hadn't prepared her for the sounds, the motion, the sight of white sails rising, snapping in the wind, then filling with it.

For a moment the boat seemed to fly, with the wind slapping her cheeks and filling the canvas to bursting. Water churned in their wake and she tasted salt.

She wanted to watch everything at once, the waves rising from blue-green water, the sea of white canvas above, the stretches and bumps of land. And the man and boy who worked so smoothly, so competently, with barely a word passing between them.

They sailed past what Seth identified as a crab shanty. It was no more than a fragile shack of beaten and weathered gray wood stilted out of the water and attached to a rickety dock. The orange floats that marked the crab pots dotted the surface. She watched a workboat rocking in the tide as a waterman—a picture in his faded pants, battered cap, and white boots—hauled up a chicken wire cage.

He paused in his work long enough to touch the brim

of his cap in greeting before tossing two snapping crabs into his water tank.

Life on the water, Anna thought and watched the workboat putt toward the next float.

"That's Little Donnie," Seth told her. "Ethan says they call him that even though he's grown up because his father's Big Donnie. Weird."

Anna laughed. It had looked to her as if Little Donnie was pushing two hundred pounds. "I guess that's the way it is when you live in a small community. It must be wonderful to live and work on the water that way."

Seth lifted a shoulder. "It's okay. But I'd rather just sail."

When she lifted her face to the wind, she decided he had a point. Just sail—fast and free, with the boat rising and falling, the gulls wheeling overhead. Cam looked so natural at the wheel, she thought, with his long legs planted apart to accommodate the roll of the boat, his hands firm, his dark hair flying. When he turned his head, was it any wonder her heart jumped? When he held out a hand, was it any wonder she rose and walked cautiously over the unfamiliar deck to take it.

"Want the wheel?"

Desperately. "Better not," she said, trying to be practical. "I don't know what I'm doing."

"I do." He tugged her in front of him, put his hands over hers. "That's Pocomoke," he told her, nodding toward a narrow channel. "If you want to slow down, we can head that way, dodge some crab pots."

The wind slapped playfully at her face. She watched a gull swoop toward the surface of the water, skim it, then rise up calling in that sharp cry that sounded like a laughing scream. The hell with practicalities. "I don't want to slow down."

She heard him laugh above her ear. "Atta girl."

"Where are we heading? What are we doing?"

"Heading south, southwest. Sailing to the luff," he told her. "On the edge of the wind."

"On the edge? It feels like we're in the middle of it. I didn't know we could go so fast. It's wonderful."

"Good. Hold on a minute."

To her shock, he stepped back and called to Seth to help him make some adjustments to the sails. As her hands white-knuckled on the wheel, she heard them laughing. She heard the creak of the masts, the shiver of the canvas as it turned. If anything, she thought the boat picked up speed. She tried to relax. After all, there was nothing but water ahead of them.

She could see to the right—starboard, she corrected herself—a small motorboat cruising out of one of the many rivers and channels. Too far away, she judged, for any traffic jams or accidents.

Just as she had herself convinced she could do the job without incident, the boat tilted. She muffled a scream and nearly whipped the wheel in the opposite direction of the tilt, but Cam's hands closed over hers again and held it steady.

"We're going over!"

"Nah. We're heeled in nicely. More speed."

Her heart stayed in her throat. "You left me at the wheel."

"Sails needed trimming. The kid knows how to work the sheets. Ethan's taught him a lot, and he catches on quick. He's a damn good sailor."

"But you left me at the wheel," she repeated.

"You did fine." He brushed an absent kiss on the top of her head. "That's Tangier Island up ahead. We'll go around it, then head north. There's some quiet spots on the Little Choptank. We'll hit there about lunchtime."

They didn't appear to be capsizing, she thought with a steadying breath. And since she hadn't run them aground, she relaxed enough to lean back against him.

She planted her feet apart, as Cam did, and let her body balance with the motion of the boat. Her newest ambition was to have a little sloop, skiff, whatever it was called, when she finally got that house on the water.

She would have the Quinn brothers build it for her, she decided, dreaming. "If I had a boat, I'd do this every chance I got."

"We'll have to teach you the basics. Before long we'll have you trapezing."

"What? Swinging from the mast in a spangled leotard?"

The image had its appeal. "Not quite. You use a rig—a trapeze—and you hang out over the water."

"For fun?"

"Well, I like it," he said with a laugh. "It's for speed, balancing power."

"Hanging out over the water," she mused, glancing to port. "I might like it too."

HE LET HER WORK THE jib, under Seth's watchful eye. She liked the feel of the line in her hand and knowing she was in charge—more or less—of the billowing white sheet. They rounded the little sandy spit of Tangier Island, and she was treated to the quick maneuvering of tacking, jibbing, the teamwork necessary to maintain speed while changing course.

Cam had stripped down to denim cutoffs, and his skin gleamed with sun and sweat and water. If her hands ached a little from the unfamiliar work, she didn't complain. Instead she got a foolish thrill when Cam told her she was a pretty good crew.

They had lunch on Hudson Creek off the Little Choptank River, near a broken-down wharf with only the birds and the lap of water for company. The sun was bright in a clear blue sky, and the temperature had soared into the eighties to give a hint of the summer that was still weeks away.

To the accompaniment of music on the radio, they took a cooling swim. Foolish paddled joyfully while Seth dived beneath the mirrorlike surface and swam like a wild dolphin.

"He's having the time of his life," Anna murmured. A layer of the sulky, defiant, angry boy she'd first interviewed was being washed away. She wondered if he knew it.

"Then I guess I can't be too annoyed that you insisted on his coming along."

She smiled. She'd bundled her hair on top of her head in a vain attempt to keep it dry. With the way Seth and the puppy were splashing, nothing was dry. "You don't really mind. And you'd never have had that smooth of a sail without him on board."

"True enough, but there's something to be said for a rough sail." He parted the water in front of him, then slid his arms around her.

Anna gripped his shoulders in automatic defense. "No dunking."

"Would I do anything that predictable?" His eyes were smoky with laughter. "Especially when this is more fun." He tilted his head and kissed her.

Their lips were wet and slippery, and Anna's pulse thrummed at the sensation of his mouth sliding over hers, then capturing, then taking. The cool water seemed to grow warmer as their legs tangled. She was weightless, sighing as she floated into the kiss.

Then she was underwater.

She surfaced sputtering, shaking wet hair out of her eyes. The first thing she heard was Seth's laughter. The first thing she saw was Cam's grin.

"It was irresistible," he claimed, then swallowed water himself as she flipped onto her stomach and kicked it into his face.

"You're next," she warned Seth, who was so stunned at the idea of an adult playing with him that she caught him easily and wrestled him under.

He struggled, spat out water, swallowed more when he laughed. "Hey, I didn't do anything."

"You laughed. Besides, as I see it, you guys work as a team. It was probably your idea."

"No way." He wiggled free, then got the bright idea to dive and pull her under the surface by the ankle.

It was a pitched battle, and when they were exhausted, they agreed to call it a draw. It was only then that they noticed Cam was no longer in the water but sitting comfortably on the side of the boat eating a sandwich.

"What are you doing up there?" Anna called out while she pushed her sopping-wet hair back.

"Watching the show." He washed the ham and cheese down with Pepsi. "A couple of goons."

"Goons?" She slid her eyes toward Seth, and in tacit agreement the foes became a unit. "I only see one goon around here, how about you?"

"Just one," he agreed as they swam slowly toward the boat.

Any idiot could have seen what they had in mind. Cam nearly lifted his legs out of reach, then he decided what the hell and let them pull him back into the water with an impressive splash.

It would be hours before it occurred to Seth that Anna and Cam had both had their hands on him. And he hadn't been scared at all.

AFTER THE BOAT WAS docked, the sails dropped, the decks swabbed, Anna rolled up her metaphorical sleeves and got to work in the kitchen. It was her mission to give the Quinn men a meal they wouldn't soon forget. She might have been a novice sailor, but here she was an expert.

"It smells like glory," Phillip told her when he wandered in.

"It'll taste better." She built the layers of her lasagna with an artist's flair. "Old family recipe."

"They're the best," he agreed. "We've got my father's

secret waffle batter recipe. I'll have to whip you up some in the morning."

"I'd like that." She glanced up to smile at him and noted what she thought was worry in his eyes. "Everything all right?"

"Sure. Just some leftover tangles from work." It had nothing to do with work, but with the latest report from the private investigator he'd hired. Seth's mother had been spotted in Norfolk—and that was entirely too close. "Need any help in here?"

"Everything's under control." She finished off her casserole with a thin layer of mozzarella before popping it in the oven. "You might want to try the wine."

Absently Phillip picked up the bottle breathing on the counter. And instantly his interest was piqued. "Nebbiolo, the best of the Italian reds."

"I think so, and I can promise my lasagna's a match for it."

Phillip grinned as he poured two glasses. His eyes were a golden brown that for some reason made Anna think of archangels. "Anna, my love, why don't you toss Cam over and run away with me?"

"Because I'd hunt you both down and kill you," Cam stated as he stepped into the kitchen. "Back off from my woman, bro, before I hurt you." Though it was said lightly, Cam wasn't entirely sure he was joking. And he wasn't entirely pleased to feel the hot little spurt of jealousy.

He wasn't the jealous type.

"He doesn't know a Barolo from a Chianti," Phillip told her as he got down another glass. "You're better off with me."

"Goodness," she said in a passable imitation of their below-the-Mason-Dixon-line drawl, "I just love being fought over by strong men. And here comes one more," she added as Ethan stepped through the back door. "You want to duel for me too, Ethan?"

He blinked and scratched his head. Women confused

him, but he was pretty sure there was a joke coming on. "Did you make whatever's cooking in there?"

"With my own little hands," she assured him.

"I'll go get my gun."

When she laughed, he shot her a quick smile, then ducked out of the room to shower off the day's work.

"Jesus, Ethan nearly flirted with a woman." Amazed, Phillip lifted his glass in a toast. "We're going to have to keep you around, Anna."

"If someone will set the table while I put the salad together, I might hang around long enough to let you sample my cannoli."

Cam and Phillip eyed each other. "Whose turn is it?" Cam demanded.

"Not mine. It must be yours."

"No way. I did it yesterday." They studied each other another moment, then both turned to the door and yelled for Seth.

Anna only shook her head. Younger brothers, she supposed, were meant to be abused in such matters.

She knew the meal was a success when Seth gobbled up a third helping. He'd lost that alley-cat boniness, she noted. And the pallor. Perhaps his eyes were still occasionally wary, peeking out under his lashes as if searching for the blow that he'd learned too young to expect. But more often, Anna thought, there was humor in his eyes. He was a bright boy who was discovering how to be amused by people.

His language was rough, and she didn't expect there would be a great deal of improvement in it as long as he lived in a household of men. Though she did see that Cam booted him lightly under the table now and again when he swore too often.

They were making it work. She'd had strong doubts in the beginning that three grown men, well set in their ways, would find a way of adjusting, of making room. And especially of opening their hearts to a boy who had been thrust upon them.

But they were making it work. When she wrote her report on the Quinn case the following week, she was going to state that Seth DeLauter was home, exactly where he belonged.

It would take time for the guardianship to move from temporary to permanent, but she would add her weight. Nothing warmed her heart quite so deeply as seeing the way Seth looked over at Cam after another under-the-table kick and grinned exactly like a ten-year-old boy caught sinning.

He would make a terrific father, she thought. Just rough enough around the edges to make it fun. He'd be the type to cart a child around on his shoulders, to wrestle in the yard. She could almost see it—the handsome dark-haired little boy, the pretty rosy-cheeked girl.

"You're in the wrong business," Phillip told her as he pushed back from the table and considered loosening his belt.

She blinked, caught daydreaming, and very nearly flushed. "I am?"

"You should own a restaurant. Any time you want to shift gears in that direction, I'll be the first in line to invest." He rose, intending to make use of his cappuccino maker to complement her dessert, and answered the phone on the first ring.

At the sound of the husky female voice with a sexy Italian accent, he raised his eyebrows. "He's right here." Phillip ran his tongue over his teeth and held out the phone to Cam. "It's for you, pal."

Cam took the phone, and after one purring sentence in his ear, almost placed the voice. "Hi, sugar," he said, searching for a name. *"Come va?"*

Because he did indeed love his brother, Phillip tried his best to distract Anna. "I just picked up this machine about six months ago," he told her, holding her chair so she would rise—and perhaps move out of earshot. "It's a beaut."

"Really?" She wasn't the least bit interested in the

working of some fancy coffee machine. Not when she'd heard just how smoothly Cam had greeted his obviously female caller. When she heard him laugh, her teeth went on edge.

It didn't occur to Cam to muffle his voice or censor the content. He'd finally put a name with the voice—Sophia of the curvy body and bedroom eyes—and was chatting lightly about mutual acquaintances. She liked racing—all manner of racing—and was a hot, sleek bullet in bed.

"No, I had to take a pass on the rest of the season this year," he told her. "I don't know when I'll get back to Rome. You'll be the first, *bella,*" he answered when she asked if he would call her when he did. "Sure, I remember—the little trattoria near the Trevi Fountain. Absolutely."

He leaned back against the counter. Her voice brought back memories. Not of her particularly, as he could barely get a clear image of her face in his head. But of Rome itself, the busy, narrow streets, the smells, the sounds, the rush.

The races.

"What?" Her question about his Porsche jerked him back to the present time and place. "Yeah, I've got it garaged in Nice until . . ."

He trailed off, his thoughts scattering as she asked him if he would consider selling it. She had a friend, she told him. Carlo. He remembered Carlo, didn't he? Carlo wondered if Cam would be interested in selling the car, since he was staying so long in the States.

"I haven't thought about it." Sell the car? A little lance of panic stabbed him. It would be like admitting he wasn't going back. Not just to Europe but to his life.

She was speaking quickly, persuasively, her Italian and English mixing and confusing him. He had her number, *si?* And could call her anytime. She would tell Carlo he was thinking about it. They were all missing Cam. Rome was so *noioso* without him. She had heard he had said no to a big race in Australia and was afraid it must be a woman holding him. Had he finally fallen for a woman?

"Yes, no—" His head was spinning. "It's complicated, sweetie. But I'll be in touch." Then she made him laugh one more time when she whispered a suggestion on how they might spend his first night back in Rome. "I'll be sure to keep that in mind. Darling, how could I forget? Yeah. *Ciao*."

Phillip was busily foaming milk and trying with the air of a desperate man to engage Anna in conversation about types of coffee beans. Ethan, with the instinct of a survivor, had already deserted the kitchen. And Seth simply sat, crumbling a heel of garlic bread for Foolish, who hid under the table.

Oblivious, Cam raised a suspicious eyebrow at the cappuccino machine. "I'll stick with regular coffee," he began and smiled when Anna walked up to him. "I remember your cannoli from—" And the air whooshed out of his lungs as she plowed a fist into his gut. Before he could suck it back in, she strode past him and outside with a slap of the screen door.

"What?" Rubbing his stomach, Cam goggled at Phillip. "Jesus, what did you say to her?"

"You're such a jerk," Phillip muttered and deftly poured the first cup.

"She looked really pissed," Seth commented and sniffed the air. "Can I try some of that junk you're making?"

"Sure." Phillip made up a latte, heavy on the milk, while Cam headed outside.

Cam caught up to Anna on the dock, where she stood fuming, her arms folded over her chest. "What the hell was that for?"

"Oh, I don't know, Cam. For the hell of it." She whirled around to face him, her eyes blazing in the starlight. "Women are peculiar creatures. They get annoyed when the man they're supposed to be with flirts over the phone, right in their damn face, with some Italian bimbo."

The light dawned, but to his credit he barely winced. "Come on, sugar—"

He broke off, unsure whether he was amused or frightened when she lifted a fist. "Don't you call me sugar. You use my name. Do you think I'm an idiot? Sugar, sweetie, honey pie—that's what you say when you can't even remember the name of the woman who's underneath you in bed."

"Wait a damn minute."

"No, *you* wait a damn minute. Do you have any idea how *insulting* it is to stand there and hear you make a date to meet your Italian squeeze in Rome when my lasagna's barely settled in your stomach?"

Worse, she thought, much, much worse, he'd done it seconds after she'd been building foolish castles in the air of him with children. Their children. Oh, it was mortifying. Infuriating.

"I wasn't making a date," he began, then paused, fascinated, while a stream of impressive Italian curses poured out of her mouth. "You didn't learn those from your grandparents." When she bared her teeth and hissed, he couldn't stop the smile. "You're jealous."

"It's not a matter of jealousy. It's a matter of courtesy." She tossed her head and tried to calm down. She was only embarrassing herself more with the outburst, she realized. But by damn, she wasn't finished yet. "You're a free agent, Cameron, and so am I. No pretenses, no promises, fine. But I won't tolerate you having phone sex while I'm standing in the same room."

"It wasn't phone sex, it was a conversation."

"The little trattoria by the Trevi Fountain?" she said, coolly now. "How could I forget? You'll be the first? You want to have some Italian *zucchero*, Cam, that's your business. But don't you ever do it in my face again."

She took a breath, then held up a hand before he could speak. "I'm sorry I hit you."

He gauged her mood. Ruffled, but calming. "No, you're not."

"Okay, I'm not. You deserved it."

"It didn't mean anything, Anna."

Yes, she thought wearily, it did. To her it meant a great deal. And that was her own fault, her own small disaster. "It was rude."

"Manners never were my strong point. I'm not interested in her. I can't even remember her face."

Anna angled her head. "Do you honestly think a statement like that goes to your credit?"

What the hell did she want him to say? he wondered with a quick, impatient hiss of breath. Sometimes, he supposed, the truth was best. "It's your face, Anna, that I can't get out of my mind."

She sighed. "Now you're trying to distract me."

"Is it working?"

"Maybe." Her emotions, she reminded herself, her problem. "Let's just agree that even casual relationships have lines that shouldn't be crossed."

He wasn't sure "casual" was the word to describe what was between them. But at the moment whatever made her happy suited him. "Okay. Starting now you're the only Italian bimbo I flirt with." Her bland, unsmiling stare made him grin. "It was terrific lasagna. None of my other bimbos could cook."

She slid her gaze to the water, back to his face. Then cocked her head consideringly. Cam was pretty sure he saw the beginnings of humor in her eyes. "We'd both end up in there," he told her. "But I don't mind if you don't."

"I suppose, all in all, I'd rather stay dry." She glanced toward the house when music slipped through the windows and into the air. "Who plays the violin?"

"That's Ethan." It was a quick and lively jig, one of their parents' favorites. The piano joined in, made him smile. "And that's Phillip."

"What do you play?"

"A little guitar."

"I'd like to hear." In a gesture of peace, she held out

a hand. He took it, drawing her closer, taking her fingers to his lips.

"You're the one I want, Anna. You're the one I think of."

For now, she thought, and let him slide her into his arms. Now was all that had to matter.

EIGHTEEN

ANNA WASN'T SURE HOW she felt about seeing Cam frown in concentration as he tuned up a battered old Gibson guitar. It was a piece of him she hadn't counted on.

It surprised her, pleased her, to see how smoothly, how easily the three men had slid into a song. Strong voices, she mused, quick and clever fingers. Teamwork once again. And unbroken family ties.

Without a doubt there had been many evenings such as this in their lives. She could imagine the three of them, years younger, melding their tunes, with the two people who had given them the music, and the purpose, and the family, sitting in the room with them.

She took that image, and the music, upstairs with her when she finally went to bed. To Cam's bed.

Reminding herself there was a child in the house, she locked the door—in case Cam came tiptoeing up from his makeshift bed on the sofa downstairs. And she told herself she wouldn't unlock it if he came tapping. No matter how sexy he'd looked strumming that old guitar to life.

Most of the tunes had been old Irish ballads and pub songs that she'd been unfamiliar with. She found them sad and heart-wrenching even when the tune beneath the words was lively. They mixed in some rock, and sneered at Seth when he suggested they play something from this century.

It had been sweet, Anna thought as she undressed. They would never think of it that way, and would likely be horrified that anyone else did. But sweet was how she'd seen it. Four males—four brothers—not of the blood but of the heart. It was easy to see how well they understood each other, and how they had come to just not accept the child but to include him.

When Seth commented that violins were for girls and wusses, Ethan merely smiled and went into a hot lick designed to capture Seth's interest and imagination. And Ethan's dry comment—*let's see a wuss do that*—earned a shrug and a grin from Seth.

When Seth had fallen asleep, they'd just left him there, sprawled on the rug with the puppy's head pillowed on his butt. Another belonging, in Anna's mind.

She slipped into her nightshirt and picked up her hairbrush. This house was an easy place to feel belonging. Big, simple rooms, lived-in furniture, noisy plumbing. She caught a few female touches that hadn't been there before. A gleam to the furniture, the odd vase of spring flowers. Compliments of the housekeeper, Anna imagined, which probably went largely unnoticed by the occupants.

If it were her house, she wouldn't change much, she decided, dreaming again as she ran the brush through her hair. Maybe spruce up some of the colors, add a bit of dash here and there with thick throw pillows and splashier flowers. She would definitely want to expand the gardens. She'd been doing some reading on perennials—what worked best in sun, what thrived in shade. There was a nice spot where the trees began to take over from the yard. She thought lily of the valley, some hostas, and periwinkles would do well there and add some interest.

Wouldn't it be lovely, she reflected, to while away a Saturday morning, digging in the earth, crowding pretty bedding plants together, planning the flow of colors and textures and heights?

And to watch them grow and spread and bloom, year after year.

A movement outside the window caught her eye in the mirror. Her heart sprang into her throat as she saw the shadow move behind the dark glass. As the window crept up, she turned slowly, holding the brush like a weapon.

And Cam stepped over the sill. "Hi." He had enjoyed watching her brush her hair, hated to see her stop. "Brought you something."

He held out a clutch of wild violets, which she tried to eye suspiciously. "Just how did you get up here?"

"Climbed." He stepped forward, she stepped back.

"Climbed what?"

"Up the side of the house mostly. Used to be able to shimmy up and down the gutter, but I weighed less then." He came closer, she moved back.

"That was clever of you. What if you'd fallen?"

He'd climbed sheer rock faces in Montana, Mexico, and France, but he smiled winningly at her concern. "You'd have felt sorry for me?"

"I don't think so." Since he had maneuvered his way to arm's length, she reached out and snatched the slightly crushed flowers. "Thanks for the violets. Good night."

Interesting, he decided. Her voice and her expression were prim despite the fact that she was standing there in nothing more than a long white T-shirt. For some reason he found the plain and practical cotton ridiculously sexy. It appeared he was finally going to get the chance to seduce her.

"I couldn't sleep." He reached over, hit the light switch, and left only the small bedside lamp burning warm and gold.

"You didn't try very long," she said, flicking the switch back on again.

"Seemed like hours." He lifted a hand to trace a finger lightly up her arm from wrist to elbow. Her skin was dusky, golden against the pure white of the nightshirt. "All I could think about was you. Beautiful Anna," he said softly, "with the Italian eyes."

Her toes seemed to curl in response to that skimming finger, which moved now to trace her jawline. Her heart was fluttering. No, it was her stomach. No, it was everything. "Cam, there's a young boy in the house."

"Who's dead asleep." His fingers dipped to her throat, tested the rapid pulse beating there. "Snoring on the living room rug."

"You should have carried him up to bed."

"Why?"

"Because . . ." There had to be a good reason, but how was she supposed to think clearly when he was looking at her, those flint-gray eyes so focused, so intense on her face? "You planned this," she said weakly.

"Not exactly. I thought I would have to talk you into going for a walk in the woods after the house quieted down. And then I would make love to you outside." He took her hand, turned it palm up, and pressed his lips to the center. "In the starlight. But rain's coming in."

"Rain?" She glanced toward the window and saw the curtains billowing in the freshening wind. When she looked back he was closer, and his arms were around her, those broad-palmed, clever hands stroking up her back.

"And I want you in bed. My bed." He tipped his head to nibble kisses along her jaw, then just under it where the skin was soft as water. "I want you, Anna. Day and night."

"Tomorrow," she began.

"Tonight. Tomorrow." And the word "always" was on the edge of his mind when his mouth found hers.

She made a small sound that might have been distress when his tongue slipped through her parted lips to deepen the kiss. It went deeper, still deeper until she had no choice but to let herself sink. The pretty little flowers drifted to the floor as her fingers went limp.

He had kissed her like this only once before, with such

unspeakable tenderness that it stripped her soul bare. If she could have formed words, she would have babbled out her love for him. But her knees were jelly, her heart lost, and words were beyond her.

He barely touched her, just those hands light on her back while his mouth drank from hers—and destroyed her.

"It's not a race this time." He heard himself murmur the words but wasn't sure if he spoke to himself or to her. All he knew was he wanted slow, painfully slow, endlessly slow, so that he could savor every moment, every move, every moan.

He reached out, dimmed the lights. "I want this spot," he whispered and let his mouth journey along the fragile skin just under her jaw again. "And this one." To the slender column of her throat, where her scent was warm and smoky.

When he stepped back and tugged his shirt over his head, she took a breath. She would get her feet back under her, she thought, and offer back some of what he was giving her. She reached for him, rose on her toes until their eyes and mouths lined up.

But he kissed her temples, her brow, her eyes when they fluttered closed. "I love looking at you," he told her. He took the hem of her nightshirt in his fingers and lifted it, inch by inch. "All of you. Even when you're not around, I have a picture of you in my head."

When her nightshirt was pooled on the floor, he kept his eyes on her face, lifted her into his arms. Felt her tremble.

And he knew, in one breath-stealing flash, that he had never wanted another woman the way he wanted Anna. This time when he laid her on the bed, it was he who sank mindlessly into the kiss.

He didn't have to order his hands to be gentle, to go slowly. He didn't have to hold back an urge to plunder. Not when she sighed so softly under his touch, not when she moved so fluidly beneath his hands, not when she gave so completely before he could ask.

He explored her with a kind of wonder, as if it were the first time. The first woman, the first need. Somehow it was new, this longing to linger. To sip instead of gulp. To glide instead of race. When her hands roamed over him, his skin quivered and warmed.

Neither of them heard the first soft patters of rain or the low, poignant moan of the wind.

She rose to peak on one long, shimmering wave. Floated down again breathing out his name.

Pleasure was liquid, soft as morning dew, wide as a dark sea. She could feel it sliding through her, shifting, spreading, taking her up on another high, curving crest where only he existed.

She pressed her mouth to his throat, his shoulder, would have absorbed him into her skin if she'd known a way. No one had ever taken her away so completely. And when she framed his face, brought his mouth to hers and poured all she was into the kiss, she knew he was with her. Absolutely hers.

When he filled her, it was only one more link. She opened, took him, and gave. They moved together slowly, breath tangling, gazes locked. Moved together silkily, rhythms matched to draw out every ounce of pleasure.

It built, dizzying and dazzling so that her lips curved even as her eyes swam. ''Kiss me,'' she demanded on one last, trembling breath.

So their mouths met, clung, as that last sweeping wave swamped them.

He didn't speak, didn't dare, when her hands slid limply from his back to the bed. He felt as if he'd tumbled off a cliff and fallen hard on his heart. Now his heart was swollen, exposed. And it was hers.

If this was love, it scared the hell out of him.

But he couldn't move, couldn't let her go. She felt so good, so right beneath him. His body was weak, sated, and his mind close to empty. It was only his heart that trembled and pumped.

He would worry about it later.

Saying nothing, nothing at all, he shifted, drew her close, possessively close, to his side, and let the rain lull him to sleep.

ANNA AWOKE WITH THE sun shooting into her eyes and was stunned to find herself wrapped up in Cam. His arms had a good strong hold on her, and hers were snug around him. Their legs were tangled, with her right hooked over his hip like an anchor.

If her mind had been clear it might have occurred to her that while they both assumed their affair was casual, even sophisticated, in sleep they'd both known better.

She slid her leg down, hoping to unknot their limbs, but he only shifted and anchored hers more firmly.

"Cam." She whispered it, feeling foolish and guilty, and when she received no response, wriggled and spoke more firmly. "Cameron, wake up."

He grunted, snuggled closer, and muttered something into her hair.

She sighed and, deciding she had no choice, lifted the leg that was caught between his until her knee pressed firmly against his crotch. Then she gave it a quick nudge.

That got his eyes open.

"Whoa! What?"

"Wake up."

"I'm awake." And his just-open eyes were all but crossed. "Would you mind moving your . . ." When the pressure eased off, he let out the breath he'd been holding. "Thanks."

"You've got to go." She was back to whispering. "You shouldn't have stayed in here all night."

"Why not?" he whispered back. "It's my bed."

"You know what I'm talking about," she hissed. "One of your brothers could get up any minute."

He exerted himself to lift his head a couple of inches and peer at the clock on the opposite nightstand. "It's after seven. Ethan's already up, has probably emptied his first crab pot. And why are we whispering?"

"Because you're not supposed to be here."

"I live here." A sleepy smile moved over his face. "Damn, you're pretty when you're all rumpled and embarrassed. I guess I have to have you again."

"Stop it." She nearly giggled, until his hand snuck around to cup her breast. "Not now."

"We're here now, naked and everything. And you're all soft and warm." He nuzzled his way to her neck.

"Don't you start."

"Too late. I'm already into the first lap."

And indeed when he shifted, she understood that the starting gun had already sounded. He was inside her in one easy move, and it was so smooth, so natural, so lovely, she could only sigh.

"No moaning," he said with a chuckle at her ear. "You'll wake up my brothers."

She snorted out a laugh and, caught between amusement and arousal, shoved and rolled until she straddled him. He looked sleepy, and dangerous, and exciting. A little breathless, she braced her hands on either side of his head. She bent down and sucked his bottom lip into her mouth.

"Okay, smart guy, let's see who moans first."

And arching back, she began to ride.

Afterward, they decided it was a tie.

SHE MADE HIM CLIMB OUT the window, which he claimed was ridiculous. But it made her feel a little less decadent. The house was quiet when she came downstairs, freshly showered and comfortable in olive-drab cotton slacks and a camp shirt. Seth was still sleeping on the rug. Foolish stood guard on the floor.

At the sight of Anna, the pup scrambled up, whining pitifully as he followed her into the kitchen. She assumed it was either an empty stomach or a full bladder. When she opened the back door, he shot out like a bullet and proved it was the latter by peeing copiously on an azalea just struggling into bloom.

Birds were singing with full, joyful throats. Dew sparkled on the grass—and the grass needed mowing. There was still a light mist on the water, but it was burning off quickly, like blown smoke, and through it she could see little diamond sparks of sunlight on calm water.

The air was fresh from the night's rain, and the leaves seemed greener, fuller than they had only a day before.

She built a little fantasy that included steaming coffee and a walk down to the dock. By the time she'd taken the first step toward brewing the coffee, Cam came in through the hallway door.

He hadn't shaved, she noted, and found that the stubble of beard suited her image of a lazy Sunday morning in the country. He lifted a brow.

She got two mugs out of the cupboard, then lifted hers. "Good morning, Cameron."

"Good morning, Anna." Deciding to play along, he walked over and gave her a chaste kiss. "How did you sleep?"

"Very well, and you?"

"Like a log." He wound a lock of her hair around his finger. "It wasn't too quiet for you?"

"Quiet?"

"City girl, country silence."

"Oh. No, I liked it. In fact, I don't think I've ever slept better."

They were grinning at each other when Seth stumbled in, rubbing his eyes. "Have we got anything to eat?"

Cam kept his gaze locked on Anna's. "Phillip ran his mouth about making waffles. Go wake him up."

"Waffles? Cool." He ran off, his bare feet slapping on the wood floor.

"Phillip's not going to appreciate that," Anna commented.

"He's the one who started the waffle rumor."

"I could make them."

"You made dinner. We take turns around here. To avoid chaos. And the shedding of blood." A loud and nasty thud sounded over their heads and made Cam grin. "Why don't we pour that coffee and take a walk out of the line of fire?"

"I was thinking the same thing."

On impulse, he grabbed a fishing pole. "Hold this." A hunt through the fridge netted him a small round of Phillip's Brie.

"I thought we were having waffles."

"We are. This is bait." He tucked the cheese in his pocket and picked up his coffee.

"You use Brie for bait?"

"You use what's handy. A fish is going to bite, it'll bite on damn near anything." He handed her a mug of coffee. "Let's see what we can catch."

"I don't know how to fish," she said as they headed out.

"Nothing to it. You drown a worm—or in this case some fancy cheese—and see what happens."

"Then why do guys go off with all that expensive, complicated gear and those funny hats?"

"Just trappings. We're not talking dry fly-fishing here. We're just dropping a line. If we can't pull up a couple of cats by the time Phillip's got waffles on the table, I've really lost my touch."

"Cats?" For one stunning moment, she was absolutely horrified. "You don't use cats as bait."

He blinked at her, saw that she was perfectly serious, then roared with laughter. "Sure we do. You catch 'em by the tail, skin their bellies, and drop them in." He took pity on her only because she went deathly pale. But it didn't stop him from laughing. "Cat*fish*, honey. We're going to bring up some catfish before breakfast."

"Very funny." She sniffed and started walking again. "Catfish are really ugly. I've seen pictures."

"You're telling me you've never eaten catfish?"

"Why in the world would I?" A little miffed, she sat on the side of the dock, feet dangling, and cupped her mug in both hands.

"Fry them fresh and fry them right, and you've never tasted better. Toss in some hush puppies, a couple ears of sweet corn, and you've got yourself a feast."

She eyed him as he settled beside her and began to bait his hook with Brie. His chin was stubbled, his hair untidy, his feet bare. "Fried catfish and hush puppies? This from the reckless Cameron Quinn, the man who races through the waters, roads, and the hearts of Europe. I don't think your little pastry from Rome would recognize you."

He grimaced and dropped his line in the water. "We're not going to get into that again, are we?"

"No." She laughed and leaned over to kiss his cheek. "I almost don't recognize you myself. But I kind of like it."

He handed her the pole. "You don't exactly look like the sober and dedicated public servant yourself this morning, Miz Spinelli."

"I take Sundays off. What do I do if I catch a fish?"

"Reel it in."

"How?"

"We'll worry about that when it happens." He leaned over to pull up the crab pot tied to the near piling. The two annoyed-looking jimmies inside made him grin. "At least we won't starve tonight."

The snapping claws had Anna lifting her feet slightly higher above the water. But she was content to sit there, sipping coffee, watching the morning bloom. When Mama Duck and her six fuzzy babies swam by, she had what Cam considered a typical city girl reaction.

"Oh, look! Look, baby ducks. Aren't they cute?"

"We get a nest down there in the bend near the edge of the woods most every year." And because she was looking so dreamy-eyed, he couldn't resist. "Makes for good hunting over the winter."

"Hunting what?" she murmured, charmed and already imagining what it would be like to hold one of those puffy ducklings in her hand. Then her eyes popped wide, horrified. "You shoot the little ducks?"

"Well, they're bigger by then." He had never shot a duck or anything else in his life. "You can sit right here and drop a couple before breakfast."

"You should be ashamed."

"Your city's showing."

"I'd call it my humanity. If they were my ducks, no one would shoot them." His quick grin had her narrowing her eyes. "You were just trying to get a rise out of me."

"It worked. You look so cute when you're outraged." He kissed her cheek to mollify her. "My mother's heart was too soft to allow hunting. Fishing never bothered her. She said that was more of an even match. And she hated guns."

"What was she like?"

"She was . . . steady," he decided. "It was hard to rock her. Once you did, she had a kick-ass temper, but it was tough to get it going. She loved her work, loved the kids. She had a lot of soft spots. She'd cry at movies or over books, and she couldn't even watch when we cleaned fish. But when there was trouble, she was a rock."

He'd taken Anna's hand without realizing it, lacing their fingers. "When I came here I was beat up pretty bad. She fixed me up. I kept thinking I'd take off as soon as I was steady on my feet again. I kept telling myself these people were a couple of assholes. I could rob them blind and take off anytime I wanted. I was going to Mexico."

"But you didn't take off," Anna said quietly.

"I fell in love with her. It was the day I got back from my first sail with Dad. This world had opened up for me. I was a little scared of it, but there it was. He went inside to grade some papers, I think. I was making bitching noises about having to wear that stupid life jacket, and just general bullshit. She took me by the hand and pulled me right into the water. She said then I'd better learn to swim. And she taught me. I fell in love with her about ten feet out from this dock. You couldn't have dragged me away from here.''

Moved, Anna lifted their joined hands to her cheek. ''I wish I'd had the chance to meet her. To meet both of them.''

He shifted, suddenly realizing that he had told her a story he'd never shared with anyone. And he remembered the way he'd sat here the night before, talking to his father. ''Do you, ah, believe that people come back?''

''From?''

''You know, ghosts, spirits, *Twilight Zone* stuff?''

''I don't not believe it,'' she said after a moment. ''After my mother died, there were times when I could smell her perfume. Just out of the blue, out of the air, this scent that was so . . . her. Maybe it was real, maybe it was my imagination, but it helped me. That's what counts, I suppose.''

''Yeah, but—''

''Oh!'' She nearly dropped the pole when she felt the tug. ''Something's on here! Take it!''

''Uh-uh. You caught it.'' He decided the distraction was for the best. Another minute or two, he might have made a total fool of himself and told her everything. He reached over to steady the pole. ''Reel it in some, then let it play out. That's it. No, don't jerk, just slow and steady.''

''It feels big.'' Her heart was thudding between her ears. ''Really big.''

''They always do. You got it now, just keep bringing it in.'' He rose to get the net that always hung over the edge of the dock. ''Bring her up, up and out.''

Anna leaned back, eyes half shut. They popped wide when the fish came flashing and wriggling out of the water and into the sunlight. ''Oh, my God.''

''Don't drop the pole, for God's sake.'' Shaking with laughter, Cam gripped her shoulder before she could pitch herself into the water. Leaning forward, he netted the flopping catfish. ''Nice one.''

''What do I do? What do I do now?''

Expertly Cam freed fish from hook, then to her horror handed her the full net. ''Hang on to it.''

''Don't leave me with this thing.'' She took one squinting look, saw whiskers and fishy eyes—and shut her own. ''Cam, come back here and take this ugly thing.''

He set the widemouthed pail he'd just filled with water on the dock, took the net, and flopped the catch into it. ''City girl.''

She let out a long breath of relief. ''Maybe.'' She peeped into the pail. ''Ugh. Throw it back. It's hideous.''

''Not on your life. It's a four-pounder easy.''

When she refused to take the pole a second time, he sacrificed the rest of his brother's Brie and settled down to catch the rest of that night's supper himself.

THE RECEPTION THAT HER morning's work received from Seth changed her attitude. Impressing a small boy by catching an indisputably ugly and possibly gourmand fish was a new kind of triumph. By the time she was driving with Cam to the boatyard, she'd decided one of her next projects would be to read up on the art of fishing.

''I think, with the proper bait, I could catch something much more attractive than a catfish.''

''Want to go dig up some night crawlers next weekend?''

She tipped down her sunglasses. ''Are those what they sound like?''

''You bet.''

She tipped them back up. ''I don't think so. I think I'd prefer using those pretty feathers and whatnot.'' She glanced at him again. ''So, do you know your father's secret waffle recipe?''

''Nope. He didn't trust me with it. He figured out pretty fast that I was a disaster in the kitchen.''

''What kind of bribe would work best on Phillip?''

"You couldn't worm it out of him with a Hermes tie. It only gets passed down to a Quinn."

They'd see about that, she decided, and tapped her fingers on her knee. She continued tapping them when he pulled into the lot beside the old brick building. She wasn't sure what reaction he expected from her. As far as she could see, there was little change here. The trash had been picked up, the broken windows replaced, but the building still looked ancient and deserted.

"You cleaned up." It seemed like a safe response, and it appeared to satisfy him as they got out of opposite doors of the car.

"The dock's going to need some work," he commented. "Phillip ought to be able to handle it." He took out keys, as shiny as the new lock on the front door. "I guess we need a sign or something," he said half to himself as he unlocked the dead bolts. When he opened the door, Anna caught the scent of sawdust, mustiness, and stale coffee. But the polite smile she'd fixed on her face widened in surprise as she stepped inside.

He flicked on lights and made her blink. They were brilliant overhead, hanging from the rafters and unshaded. The newly repaired floor had been swept clean—or nearly so. Bare drywall angled out on the near side to form a partition. The stairs had been replaced, the banister of plain wood oiled. The loft overhead still looked dangerous, but she began to see the potential.

She saw pulleys and wenches, enormous power tools with wicked teeth, a metal chest with many drawers that she assumed held baffling tools. New steel locks glinted on the wide doors leading to the dock.

"This is wonderful, Cam. You do work fast."

"Speed's my business." He said it lightly, but it pleased him to see that she was genuinely impressed.

"You had to work like dogs to get this much done." Though she wanted to see everything, it was the huge platform in the center of the building that pulled her forward.

Drawn on it in dark pencil or chalk were curves and lines and angles.

"I don't understand this." Fascinated, she circled around it. "Is this supposed to be a boat?"

"It is a boat. The boat. It's lofting. You draw the hull, full size. The mold section, transverse forms. Then you test them out by sketching in some longitudinal curves—like the sheer. Some of the waterlines."

He was on his knees on the platform as he spoke, using his hands to show her. And still leaving her in the dark.

But it didn't matter whether she understood the technique he described or not. She understood him. He might not realize it yet, but he had fallen in love with this place, and with the work he would do here.

"We need to add the bow lines, and the diagonals. We may want to use this design again, and this is the only way to reproduce it with real accuracy. It's a damn good design. I'm going to want to add in the structural details, full size. The more detail, the better."

He looked up and saw her smiling at him, swinging her sunglasses by the earpiece. "Sorry. You don't know what the hell I'm talking about."

"I think it's wonderful. I mean it. You're building more than boats here."

Faintly embarrassed, he got to his feet. "Boats is the idea." He jumped nimbly off the platform. "Come take a look at these."

He caught her hand, led her to the opposite walls. There were two framed sketches now, one of Ethan's beloved skipjack and the other of the boat yet to be built.

"Seth did them." The pride in his voice was just there. He didn't even notice it. "He's the only one of us who can really draw worth a damn. Phil's adequate, but the kid is just great. He's doing Ethan's workboat next, then the sloop. I've got to get some pictures of a couple of boats I worked on so he can copy them. We'll hang them all in here—and add drawings of the others we build. Kind of like a gallery. A trademark."

There were tears in her eyes when she turned and wrapped her arms around him. Her fierce grip surprised him, but he returned it.

''More than boats,'' she murmured, then drew back to frame his face in her hands. ''It's wonderful,'' she said again and pulled his mouth down to hers.

The kiss swarmed through him, swamped him, staggered him. Everything about her, about them, spun around in his heart. Questions, dozens of them, buzzed like bees in his head. And the answer, the single answer to all of them, was nearly within his reach.

He said her name, just once, then drew her unsteadily away. He had to look at her, really look, but nothing about him seemed quite on balance.

''Anna,'' he said again. ''Wait a minute.''

Before he could get a firm grip on the answer, before he could get his feet back under him again, the door creaked open, letting in sunlight.

''Excuse me, folks,'' Mackensie said pleasantly. ''I saw the car out front.''

NINETEEN

CAM'S FIRST REACTION was pure annoyance. Something was happening here, something monumental, and he didn't want any interruptions.

"We're not open for business, Mackensie." He kept his grip on Anna's arms firm and turned his back to the man he considered no more than a paper-pushing pest.

"Didn't think you were." With his voice still mild and friendly, Mackensie wandered in. In his line of work he rarely received a warm welcome. "Door was unlocked. Well, this is going to be quite a place."

He was a Harry Homemaker at heart, and the sight of all those spanking-new power tools stirred the juices. "Got yourself some top-grade equipment here."

"You want a boat, come back tomorrow and we'll talk."

"I get seasick," Mackensie confessed with a quick grimace. "Can't even stand on a dock without getting queasy."

"That's tough. Go away."

"But I sure do admire the looks of boats. Can't say I ever gave much thought to what went into building them.

That's some band saw over there. Must've set you back some."

This time Cam did turn, the fury in his eyes as dangerous as a cocked gun. "It's my business how I spend my money."

Baffled by the exchange, Anna laid a hand on Cam's arm. She wasn't surprised that he was being rude—she'd seen him be rude before—but the snap and hiss of his anger over what appeared to be no more than a nuisance puzzled her.

If this is the way he intends to treat potential clients, she thought, he might as well close the doors now.

Before she could think of the proper calming words, Cam shook her off. "What the hell do you want now?"

"Just a couple of questions." He nodded politely to Anna. "Ma'am. Larry Mackensie, claim investigator for True Life Insurance."

In the dark, Anna automatically accepted the hand he held out. "Mr. Mackensie. I'm Anna Spinelli."

Mackensie did a quick flip through his mental file. It took only a moment for him to tag her as Seth DeLauter's caseworker. As she had come on the scene after the death of the insured, he'd had no need to contact her, but she was in his records. And the cozy little scene he'd walked in on told him she was pretty tight with at least one of the Quinns. He wasn't sure if or how that little bit of information would apply, but he would just make a note of it.

"Pleased to meet you."

"If you two have business to discuss," Anna began, "I'll just wait outside."

"I don't have anything to discuss with him, now or later. Go file your report, Mackensie. We're done."

"Just about. I figured you'd like to know I'll be heading back to the home office. Got a lot of mixed results on my interviews, Mr. Quinn. Not much of what you'd call hard facts, though." He glanced toward the band saw again, wished fleetingly he could afford one like it. "There's the letter that was found in your father's car—that goes to state of mind. Single-car accident, driver a physically fit man, no traces of alcohol or drugs.'' He lifted his shoulders. ''Then there's the fact that the insured increased his policy and added a beneficiary shortly before the accident. The company looks hard at that kind of thing.''

''You go ahead and look.'' Cam's voice had lowered, like the warning growl of an attack dog. ''But not here. Not in my place.''

''Just letting you know how things stand. Starting a new business,'' Mackensie said conversationally, ''takes a good chunk of capital. You been planning this for long?''

Cam sprang quickly, had Mackensie by the lapels and up on the toes of his shiny, lace-up shoes. ''You son of a bitch.''

''Cam, stop it!'' The order was quick and sharp, and Anna punctuated it by stepping forward and shoving a hand on each man's chest. She thought it was like moving between a wolf and a bull, but she held her ground. ''Mr. Mackensie, I think you'd better go now.''

''On my way.'' His voice was steady enough, despite the cold sweat that had pooled at the base of his neck and was even now dripping down his spine. ''It's just details, Mr. Quinn. The company pays me to gather the details.''

But it didn't pay him, he reminded himself as he walked outside where he could gulp in air, to be beaten to a pulp by a furious beneficiary.

''Bastard, fucking bastard.'' Cam desperately wanted to hit something, anything, but there was too much empty air. ''Does he really think my father plowed into a telephone pole so I could start building boats? I should have decked him. Goddamn it. First they say he did it because he couldn't face the scandal, now it's because he wanted us to have a pile of money. The hell with their dead money. They didn't know him. They don't know any of us.''

Anna let him rant, let him prowl around the building looking for something to damage. Her heart was frozen in her chest. Suicide was suspected, she thought numbly. An investigation was in place.

And Cam had known, must have known all along.

"That was a claim investigator from the company who holds your father's life insurance policy?"

"That was a fucking moron." Cam whirled, more oaths stinging his tongue. Then he saw her face—set and entirely too cool. "It's nothing. Just a hassle. Let's get out of here."

"It's suspected that your father committed suicide."

"He didn't kill himself."

She held up a hand. She had to keep the hurt buried for now and lead with the practical. "You've spoken with Mackensie before. And I assume you—your lawyer at any rate—has been in contact with the insurance company about this matter for some time."

"Phillip's handling it."

"You knew, but you didn't tell me."

"It has nothing to do with you."

No, she realized, it wasn't possible to keep all the hurt buried. "I see." That was personal, she reminded herself. She would deal with that later. "And as to how it affects Seth?"

Fury sprang up again, clawed at his throat. "He doesn't know anything about it."

"If you actually believe that, you're deluding yourself. Gossip runs thick in small towns, close communities. And young boys hear a great deal."

It was the caseworker now, Cam thought with rising resentment. She might as well be carrying her briefcase and wearing one of her dumpy suits. "Gossip's all it is. It doesn't matter."

"On the contrary, gossip can be very damaging. You'd be wiser to be open with him, to be honest. Though that seems to be difficult for you."

"Don't twist this around on me, Anna. It's goddamn insurance. It's nothing."

"It's your father," she corrected. "His reputation. I don't imagine there's much that means more to you." She drew a deep breath. "But as you said, it's nothing to do with me on a personal level. I think we're finished here.''

''Wait a minute.'' He stepped in front of her, blocking her exit. He had the sinking feeling that if she walked, she meant to walk a lot farther than his car.

''Why? So you can explain? It's family business? I'm not family. You're absolutely right.'' It amazed her that her voice was so calm, so detached, so utterly reasonable when she was boiling inside. ''And I imagine you felt it best to hold the matter back from Seth's caseworker. Much wiser to show her only the positive angles, lock up any negatives.''

''My father didn't kill himself. I don't have to defend him to you, or anyone.''

''No, you don't. And I'd never ask you to.'' She stepped around him and started for the door. He caught her before she reached it, but she'd expected that and turned calmly. ''There's no point in arguing, Cam, when essentially we agree.''

''There's no point in you being pissed off,'' he shot back. ''We're handling the insurance company. We're handling the gossip about Seth being his love child, for Christ's sake.''

''What?'' Stunned, she pressed a hand to her head. ''There's speculation that Seth is your father's illegitimate son?''

''It's nothing but bull and small minds,'' Cam replied.

''My God, have you considered, even for a moment, what it could do to Seth to hear that kind of talk? Have you considered, even for a moment, that this was something I needed to know in order to evaluate, in order to help Seth properly?''

His thumbs went into his pockets. ''Yeah, I considered it—and I didn't tell you. Because we're handling it. We're talking about my father here.''

''We're also talking about a minor child in your care.''

''He is in my care,'' Cam said evenly. ''And that's the point. I'm doing what I thought was best all around. I didn't tell you about the insurance thing or about the gossip because they're both lies."

"Perhaps they are, but by not telling me, you lied."

"I wasn't going to go around feeding anybody this crap that the kid was my father's bastard."

She nodded slowly. "Well, take it from some other man's bastard, it doesn't make Seth less of a person."

"I didn't mean it like that," he began and reached out for her. But she stepped away. "Don't do that." He exploded with it and grabbed her arms. "Don't back off from me. For Christ's sake, Anna, my life has turned inside out in the past couple of months, and I don't know how long it's going to be before I can turn it back around. I've got the kid to worry about, the business, you. Mackensie's coming around, people are speculating about my father's morals over the fresh fruit at the supermarket, Seth's bitch of a mother's down in Norfolk—"

"Wait." She didn't move away this time, she yanked away. "Seth's mother has contacted you?"

"No. No." Jesus, his brain was on fire. "We hired a detective to track her down. Phillip figured we'd be better off knowing where she is, what she's up to."

"I see." Her heart broke in two halves, one for the woman, one for the professional. Both sides bled. "And she's in Norfolk, but you didn't bother to tell me that either."

"No, I didn't tell you." He'd backed himself into this corner, Cam realized. And there was no way out. "We only know she was there a couple of days ago."

"Social Services would expect to be notified of this information."

He kept his eyes on hers, nodded slowly. "I guess they just were. My mistake."

There was a line between them now, she realized, very thick and very darkly drawn. "Obviously you don't think very much of me—or of yourself, for that matter. Let me explain something to you. However I may be feeling about you on a personal level at this moment, it's my professional opinion that you and your brothers are the right guardians for Seth.''

''Okay, so—''

''I will have to take this information I've just learned into consideration,'' she continued. ''It will have to be documented.''

''All that's going to do is screw things up for the kid.'' He hated the fact that his stomach clenched at the thought. Hated the idea that he might see that look of white-faced fear on Seth's face again. ''I'm not going to let some sick gossip mess things up for him.''

''Well, on that we can agree.'' She'd gotten her wish on one level, Anna realized. She'd been around to see how much Seth would come to matter to him. Just long enough, she thought hollowly.

''It's my professional opinion that Seth is well cared for both physically and emotionally.'' Her voice was brisk now, professional. ''He's happy and is beginning to feel secure. Added to that is the fact that he loves you, and you love him, though neither one of you may fully realize it. I still believe counseling would benefit all of you, and that, too, will go into my report and recommendation when the court rules on permanent guardianship. As I told you from the beginning, my concern—my primary concern—is the best welfare of the child.''

She was solidly behind them, Cam realized. And would have been no matter what he'd told her. Or hadn't told her. Guilt struck him a sharp, backhanded blow.

''I was never less than honest with you,'' she said before he could speak.

''Damn it, Anna—''

''I'm not through,'' she said coolly. ''I have no doubt that you'll see Seth is well settled, and that this new business is secure before—as you put it—you turn your life back around. Which I assume means picking up your racing career in Europe. You'll have to find a way to juggle your needs, but that's not my concern. But there may come a time when the guardianship is contested, if indeed Seth's mother makes her way back here. At that time, the case file will be reevaluated. If he remains happy and well cared for under your guardianship, I'll do whatever I can to see to it that he remains with you. I'm on his side, which appears to put me on yours. That's all."

Shame layered onto guilt, with a sprinkling of relief between. "Anna, I know how much you've done. I'm grateful."

She shook her head when he lifted a hand. "I'm not feeling very friendly toward you at the moment. I don't want to be touched."

"Fine. I won't touch you. Let's find somewhere to sit down and talk the rest of this out."

"I thought we just had."

"Now you're being stubborn."

"No, now I'm being realistic. You slept with me, but you didn't trust me. The fact that I was honest with you and you weren't with me is my problem. The fact that I went to bed with a man who saw me as an enjoyment on one hand and an obstacle on the other is my mistake."

"That's not the way it was." His temper began to rise again, pumped by a slick panic. "That's not the way it is."

"It's the way I see it. Now I need to take some time and see how I feel about that. I'd appreciate it if you'd drive me back to my car."

She turned and walked away.

HE PREFERRED FIRE TO ice, but he couldn't break through the frigid shield she'd wrapped around her temper. It scared him, a sensation that he didn't appreciate. She was perfectly polite, even friendly, to Seth and Phillip when she returned to the house to gather her things.

She was perfectly polite to Cam—so polite that he imagined he would feel the chill of it for days.

He told himself it didn't matter. She'd get over it. She was just in a snit because he hadn't bared his soul, shared all the intimate details of his life with her. It was a woman thing.

After all, women had invented the cold shoulder just to make men feel like slugs.

He would give her a couple of days, he decided. Let her stew. Let her come to her senses. Then he would take her flowers.

"She's ticked off at you," Seth commented as Cam stood by the front door staring out.

"What do you know?"

"She's ticked off," Seth repeated, entertaining himself with his sketchbook while sitting cross-legged on the front porch. "She didn't let you kiss her good-bye, and you're all the time locking lips."

"Shut up."

"What'd you do?"

"I didn't do anything." Cam kicked the door open and stomped out. "She's just being female."

"You did something." Seth eyed him owlishly. "She's not a jerk."

"She'll get over it." Cam dropped down into the rocker. He wasn't going to worry about it. He never worried about women.

HE LOST HIS APPETITE. How was he supposed to eat fried fish without remembering how he and Anna had sat on the dock that morning?

He couldn't sleep. How was he supposed to sleep in his own bed without remembering how they'd made love on those same sheets?

He couldn't concentrate on work. How was he supposed to detail diagonals without remembering how she'd beamed at him when he showed her the lofting platform?

By mid-morning, he gave up and drove to Princess

Anne. But he didn't take her flowers. Now *he* was ticked off.

He strode through the reception area, straight back into her office. Then fumed when he found it empty. Typical, was all he could think. His luck had turned all bad.

"Mr. Quinn." Marilou stood in the doorway, her hands folded. "Is there something I can do for you?"

"I'm looking for Anna—Ms. Spinelli."

"I'm sorry, she's not available."

"I'll wait."

"It'll be a long one. She won't be in until next week."

"Next week?" His narrowed eyes reminded Marilou of steel sharpened to the killing point. "What do you mean, she won't be in?"

"Ms. Spinelli is taking the week off." And Marilou figured the reason for it was even now boring holes through her with furious gray eyes. She'd thought the same when Anna had dropped off her report that morning and requested the time. "I'm familiar with the case file, if there's something I can do."

"No, it's personal. Where did she go?"

"I can't give you that information, Mr. Quinn, but you're free to leave a message, either a written one or one on her voice mail. Of course, if she checks in, I'll be happy to tell her you'd like to speak with her."

"Yeah, thanks."

He couldn't get out fast enough. She was probably in her apartment, he decided as he hopped back in his car. Sulking. So he would let her yell at him, get it all out of her system. Then he'd nudge her along to bed so they could put this ridiculous little episode behind them.

He ignored the nerves dancing in his stomach as he walked down the hall to her apartment. He knocked briskly, then tucked his hands into his pockets. He knocked louder, banged his fist on the door.

"Damn it, Anna. Open up. This is stupid. I saw your car out front."

The door behind him creaked open. One of the sisters

peered out. The jingling sound of a morning game show filled the hallway. "She not in there, Anna's Young Man."

"Her car's out front," he said.

"She took a cab."

He bit back an oath, pasted on a charming smile, and walked across the hall. "Where to?"

"To the train station—or maybe it was the airport." She beamed up at him. Really, he was such a handsome boy. "She said she'd be gone for a few days. She promised to call to make sure Sister and I were getting on. Such a sweet girl, thinking of us when she's on vacation."

"Vacation to . . ."

"Did she say?" The woman bit her lip and her eyes unfocused in thought. "I don't think she mentioned it. She was in an awful hurry, but she stopped by just the same so we wouldn't be worried. She's such a considerate girl."

"Yeah." The sweet, considerate girl had left him high and dry.

SHE'D HAD NO BUSINESS flying to Pittsburgh; the airfare had eaten a large hole in her budget. But she'd wanted to get there. Had needed to get there. The minute she walked into her grandparents' cramped row house, half her burden lifted.

"Anna Louisa!" Theresa Spinelli was a tiny, slim woman with steel-gray hair ruthlessly waved, a face that fell into dozens of comfortable wrinkles, and a smile as wide as the Mediterranean Sea. Anna had to bend low to be clasped and kissed. "Al, Al, our bambina's home."

"It's good to be home, Nana."

Alberto Spinelli hurried to the door. He was a foot taller than his wife's tidy five-three, with a broad chest and a spare tire that pressed cozily against Anna as they embraced. His hair was thin and white, his eyes dark and merry behind his thick glasses.

He all but carried her into the living room, where they could begin to fuss over her in earnest.

They spoke rapidly, and in a mix of Italian and English. Food was the first order of business. Theresa always thought her baby was starving. After they'd plied her with minestrone, and fresh bread and an enormous cube of tiramisu, Theresa was almost satisfied that her chick wouldn't perish of malnutrition.

"Now." Al sat back, puffing to life one of his thick cigars. "You'll tell us why you're here."

"Do I need a reason to come home?" Struggling to relax fully, Anna stretched out in one of a pair of ancient wing chairs. It had been recovered, she knew, countless times. Just now it was in a gay striped pattern, but the cushion still gave way beneath her butt like butter.

"You called three days ago. You didn't say you were coming home."

"It was an impulse. I've been swamped at work, up to my ears. I'm tired and wanted a break. I wanted to come home and eat Nana's cooking for a while."

It was true enough, if not the whole truth. She didn't think it would be wise to tell her doting grandparents that she'd walked into an affair, eyes wide open, and ended up with her heart broken.

"You work too hard," Theresa said. "Al, don't I tell you the girl works too hard?"

"She likes to work hard. She likes to use her brain. It's a good brain. Me, I've got a good brain, too, and I say she's not here just to eat your manicotti."

"Are we having manicotti for dinner?" Anna beamed, knowing it wouldn't distract them for long. They'd seen her through the worst, stuck by her when she'd done her best to hurt them, and herself. And they knew her.

"I started the sauce the minute you called to say you were coming. Al, don't nag the girl."

"I'm not nagging, I'm asking."

Theresa rolled her eyes. "If you have such a good brain in that big head of yours, you'd know it's a boy that sent her running home. Is he Italian?'' Theresa demanded, fixing Anna with those bright bird eyes.

And she had to laugh. God, it was good to be home. ''I have no idea, but he loves my red sauce.''

''Then he's got good taste. Why don't you bring him home, let us get a look at him?''

''Because we're having some problems, and I need to work them out.''

''Work them out?'' Theresa waved a hand. ''How do you work them out when you're here and he's not? Is he good-looking?''

''Gorgeous.''

''Does he have work?'' Al wanted to know.

''He's starting his own business—with his brothers.''

''Good, he knows family.'' Theresa nodded, pleased. ''You bring him next time, we'll see for ourselves.''

''All right,'' she said because it was easier to agree than to explain. ''I'm going to go unpack.''

''He's hurt her heart,'' Theresa murmured when Anna left the room.

Al reached over and patted her hand. ''It's a strong heart.''

ANNA TOOK HER TIME, hanging her clothes in the closet, folding them into the drawers of the old dresser she'd used as a child. The room was so much the same. The wallpaper had faded a bit. She remembered that her grandfather had hung it himself, to brighten the room when she'd come to live with them.

And she'd hated the pretty roses on the wall because they looked so fresh and alive, and everything inside her was dead.

But the roses were still there, a little older but still there. As were her grandparents. She sat on the bed, hearing the familiar creak of springs.

The familiar, the comforting, the secure.

That, she admitted, was what she wanted. Home, children, routine—with the surprises that family always provided thrown in. To some, she supposed, it would have sounded ordinary. At one time, she had told herself the same thing.

But she knew better now. Home, marriage, family. There was nothing ordinary there. The three elements formed a unit that was unique and precious.

She wanted, needed that, for herself.

Maybe she had been playing games after all. Maybe she hadn't been completely honest. Not with Cam, and not with herself. She hadn't tried to trap him into her dreams, but underneath it all, hadn't she begun to hope he'd share them? She'd maintained a front of casual, no-strings sex, but her heart had been reckless enough to yearn for more.

Maybe she deserved to have it broken.

The hell she did, she thought, springing up. She'd been making it enough, she'd accepted the limitations of their relationship. And still, he hadn't trusted her. That she wouldn't tolerate.

Damned if she'd take the blame for this, she decided, and stalking to the streaked mirror over her dresser, she began to freshen her makeup.

She would have what she wanted one day. A strong man who loved her, respected her, *and* trusted her. She would have a man who saw her as a partner, not as the enemy. She'd have that home in the country near the water, and children of her own, and a goddamn stupid dog if she wanted. She would have it all.

It just wouldn't be with Cameron Quinn.

If anything, she should thank him for opening her eyes, not only to the flaws in their so-called relationship but to her own needs and desires.

She would rather choke.

TWENTY

A WEEK COULD BE A long time, Cam discovered. Particularly when you had a great deal stuck in your craw that you couldn't spit out.

It helped that he'd been able to pick fights with both Phillip and Ethan. But it wasn't quite the same as having a showdown with Anna.

It helped, too, that beginning work on the hull of the boat took so much of his time and concentration. He couldn't afford to think about her when he was planking.

He thought of her anyway.

He'd had a few bad moments imagining her running around on some Caribbean beach—in that little bikini—and having some overmuscled, overtanned type rubbing sunscreen on her back and buying her mai tais.

Then he'd told himself that she'd gone off somewhere to lick her imaginary wounds and was probably in some hotel room, drapes drawn, sniffing into a hankie.

But that image didn't make him feel any better.

When he got home from a full Saturday at the boatyard, he was ready for a beer. Maybe two. He and Ethan headed straight for the refrigerator and had already popped tops when Phillip came in.

"Seth isn't with you?"

"Over at Danny's." Cam guzzled from the bottle to wash the sawdust out of his throat. "Sandy's dropping him off later."

"Good." Phillip got a beer for himself. "Sit down."

"What?"

"I got a letter from the insurance company this morning." Phillip pulled out a chair. "The gist is, they're stalling. They used a bunch of legal terms, cited clauses, but the upshot is they're casting doubt on cause of death and are continuing to investigate."

"Fuck that. Cheapscate bastards just don't want to shell out." Annoyed, Cam kicked out a chair—and wished with all his heart it had been Mackensie.

"I talked to our lawyer," Phil continued, grimacing. "He may start rethinking our friendship if I keep calling him on weekends. He says we have some choices. We can sit tight, let the insurance company continue its investigation, or we can file suit against them for nonpayment of claim."

"Let them keep their fucking money, I don't want it anyway."

"No." Ethan spoke quietly in the echo of Cam's outburst. He continued to brood into his beer, shaking his head. "It's not right. Dad paid the premiums, year after year. He added to the policy for Seth. It's not right that they don't pay. And if they don't pay, it's going to go down somewhere that he killed himself. That's not right either. They've been doing all the pushing up to now," he added and raised his somber eyes. "Let's push back."

"If it ends up going to court," Phillip warned him, "it could get messy."

"So we turn away from a fight because it could get messy?" For the first time, amusement flickered over Ethan's face. "Well, fuck that."

"Cam?"

Cam sipped again. "I've been wanting a good fight for a while. I guess this is it."

"Then we're agreed. We'll have the papers drawn up next week, and we'll go after their asses." Revved and ready, Phillip lifted his bottle. "Here's to a good fight."

"Here's to winning," Cam corrected.

"I'm for that. It's going to cost us some," Phillip added. "Filing fees, legal fees. Most of the capital we've pooled is sunk into the business." He blew out a breath. "I guess we need another pool."

With less regret than he'd expected, Cam thought of his beloved Porsche waiting patiently for him in Nice. Just a car, he told himself. Just a damn car. "I can get my hands on some fresh cash. It'll take a couple of days."

"I can sell my house." Ethan shrugged his shoulders. "I've had some people asking about it, and it's just sitting there."

"No." The thought of it twisted in Cam's gut. "You're not selling your house. Rent it out. We'll get through this."

"I've got some stocks." Phillip sighed and waved goodbye to a chunk of his growing portfolio. "I'll tell my broker to cash them in. We'll open a joint account next week—the Quinn Legal Defense Fund."

The three of them managed weak smiles.

"The kid ought to know," Ethan said after a moment. "If we're going to take this to the wall, he ought to know what's going on."

Cam looked up in time to see both of his brothers' eyes focus on him. "Oh, come on. Why does it have to be me?"

"You're the oldest." Phillip grinned at him. "Besides, it'll take your mind off Anna."

"I'm not brooding about her—or any woman."

"Been edgy and broody all week," Ethan mumbled. "Making me nuts."

"Who asked you? We had a little disagreement, that's all. I'm giving her time to simmer down."

"Seems to me she'd simmered down to frozen the last

time I saw her." Phillip examined his beer. "That was a week ago."

"It's my business how I handle a woman."

"Sure is. But let me know when you're done with her, will you? She's—"

Phillip broke off when Cam all but leaped over the table and grabbed him by the throat. Beer bottles flew and shattered on the floor.

Resigned, Ethan raked his hand through his hair, scattering drops of spilled beer. Cam and Phillip were on the floor, pounding hell out of each other. He got himself a fresh beer before filling a pitcher with cold water.

His work boots crunched over broken glass, which he kicked out of the way in hopes that he wouldn't have to run anybody to the hospital for stitches. With malice toward neither, he emptied the pitcher on both his brothers.

It got their attention.

Phillip's lip was split, Cam's ribs throbbed, and both of them were bleeding from rolling around on broken glass. Drenched and panting, they eyed each other warily. Gingerly, Phillip wiped a knuckle over his bloody lip.

"Sorry. Bad joke. I didn't know things were serious between you."

"I never said they were serious."

Phillip laughed, then winced as his lip wept. "Brother, did you ever. I guess I never figured you'd be the first of us to fall in love with a woman."

The stomach that Phillip's fists had abused jittered wildly. "Who said I'm in love with her?"

"You didn't punch me in the face because you're in like." He looked down at his pleated slacks. "Shit. Do you know how hard it is to get bloodstains out of a cotton blend?" He rose, held out a hand to Cam. "She's a terrific lady," he said as he hauled Cam to his feet. "Hope you work it out."

"I don't have to work out anything," Cam said desperately. "You're way off here."

"If you say so. I'm going to get cleaned up."

He headed out, limping only a little.

"I ain't mopping the damn floor," Ethan stated, "because your glands got in an uproar."

"He started it," Cam muttered, not caring how ridiculous it sounded.

"No, I figure you did, with whatever you did to piss Anna off." Ethan opened the broom closet, took out a mop, and tossed it to Cam. "Now I guess you got to clean it up."

He slipped out the back door.

"The two of you think you know so goddamn much." Furious, he kicked a chair over on his way to fetch a bucket. "I ought to know what's going on in my own life. Insanity, that's what. I should be in Australia, prepping for the race of my life, that's where I should be."

He dragged the mop through water, beer, glass, and blood, muttering to himself. "Australia's just where I'd be if I had any sense left. Damn woman's complicating things. Better off just cutting loose there."

He kicked over another chair because it felt good, then shook shards of glass from the mop into the bucket.

"Who had a fight?" Seth wanted to know.

Cam turned and narrowed his eyes at the boy standing in the doorway. "I kicked Phillip's ass."

"What for?"

"Because I wanted to."

With a nod, Seth walked around the puddle and got a Pepsi out of the fridge. "If you kicked his ass, how come you're bleeding?"

"Maybe I like to bleed." He finished mopping up while the boy stood watching him. "What's your problem?" Cam demanded.

"I got no problem."

Cam shoved the bucket aside with his foot. The least Phillip could do was empty it somewhere. He went to the sink and bad-temperedly picked glass out of his arm. Then he got out the whiskey, righted a chair, and sat down with the bottle and a glass.

He saw Seth's eyes slide over the bottle and away. Deliberately Cam poured two fingers of Johnnie Walker into a glass. "Not everybody who drinks gets drunk," he said. "Not everybody who gets drunk—as I may decide to do—knocks kids around."

"Don't know why anybody drinks that shit anyway."

Cam knocked back the whiskey. "Because we're weak, and stupid, and it feels good at the time."

"Are you going to Australia?"

Cam poured another shot. "Doesn't look like it."

"I don't care if you go. I don't care where the hell you go." The underlying fury in the boy's voice surprised them both. Flushing, Seth turned and raced out the door.

Well, hell, Cam thought and shoved the whiskey aside. He pushed away from the table and hit the door as Seth streaked across the yard to the woods.

"Hold it!" When that didn't slow the boy down, Cam put some mean into it. "Goddamn it, I said hold it!"

This time Seth skidded to a halt. When he turned around, they stared at each other across the expanse of grass, temper and nerves vibrating from them in all but visible waves.

"Get your butt back over here. Now."

He came, fists clenched, chin jutting out. They both knew he had nowhere to run. "I don't need you."

"Oh, the hell you don't. I ought to kick your ass for being stupid. Everybody says you've got some genius brain in there, but if you ask me you're dumb as dirt. Now sit down. There," he added, jabbing a finger at the steps. "And if you don't do what I tell you when I tell you, I might just kick your ass after all."

"You don't scare me," Seth said, but he sat.

"I scare you white, and that gives me the hammer." Cam sat as well, watched the puppy come crawling toward them on his belly. And I scare little dogs too, he thought in disgust. "I'm not going anywhere," he began.

"I said I don't care."

"Fine, but I'm telling you anyway. I figured I would,

once everything settled down. I told myself I would. I guess I needed to. Never figured on coming back here to stay."

"Then why don't you go?"

Cam gave him a halfhearted boot on the top of his head with the heel of one hand. "Why don't you shut up until I say what I have to say?"

The painless smack and impatient order were more comforting to Seth than a thousand promises.

"I've been coming to the fact that I've been running long enough. I liked what I was doing while I was doing it, but I guess I'm pretty well finished with it. It looks like I've got a place here, and a business here, maybe a woman here," he murmured, thinking of Anna.

"So you're staying to work and poke at a girl."

"Those are damn good reasons for hanging in one place. Then there's you." Cam leaned back on the upper steps, bracing with his elbows. "I can't say I cared much for you when I first came back. There's that crappy attitude of yours, and you're ugly, but you kind of grow on a guy."

Immensely cheered, Seth snickered. "You're uglier."

"I'm bigger, I'm entitled. So I guess I'll hang around to see if you get any prettier as time goes on."

"I didn't really want you to go," Seth said under his breath after a long moment. It was the closest he could get to speaking his heart.

"I know." Cam sighed. "Now that we've got that settled, we've got this other thing. Nothing to worry about, it's just some legal bullshit. Phil and the lawyer'll handle most of it, but there might be some talk. You shouldn't pay any attention to it if you hear it."

"What kind of talk?"

"Some people—some idiots—think Dad aimed for that pole. Killed himself."

"Yeah, and now this asshole from the insurance company's asking questions."

Cam hissed out a breath. He knew he should probably

tell the kid not to call adults assholes, but there were bigger issues here. "You knew that?"

"Sure, it goes around. He talked to Danny and Will's mother. Danny said she gave him an earful. She didn't like some guy coming around asking questions about Ray. That butthead Chuck up at the Dairy Queen told the detective guy that Ray was screwing around with his students, then had a crisis of conscience and killed himself."

"Crisis of conscience." Jesus, where did the kid come up with this stuff? "Chuck Kimball? He always was a butthead. Word is he got caught cheating on a lit exam and got booted out of college. And it seems to me Phillip beat the crap out of him once. Can't remember why, though."

"He's got a face like a carp."

Cam laughed. "Yeah, I guess he does. Dad—Ray—never touched a student, Seth."

"He was square with me." And that counted for everything. "My mother . . ."

"Go ahead," Cam prompted.

"She told me he was my father. But another time she said this other guy was, and once when she was really loaded she said my old man was some guy named Keith Richards."

Cam couldn't help it, the laugh just popped out. "Jesus, now she's hitting on the Stones?"

"Who?"

"I'll see to your music education later."

"I don't know if Ray was my father." Seth looked up. "She's a liar, so I don't go with anything she said, but he took me. I know he gave her money, a lot of it. I don't know if he'd have told me if he was. He said there were things we had to talk about, but he had stuff to work out first. I know you don't want him to be."

It couldn't matter, Cam realized. Not anymore. "Do you want him to be?"

"He was decent," the boy said so simply that Cam

draped an arm around his shoulders. And Seth leaned against him.

"Yeah, he was."

EVERYTHING HAD CHANGED. Everything was different. And he was desperate to tell her. Cam knew his life had turned on its axis yet again. And somehow he'd ended up exactly where he needed to be.

The only thing missing was Anna.

He took a chance and drove to her apartment. It was Saturday night, he thought. She was due back at work on Monday. She was a practical woman and would want to take Sunday to catch up, sort her laundry, answer her mail. Whatever.

If she wasn't home, he was going to by God sit on her doorstep until she got there.

But when she answered his knock and stood there looking so fresh, so gorgeous, he was caught off balance.

Anna, on the other hand, had prepared for this meeting all week. She knew exactly how she would handle it. "Cam, this is a surprise. You just caught me."

"Caught you?" he said stupidly.

"Yes, but I've got a few minutes. Would you like to come in?"

"Yeah, I—where the hell have you been?"

She lifted her brows. "Excuse me?"

"You took off, out of the blue."

"I wouldn't say that. I arranged leave from work, checked in with my neighbors, had my plants watered while I was gone. I was hardly abducted by aliens, I simply took a few days of personal time. Do you want some coffee?"

"No." Okay, he thought, she was going to keep playing it cool. He could do that. "I want to talk to you."

"That's good, because I want to talk to you, too. How's Seth?"

"He's fine. Really. We got a lot of things ironed out. Just today—"

"What have you done to your arm?"

Impatient, he glanced down at the raw nicks and scrapes. "Nothing. It's nothing. Listen, Anna—"

"Why don't you sit down? I'd really like to apologize if I was hard on you last weekend."

"Apologize?" Well, that was more like it. Willing to be forgiving, he sat on the sofa. "Why don't we just forget it? I've got a lot to tell you."

"I'd really like to clear this up." Smiling pleasantly, she sat across from him. "I suppose we were both in a difficult position. A great deal of that was my fault. Becoming involved with you was a calculated risk. But I was attracted and didn't weigh the potential problems as carefully as I should have. Obviously something like last weekend's disagreement was bound to happen. And as we both have Seth's interests at heart, and will continue to, I would hate for us to be at odds."

"Good, then we won't." He reached for her hand, but she evaded his gesture and merely patted his.

"Now that that's settled, you really have to excuse me. I hate to rush you along, Cam, but I have a date."

"A what?"

"A date." She glanced at the watch on her wrist. "Shortly, as it happens, and I have to change."

Very slowly he got to his feet. "You have a date? Tonight? What the hell is that supposed to mean?"

"What it generally does." She blinked twice, as if confused, then let her eyes fill with apology. "Oh, I'm sorry. I thought we both understood that we'd ended the . . . well, the more personal aspect of our relationship. I assumed it was clear that it wasn't working out for either of us."

It felt as though someone had blown past his guard and rammed an iron fist into his solar plexus. "Look, if you're still pissed off—"

"Do I look pissed off?" she asked coolly.

"No." He stared at her, shaking his head while his

stomach did a quick pitch and roll. "No, you don't. You're dumping me."

"Don't be melodramatic. We're simply ending an affair that both of us entered freely and without promises or expectations. It was good while it lasted, really good. I'd hate to spoil that. Now as far as our professional relationship goes, I've told you that I'll do all I can to support your permanent guardianship of Seth. However, I do expect you to be more forthcoming with information from now on. I'll also be happy to consult with you or advise you on any area of that guardianship. You and your brothers are doing a marvelous job with him."

He waited, certain there would be more. "That's it?"

"I can't think of anything else—and I am a little pressed for time."

"You're pressed for time." She'd just stabbed him dead center of the heart, and she was pressed for time. "That's too damn bad, because I'm not finished."

"I'm sorry if your ego's bruised."

"Yeah, my ego's bruised. I got a lot of bruises right now. How the hell can you stand there and brush me off after what we had together?"

"We had great sex. I'm not denying it. We're just not going to have it any longer."

"Sex?" He grabbed her arms and shook her, and had the small satisfaction of seeing a flash of anger heat through the chill in her eyes. "That's all it was for you?"

"That's what it was for both of us." It wasn't going the way she'd planned. She'd expected him to be angry and storm out. Or to be relieved that she'd backed away first and walk away whistling. But he wasn't supposed to confront her like this. "Let go of me."

"The hell I will. I've been half crazy for you to get back. You turned my life upside down, and I'll be damned if you'll just stroll away because you're through with me."

"We're through with each other. I don't want you anymore, and it's your bad luck I said it first. Now take your hands off me."

He released her as if her skin had burned his palms. There'd been a hitch in her voice, a suspicious one. "What makes you think I'd have said it at all?"

"We don't want the same things. We were going nowhere, and I'm not going to keep heading there, no matter how I feel about you."

"How do you feel about me?"

"Tired of you!" she shouted. "Tired of me, tired of us. Sick and tired of telling myself fun and games could be enough. Well, it's not. Not nearly, and I want you out."

He felt the temper and panic that had gripped him ease back into delight. "You're in love with me, aren't you?"

He'd never seen a woman go from simmer to boil so fast. And seeing it, he wondered why it had taken him so long to realize he adored her. She whirled, grabbed a lamp, and hurled it.

He gave her credit for aim and gave thanks that he was light on his feet, as the base whistled by his head before it crashed into the wall.

"You arrogant, conceited, cold-blooded son of a bitch." She grabbed a vase now, a new one she'd bought on the way home to cheer herself up. She let it fly.

"Jesus, Anna." It was admiration, pure and simple, that burst through him as he was forced to catch the vase before it smashed into his face. "You must be nuts about me."

"I despise you." She looked frantically for something else to throw at him and snagged a bowl of fruit off the kitchen counter. The fruit went first. Apples. "Loathe you." Pears. "Hate you." Bananas. "I can't believe I ever let you touch me." Then the bowl. But she was more clever this time, feinted first, then heaved in the direction of his dodge.

The stoneware caught him just above the ear and had stars spinning in front of his eyes.

"Okay, game over." He made a dive for her, caught her around the waist. His already abused body suffered from kicks and punches, but he hauled her to the couch and held her down. "Get ahold of yourself before you kill me."

"I want to kill you," she said between gritted teeth.

"Believe me, I get the picture."

"You don't get anything." She bucked under him and sent his system into a tangled mess of lust and laughter. Sensing both, she reared up and bit him, hard.

"Ouch. Goddamn it. Okay, that's it." He dragged her up and threw her over his shoulder. "You still packed? Tells me she's got a damn date. Like hell she does. Tells me we're finished. What bullshit." He marched her into the bedroom, saw her bag on the bed, and grabbed it.

"What are you doing? Put me down. Put that down."

"I'm not letting loose of either until we're in Vegas."

"Vegas? Las Vegas?" She thudded both fists on his back. "I'm not going anywhere with you, much less Vegas."

"That's exactly where we're going. It's the quickest place to get married, and I'm in a hurry."

"And how the hell do you expect to get me on a plane when I'm screaming my lungs out? I'll have you in jail in five minutes flat."

At his wits' end because she was inflicting considerable damage, he dumped her at the front door and held her arms. "We're getting married, and that's the end of it."

"You can just—" Her body sagged, and her head reeled. "Married?" The word finally pierced her temper. "You don't want to get married."

"Believe me, I've been rethinking the idea since you beaned me with the fruit bowl. Now, are you going to come along reasonably, or do I have to sedate you?"

"Please let me go."

"Anna." He lowered his brow to hers. "Don't ask me to do that, because I don't think I can live without you. Take a chance, roll the dice. Come with me."

"You're angry and you're hurt," she said shakily. "And you think rushing off to Vegas to have some wild, plastic-coated instant marriage is going to fix everything."

He framed her face, gently now. Tears were shimmering in her eyes, and he knew he'd be on his knees if she let them spill over. "You can't tell me you don't love me. I won't believe you."

"Oh, I'm in love with you, Cam, but I'll survive it. There are things I need. I had to be honest with myself and admit that. You broke my heart."

"I know." He pressed his lips to her forehead. "I know I did. I was shortsighted, I was selfish, I was stupid. And damn it, I was scared. Of me, of you, of everything that was going on around me. I messed it up, and now you don't want to give me another chance."

"It's not a matter of chances. It's a matter of being practical enough to admit that we want different things."

"I finally figured out today what it is I want. Tell me what you want."

"I want a home."

He had one for her, he thought.

"I want marriage."

Hadn't he just asked her?

"I want children."

"How many?"

Her tears dried up, and she shoved at him. "It isn't a joke."

"I'm not joking. I was thinking two with an option for three." His mouth quirked at the look of blank-eyed shock on her face. "There, now *you're* getting scared because you're beginning to realize I'm serious."

"You—you're going back to Rome, or wherever, as soon as you can."

"*We* can go to Rome, or wherever, on our honeymoon. We're not taking the kid. I draw the line there. I might like to get in a couple of races from time to time. Just to keep my hand in. But basically I'm in the boat building business. Of course, it might go belly-up. Then you'd be stuck with a househusband who really hates housework."

She wanted to press her fingers to her temples, but he still had her by the arms. "I can't think."

"Good. Just listen. You cut a hole in me when you left, Anna. I wouldn't admit it, but it was there. Big and empty."

He rested his brow on hers for a moment. "You know what I did today? I worked on building a boat. And it felt good. I came home, the only home I've ever had, and it felt right. Had a family meeting and decided that we'd take on the insurance company and do what's right for our father. By the way, I've been talking to him."

She couldn't stop staring at him, even though her head was reeling. "What? Who?"

"My father. Had some conversations with him—three of them—since he died. He looks good."

Her breath was clogged right at the base of her throat. "Cam."

"Yeah, yeah," he said with a quick grin. "I need counseling. We can talk about that later—didn't mean to get off the track. I was telling you what I did today, right?"

Very slowly she nodded. "Yes."

"Okay, after the meeting, Phil made some smart remark, so I punched him, and we beat on each other for a bit. That felt good too. Then I talked to Seth about the things I should have talked to him about before, and I listened to him the way I should have listened before, then we just sat for a while. That felt good, Anna, and it felt right."

Her lips curved. "I'm glad."

"There's more. I knew when I was sitting there that that was where I wanted to be, needed to be. Only one thing was missing, and that was you. So I came to find you and take you back." He pressed his lips gently to her forehead. "To take you home, Anna."

"I think I want to sit down."

"No, I want your knees weak when I tell you I love you. Are you ready?"

"Oh, God."

"I've been real careful never to tell a woman I loved her—except my mother. I didn't tell her often enough.

Take a chance on me, Anna, and I'll tell you as often as you can stand hearing it."

She hitched in a breath. "I'm not getting married in Vegas."

"Spoilsport." He watched her lips bow up before he closed his over them. And the taste of her soothed every ache in his body and soul. "God, I missed you. Don't go away again."

"It brought you to your senses." She wrapped her arms tight around him. And it felt good, she thought giddily. It felt right. "Oh, Cam, I want to hear it, right now."

"I love you. It feels so damn perfect loving you. I can't believe I wasted so much time."

"Less than three months," she reminded him.

"Too much time. But we'll make it up."

"I want you to take me home," she murmured. "After."

He eased back, cocked his head. "After what?" Then he made her laugh by lifting her into his arms.

He picked his way through the wreckage, kicked a very sad-looking banana out of the way. "You know, I can't figure out why I used to think marriage would be boring."

"Ours won't be." She kissed his bruised head. It was still bleeding a little. "Promise."

Turn the page for a preview of

Rising Tides

Nora Roberts's trilogy continues with a captivating novel about the lives and loves of three brothers...

Months after their father's death, Ethan Quinn and his brothers were settled into the family home on Chesapeake Bay. But something kept Ethan from working through his grief: People were talking about the late Mighty Quinn—and his young son Seth. To honor the memory of the greatest man he ever knew, Ethan must clear his father's name once and for all...

"GOT US SOME NICE peelers here, Cap'n." Jim Bodine culled crabs from the pot, tossing the marketable catch in the tank. He didn't mind the snapping claws—and had the scars on his thick hands to prove it. He wore the traditional gloves of his profession, but as any waterman could tell you, they wore out quick. And if there was a hole in them, by God, a crab would find it.

He worked steadily, his legs braced apart for balance on the rocking boat, his dark eyes squinting in a face weathered with age and sun and living. He might have been taken for fifty or eighty, and Jim didn't much care which end you stuck him in.

He always called Ethan "Cap'n," and rarely said more than one declarative sentence at a time.

Ethan altered course toward the next pot, his right hand nudging the steering stick most watermen used rather than a wheel. At the same time, he nudged the throttle and gear levels with his left hand. There were constant small adjustments to be made with every foot of progress up the line of traps.

The Chesapeake Bay could be generous when she chose,

but she liked to be tricky and make you work for it.

Ethan knew the Bay as well as he knew himself. Often he thought he knew it better—the fickle moods and movements of the continent's largest estuary. For two hundred miles it flowed from north to south, yet it measured only four miles across where it brushed by Annapolis and thirty at the mouth of the Potomac River. St. Christopher sat snug on Maryland's southeastern shore, depending on its generosity, cursing its caprices.

Ethan's waters—his home waters—were edged with marshland, strung with flatland rivers with sharp shoulders that shimmered through thickets of gum and oak.

It was a world of tidal creeks and sudden shallows where wild celery and widgeongrass rooted.

It had become his world—with its changing seasons, sudden storms and always, always, the sounds and scents of the water.

Timing it, Ethan grabbed his gaffing pole and, in a practiced motion as smooth as a dance, hooked the pot line and drew it into the pot puller.

In seconds, the pot rose out of the water, streaming with weeds and pieces of old bait, and crowded with crabs.

He saw the bright-red pinchers of the full-grown females, or sooks, and the scowling eyes of Jimmies.

"Right smart bunch of crabs," was all Jim had to say as he went to work, heaving the pot onboard as if it weighed ounces rather than pounds.

The water was rough today, and Ethan could smell a storm coming in. He worked the controls with his knees when he needed his hands for other work, and he eyed the clouds beginning to boil together in the far western sky.

Time enough, he judged, to move down the line of traps in the gut of the Bay and see how many more crabs had crawled into the pots. He knew Jim was hurting some for cash—and he needed all he could come by himself in order to keep afloat the fledgling boat building business he and his brothers had started.

Time enough, he thought again, as Jim rebaited a pot

with thawing fish parts and tossed it overboard. In leapfrog fashion, Ethan gaffed the next buoy.

Ethan's sleek Chesapeake Bay retriever, Simon, stood with his front paws on the gunwhale, tongue lolling. Like his master, he was rarely happier than when out on the water.

The men worked in tandem, and in near silence, communicating with grunts, shrugs and the occasional oath. The work was a comfort, since the crabs were plentiful. There were years when they weren't, years when it seemed the winter had killed them off or that the waters would never warm enough to tempt them to swim.

In those years, the waterman suffered—unless he had another source of income. Ethan intended to have one building boats.

The first boat by Quinn was nearly finished. And a little beauty it was, Ethan thought. Cameron had another client on the line—some rich guy from Cam's racing days—so they would start another before long. Ethan never doubted that his brother would reel the money in.

They'd do it, he told himself, however doubtful and full of complaints Philip was.

He glanced up at the sun and the clouds sailing slowly, steadily eastward, and gauged the time.

"We'll take them in, Jim."

They'd been eight hours on the water, a short day, but Jim didn't complain. He knew it wasn't so much the oncoming storm that had Ethan piloting the boat back up the gut. "Boy's home from school by now," he said.

"Yeah." And though Seth was self-sufficient enough to stay home alone for a time in the afternoon, Ethan didn't like to dare fate. A boy of ten, with Seth's temperament, was a magnet for trouble.

When Cam returned from Europe in a couple weeks, they'd juggle Seth between them. But for now the boy was Ethan's responsibility.

The water in the Bay kicked, turning gunmetal-gray now to mirror the sky, but neither the men nor the dog worried about the rocky ride as the boat crept up the steep fronts of the waves then slid back down in the troughs. Simon stood at the bow now, head lifted, the wind blowing his ears back, grinning his doggie grin. Ethan had built the workboat himself, and knew she would do. As confident as the dog, Jim moved to the protection of the awning, and cupped his hands to light a cigarette.

The waterfront of St. Chris was alive with tourists. The early days of June lured them out of the city, tempted them to drive from the suburbs of D.C. and Baltimore. He imagined they thought of the little town of St. Christopher's as quaint, with its narrow streets, clapboard houses and tiny shops. They liked to watch the crab pickers' fingers fly, and eat the flaky crab cakes or tell their friends they'd had a bowl of she-crab soup. They stayed in the bed-and-breakfasts—St. Chris was the proud home of no less than four—and they spent their money in the restaurants and gift shops.

Ethan didn't mind them. During the times when the Bay was stingy, tourism kept the town alive. And he thought there would come a time when some of those same tourists might decide having a hand built wooden sailboat was their heart's desire.

The wind picked up as Ethan moored at the dock. Jim jumped nimbly out to secure lines, his short legs and squat body giving him the look of a leaping frog wearing white rubber boots and a grease-smeared gimme cap.

At Ethan's careless hand signal, Simon plopped his butt down and stayed in the boat as the men worked to unload the day's catch. The wind made the boat's sun-faded green awning dance. Ethan watched Pete Monroe walk toward them, iron-gray hair crushed under a battered billed hat, stocky body outfitted in baggy khakis and a red-checked shirt.

"Good catch today, Ethan?"

Ethan smiled. He liked Mr. Monroe well enough, though the man had a bone-deep stingy streak. He ran Monroe's Crab House with a tightly closed fist. But, as far as Ethan could tell, every man's son who ran a picking plant complained about profits.

Ethan pushed his own cap back, scratched the nape of his neck where sweat and damp hair tickled. "Good enough."

"You're in early today."

"Storm's coming."

Monroe nodded. Already his crab pickers who worked under the shade of striped awnings were preparing to move inside. Rain would drive the tourists inside as well, he knew, to drink coffee or eat ice cream sundaes. Since he was half owner of The Bayside Cafe, he didn't mind.

"Looks like you got about seventy bushels there."

Ethan let his smile widen. Some might have said there was a hint of the pirate in the look. Ethan wouldn't have been insulted, but he'd have been surprised. "Closer to ninety, I'd say." He knew the market price, to the penny, but understood they would, as always, negotiate. He took out his negotiating cigar, lit it and got to work.

THE FIRST FAT DROPS OF rain began to fall as Ethan motored toward home. He figured he'd gotten a fair price for his crabs—his eighty-seven bushels of crabs. If the rest of the summer was as good, he was going to consider dropping another hundred pots next year, maybe hiring on a part-time crew.

Oystering wasn't what it had been on the Bay, not since parasites had killed off so many. That made the winters hard. A few good crabbing seasons were what he needed to dump the lion's share of the profits into the new business—and to help pay the lawyer's fee. His mouth tightened at that thought as he rode out the swells toward home.

They shouldn't need a damn lawyer. They shouldn't have to pay some slick, suited talker to clear their father's good name. It wouldn't stop the whispers around town anyway. Those would only stop when people found something juicier to chew on than Ray Quinn's life and death.

And the boy, Ethan mused, staring out over the water that trembled under the steady pelting of rain. There were some who liked to whisper about the boy who looked back at them with Ray Quinn's dark-blue eyes.

He didn't mind for himself. As far as Ethan was concerned they could wag their tongues about him until they fell out of their flapping mouths. But he minded, deeply, that anyone would speak a dark word about the man he'd loved with every beat of his heart.

So he would work his fingers numb to pay the lawyer. And he would do whatever it took to guard the child.

Thunder shook the sky, booming off the water like cannon fire. The light went dim as dusk, and those dark clouds burst wide to pour out solid sheets of rain. Still he didn't hurry as he docked at his home pier. A little more wet, to his mind, wouldn't kill him.

As if in agreement with the sentiment, Simon leaped out to swim to shore while Ethan secured the lines. He gathered up his lunch pail, and with his waterman's boots *thwack*ing wetly against the dock, he headed for home.

Ethan removed the boots on the back porch. His mother had scalded his skin about tracking mud often enough in his youth for the habit to stick to the man. Still, he didn't think anything of letting the wet dog nose in the door ahead of him.

Until he saw the gleaming floor and counters.

Shit, was all he could think as he studied the paw prints, and heard Simon's happy bark of greeting. There was a squeal, more barking, then laughter.

"You're soaking wet!" The female voice was low and smooth and amused. It was also very firm and made Ethan wince in guilt. "Out, Simon! Out you go. You just dry off on the front porch."

There was another squeal, baby giggles, and the accompanying laughter of a young boy. *The gang's all here,* Ethan thought, rubbing rain from his hair. The minute he heard footsteps heading in his direction, he made a beeline for the broom closet and a mop.

He didn't often move fast, but he could when he had to.

"Oh, Ethan." Grace Monroe stood with her hands on her narrow hips, looking from him to the paw prints on her just-waxed floor.

"I'll get it. Sorry." He could see that the mop was still damp and decided it was best not to look at her directly. "Wasn't thinking," he muttered, filling a bucket at the sink. "Didn't know you were coming by today."

"Oh, so you let wet dogs run through the house and dirty up the floors when I'm not coming by?"

He jerked a shoulder. "Floor was dirty when I left this morning, didn't figure a little wet would hurt it any." Then he relaxed a little. It always seemed to take him a few minutes to relax around Grace these days. "But if I'd known you were here to skin me over it, I'd have left him on the porch."

He was grinning when he turned, and made her sigh.

"Oh, give me the mop. I'll do it."

"Nope. My dog, my mess. I heard Aubrey."

Absently Grace leaned on the doorjamb. She was tired, but she often was. She'd put in eight hours that day, too. And she would put in another four at Shiney's Pub that night serving drinks.

There were nights when she crawled into bed that she would have sworn she heard her feet crying.

"Seth's minding her for me. I had to switch my days. Mrs. Lynley called this morning and asked if I'd shift doing her house till tomorrow because her mother-in-law called her from D.C. and invited herself down to dinner. Mrs. Lynley claims her mother-in-law is a woman who looks at a speck of dust like it's a sin against God and man. I didn't think you'd mind if I did y'all today instead of tomorrow."

"You fit us in whenever you can manage it, Grace, and we're grateful."

He was watching her from under his lashes as he mopped. He'd always thought she was a pretty thing. Like a palomino—all gold and long-legged. She chopped her hair off short as a boy's, but he liked the way it sat on her head, like a shiny cap with fringes.

She was as thin as one of those million-dollar models, but he knew Grace's long, lean form wasn't for fashion. She'd been a gangly, skinny kid as he recalled. She'd have been about seven or eight when he'd first come to St. Chris and the Quinns. He supposed she was twenty and a couple now—and skinny wasn't exactly the word for her.

She was like a willow slip, he thought and then very nearly flushed.

She smiled at him, and her mermaid-green eyes warmed, faint dimples flirted in her cheeks. For reasons she couldn't name, seeing such a healthy male specimen wielding a mop entertained her.

"Did you have a good day, Ethan?"

"Good enough." He did a thorough job with the floor. He was a thorough man. Then he went to the sink again to rinse bucket and mop. "Sold a mess of crabs to your daddy."

At the mention of her father, Grace's smile dimmed a little. There was distance between them, and had been since she'd become pregnant with Aubrey and had married Jack Casey, the man her father had called "that no-account grease monkey from upstate."

Her father had turned out to be right about Jack. The man had left her high and dry a month before Aubrey had been born. And he'd taken her savings, her car, and most of her self-respect with him.

But she'd gotten through it, Grace reminded herself. And she was doing just fine. She'd keep right on doing fine, on her own, without a single penny from her family—if she had to work herself to death to prove it.

She heard Aubrey laugh again, a long rolling gut laugh, and her resentment vanished. She had everything that mattered. It was all tied up in a bright-eyed, curly headed little angel just in the next room.

"I'll make you up some dinner before I go."

Ethan turned back, took another look at her. She was getting some sun, and it looked good on her. Warmed her skin. She had a long face that went well with her long body—though the chin tended to be stubborn. A man could take a glance and he'd see a long, cool blonde—a pretty body, a face that made you want to glance back just a little longer.

And if you did, you'd see shadows under the big green eyes, and weariness around that soft mouth.

"You don't have to do that, Grace. You ought to go on home and relax a while. You're on at Shiney's tonight, aren't you?"

"I've got time—and I promised Seth sloppy joes. It won't take me long." She shifted as Ethan continued to stare at her. She'd long ago accepted that those long thoughtful looks from him would stir her blood. Just another of life's little problems, she supposed. "What?" she demanded, and rubbed a hand over her cheek as if expecting to find a smudge.

"Nothing. Well, if you're going to cook, you ought to hang around and help us eat it."

"I'd like that." She relaxed again and moved forward to take the bucket and mop from him and put them away herself. "Aubrey loves being here with you and Seth. Why don't you go on in with them? I've got some laundry to finish up, then I'll start dinner."

"I'll give you a hand."

"No, you won't." It was another point of pride for her. They paid her, she did the work. All the work. "Go on in the front room—and be sure to ask Seth about the math test he got back today."

"How'd he do?"

"Another *A*." She winked and shooed Ethan away. Seth had such a sharp brain, she thought as she headed into the laundry room off the kitchen. If she'd had a better head for figures, for practical matters when she'd been younger, she wouldn't have dreamed her way through school.

She'd have learned a skill, a real one, not just serving drinks and tending house or picking crabs. She'd have had a career to fall back on when she'd found herself alone and pregnant with all her hopes of running off to New York to be a dancer dashed like glass on brick.

It had been a silly dream anyway, she told herself, unloading the dryer and shifting the wet clothes from the washer into it. Pie in the sky, her mama would say. But the fact was, growing up there had only been two things she'd wanted: the dance and Ethan Quinn.

HIGH NOON

Nora Roberts

Those closest to you can do the most harm

Phoebe MacNamara first comes face to face with Duncan Swift high up on a rooftop, as she tries to stop one of his ex-employees from jumping. As Savannah's chief hostage negotiator, Phoebe is talented, courageous and willing to risk her life to save others – and Duncan is determined to keep this intriguing woman in his life.

But Phoebe has made enemies too. When she is viciously assaulted and sent threatening messages, she realises that someone is out to destroy her – both professionally and personally. With Duncan by her side, Phoebe must discover just who is pursuing her, before it's too late . . .

'Women are addicted to her contemporary novels as chocoholics are to Godiva . . . Roberts is a superstar'
New York Times

978-0-7499-3898-7

Nora Roberts is the *New York Times* bestselling author of more than 190 novels. Under the pen name J. D. Robb, she is the author of the *New York Times* bestselling futuristic suspense series, which features Lieutenant Eve Dallas and Roarke. There are more than 300 million copies of her books in print, and she has had more than 150 *New York Times* bestsellers.

Visit her website at www.nora-roberts.co.uk

By Nora Roberts

Homeport
The Reef
River's End
Carolina Moon
The Villa
Midnight Bayou
Three Fates
Birthright
Northern Lights
Blue Smoke
Montana Sky
Angels Fall
High Noon
Divine Evil
Tribute
Sanctuary

Three Sisters Island Trilogy:
Dance Upon the Air
Heaven and Earth
Face the Fire

Chesapeake Bay Quartet:
Sea Swept
Rising Tides
Inner Harbour
Chesapeake Blue

The Key Trilogy:
Key of Light
Key of Knowledge
Key of Valour

In the Garden Trilogy:
Blue Dahlia
Black Rose
Red Lily

The Irish Trilogy:
Jewels of the Sun
Tears of the Moon
Heart of the Sea

The Circle Trilogy:
Morrigan's Cross
Dance of the Gods
Valley of Silence

The Dream Trilogy:
Daring to Dream
Holding the Dream
Finding the Dream

The Sign of Seven Trilogy:
Blood Brothers
The Hollow
The Pagan Stone

As J. D. Robb:

Naked in Death
Glory in Death
Immortal in Death
Rapture in Death
Ceremony in Death
Vengeance in Death
Holiday in Death
Conspiracy in Death
Loyalty in Death
Witness in Death
Judgement in Death
Betrayal in Death
Seduction in Death
Reunion in Death
Purity in Death
Portrait in Death
Imitation in Death
Divided in Death
Visions in Death
Survivor in Death
Origin in Death
Memory in Death
Born in Death
Innocent in Death
Creation in Death
Strangers in Death

By Nora Roberts and J. D. Robb

Remember When

Blood Brothers

Nora Roberts

PIATKUS

First published in the US in 2007 by The Berkley Publishing Group, a member of Penguin Group (USA) Inc., New York.
First published in Great Britain in 2007 by Piatkus Books
This paperback edition published in 2007 by Piatkus Books
Reprinted 2008 (three times), 2009

All characters and events in this publication, other than those clearly in the public domain, are fictitious and any resemblance to real persons, living or dead, is purely coincidental.

A CIP catalogue record for this book is available from the British Library

ISBN 978-0-7499-3843-7

Data manipulation by Phoenix Photosetting, Chatham, Kent
www.phoenixphotosetting.co.uk
Printed and bound in the UK by CPI Mackays, Chatham, ME5 8TD

Papers used by Piatkus Books are natural, renewable and recyclable products made from wood grown in sustainable forests and certified in accordance with the rules of the Forest Stewardship Council.

Piatkus Books
An imprint of
Little, Brown Book Group
100 Victoria Embankment
London EC4Y 0DY

An Hachette Livre UK Company
www.hachettelivre.co.uk

www.piatkus.co.uk

To my boys,
who roamed the woods,
even when they weren't supposed to.

Where God hath a temple,
the Devil will have a chapel.

—ROBERT BURTON

The childhood shows the man
As morning shows the day.

—JOHN MILTON

Blood Brothers

Prologue

Hawkins Hollow
Maryland Province
1652

IT CRAWLED ALONG THE AIR THAT HUNG HEAVY as wet wool over the glade. Through the snakes of fog that slid silent over the ground, its hate crept. It came for him through the heat-smothered night.

It wanted his death.

So he waited as it pushed its way through the woods, its torch raised toward the empty sky, as it waded across the streams, around the thickets where small animals huddled in fear of the scent it bore with it.

Hellsmoke.

He had sent Ann and the lives she carried in her womb away, to safety. She had not wept, he thought now as he sprinkled the herbs he'd selected over water. Not his Ann. But he had seen the grief on her face, in the deep, dark eyes he loved through this lifetime, and all the others before.

The three would be born from her, raised by her, and taught by her. And from them, when the time came, there would be three more.

What power he had would be theirs, these sons, who

would loose their first cry long, long after this night's work was done. To leave them what tools they would need, the weapons they would wield, he risked all he had, all he was.

His legacy to them was in blood, in heart, in vision.

In this last hour he would do all he could to provide them with what was needed to carry the burden, to remain true, to see their destiny.

His voice was strong and clear as he called to wind and water, to earth and fire. In the hearth the flames snapped. In the bowl, the water trembled.

He laid the bloodstone on the cloth. Its deep green was generously spotted with red. He had treasured this stone, as had those who'd come before him. He had honored it. And now he poured power into it as one would pour water into a cup.

So his body shook and sweat and weakened as light hovered in a halo around the stone.

"For you now," he murmured, "sons of sons. Three parts of one. In faith, in hope, in truth. One light, united, to strike back dark. And here, my vow. I will not rest until destiny is met."

With the athame, he scored his palm so his blood fell onto the stone, into the water, and into flame.

"Blood of my blood. Here I will hold until you come for me, until you loose what must be loosed again on the world. May the gods keep you."

For a moment there was grief. Even through his purpose, there was grief. Not for his life, as the sands of it were dripping down the glass. He had no fear of death. No fear of what he would soon embrace that was not death. But he grieved that he would never lay his lips on Ann's again in this life. He would not see his children born, nor the children of his children. He grieved that he would not be able to stop the suffering to come, as he had been unable to stop the suffering that had come before, in so many other lifetimes.

He understood that he was not the instrument, but only the vessel to be filled and emptied at the needs of the gods.

So weary from the work, saddened by the loss, he stood outside the little hut, beside the great stone, to meet his fate.

It came in the body of a man, but that was a shell. As his own body was a shell. It called itself Lazarus Twisse, an elder of "the godly." He and those who followed had settled in the wilderness of this province when they broke with the Puritans of New England.

He studied them now in their torchlight, these men and the one who was not a man. These, he thought, who had come to the New World for religious freedom, and then persecuted and destroyed any who did not follow their single, narrow path.

"You are Giles Dent."

"I am," he said, "in this time and this place."

Lazarus Twisse stepped forward. He wore the unrelieved formal black of an elder. His high-crowned, wide-brimmed hat shadowed his face. But Giles could see his eyes, and in his eyes, he saw the demon.

"Giles Dent, you and the female known as Ann Hawkins have been accused and found guilty of witchcraft and demonic practices."

"Who accuses?"

"Bring the girl forward!" Lazarus ordered.

They pulled her, a man on each arm. She was a slight girl, barely six and ten by Giles's calculation. Her face was wax white with fear, her eyes drenched with it. Her hair had been shorn.

"Hester Deale, is this the witch who seduced you?"

"He and the one he calls wife laid hands on me." She spoke as if in a trance. "They performed ungodly acts upon my body. They came to my window as ravens, flew into my room in the night. They stilled my throat so I could not speak or call for help."

"Child," Giles said gently, "what has been done to you?"

Those fear-swamped eyes stared through him. "They called to Satan as their god, and cut the throat of a cock in sacrifice. And drank its blood. They forced its blood on me. I could not stop them."

"Hester Deale, do you renounce Satan?"

"I do renounce him."

"Hester Deale, do you renounce Giles Dent and the woman Ann Hawkins as witches and heretics?"

"I do." Tears spilled down her cheeks. "I do renounce them, and pray to God to save me. Pray to God to forgive me."

"He will," Giles whispered. "You are not to blame."

"Where is the woman Ann Hawkins?" Lazarus demanded, and Giles turned his clear gray eyes to him.

"You will not find her."

"Stand aside. I will enter this house of the devil."

"You will not find her," Giles repeated. For a moment he looked beyond Lazarus to the men and the handful of women who stood in his glade.

He saw death in their eyes, and more, the hunger for it. This was the demon's power, and his work.

Only in Hester's did Giles see fear or sorrow. So he used what he had to give, pushed his mind toward hers. *Run!*

He saw her jolt, stumble back, then he turned to Lazarus.

"We know each other, you and I. Dispatch them, release them, and it will be between us alone."

For an instant he saw the gleam of red in Lazarus's eyes. "You are done. Burn the witch!" he shouted. "Burn the devil house and all within it!"

They came with torches, and with clubs. Giles felt the blows rain on him, and the fury of the hate that was the demon's sharpest weapon.

They drove him to his knees, and the wood of the hut began to flame and smoke. Screams rang in his head, the madness of them.

With the last of his power he reached out toward the demon inside the man, with red rimming its dark eyes as it fed on the hate, the fear, the violence. He felt it gloat, he felt it *rising*, so sure of its victory, and the feast to follow.

And he ripped it to him, through the smoking air. He heard it scream in fury and pain as the flames bit into flesh. And he held it to him, close as a lover as the fire consumed them.

And with that union the fire burst, spread, destroyed every living thing in the glade.

It burned for a day and a night, like the belly of hell.

One

Hawkins Hallow
Maryland
July 6, 1987

INSIDE THE PRETTY KITCHEN OF THE PRETTY house on Pleasant Avenue, Caleb Hawkins struggled not to squirm as his mother packed her version of campout provisions.

In his mother's world, ten-year-old boys required fresh fruit, homemade oatmeal cookies (they weren't so bad), half a dozen hard-boiled eggs, a bag of Ritz crackers made into sandwiches with Jif peanut butter for filling, some celery and carrot sticks (yuck!), and hearty ham-and-cheese sandwiches.

Then there was the thermos of lemonade, the stack of paper napkins, and the two boxes of Pop-Tarts she wedged into the basket for breakfast.

"Mom, we're not going to *starve* to death," he complained as she stood deliberating in front of an open cupboard. "We're going to be right in Fox's backyard."

Which was a lie, and kinda hurt his tongue. But she'd never let him go if he told her the truth. And, sheesh, he was ten. Or would be the very next day.

Frannie Hawkins put her hands on her hips. She was a pert, attractive blonde with summer blue eyes and a stylish curly perm. She was the mother of three, and Cal was her baby and only boy. "Now, let me check that backpack."

"Mom!"

"Honey, I just want to be sure you didn't forget anything." Ruthless in her own sunny way, Frannie unzipped Cal's navy blue pack. "Change of underwear, clean shirt, socks, good, good, shorts, toothbrush. Cal, where are the Band-Aids I told you to put in, and the Bactine, the bug repellant."

"Sheesh, we're not going to Africa."

"All the same," Frannie said, and did her signature finger wave to send him along to gather up the supplies. While he did, she slipped a card out of her pocket and tucked it into the pack.

He'd been born—after eight hours and twelve minutes of vicious labor—at one minute past midnight. Every year she stepped up to his bed at twelve, watched him sleep for that minute, then kissed him on the cheek.

Now he'd be ten, and she wouldn't be able to perform the ritual. Because it made her eyes sting, she turned away to wipe at her spotless counter as she heard his tromping footsteps.

"I got it all, okay?"

Smiling brightly, she turned back. "Okay." She stepped over to rub a hand over his short, soft hair. He'd been her towheaded baby boy, she mused, but his hair was darkening, and she suspected it would be a light brown eventually.

Just as hers would be without the aid of Born Blonde.

In a habitual gesture, Frannie tapped his dark-framed glasses back up his nose. "You make sure you thank Mrs. Barry and Mr. O'Dell when you get there."

"I will."

"*And* when you leave to come home tomorrow."

"Yes, ma'am."

She took his face in her hands, looked through the thick lenses into eyes the same color as his father's calm gray ones. "Behave," she said and kissed his cheek. "Have fun." Then the other. "Happy birthday, my baby."

Usually it mortified him to be called her *baby*, but for some reason, just then, it made him feel sort of gooey and good.

"Thanks, Mom."

He shrugged on the backpack, then hefted the loaded picnic basket. How the hell was he going to ride all the way out to Hawkins Wood with half the darn grocery store on his bike?

The guys were going to razz him something fierce.

Since he was stuck, he carted it into the garage where his bike hung tidily—by Mom decree—on a rack on the wall. Thinking it through, he borrowed two of his father's bungee cords and secured the picnic basket to the wire basket of his bike.

Then he hopped on his bike and pedaled down the short drive.

FOX FINISHED WEEDING HIS SECTION OF THE vegetable garden before hefting the spray his mother mixed up weekly to discourage the deer and rabbits, from invading for an all-you-can-eat buffet. The garlic, raw egg, and cayenne pepper combination stank so bad he held his breath as he squirted it on the rows of snap beans and limas, the potato greens, the carrot and radish tops.

He stepped back, took a clear breath, and studied his work. His mother was pretty damn strict about the gardening. It was all about respecting the Earth, harmonizing with Nature, and that stuff.

It was also, Fox knew, about eating, and making enough food and money to feed a family of six—and whoever dropped by. Which was why his dad and his older sister, Sage, were down at their stand selling fresh eggs, goat's milk, honey, and his mother's homemade jams.

He glanced over to where his younger brother Ridge

was stretched out between the rows playing with the weeds instead of yanking them. And because his mother was inside putting their baby sister, Sparrow, down for her nap, he was on Ridge duty.

"Come on, Ridge, pull the stupid things. I wanna go."

Ridge lifted his face, turned his I'm-dreaming eyes on his brother. "Why can't I go with you?"

"Because you're eight and you can't even weed the dumb tomatoes." Annoyed, Fox stepped over the rows to Ridge's section and, crouching, began to yank.

"Can, too."

As Fox hoped, the insult had Ridge weeding with a vengeance. Fox straightened, rubbed his hands on his jeans. He was a tall boy with a skinny build, a mass of bark-brown hair worn in a waving tangle around a sharp-boned face. His eyes were tawny and reflected his satisfaction now as he trooped over for the sprayer.

He dumped it beside Ridge. "Don't forget to spray this shit."

He crossed the yard, circling what was left—three short walls and part of a chimney—of the old stone hut on the edge of the vegetable garden. It was buried, as his mother liked it best, in honeysuckle and wild morning glory.

He skirted past the chicken coop and the cluckers that were pecking around, by the goat yard where the two nannies stood slack-hipped and bored, edged around his mother's herb garden. He headed toward the kitchen door of the house his parents had mostly built. The kitchen was big, and the counters loaded with projects—canning jars, lids, tubs of candle wax, bowls of wicks.

He knew most of the people in and around the Hollow thought of his family as the weird hippies. It didn't bother him. For the most part they got along, and people were happy to buy their eggs and produce, his mother's needlework and handmade candles and crafts, or hire his dad to build stuff.

Fox washed up at the sink before rooting through the

cupboards, poking in the big pantry searching for *something* that wasn't health food.

Fat chance.

He'd bike over to the market—the one right outside of town just in case—and use some of his savings to buy Little Debbies and Nutter Butters.

His mother came in, tossing her long brown braid off the shoulder bared by her cotton sundress. "Finished?"

"I am. Ridge is almost."

Joanne walked to the window, her hand automatically lifting to brush down Fox's hair, staying to rest on his neck as she studied her younger son.

"There's some carob brownies and some veggie dogs, if you want to take any."

"Ah." Barf. "No, thanks. I'm good."

He knew that she knew he'd be chowing down on meat products and refined sugar. And he knew she knew he knew. But she wouldn't rag him about it. Choices were big with Mom.

"Have a good time."

"I will."

"Fox?" She stood where she was, by the sink with the light coming in the window and haloing her hair. "Happy birthday."

"Thanks, Mom." And with Little Debbies on his mind, he bolted out to grab his bike and start the adventure.

THE OLD MAN WAS STILL SLEEPING WHEN GAGE shoved some supplies into his pack. Gage could hear the snoring through the thin, crappy walls of the cramped, crappy apartment over the Bowl-a-Rama. The old man worked there cleaning the floors, the johns, and whatever else Cal's father found for him to do.

He might've been a day shy of his tenth birthday, but Gage knew why Mr. Hawkins kept the old man on, why they had the apartment rent-free with the old man supposedly being the maintenance guy for the building. Mr. Hawkins felt sorry for them—and mostly sorry for Gage because he was stuck as the motherless son of a mean drunk.

Other people felt sorry for him, too, and that put Gage's back up. Not Mr. Hawkins though. He never let the pity show. And whenever Gage did any chores for the bowling alley, Mr. Hawkins paid him in cash, on the side. And with a conspirator's wink.

He knew, hell, everybody knew, that Bill Turner knocked his kid around from time to time. But Mr. Hawkins was the *only* one who'd ever sat down with Gage and asked *him* what he wanted. Did he want the cops, Social Services, did he want to come stay with him and his family for a while?

He hadn't wanted the cops or the do-gooders. They only made it worse. And though he'd have given anything to live in that nice house with people who lived decent lives, he'd only asked if Mr. Hawkins would please, please, not fire his old man.

He got knocked around less whenever Mr. Hawkins kept his father busy and employed. Unless, of course, good old Bill went on a toot and decided to whale in.

If Mr. Hawkins knew how bad it could get during those times, he would call the cops.

So he didn't tell, and he learned to be very good at hiding beatings like the one he'd taken the night before.

Gage moved carefully as he snagged three cold ones out of his father's beer supply. The welts on his back and butt were still raw and angry and they stung like fire. He'd expected the beating. He always got one around his birthday. He always got another one around the date of his mother's death.

Those were the big, traditional two. Other times, the whippings came as a surprise. But mostly, mostly when the old man was working steady, the hits were just a careless cuff or shove.

He didn't bother to be quiet when he turned toward his

father's bedroom. Nothing short of a raid by the A-Team would wake Bill Turner when he was in a drunken sleep.

The room stank of beer sweat and stale smoke, causing Gage to wrinkle his handsome face. He took the half pack of Marlboros off the dresser. The old man wouldn't remember if he'd had any, so no problem there.

Without a qualm, he opened his father's wallet and helped himself to three singles and a five.

He looked at his father as he stuffed the bills in his pocket. Bill sprawled on the bed, stripped down to his boxers, his mouth open as the snores pumped out.

The belt he'd used on his son the night before lay on the floor along with dirty shirts, socks, jeans.

For a moment, just a moment, it rippled through Gage with a kind of mad glee—the image of himself picking up that belt, swinging it high, laying it snapping hard over his father's bare, sagging belly.

See how you like it.

But there on the table with its overflowing ashtray, the empty bottle, was the picture of Gage's mother, smiling out.

People said he looked like her—the dark hair, the hazy green eyes, the strong mouth. It had embarrassed him once, being compared to a woman. But lately, since everything but that one photograph was so faded in his head, when he couldn't hear her voice in his head or remember how she'd smelled, it steadied him.

He looked like his mother.

Sometimes he imagined the man who drank himself into a stupor most nights wasn't his father.

His father was smart and brave and sort of reckless.

And then he'd look at the old man and know that was all bullshit.

He shot the old bastard the finger as he left the room. He had to carry his backpack. No way he could put it on with the welts riding his back.

He took the outside steps down, went around the back where he chained up his thirdhand bike.

Despite the pain, he grinned as he got on.

For the next twenty-four hours, he was free.

THEY'D AGREED TO MEET ON THE WEST EDGE OF town where the woods crept toward the curve of the road. The middle-class boy, the hippie kid, and the drunk's son.

They shared the same birthday, July seventh. Cal had let out his first shocked cry in the delivery room of Washington County Hospital while his mother panted and his father wept. Fox had shoved his way into the world and into his laughing father's waiting hands in the bedroom of the odd little farmhouse while Bob Dylan sang "Lay, Lady, Lay" on the record player, and lavender-scented candles burned. And Gage had struggled out of his terrified mother in an ambulance racing up Maryland Route Sixty-five.

Now, Gage arrived first, sliding off his bike to walk it into the trees where nobody cruising the road could spot it, or him.

Then he sat on the ground and lit his first cigarette of the afternoon. They always made him a little sick to his stomach, but the defiant act of lighting up made up for the queasiness.

He sat and smoked in the shady woods, and imagined himself on a mountain path in Colorado or a steamy South American jungle.

Anywhere but here.

He'd taken his third puff, and his first cautious inhale, when he heard the bumps of tires over dirt and rock.

Fox pushed through the trees on Lightning, his bike so named because Fox's father had painted lightning bolts on the bars.

His dad was cool that way.

"Hey, Turner."

"O'Dell." Gage held out the cigarette.

They both knew Fox took it only because to do otherwise made him a dweeb. So he took a quick drag, passed it back. Gage nodded to the bag tied to Lightning's handlebars. "What'd you get?"

"Little Debbies, Nutter Butters, some TastyKake pies. Apple and cherry."

"Righteous. I got three cans of Bud for tonight."

Fox's eyes didn't pop out of his head, but they were close. "No shit?"

"No shit. Old man was trashed. He'll never know the difference. I got something else, too. Last month's *Penthouse* magazine."

"No way."

"He keeps them buried under a bunch of crap in the bathroom."

"Lemme see."

"Later. With the beer."

They both looked over as Cal dragged his bike down the rough path. "Hey jerkwad," Fox greeted him.

"Hey, dickheads."

That said with the affection of brothers, they walked their bikes deeper into the trees, then off the narrow path.

Once the bikes were deemed secure, supplies were untied and divvied up.

"Jesus, Hawkins, what'd your mom put in here?"

"You won't complain when you're eating it." Cal's arms were already protesting at the weight as he scowled at Gage. "Why don't you put your pack on, and give me a hand?"

"Because I'm carrying it." But he flipped the top on the basket and after hooting at the Tupperware, shoved a couple of the containers into his pack. "Put something in yours, O'Dell, or it'll take us all day just to get to Hester's Pool."

"Shit." Fox pulled out a thermos, wedged it in his pack. "Light enough now, Sally?"

"Screw you. I got the basket and my pack."

"I got the supplies from the market and my pack." Fox pulled his prized possession from his bike. "You carry the boom box, Turner."

Gage shrugged, took the radio. "Then I pick the tunes."

"No rap," Cal and Fox said together, but Gage only grinned as he walked and tuned until he found some Run-D.M.C.

With a lot of bitching and moaning, they started the hike.

The leaves, thick and green, cut the sun's glare and summer heat. Through the thick poplars and towering oaks, slices and dabs of milky blue sky peeked. They aimed for the wind of the creek while the rapper and Aerosmith urged them to walk this way.

"Gage has a *Penthouse*," Fox announced. "The skin magazine, numbnut," he said at Cal's blank stare.

"Uh-uh."

"Uh-huh. Come on, Turner, break it out."

"Not until we're camped and pop the beer."

"Beer!" Instinctively, Cal sent a look over his shoulder, just in case his mother had magically appeared. "You got beer?"

"Three cans of suds," Gage confirmed, strutting. "Smokes, too."

"Is this far-out or what?" Fox gave Cal a punch in the arm. "It's the best birthday ever."

"Ever," Cal agreed, secretly terrified. Beer, cigarettes, and pictures of naked women. If his mother ever found out he'd be grounded until he was thirty. That didn't even count the fact he'd lied. Or that he was hiking his way through Hawkins Wood to camp out at the expressly forbidden Pagan Stone.

He'd be grounded until he died of old age.

"Stop worrying." Gage shifted his pack from one arm to the other, with a wicked glint of what-the-hell in his eyes. "It's all cool."

"I'm not worried." Still, Cal jolted when a fat jay zoomed out of the trees and let out an irritated call.

Two

HESTER'S POOL WAS ALSO FORBIDDEN IN CAL'S world, which was only one of the reasons it was irresistible.

The scoop of brown water, fed by the winding Antietam Creek and hidden in the thick woods, was supposed to be haunted by some weird Pilgrim girl who'd drowned in it way back whenever.

He'd heard his mother talk about a boy who'd drowned there when she'd been a kid, which in Mom Logic was the number one reason Cal was *never allowed* to swim there. The kid's ghost was supposed to be there, too, lurking under the water, just waiting to grab another kid's ankle and drag him down to the bottom so he'd have somebody to hang out with.

Cal had swum there twice that summer, giddy with fear and excitement. And both times he'd *sworn* he'd felt bony fingers brush over his ankle.

A dense army of cattails trooped along the edges, and around the slippery bank grew bunches of the wild orange lilies his mother liked. Fans of ferns climbed up the rocky slope, along with brambles of wild berries, which when ripe would stain the fingers a kind of reddish purple that looked a little like blood.

The last time they'd come, he'd seen a black snake slither its way up the slope, barely stirring the ferns.

Fox let out a shout, dumped his pack. In seconds he'd dragged off his shoes, his shirt, his jeans and was sailing over the water in a cannonball without a thought for snakes or ghosts or whatever else might be under that murky brown surface.

"Come on, you pussies!" After a slick surface dive, Fox bobbed around the pool like a seal.

Cal sat, untied his Converse All Stars, carefully tucked his socks inside them. While Fox continued to whoop and splash, he glanced over where Gage simply stood looking out over the water.

"You going in?"

"I dunno."

Cal pulled off his shirt, folded it out of habit. "It's on the agenda. We can't cross it off unless we all do it."

"Yeah, yeah." But Gage only stood as Cal stripped down to his Fruit of the Looms.

"We have to all go in, dare the gods and stuff."

With a shrug, Gage toed off his shoes. "Go on, what are you, a homo? Want to watch me take my clothes off?"

"Gross." And slipping his glasses inside his left shoe, Cal sucked in breath, gave thanks his vision blurred, and jumped.

The water was a quick, cold shock.

Fox immediately spewed water in his face, fully blinding him, then stroked off toward the cattails before retaliation. Just when he'd managed to clear his myopic eyes, Gage jumped in and blinded him all over again.

"Sheesh, you guys!"

Gage's choppy dog paddle worked up the water so Cal swam clear of the storm. Of the three, he was the best swimmer. Fox was fast, but he ran out of steam. And Gage, well, Gage sort of attacked the water like he was in a fight with it.

Cal worried—even as part of him thrilled at the idea—that he'd one day have to use the lifesaving techniques his dad had taught him in their above-ground pool to save Gage from drowning.

He was picturing it, and how Gage and Fox would stare at him with gratitude and admiration, when a hand grabbed his ankle and yanked him underwater.

Even though he *knew* it was Fox who pulled him down, Cal's heart slammed into his throat as the water closed over his head. He floundered, forgetting all his training in that first instant of panic. Even as he managed to kick off the hold on his ankle and gather himself to push to the surface, he saw a movement to the left.

It—she—seemed to glide through the water toward him. Her hair streamed back from her white face, and her eyes were cave black. As her hand reached out, Cal opened his mouth to scream. Gulping in water he clawed his way to the surface.

He could hear laughter all around him, tinny and echoing like the music out of the old transistor radio his father sometimes used. With terror biting inside his throat, he slapped and clawed his way to the edge of the pool.

"I saw her, I saw her, in the water, I saw her." He choked out the words while fighting to climb out.

She was coming for him, fast as a shark in his mind, and in his mind he saw her mouth open, and the teeth gleam sharp as knives.

"Get out! Get out of the water!" Panting, he crawled through the slippery weeds and rolling, saw his friends treading water. "She's in the water." He almost sobbed it, bellying over to fumble his glasses out of his shoe. "I *saw* her. Get out. Hurry up!"

"Oooh, the ghost! Help me, help me!" With a mock gurgle, Fox sank underwater.

Cal lurched to his feet, balled his hands into fists at his

sides. Fury tangled with terror to have his voice lashing through the still summer air. "Get the fuck out."

The grin on Gage's face faded. Eyes narrowed on Cal, he gripped Fox by the arm when Fox surfaced laughing.

"We're getting out."

"Come *on*. He's just being spaz because I dunked him."

"He's not bullshitting."

The tone got through, or when he bothered to look, the expression on Cal's face tripped a chord. Fox shot off toward the edge, spooked enough to send a couple of wary looks over his shoulder.

Gage followed, a careless dog paddle that made Cal think he was daring something to happen.

When his friends hauled themselves out, Cal sank back down to the ground. Drawing his knees up, he pressed his forehead to them and began to shake.

"Man." Dripping in his underwear, Fox shifted from foot to foot. "I just gave you a tug, and you freak out. We were just fooling around."

"I saw her."

Crouching, Fox shoved his sopping hair back from his face. "Dude, you can't see squat without those Coke bottles."

"Shut up, O'Dell." Gage squatted down. "What did you see, Cal?"

"*Her*. She had all this hair swimming around her, and her eyes, oh man, her eyes were black like the shark in *Jaws*. She had this long dress on, long sleeves and all, and she reached out like she was going to grab me—"

"With her bony fingers," Fox put in, falling well short of his target of disdain.

"They weren't bony." Cal lifted his head now, and behind the lenses his eyes were fierce and frightened. "I thought they would be, but she looked, all of her, looked just . . . real. Not like a ghost or a skeleton. Oh man, oh God, I saw her. I'm not making it up."

"Well Jee-sus." Fox crab-walked another foot away

from the pond, then cursed breathlessly when he tore his forearm on berry thorns. "Shit, now I'm bleeding." Fox yanked a handful of weedy grass, swiped at the blood seeping from the scratches.

"Don't even think about it." Cal saw the way Gage was studying the water—that thoughtful, wonder-what'll-happen gleam in his eye. "Nobody's going in there. You don't swim well enough to try it anyway."

"How come you're the only one who saw her?"

"I don't know and I don't care. I just want to get away from here."

Cal leaped up, grabbed his pants. Before he could wiggle into them, he saw Gage from behind. "Holy cow. Your back is messed up bad."

"The old man got wasted last night. It's no big deal."

"Dude." Fox walked around to get a look. "That's gotta hurt."

"The water cooled it off."

"I've got my first aid kit—" Cal began, but Gage cut him off.

"I said no big deal." He grabbed his shirt, pulled it on. "If you two don't have the balls to go back in and see what happens, we might as well move on."

"I don't have the balls," Cal said in such a deadpan, Gage snorted out a laugh.

"Then put your pants on so I don't have to wonder what that is hanging between your legs."

Fox broke out the Little Debbies, and one of the six-pack of Coke he'd bought at the market. Because the incident in the pond and the welts on Gage's back were too important, they didn't speak of them. Instead, hair still dripping, they resumed the hike, gobbling snack cakes and sharing a can of warm soda.

But with Bon Jovi claiming they were halfway there, Cal thought of what he'd seen. Why had he been the only one? How had her face been so clear in the murky water, and with his glasses tucked in his shoe? How could he have seen her? With every step he took away from the pond, it was easier to convince himself he'd just imagined it.

Not that he'd ever, *ever* admit that maybe he'd just freaked out.

The heat dried his damp skin and brought on the sweat. It made him wonder how Gage could stand having his shirt clinging to his sore back. Because, man, those marks were all red and bumpy, and really had to hurt. He'd seen Gage after Old Man Turner had gone after him before, and it hadn't ever, ever been as bad as this. He wished Gage had let him put some salve on his back.

What if it got infected? What if he got blood poisoning, got all delirious or something when they were all the way in to the Pagan Stone?

He'd have to send Fox for help, yeah, that's what he'd do—send Fox for help while he stayed with Gage and treated the wounds, got him to drink something so he didn't—what was it?—dehydrate.

Of course, all their butts would be in the sling when his dad had to come get them, but Gage would get better.

Maybe they'd put Gage's father in jail. Then what would happen? Would Gage have to go to an orphanage?

It was almost as scary to think about as the woman in the pond.

They stopped to rest, then sat in the shade to share one of Gage's stolen Marlboros. They always made Cal dizzy, but it was kind of nice to sit there in the trees with the water sliding over rocks behind them and a bunch of crazy birds calling out to each other.

"We could camp right here," Cal said half to himself.

"No way." Fox punched his shoulder. "We're turning ten at the Pagan Stone. No changing the plan. We'll be there in under an hour. Right, Gage?"

Gage stared up through the trees. "Yeah. We'd be moving faster if you guys hadn't brought so much shit with you."

"Didn't see you turn down a Little Debbie," Fox reminded him.

"Nobody turns down Little Debbies. Well . . ." He crushed out the cigarette, then planted a rock over the butt. "Saddle up, troops."

Nobody came here. Cal knew it wasn't true, knew when deer was in season these woods were hunted.

But it *felt* like nobody came here. The two other times he'd been talked into hiking all the way to the Pagan Stone he'd felt exactly the same. And both those times they'd started out early in the morning instead of afternoon. They'd been back out before two.

Now, according to his Timex it was nearly four. Despite the snack cake, his stomach wanted to rumble. He wanted to stop again, to dig into what his mother had packed in the stupid basket.

But Gage was pushing on, anxious to get to the Pagan Stone.

The earth in the clearing had a scorched look about it, as if a fire had blown through the trees there and turned them all to ash. It was almost a perfect circle, ringed by oaks and locus and the bramble of wild berries. In its center was a single rock that jutted two feet out of the burned earth and flattened at the top like a small table.

Some said altar.

People, when they spoke of it at all, said the Pagan Stone was just a big rock that pushed out of the ground. Ground so colored because of minerals, or an underground stream, or maybe caves.

But others, who were usually more happy to talk about it, pointed to the original settlement of Hawkins Hollow and the night thirteen people met their doom, burned alive in that very clearing.

Witchcraft, some said, and others devil worship.

Another theory was an inhospitable band of Indians had killed them, then burned the bodies.

But whatever the theory, the pale gray stone rose out of the soot-colored earth like a monument.

"We made it!" Fox dumped his pack to dash forward and do a dancing run around the rock. "Is this cool? Is this cool? Nobody knows where we are. And we've got *all* night to do anything we want."

"Anything we want in the middle of the woods," Cal added. Without a TV, or a refrigerator.

Fox threw back his head and let out a shout that echoed away. "See that? Nobody can hear us. We could be attacked by mutants or ninjas or space aliens, and nobody would hear us."

That, Cal realized, didn't make his stomach feel any steadier. "We need to get wood for a campfire."

"The Boy Scout's right," Gage decided. "You guys find some wood. I'll go put the beer and the Coke in the stream. Cool off the cans."

In his tidy way, Cal organized the campsite first. Food in one area, clothes in another, tools in another still. With his Scout knife and compass in his pocket, he set off to gather twigs and small branches. The brambles nipped and scratched as he picked his way through them. With his arms loaded he didn't notice a few drops of his blood drip onto the ground at the edge of the circle.

Or the way the blood sizzled, smoked, then was sucked into that scarred earth.

Fox set the boom box on the rock so they set up camp with Madonna and U2 and the Boss. Following Cal's advice, they built the fire, but didn't set it to light while they had the sun.

Sweaty and filthy, they sat on the ground and tore into the picnic basket with grubby hands and huge appetites. As the familiar flavors of the food filled his belly and soothed his system, Cal decided it had been worth hauling the basket for a couple of hours.

Replete, they stretched out on their backs, faces to the sky.

"Do you really think all those people died right here?" Gage wondered.

"There are books about it in the library," Cal told him. "About a fire of, like, 'unknown origin' breaking out and these people burned up."

"Kind of a weird place for them to be."

"We're here."

Gage only grunted at that.

"My mom said how the first white people to settle here were Puritans." Fox blew a huge pink bubble with the Bazooka he'd bought at the market. "A sort of radical Puritan or something. How they came over here looking for religious freedom, but really only meant it was free if it was, you know, their way. Mom says lots of people are like that about religion. I don't get it."

Gage thought he knew, or knew part. "A lot of people are mean, and even if they're not, a lot more people think they're better than you." He saw it all the time, in the way people looked at him.

"But do you think they were witches, and the people from the Hollow back then burned them at the stake or something?" Fox rolled over on his belly. "My mom says that being a witch is like a religion, too."

"Your mom's whacked."

Because it was Gage, and because it was said jokingly, Fox grinned. "We're all whacked."

"I say this calls for a beer." Gage pushed up. "We'll share one, let the others get colder." As Gage walked off to the stream, Cal and Fox exchanged looks.

"You ever had beer before?" Cal wanted to know.

"No. You?"

"Are you kidding? I can only have Coke on special occasions. What if we get drunk and pass out or something?"

"My dad drinks beer sometimes. He doesn't. I don't think."

They went quiet when Gage walked back with the dripping can. "Okay. This is to, you know, celebrate that we're going to stop being kids at midnight."

"Maybe we shouldn't drink it until midnight," Cal supposed.

"We'll have the second one after. It's like . . . it's like a ritual."

The sound of the top popping was loud in the quiet

woods, a quick *crack*, almost as shocking to Cal as a gunshot might have been. He smelled the beer immediately, and it struck him as a sour smell. He wondered if it tasted the same.

Gage held the beer up in one hand, high, as if he gripped the hilt of a sword. Then he lowered it, took a long, deep gulp from the can.

He didn't quite mask the reaction, a closing in of his face as if he'd swallowed something strange and unpleasant. His cheeks flushed as he let out a short, gasping breath.

"It's still pretty warm but it . . ." He coughed once. "It hits the spot. Now you."

He passed the can to Fox. With a shrug Fox took the can, mirrored Gage's move. Everyone knew if there was anything close to a dare, Fox would jump at it. "Ugh. It tastes like piss."

"You been drinking piss lately?"

Fox snorted at Gage's question and passed the can to Cal. "Your turn."

Cal studied the can. It wasn't like a sip of beer would kill him or anything. So he sucked in a breath and swallowed some down.

It made his stomach curl and his eyes water. He shoved the can back at Gage. "It does taste like piss."

"I guess people don't drink it for how it tastes. It's how it makes you feel." Gage took another sip, because he wanted to know how it made him feel.

They sat cross-legged in the circular clearing, knees bumping, passing the can from hand to hand.

Cal's stomach pitched, but it didn't feel sick, not exactly. His head pitched, too, but it felt sort of goofy and fun. And the beer made his bladder full. When he stood, the whole world pitched and made him laugh helplessly as he staggered toward a tree.

He unzipped, aimed toward the tree but the tree kept moving.

Fox was struggling to light one of the cigarettes when

Cal stumbled back. They passed that around the circle as well until Cal's almost ten-year-old stomach revolted. He crawled off to sick it all up, crawled back, and just lay flat, closing his eyes and willing the world to go still again.

He felt as if he were once again swimming in the pond, and being slowly pulled under.

When he surfaced again it was nearly dusk.

He eased up, hoping he wouldn't be sick again. He felt a little hollow inside—belly and head—but not like he was going to puke. He saw Fox curled against the stone, sleeping. He crawled over on all fours for the thermos and as he washed the sick and beer out of his throat, he was never so grateful for his mother and her lemonade.

Steadier, he rubbed his fingers on his eyes under his glasses, then spotted Gage sitting, staring at the tented wood of the campfire they'd yet to light.

" 'Morning, Sally."

With a wan smile, Cal scooted over.

"I don't know how to light this thing. I figured it was about time to, but I needed a Boy Scout."

Cal took the book of matches Gage handed him, and set fire to several spots on the pile of dried leaves he'd arranged under the wood. "That should do it. Wind's pretty still, and there's nothing to catch in the clearing. We can keep feeding it when we need to, and just make sure we bury it before we go tomorrow."

"Smokey the Bear. You all right?"

"Yeah. I guess I threw most everything up."

"I shouldn't have brought the beer."

Cal lifted a shoulder, glanced toward Fox. "We're okay, and now we won't have to wonder what it tastes like. We know it tastes like piss."

Gage laughed a little. "It didn't make me feel mean." He picked up a stick, poked at the little flames. "I wanted to know if it would, and I figured I could try it with you and Fox. You're my best friends, so I could try it with you and see if it made me feel mean."

"How did it make you feel?"

"It made my head hurt. It still does a little. I didn't get sick like you, but I sorta wanted to. I went and got one of the Cokes and drank that. It felt better then. Why does he drink so goddamn much if it makes him feel like that?"

"I don't know."

Gage dropped his head on his knees. "He was crying when he went after me last night. Blubbering and crying the whole time he used the belt on me. Why would anybody want to feel like that?"

Careful to avoid the welts on Gage's back, Cal draped an arm over his shoulders. He wished he knew what to say.

"Soon as I'm old enough I'm getting out. Join the army maybe, or get a job on a freighter, maybe an oil rig."

Gage's eyes gleamed when he lifted his head, and Cal looked away because he knew the shine was tears. "You can come stay with us when you need to."

"It'd just be worse when I went back. But I'm going to be ten in a few hours. And in a few years I'll be as big as he is. Bigger maybe. I won't let him come after me then. I won't let him hit me. Screw it." Gage rubbed his face. "Let's wake Fox up. Nobody sleeps tonight."

Fox moaned and grumbled, and he got himself up to pee and fetch a cool Coke from the stream. They shared it with another round of Little Debbies. And, at last, the copy of *Penthouse*.

Cal had seen naked breasts before. You could see them in the *National Geographic* in the library, if you knew where to look.

But these were different.

"Hey guys, did you ever think about doing it?" Cal asked.

"Who doesn't?" they both replied.

"Whoever does it first has to tell the other two everything. All about how it feels," Cal continued. "And how you did it, and what she does. Everything. I call for an oath."

A call for an oath was sacred. Gage spat on the back of his hand, held it out. Fox slapped his palm on, spat on the back of his hand, and Cal completed the contact.

"And so we swear," they said together.

They sat around the fire as the stars came out, and deep in the woods an owl hooted its night call.

The long, sweaty hike, ghostly apparitions, and beer puke were forgotten.

"We should do this every year on our birthday," Cal decided. "Even when we're old. Like thirty or something. The three of us should come here."

"Drink beer and look at pictures of naked girls," Fox added. "I call for—"

"Don't." Gage spoke sharply. "I can't swear. I don't know where I'm going to go, but it'll be somewhere else. I don't know if I'll ever come back."

"Then we'll go where you are, when we can. We're always going to be best friends." Nothing would change that, Cal thought and took his own, personal oath on it. Nothing ever could. He looked at his watch. "It's going to be midnight soon. I have an idea."

He took out his Boy Scout knife and, opening the blade, held it in the fire.

"What's up?" Fox demanded.

"I'm sterilizing it. Like, ah, purifying it." It got so hot he had to pull back, blow on his fingers. "It's like Gage said about ritual and stuff. Ten years is a decade. We've known each other almost the whole time. We were born on the same day. It makes us . . . different," he said, searching for words he wasn't quite sure of. "Like special, I guess. We're best friends. We're like brothers."

Gage looked at the knife, then into Cal's face. "Blood brothers."

"Yeah."

"Cool." Already committed, Fox held out his hand.

"At midnight," Cal said. "We should do it at midnight, and we should have some words to say."

"We'll swear an oath," Gage said. "That we mix our blood, um, three into one? Something like that. In loyalty."

"That's good. Write it down, Cal."

Cal dug pencil and paper out of his pack. "We'll write

words down, and say them together. Then we'll do the cut and put our wrists together. I've got Band-Aids for after if we need them."

Cal wrote the words with his Number Two pencil on the blue lined paper, crossing out when they changed their minds.

Fox added more wood to the fire so that the flames crackled as they stood by the Pagan Stone.

At moments to midnight, they stood, three young boys with faces lit by fire and starlight. At Gage's nod, they spoke together in voices solemn and achingly young.

"We were born ten years ago, on the same night, at the same time, in the same year. We are brothers. At the Pagan Stone we swear an oath of loyalty and truth and brotherhood. We mix our blood."

Cal sucked in a breath and geared up the courage to run the knife across his wrist first. "Ouch."

"We mix our blood." Fox gritted his teeth as Cal cut his wrist.

"We mix our blood." And Gage stood unflinching as the knife drew over his flesh.

"Three into one, and one for the three."

Cal held his arm out. Fox, then Gage pressed their scored wrists down to his. "Brothers in spirit, in mind. Brothers in blood for all time."

As they stood, clouds shivered over the fat moon, misted over the bright stars. Their mixed blood dripped and fell onto the burnt ground.

The wind exploded with a voice like a raging scream. The little campfire spewed up flame in a spearing tower. The three of them were lifted off their feet as if a hand gripped them, tossed them. Light burst as if the stars had shattered.

As he opened his mouth to shout, Cal felt something shove inside him, hot and strong, to smother his lungs, to squeeze his heart in a stunning agony of pain.

The light shut off. In the thick dark blew an icy cold that numbed his skin. The sound the wind made now was like an animal, like a monster that only lived inside books. Beneath him the ground shook, heaving him back as he tried to crawl away.

And something came out of that icy dark, out of that quaking ground. Something huge and horrible.

Eyes bloodred and full of . . . hunger. It looked at him. And when it smiled its teeth glittered like silver swords.

He thought he died, and that it took him in, in one gulp.

But when he came to himself again, he could hear his own heart. He could hear the shouts and calls of his friends.

Blood brothers.

"Jesus, Jesus, what was that? Did you see?" Fox called out in a voice thin as a reed. "Gage, God, your nose is bleeding."

"So's yours. Something . . . Cal. God, Cal."

Cal lay where he was, flat on his back. He felt the wet warmth of blood on his face. He was too numb to be frightened by it. "I can't see." He croaked out a weak whisper. "I can't see."

"Your glasses are broken." Face filthy with soot and blood, Fox crawled to him. "One of the lenses is cracked. Dude, your mom's going to kill you."

"Broken." Shaking, Cal reached up to pull off his glasses.

"Something. Something was here." Gage gripped Cal's shoulder. "I felt something happen, after everything went crazy, I felt something happen inside me. Then . . . did you see it? Did you see that thing?"

"I saw its eyes," Fox said, and his teeth chattered. "We need to get out of here. We need to get out."

"Where?" Gage demanded. Though his breath still wheezed, he grabbed Cal's knife from the ground, gripped it. "We don't know where it went. Was it some kind of bear? Was it—"

"It wasn't a bear." Cal spoke calmly now. "It was what's been here, in this place, a long time. I can see . . . I can see it. It looked like a man once, when it wanted. But it wasn't."

"Man, you hit your head."

Cal turned his eyes on Fox, and the irises were nearly black. "I can see it, and the other." He opened the hand of the wrist he'd cut. In the palm was a chunk of a green stone spotted with red. "His."

Fox opened his hand, and Gage his. In each was an identical third of the stone. "What is it?" Gage whispered. "Where the hell did it come from?"

"I don't know, but it's ours now. Uh, one into three, three into one. I think we let something out. And something came with it. Something bad. I can see."

He closed his eyes a moment, then opened them to look at his friends. "I can see, but not with my glasses. I can see without them. It's not blurry. I can see without my glasses."

"Wait." Trembling, Gage pulled up his shirt, turned his back.

"Man, they're gone." Fox reached out to touch his fingers to Gage's unmarred back. "The welts. They're gone. And . . ." He held out his wrist where the shallow cut was already healing. "Holy cow, are we like superheroes now?"

"It's a demon," Cal said. "And we let it out."

"Shit." Gage stared off into the dark woods. "Happy goddamn birthday to us."

Three

Hawkins Hollow
February 2008

IT WAS COLDER IN HAWKINS HOLLOW, MARYLAND, than it was in Juno, Alaska. Cal liked to know little bits like that, even though at the moment he was in the Hollow where the damp, cold wind blew like a mother and froze his eyeballs.

His eyeballs were about the only thing exposed as he zipped across Main Street from Coffee Talk, with a to-go cup of mochaccino in one gloved hand, to the Bowl-a-Rama.

Three days a week, he tried for a counter breakfast at Ma's Pantry a couple doors down, and at least once a week he hit Gino's for dinner.

His father believed in supporting the community, the other merchants. Now that his dad was semi-retired and Cal oversaw most of the businesses, he tried to follow that Hawkins tradition.

He shopped the local market even though the chain supermarket a couple miles outside town was cheaper. If he wanted to send a woman flowers, he resisted doing so with a couple of clicks on his computer and hauled himself down to the Flower Pot.

He had relationships with the local plumber, electrician, painter, the area craftsmen. Whenever possible, he hired for the town from the town.

Except for his years away at college, he'd always lived in the Hollow. It was his place.

Every seven years since his tenth birthday, he lived through the nightmare that visited his place. And every seven years, he helped clean up the aftermath.

He unlocked the front door of the Bowl-a-Rama, relocked it behind him. People tended to walk right in, whatever the posted hours, if the door wasn't locked.

He'd once been a little more casual about that, until one fine night while he'd been enjoying some after-hours Strip Bowling with Allysa Kramer, three teenage boys had wandered in, hoping the video arcade was still open.

Lesson learned.

He walked by the front desk, the six lanes and ball returns, the shoe rental counter and the grill, turned and jogged up the stairs to the squat second floor that held his (or his father's if his father was in the mood) office, a closet-sized john, and a mammoth storage area.

He set the coffee on the desk, stripped off gloves, scarf, watch cap, coat, insulated vest.

He booted up his computer, put on the satellite radio, then sat down to fuel up on caffeine and get to work.

The bowling center Cal's grandfather had opened in the postwar forties had been a tiny, three-lane gathering spot with a couple of pinball machines and counter Cokes. It expanded in the sixties, and again, when Cal's father took the reins, in the early eighties.

Now, with its six lanes, its video arcade, and its private party room, it was *the* place to gather in the Hollow.

Credit to Grandpa, Cal thought as he looked over the party reservations for the next month. But the biggest chunk of credit went to Cal's father, who'd morphed the lanes into a family center, and had used its success to dip into other areas of business.

The town bears our name, Jim Hawkins liked to say. *Respect the name, respect the town.*

Cal did both. He'd have left long ago otherwise.

An hour into the work, Cal glanced up at the rap on his doorjamb.

"Sorry, Cal. Just wanted you to know I was here. Thought I'd go ahead and get that painting done in the rest rooms since you're not open this morning."

"Okay, Bill. Got everything you need?"

"Sure do." Bill Turner, five years, two months and six days sober, cleared his throat. "Wonder if maybe you'd heard anything from Gage."

"Not in a couple months now."

Tender area, Cal thought when Bill just nodded. Boggy ground.

"I'll just get started then."

Cal watched as Bill moved away from the doorway. Nothing he could do about it, he told himself. Nothing he was sure he should do.

Did five years clean and sober make up for all those whacks with a belt, for all those shoves and slaps, all those curses? It wasn't for him to judge.

He glanced down at the thin scar that ran diagonally across his wrist. Odd how quickly that small wound had healed, and yet the mark of it remained—the only scar he carried. Odd how so small a thing had catapulted the town and people he knew into seven days of hell every seven years.

Would Gage come back this summer, as he had every seventh year? Cal couldn't see ahead, that wasn't his gift or his burden. But he knew when he, Gage, and Fox turned thirty-one, they would all be together in the Hollow.

They'd sworn an oath.

He finished up the morning's work, and because he couldn't get his mind off it, composed a quick e-mail to Gage.

Hey. Where the hell are you? Vegas? Mozambique? Duluth? Heading out to see Fox. There's a writer coming into the Hollow to do research on the history, the legend, and what they're calling the anomalies. Probably got it handled, but thought you should know.

It's twenty-two degrees with a windchill factor of fifteen. Wish you were here and I wasn't.

Cal

He'd answer eventually, Cal thought as he sent the e-mail, then shut down the computer. Could be in five minutes or in five weeks, but Gage would answer.

He began to layer on the outer gear again over a long and lanky frame passed down by his father. He'd gotten his outsized feet from dear old Dad, too.

The dark blond hair that tended to go as it chose was from his mother. He knew that only due to early photos of her, as she'd been a soft, sunny blonde, perfectly groomed, throughout his memory.

His eyes, a sharp, occasionally stormy gray, had been twenty-twenty since his tenth birthday.

Even as he zipped up his parka to head outside, he thought that the coat was for comfort only. He hadn't had so much as a sniffle in over twenty years. No flu, no virus, no hay fever.

He'd fallen out of an apple tree when he'd been twelve. He'd heard the bone in his arm snap, had felt the breathless pain.

And he'd felt it knit together again—with more pain—before he'd made it across the lawn to the house to tell his mother.

So he'd never told her, he thought as he stepped outside into the ugly slap of cold. Why upset her?

He covered the three blocks to Fox's office quickly, shooting out waves or calling back greetings to neighbors and friends. But he didn't stop for conversation. He might not get pneumonia or postnasal drip, but he was *freaking* tired of winter.

Gray, ice-crusted snow lay in a dirty ribbon along the curbs, and above, the sky mirrored the brooding color. Some of the houses or businesses had hearts and Valentine wreaths on doors and windows, but they didn't add a lot of cheer with the bare trees and winter-stripped gardens.

The Hollow didn't show to advantage, to Cal's way of thinking, in February.

He walked up the short steps to the little covered porch of the old stone townhouse. The plaque beside the door read: FOX B. O'DELL, ATTORNEY AT LAW.

It was something that always gave Cal a quick jolt and a quick flash of amusement. Even after nearly six years, he couldn't quite get used to it.

The long-haired hippie freak was a goddamn lawyer.

He stepped into the tidy reception area, and there was Alice Hawbaker at the desk. Trim, tidy in her navy suit with its bowed white blouse, her snow-cap of hair and no-nonsense bifocals, Mrs. Hawbaker ran the office like a Border collie ran a herd.

She looked sweet and pretty, and she'd bite your ankle if you didn't fall in line.

"Hey, Mrs. Hawbaker. Boy, it is *cold* out there. Looks like we might get some more snow." He unwrapped his scarf. "Hope you and Mr. Hawbaker are keeping warm."

"Warm enough."

He heard something in her voice that had him looking more closely as he pulled off his gloves. When he realized she'd been crying he instinctively stepped to the desk. "Is everything okay? Is—"

"Everything's fine. Just fine. Fox is between appointments. He's in there sulking, so you go right on back."

"Yes, ma'am. Mrs. Hawbaker, if there's anything—"

"Just go right on back," she repeated, then made herself busy with her keyboard.

Beyond the reception area a hallway held a powder room on one side and a library on the other. Straight back,

Fox's office was closed off by a pair of pocket doors. Cal didn't bother to knock.

Fox looked up when the doors slid open. He did appear to be sulking as his gilded eyes were broody and his mouth was in full scowl.

He sat behind his desk, his feet, clad in hiking boots, propped on it. He wore jeans and a flannel shirt open over a white insulated tee. His hair, densely brown, waved around his sharp-featured face.

"What's going on?"

"I'll tell you what's going on. My administrative assistant just gave me her notice."

"What did you do?"

"Me?" Fox shoved back from the desk and opened the minifridge for a can of Coke. He'd never developed a taste for coffee. "Try *we*, brother. We camped out at the Pagan Stone one fateful night, and screwed the monkey."

Cal dropped into a chair. "She's quitting because—"

"Not just quitting. They're leaving the Hollow, she and Mr. Hawbaker. And yeah, because." He took a long, greedy drink the way some men might take a pull on a bottle of whiskey. "That's not the reason she gave me, but that's the reason. She said they decided to move to Minneapolis to be close to their daughter and grandchildren, and that's bogus. Why does a woman heading toward seventy, married to a guy older than dirt, pick up and move north? They've got another kid lives outside of D.C., and they've got strong ties here. I could tell it was bull."

"Because of what she said, or because you took a cruise through her head?"

"First the one, then the other. Don't start on me." Fox gestured with the Coke, then slammed it down on his desk. "I don't poke around for the fun of it. Son of a bitch."

"Maybe they'll change their minds."

"They don't want to go, but they're afraid to stay. They're afraid it'll happen again—which I could tell her it will—and they just don't want to go through it again. I offered her a raise—like I could afford it—offered her the whole month of July off, letting her know that I knew what was at the bottom of it. But they're going. She'll give me until April first. April frickin' Fools," he ranted. "To find somebody else, for her to show them the ropes. I don't know where the damn ropes are, Cal. I don't know half the stuff she does. She just does it. Anyway."

"You've got until April, maybe we'll think of something."

"We haven't thought of the solution to this in twenty years plus."

"I meant your office problem. But yeah, I've been thinking a lot about the other." Rising, he walked to Fox's window, looked out on the quiet side street. "We've got to end it. This time we've got to end it. Maybe talking to this writer will help. Laying it out to someone objective, someone not involved."

"Asking for trouble."

"Maybe it is, but trouble's coming anyway. Five months to go. We're supposed to meet her at the house." Cal glanced at his watch. "Forty minutes."

"We?" Fox looked blank for a moment. "That's today? See, see, I didn't tell Mrs. H, so it didn't get written down somewhere. I've got a deposition in an hour."

"Why don't you use your damn BlackBerry?"

"Because it doesn't follow my simple Earth logic. Reschedule the writer. I'm clear after four."

"It's okay, I can handle it. If she wants more, I'll see about setting up a dinner, so keep tonight open."

"Be careful what you say."

"Yeah, yeah, I'm going to. But I've been thinking. We've been careful about that for a long time. Maybe it's time to be a little reckless."

"You sound like Gage."

"Fox . . . I've already started having the dreams again."

Fox blew out a breath. "I was hoping that was just me."

"When we were seventeen they started about a week before our birthday, then when we were twenty-four, over a month. Now, five months out. Every time it gets stronger.

I'm afraid if we don't find the way, this time could be the last for us, and the town."

"Have you talked to Gage?"

"I just e-mailed him. I didn't tell him about the dreams. You do it. Find out if he's having them, too, wherever the hell he is. Get him home, Fox. I think we need him back. I don't think we can wait until summer this time. I gotta go."

"Watch your step with the writer," Fox called out as Cal started for the door. "Get more than you give."

"I can handle it," Cal repeated.

QUINN BLACK EASED HER MINI COOPER OFF THE exit ramp and hit the usual barrage at the interchange. Pancake House, Wendy's, McDonald's, KFC.

With great affection, she thought of a Quarter Pounder, with a side of really salty fries, and—natch—a Diet Coke to ease the guilt. But since that would be breaking her vow to eat fast food no more than once a month, she wasn't going to indulge.

"There now, don't you feel righteous?" she asked herself with only one wistful glance in the rearview at the lovely Golden Arches.

Her love of the quick and the greasy had sent her on an odyssey of fad diets, unsatisfying supplements, and miracle workout tapes through her late teens and early twenties. Until she'd finally slapped herself silly, tossed out all her diet books, her diet articles, her I LOST TWENTY POUNDS IN TWO WEEKS—AND YOU CAN, TOO! ads, and put herself on the path to sensible eating and exercising.

Lifestyle change, she reminded herself. She'd made a lifestyle change.

But boy, she missed those Quarter Pounders more than she missed her ex-fiance.

Then again, who wouldn't?

She glanced at the GPS hooked to her dashboard, then

over at the directions she'd printed out from Caleb Hawkins's e-mail. So far, they were in tandem.

She reached down for the apple serving as her mid-morning snack. Apples were filling, Quinn thought as she bit in. They were good for you, and they were tasty.

And they were no Quarter Pounder.

In order to keep her mind off the devil, she considered what she hoped to accomplish on this first face-to-face interview with one of the main players in the odd little town of Hawkins Hollow.

No, not fair to call it odd, she reminded herself. Objectivity first. Maybe her research leaned her toward the odd label, but there would be no making up her mind until she'd seen for herself, done her interviews, taken her notes, scoped out the local library. And, maybe most important, seen the Pagan Stone in person.

She loved poking at all the corners and cobwebs of small towns, digging down under the floorboards for secrets and surprises, listening to the gossip, the local lore and legend.

She'd made a tiny name for herself doing a series of articles on quirky, off the mainstream towns for a small press magazine called *Detours*. And as her professional appetite was as well-developed as her bodily one, she'd taken a risky leap and written a book, following the same theme, but focussing on a single town in Maine reputed to be haunted by the ghosts of twin sisters who'd been murdered in a boardinghouse in 1843.

The critics had called the result "engaging" and "good, spooky fun," except for the ones who'd deemed it "preposterous" and "convoluted."

She'd followed it up with a book highlighting a small town in Louisiana where the descendent of a voodoo priestess served as mayor and faith healer. And, Quinn had discovered, had been running a very successful prostitution ring.

But Hawkins Hollow—she could just feel it—was going to be bigger, better, meatier.

She couldn't wait to sink her teeth in.

The fast-food joints, the businesses, the ass-to-elbow houses gave way to bigger lawns, bigger homes, and to fields sleeping under the dreary sky.

The road wound, dipped and lifted, then veered straight again. She saw a sign for the Antietam Battlefield, something else she meant to investigate and research firsthand. She'd found little snippets about incidents during the Civil War in and around Hawkins Hollow.

She wanted to know more.

When her GPS and Caleb's directions told her to turn, she turned, following the next road past a grove of naked trees, a scatter of houses, and the farms that always made her smile with their barns and silos and fenced paddocks.

She'd have to find a small town to explore in the Midwest next time. A haunted farm, or the weeping spirit of a milkmaid.

She nearly ignored the directions to turn when she saw the sign for Hawkins Hollow (est. 1648). As with the Quarter Pounder, her heart longed to indulge, to drive into town rather than turn off toward Caleb Hawkins's place. But she hated to be late, and if she got caught up exploring the streets, the corners, the *look* of the town, she certainly would be late for her first appointment.

"Soon," she promised, and turned to take the road winding by the woods she knew held the Pagan Stone at their heart.

It gave her a quick shiver, and that was strange. Strange to realize that shiver had been fear and not the anticipation she always felt with a new project.

As she followed the twists of the road, she glanced with some unease toward the dark and denuded trees. And hit the brakes hard when she shifted her eyes back to the road and saw something rush out in front of her.

She thought she saw a child—oh God, oh God—then thought it was a dog. And then . . . it was nothing. Nothing at all on the road, nothing rushing to the field beyond. Nothing there but herself and her wildly beating heart in the little red car.

"Trick of the eye," she told herself, and didn't believe it. "Just one of those things."

But she restarted the car that had stalled when she'd slammed the brakes, then eased to the strip of dirt that served as the shoulder of the road. She pulled out her notebook, noted the time, and wrote down exactly what she thought she'd seen.

Young boy, abt ten. Lng blck hair, red eyes. He LOOKED right at me. Did I blink? Shut my eyes? Opened, & saw lrg blck dog, not boy. Then poof. Nothing there.

Cars passed her without incident as she sat a few moments more, waited for the trembling to stop.

Intrepid writer balks at first possible phenomenom, she thought, turns around and drives her adorable red car to the nearest Mickey D's for a fat-filled antidote to nerves.

She could do that, she considered. Nobody could charge her with a felony and throw her into prison. And if she did that, she wouldn't have her next book, or any self-respect.

"Man up, Quinn," she ordered. "You've seen spooks before."

Steadier, she swung back out on the road, and made the next turn. The road was narrow and twisty with trees looming on both sides. She imagined it would be lovely in the spring and summer, with the green dappling, or after a snowfall with all those trees ermine drenched. But under a dull gray sky the woods seemed to crowd the road, bare branches just waiting to reach out and strike, as if they and only they were allowed to live there.

As if to enforce the sensation, no other car passed, and when she turned off her radio as the music seemed too loud, the only sound was the keening curse of the wind.

Should've called it Spooky Hollow, she decided, and nearly missed the turn into the gravel lane.

Why, she wondered, would anyone *choose* to live here? Amid all those dense, thrusting trees where bleak pools of snow huddled to hide from the sun? Where the only sound was the warning growl of Nature. Everything was brown and gray and moody.

She bumped over a little bridge spanning a curve of a creek, followed the slight rise of the stingy lane.

There was the house, exactly as advertised.

It sat on what she would have termed a knoll rather than a hill with the front slope tamed into step-down terraces decked with shrubs she imagined put on a hell of a show in the spring and summer.

There wasn't a lawn, so to speak, and she thought Hawkins had been smart to go with the thick mulch and shrubs and trees skirting the front instead of the traditional grass that would probably be a pain in the ass to mow and keep clear of weeds.

She approved of the deck that wrapped around the front and sides, and she'd bet the rear as well. She liked the earthy tones of the stone and the generous windows.

It sat like it belonged there, content and well-settled in the woods.

She pulled up beside an aging Chevy pickup, got out of her car to stand and take a long view.

And understood why someone would choose this spot. There was, unquestionably, an aura of spookiness, especially for one who was inclined to see and feel such things. But there was considerable charm as well, and a sense of solitude that was far from lonely. She could imagine very well sitting on that front deck some summer evening, drinking a cold one, and wallowing in the silence.

Before she could move toward the house, the front door opened.

The sense of *déjà vu* was vivid, almost dizzying. He stood there at the door of the cabin, the blood like red flowers on his shirt.

We can stay no longer.

The words sounded in her head, clear, and in a voice she somehow knew.

"Miss Black?"

She snapped back. There was no cabin, and the man standing on the lovely deck of his charming house had no blood blooming on him. There was no force of great love and great grief shining in his eyes.

And still, she had to lean back against her car for a minute and catch her breath. "Yeah, hi. I was just . . . admiring the house. Great spot."

"Thanks. Any trouble finding it?"

"No, no. Your directions were perfect." And, of course, it was ridiculous to be having this conversation outside in the freezing wind. From the quizzical look on his face, he obviously felt the same.

She pushed off the car, worked up what she hoped was a sane and pleasant expression as she walked to the trio of wooden steps.

And wasn't he a serious cutie? she realized as she finally focused on the reality. All that windblown hair and those strong gray eyes. Add the crooked smile, the long, lean body in jeans and flannel, and a woman might be tempted to hang a SOLD! sign around his neck.

She stepped up, held out a hand. "Quinn Black, thanks for meeting with me, Mr. Hawkins."

"Cal." He took her hand, shook it, then held it as he gestured to the door. "Let's get you out of the wind."

They stepped directly into a living room that managed to be cozy and male at the same time. The generous sofa faced the big front windows, and the chairs looked as though they'd allow an ass to sink right in. Tables and lamps probably weren't antiques, but looked to be something a grandmother might have passed down when she got the urge to redecorate her own place.

There was even a little stone fireplace with the requisite large mutt sprawled sleeping in front of it.

"Let me take your coat."

"Is your dog in a coma?" Quinn asked when the dog didn't move a muscle.

"No. Lump leads an active and demanding internal life that requires long periods of rest."

"I see."

"Want some coffee?"

"That'd be great. So would the bathroom. Long drive."

"First right."

"Thanks."

She closed herself into a small, spotlessly clean powder room as much to pull herself back together from a couple of psychic shocks as to pee.

"Okay, Quinn," she whispered. "Here we go."

Four

HE'D READ HER WORK; HE'D STUDIED HER AUthor photos and used Google to get some background, to read her interviews. Cal wasn't one to agree to talk to any sort of writer, journalist, reporter, Internet blogger about the Hollow, himself, or much of anything else without doing a thorough check.

He'd found her books and articles entertaining. He'd enjoyed her obvious affection for small towns, had been intrigued by her interest and treatment of lore, legend, and things that went bump in the night.

He liked the fact that she still wrote the occasional article for the magazine that had given her a break when she'd still been in college. It spoke of loyalty.

He hadn't been disappointed that her author photo had shown her to be a looker, with a sexy tumble of honey blond hair, bright blue eyes, and the hint of a fairly adorable overbite.

The photo hadn't come close.

She probably wasn't beautiful, he thought as he poured coffee. He'd have to get another look when, hopefully, his brain wouldn't go to fuzz, then decide about that.

What he did know, unquestionably, was she just plain radiated energy and—to his fuzzed brain—sex.

But maybe that was because she was built, another thing the photo hadn't gotten across. The lady had some truly excellent curves.

And it wasn't as if he hadn't seen curves on a woman before or, in fact, seen his share of naked female curves alive and in person. So why was he standing in his own kitchen frazzled because an attractive, fully dressed woman was in his house? For professional purposes.

"Jesus, grow up, Hawkins."

"Sorry?"

He actually jumped. She was in the kitchen, a few steps behind him, smiling that million-watt smile.

"Were you talking to yourself? I do that, too. Why do people think we're crazy?"

"Because they want to suck us into talking to them."

"You're probably right." Quinn shoved back that long spill of blond.

Cal saw he was right. She wasn't beautiful. The top-heavy mouth, the slightly crooked nose, the oversized eyes weren't elements of traditional beauty. He couldn't label her pretty, either. It was too simple and sweet a word. Cute didn't do it.

All he could think of was *hot*, but that might have been his brain blurring again.

"I didn't ask how you take your coffee."

"Oh. I don't suppose you have two percent milk."

"I often wonder why anybody does."

With an easy laugh that shot straight to his bloodstream, she wandered over to study the view outside the glass doors that led—as she'd suspected—to the rear portion of the circling deck. "Which also means you probably don't have any fake sugar. Those little pink, blue, or yellow packets?"

"Fresh out. I could offer you actual milk and actual sugar."

"You could." And hadn't she eaten an apple like a good girl? "And I could accept. Let me ask you something else, just to satisfy my curiosity. Is your house always so clean and tidy, or did you do all this just for me?"

He got out the milk. "*Tidy*'s a girlie word. I prefer the term *organized*. I like organization. Besides." He offered her a spoon for the sugar bowl. "My mother could—and does—drop by unexpectedly. If my house wasn't clean, she'd ground me."

"If I don't call my mother once a week, she assumes I've been hacked to death by an ax murderer." Quinn held herself to one scant spoon of sugar. "It's nice, isn't it? Those long and elastic family ties."

"I like them. Why don't we go sit in the living room by the fire?"

"Perfect. So, how long have you lived here? In this particular house," she added as they carried their mugs out of the kitchen.

"A couple of years."

"Not much for neighbors?"

"Neighbors are fine, and I spend a lot of time in town. I like the quiet now and then."

"People do. I do myself, now and again." She took one of the living room chairs, settled back. "I guess I'm surprised other people haven't had the same idea as you, and plugged in a few more houses around here."

"There was talk of it a couple of times. Never panned out."

He's being cagey, Quinn decided. "Because?"

"Didn't turn out to be financially attractive, I guess."

"Yet here you are."

"My grandfather owned the property, some acres of Hawkins Woods. He left it to me."

"So you had this house built."

"More or less. I'd liked the spot." Private when he needed to be private. Close to the woods where everything had changed. "I know some people in the trade, and we put the house up. How's the coffee?"

"It's terrific. You cook, too?"

"Coffee's my specialty. I read your books."

"How were they?"

"I liked them. You probably know you wouldn't be here if I hadn't."

"Which would've made it a lot tougher to write the book I want to write. You're a Hawkins, a descendent of the founder of the settlement that became the village that became the town. And one of the main players in the more recent unexplained incidents related to the town. I've done a lot of research on the history, the lore, the legends, and the various explanations," she said, and reached in the bag that served as her purse and her briefcase. Taking out a minirecorder, she switched it on, set it on the table between them.

Her smile was full of energy and interest when she set her notebook on her lap, flipped pages to a clear one. "So, tell me, Cal, about what happened the week of July seventh, nineteen eighty-seven, ninety-four, and two thousand one."

The tape recorder made him . . . itchy. "Dive right in, don't you?"

"I love knowing things. July seventh is your birthday. It's also the birthday of Fox O'Dell and Gage Turner—born the same year as you, who grew up in Hawkins Hollow with you. I read articles that reported you, O'Dell, and Turner were responsible for alerting the fire department on July eleventh, 1987, when the elementary school was set on fire, and also responsible for saving the life of one Marian Lister who was inside the school at the time."

She continued to look straight into his eyes as she spoke. He found it interesting she didn't need to refer to notes, and that she didn't appear to need the little breaks from direct eye contact.

"Initial reports indicated the three of you were originally suspected of starting the fire, but it was proven Miss

Lister herself was responsible. She suffered second degree burns on nearly thirty percent of her body as well as a concussion. You and your friends, three ten-year-old boys, dragged her out and called the fire department. Miss Lister was, at that time, a twenty-five-year-old fourth-grade teacher with no history of criminal behavior or mental illness. Is that all correct information?"

She got her facts in order, Cal noted. Such as the facts were known. They fell far short of the abject terror of entering that burning school, of finding the pretty Miss Lister cackling madly as she ran through the flames. Of how it felt to chase her through those hallways as her clothes burned.

"She had a breakdown."

"Obviously." Smile in place, Quinn lifted her eyebrows. "There were also over a dozen nine-one-one calls on domestic abuse during that single week, more than previously had been reported in Hawkins Hollow in the six preceding months. There were two suicides and four attempted suicides, numerous accounts of assault, three reported rapes, and a hit-and-run. Several homes and businesses were vandalized. None—virtually none—of the people involved in any of the reported crimes or incidents has a clear memory of the events. Some speculate the town suffered from mass hysteria or hallucinations or an unknown infection taken through food or water. What do you think?"

"I think I was ten years old and pretty much scared shitless."

She offered that brief, sunny smile. "I bet." Then it was gone. "You were seventeen in nineteen ninety-four when during the week of July seventh another—let's say outbreak—occurred. Three people were murdered, one of them apparently hanged in the town park, but no one came forward as a witness or to admit participation. There were more rapes, more beatings, more suicides, two houses burned to the ground. There were reports that you, O'Dell, and Turner were able to get some of the wounded and traumatized onto a school bus and transport them to the hospital. Is that accurate?"

"As far as it goes."

"I'm looking to go further. In two thousand one—"

"I know the pattern," Cal interrupted.

"Every seven years," Quinn said with a nod. "For seven nights. Days—according again to what I can ascertain—little happens. But from sundown to sunset, all hell breaks loose. It's hard to believe that it's a coincidence this anomaly happens every seven years, with its start on your birthday. Seven's considered a magickal number by those who profess to magicks, black and white. You were born on the seventh day of the seventh month of nineteen seventy-seven."

"If I knew the answers, I'd stop it from happening. If I knew the answers, I wouldn't be talking to you. I'm talking to you because maybe, just maybe, you'll find them, or help find them."

"Then tell me what happened, tell me what you *do* know, even what you think or sense."

Cal set his coffee aside, leaned forward to look deep into her eyes. "Not on a first date."

Smart-ass, she thought with considerable approval. "Fine. Next time I'll buy you dinner first. But now, how about playing guide and taking me to the Pagan Stone."

"It's too late in the day. It's a two-hour hike from here. We wouldn't make it there and back before dark."

"I'm not afraid of the dark."

His eyes went very cool. "You would be. I'll tell you this, there are places in these woods no one goes after dark, not any time of the year."

She felt the prick of ice at the base of her spine. "Have you ever seen a boy, about the age you'd have been in '87. A boy with dark hair. And red eyes." She saw by the way Cal paled she'd flicked a switch. "You have seen him."

"Why do you ask about that?"

"Because I saw him."

Now Cal pushed to his feet, paced to the window, stared

out at the woods. The light was dimmer, duller already than it had been an hour before.

They'd never told anyone about the boy—or the man—whatever form the thing chose to take. Yes, he'd seen him, and not only during that one hellish week every seven years.

He'd seen it in dreams. He'd seen it out of the corner of his eye, or loping through the woods. Or with its face pressed to the dark glass of his bedroom window . . . and its mouth grinning.

But no one, no one but he, Fox, and Gage had ever seen it in the between times.

Why had she?

"When and where did you see him?"

"Today, just before I turned off on to Pagan Road. He ran in front of my car. Came out of nowhere. That's what people always say, but this time it's true. A boy, then it wasn't a boy but a dog. Then it wasn't anything. There was nothing there."

He heard her rise, and when he turned was simply stunned to see that brilliant smile on her face. "And this kind of thing makes you happy?"

"It makes me thrilled. Excited. I'm saying wow! I had myself what we could call a close encounter with an unspecified phenomenon. Scary, I grant you, but again, wow. This sort of thing completely winds me up."

"I can see that."

"I knew there was something here, and I thought it was big. But to have it confirmed, the first day out, that's hitting the mother lode with the first whack of the pick."

"I haven't confirmed anything."

"Your face did." She picked up her recorder, turned it off. He wasn't going to tell her anything today. Cautious man, Caleb Hawkins. "I need to get into town, check into the hotel, get a lay of the land. Why don't I buy you that dinner tonight?"

She moved fast, and he made a habit of taking his time. "Why don't you take some time to settle in? We can talk about dinner and so on in a couple days."

"I love a man who's hard to get." She slipped her recorder, her notepad back in her bag. "I guess I'll need my coat."

After he'd brought it to her, she studied him as she shrugged it on. "You know, when you first came outside, I had the strangest sensation. I thought I recognized you, that I'd known you before. That you'd waited for me before. It was very strong. Did you feel anything like that?"

"No. But maybe I was too busy thinking, she looks better than her picture."

"Really? Nice, because I looked terrific in that picture. Thanks for the coffee." She glanced back to the dog who'd snored lightly the entire time they'd talked. "See you later, Lump. Don't work so hard."

He walked her out. "Quinn," he said as she started down the stairs. "Don't get any ideas about Lois Laning it and trying to find the Pagan Stone on your own. You don't know the woods. I'll take you there myself, sometime this week."

"Tomorrow?"

"I can't, I've got a full plate. Day after if you're in a hurry."

"I almost always am." She walked backward toward her car so she could keep him in view. "What time?"

"Let's say we'll meet here at nine, weather permitting."

"That's a date." She opened her car door. "The house suits you, by the way. Country boy with more style than pretention. I like it."

He watched her drive off—strange and sexy Quinn Black.

And he stood for a long time watching the light go dimmer in the woods where he'd made his home.

CAL HEADED FOX OFF WITH A PHONE CALL AND arranged to meet him at the bowling alley. Since the Pin Boys and the Alley Cats were having a league game on lanes one and two, he and Fox could have dinner and a show at the grill.

Added to it, there was little as noisy as a bowling alley, so their conversation would be covered by the crash of ball, against pins, the hoots and hollers.

"First, let's backtrack into the land of logic for a minute." Fox took a swig of his beer. "She could've made it up to get a reaction."

"How did she know what to make up?"

"During the Seven, there are people who see it—who've said they did before it starts to fade on them. She got wind."

"I don't think so, Fox. Some talked about seeing something—boy, man, woman, dog, wolf—"

"The rat the size of a Doberman," Fox remembered.

"Thanks for bringing that one back. But no one ever claimed they'd seen it before or after the Seven. No one but us, and we've never told anyone." Cal arched his brow in question.

"No. You think I'm going to spread it around that I see red-eyed demons? I'd just rake in the clients that way."

"She's smart. I don't see why she'd claim to have seen it, outside the norm—ha-ha—if she hadn't. Plus she was psyched about it. Juiced up. So, let's accept she did and continue to dwell in the land of logic. One logical assumption is that the bastard's stronger, we know he will be. But strong enough to push out of the Seven into the between time."

Fox brooded over his beer. "I don't like that logic."

"Second option could be she's somehow connected. To one of us, the town, the incident at the Pagan Stone."

"I like that better. Everyone's connected. It's not just Kevin Bacon. If you work at it, you can put a handful of degrees between almost any two people." Thoughtful, Fox picked up his second slice of pizza. "Maybe she's a distant cousin. I've got cousins up the wazoo and so do you. Gage, not so much, but there's some out there."

"Possible. But why would a distant cousin see something none of our immediate family has? They'd tell us, Fox. They all know what's coming better and clearer than anyone else."

"Reincarnation. That's not off the Planet Logic, considering. Besides, reincarnation's big in the family O'Dell. Maybe she was there when it all happened. Another life."

"I don't discount anything. But more to the point, why is she here, now? And will it help us put a goddamn end to this?"

"It's going to take more than an hour's chat in front of the fire to figure that out. I don't guess you heard from Gage."

"Not yet. He'll be in touch. I'm going to take her out to the stone day after tomorrow."

"Leaping forward fast, Cal."

Cal shook his head. "If I don't take her soon enough, she'll try it on her own. If something happened . . . We can't be responsible for that."

"We are responsible—isn't that the point? On some level it's on us." Frowning now, he watched Don Myers, of Myers Plumbing, make a seven-ten split to appropriate hoots and shouts. All three hundred and twenty pounds of Myers did a flab-wriggling victory dance that was not a pretty sight.

"You go on," Fox said quietly, "day after day, doing what you do, living your life, making your life. Eating pizza, scratching your ass, getting laid if you're lucky. But you know, on some level you try to keep buried just to get through, that it's coming back. That some of the people you see on the street every day, maybe they won't make it through the next round. Maybe we won't. What the hell." He rapped his beer against Cal's. "We've got the now, plus five months to figure this out."

"I can try to go back again."

"Not unless Gage is here. We can't risk it unless we're together. It's not worth it, Cal. The other times you only got bits and pieces, and took a hell of a beating for it."

"Older and wiser now. And I'm thinking, if it's showing itself now—our dreams, what happened to Quinn—it's expending energy. I might get more than I have before."

"Not without Gage. That's . . . Hmm," he said as his attention wandered over his friend's shoulder. "Fresh flowers."

Glancing back, Cal saw Quinn standing behind lane one, her coat open and a bemused expression on her face as she watched Myers, graceful as a hippo in toe shoes, make his approach and release his lucky red ball.

"That's Quinn."

"Yeah, I recognized her. I read the books, too. She's hotter than her picture, and that was pretty hot."

"I saw her first."

Fox snorted, shifted his eyes to sneer at Cal. "Dude, it's not about who saw her first, it's who *she* sees. I pull out the full power of my sexual charm, and you'll be the Invisible Man."

"Shit. The full power of your sexual charm wouldn't light up a forty-watt bulb."

Cal pushed off the stool when Quinn walked toward him.

"So this is why I got the brush-off tonight," she said. "Pizza, beer, and bowling."

"The Hawkins Hollow hat trick. I'm on manager duty tonight. Quinn, this is Fox O'Dell."

"The second part of the triad." She shook Fox's hand. "Now I'm doubly glad I decided to check out what seems to be the town's hot spot. Mind if I join you?"

"Wouldn't have it any other way. Buy you a beer?" Fox asked.

"Boy, could you, but . . . make it a light one."

Cal stepped back to swing around the counter. "I'll take care of it. Anything to go with it? Pizza?"

"Oh." She looked at the pizza on the counter with eyes that went suddenly dewy. "Um, I don't suppose you have any with whole-wheat crust and low-fat mozzarella?"

"Health nut?" Fox asked.

"Just the opposite." Quinn bit her bottom lip. "I'm in a lifestyle change. Damn it, that really looks good. How about if we cut one of those slices in half." She sawed the side of her hand over the plate.

"No problem."

Cal got a pizza cutter and slid it down a slice.

"I love fat and sugar like a mother loves her child," Quinn told Fox. "I'm trying to eat more sensibly."

"My parents are vegetarians," Fox said as they each picked up a half slice. "I grew up on tofu and alfalfa."

"God. That's so sad."

"Which is why he ate at my house whenever he could manage it, and spent all his money on Little Debbies and Slim Jims."

"Little Debbies are food for the gods." She smiled at Cal when he set her beer on the counter. "I like your town. I took a walk up and down several blocks of Main Street. And since I was freezing my ass off, went back to the really charming Hotel Hollow, sat on my windowsill and watched the world go by."

"Nice world," Cal said, "that moves a little slow this time of year."

"Umm," was her agreement as she took a minute bite of the point of her narrow triangle of pizza. She closed her eyes on a sigh. "It *is* good. I was hoping, being bowling-alley pizza, it wouldn't be."

"We do okay. Gino's across the street is better, and has more selections."

She opened her eyes to find him smiling at her. "That's a lousy thing to tell a woman in the middle of a lifestyle change."

Cal leaned on the counter, bringing that smile a little closer, and Quinn found herself losing her train of thought. He had the best quick and crooked grin, the kind a woman wanted to take a testing nibble of.

Before he could speak, someone hailed him, and those eyes of quiet gray glanced away from hers toward the end of the counter. "Be right back."

"Well." Jeez, her pulse had actually tripped. "Alone at last," she said to Fox. "So you and Cal and the as-yet-absent Gage Turner have been friends since you were kids."

"Babies, actually. In utero, technically. Cal's and Gage's mother got together with mine when my mother was teaching a Lamaze class. They had a kind of roundup with the class a couple months after everyone delivered the packages, and the deal about the three of us being born on the same day, same time came out."

"Instant mommy bonding."

"I don't know. They always got along, even though you could say they all came from different planets. They were friendly without being friends. My parents and Cal's still get along fine, and Cal's dad kept Gage's employed when nobody else in town would've hired him."

"Why wouldn't anyone have hired him?"

Fox debated for a minute, drank some of his beer. "It's no secret," he decided. "He drank. He's been sober for a while now. About five years, I guess. I always figured Mr. Hawkins gave him work because that's just the way he is, and, in a big part, he did it for Gage. Anyway, I don't remember the three of us not being friends."

"No 'you like him better than me,' major falling-outs or your basic and usual drifting apart?"

"We fought—fight still—now and then." Didn't all brothers? Fox thought. "Had your expected pissy periods, but no. We're connected. Nothing can snap that connection. And the 'you like him better than me'? Mostly a girl thing."

"But Gage doesn't live here anymore."

"Gage doesn't live anywhere, really. He's the original footloose guy."

"And you? The hometown boy."

"I thought about the bright lights, big city routine, even gave it a short try." He glanced over in the direction of the moans coming from one of the Alley Cats who had failed to pick up a spare. "I like the Hollow. I even like my family, most of the time. And I like, as it turns out, practicing small-town law."

Truth, Quinn decided, but not the whole truth of it. "Have you seen the kid with the red eyes?"

Off-balance, Fox set down the beer he'd lifted to drink. "That's a hell of a segue."

"Maybe. But that wasn't an answer."

"I'm going to postpone my answer until further deliberation. Cal's taking point on this."

"And you're not sure you like the idea of him, or anyone, talking to me about what may or may not go on here."

"I'm not sure what purpose it serves. So I'm weighing the information as it comes in."

"Fair enough." She glanced over as Cal came back. "Well, boys, thanks for the beer and the slice. I should get back to my adorable room."

"You bowl?" Cal asked her, and she laughed.

"Absolutely not."

"Oh-oh," Fox said under his breath.

Cal walked around the counter, blocking Quinn before she could slide off the stool. He took a long, considering look at her boots. "Seven and a half, right?"

"Ah . . ." She looked down at her boots herself. "On the money. Good eye."

"Stay." He tapped her on the shoulder. "I'll be right back."

Quinn frowned after him, then looked at Fox. "He is *not* going to get me a pair of bowling shoes."

"Oh yeah, he is. You mocked the tradition, which—if you give him any tiny opening—he'll tell you started five thousand years ago. Then he'll explain its evolution and so on and so on."

"Well, Christ," was all Quinn could think to say.

Cal brought back a pair of maroon and cream bowling shoes, and another, larger pair of dark brown ones, which were obviously his. "Lane Five's open. You want in, Fox?"

"Sadly, I have a brief to finish writing. I'll rain-check it. See you later, Quinn."

Cal tucked the shoes under his arm, then, taking Quinn's hand, pulled her off the stool. "When's the last time you bowled?" he asked as he led her across the alley to an open lane.

"I think I was fourteen. Group date, which didn't go well as the object of my affection, Nathan Hobbs, only had eyes for the incessantly giggly and already well-developed Missy Dover."

"You can't let previous heartbreak spoil your enjoyment."

"But I didn't like the bowling part either."

"That was then." Cal sat her down on the smooth wooden bench, slid on beside her. "You'll have a better time with it tonight. Ever make a strike?"

"Still talking bowling? No."

"You will, and there's nothing much that beats the feeling of that first strike."

"How about sex with Hugh Jackman?"

He stopped tying his bowling shoe to stare over at her. "You had sex with Hugh Jackman?"

"No, but I'm willing to bet any amount of money that having sex with Hugh Jackman would, for me, beat out the feeling of knocking down ten pins with one ball."

"Okay. But I'm willing to bet—let's make it ten bucks—that when you throw a strike, you'll admit it's up there on the Thrill-O-Meter."

"First, it's highly unlikely I'll throw anything resembling a strike. Second, I could lie."

"You will. And you won't. Change your shoes, Blondie."

Five

IT WASN'T AS RIDICULOUS AS SHE'D ASSUMED IT would be. Silly, yes, but she had plenty of room for silly.

The balls were mottled black—the small ones without the three holes. The job was to heave it down the long polished alley toward the red-necked pins he called Duck Pins.

He watched as she walked up to the foul line, swung back, and did the heave.

The ball bounced a couple of times before it toppled into the gutter.

"Okay." She turned, tossed back her hair. "Your turn."

"You get two more balls per frame."

"Woo-hoo."

He shot her the quick grin. "Let's work on your delivery and follow-through, then we'll tackle approach." He walked toward her with another ball as he spoke. He handed her the ball. "Hold it with both hands," he instructed as he turned her around to face the pins. "Now you want to take a step forward with your left foot, bend your knees like you were doing a squat, but bend over from the waist."

He was snuggled up right behind her now, his front sort of bowing over her back. She tipped her face around to meet his eyes.

"You use this routine to hit on women, right?"

"Absolutely. Eighty-five percent success ratio. You're going to want to aim for the front pin. You can worry about the pockets and the sweet spot later. Now you're just going to bring your right arm back, then sweep it forward with your fingers aimed at the front pin. Let the ball go, following your fingers."

"Hmm." But she tried it. This time the ball didn't bounce straight into the gutter, but actually stayed on the lane long enough to bump down the two pins on the far right.

Since the woman in the next lane, who *had* to be sixty if she was a day, slid gracefully to the foul line, released, and knocked down seven pins, Quinn didn't feel like celebrating.

"Better."

"Two balls, two pins. I don't think that earns my bootie dance."

"Since I'm looking forward to your bootie dance, I'll help you do better yet. More from your shoulder down this time. Nice perfume," he added before he walked back to get her another ball.

"Thanks." Stride, bend, swing, release, she thought. And actually managed to knock down the end pin on the other side of the alley.

"Overcompensated." He hit the reset button. The grate came down, pins were swept off with a lot of clattering, and another full triangle thudded into place.

"She knocked them all down." Quinn gave a head nod toward the woman in the next lane who'd taken her seat. "She didn't seem all that excited."

"Mrs. Keefafer? Bowls twice a week, and has become

jaded. On the outside. Inside, believe me, she's doing her bootie dance."

"If you say so."

He adjusted Quinn's shoulders, shifted her hips. And yeah, she could see why he had such a high success rate with this routine. Eventually, after countless attempts she was able to take down multiple pins that took odd bites out of the triangle.

There was a wall of noise, the low thunder of balls rolling, the sharp clatter of pins, hoots and cheers from bowlers and onlookers, the bright bells of a pinball machine.

She smelled beer and wax, and the gooey orange cheese—a personal favorite—from the nachos someone munched on in the next lane.

Timeless, all-American, she mused, absently drafting an article on the experience. Centuries-old sport—she'd need to research that part—to good, clean, family fun.

She thought she had the hang of it, more or less, though she was shallow enough to throw a deliberate gutter ball here and there so Cal would adjust her stance.

As he did, she considered changing the angle of the article from family fun to the sexiness of bowling. The idea made her grin as she took her position.

Then it happened. She released the ball and it rolled down the center of the alley. Surprised, she took a step back. Then another with her arms going up to clamp on the sides of her head.

Something tingled in her belly as her heartbeat sped up.

"Oh. Oh. Look! It's going to—"

There was a satisfying *crack* and *crash* as ball slapped pins and pins tumbled in all directions. Bumping into each other, rolling, spinning, until the last fell with a slow, drunken sway.

"Well, my *God!*" She actually bounced on the toes of her rented shoes. "Did you see that? Did you—" And when she spun around, a look of stunned delight on her face, he was grinning at her.

"Son of a bitch," she muttered. "I owe you ten bucks."

"You learn fast. Want to try an approach?"

She wandered back toward him. "I believe I'm . . . spent. But I may come by some evening for lesson number two."

"Happy to oblige." Sitting hip-to-hip, they changed shoes. "I'll walk you back to the hotel."

"All right."

He got his coat, and on the way out shot a wave at the skinny young guy behind the shoe rental counter. "Back in ten."

"Quiet," she said the minute they stepped outside. "Just listen to all that quiet."

"The noise is part of the fun and the quiet after part of the reward."

"Did you ever want to do anything else, or did you grow up with a burning desire to manage a bowling alley?"

"Family fun center," he corrected. "We have an arcade—pinball, skee-ball, video games, and a section for kids under six. We do private parties—birthday parties, bachelor parties, wedding receptions—"

"Wedding receptions?"

"Sure. Bar mitzvahs, bat mitzvahs, anniversaries, corporate parties."

Definitely meat for an article, she realized. "A lot of arms on one body."

"You could say that."

"So why aren't you married and raising the next generation of Bowl-a-Rama kingpins, pun intended."

"Love has eluded me."

"Aw."

Despite the biting cold, it was pleasant to walk beside a man who naturally fit his stride to hers, to watch the clouds of their breath puff out, then merge together before the wind tore them to nothing.

He had an easy way about him and killer eyes, so there were worse things than feeling her toes go numb with cold in boots she knew were more stylish than practical.

"Are you going to be around if I think of some pertinent question to ask you tomorrow?"

" 'Round and about," he told her. "I can give you my cell phone number if—"

"Wait." She dug into her bag and came out with her own phone. Still walking, she punched a few keys. "Shoot."

He rattled it off. "I'm aroused by a woman who not only immediately finds what she's looking for in the mysterious depths of her purse, but who can skillfully operate electronic devices."

"Is that a sexist remark?"

"No. My mother always knows where everything is, but is still defeated by the universal remote. My sister Jen can operate anything from a six-speed to a wireless mouse, but can never find anything without a twenty-minute hunt, and my other sister, Marly, can't find anything, ever, and gets intimidated by her electric can opener. And here you are, stirring me up by being able to do both."

"I've always been a siren." She tucked her phone back in her bag as they turned to the steps leading to the long front porch of the hotel. "Thanks for the escort."

"No problem."

There was one of those beats; she recognized it. Both of them wondering, did they shake hands, just turn and go, or give in to curiosity and lean into a kiss.

"Let's stay to the safe road for now," she decided. "I admit, I like the look of your mouth, but moving on that's bound to tangle things up before I really get started on what brought me here."

"It's a damn shame you're right about that." He dipped his hands into his pockets. "So I'll just say good night. I'll wait, make sure you get inside."

"Good night." She walked up the steps to the door, eased it open. Then glanced back to see him standing, hands still in his pockets, with the old-fashioned streetlight spotlighting him.

Oh, yeah, she thought, it was a damn shame.

"See you soon."

He waited until the door shut behind her, then taking a couple of steps, studied the windows of the second and third floor. She'd said her window faced Main Street, but he wasn't sure what level she was on.

After a few moments, a light flashed on in a second-floor window, telling him Quinn was safe in her room.

He turned and had taken two steps when he saw the boy. He stood on the sidewalk half a block down. He wore no coat, no hat, no protection against the bite of wind. The long stream of his hair didn't stir in it.

His eyes gleamed, eerily red, as his lips peeled back in a snarl.

Cal heard the sound inside his head while ice balled in his belly.

Not real, he told himself. Not yet. A projection only, like in the dreams. But even in the dreams, it could hurt you or make you think you were hurt.

"Go back where you came from, you bastard." Cal spoke clearly, and as calmly as his shaken nerves would allow. "It's not your time yet."

When it is, I'll devour you, all of you, and everything you hold precious.

The lips didn't move with the words, but stayed frozen in that feral snarl.

"We'll see who feels the bite this round." Cal took another step forward.

And the fire erupted. It spewed out of the wide brick sidewalk, fumed across the street in a wall of wild red. Before he could register that there was no heat, no burn, Cal had already stumbled back, thrown up his hands.

The laughter rang in his head, as wild as the flames. Then both snapped off.

The street was quiet, the brick and buildings unmarred.

Tricks up his sleeve, Cal reminded himself. Lots of tricks up his sleeve.

He made himself stride forward, through where the false fire had run. There was a strong acrid odor that puffed then vanished like the vapor of his own breath. In that instant he recognized it.

Brimstone.

UPSTAIRS IN THE ROOM THAT MADE HER BLISSfully happy with its four-poster bed and fluffy white duvet, Quinn sat at the pretty desk with its curved legs and polished surface writing up the day's notes, data, and impressions on her laptop.

She loved that there were fresh flowers in the room, and a little blue bowl of artfully arranged fresh fruit. The bath held a deep and delightful claw-foot tub and a snowy white pedestal sink. There were thick, generous towels, two bars of soap, and rather stylish minibottles of shampoo, body cream, and bath gel.

Instead of boring, mass-produced posters, the art on the walls were original paintings and photos, which the discreet note on the desk identified as works by local artists available at Artful, a shop on South Main.

The room was full of homey welcoming touches, *and* provided high-speed Internet access. She made a note to reserve the same room after her initial week was up, for the return trips she planned in April, then again in July.

She'd accomplished quite a bit on her first day, which was a travel day on top of it. She'd met two of the three focal players, had an appointment to hike to the Pagan Stone. She'd gotten a feel for the town, on the surface in any case. And had, she believed, a personal experience with the manifestation of an unidentified (as yet) force.

And she had the bare bones for a bowling article that should work for her friends at *Detour*.

Not bad, especially when you added in she'd dined

sensibly on the grilled chicken salad in the hotel dining room, had *not* given in to temptation and inhaled an entire pizza but had limited herself to half a slice. And she'd bowled a strike.

On the personal downside, she supposed, as she shut down to prepare for bed, she'd also resisted the temptation to lock lips with the very appealing Caleb Hawkins.

Wasn't she all professional and unsatisfied?

Once she'd changed into her bedtime flannel pants and T-shirt, she nagged herself into doing fifteen minutes of pilates (okay, ten), then fifteen of yoga, before burrowing under the fabulous duvet with her small forest of down pillows.

She took her current book off the nightstand, burrowed into that as well until her eyes began to droop.

Just past midnight, she marked the novel, switched off the lamp, and snuggled into her happy nest.

As was her habit, she was asleep in a finger snap.

Quinn recognized the dream as a dream. Always, she enjoyed the sensation of the disjointed, carnival world of dreamscapes. It was, for her, like having some crazy adventure without any physical exertion. So when she found herself on a crooked path through a thick wood where the moonshine silvered the leaves and the curling fog rippled along the ground, a part of her mind thought: Oh boy! Here we go.

She thought she heard chanting, a kind of hoarse and desperate whisper, but the words themselves were indiscernible.

The air felt like silk, so soft, as she waded through the pools of fog. The chanting continued, drawing her toward it. A single word seemed to fly out of that moonstruck night, and the word was *bestia.*

She heard it over and over as she followed the crooked path through the silken air and the silver-laced trees. She felt a sexual pull, a heat and reaching in the belly toward whatever, whoever called out in the night.

Twice, then three times, the air seemed to whisper. *Bea-*

tus. The murmur of that warmed her skin. In the dream, she quickened her steps.

Out of the moon-drenched trees swam a black owl, its great wings stirring a storm in that soft air, chilling it until she shivered. And was, even in the dream, afraid.

With that cold wind stirring, she saw, stretched across the path, a golden fawn. The blood from its slit throat drenched the ground so it gleamed wet and black in the night.

Her heart squeezed with pity. So young, so sweet, she thought as she made herself approach it. Who could have done such a thing?

For a moment, the dead, staring eyes of the fawn cleared, shone as gold as its hind. It looked at her with such sorrow, such wisdom, tears gathered in her throat.

The voice came now, not through the whipped air, but in her mind. The single word: *devoveo*.

Then the trees were bare but for the ice that sheathed trunk and branch, and the silver moonlight turned gray. The path had turned, or she had, so now she faced a small pond. The water was black as ink, as if any light the sky pushed down was sucked into its depths and smothered there.

Beside the pond was a young woman in a long brown dress. Her hair was chopped short, with the strings and tufts of it sticking out wildly. Beside the black pond she bent to fill the pockets of her brown dress with stones.

Hello! Quinn called out. *What are you doing?*

The girl only continued to fill her pockets. As Quinn walked closer, she saw the girl's eyes were full of tears, and of madness.

Crap. You don't want to do that. You don't want to go Virginia Woolf. Wait. Just wait. Talk to me.

The girl turned her head, and for one shocked moment, Quinn saw the face as her own. *He doesn't know everything,* the mad girl said. *He didn't know you.*

She threw out her arms, and her slight body, weighed heavy with her cache of stones, tipped, tipped, tipped until it met the black water. The pond swallowed it like a waiting mouth.

Quinn leaped—what else could she do? Her body braced for the shock of cold as she filled her lungs with air.

There was a flash of light, a roar that might have been thunder or something alive and hungry. She was on her knees in a clearing where a stone rose out of the earth like an altar. Fire spewed around her, above her, through her, but she felt none of its heat.

Through the flames she saw two shapes, one black, one white, grappling like mad animals. With a terrible rending sound, the earth opened up, and like the waiting mouth of the pond, swallowed everything.

The scream ripped from her throat as that maw widened to take her. Clawing, she dragged herself toward the stone, fought to wrap her arms around it.

It broke into three equal parts, sending her tumbling, tumbling into that open, avid mouth.

She woke, huddled on the lovely bed, the linens tangled around her legs as she gripped one of the bedposts as if her life depended on it.

Her breath was an asthmatic's wheeze, and her heart beat so fast and hard it had her head spinning.

A dream, just a dream, she reminded herself, but couldn't force herself—not quite yet—to release her hold on the bedpost.

Clinging to it, she let her cheek rest on the wood, closed her eyes until the shaking had lessened to an occasional quiver.

"Hell of a ride," she mumbled.

The Pagan Stone. That's where she'd been at the end of the dream, she was certain of it. She recognized it from pictures she'd seen. Small wonder she'd have a scary dream about it, about the woods. And the pond . . . Wasn't there something in her research about a woman drowning in the pond? They'd named it after her. Hester's Pond. No, pool. Hester's Pool.

It all made sense, in dream logic.

Yeah, a hell of a ride, and she'd die happy if she never took another like it.

She glanced at her travel alarm, and saw by its luminous dial it was twenty after three. Three in the morning, she thought, was the dead time, the worst time to be wakeful. So she'd go back to sleep, like a sensible woman. She'd straighten the bed, get herself a nice cool drink of water, then tune out.

She'd had enough jolts and jumps for her first day.

She slid out of bed to tug the sheets and duvet back into some semblance of order, then turned, intending to go to the adjoining bath for a glass of water.

The scream wouldn't sound. It tore through her head like scrabbling claws, but nothing could tear its way out of the hot lock of her throat.

The boy grinned obscenely through the dark window. His face, his hands pressed against the glass bare inches away from her own. She saw its tongue flick out to roll across those sharp, white teeth, and those eyes, gleaming red, seemed as bottomless and hungry as the mouth of earth that had tried to swallow her in her dream.

Her knees wanted to buckle, but she feared if she dropped to the ground it would come crashing through the glass to latch those teeth on her throat like a wild dog.

Instead, she lifted her hand in the ancient sign against evil. "Get away from here," she whispered. "Stay away from me."

It laughed. She heard the horrible, giddy sound of it, saw its shoulders shake with mirth. Then it pushed off the glass into a slow, sinuous somersault. It hung suspended for a moment above the sleeping street. Then it . . . condensed, was all she could think. It shrank into itself, into a pinpoint of black, and vanished.

Quinn launched herself at the window, yanked the shade down to cover every inch of glass. And lowering to the floor at last, she leaned back against the wall, trembling.

When she thought she could stand, she used the wall as

a brace, quick-stepping to the other windows. She was out of breath again by the time all the shades were pulled, and tried to tell herself the room didn't feel like a closed box.

She got the water—she needed it—and gulped down two full glasses. Steadier, she stared at the covered windows.

"Okay, screw you, you little bastard."

Picking up her laptop, she went back to her position on the floor—it just felt safer under the line of the windowsills—and began to type up every detail she remembered from the dream, and from the thing that pressed itself to the night glass.

WHEN SHE WOKE, THE LIGHT WAS A HARD YELlow line around the cream linen of the shades. And the battery of her laptop was stone dead. Congratulating herself on remembering to back up before she'd curled onto the floor to sleep, she got her creaky self up.

Stupid, of course, she told herself as she tried to stretch out the worst of the stiffness. Stupid not to turn off her machine, then crawl back into that big, cozy bed. But she'd forgotten the first and hadn't even considered the second.

Now, she put the computer back on the pretty desk, plugged it in to recharge the batteries. With some caution—after all, it had been broad daylight when she'd seen the boy the first time—she approached the first window. Eased up the shade.

The sun was lancing down out of a boiled blue sky. On the pavement, on awnings, and roofs a fresh white carpet of snow shimmered.

She spotted a few merchants or their employees busily shoveling sidewalks or porches and steps. Cars putted along the plowed street. She wondered if school had been called or delayed due to the snow.

She wondered if the boy had demon classes that day.

For herself, Quinn decided she was going to treat her abused body to a long soak in the charming tub. Then she'd try Ma's Pantry for breakfast, and see who she could get to talk to her over her fruit and granola about the legends of Hawkins Hollow.

Six

CAL SAW HER COME IN WHILE HE CUT INTO HIS short stack at the counter. She had on those high, sharp-heeled boots, faded jeans, and a watch cap, bright as a cardinal, pulled over her hair.

She'd wound on a scarf that made him think of Joseph's coat of many colors, which added a jauntiness with her coat opened. Under it was a sweater the color of ripe blueberries.

There was something about her, he mused, that would have been bright and eye-catching even in mud brown.

He watched her eyes track around the diner area, and decided she was weighing where to sit, whom to approach. Already working, he concluded. Maybe she always was. He was damn sure, even on short acquaintance, that her mind was always working.

She spotted him. She aimed that sunbeam smile of hers, started over. He felt a little like the kid in the pickup game of ball, who got plucked from all the others waving their arms and shouting: Me! Me! Pick me!

"Morning, Caleb."

"Morning, Quinn. Buy you breakfast?"

"Absolutely." She leaned over his plate, took a long, dramatic sniff of his butter-and-syrup-loaded pancakes. "I bet those are fabulous."

"Best in town." He stabbed a thick bite with his fork, held it out. "Want a sample?"

"I can never stop at a taste. It's a sickness." She slid onto the stool, swiveled around to beam at the waitress as she unwound her scarf. "Morning. I'd love some coffee, and do you have any granola-type substance that could possibly be topped with any sort of fruit?"

"Well, we got Special K, and I could slice you up some bananas with it."

"Perfect." She reached over the counter. "I'm Quinn."

"The writer from up in PA." The waitress nodded, took Quinn's hand in a firm grip. "Meg Stanley. You watch this one here, Quinn," Meg said with a poke at Cal. "Some of those quiet types are sneaky."

"Some of us mouthy types are fast."

That got a laugh out of Meg as she poured Quinn's coffee. "Being quick on your feet's a strong advantage. I'll get that cereal for you."

"Why," Cal wondered aloud as he forked up another dripping bite of pancake, "would anyone willingly choose to eat trail mix for breakfast?"

"It's an acquired taste. I'm still acquiring it. But knowing myself, and I do, if I keep coming in here for breakfast, I'll eventually succumb to the allure of the pancake. Does the town have a gym, a health club, a burly guy who rents out his Bowflex?"

"There's a little gym down in the basement of the community center. You need a membership, but I can get you a pass on that."

"Really? You're a handy guy to know, Cal."

"I am. You want to change your order? Go for the gold, then the treadmill?"

"Not today, but thanks. So." After she'd doctored her

coffee, she picked up the cup with both hands, sipping as she studied him through the faint rise of steam. "Now that we're having our second date—"

"How'd I miss the first one?"

"You bought me pizza and a beer and took me bowling. In my dictionary, that falls under the definition of date. Now you're buying me breakfast."

"Cereal and bananas. I do appreciate a cheap date."

"Who doesn't? But since we're dating and all . . ." She took another sip as he laughed. "I'd like to share an experience with you."

She glanced over as Meg brought her a white stoneware bowl heaped with cereal and sliced bananas. "Figured you'd be going for the two percent milk with this."

"Perceptive and correct, thanks."

"Get you anything else?"

"We're good for now, Meg," Cal told her. "Thanks."

"Just give a holler."

"An experience," Cal prompted, as Meg moved down the counter.

"I had a dream."

His insides tensed even before she began to tell him, in a quiet voice and in careful detail of the dream she'd had during the night.

"I knew it was a dream," she concluded. "I always do, even during them. Usually I get a kick out of them, even the spooky ones. Because, you know, they're not really happening. I haven't actually grown a second head so I can argue with myself, nor am I jumping out of a plane with a handful of red balloons. But this . . . I can't say I got a charge out of it. I didn't just think I felt cold, for instance. I *was* cold. I didn't just think I felt myself hit and roll on the ground. I found bruises this morning that weren't there when I went to bed. Fresh bruises on my hip. How do you get hurt in a dream, if it's just a dream?"

You could, he thought, in Hawkins Hollow. "Did you fall out of bed, Quinn?"

"No, I didn't fall out of bed." For the first time, there

was a whiff of irritation in her voice. "I woke up with my arms locked around the bedpost like it was my long-lost lover. And all this was before I saw that red-eyed little bastard again."

"Where?"

She paused long enough to spoon up some cereal. He wasn't sure if the expression of displeasure that crossed her face was due to the taste, or her thoughts. "Did you ever read King's *Salem's Lot*?"

"Sure. Small town, vampires. Great stuff."

"Remember that scene? The little boys, brothers. One's been changed after they snatched him off the path in the woods. He comes to visit his brother one night."

"Nothing scarier than kiddie vampires."

"Not much, anyway. And the vampire kid's just *hanging* outside the window. Just floating out there, scratching on the glass. It was like that. He was pressed to the glass, and I'll point out I'm on the second floor. Then he did a stylish back flip in the air, and poofed."

He laid a hand over hers, found it cold, rubbed some warmth into it. "You have my home and cell numbers, Quinn. Why didn't you call me?"

She ate a little more, then, smiling at Meg, held up her cup for a top-off. "I realize we're dating, Cal, but I don't call all the guys I go bowling with at three thirty in the morning to go: eek! I slogged through swamps in Louisiana on the trail of the ghost of a voodoo queen—and don't think I don't know how that sounds. I spent the night, alone, in a reputedly haunted house on the coast of Maine, and interviewed a guy who was reported to be possessed by no less than thirteen demons. Then there was the family of werewolves in Tallahassee. But this kid . . ."

"You don't believe in werewolves and vampires, Quinn."

She turned on the stool to face him directly. "My mind's as open as a twenty-four hour deli, and considering the circumstances, yours should be, too. But no, I don't think this thing is a vampire. I saw him in broad daylight, after all.

But he's not human, and just because he's not human doesn't make him less than real. He's part of the Pagan Stone. He's part of what happens here every seven years. And he's early, isn't he?"

Yeah, he thought, her mind was always working and it was sharp as a switchblade. "This isn't the best place to go into this any deeper."

"Say where."

"I said I'd take you to the stone tomorrow, and I will. We'll get into more detail then. Can't do it today," he said, anticipating her. "I've got a full plate, and tomorrow's better anyway. They're calling for sun and forties today and tomorrow." He hitched up a hip to take out his wallet. "Most of this last snow'll be melted." He glanced down at her boots as he laid bills on the counter to cover both their tabs. "If you don't have anything more suitable to hike in than those, you'd better buy something. You won't last a half mile otherwise."

"You'd be surprised how long I can last."

"Don't know as I would. I'll see you tomorrow if not before."

Quinn frowned at him as he walked out, then turned back as Meg slid her rag down the counter. "Sneaky. You were right about that."

"Known the boy since before he was born, haven't I?"

Amused, Quinn propped an elbow back on the bar as she toyed with the rest of her cereal. Apparently a serious scare in the night and mild irritation with a man in the morning was a more effective diet aid than any bathroom scale. Meg struck her as a comfortable woman, wide-hipped in her brown cords and flannel shirt, sleeves rolled up at the elbows. Her hair curled tight as a poodle's fur in a brown ball around a soft and lined face. And there was a quick spark in her hazel eyes that told Quinn she'd be inclined to talk.

"So, Meg, what else do you know? Say about the Pagan Stone."

"Buncha nonsense, you ask me."

"Really?"

"People just get a little"—she circled her finger at her ear—"now and again. Tip too much at the bottle, get all het up. One thing leads to another. Good for business though, the speculation, if you follow me. Get plenty of flatlanders in here wondering about it, asking about it, taking pictures, buying souvenirs."

"You never had any experiences?"

"Saw some people usually have good sense acting like fools, and some who got a mean streak in them acting meaner for a spell of time." She shrugged. "People are what people are, and sometimes they're more so."

"I guess that's true."

"If you want more about it, you should go on out to the library. There's some books there written about the town, the history and whatnot. And Sally Keefafer—"

"Bowling Sally?"

Meg snorted a laugh. "She does like to bowl. Library director. She'll bend your ear plenty if you ask her questions. She loves to talk, and never found a subject she couldn't expound on 'til you wanted to slap some duct tape over her mouth."

"I'll do that. You sell duct tape here?"

Meg hooted out another laugh, shook her head. "If you really want to talk, and get some sense out of it, you want Mrs. Abbott. She ran the old library, and she's at the new one for a spell most every day."

Then scooping up the bills Cal left, she went to refill waiting cups at the other end of the counter.

CAL HEADED STRAIGHT TO HIS OFFICE. HE HAD the usual morning's paperwork, phone calls, e-mails. And he had a morning meeting scheduled with his father and the arcade guy before the center opened for the afternoon leagues.

He thought of the wall of fire across Main Street the night before. Add that to two sightings by Quinn—an outsider—and it sure as hell seemed the *entity* that plagued the town was starting its jollies early.

Her dream troubled him as well. The details—he'd recognized where she'd been, what she'd seen. For her to have dreamed so lucidly about the pond, about the clearing, to have bruises from it, meant, in his opinion, she had to be connected in some way.

A distant relation wasn't out of the question, and there should be a way to do a search. But he had other relations, and none but his immediate family had ever spoken of any effects, even during the Seven.

As he passed through the bowling center, he sent a wave toward Bill Turner, who was buffing the lanes. The big, burly machine's throaty hum echoed through the empty building.

The first thing he checked in his office was his e-mail, and he let out a breath of relief when he saw one from Gage.

Prague. Got some business to clear up. Should be back in the U.S. of A. inside a couple weeks. Don't do anything stupider than usual without me.

No salutation, no signature. Very Gage, Cal thought. And it would have to do, for now.

Contact me as soon as you're Stateside, Cal wrote back. *Things are already rumbling. Will always wait for you to do the stupid, because you're better at it.*

After clicking Send, he dashed another off to Fox.

Need to talk. My place, six o'clock. Got beer. Bring food that's not pizza.

Best he could do, for now, Cal thought. Because life just had to keep rolling on.

QUINN WALKED BACK TO THE HOTEL TO RE-trieve her laptop. If she was going to the library, she might as well use it for a couple hours' work. And while she expected she had most, if not all, of the books tucked into the town's library already, maybe this Mrs. Abbott would prove to be a valuable source.

Caleb Hawkins, it appeared, was going to be a clam until the following day.

As she stepped into the hotel lobby she saw the pert blond clerk behind the desk—Mandy, Quinn thought after a quick scroll through her mental PDA—and a brunette in the curvy chair being checked in.

Quinn's quick once-over registered the brunette with the short, sassy do as mid to late twenties, with a travel-weary look about her that didn't do anything much to diminish the seriously pretty face. Jeans and a black sweater fit well over an athletic build. Pooled at her feet were a suitcase, a laptop case, a smaller bag probably for cosmetics and other female necessities, and an excellent and roomy hobo in slick red leather.

Quinn had a moment of purse envy as she aimed a smile.

"Welcome back, Miss Black. If you need anything, I'll be with you in just a minute."

"I'm fine, thanks."

Quinn turned to the stairs and, starting up, heard Mandy's cheerful, "You're all checked in, Miss Darnell. I'm just going to call Harry to help with your bags."

As was her way, Quinn speculated on Miss Gorgeous Red Bag Darnell as she climbed up to her room. Passing through on her way to New York. No, too odd a place to stop over, and too early in the day to stop a road trip.

Visiting relatives or friends, but why wouldn't she just bunk with said relatives or friends? Then again, she had some of both she'd rather not bunk with.

Maybe a business trip, Quinn mused as she let herself into her room.

Well, if Red Bag I Want for My Very Own stayed more than a few hours, Quinn would find out just who and what and why. It was, after all, what she was best at.

Quinn packed up her laptop, added a spare notebook and extra pencils in case she got lucky. Digging out her phone she set it on vibrate. Little was more annoying, to her mind, than ringing cell phones in libraries and theaters.

She slipped a county map into her case in the event she decided to explore.

Armed, she headed down for the drive to the other end of town and the Hawkins Hollow Library.

From her own research, Quinn knew that the original stone building tucked on Main Street now housed the community center, and the gym she intended to make use of. At the turn of the current century the new library had been built on a pretty rise of land on the south end of town. It, too, was stone, though Quinn was pretty sure it was the facing used on concrete and such rather than quarried. It was two levels with short wings on either side and a portico-style entrance. The style, she thought, was attractively old-fashioned. One, she guessed, the local historic society had likely fought a war to win.

She admired the benches, and the trees she imagined made shady reading nooks in season as she pulled up to park in the side lot.

It smelled like a library, she thought. Of books and a little dust, of silence.

She saw a brightly lettered sign announcing a Story Hour in the Children's section at ten thirty.

She wound her way through. Computers, long tables, carts, a few people wandering the stacks, a couple of old men paging through newspapers. She heard the soft *hum-chuck* of a copier and the muted ringing of a phone from the Information Desk.

Reminding herself to focus because if she wandered she'd be entranced by the spell she believed all libraries wove, she aimed straight for Information. And in the hushed tone reserved for libraries and churches, addressed the stringy man on duty. "Good morning, I'm looking for books on local history."

"That would be on the second floor, west wing. Steps over to the left, elevator straight back. Anything in particular you're after?"

"Thanks, but I'm just going to poke. Is Mrs. Abbott in

today?"

"Mrs. Abbott is retired, but she's in most every day by eleven. In a volunteer capacity."

"Thanks again."

Quinn used the stairs. They had a nice curve to them, she thought, almost a *Gone with the Wind* sort of swish. She put on mental blinders so as not to be tempted by stacks and reading areas until she found herself in Local Interest.

It was more a room—a mini-library—than a section. Nice cozy chairs, tables, amber-shaded lamps, even footrests. And it was larger than she'd expected.

Then again, she should have accounted for the fact that there had been battles fought in and around the Hollow in both the Revolutionary and Civil Wars.

Books pertaining to those were arranged in separate areas, as were books on the county, the state, and the town.

In addition there was a very healthy section for local authors.

She tried that section first and saw she'd hit a treasure trove. There had to be over a dozen she hadn't come across on her own hunt before coming to town. They were self-published, vanity-pressed, small local publishers.

Titles like *Nightmare Hollow* and *The Hollow, The Truth* had her giddy with anticipation. She set up her laptop, her notebook, her recorder, then pulled out five books. It was then she noticed the discreet bronze plaque.

The Hawkins Hollow Library

gratefully acknowledges the generosity of
the Franklin and Maybelle Hawkins Family

Franklin and Maybelle. Very probably Cal's ancestors. It struck Quinn as both suitable and generous that they would have donated the funds to sponsor this room. This particular room.

She settled at the table, chose one of the books at random, then began to read.

She'd covered pages of her notebook with names, locations, dates, reputed incidents, and any number of theories when she scented lavender and baby powder.

Surfacing, she saw a trim and tidy old woman standing in black, sensible shoes with her hands folded neatly at the waist of her purple suit.

Her hair was a thinning snowball; her clear framed glasses so thickly lensed Quinn wondered how the tiny nose and ears supported their weight.

She wore pearls around her neck, a gold wedding band on her finger, and a leather-banded watch with a huge face that looked to be as practical as her thick-soled shoes.

"I'm Estelle Abbott," she said in her creaky voice. "Young Dennis said you asked after me."

As Quinn had gauged Dennis at Information as tumbling down the back end of his sixties, she imagined the woman who termed him young must have him by a good two decades.

"Yes." Quinn got to her feet, crossed over to offer her hand. "I'm Quinn Black, Mrs. Abbott. I'm—"

"Yes, I know. The writer. I've enjoyed your books."

"Thank you very much."

"No need. If I hadn't liked them I'd've told you straight-out. You're researching for a book on the Hollow."

"Yes, ma'am, I am."

"You'll find quite a bit of information here. Some of it useful." She peered at the books on the table. "Some of it nonsense."

"Then in the interest of separating the wheat from the chaff, maybe you could find some time to talk to me at some point. I'd be happy to take you to lunch or dinner whenever you—"

"That's very nice of you, but unnecessary. Why don't we sit down for a while, and we'll see how things go?"

"That would be great."

Estelle crossed to a chair, sat, then with her back ruler-straight and her knees glued together, folded her hands in her lap. "I was born in the Hollow," she began, "lived here all of my ninety-seven years."

"Ninety-seven?" Quinn didn't have to feign the surprise. "I'm usually pretty good at gauging age, and I'd put you a solid decade under that."

"Good bones," Estelle said with an easy smile. "I lost my husband, John, also born and raised here, eight years back come the fifth of next month. We were married seventy-one years."

"What was your secret?"

That brought on another smile. "Learn to laugh, otherwise, you'll beat them to death with a hammer first chance."

"Just let me write that down."

"We had six children—four boys, two girls—and all of them living still and not in jail, thank the lord. Out of them, we had ourselves nineteen grandchildren, and out of them got ourselves twenty-eight greats—last count, and five of the next generation with two on the way."

Quinn simply goggled. "Christmas must be insane in a good way."

"We're scattered all over, but we've managed to get most everybody in one place at one time a few times."

"Dennis said you were retired. You were a librarian?"

"I started working in the library when my youngest started school. That would be the old library on Main Street. I worked there more than fifty years. Went back to school myself and got my degree. Johnnie and I traveled, saw a lot of the world together. For a time we thought about moving on down to Florida. But our roots here were too deep for that. I went to part-time work, then I retired when my Johnnie got sick. When he passed, I came back—still the old one while this was being built—as a volunteer or as an artifact, however you look at it. I tell you this so you'll have some idea about me."

"You love your husband and your children, and the children who've come from them. You love books, and you're proud of the work you've done. You love this town, and respect the life you've lived here."

Estelle gave her a look of approval. "You have an efficient and insightful way of summing up. You didn't say I loved my husband, but used the present tense. That tells me you're an observant and sensitive young woman. I sensed from your books that you have an open and seeking mind. Tell me, Miss Black, do you also have courage?"

Quinn thought of the thing outside the window, the way its tongue had flicked over its teeth. She'd been afraid, but she hadn't run. "I like to think so. Please call me Quinn."

"Quinn. A family name."

"Yes, my mother's maiden."

"Irish Gaelic. I believe it means counselor."

"It does, yes."

"I have a well of trivial information," Estelle said with a tap of her finger to her temple. "But I wonder if your name isn't relevant. You'll need to have the objectivity, and the sensitivity of a counselor to write the book that should be written on Hawkins Hollow."

"Why haven't you written it?"

"Not everyone who loves music can play the tune. Let me tell you a few things, some of which you may already know. There is a place in the woods that borders the west of this town, and that place was sacred ground, sacred and volatile ground long before Lazarus Twisse sought it out."

"Lazarus Twisse, the leader of the Puritan sect—the radical sect—which broke off, or more accurately, was cut off, from the godly in Massachusetts."

"According to the history of the time, yes. The Native Americans held that ground as sacred. And before them, it's said, powers battled for that circle of ground, both—the dark and the light, good and evil, whatever terms you prefer—left some seeds of that power there. They lay dormant, century by century, with only the stone to mark what had passed there. Over time the memories of the battle were forgotten or bastardized in folklore, and only the sense many felt that this ground and its stone were not ordinary dirt and rock remained."

Estelle paused, fell into silence so that Quinn heard the click and hum of the heater, and the light slap of leather shoes on the floor as someone passed by the room toward other business.

"Twisse came to the Hollow, already named for Richard Hawkins who, with his wife and children, had carved a small settlement in 1648. You should remark that Richard's eldest daughter was Ann. When Twisse came, Hawkins, his family, and a handful of others—some who'd fled Europe as criminals, political or otherwise—had made their life here. As had a man calling himself Giles Dent. And Dent built a cabin in the woods where the stone rose out of the ground."

"What's called the Pagan Stone."

"Yes. He troubled no one, and as he had some skill and knowledge of healing, was often sought out for sickness or injury. There are some accounts that claim he was known as the Pagan, and that this was the basis of the name the Pagan Stone."

"You're not convinced those accounts are accurate."

"It may be that the term stuck, entered the language and the lexicon at that time. But it was the Pagan Stone long before the arrival of Giles Dent or Lazarus Twisse. There are other accounts that claim Dent dabbled in witchcraft, that he enspelled Ann Hawkins, seduced and impregnated her. Others state that Ann and Dent were indeed lovers, but that she went to his bed of her own free will, and left her family home to live with him in the little cabin with the Pagan Stone."

"It would've been difficult for her—for Ann Hawkins—either way," Quinn speculated. "Enspelled or free will, to live with a man, unmarried. If it was free will, if it was love, she must have been very strong."

"The Hawkinses have always been strong. Ann had to be strong to go to Dent, to stay with him. Then she had to be strong enough to leave him."

"There are a lot of conflicting stories," Quinn began. "Why do you believe Ann Hawkins left Giles Dent?"

"I believe she left to protect the lives growing inside her."

"From?"

"Lazarus Twisse. Twisse and those who followed him came to Hawkins Hollow in sixteen fifty-one. He was a powerful force, and soon the settlement was under his rule. His rule decreed there would be no dancing, no singing, no music, no books but the Bible. No church but his church, no god but his god."

"So much for freedom of religion."

"Freedom was never Twisse's goal. In the way of those thirsty for power above all else, he intimidated, terrorized, punished, banished, and used as his visible weapon, the wrath of his chosen god. As Twisse's power grew, so did his punishments and penalties. Stocks, lashings, the shearing of a woman's hair if she was deemed ungodly, the branding of a man should he be accused of a crime. And finally, the burning of those he judged to be witches. On the night of July the seventh, 1652, on the accusation of a young woman, Hester Deale, Twisse led a mob from the settlement to the Pagan Stone, and to Giles Dent. What happened there . . ."

Quinn leaned forward. But Estelle sighed and shook her head. "Well, there are many accounts. As there were many deaths. Seeds planted long before stirred in the ground. Some may have sprouted, only to die in the blaze that scorched the clearing.

"There are . . . fewer reports of what immediately followed, or followed over the next days and weeks. But in time, Ann Hawkins returned to the settlement with her three sons. And Hester Deale gave birth to a daughter eight months after the killing blaze at the Pagan Stone. Shortly, very shortly after her child, whom she claimed was sired by the devil, was born, Hester drowned herself in a small pond in Hawkins Wood."

Loading her pockets with stones, Quinn thought with a suppressed shudder. "Do you know what happened to her child? Or the children of Ann Hawkins?"

"There are some letters, some journals, family Bibles. But most concrete information has been lost, or has never come to light. It will take considerable time and effort to dig out the truth. I can tell you this, those seeds stayed dormant until a night twenty-one years ago this July. They were awakened, and what sowed them awakened. They bloom for seven nights every seven years, and they strangle Hawkins Hollow. I'm sorry, I tire so quickly these days. It's irritating."

"Can I get you something? Or drive you home?"

"You're a good girl. My grandson will be coming along to pick me up. You'll have spoken, I imagine, to his son by now. To Caleb."

Something in the smile turned a switch in Quinn's brain. "Caleb would be your—"

"Great-grandson. Honorary, you could say. My brother Franklin and his wife, my dearest friend, Maybelle, were killed in an accident just before Jim—Caleb's father was born. My Johnnie and I stood as grandparents to my brother's grandchildren. I'd have counted them and theirs in that long list of progeny before."

"You're a Hawkins by birth then."

"I am, and our line goes back, in the Hollow, to Richard Hawkins, the founder—and through him to Ann." She paused a moment as if to let Quinn absorb, analyze. "He's a good boy, my Caleb, and he carries more than his share of weight on his shoulders."

"From what I've seen, he carries it well."

"He's a good boy," Estelle repeated, then rose. "We'll talk again, soon."

"I'll walk you downstairs."

"Don't trouble. They'll have tea and cookies for me in the staff lounge. I'm a pet here—in the nicest sense of the word. Tell Caleb we spoke, and that I'd like to speak with you again. Don't spend all this pretty day inside a book. As much as I love them, there's life to be lived."

"Mrs. Abbott?"

"Yes?"

"Who do you think planted the seeds at the Pagan Stone?"

"Gods and demons." Estelle's eyes were tired, but clear. "Gods and demons, and there's such a thin line between the two, isn't there?"

Alone, Quinn sat again. Gods and demons. Those were a big, giant step up from ghosts and spirits, and other bump-in-the-night residents. But didn't it fit, didn't it click right together with the words she remembered from her dreams?

Words she'd looked up that morning.

Bestia, Latin for beast.

Beatus, Latin for blessed.

Devoveo, Latin for sacrifice.

Okay, okay, she thought, if we're heading down that track, it might be a good time to call in the reserves.

She pulled out her phone. When she was greeted by voice mail, Quinn pushed down impatience and waited for her cue to leave a message.

"Cyb, it's Q. I'm in Hawkins Hollow, Maryland. And, wow, I've hooked a big one. Can you come? Let me know if you can come. Let me know if you can't come so I can talk you into it."

She closed the phone, and for the moment she ignored the stack of books she'd selected. Instead, she began to busily type up notes from Estelle Hawkins Abbott's recitation.

Seven

CAL DID WHAT HE THOUGHT OF AS THE PASS OFF to his father. Since the meetings and the morning and afternoon league games were over and there was no party or event scheduled, the lanes were empty but for a couple of old-timers having a practice game on lane one.

The arcade was buzzing, as it tended to between the last school bell and the dinner hour. But Cy Hudson was running herd there, and Holly Lappins manned the front desk. Jake and Sara worked the grill and fountain, which would start hopping in another hour.

Everything, everyone was in its place, so Cal could sit with his father at the end of the counter over a cup of coffee before he headed for home, and his dad took over the center for the night.

They could sit quietly for a while, too. Quiet was his father's way. Not that Jim Hawkins didn't like to socialize. He seemed to like crowds as much as his alone time, remembered names, faces, and could and would converse on any subject, including politics and religion. The fact that he could do so without pissing anyone off was, in Cal's opinion, one of his finest skills.

His sandy-colored hair had gone a pure and bright silver over the last few years, and was trimmed every two weeks at the local barbershop. He rarely altered his uniform of khakis, Rockports, and oxford shirts on workdays.

Some would have called Jim Hawkins habitual, even boring. Cal called him reliable.

"Having a good month so far," Jim said in his take-your-time drawl. He took his coffee sweet and light, and by his wife's decree, cut off the caffeine at six p.m. sharp. "Kind of weather we've been having, you never know if people are going to burrow in, or get cabin fever so bad they want to be anywhere but home."

"It was a good idea, running the three-game special for February."

"I get one now and again." Jim smiled, lines fanning out and deepening around his eyes. "So do you. Your mom's wishing you'd come by, have dinner some night soon."

"Sure. I'll give her a call."

"Heard from Jen yesterday."

"How's she doing?"

"Fine enough to flaunt that it was seventy-four in San Diego. Rosie's learning to write her letters, and the baby's getting another tooth. Jen said she'd send us pictures."

Cal heard the wistfulness. "You and Mom should take another trip out there."

"Maybe, maybe in a month or two. We're heading to Baltimore on Sunday to see Marly and her brood. I saw your great-gran today. She told me she had a nice chat with that writer who's in town."

"Gran talked with Quinn?"

"In the library. She liked the girl. Likes the idea of this book, too."

"And how about you?"

Jim shook his head, contemplated as Sara drew off Cokes for a couple of teenagers taking a break from the arcade. "I don't know what I think, Cal, that's the plain truth.

I ask myself what good's it going to do to have somebody—and an outsider at that—write all this down so people can read about it. I tell myself that what happened before won't happen again—"

"Dad."

"I know that's not true, or most likely not true."

For a moment Jim just listened to the voices from the boys at the other end of the counter, the way they joked and poked at each other. He knew those boys, he thought. He knew their parents. If life worked as it ought to work, he'd know their wives and kids one day.

Hadn't he joked and poked at his own friends here once upon a time, over fountain Cokes and fries? Hadn't his own children run tame through this place? Now his girls were married and gone, with families of their own. And his boy was a man, sitting with worry in his eyes over problems too big to be understood.

"You have to prepare for it to happen again," Jim continued. "But for most of us, it all hazes up, it just hazes up so you can barely remember what did happen. Not you, I know. It's clear for you, and I wish that wasn't so. I guess if you believe this writer can help find the answers, I'm behind you on that."

"I don't know what I believe. I haven't worked it out yet."

"You will. Well. I'm going to go check on Cy. Some of the evening rollers'll be coming in before long, wanting a bite before they suit up."

He pushed away from the counter, took a long look around. He heard the echoes of his boyhood, and the shouts of his children. He saw his son, gangly with youth, sitting at the counter with the two boys Jim knew were the same as brothers to him.

"We've got a good place here, Cal. It's worth working for. Worth fighting to hold it steady."

Jim gave Cal a pat on the shoulder, then strolled away.

Not just the center, Cal thought. His father had meant the town. And Cal was afraid that holding it steady this time was going to be one hell of a battle.

He went straight home where most of the snow had melted off the shrubs and stones. Part of him had wanted to hunt Quinn down, pump out of her what she and his great-grandmother had talked about. Better to wait, he thought as he jingled his keys, better to wait then ease it out of her the next day. When they went to the Pagan Stone.

He glanced toward the woods where trees and shadows held pockets and rivers of snow, where he knew the path would be muddy from the melt.

Was it in there now, gathering itself? Had it somehow found a way to strike outside the Seven? Maybe, maybe, but not tonight. He didn't feel it tonight. And he always did.

Still, he couldn't deny he felt less exposed when he was inside the house, after he'd put on lights to push away the gloom.

He went through to the back door, opened it, and gave a whistle.

Lump took his time as Lump was wont to do. But the dog eased his way out of the doghouse and even stirred up the energy for a couple of tail wags before he moseyed across the backyard to the bottom of the deck stairs.

He gave a doggie sigh before clumping up the short flight. Then he leaned his whole body against Cal.

And that, Cal thought, was love. That was welcome home, how ya doing, in Lump's world.

He crouched down to stroke and ruffle the fur, to scratch between the floppy ears while Lump gazed at him soulfully. "How's it going? Get all your work done? What do you say we have a beer?"

They went inside together. Cal filled the dog bowl from the bin of chow while Lump sat politely, though Cal assumed a large portion of his dog's manners were sheer laziness. When the bowl was set in front of him, Lump ate slowly, and with absolute focus on the task at hand.

Cal pulled a beer out of the fridge and popped the top. Leaning back on the counter he took that first long swallow that signaled the end of the workday.

"Got some serious shit on my mind, Lump. Don't know what to do about it, think about it. Should I have found a way to stop Quinn from coming here? Not sure that would've worked since she seems to go where the hell she wants, but I could've played it different. Laughed it off, or pushed it higher, so the whole thing came off as bogus. Played it straight, so far, and I don't know where that's going to lead."

He heard the front door open, then Fox shouted, "Yo!" and Fox came in carrying a bucket of chicken and a large white takeout bag. "Got tub-o-cluck, got fries. Want beer."

After dumping the food on the table, Fox pulled out a beer. "Your summons was pretty abrupt, son. I might've had a hot date tonight."

"You haven't had a hot date in two months."

"I'm storing it up." After the first swig, Fox shrugged off his coat, tossed it over a chair. "What's the deal?"

"Tell you while we eat."

As he'd been too brainwashed by his mother to fall back on the single-man's friend of paper plates, Cal set out two of stoneware in dull blue. They sat down to fried chicken and potatoes with Lump—as the only thing that lured the dog from food was more food—caging fries by leaning against Cal's knee or Fox's.

He told Fox everything, from the wall of fire, through Quinn's dream, and up to the conversation she'd had with his great-grandmother.

"Seeing an awful lot of the fucker for February," Fox mused. "That's never happened before. Did you dream last night?"

"Yeah."

"Me, too. Mine was a replay of the first time, the first summer. Only we didn't get to the school in time, and it wasn't just Miss Lister inside. It was everybody." He scrubbed a hand over his face before taking a long pull of beer. "Everybody in town, my family, yours, all inside. Trapped, beating on the windows, screaming, their faces at the windows while the place burned." He offered Lump another fry, and his eyes were as dark and soulful as the dog's. "Didn't happen that way, thank Christ. But it felt like it did. You know how that goes."

"Yeah." Cal let out a breath. "Yeah, I know how that goes. Mine was from that same summer, and we were all riding our bikes through town the way we did. Buildings were burned out, windows broken, cars wrecked and smoking. Bodies everywhere."

"It didn't happen that way," Fox repeated. "We're not ten anymore, and we're not going to let it happen that way."

"I've been asking myself how long we can do this, Fox. How long can we hold it back as much as we do? This time, the next. Three more times? How many more times are we going to watch people we know, people we see most every day turn? Go crazy, go mean. Hurt each other, hurt themselves?"

"As long as it takes."

Cal shoved his plate aside. "Not good enough."

"It's all we've got, for now."

"It's like a virus, an infection, passing from one person to another. Where's the goddamn antidote?"

"Not everyone's affected," Fox reminded him. "There has to be a reason for that."

"We've never found it."

"No, so maybe you were right. Maybe we do need fresh eyes, an outsider, objectivity we just don't have. Are you still planning to take Quinn to the stone tomorrow?"

"If I don't, she'll go anyway. So yeah, it's better I'm there."

"You want me? I can cancel some stuff."

"I can handle it." Had to handle it.

QUINN STUDIED THE MENU IN THE HOTEL'S ALmost empty dining room. She'd considered getting some takeout and eating in her room over her laptop, but she fell too easily into that habit, she knew. And to write about a town, she had to experience the town, and couldn't do that closed up in her pretty room eating a cold-cut sub.

She wanted a glass of wine, something chilly with a subtle zip. The hotel's cellar was more extensive than she'd expected, but she didn't want a whole bottle. She was frowning over the selections offered by the glass when Miss Fabulous Red Bag stepped in.

She'd changed into black pants, Quinn noted, and a cashmere sweater in two tissue-thin layers of deep blue under pale. The hair was great, she decided, pin straight with those jagged ends just past chin length. What Quinn knew would look messy on her came off fresh and stylish on the brunette.

Quinn debated catching her eye, trying a wave. She could ask Red Purse to join her for dinner. After all, who didn't hate to eat alone? Then she could pump her dinner companion for the really important details. Like where she got that bag.

Even as she charged up her smile, Quinn saw it.

It *slithered* across the glossy planks of the oak floor, leaving a hideous trail of bloody ooze behind it. At first she thought snake, then slug, then could barely think at all as she watched it slide up the legs of a table where an attractive young couple were enjoying cocktails by candlelight.

Its body, thick as a truck tire, mottled red over black, wound its way over the table, leaving that ugly smear on the snowy linen while the couple laughed and flirted.

A waitress walked briskly in, stepped in and through the sludge on the floor, to serve the couple their appetizers.

Quinn swore she could hear the table creak under its weight.

And its eyes when they met hers were the eyes of the boy, the red gleam in them bright and somehow *amused*. Then it began to wiggle wetly down the skirt of the tablecloth, and toward the brunette.

The woman stood frozen in place, her face bone white. Quinn pushed to her feet and, ignoring the surprised look from the waitress, leaped over the ugly path. She gripped the brunette's arm, pulled her out of the dining room.

"You saw it, too," Quinn said in a whisper. "You saw that thing. Let's get out of here."

"What? What?" The brunette cast shocked glances over her shoulder as she and Quinn stumbled for the door. "You saw it?"

"Sluggy, red-eyed, very nasty wake. Jesus. Jesus." She gulped in the raw February air on the hotel's porch. "They didn't see it, but you did. I did. Why is that? Fuck if I know, but I have an idea who might. That's my car right there. Let's go. Let's just go."

The brunette didn't say another word until they were in the car and Quinn was squealing away from the curb. "Who the hell are you?"

"Quinn. Quinn Black. I'm a writer, mostly on the spooky. Of which there is a surplus in this town. Who are you?"

"Layla Darnell. What *is* this place?"

"That's what I want to find out. I don't know if it's nice to meet you or not, Layla, under the circumstances."

"Same here. Where are we going?"

"To the source, or one of them." Quinn glanced over, saw Layla was still pale, still shaky. Who could blame her? "What are you doing in Hawkins Hollow?"

"I'm damned if I know, but I think I've decided to cut my visit short."

"Understandable. Nice bag, by the way."

Layla worked up a wan smile. "Thanks."

"Nearly there. Okay, you don't know why you're here, so where did you come from?"

"New York."

"I knew it. It's the polish. Do you love it?"

"Ah." Layla combed her fingers through her hair as she swiveled to look back. "Most of the time. I manage a boutique in SoHo. Did. Do. I don't know that anymore either."

Nearly there, Quinn thought again. *Let's keep calm.* "I bet you get great discounts."

"Yeah, part of the perks. Have you seen anything like that before. Like that *thing*?"

"Yeah. Have you?"

"Not when I was awake. I'm not crazy," Layla stated. "Or I am, and so are you."

"We're not crazy, which is what crazy people tend to say, so you'll just have to take my word." She swung onto Cal's lane, and aimed the car over the little bridge toward the house where lights—thank God—glowed in the windows.

"Whose house is this?" Layla gripped the front edge of her seat. "Who lives here?"

"Caleb Hawkins. His ancestors founded the town. He's okay. He knows about what we saw."

"How?"

"It's a long story, with a lot of holes in it. And now you're thinking, what am I doing in this car with a complete stranger who's telling me to go into this house pretty much in the middle of nowhere."

Layla took firm hold on the short strap of her bag, as if she might use it as a weapon. "The thought's crossed."

"Your instinct put you in the car with me, Layla. Maybe you could follow along with that for the next step. Plus, it's cold. We didn't bring our coats."

"All right. Yes, all right." With a bracing breath, Layla opened the door, and with Quinn walked toward the house. "Nice place. If you like isolated houses in the woods."

"Culture shock for the New Yorker."

"I grew up in Altoona, Pennsylvania."

"No kidding. Philadelphia. We're practically neighbors." Quinn knocked briskly on the door, then just opened the door and called in, "Cal!"

She was halfway across the living room when he hurried in. "Quinn? What?" Spotted Layla. "Hello. What?"

"Who's here?" Quinn demanded. "I saw another car in the drive."

"Fox. What's going on?"

"The bonus-round question." She sniffed. "Do I smell

fried chicken? Is there food? Layla—this is Layla Darnell, Layla, Cal Hawkins—Layla and I haven't had dinner."

She moved right by him, and walked toward the kitchen.

"I'm sorry, I think, to bust in on you," Layla began. It passed through her mind that he didn't look like a serial killer. But then again, how would she know? "I don't know what's happening, or why I'm here. I've had a confusing few days."

"Okay. Well, come on back."

Quinn already had a drumstick in her hand, and was taking a swig of Cal's beer. "Layla Darnell, Fox O'Dell. I'm not really in the mood for beer," she said to Cal. "I was about to order some wine when Layla and I were disgustingly interrupted. Got any?"

"Yeah. Yeah."

"Is it decent? If you run to jug or twist caps, I'll stick with beer."

"I've got some damn decent wine." He yanked a plate out, pushed it at her. "Use a plate."

"He's completely Sally about things like that," Fox told her. He'd risen, and pulled out a chair. "You look a little shaken up—Layla, right? Why don't you sit down?"

She just couldn't believe psycho killers sat around a pretty kitchen eating bucket chicken and debating wine over beer. "Why don't I? I'm probably not really here." She sat, dropped her head in her hands. "I'm probably in some padded room imagining all this."

"Imagining all what?" Fox asked.

"Why don't I take it?" Quinn glanced at Layla as Cal got out wineglasses. "Then you can fill in as much of your own backstory as you want."

"Fine. That's fine."

"Layla checked into the hotel this morning. She's from New York. Just a bit ago, I was in the hotel dining room, considering ordering the green salad and the haddock, along with a nice glass of white. Layla was just coming in, I assume, to have her own dinner. I was going to ask you to join me, by the way."

"Oh. Ah, that's nice."

"Before I could issue the invite, what I'd describe as a sluglike creature thicker than my aunt Christine's thigh and about four feet in length oozed its way across the dining room, up over the table where a couple happily continued their dining foreplay, then oozed down again, leaving a revolting smear of God-knows-what behind it. She saw it."

"It looked at me. It looked right at me," Layla whispered.

"Don't be stingy with the wine, Cal." Quinn stepped over to rub a hand on Layla's shoulder. "We were the only ones who saw it, and no longer wishing to dine at the hotel, and believing Layla felt the same, we booked. And I'm now screwing my caloric intake for the day with this drumstick."

"You're awfully . . . blithe. Thanks." Layla accepted the wineglass Cal offered, then drank half the contents at one go.

"Not really. Defense mechanism. So here we are, and I want to know if either of you have ever seen anything like I just described."

There was a moment of silence, then Cal picked up his beer, drank. "We've seen a lot of things. The bigger question for me is, why are you seeing them, and part two, why are you seeing them now?"

"Got a theory."

Cal turned to Fox. "Such as?"

"Connections. You said yourself there had to be some connection for Quinn to see it, to have the dream—"

"Dreams." Layla's head came up. "You've had dreams?"

"And so, apparently, have you," Fox continued. "So we'll connect Layla. Figuring out how they're connected may take a while, but let's just go with the hypothesis that they are, and say, what if. What if, due to this connection, due to Quinn, then Layla being in the Hollow, particularly during the seventh year, gives it some kind of psychic boost? Gives it the juice to manifest?"

"That's not bad," Cal replied.

"I'd say it's damn good." Quinn cocked her head as she considered. "Energy. Most paranormal activity stems from energy. The energy the . . . well, entity or entities, the actions, the emotions thereof, leave behind, and the energy of the people within its sphere, let's say. And we could speculate that this psychic energy has built over time, strengthened, so that now, with the addition of other connected energies, it's able to push out into our reality, to some extent, outside of its traditional time frame."

"What in God's name are you people talking about?" Layla demanded.

"We'll get to that, I promise." Quinn offered her a bolstering smile. "Why don't you eat something, settle the nerves?"

"I think it's going to be a while before food holds any appeal for me."

"Mr. Slug slimed right over the bread bowl," Quinn explained. "It was pretty damn gross. Sadly, nothing puts me off food." She snagged a couple of cold fries. "So, if we run with Fox's theory, where is its counterpoint? The good to its bad, the white to its dark. All my research on this points to both sides."

"Maybe it can't pull out yet, or it's hanging back."

"Or the two of you connect to the dark, and not the light," Cal added.

Quinn narrowed her eyes at him, with something glinting between her lashes. Then she shrugged. "Insulting, but unarguable at this time. Except for the fact that, logically, if we were more a weight on the bad side, why is said bad side trying to scare the living daylights out of us?"

"Good point," Cal conceded.

"I want some answers."

Quinn nodded at Layla. "I bet you do."

"I want some serious, sensible answers."

"Thumbnail: The town includes an area in the woods known as the Pagan Stone. Bad stuff happened there. Gods, demons, blood, death, fire. I'm going to lend you a couple of books on the subject. Centuries pass, then something opened it up again. Since 1987, for seven nights in July, every seventh year, it comes out to play. It's mean, it's ugly, and it's powerful. We're getting a preview."

Gratefully, Layla held out her glass for more wine as she studied Quinn. "Why haven't I ever heard of this? Or this place?"

"There have been some books, some articles, some reports—but most of them hit somewhere between alien abductions and sightings of Bigfoot," Quinn explained. "There's never been a serious, thorough, fully researched account published. That's going to be my job."

"All right. Say I believe all this, and I'm not sure I'm not just having the mother of all hallucinations, why you, and you?" she said to Fox and Cal. "Where do you come in?"

"Because we're the ones who opened it," Fox told her. "Cal, me, and a friend who's currently absent. Twenty-one years ago this July."

"But you'd have been kids. You'd have had to have been—"

"Ten," Cal confirmed. "We share a birthday. It was our tenth birthday. Now, we showed some of ours. How about seeing some of yours. Why did you come here?"

"Fair enough." Layla took another slow sip of her wine. Whether it was that or the brightly lit kitchen with a dog snoring under the table or just having a group of strangers who were likely to believe what she was about to tell them, her nerves were steadier.

"I've been having dreams for the last several nights. Nightmares or night terrors. Sometimes I'd wake up in my bed, sometimes I'd wake up trying to get out the door of my apartment. You said blood and fire. There was both in the dreams, and a kind of altar in a clearing in the woods. I think it was stone. And there was water, too. Black water. I was drowning in it. I was captain of the swim team in high school, and I was drowning."

She shuddered, took another breath. "I was afraid to sleep. I thought I heard voices even when I wasn't asleep. I couldn't understand them, but I'd be at work, doing my job, or stopping by the dry cleaners on the way home, and these voices would just *fill* my head. I thought I was having a breakdown. But why? Then I thought maybe I had a brain tumor. I even thought about making an appointment with a neurologist. Then last night, I took a sleeping pill. Maybe I could just drug my way out of it. But it came, and in the dream something was in bed with me."

Her breath trembled out this time. "Not my bed, but somewhere else. A small room, a small hot room with a tiny window. I was someone else. I can't explain it, really."

"You're doing fine," Quinn assured her.

"It was happening to me, but I wasn't me. I had long hair, and the shape of my body, it was different. I was wearing a long nightgown. I know because it . . . it pulled it up. It was touching me. It was cold, it was so cold. I couldn't scream, I couldn't fight, even when it raped me. It was inside me, but I couldn't see, I couldn't move. I felt it, all of it, as if it were happening, but I couldn't stop it."

She wasn't aware of the tears until Fox pressed a napkin into her hand. "Thanks. When it was over, when it was gone, there was a voice in my head. Just one voice this time, and it calmed me, it made me warm again and took away the pain. It said: 'Hawkins Hollow.' "

"Layla, were you raped?" Fox spoke very quietly. "When you came out of the dream, was there any sign you'd been raped?"

"No." She pressed her lips together, kept her gaze on his face. His eyes were golden brown, and full of compassion. "I woke up in my own bed, and I made myself go . . . check. There was nothing. It hurt me, so there would've been bruises, there would've been marks, but there was nothing. It was early in the morning, not quite four in the morning, and I kept thinking Hawkins Hollow. So I packed, and I took a cab out to the airport to rent a car. Then I drove here. I've never been here."

She paused to look at Quinn now, at Cal. "I've never heard of Hawkins Hollow that I can remember, but I *knew* what roads to take. I knew how to get here, and how to get to the hotel. I checked in this morning, went up to the room they gave me, and I slept like the dead until nearly six. When I walked into the dining room and saw that thing, I thought I was still asleep. Dreaming again."

"It's a wonder you didn't bolt," Quinn commented.

Layla sent her an exhausted look. "To where?"

"There's that." Quinn put a hand on Layla's shoulder, rubbing gently as she spoke. "I think we all need as much information as there is to be had, from every source there is. I think, from this point, it's share and share alike, one for goddamn all and all for goddamn one. You don't like that," she said with a nod toward Cal, "but I think you're going to have to get used to it."

"You've been in this for days. Fox and I have lived with it for years. Lived *in* it. So, don't put on your badge and call yourself captain yet, Blondie."

"Living in it for twenty-one years gives you certain advantages. But you haven't figured it out, you haven't stopped it or even identified it, as far as I can tell, in your twenty-one-year experience. So loosen up."

"You poked at my ninety-seven-year-old great-grandmother today."

"Oh, bull. Your remarkable and fascinating ninety-seven-year-old great-grandmother came up to where I was researching in the library, sat down, and had a conversation with me of her own free will. There was no poking. My keen observation skills tell me you didn't inherit your tight-ass tendencies from her."

"Kids, kids." Fox held up a hand. "Tense situation, agreed, but we're all on the same side, or are on the same side potentially. So chill. Cal, Quinn makes a good point, and it bears consideration. At the same time, Quinn, you've been in the Hollow a couple of days, and Layla less than that. You're going to have to be patient, and accept the fact that some areas of information are more sensitive than others, and may take time to be offered. Even if we start with what can and has been corroborated or documented—"

"What are you, a lawyer?" Layla asked.

"Yeah."

"Figures," she said under her breath.

"Let's just table this," Cal suggested. "Let's let it sit, so we can all think about it for the night. I said I'd take you to the Pagan Stone tomorrow, and I will. Let's see how it goes."

"Accepted."

"Are you two all right at the hotel? You can stay here if you're not easy about going back."

The fact that he'd offered had Quinn's hackles smoothing down again. "We're not wimps, are we, Layla?"

"I wouldn't have said I was a few days ago. Now, I'm not so sure. But I'll be all right at the hotel." In fact, she wanted to go back, crawl into that big, soft bed and pull the covers over her head. "I slept better there than I have all week, so that's something."

Quinn decided she'd wait until they were back before she advised Layla to lower all the shades, and maybe leave a light burning.

Eight

IN THE MORNING, QUINN PRESSED AN EAR against the door to Layla's room. Since she heard the muted sounds of the *Today* show, she gave the door a knuckle rap. "It's Quinn," she added, in case Layla was still jumpy.

Layla opened the door in a pretty damn cute pair of purple-and-white-striped pajama pants and a purple sleep tank. There was color in her cheeks, and her quiet green eyes had the clarity that told Quinn she'd been awake awhile.

"I'm about to head out to Cal's. Mind if I come in a minute?"

"No." She stepped back. "I was trying to figure out what I'm supposed to do with myself today."

"You can come with me if you want."

"Into the woods? Not quite ready for that, thanks. You know . . ." Layla switched off the TV before dropping into a chair. "I was thinking about the wimp statement you made last night. I've never been a wimp, but it occurred to me as I was huddled in bed with the shades drawn and this stupid chair under the doorknob that I've never had anything happen that tested that before. My life's been pretty normal."

"You came here, and you're still here. So I'm thinking that puts you pretty low on the wimp scale. How'd you sleep?"

"Good. Once I got there, good. No dreams, no visitations, no bumps in the night. So, of course, now I'm wondering why."

"No dreams for me either." Quinn glanced around the room. Layla's bed was a sleigh style and the color scheme was muted greens and creams. "We could theorize that your room here's a safe zone, but that's off because mine isn't, and it's two doors down. It could be that whatever it is just took the night off. Maybe needed to recharge some expended energy."

"Happy thought."

"You've got my cell number, Cal's, Fox's. We've got yours. We're—connected. I wanted to let you know that the diner across the street, figuring you're not going to try the dining room here again, has a nice breakfast."

"I'm thinking I might try room service, and start on the books that you gave me last night. I didn't want to try them for bedtime reading."

"Wise. Okay. If you head out, it's a nice town. Some cute little shops, a little museum I haven't had time to explore so can't give you a rating, and there's always the Bowl-a-Rama."

A hint of a smile appeared around Layla's mouth. "Is there?"

"It's Cal's family's place. Interesting, and it feels like the hub of the town. So, I'll look you up when I get back?"

"Okay. Quinn?" Layla added as Quinn reached for the door. "Wimp scale or not, I'm not sure I'd still be here if I hadn't run into you."

"I know how you feel. I'll see you later."

CAL WAS WAITING FOR HER WHEN SHE DROVE UP. He stepped out, started down the steps, the dog wandering behind him, as she got out of the car. He took a scan, starting with her feet. Good, sturdy hiking boots that showed some scars and wear, faded jeans, tough jacket in I'm-Not-a-Deer red, and a multistriped scarf that matched the cloche-style cap on her head. Silly hat, he mused, that was unaccountably appealing on her.

In any case, he decided she knew what to wear on a hike through the winter woods.

"Do I pass muster, Sergeant?"

"Yeah." He came down the rest of the steps. "Let's start this off with me saying I was off base by a couple inches last night. I haven't completely resolved dealing with you, and now there's another person in the mix, another unknown. When you live with this as long as I have, part of you gets used to it, and other parts just get edgier. Especially when you're into the seventh year. So, I'll apologize, if you need it."

"Well. Wind, sails sucked out. Okay, I can't be pissed off after that or it's just bitchy instead of righteous. So let me say this. Before I came here, this was an idea for a book, a job I enjoy on a level some might consider twisted, and that I consider vastly fascinating. Now, it's more personal. While I can appreciate you being somewhat edgy, and somewhat proprietary, I'm bringing something important to the table. Experience and objectivity. And guts. I've got some impressive guts."

"I've noticed."

"So, we're going to do this thing?"

"Yeah, we're going to do it."

She gave the dog who came over to lean on her a rub. "Is Lump seeing us off on our adventure?"

"He's coming. He likes to walk in the woods when the mood strikes. And if he's had enough, he'll just lie down and sleep until he's in the mood to walk back home again."

"Strikes me as a sensible attitude." She picked up a small pack, hitched it on, then drew her tape recorder out of her pocket. It was attached to the pocket with a small clamp. "I'm going to want to record observations, and whatever you tell me. Okay with that?"

"Yeah." He'd given it a lot of thought overnight. "I'm okay with that."

"Then I'm ready when you are, Tonto."

"Trail's going to be sloppy," he said as they started toward the woods. "Given that, from this point it'll take about two hours—a little more depending—to reach the clearing."

"I'm in no hurry."

Cal glanced up at the sky. "You will be if the weather turns, or anything holds us up after sundown."

She clicked on her recorder, and hoped she'd been generous enough with her cache of extra tapes and batteries. "Why?"

"Years back people hiked or hunted in this section of the woods routinely. Now they don't. People got lost, turned around, spooked. Some reported hearing what they thought were bear or wolves. We don't have wolves and it's rare for bear to come this far down the mountains. Kids, teens mostly, used to sneak in to swim in Hester's Pool in the summer, or to screw around. Now they don't. People used to say the pool was haunted, it was kind of a local legend. Now, people don't like to talk about it."

"Do you think it's haunted?"

"I know there's something in it. I saw it myself. We'll talk about that once we get to the pool. No point in going into it now."

"All right. Is this the way the three of you came in on your birthday twenty-one years ago?"

"We came in from the east." He gestured. "Track closest to town. This way's shorter, but it would've been a longer ride around for us from town. There wasn't anything . . . off about it, until we got to the pool."

"Have the three of you been back together since that night?"

"Yeah, we went back. More than once." He glanced toward her. "I can tell you that going back anytime near the Seven isn't an experience I look forward to repeating."

"The Seven?"

"That's what we call the week in July."

"Tell me more about what happens during the Seven."

It was time to do just that, he thought. To say it straightout to someone who wanted to know. To someone, maybe, who was part of the answer.

"People in the Hollow get mean, violent, even murderous. They do things they'd never do at any other time. Destroy property, beat the hell out of each other, start fires. Worse."

"Murders, suicides."

"Yeah. After the week's up, they don't remember clearly. It's like watching someone come out of a trance, or a long illness. Some of them are never the same. Some of them leave town. And some fix up their shop or their house, and just go on. It doesn't hit everyone, and it doesn't hit those it does all in the same way. The best I can explain is it's like a mass psychotic episode, and it gets stronger each time."

"What about the police?"

Out of habit, Cal reached down, picked up a stick. There was no point in tossing it for Lump, that would only embarrass them both. So he held it down so Lump could take it into his mouth and plod contentedly along.

"Chief Larson was in charge last time. He was a good man, went to school with my father. They were friends. The third night, he locked himself in his office. I think he, some part of him anyway, knew what was happening to him, and didn't want to risk going home to his wife and kids. One of the deputies, guy named Wayne Hawbaker, nephew to Fox's secretary, came in looking for him, needed help. He heard Larson crying in the office. Couldn't get him to come out. By the time Wayne knocked down the door, Larson had shot himself. Wayne's chief of police now. He's a good man, too."

How much loss had he seen? Quinn wondered. How many losses had he suffered since his tenth birthday? And yet he was walking back into these woods, back where it all began for him. She didn't think she'd ever known a braver stand.

"What about the county cops, the state cops?"

"It's like we're cut off for that week." A cardinal winged by, boldly red, carelessly free. "Sometimes people get out, sometimes they get in, but by and large, we're on our own. It's like . . ." He groped for words. "It's like this veil comes down, and nobody sees, not clearly. Help doesn't come, and after, nobody questions it too closely. Nobody looks straight on at what happened, or why. So it ends up being lore, or *Blair Witch* stuff. Then it fades off until it happens again."

"You stay, and you look at it straight on."

"It's my town," he said simply.

No, Quinn thought, *that* was the bravest stand she'd ever known.

"How'd you sleep last night?" he asked her.

"Dreamlessly. So did Layla. You?"

"The same. Always before, once it started, it didn't stop. But then, things are different this time around."

"Because I saw something, and so did Layla."

"That's the big one. And it's never started this early, or this strong." As they walked, he studied her face. "Have you ever had a genealogy done?"

"No. You think we're related back when, or I'm related to someone who was involved in whatever happened at the Pagan Stone way back when?"

"I think, we've always thought, this was about blood." Absently, he glanced at the scar on his wrist. "So far, knowing or sensing that hasn't done any good. Where are your ancestors from?"

"England primarily, some Irish tossed in."

"Mine, too. But then a lot of Americans have English ancestry."

"Maybe I should start researching and find out if there are any Dents or Twisses in my lineage?" She shrugged when he frowned at her. "Your great-grandmother sent me down that path. Have you tried to trace them? Giles Dent and Lazarus Twisse?"

"Yeah. Dent may be an ancestor, if he did indeed father the three sons of Ann Hawkins. There's no record of him. And other than accounts from the time, some old family letters and diaries, no Giles Dent on anything we've dug up. No record of birth, death. Same for Twisse. They could've dropped down from Pluto as far as we've been able to prove."

"I have a friend who's a whiz on research. I sent her a heads-up. And don't get that look on your face again. I've known her for years, and we've worked together on other projects. I don't know as yet if she can or will come in on this, but trust me, if she does you'll be grateful. She's brilliant."

Rather than respond, he chewed on it. How much of his resistance was due to this feeling of losing control over the situation? And had he ever had any control to begin with? Some, he knew, was due to the fact that the more people who became involved, the more people he felt responsible for.

And maybe most of all, how much was all this exposure going to affect the town?

"The Hollow's gotten some publicity over the years, focused on this whole thing. That's how you found out about us to begin with. But it's been mild, and for the most part, hasn't done much more than bring interested tourists through. With your involvement, and now potentially two others, it could turn the Hollow into some sort of lurid or ridiculous caption in the tourist guides."

"You knew that was a risk when you agreed to talk to me."

She was keeping pace with him, stride-by-stride on the sloppy ground. And, she was striding into the unknown without a quake or a quiver. "You'd have come whether or not I agreed."

"So part of your cooperation is damage control." She nodded. "Can't blame you. But maybe you should be thinking bigger picture, Cal. More people invested means more brains and more chance of figuring out how to stop what's been happening. Do you want to stop it?"

"More than I can possibly tell you."

"I want a story. There's no point in bullshitting you about that. But I want to stop it, too. Because despite my famous guts, this thing scares me. Better shot at that, it seems to me, if we work together and utilize all our resources. Cybil's one of mine, and she's a damn good one."

"I'll think about it." For now, he thought, he'd given her enough. "Why don't you tell me what made you head down the woo-woo trail, writing-wise."

"That's easy. I always liked spooky stuff. When I was a kid and had a choice between say, *Sweet Valley High* or Stephen King, King was always going to win. I used to write my own horror stories and give my friends nightmares. Good times," she said and made him laugh. "Then, the turning point, I suppose, was when I went into this reputed haunted house with a group of friends. Halloween. I was twelve. Big dare. Place was falling down and due to be demolished. We were probably lucky we didn't fall through floorboards. So we poked around, squealed, scared ourselves and had some laughs. Then I saw her."

"Who?"

"The ghost, of course." She gave him a friendly elbow poke. "Keep up. None of the others did. But I saw her, walking down the stairs. There was blood all over her. She looked at me," Quinn said quietly now. "It seemed like she looked right at me, and walked right by. I felt the cold she carried with her."

"What did you do? And if I get a guess, I'm guessing you followed her."

"Of course, I followed her. My friends were running around, making spooky noises, but I followed her into the falling-down kitchen, down the broken steps to the basement by the beam of my Princess Leia flashlight. No cracks."

"How can I crack when I had a Luke Skywalker flashlight?"

"Good. What I found were a lot of spiderwebs, mouse droppings, dead bugs, and a filthy floor of concrete. Then the concrete was gone and it was just a dirt floor with a hole—a grave—dug in it. A black-handled shovel beside it. She went to it, looked at me again, then slid down, hell, like a woman might slide into a nice bubble bath. Then I was standing on the concrete floor again."

"What did you do?"

"Your guess?"

"I'd guess you and Leia got the hell out of there."

"Right again. I came out of the basement like a rocket. I told my friends, who didn't believe me. Just trying to spook them out as usual. I didn't tell anyone else, because if I had, our parents would have known we were in the house and we'd have been grounded till our Social Security kicked in. But when they demolished the house, started jackhammering the concrete floor, they found her. She'd been in there since the thirties. The wife of the guy who'd owned the house had claimed she'd run off. He was dead by then, so nobody could ask him how or why he'd done it. But I knew. From the time I saw her until they found her bones, I dreamed about her murder, I saw it happen.

"I didn't tell anyone. I was too afraid. Ever since, I've told what I find, confirming or debunking. Maybe partly to make it up to Mary Bines—that was her name. And partly because I'm not twelve anymore, and nobody's going to ground me."

He said nothing for a long time. "Do you always see what happened?"

"I don't know if it's seeing or just intuiting, or just my imagination, which is even more far-famed than my guts. But I've learned to trust what I feel, and go with it."

He stopped, gestured. "This is where the tracks cross.

We came in from that direction, picked up the cross trail here. We were loaded down. My mother had packed a picnic basket, thinking we were camping out on Fox's family farm. We had his boom box, his load from the market, our backpacks full of the stuff we figured we couldn't live without. We were still nine years old. Kids, pretty much fearless. That all changed before we came out of the woods again."

When he started to walk once more, she put a hand on his arm, squeezed. "Is that tree bleeding, or do you just have really strange sap in this part of the world?"

He turned, looked. Blood seeped from the bark of the old oak, and seeped into the soggy ground at its trunk.

"That kind of thing happens now and again. It puts off the hikers."

"I bet." She watched Lump plod by the tree after only a cursory sniff. "Why doesn't he care?"

"Old hat to him."

She started to give the tree a wide berth, then stopped. "Wait, wait. This is the spot. This is the spot where I saw the deer across the path. I'm sure of it."

"He called it, with magic. The innocent and pure."

She started to speak, then looking at Cal's face, held her tongue. His eyes had darkened; his cheeks had paled.

"Its blood for the binding. Its blood, his blood, the blood of the dark thing. He grieved when he drew the blade across its neck, and its life poured onto his hands and into the cup."

As his head swam, Cal bent over from the waist. Prayed he wouldn't be sick. "Need a second to get my breath."

"Take it easy." Quickly, Quinn pulled off her pack and pulled out her water bottle. "Drink a little."

Most of the queasiness passed when she took his hand, pressed the bottle into it. "I could see it, *feel* it. I've gone by this tree before, even when it's bled, and I never saw that. Or felt that."

"Two of us this time. Maybe that's what opened it up."

He drank slowly. Not just two, he thought. He'd walked this path with Fox and Gage. We two, he decided. Something about being here with her. "The deer was a sacrifice."

"I get that. *Devoveo*. He said it in Latin. Blood sacrifice. White witchery doesn't ascribe to that. He had to cross over the line, smear on some of the black to do what he felt he needed to do. Was it Dent? Or someone who came long before him?"

"I don't know."

Because she could see his color was eking back, her own heart rate settled. "Do you see what came before?"

"Bits, pieces, flashes. Not all of it. I generally come back a little sick. If I push for more, it's a hell of a lot worse."

"Let's not push then. Are you okay to go on?"

"Yeah. Yeah." His stomach was still mildly uneasy, but the light-headedness had passed. "We'll be coming to Hester's Pool soon."

"I know. I'm going to tell you what it looks like before we get there. I'm telling you I've never been there before, not in reality, but I've seen it, and I stood there night before last. There are cattails and wild grass. It's off the path, through some brush and thorny stuff. It was night, so the water looked black. Opaque. Its shape isn't quite round, not really oval. It's more of a fat crescent. There were a lot of rocks. Some more like boulders, some no more than pebbles. She filled her pockets with them—they looked to be about hand-sized or smaller—until her pockets were sagging with the weight. Her hair was cut short, like it'd been hacked at, and her eyes looked mad."

"Her body didn't stay down, not according to reports."

"I've read them," Quinn acknowledged. "She was found floating in the pool, which came to bear her name, and because it was suicide, they buried her in unconsecrated ground. Records I've dug up so far don't indicate what happened to the infant daughter she left behind."

Before replacing the pack, she took out a bag of trail mix. Opened it, offered. Cal shook his head. "There's plenty of bark and twigs around if I get that desperate."

"This isn't bad. What did your mother pack for you that day?"

"Ham-and-cheese sandwiches, hard-boiled eggs, apple slices, celery and carrot sticks, oatmeal cookies, lemonade." Remembering made him smile. "Pop-Tarts, snack pack cereal for breakfast."

"Uppercase *M* Mom."

"Yeah, always has been."

"How long do we date before I meet the parents?"

He considered. "They want me to come for dinner some night soon if you want in."

"A home-cooked meal by Mom? I'm there. How does she feel about all this?"

"It's hard for them, all of this is hard. And they've never let me down in my life."

"You're a lucky man, Cal."

He broke trail, skirting the tangles of blackberry bushes, and following the more narrow and less-trod path. Lump moved on ahead, as if he understood where they were headed. The first glint of the pool brought a chill down his spine. But then, it always did.

Birds still called, and Lump—more by accident than design, flushed a rabbit that ran across the path and into another thicket. Sunlight streamed through the empty branches onto the leaf-carpeted ground. And glinted dully on the brown water of Hester's Pool.

"It looks different during the day," Quinn noted. "Not nearly as ominous. But I'd have to be very young and very hot to want to go splashing around in that."

"We were both. Fox went in first. We'd snuck out here before to swim, but I'd never much liked it. Who knew what was swimming under there? I always thought Hester's bony hand was going to grab my ankle and pull me under. Then it did."

Quinn's eyebrows shot up, and when he didn't continue, she sat on one of the rocks. "I'm listening."

"Fox was messing with me. I was a better swimmer, but he was sneaky. Gage couldn't swim for crap, but he was game. I thought it was Fox again, dunking me, but it was her. I saw her when I went under. Her hair wasn't short the way you saw her. I remember how her hair streamed out. She didn't look like a ghost. She looked like a woman. Girl," he corrected. "I realized when I got older she was just a girl. I couldn't get out fast enough, and I made Fox and Gage get out. They hadn't seen anything."

"But they believed you."

"That's what friends do."

"Did you ever go back in?"

"Twice. But I never saw her again."

Quinn gave Lump, who wasn't as particular as his master, a handful of trail mix. "It's too damn cold to try now, but come June, I'd like to take a dip and see what happens." She munched some mix as she looked around. "It's a nice spot, considering. Primitive, but still picturesque. Seems like a great place for three boys to run a little wild."

She cocked her head. "So do you usually bring your women here on dates?"

"You'd be the first."

"Really? Is that because they haven't been interested, or you haven't wanted to answer questions pertaining."

"Both."

"So I'm breaking molds here, which is one of my favorite hobbies." Quinn stared out over the water. "She must've been so sad, so horribly sad to believe there was no other way for her. Crazy's a factor, too, but I think she must've been weighed down by sadness and despair before she weighed herself down with rocks. That's what I felt in the dream, and it's what I feel now, sitting here. Her horrible, heavy sadness. Even more than the fear when it raped her."

She shuddered, rose. "Can we move on? It's too much, sitting here. It's too much."

It would be worse, he thought. If she felt already, sensed or understood this already, it would be worse. He took her hand to lead her back to the path. Since, at least for the moment, it was wide enough to walk abreast, he kept ahold of her hand. It almost seemed as if they were taking a simple walk in the winter woods.

"Tell me something surprising about you. Something I'd never guess."

He cocked his head. "Why would I tell you something about me you'd never guess?"

"It doesn't have to be some dark secret." She bumped her hip against his. "Just something unexpected."

"I lettered in track and field."

Quinn shook her head. "Impressive, but not surprising. I might've guessed that. You've got a yard or so of leg."

"All right, all right." He thought it over. "I grew a pumpkin that broke the county record for weight."

"The fattest pumpkin in the history of the county?"

"It missed the state record by ounces. It got written up in the paper."

"Well, that is surprising. I was hoping for something a bit more salacious, but am forced to admit, I'd never have guessed you held the county record for fattest pumpkin."

"How about you?"

"I'm afraid I've never grown a pumpkin of any size or weight."

"Surprise me."

"I can walk on my hands. I'd demonstrate, but the ground's not conducive to hand-walking. Come on. You wouldn't have guessed that."

"You're right. I will, however, insist on a demo later. I, after all, have documentation of the pumpkin."

"Fair enough."

She kept up the chatter, light and silly enough to make him laugh. He wasn't sure he'd laughed along this path since that fateful hike with his friends. But it seemed natural enough now, with the sun beaming down through the trees, the birds singing.

Until he heard the growl.

She'd heard it, too. He couldn't think of another reason her voice would have stopped so short, or her hand would have gripped his arm like a vise. "Cal—"

"Yeah, I hear it. We're nearly there. Sometimes it makes noise, sometimes it makes an appearance." Never this time of year, he thought, as he hitched up the back of his jacket. But these, apparently, were different times. "Just stay close."

"Believe me, I . . ." Her voice trailed off this time as he drew the large, jagged-edged hunting knife. "Okay. Okay. Now *that* would have been one of those unexpected things about you. That you, ah, carry a Crocodile Dundee around."

"I don't come here unarmed."

She moistened her lips. "And you probably know how to use it, if necessary."

He shot her a look. "I probably do. Do you want to keep going, or do you want to turn around and go back?"

"I'm not turning tail."

He could hear it rustling in the brush, could hear the slide of mud underfoot. Stalking them, he thought. He imagined the knife was as useless as a few harsh words if the thing meant business, but he felt better with it in his hand.

"Lump doesn't hear it," Quinn murmured, lifting her chin to where the dog slopped along the path a few feet ahead. "Even he can't be that lazy. If he heard it, scented it, he'd show some concern. So it's not real." She took a slow breath. "It's just show."

"Not real to him, anyway."

When the thing howled, Cal took her firmly by the arm and pulled her through the edge of the trees into the clearing where the Pagan Stone speared up out of the muddy earth.

"I guess, all things considered, I was half expecting something along the lines of the king stone from Stonehenge." Quinn stepped away from Cal to circle the stone.

"It's amazing enough though, when you take a good look, the way it forms a table, or altar. How flat and smooth the top is." She laid her hand on it. "It's warm," she added. "Warmer than stone should be in a February wood."

He put his hand beside hers. "Sometimes it's cold." He fit the knife back into its sheath. "Nothing to worry about when it's warm. So far." He shoved his sleeve back, examined the scar on his wrist. "So far," he repeated.

Without thinking, he laid his hand over hers. "As long as—"

"It's heating up! Feel that? Do you feel that?"

She shifted, started to place her other hand on the stone. He moved, felt himself move as he might have through that wall of fire. Madly.

He gripped her shoulders, spinning her around until her back was pressed to the stone. Then sated the sudden, desperate appetite by taking her mouth.

For an instant, he was someone else, as was she, and the moment was full of grieving desperation. Her taste, her skin, the beat of her heart.

Then he was himself, feeling Quinn's lips heat under his as the stone had heated under their hands. It was her body quivering against his, and her fingers digging into his hips.

He wanted more, wanted to shove her onto the table of rock, to cover her with his body, to surround himself with all she was.

Not him, he thought dimly, or not entirely him. And so he made himself pull back, forced himself to break that connection.

The air wavered a moment. "Sorry," he managed. "Not altogether sorry, but—"

"Surprised." Her voice was hoarse. "Me, too. That was definitely unexpected. Made me dizzy," she whispered. "That's not a complaint. It wasn't us, then it was." She took another steadying breath. "Call me a slut, but I liked it both ways." With her eyes on his, she placed her hand on the stone again. "Want to try it again?"

"I think I'm still a man, so damn right I do. But I don't think it'd be smart, or particularly safe. Plus, I don't care for someone—something—else yanking on my hormones. Next time I kiss you, it's just you and me."

"All right. Connections." She nodded. "I'm more in favor than ever about the theory regarding connections. Could be blood, could be a reincarnation thing. It's worth exploring."

She sidestepped away from the stone, and him. "So, no more contact with each other and that thing for the time being. And let's take it back to the purpose at hand."

"Are you okay?"

"Stirred me up, I'll admit. But no harm, no foul." She took out her water bottle, and this time drank deep.

"I wanted you. Both ways."

Lowering the bottle, she met those calm gray eyes. She'd just gulped down water, she thought, but now her throat was dry again. "I know. What I don't know is if that's going to be a problem."

"It's going to be a problem. I'm not going to care about that."

Her pulse gave a couple of quick jumps. "Ah . . . This probably isn't the place to—"

"No, it's not." He took a step forward, but didn't touch her. And still her skin went hot. "There's going to be another place."

"Okay." She cleared her throat. "All right. To work."

She did another circle while he watched her. He'd made her a little jumpy. He didn't mind that. In fact, he considered it a point for his side. Something might have pushed him to kiss her that way, but he knew what he'd felt as that *something* released its grip. He knew what he'd been feeling since she'd stepped out of her car at the top of his lane.

Plain and simple lust. Caleb Hawkins for Quinn Black.

"You camped here, the three of you, that night." Apparently taking Cal at his word about the safety of the area,

Quinn moved easily around the clearing. "You—if I have any understanding of young boys—ate junk food, ragged on each other, maybe told ghost stories."

"Some. We also drank the beer Gage stole from his father, and looked at the skin mags he'd swiped."

"Of course, though I'd have pegged those activities for more like twelve-year-olds."

"Precocious." He ordered himself to stop thinking about her, to take himself back. "We built a fire. We had the boom box on. It was a pretty night, still hot, but not oppressive. And it was our night. It was, we thought, our place. Sacred ground."

"So your great-grandmother said."

"It called for ritual." He waited for her to turn to him. "We wrote down words. Words we made. We swore an oath, and at midnight, I used my Boy Scout knife to cut our wrists. We said the words we'd made and pressed our wrists together to mix the blood. To make us blood brothers. And hell opened up."

"What happened?"

"I don't know, not exactly. None of us do, not that we can remember. There was a kind of explosion. It seemed like one. The light was blinding, and the force of it knocked me back. Lifted me right off my feet. Screams, but I've never known if they were mine, Fox's, Gage's, or something else. The fire shot straight up, there seemed to be fire everywhere, but we weren't burned. Something *pushed* out, pushed into me. Pain, I remember pain. Then I saw some kind of dark mass rising out, and felt the cold it brought with it. Then it was over, and we were alone, scared, and the ground was scorched black."

Ten years old, she thought. Just a little boy. "How did you get out?"

"We hiked out the next morning pretty much as we'd hiked in. Except for a few changes. I came into this clearing when I was nine. I was wearing glasses. I was nearsighted."

Her brows rose. "Was?"

"Twenty-one hundred in my left eye, twenty-ninety in my right. I walked out ten, and twenty-twenty. None of us had a mark on him when we left, though Gage especially had some wounds he brought in with him. Not one of us has been sick a day since that night. If we're injured, it heals on its own."

There was no doubt on her face, only interest with a touch, he thought, of fascination. It struck him that other than his family she was the only one who knew. Who believed.

"You were given some sort of immunity."

"You could call it that."

"Do you feel pain?"

"Damn right. I came out with perfect vision, not X-ray. And the healing can hurt like a mother, but it's pretty quick. I can see things that happened before, like out on the trail. Not all the time, not every time, but I can see events of the past."

"A reverse clairvoyance."

"When it's on. I've seen what happened here on July seventh, sixteen fifty-two."

"What happened here, Cal?"

"The demon was bound under the stone. And Fox, Gage, and I, we cut the bastard loose."

She moved to him. She wanted to touch him, to soothe that worry from his face, but was afraid to. "If you did, you weren't to blame."

"Blame and responsibility aren't much different."

The hell with it. She laid her hands on his cheeks even when he flinched. Then touched her lips gently to his. "That was normal. You're responsible because, to my mind, you're willing to take responsibility. You've stayed when a lot of other men would've walked, if not run, away from here. So I say there's a way to beat it back where it belongs. And I'm going to do whatever I can to help you do just that."

She opened her pack. "I'm going to take photos, some measurements, some notes, and ask a lot of annoying questions."

She'd shaken him. The touch, the words, the faith. He wanted to draw her in, hold on to her. Just hold on. Normal, she'd said, and looking at her now, he craved the bliss of normality.

Not the place, he reminded himself, and stepped back. "You've got an hour. We start back in an hour. We're going to be well out of the woods before twilight."

"No argument." This time, she thought, and went to work.

Nine

SHE SPENT A LOT OF TIME, TO CAL'S MIND, WANdering around, taking what appeared to be copious notes and a mammoth number of photographs with her tiny little digital, and muttering to herself.

He didn't see how any of that was particularly helpful, but since she seemed to be absorbed in it all, he sat under a tree with the snoring Lump and let her work.

There was no more howling, no more sense of anything stalking the clearing, or them. Maybe the demon had something else to do, Cal thought. Or maybe it was just hanging back, watching. Waiting.

Well, he was doing the same, he supposed. He didn't mind waiting, especially when the view was good.

It was interesting to watch her, to watch the way she moved. Brisk and direct one minute, slow and wandering the next. As if she couldn't quite make up her mind which approach to take.

"Have you ever had this analyzed?" she called out. "The stone itself? A scientific analysis?"

"Yeah. We took scrapings when we were teenagers, and took them to the geology teacher at the high school. It's limestone. Common limestone. And," he continued, anticipating her, "we took another sample a few years later, that Gage took to a lab in New York. Same results."

"Okay. Any objection if I take a sample, send it to a lab I've used, just for one more confirmation?"

"Help yourself." He started to hitch up a hip for his knife, but she was already taking a Swiss Army out of her pocket. He should've figured her for it. Still, it made him smile.

Most of the women he knew might have lipstick in their pocket, but wouldn't consider a Swiss Army. He was betting Quinn had both.

He watched her hands as she scraped stone dust into a Baggie she pulled out of her pack. A trio of rings circled two fingers and the thumb of her right hand to catch quick glints of the sun with the movement.

The glints brightened, beamed into his eyes.

The light changed, softened like a summer morning even as the air warmed and took on a weight of humidity. Leaves budded, unfurled, then burst into thick green on the trees, casting shade and light in patterns on the ground, on the stone.

On the woman.

Her hair was long and loose, the color of raw honey. Her face was sharp-featured with eyes long and tipped up slightly. She wore a long dress of dusky blue under a white apron. She moved with care, and still with grace, though her body was heavily pregnant. And she carried two pails across the clearing toward a little shed behind the stone.

As she walked she sang in a voice clear and bright as the summer morning.

All in a garden green where late I laid me down upon a bank of chamomile where I saw upon a style sitting, a country clown . . .

Hearing her, seeing her, Cal was filled with love so urgent, so ripe, he thought his heart might burst from it.

The man stepped through the door of the shed, and that love was illuminated on his face. The woman stopped, gave a knowing, flirtatious toss of her head, and sang as the man walked toward her.

. . . holding in his arms a comely country maid. Courting her with all his skill, working her unto his will. Thus to her he said, Kiss me in kindness, sweetheart.

She lifted her face, offered her lips. The man brushed them with his, and as her laugh burst like a shooting star, he took the pails from her, setting them on the ground before wrapping her in an embrace.

Have I not told you, you are not to carry water or wood? You carry enough.

His hands stroked over the mound of her belly, held there when hers covered them. *Our sons are strong and well. I will give you sons, my love, as bright and brave as their father. My love, my heart.* Now Cal saw the tears glimmer in those almond-shaped eyes. *Must I leave you?*

You will never leave me, not truly, nor I you. No tears. He kissed them away, and Cal felt the wrench of his own heart. *No tears.*

No. I swore an oath against them. So she smiled. *There is time yet. Soft mornings and long summer days. It is not death. You swear to me?*

It is not death. Come now. I will carry the water.

When they faded, he saw Quinn crouched in front of him, heard her saying his name sharply, repeatedly.

"You're back. You went somewhere. Your eyes . . . Your eyes go black and . . . *deep* is the only word I can think of when you go somewhere else. Where did you go, Cal?"

"She's not you."

"Okay." She'd been afraid to touch him before, afraid if she did she'd push them both into that somewhere else, or yank him back before he was done. Now she reached out to rest her hand on his knee. "I'm not who?"

"Whoever I was kissing. Started to, then it was you, but before, at first . . . Jesus." He clamped the heels of his hands at his temple. "Headache. Bitch of a headache."

"Lean back, close your eyes. I'll—"

"It'll pass in a minute. They always do. We're not them. It's not a reincarnation deal. It doesn't feel right. Sporadic possession maybe, which is bad enough."

"Who?"

"How the hell do I know?" His head screamed until he had to lower his head between his knees to fight off the sudden, acute nausea. "I'd draw you a damn picture if I could draw. Give me a minute."

Rising, Quinn went behind him and, kneeling, began to massage his neck, his shoulders.

"Okay, all right. Sorry. Christ. It's like having an electric drill inside my head, biting its way out through my temples. It's better. I don't know who they were. They didn't call each other by name. But best guess is Giles Dent and Ann Hawkins. They were obviously living here, and she was really, really pregnant. She was singing," he said and told her what he'd seen.

Quinn continued to rub his shoulders while she listened. "So they knew it was coming, and from what you say, he was sending her away before it did. Not death. That's interesting, and something to look into. But for now, I think you've had enough of this place. And so have I."

She sat on the ground then, hissed a breath out, sucked one in. "While you were out, let's say, it came back."

"Jesus Christ." He started to spring up, but she gripped his arm.

"It's gone. Let's just sit here until we both get our legs back under us. I heard it growling, and I spun around. You were taking a trip, and I quashed my first instinct to grab you, shake you out of it, in case doing that pulled me in with you."

"And we'd both be defenseless," he said in disgust.

"And now Mr. Responsibility is beating himself up because he didn't somehow see this coming, fight off the magickal forces so he could stay in the here and now and protect the girl."

Even with the headache, he could manage a cool, steely stare. "Something like that."

"Something like that is appreciated, even if it is annoying. I had my handy Swiss Army knife, which, while it isn't up to Jim Bowie standards, does include a nice corkscrew and tweezers, both of which you never know when you may need."

"Is that spunk? Are you being spunky?"

"I'm babbling until I level out and I'm nearly there. The thing is, it just circled, making its nasty 'I'll eat you, my pretty and your big, lazy dog, too.' Rustling, growling, snarling. But it didn't show itself. Then it stopped, and you came back."

"How long?"

"I don't know. I think just a couple minutes, though it seemed longer at the time. However long, I'm so ready to get gone. I hope to hell you can walk back, Cal, because strong and resilient as I am, there's no way I can carry you piggyback."

"I can walk."

"Good, then let's get the hell out of here, and when we get to civilization, Hawkins, you're buying me a really big drink."

They gathered their packs; Cal whistled Lump awake. As they started back he wondered why he hadn't told her of the bloodstone—the three pieces he, Fox, and Gage held. The three pieces that he now knew formed the stone in the amulet Giles Dent had worn when he'd lived at the Pagan Stone.

WHILE CAL AND QUINN WERE HIKING OUT OF Hawkins Wood, Layla was taking herself out for an aimless walk around town. It was odd to just let her feet choose any direction. During her years in New York she'd always had a specific destination, always had a specific task, or several specific tasks to accomplish within a particular time frame.

Now, she'd let the morning stretch out, and had accomplished no more than reading sections of a few of the odd books Quinn had left with her. She might have stayed right there, inside her lovely room, inside that safe zone as Quinn had termed it.

But she'd needed to get away from the books. In any case, it gave the housekeeper an opportunity to set the room to rights, she supposed. And gave herself an opportunity to take a real look at the town she'd been compelled to visit.

She didn't have the urge to wander into any of the shops, though she thought Quinn's assessment was on the mark. There were some very interesting possibilities.

But even window shopping made her feel guilty for leaving the staff of the boutique in the lurch. Taking off the way she had, barely taking the time to call in from the road to tell the owner she'd had a personal emergency and wouldn't be in for the next several days.

Personal emergency covered it, Layla decided.

And it could very well get her fired. Still, even knowing that, she couldn't go back, pick things up, forget what had happened.

She'd get another job if she had to. When and if, she'd find another. She had some savings, she had a cushion. If her boss couldn't cut her some slack, she didn't want that stupid job anyway.

And, oh God, she was already justifying being unemployed.

Don't think about it, she ordered herself. Don't think about that right this minute.

She didn't think about it, and didn't think twice when her feet decided to continue on beyond the shops. She couldn't have said why they wanted to stop at the base of the building. LIBRARY was carved into the stone lintel over the door, but the glossy sign read HAWKINS HOLLOW COMMUNITY CENTER.

Innocuous enough, she told herself. But when a chill danced over her skin she ordered her feet to keep traveling.

She considered going into the museum, but couldn't work up the interest. She thought about crossing the street to Salon A and whiling away some time with a manicure, but simply didn't care about the state of her nails.

Tired and annoyed with herself, she nearly turned around and headed back. But the sign that caught her eye this time drew her forward.

FOX O'DELL, ATTORNEY AT LAW.

At least he was someone she knew—more or less. The hot lawyer with the compassionate eyes. He was probably busy with a client or out of the office, but she didn't care. Going in was something to do other than wander around feeling sorry for herself.

She stepped into the attractive, homespun reception area. The woman behind the gorgeous old desk offered a polite smile.

"Good morning—well, afternoon now. Can I help you?"

"I'm actually . . ." What? Layla wondered. What exactly was she? "I was hoping to speak to Mr. O'Dell for a minute if he's free."

"Actually, he's with a client, but they shouldn't be much longer if you'd like to . . ."

A woman in tight jeans, a snug pink sweater, and an explosion of hair in an improbable shade of red marched out on heeled boots. She dragged on a short leather jacket. "I want him skinned, Fox, you hear? I gave that son of a bitch the best two years and three months of my life, and I want him skinned like a rabbit."

"So noted, Shelley."

"How could he do that to me?" On a wail she collapsed into Fox's arms.

He wore jeans as well, and an untucked pinstriped shirt, along with an expression of resignation as he glanced over at Layla. "There, there," he said, patting the sobbing Shelley's back. "There, there."

"I just bought him new tires for his truck! I'm going to go slash every one of them."

"Don't." Fox took a good hold of her before Shelley, tears streaming away in fresh rage, started to yank back. "I don't want you to do that. You don't go near his truck, and for now, honey, try to stay away from him, too. And Sami."

"That turncoat slut of a bitch."

"That's the one. Leave this to me for now, okay? You go on back to work and let me handle this. That's why you hired me, right?"

"I guess. But you skin him raw, Fox. You crack that bastard's nuts like pecans."

"I'm going to get right on that," he assured her as he led her to the door. "You just stay above it all, that's the way. I'll be in touch."

After he'd closed the door, leaned back on it, he heaved out a breath. "Holy Mother of God."

"You should've referred that one," Alice told him.

"You can't refer off the first girl you got to second base with when she's filing for divorce. It's against the laws of God and Man. Hello, Layla, need a lawyer?"

"I hope not." He was better looking than she remembered, which just went to show the shape she'd been in the night before. Plus he didn't look anything like a lawyer. "No offense."

"None taken. Layla . . . It's Darnell, right?"

"Yes."

"Layla Darnell, Alice Hawbaker. Mrs. H, I'm clear for a while?"

"You are."

"Come on back, Layla." He gestured. "We don't usually put a show on this early in the day, but my old pal Shelley walked into the back room over at the diner to visit her twin sister, Sami, and found her husband—that would be Shelley's husband, Block—holding Sami's tip money."

"I'm sorry, she's filing for divorce because her husband was holding her sister's tip money?"

"It was in Sami's Victoria's Secret Miracle Bra at the time."

"Oh. Well."

"That's not privileged information as Shelley chased them both out of the back room and straight out onto Main

Street—with Sami's miraculous bra in full view—with a rag mop. Want a Coke?"

"No, I really don't. I don't think I need anything to give me an edge."

Since she looked inclined to pace, he didn't offer her a chair. Instead, he leaned back against his desk. "Rough night?"

"No, the opposite. I just can't figure out what I'm doing here. I don't understand any of this, and I certainly don't understand my place in it. A couple hours ago I told myself I was going to pack and drive back to New York like a sane person. But I didn't." She turned to him. "I couldn't. And I don't understand that either."

"You're where you're supposed to be. That's the simplest answer."

"Are you afraid?"

"A lot of the time."

"I don't think I've ever been really afraid. I wonder if I'd be so damned edgy if I had something to *do*. An assignment, a task."

"Listen, I've got to drive to a client a few miles out of town, take her some papers."

"Oh, sorry. I'm in the way."

"No, and when I start thinking beautiful women are in my way, please notify my next of kin so they can gather to say their final good-byes before my death. I was going to suggest you ride out with me, which is something to do. And you can have chamomile tea and stale lemon snaps with Mrs. Oldinger, which is a task. She likes company, which is the real reason she had me draw up the fifteenth codicil to her will."

He kept talking, knowing that was one way to help calm someone down when she looked ready to bolt. "By the time that's done, I can swing by another client who's not far out of the way and save him a trip into town. By my way of thinking, Cal and Quinn should be just about back home by the time we're done with all that. We'll go by, see what's what."

"Can you be out of the office all that time?"

"Believe me." He grabbed his coat, his briefcase. "Mrs. H will holler me back if I'm needed here. But unless you've got something better to do, I'll have her pull out the files I need and we'll take a drive."

It was better than brooding, Layla decided. Maybe she thought it was odd for a lawyer, even a small-town lawyer to drive an old Dodge pickup with a couple of Ring Ding wrappers littering the floorboards.

"What are you doing for the second client?"

"That's Charlie Deen. Charlie got clipped by a DUI when he was driving home from work. Insurance company's trying to dance around some of the medical bills. Not going to happen."

"Divorce, wills, personal injury. So you don't specialize?"

"All law, all the time," he said and sent her a smile that was a combination of sweet and cocky. "Well, except for tax law if I can avoid it. I leave that to my sister. She's tax and business law."

"But you don't have a practice together."

"That'd be tough. Sage went to Seattle to be a lesbian."

"I beg your pardon?"

"Sorry." He boosted the gas as they passed the town limits. "Family joke. What I mean is my sister Sage is gay, and she lives in Seattle. She's an activist, and she and her partner of, hmm, I guess about eight years now run a firm they call Girl on Girl. Seriously," he added when Layla said nothing. "They specialize in tax and business law for gays."

"Your family doesn't approve?"

"Are you kidding? My parents eat it up like tofu. When Sage and Paula—that's her partner—got married. Or had their life-partner affirmation, whatever—we all went out there and celebrated like mental patients. She's happy and that's what counts. The alternate lifestyle choice is just kind of a bonus for my parents. Speaking of family, that's my little brother's place."

Layla saw a log house all but buried in the trees, with a sign near the curve of the road reading HAWKINS CREEK POTTERY.

"Your brother's a potter."

"Yeah, a good one. So's my mother when she's in the mood. Want to stop in?"

"Oh, I . . ."

"Better not," he decided. "Ridge'll get going and Mrs. H has called Mrs. Oldinger by now to tell her to expect us. Another time."

"Okay." Conversation, she thought. Small talk. Relative sanity. "So you have a brother and sister."

"Two sisters. My baby sister owns the little vegetarian restaurant in town. It's pretty good, considering. Of the four of us I veered the farthest off the flower-strewn path my counterculture parents forged. But they love me anyway. That's about it for me. How about you?"

"Well . . . I don't have any relatives nearly as interesting as yours sound, but I'm pretty sure my mother has some old Joan Baez albums."

"There, that strange and fateful crossroads again."

She started to laugh, then gasped with pleasure as she spotted the deer. "Look! Oh, look. Aren't they gorgeous, just grazing there along the edge of the trees?"

To accommodate her, Fox pulled over to the narrow shoulder so she could watch. "You're used to seeing deer, I suppose," she said.

"Doesn't mean I don't get a kick out of it. We had to run herds off the farm when I was a kid."

"You grew up on a farm."

There was that urban-dweller wistfulness in her voice. The kind that said she saw the pretty deer, the bunnies, the sunflowers, and happy chickens. And not the plowing, the hoeing, weeding, harvesting. "Small, family farm. We grew our own vegetables, kept chickens and goats, bees. Sold some of the surplus, some of my mother's crafts, my father's woodwork."

"Do they still have it?"

"Yeah."

"My parents owned a little dress shop when I was a kid. They sold out about fifteen years ago. I always wished—Oh God, oh my God!"

Her hand whipped over to clamp on his arm.

The wolf leaped out of the trees, onto the back of a young deer. It bucked, it screamed—she could hear its high-pitched screams of fear and pain—it bled while the others in the small herd continued to crop at grass.

"It's not real."

His voice sounded tinny and distant. In front of her horrified eyes the wolf took the deer down, then began to tear and rip.

"It's not real," he repeated. He put his hands on her shoulders, and she felt something click. Something inside her pushed toward him and away from the horror at the edge of the trees. "Look at it, straight on," he told her. "Look at it and *know* it's not real."

The blood was so red, so wet. It flew in ugly rain, smearing the winter grass of the narrow field. "It's not real."

"Don't just say it. Know it. It lies, Layla. It lives in lies. It's not real."

She breathed in, breathed out. "It's not real. It's a lie. It's an ugly lie. A small, cruel lie. It's not real."

The field was empty; the winter grass ragged and unstained.

"How do you live with this?" Shoving around in her seat, Layla stared at him. "How do you stand this?"

"By knowing—the way I knew that was a lie—that some day, some way, we're going to kick its ass."

Her throat burned dry. "You did something to me. When you took my shoulders, when you were talking to me, you did something to me."

"No." He denied it without a qualm. He'd done something *for* her, Fox told himself. "I just helped you remember it wasn't real. We're going on to Mrs. Oldinger. I bet you could use that chamomile tea about now."

"Does she have any whiskey to go with it?"
"Wouldn't surprise me."

QUINN COULD SEE CAL'S HOUSE THROUGH THE trees when her phone signaled a waiting text-message. "Crap, why didn't she just call me?"

"Might've tried. There are lots of pockets in the woods where calls drop out."

"Color me virtually unsurprised." She brought up the message, smiling a little as she recognized Cybil's shorthand.

Bzy, but intrig'd. Tell u more when. Cn B there in a wk, 2 latest. Tlk whn cn. Q? B-ware. Serious. C.

"All right." Quinn replaced the phone and made the decision she'd been weighing during the hike back. "I guess we'll call Fox and Layla when I'm having that really big drink by the fire you're going to build."

"I can live with that."

"Then, seeing as you're a town honcho, you'd be the one to ask about finding a nice, attractive, convenient, and somewhat roomy house to rent for the next, oh, six months."

"And the tenant would be?"

"Tenants. They would be me, my delightful friend Cybil, whom I will talk into digging in, and most likely Layla, whom—I believe—will take a bit more convincing. But I'm very persuasive."

"What happened to staying a week for initial research, then coming back in April for a follow-up."

"Plans change," she said airily, and smiled at him as they stepped onto the gravel of his driveway. "Don't you just love when that happens?"

"Not really." But he walked with her onto the deck and opened the door so she could breeze into his quiet home ahead of him.

Ten

THE HOUSE WHERE CAL HAD GROWN UP WAS, IN his opinion, in a constant state of evolution. Every few years his mother would decide the walls needed "freshening," which meant painting—or often in his mother's vocabulary a new "paint treatment."

There was ragging, there was sponging, there was combing, and a variety of other terms he did his best to tune out.

Naturally, new paint led to new upholstery or window treatments, certainly to new bed linens when she worked her way to bedrooms. Which invariably led to new "arrangements."

He couldn't count the number of times he'd hauled furniture around to match the grafts his mother routinely generated.

His father liked to say that as soon as Frannie had the house the way she wanted, it was time for her to shake it all up again.

At one time, Cal had assumed his mother had fiddled, fooled, painted, sewed, arranged, and re-arranged out of boredom. Although she volunteered, served on various committees, or stuck her oar in countless organizations, she'd never worked outside the home. He'd gone through a period in his late teens and early twenties where he'd imagined her (pitied her) as an unfulfilled, semi-desperate housewife.

At one point he, in his worldliness of two college semesters, got her alone and explained his understanding of her sense of repression. She'd laughed so hard she'd had to set down her upholstery tacks and wipe her eyes.

"Honey," she'd said, "there's not a single bone of repression in my entire body. I love color and texture and patterns and flavors. And oh, just all sorts of things. I get to use this house as my studio, my science project, my laboratory, and my showroom. I get to be the director, the designer, the set builder, and the star of the whole show. Now, why would I want to go out and get a job or a career—since we don't need the money—and have somebody else tell me what to do and when to do it?"

She'd crooked her finger so he leaned down to her. And she'd laid a hand on his cheek. "You're such a sweetheart, Caleb. You're going to find out that not everybody wants what society—in whatever its current mood or mode might be—tells them they should want. I consider myself lucky, even privileged, that I was able to make the choice to stay home and raise my children. And I'm lucky to be able to be married to a man who doesn't mind if I use my talents—and I'm damned talented—to disrupt his quiet home with paint samples and fabric swatches every time he turns around. I'm happy. And I love knowing you worried I might not be."

He'd come to see she was exactly right. She did just as she liked, and was terrific at what she did. And, he'd come to see that when it came down to the core, she was the power in the house. His father brought in the money, but his mother handled the finances. His father ran his business, his mother ran the home.

And that was exactly the way they liked it.

So he didn't bother telling her not to fuss over Sunday dinner—just as he hadn't attempted to talk her out of extending the invitation to Quinn, Layla, and Fox. She lived to fuss, and enjoyed putting on elaborate meals for people, even if she didn't know them.

Since Fox volunteered to swing into town and pick up the women, Cal went directly to his parents' house, and went early. It seemed wise to give them some sort of groundwork—and hopefully a few basic tips on how to deal with a woman who intended to write a book on the Hollow, since the town included people, and those people included his family.

Frannie stood at the stove, checking the temperature of her pork tenderloin. Obviously satisfied with that, she crossed to the counter to continue the layers of her famous antipasto squares.

"So, Mom," Cal began as he opened the refrigerator.

"I'm serving wine with dinner, so don't go hunting up any beer."

Chastised, he shut the refrigerator door. "Okay. I just wanted to mention that you shouldn't forget that Quinn's writing a book."

"Have you noticed me forgetting things?"

"No." The woman forgot nothing, which could be a little daunting. "What I mean is, we should all be aware that things we say and do may end up in a book."

"Hmm." Frannie layered pepperoni over provolone. "Do you expect me or your father to say or do something embarrassing over appetizers? Or maybe we'll wait until dessert. Which is apple pie, by the way."

"No, I— You made apple pie?"

She spared him a glance, and a knowing smile. "It's your favorite, isn't it, my baby?"

"Yeah, but maybe you've lost your knack. I should sample a piece before company gets here. Save you any embarrassment if it's lousy pie."

"That didn't work when you were twelve."

"I know, but you always pounded the whole if-you-don't-succeed chestnut into my head."

"You just keep trying, sweetie. Now, why are you worried about this girl, who I'm told you've been seen out and about with a few times, coming around for dinner?"

"It's not like that." He wasn't sure what it was like. "It's about why she's here at all. We can't forget that, that's all I'm saying."

"I never forget. How could I? We have to live our lives, peel potatoes, get the mail, sneeze, buy new shoes, in spite of it all, maybe because of it all." There was a hint of fierceness in her voice he recognized as sorrow. "And that living includes being able to have a nice company meal on a Sunday."

"I wish it were different."

"I know you do, but it's not." She kept layering, but her eyes lifted to his. "And, Cal, my handsome boy, you can't do more than you do. If anything, there are times I wish you could do less. But . . . tell me, do you like this girl? Quinn Black?"

"Sure." Like to get a taste of that top-heavy mouth again, he mused. Then broke off that train of thought quickly since he knew his mother's skill at reading her children's minds.

"Then I intend to give her and the others a comfortable evening and an excellent meal. And, Cal, if you didn't want her here, didn't want her to speak with me or your dad, you wouldn't let her in the door. I wouldn't be able, though my powers are fierce, to shove you aside and open it myself."

He looked at her. Sometimes when he did, it surprised him that this pretty woman with her short, streaked blond hair, her slim build and creative mind could have given birth to him, could have raised him to be a man. He could look and think she was delicate, and then remember she was almost terrifyingly strong.

"I'm not going to let anything hurt you."

"Back at you, doubled. Now get out of my kitchen. I need to finish up the appetizers."

He'd have offered to lend her a hand, but would have earned one of her pitying stares. Not that she didn't allow kitchen help. His father was not only allowed to grill, but encouraged to. And any and all could and were called in as line chefs from time to time.

But when his mother was in full-out company-coming mode, she wanted the kitchen to herself.

He passed through the dining room where, naturally, the table was already set. She'd used festive plates, which meant she wasn't going for elegant or drop-in casual. Tented linen napkins, tea lights in cobalt rounds, inside a centerpiece of winter berries.

Even during the worst time, even during the Seven, he could come here and there would be fresh flowers artfully arranged, furniture free of dust and gleaming with polish and intriguing little soaps in the dish in the downstairs powder room.

Even hell didn't cause Frannie Hawkins to break stride.

Maybe, Cal thought as he wandered into the living room, that was part of the reason—even the most important reason—he got through it himself. Because whatever else happened, his mother would be maintaining her own brand of order and sanity.

Just as his father would be. They'd given him that, Cal thought. That rock-solid foundation. Nothing, not even a demon from hell had ever shaken it.

He started to go upstairs, hunt down his father who, he suspected, would be in his home office. But saw Fox's truck pull in when he glanced out the window.

He stood where he was, watched Quinn jump out first, cradling a bouquet wrapped in green florist paper. Layla slid out next, holding what looked to be a wine gift bag. His mother, Cal thought, would approve of the offerings. She herself had shelves and bins in her ruthlessly organized workroom that held carefully selected emergency hostess gifts, gift bags, colored tissue paper, and an assortment of bows and ribbons.

When Cal opened the door, Quinn strode straight in. "Hi. I love the house and the yard! Shows where you came by your eye for landscaping. What a great space. Layla, look at these walls. Like an Italian villa."

"It's their latest incarnation," Cal commented.

"It looks like home, but with a kick of style. Like you could curl up on that fabulous sofa and take a snooze, but you'd probably read *Southern Homes* first."

"Thank you." Frannie stepped out. "That's a lovely compliment. Cal, take everyone's coats, will you? I'm Frannie Hawkins."

"It's so nice to meet you. I'm Quinn. Thanks so much for having us. I hope you like mixed bouquets. I have a hard time deciding on one type of mostly anything."

"They're wonderful, thank you." Frannie accepted the flowers, smiled expectantly at Layla.

"I'm Layla Darnell, thank you for having us in your home. I hope the wine's appropriate."

"I'm sure it is." Frannie took a peek inside the gift bag. "Jim's favorite cabernet. Aren't you clever girls? Cal, go up and tell your father we have company. Hello, Fox."

"I brought you something, too." He grabbed her, lowered her into a stylish dip, and kissed both her cheeks. "What's cooking, sweetheart?"

As she had since he'd been a boy, Frannie ruffled his hair. "You won't have long to wait to find out. Quinn and Layla, you make yourselves comfortable. Fox, you come with me. I want to put these flowers in water."

"Is there anything we can do to help?"

"Not a thing."

When Cal came down with his father, Fox was doing his version of snooty French waiter as he served appetizers. The women were laughing, candles were lit, and his mother carried in her grandmother's best crystal vase with Quinn's flowers a colorful filling.

Sometimes, Cal mused, all really was right with the world.

HALFWAY THROUGH THE MEAL, WHERE THE CONversation stayed in what Cal considered safe territories, Quinn set down her fork, shook her head. "Mrs. Hawkins, this is the most amazing meal, and I have to ask. Did you study? Did you have a career as a gourmet chef at some point or did we just hit you on a really lucky day?"

"I took a few classes."

"Frannie's taken a lot of 'a few classes,'" Jim said. "In all kinds of things. But she's just got a natural talent for cooking and gardening and decorating. What you see around here, it's all her doing. Painted the walls, made the curtains—sorry, window treatments," he corrected with a twinkle at his wife.

"Get out. You did all the faux and fancy paintwork? Yourself?"

"I enjoy it."

"Found that sideboard there years back at some flea market, had me haul it home." Jim gestured toward the gleaming mahogany sideboard. "A few weeks later, she has me haul it in here. Thought she was pulling a fast one, had snuck out and bought something from an antique store."

"Martha Stewart eats your dust," Quinn decided. "I mean that as a compliment."

"I'll take it."

"I'm useless at all of that. I can barely paint my own nails. How about you?" Quinn asked Layla.

"I can't sew, but I like to paint. Walls. I've done some ragging that turned out pretty well."

"The only ragging I've done successfully was on my exfiance."

"You were engaged?" Frannie asked.

"I thought I was. But our definition of same differed widely."

"It can be difficult to blend careers and personal lives."

"Oh, I don't know. People do it all the time—with varying degrees of success, sure, but they do. I think it just has to be the right people. The trick, or the first of probably many tricks, is recognizing the right person. Wasn't it like that for you? Didn't you have to recognize each other?"

"I knew the first time I saw Frannie. There she is." Jim beamed down the table at his wife. "Frannie now, she was a little more shortsighted."

"A little more practical," Frannie corrected, "seeing as we were eight and ten at the time. Plus I enjoyed having you moon over and chase after me. Yes, you're right." Frannie looked back at Quinn. "You have to see each other, and see in each other something that makes you want to take the chance, that makes you believe you can dig down for the long haul."

"And sometimes you think you see something," Quinn commented, "but it was just a—let's say—trompe l'oeil."

ONE THING QUINN KNEW HOW TO DO WAS FINAgle. Frannie Hawkins wasn't an easy mark, but Quinn managed to charm her way into the kitchen to help put together dessert and coffee.

"I love kitchens. I'm kind of a pathetic cook, but I love all the gadgets and tools, all the shiny surfaces."

"I imagine with your work, you eat out a lot."

"Actually, I eat in most of the time or call for takeout. I implemented a lifestyle change—nutrition-wise—a couple of years ago. Determined to eat healthier, depend less on fast or nuke-it-out-of-a-box food. I make a really good salad these days. That's a start. Oh God, oh God, that's apple pie. Homemade apple pie. I'm going to have to do double duty in the gym as penance for the huge piece I'm going to ask for."

Her enjoyment obvious, Frannie shot her a wicked smile. "À la mode, with vanilla bean ice cream?"

"Yes, but only to show my impeccable manners." Quinn hesitated a moment, then jumped in. "I'm going to ask you, and if you want this off-limits while I'm enjoying your hospitality, just tell me to back off. Is it hard for you to nurture this normal life, to hold your family, yourself, your home together when you know all of it will be threatened?"

"It's very hard." Frannie turned to her pies while the coffee brewed. "Just as it's very necessary. I wanted Cal to go, and if he had I would have convinced Jim to leave. I could do that, I could turn my back on it all. But Cal couldn't. And I'm so proud of him for staying, for not giving up."

"Will you tell me what happened when he came home that morning, the morning of his tenth birthday?"

"I was in the yard." Frannie walked over to the window that faced the back. She could see it all, every detail. How green the grass was, how blue the sky. Her hydrangeas were headed up and beginning to pop, her delphiniums towering spears of exotic blue.

Deadheading her roses, and some of the coreopsis that had bloomed off. She could even hear the busy *snip*, *snip* of her shears, and the hum of the neighbor's—it had been the Petersons, Jack and Lois then—lawn mower. She remembered, too, she'd been thinking about Cal, and his birthday party. She'd had his cake in the oven.

A double-chocolate sour cream cake, she remembered. She'd intended to do a white frosting to simulate the ice planet from one of the *Star Wars* movies. Cal had loved *Star Wars* for years and years. She'd had the little action figures to arrange on it, the ten candles all ready in the kitchen.

Had she heard him or sensed him—probably some of both—but she'd looked around as he'd come barreling up on his bike, pale, filthy, sweaty. Her first thought had been accident, there'd been an accident. And she'd been on her feet and rushing to him before she'd noticed he wasn't wearing his glasses.

"The part of me that registered that was ready to give him a good tongue-lashing. But the rest of me was still running when he climbed off his bike, and ran to me. He ran to me and he grabbed on so tight. He was shaking—my little boy—shaking like a leaf. I went down on my knees, pulling him back so I could check for blood or broken bones."

What is it, what happened, are you hurt? All of that, Frannie remembered had flooded out of her, so fast it was like one word. *In the woods,* he'd said. *Mom. Mom. In the woods.*

"There was that part of me again, the part that thought what were you doing in the woods, Caleb Hawkins? It all came pouring out of him, how he and Fox and Gage planned this adventure, what they'd done, where they'd gone. And that same part was coldly devising the punishment to fit the crime, even while the rest of me was terrified, and relieved, so pitifully relieved I was holding my dirty, sweaty boy. Then he told me the rest."

"You believed him?"

"I didn't want to. I wanted to believe he'd had a nightmare, which he richly deserved, that he'd stuffed himself on sweets and junk food and had a nightmare. Even, that someone had gone after them in the woods. But I couldn't look at his face and believe that. I couldn't believe the easy that, the fixable that. And then, of course, there were his eyes. He could see a bee hovering over the delphiniums across the yard. And under the dirt and sweat, there wasn't a bruise on him. The nine-year-old I'd sent off the day before had scraped knees and bruised shins. The one who came back to me hadn't a mark on him, but for the thin white scar across his wrist he hadn't had when he left."

"Even with that, a lot of adults, even mothers, wouldn't have believed a kid who came home with a story like that."

"I won't say Cal never lied to me, because obviously he did. He had. But I knew he wasn't lying. I knew he was telling me the truth, all the truth he knew."

"What did you do?"

"I took him inside, told him to clean up, change his clothes. I called his father, and got his sisters home. I burned his birthday cake—completely forgot about it, never heard the timer. Might've burned the house down if Cal himself hadn't smelled the burning. So he never got his ice planet or his ten candles. I hate remembering that. I burned his cake and he never got to blow out his birthday candles. Isn't that silly?"

"No, ma'am. No," Quinn said with feeling when Frannie looked at her, "it's not."

"He was never really, not wholly, a little boy again." Frannie sighed. "We went straight over to the O'Dells, because Fox and Gage were already there. We had what I guess you could call our first summit meeting."

"What did—"

"We need to take in the dessert and coffee. Can you handle that tray?"

Understanding the subject was closed for now, Quinn stepped over. "Sure. It looks terrific, Mrs. Hawkins."

In between moans and tears of joy over the pie, Quinn aimed her charm at Jim Hawkins. Cal, she was sure, had been dodging and weaving, avoiding and evading her since their hike to the Pagan Stone.

"Mr. Hawkins, you've lived in the Hollow all your life."

"Born and raised. Hawkins have been here since the town was a couple of stone cabins."

"I met your grandmother, and she seems to know town history."

"Nobody knows more."

"People say you're the one who knows real estate, business, local politics."

"I guess I do."

"Then you may be able to point me in the right direction." She slid a look at Cal, then beamed back at his father. "I'm looking to rent a house, something in town or close to it. Nothing fancy, but I'd like room. I have a friend coming in soon, and I've nearly talked Layla into staying longer. I think we'd be more comfortable, and it would be more efficient, for the three of us to have a house instead of using the hotel."

"How long are you looking for?"

"Six months." She saw it register on his face, just as she noticed the frown form on Cal's. "I'm going to stay through July, Mr. Hawkins, and I'm hoping to find a house that would accommodate three women—potentially three—" she said with a glance at Layla.

"I guess you've thought that over."

"I have. I'm going to write this book, and part of the angle I'm after is the fact that the town remains, the people—a lot of them—stay. They stay and they make apple pie and have people over to Sunday dinner. They bowl, and they shop. They fight and they make love. They live. If I'm going to do this right, I want to be here, before, during, and after. So I'd like to rent a house."

Jim scooped up some pie, chased it with coffee. "It happens I know a place on High Street, just a block off Main. It's old, main part went up before the Civil War. It's got four bedrooms, three baths. Nice porches, front and back. Had a new roof on her two years ago. Kitchen's eat-in size, though there's a little dining room off it. Appliances aren't fancy, but they've only got five years on them. Just been painted. Tenants moved out just a month ago."

"It sounds perfect. You seem to know it well."

"Should. We own it. Cal, you should take Quinn by. Maybe run her and Layla over there on the way home. You know where the keys are."

"Yeah," he said when Quinn gave him a big, bright smile. "I know where the keys are."

AS IT MADE THE MOST SENSE, QUINN HITCHED A ride with Cal, and left Fox and Layla to follow. She stretched out her legs, let out a sigh.

"Let me start off by saying your parents are terrific, and you're lucky to have grown up in such a warm, inviting home."

"I agree."

"Your dad's got that Ward Cleaver meets Jimmy Stewart thing going. I could've eaten him up like your mother's—Martha Stewart meets Grace Kelly by way of Julia Child—apple pie."

His lips twitched. "They'd both like those descriptions."

"You knew about the High Street house."

"Yeah, I did."

"You knew about the High Street house, and avoided telling me about it."

"That's right. You found out about it, too, before dinner, which is why you did the end-run around me to my father."

"Correct." She tapped her finger on his shoulder. "I figured he'd point me there. He likes me. Did you avoid telling me because you're not comfortable with what I might write about Hawkins Hollow?"

"Some of that. More, I was hoping you'd change your mind and leave. Because I like you, too."

"You like me, so you want me gone?"

"I like you, Quinn, so I want you safe." He looked at her again, longer. "But some of the things you said about the Hollow over apple pie echoed pretty closely some of the things my mother said to me today. It all but eliminates any discomfort with what you may decide to write. But it makes me like you more, and that's a problem."

"You had to know, after what happened to us in the woods, I wouldn't be leaving."

"I guess I did." He pulled off into a short, steep driveway.

"Is this the house? It *is* perfect! Look at the stonework, and the big porch, the windows have shutters."

They were painted a deep blue that stood out well against the gray stone. The little front yard was bisected by a trio of concrete steps and the narrow walkway. A trim tree Quinn thought might be a dogwood highlighted the left square of front yard.

As Fox's truck pulled in behind, Quinn popped out to stand, hands on hips. "Pretty damned adorable. Don't you think, Layla?"

"Yes, but—"

"No buts, not yet. Let's take a look inside." She cocked her head at Cal. "Okay, landlord?"

As they trooped up to the porch, Cal took out the keys he'd grabbed off their hook from his father's home office. The ring was clearly labeled with the High Street address.

The fact that the door opened without a creak told Quinn the landlords were vigilant in the maintenance department.

The door opened straight into the living area that stood twice as long as it was wide, with the steps to the second floor a couple of strides in on the left. The wood floors showed wear, but were spotlessly clean. The air was chilly and carried the light sting of fresh paint.

The small brick fireplace delighted her.

"Could use your mother's eye in the paint department," Quinn commented.

"Rental properties get eggshell, through and through. It's the Hawkins's way. Tenants want to play around with that, it's their deal."

"Reasonable. I want to start at the top, work down. Layla, do you want to go up and fight over who gets which bedroom?"

"No." Cal thought there was mutiny, as well as frustration on her face. "I *have* a bedroom. In New York."

"You're not in New York," Quinn said simply, then dashed up the steps.

"She's not listening to me," Layla muttered. "I don't seem to be listening to me either about going back."

"We're here." Fox gave a shrug. "Might as well poke around. I really dig empty houses."

"I'll be up." Cal started up the stairs.

He found her in one of the bedrooms, one that faced the tiny backyard. She stood at the long, narrow window, the fingertips of her right hand pressed to the glass. "I thought I'd go for one of the rooms facing the street, catch the who's going where when and with who. I usually go for that. Just have to know what's going on. But this is the one for me. I bet, in the daylight, you can stand here, see backyards, other houses, and wow, right on to the mountains."

"Do you always make up your mind so fast?"

"Yeah, usually. Even when I surprise myself like now. Bathroom's nice, too." She turned enough to gesture to the door on the side of the room. "And since it's girls, if any of us share that one, it won't be too weird having it link up the two bedrooms on this side."

"You're sure everyone will fall in line."

Now she turned to him, fully. "Confidence is the first step to getting what you want, or need. But we'll say I'm hoping Layla and Cyb will agree it's efficient, practical, and would be more comfortable to share the house for a few months than to bunk at the hotel. Especially considering the fact that both Layla and I are pretty well put off of the dining room there after Slugfest."

"You don't have any furniture."

"Flea markets. We'll pick up the essentials. Cal, I've stayed in less stellar accommodations and done it for one thing. A story. This is more. Somehow or other I'm connected to this story, this place. I can't turn that off and walk away."

He wished she could, and knew if she could his feelings for her wouldn't be as strong or as complex. "Okay, but let's agree, here and now, that if you change your mind and do just that, no explanations needed."

"That's a deal. Now, let's talk rent. What's this place going to run us?"

"You pay the utilities—heat, electric, phone, cable."

"Naturally. And?"

"That's it."

"What do you mean, that's it?"

"I'm not going to charge you rent, not when you're staying here, at least in part, because of me. My family, my friends, my town. We're not going to make a profit off that."

"Straight arrow, aren't you, Caleb?"

"About most."

"I'll make a profit, she says optimistically, from the book I intend to write."

"If we get through July and you write a book, you'll have earned it."

"Well, you drive a hard bargain, but it looks like we have a deal." She stepped forward, offered a hand.

He took it, then cupped his other at the back of her neck. Surprise danced in her eyes, but she didn't resist as he eased her toward him.

He moved slow, the closing together of bodies, the meeting of lips, the testing slide of tongues. There was no explosion of need as there had been in that moment in the clearing. No sudden, almost painful shock of desire. Instead, it was a long and gradual glide from interest to pleasure to ache while her head went light and her blood warmed. It seemed everything inside her went quiet so that she heard, very clearly, the low hum in her own throat as he changed the angle of the kiss.

He felt her give, degree by degree, even as he felt the hand he held in his go lax. The tension that had dogged him throughout the day drained away, so there was only the moment, the quiet, endless moment.

Even when he drew back, that inner stillness held. And she opened her eyes, met his.

"That was just you and me."

"Yeah." He stroked his fingers over the back of her neck. "Just you and me."

"I want to say that I have a policy against becoming romantically, intimately, or sexually—just to cover all my bases—involved with anyone directly associated with a story I'm researching."

"That's probably smart."

"I am smart. I also want to say I'm going to negate that policy in this particular case."

He smiled. "Damn right you are."

"Cocky. Well, mixed with the straight arrow, I have to like it. Unfortunately, I should get back to the hotel. I have a lot of . . . things. Details to see to before I can move in here."

"Sure. I can wait."

He kept her hand in his, switching off the light as he led her out.

Eleven

CAL SENT A DOZEN PINK ROSES TO HIS MOTHER. She liked the traditional flower for Valentine's Day, and he knew his father always went for the red. If he hadn't known, Amy Yost in the flower shop would have reminded him as she did every blessed year.

"Your dad ordered a dozen red last week, for delivery today, potted geranium to his grandma, *and* he sent the Valentine's Day Sweetheart Special to your sisters."

"That suck-up," Cal said, knowing it would make Amy gasp and giggle. "How about a dozen yellow for my gran. In a vase, Amy. I don't want her to have to fool with them."

"Aw, that's sweet. I've got Essie's address on file, you just fill out the card."

He picked one out of the slot, gave it a minute's thought before writing: Hearts are red, these roses are yellow. Happy Valentine's Day from your best fellow.

Corny, sure, he decided, but Gran would love it.

He reached for his wallet to pay when he noticed the

red-and-white-striped tulips behind the glass doors of the refrigerated display. "Ah, those tulips are . . . interesting."

"Aren't they pretty? And they just make me feel like spring. It's no problem if you want to change either of the roses for them. I can just—"

"No, no, maybe . . . I'll take a dozen of them, too. Another delivery in a vase, Amy."

"Sure." Her cheerful round face lit up with curiosity and the anticipation of good gossip. "Who's your valentine, Cal?"

"It's more a housewarming kind of thing." He couldn't think of any reason why *not* to send Quinn flowers. Women liked flowers, he thought as he filled out the delivery form. It was Valentine's Day, and she was moving into the High Street house. It wasn't like he was buying her a ring and picking out a band for the wedding.

It was just a nice gesture.

"Quinn Black." Amy wiggled her eyebrows as she read the name on the form. "Meg Stanley ran into her at the flea market yesterday, along with that friend of hers from New York. They bought a bunch of stuff, according to Meg. I heard you were going around with her."

"We're not . . ." Were they? Either way, it was best to leave it alone. "Well, what's the damage, Amy?"

With his credit card still humming, he stepped outside, hunched his shoulders against the cold. There might be candy-striped tulips, but it didn't feel as if Mother Nature was giving so much as a passing thought to spring. The sky spat out a thin and bitter sleet that lay slick as grease on the streets and sidewalks.

He'd walked down from the bowling center as was his habit, timing his arrival at the florist to their ten o'clock opening. It was the best way to avoid the panicked rush of others who had waited until the last minute to do the Valentine's thing.

It didn't appear he'd needed to worry. Not only had no other customers come in while he'd been buying his roses and impulsive tulips, but there was no one on the sidewalks, no cars creeping cautiously toward the curb in front of the Flower Pot.

"Strange." His voice sounded hollow against the sizzle of sleet striking asphalt. Even on the crappiest day, he'd pass any number of people on his walks around town. He shoved his gloveless hands into his pockets and cursed himself for not breaking his routine and driving.

"Creatures of habit freeze their asses off," he muttered. He wanted to be inside in his office, drinking a cup of coffee, even preparing to start the cancellation process on the evening's scheduled Sweetheart Dance if the sleet worsened. If he'd just taken the damn truck, he'd already be there.

So thinking, he looked up toward the center, and saw the stoplight at the Town Square was out.

Power down, Cal thought, and that was a problem. He quickened his steps. He knew Bill Turner would make certain the generator kicked on for the emergency power, but he needed to be there. School was out, and that meant kids were bound to be scattered around in the arcade.

The hissing of the sleet increased until it sounded like the forced march of an army of giant insects. Despite the slick sidewalk, Cal found himself breaking into a jog when it struck him.

Why weren't there any cars at the Square, or parked at the curbs? Why weren't there any cars anywhere?

He stopped, and so did the hiss of the sleet. In the ensuing silence, he heard his own heart thumping like a fist against steel.

She stood so close he might have reached out to touch her, and knew if he tried, his hand would pass through her as it would through water.

Her hair was deep blond, worn long and loose as it had been when she'd carried the pails toward the little cabin in Hawkins Wood. When she'd sung about a garden green. But her body was slim and straight in a long gray dress.

He had the ridiculous thought that if he had to see a ghost, at least it wasn't a pregnant one.

As if she heard his thoughts, she smiled. "I am not your fear, but you are my hope. You and those who make up the whole of you. What makes you, Caleb Hawkins, is of the past, the now, and the yet to come."

"Who are you? Are you Ann?"

"I am what came before you, and you are formed through love. Know that, know that long, long before you came into the world, you were loved."

"Love isn't enough."

"No, but it is the rock on which all else stands. You have to look; you have to see. This is the time, Caleb. This was always to be the time."

"The time for what?"

"The end of it. Seven times three. Death or life."

"Just tell me what I need to do. Goddamn it."

"If I could. If I could spare you." She lifted a hand, let it fall again. "There must be struggle, and sacrifice, and great courage. There must be faith. There must be love. It is courage, faith, love that holds it so long, that prevents it from taking all who live and breathe within this place. Now it is for you."

"We don't know *how*. We've tried."

"This is the time," she repeated. "It is stronger, but so are you, and so are we. Use what you were given, take what it sowed but could never own. You cannot fail."

"Easy for you to say. You're dead."

"But you are not. They are not. Remember that."

When she started to fade, he did reach out, uselessly. "Wait, damn it. Wait. Who are you?"

"Yours," she said. "Yours as I am and always will be his."

She was gone, and the sleet sizzled on the pavement again. Cars rumbled by as the traffic light on the Square glowed green.

"Not the spot for daydreaming." Meg Stanley skidded by, giving him a wink as she pulled open the door of Ma's Pantry.

"No," Cal muttered. "It's not."

He started toward the center again, then veered off to take a detour to High Street.

Quinn's car was in the drive, and through the windows he could see the lights she must've turned on to chase back the gloom. He knocked, heard a muffled call to come in.

When he did, he saw Quinn and Layla trying to muscle something that resembled a desk up the stairs.

"What are you doing? Jesus." He stepped over to grip the side of the desk beside Quinn. "You're going to hurt yourselves."

In an annoyed move, she tossed her head to flip the hair away from her face. "We're managing."

"You'll be managing a trip to the ER. Go on up, take that end with Layla."

"Then we'll both be walking backward. Why don't you take that end?"

"Because I'm going to be taking the bulk of the weight this way."

"Oh." She let go, squeezed between the wall and the desk.

He didn't bother to ask why it had to go up. He'd lived with his mother too long to waste his breath. Instead he grunted out orders to prevent the edge of the desk from bashing into the wall as they angled left at the top of the stairs. Then followed Quinn as she directed the process to the window in the smallest bedroom.

"See, we were right." Quinn panted, and tugged down a Penn State sweatshirt. "This is the spot for it."

There was a seventies chair that had seen better days, a pole lamp with a rosy glass shade that dripped long crystals, and a low bookshelf varnished black over decades that wobbled when he set a hand on it.

"I know, I know." Quinn waved away his baleful look. "But it just needs a little hammering or something, and it's really just to fill things out. We were thinking about making it a little sitting room, then decided it would be better as a little office. Hence the desk we originally thought should be in the dining room."

"Okay."

"The lamp looks like something out of *The Best Little Whorehouse in Texas*." Layla gave one of the crystals a flick with her fingers. "But that's what we like about it. The chair is hideous."

"But comfortable," Quinn inserted.

"But comfortable, and that's what throws are for."

Cal waited a beat as both of them looked at him expectantly. "Okay," he repeated, which was generally how he handled his mother's decorating explanations.

"We've been busy. We turned in Layla's rental car, then hit the flea market just out of town. Bonanza. Plus we agreed no secondhand mattresses. The ones we ordered should be here this afternoon. Anyway, come see what we've got going so far."

Quinn grabbed his hand, pulled him across the hall to the room she'd chosen. There was a long bureau desperately in need of refinishing, topped by a spotted mirror. Across the room was a boxy chest someone had painted a murderous and shiny red. On it stood a Wonder Woman lamp.

"Homey."

"It'll be very livable when we're done."

"Yeah. You know I think that lamp might've been my sister Jen's twenty, twenty-five years ago."

"It's classic," Quinn claimed. "It's kitschy."

He fell back on the standard. "Okay."

"I think I have Danish modern," Layla commented from the doorway. "Or possibly Flemish. It's absolutely horrible. I have no idea why I bought it."

"Did you two haul this stuff up here?"

"Please." Quinn tossed her head.

"We opted for brain over brawn."

"Every time. That and a small investment. Do you know how much a couple of teenage boys will cart and carry for twenty bucks each and the opportunity to ogle a couple of hot chicks such as we?" Quinn fisted a hand on her hip, struck a pose.

"I'd've done it for ten. You could have called."

"Which was our intention, actually. But the boys were handy. Why don't we go down and sit on our new third- or fourthhand sofa?"

"We did splurge," Layla added. "We have an actual new coffeemaker and a very eclectic selection of coffee mugs."

"Coffee'd be good."

"I'll get it started."

Cal glanced after Layla. "She seems to have done a one-eighty on all this."

"I'm persuasive. And you're generous. I think I should plant one on you for that."

"Go ahead. I can take it."

Laughing, she braced her hands on his shoulders, gave him a firm, noisy kiss."

"Does that mean I don't get ten bucks?"

Her smile beamed as she poked him in the belly. "You'll take the kiss and like it. Anyway, part of the reason for Layla hanging back was the money. The idea of staying was—is—difficult for her. But the idea of taking a long leave, unpaid, from her job, coming up with rent money here, keeping her place in New York, that was pretty much off the table."

She stepped up to the bright red chest to turn her Wonder Woman lamp on and off. From the look on her face, Cal could see the act pleased her.

"So, the rent-free aspect checked one problem off her list," Quinn went on. "She hasn't completely committed. Right now, it's a day at a time for her."

"I've got something to tell you, both of you, that may make this her last day."

"Something happened." She dropped her hand, turned. "What happened?"

"I'll tell you both. I want to call Fox first, see if he can swing by. Then I can tell it once."

HE HAD TO DO IT WITHOUT FOX, WHO, ACCORDing to Mrs. Hawbaker, was at the courthouse being a lawyer. So he sat in the oddly furnished living room on a couch so soft and saggy he was already wishing for the opportunity to get Quinn naked on it, and told them about the visitation on Main Street.

"An OOB," Quinn decided.

"An oob?"

"No, no. Initials, like CYA. Out of body—experience. It sounds like that might be what you had, or maybe there was a slight shift in dimensions and you were in an alternate Hawkins Hollow."

He might have spent two-thirds of his life caught up in something beyond rational belief, but he'd never heard another woman talk like Quinn Black. "I was not in an alternate anything, and I was right inside my body where I belong."

"I've been studying, researching, and writing about the paranormal for some time now." Quinn drank some coffee and brooded over it.

"It could be he was talking to a ghost who caused the illusion that they were alone on the street, and caused everyone else out there to—I don't know—blip out for a few minutes." Layla shrugged at Quinn's narrowed look. "I'm new at this, and I'm still working really hard not to hide under the covers until somebody wakes me up and tells me this was all a dream."

"For the new kid, your theory's pretty good," Quinn told her.

"How about mine? Which is what she said is a hell of a lot more important right now than how she said it."

"Point taken." Quinn nodded at Cal. "This is the time, she said. Three times seven. That one's easy enough to figure."

"Twenty-one years." Cal pushed up to pace. "This July makes twenty-one years."

"Three, like seven, is considered a magickal number. It sounds like she was telling you it was always going to come now, this July, this year. It's stronger, you're stronger, they're stronger." Quinn squeezed her eyes shut.

"So, it and this woman—this spirit—have both been able to . . ."

"Manifest." Quinn finished Layla's thought. "That follows the logic."

"Nothing about this is logical."

"It is, really." Opening her eyes again, Quinn gave Layla a sympathetic look. "Inside this sphere, there's logic. It's just not the kind we deal with, or most of us deal with, every day. The past, the now, the yet to be. Things that happened, that are happening, and that will or may are all part of the solution, the way to end it."

"I think there's more to that part." Cal turned back from the window. "After that night in the clearing, the three of us were different."

"You don't get sick, and you heal almost as soon as you're hurt. Quinn told me."

"Yeah. And I could see."

"Without your glasses."

"I could also see before. I started—right there minutes afterward—to have flashes of the past."

"The way you did—both of us did," Quinn corrected, "when we touched the stone together. And later, when we—"

"Like that, not always that clear, not always so intense. Sometimes awake, sometimes like a dream. Sometimes completely irrelevant. And Fox . . . It took him a while to understand. Jesus, we were ten. He can see now." Annoyed with himself, Cal shook his head. "He can see, or sense what you're thinking, or feeling."

"Fox is psychic?" Layla demanded.

"Psychic lawyer. He's so hired."

Despite everything, Quinn's announcement made Cal's lips twitch. "Not like that, not exactly. It's never been something we can completely control. Fox has to deliberately push it, and it doesn't always work then. But since then he has an instinct about people. And Gage—"

"He sees what could happen," Quinn added. "He's the soothsayer."

"It's hardest for him. That's why—one of the reasons why—he doesn't spend much time here. It's harder here.

He's had some pretty damn vicious dreams, visions, nightmares, whatever the hell you want to call them."

And it hurts you when he hurts, Quinn thought. "But he hasn't seen what you're meant to do?"

"No. That would be too easy, wouldn't it?" Cal said bitterly. "Has to be more fun to mess up the lives of three kids, to let innocent people die or kill and maim each other. Stretch that out for a couple of decades, then say: okay, boys, now's the time."

"Maybe there was no choice." Quinn held up a hand when Cal's eyes fired. "I'm not saying it's fair. In fact, it sucks. Inside and out, it sucks. I'm saying maybe it couldn't be another way. Whether it was something Giles Dent did, or something set in motion centuries before that, there may have been no other choice. She said he was holding it, that he was preventing it from destroying the Hollow. If it was Ann, and she meant Giles Dent, does that mean he trapped this thing, this *bestia*, and in some form—*beatus*—has been trapped with it, battling it, all this time? Three hundred and fifty years and change. That sucks, too."

Layla jumped at the brisk knock on the door, then popped up. "I'll get it. Maybe it's the delivery."

"You're not wrong," Cal said quietly. "But it doesn't make it easier to live through it. It doesn't make it easier to know, in my gut, that we're coming up to our last chance."

Quinn got to her feet. "I wish—"

"It's flowers!" Layla's voice was giddy with delight as she came in carrying the vase of tulips. "For you, Quinn."

"Jesus, talk about weird timing," Cal muttered.

"For me? Oh God, they look like lollipop cups. They're gorgeous!" Quinn set them on the ancient coffee table. "Must be a bribe from my editor so I'll finish that article on—" She broke off as she ripped open the card. Her face was blank with shock as she lifted her eyes to Cal. "You sent me flowers?"

"I was in the florist before—"

"You sent me flowers on Valentine's Day."

"I hear my mother calling," Layla announced. "Coming, Mom!" She made a fast exit.

"You sent me tulips that look like blooming candy canes on Valentine's Day."

"They looked like fun."

"That's what you wrote on the card. 'These look like fun.' Wow." She scooped a hand through her hair. "I have to say that I'm a sensible woman, who knows very well Valentine's Day is a commercially generated holiday designed to sell greeting cards, flowers, and candy."

"Yeah, well." He slid his hands into his pockets. "Works."

"And I'm not the type of woman who goes all mushy and gooey over flowers, or sees them as an apology for an argument, a prelude to sex, or any of the other oft perceived uses."

"I just saw them, thought you'd get a kick out of them. Period. I've got to get to work."

"But," she continued and moved toward him, "strangely, I find none of that applies in the least in this particular case. They are fun." She rose up on her toes, kissed his cheek. "And they're beautiful." Then his other cheek. "And thoughtful." Now his lips. "Thank you."

"You're welcome."

"I'd like to add that . . ." She trailed her hands down his shirt, up again. "If you'll tell me what time you finish up tonight, I'll have a bottle of wine waiting in my bedroom upstairs, where I can promise you, you're going to get really, really lucky."

"Eleven," he said immediately. "I can be here at eleven-oh-five. I— Oh shit. Sweetheart Dance, that's midnight. Special event. No problem. You'll come."

"That's my plan." When he grinned, she rolled her eyes. "You mean to this dance. At the Bowl-a-Rama. A Sweetheart Dance at the Bowl-a-Rama. God, I'd *love* that. But, I can't leave Layla here, not at night. Not alone."

"She can come, too—to the dance."

Now her eyeroll was absolutely sincere. "Cal, no woman wants to tag along with a couple to a dance on

Valentine's Day. It paints a big *L* for loser in the middle of her forehead, and they're so damn hard to wash off."

"Fox can take her. Probably. I'll check."

"That's a possibility, especially if we make it all for fun. You check, then I'll check, then we'll see. But either way." She grabbed a fistful of his shirt, and this time brought him to her for a long, long kiss. "My bedroom, twelve-oh-five."

LAYLA SAT ON HER BRAND-NEW DISCOUNT MATtress while Quinn busily checked out the clothes she'd recently hung in her closet.

"Quinn, I appreciate the thought, I really do, but put yourself in my place. The third-wheel position."

"It's perfectly acceptable to be the third wheel when there're four wheels altogether. Fox is going."

"Because Cal asked him to take pity on the poor dateless V-Day loser. Probably told him or bribed him or—"

"You're right. Fox certainly had to have his arm twisted to go out with such an ugly hag like yourself. I admit every time I look at you, I'm tempted to go: woof, woof, what a dog. Besides . . . Oh, I love this jacket! You have the best clothes. But this jacket is seriously awesome. Mmm." Quinn stroked it like a cat. "Cashmere."

"I don't know why I packed it. I don't know why I packed half the stuff I did. I just started grabbing things. And you're trying to distract me."

"Not really, but it's a nice side benefit. What was I saying? Oh, yeah. Besides, it's not a date. It's a gang bang," she said and made Layla laugh. "It's just the four of us going to a bowling alley, for God's sake, to hear some local band play and dance a little."

"Sure. After which, you'll be hanging a scarf over the doorknob of your bedroom. I went to college, Quinn. I had a roommate. Actually, I had a nympho of a roommate who had an endless supply of scarves."

"Is it a problem?" Quinn stopped poking in the closet

long enough to look over her shoulder. "Cal and me, across the hall?"

"No. No." And now didn't she feel stupid and petty? "I think it's great. Really, I do. Anybody can tell the two of you rev like engines when you're within three feet of each other."

"They can?" Quinn turned all the way around now. "We do?"

"*Vroom, vroom.* He's great, it's great. I just feel . . ." Layla rolled her shoulders broadly. "In the way."

"You're not. I couldn't stay here without you. I'm pretty steady, but I couldn't stay in this house alone. The dance isn't a big deal. We don't have to go, but I think it'd be fun, for all of us. And a chance to do something absolutely normal to take our minds off everything that isn't."

"That's a good point."

"So get dressed. Put on something fun, maybe a little sexy, and let's hit the Bowl-a-Rama."

THE BAND, A LOCAL GROUP NAMED HOLLOWED Out, was into its first set. They were popular at weddings and corporate functions, and regularly booked at the center's events because their playlist ran the gamut from old standards to hip-hop. The something-for-everybody kept the dance floor lively while those sitting one out could chat at one of the tables circling the room, sip drinks, or nibble from the light buffet set up along one of the side walls.

Cal figured it was one of the center's most popular annual events for good reason. His mother headed up the decorating committee, so there were flowers and candles, red and white streamers, glittering red hearts. It gave people a chance to get a little dressed up in the dullness that was February, get out and socialize, hear some music, show off their moves if they had them. Or like Cy Hudson, even if they didn't.

It was a little bright spot toward the end of a long winter, and they never failed to have a full house.

Cal danced with Essie to "Fly Me to the Moon."

"Your mother was right to make you take those dance lessons."

"I was humiliated among my peers," Cal said. "But light on my feet."

"Women tend to lose their heads over a good dancer."

"A fact I've exploited whenever possible." He smiled down at her. "You look so pretty, Gran."

"I look dignified. Now, there was a day when I turned plenty of heads."

"You still turn mine."

"And you're still the sweetest of my sweethearts. When are you going to bring that pretty writer to see me?"

"Soon, if that's what you want."

"It feels like time. I don't know why. And speaking of—" She nodded toward the open double doors. "Those two turn heads."

He looked. He noticed Layla, in that she was there. But his focus was all for Quinn. She'd wound that mass of blond hair up, a touch of elegance, and wore an open black jacket over some kind of lacey top—camisole, he remembered. They called them camisoles, and God bless whoever invented them.

Things glittered at her ears, at her wrists, but all he could think was she had the sexiest collarbone in the history of collarbones, and he couldn't wait to get his mouth on it.

"You're about to drool, Caleb."

"What?" He blinked his attention back to Essie. "Oh. Jeez."

"She does look a picture. You take me on back to my table now and go get her. Bring her and her friend around to say hello before I leave."

By the time he got to them, Fox had already scooped them up to one of the portable bars and sprung for champagne. Quinn turned to Cal, glass in hand, and pitched her voice over the music. "This is great! The band's hot, the bubbly's cold, and the room looks like a love affair."

"You were expecting a couple of toothless guys with a washboard and a jug, some hard cider, and a few plastic hearts."

"No." She laughed, jabbed him with her finger. "But something between that and this. It's my first bowling alley dance, and I'm impressed. And look! Isn't that His Honor, the mayor, getting down?"

"With his wife's cousin, who is the choir director for the First Methodist Church."

"Isn't that your assistant, Fox?" Layla gestured to a table.

"Yeah. Fortunately, the guy she's kissing is her husband."

"They look completely in love."

"Guess they are. I don't know what I'm going to do without her. They're moving to Minneapolis in a couple months. I wish they'd just take off for a few weeks in July instead of—" He caught himself. "No shop talk tonight. Do you want to scare up a table?"

"Perfect for people-watching," Quinn agreed, then spun toward the band. " 'In the Mood'!"

"Signature piece for them. Do you swing?" Cal asked her.

"Damn right." She glanced at him, considered. "Do you?"

"Let's go see what you've got, Blondie." He grabbed her hand, pulled her out to the dance floor.

Fox watched the spins and footwork. "I absolutely can't do that."

"Neither can I. Wow." Layla's eyes widened. "They're really good."

On the dance floor, Cal set Quinn up for a double spin, whipped her back. "Lessons?"

"Four years. You?"

"Three." When the song ended and bled into a slow number, he fit Quinn's body to his and blessed his mother. "I'm glad you're here."

"Me, too." She nuzzled her cheek to his. "Everything feels good tonight. Sweet and shiny. And mmm," she murmured when he led her into a stylish turn. "Sexy." Tipping back her head, she smiled at him. "I've completely reversed my cynical take on Valentine's Day. I now consider it the perfect holiday."

He brushed his lips over hers. "After this dance, why don't we sneak off to the storeroom upstairs and neck?"

"Why wait?"

With a laugh, he started to bring her close again. And froze.

The hearts bled. The glittery art board dripped, and splattered red on the dance floor, plopped on tables, slid down the hair and faces of people while they laughed, or chatted, strolled or swayed.

"Quinn."

"I see it. Oh God."

The vocalist continued to sing of love and longing as the red and silver balloons overhead popped like gunshots. And from them rained spiders.

Twelve

QUINN BARELY MANAGED TO MUFFLE A SCREAM, and would have danced back as the spiders skittered over the floor if Cal hadn't gripped her.

"Not real." He said it with absolute and icy calm. "It's not real."

Someone laughed, and the sound spiked wildly. There were shouts of approval as the music changed tempo to hip-grinding rock.

"Great party, Cal!" Amy from the flower shop danced by with a wide, blood-splattered grin.

With his arm still tight around Quinn, Cal began to back off the floor. He needed to see his family, needed to see . . . And there was Fox, gripping Layla's hand as he wound his way through the oblivious crowd.

"We need to go," Fox shouted.

"My parents—"

Fox shook his head. "It's only happening because we're here. I think it only can happen because we're here. Let's move out. Let's move."

As they pushed between tables, the tiny tea lights in the centerpieces flashed like torches, belching a volcanic spew of smoke. Cal felt it in his throat, stinging, even as his foot crunched down on a fist-sized spider. On the little stage, the drummer swung into a wild solo with bloodied sticks. When they reached the doors, Cal glanced back.

He saw the boy floating above the dancers. Laughing.

"Straight out." Following Fox's line of thought, Cal pulled Quinn toward the exit. "Straight out of the building. Then we'll see. Then we'll damn well see."

"They didn't see." Out of breath, Layla stumbled outside. "Or feel. It wasn't happening for them."

"It's outside the box, okay, it's pushed outside the lines. But only for us." Fox stripped off his jacket and tossed it over Layla's shaking shoulders. "Giving us a preview of coming attractions. Arrogant bastard."

"Yes." Quinn nodded, even as her stomach rolled. "I think you're right, because every time it puts on a show, it costs energy. So we get that lull between production numbers."

"I have to go back." He'd left his family. Even if retreat was to defend, Cal couldn't stand and do nothing while his family was inside. "I need to be in there, need to close down when the event's over."

"We'll all go back," Quinn linked her cold fingers with Cal's. "These performances are always of pretty short duration. It lost its audience, and unless it's got enough for a second act, it's done for tonight. Let's go back. It's freezing out here."

Inside, the tea lights glimmered softly, and the hearts glittered. The polished dance floor was unstained. Cal saw his parents dancing, his mother's head resting on his father's shoulder. When she caught his eye and smiled at him, Cal felt the fist twisting in his belly relax.

"I don't know about you, but I'd really like another glass of champagne." Quinn blew out a breath, as her eyes went sharp and hard. "Then you know what? Let's dance."

FOX WAS SPRAWLED ON THE COUCH WATCHING some drowsy black-and-white movie on TV when Cal and Quinn came into the rental house after midnight. "Layla went up," he said as he shoved himself to sitting. "She was beat."

The subtext, that she'd wanted to be well tucked away before her housemate and Cal came up, was perfectly clear.

"Is she all right?" Quinn asked.

"Yeah. Yeah, she handles herself. Anything else happen after we left?"

Cal shook his head as his gaze tracked over to the window, and the dark. "Just a big, happy party momentarily interrupted for some of us by supernatural blood and spiders. Everything okay here?"

"Yeah, except for the fact these women buy Diet Pepsi. Classic Coke," he said to Quinn. "A guy has to have some standards."

"We'll look right into that. Thanks, Fox." She stepped up and kissed his cheek. "For hanging out until we got back."

"No big. It got me out of cleanup duty and let me watch . . ." He looked back at the little TV screen. "I have no idea. You ought to think about getting cable. ESPN."

"I don't know how I've lived without it these last few days."

He grinned as he pulled on his coat. "Humankind shouldn't live by network alone. Call me if you need anything," he added as he headed for the door.

"Fox." Cal trailed behind him. After a murmured conversation, Fox sent Quinn a quick wave and left.

"What was that?"

"I asked if he'd bunk at my place tonight, check on Lump. It's no problem. I've got Coke and ESPN."

"You've got worry all over you, Cal."

"I'm having a hard time taking it off."

"It can't hurt us, not yet. It's all head games. Mean, disgusting, but just psychological warfare."

"It means something, Quinn." He gave her arms a quick, almost absent rub before turning to check the dark, again. "That it can do it now, with us. That I had that episode with Ann. It means something."

"And you have to think about it. You think a lot, have all sorts of stores up here." She tapped her temple. "The fact that you do is, well, it's comforting to me and oddly attractive. But you know what? After this really long, strange day, it might be good for us not to think at all."

"That's a good idea." Take a break, he told himself. Take some normal. Walking back to her, he skimmed his fingers over her cheek, then let them trail down her arm until they linked with hers. "Why don't we try that?"

He drew her toward the steps, started up. There were a few homey creaks, the click and hum of the furnace, and nothing else.

"Do you—"

He cut her off by cupping a hand on her cheek, then laying his lips on hers. Soft and easy as a sigh. "No questions either. Then we'd have to think of the answers."

"Good point."

Just the room, the dark, the woman. That was all there would be, all he wanted for the night. Her scent, her skin, the fall of her hair, the sounds two people made when they discovered each other.

It was enough. It was more than enough.

He closed the door behind him.

"I like candles." She drew away to pick up a long, slim lighter to set the candles she'd scattered around the room to flame.

In their light she looked delicate, more delicate than she was. He enjoyed the contrast of reality and illusion. The mattress and box spring sat on the floor, covered by sheets that looked crisp and pearly against a blanket of deep, rich purple. His tulips sat like a cheerful carnival on the scarred wood of her flea market dresser.

She'd hung fabric in a blurry blend of colors over the windows to close out the night. And when she turned from them, she smiled.

It was, for him, perfect.

"Maybe I should tell you—"

He shook his head, stepped toward her.

"Later." He did the first thing that came to mind, lifting his hands to her hair. He drew the pins out, let them fall. When the weight of it tumbled free, over her shoulders, down her back, he combed his fingers through it. With his eyes on hers, he wrapped her hair around his fist like a rope, gave a tug.

"There's still a lot of later," he said, and took her mouth with his.

Her lips, for him, were perfect. Soft and full, warm and generous. He felt a quick tremble from her as her arms wound around him, as she pressed her body to his. She didn't yield, didn't soften—not yet. Instead she met his slow, patient assault with one of her own.

He slid the jacket from her shoulders, let it fall like the pins so his hands, his fingertips could explore silk and lace and flesh. While their lips brushed, rubbed, pressed, her hands came to his shoulders, then shoved at his jacket until it dropped away.

He tasted her throat, heard her purr of approval. As he eased back, he danced his fingers over the alluring line of her collarbone. Her eyes were vivid, alight with anticipation. He wanted to see them heavy. He wanted to see them go blind. Watching them, watching her, he let his fingers trail down to the swell of her breast where the lace flirted. And watching her still, glided them over the lace, over the silk to cup her while his thumb lightly rubbed, rubbed to tease her nipple.

He heard her breath catch, release, felt her shiver even

as she reached to him to unbutton his shirt. Her hands slid up his torso, spread. He knew his heartbeat skipped, but his own hand made the journey almost lazily to the waistband of her pants. The flesh there was warm, and her muscles quivered as his fingers did a testing sweep. Then with a flick and a tug, her pants floated down her legs.

The move was so sudden, so unexpected, she couldn't anticipate or prepare. Everything had been so slow, so dreamy, then his hands hooked under her arms, lifted her straight off her feet. The quick, careless show of strength shocked her system, made her head swim. Even when he set her back down, her knees stayed weak.

His gaze skimmed down, over the camisole, over the frothy underwear she'd donned with the idea of making him crazy. His lips curved as his eyes came back to hers.

"Nice."

It was all he said, and her mouth went dry. It was ridiculous. She'd had other men look at her, touch her, want her. But he did, and her throat went dry. She tried to find something clever and careless to say back, but could barely find the wit to breathe.

Then he hooked his finger in the waist of her panties, gave one easy tug. She stepped toward him like a woman under a spell.

"Let's see what's under here," he murmured, and lifted the camisole over her head. "Very nice," was his comment as he traced his fingertip along the edge of her bra.

She couldn't remember her moves, had to remind herself she was *good* at this—actively good, not just the type who went limp and let a guy do all the work. She reached for the hook of his trousers, fumbled.

"You're shaking."

"Shut up. I feel like an idiot."

He took her hands, brought them both to his lips and she knew she was as sunk as the *Titanic*. "Sexy," he corrected. "What you are is stupendously sexy."

"Cal." She had to concentrate to form the words. "I really need to lie down."

There was that smile again, and though it might have transmitted *self-satisfied male*, she really didn't give a damn.

Then they were on the bed, aroused bodies on cool, crisp sheets, candlelight flickering like magic in the dark. And his hands, his mouth, went to work on her.

He runs a bowling alley, she thought as he simply saturated her with pleasure. How did he get hands like this? Where did he learn to . . . Oh my God.

She came in a long, rolling wave that seemed to curl up from her toes, ride over her legs, burst in her center then wash over heart and mind. She clung to it, greedily wringing every drop of shock and delight until she was both limp and breathless.

Okay, okay, was all her brain could manage. Okay, wow.

Her body was a feast of curves and quivers. He could have lingered over those lovely breasts, the strong line of torso, that feminine flare of hip for days. Then there were her legs, smooth and strong and . . . sensitive. So many places to touch, so much to taste, and all the endless night to savor.

She rose to him, wrapped around him, arched and flowed and answered. He felt her heart thundering under his lips, heard her moan as he used his tongue to torment. Her fingers dug into his shoulders, his hips, her hands squeezing then gliding to fray the taut line of his control.

Kisses became more urgent. The cool air of the room went hot, went thick as smoke. When the need became a blur, he slipped inside her. And yes, watched her eyes go blind.

He gripped her hands to anchor himself, to stop himself from simply plunging, from bulleting by the aching pleasure to release. Her fingers tightened on his, and that pleasure glowed on her face with each long, slow thrust. Stay with me, he thought, and she did, beat for beat. Until it built and built in her ragged breaths, in the shivering of her body. She made a helpless sound as she closed her eyes, turned her head on the pillow. When her body melted under him, he pressed his face to that exposed curve of her neck. And let himself go.

HE LAY QUIET, THINKING SHE MIGHT HAVE fallen asleep. She'd rolled so that her head was on his shoulder, her arm tossed across his chest, and her leg hooked around his. It was, he thought, a little like being tied up with a Quinn bow. And he couldn't find anything not to like about it.

"I was going to say something."

Not asleep, he realized, though her words were drunk and slurry.

"About what?"

"Mmm. I was going to say, when we first came into the room. I was going to say something." She curled closer, and he realized the heat sex had generated had ebbed, and she was cold.

"Hold on." He had to unwind her, to which she gave a couple of halfhearted mutters of protest. But when he pulled up the blanket, she snuggled right in. "Better?"

"Couldn't be any. I was going to say that I've been—more or less—thinking about getting you naked since I met you."

"That's funny. I've been more or less thinking the same about you. You've got an amazing body there, Quinn."

"Lifestyle change, for which I could now preach like an evangelist. However." She levered up so she could look down into his face. "Had I known what it would be like, I would've had you naked in five minutes flat."

He grinned. "Once again, our thoughts run on parallel lines. Do that thing again. No," he said with a laugh when her eyebrows wiggled. "This thing."

He tugged her head down again until it rested on his shoulder, then drew her arm over his chest. "And the leg. That's it," he said when she obliged. "That's perfect."

The fact that it was gave her a nice warm glow under her

heart. Quinn closed her eyes, and without a worry in the world, drifted off to sleep.

IN THE DARK, SHE WOKE WHEN SOMETHING FELL on her. She managed a breathless squeal, shoved herself to sitting, balled her hands into fists.

"Sorry, sorry."

She recognized Cal's whisper, but it was too late to stop the punch. Her fist jabbed into something hard enough to sting her knuckles. "Ow! Ow! Shit."

"I'll say," Cal muttered.

"What the hell are you doing?"

"Tripping, falling down, and getting punched in the head."

"Why?"

"Because it's pitch-dark." He shifted, rubbed his sore temple. "And I was trying not to wake you up, and you hit me. In the head."

"Well, I'm sorry," she hissed right back. "For all I knew you could've been a mad rapist, or more likely, given the location, a demon from hell. What are you doing milling around in the dark?"

"Trying to find my shoes, which I think is what I tripped over."

"You're leaving?"

"It's morning, and I've got a breakfast meeting in a couple hours."

"It's dark."

"It's February, and you've got those curtain deals over the windows. It's about six thirty."

"Oh God." She plopped back down. "Six thirty isn't morning, even in February. Or maybe especially."

"Which is why I was trying not to wake you up."

She shifted. She could make him out now, a little, as her eyes adjusted. "Well, I'm awake, so why are you still whispering?"

"I don't know. Maybe I have brain damage from getting punched in the head."

Something about the baffled irritation in his voice stirred her juices. "Aw. Why don't you crawl back in here with me where it's all nice and warm? I'll kiss it and make it better."

"That's a cruel thing to suggest when I have a breakfast meeting with the mayor, the town manager, and the town council."

"Sex and politics go together like peanut butter and jelly."

"That may be, but I've got to go home, feed Lump, drag Fox out of bed as he's in on this meeting. Shower, shave, and change so it doesn't look like I've been having hot sex."

As he dragged on his shoes, she roused herself to push up again, then slither around him. "You could do all that after."

Her breasts, warm and full, pressed against his back as she nibbled on the side of his throat. And her hand snuck down to where he'd already gone rock hard.

"You've got a mean streak, Blondie."

"Maybe you ought to teach me a lesson." She let out a choked laugh when he swiveled and grabbed her.

This time when he fell on her, it was on purpose.

HE WAS LATE FOR THE MEETING, BUT HE WAS feeling too damn good to care. He ordered an enormous breakfast—eggs, bacon, hash browns, two biscuits. He worked his way through it while Fox gulped down Coke as if it were the antidote to some rare and fatal poison in his bloodstream, and the others engaged in small talk.

Small talk edged into town business. It may have been February, but plans for the annual Memorial Day parade had to be finalized. Then there was the debate about installing new benches in the park. Most of it washed over Cal as he ate, as he thought about Quinn.

He tuned back in, primarily because Fox kicked him under the table.

"The Branson place is only a couple doors down from the Bowl-a-Rama," Mayor Watson continued. "Misty said it looked like the house on either side went dark, too, but across the street, the lights were on. Phones went out, too. Spooked her pretty good, she said when Wendy and I picked her up after the dance. Only lasted a few minutes."

"Maybe a breaker," Jim Hawkins suggested, but he looked at his son.

"Maybe, but Misty said it all flickered and snapped for a few seconds. Power surge maybe. But I think I'm going to urge Mike Branson to get his wiring checked out. Could be something's shorting out. We don't want an electrical fire."

How did they manage to forget? Cal wondered. Was it a defense mechanism, amnesia, or simply part of the whole ugly situation?

Not all of them. He could see the question, the concern in his father's eyes, in one or two of the others. But the mayor and most of the council were moving on to a discussion of painting the bleachers in the ballpark before Little League season began.

There had been other odd power surges, other strange power outages. But never until June, never before that final countdown to the Seven.

When the meeting was over, Fox walked to the bowling center with Cal and his father. They didn't speak until they were inside, and the door closed behind them.

"It's too early for this to happen," Jim said immediately. "It's more likely a power surge, or faulty wiring."

"It's not. Things have been happening already," Cal told him. "And it's not just Fox and I who've seen them. Not this time."

"Well." Jim sat down heavily at one of the tables in the grill section. "What can I do?"

Take care of yourself, Cal thought. Take care of Mom. But it would never be enough. "Anything feels off, you tell me. Tell Fox, or Gage when he gets here. There are more of us this time. Quinn and Layla, they're part of it. We need to figure out how and why."

His great-grandmother had known Quinn was connected, Cal thought. She'd sensed something. "I need to talk to Gran."

"Cal, she's ninety-seven. I don't care how spry she is, she's still ninety-seven."

"I'll be careful."

"You know, I'm going to talk to Mrs. H again." Fox shook his head. "She's jumpy, nervous. Making noises about leaving next month instead of April. I figured it was just restlessness now that she's decided to move. Maybe it's more."

"All right." Jim blew out a breath. "You two go do what you need to do. I'll handle things here. I know how to run the center," he said before Cal could protest. "Been doing it awhile now."

"Okay. I'll run Gran to the library if she wants to go today. I'll be back after, and we can switch off. You can pick her up, take her home."

CAL WALKED TO ESSIE'S HOUSE. SHE ONLY LIVED a block away in the pretty little house she shared with his cousin Ginger. Essie's concession to her age was to have Ginger live in, take care of the house, the grocery shopping, most of the cooking, and be her chauffeur for duties like doctors' and dentist's appointments.

Cal knew Ginger to be a sturdy, practical sort who stayed out of his gran's way—and her business—unless she needed to do otherwise. Ginger preferred TV to books, and lived for a trio of afternoon soaps. Her disastrous and childless marriage had turned her off men, except television beefcake or those within the covers of *People* magazine.

As far as Cal could tell, his gran and his cousin bumped along well enough in the little dollhouse with its trim front yard and cheerful blue porch.

When he arrived he didn't see Ginger's car at the curb, and wondered if his gran had an early medical appointment. His father kept Essie's schedule in his head, as he kept so much else, but he'd been upset that morning.

Still, it was more likely that Ginger had taken a run to the grocery store.

He crossed the porch and knocked. It didn't surprise him when the door opened. Even upset, his father rarely forgot anything.

But it did surprise him to see Quinn at the threshold.

"Hi. Come on in. Essie and I are just having some tea in the parlor."

He gripped her arm. "Why are you here?"

The greeting smile faded at the sharp tone. "I have a job to do. And Essie called me."

"Why?"

"Maybe if you come in instead of scowling at me, we'll both find out."

Seeing no other choice, Cal walked into his great-grandmother's lovely living room where African violets bloomed in purple profusion in the windows, where built-in shelves Fox's father had crafted were filled with books, family pictures, little bits and bobs of memories. Where the company tea set was laid out on the low table in front of the high-backed sofa his mother had reupholstered only the previous spring.

Where his beloved gran sat like a queen in her favored wingback chair. "Cal." She lifted her hand for his, and her cheek for his kiss. "I thought you'd be tied up all morning between the meeting and center business."

"Meeting's over, and Dad's at the center. I didn't see Ginger's car."

"She's off running some errands since I had company. Quinn's just pouring the tea. Go get yourself a cup out of the cupboard."

"No, thanks. I'm fine. Just had breakfast."

"I would've called you, too, if I'd realized you'd have time this morning."

"I've always got time for you, Gran."

"He's my boy," she said to Quinn, squeezing Cal's hand

before she released it to take the tea Quinn offered. "Thank you. Please, sit down, both of you. I might as well get right to it. I need to ask you if there was an incident last night, during the dance. An incident just before ten."

She looked hard at Cal's face as she asked, and what she saw had her closing her eyes. "So there was." Her thin voice quivered. "I don't know whether to be relieved or afraid. Relieved because I thought I might be losing my mind. Afraid because I'm not. It was real then," she said quietly. "What I saw."

"What did you see?"

"It was as if I were behind a curtain. As if a curtain had dropped, or a shroud, and I had to look through it. I thought it was blood, but no one seemed to notice. No one noticed all the blood, or the things that crawled and clattered over the floor, over the tables." Her hand lifted to rub at her throat. "I couldn't see clearly, but I saw a shape, a black shape. It seemed to float in the air on the other side of the curtain. I thought it was death."

She smiled a little as she lifted her tea with a steady hand. "You prepare for death at my age, or you damn well should. But I was afraid of that shape. Then it was gone, the curtain lifted again, and everything was exactly as it should be."

"Gran—"

"Why didn't I tell you last night?" she interrupted. "I can read your face like a book, Caleb. Pride, fear. I simply wanted to get out, to be home, and your father drove me. I needed to sleep, and I did. This morning, I needed to know if it was true."

"Mrs. Hawkins—"

"You'll call me Essie now," she said to Quinn.

"Essie, have you ever had an experience like this before?"

"Yes. I didn't tell you," she said when Cal cursed. "Or anyone. It was the summer you were ten. That first summer. I saw terrible things outside the house, things that couldn't be. That black shape that was sometimes a man, sometimes a dog. Or a hideous combination of both. Your grandfather didn't see, or wouldn't. I always thought he simply wouldn't see. There were horrible things that week."

She closed her eyes a moment, then took another soothing sip of tea. "Neighbors, friends. Things they did to themselves and each other. After the second night, you came to the door. Do you remember, Cal?"

"Yes, ma'am, I remember."

"Ten years old." She smiled at Quinn. "He was only a little boy, with his two young friends. They were so afraid. You could see and feel the fear and the, valor, I want to say, coming off them like light. You told me we had to pack up, your grandfather and I. We had to come stay at your house. That it wasn't safe in town. Didn't you ever wonder why I didn't argue, or pat you on the head and shoo you on home?"

"No. I guess there was too much else going on. I just wanted you and Pop safe."

"And every seven years, I packed for your grandfather and me, then when he died, just for me, now this year it'll be Ginger and me. But it's coming sooner and stronger this time."

"I'll pack for you, Gran, for you and Ginger right now."

"Oh, I think we're safe enough for now," she said to Cal. "When it's time, Ginger and I can put what we'll need together. I want you to take the books. I know I've read them, you've read them. It seems countless times. But we've missed something, somehow. And now, we have fresh eyes."

Quinn turned toward Cal, narrowed her eyes. "Books?"

Thirteen

Fox made a run to the bank. It was completely unnecessary since the papers in his briefcase could have been dropped off at any time—or more efficiently, the client could have come into his office to ink them.

But he'd wanted to get out, get some air, walk off his frustration.

It was time to admit that he'd still held on to the hope that Alice Hawbaker would change her mind, or that he could change it for her. Maybe it was selfish, and so what? He depended on her, he was used to her. And he loved her.

The love meant he had no choice but to let her go. The love meant if he could take back the last twenty minutes he'd spent with her, he would.

She'd nearly broken down, he remembered as he strode along in his worn-down hiking boots (no court today). She never broke. She never even cracked, but he'd pushed her hard enough to cause fissures. He'd always regret it.

If we stay, we'll die. She'd said that with tears in her voice, with tears glimmering in her eyes.

He'd only wanted to know why she was so set to leave, why she was jumpier every day to the point she wanted to go sooner than originally planned.

So he'd pushed. And finally, she'd told him.

She'd seen their deaths, over and over, every time she closed her eyes. She'd seen herself getting her husband's deer rifle out of the locked case in his basement workroom. Seen herself calmly loading it. She'd watched herself walk upstairs, through the kitchen where the dinner dishes were loaded into the dishwasher, the counters wiped clean. Into the den where the man she'd loved for thirty-six years, had made three children with, was watching the Orioles battle the Red Sox. The O's were up two-zip, but the Sox were at the plate, with a man on second, one out. Top of the sixth. The count was one and two.

When the pitcher wound up, she pumped a bullet through the back of her husband's head as he sat in his favorite recliner.

Then she'd put the barrel under her own chin.

So, yes, he had to let her go, just as he'd had to make an excuse to leave the office because he knew her well enough to understand she didn't want him around until she was composed again.

Knowing he'd given her what she wanted and needed didn't stop him from feeling guilty, frustrated, and inadequate.

He ducked in to buy flowers. She'd accept them as a peace offering, he knew. She liked flowers in the office, and often picked them up herself as he tended to forget.

He came out with an armload of mixed blooms, and nearly ran over Layla.

She stumbled back, even took a couple extra steps in retreat. He saw upset and unhappiness on her face, and wondered if it was his current lot to make women nervous and miserable.

"Sorry. Wasn't looking."

She didn't smile, just started fiddling with the buttons of her coat. "It's okay. Neither was I."

He should just go. He didn't have to tap in to her mind to feel the jangle of nerves and misery surrounding her. It seemed to him she never relaxed around him, was always making that little move away. Or maybe she never relaxed ever. Could be a New York thing, he mused. He sure as hell hadn't been able to relax there.

But there was too much of the how-can-I-fix-this in him. "Problem?"

Now *her* eyes glimmered with tears, and Fox quite simply wanted to step into the street into the path of a passing truck.

"Problem? How could there possibly be a problem? I'm living in a strange house in a strange town, seeing things that aren't there—or worse, *are* there and want me dead. Nearly everything I own is sitting in my apartment in New York. An apartment I have to pay for, and my very understanding and patient boss called this morning to tell me, regretfully, that if I couldn't come back to work next week, she'll have to replace me. So do you know what I did?"

"No."

"I started to pack. Sorry, really, sorry, but I've got a *life* here. I have responsibilities and bills and a goddamn routine." She gripped her elbows in opposite hands as if to hold herself in place. "I need to get back to them. And I couldn't. I just couldn't do it. I don't even know why, not on any reasonable level, but I couldn't. So now I'm going to be out of a job, which means I won't be able to afford my apartment. And I'm probably going to end up dead or institutionalized, and that's after my landlord sues me for back rent. So problems? No, not me."

He listened all the way through without interruption, then just nodded. "Stupid question. Here." He shoved the flowers at her.

"What?"

"You look like you could use them."

Flummoxed, she stared at him, stared at the colorful blooms in her arms. And felt the sharpest edge of what might have been hysteria dulling into perplexity. "But . . . you bought them for someone."

"I can buy more." He waved a thumb at the door of the flower shop. "And I can help with the landlord if you get me the information. The rest, well, we're working on it. Maybe something pushed you to come here, and maybe something's pushing you to stay, but at the bottom of it, Layla, it's your choice. If you decide you have to leave . . ." He thought of Alice again, and some of his own frustration ebbed. "Nobody's going to blame you for it. But if you stay, you need to commit."

"I've—"

"No, you haven't." Absently, he reached out to secure the strap of her bag that had slipped down to the crook of her elbow back on her shoulder. "You're still looking for the way out, the loophole in the deal that means you can pack your bags and go without consequences. Just go back to the way things were. Can't blame you for it. But choose, then stick. That's all. I've got to finish up and get back. Talk to you later."

He stepped back into the florist and left her standing speechless on the sidewalk.

QUINN SHOUTED DOWN FROM THE SECOND floor when Layla came in.

"It's me," Layla called up, and still conflicted, walked back to the kitchen with the flowers and the bottles and pots she'd bought in a gift shop on the walk home.

"Coffee." Quinn bustled in a few moments later. "Going to need lots and lots of . . . Hey, pretty," she said when she saw the flowers Layla was clipping to size and arranging in various bottles.

"They really are. Quinn, I need to talk to you."

"Need to talk to you, too. You go first."

"I was going to leave this morning."

Quinn stopped on the way to fill the coffeepot. "Oh."

"And I was going to do my best to get out before you came back, and talked me out of it. I'm sorry."

"Okay. It's okay." Quinn busied herself making the coffee. "I'd avoid me, too, if I wanted to do something I didn't want me to do. If you get me."

"Oddly enough, I do."

"Why aren't you gone?"

"Let me backtrack." While she finished fussing with the flowers, Layla related the telephone conversation she'd had with her boss.

"I'm sorry. It's so unfair. I don't mean your boss is unfair. She's got a business to run. But that this whole thing is unfair." Quinn watched Layla arrange multicolored daisies in an oversized teacup. "On a practical level I'm okay, because this is my job, or the job I picked. I can afford to take the time to be here and supplement that with articles. I could help—"

"That's not what I'm looking for. I don't want you to loan me money, or to carry my share of the expenses. If I stay, it's because I've chosen to stay." Layla looked at the flowers, thought of what Fox had said. "I think, until today, I didn't accept that, or want to accept it. Easier to think I'd been driven to come here, and that I was being pressured to stay. I wanted to go because I didn't want any of this to be happening. But it is. So I'm staying because I've decided to stay. I'll just have to figure out the practicalities."

"I've got a couple of ideas on that, maybe just a thumb in the dike. Let me think about them. The flowers were a nice idea. Cheer up a bad news day."

"Not my idea. Fox gave them to me when I ran into him outside the florist. I cut loose on him." Layla shrugged, then gathered up the bits of stems she'd cut off, the florist wrappings. "He's basically, 'how are you doing,' and I'm 'how am I doing? I'll tell you how I'm doing.' " She tossed the leavings in the trash, then leaned back and laughed. "God, I just blasted him. So he gives me the flowers he'd just bought, thrusted them at me, really, and gave me a short, pithy lecture. I guess I deserved it."

"Hmm." Quinn added the information to the think-pot she was stirring. "And you feel better?"

"Better?" Layla walked into the little dining room to arrange a trio of flowers on the old, drop-leaf table they'd picked up at the flea market. "I feel more resolved. I don't know if that's better."

"I've got something to keep you busy."

"Thank God. I'm used to working, and all this time on my hands makes me bitchy."

"Come with me. Don't leave all the flowers, you should have some of them in your room."

"I thought they'd be for the house. He didn't buy them for me or—"

"He gave them to you. Take some of them up. You made me take the tulips up to mine." To solve the matter, Quinn picked up one of the little pots and a slender bottle herself. "Oh, coffee."

"I'll get it." Layla poured one of the mugs for Quinn, doctored it, then got a bottle of water for herself. "What's the project that's going to keep me busy?"

"Books."

"We already have the books from the library."

"Now we have some from Estelle Hawkins's personal store. Some of them are journals. I haven't really scratched the surface yet," Quinn explained as they headed up. "I'd barely gotten home ahead of you. But there are three of them written by Ann Hawkins. After her children were born. Her children with Giles Dent."

"But Mrs. Hawkins must have read them before, shown them to Cal."

"Right, and right. They've all been read, studied, pondered over. But not by us, Layla. Fresh eyes, different angle." She detoured to Layla's room to set the flowers down, then took the coffee mug on her way to the office. "And I've already got the first question on my notes. Where are the others?"

"Other journals?"

"Ann's other journals, because I'm betting there are

more, or were. Where's the journal she kept when she lived with Dent, when she was carrying her triplets? That's one of the new angles I hope our fresh eyes can find. Where would they be, and why aren't they with the others?"

"If she did write others, they might have been lost or destroyed."

"Let's hope not." Quinn's eyes were sharp as she sat, lifted a small book bound in brown leather. "Because I think she had some of the answers we need."

CAL COULDN'T REASONABLY BREAK AWAY FROM the center until after seven. Even then he felt guilty leaving his father to handle the rest of the night. He'd called Quinn in the late afternoon to let her know he'd be by when he could. And her absent response had been for him to bring food with him.

She'd have to settle for pizza, he thought as he carried the takeout boxes up the steps. He hadn't had the time or inclination to figure out what her lifestyle-change option might be.

As he knocked, the wind whistled across the back of his neck, had him glancing uneasily behind him. Something coming, he thought. Something's in the wind.

Fox answered the door. "Thank God, pizza and a testosterone carrier. I'm outnumbered here, buddy."

"Where's the estrogen?"

"Up. Buried in books and notes. Charts. Layla makes charts. I made the mistake of telling them I had a dry-wipe board down at the office. They made me go get it, haul it in here, haul it upstairs." The minute Cal set the pizza down on the kitchen counter, Fox shoved up the lid and took out a slice. "There's been talk of index cards. Colored index cards. Don't leave me here alone again."

Cal grunted, opened the fridge and found, as he'd hoped and dreamed, Fox had stocked beer. "Maybe we were never organized enough, so we missed some detail. Maybe—"

He broke off as Quinn rushed in. "Hi! Pizza. Oh-oh. Well, I'll work it off with the power of my mind and with a session in the gym tomorrow morning."

She got down plates, passed one to Fox, who was already halfway through with his first slice. Then she smiled that smile at Cal. "Got anything else for me?"

He leaned right in, laid his mouth on hers. "Got that."

"Coincidentally, exactly what I wanted. So how about some more." She got a fistful of his shirt and tugged him down for another, longer kiss.

"You guys want me to leave? Can I take the pizza with me?"

"As a matter of fact," Cal began.

"Now, now." Quinn patted Cal's chest to ease him back. "Mommy and Daddy were just saying hello," she told Fox. "Why don't we eat in the dining room like the civilized. Layla's coming right down."

"How come I can't say hello to Mommy?" Fox complained as Quinn sailed off with the plates.

"Because then I'd have to beat you unconscious."

"As if." Amused, Fox grabbed the pizza boxes and started after Quinn. "Beverages on you, bro."

Shortly after they were seated, drinks, plates, napkins, pizza passed around, Layla came in with a large bowl and a stack of smaller ones. "I put this together earlier. I wasn't sure what you might bring," she said to Cal.

"You made salad?" Quinn asked.

"My specialty. Chop, shred, mix. No cooking."

"Now, I'm forced to be good." Quinn gave up the dream of two slices of pizza, settled on one and a bowl of Layla's salad. "We made progress," she began as she forked up the first bite.

"Yeah, ask the ladies here how to make tallow candles or black raspberry preserves," Fox suggested. "They've got it down."

"So, some of the information contained in the books we're going through may not currently apply to our situation." Quinn raised her eyebrows at Fox. "But one day I may be called on in some blackout emergency to make a tallow candle. By progress, however, I mean that there's a lot of interesting information in Ann's journals."

"We've read them," Cal pointed out. "Multiple times."

"You're not women." She held up a finger. "And, yes, Essie is. But Essie's a woman who's a descendent, who's part of this town and its history. And however objective she might try to be, she may have missed some nuances. First question, where are the others?"

"There aren't any others."

"I disagree. There aren't any others that were found. Essie said these books were passed to her by her father, because she loved books. I called her to be sure, but he never said if there were more."

"If there'd been more," Cal insisted, "he'd have given them to her."

"If he had them. There's a long span between the sixteen hundreds and the nineteen hundreds," Quinn pointed out. "Things get misplaced, lost, tossed out. According to the records and your own family's oral history, Ann Hawkins lived most of her life in what's now the community center on Main Street, which was previously the library. Books, library. Interesting."

"A library Gran knew inside and out," Cal returned. "There couldn't have been a book in there she didn't know about. And something like this?" He shook his head. "She'd have it if it was to be had."

"Unless she never saw it. Maybe it was hidden, or maybe, for the sake of argument, she wasn't *meant* to find it. It wasn't meant to be found, not by her, not then."

"Debatable," Fox commented.

"And something to look into. Meanwhile, she didn't date her journals, so Layla and I are dating them, more or less, by how she writes about her sons. In what we're judging to be the first, her sons are about two to three. In the next they're five because she writes about their fifth birthday very specifically, and about seven, we think, when that one ends. The third it seems that they're young men. We think about sixteen."

"A lot of years between," Layla said.

"Maybe she didn't have anything worth writing about during those years."

"Could be," Quinn said to Cal. "But I'm betting she did, even if it was just about blackberry jam and a trio of active sons. More important now, at least I think so, is where is the journal or journals that cover her time with Dent, to the birth of her sons through to the first two years of their lives? Because you can just bet your ass those were interesting times."

"She writes of him," Layla said quietly. "Of Giles Dent. Again and again, in all the journals we have. She writes about him, of her feelings for him, her dreams about him."

"And always in the present tense," Quinn added.

"It's hard to lose someone you love." Fox turned his beer bottle in his hand.

"It is, but she writes of him, consistently, as if he were alive." Quinn looked at Cal. "It is not death. We talked about this, how Dent found the way to exist, with this thing. To hold it down or through or inside. Whatever the term. Obviously he couldn't—or didn't—kill or destroy it, but neither could it kill or destroy him. He found a way to keep it under, and to continue to exist. Maybe only for that single purpose. She knew it. Ann knew what he did, and I'm betting she knew how he did it."

"You're not taking into account love and grief," Cal pointed out.

"I'm not discounting them, but when I read her journals, I get the sense of a strong-minded woman. And one who shared a very deep love with a strong-minded man. She defied convention for him, risked shunning and censure. Shared his bed, but I believe, shared his obligations, too. Whatever he planned to do, attempted to do, felt bound to do, he would have shared it with her. They were a unit.

Isn't that what you felt, what we both felt, when we were in the clearing?"

"Yeah." He couldn't deny it, Cal thought. "That's what I felt."

"Going off that, Ann knew, and while she may have told her sons when they were old enough, that part of the Hawkins's oral history could have been lost or bastardized. It happens. I think she would have written it out, too. And put the record somewhere she believed would be safe and protected, until it was needed."

"It's been needed for twenty-one years."

"Cal, that's your responsibility talking, not logic. At least not the line of logic that follows this route. She told you this was the time. That it was always to be this time. Nothing you had, nothing you could have done would have stopped it before this time."

"We let it out," Fox said. "Nothing would have been needed if we hadn't let it out."

"I don't think that's true." Layla shifted toward him, just a little. "And maybe, if we find the other journals, we'll understand. But, we noticed something else."

"Layla caught it right off the bat," Quinn put in.

"Because it was in front of me first. But in any case, it's the names. The names of Ann's sons. Caleb, Fletcher, and Gideon."

"Pretty common for back then." Cal gave a shrug as he pushed his plate away. "Caleb stuck in the Hawkins line more than the other two did. But I've got a cousin Fletch and an uncle Gideon."

"No, first initials," Quinn said impatiently. "I told you they'd missed it," she added to Layla. "C, F, G. Caleb, Fox, Gage."

"Reaching," Fox decided. "Especially when you consider I'm Fox because my mother saw a pack of red foxes running across the field and into the woods about the time she was going into labor with me. My sister Sage? Mom smelled the sage from her herb garden right after Sage was born. It was like that with all four of us."

"You were named after an actual fox? Like a . . . release-the-hounds fox?" Layla wanted to know.

"Well, not a specific one. It was more a . . . You have to meet my mother."

"However Fox got his famous name, I don't think we discount coincidences." Quinn studied Cal's face, saw he was considering it. "And I think there's more than one of Ann Hawkins's descendents at this table."

"Quinn, my father's people came over from Ireland, four generations back," Fox told her. "They weren't here in Ann Hawkins's time because they were plowing fields in Kerry."

"What about your mother's?" Layla asked.

"Wider mix. English, Irish. I think some French. Nobody ever bothered with a genealogy, but I've never heard of any Hawkins on the family tree."

"You may want to take a closer look. How about Gage?" Quinn wondered.

"No idea." And Cal was more than considering it now. "I doubt he does either. I can ask Bill, Gage's father. If it's true, if we're direct descendents, it could explain one of the things we've never understood."

"Why it was you," Quinn said quietly. "You three, the mix of blood from you, Fox, and Gage that opened the door."

"I ALWAYS THOUGHT IT WAS ME."

With the house quiet, and night deep, Cal lay on Quinn's bed with her body curled warm to his. "Just you?"

"They helped trigger it maybe, but yes, me. Because it was my blood—not just that night, but my heritage, you could say. I was the Hawkins. They weren't from here, not the same way I was. Not forever, like I was. Generations back. But if this is true . . . I still don't know how to feel about it."

"You could give yourself a tiny break." She stroked her hand over his heart. "I wish you would."

"Why did he let it happen? Dent? If he'd found a way to stop it, why did he let it come to this?"

"Another question." She pushed herself up until they were eye-to-eye. "We'll figure it out, Cal. We're supposed to. I believe that."

"I'm closer to believing it, with you." He touched her cheek. "Quinn, I can't stay again tonight. Lump may be lazy, but he depends on me."

"Got another hour to spare?"

"Yeah." He smiled as she lowered to him. "I think he'll hold out another hour."

LATER, WHEN HE WALKED OUT TO HIS CAR, THE air shivered so that the trees rattled their empty branches. Cal searched the street for any sign, anything he needed to defend against. But there was nothing but empty road.

Something's in the wind, he thought again, and got in his car to drive home.

IT WAS AFTER MIDNIGHT WHEN THE LOW-GRADE urge for a cigarette buzzed through Gage's brain. He'd given them up two years, three months, and one week before, a fact that could still piss him off.

He turned up the radio to take his mind off it, but the urge was working its way up to craving. He could ignore that, too; he did so all the time. To do otherwise was to believe there was solid truth in the old adage: like father, like son.

He was nothing like his father.

He drank when he wanted a drink, but he never got drunk. Or hadn't since he'd been seventeen, and then the drunkenness had been with absolute purpose. He didn't blame others for his shortcomings, or lash out with his fists on something smaller and weaker so he could feel bigger and stronger.

He didn't even blame the old man, not particularly. You

played the cards you were dealt, to Gage's mind. Or you folded and walked away with your pockets empty.

Luck of the draw.

So he was fully prepared to ignore this sudden, and surprisingly intense desire for a cigarette. But when he considered he was within miles of Hawkins Hollow, a place where he was very likely to die an ugly and painful death, the surgeon general's warnings seemed pretty goddamn puny, and his own self-denial absolutely useless.

When he saw the sign for the Sheetz, he decided what the hell. He didn't want to live forever. He swung into the twenty-four-hour mart, picked up coffee, black, and a pack of Marlboros.

He strode back to the car he'd bought that very evening in D.C. after his plane had landed, and before he'd paid off a small debt. The wind whipped through his hair. The hair was dark as the night, a little longer than he usually wore it, a little shaggy, as he hadn't trusted the barbers in Prague.

There was stubble on his face since he hadn't bothered to shave. It added to the dark, dangerous look that had had the young female clerk who rung up the coffee and cigarettes shivering inwardly with lust.

He'd topped off at six feet, and the skinny build of his youth had filled out. Since his profession was usually sedentary, he kept his muscles toned and his rangy build with regular, often punishing workouts.

He didn't pick fights, but he rarely walked away from one. And he liked to win. His body, his face, his mind, were all tools of his trade. As were his eyes, his voice, and the control he rarely let off the leash.

He was a gambler, and a smart gambler kept all of his tools well honed.

Swinging back onto the road, Gage let the Ferrari rip. Maybe it had been foolish to toss so much of his winnings into a car, but Jesus, it *moved.* And fucking A, he'd ridden his thumb out of the Hollow all those years ago. It felt damn good to ride back in in style.

Funny, now that he'd bought the damn cigarettes, the urge for one had passed. He didn't even want the coffee, the speed was kick enough.

He flew down the last miles of the interstate, whipped onto the exit that would take him to the Hollow. The dark rural road was empty—no surprise to him, not this time of night. There were shadows and shapes—houses, hills, fields, trees. There was a twisting in his gut that he was heading back instead of away, and yet that pull—it never quite left him—that pull toward home was strong.

He reached toward his coffee more out of habit than desire, then was forced to whip the wheel, slam the brakes as headlights cut across the road directly into his path. He blasted the horn, saw the other car swerve.

He thought: Fuck, fuck, *fuck!* I just bought this sucker.

When he caught his breath, and the Ferrari sat sideways in the middle of the road, he thought it was a miracle the crash hadn't come. Inches, he realized. Less than inches.

His lucky goddamn day.

He reversed, pulled to the shoulder, then got out to check on the other driver he assumed was stinking drunk.

She wasn't. What she was, was hopping mad.

"Where the hell did you come from?" she demanded. She slammed out of her car, currently tipped into the shallow ditch along the shoulder, in a blur of motion. He saw a mass of dark gypsy curls wild around a face pale with shock.

Great face, he decided in one corner of his brain. Huge eyes that looked black against her white skin, a sharp nose, a wide mouth, sexily full that may have owned its sensuality to collagen injections.

She wasn't shaking, and he didn't sense any fear along with the fury as she stood on a dark road facing down a complete stranger.

"Lady," he said with what he felt was admirable calm, "where the hell did *you* come from?"

"From that stupid road that looks like all the other stupid roads around here. I looked both damn ways, and you weren't there. Then. How did you . . . Oh never mind. We didn't die."

"Yay."

With her hands on her hips she turned around to study her car. "I can get out of there, right?"

"Yeah. Then there's the flat tire."

"What flat . . . Oh for God's sake! You have to change it." She gave the flat tire on the rear of her car an annoyed kick. "It's the least you can do."

Actually, it wasn't. The least he could do was stroll back to his car and wave good-bye. But he appreciated her bitchiness, and preferred it over quivering. "Pop the trunk. I need the spare and the jack."

When she had, and he'd lifted a suitcase out, set it on the ground, he took one look at her spare. And shook his head. "Not your day. Your spare's toast."

"It can't be. What the hell are you talking about?" She shoved him aside, peered in herself by the glow of the trunk light. "Damn her, damn her, damn her. My sister." She whirled away, paced down the shoulder a few feet, then back. "I loaned her my car for a couple of weeks. This is so typical. She ruins a tire, but does she get it fixed, does she even bother to mention it? No."

She pushed her hair back from her face. "I'm not calling a tow truck at this time of night, then sitting in the middle of nowhere. You're just going to have to give me a ride."

"Am I?"

"It's your fault. At least part of it is."

"Which part?"

"I don't know, and I'm too tired, I'm too mad, I'm too lost in this foreign wilderness to give a damn. I need a ride."

"At your service. Where to?"

"Hawkins Hollow."

He smiled, and there was something dark in it. "Handy. I'm heading there myself." He gestured toward his car. "Gage Turner," he added.

She gestured in turn, rather regally, toward her suitcase. "Cybil Kinski." She lifted her eyebrows when she got her first good look at his car. "You have very nice wheels, Mr. Turner."

"Yeah, and they all work."

Fourteen

CAL WASN'T PARTICULARLY SURPRISED TO SEE Fox's truck in his driveway, despite the hour. Nor was he particularly surprised when he walked in to see Fox blinking sleepily on the couch in front of the TV, with Lump stretched out and snoring beside him.

On the coffee table were a can of Coke, the last of Cal's barbecue potato chips, and a box of Milk Bones. The remains, he assumed, of a guy-dog party.

"Whatcha doing here?" Fox asked groggily.

"I live here."

"She kick you out?"

"No, she didn't kick me out. I came home." Because they were there, Cal dug into the bag of chips and managed to pull out a handful of crumbs. "How many of those did you give him?"

Fox glanced at the box of dog biscuits. "A couple. Maybe five. What're you so edgy about?"

Cal picked up the Coke and gulped down the couple of

warm, flat swallows that were left. "I got a feeling, a . . . thing. You haven't felt anything tonight?"

"I've had feelings and things pretty much steady the last couple weeks." Fox scrubbed his hands over his face, back into his hair. "But yeah, I got something just before you drove up. I was half asleep, maybe all the way. It was like the wind whooshing down the flue."

"Yeah." Cal walked over to stare out the window. "Have you checked in with your parents lately?"

"I talked to my father today. It's all good with them. Why?"

"If all three of us are direct descendents, then one of your parents is in the line," Cal pointed out.

"I figured that out on my own."

"None of our family was ever affected during the Seven. We were always relieved by that." He turned back. "Maybe relieved enough we didn't really ask why."

"Because we figured it, at least partly, was because they lived outside of town. Except for Bill Turner, and who the hell could tell what was going on with him?"

"My parents and yours, they came into town during the Seven. And there were people, you remember what happened out at the Poffenberger place last time?"

"Yeah. Yeah, I remember." Fox rubbed at his eyes. "Being five miles out of town didn't stop Poffenberger from strangling his wife while she hacked at him with a butcher knife."

"Now we know Gran felt things, saw things that first summer, and she saw things the other night. Why is that?"

"Maybe it picks and chooses, Cal." Rising, Fox walked over to toss another log on the fire. "There have always been people who weren't affected, and there have always been degrees with those who were."

"Quinn and Layla are the first outsiders. We figured a connection, but what if that connection is as simple as blood ties?"

Fox sat again, leaned back, stroked a hand over Lump's head as the dog twitched in his sleep. "Good theory. It shouldn't weird you out if you happen to be rolling naked with your cousin a couple hundred times removed."

"Huh." That was a thought. "If they're descendents, the next point to figure is if having them here gives us more muscle, or makes us more vulnerable. Because it's pretty clear this one's it. This one's going to be the all or nothing. So . . . Someone's coming."

Fox pushed off the couch, strode quickly over to stand by Cal. "I don't think the Big Evil's going to drive up to your house, and in a . . ." He peered closer as the car set off Cal's motion lights. "Holy Jesus, is that a Ferrari?" He shot a grin at Cal.

"Gage," they said together.

They went on the front porch, in shirtsleeves, leaving the door open behind them. Gage climbed out of the car, his eyes skimming over them both as he walked back to get his bag out of the trunk. He slung its strap over his shoulder, started up the steps. "You girls having a slumber party?"

"Strippers just left," Fox told him. "Sorry you missed them." Then he rushed forward, flung his arms around Gage in a hard hug. "Man, it's good to see you. When can I drive your car?"

"I was thinking never. Cal."

"Took your goddamn time." The relief, the love, the sheer pleasure pushed him forward to grip Gage just as Fox had.

"Had some business here and there. Want a drink. Need a room."

"Come on in."

In the kitchen, Cal poured whiskey. All of them understood it was a welcome-home toast for Gage, and very likely a drink before war.

"So," Cal began, "I take it you came back flush."

"Oh yeah."

"How much you up?"

Gage turned the glass around in his hand. "Considering expenses, and my new toy out there, about fifty."

"Nice work if you can get it," Fox commented.

"And I can."

"Look a little worn there, brother."

Gage shrugged at Cal. "Long couple of days. Which nearly ended with me in a fiery crash right out on sixty-seven."

"Toy get away from you?" Fox asked.

"Please." Gage smirked at the idea. "Some ditz, of the female and very hot variety, pulled out in front of me. Not another car on the road, and she pulls out in this ancient Karmann Ghia—nice wheels, actually—then she jumps out and goes at me like it was my fault."

"Women," Fox said, "are an endless source of every damn thing."

"And then some. So she's tipped down in the little runoff," Gage went on, gesturing with his free hand. "No big deal, but she's popped a flat. No big deal either, except her spare's a pancake. Turns out she's heading into the Hollow, so I manage to load her two-ton suitcase into my car. Then she's rattling off an address and asking me, like I'm MapQuest, how long it'll take to get there."

He took a slow sip of whiskey. "Lucky for her I grew up here and could tell her I'd have her there in five. She snaps out her phone, calls somebody she calls Q, like James freaking Bond, tells her, as it turns out from the look I got of Q in the doorway—very nice, by the way—to wake up, she'll be there in five minutes. Then—"

Cal rattled off an address. "That the one?"

Gage lowered his glass. "As a matter of fact."

"Something in the wind," Cal murmured. "I guess it was you, and Quinn's Cybil."

"Cybil Kinski," Gage confirmed. "Looks like a gypsy by way of Park Avenue. Well, well." He downed the rest of the whiskey in his glass. "Isn't this a kick in the ass?"

"HE CAME OUT OF NOWHERE." THERE WAS A glass of red wine on the dresser Quinn had picked up in anticipation of Cybil's arrival.

As that arrival had woken Layla, Quinn sat beside her on what would be Cybil's bed while the woman in question swirled around the room, hanging clothes, tucking them in drawers, taking the occasional sip of wine.

"I thought that was it, just it, even though I've never seen any death by car in my future. I swear, I don't know how we missed being bloody pulps tangled in burning metal. I'm a good driver," Cybil said to Quinn.

"You are."

"But I must be better than I thought, and so—fortunately—was he. I know I'm lucky all I got was a scare and a flat tire out of it, but damn Rissa for, well, being Rissa."

"Rissa?" Layla looked blank.

"Cyb's sister Marissa," Quinn explained. "You loaned her your car again."

"I know, I know. I *know*," she said, puffing out a breath that blew curls off her forehead. "I don't know how she manages to talk me into these things. My spare was flat, thanks to Rissa."

"Which explains why you were dropped off from a really sexy sports car."

"He could hardly leave me there, though he looked like the type who'd consider it. All scruffy, gorgeous, and dangerous looking."

"Last time I had a flat," Quinn remembered, "the very nice guy who stopped to help had a paunch over his belt the size of a sack of cement, and ass crack reveal."

"No paunch on this one, and though his coat prevented me from a good look, I'm betting Gage Turner has a superior ass."

"Gage Turner." Layla put a hand on Quinn's thigh. "Quinn."

"Yeah." Quinn let out a breath. "Okay, I guess it's hail, hail, the gang's all here."

IN THE MORNING, QUINN LEFT HER HOUSEMATES sleeping while she jogged over to the community center.

She already knew she'd regret jogging over, because that meant she'd have to jog back—after her workout. But it seemed a cheat on the lifestyle change to drive three blocks to the gym.

And she wanted the thinking time.

There was no buying, for any price, Cybil and Gage Turner had run into each other—almost literally—in the middle of the night just outside of town as a coincidence.

One more thing to add to the list of oddities, Quinn thought as she puffed out air in frosty vapors.

Another addition would be the fact that Cybil had a very sharp sense of direction, but had apparently made wrong turn after wrong turn to end up on that side road at the exact moment Gage was coming up the main.

One more, Quinn decided as she approached the back entrance of the community center, would be Cybil saying "he came out of nowhere." Quinn was willing to take that literally. If Cybil didn't see him, then maybe—in her reality, for just those vital moments—he *hadn't* been there.

So why had it been important for them to meet separately, outside the group? Wasn't it strange enough that they'd both arrived on the same night, at the same time?

She dug out her membership key—thanks Cal—to open the door to the fitness area, pressed her guest pass number on the keypad.

The lights were still off, which was a surprise. Normally when she arrived, they were already on, and at least one of the trio of swivel TVs was tuned to CNN or ESPN or one of the morning talk shows. Very often there was somebody on one of the treadmills or bikes, or pumping weights.

She flipped on the lights, called out. And her voice echoed hollowly. Curious, she walked through, pushed open the door, and saw the lights were also off in the tiny attendant's office, and in the locker room.

Maybe somebody had a late date the night before, she decided. She helped herself to a locker key, stripped down to her workout gear, then grabbed a towel. Opting to start her session with cardio, she switched on the *Today* show before climbing onto the single elliptical trainer the club boasted.

She programmed it, resisting the urge to cheat a few pounds off her weight. As if it mattered, Quinn reminded herself. (Of course, it mattered.)

She started her warm-up pleased with her discipline, and her solitude. Still, she expected the door to slam open any minute, for Matt or Tina, who switched off as attendants, to rush in. By the time she was ten minutes in, she'd kicked up the resistance and was focused on the TV screen to help her get through the workout.

When she hit the first mile, Quinn took a long gulp of water from the sports bottle she'd brought with her. As she started on mile two, she let her mind drift to what she hoped to accomplish that day. Research, the foundation of any project. And she wanted to draft what she thought would be the opening of her book. Writing it out might spark some idea. At some point, she wanted to walk around the town again, with Cybil—and Layla if she was up for it.

A visit to the cemetery was in order with Cybil in tow. Time to pay a call on Ann Hawkins.

Maybe Cal would have time to go with them. Needed to talk to him anyway, discuss how he felt, what he thought, about Gage—whom she wanted to get a look at—and Cybil's arrival. Mostly, she admitted, she just wanted to see him again. Show him off to Cybil.

Look! Isn't he cute? Maybe it was completely high school, but it didn't seem to matter. She wanted to touch him again, even if it was just a quick squeeze of hands. And she was looking forward to a hello kiss, and finding a way to turn that worried look in his eyes into a glint of amusement. She *loved* the way his eyes laughed before the rest of him did, and the way he . . .

Well. Well, well, well. She was absolutely gone over him, she realized. Seriously hooked on the hometown boy. That was kind of cute, too, she decided, except it made her stomach jitter. Still, the jitter wasn't altogether a bad thing.

It was a combination of *oh-oh* and *oh boy!*, and wasn't that interesting?

Quinn's falling in love, she thought, and hit mile two with a dopey smile on her face. She might've been puffing, sweat might have been dribbling down her temples, but she felt just as fresh and cheerful as a spring daisy.

Then the lights went out.

The machine stopped; the TV went blank and silent.

"Oh, shit." Her first reaction wasn't alarm as much as, what now? The dark was absolute, and though she could draw a reasonable picture in her mind where she was in relation to the outside door—and what was between her and the door—she was wary about making her way to it blind.

And then what? she wondered as she waited for her breathing to level. She couldn't possibly fumble her way to the locker room, to her locker and retrieve her clothes. So she'd have to go out in a damn sports bra and bike pants.

She heard the first thud; the chill washed over her skin. And she understood she had much bigger problems than skimpy attire.

She wasn't alone. As her pulse began to bang, she hoped desperately whatever was in the dark with her was human. But the sounds, that unholy thudding that shook the walls, the floor, the awful *scuttling* sounds creeping under it weren't those of a man. Gooseflesh pricked her skin, partly from fear, partly from the sudden and intense cold.

Keep your head, she ordered herself. For God's sake, keep your head. She gripped the water bottle—pitiful weapon, but all she had—and started to ease off the foot pads on the machine to the floor.

She went flying blindly in the black. She hit the floor, her shoulder and hip taking the brunt. Everything shook and rolled as she fought to scramble up. Disoriented, she had no idea which direction to run. There was a voice behind her, in front of her, inside her head—she couldn't tell—and it whispered gleefully of death.

She knew she screamed as she clawed her way across the quaking floor. Teeth chattering against terror and cold, she rapped her shoulder against another machine. Think, think, think! she told herself, because something was coming, something was coming in the dark. She ran her shaking hands over the machine—recumbent bike—and with every prayer she knew ringing in her head, used its placement in the room to angle toward the door.

There was a crash behind her, and something thudded against her foot. She jerked up, tripped, jerked up again. No longer caring what might stand between herself and the door, she flung herself toward where she hoped it would be. With her breath tearing out of her lungs, she ran her hands over the wall.

"Find it, goddamn it, Quinn. Find the goddamn door!"

Her hand bumped the hinges, and on a sob she found the knob. Turned, pulled.

The light burst in front of her eyes, and Cal's body—already in motion—rammed hers. If she'd had any breath left, she'd have lost it. Her knees didn't get a chance to buckle as he wrapped his arms around her, swung her around to use his body as a shield between hers and the room beyond.

"Hold on, now. Can you hold on to me?" His voice was eerily calm as he reached behind him and pulled the door closed. "Are you hurt? Tell me if you're hurt." His hands were already skimming over her, before they came up to her face, gripped it.

Before his mouth crushed down on hers.

"You're all right," he managed, propping her against the stone of the building as he dragged off his coat. "You're okay. Here, get into this. You're freezing."

"You were there." She stared up into his face. "You were there."

"Couldn't get the door open. Key wouldn't work." He took her hands, rubbed them warm between his. "My truck's right up there, okay. I want you to go up, sit in my truck. I left the keys in it. Turn on the heat. Sit in my truck and turn on the heat. Can you do that?"

She wanted to say yes. There was something in her that

wanted to say yes to anything he asked. But she saw, in his eyes, what he meant to do.

"You're going in there."

"That's what I have to do. What you have to do is go sit in the truck for a few minutes."

"If you go in, I go in."

"Quinn."

How, she wondered, did he manage to sound patient and annoyed at the same time? "I need to as much as you, and I'd hate myself if I huddled in your truck while you went in there. I don't want to hate myself. Besides, it's better if there's two of us. It's better. Let's just do it. Just do it, and argue later."

"Stay behind me, and if I say get out, you get out. That's the deal."

"Done. Believe me, I'm not ashamed to hide behind you."

She saw it then, just the faintest glimmer of a smile in his eyes. Seeing it settled her nerves better than a quick shot of brandy.

He turned his key again, keyed in the touch pad. Quinn held her breath. When Cal opened the door, the lights were on. Al Roker's voice cheerily announced the national weather forecast. The only sign anything had happened was her sports bottle under the rack of free weights.

"Cal, I swear, the power went out, then the room—"

"I saw it. It was pitch-black in here when you came through the door. Those weights were all over the floor. I could see them rolling around from the light coming in the door. The floor was heaving. I saw it, Quinn. And I heard it from outside the door."

He'd rammed that door twice, he remembered, put his full weight into it, because he'd heard her screaming, and it had sounded like the roof was caving in.

"Okay. My things are in the locker room. I really want to get my things out of the locker."

"Give me the key, and I'll—"

"Together." She gripped his hand. "There's a scent, can

you smell it? Over and above my workout and panic sweat."

"Yeah. I always thought it must be what brimstone smells like. It's fading." He smiled, just a little as she stopped to pick up a ten-pound free weight, gripped it like a weapon.

He pushed open the door of the women's locker room. It was as ordered and normal as the gym. Still, he took her key, nudged her behind him before he opened her locker. Moving quickly, she dragged on her sweats, exchanged coats. "Let's get out of here."

He had her hand as they walked back out and Matt walked in.

He was young, the college-jock type, doing the part-time attendant, occasional personal trainer gig. A quick, inoffensive smirk curved on his lips as he saw them come out of the women's locker room together. Then he cleared his throat.

"Hey, sorry I'm late. Damnedest thing. First my alarm didn't go off and I know how that sounds. Then my car wouldn't start. One of those mornings."

"Yeah," Quinn agreed as she put back the weight, retrieved her water bottle. "One of those. I'm done for the day." She tossed him the locker key. "See you later."

"Sure."

She waited until they were out of the building. "He thought we'd been—"

"Yeah, yeah."

"Ever do it in a locker room?"

"As that was actually my first foray into a girl's locker room, I have to say no."

"Me, either. Cal, have you got time to come over, have coffee—God, I'll even cook breakfast—and talk about this?"

"I'm making time."

SHE TOLD HIM EVERYTHING THAT HAD HAPPENED while she scrambled eggs. "I was scared out of my mind," she finished as she carried the coffee into the little dining room.

"No, you weren't." Cal set the plates of eggs and whole-wheat toast on the table. "You found the door, in the pitch-black, and with all that going on, you kept your head and found the door."

"Thanks." She sat. She wasn't shaking any longer, but the inside of her knees still felt like half-set Jell-O. "Thanks for saying that."

"It's the truth."

"You were there when I opened the door, and that was one of the best moments of my life. How did you know to be there?"

"I came in early because I wanted to swing by here, see how you were. Talk to you. Gage—"

"I know about that. Tell me the rest of this first."

"Okay. I turned off Main to come around the back way, come here, and I saw Ann Hawkins. I saw her standing in front of the door. I heard you screaming."

"From inside your truck, on the street. That far away—through stone walls, you heard me?"

"I heard you." It hadn't been one of the best moments of his life. "When I jumped out, ran toward the door, I heard crashing, thumping, God knows what from inside. I couldn't get the goddamn door open."

She heard it now, the emotion in his voice, the fear he hadn't let show while they were doing what needed doing. She rose, did them both a favor and crawled right into his lap.

She was still there, cradled in his arms, when Cybil strolled in.

"Hi. Don't get up." She took Quinn's chair. "Anyone eating this?" Studying them, Cybil took a forkful of eggs. "You must be Cal."

"Cybil Kinski, Caleb Hawkins. We had a rough morning."

Layla stepped in with a coffee mug and sleepy eyes that clouded with concern the minute she saw Quinn. "What happened?"

"Have a seat, and we'll run it through for both of you."

"I need to see the place," Cybil said as soon as the story was told. "And the room in the bowling alley, any place there's been an incident."

"Try the whole town," Quinn said dryly.

"And I need to see the clearing, this stone, as soon as possible."

"She's bossy," Quinn told Cal.

"I thought you were, but I think she beats you out. You can come into the bowling center anytime you like. Quinn can get you into the fitness center, but if I can't be there, I'll make sure either Fox or Gage is. Better, both of them. As far as the Pagan Stone goes, I talked with Fox and Gage about that last night. We're agreed that the next time we go, we all go. All of us. I can't make it today and neither can Fox. Sunday's going to be best."

"He's organized and take-charge," Cybil said to Quinn.

"Yes." She pressed a kiss to Cal's cheek. "Yes, he is. And I've made you let your eggs get cold."

"It was a worthwhile trade-off. I'd better get going."

"We still have a lot to talk about. Listen, maybe the three of you should come to dinner."

"Is someone cooking?" Cal asked.

"Cyb is."

"Hey!"

"You ate my breakfast. Plus you actually cook. But in the meantime, just one thing." She slid out of his lap so he could stand. "Would Fox hire Layla?"

"What? Who? Why?" Layla sputtered.

"Because you need a job," Quinn reminded her. "And he needs an office manager."

"I don't know anything about—you just can't—"

"You managed a boutique," Quinn reminded her, "so that's half the job. Managing. You're on the anal side of organized, Miss Colored Index Cards and Charts, so I say you can file, keep a calendar, and whatever with the best of them. Anything else, you'll pick up as you go. Ask Fox, okay, Cal?"

"Sure. No problem."

"She calls me bossy," Cybil commented as she finished Quinn's coffee.

"I call it creative thinking and leadership. Now, go fill that mug up again while I walk Cal to the door so I can give him a big, sloppy you're-my-hero kiss."

Cybil smiled after them as Quinn pulled Cal out of the room. "She's in love."

"Really?"

Now Cybil turned her smile on Layla. "That got your mind off taking a bite out of her for pushing that job in your face."

"I'll get back to that. Do you think she's in love with Cal—the uppercase *L*?"

"About to be all caps, in bold letters." She picked up the mug and rose. "Q likes to direct people," she said, "but she's careful to try to direct them toward something helpful, or at least interesting. She wouldn't push this job business if she didn't think you could handle it."

She blew out a breath as she walked back toward the kitchen. "What the hell am I supposed to fix for dinner?"

Fifteen

IT WAS HARD FOR CAL TO SEE BILL TURNER AND say nothing about Gage being in town. But Cal knew his friend. When and if Gage wanted his father to know, Gage would tell him. So Cal did his best to avoid Bill by closing himself in his office.

He dealt with orders, bills, reservations, contacted their arcade guy to discuss changing out one of their pinball machines for something jazzier.

Checking the time, he judged if Gage wasn't awake by now, he should be. And so picked up the phone.

Not awake, Cal decided, hearing the irritation in Gage's voice, hasn't had coffee. Ignoring all that, Cal launched into an explanation of what happened that morning, relayed the dinner plans, and hung up.

Now, rolling his eyes, Cal called Fox to run over the same information, and to tell Fox that Layla needed a job and he should hire her to replace Mrs. Hawbaker.

Fox said, "Huh?"

Cal said, "Gotta go," and hung up.

There, duty done, he considered. Satisfied, he turned to his computer and brought up the information on the automatic scoring systems he wanted to talk his father into installing.

It was past time for the center to do the upgrade. Maybe it was foolish to think about that kind of investment if everything was going to hell in a few months. But, if everything was going to hell in a few months, the investment wouldn't hurt a thing.

His father would say some of the old-timers would object, but Cal didn't think so. If they wanted to keep score by hand, the center would provide the paper score sheets and markers. But he thought having someone show them how it worked, give them a few free games to get used to the new system, they'd jump on.

They could get them used and reconditioned, which was part of the argument he was prepared to make. They had Bill onboard, and he could fix damn near anything.

It was one thing to be a little kitschy and traditional, another to be old-fashioned.

No, no, that wasn't the tack to take with his father. His father liked old-fashioned. Better to use figures. Bowling accounted for more than half, closer to sixty percent, of their revenue, so—

He broke off at the knock on his door and inwardly winced thinking it was Bill Turner.

But it was Cal's mother who popped her head in. "Too busy for me?"

"Never. Here to bowl a few games before the morning league?"

"Absolutely not." Frannie loved her husband, but she liked to say she hadn't taken a vow to love, honor, and bowl. She came in to sit down, then angled her head so she could see his computer screen. Her lips twitched. "Good luck with that."

"Don't say anything to Dad, okay?"

"My lips are sealed."

"Who are you having lunch with?"

"How do you know I'm having lunch with anyone?"

He gestured to her pretty fitted jacket, trim pants, heeled boots. "Too fancy for shopping."

"Aren't you smart? I do have a few errands, then I'm meeting a friend for lunch. Joanne Barry."

Fox's mother, Cal thought, and just nodded.

"We have lunch now and then, but she called me yesterday, specifically to see if I could meet her today. She's worried. So I'm here to ask you if there's anything I should know, anything you want to tell me before I see her."

"Things are as under control as I can make them, Mom. I don't have the answers yet. But I have more questions, and I think that's progress. In fact, I have one you could ask Fox's mom for me."

"All right."

"You could ask if there's a way she could find out if any of her ancestors were Hawkins."

"You think we might be related somehow? Would it help if we are?"

"It would be good to know the answer."

"Then I'll ask the question. Now answer one for me. Are you all right? Just a yes or no is good enough."

"Yes."

"Okay then." She rose. "I have half a dozen things on my list before I meet Jo." She started for the door, said, *"damn it"* very quietly under her breath, and turned back. "I wasn't going to ask, but I have no willpower over something like this. Are you and Quinn Black serious?"

"About what?"

"Caleb James Hawkins, don't be dense."

He would've laughed, but that tone brought on the Pavlovian response of hunched shoulders. "I don't exactly know the answer. And I'm not sure it's smart to get serious, in that way, with so much going on. With so much at stake."

"What better time?" Frannie replied. "My levelheaded

Cal." She put her hand on the knob, smiled at him. "Oh, and those fancy scoring systems? Try reminding your father how much his father resisted going to projection-screen scoreboards thirty-five years ago, give or take."

"I'll keep that in mind."

Alone, Cal printed out the information on the automatic systems, new and reconditioned, then shut down long enough to go downstairs and check in with the front desk, the grill, the play area during the morning leagues games.

The scents from the grill reminded him he'd missed breakfast, so he snagged a hot pretzel and a Coke before he headed back up to his office.

So armed, he decided since everything was running smoothly, he could afford to take a late-morning break. He wanted to dig a little deeper into Ann Hawkins.

She'd appeared to him twice in three days. Both times, Cal mused, had been a kind of warning. He'd seen her before, but only in dreams. He'd wanted her in dreams, Cal admitted—or Giles Dent had, working through him.

These incidents had been different, and his feelings different.

Still, that wasn't the purpose, that wasn't the point, he reminded himself as he gnawed off a bite of pretzel.

He was trusting Quinn's instincts about the journals. Somewhere, at some time, there had been more. Maybe they were in the old library. He certainly intended to get in there and search the place inch by inch. If, God, they'd somehow gotten transferred into the new space and mis-shelved or put in storage, the search could be a nightmare.

So he wanted to know more about Ann, to help lead him to the answers.

Where had she been for nearly two years? All the information, all the stories he'd heard or read indicated she'd vanished the night of the fire in the clearing and hadn't returned to the Hollow until her sons were almost two.

"Where did you go, Ann?"

Where would a woman, pregnant with triplets, go during the last weeks before their births? Traveling had to have been extremely difficult. Even for a woman without the pregnancy to weigh her down.

There had been other settlements, but nothing as far as he remembered for a woman in her condition to have walked, or even ridden. So logically, she'd had somewhere to go close by, and someone had taken her in.

Who was most likely to take a young, unmarried woman in? A relative would be his first guess.

Maybe a friend, maybe some kindly old widow, but odds were on family.

"That's where you went first, when there was trouble, wasn't it?"

While it wasn't easy to find specifics on Ann Hawkins, there was plenty of it on her father—the founder of the Hollow.

He'd read it, of course. He'd studied it, but he'd never read or studied it from this angle. Now, he brought up all the information he'd previously downloaded on his office computer relating to James Hawkins.

He took side trips, made notes on any mention of relatives, in-laws. The pickings were slim, but at least there was something to pick from. Cal was rolling with it when someone knocked on his door. He surfaced as Quinn poked her head in just as his mother had that morning.

"Working. I bet you hate to be interrupted. But . . ."

"It's okay." He glanced at the clock, saw with a twinge of guilt his break had lasted more than an hour. "I've been at it longer than I meant to."

"It's dog-eat-dog in the bowling business." She said it with a smile as she came in. "I just wanted you to know we were here. We took Cyb on a quick tour of the town. Do you know there's no place to buy shoes in Hawkins Hollow? Cyb's saddened by that as she's always on the hunt. Now she's making noises about bowling. She has a vicious competitive streak. So I escaped up here before she drags me into that. The hope was to grab a quick bite at your grill—maybe you could join us—before Cyb . . ."

She trailed off. Not only hadn't he said a word, but he was staring at her. Just staring. "What?" She brushed a hand over her nose, then up over her hair. "Is it my hair?"

"That's part of it. Probably part of it."

He got up, came around the desk. He kept his eyes on her face as he moved past her. As he shut and locked the door.

"Oh. *Oh.* Really? Seriously? Here? Now?"

"Really, seriously. Here and now." She looked flustered, and that was a rare little treat. She looked, every inch of her, amazing. He couldn't say why he'd gone from pleased to see her to aroused in the snap of a finger, and he didn't much care. What he knew, without question, was he wanted to touch her, to draw in her scent, to feel her body go tight, go loose. Just go.

"You're not nearly as predictable as you should be." Watching him now, she pulled off her sweater, unbuttoned the shirt beneath it.

"I should be predictable?" Without bothering with buttons, he pulled his shirt over his head.

"Hometown boy from a nice, stable family, who runs a third-generation family business. You should be predictable, Caleb," she said as she unbuttoned her jeans. "I like that you're not. I don't mean just the sex, though major points there."

She bent down to pull off her boots, tossing her hair out of her eyes so she could look up at him. "You should be married," she decided, "or on your way to it with your college sweetheart. Thinking about 401(k)s."

"I think about 401(k)s. Just not right now. Right now, Quinn, all I can think about is you."

That gave her heart a bounce, even before he reached out, ran his hands down her bare arms. Even before he drew her to him and seduced her mouth with his.

She may have laughed when they lowered to the floor,

but her pulse was pounding. There was a different tone from when they were in bed. More urgency, a sense of recklessness as they tangled together in a giddy heap on the office floor. He tugged her bra down so he could use his lips, his teeth, his tongue on her breasts until her hips began to pump. She closed her hand around him, found him hard, made him groan.

He couldn't wait, not this time. He couldn't savor; needed to take. He rolled, dragging her over so she could straddle him. Even as he gripped her hips, she was rising. She was taking him in. When she leaned forward for a greedy kiss, her hair fell to curtain their faces. Surrounded by her, he thought. Her body, her scent, her energy. He stroked the line of her back, the curve of her hips as she rocked and rocked and rocked him through pleasure toward desperation.

Even when she arched back, even with his vision blurred, the shape of her, the tones of her enthralled him.

She let herself go, simply steeped herself in sensation. Hammering pulses and speed, slick bodies and dazzling friction. She felt him come, that sudden, sharp jerk of his hips, and was thrilled. She had driven him to lose control first, she had taken him over. And now she used that power, that thrill, to drive herself over that same edgy peak.

She slid down from it, and onto him so they could lie there, heated, a little stunned, until they got their breath back. And she began to laugh.

"God, we're like a couple of teenagers. Or rabbits."

"Teenage rabbits."

Amused, she levered up. "Do you often multitask in your office like this?"

"Ah . . ."

She gave him a little poke as she tugged her bra back in place. "See, unpredictable."

He held out her shirt. "It's the first time I've multitasked in this way during working hours."

Her lips curved as she buttoned her shirt. "That's nice."

"And I haven't felt like a teenage rabbit since I was."

She leaned over to give him a quick peck on the lips. "Even nicer." Still on the floor, she scooted into her pants as he did the same. "I should tell you something." She reached for her boots, pulled one on. "I think . . . No, saying 'I think' is a cop-out, it's the coward's way."

She took a deep breath, yanked on the other boot then looked him dead in the eye. "I'm in love with you."

The shock came first—fast, arrow-point shock straight to the gut. Then the concern wrapped in a slippery fist of fear. "Quinn—"

"Don't waste your breath with the 'we've only known each other a couple of weeks' gambit. And I really don't want to hear the 'I'm flattered, but,' either. I didn't tell you so you could say anything. I told you because you should know. So first, it doesn't matter how long we've known each other. I've known me a long time, and I know me very well. I know what I feel when I feel it. Second, you should be flattered, goes without saying. And there's no need to freak out. You're not obligated or expected to feel what I feel."

"Quinn, we're—all of us—are under a lot of pressure. We don't even know if we'll make it through to August. We can't—"

"Exactly so. Nobody ever knows that, but we have more reason to worry about it. So, Cal." She framed his face with her hands. "The moment's important. The right-this-minute matters a whole hell of a lot. I doubt I'd have told you otherwise, though I can be impulsive. But I think, under other circumstances, I'd have waited for you to catch up. I hope you do, but in the meantime, things are just fine the way they are."

"You have to know I—"

"Don't, absolutely don't tell me you care about me." The first hint of anger stung her voice. "Your instinct is to say all the cliches people babble out in cases like this. They'll only piss me off."

"Okay, all right, let me just ask this, without you getting pissed off. Have you considered what you're feeling might be something like what happened in the clearing? That it's, say, a reflection of what Ann felt for Dent?"

"Yes, and it's not." She pushed to her feet, drew on her sweater. "Good question though. Good questions don't piss me off. What she felt, and I felt through that, was intense and consuming. I'm not going to say some of what I feel for you isn't like that. But it was also painful, and wrenching. Under the joy was grief. That's not this, Cal. This isn't painful. I don't feel sad. So . . . do you have time to come down and grab some lunch before Cyb and Layla and I head out?"

"Ah . . . sure."

"Great. Meet you down there. I'm going to pop in the bathroom and fix myself up a little."

"Quinn." He hesitated as she opened the door, turned back. "I've never felt like this about anyone before."

"Now that is a very acceptable thing to say."

She smiled as she strolled away. If he'd said it, he meant it because that was the way he was. Poor guy, she thought. Didn't even know he was caught.

A THICK GROVE OF TREES SHIELDED THE OLD cemetery on the north side. It fanned out over bumpy ground, with hills rolling west, at the end of a dirt road barely wide enough for two cars to pass. An historical marker faded by weather stated the First Church of the Godly had once stood on the site, but had been destroyed when it had been struck by lightning and razed by fire on July 7, 1652.

Quinn had read that fact in her research, but it was different to stand here now, in the wind, in the chill and imagine it. She'd read, too, as the plaque stated, that a small chapel had stood as a replacement until it was damaged during the Civil War, and gone to ruin.

Now, there were only the markers here, the stones, the winter-hardy weeds. Beyond a low stone wall were the graves of the newer dead. Here and there she saw bright blots of color from flowers that stood out like grief against the dull grays and winter browns.

"We should've brought flowers," Layla said quietly as she looked down at the simple and small stone that read only:

ANN HAWKINS

"She doesn't need them," Cybil told her. "Stones and flowers, they're for the living. The dead have other things to do."

"Cheery thought."

Cybil only shrugged at Quinn. "I think so, actually. No point in being dead *and* bored. It's interesting, don't you think, that there are no dates. Birth or death. No sentiment. She had three sons, but they didn't have anything but her name carved in her gravestone. Even though they're buried here, too, with their wives, and I imagine at least some of their children. Wherever they went in life, they came home to be buried with Ann."

"Maybe they knew, or believed, she'd be back. Maybe she told them death isn't the end." Quinn frowned at the stone. "Maybe they just wanted to keep it simple, but I wonder, now that you mention it, if it was deliberate. No beginning, no end. At least not until . . ."

"This July," Layla finished. "Another cheery thought."

"Well, while we're all getting cheered up, I'm going to get some pictures." Quinn pulled out her camera. "Maybe you two could write down some of the names here. We may want to check on them, see if any have any direct bearing on—"

She tripped while backing up to get a shot, fell hard on her ass. "Ouch, goddamn it! Shit. Right on the bruise I got this morning. Perfect."

Layla rushed over to help her up. Cybil did the same, even as she struggled with laughter.

"Just shut up," Quinn grumbled. "The ground's all bumpy here, and you can hardly see some of these stones popping out." She rubbed her hip, scowled down at the stone that had tripped her up. "Ha. That's funny. Joseph Black, died 1843." The color annoyance brought to her face faded. "Same last name as mine. Common name Black, really. Until you consider it's here, and that I just happened to trip over his grave."

"Odds are he's one of yours," Cybil agreed.

"And one of Ann's?"

Quinn shook her head at Layla's suggestion. "I don't know. Cal's researched the Hawkins's family tree, and I've done a quick overview. I know some of the older records are lost, or just buried deeper than we've dug, but I don't see how we'd both have missed branches with my surname. So. I think we'd better see what we can find out about Joe."

HER FATHER WAS NO HELP, AND THE CALL HOME kept her on the phone for forty minutes, catching up on family gossip. She tried her grandmother next, who had a vague recollection about her mother-in-law mentioning an uncle, possibly a great-uncle, maybe a cousin, who'd been born in the hills of Maryland. Or it might've been Virginia. His claim to fame, family-wise, had been running off with a saloon singer, deserting his wife and four children and taking the family savings held inside a cookie tin with him.

"Nice guy, Joe," Quinn decided. "Should you be my Joe."

She decided, since it would get her out of any type of food preparation, she had enough time to make a trip to Town Hall, and start digging on Joseph Black. If he'd died here, maybe he'd been born here.

WHEN QUINN GOT HOME SHE WAS GLAD TO FIND the house full of people, sound, the scents of food. Cybil, being Cybil, had music on, candles lit, and wine poured. She had everyone piled in the kitchen, whetting appetites with marinated olives. Quinn popped one, took Cal's wine and washed it down.

"Are my eyes bleeding?" she asked.

"Not so far."

"I've been searching records for nearly three hours. I think I bruised my brain."

"Joseph Black." Fox got her a glass of wine for her own. "We've been filled in."

"Good, saves me. I could only trace him back to his grandfather—Quinton Black, born 1676. Nothing on record before that, not here anyway. And nothing after Joe, either. I went on side trips, looking for siblings or other relatives. He had three sisters, but I've got nothing on them but birth records. He had aunts, uncles, and so on, and not much more there. It appears the Blacks weren't a big presence in Hawkins Hollow."

"Name would've rung for me," Cal told her.

"Yeah. Still, I got my grandmother's curiosity up, and she's now on a hunt to track down the old family Bible. She called me on my cell. She thinks it went to her brother-in-law when his parents died. Maybe. Anyway, it's a line."

She focused on the man leaning back against the counter toying with a glass of wine. "Sorry? Gage, right?"

"That's right. Roadside service a specialty."

Quinn grinned as Cybil rolled her eyes and took a loaf of herbed bread out of the oven.

"So I hear, and that looks like dinner's ready. I'm starved. Nothing like searching through the births and deaths of Blacks, Robbits, Clarks to stir up the appetite."

"Clark." Layla lowered the plate she'd taken out to offer Cybil for the bread. "There were Clarks in the records?"

"Yeah, an Alma and a Richard Clark in there, as I remember. Need to check my notes. Why?"

"My grandmother's maiden name was Clark." Layla managed a wan smile. "That's probably not a coincidence either."

"Is she still living?" Quinn asked immediately. "Can you get in touch and—"

"We're going to eat while it's hot," Cybil interrupted. "Time enough to give family trees a good shake later. But when I cook—" She pushed the plate of hot bread into Gage's hand. "We eat."

Sixteen

IT HAD TO BE IMPORTANT. IT HAD TO MATTER. Cal rolled it over and over and over, carving time out of his workday and his off time to research the Hawkins-Black lineage himself. Here was something new, he thought, some door they hadn't known existed, much less tried to break down.

He told himself it was vital, and time-consuming work, and that was why he and Quinn hadn't managed to really connect for the last couple of days. He was busy; she was busy. Couldn't be helped.

Besides, it was probably a good time for them to have this break from each other. Let things just simmer down a little. As he'd told his mother, this wasn't the time to get serious, to think about falling in love. Because big, life-altering things were supposed to happen after people fell seriously in love. And he had enough, big, life-altering things to worry about.

He dumped food in Lump's bowl as his dog waited for breakfast with his usual unruffled patience. Because it was

Thursday, he'd tossed a load of laundry in the washer when he'd let Lump out for his morning plod and pee. He continued his habitual weekday morning routine, nursing his first cup of coffee while he got out a box of Chex.

But when he reached for the milk it made him think of Quinn. Two percent milk, he thought with a shake of his head. Maybe she was fixing her version of a bowl of cereal right now. Maybe she was standing in her kitchen with the smell of coffee in the air, thinking of him.

Because the idea of that held such appeal, he reached for the phone to call her, when he heard the sound behind him and turned.

Gage got the coffee mug out of the cupboard he opened. "Jumpy."

"No. I didn't hear you come in."

"You were mooning over a woman."

"I have a lot of things on my mind."

"Especially the woman. You've got tells, Hawkins. Starting with the wistful, cocker spaniel eyes."

"Up yours, Turner."

Gage merely grinned and poured coffee. "Then there's that fish hook in the corner of your mouth." He hooked his finger in his own, gave a tug. "Unmistakable."

"You're jealous because you're not getting laid regular."

"No question about that." Gage sipped his black coffee, used one bare foot to rub Lump's flank as the dog concentrated his entire being on his kibble. "She's not your usual type."

"Oh?" Irritation crawled up Cal's back like a lizard. "What's my usual type?"

"Pretty much same as mine. Keep it light, no deep thinking, no strings, no worries. Who could blame us, considering?" He picked up the cereal, dug right into the box. "But she breaks your mold. She's smart, she's steady, and she's got a big, fat ball of string in her back pocket. She's already started wrapping you in it."

"Does that cynicism you carry around everywhere ever get heavy?"

"Realism," Gage corrected as he munched on cereal. "And it keeps me light on my feet. I like her."

"I do, too." Cal forgot the milk and just took a handful of cereal out of the bowl he'd poured. "She . . . she told me she's in love with me."

"Fast work. And now she's suddenly pretty damn busy, and you're sleeping alone, pal. I said she was smart."

"Jesus, Gage." Insult bloomed on two stalks—one for himself, one for Quinn. "She's not like that. She doesn't use people like that."

"And you know this because you know her so well."

"I do." Any sign of irritation faded as that simple truth struck home. "That's just it. I do know her. There may be dozens, hell, hundreds of things I don't know, but I know who—how—she is. I don't know if some of that's because of this connection, because of what we're all tied to, but I know it's true. The first time I met her, things changed. I don't know. Something changed for me. So you can make cracks, but that's the way it is."

"I'm going to say you're lucky," Gage said after a moment. "That I hope it works out the way you want. I never figured any of us had a decent shot at normal." He shrugged. "Wouldn't mind being wrong. Besides, you look real cute with that hook in your mouth."

Cal lifted his middle finger off the bowl and into the air.

"Right back atcha," Fox said as he strolled in. He went straight to the refrigerator for a Coke. "What's up?"

"What's up is you're mooching my Cokes again, and you never bring any to replace them."

"I brought beer last week. Besides, Gage told me to come over this morning, and when I come over in the morning, I expect a damn Coke."

"You told him to come over?"

"Yeah. So, O'Dell, Cal's in love with the blonde."

"I didn't say I—"

"Tell me something I don't know." Fox popped the top on the can of Coke and gulped.

"I never said I was in love with anyone."

Fox merely shifted his gaze to Cal. "I've known you my whole life. I know what those shiny little hearts in your eyes mean. It's cool. She was, like, made for you."

"He says she's not my usual type, you say she's made for me."

"We're both right. She's not the type you usually fish for." Fox gulped down more soda, then took the box of cereal from Gage. "Because you didn't want to find the one who fit. She fits, but she was sort of a surprise. Practically an ambush. Did I get up an hour early to come over here before work so we could talk about Cal's love life?"

"No, it was just an interesting sidebar. I got some information when I was in the Czech Republic. Rumors, lore, mostly, which I followed up when I had time. I got a call from an expert last night, which is why I told you to come over this morning. I might have ID'd our Big Evil Bastard."

They sat down at the kitchen table with coffee and dry cereal—Fox in one of his lawyer suits, Gage in a black T-shirt and loose pants, Cal in jeans and a flannel shirt.

And spoke of demons.

"I toured some of the smaller and outlying villages," Gage began. "I always figure I might as well pick up some local color, maybe a local skirt while I'm stacking up poker chips and markers."

He'd been doing the same for years, Cal knew. Following any whiff of information about devils, demons, unexplained phenomenon. He always came back with stories, but nothing that had ever fit the, well, the profile, Cal supposed, of their particular problem.

"There was talk about this old demon who could take other forms. You get werewolf stuff over there, and initially, I figured that was this deal. But this wasn't about biting throats out and silver bullets. The talk was about how this thing hunted humans to enslave them, and feed off their . . . the translation was kind of vague, and the best I got was essence, or humanity."

"Feed how?"

"That's vague, too—or colorful as lore tends to be. Not on flesh and bone, not with fang and claw—that kind of thing. The legend is this demon, or creature, could take people's minds as well as their souls, and cause them to go mad, cause them to kill."

"Could be the root of ours," Fox decided.

"It rang close enough that I followed it up. It was a lot to wade through; that area's ripe with stories like this. But in this place in the hills, with this thick forest that reminded me of home, I hit something. Its name is *Tmavy*. Translates to Dark. The Dark."

He thought, they all thought of what had come out of the ground at the Pagan Stone. "It came like a man who wasn't a man, hunted like a wolf that wasn't a wolf. And sometimes it was a boy, a boy who lured women and children in particular into the forest. Most never came back, and those who did were mad. The families of those who did went mad, too. Killed each other, or themselves, their neighbors."

Gage paused, rose to get the coffeepot. "I got some of this when I was there, but I found a priest who gave me the name of a guy, a professor, who studied and publishes on Eastern European demonology. He got in touch last night. He claims this particular demon—and he isn't afraid to use the word—roamed Europe for centuries. He, in turn, was hunted by a man—some say another demon, or a wizard, or just a man with a mission. Legend has it that they battled in the forest, and the wizard was mortally wounded, left for dead. And that, according to Professor Linz, was its mistake. Someone came, a young boy, and the wizard passed the boy his power before he died."

"What happened?" Fox demanded.

"No one, including Linz, is sure. The stories claim the thing vanished, or moved on, or died, somewhere in the early- to mid-seventeenth century."

"When he hopped a goddamn boat for the New World," Cal added.

"Maybe. That may be."

"So did the boy," Cal continued, "or the man he'd become, or his descendent. But he nearly had him over there, nearly did at some point in time—that's something I've seen. I think. Him and the woman, a cabin. Him holding a bloody sword, and knowing nearly all were dead. He couldn't stop it there, so he passed what he had to Dent, and Dent tried again. Here."

"What did he pass to us?" Fox demanded. "What power? Not getting a freaking head cold, having a broken arm knit itself? What good does that do?"

"Keeps us healthy and whole when we face it down. And there's the glimmers I see, that we all see in different ways." Cal shoved at his hair. "I don't know. But it has to be something that matters. The three parts of the stone. They have to be. We've just never figured it out."

"And time's almost up."

Cal nodded at Gage. "We need to show the stones to the others. We took an oath, we all have to agree to that. If we hadn't, I'd have—"

"Shown yours to Quinn already," Fox finished. "And yeah, maybe you're right. It's worth a shot. It could be it needs all six of us to put it back together."

"Or it could be that when whatever happened at the Pagan Stone happened, the bloodstone split because its power was damaged. Destroyed."

"Your glass is always half empty, Turner," Fox commented. "Either way, it's worth the try. Agreed?"

"Agreed." Cal looked at Gage, who shrugged.

"What the hell."

CAL DEBATED WITH HIMSELF ALL THE WAY INTO town. He didn't need an excuse to stop by to see Quinn. For God's sake, they were sleeping together. It wasn't as if he needed an appointment or clearance or a specific reason to knock on her door, to see how she was doing. To ask what the hell was going on.

There was no question she'd been distracted every time he'd managed to reach her by phone the last couple of days. She hadn't dropped into the center since they'd rolled around his office floor.

And she'd told him she was in love with him.

That was the problem. The oil on the water, the sand in the shoe, or whatever goddamn analogy made the most sense. She'd told him she loved him, he hadn't said "me, too," which she claimed she didn't expect. But any guy who actually believed a woman always meant exactly what she said was deep in dangerous delusion.

Now, she was avoiding him.

They didn't have *time* for games, for bruised feelings and sulks. There were more important things at stake. Which, he was forced to admit, was why he shouldn't have touched her in the first place. By adding sex to the mix, they'd clouded and complicated the issue, and the issue was already clouded and complicated enough. They had to be practical; they had to be smart. Objective, he added as he pulled up in front of the rental house. Cold-blooded, clear-minded.

Nobody was any of those things when they were having sex. Not if they were having really good sex.

He jammed his hands in his pockets as he walked up to her door, then dragged one out to knock. The fact that he'd worked himself up to a mad might not have been objective or practical, but it felt absolutely right.

Until she opened the door.

Her hair was damp. She'd pulled it back from her face in a sleek tail, and he could see it wasn't quite dry. He could smell the girly shampoo and soap, and the scents wound their way into him until the muscle in his gut tightened in response.

She wore fuzzy purple socks, black flannel pants and a hot pink sweatshirt that announced: T.G.I.F. THANK GOD I'M FEMALE.

He could add his own thanks.

"Hi!"

The idea she was sulking was hard to hang on to when he was blasted by her sunbeam smile and buzzing energy.

"I was just thinking about you. Come inside. Jesus, it's cold. I've so had it with winter. I was about to treat myself to a low-fat mug of hot chocolate. Want in on that?"

"Ah—I really don't."

"Well, come on back, because I've got the yen." She rose up on her toes to give him a long, solid kiss, then grabbed his hand to pull him back to the kitchen. "I nagged Cyb and Layla into going to the gym with me this morning. Took some doing with Cyb, but I figured safety in numbers. Nothing weird happened, unless you count watching Cyb twist herself into some advanced yoga positions. Which Matt did, let me tell you. Things have been quiet in the otherworldly sense the last couple days."

She got out a packet of powdered mix, slapped it against her hand a couple of times to settle it before ripping it open to pour it into a mug. "Sure you don't want some?"

"Yeah, go ahead."

"We've been a busy hive around here," she went on as she filled the mug, half with water, half with two percent milk. "I'm waiting to hear something about the family Bible, or whatever else my grandmother might dig up. Today, maybe, hopefully by tomorrow. Meanwhile, we've got charts of family trees as we know them, and Layla's trying to shake some ancestry out of her relatives."

She stirred up the liquid and mix, stuck it in the microwave. "I had to leave a lot of the research up to my partners in crime and finish an article for the magazine. Gotta pay the doorman, after all. So?" She turned back as the microwave hummed. "How about you?"

"I missed you." He hadn't planned to say it, certainly hadn't expected it to be the first thing out of his mouth. Then he realized, it was obviously the first thing on his mind.

Her eyes went soft; that sexy mouth curved up. "That's nice to hear. I missed you, too, especially last night when I crawled into bed about one in the morning. My cold, empty bed."

"I didn't just mean the sex, Quinn." And where had *that* come from?

"Neither did I." She angled her head, ignoring the beep of the microwave. "I missed having you around at the end of the day, when I could finally come down from having to hammer out that article, when I wanted to stop thinking about what I had to do, and what was going to happen. You're irritated about something. Why don't you tell me what it is?"

She turned toward the microwave as she spoke to get her mug out. Cal saw immediately she'd made the move as Cybil was stepping through the kitchen doorway. Quinn merely shook her head, and Cybil stepped back and retreated without a word.

"I don't know, exactly." He pulled off his coat now, tossed it over one of the chairs around a little cafe table that hadn't been there on his last visit. "I guess I thought, after the other day, after . . . what you said—"

"I said I was in love with you. That makes you quiver inside," she noted. "Men."

"I didn't start avoiding you."

"You think—" She took a deep inhale through her nose, exhaled in a huff. "Well, you have a really high opinion of yourself, and a crappy one of me."

"No, it's just—"

"I had things to do, I had work. I am not at your beck any more than you're at mine."

"That's not what I meant."

"You think I'd play games like that? Especially now?"

"Especially now's the point. This isn't the time for big personal issues."

"If not now, when?" she demanded. "Do you really, do you honestly think we can label and file all our personal business and close it in a drawer until it's *convenient*? I like things in their place, too. I want to know where things are, so I put them where I want or need them to be. But feelings and thoughts are different from the goddamn car keys, Cal."

"No argument, but—"

"And my feelings and thoughts are as cluttered and messy as Grandma's attic," she snapped out, far from winding down. "That's just the way I like it. If things were normal every day, bopping right along, I probably wouldn't have told you. Do you think this is my first cannonball into the Dating and Relationship Pool? I was engaged, for God's sake. I told you because—because I think, maybe *especially* now, that feelings are what matter most. If that screws you up, too damn bad."

"I wish you'd shut up for five damn minutes."

Her eyes went to slits. "Oh, really?"

"Yeah. The fact is I don't know how to react to all of this, because I never let myself consider being in this position. How could I, with this hanging over my head? Can't risk falling for someone. How much could I tell her? How much is too much? We're—Fox and Gage and I—we're used to holding back, to keeping big pieces of this to ourselves."

"Keeping secrets."

"That's right," he said equably. "That's exactly right. Because it's safer that way. How could I ever think about falling in love, getting married, having kids? Bringing a kid into this nightmare's out of the question."

Those slitted blue eyes went cold as winter. "I don't believe I've yet expressed the wish to bear your young."

"Remember who you're talking to," he said quietly. "You take this situation out of the equation you've got a normal guy from a normal family. The kind who gets married, raises a family, has a mortgage and a big sloppy dog. If I let myself fall in love with a woman, that's how it's going to work."

"I guess you told me."

"And it's irresponsible to even consider any of that."

"We disagree. I happen to think considering that, moving toward that, is shooting the bird at the dark. In the end, we're each entitled to our own take on it. But understand me, get this crystal, telling you I love you didn't mean I expected you to pop a ring on my finger."

"Because you've been there."

She nodded. "Yes, I have. And you're wondering about that."

"None of my business." Screw it. "Yes."

"Okay, it's simple enough. I was seeing Dirk—"

"Dirk—"

"Shut up." But her lips twitched. "I was seeing him exclusively for about six months. We enjoyed each other. I thought I was ready for the next stage in my life, so I said yes when he asked me to marry him. We were engaged for two months when I realized I'd made a mistake. I didn't love him. Liked him just fine. He didn't love me, either. He didn't really get me—not the whole of me, which was why he figured the ring on my finger meant he could begin to advise me on my work, on my wardrobe, habits and career options. There were a lot of little things, and they're not really important. The fact was we weren't going to make it work, so I broke it off."

She blew out another breath because it wasn't pleasant to remember she'd made that big a mistake. That she'd failed at something she knew she'd be good at. "He was more annoyed than brokenhearted, which told me I'd done the right thing. And the truth is, it stung to know I'd done the right thing, because it meant I'd done the wrong thing first. When I suggested he tell his friends he'd been the one to end it, he felt better about it. I gave him back the ring, we each boxed up things we'd kept in each other's apartments, and we walked away."

"He didn't hurt you."

"Oh, Cal." She took a step closer so she could touch his face. "No, he didn't. The situation hurt me, but he didn't. Which is only one of the reasons I knew he wasn't the one. If you want me to reassure you that you can't, that you won't break my heart, I just can't do it. Because you can, you might, and that's how I know you are. The one." She slipped her arms around him, laid her lips on his. "That must be scary for you."

"Terrifying." He pulled her against him, held her hard. "I've never had another woman in my life who's given me as many bad moments as you."

"I'm delighted to hear it."

"I thought you would be." He laid his cheek on top of her head. "I'd like to stay here, just like this, for an hour or two." He replaced his cheek with his lips, then eased back. "But I've things I have to do, and so do you. Which I knew before I walked in here and used it as an excuse to pick a fight."

"I don't mind a fight. Not when the air's clear afterward."

He framed her face with his hands, kissed her softly. "Your hot chocolate's getting cold."

"Chocolate's never the wrong temperature."

"The one thing I said before? Absolute truth. I missed you."

"I believe I can arrange some free time in my busy schedule."

"I have to work tonight. Maybe you could stop in. I'll give you another bowling lesson."

"All right."

"Quinn, we—all of us—have to talk. About a lot of things. As soon as we can."

"Yes, we do. One thing before you go. Is Fox going to offer Layla a job?"

"I said something to him." Cal swore under his breath at her expression. "I'll give him another push on it."

"Thanks."

Alone, Quinn picked up her mug, thoughtfully sipped at her lukewarm chocolate. Men, she thought, were such interesting beings.

Cybil came in. "All clear?"

"Yeah, thanks."

"No problem." She opened a cupboard and chose a small tin of loose jasmine tea from her supply. "Discuss or mind my own?"

"Discuss. He was worked up because I told him I love him."

"Annoyed or panicked?"

"Some of both, I think. More worried because we've all got scary things to deal with, and this is another kind of scary thing."

"The scariest, when you come down to it." Cybil filled the teakettle with water. "How are you handling it?"

"It feels . . . great," she decided. "Energizing and bouncy and bright, then sort of rich and glimmering. You know, with Dirk it was all . . ." Quinn held out a hand, drawing it level through the air. "This was—" She shot her hand up, down, then up again. "Here's a thing. When he's telling me why this is crazy, he says how he's never been in a position—or so he thinks—to let himself think about love, marriage, family."

"Whoa, point A to Z in ten words or less."

"Exactly." Quinn gestured with her mug. "And he was rolling too fast to see that the *M* word gave me a serious jolt. I practically just jumped off that path, and whoops, there it is again, under my feet."

"Hence the jolt." Cybil measured out her tea. "But I don't see you jumping off."

"Because you know me. I like where my feet are, as it turns out. I like the idea of heading down that path with Cal, toward wherever it ends up. He's in trouble now," she murmured and took another sip.

"So are you, Q. But then trouble's always looked good on you."

"Better than a makeover at the Mac counter at Saks." Quinn answered the kitchen phone on its first ring. "Hello. Hello, Essie. Oh. Really? No, it's great. It's perfect. Thanks so much. I absolutely will. Thanks again. Bye." She hung up, grinned. "Essie Hawkins got us into the community center. No business there today on the main level. We can go in, poke around to our hearts' content."

"Won't that be fun?" Cybil said it dryly as she poured boiling water for her tea.

ARMED WITH THE KEY, CYBIL OPENED THE MAIN door of the old library. "We're here, on the surface, for research. One of the oldest buildings in town, home of the Hawkins family. But . . ." She switched on the lights. "Primarily we're looking for hidey-holes. A hiding place that was overlooked."

"For three and a half centuries," Cybil commented.

"If something's overlooked for five minutes, it can be overlooked forever." Quinn pursed her lips as she looked around. "They modernized it, so to speak, when they turned it into a library, but when they built the new one, they stripped out some of the newfangled details. It's not the way it was, but it's closer."

There were some tables and chairs set up, and someone had made an attempt at some old-timey decor in the antique old lamps, old pottery, and wood carvings on shelves. Quinn had been told groups like the Historical Society or the Garden Club could hold meetings or functions here. At election times it was a voting center.

"Stone fireplace," she said. "See, that's an excellent place to hide something." After crossing to it, she began to poke at the stones. "Plus there's an attic. Essie said they used it for storage. Still do. They keep the folding tables and chairs up there, and that kind of thing. Attics are treasure troves."

"Why is it buildings like this are so cold and creepy when no one's in them?" Layla wondered.

"We're in this one. Let's start at the top," Quinn suggested, "work our way down."

"ATTICS ARE TREASURE TROVES," CYBIL SAID twenty minutes later, "of dust and spiders."

"It's not that bad." Quinn crawled along, hoping for a loose floorboard.

"Not that good either." Courageously, Layla stood on a folding chair, checking rafters. "I don't understand why people don't think storage spaces shouldn't be cleaned as regularly as anyplace else."

"It was clean once. She kept it clean."

"Who—" Layla began, but Cybil waved a hand at her, frowned at Quinn.

"Ann Hawkins?"

"Ann and her boys. She brought them home, and shared the attic with them. Her three sons. Until they were old enough to have a room downstairs. But she stayed here. She wanted to be high, to be able to look out of her window. Even though she knew he wouldn't come, she wanted to look out for him. She was happy here, happy enough. And when she died here, she was ready to go."

Abruptly, Quinn sat back on her heels. "Holy shit, was that me?"

Cybil crouched down to study Quinn's face. "You tell us."

"I guess it was." She pressed her fingers to her forehead. "Damn, got one of those I-drank-my-frozen-margarita-too-fast-and-now-have-an-ice pick-through-my-brain headaches. I saw it, her, them, in my head. Just as clear. Everything moving, like a time-action camera. Years in seconds. But more, I felt it. That's the way it is for you, isn't it—going the other way?"

"Often," Cybil agreed.

"I saw her writing in her journal, and washing her sons' faces. I saw her laughing, or weeping. I saw her standing at the window looking into the dark. I felt . . ." Quinn laid a hand on her heart. "I felt her longing. It was . . . brutal"

"You don't look well." Layla touched her shoulder. "We should go downstairs, get you some water."

"Probably. Yeah." She took the hand Layla offered to help her up. "Maybe I should try it again. Try to bring it back, get more."

"You're awfully pale," Layla told her. "And, honey, your hand's like ice."

"Plenty for one day," Cybil agreed. "You don't want to push it."

"I didn't see where she put the journals. If she put anything here, I didn't see."

Seventeen

IT WASN'T THE TIME, CAL DETERMINED, TO TALK about a broken stone or property searches when Quinn was buzzed about her trip to the past with Ann Hawkins. In any case, the bowling center wasn't the place for that kind of exchange of information.

He considered bringing it up after closing when she dragged him into her home office to show him the new chart Layla had generated that listed the time, place, approximate duration, and involved parties in all known incidents since Quinn's arrival.

He forgot about it when he was in bed with her, when she was moving with him, when everything felt right again.

Then he told himself it was too late to bring it up, to give the topics the proper time when she was curled up warm with him.

Maybe it was avoidance, but he opted for the likelihood it was just his tendency to prefer things at the right time, in the right place. He'd arranged to take Sunday off so the entire group could hike to the Pagan Stone. That, to his mind, was the right time and place.

Then Nature screwed with his plans.

When forecasters began to predict an oncoming blizzard, he kept a jaundiced eye on the reports. They were, in his experience, wrong at least as often as they were right. Even when the first flakes began to fall mid-morning, he remained unconvinced. It was the third blizzard hype of the year, and so far the biggest storm had dumped a reasonable eight inches.

He shrugged it off when the afternoon leagues canceled. It had gotten so people canceled everything at the first half inch, then went to war over bread and toilet paper in the supermarket. And since the powers-that-be canceled school before noon, the arcade and the grill were buzzing.

But when his father came in about two in the afternoon, looking like Sasquatch, Cal paid more attention.

"I think we're going to close up shop," Jim said in his easy way.

"It's not that bad. The arcade's drawing the usual suspects, the grill's been busy. We've had some lanes booked. A lot of towners will come in later in the afternoon, looking for something to do."

"It's bad enough, and it's getting worse." Jim shoved his gloves in the pocket of his parka. "We'll have a foot by sundown the way it's going. We need to send these kids home, haul them there if they don't live within easy walking distance. We'll close up, then you go on home, too. Or you get your dog and Gage and come on over and stay with us. Your mother'll worry sick if she thinks you're out driving in this at night."

He started to remind his father that he was thirty, had four-wheel drive, and had been driving nearly half his life. Knowing it was pointless, Cal just nodded. "We'll be fine. I've got plenty of supplies. I'll clear out the customers, close up, Dad. You go on home. She'll worry about you, too."

"There's time enough to close down and lock up." Jim glanced over at the lanes where a six-pack of teenagers sent off energy and hormones in equal measure. "Had a hell of a storm when I was a kid. Your grandfather kept her open. We stayed here for three days. Time of my life."

"I bet." Cal grinned. "Want to call Mom, say we're stuck? You and me can ride it out. Have a bowling marathon."

"Damned if I wouldn't." The lines around Jim's eyes crinkled at the idea. "Of course, she'll kick my ass for it and it'd be the last time I bowled."

"Better shut down then."

Though there were protests and moans, they moved customers along, arranging for rides when necessary with some of the staff. In the silence, Cal shut down the grill himself. He knew his father had gone back to check with Bill Turner. Not just to give instructions, he thought, but to make sure Bill had whatever he needed, to slip him a little extra cash if he didn't.

As he shut down, Cal pulled out his phone and called Fox's office. "Hey. Wondered if I'd catch you."

"Just. I'm closing. Already sent Mrs. H home. It's getting bad out there."

"Head over to my place. If this comes in like they're whining about, it might be a couple days before the roads are clear. No point wasting them. And maybe you should stop and pick up, you know, toilet paper, bread."

"Toilet . . . You're bringing the women?"

"Yeah." He'd made up his mind on that when he'd taken a look outside. "Get . . . stuff. Figure it out. I'll be home as soon as I can."

He clicked off, then shut down the alley lights as his father came out.

"Everything set?" Cal asked.

"Yep."

The way his father looked around the darkened alley told Cal he was thinking they weren't just going to lose their big Friday night, but likely the entire weekend.

"We'll make it up, Dad."

"That's right. We always do." He gave Cal a slap on the shoulder. "Let's get home."

QUINN WAS LAUGHING WHEN SHE OPENED THE door. "Isn't this great! They say we could get three feet, maybe more! Cyb's making goulash, and Layla went out and picked up extra batteries and candles in case we lose power."

"Good. Great." Cal stomped snow off his boots. "Pack it up and whatever else you all need. We're going to my place."

"Don't be silly. We're fine. You can stay, and we'll—"

As clear of snow as he could manage, he stepped in, shut the door behind him. "I have a small gas generator that'll run little things—such as the well, which means water to flush the toilets."

"Oh. Toilets. I hadn't thought of that one. But how are we all going to fit in your truck?"

"We'll manage. Get your stuff."

It took them half an hour, but he'd expected that. In the end, the bed of his truck was loaded with enough for a week's trek through the wilderness. And three women were jammed with him in the cab.

He should've had Fox swing by, get one of them, he realized. Then Fox could've hauled half the contents of their house in *his* truck. And it was too late now.

"It's gorgeous." Layla perched on Quinn's lap, bracing a hand on the dash while the Chevy's windshield wipers worked overtime to clear the snow from the glass. "I know it's going to be a big mess, but it's so beautiful, so different than it is in the city."

"Remember that when we're competing for bathroom time with three men," Cybil warned her. "And let me say right now, I refuse to be responsible for all meals just because I know how to turn on the stove."

"So noted," Cal muttered.

"It *is* gorgeous," Quinn agreed, shifting her head from side to side to see around Layla. "Oh, I forgot. I heard from my grandmother. She tracked down the Bible. She's having her sister-in-law's granddaughter copy and scan the appropriate pages, and e-mail them to me." Quinn wiggled to try for more room. "At least that's the plan, as the granddaughter's the only one of them who understands how to scan and attach files. E-mail and online poker's as far as Grandma goes on the Internet. I hope to have the information by tomorrow. Isn't this great?"

Wedged between Quinn's butt and the door, Cybil dug in to protect her corner of the seat. "It'd be better if you'd move your ass over."

"I've got Layla's space, too, so I get more room. I want popcorn," Quinn decided. "Doesn't all this snow make everyone want popcorn? Did we pack any? Do you have any?" she asked Cal. "Maybe we could stop and buy some Orville's."

He kept his mouth shut, and concentrated on surviving what he thought might be the longest drive of his life.

He plowed his way down the side roads, and though he trusted the truck and his own driving, was relieved when he turned onto his lane. As he'd been outvoted about the heat setting, the cab of the truck was like a sauna.

Even under the circumstances, Cal had to admit his place, his woods, did look like a picture. The snow-banked terraces, the white-decked trees and huddles of shrubs framed the house where smoke was pumping from the chimney, and the lights were already gleaming against the windows.

He followed the tracks of Fox's tires across the little bridge over his snow- and ice-crusted curve of the creek.

Lump padded toward the house from the direction of the winter-postcard woods, leaving deep prints behind him. His tail swished once as he let out a single, hollow bark.

"Wow, look at Lump." Quinn managed to poke Cal with her elbow as the truck shoved its way along the lane. "He's positively frisky."

"Snow gets him going." Cal pulled behind Fox's truck, smirked at the Ferrari, slowly being buried, then laid on the horn. He'd be damned if he was going to haul the bulk of what three women deemed impossible to live without for a night or two.

He dragged bags out of the bed.

"It's a beautiful spot, Cal." Layla took the first out of his hands. "Currier and Ives for the twenty-first century. Is it all right if I go right in?"

"Sure."

"Pretty as a picture." Cybil scanned the bags and boxes, chose one for herself. "Especially if you don't mind being isolated."

"I don't."

She glanced over as Gage and Fox came out of the house. "I hope you don't mind crowds either."

They got everything inside, trailing snow everywhere. Cal decided it must have been some sort of female telepathy that divided them all into chores without discussion. Layla asked him for rags or old towels and proceeded to mop up the wet, Cybil took over the kitchen with her stew pot and bag of kitchen ingredients. And Quinn dug into his linen closet, such as it was, and began assigning beds, and ordering various bags carried to various rooms.

There wasn't anything for him to do, really, but have a beer.

Gage strode in as Cal poked at the fire. "There are bottles of girl stuff all over both bathrooms up there." Gage jerked a thumb at the ceiling. "What have you done?"

"What had to be done. I couldn't leave them. They could've been cut off for a couple of days."

"And what, turned into the next Donner Party? Your woman has Fox making my bed, which is now the pullout in your office. And which I'm apparently supposed to share with him. You know that son of a bitch is a bed hog."

"Can't be helped."

"Easy for you to say, seeing as you'll be sharing yours with the blonde."

This time Cal grinned, smugly. "Can't be helped."

"Esmerelda's brewing up something in the kitchen."

"Goulash—and it's Cybil."

"Whatever, it smells good, I'll give her that. She smells better. But the point is I got the heave-ho when I tried to get a damn bag of chips to go with the beer."

"You want to cook for six people?"

Gage only grunted, sat, propped his feet on the coffee table. "How much are they calling for?"

"About three feet." Cal dropped down beside him, mirrored his pose. "Used to be we liked nothing better. No school, haul out the sleds. Snowball wars."

"Those were the days, my friend."

"Now we're priming the generator, loading in firewood, buying extra batteries and toilet paper."

"Sucks to be grown up."

Still, it was warm, and while the snow fell in sheets outside, there was light, and there was food. It was hard to complain, Cal decided, when he was digging into a bowl of hot, spicy stew he had nothing to do with preparing. Plus, there were dumplings, and he was weak when it came to dumplings.

"I was in Budapest not that long ago." Gage spooned up goulash as he studied Cybil. "This is as good as any I got there."

"Actually, this isn't Hungarian goulash. It's a Serbo-Croatian base."

"Damn good stew," Fox commented, "wherever it's based."

"Cybil's an Eastern European stew herself." Quinn savored the half dumpling she'd allowed herself. "Croatian, Ukrainian, Polish—with a dash of French for fashion sense and snottiness."

"When did your family come over?" Cal wondered.

"As early as the seventeen hundreds, as late as just before World War II, depending on the line." But she understood the reason for the question. "I don't know if there is a connection to Quinn or Layla, or any of this, where it might root from. I'm looking into it."

"We had a connection," Quinn said, "straight off."

"We did."

Cal understood that kind of friendship, the kind he saw when the two women looked at each other. It had little to do with blood, and everything to do with the heart.

"We hooked up the first day—evening really—of college." Quinn spooned off another minuscule piece of dumpling with the stew. "Met in the hall of the dorm. We were across from each other. Within two days, we'd switched. Our respective roommates didn't care. We bunked together right through college."

"And apparently still are," Cybil commented.

"Remember you read my palm that first night?"

"You read palms?" Fox asked.

"When the mood strikes. My gypsy heritage," Cybil added with a flourishing gesture of her hands.

And Cal felt a knot form in his belly. "There were gypsies in the Hollow."

"Really?" Carefully, Cybil lifted her wineglass, sipped. "When?"

"I'd have to check to be sure. This is from stories my gran told me that her grandmother told her. Like that. About how gypsies came one summer and set up camp."

"Interesting. Potentially," Quinn mused, "someone local could get cozy with one of those dark-eyed beauties or hunks, and nine months later, oops. Could lead right to you, Cyb."

"Just one big, happy family," Cybil muttered.

After the meal, chores were divvied up again. Wood needed to be brought in, the dog let out, the table cleared, dishes dealt with.

"Who else cooks?" Cybil demanded.

"Gage does," Cal and Fox said together.

"Hey."

"Good." Cybil sized him up. "If there's a group breakfast on the slate, you're in charge. Now—"

"Before we . . . whatever," Cal decided, "there's something we have to go over. Might as well stick to the dining room. We have to get something," he added, looking at Fox and Gage. "You might want to open another bottle of wine."

"What's all this?" Quinn frowned as the men retreated. "What are they up to?"

"It's more what haven't they told us," Layla said. "Guilt and reluctance, that's what I'm picking up. Not that I know any of them that well."

"You know what you know," Cybil told her. "Get another bottle, Q." She gave a little shudder. "Maybe we should light a couple more candles while we're at it, just in case. It already feels . . . dark."

THEY LEFT IT TO HIM, CAL SUPPOSED, BECAUSE IT was his house. When they were all back around the table, he tried to find the best way to begin.

"We've gone over what happened that night in the clearing when we were kids, and what started happening after. Quinn, you got some of it yourself when we hiked there a couple weeks ago."

"Yeah. Cyb and Layla need to see it, as soon as the snow's cleared enough for us to make the hike."

He hesitated only a beat. "Agreed."

"It ain't a stroll down the Champs Élysées," Gage commented, and Cybil cocked an eyebrow at him.

"We'll manage."

"There was another element that night, another aspect we haven't talked about with you."

"With anyone," Fox added.

"It's hard to explain why. We were ten, everything went

to hell, and . . . Well." Cal set his part of the stone on the table.

"A piece of rock?" Layla said.

"Bloodstone." Cybil pursed her lips, started to reach for it, stopped. "May I?"

Gage and Fox set theirs down beside Cal's. "Take your pick," Gage invited.

"Three parts of one." Quinn picked up the one closest to her. "Isn't that right? These are three parts of one stone."

"One that had been rounded, tumbled, polished," Cybil continued. "Where did you get the pieces?"

"We were holding them," Cal told her. "After the light, after the dark, when the ground stopped shaking, each one of us was holding his part of this stone." He studied his own hand, remembering how his fist had clenched around the stone as if his life depended on it.

"We didn't know what they were. Fox looked it up. His mother had books on rocks and crystals, and he looked it up. Bloodstone," Cal repeated. "It fit."

"It needs to be put back together," Layla said. "Doesn't it? It needs to be whole again."

"We've tried. The breaks are clean," Fox explained. "They fit together like a puzzle." He gestured, and Cal took the pieces, fit them into a round.

"But it doesn't do anything."

"Because you're holding them together?" Curious, Quinn held out her hand until Cal put the three pieces into it. "They're not . . . fused would be the word, I guess."

"Tried that, too. MacGyver over there tried superglue."

Cal sent Gage a bland stare. "Which should've worked—at least as far as holding the pieces together. But I might as well have used water. No stick. We've tried banding them, heating them, freezing them. No dice. In fact, they don't even change temperature."

"Except—" Fox broke off, got the go-ahead nod. "During the Seven, they heat up. Not too hot to hold, but right on the edge."

"Have you tried putting them back together during that week?" Quinn demanded.

"Yeah. No luck. The one thing we know is that Giles Dent was wearing this, like an amulet around his neck, the night Lazarus Twisse led that mob into the clearing. I saw it. Now we have it."

"Have you tried magickal means?" Cybil asked.

Cal squirmed a little, cleared his throat.

"Jesus, Cal, loosen up." Fox shook his head. "Sure. I got some books on spells, and we gave that a try. Down the road, Gage has talked to some practicing witches, and we've tried other rites and so on."

"But you never showed them to anyone." Quinn set the pieces down carefully before picking up her wine. "Anyone who might have been able to work with them, or understand the purpose. Maybe the history."

"We weren't meant to." Fox lifted his shoulders. "I know how it sounds, but I knew we weren't supposed to take it to, what, a geologist or some Wiccan high priestess, or the damn Pentagon. I just . . . Cal voted for the science angle right off."

"MacGyver," Gage repeated.

"Fox was sure that was off-limits, and that was good enough. That was good enough for the three of us." Cal looked at his friends. "It's been the way we've handled it, up till now. If Fox felt we shouldn't show you, we wouldn't be."

"Because you feel it the strongest?" Layla asked Fox.

"I don't know. Maybe. I know I believed—I believe—we survived that night, that we came out of it the way we came out of it because we each had a piece of that stone. And as long as we do, we've got a chance. It's just something I know, the same way Cal saw it, that he recognized it as the amulet Dent wore."

"How about you?" Cybil asked Gage. "What do you know? What do you see?"

His eyes met hers. "I see it whole, on top of the Pagan

Stone. The stone on the stone. And the flames flick up from it, kindling in the blood spots. Then they consume it, ride over the flat, down the pedestal like a sheath of fire. I see the fire race across the ground, fly into the trees until they burst from the heat. And the clearing's a holocaust even the devil himself couldn't survive."

He took a drink of wine. "That's what I see when it's whole again, so I'm in no big hurry to get there."

"Maybe that's how it was formed," Layla began.

"I don't see back. That's Cal's gig. I see what might be coming."

"That'd be handy in your profession."

Gage shifted his gaze back to Cybil, smiled slowly. "It doesn't hurt." He picked up his stone, tossed it lightly in his hand. "Anyone interested in a little five-card draw?"

As soon as he spoke, the light snapped off.

Rather than romance or charm, the flickering candles they'd lit as backup lent an eeriness to the room. "I'll go fire up the generator." Cal pushed up. "Water, refrigerator, and stove for now."

"Don't go out alone." Layla blinked as if surprised the words had come out of her mouth. "I mean—"

"I'm going with you."

As Fox rose, something howled in the dark.

"Lump." Cal was out of the room, through the kitchen, and out the back door like a bullet. He barely broke stride to grab the flashlight off the wall, punch it on.

He swept it toward the sound. The beam struggled against the thick, moving curtain of snow, did little but bounce the light back at him.

The blanket had become a wall that rose past his knees. Calling his dog, Cal pushed through it, trying to pinpoint the direction of the howling. It seemed to come from everywhere, from nowhere.

As he heard sounds behind him, he whirled, gripping the flashlight like a weapon.

"Don't clock the reinforcements," Fox shouted. "Christ,

it's insane out here." He gripped Cal's arm as Gage moved to Cal's other side. "Hey, Lump! Come on, Lump! I've never heard him like that."

"How do you know it's the dog?" Gage asked quietly.

"Get back inside," Cal said grimly. "We can't leave the women alone. I'm going to find my dog."

"Oh yeah, we'll just leave you out here, stumbling around in a fucking blizzard." Gage jammed his freezing hands in his pockets, glanced back. "Besides."

They came, arms linked and gripping flashlights. Which showed sense, Cal was forced to admit. And they'd taken the time to put on coats, probably boots as well, which is more than he or his friends had done.

"Go back in." He had to shout now, over the rising wind. "We're just going to round up Lump. Be right there."

"We all go in or nobody does." Quinn unhooked her arm from Layla's, hooked it to Cal's. "That includes Lump. Don't waste time," she said before he could argue. "We should spread out, shouldn't we?"

"In pairs. Fox, you and Layla try that way, Quinn and I'll take this way. Gage and Cybil toward the back. He's got to be close. He never goes far."

He sounded scared, that's what Cal didn't want to say out loud. His stupid, lazy dog sounded scared. "Hook your hand in my pants—the waistband. Keep a good hold."

He hissed against the cold as her gloves hit his skin, then began to trudge forward. He'd barely made it two feet when he heard something under the howls.

"You catch that?"

"Yes. Laughing. The way a nasty little boy might laugh."

"Go—"

"I'm not leaving that dog out here any more than you are."

A vicious gush of wind rose up like a tidal wave, spewing huge clumps of snow, and what felt like pellets of ice. Cal heard branches cracking, like gunfire in the dark. Behind him, Quinn lost her footing in the force of the wind and nearly took them both down.

He'd get Quinn back into the house, he decided. Get her the hell in, lock her in a damn closet if necessary, then come back out and find his dog.

Even as he turned to get a grip on her arm, he saw them.

His dog sat on his haunches, half buried in the snow, his head lifted as those long, desperate howls worked his throat.

The boy floated an inch above the surface of the snow. Chortling, Cal thought. There was a word you didn't use every day, but it sure as hell fit the filthy sound it made.

It grinned as the wind blasted again. Now Lump was buried to his shoulders.

"Get the fuck away from my dog."

Cal lurched forward; the wind knocked him back so that both he and Quinn went sprawling.

"Call him," Quinn shouted. "Call him, make him come!" She dragged off her gloves as she spoke. Using her fingers to form a circle between her lips, she whistled shrilly as Cal yelled at Lump.

Lump quivered; the thing laughed.

Cal continued to call, to curse now, to crawl while the snow flew into his eyes, numbed his hands. He heard shouting behind him, but he focused everything he had on pushing ahead, on getting there before the next gust of wind put the dog under.

He'd drown, Cal thought as he pushed, shoved, slid forward. If he didn't get to Lump, his dog would drown in that ocean of snow.

He felt a hand lock on his ankle, but kept dragging himself forward.

Gritting his teeth, he flailed out, got a slippery hold on Lump's collar. Braced, he looked up into eyes that glittered an unholy green rimmed with red. "You can't have him."

Cal yanked. Ignoring Lump's yelp, he yanked again, viciously, desperately. Though Lump howled, whimpered, it was as if his body was sunk in hardened cement.

And Quinn was beside him, belly down, digging at the snow with her hands.

Fox skidded down, shooting snow like shrapnel. Cal gathered everything he had, looked once more into those monstrous eyes in the face of a young boy. "I said you can't have him."

With the next pull, Cal's arms were full of quivering, whimpering dog.

"It's okay, it's okay." He pressed his face against cold, wet fur. "Let's get the hell out of here."

"Get him in by the fire." Layla struggled to help Quinn up as Cybil pushed up from her knees. Shoving the butt of a flashlight in his back pocket, Gage pulled Cybil to her feet, then plucked Quinn out of the snow.

"Can you walk?" he asked her.

"Yeah, yeah. Let's get in, let's get inside, before somebody ends up with frostbite."

Towels and blankets, dry clothes, hot coffee. Brandy—even for Lump—warmed chilled bones and numbed flesh. Fresh logs had the fire blazing.

"It was holding him. He couldn't get away." Cal sat on the floor, the dog's head in his lap. "He couldn't get away. It was going to bury him in the snow. A stupid, harmless dog."

"Has this happened before?" Quinn asked him. "Has it gone after animals this way?"

"A few weeks before the Seven, animals might drown, or there's more roadkill. Sometimes pets turn mean. But not like this. This was—"

"A demonstration." Cybil tucked the blanket more securely around Quinn's feet. "He wanted us to see what he could do."

"Maybe wanted to see what we could do," Gage countered, and earned a speculative glance from Cybil.

"That may be more accurate. That may be more to the point. Could we break the hold? A dog's not a person, has to be easier to control. No offense, Cal, but your dog's brainpower isn't as high as most toddlers'."

Gently, affectionately, Cal pulled on one of Lump's floppy ears. "He's thick as a brick."

"So it was showing off. It hurt this poor dog for sport." Layla knelt down and stroked Lump's side. "That deserves some payback."

Intrigued, Quinn cocked her head. "What do you have in mind?"

"I don't know yet, but it's something to think about."

Eighteen

CAL DIDN'T KNOW WHAT TIME THEY'D FALLEN into bed. But when he opened his eyes the thin winter light eked through the window. Through it, he saw the snow was still falling in the perfect, fat, white flakes of a Hollywood Christmas movie.

In the hush only a snowfall could create, was steady and somehow satisfied snoring. It came from Lump, who was stretched over the foot of the bed like a canine blanket. That was something Cal generally discouraged, but right now, the sound, the weight, the warmth were exactly right.

From now on, he determined, the damn dog was going everywhere with him.

Because his foot and ankle were currently under the bulk of the dog, Cal shifted to pull free. The movement had Quinn stirring, giving a little sigh as she wiggled closer and managed to wedge her leg between his. She wore flannel, which shouldn't have been remotely sexy, and she'd managed to pin his arm during the night so it was now alive with needles and pins. And that should've been, at least mildly, annoying.

Instead, it was exactly right, too.

Since it was, since they were cuddled up together in bed with Hollywood snow falling outside the window, he couldn't think of a single reason not to take advantage of it.

Smiling, he slid a hand under her T-shirt, over warm, smooth flesh. When he cupped her breast he felt her heart beat under his palm, slow and steady as Lump's snoring. He stroked, a lazy play of fingertips as he watched her face. Lightly, gently, he teased her nipple, arousing himself as he imagined taking it into his mouth, sliding his tongue over her.

She sighed again.

He trailed his hand down, tracing those fingertips over her belly, under the flannel to skim down her thigh. Up again. Down, then up, a whispering touch that eased closer, closer to her center.

And the sound she made in sleep was soft and helpless.

She was wet when he brushed over her, hot when he dipped inside her. When he pressed, he lowered his mouth to hers to take her gasp.

She came as she woke, her body simply erupting as her mind leaped out of sleep and into shock and pleasure.

"Oh God!"

"Shh." He laughed against her lips. "You'll wake the dog."

He tugged down her pants as he rolled. Before she could clear her mind, he pinned her, and he filled her.

"Oh. Well. Jesus." The words hitched and shook. "Good morning."

He laughed again, and bracing himself, set a slow and torturous pace. She fought to match it, to hold back and take that slow climb with him, but it flashed through her again, and flung her up.

"God. God. God. I don't think I can—"

"Shh, shh," he repeated, and brought his mouth down to toy with hers. "I'll go slow," he whispered. "You just go."

She could do nothing else. Her system was already wrecked, her body already his. Utterly his. When he took her up again, she was too breathless to cry out.

THOROUGHLY PLEASURED, THOROUGHLY USED, Quinn lay under Cal's weight. He'd eased down so that his head rested between her breasts, and she could play with his hair. She imagined it was some faraway Sunday morning where they had nothing more pressing to worry about than if they'd make love again before breakfast, or make love after.

"Do you take some kind of special vitamin?" she wondered.

"Hmm?"

"I mean, you've got some pretty impressive stamina going for you."

She felt his lips curve against her. "Just clean living, Blondie."

"Maybe it's the bowling. Maybe bowling . . . Where's Lump?"

"He got embarrassed about halfway through the show." Cal turned his head, gestured. "Over there."

Quinn looked, saw the dog on the floor, his face wedged in the corner. She laughed till her sides ached. "We embarrassed the dog. That's a first for me. God! I feel good. How can I feel so good after last night?" Then she shook her head, stretched up her arms before wrapping them around Cal. "I guess that's the point, isn't it? Even in a world gone to hell, there's still this."

"Yeah." He sat up then, reached down to brush her tumbled hair as he studied her. "Quinn." He took her hand now, played with her fingers.

"Cal," she said, imitating his serious tone.

"You crawled through a blizzard to help save my dog."

"He's a good dog. Anyone would have done the same."

"No. You're not naive enough to think that. Fox and Gage, yeah. For the dog, and for me. Layla and Cybil, maybe. Maybe it was being caught in the moment, or maybe they're built that way."

She touched his face, skimmed her fingers under those patient gray eyes. "No one was going to leave that dog out there, Cal."

"Then I'd say that dog is pretty lucky to have people like you around. So am I. You crawled through the snow, toward that thing. You dug in the snow with your bare hands."

"If you're trying to make a hero out of me . . . Go ahead," she decided. "I think I like the fit."

"You whistled with your fingers."

Now she grinned. "Just a little something I picked up along the way. I can actually whistle a lot louder than that, when I'm not out of breath, freezing, and quivering with terror."

"I love you."

"I'll demonstrate sometime when . . . What?"

"I never thought to say those words to any woman I wasn't related to. I was just never going to go there."

If she'd been given a hard, direct jolt of electricity to her heart, it couldn't have leaped any higher. "Would you mind saying them again, while I'm paying better attention?"

"I love you."

There it went again, she thought. Leaps and bounds. "Because I can whistle with my fingers?"

"That might've been the money shot."

"God." She shut her eyes. "I want you to love me, and I really like to get what I want. But." She took a breath. "Cal, if this is because of last night, because I helped get Lump, then—"

"This is because you think if you eat half my slice of pizza it doesn't count."

"Well, it doesn't, technically."

"Because you always know where your keys are, and you can think about ten things at the same time. Because you don't back down, and your hair's like sunlight. Because you tell the truth and you know how to be a friend. And for dozens of reasons I haven't figured out yet. Dozens more I may never figure out. But I know I can say to you what I never thought to say to anyone."

She hooked her arms around his neck, rested her forehead on his. She had to just breathe for a moment, just breathe her way through the beauty of it as she often did with a great work of art or a song that brought tears to her throat.

"This is a really good day." She touched her lips to his. "This is a truly excellent day."

They sat for a while, holding each other while the dog snored in the corner, and the snow fell outside the windows.

When Cal went downstairs, he followed the scent of coffee into the kitchen, and found Gage scowling as he slapped a skillet onto the stove. They grunted at each other as Cal got a clean mug out of the dishwasher.

"Looks like close to three out there already, and it's still coming."

"I got eyes." Gage ripped open a pound of bacon. "You sound chipper about it."

"It's a really good day."

"I'd probably think so, too, if I started it off with some morning nookie."

"God, men are crude." Cybil strolled in, her dark eyes bleary.

"Then you ought to plug your ears when you're around our kind. Bacon gets fried, eggs get scrambled," Gage told them. "Anybody doesn't like the options should try another restaurant."

Cybil poured her coffee, stood studying him over the rim as she took the first sip. He hadn't shaved or combed that dark mass of hair. He was obviously morning irritable, and none of that, she mused, made him any less attractive.

Too bad.

"You know what I've noticed about you, Gage?"

"What's that?"

"You've got a great ass, and a crappy attitude. Let me

know when breakfast is ready," she added as she strolled out of the kitchen.

"She's right. I've often said that about your ass and attitude."

"Phones are out," Fox announced as he came in, yanked open the refrigerator and pounced on a Coke. "Got ahold of my mother by cell. They're okay over there."

"Knowing your parents, they probably just had sex," Gage commented.

"Hey! True," Fox said after a moment, "but, hey."

"He's got sex on the brain."

"Why wouldn't he? He's not sick or watching sports, the only two circumstances men don't necessarily have sex on the brain."

Gage laid bacon in the heated skillet. "Somebody make some toast or something. And we're going to need another pot of coffee."

"I've got to take Lump out. I'm not just letting him out on his own."

"I'll take him." Fox leaned down to scratch Lump's head. "I want to walk around anyway." He turned, nearly walked into Layla. "Hi, sorry. Ah . . . I'm going to take Lump out. Why don't you come along?"

"Oh. I guess. Sure. I'll just get my things."

"Smooth," Gage commented when Layla left. "You're a smooth one, Fox."

"What?"

"Good morning, really attractive woman. How would you like to trudge around with me in three feet of snow and watch a dog piss on a few trees? Before you've even had your coffee?"

"It was just a suggestion. She could've said no."

"I'm sure she would have if she'd had a hit of caffeine so her brain was in gear."

"That must be why you only get lucky with women without brains."

"You're just spreading sunshine," Cal commented when Fox steamed out.

"Make another damn pot of coffee."

"I need to bring in some wood, feed the generator, and start shoveling three feet of snow off the decks. Let me know when breakfast is ready."

Alone, Gage snarled, and turned the bacon. He still had the snarl when Quinn came in.

"I thought I'd find everyone in here, but they're all scattered." She got out a mug. "Looks like we need another pot of coffee."

Because she got the coffee down, Gage didn't have time to snap at her.

"I'll take care of that. Anything else I can do to help?"

He turned his head to look at her. "Why?"

"Because I figure if I help you with breakfast, it takes us both off the cooking rotation for the next couple of meals."

He nodded, appreciating the logic. "Smart. You're the toast and additional coffee."

"Check."

He beat a dozen eggs while she got to work. She had a quick, efficient way about her, Gage noted. The quick wouldn't matter so much to Cal, but the efficient would be a serious plus. She was built, she was bright, and as he'd seen for himself last night, she had a wide streak of brave.

"You're making him happy."

Quinn stopped, looked over. "Good, because he's making me happy."

"One thing, if you haven't figured it out by now. He's rooted here. This is his place. Whatever happens, the Hollow's always going to be Cal's place."

"I figured that out." She plucked toast when it popped, dropped more bread in. "All things considered, it's a nice town."

"All things considered," Gage agreed, then poured the eggs into the second skillet.

OUTSIDE, AS GAGE PREDICTED, FOX WATCHED Lump piss on trees. More entertaining, he supposed, had been watching the dog wade, trudge, and occasionally leap through the waist-high snow. It was the waist-high factor that had Fox and Layla stopping on the front deck, and Fox going to work with the shovel Cal had shoved into his hands on their way out.

Still, it was great to be out in the snow globe of the morning, tossing the white stuff around while more of it pumped out of the sky.

"Maybe I should go down, knock the snow off some of Cal's shrubs."

Fox glanced over at her. She had a ski cap pulled over her head, a scarf wrapped around her neck. Both had already picked up a layer of white. "You'll sink, then we'll be tossing you a lifeline to get you back. We'll dig out a path eventually."

"He doesn't seem to be spooked." She kept an eagle eye on Lump. "I thought, after last night, he'd be skittish about going out."

"Short-term doggie memory. Probably for the best."

"I won't forget it."

"No." He shouldn't have asked her to come out, Fox realized. Especially since he couldn't quite figure out how to broach the whole job deal, which had been part of the idea for having her tag along.

He was usually better at this stuff, dealing with people. Dealing with women. Now, he worked on carving down a shovel-width path across the deck to the steps, and just jumped in.

"So, Cal said you're looking for a job."

"Not exactly. I mean I'm going to have to find some work, but I haven't been looking."

"My secretary—office manager—assistant." He dumped snow, dug the shovel back down. "We never settled on a title, now that I think about it. Anyway, she's moving to Minneapolis. I need somebody to do the stuff she does."

Damn Quinn, she thought. "The stuff."

It occurred to Fox that he was considered fairly articulate in court. "Filing, billing, answering phones, keeping the calendar, rescheduling when necessary, handling clients, typing documents and correspondence. She's a notary, too, but that's not a necessity right off."

"What software does she use?"

"I don't know. I'd have to ask her." Did she use any software? How was he supposed to know?

"I don't know anything about secretarial work, or office management. I don't know anything about the law."

Fox knew tones, and hers was defensive. He kept shoveling. "Do you know the alphabet?"

"Of course I know the alphabet, but the point—"

"Would be," he interrupted, "if you know the alphabet you can probably figure out how to file. And you know how to use a phone, which means you can answer one and make calls from one. Those would be essential job skills for this position. Can you use a keyboard?"

"Yes, but it depends on—"

"She can show you whatever the hell she does in that area."

"It doesn't sound as if you know a lot about what she does."

He also knew disapproval when he heard it. "Okay." He straightened, leaned on the shovel, and looked dead into her eyes. "She's been with me since I set up. I'm going to miss her like I'd miss my arm. But people move on, and the rest of us have to deal. I need somebody to put papers where they belong and find them when I need to have them, to send out bills so I can pay mine, to tell me when I'm due in court, to answer the phone we hope rings so I'll have somebody to bill, and basically maintain some kind of order so I can practice law. You need a job and a paycheck. I think we could help each other out."

"Cal asked you to offer me a job because Quinn asked him to ask you."

"That would be right. Doesn't change the bottom line."

No, it didn't, she supposed. But it still griped. "It wouldn't be permanent. I'm only looking for something to fill in until . . ."

"You move on." Fox nodded. "Works for me. That way, neither of us are stuck. We're just helping each other out for a while." He shoveled off two more blades of snow, then stopped just to lean on it with his eyes on hers.

"Besides, you knew I was going to offer you the job because you pick up that sort of thing."

"Quinn asked Cal to ask you to offer it to me right in front of me."

"You pick up on that sort of thing," he repeated. "That's your part in this, or part of your part. You get a sense of people, of situations."

"I'm not psychic, if that's what you're saying." The defensive was back in her tone.

"You drove to the Hollow, when you'd never been here before. You knew where to go, what roads to take."

"I don't know what that was." She crossed her arms, and the move wasn't just defensive, Fox thought. It was stubborn.

"Sure you do, it just freaks you. You took off with Quinn that first night, went with her, a woman you'd never met."

"She was a sane alternative to a big, evil slug," Layla said dryly.

"You didn't just run, didn't haul ass to your room and lock the door. You got in her car with her, came with her out here—where you'd also never been, and walked into a house with two strange men in it."

"*Strange* might be the operative word. I was scared, confused, and running on adrenaline." She looked away from him, toward where Lump was rolling in the snow as if it was a meadow of daisies. "I trusted my instincts."

"Instincts is one word for it. I bet when you were working in that clothes shop you had really good instincts about what your customers wanted, what they'd buy. Bet you're damn good at that."

He went back to shoveling when she said nothing. "Bet you've always been good at that sort of thing. Quinn gets flashes from the past, like Cal. Apparently Cybil gets them of possible future events. I'd say you're stuck with me, Layla, in the now."

"I can't read minds, and I don't want anyone reading mine."

"It's not like that, exactly." He was going to have to work with her, he decided. Help her figure out what she had and how to use it. And he was going to have to give her some time and some space to get used to the idea.

"Anyway, we're probably going to be snowed in here for the weekend. I've got stuff next week, but when we can get back to town, you could come in when it suits you, let Mrs. H show you the ropes. We'll see how you feel about the job then."

"Look, I'm grateful you'd offer—"

"No, you're not." Now he smiled and tossed another shovel of snow off the deck. "Not so much. I've got instincts, too."

It wasn't just humor, but understanding. The stiffness went out of her as she kicked at the snow. "There's gratitude, it's just buried under the annoyance."

Cocking his head, he held out the shovel. "Want to dig it out?"

And she laughed. "Let's try this. If I do come in, and do decide to take the job, it's with the stipulation that if either of us decide it's not working, we just say so. No hard feelings."

"That's a deal." He held out a hand, took hers to seal it. Then just held it while the snow swirled around them.

She had to feel it, he thought, had to feel that immediate and tangible link. That recognition.

Cybil cracked the door an inch. "Breakfast is ready."

Fox released Layla's hand, turned. He let out a quiet breath before calling the dog home.

PRACTICAL MATTERS HAD TO BE SEEN TO. SNOW needed to be shoveled, firewood hauled and stacked. Dishes had to be washed and food prepared. Cal might have felt like the house, which had always seemed roomy, grew increasingly tight with six people and one dog stuck inside it. But he knew they were safer together.

"Not just safer." Quinn took her turn plying the shovel. She considered digging out a path to Cal's storage shed solid exercise in lieu of a formal workout. "I think all this is meant. This enforced community. It's giving us time to get used to each other, to learn how to function as a group."

"Here, let me take over there." Cal set aside the gas can he'd used to top off the generator.

"No, see, that's not working as a group. You guys have to learn to trust the females to carry their load. Gage being drafted to make breakfast today is an example of the basics in non-gender-specific teamwork."

Non-gender-specific teamwork, he thought. How could he not love a woman who'd use a term like that?

"We can all cook," she went on. "We can all shovel snow, haul firewood, make beds. We can all do what we have to do—play to our strengths, okay, but so far it's pretty much been like a middle school dance."

"How?"

"Boys on one side, girls on the other, and nobody quite sure how to get everyone together. Now we are." She stopped, rolled her shoulders. "And we have to figure it out. Even with us, Cal, even with how we feel about each other, we're still figuring each other out, learning how to trust each other."

"If this is about the stone, I understand you might be annoyed I didn't tell you sooner."

"No, I'm really not." She shoveled a bit more, but it was mostly for form now. Her arms were *killing* her. "I started to be, even wanted to be, but I couldn't stir it up. Because I get that the three of you have been a unit all your lives. I don't imagine you remember a time when you weren't. Added to that you went through together—I don't think it's an exaggeration to say an earth-shattering experience. The three of you are like a . . . a body with three heads isn't right," she said and passed off the shovel.

"We're not the damn Borg."

"No, but that's closer. You're a fist, tight, even closed off to a certain extent, but—" She wiggled her gloved fingers. "Individual. You work together, it's instinctive. And now." She held up her other hand. "This other part comes along. So we're figuring out how to make them mesh." She brought her hands together, fingers linked.

"That actually makes sense." And brought on a slight twinge of guilt. "I've been doing a little digging on my own."

"You don't mean in the snow. And on your own equals you've told Fox and Gage."

"I probably mentioned it. We don't know where Ann Hawkins was for a couple of years, where she gave birth to her sons, where she stayed before she came back to the Hollow—to her parents' house. So I was thinking about extended family. Cousins, aunts, uncles. And figuring a woman that pregnant might not be able to travel very far, not back then. So maybe she'd have been in the general area. Ten, twenty miles in the sixteen hundreds was a hell of lot farther than ten or twenty miles is today."

"That's a good idea. I should have had it."

"And I should've brought it up before."

"Yeah. Now that you have, you should give it to Cyb, give her whatever information you have. She's the research queen. I'm good, she's better."

"And I'm a rank amateur."

"Nothing rank about you." Grinning she took a leap, bounced up into his arms. The momentum had him skidding. She squealed, as much with laughter as alarm as he tipped backward. He flopped; she landed face-first.

Breathless, she dug in, got two handsful of snow to mash into his face before she tried to roll away. He caught her at the waist, dragged her back while she screamed with helpless laughter.

"I'm a champion snow wrestler," he warned her. "You're out of your league, Blondie. So—"

She managed to get a hand between his legs for a nice,

firm stroke. Then taking advantage of the sudden and dramatic dip of his IQ, shoved a messy ball of snow down the back of his neck.

"Those moves are against the rules of the SWF."

"Check the book, buddy. This is intergender play."

She tried to scramble up, fell, then whooshed out a breath when his weight pinned her. "And still champion," he announced, and was about to lower his mouth to hers when the door opened.

"Kids," Cybil told them, "there's a nice warm bed upstairs if you want to play. And FYI? The power just came back on." She glanced back over her shoulder. "Apparently the phones are up, too."

"Phones, electricity. Computer." Quinn wiggled out from under Cal. "I have to check my e-mail."

CYBIL LEANED ON THE DRYER AS LAYLA LOADED towels into the washing machine in Cal's laundry room. "They looked like a couple of horny snow people. Covered, crusted, pink-cheeked, and groping."

"Young love is immune to climatic conditions."

Cybil chuckled. "You know, you don't have to take on the laundry detail."

"Clean towels are a memory at this point, and the power may not stay on. Besides, I'd rather be warm and dry in here washing towels than cold and wet out there shoveling snow." She tossed back her hair. "Especially since no one's groping me."

"Good point. But I was bringing that up as, by my calculations, you and Fox are going to have to flip for cooking detail tonight."

"Quinn hasn't cooked yet, or Cal."

"Quinn helped with breakfast. It's Cal's house."

Defeated, Layla stared at the machine. "Hell. I'll take dinner."

"You can dump it on Fox, using laundry detail as a lever."

"No, we don't know if he can cook, and I can."

Cybil narrowed her eyes. "You can cook? This hasn't been mentioned before."

"If I'd mentioned it, I'd have had to cook."

Lips pursed, Cybil nodded slowly. "Diabolical and self-serving logic. I like it."

"I'll check the supplies, see what I can come up with. Something—" She broke off, stepped forward. "Quinn? What is it?"

"We have to talk. All of us." So pale her eyes looked bruised, Quinn stood in the doorway.

"Q? Honey." Cybil reached out in support. "What's happened?" She remembered Quinn's dash to the computer for e-mail. "Is everyone all right? Your parents?"

"Yes. Yes. I want to tell it all at once, to everyone. We need to get everyone."

She sat in the living room with Cybil perched on the arm of her chair for comfort. Quinn wanted to curl up in Cal's lap as she'd done once before. But it seemed wrong.

It all seemed wrong now.

She wished the power had stayed off forever. She wished she hadn't contacted her grandmother and prodded her into seeking out family history.

She didn't want to know what she knew now.

No going back, she reminded herself. And what she had to say could change everything that was to come.

She glanced at Cal. She knew she had him worried. It wasn't fair to drag it out. How would he look at her afterward? she wondered.

Yank off the bandage, Quinn told herself, and get it over with.

"My grandmother got the information I'd asked her about. Pages from the family Bible. There were even some records put together by a family historian in the late eighteen hundreds. I, ah, have some information on the Clark branch, Layla, that may help you. No one ever pursued that end very far, but you may be able to track back, or out from what I have now."

"Okay."

"The thing is, it looks like the family was, we'll say, pretty religious about their own tracking back. My grandfather, not so much, but his sister, a couple of cousins, they were more into it. They, apparently, get a lot of play out of the fact their ancestors were among the early Pilgrims who settled in the New World. So there isn't just the Bible, and the pages added to that over time. They've had genealogies done tracing roots back to England and Ireland in the fifteen hundreds. But what applies to us, to this, is the branch that came over here. Here to Hawkins Hollow," she said to Cal.

She braced herself. "Sebastian Deale brought his wife and three daughters to the settlement here in sixteen fifty-one. His eldest daughter's name was Hester. Hester Deale."

"Hester's Pool," Fox murmured. "She's yours."

"That's right. Hester Deale, who according to town lore denounced Giles Dent as a witch on the night of July 7, sixteen fifty-two. Who eight months later delivered a daughter, and when that daughter was two weeks old, drowned herself in the pond in Hawkins Wood. There's no father documented, nothing on record. But we know who fathered her child. We know what fathered her child."

"We can't be sure of that."

"We know it, Caleb." However much it tore inside her, Quinn knew it. "We've seen it, you and I. And Layla, Layla experienced it. He raped her. She was barely sixteen. He lured her, he overpowered her—mind and body, and he got her with child. One that carried his blood." To keep them still, Quinn gripped her hands together. "A half-demon child. She couldn't live with it, with what had been done to her, with what she'd brought into the world. So she filled her pockets with stones and went into the water to drown."

"What happened to her daughter?" Layla asked.

"She died at twenty, after having two daughters of her own. One of them died before her third birthday, the other went on to marry a man named Duncan Clark. They had three sons and a daughter. Both she, her husband, and her youngest son were killed when their house burned down. The other children escaped."

"Duncan Clark must be where I come in," Layla said.

"And somewhere along the line, one of them hooked up with a gypsy from the Old World," Cybil finished. "Hardly seems fair. They get to descend from a heroic white witch, and we get the demon seed."

"It's not a joke," Quinn snapped.

"No, and it's not a tragedy. It just is."

"Damn it, Cybil, don't you see what this means? That *thing* out there is my—probably our—great-grandfather times a dozen generations. It means we're carrying some part of that in us."

"And if I start to sprout horns and a tail in the next few weeks, I'm going to be very pissed off."

"Oh, fuck that!" Quinn pushed up, rounded on her friend. "Fuck the Cybilese. He raped that girl to get to us, three and a half centuries ago, but what he planted led to this. What if we're not here to stop it, not here to help this end? What if we're here to see that it doesn't stop? To play some part in hurting them?"

"If your brain wasn't mushy with love you'd see that's a bullshit theory. Panic reaction with a heavy dose of self-pity to spice it up." Cybil's voice was brutally cool. "We're not under some demon's thumb. We're not going to suddenly jump sides and put on the uniform of some *dark entity* who tries to kill a dog to get his rocks off. We're exactly who we were five minutes ago, so stop being stupid, and pull yourself together."

"She's right. Not about being stupid," Layla qualified. "But about being who we are. If all this is part of it, then we have to find a way to use it."

"Fine. I'll practice getting my head to do three-sixties."

"Lame," Cybil decided. "You'd do better with the sarcasm, Q, if you weren't so worried Cal's going to dump you because of the big *D* for demon on your forehead."

"Cut it out," Layla commanded, and Cybil only shrugged.

"If he does," Cybil continued equably, "he's not worth your time anyway."

In the sudden, thundering silence a log fell in the grate and shot sparks.

"Did you print out the attachment?" Cal asked.

"No, I . . ." Quinn trailed off, shook her head.

"Let's go do that now, then we can take a look." He rose, put a hand on Quinn's arm and drew her from the room.

"Nice job," Gage commented to Cybil. Before she could snarl, he angled his head. "That wasn't sarcasm. It was either literally or verbally give her a slap across the face. Verbally's trickier, but a lot less messy."

"Both are painful." Cybil pushed to her feet. "If he hurts her, I'll twist off his dick and feed it to his dog." With that, she stormed out of the room.

"She's a little scary," Fox decided.

"She's not the only one. I'm the one who'll be roasting his balls for dessert." Layla headed out behind Cybil. "I have to find something to make for dinner."

"Oddly, I don't have much of an appetite right now." Fox glanced at Gage. "How about you?"

Upstairs, Cal waited until they'd stepped into the office currently serving as the men's dorm. He pushed Quinn's back to the door. The first kiss was hard, with sharp edges of anger. The second frustrated. And the last soft.

"Whatever's in your head about you and me, because of this, get it out. Now. Understand?"

"Cal—"

"It's taken me my whole life to say what I said to you this morning. I love you. This doesn't change that. So pitch that out, Quinn, or you're going to piss me off."

"It wasn't—that isn't . . ." She closed her eyes as a storm of emotions blew through her. "All right, that was in there, part of it, but it's all of it, the whole. When I read the file she sent it just . . ."

"It kicked your feet out from under you. I get that. But you know what? I'm right here to help you up." He lifted a hand, made a fist, then opened it.

Understanding, she fought back tears. Understanding, she put her palm to his, interlaced fingers.

"Okay?"

"Not okay," she corrected. "Thank God about covers it."

"Let's print it out, see what we've got."

"Yeah." Steadier, she glanced at the room. The messy, unmade pullout, the piles of clothes. "Your friends are slobs."

"Yes. Yes, they are."

Together, they picked their way through the mess to the computer.

Nineteen

IN THE DINING ROOM, QUINN SET COPIES OF THE printouts in front of everyone. There were bowls of popcorn on the table, she noted, a bottle of wine, glasses, and paper towels folded into triangles. Which would all be Cybil's doing, she knew.

Just as she knew Cybil had made the popcorn for her. Not a peace offering, they didn't need peace offerings between them. It was just because.

She touched a hand to Cybil's shoulder before she took her seat.

"Apologies for the big drama," Quinn began.

"If you think that was drama, you need to come over to my parents' house during one of the family gatherings." Fox gave her a smile as he took a handful of popcorn. "The Barry-O'Dells don't need demon blood to raise hell."

"We'll all accept the demon thing is going to be a running gag from now on." Quinn poured a glass of wine. "I don't know how much all this will tell everyone, but it's more than we had before. It shows a direct line from the other side."

"Are you sure Twisse is the one who raped Hester Deale?" Gage asked. "Certain he's the one who knocked her up?"

Quinn nodded. "Believe me."

"I experienced it." Layla twisted the paper towel in her hands as she spoke. "It wasn't like the flashes Cal and Quinn get, but . . . Maybe the blood tie explains it. I don't know. But I know what he did to her. And I know she was a virgin before he—it—raped her."

Gently, Fox took the pieces of the paper towel she'd torn, gave her his.

"Okay," Gage continued, "are we sure Twisse is what we're calling the demon for lack of better?"

"He never liked that term," Cal put in. "I think we can go affirmative on that."

"So, Twisse uses Hester to sire a child, to extend his line. If he's been around as long as we think—going off some of the stuff Cal's seen and related, it's likely he'd done the same before."

"Right." Cybil acknowledged. "Maybe that's where we get people like Hitler or Osama bin Laden, Jack the Ripper, child abusers, serial killers."

"If you look at the lineage, you'll see there were a lot of suicides and violent deaths, especially in the first hundred, hundred and twenty years after Hester. I think," Quinn said slowly, "if we're able to dig a little deeper on individuals, we might find more than the average family share of murder, insanity."

"Anything that stands out in recent memory?" Fox asked. "Major family skeletons?"

"Not that I know of. I have the usual share of kooky or annoying relatives, but nobody's been incarcerated or institutionalized."

"It dilutes." Fox narrowed his eyes as he paged through the printouts. "This wasn't his plan, wasn't his strategy. I know strategy. Consider. Twisse doesn't know what Dent's got cooking that night. He's got Hester—got her mind under control, got the demon bun in the oven, but he doesn't know that's going to be it."

"That Dent's ready for him, and has his own plans," Layla continued. "I see where you're going. He thought—planned—to destroy Dent that night, or at least damage him, drive him away."

"Then he gets the town," Fox continued, "uses it up, moves on. Leaves progeny, before he finds the next spot that suits him to do the same."

"Instead Dent takes him down, holds him down until . . ." Cal turned over his hand, exposed the thin scar on his wrist. "Until Dent's progeny lets him out. Why would he want that? Why would he allow it?"

"Could be Dent figured keeping a demon in a headlock for three centuries was long enough." Gage helped himself to popcorn. "Or that's as long as he could hold him, and he called out some reinforcements."

"Ten-year-old boys," Cal said in disgust.

"Children are more likely to believe, to accept what adults can't. Or won't," Cybil added. "And hell, nobody said any of this was fair. He gave you what he could. Your ability to heal quickly, your insights into what was, is, will be. He gave you the stone, in three parts."

"And time to grow up," Layla added. "Twenty-one years. Maybe he found the way to bring us here. Quinn, Cybil, and me. Because I can't see the logic, the purpose of having me compelled to come here, then trying to scare me away."

"Good point." And it loosened something inside Quinn's belly. "That's a damn good point. Why scare if he could seduce? Really good point."

"I can look deeper into the family tree for you, Q. And I'll see what I can find on Layla's and my own. But that's just busywork at this point. We know the root."

Cybil turned one of the pages over, used a pencil on the back. She drew two horizontal lines at the bottom. "Giles Dent and Ann Hawkins here, Lazarus Twisse and the doomed Hester here. Each root sends up a tree, and the trees their branches." She drew quickly, simply. "And at the right point, branches from each tree cross each other. In palmistry the crossing of lines is a sign of power."

She completed the sketch, three branches, crossing three branches. "So we have to find the power, and use it."

THAT EVENING, LAYLA DID SOMETHING FAIRLY tasty with chicken breasts, stewed tomatoes, and white beans. By mutual agreement they channeled the conversation into other areas. Normal, Quinn thought as it ranged from dissecting recent movies to bad jokes to travel. They all needed a good dose of normal.

"Gage is the one with itchy feet," Cal commented. "He's been traveling that long, lonesome highway since he hit eighteen."

"It's not always lonesome."

"Cal said you were in Prague." Quinn considered. "I think I'd like to see Prague."

"I thought it was Budapest."

Gage glanced at Cybil. "There, too. Prague was the last stop before heading back."

"Is it fabulous?" Layla wondered. "The art, the architecture, the food?"

"It's got all that. The palace, the river, the opera. I got a taste of it, but mostly I was working. Flew in from Budapest for a poker game."

"You spent your time in—what do they call it—the Paris of Eastern Europe playing poker?" Quinn demanded.

"Not all of it, just the lion's share. The game went for just over seventy-three hours."

"Three days, playing poker?" Cybil's eyebrow winged up. "Wouldn't that be a little obsessive?"

"Depends on where you stand, doesn't it?"

"But don't you need to sleep, eat? Pee?" Layla wondered.

"Breaks are worked in. The seventy-three hours was

actual game time. This was a private game, private home. Serious money, serious security."

"Win or lose?" Quinn asked him with a grin.

"I did okay."

"Do you use your precognition to help you do okay?" Cybil asked.

"That would be cheating."

"Yes, it would, but that didn't answer the question."

He picked up his wine, kept his eyes on hers. "If I had to cheat to win at poker, I should be selling insurance. I don't have to cheat."

"We took an oath." Fox held up his hands when Gage scowled at him. "We're in this together now. They should understand how it works for us. We took an oath when we realized we all had something extra. We wouldn't use it against anyone, or to hurt anyone, or, well, to screw anyone. We don't break our word to each other."

"In that case," Cybil said to Gage, "you ought to be playing the ponies instead of cards."

He flashed a grin. "Been known to, but I like cards. Wanna play?"

"Maybe later."

When Cybil glanced at Quinn with a look of apology, Quinn knew what was coming. "I guess we should get back to it," Cybil began. "I have a question, a place I'd like to start."

"Let's take fifteen." Quinn pushed to her feet. "Get the table cleared off, take the dog out. Just move a little. Fifteen."

Cal brushed a hand over her arm as he rose with her. "I need to check the fire anyway, probably bring in more wood. Let's do this in the living room when we're finished up."

THEY LOOKED LIKE ORDINARY PEOPLE, CAL thought. Just a group of friends hanging out on a winter night. Gage had switched to coffee, and that was usual. Cal hadn't known Gage to indulge in more than a couple drinks at a time since the summer they'd been seventeen. Fox was back on Coke, and he himself had opted for water.

Clear heads, he mused. They wanted clear heads if there were questions to be answered.

They'd gone back to gender groups. Had that been automatic, even intrinsic? he wondered. The three women on the couch, Fox on the floor with Lump. He'd taken a chair, and Gage stood by the fire as if he might just walk out if the topic didn't suit his mood.

"So." Cybil tucked her legs under her, let her dark eyes scan the room. "I'm wondering what was the first thing, event, instance, the first happening, we'll say, that alerted you something was wrong in town. After your night in the clearing, after you went home."

"Mr. Guthrie and the fork." Fox stretched out, propped his head on Lump's belly. "That was a big clue."

"Sounds like the title of a kid's book." Quinn made a note on her pad. "Why don't you fill us in?"

"You take it, Cal," Fox suggested.

"It would've been our birthday—the night, or really the evening of it. We were all pretty spooked. It was worse being separated, each of us in our own place. I talked my mother into letting me go into the bowling center, so I'd have something to do, and Gage would be there. She couldn't figure out whether to ground me or not," he said with a half smile. "First and last time I remember her being undecided on that kind of issue. So she let me go in with my father. Gage?"

"I was working. Mr. Hawkins let me earn some spending money at the center, mopping up spills or carrying grill orders out to tables. I know I felt a hell of a lot better when Cal came in. Then Fox."

"I nagged my parents brainless to let me go in. My father finally caved, took me. I think he wanted to have a confab with Cal's dad, and Gage's if he could."

"So, Brian—Mr. O'Dell—and my dad sat down at the

end of the counter, having coffee. They didn't bring Bill, Gage's father, into it at that point."

"Because he didn't know I'd been gone in the first place," Gage said. "No point getting me in trouble until they'd decided what to do."

"Where was your father?" Cybil asked.

"Around. Behind the pins. He was having a few sober hours, so Mr. Hawkins had him working on something."

"Ball return, lane two," Cal murmured. "I remember. It seemed like an ordinary summer night. Teenagers, some college types on the pinballs and video games. Grill smoking, pins crashing. There was a kid—two or three years old, I guess—with a family in the four lane. Major tantrum. The mother hauled him outside right before it happened."

He took a swig of water. He could see it, bell clear. "Mr. Guthrie was at the counter, drinking a beer, eating a dog and fries. He came in once a week. Nice enough guy. Sold flooring, had a couple of kids in high school. Once a week, he came in when his wife went to the movies with girlfriends. It was clockwork. And Mr. Guthrie would order a dog and fries, and get steadily trashed. My dad used to say he did his drinking there because he could tell himself it wasn't real drinking if he wasn't in a bar."

"Troublemaker?" Quinn asked as she made another note.

"Anything but. He was what my dad called an affable drunk. He never got mean, or even sloppy. Tuesday nights, Mr. Guthrie came in, got a dog and fries, drank four or five beers, watched some games, talked to whoever was around. Somewhere around eleven, he'd leave a five-dollar tip on the grill and walk home. Far as I know he didn't so much as crack a Bud otherwise. It was a Tuesday night deal."

"He used to buy eggs from us," Fox remembered. "A dozen brown eggs, every Saturday morning. Anyway."

"It was nearly ten, and Mr. Guthrie was having another beer. He was walking by the tables with it," Cal said.

"Probably going to take it and stand behind the lanes, watch some of the action. Some guys were having burgers. Frank Dibbs was one of them—held his league's record for high game, coached Little League. We were sitting at the next table, eating pizza. Dad told us to take a break, so we were splitting a pizza. Dibbs said, 'Hey, Guth, the wife wants new vinyl in the kitchen. What kind of deal can you give me?'

"And Guthrie, he just smiles. One of those tight-lipped smiles that don't show any teeth. He picks up one of the forks sitting on the table. He jammed it into Dibbs's cheek, just stabbed it into his face, and kept walking. People are screaming and running, and, Christ, that fork is just sticking out of Mr. Dibbs's cheek, and blood's sliding down his face. And Mr. Guthrie strolls over behind lane two, and drinks his beer."

To give himself a moment, Cal took a long drink. "My dad wanted us out. Everything was going crazy, except Guthrie, who apparently *was* crazy. Your dad took care of Dibbs," Cal said to Fox. "I remember how he kept his head. Dibbs had already yanked the fork out, and your father grabbed this stack of napkins and got the bleeding stopped. There was blood on his hands when he drove us home."

Cal shook his head. "Not the point. Fox's dad took us home. Gage came with me, my father took care of that. He didn't get home until it was light out. I heard him come home; my mother had waited for him. I heard him tell her they had Guthrie locked up, and he was just sitting in his cell laughing. Laughing like it was all a big joke. Later, when it was all over, he didn't even remember. Nobody remembered much of what went on that week, or if they did, they put it away. He never came in the center again. They moved away the next winter."

"Was that the only thing that happened that night?" Cybil asked after a moment.

"Girl was raped." Gage set his empty mug on the mantel. "Making out with her boyfriend out on Dog Street. He didn't stop when she said stop, didn't stop when she started to cry, to scream. He raped her in the backseat of his secondhand Buick, then shoved her out on the side of the road and drove off. Wrapped his car around a tree a couple hours later. Ended up in the same hospital as she did. Only he didn't make it."

"Family mutt attacked an eight-year-old boy," Fox added. "Middle of that night. The dog had slept with the kid every night for three years. The parents woke up hearing the kid screaming, and when they got to the bedroom, the dog went for them, too. The father had to beat it off with the kid's baseball bat."

"It just got worse from there. That night, the next night." Cal took a long breath. "Then it didn't always wait for night. Not always."

"There's a pattern to it." Quinn spoke quietly, then glanced up when Cal's voice cut through her thoughts.

"Where? Other than ordinary people turn violent or psychotic?"

"We saw what happened with Lump. You've just told us about another family pet. There have been other incidents like that. Now you've said the first overt incident all of you witnessed involved a man who'd had several beers. His alcohol level was probably over the legal limit, meaning he was impaired. Mind's not sharp after drinking like that. You're more susceptible."

"So Guthrie was easier to influence or infect because he was drunk or well on the way?" Fox pushed up to sitting. "That's good. That makes good sense."

"The boy who raped his girlfriend of three months then drove into a tree hadn't been drinking." Gage shook his head. "Where's that in the pattern?"

"Sexual arousal and frustration tend to impair the brain." Quinn tapped her pencil on her pad. "Put those into a teenage boy, and that says susceptible to me."

"It's a valid point." Cal shoved his hand through his hair. Why hadn't they seen it themselves? "The dead crows. There were a couple dozen dead crows all over Main Street the morning of our birthday that year. Some broken windows where they'd repeatedly flown into the glass. We always figured that was part of it. But nobody got hurt."

"Does it always start that way?" Layla asked. "Can you pinpoint it?"

"The first I remember from the next time when the Myers found their neighbor's dog drowned in a backyard swimming pool. There was the woman who left her kid locked in the car and went into the beauty salon, got a manicure and so on. It was in the nineties that day," Fox added. "Somebody heard the kid crying, called the cops. They got the kid out, but when they went in to get the woman, she said she didn't have a baby. Didn't know what they were talking about. It came out she'd been up two nights running because the baby had colic."

"Sleep deprivation." Quinn wrote it down.

"But we knew it was happening again," Cal said slowly, "we knew for sure on the night of our seventeenth when Lisa Hodges walked out of the bar at Main and Battlefield, stripped down naked, and started shooting at passing cars with the twenty-two she had in her purse."

"We were one of the cars," Gage added. "Good thing for all concerned her aim was lousy."

"She caught your shoulder," Fox reminded him.

"She *shot* you?"

Gage smiled easily at Cybil. "Grazed me, and we heal fast. We managed to get the gun from her before she shot anyone else, or got hit by a car as she was standing buck naked in the middle of the street. Then she offered us blow jobs. Rumor was she gave a doozy, but we weren't much in the mood to find out."

"All right, from pattern to theory." Quinn rose to her feet to work it out. "The thing we'll call Twisse, because it's better to have a name for it, requires energy. We're all made up of energy, and Twisse needs it to manifest, to work. When he's out, during this time Dent is unable to hold him, he seeks out the easiest sources of energy first.

Birds and animals, people who are most vulnerable. As he gets stronger, he's able to move up the chain."

"I don't think the way to stop him is to clear out all the pets," Gage began, "ban alcohol, drugs, and sex and make sure everyone gets a good night's sleep."

"Too bad," Cybil tossed back, "because it might buy us some time. Keep going, Q."

"Next question would be, how does he generate the energy he needs?"

"Fear, hate, violence." Cal nodded. "We've got that. We can't cut off his supply because you can't block those emotions out of the population. They exist."

"So do their counterparts, so we can hypothesize that those are weapons or countermeasures against him. You've all gotten stronger over time, and so has he. Maybe he's able to store some of this energy he pulls in during the dormant period."

"And so he's able to start sooner, start stronger the next time. Okay," Cal decided. "Okay, it makes sense."

"He's using some of that store now," Layla put in, "because he doesn't want all six of us to stick this out. He wants to fracture the group before July."

"He must be disappointed." Cybil picked up the wine she'd nursed throughout the discussion. "Knowledge is power and all that, and it's good to have logical theories, more areas to research. But it seems to be we need to move. We need a strategy. Got any, Mr. Strategy?"

From his spot on the floor, Fox grinned. "Yeah. I say as soon as the snow melts enough for us to get through it, we go to the clearing. We go to the Pagan Stone, all of us together. And we double-dog dare the son of a bitch."

IT SOUNDED GOOD IN THEORY. IT WAS A DIFFERent matter, in Cal's mind, when you added the human factor. When you added Quinn. He'd taken her there once before, and he'd zoned out, leaving her alone and vulnerable.

And he hadn't loved her then.

He knew there was no choice, that there were bigger stakes involved. But the idea of putting her at risk, at deliberately putting her at the center of it with him, kept him awake and restless.

He wandered the house, checking locks, staring out windows for any glimpse of the thing that stalked them. The moon was out, and the snow tinted blue under it. They'd be able to shovel their way out the next day, he thought, dig out the cars. Get back to what passed for normal within a day or two.

He already knew if he asked her to stay, just stay, she'd tell him she couldn't leave Layla and Cybil on their own. He already knew he'd have to let her go.

He couldn't protect her every hour of every day, and if he tried they'd end up smothering each other.

As he moved through the living room, he saw the glow of the kitchen lights. He headed back to turn them off and check locks. And there was Gage, sitting at the counter playing solitaire with a mug of coffee steaming beside the discard pile.

"A guy who drinks black coffee at one a.m. is going to be awake all night."

"It never keeps me up." Gage flipped a card, made his play. "When I want to sleep, I sleep. You know that. What's your excuse?"

"I'm thinking it's going to be a long, hard, messy hike into the woods even if we wait a month. Which we probably should."

"No. Red six on black seven. You're trying to come up with a way to go in without Quinn. Without any of them, really, but especially the blonde."

"I told you how it was when we went in before."

"And she walked out again on her own two sexy legs. Jack of clubs on queen of diamonds. I'm not worried about her. I'm worried about you."

Cal's back went up. "Is there a time I didn't handle myself?"

"Not up until now. But you've got it bad, Hawkins. You've got it bad for the blonde, and being you, your first and last instinct is going to be to cover her ass if anything goes down."

"Shouldn't it be?" He didn't want any damn coffee, but since he doubted he'd sleep anyway, he poured some. "Why wouldn't it be?"

"I'd lay money that your blonde can handle herself. Doesn't mean you're wrong, Cal. I imagine if I had a woman inside me the way she's inside you, I wouldn't want to put how she handled herself to the test. The trouble is, you're going to have to."

"I never wanted to feel this way," Cal said after a moment. "This is a good part of the reason why. We're good together, Gage."

"I can see that for myself. Don't know what she sees in a loser like you, but it's working for her."

"We could get better. I can feel we'd just get better, make something real and solid. If we had the chance, if we had the time, we'd make something together."

Casually, Gage gathered up the cards, shuffled them with a blur of speed. "You think we're going down this time."

"Yeah." Cal looked out the window at the cold, blue moonlight. "I think we're going down. Don't you?"

"Odds are." Gage dealt them both a hand of blackjack. "But hell, who wants to live forever?"

"That's the problem. Now that I've found Quinn, forever sounds pretty damn good." Cal glanced at his hold card, noted the king to go with his three. "Hit me."

With a grin, Gage flipped over a nine. "Sucker."

Twenty

CAL HOPED FOR A WEEK, TWO IF HE COULD MANAGE it. And got three days. Nature screwed his plans again, this time shooting temperatures up into the fifties. Mountains of snow melted into hills while the February thaw brought the fun of flash flooding, swollen creeks, and black ice when the thermometer dropped to freezing each night.

But three days after he'd had his lane plowed and the women were back in the house on High Street, the weather stabilized. Creeks ran high, but the ground sucked up most of the runoff. And he was coming up short on excuses to put off the hike to the Pagan Stone.

At his desk, with Lump contentedly sprawled on his back in the doorway, feet in the air, Cal put his mind into work. The winter leagues were winding up, and the spring groups would go into gear shortly. He knew he was on the edge of convincing his father the center would profit from the automatic scoring systems, and wanted to give it one more solid push. If they moved on it soon, they could have the systems up and running for the spring leagues.

They'd want to advertise, run a few specials. They'd have to train the staff, which meant training themselves.

He brought up the spreadsheet for February, noted that the month so far had been solid, even up a bit from last year. He'd use that as more ammunition. Which, of course, his father could and would counter that if they were up the way things were, why change it?

As he was holding the conversation in his head, Cal heard the click that meant a new e-mail had come in. He toggled over, saw Quinn's address.

Hi, Love of My Life,

I didn't want to call in case you were knee-deep in whatever requires you to be knee-deep. Let me know when you're not.

Meanwhile, this is Black's Local Weather Service reporting: Temperatures today should reach a high of forty-eight under partly sunny skies. Lows in the upper thirties. No precipitation is expected. Tomorrow's forecast is for sunny with a high of fifty.

Adding the visual, I can see widening patches of grass in both the front and backyard. Realistically, there's probably more snow, more mud in the woods, but, baby, it's time to saddle up and move out.

My team can be ready bright and early tomorrow and will bring suitable provisions.

Also, Cyb's confirmed the Clark branch connection, and is currently climbing out on some Kinski limbs to verify that. She thinks she may have a line on a couple of possibilities where Ann Hawkins stayed, or at least where she might have gone to give birth. I'll fill you in when I see you.

Let me know, soon as you can, if tomorrow works.

XXOO Quinn.

(I know that whole XXOO thing is dopey, but it seemed more refined than signing off with: I wish you could come over and do me. Even though I do.)

The last part made him smile even though the text of the post had a headache sneaking up the back of his skull.

He could put her off a day or two, and put her off honestly. He couldn't expect Fox to dump his scheduled clients or any court appearances at the snap of a finger, and she'd understand that. But if he were to use that, and his own schedule, he had to do it straight.

With some annoyance, he shot an e-mail to Fox, asking when he could clear time for the trip to the clearing. The annoyance increased when Fox answered back immediately.

Fri's good. Morning's clear, can clear full day if nec.

"Well, fuck." Cal pushed on the ache at the back of his head. Since e-mail wasn't bringing him any luck, he'd go see Quinn in person when he broke for lunch.

AS CAL PREPARED TO CLOSE OUT FOR THE MORNing, Bill Turner stopped in the office doorway.

"Ah, got that toilet fixed in the ladies room downstairs, and the leak in the freezer was just a hose needed replacing."

"Thanks, Bill." He swung his coat on as he spoke. "I've got a couple of things to do in town. Shouldn't be above an hour."

"Okay, then. I was wondering if, ah . . ." Bill rubbed a hand over his chin, let it drop. "I was wondering if you think Gage'll be coming in, maybe the next day or two. Or if maybe I could, maybe I could run over to your place to have a word with him."

Rock and a hard place, Cal thought, and bought himself some time by adjusting his jacket. "I don't know if he's thinking about dropping by, Bill. He hasn't mentioned it. I think . . . Okay, look, I'd give him some time. I'd just give it some time before you made that first move. I know you want—"

"It's okay. That's okay. Appreciate it."

"Shit," Cal said under his breath as Bill walked away. Then, "Shit, shit, shit," as he headed out himself.

He had to take Gage's side in this, how could he not? He'd seen firsthand what Bill's belt had done to Gage when they'd been kids. And yet, he'd also witnessed, firsthand, the dozens of ways Bill had turned himself around in the last few years.

And, hadn't he just seen the pain, guilt, even the grief on Bill's face just now? So either way he went, Cal knew he was going to feel guilty and annoyed.

He walked straight out and over to Quinn's.

She pulled open the door, yanked him in. Before he could say a word her arms were locked around his neck and her mouth was very busy on his. "I was hoping that was you."

"Good thing it was, because Greg, the UPS guy on this route, might get the wrong idea if you greeted him that way."

"He is kind of cute. Come on back to the kitchen. I'd just come down to do a coffee run. We're all working on various projects upstairs. Did you get my e-mail?"

"Yeah."

"So, we're all set for tomorrow?" She glanced back as she reached up for the coffee.

"No, tomorrow's no good. Fox can't clear his slate until Friday."

"Oh." Her lips moved into a pout, quickly gone. "Okay then, Friday it is. Meanwhile we'll keep reading, researching, working. Cyb thinks she's got a couple of good possibilities on . . . What?" she asked when she got a good look at his face. "What's going on?"

"Okay." He took a couple paces away, then back. "Okay, I'm just going to say it. I don't want you going back in there. Just be quiet a minute, will you?" he said when he saw the retort forming. "I wish there was a way I could stop you from going, that there was a way I could ignore the fact that we all need to go. I know you're a part of this, and I know you have to go back to the Pagan Stone. I know there's going to be more you have to be a part of than I'd wish otherwise. But I can wish you weren't part of this, Quinn, and that you were somewhere safe until this is over. I can want that, just as I know I can't have what I want.

"If you want to be pissed off about that, you'll have to be pissed off."

She waited a beat. "Have you had lunch?"

"No. What does that have to do with anything?"

"I'm going to make you a sandwich—an offer I never make lightly."

"Why are you making it now?"

"Because I love you. Take off your coat. I love that you'd say all that to me," she began as she opened the refrigerator for fixings. "That you'd need to let me know how you felt about it. Now if you'd tried ordering me to stay out of it, if you'd lied or tried to do some sort of end-run around me, I'd feel different. I'd still love you, because that sort of thing sticks with me, but I'd be mad, and more, I'd be disappointed in you. As it is, Cal, I'm finding myself pretty damn pleased and a hell of a lot smug that my head and heart worked so well together and picked the perfect guy. The perfect guy for me."

She cut the sandwich into two tidy triangles, offered it. "Do you want coffee or milk?"

"You don't have milk, you have white water. Coffee'd be fine, thanks." He took a bite of the turkey and Swiss with alfalfa on whole wheat. "Pretty good sandwich."

"Don't get used to the service." She glanced over as she poured out coffee. "We should get an early start on Friday, don't you think? Like dawn?"

"Yeah." He touched her cheek with his free hand. "We'll head in at first light."

SINCE HE'D HAD GOOD LUCK WITH QUINN, AND gotten lunch out of it, Cal decided he was going to speak his mind to Gage next. The minute he and Lump stepped into the house, he smelled food. And when they wandered back Cal found Gage in the kitchen, taking a pull off a beer as he stirred something in a pot.

"You made food."

"Chili. I was hungry. Fox called. He tells me we're taking the ladies for a hike Friday."

"Yeah. First light."

"Should be interesting."

"Has to be done." Cal dumped out food for Lump before getting a beer of his own. And so, he thought, did this have to be done. "I need to talk to you about your father."

Cal saw Gage close off. Like a switch flipped, a finger snapped, his face simply blanked out. "He works for you; that's your business. I've got nothing to say."

"You've got every right to shut him out. I'm not saying different. I'm letting you know he asks about you. He wants to see you. Look, he's been sober five years now, and if he'd been sober fifty it wouldn't change the way he treated you. But this is a small town, Gage, and you can't dodge him forever. My sense is he's got things to say to you, and you may want to get it done, put it behind you. That's it."

There was a reason Gage made his living at poker. It showed now in a face, a voice, completely devoid of expression. "My sense is you should take yourself out of the middle. I haven't asked you to stand there."

Cal held up a hand for peace. "Fine."

"Sounds like the old man's stuck on Steps Eight and Nine with me. He can't make amends on this, Cal. I don't give a damn about his amends."

"Okay. I'm not trying to convince you otherwise. Just letting you know."

"Now I know."

IT OCCURRED TO CAL WHEN HE STOOD AT THE window on Friday morning, watching the headlights cut through the dim predawn that it had been almost a month exactly since Quinn had first driven up to his house.

How could so much have happened? How could so much have changed in such a short time?

It had been slightly less than that month since he'd led her into the woods the first time. When he'd led her to the Pagan Stone.

In those short weeks of the shortest month he'd learned it wasn't only himself and his two blood brothers who were destined to face this threat. There were three women now, equally involved.

And he was completely in love with one of them.

He stood just as he was to watch her climb out of Fox's truck. Her bright hair spilled out from under the dark watch cap. She wore a bold red jacket and scarred hiking boots. He could see the laugh on her face as she said something to Cybil, and her breath whisked out in clouds in the early morning chill.

She knew enough to be afraid, he understood that. But she refused to allow fear to dictate her moves. He hoped he could say the same as he had more to risk now. He had her.

He stood watch until he heard Fox use his key to unlock the front door, then Cal went down to join them, and to gather his things for the day.

Fog smoked the ground that the cold had hardened like stone overnight. By midday, Cal knew the path would be sloppy again, but for now it was quick and easy going.

There were still pockets and lumpy hills of snow, and he identified the hoofprints of the deer that roamed the woods, to Layla's delight. If any of them were nervous they hid it well, at least on this first leg of the hike.

It was so different from that long-ago day in July when he and Fox and Gage had made this trip. No boom box pumping out rap or heavy metal, no snacks of Little Debbies, no innocent, youthful excitement of a stolen day, and the night to come.

None of them had ever been so innocent again.

He caught himself lifting a hand to his face, where his glasses used to slide down the bridge of his nose.

"How you doing, Captain?" Quinn stepped up to match her pace to his, gave him a light arm bump.

"Okay. I was just thinking about that day. Everything hot and green, Fox hauling that stupid boom box. My mother's lemonade, snack cakes."

"Sweat rolling," Fox continued from just behind him.

"We're coming up on Hester's Pool," Gage said, breaking the memory.

The water made Cal think of quicksand rather than the cool and forbidden pool he and his friends had leaped into so long ago. He could imagine going in now, being sucked in, deeper and deeper until he never saw light again.

They stopped as they had before, but now it was coffee instead of lemonade.

"There's been deer here, too." Layla pointed at the ground. "Those are deer prints, right?"

"Some deer," Fox confirmed. "Raccoon." He took her arm to turn her, pointed to the prints on the ground.

"Raccoons?" Grinning, she bent to take a closer look. "What else might be in here?"

"Some of my namesakes, wild turkey, now and then—though mostly north of here—you might see bear."

She straightened quickly. "Bear."

"Mostly north," he repeated, but found it as good an excuse as any to take her hand.

Cybil crouched by the edge of the pool, stared at the water.

"A little cold to think about taking a dip," Gage told her.

"Hester drowned herself here." She glanced up, then looked over at Cal. "And when you went in that day, you saw her."

"Yeah. Yeah, I saw her."

"And you and Quinn have both seen her in your heads. Layla's dreamed of her, vividly. So . . . maybe I can get something."

"I thought yours was precog, not the past," Cal began.

"It is, but I still get vibes from people, from places that

are strong enough to send them out. How about you?" She looked back at Gage. "We might stir up more in tandem. Are you up for that?"

Saying nothing, he held out a hand. She took it, rose to her feet. Together, they stared at that still, brown surface.

The water began to beat and froth. It began to spin, to spew up white-tipped waves. It roared like a sea mating with a wild and vicious storm.

And a hand shot out to claw at the ground.

Hester pulled herself out of that churning water—bone white skin, a mass of wet, tangled hair, dark, glassy eyes. The effort, or her madness, peeled her lips back from her teeth.

Cybil heard herself scream as Hester Deale's arms opened, as they locked around her and dragged her toward that swirling brown pool.

"Cyb! Cyb! Cybil!"

She came back struggling, and found herself locked not in Hester's arms, but Gage's. "What the hell was that?"

"You were going in."

She stayed where she was, feeling her heart hammer against his as Quinn gripped her shoulder. Cybil took another look at the still surface of the pool. "That would've been really unpleasant."

She was trembling, one hard jolt after the next, but Gage had to give her points for keeping her voice even.

"Did you get anything?" she asked him.

"Water kicked up; she came up. You started to tip."

"She grabbed me. She . . . embraced me. That's what I think, but I wasn't focused enough to feel or sense what she felt. Maybe if we tried it again—"

"We've got to get moving now," Cal interrupted.

"It only took a minute."

"Try nearly fifteen," Fox corrected.

"But . . ." Cybil eased back from Gage when she realized she was still in his arms. "Did it seem that long to you?"

"No. It was immediate."

"It wasn't." Layla held out another thermos lid of coffee. "We were arguing about whether we should pull you back, and how we should if we did. Quinn said to leave you be for another few minutes, that sometimes it took you a while to warm up."

"Well, it felt like a minute, no more than, for the whole deal. And it didn't feel like something from before." Again, Cybil looked at Gage.

"No, it didn't. So if I were you, I wouldn't think about taking a dip anytime soon."

"I prefer a nice blue pool, with a swim-up bar."

"Bikini margaritas." Quinn rubbed her hand up and down Cybil's arm.

"Spring break, two thousand." Cybil caught Quinn's hand, squeezed. "I'm fine, Q."

"I'll buy the first round of those margaritas when this is done. Ready to move on?" Cal asked.

He hitched up his pack, turned. Then shook his head. "This isn't right."

"We're leaving the haunted pool to walk through the demonic woods." Quinn worked up a smile. "What could be wrong?"

"That's not the path." He gestured toward the thawing track. "That's not the direction." He squinted up at the sun as he pulled his old Boy Scout compass out of his pocket.

"Ever thought about upgrading to a GPS?" Gage asked him.

"This does the job. See, we need to head west from here. That trail's leading north. That trail shouldn't even be there."

"It's not there." Fox's eyes narrowed, darkened. "There's no trail, just underbrush, a thicket of wild blackberries. It's not real." He shifted, angled himself. "It's that way." He gestured west. "It's hard to see, it's like looking through mud, but . . ."

Layla stepped forward, took his hand.

"Okay, yeah. That's better."

"You're pointing at a really big-ass tree," Cybil told him.

"That isn't there." Still holding Layla's hand, Fox walked forward. The image of the large oak broke apart as he walked through it.

"Nice trick." Quinn let out a breath. "So, Twisse doesn't want us to go to the clearing. I'll take point."

"I'll take point." Cal took her arm to tug her behind him. "I've got the compass." He had only to glance back at his friends to have them falling in line. Fox taking center, Gage the rear with the women between.

As soon as the track widened enough to allow it, Quinn moved up beside Cal. "This is the way it has to work." She glanced back to see the other women had followed her lead, and now walked abreast with their partners. "We're linked up this way, Cal. Two-by-two, trios, the group of six. Whatever the reasons are, that's the way it is."

"We're walking into something. I can't see what it is, but I'm walking you and the others right into it."

"We're all on our own two feet, Cal." She passed him the bottle of water she carried in her coat pocket. "I don't know if I love you because you're Mr. Responsibility or in spite of it."

"As long as you do. And since you do, maybe we should think about the idea of getting married."

"I like the idea," she said after a moment. "If you want my thoughts on it."

"I do." Stupid, he thought, stupid way to propose, and a ridiculous place for it, too. Then again, when they couldn't be sure what was around the bend, it made sense to grab what you did now, tight and quick. "As it happens, I agree with you. More thoughts on the idea would be that my mother, especially, will want the splash—big deal, big party, bells and whistles."

"I happen to agree with that, too. How is she with communication by phone and/or e-mail?"

"She's all about that."

"Great. I'll hook her up with my mother and they can go for it. How's your September schedule?"

"September?"

She studied the winter woods, watched a squirrel scamper up a tree and across a thick branch. "I bet the Hollow's beautiful in September. Still green, but with just a hint of the color to come."

"I was thinking sooner. Like April, or May." Before, Cal thought. Before July, and what might be the end of everything he knew and loved.

"It takes a while to organize those bells and whistles." When she looked at him he understood she read him clearly. "After, Cal, after we've won. One more thing to celebrate. When we're—"

She broke off when he touched a finger to her lips.

The sound came clearly now as all movement and conversation stopped. The wet and throaty snarl rolled across the air, and shot cold down the spine. Lump curled down on his haunches and whined.

"He hears it, too, this time." Cal shifted, and though the movement was slight, it put Quinn between him and Fox.

"I don't guess we could be lucky, and that's just a bear." Layla cleared her throat. "Either way, I think we should keep moving. Whatever it is doesn't want us to, so . . ."

"We're here to flip it the bird," Fox finished.

"Come on, Lump, come on with me."

The dog shivered at Cal's command, but rose, and with its side pressed to Cal's legs, walked down the trail toward the Pagan Stone.

The wolf, Cal would never have referred to the thing as a dog, stood at the mouth of the clearing. It was huge and black, with eyes that were somehow human. Lump tried a half-hearted snarl in answer to the low, warning growl, then cowered against Cal.

"Are we going to walk through that, too?" Gage asked from the rear.

"It's not like the false trail." Fox shook his head. "It's not real, but it's there."

"Okay." Gage started to pull off his pack.

And the thing leaped.

It seemed to fly, Cal thought, a mass of muscle and teeth. He fisted his hands to defend, but there was nothing to fight.

"I felt . . ." Slowly, Quinn lowered the arms she'd thrown up to protect her face.

"Yeah. Not just the cold, not that time." Cal gripped her arm to keep her close. "There was weight, just for a second, and there was substance."

"We never had that before, not even during the Seven." Fox scanned the woods on both sides. "Whatever form Twisse took, whatever we saw, it wasn't really *there*. It's always been mind games."

"If it can solidify, it can hurt us directly," Layla pointed out.

"And be hurt." From behind her Gage pulled a 9mm Glock out of his pack.

"Good thinking," was Cybil's cool opinion.

"Jesus Christ, Gage, where the hell did you get that?"

Gage lifted his eyebrows at Fox. "Guy I know down in D.C. Are we going to stand here in a huddle, or are we going in?"

"Don't point that at anybody," Fox demanded.

"Safety's on."

"That's what they always say before they accidentally blow a hole in the best friend."

They stepped into the clearing, and the stone.

"My God, it's beautiful." Cybil breathed the words reverently as she moved toward it. "It can't possibly be a natural formation, it's too perfect. It's designed, and for worship, I'd think. And it's warm. Feel it. The stone's warm." She circled it. "Anyone with any sensitivity has to feel, has to know this is sacred ground."

"Sacred to who?" Gage countered. "Because what came up out of here twenty-one years ago wasn't all bright and friendly."

"It wasn't all dark either. We felt both." Cal looked at Fox. "We saw both."

"Yeah. It's just the big, black scary mass got most of our attention while we were being blasted off our feet."

"But the other gave us most of his, that's what I think. I walked out of here not only without a scratch, but with twenty-twenty vision and a hell of an immune system."

"The scratches on my arms had healed up, and the bruises from my most recent tussle with Napper." Fox shrugged. "Never been sick a day since."

"How about you?" Cybil asked Gage. "Any miraculous healing?"

"None of us had a mark on him after the blast," Cal began.

"It's no deal, Cal. No secrets from the team. My old man used his belt on me the night before we were heading in here. A habit of his when he'd get a drunk on. I was carrying the welts when I came in, but not when I walked out."

"I see." Cybil held Gage's eyes for several beats. "The fact that you were given protection, and your specific abilities enabled you to defend your ground, so to speak. Otherwise, you'd have been three helpless little boys."

"It's clean." Layla's comment had everyone turning to where she stood by the stone. "That's what comes to my mind. I don't think it was ever used for sacrifice. Not blood and death, not for the dark. It feels clean."

"I've seen the blood on it," Gage said. "I've seen it burn. I've heard the screams."

"That's not its purpose. Maybe that's what Twisse wants." Quinn laid her palm on the stone. "To defile it, to twist its power. If he can, well, he'll own it, won't he? Cal."

"Okay." His hand hovered over hers. "Ready?" At her nod, he joined his hand to hers on the stone.

At first there was only her, only Quinn. Only the courage in her eyes. Then the world tumbled back, five years, twenty, so that he saw the boy he'd been with his friends, scoring his knife over their wrists to bind them together. Then rushing back, decades, centuries, to the blaze and the screams while the stone stood cool and white in the midst of hell.

Back to another waning winter where Giles Dent stood with Ann Hawkins as he stood with Quinn now. Dent's words came from his lips.

"We have only until summer. This I cannot change, even for you. Duty outstrips even my love for you, and for the lives we have made." He touched a hand to her belly. "I wish, above all, that I could be with you when they come into the world."

"Let me stay. Beloved."

"I am the guardian. You are the hope. I cannot destroy the beast, only chain it for a time. Still, I do not leave you. It is not death, but an endless struggle, a war only I can wage. Until what comes from us makes the end. They will have all I can give, this I swear to you. If they are victorious in their time, I will be with you again."

"What will I tell them of their father?"

"That he loved their mother, and them, with the whole of his heart."

"Giles, it has a man's form. A man can bleed, a man can die."

"It is not a man, and it is not in my power to destroy it. That will be for those who come after us both. It, too, will make its own. Not through love. They will not be what it intends. It cannot own them if they are beyond its reach, even its ken. This is for me to do. I am not the first, Ann, only the last. What comes from us is the future."

She pressed a hand to her side. "They quicken," she whispered. "When, Giles, when will it end? All the lives we have lived before, all the joy and the pain we have known? When will there be peace for us?"

"Be my heart." He lifted her hands to his lips. "I will be your courage. And we will find each other once more."

Tears slid down Quinn's cheeks even as she felt the images fade. "We're all they have. If we don't find the way, they're lost to each other. I felt her heart breaking inside me."

"He believed in what he'd done, what he had to do. He believed in us, though he couldn't see it clearly. I don't think he could see us, all of us," Cal said as he looked around. "Not clearly. He took it on faith."

"Fine for him." Gage shifted his weight. "But I put a little more of mine in this Glock."

It wasn't the wolf, but the boy that stood on the edge of the clearing. Grinning, grinning. He lifted his hands, showed fingernails that were sharpened to claws.

The sun dimmed from midday to twilight; the air from cool to frigid. And thunder rumbled in the late winter sky.

In a lightning move so unexpected Cal couldn't prevent it, Lump sprang. The thing who masked as a boy squealed with laughter, shinnied up a tree like a monkey.

But Cal had seen it, in a flash of an instant. He'd seen the shock, and what might have been fear.

"Shoot it," Cal shouted to Gage, even as he dashed forward to grab Lump's collar. "Shoot the son of a bitch."

"Jesus, you don't actually think a bullet's going to—"

Over Fox's objection, Gage fired. Without hesitation he aimed for the boy's heart.

The bullet cracked the air, struck the tree. This time no one could miss the look of shock on the boy's face. His howl of pain and fury gushed across the clearing and shook the ground.

With ruthless purpose, Gage emptied the clip into it.

It changed. It grew. It twisted itself into something massive and black and sinuous that rose over Cal as he stood his ground, fighting to hold back his dog who strained and barked like a mad thing.

The stench of it, the *cold* of it hammered down on him like stones. "We're still here," Cal shouted. "This is our place, and you can go to hell."

He staggered against a blast of sound and slapping air.

"Better reload, Deadeye," Cybil commanded.

"Knew I should've bought a howitzer." But Gage slapped in a full clip.

"This isn't your place," Cal shouted again. The wind threatened to knock him off his feet, seemed to tear at his clothes and his skin like a thousand knives. Through the scream of it, he heard the crack of gunfire, and the rage it spewed out clamped on his throat like claws.

Then Quinn braced against his side. And Fox shouldered in at his other. They formed a line, all six.

"This," Cal called out, "is ours. Our place and our time. You couldn't have my dog, and you can't have my town."

"So fuck off," Fox suggested, and bending picked up a rock. He hurled it, a straightaway fast ball.

"Hello, got a gun here."

Fox's grin at Gage was wild and wide as the feral wind battered them. "Throwing rocks is an insult. It'll undermine its confidence."

Die here!

It wasn't a voice, but a tidal wave of sound and wind that knocked them to the ground, scattered them like bowling pins.

"Undermine, my ass." Gage shoved to his knees and began firing again.

"You'll die here." Cal spoke coolly as the others took Fox's tack and began to hurl stones and sticks.

Fire swept across the clearing, its flames like shards of ice. Smoke belched up in fetid clouds as it roared its outrage.

"You'll die here," Cal repeated. Pulling his knife from its sheath, he rushed foward to plunge it into the boiling black mass.

It screamed. He thought it screamed, thought the sound held something of pain as well as fury. The shock of power sang up his arm, stabbed through him like a blade, twin edges of scorching heat and impossible cold. It flung him away, sent him flying through the smoke like a pebble from a sling. Breathless, bones jarred from the fall, Cal scrambled to his feet.

"You'll die here!" This time he shouted it as he gripped the knife, as he charged forward.

The thing that was a wolf, a boy, a man, a demon looked at him with eyes of hate.

And vanished.

"But not today." The fire died, the smoke cleared as he bent over to suck in air. "Anybody hurt? Is everybody okay? Quinn. Hey, Lump, hey." He nearly toppled backward when Lump leaped up, paws on shoulders to lap his face.

"Your nose is bleeding." Scurrying over on her hands and knees, Quinn gripped his arm to pull herself to her feet. "Cal." Her hands rushed over his face, his body. "Oh God, Cal. I've never seen anything so brave, or so goddamn stupid."

"Yeah, well." In a defiant move, he swiped at the blood. "It pissed me off. If that was its best shot, it fell way short."

"It didn't dish out anything a really big drink and a long hot bath won't cure," Cybil decided. "Layla? Okay?"

"Okay." Face fierce, Layla brushed at her stinging cheeks. "Okay." She took Fox's outstretched hand and got to her feet. "We scared it. We scared it, and it ran away."

"Even better. We hurt it." Quinn took a couple of shuddering breaths, then much as Lump had, leaped at Cal. "We're all right. We're all okay. You were amazing. You were beyond belief. Oh God, God, give me a really big kiss."

As she laughed and wept, he took her mouth. He held her close, understanding that of all the answers they needed, for him she was the first.

They weren't going down this time, he realized.

"We're going to win this." He drew her away so he could look into her eyes. His were calm, steady, and clear. "I never believed it before, not really. But I do now. I know it now. Quinn." He pressed his lips to her forehead. "We're going to win this, and we're getting married in September."

"Damn straight."

When she wrapped around him again, it was victory enough for now. It was enough to stand on until the next time. And the next time, he determined, they'd be better armed.

"Let's go home. It's a long walk back, and we've got a hell of a lot to do."

She held on another moment, held tight while he looked over her head into the eyes of his brothers. Gage nodded, then shoved the gun back in his pack. Swinging it on, he crossed the clearing to the path beyond.

The sun bloomed overhead, and the wind died. They walked out of the clearing, through the winter woods, three men, three women, and a dog.

On its ground the Pagan Stone stood silent, waiting for their return.

Turn the page for an exclusive sneak preview of the next book in the *Sign of Seven Trilogy*!

The Hollow

Coming soon from Piatkus Books.

7

Hawkins Hollow
June 1994

ON A BRIGHT SUMMER MORNING, A TEACUP POOdle drowned in the Bestlers' backyard swimming pool. At first Lynne Bestler, who'd gone out to sneak in a solitary swim before her kids woke, thought it was a dead squirrel. Which would've been bad enough. But when she steeled herself to scoop out the tangle of fur with the net, she recognized her neighbor's beloved Marcell.

Squirrels generally didn't wear rhinestone collars.

Her shouts, and the splash as Lynne tossed the hapless dog, net and all, back into the pool, brought Lynne's husband rushing out in his boxers. Their mother's sobs and their father's curses as he jumped in to grab the pole and tow the body to the side, woke the Bestler twins, who stood screaming in their matching My Little Pony nightgowns. Within moments, the backyard hysteria had neighbors hurrying to fences just as Bestler dragged himself and his burden out of the water. As, like many men, Bestler had developed an attachment to ancient underwear, the weight of the water was too much for the worn elastic.

So Bestler came out of his pool with a dead dog, and no boxers.

The bright summer morning in the little town of Hawkins Hollow began with shock, grief, farce and drama.

Fox learned of Marcell's untimely death minutes after he stepped into Ma's Pantry to pick up a sixteen-ounce bottle of Coke and a couple of Slim Jims.

He'd copped a quick break from working with his father on a kitchen remodel down Main Street. Mrs. Larson wanted new countertops, cabinet doors, new floors, new paint. She called it freshening things up, and Fox called it a way to earn enough money to take Allyson Brendon out for pizza and the movies on Saturday night. He hoped to use that gateway to talk her into the backseat of his ancient VW Bug.

He didn't mind working with his dad. He hoped to hell he wouldn't spend the rest of his life swinging a hammer or running a power saw, but he didn't mind it. His father's company was always easy, and the job got Fox out of gardening and animal duty on their little farm. It also provided easy access to Cokes and Slim Jims—two items which would never, never be found in the O'Dell-Barry household.

His mother ruled there.

So he heard about the dog from Susan Keefaffer, who rang up his purchases while a few people with nothing better to do on a June afternoon sat at the counter over coffee and gossip.

He didn't know Marcell, but Fox had a soft spot for animals so he suffered a twist of grief for the unfortunate poodle. That was leavened somewhat by the idea of Mr. Bestler, whom he *did* know, standing "naked as a jaybird," in Susan Keefaffer's words, beside his backyard pool.

While it made Fox sad to imagine some poor dog drowning in a swimming pool, he didn't connect it—not then—to the nightmare he and his two closest friends had lived through seven years before.

He'd had a dream the night before, a dream of blood

and fire, of voices chanting in a language he didn't understand. But then he'd watched a double feature of videos—*The Night of the Living Dead* and *The Texas Chainsaw Massacre*—with his friends Cal and Gage.

He didn't connect a dead French poodle with the dream, or with what had burned through Hawkins Hollow for a week after his tenth birthday. After the night he and Cal and Gage had spent at the Pagan Stone in Hawkins Wood—and everything had changed for them, and for the Hollow.

In a few weeks he and Cal and Gage would all turn seventeen—and that was on his mind. Baltimore had a damn good chance at a pennant this year, so that was on his mind. He'd be going back to high school as a senior, which meant top of the food chain at last, and planning for college.

What occupied a sixteen-year-old boy was considerably different than what occupied a ten-year-old. Including rounding second and heading for home with Allyson Brendon.

So when he walked back down the street, a lean boy not quite beyond the gangly stage of adolescence, his dense brown hair tied back in a stubby tail, golden brown eyes shaded with Oakleys, it was, for him, just another ordinary day.

The town looked as it always did. Tidy, a little old-timey, with the old stone townhouses or shops, the painted porches, the high curbs. He glanced back over his shoulder toward the Bowl-A-Rama on the square. It was the biggest building in town, and where Cal and Gage were both working.

When he and his father knocked off for the day, he thought, he'd head on up, see what was happening.

He crossed over to the Larson place, walked into the unlocked house where Bonnie Raitt's smooth Delta Blues slid smoothly out of the kitchen. His father sang along with her in his clear and easy voice as he checked the level on the shelves Mrs. Larson wanted in her utility closet. Though the windows and back door were open to their screens, the room smelled of sawdust, sweat and the glue they'd used that morning to lay the new Formica.

His father worked in old Levis and his Give Peace a Chance T-shirt. His hair was six inches longer than Fox's, worn in a tail under a blue bandanna. He'd shaved off the beard and moustache he'd had as long as Fox remembered. Fox still wasn't quite used to seeing so much of his father's face—or so much of himself in it.

"A dog drowned in the Bestlers' swimming pool over on Laurel Lane," Fox told him, and Brian stopped working to turn.

"That's a damn shame. Anybody know how it happened?"

"Not really. It was one of those little poodles, so think it must've fallen in, then it couldn't get out again."

"You'd think somebody would've heard it barking. That's a lousy way to go." Brian set down his tools, smiled at his boy. "Gimme one of those Slim Jims."

"What Slim Jims?"

"The ones you've got in your back pocket. You're not carrying a bag, and you weren't gone long enough to scarf down Hostess Pies or Twinkies. I'm betting you're packing the Jims. I get one, and your mom never has to know we ate chemicals and meat byproducts. It's called blackmail, kid of mine."

Fox snorted, pulled them out. He'd bought two for just this purpose. Father and son unwrapped, bit off, chewed in perfect harmony. "The counter looks good, Dad."

"Yeah, it does." Brian ran a hand over the smooth, eggshell surface. "Mrs. Larson's not much for color, but it's good work. I don't know who I'm going to get to be my lapdog when you head off to college."

"Ridge is next in line," Fox said, thinking of his younger brother.

"Ridge wouldn't keep measurements in his head for two minutes running, and he'd probably cut off a finger dreaming while he was using a band saw. No." Brian smiled, shrugged. "This kind of work isn't for Ridge, or for you, for that matter. Or either of your sisters. I guess I'm going to have to rent a kid to get one who wants to work with wood."

"I never said I didn't want to." Not out loud.

His father looked at him the way he sometimes did, as if he saw more than what was there. "You've got a good eye, you've got good hands. You'll be handy around your own house once you get one. But you won't be strapping on a tool belt to make a living. But until you figure out just what it is you want, you can haul these scraps on out to the Dumpster."

"Sure." Fox gathered up scraps, trash, began to cart them out the back, across the narrow yard to the Dumpster the Larsons had rented for the duration of the remodel.

He glanced toward the adjoining yard and the sound of kids playing. And the armload he carried thumped and bounced on the ground as his body went numb.

The little boys played with trucks and shovels and pails in a bright blue sandbox. But it wasn't filled with sand. Blood covered their bare arms as they pushed their Tonka trucks through the muck inside the box. He stumbled back as the boys made engine sounds, as red lapped over the bright blue sides and dripped onto the green grass.

On the fence between the yards where hydrangeas headed up toward bloom, crouched a boy that wasn't a boy. He bared its teeth in a grin as Fox backed toward the house.

"Dad! Dad!"

The tone, the breathless fear had Brian rushing outside. "What? What is it?"

"Don't you—can't you see?" But even as he said it, as he pointed, something inside Fox knew. It wasn't real.

"What?" Firmly now, Brian took his son's shoulders. "What do you see?"

The boy that wasn't a boy danced along the top of the chain-link fence while flames spurted up below and burned the hydrangeas to cinders.

"I have to go. I have to go see Cal and Gage. Right now, Dad. I have to—"

"Go." Brian released his hold on Fox, stepped back. He didn't question. "Go."

He all but flew through the house and out again, up the sidewalk to the square. The town no longer looked as it usually did to him. In his mind's eye Fox could see it as it had been that horrible week in July seven years before.

Fire and blood, he remembered, thinking of the dream.

He burst into the Bowl-A-Rama where the summer afternoon leagues were in full swing. The thunder of balls, the crash of pins pounded in his head as he ran straight to the front desk where Cal worked.

"Where's Gage?" Fox demanded.

"Jesus, what's up with you?"

"Where's Gage?" Fox repeated, and Cal's amused gray eyes sobered. "Working the arcade. He's . . . he's coming out now."

At Cal's quick signal, Gage sauntered over. "Hello, ladies. What . . ." The smirk died after one look at Fox's face. "What happened?"

"It's back," Fox said. "It's come back."

THE REEF

Nora Roberts

The *New York Times* bestseller

Tate Beaumont, a beautiful student of marine archaeology, and Matthew Lassiter, a sea-scarred young man, share a dream of finding Angelique's Curse, the jewelled amulet surrounded by legend and said to be long lost at the bottom of the Caribbean.

Forced into a reluctant partnership with Matthew and his uncle, Tate soon learns that her arrogant but attractive fellow diver holds as many secrets as the sea itself. And when the truth emerges about the mysterious death of Matthew's father eight years earlier, desire – and danger – begin to rise to the surface.

'Nora Roberts is at the top of her game'
People

'A consistently entertaining writer'
USA Today

'The publishing world might be hard-pressed to find an author with a more diverse style or fertile imagination than Roberts'
Publishers Weekly

978-0-7499-3159-9

Swift high up [illegible] rooftop, as she tries [illegible] one of his
ex-employees [illegible] jumping. As Savann[illegible] hostage

HIGH NOON

Nora Roberts

Those closest to you can do the most harm

Phoebe MacNamara first comes face to face with Duncan Swift high up on a rooftop, as she tries to stop one of his ex-employees from jumping. As Savannah's chief hostage negotiator, Phoebe is talented, courageous and willing to risk her life to save others – and Duncan is determined to keep this intriguing woman in his life.

But Phoebe has made enemies too. When she is viciously assaulted and sent threatening messages, she realises that someone is out to destroy her – both professionally and personally. With Duncan by her side, Phoebe must discover just who is pursuing her, before it's too late . . .

'Women are addicted to her contemporary novels as chocoholics are to Godiva . . . Roberts is a superstar'
New York Times

978-0-7499-3898-7

BLUE DAHLIA

Nora Roberts is the *New York Times* bestselling author of more than 190 novels. Under the pen name J. D. Robb, she is the author of the *New York Times* bestselling futuristic suspense series, which features Lieutenant Eve Dallas and Roarke. There are more than 300 million copies of her books in print, and she has had more than 150 *New York Times* bestsellers.

Visit her website at www.nora-roberts.co.uk

By Nora Roberts

Homeport
The Reef
River's End
Carolina Moon
The Villa
Midnight Bayou
Three Fates
Birthright
Northern Lights
Blue Smoke
Montana Sky
Angels Fall
High Noon
Divine Evil
Tribute
Sanctuary

Three Sisters Island Trilogy:
Dance Upon the Air
Heaven and Earth
Face the Fire

Chesapeake Bay Quartet:
Sea Swept
Rising Tides
Inner Harbour
Chesapeake Blue

The Key Trilogy:
Key of Light
Key of Knowledge
Key of Valour

In the Garden Trilogy:
Blue Dahlia
Black Rose
Red Lily

The Irish Trilogy:
Jewels of the Sun
Tears of the Moon
Heart of the Sea

The Circle Trilogy:
Morrigan's Cross
Dance of the Gods
Valley of Silence

The Dream Trilogy:
Daring to Dream
Holding the Dream
Finding the Dream

The Sign of Seven Trilogy:
Blood Brothers
The Hollow
The Pagan Stone

As J. D. Robb:

Naked in Death
Glory in Death
Immortal in Death
Rapture in Death
Ceremony in Death
Vengeance in Death
Holiday in Death
Conspiracy in Death
Loyalty in Death
Witness in Death
Judgement in Death
Betrayal in Death
Seduction in Death
Reunion in Death
Purity in Death
Portrait in Death
Imitation in Death
Divided in Death
Visions in Death
Survivor in Death
Origin in Death
Memory in Death
Born in Death
Innocent in Death
Creation in Death
Strangers in Death

By Nora Roberts and J. D. Robb

Remember When

Dear Reader:

I don't have hobbies. I have passions. Gardening is one of my passions, and spring—when it's time to get out there and dig in the dirt—is my favorite season.

I live in the woods, in the foothills of the Blue Ridge Mountains, and my land is rough and rocky. A tough field for a passionate gardener to play in. I've solved part of the problem with many raised beds, but the rocks still find a way. Every spring, it's a battle—me against rock, and most years I win.

I'm fortunate to be married to a man who enjoys yard work. Because if I want to plant a daffodil bulb in the stony ground, I've got to call my guy with the pick. But it's worth it. Every spring when I see my daffodils popping, watch my willows greening, see the perennials I've planted in place of rock spearing up, I'm happy. Just as I'm happy to get out there with my spade and cultivator to start prepping the soil for what I might plant this season.

It's hard, sweaty, dirty work, and it pleases me to do it, year after year. For me, a garden is always a work in progress, never quite finished, and always a delight to the eye. Nearly twenty years ago, my guy planted a tulip magnolia in front of our house. Now, every spring, my bedroom windows are full of those gorgeous pink blooms. And when they fade and drop, something else will flower to make me smile.

At the end of a long day, whether it's writing or gardening, or just dealing with the dozens of chores life hands out, there's nothing quite like a walk in the garden to soothe the mind and heart.

So plant some flowers, watch them grow. The rewards far outreach the toil.

NORA ROBERTS

Blue Dahlia

Nora Roberts

PIATKUS

PIATKUS

First published in the US in 2004 by
The Berkley Publishing Group, a division of Penguin Group (USA) Inc.
First published in Great Britain in 2004 by Piatkus Books
Reprinted 2005 (three times), 2006 (four times), 2007, 2009

A CIP catalogue record for this book
is available from the British Library

ISBN 978-0-7499-3533-7

Printed and bound in Great Britain by
CPI Mackays, Chatham, ME5 8TD

Papers used by Piatkus Books are natural, renewable and recyclable products made from wood grown in sustainable forests and certified in accordance with the rules of the Forest Stewardship Council.

Piatkus Books
An imprint of
Little, Brown Book Group
100 Victoria Embankment
London EC4Y 0DY

An Hachette Livre UK Company
www.hachettelivre.co.uk

www.piatkus.co.uk

For Dan and Jason.
You may be men, but you'll always be my boys.

If the plant root ball is tightly packed with roots,
these should be gently loosened.
They need to spread out after planting,
rather than continue to grow in a tight mass.

—FROM THE *TREASURY OF GARDENING*,
ON TRANSPLANTING POTTED PLANTS

And 'tis my faith that every flower
Enjoys the air it breathes.

—WORDSWORTH

PROLOGUE

Memphis, Tennessee

August 1892

BIRTHING A BASTARD WASN'T IN THE PLANS. WHEN she'd learned she was carrying her lover's child, the shock and panic turned quickly to anger.

There were ways of dealing with it, of course. A woman in her position had contacts, had avenues. But she was afraid of them, nearly as afraid of the abortionists as she was of what was growing, unwanted, inside her.

The mistress of a man like Reginald Harper couldn't afford pregnancy.

He'd kept her for nearly two years now, and kept her well. Oh, she knew he kept others—including his wife—but they didn't concern her.

She was still young, and she was beautiful. Youth and beauty were products that could be marketed. She'd done so, for nearly a decade, with steely mind and heart. And she'd profited by them, polished them with the grace and charm she'd learned by watching and emulating the fine ladies who'd visited the grand house on the river where her mother had worked.

She'd been educated—a bit. But more than books and music, she'd learned the arts of flirtation.

She'd sold herself for the first time at fifteen and had pocketed knowledge along with the coin. But prostitution wasn't her goal, any more than domestic work or trudging off to the factory day after day. She knew the difference between whore and mistress. A whore traded quick and cold sex for pennies and was forgotten before the man's fly was buttoned again.

But a mistress—a clever and successful mistress—offered romance, sophistication, conversation, gaiety along with the commodity between her legs. She was a companion, a wailing wall, a sexual fantasy. An ambitious mistress knew to demand nothing and gain much.

Amelia Ellen Conner had ambitions.

And she'd achieved them. Or most of them.

She'd selected Reginald quite carefully. He wasn't handsome or brilliant of mind. But he was, as her research had assured her, very rich and very unfaithful to the thin and proper wife who presided over Harper House.

He had a woman in Natchez, and it was said he kept another in New Orleans. He could afford another, so Amelia set her sights on him. Wooed and won him.

At twenty-four, she lived in a pretty house on South Main and had three servants of her own. Her wardrobe was full of beautiful clothes, and her jewelry case sparkled.

It was true she wasn't received by the fine ladies she'd once envied, but there was a fashionable half world where a woman of her station was welcome. Where *she* was envied.

She threw lavish parties. She traveled. She *lived.*

Then, hardly more than a year after Reginald had tucked her into that pretty house, her clever, craftily designed world crashed.

She would have hidden it from him until she'd gathered the courage to visit the red-light district and end the thing. But he'd caught her when she was violently ill, and he'd studied her face with those dark, shrewd eyes.

And he'd known.

He'd not only been pleased but had forbidden her to end

the pregnancy. To her shock, he'd bought her a sapphire bracelet to celebrate her situation.

She hadn't wanted the child, but he had.

So she began to see how the child could work for her. As the mother of Reginald Harper's child—bastard or no—she would be cared for in perpetuity. He might lose interest in coming to her bed as she lost the bloom of youth, as beauty faded, but he would support her, and the child.

His wife hadn't given him a son. But she might. She *would.*

Through the last chills of winter and into the spring, she carried the child and planned for her future.

Then something strange happened. It moved inside her. Flutters and stretches, playful kicks. The child she hadn't wanted became her child.

It grew inside her like a flower that only she could see, could feel, could know. And so did a strong and terrible love.

Through the sweltering, sticky heat of the summer she bloomed, and for the first time in her life she knew a passion for something other than herself and her own comfort.

The child, her son, needed her. She would protect it with all she had.

With her hands resting on her great belly, she supervised the decorating of the nursery. Pale green walls and white lace curtains. A rocking horse imported from Paris, a crib handmade in Italy.

She tucked tiny clothes into the miniature wardrobe. Irish and Breton lace, French silks. All were monogrammed with exquisite embroidery with the baby's initials. He would be James Reginald Conner.

She would have a son. Something at last of her own. Someone, at last, to love. They would travel together, she and her beautiful boy. She would show him the world. He would go to the best schools. He was her pride, her joy, and her heart. And if through that steamy summer, Reginald came to the house on South Main less and less, it was just as well.

He was only a man. What grew inside her was a son.

She would never be alone again.

When she felt the pangs of labor, she had no fear. Through the sweaty hours of pain, she held one thing in the front of her mind. Her James. Her son. Her child.

Her eyes blurred with exhaustion, and the heat, a living, breathing monster, was somehow worse than the pain.

She could see the doctor and the midwife exchange looks. Grim, frowning looks. But she was young, she was healthy, and she *would* do this thing.

There was no time; hour bled into hour with gaslight shooting flickering shadows around the room. She heard, through the waves of exhaustion, a thin cry.

"My son." Tears slid down her cheeks. "My son."

The midwife held her down, murmuring, murmuring, "Lie still now. Drink a bit. Rest now."

She sipped to soothe her fiery throat, tasted laudanum. Before she could object, she was drifting off, deep down. Far away.

When she woke, the room was dim, the draperies pulled tight over the windows. When she stirred, the doctor rose from his chair, came close to lift her hand, to check her pulse.

"My son. My baby. I want to see my baby."

"I'll send for some broth. You slept a long time."

"My son. He'll be hungry. Have him brought to me."

"Madam." The doctor sat on the side of the bed. His eyes seemed very pale, very troubled. "I'm sorry. The child was stillborn."

What clutched her heart was monstrous, vicious, rending her with burning talons of grief and fear. "I heard him cry. This is a lie! Why are you saying such an awful thing to me?"

"She never cried." Gently, he took her hands. "Your labor was long and difficult. You were delirious at the end of it. Madam, I'm sorry. You delivered a girl, stillborn."

She wouldn't believe it. She screamed and raged and

wept, and was sedated only to wake to scream and rage and weep again.

She hadn't wanted the child. And then she'd wanted nothing else.

Her grief was beyond name, beyond reason.

Grief drove her mad.

ONE

Southfield, Michigan

September 2001

SHE BURNED THE CREAM SAUCE. STELLA WOULD always remember that small, irritating detail, as she would remember the roll and boom of thunder from the late-summer storm and the sound of her children squabbling in the living room.

She would remember the harsh smell, the sudden scream of the smoke alarms, and the way she'd mechanically taken the pan off the burner and dumped it in the sink.

She wasn't much of a cook, but she was—in general—a *precise* cook. For this welcome-home meal, she'd planned to prepare the chicken Alfredo, one of Kevin's favorites, from scratch and match it with a nice field greens salad and some fresh, crusty bread with pesto dipping sauce.

In her tidy kitchen in her pretty suburban house she had all the ingredients lined up, her cookbook propped on its stand with the plastic protector over the pages.

She wore a navy-blue bib apron over her fresh pants and shirt and had her mass of curling red hair bundled up on top of her head, out of her way.

She was getting started later than she'd hoped, but work had been a madhouse all day. All the fall flowers at the garden center were on sale, and the warm weather brought customers out in droves.

Not that she minded. She loved the work, absolutely loved her job as manager of the nursery. It felt good to be back in the thick of it, full-time now that Gavin was in school and Luke old enough for a play group. How in the world had her baby grown up enough for first grade?

And before she knew it, Luke would be ready for kindergarten.

She and Kevin should start getting a little more proactive about making that third child. Maybe tonight, she thought with a smile. When she got into *that* final and very personal stage of her welcome-home plans.

As she measured ingredients, she heard the crash and wail from the next room. Glutton for punishment, she thought as she dropped what she was doing to rush in. Thinking about having another baby when the two she had were driving her crazy.

She stepped into the room, and there they were. Her little angels. Gavin, sunny blond with the devil in his eyes, sat innocently bumping two Matchbox cars into each other while Luke, his bright red hair a dead ringer for hers, screamed over his scattered wooden blocks.

She didn't have to witness the event to *know.* Luke had built; Gavin had destroyed.

In their house it was the law of the land.

"Gavin. Why?" She scooped up Luke, patted his back. "It's okay, baby. You can build another."

"My house! My house!"

"It was an accident," Gavin claimed, and that wicked twinkle that made a bubble of laughter rise to her throat remained. "The car wrecked it."

"I bet the car did—after you aimed it at his house. Why can't you play nice? He wasn't bothering you."

"I was playing. He's just a baby."

"That's right." And it was the look that came into her eyes that had Gavin dropping his. "And if you're going to be a baby, too, you can be a baby in your room. Alone."

"It was a stupid house."

"Nuh-uh! Mom." Luke took Stella's face in both his hands, looked at her with those avid, swimming eyes. "It was good."

"You can build an even better one. Okay? Gavin, leave him alone. I'm not kidding. I'm busy in the kitchen, and Daddy's going to be home soon. Do you want to be punished for his welcome home?"

"No. I can't do *anything*."

"That's too bad. It's really a shame you don't have any toys." She set Luke down. "Build your house, Luke. Leave his blocks alone, Gavin. If I have to come in here again, you're not going to like it."

"I want to go *outside*!" Gavin mourned at her retreating back.

"Well, it's raining, so you can't. We're all stuck in here, so behave."

Flustered, she went back to the cookbook, tried to clear her head. In an irritated move, she snapped on the kitchen TV. God, she missed Kevin. The boys had been cranky all afternoon, and she felt rushed and harried and overwhelmed. With Kevin out of town these last four days she'd been scrambling around like a maniac. Dealing with the house, the boys, her job, all the errands alone.

Why was it that the household appliances waited, just waited, to go on strike when Kevin left town? Yesterday the washer had gone buns up, and just that morning the toaster oven had fried itself.

They had such a nice rhythm when they were together, dividing up the chores, sharing the discipline and the pleasure in their sons. If he'd been home, he could have sat down to play with—and referee—the boys while she cooked.

Or better, he'd have cooked and she'd have played with the boys.

She missed the smell of him when he came up behind her to lean down and rub his cheek over hers. She missed curling up to him in bed at night, and the way they'd talk in the dark about their plans, or laugh at something the boys had done that day.

For God's sake, you'd think the man had been gone four months instead of four days, she told herself.

She listened with half an ear to Gavin trying to talk Luke into building a skyscraper that they could both wreck as she stirred her cream sauce and watched the wind swirl leaves outside the window.

He wouldn't be traveling so much after he got his promotion. Soon, she reminded herself. He'd been working so hard, and he was right on the verge of it. The extra money would be handy, too, especially when they had another child—maybe a girl this time.

With the promotion, and her working full-time again, they could afford to take the kids somewhere next summer. Disney World, maybe. They'd love that. Even if she were pregnant, they could manage it. She'd been squirreling away some money in the vacation fund—and the new-car fund.

Having to buy a new washing machine was going to seriously damage the emergency fund, but they'd be all right.

When she heard the boys laugh, her shoulders relaxed again. Really, life was good. It was perfect, just the way she'd always imagined it. She was married to a wonderful man, one she'd fallen for the minute she'd set eyes on him. Kevin Rothchild, with his slow, sweet smile.

They had two beautiful sons, a pretty house in a good neighborhood, jobs they both loved, and plans for the future they both agreed on. And when they made love, bells still rang.

Thinking of that, she imagined his reaction when, with the kids tucked in for the night, she slipped into the sexy new lingerie she'd splurged on in his absence.

A little wine, a few candles, and . . .

The next, bigger crash had her eyes rolling toward the ceiling. At least this time there were cheers instead of wails.

"Mom! Mom!" Face alive with glee, Luke rushed in. "We wrecked the *whole* building. Can we have a cookie?"

"Not this close to dinner."

"Please, please, please, *please*!"

He was pulling on her pants now, doing his best to climb up her leg. Stella set the spoon down, nudged him away from the stove. "No cookies before dinner, Luke."

"We're starving." Gavin piled in, slamming his cars together. "How come we can't eat something when we're hungry? Why do we have to eat the stupid fredo anyway?"

"Because." She'd always hated that answer as a child, but it seemed all-purpose to her now.

"We're all eating together when your father gets home." But she glanced out the window and worried that his plane would be delayed. "Here, you can split an apple."

She took one out of the bowl on the counter and grabbed a knife.

"I don't like the peel," Gavin complained.

"I don't have time to peel it." She gave the sauce a couple of quick stirs. "The peel's good for you." Wasn't it?

"Can I have a drink? Can I have a drink, too?" Luke tugged and tugged. "I'm thirsty."

"God. Give me five minutes, will you? Five minutes. Go, go *build* something. Then you can have some apple slices and juice."

Thunder boomed, and Gavin responded to it by jumping up and down and shouting, "Earthquake!"

"It's not an earthquake."

But his face was bright with excitement as he spun in circles, then ran from the room. "Earthquake! Earthquake!"

Getting into the spirit, Luke ran after him, screaming.

Stella pressed a hand to her pounding head. The noise was insane, but maybe it would keep them busy until she got the meal under control.

She turned back to the stove, and heard, without much interest, the announcement for a news bulletin.

It filtered through the headache, and she turned toward the set like an automaton.

Commuter plane crash. En route to Detroit Metro from Lansing. Ten passengers on board.

The spoon dropped out of her hand. The heart dropped out of her body.

Kevin. Kevin.

Her children screamed in delighted fear, and thunder rolled and burst overhead. In the kitchen, Stella slid to the floor as her world fractured.

THEY CAME TO TELL HER KEVIN WAS DEAD. STRANGERS at her door with solemn faces. She couldn't take it in, couldn't believe it. Though she'd known. She'd known the minute she heard the reporter's voice on her little kitchen television.

Kevin couldn't be dead. He was young and healthy. He was coming home, and they were having chicken Alfredo for dinner.

But she'd burned the sauce. The smoke had set off the alarms, and there was nothing but madness in her pretty house.

She had to send her children to her neighbor's so it could be explained to her.

But how could the impossible, the unthinkable ever be explained?

A mistake. The storm, a strike of lightning, and everything changed forever. One instant of time, and the man she loved, the father of her children, no longer lived.

Is there anyone you'd like to call?

Who would she call but Kevin? He was her family, her friend, her life.

They spoke of details that were like a buzz in her brain, of arrangements, of counseling. They were sorry for her loss.

They were gone, and she was alone in the house she and Kevin had bought when she'd been pregnant with Luke. The house they'd saved for, and painted, and decorated together. The house with the gardens she'd designed herself.

The storm was over, and it was quiet. Had it ever been so quiet? She could hear her own heartbeat, the hum of the heater as it kicked on, the drip of rain from the gutters.

Then she could hear her own keening as she collapsed on the floor by her front door. Lying on her side, she gathered herself into a ball in defense, in denial. There weren't tears, not yet. They were massed into some kind of hard, hot knot inside her. The grief was so deep, tears couldn't reach it. She could only lie curled up there, with those wounded-animal sounds pouring out of her throat.

It was dark when she pushed herself to her feet, swaying, light-headed and ill. Kevin. Somewhere in her brain his name still, over and over and over.

She had to get her children, she had to bring her children home. She had to tell her babies.

Oh, God. Oh, God, how could she tell them?

She groped for the door, stepped out into the chilly dark, her mind blessedly blank. She left the door open at her back, walked down between the heavy-headed mums and asters, past the glossy green leaves of the azaleas she and Kevin had planted one blue spring day.

She crossed the street like a blind woman, walking through puddles that soaked her shoes, over damp grass, toward her neighbor's porch light.

What was her neighbor's name? Funny, she'd known her for four years. They carpooled, and sometimes shopped together. But she couldn't quite remember. . . .

Oh, yes, of course. Diane. Diane and Adam Perkins, and their children, Jessie and Wyatt. Nice family, she thought dully. Nice, normal family. They'd had a barbecue together just a couple weeks ago. Kevin had grilled chicken.

He loved to grill. They'd had some good wine, some good laughs, and the kids had played. Wyatt had fallen and scraped his knee.

Of course she remembered.

But she stood in front of the door not quite sure what she was doing there.

Her children. Of course. She'd come for her children. She had to tell them. . . .

Don't think. She held herself hard, rocked, held in. Don't think yet. If you think, you'll break apart. A million pieces you can never put together again.

Her babies needed her. Needed her now. Only had her now.

She bore down on that hot, hard knot and rang the bell.

She saw Diane as if she were looking at her through a thin sheen of water. Rippling, and not quite there. She heard her dimly. Felt the arms that came around her in support and sympathy.

But your husband's alive, you see, Stella thought. Your life isn't over. Your world's the same as it was five minutes ago. So you can't know. You can't.

When she felt herself begin to shake, she pulled back. "Not now, please. I can't now. I have to take the boys home."

"I can come with you." There were tears on Diane's cheeks as she reached out, touched Stella's hair. "Would you like me to come, to stay with you?"

"No. Not now. I need . . . the boys."

"I'll get them. Come inside, Stella."

But she only shook her head.

"All right. They're in the family room. I'll bring them. Stella, if there's anything, anything at all. You've only to call. I'm sorry. I'm so sorry."

She stood in the dark, looking in at the light, and waited.

She heard the protests, the complaints, then the scrambling of feet. And there were her boys—Gavin with his father's sunny hair, Luke with his father's mouth.

"We don't want to go yet," Gavin told her. "We're playing a game. Can't we finish?"

"Not now. We have to go home now."

"But I'm winning. It's not fair, and—"

"Gavin. We have to go."

"Is Daddy home?"

She looked down at Luke, his happy, innocent face, and nearly broke. "No." Reaching down, she picked him up, touched her lips to the mouth that was so like Kevin's. "Let's go home."

She took Gavin's hand and began the walk back to her empty house.

"If Daddy was home, he'd let me finish." Cranky tears smeared Gavin's voice. "I want Daddy."

"I know. I do too."

"Can we have a dog?" Luke wanted to know, and turned her face to his with his hands. "Can we ask Daddy? Can we have a dog like Jessie and Wyatt?"

"We'll talk about it later."

"I want Daddy," Gavin said again, with a rising pitch in his voice.

He knows, Stella thought. He knows something is wrong, something's terribly wrong. I have to do this. I have to do it now.

"We need to sit down." Carefully, very carefully, she closed the door behind her, carried Luke to the couch. She sat with him in her lap and laid her arm over Gavin's shoulder.

"If I had a dog," Luke told her soberly, "I'd take care of him. When's Daddy coming?"

"He can't come."

"'Cause of the busy trip?"

"He . . ." Help me. God, help me do this. "There was an accident. Daddy was in an accident."

"Like when the cars smash?" Luke asked, and Gavin said nothing, nothing at all as his eyes burned into her face.

"It was a very bad accident. Daddy had to go to heaven."

"But he has to come home after."

"He can't. He can't come home anymore. He has to stay in heaven now."

"I don't want him there." Gavin tried to wrench away, but she held him tightly. "I want him to come home *now*."

"I don't want him there either, baby. But he can't come back anymore, no matter how much we want it."

Luke's lips trembled. "Is he mad at us?"

"No. No, no, no, baby. No." She pressed her face to his hair as her stomach pitched and what was left of her heart throbbed like a wound. "He's not mad at us. He loves us. He'll always love us."

"He's dead." There was fury in Gavin's voice, rage on his face. Then it crumpled, and he was just a little boy, weeping in his mother's arms.

She held them until they slept, then carried them to her bed so none of them would wake alone. As she had countless times before, she slipped off their shoes, tucked blankets around them.

She left a light burning while she walked—it felt like floating—through the house, locking doors, checking windows. When she knew everything was safe, she closed herself into the bathroom. She ran a bath so hot the steam rose off the water and misted the room.

Only when she slipped into the tub, submerged herself in the steaming water, did she allow that knot to snap. With her boys sleeping, and her body shivering in the hot water, she wept and wept and wept.

SHE GOT THROUGH IT. A FEW FRIENDS SUGGESTED SHE might take a tranquilizer, but she didn't want to block the feelings. Nor did she want to have a muzzy head when she had her children to think of.

She kept it simple. Kevin would have wanted simple. She chose every detail—the music, the flowers, the photographs—of his memorial service. She selected a silver box for his ashes and planned to scatter them on the lake. He'd proposed to her on the lake, in a rented boat on a summer afternoon.

She wore black for the service, a widow of thirty-one, with two young boys and a mortgage, and a heart so broken she wondered if she would feel pieces of it piercing her soul for the rest of her life.

She kept her children close, and made appointments with a grief counselor for all of them.

Details. She could handle the details. As long as there was something to do, something definite, she could hold on. She could be strong.

Friends came, with their sympathy and covered dishes and teary eyes. She was grateful to them more for the distraction than the condolences. There was no condolence for her.

Her father and his wife flew up from Memphis, and them she leaned on. She let Jolene, her father's wife, fuss over her, and soothe and cuddle the children, while her own mother complained about having to be in the same room as *that woman.*

When the service was over, after the friends drifted away, after she clung to her father and Jolene before their flight home, she made herself take off the black dress.

She shoved it into a bag to send to a shelter. She never wanted to see it again.

Her mother stayed. Stella had asked her to stay a few days. Surely under such circumstances she was entitled to her mother. Whatever friction was, and always had been, between them was nothing compared with death.

When she went into the kitchen, her mother was brewing coffee. Stella was so grateful not to have to think of such a minor task, she crossed over and kissed Carla's cheek.

"Thanks. I'm so sick of tea."

"Every time I turned around that woman was making more damn tea."

"She was trying to help, and I'm not sure I could've handled coffee until now."

Carla turned. She was a slim woman with short blond hair. Over the years, she'd battled time with regular trips to the surgeon. Nips, tucks, lifts, injections had wiped away some of the years. And left her looking whittled and hard, Stella thought.

She might pass for forty, but she'd never look happy about it.

"You always take up for her."

"I'm not taking up for Jolene, Mom." Wearily, Stella sat. No more details, she realized. No more something that has to be done.

How would she get through the night?

"I don't see why I had to tolerate her."

"I'm sorry you were uncomfortable. But she was very kind. She and Dad have been married for, what, twenty-five years or so now. You ought to be used to it."

"I don't like having her in my face, her and that twangy voice. Trailer trash."

Stella opened her mouth, closed it again. Jolene hadn't come from a trailer park and was certainly not trash. But what good would it do to say so? Or to remind her mother that she'd been the one who'd wanted a divorce, the one to leave the marriage. Just as it wouldn't do any good to point out that Carla had been married twice since.

"Well, she's gone now."

"Good riddance."

Stella took a deep breath. No arguments, she thought, as her stomach clenched and unclenched like a fist. Too tired to argue.

"The kids are sleeping. They're just worn out. Tomorrow . . . we'll just deal with tomorrow. I guess that's the way it's going to be." She let her head fall back, closed her eyes. "I keep thinking this is a horrible dream, and I'll wake up any second. Kevin will be here. I don't . . . I can't imagine life without him. I can't stand to imagine it."

The tears started again. "Mom, I don't know what I'm going to do."

"Had insurance, didn't he?"

Stella blinked, stared as Carla set a cup of coffee in front of her. "What?"

"Life insurance. He was covered?"

"Yes, but—"

"You ought to talk to a lawyer about suing the airline. Better start thinking of practicalities." She sat with her own coffee. "It's what you're best at, anyway."

"Mom"—she spoke slowly as if translating a strange foreign language—"Kevin's dead."

"I know that, Stella, and I'm sorry." Reaching over, Carla gave Stella's hand a pat. "I dropped everything to come here and give you a hand, didn't I?"

"Yes." She had to remember that. Appreciate that.

"It's a damn fucked-up world when a man of his age dies for no good reason. Useless waste. I'll never understand it."

"No." Pulling a tissue out of her pocket, Stella rubbed the tears away. "Neither will I."

"I liked him. But the fact is, you're in a fix now. Bills, kids to support. Widowed with two growing boys. Not many men want to take on ready-made families, let me tell you."

"I don't want a man to take us on. God, Mom."

"You will," Carla said with a nod. "Take my advice and make sure the next one's got money. Don't make my mistakes. You lost your husband, and that's hard. It's really hard. But women lose husbands every day. It's better to lose one this way than to go through a divorce."

The pain in Stella's stomach was too sharp for grief, too cold for rage. "Mom. We had Kevin's memorial service today. I have his ashes in a goddamn box in my bedroom."

"You want my help." She waggled the spoon. "I'm trying to give it to you. You sue the pants off the airline, get yourself a solid nest egg. And don't hook yourself up with some loser like I always do. You don't think divorce is a hard knock, too? Haven't been through one, have you? Well, I have. Twice. And I might as well tell you it's coming up on three. I'm done with that stupid son of a bitch.

You've got no idea what he's put me through. Not only is he an inconsiderate, loudmouthed asshole, but I think he's been cheating on me."

She pushed away from the table, rummaged around, then cut herself a piece of cake. "He thinks I'm going to tolerate that, he's mistaken. I'd just love to see his face when he gets served with the papers. Today."

"I'm sorry your third marriage isn't working out," Stella said stiffly. "But it's a little hard for me to be sympathetic, since both the third marriage and the third divorce were your choice. Kevin's dead. My husband is dead, and that sure as hell wasn't my choice."

"You think I want to go through this again? You think I want to come here to help you out, then have your father's bimbo shoved in my face?"

"She's his wife, who has never been anything but decent to you and who has always treated me kindly."

"To your face." Carla stuffed a bite of cake into her mouth. "You think you're the only one with problems? With heartache? You won't be so quick to shrug it off when you're pushing fifty and facing life alone."

"You're pushing fifty from the back end, Mom, and being alone is, again, your choice."

Temper turned Carla's eyes dark and sharp. "I don't appreciate that tone, Stella. I don't have to put up with it."

"No, you don't. You certainly don't. In fact, it would probably be best for both of us if you left. Right now. This was a bad idea. I don't know what I was thinking."

"You want me gone, fine." Carla shoved up from the table. "I'd just as soon get back to my own life. You never had any gratitude in you, and if you couldn't be on my back about something you weren't happy. Next time you want to cry on somebody's shoulder, call your country bumpkin stepmother."

"Oh, I will," Stella murmured as Carla sailed out of the room. "Believe me."

She rose to carry her cup to the sink, then gave in to the petty urge and smashed it. She wanted to break everything as she'd been broken. She wanted to wreak havoc on the world as it had been on her.

Instead she stood gripping the edge of the sink and praying that her mother would pack and leave quickly. She wanted her out. Why had she ever thought she wanted her to stay? It was always the same between them. Abrasive, combative. No connection, no common ground.

But God, she'd wanted that shoulder. Needed it so much, just for one night. Tomorrow she would do whatever came next. But she'd wanted to be held and stroked and comforted tonight.

With trembling fingers she cleaned the broken shards out of the sink, wept over them a little as she poured them into the trash. Then she walked to the phone and called a cab for her mother.

They didn't speak again, and Stella decided that was for the best. She closed the door, listened to the cab drive away.

Alone now, she checked on her sons, tucked blankets over them, laid her lips gently on their heads.

They were all she had now. And she was all they had.

She would be a better mother. She swore it. More patient. She would never, never let them down. She would never walk away when they needed her.

And when they needed her shoulder, by God, she would give it. No matter what. No matter when.

"You're first for me," she whispered. "You'll always be first for me."

In her own room, she undressed again, then took Kevin's old flannel robe out of the closet. She wrapped herself in it, in the familiar, heartbreaking smell of him.

Curling up on the bed, she hugged the robe close, shut her eyes, and prayed for morning. For what happened next.

two

Harper House
January 2004

She couldn't afford to be intimidated by the house, or by its mistress. They both had reputations.

The house was said to be elegant and old,with gardens that rivaled Eden. She'd just confirmed that for herself.

The woman was said to be interesting, somewhat solitary, and perhaps a bit "difficult." A word, Stella knew, that could mean anything from strong-willed to stone bitch.

Either way, she could handle it, she reminded herself as she fought the need to get up and pace. She'd handled worse.

She needed this job. Not just for the salary—and it was generous—but for the structure, for the challenge, for the doing. Doing more, she knew, than circling the wheel she'd fallen into back home.

She needed a life, something more than clocking time, drawing a paycheck that would be soaked up by bills. She needed, however self-help-book it sounded, something that fulfilled and challenged her.

Rosalind Harper was fulfilled, Stella was sure. A beautiful ancestral home, a thriving business. What was it like, she wondered, to wake up every morning knowing exactly where you belonged and where you were going?

If she could earn one thing for herself, and give that gift to her children, it would be the sense of knowing. She was afraid she'd lost any clear sight of that with Kevin's death. The sense of doing, no problem. Give her a task or a challenge and the room to accomplish or solve it, she was your girl.

But the sense of knowing who she was, in the heart of herself, had been mangled that day in September of 2001 and had never fully healed.

This was her start, this move back to Tennessee. This final and face-to-face interview with Rosalind Harper. If she didn't get the job—well, she'd get another. No one could accuse her of not knowing how to work or how to provide a living for herself and her kids.

But, God, she wanted *this* job.

She straightened her shoulders and tried to ignore all the whispers of doubt muttering inside her head. She'd *get* this one.

She'd dressed carefully for this meeting. Businesslike but not fussy, in a navy suit and starched white blouse. Good shoes, good bag, she thought. Simple jewelry. Nothing flashy. Subtle makeup, to bring out the blue of her eyes. She'd fought her hair into a clip at the nape of her neck. If she was lucky, the curling mass of it wouldn't spring out until the interview was over.

Rosalind was keeping her waiting. It was probably a mind game, Stella decided as her fingers twisted, untwisted her watchband. Letting her sit and stew in the gorgeous parlor, letting her take in the lovely antiques and paintings, the sumptuous view from the front windows.

All in that dreamy and gracious southern style that reminded her she was a Yankee fish out of water.

Things moved slower down here, she reminded herself. She would have to remember that this was a different pace from the one she was used to, and a different culture.

The fireplace was probably an Adams, she decided. That lamp was certainly an original Tiffany. Would they call those drapes portieres down here, or was that too Scarlett O'Hara? Were the lace panels under the drapes heirlooms?

God, had she ever been more out of her element? What was a middle-class widow from Michigan doing in all this southern splendor?

She steadied herself, fixed a neutral expression on her face, when she heard footsteps coming down the hall.

"Brought coffee." It wasn't Rosalind, but the cheerful man who'd answered the door and escorted Stella to the parlor.

He was about thirty, she judged, average height, very slim. He wore his glossy brown hair waved around a movie-poster face set off by sparkling blue eyes. Though he wore black, Stella found nothing butlerlike about it. Much too artsy, too stylish. He'd said his name was David.

He set the tray with its china pot and cups, the little linen napkins, the sugar and cream, and the tiny vase with its clutch of violets on the coffee table.

"Roz got a bit hung up, but she'll be right along, so you just relax and enjoy your coffee. You comfortable in here?"

"Yes, very."

"Anything else I can get you while you're waiting on her?"

"No. Thanks."

"You just settle on in, then," he ordered, and poured coffee into a cup. "Nothing like a fire in January, is there? Makes you forget that a few months ago it was hot enough to melt the skin off your bones. What do you take in your coffee, honey?"

She wasn't used to being called "honey" by strange men who served her coffee in magnificent parlors. Especially since she suspected he was a few years her junior.

"Just a little cream." She had to order herself not to stare at his face—it was, well, delicious, with that full mouth, those sapphire eyes, the strong cheekbones, the sexy little dent in the chin. "Have you worked for Ms. Harper long?"

"Forever." He smiled charmingly and handed her the coffee. "Or it seems like it, in the best of all possible ways. Give her a straight answer to a straight question, and don't take any bullshit." His grin widened. "She *hates* it when people kowtow. You know, honey, I love your hair."

"Oh." Automatically, she lifted a hand to it. "Thanks."

"Titian knew what he was doing when he painted that color. Good luck with Roz," he said as he started out. "Great shoes, by the way."

She sighed into her coffee. He'd noticed her hair *and* her shoes, complimented her on both. Gay. Too bad for her side.

It was good coffee, and David was right. It was nice having a fire in January. Outside, the air was moist and raw, with a broody sky overhead. A woman could get used to a winter hour by the fire drinking good coffee out of—what was it? Meissen, Wedgwood? Curious, she held the cup up to read the maker's mark.

"It's Staffordshire, brought over by one of the Harper brides from England in the mid-nineteenth century."

No point in cursing herself, Stella thought. No point in cringing about the fact that her redhead's complexion would be flushed with embarrassment. She simply lowered the cup and looked Rosalind Harper straight in the eye.

"It's beautiful."

"I've always thought so." She came in, plopped down in the chair beside Stella's, and poured herself a cup.

One of them, Stella realized, had miscalculated the dress code for the interview.

Rosalind had dressed her tall, willowy form in a baggy olive sweater and mud-colored work pants that were frayed at the cuffs. She was shoeless, with a pair of thick brown socks covering long, narrow feet. Which accounted, Stella supposed, for her silent entry into the room.

Her hair was short, straight, and black.

Though to date all their communications had been via phone, fax, or e-mail, Stella had Googled her. She'd wanted background on her potential employer—and a look at the woman.

Newspaper and magazine clippings had been plentiful. She'd studied Rosalind as a child, through her youth. She'd marveled over the file photos of the stunning and delicate bride of eighteen and sympathized with the pale, stoic-looking widow of twenty-five.

There had been more, of course. Society-page stuff, gossipy speculation on when and if the widow would marry again. Then quite a bit of press surrounding the forging of the nursery business, her gardens, her love life. Her brief second marriage and divorce.

Stella's image had been of a strong-minded, shrewd woman. But she'd attributed those stunning looks to camera angles, lighting, makeup.

She'd been wrong.

At forty-six, Rosalind Harper was a rose in full bloom. Not the hothouse sort, Stella mused, but one that weathered the elements, season after season, and came back, year after year, stronger and more beautiful.

She had a narrow face angled with strong bones and deep, long eyes the color of single-malt scotch. Her mouth, full, strongly sculpted lips, was unpainted—as, to Stella's expert eye, was the rest of that lovely face.

There were lines, those thin grooves that the god of time reveled in stamping, fanning out from the corners of the dark eyes, but they didn't detract.

All Stella could think was, Could I be you, please, when I grow up? Only I'd like to dress better, if you don't mind.

"Kept you waiting, didn't I?"

Straight answers, Stella reminded herself. "A little, but it's not much of a hardship to sit in this room and drink good coffee out of Staffordshire."

"David likes to fuss. I was in the propagation house, got caught up."

Her voice, Stella thought, was brisk. Not clipped—you

just couldn't clip Tennessee—but it was to the point and full of energy. "You look younger than I expected. You're what, thirty-three?"

"Yes."

"And your sons are . . . six and eight?"

"That's right."

"You didn't bring them with you?"

"No. They're with my father and his wife right now."

"I'm very fond of Will and Jolene. How are they?"

"They're good. They're enjoying having their grandchildren around."

"I imagine so. Your daddy shows off pictures of them from time to time and just about bursts with pride."

"One of my reasons for relocating here is so they can have more time together."

"It's a good reason. I like young boys myself. Miss having them around. The fact that you come with two played in your favor. Your résumé, your father's recommendation, the letter from your former employer—well, none of that hurt."

She picked up a cookie from the tray, bit in, without her eyes ever leaving Stella's face. "I need an organizer, someone creative and hardworking, personable and basically tireless. I like people who work for me to keep up with me, and I set a strong pace."

"So I've been told." Okay, Stella thought, brisk and to the point in return. "I have a degree in nursery management. With the exception of three years when I stayed home to have my children—and during which time I landscaped my own yard and two neighbors'—I've worked in that capacity. For more than two years now, since my husband's death, I've raised my sons and worked outside the home in my field. I've done a good job with both. I can keep up with you, Ms. Harper. I can keep up with anyone."

Maybe, Roz thought. Just maybe. "Let me see your hands."

A little irked, Stella held them out. Roz set down her

coffee, took them in hers. She turned them palms up, ran her thumbs over them. "You know how to work."

"Yes, I do."

"Banker suit threw me off. Not that it isn't a lovely suit." Roz smiled, then polished off the cookie. "It's been damp the last couple of days. Let's see if we can put you in some boots so you don't ruin those very pretty shoes. I'll show you around."

THE BOOTS WERE TOO BIG, AND THE ARMY-GREEN rubber hardly flattering, but the damp ground and crushed gravel would have been cruel to her new shoes.

Her own appearance hardly mattered when compared with the operation Rosalind Harper had built.

In the Garden spread over the west side of the estate. The garden center faced the road, and the grounds at its entrance and running along the sides of its parking area were beautifully landscaped. Even in January, Stella could see the care and creativity put into the presentation with the selection and placement of evergreens and ornamental trees, the mulched rises where she assumed there would be color from bulbs and perennials, from splashy annuals through the spring and summer and into fall.

After one look she didn't want the job. She was desperate for it. The lust tied knots of nerves and desire in her belly, the kinds that were usually reserved for a lover.

"I didn't want the retail end of this near the house," Roz said as she parked the truck. "I didn't want to see commerce out my parlor window. Harpers are, and always have been, business-minded. Even back when some of the land around here was planted with cotton instead of houses."

Because Stella's mouth was too dry to speak, she only nodded. The main house wasn't visible from here. A wedge of natural woods shielded it from view and kept the long, low outbuildings, the center itself, and, she imagined, most of the greenhouses from intruding on any view from Harper House.

And just look at that gorgeous old ruby horse chestnut!

"This section's open to the public twelve months a year," Roz continued. "We carry all the sidelines you'd expect, along with houseplants and a selection of gardening books. My oldest son's helping me manage this section, though he's happier in the greenhouses or out in the field. We've got two part-time clerks right now. We'll need more in a few weeks."

Get your head in the game, Stella ordered herself. "Your busy season would start in March in this zone."

"That's right." Roz led the way to the low-slung white building, up an asphalt ramp, across a spotlessly clean porch, and inside.

Two long, wide counters on either side of the door, Stella noted. Plenty of light to keep it cheerful. There were shelves stocked with soil additives, plant foods, pesticides, spin racks of seeds. More shelves held books or colorful pots suitable for herbs or windowsill plants. There were displays of wind chimes, garden plaques, and other accessories.

A woman with snowy white hair dusted a display of sun catchers. She wore a pale blue cardigan with roses embroidered down the front over a white shirt that looked to have been starched stiff as iron.

"Ruby, this is Stella Rothchild. I'm showing her around."

"Pleased to meet you."

The calculating look told Stella the woman knew she was in about the job opening, but the smile was perfectly cordial. "You're Will Dooley's daughter, aren't you?"

"Yes, that's right."

"From . . . up north."

She said it, to Stella's amusement, as if it were a Third World country of dubious repute. "From Michigan, yes. But I was born in Memphis."

"Is that so?" The smile warmed, fractionally. "Well,

that's something, isn't it? Moved away when you were a little girl, didn't you?"

"Yes, with my mother."

"Thinking about moving back now, are you?"

"I have moved back," Stella corrected.

"Well." The one word said they'd see what they'd see. "It's a raw one out there today," Ruby continued. "Good day to be inside. You just look around all you want."

"Thanks. There's hardly anywhere I'd rather be than inside a nursery."

"You picked a winner here. Roz, Marilee Booker was in and bought the dendrobium. I just couldn't talk her out of it."

"Well, *shit*. It'll be dead in a week."

"Dendrobiums are fairly easy care," Stella pointed out.

"Not for Marilee. She doesn't have a black thumb. Her whole arm's black to the elbow. That woman should be barred by law from having anything living within ten feet of her."

"I'm sorry, Roz. But I did make her promise to bring it back if it starts to look sickly."

"Not your fault." Roz waved it away, then moved through a wide opening. Here were the houseplants, from the exotic to the classic, and pots from thimble size to those with a girth as wide as a manhole cover. There were more accessories, too, like stepping-stones, trellises, arbor kits, garden fountains, and benches.

"I expect my staff to know a little bit about everything," Roz said as they walked through. "And if they don't know the answer, they need to know how to find it. We're not big, not compared to some of the wholesale nurseries or the landscaping outfits. We're not priced like the garden centers at the discount stores. So we concentrate on offering the unusual plants along with the basic, and customer service. We make house calls."

"Do you have someone specific on staff who'll go do an on-site consult?"

"Either Harper or I might go if you're talking about a

customer who's having trouble with something bought here. Or if they just want some casual, personal advice."

She slid her hands into her pockets, rocked back and forth on the heels of her muddy boots. "Other than that, I've got a landscape designer. Had to pay him a fortune to steal him away from a competitor. Had to give him damn near free rein, too. But he's the best. I want to expand that end of the business."

"What's your mission statement?"

Roz turned, her eyebrows lifted high. There was a quick twinkle of amusement in those shrewd eyes. "Now, there you are—that's just why I need someone like you. Someone who can say 'mission statement' with a straight face. Let me think."

With her hands on her hips now, she looked around the stocked area, then opened wide glass doors into the adjoining greenhouse. "I guess it's two-pronged—this is where we stock most of our annuals and hanging baskets starting in March, by the way. First prong would be to serve the home gardener. From the fledgling who's just dipping a toe in to the more experienced who knows what he or she wants and is willing to try something new or unusual. To give that customer base good stock, good service, good advice. Second would be to serve the customer who's got the money but not the time or the inclination to dig in the dirt. The one who wants to beautify but either doesn't know where to start or doesn't want the job. We'll go in, and for a fee we'll work up a design, get the plants, hire the laborers. We'll guarantee satisfaction."

"All right." Stella studied the long, rolling tables, the sprinkler heads of the irrigation system, the drains in the sloping concrete floor.

"When the season starts we have tables of annuals and perennials along the side of this building. They'll show from the front as people drive by, or in. We've got a shaded area for ones that need shade," she continued as she walked through, boots slapping on concrete. "Over here we keep our herbs, and through there's a storeroom for extra pots and plastic flats, tags. Now, out back here's greenhouses for stock plants, seedlings, preparation areas. Those two will open to the public, more annuals sold by the flat."

She crunched along gravel, over more asphalt. Shrubs and ornamental trees. She gestured toward an area on the side where the stock wintering over was screened. "Behind that, closed to the public, are the propagation and grafting areas. We do mostly container planting, but I've culled out an acre or so for field stock. Water's no problem with the pond back there."

They continued to walk, with Stella calculating, dissecting. And the lust in her belly had gone from tangled knot to rock-hard ball.

She could *do* something here. Make her mark over the excellent foundation another woman had built. She could help improve, expand, refine.

Fulfilled? she thought. Challenged? Hell, she'd be so busy, she'd be fulfilled and challenged every minute of every day.

It was perfect.

There were the white scoop-shaped greenhouses, worktables, display tables, awnings, screens, sprinklers. Stella saw it brimming with plants, thronged with customers. Smelling of growth and possibilities.

Then Roz opened the door to the propagation house, and Stella let out a sound, just a quiet one she couldn't hold back. And it was pleasure.

The smell of earth and growing things, the damp heat. The air was close, and she knew her hair would frizz out insanely, but she stepped inside.

Seedlings sprouted in their containers, delicate new growth spearing out of the enriched soil. Baskets already planted were hung on hooks where they'd be urged into early bloom. Where the house teed off there were the stock plants, the parents of these fledglings. Aprons hung on pegs, tools were scattered on tables or nested in buckets.

Silently she walked down the aisles, noting that the containers were marked clearly. She could identify some of the plants without reading the tags. Cosmos and columbine, petunias and penstemon. This far south, in a few short weeks they'd be ready to be laid in beds, arranged in patio pots, tucked into sunny spaces or shady nooks.

Would she? Would she be ready to plant herself here, to root here? To bloom here? Would her sons?

Gardening was a risk, she thought. Life was just a bigger one. The smart calculated those risks, minimized them, and worked toward the goal.

"I'd like to see the grafting area, the stockrooms, the offices."

"All right. Better get you out of here. Your suit's going to wilt."

Stella looked down at herself, spied the green boots. Laughed. "So much for looking professional."

The laugh had Roz angling her head in approval. "You're a pretty woman, and you've got good taste in clothes. That kind of image doesn't hurt. You took the time to put yourself together well for this meeting, which I neglected to do. I appreciate that."

"You hold the cards, Ms. Harper. You can put yourself together any way you like."

"You're right about that." She walked back to the door, gestured, and they stepped outside into a light, chilly drizzle. "Let's go into the office. No point hauling you around in the wet. What are your other reasons for moving back here?"

"I couldn't find any reason to stay in Michigan. We moved there after Kevin and I were married—his work. I think, I suppose, I've stayed there since he died out of a kind of loyalty to him, or just because I was used to it. I'm not sure. I liked my work, but I never felt—it never felt like my place. More like I was just getting from one day to the next."

"Family?"

"No. No, not in Michigan. Just me and the boys.

Kevin's parents are gone, were before we married. My mother lives in New York. I'm not interested in living in the city or raising my children there. Besides that, my mother and I have . . . tangled issues. The way mothers and daughters often do."

"Thank God I had sons."

"Oh, yeah." She laughed again, comfortably now. "My parents divorced when I was very young. I suppose you know that."

"Some of it. As I said, I like your father, and Jolene."

"So do I. So rather than stick a pin in a map, I decided to come here. I was born here. I don't really remember, but I thought, hoped, there might be a connection. That it might be the place."

They walked back through the retail center and into a tiny, cluttered office that made Stella's organized soul wince. "I don't use this much," Roz began. "I've got stuff scattered between here and the house. When I'm over here, I end up spending my time in the greenhouses or the field."

She dumped gardening books off a chair, pointed to it, then sat on the edge of the crowded desk when Stella took the seat.

"I know my strengths, and I know how to do good business. I've built this place from the ground up, in less than five years. When it was smaller, when it was almost entirely just me, I could afford to make mistakes. Now I have up to eighteen employees during the season. People depending on me for a paycheck. So I can't afford to make mistakes. I know how to plant, what to plant, how to price, how to design, how to stock, how to handle employees, and how to deal with customers. I know how to organize."

"I'd say you're absolutely right. Why do you need me—or someone like me?"

"Because of all those things I can—and have done—there are some I don't like. I don't like to organize. And we've gotten too big for it to fall only to me how and what to stock. I want a fresh eye, fresh ideas, and a good head."

"Understood. One of your requests was that your nursery manager live in your house, at least for the first several months. I—"

"It wasn't a request. It was a requirement." In the firm tone, Stella recognized the *difficult* attributed to Rosalind Harper. "We start early, we work late. I want someone on hand, right on hand, at least until I know if we're going to find the rhythm. Memphis is too far away, and unless you're ready to buy a house within ten miles of mine pretty much immediately, there's no other choice."

"I have two active young boys, and a dog."

"I like active young boys, and I won't mind the dog unless he's a digger. He digs in my gardens, we'll have a problem. It's a big house. You'll have considerable room for yourself and your sons. I'd offer you the guest cottage, but I couldn't pry Harper out of it with dynamite. My oldest," she explained. "Do you want the job, Stella?"

She opened her mouth, then took a testing breath. Hadn't she already calculated the risks in coming here? It was time to work toward the goal. The risk of the single condition couldn't possibly outweigh the benefits.

"I do. Yes, Ms. Harper, I very much want the job."

"Then you've got it." Roz held out a hand to shake. "You can bring your things over tomorrow—morning's best—and we'll get y'all settled in. You can take a couple of days, make sure your boys are acclimated."

"I appreciate that. They're excited, but a little scared too." And so am I, she thought. "I have to be frank with you, Ms. Harper. If my boys aren't happy—after a reasonable amount of time to adjust—I'll have to make other arrangements."

"If I thought differently, I wouldn't be hiring you. And call me Roz."

SHE CELEBRATED BY BUYING A BOTTLE OF CHAMPAGNE and a bottle of sparkling cider on the way back to her father's home. The rain, and the detour, put her in a nasty knot of mid-afternoon traffic. It occurred to her that however awkward it might be initially, there were advantages to living essentially where she worked.

She got the job! A dream job, to her point of view. Maybe she didn't know how Rosalind—call me Roz—Harper would be to work for, and she still had a lot of boning up to do about the nursery process in this zone—and she couldn't be sure how the other employees would handle taking orders from a stranger. A Yankee stranger at that.

But she couldn't wait to start.

And her boys would have more room to run around at the Harper . . . estate, she supposed she'd call it. She wasn't ready to buy a house yet—not before she was sure they'd stay, not before she had time to scout out neighborhoods and communities. The fact was, they were crowded in her father's house. Both he and Jolene were more than accommodating, more than welcoming, but they couldn't stay indefinitely jammed into a two-bedroom house.

This was the practical solution, at least for the short term.

She pulled her aging SUV beside her stepmother's snappy little roadster and, grabbing the bag, dashed through the rain to the door.

She knocked. They'd given her a key, but she wasn't comfortable just letting herself in.

Jolene, svelte in black yoga pants and a snug black top, looking entirely too young to be chasing sixty, opened the door.

"I interrupted your workout."

"Just finished. Thank God!" She dabbed at her face with a little white towel, shook back her cloud of honey-blond hair. "Misplace your key, honey?"

"Sorry. I can't get used to using it." She stepped in, listened. "It's much too quiet. Are the boys chained in the basement?"

"Your dad took them into the Peabody to see the afternoon duck walk. I thought it'd be nice for just the three of them, so I stayed here with my yoga tape." She cocked her head to the side. "Dog's snoozing out on the screened porch. You look smug."

"I should. I'm hired."

"I knew it, I knew it! Congratulations!" Jolene threw out her arms for a hug. "There was never any question in my mind. Roz Harper's a smart woman. She knows gold when she sees it."

"My stomach's jumpy, and my nerves are just plain shot. I should wait for Dad and the boys, but . . ." She pulled out the champagne. "How about an early glass of champagne to toast my new job?"

"Oh, twist my arm. I'm so excited for you I could just pop!" Jolene slung an arm around Stella's shoulders as they turned into the great room. "Tell me what you thought of Roz."

"Not as scary in person." Stella set the bottle on the counter to open while Jolene got champagne flutes out of her glass-front display cabinet. "Sort of earthy and direct, confident. And that house!"

"It's a beaut." Jolene laughed when the cork popped. "My, my, what a decadent sound in the middle of the afternoon. Harper House has been in her family for generations. She's actually an Ashby by marriage—the first one. She went back to Harper after her second marriage fizzled."

"Give me the dish, will you, Jolene? Dad won't."

"Plying me with champagne to get me to gossip? Why, thank you, honey." She slid onto a stool, raised her glass. "First, to our Stella and brave new beginnings."

Stella clinked glasses, drank. "Mmmmm. Wonderful. Now, dish."

"She married young. Just eighteen. What you'd call a good match—good families, same social circle. More important, it was a love match. You could see it all over them. It was about the time I fell for your father, and a woman recognizes someone in the same state she's in. She was a late baby—I think her mama was near forty and her daddy heading to fifty when she came along. Her mama was never well after, or she enjoyed playing the frail wife—depending on who you talk to. But in any case, Roz lost them both within two years. She must've been pregnant with her second son. That'd be . . . shoot. Austin, I think. She and John took over Harper House. She had the three boys, and the youngest barely a toddler, when John was killed. You know how hard that must've been for her."

"I do."

"Hardly saw her outside that house for two, three years, I guess. When she did start getting out again, socializing, giving parties and such, there was the expected speculation. Who she'd marry, when. You've seen her. She's a beautiful woman."

"Striking, yes."

"And down here, a lineage like hers is worth its weight and then some. Her looks, her bloodline, she could've had any man she wanted. Younger, older, or in between, single, married, rich, or poor. But she stayed on her own. Raised her boys."

Alone, Stella thought, sipping champagne. She understood the choice very well.

"Kept her private life private," Jolene went on, "much to Memphis society's consternation. Biggest to-do I recall was when she fired the gardener—well, both of them. Went after them with a Weedwacker, according to some reports, and ran them right off the property."

"Really?" Stella's eyes widened in shocked admiration. "Really?"

"That's what I heard, and that's the story that stuck, truth or lie. Down here, we often prefer the entertaining lie to the plain truth. Apparently they'd dug up some of her plants or something. She wouldn't have anybody else after that. Took the whole thing over herself. Next thing you know—though I guess it was about five years later—she's building that garden place over on her west end. She got married about three years ago, and divorced—well, all you had to do was blink. Honey, why don't we make that two early glasses of champagne?"

"Why don't we?" Stella poured. "So, what was the deal with the second husband?"

"Hmmm. Very slick character. Handsome as sin and twice as charming. Bryce Clerk, and he *says* his people are from Savannah, but I don't know as I'd believe a word coming out of his mouth if it was plated with gold. Anyway, they looked stunning together, but it happened he enjoyed looking stunning with a variety of women, and a wedding ring didn't restrict his habits. She booted him out on his ear."

"Good for her."

"She's no pushover."

"That came through loud and clear."

"I'd say she's proud, but not vain, tough-minded but not hard—or not too hard, though there are some who would disagree with that. A good friend, and a formidable enemy. You can handle her, Stella. You can handle anything."

She liked people to think so, but either the champagne or fresh nerves was making her stomach a little queasy. "Well, we're going to find out."

three

SHE HAD A CAR FULL OF LUGGAGE, A BRIEFCASE stuffed with notes and sketches, a very unhappy dog who'd already expressed his opinion of the move by vomiting on the passenger seat, and two boys bickering bitterly in the back.

She'd already pulled over to deal with the dog and the seat, and despite the January chill had the windows wide open. Parker, their Boston terrier, sprawled on the floor looking pathetic.

She didn't know what the boys were arguing about, and since it hadn't come to blows yet, let them go at it. They were, she knew, as nervous as Parker about yet another move.

She'd uprooted them. No matter how carefully you dug, it was still a shock to the system. Now all of them were about to be transplanted. She believed they would thrive. She had to believe it or she'd be as sick as the family dog.

"I hate your slimy, stinky guts," eight-year-old Gavin declared.

"I hate your big, stupid butt," six-year-old Luke retorted.

"I hate your ugly elephant ears."

"I hate your whole ugly *face*!"

Stella sighed and turned up the radio.

She waited until she'd reached the brick pillars that flanked the drive to the Harper estate. She nosed in, out of the road, then stopped the car. For a moment, she simply sat there while the insults raged in the backseat. Parker sent her a cautious look, then hopped up to sniff at the air through the window.

She turned the radio off, sat. The voices behind her began to trail off, and after a last, harshly whispered, "And I hate your entire body," there was silence.

"So, here's what I'm thinking," she said in a normal, conversational tone. "We ought to pull a trick on Ms. Harper."

Gavin strained forward against his seat belt. "What kind of trick?"

"A tricky trick. I'm not sure we can pull it off. She's pretty smart; I could tell. So we'd have to be really sneaky."

"I can be sneaky," Luke assured her. And her glance in the rearview mirror told her the battle blood was already fading from his cheeks.

"Okay, then, here's the plan." She swiveled around so she could face both her boys. It struck her, as it often did, what an interesting meld of herself and Kevin they were. Her blue eyes in Luke's face, Kevin's gray-green ones in Gavin's. Her mouth to Gavin, Kevin's to Luke. Her coloring—poor baby—to Luke, and Kevin's sunny blond to Gavin.

She paused, dramatically, noted that both her sons were eagerly focused.

"No, I don't know." She shook her head regretfully. "It's probably not a good idea."

There was a chorus of pleas, protests, and a great deal of seat bouncing that sent Parker into a spate of enthusiastic barking.

"Okay, okay." She held up her hands. "What we do is,

we drive up to the house, and we go up to the door. And when we're inside and you meet Ms. Harper—this is going to have to be really sneaky, really clever."

"We can do it!" Gavin shouted.

"Well, when that happens, you have to pretend to be . . . this is tough, but I think you can do it. You have to pretend to be polite, well-behaved, well-mannered boys."

"We can do it! We . . ." Luke's face scrunched up. "Hey!"

"And I have to pretend not to be a bit surprised by finding myself with two well-behaved, well-mannered boys. Think we can pull it off?"

"Maybe we won't like it there," Gavin muttered.

Guilt roiled up to churn with nerves. "Maybe we won't. Maybe we will. We'll have to see."

"I'd rather live with Granddad and Nana Jo in their house." Luke's little mouth trembled, and wrenched at Stella's heart. "Can't we?"

"We really can't. We can visit, lots. And they can visit us, too. Now that we're going to live down here, we can see them all the time. This is supposed to be an adventure, remember? If we try it, really try it, and we're not happy, we'll try something else."

"People talk funny here," Gavin complained.

"No, just different."

"And there's no snow. How are we supposed to build snowmen and go sledding if it's too stupid to snow?"

"You've got me there, but there'll be other things to do." Had she seen her last white Christmas? Why hadn't she considered that before?

He jutted his chin out. "If she's mean, I'm not staying."

"That's a deal." Stella started the car, took a steadying breath, and continued down the drive.

Moments later she heard Luke's wondering: "It's big!"

No question about that, Stella mused, and wondered how her children saw it. Was it the sheer size of the three-storied structure that overwhelmed them? Or would they notice the details? The pale, pale yellow stone, the majestic columns, the charm of the entrance that was covered by the double stairway leading to the second floor and its pretty wraparound terrace?

Or would they just see the bulk of it—triple the size of their sweet house in Southfield?

"It's really old," she told them. "Over a hundred and fifty years old. And Ms. Harper's family's lived here always."

"Is she a hundred and fifty?" Luke wanted to know and earned a snort and an elbow jab from his brother.

"Dummy. Then she'd be *dead.* And there'd be worms crawling all over her—"

"I have to remind you, polite, well-mannered, well-behaved boys don't call their brothers dummy. See all the lawn? Won't Parker love being taken for walks out here? And there's so much room for you to play. But you have to stay out of the gardens and flower beds, just like at home. Back in Michigan," she corrected herself. "And we'll have to ask Ms. Harper where you're allowed to go."

"There's really big trees," Luke murmured. "Really big."

"That one there? That's a sycamore, and I bet it's even older than the house."

She pulled around the parking circle, admiring the use of Japanese red maple and golden mop cedar along with azaleas in the island.

She clipped on Parker's leash with hands that were a lot more steady than her heart rate. "Gavin, you take Parker. We'll come out for our things after we go in and see Ms. Harper."

"Does she get to boss us?" he demanded.

"Yes. The sad and horrible fate of children is to be bossed by adults. And as she's paying my salary, she gets to boss me, too. We're all in the same boat."

Gavin took Parker's leash when they got out. "I don't like her."

"That's what I love about you, Gavin." Stella ruffled his wavy blond hair. "Always thinking positive. Okay, here we go." She took his hand, and Luke's, gave each a gentle squeeze. The four of them started toward the covered entry.

The doors, a double set painted the same pure and glossy white as the trim, burst open.

"At last!" David flung out his arms. "Men! I'm no longer outnumbered around here."

"Gavin, Luke, this is Mr.—I'm sorry, David, I don't know your last name."

"Wentworth. But let's keep it David." He crouched down, looked the rapidly barking Parker in the eye. "What's your problem, buddy?"

In response, Parker planted his front paws on David's knee and lapped, with great excitement, at his face.

"That's more like it. Come on in. Roz'll be right along. She's upstairs on the phone, skinning some supplier over a delivery."

They stepped into the wide foyer, where the boys simply stood and goggled.

"Pretty ritzy, huh?"

"Is it like a church?"

"Nah." David grinned at Luke. "It's got fancy parts, but it's just a house. We'll get a tour in, but maybe you need some hot chocolate to revive you after your long journey."

"David makes wonderful hot chocolate." Roz started down the graceful stairs that divided the foyer. She was dressed in work clothes, as she'd been the day before. "With lots of whipped cream."

"Ms. Harper, my boys. Gavin and Luke."

"I'm very pleased to meet you. Gavin." She offered a hand to him.

"This is Parker. He's our dog. He's one and a half."

"And very handsome. Parker." She gave the dog a friendly pat.

"I'm Luke. I'm six, and I'm in first grade. I can write my name."

"He cannot either." Gavin sneered in brotherly disgust. "He can only print it."

"Have to start somewhere, don't you? It's very nice to

meet you, Luke. I hope you're all going to be comfortable here."

"You don't look really old," Luke commented, and had David snorting out a laugh.

"Why, thank you. I don't feel really old either, most of the time."

Feeling slightly ill, Stella forced a smile. "I told the boys how old the house was, and that your family's always lived here. He's a little confused."

"I haven't been here as long as the house. Why don't we have that hot chocolate, David? We'll sit in the kitchen, get acquainted."

"Is he your husband?" Gavin asked. "How come you have different last names?"

"She won't marry me," David told him, as he herded them down the hall. "She just breaks my poor, weeping heart."

"He's teasing you. David takes care of the house, and most everything else. He lives here."

"Is she the boss of you, too?" Luke tugged David's hand. "Mom says she's the boss of all of us."

"I let her think so." He led the way into the kitchen with its granite counters and warm cherry wood. A banquette with sapphire leather cushions ranged under a wide window.

Herbs thrived in blue pots along the work counter. Copper pots gleamed.

"This is my domain," David told them. "I'm boss here, just so you know the pecking order. You like to cook, Stella?"

"I don't know if 'like's' the word, but I do know I can't manage anything that would earn a kitchen like this."

Two Sub-Zero refrigerators, what looked to be a restaurant-style stove, double ovens, acres of counter.

And the little details that made a serious work space homey, she noted with relief. The brick hearth with a pretty fire simmering, the old china cupboard filled with antique glassware, forced bulbs of tulips and hyacinths blooming on a butcher block table.

"I live to cook. I can tell you it's pretty frustrating to waste my considerable talents on Roz. She'd just as soon eat cold cereal. And Harper rarely makes an appearance."

"Harper's my oldest son. He lives in the guest house. You'll see him sometimes."

"He's the mad scientist." David got out a pot and chunks of chocolate.

"Does he make monsters? Like Frankenstein?" As he asked, Luke snuck his hand into his mother's again.

"Frankenstein's just pretend," Stella reminded him. "Ms. Harper's son works with plants."

"Maybe one day he'll make a giant one that talks."

Delighted, Gavin sidled over toward David. "Nuh-uh."

" 'There are more things in heaven and earth, Horatio.' Bring that stool over, my fine young friend, and you can watch the master make the world's best hot chocolate."

"I know you probably want to get to work shortly," Stella said to Roz. "I have some notes and sketches I worked on last night I'd like to show you at some point."

"Busy."

"Eager." She glanced over as Luke let go of her hand and went over to join his brother on the stool. "I have an appointment this morning with the principal at the school. The boys should be able to start tomorrow. I thought I could ask at the school office for recommendations for before- and after-school care, then—"

"Hey!" David whipped chocolate and milk in the pot. "These are my men now. I figured they'd hang out with me, providing me with companionship as well as slave labor, when they're not in school."

"I couldn't ask you to—"

"We could stay with David," Gavin piped up. "That'd be okay."

"I don't—"

"Of course, it all depends." David spoke easily as he

added sugar to the pot. "If they don't like PlayStation, the deal's off. I have my standards."

"I like PlayStation," Luke said.

"Actually, they have to *love* PlayStation."

"I do! I do!" They bounced in unison on the stool. "I *love* PlayStation."

"Stella, while they're finishing up here, why don't we get some of your things out of the car?"

"All right. We'll just be a minute. Parker—"

"Dog's fine," David said.

"Well. Be right back, then."

Roz waited until they were at the front door. "David's wonderful with kids."

"Anyone could see." She caught herself twisting the band of her watch, made herself stop. "It just feels like an imposition. I'd pay him, of course, but—"

"You'll work that out between you. I just wanted to say—from one mother to another—that you can trust him to look after them, to entertain them, and to keep them—well, no, you can't trust him to keep them out of trouble. I'll say serious trouble, yes, but not the ordinary sort."

"He'd have to have superpowers for that."

"He practically grew up in this house. He's like my fourth son."

"It would be tremendously easy this way. I wouldn't have to haul them to a sitter." Yet another stranger, she thought.

"And you're not used to things being easy."

"No, I'm not." She heard squeals of laughter rolling out from the kitchen. "But I want my boys to be happy, and I guess that's the deciding vote right there."

"Wonderful sound, isn't it? I've missed it. Let's get your things."

"You have to give me the boundaries," Stella said as they went outside. "Where the boys can go, where they can't. They need chores and rules. They're used to having them at home. Back in Michigan."

"I'll give that some thought. Though David—despite

the fact that I'm the boss of all of you—probably has ideas on all that already. Cute dog, too, by the way." She hauled two suitcases out of the back of the SUV. "My dog died last year, and I haven't had the heart to get another. It's nice having a dog around. Clever name."

"Parker—for Peter Parker. That's—"

"Spider-Man. I did raise three boys of my own."

"Right." Stella grabbed another suitcase and a cardboard carton. She felt her muscles strain even as Roz carried her load with apparent ease.

"I meant to ask who else lives here, or what other staff you have."

"It's just David."

"Oh? He said something about being outnumbered by women before we got here."

"That's right. It would be David, and me, and the Harper Bride."

Roz carried the luggage inside and started up the steps with it. "She's our ghost."

"Your . . ."

"A house this old isn't haunted, it would be a damn shame, I'd think."

"I guess that's one way to look at it."

She decided Roz was amusing herself with a little local color for the new kid on the block. Ghosts would add to the family lore. So she dismissed it.

"You can have your run of the west wing. I think the rooms we've earmarked will suit best. I'm in the east wing, and David's rooms are off the kitchen. Everyone has plenty of privacy, which I've always felt is vital to good relations."

"This is the most beautiful house I've ever seen."

"It is, isn't it?" Roz stopped a moment, looking out the windows that faced one of her gardens. "It can be damp in the winter, and we're forever calling the plumber, the electrician, someone. But I love every inch of it. Some might think it's a waste for a woman on her own."

"It's yours. Your family home."

"Exactly. And it'll stay that way, whatever it takes. You're just down here. Each room opens to the terrace. I'll leave it to you to judge if you need to lock the one in the boys' room. I assumed they'd want to share at this age, especially in a new place."

"Bull's-eye." Stella walked into the room behind Roz. "Oh, they'll love this. Lots of room, lots of light." She laid the carton and the suitcase on one of the twin beds. But antiques." She ran her fingers over the child-size chest of drawers. "I'm terrified."

"Furniture's meant to be used. And good pieces respected."

"Believe me, they'll get the word." Please, God, don't let them break anything.

"You're next door. The bath connects." Roz gestured, angled her head. "I thought, at least initially, you'd want to be close."

"Perfect." She walked into the bath. The generous claw-foot tub stood on a marble platform in front of the terrace doors. Roman shades could be pulled down for privacy. The toilet sat in a tall cabinet built from yellow pine and had a chain pull—wouldn't the boys get a kick out of that!

Beside the pedestal sink was a brass towel warmer already draped with fluffy sea-green towels.

Through the connecting door, her room was washed with winter light. Rhizomes patterned the oak floor.

A cozy sitting area faced the small white-marble fireplace, with a painting of a garden in full summer bloom above it.

Draped in gauzy white and shell pink, the canopy bed was accented with a generous mountain of silk pillows in dreamy pastels. The bureau with its long oval mirror was gleaming mahogany, as was the charmingly feminine dressing table and the carved armoire.

"I'm starting to feel like Cinderella at the ball."

"If the shoe fits." Roz set down the suitcases. "I want you to be comfortable, and your boys to be happy because I'm going to work you very hard. It's a big house, and

David will show you through at some point. We won't bump into each other, unless we want to."

She shoved up the sleeves of her shirt as she looked around. "I'm not a sociable woman, though I do enjoy the company of people I like. I think I'm going to like you. I already like your children."

She glanced at her watch. "I'm going to grab that hot chocolate—I can't ever resist it—then get to work."

"I'd like to come in, show you some of my ideas, later today."

"Fine. Hunt me up."

SHE DID JUST THAT. THOUGH SHE'D INTENDED TO bring the kids with her after the school meeting, she hadn't had the heart to take them away from David.

So much for her worries about their adjustment to living in a new house with strangers. It appeared that most of the adjustments were going to be on her end.

She dressed more appropriately this time, in sturdy walking shoes that had already seen their share of mud, jeans with considerable wear, and a black sweater. With her briefcase in hand, she headed into the main entrance of the garden center.

The same woman was at the counter, but this time she was waiting on a customer. Stella noted a small dieffenbachia in a cherry-red pot and a quartet of lucky bamboo, tied with decorative hemp, already in a shallow cardboard box.

A bag of stones and a square glass vase were waiting to be rung up.

Good.

"Is Roz around?" Stella asked.

"Oh . . ." Ruby gestured vaguely. "Somewhere or the other."

She nodded to the two-ways behind the counter. "Would she have one of those with her?"

The idea seemed to amuse Ruby. "I don't think so."

"Okay, I'll find her. That's so much fun," she said to the

customer, with a gesture toward the bamboo. "Carefree and interesting. It's going to look great in that bowl."

"I was thinking about putting it on my bathroom counter. Something fun and pretty."

"Perfect. Terrific hostess gifts, too. More imaginative than the usual flowers."

"I hadn't thought of that. You know, maybe I'll get another set."

"You couldn't go wrong." She beamed a smile, then started out toward the greenhouses, congratulating herself as she went. She wasn't in any hurry to find Roz. This gave her a chance to poke around on her own, to check supplies, stock, displays, traffic patterns. And to make more notes.

She lingered in the propagation area, studying the progress of seedlings and cuttings, the type of stock plants, and their health.

It was nearly an hour before she made her way to the grafting area. She could hear music—the Corrs, she thought—seeping out the door.

She peeked in. There were long tables lining both sides of the greenhouse, and two more shoved together to run down the center. It smelled of heat, vermiculite, and peat moss.

There were pots, some holding plants that had been or were being grafted. Clipboards hung from the edges of tables, much like hospital charts. A computer was shoved into a corner, its screen a pulse of colors that seemed to beat to the music.

Scalpels, knives, snippers, grafting tape and wax, and other tools of this part of the trade lay in trays.

She spotted Roz at the far end, standing behind a man on a stool. His shoulders were hunched as he worked. Roz's hands were on her hips.

"It can't take more than an hour, Harper. This place is as much yours as mine, and you need to meet her, hear what she has to say."

"I will, I will, but damn it, I'm in the middle of things here. You're the one who wants her to manage, so let her manage. I don't care."

"There's such a thing as manners." Exasperation rolled into the overheated air. "I'm just asking you to pretend, for an hour, to have a few."

The comment brought Stella's own words to her sons back to her mind. She couldn't stop the laugh, but did her best to conceal it with a cough as she walked down the narrow aisle.

"Sorry to interrupt. I was just . . ." She stopped by a pot, studying the grafted stem and the new leaves. "I can't quite make this one."

"Daphne." Roz's son spared her the briefest glance.

"Evergreen variety. And you've used a splice side-veneer graft."

He stopped, swiveled on his stool. His mother had stamped herself on his face—the same strong bones, rich eyes. His dark hair was considerably longer than hers, long enough that he tied it back with what looked to be a hunk of raffia. Like her, he was slim and seemed to have at least a yard of leg, and like her he dressed carelessly in jeans pocked with rips and a soil-stained Memphis University sweatshirt.

"You know something about grafting?"

"Just the basics. I cleft-grafted a camellia once. It did very well. Generally I stick with cuttings. I'm Stella. It's nice to meet you, Harper."

He rubbed his hand over his jeans before shaking hers. "Mom says you're going to organize us."

"That's the plan, and I hope it's not going to be too painful for any of us. What are you working on here?" She stepped over to a line of pots covered with clean plastic bags held clear of the grafted plant by four split stakes.

"Gypsophilia—baby's breath. I'm shooting for blue, as well as pink and white."

"Blue. My favorite color. I don't want to hold you up. I

was hoping," she said to Roz, "we could find somewhere to go over some of my ideas."

"Back in the annual house. The office is hopeless. Harper?"

"All right, okay. Go ahead. I'll be there in five minutes."

"Harper."

"Okay, ten. But that's my final offer."

With a laugh, Roz gave him a light cuff on the back of the head. "Don't make me come back in here and get you."

"Nag, nag, nag," he muttered, but with a grin.

Outside, Roz let out a sigh. "He plants himself in there, you have to jab a pitchfork in his ass to budge him. He's the only one of my boys who has an interest in the place. Austin's a reporter, works in Atlanta. Mason's a doctor, or will be. He's doing his internship in Nashville."

"You must be proud."

"I am, but I don't see nearly enough of either of them. And here's Harper, practically under my feet, and I have to hunt him like a dog to have a conversation."

Roz boosted herself onto one of the tables. "Well, what've you got?"

"He looks just like you."

"People say. I just see Harper. Your boys with David?"

"Couldn't pry them away with a crowbar." Stella opened her briefcase. "I typed up some notes."

Roz looked at the stack of papers and tried not to wince. "I'll say."

"And I've made some rough sketches of how we might change the layout to improve sales and highlight non-plant purchases. You have a prime location, excellent landscaping and signage, and a very appealing entrance."

"I hear a 'but' coming on."

"But . . ." Stella moistened her lips. "Your first-level retail area is somewhat disorganized. With some changes it would flow better into the secondary area and on through to your main plant facilities. Now, a functional organizational plan—"

"A functional organizational plan. Oh, my God."

"Take it easy, this really won't hurt. What you need is a chain of responsibility for your functional area. That's sales, production, and propagation. Obviously you're a skilled propagator, but at this point you need me to head production and sales. If we increase the volume of sales as I've proposed here—"

"You did charts." There was a touch of wonder in Roz's voice. "And graphs. I'm . . . suddenly afraid."

"You are not," Stella said with a laugh, then looked at Roz's face. "Okay, maybe a little. But if you look at this chart, you see the nursery manager—that's me—and you as you're in charge of everything. Forked out from that is your propagator—you and, I assume, Harper; production manager, me; and sales manager—still me. For now, anyway. You need to delegate and/or hire someone to be in charge of container and/or field production. This section here deals with staff, job descriptions and responsibilities."

"All right." On a little breath, Roz rubbed the back of her neck. "Before I give myself eyestrain reading all that, let me say that while I may consider hiring on more staff, Logan, my landscape designer, has a good handle on the field production at this point. I can continue to head up the container production. I didn't start this place to sit back and have others do all the work."

"Great. Then at some point I'd like to meet with Logan so we can coordinate our visions."

Roz's smile was thin, and just a little wicked. "That ought to be interesting."

"Meanwhile, since we're both here, why don't we take my notes and sketches of the first-level sales section and go through it on the spot? You can see better what I have in mind, and it'll be simpler to explain."

Simpler? Roz thought as she hopped down. She didn't think anything was going to be simpler now.

But it sure as holy hell wasn't going to be boring.

four

Everything was perfect. She worked long hours, but much of it was planning at this stage. There was little Stella loved more than planning. Unless it was *arranging*. She had a vision of things, in her head, of how things could and should be.

Some might see it as a flaw, this tendency to organize and project, to nudge those visions of things into place even when—maybe particularly when—others didn't quite get the picture.

But she didn't see it that way.

Life ran smoother when everything was where it was meant to be.

Her life had—she'd made certain of it—until Kevin's death. Her childhood had been a maze of contradictions, of confusions and irritations. In a very real way she'd lost her father at the age of three when divorce had divided her family.

The only thing she clearly remembered about the move from Memphis was crying for her daddy.

From that point on, it seemed she and her mother had butted heads over everything, from the color of paint on the walls to finances to how to spend holidays and vacations. Everything.

Those same *some people* might say that's what happened with two headstrong women living in the same house. But Stella knew different. While she was practical and organized, her mother was scattered and spontaneous. Which accounted for the four marriages and three broken engagements.

Her mother liked flash and noise and wild romance. Stella preferred quiet and settled and committed.

Not that she wasn't romantic. She was just sensible about it.

It had been both sensible and romantic to fall in love with Kevin. He'd been warm and sweet and steady. They'd wanted the same things. Home, family, future. He'd made her happy, made her feel safe and cherished. And God, she missed him.

She wondered what he'd think about her coming here, starting over this way. He'd have trusted her. He'd always believed in her. They'd believed in each other.

He'd been her rock, in a very real way. The rock that had given her a solid base to build on after a childhood of upheaval and discontent.

Then fate had kicked that rock out from under her. She'd lost her base, her love, her most cherished friend, and the only person in the world who could treasure her children as much as she did.

There had been times, many times, during the first months after Kevin's death when she'd despaired of ever finding her balance again.

Now she was the rock for her sons, and she would do whatever she had to do to give them a good life.

With her boys settled down for the night, and a low fire burning—she was *definitely* having a bedroom fireplace in her next house—she sat on the bed with her laptop.

It wasn't the most businesslike way to work, but she didn't feel right asking Roz to let her convert one of the bedrooms into a home office.

Yet.

She could make do this way for now. In fact, it was cozy and for her, relaxing, to go over the order of business for the next day while tucked into the gorgeous old bed.

She had the list of phone calls she intended to make to suppliers, the reorganization of garden accessories and the houseplants. Her new color-coordinated pricing system to implement. The new invoicing program to install.

She had to speak with Roz about the seasonal employees. Who, how many, individual and group responsibilities.

And she'd yet to corner the landscape designer. You'd think the man could find time in a damn week to return a phone call. She typed in "Logan Kitridge," bolding and underlining the name.

She glanced at the clock, reminded herself that she would put in a better day's work with a good night's sleep.

She powered down the laptop, then carried it over to the dressing table to set it to charge. She really was going to need that home office.

She went through her habitual bedtime routine, meticulously creaming off her makeup, studying her naked face in the mirror to see if the Time Bitch had snuck any new lines on it that day. She dabbed on her eye cream, her lip cream, her nighttime moisturizer—all of which were lined, according to point of use, on the counter. After slathering more cream on her hands, she spent a few minutes searching for gray hairs. The Time Bitch could be sneaky.

She wished she was prettier. Wished her features were more even, her hair straight and a reasonable color. She'd dyed it brown once, and *that* had been a disaster. So, she'd just have to live with . . .

She caught herself humming, and frowned at herself in the mirror. What song was that? How strange to have it stuck in her head when she didn't even know what it was.

Then she realized it wasn't stuck in her head. She *heard* it. Soft, dreamy singing. From the boys' room.

Wondering what in the world Roz would be doing

singing to the boys at eleven at night, Stella reached for the connecting door.

When she opened it, the singing stopped. In the subtle glow of the Harry Potter night-light, she could see her sons in their beds.

"Roz?" she whispered, stepping in.

She shivered once. Why was it so cold in there? She moved, quickly and quietly to the terrace doors, checked and found them securely closed, as were the windows. And the hall door, she thought with another frown.

She could have sworn she'd heard something. *Felt* something. But the chill had already faded, and there was no sound in the room but her sons' steady breathing.

She tucked up their blankets as she did every night, brushed kisses on both their heads.

And left the connecting doors open.

BY MORNING SHE'D BRUSHED IT OFF. LUKE COULDN'T find his lucky shirt, and Gavin got into a wrestling match with Parker on their before-school walk and had to change his. As a result, she barely had time for morning coffee and the muffin David pressed on her.

"Will you tell Roz I went in early? I want to have the lobby area done before we open at ten."

"She left an hour ago."

"An hour ago?" Stella looked at her watch. Keeping up with Roz had become Stella's personal mission—and so far she was failing. "Does she *sleep*?"

"With her, the early bird doesn't just catch the worm, but has time to sauté it with a nice plum sauce for breakfast."

"Excuse me, but *eeuw*. Gotta run." She dashed for the doorway, then stopped. "David, everything's going okay with the kids? You'd tell me otherwise, right?"

"Absolutely. We're having nothing but fun. Today, after school, we're going to practice running with scissors, then find how many things we can roughhouse with that can poke our eyes out. After that, we've moving on to flammables."

"Thanks. I feel very reassured." She bent down to give Parker a last pat. "Keep an eye on this guy," she told him.

LOGAN KITRIDGE WAS PRESSED FOR TIME. RAIN HAD delayed his personal project to the point where he was going to have to postpone some of the fine points—again—to meet professional commitments.

He didn't mind so much. He considered landscaping a perpetual work in progress. It was never finished. It *should* never be finished. And when you worked with Nature, Nature was the boss. She was fickle and tricky, and endlessly fascinating.

A man had to be continually on his toes, be ready to flex, be willing to compromise and swing with her moods. Planning in absolutes was an exercise in frustration, and to his mind there were enough other things to be frustrated about.

Since Nature had deigned to give him a good, clear day, he was taking it to deal with his personal project. It meant he had to work alone—he liked that better in any case—and carve out time to swing by the job site and check on his two-man crew.

It meant he had to get over to Roz's place, pick up the trees he'd earmarked for his own use, haul them back to his place, and get them in the ground before noon.

Or one. Two at the latest.

Well, he'd see how it went.

The one thing he couldn't afford to carve out time for was this new manager Roz had taken on. He couldn't figure out why Roz had hired a manager in the first place, and for God's sake a Yankee. It seemed to him that Rosalind Harper knew how to run her business just fine and didn't need some fast-talking stranger screwing with the system.

He liked working with Roz. She was a woman who got things done, and who didn't poke her nose into his end of things any more than was reasonable. She loved the work, just as he did, had an instinct for it. So when she did make a suggestion, you tended to listen and weigh it in.

She paid well and didn't hassle a man over every detail.

He could tell, just *tell*, that this manager was going to be nothing but bumps and ruts in his road.

Wasn't she already leaving messages for him in that cool Yankee voice about time management, invoice systems, and equipment inventory?

He didn't give a shit about that sort of thing, and he wasn't going to start giving one now.

He and Roz had a system, damn it. One that got the job done and made the client happy.

Why mess with success?

He drove his full-size pickup through the parking area, wove through the piles of mulch and sand, the landscape timbers, and around the side loading area.

He'd already eyeballed and tagged what he wanted—but before he loaded them up, he'd take one more look around. Plus there were some young evergreens in the field and a couple of hemlocks in the balled and burlapped area that he thought he could use.

Harper had grafted him a couple of willows and a hedgerow of peonies. They'd be ready to dig in this spring, along with the various pots of cuttings and layered plants Roz had helped him with.

He moved through the rows of trees, then turned around and backtracked.

This wasn't right, he thought. Everything was out of place, changed around. Where were his dogwoods? Where the hell were the rhododendrons, the mountain laurels he'd tagged? Where was his goddamn frigging magnolia?

He scowled at a pussy willow, then began a careful, step-by-step search through the section.

It was all different. Trees and shrubs were no longer in

what he'd considered an interesting, eclectic mix of type and species, but lined up like army recruits, he decided. Alphabetized, for Christ's sweet sake. In frigging Latin.

Shrubs were segregated, and organized in the same anal fashion.

He found his trees and, stewing, carted them to his truck. Muttering to himself, he decided to head into the field, dig up the trees he wanted there. They'd be safer at his place. Obviously.

Bur first he was going to hunt up Roz and get this mess straightened out.

STANDING ON A STEPLADDER, ARMED WITH A BUCKET of soapy water and a rag, Stella attacked the top of the shelf she'd cleared off. A good cleaning, she decided, and it would be ready for her newly planned display. She envisioned it filled with color-coordinated decorative pots, some mixed plantings scattered among them. Add other accessories, like raffia twine, decorative watering spikes, florist stones and marbles, and so on, and you'd have something.

At point of purchase, it would generate impulse sales.

She was moving the soil additives, fertilizers, and animal repellents to the side wall. Those were basics, not impulse. Customers would walk back there for items of that nature, and pass the wind chimes she was going to hang, the bench and concrete planter she intended to haul in. With the other changes, it would all tie together, and with the flow, draw customers into the houseplant section, across to the patio pots, the garden furniture, all before they moved through to the bedding plants.

With an hour and a half until they opened, and if she could shanghai Harper into helping her with the heavy stuff, she'd have it done.

She heard footsteps coming through from the back, blew her hair out of her eyes. "Making progress," she began. "I know it doesn't look like it yet, but . . ."

She broke off when she saw him.

Even standing on the ladder, she felt dwarfed. He had to be six-five. All tough and rangy and fit in faded jeans with bleach stains splattered over one thigh. He wore a flannel shirt jacket-style over a white T-shirt and a pair of boots so dinged and scored she wondered he didn't take pity and give them a decent burial.

His long, wavy, unkempt hair was the color she'd been shooting for the one time she'd dyed her own.

She wouldn't have called him handsome—everything about him seemed rough and rugged. The hard mouth, the hollowed cheeks, the sharp nose, the expression in his eyes. They were green, but not like Kevin's had been. These were moody and deep, and seemed somehow *hot* under the strong line of brows.

No, she wouldn't have said handsome, but arresting, in a big and tough sort of way. The sort of tough that looked like a bunched fist would bounce right off him, doing a lot more damage to the puncher than the punchee.

She smiled, though she wondered where Roz was, or Harper. Or somebody.

"I'm sorry. We're not open yet this morning. Is there something I can do for you?"

Oh, he knew that voice. That crisp, cool voice that had left him annoying messages about functional organizational plans and production goals.

He'd expected her to look like she'd sounded—a usual mistake, he supposed. There wasn't much cool and crisp about that wild red hair she was trying to control with that stupid-looking kerchief, or the wariness in those big blue eyes.

"You moved my damn trees."

"I'm sorry?"

"Well, you ought to be. Don't do it again."

"I don't know what you're talking about." She kept a grip on the bucket—just in case—and stepped down the ladder. "Did you order some trees? If I could have your name, I'll see if I can find your order. We're implementing a new system, so—"

"I don't have to order anything, and I don't like your new system. And what the hell are you doing in here? Where *is* everything?"

His voice sounded local to her, with a definite edge of nasty impatience. "I think it would be best if you came back when we're open. Winter hours start at ten A.M. If you'd leave me your name . . ." She edged toward the counter and the phone.

"It's Kitridge, and you ought to know since you've been nagging me brainless for damn near a week."

"I don't know . . . oh. Kitridge." She relaxed, fractionally. "The landscape designer. And I haven't been nagging," she said with more heat when her brain caught up. "I've been trying to contact you so we could schedule a meeting. You haven't had the courtesy to return my calls. I certainly hope you're not as rude with clients as you are with coworkers."

"Rude? Sister, you haven't seen rude."

"I have two sons," she snapped back. "I've seen plenty of rude. Roz hired me to put some order into her business, to take some of the systemic load off her shoulders, to—"

"Systemic?" His gaze rose to the ceiling like a man sending out a prayer. "Jesus, are you always going to talk like that?"

She took a calming breath. "Mr. Kitridge, I have a job to do. Part of that job is dealing with the landscaping arm of this business. It happens to be a very important and profitable arm."

"Damn right. And it's my frigging arm."

"It also happens to be ridiculously disorganized and apparently run like a circus. I've been finding little scraps of paper and hand-scribbled orders and invoices—if you can call them that—all week."

"So?"

"So, if you'd bothered to return my calls and arrange for

a meeting, I could have explained to you how this arm of the business will now function."

"Oh, is that right?" That west Tennessee tone took on a soft and dangerous hue. "You're going to explain it to me."

"That's exactly right. The system I'm implementing will, in the end, save you considerable time and effort with computerized invoices and inventory, client lists and designs, with—"

He was sizing her up. He figured he had about a foot on her in height, probably a good hundred pounds in bulk. But the woman had a mouth on her. It was what his mother would have called bee stung—pretty—and apparently it never stopped flapping.

"How the hell is having to spend half my time on a computer going to save me anything?"

"Once the data is inputted, it will. At this point, you seem to be carrying most of this information in some pocket, or inside your head."

"So? If it's in a pocket, I can find it. If it's in my head, I can find it there, too. Nothing wrong with my memory."

"Maybe not. But tomorrow you may be run over by a truck and spend the next five years in a coma." That pretty mouth smiled, icily. "Then where will we be?"

"Being as I'd be in a coma, I wouldn't be worried about it. Come out here."

He grabbed her hand, pulled her toward the door. "Hey!" she managed. Then, *"Hey!"*

"This is business." He yanked open the door and kept pulling her along. "I'm not dragging you off to a cave."

"Then let go." His hands were hard as rock, and just as rough. And his legs, she realized, as he strode away from the building, ate up ground in long, hurried bites and forced her into an undignified trot.

"Just a minute. Look at that."

He gestured toward the tree and shrub area while she struggled to get her breath back. "What about it?"

"It's messed up."

"It certainly isn't. I spent nearly an entire day on this area." And had the aching muscles to prove it. "It's cohesively arranged so if a customer is looking for an ornamental tree, he—or a member of the staff—can find the one that suits. If the customer is looking for a spring-blooming shrub or—"

"They're all lined up. What did you use, a carpenter's level? People come in here now, how can they get a picture of how different specimens might work together?"

"That's your job and the staff's. We're here to help and direct the customer to possibilities as well as their more definite wants. If they're wandering around trying to find a damn hydrangea—"

"They might just spot a spirea or camellia they'd like to have, too."

He had a point, and she'd considered it. She wasn't an idiot. "Or they may leave empty-handed because they couldn't easily find what they'd come for in the first place. Attentive and well-trained staff should be able to direct and explore with the customer. Either way has its pros and cons, but I happen to like this way better. And it's my call.

"Now." She stepped back. "If you have the time, we need to—"

"I don't." He stalked off toward his truck.

"Just wait." She jogged after him. "We need to talk about the new purchase orders and invoicing system."

"Send me a frigging memo. Sounds like your speed."

"I don't want to send you a frigging memo, and what are you doing with those trees?"

"Taking them home." He pulled open the truck door, climbed in.

"What do you mean you're taking them home? I don't have any paperwork on these."

"Hey, me neither." After slamming the door, he rolled the window down a stingy inch. "Step back, Red. Wouldn't want to run over your toes."

"Look. You can't just take off with stock whenever you feel like it."

"Take it up with Roz. If she's still the boss. Otherwise, better call the cops." He gunned the engine, and when she stumbled back, zipped into reverse. And left her staring after him.

Cheeks pink with temper, Stella marched back toward the building. Serve him right, she thought, just serve him right if she did call the police. She snapped her head up, eyes hot, as Roz opened the door.

"Was that Logan's truck?"

"Does he work with clients?"

"Sure. Why?"

"You're lucky you haven't been sued. He storms in, nothing but complaints. Bitch, bitch, bitch," Stella muttered as she swung past Roz and inside. "He doesn't like this, doesn't like that, doesn't like any damn thing as far as I can tell. Then he drives off with a truckload of trees and shrubs."

Roz rubbed her earlobe thoughtfully. "He does have his moods."

"Moods? I only saw one, and I didn't like it." She yanked off the kerchief, tossed it on the counter.

"Pissed you off, did he?"

"In spades. I'm trying to do what you hired me to do, Roz."

"I know. And so far I don't believe I've made any comments or complaints that could qualify as bitch, bitch, bitch."

Stella sent her a horrified look. "No! Of course not. I didn't mean—God."

"We're in what I'd call an adjustment period. Some don't adjust as smoothly as others. I like most of your ideas, and others I'm willing to give a chance. Logan's used to doing things his own way, and that's been fine with me. It works for us."

"He took stock. How can I maintain inventory if I don't know what he took, or what it's for? I need paperwork, Roz."

"I imagine he took the specimens he'd tagged for his

personal use. If he took others, he'll let me know. Which is not the way you do things," she continued before Stella could speak. "I'll talk to him, Stella, but you might have to do some adjusting yourself. You're not in Michigan anymore. I'm going to let you get back to work here."

And she was going back to her plants. They generally gave her less trouble than people.

"Roz? I know I can be an awful pain in the ass, but I really do want to help you grow your business."

"I figured out both those things already."

Alone, Stella sulked for a minute. Then she got her bucket and climbed up the ladder again. The unscheduled meeting had thrown her off schedule.

"I DON'T LIKE HER." LOGAN SAT IN ROZ'S PARLOR with a beer in one hand and a boatload of resentment in the other. "She's bossy, rigid, smug, and shrill." At Roz's raised brows, he shrugged. "Okay, not shrill—so far—but I stand by the rest."

"I do like her. I like her energy and her enthusiasm. And I need someone to handle the details, Logan. I've outgrown myself. I'm just asking that the two of you try to meet somewhere in the middle of things."

"I don't think she has any middle. She's extreme. I don't trust extreme women."

"You trust me."

He brooded into his beer. That was true enough. If he hadn't trusted Roz, he wouldn't have come to work for her, no matter what salary and perks she'd dangled under his nose. "She's going to have us filling out forms in triplicate and documenting how many inches we prune off a damn bush."

"I don't think it'll come to that." Roz propped her feet comfortably on the coffee table and sipped her own beer.

"If you had to go and hire some sort of manager, Roz, why the hell didn't you hire local? Get somebody in who understands how things work around here."

"Because I didn't want a local. I wanted her. When she comes down, we're going to have a nice civilized drink followed by a nice civilized meal. I don't care if the two of you don't like each other, but you will learn how to get along."

"You're the boss."

"That's a fact." She gave him a companionable pat on the thigh. "Harper's coming over, too. I browbeat him into it."

Logan brooded a minute longer. "You really like her?"

"I really do. And I've missed the company of women. Women who aren't silly and annoying, anyway. She's neither. She had a tough break, Logan, losing her man at such a young age. I know what that's like. She hasn't broken under it, or gone brittle. So yes, I like her."

"Then I'll tolerate her, but only for you."

"Sweet talker." With a laugh, Roz leaned over to kiss his cheek.

"Only because I'm crazy about you."

Stella came to the door in time to see Logan take Roz's hand in his, and thought, Oh, shit.

She'd gone head-to-head, argued with, insulted, and complained about her boss's lover.

With a sick dread in her stomach, she nudged her boys forward. She stepped inside, plastered on a smile. "Hope we're not late," she said cheerily. "There was a small homework crisis. Hello, Mr. Kitridge. I'd like you to meet my sons. This is Gavin, and this is Luke."

"How's it going?" They looked like normal kids to him rather than the pod-children he'd expected someone like Stella to produce.

"I have a loose tooth," Luke told him.

"Yeah? Let's have a look, then." Logan set down his beer to take a serious study of the tooth Luke wiggled with his tongue. "Cool. You know, I've got me some pliers in my toolbox. One yank and we'd have that out of there."

At the small horrified sound from behind him, Logan turned to smile thinly at Stella.

"Mr. Kitridge is just joking," Stella told a fascinated Luke. "Your tooth will come out when it's ready."

"When it does, the Tooth Fairy comes, and I get a *buck.*"

Logan pursed his lips. "A buck, huh? Good deal."

"It makes blood when it comes out, but I'm not scared."

"Miss Roz? Can we go see David in the kitchen?" Gavin shot a look at his mother. "Mom said we had to ask you."

"Sure. You go right on."

"No sweets," Stella called out as they dashed out.

"Logan, why don't you pour Stella a glass of wine?"

"I'll get it. Don't get up," Stella told him.

He didn't look quite as much like an overbearing jerk, she decided. He cleaned up well enough, and she could see why Roz was attracted. If you went for the *über*virile sort.

"Did you say Harper was coming?" Stella asked her.

"He'll be along." Roz gestured with her beer. "Let's see if we can all play nice. Let's get this business out of the way so we can have an enjoyable meal without ruining our digestion. Stella's in charge of sales and production, of managing the day-to-day business. She and I will, for now anyway, share personnel management while Harper and I head up propagation."

She sipped her beer, waited, though she knew her own power and didn't expect an interruption. "Logan leads the landscaping design, both on- and off-site. As such, he has first choice of stock and is authorized to put in for special orders, or arrange trades or purchases or rentals of necessary equipment, material or specimens for outside designs. The changes Stella has already implemented or proposed—and which have been approved by me—will stay or be put in place. Until such time as I decide they don't work. Or if I just don't like them. Clear so far?"

"Perfectly," Stella said coolly.

Logan shrugged.

"Which means you'll cooperate with each other, do what's necessary to work together in such a way for both of you to function in the areas you oversee. I built In the

Garden from the ground up, and I can run it myself if I have to. But I don't choose to. I choose to have the two of you, and Harper, shoulder the responsibilities you've been given. Squabble all you want. I don't mind squabbles. But get the job done."

She finished off her beer. "Questions? Comments?" After a beat of silence, she rose. "Well, then, let's eat."

five

It was, all things considered, a pleasant evening. Neither of her kids threw any food or made audible gagging noises. Always a plus, in Stella's book. Conversation was polite, even lively—particularly when the boys learned Logan's first name—the same name used by the X-Men's Wolverine.

It was instant hero status, given polish when it was discovered that Logan shared Gavin's obsession with comic books.

The fact that Logan seemed more interested in talking to her sons than her was probably another plus.

"If, you know, the Hulk and Spider-Man ever got into a fight, I think Spider-Man would win."

Logan nodded as he cut into rare roast beef. "Because Spider-Man's quicker, and more agile. But if the Hulk ever caught him, Spidey'd be toast."

Gavin speared a tiny new potato, then held it aloft on his fork like a severed head on a pike. "If he was under the influence of some evil guy, like . . ."

"Maybe Mr. Hyde."

"Yeah! Mr. Hyde, then the Hulk could be *forced* to go after Spider-Man. But I still think Spidey would win."

"That's why he's amazing," Logan agreed, "and the Hulk's incredible. It takes more than muscle to battle evil."

"Yeah, you gotta be smart and brave and stuff."

"Peter Parker's the smartest." Luke emulated his brother with the potato head.

"Bruce Banner's pretty smart, too." Since it made the kids laugh, Harper hoisted a potato, wagged it. "He always manages to get new clothes after he reverts from Hulk form."

"If he was really smart," Harper commented, "he'd figure out a way to make his clothes stretch and expand."

"You scientists," Logan said with a grin for Harper. "Never thinking about the mundane."

"Is the Mundane a supervillain?" Luke wanted to know.

"It means the ordinary," Stella told him. "As in, it's more mundane to eat your potatoes than to play with them, but that's the polite thing to do at the table."

"Oh." Luke smiled at her, an expression somewhere between sweet and wicked, and chomped the potato off the fork. "Okay." After the meal, she used the excuse of the boys' bedtime to retreat upstairs. There were baths to deal with, the usual thousand questions to answer, and all that end-of-day energy to burn off, which included one or both of them running around mostly naked.

Then came her favorite time, when she drew a chair between their beds and read to them while Parker began to snore at her feet. The current pick was *Mystic Horse*, and when she closed the book, she got the expected moans and pleas for just a little more.

"Tomorrow, because now I'm afraid it's time for sloppy kisses."

"Not sloppy kisses." Gavin rolled onto his belly to bury his face in the pillow. "Not that!"

"Yes, and you must succumb." She covered the back of his head, the base of his neck with kisses while he giggled.

"And now, for my second victim." She turned to Luke and rubbed her hands together.

"Wait, wait!" He threw out his hand to ward off the attack. "Do you think my tooth will fall out tomorrow?"

"Let's have another look." She sat on the side of his bed, studying soberly as he wiggled the tooth with his tongue. "I think it just might."

"Can I have a horse?"

"It won't fit under your pillow." When he laughed, she kissed his forehead, his cheeks, and his sweet, sweet mouth.

Rising, she switched off the lamp, leaving them in the glow of the night-light. "Only fun dreams allowed."

"I'm gonna dream I get a horse, because dreams come true sometimes."

"Yes, they do. 'Night now."

She walked back to her room, heard the whispers from bed to bed that were also part of the bedtime ritual.

It had become their ritual, over the last two years. Just the three of them at nighttime, where they had once been four. But it was solid now, and good, she thought, as a few giggles punctuated the whispers.

Somewhere along the line she'd stopped aching every night, every morning, for what had been. And she'd come to treasure what was.

She glanced at her laptop, thought about the work she'd earmarked for the evening. Instead, she went to the terrace doors.

It was still too cool to sit out, but she wanted the air, and the quiet, and the night.

Imagine, just imagine, she was standing outside at night in January. And not freezing. Though the forecasters were calling for more rain, the sky was star-studded and graced with a sliver of moon. In that dim light she could see a camellia in bloom. Flowers in winter—now that was something to add to the plus pile about moving south.

She hugged her elbows and thought of spring, when the air would be warm and garden-scented.

She wanted to be here in the spring, to see it, to be part of the awakening. She wanted to keep her job. She hadn't realized how much she wanted to keep it until Roz's firm, no-nonsense sit-down before dinner.

Less than two weeks, and she was already caught up. Maybe too much caught, she admitted. That was always a problem. Whatever she began, she needed to finish. Stella's religion, her mother called it.

But this was more. She was emotional about the place. A mistake, she knew. She was half in love with the nursery, and with her own vision of how it could be. She wanted to see tables alive with color and green, cascading flowers spilling from hanging baskets that would drop down along the aisles to make arbors. She wanted to see customers browsing and buying, filling the wagons and flatbeds with containers.

And, of course, there was that part of her that wanted to go along with each one of them and show them exactly how everything should be planted. But she could control that.

She could admit she also wanted to see the filing system in place, and the spreadsheets, the weekly inventory logs.

And whether he liked it or not, she intended to visit some of Logan's jobs. To get a feel for that end of the business.

That was supposing he didn't talk Roz into firing her.

He'd gotten slapped back, too, Stella admitted. But he had home-field advantage.

In any case, she wasn't going to be able to work, or relax, or think about anything else until she'd straightened things out.

She would go downstairs, on the pretext of making a cup of tea. If his truck was gone, she'd try to have a minute with Roz.

It was quiet, and she had a sudden sinking feeling that they'd gone up to bed. She didn't want that picture in her head. Tiptoeing into the front parlor, she peeked out the window. Though she didn't see his truck, it occurred to her she didn't know where he'd parked, or what he'd driven in the first place.

She'd leave it for morning. That was best. In the morning, she would ask for a short meeting with Roz and get everything back in place. Better to sleep on it, to plan exactly what to say and how to say it.

Since she was already downstairs, she decided to go ahead and make that tea. Then she would take it upstairs and focus on work. Things would be better when she was focused.

She walked quietly back into the kitchen, and let out a yelp when she saw the dim figure in the shaded light. The figure yelped back, then slapped at the switch beside the stove.

"Just draw and shoot next time," Roz said, slapping a hand to her heart.

"I'm sorry. God, you scared me. I knew David was going into the city tonight and I didn't think anyone was back here."

"Just me. Making some coffee."

"In the dark?"

"Stove light was on. I know my way around. You come down to raid the refrigerator?"

"What? No. No!" She was hardly that comfortable here, in another woman's home. "I was just going to make some tea to take up while I do a little work."

"Go ahead. Unless you want some of this coffee."

"If I drink coffee after dinner, I'm awake all night."

It was awkward, standing here in the quiet house, just the two of them. It wasn't her house, Stella thought, her kitchen, even her quiet. She wasn't a guest, but an employee.

However gracious Roz might be, everything around them belonged to her.

"Did Mr. Kitridge leave?"

"You can call him Logan, Stella. You only sound pissy otherwise."

"Sorry. I don't mean to be." Maybe a little. "We got off

on the wrong foot, that's all, and I . . . oh, thanks," she said when Roz handed her the teakettle. "I realize I shouldn't have complained about him."

She filled the kettle, wishing she'd thought through what she wanted to say. Practiced it a few times.

"Because?" Roz prompted.

"Well, it's hardly constructive for your manager and your landscape designer to start in on each other after one run-in, and less so to whine to you about it."

"Sensible. Mature." Roz leaned back on the counter, waiting for her coffee to brew. Young, she thought. She had to remember that despite some shared experiences, the girl was more than a decade younger than she. And a bit tender yet.

"I try to be both," Stella said, and put the kettle on to boil.

"So did I, once upon a time. Then I decided, screw that. I'm going to start my own business."

Stella pushed back her hair. Who was this woman who was elegant to look at even in the hard lights? Who spoke frank words in that debutante-of-the-southern-aristocracy voice and wore ancient wool socks in lieu of slippers? "I can't get a handle on you. I can't figure you out."

"That's what you do, isn't it? Get handles on things." She shifted to reach up and behind into a cupboard for a coffee mug. "That's a good quality to have in a manager. Might be irritating on a personal level."

"You wouldn't be the first." Stella let out a breath. "And on that personal level, I'd like to add a separate apology. I shouldn't have said those things about Logan to you. First off, because it's bad form to fly off about another employee. And second, I didn't realize you were involved."

"Didn't you?" The moment, Roz decided, called for a cookie. She reached into the jar David kept stocked, pulled out a snickerdoodle. "And you realized it when . . ."

"When we came downstairs—before dinner. I didn't mean to eavesdrop, but I happened to notice . . ."

"Have a cookie."

"I don't really eat sweets after—"

"Have a cookie," Roz insisted and handed one over. "Logan and I are involved. He works for me, though he doesn't quite see it that way." An amused smile brushed over her lips. "It's more a *with me* from his point of view, and I don't mind that. Not as long as the work gets done, the money comes in, and the customers are satisfied. We're also friends. I like him very much. But we don't sleep together. We're not, in any way, romantically involved."

"Oh." This time she huffed out a breath. "Oh. Well, I've used up my own, so I'll have to borrow someone else's foot to stuff in my mouth."

"I'm not insulted, I'm flattered. He's an excellent, specimen. I can't say I've ever thought about him in that way."

"Why?"

Roz poured her coffee while Stella took the sputtering kettle off the burner. "I've got ten years on him."

"And your point would be?"

Roz glanced back, a little flicker of surprise running over her face, just ahead of humor. "You're right. That doesn't, or shouldn't, apply. However, I've been married twice. One was good, very good. One was bad, very bad. I'm not looking for a man right now. Too damn much trouble. Even when it's good, they take a lot of time, effort, and energy. I'm enjoying using all that time, effort, and energy on myself."

"Do you get lonely?"

"Yes. Yes, I do. There was a time I didn't think I'd have the luxury of being lonely. Raising my boys, all the running around, the mayhem, the responsibilities."

She glanced around the kitchen, as if surprised to find it quiet, without the noise and debris generated by young boys. "When I'd raised them—not that you're ever really done, but there's a point where you have to step back—I thought I wanted to share my life, my home, myself with someone. That was a mistake." Though her expression stayed easy and pleasant, her tone went hard as granite. "I corrected it."

"I can't imagine being married again. Even a good marriage is a balancing act, isn't it? Especially when you toss in careers, family."

"I never had all of them at once to juggle. When John was alive, it was home, kids, him. I wrapped my life around them. Only wrapped it tighter when it was just me and the boys. I'm not sorry for doing that," she said after a sip of coffee. "It was the way I wanted things. The business, the career, that started late for me. I admire women who can handle all those balls."

"I think I was good at it." There was a pang at remembering, a sweet little slice in the heart. "It's exhausting work, but I hope I was good at it. Now? I don't think I have the skill for it anymore. Being with someone every day, at the end of it." She shook her head. "I can't see it. I could always picture Kevin and me, all the steps and stages. I can't picture anyone else."

"Maybe he just hasn't come into the viewfinder yet."

Stella lifted a shoulder in a little shrug. "Maybe. But I could picture you and Logan together."

"Really?"

There was such humor, with a bawdy edge to it, that Stella forgot any sense of awkwardness and just laughed. "Not that way. Or I started to, then engaged the impenetrable mind block. I meant you looked good together. So attractive and easy. I thought it was nice. It's nice to have someone you can be easy with."

"And you and Kevin were easy together."

"We were. Sort of flowed on the same current."

"I wondered. You don't wear a wedding ring."

"No." Stella looked at her bare finger. "I took it off about a year ago, when I started dating again. It didn't seem right to wear it when I was with another man. I don't feel married anymore. It was gradual, I guess."

At the half question, Roz nodded. "Yes, I know."

"Somewhere along the line I stopped thinking, What would Kevin say about this. Or, What would Kevin do, or think, or want. So I took off my ring. It was hard. Almost as hard as losing him."

"I took mine off on my fortieth birthday," Roz murmured. "I realized I'd stopped wearing it as a tribute. It had become more of a shield against relationships. So I took it off on that black-letter day," she said with a half smile. "Because we move on, or we fade away."

"I'm too busy to worry about all of this most of the time, and I didn't mean to get into it now. I only wanted to apologize."

"Accepted. I'm going to take my coffee up. I'll see you in the morning."

"All right. Good night."

Feeling better, Stella finished making her tea. She would get a good start in the morning, she decided as she carried it upstairs. She'd get a good chunk of the reorganizing done, she'd talk with Harper and Roz about which cuttings should be added to inventory, *and* she'd find a way to get along with Logan.

She heard the singing, quiet and sad, as she started down the hall. Her heart began to trip, and china rattled on the tray as she picked up her pace. She was all but running by the time she got to the door of her sons' room.

There was no one there, just that same little chill to the air. Even when she set her tea down, searched the closet, under the bed, she found nothing.

She sat on the floor between the beds, waiting for her pulse to level. The dog stirred, then climbed up in her lap to lick her hand.

Stroking him, she stayed there, sitting between her boys while they slept.

ON SUNDAY, SHE WENT TO HER FATHER'S FOR brunch. She was more than happy to be handed a mimosa and ordered out of the kitchen by Jolene.

It was her first full day off since she'd started at In the Garden, and she was scheduled to relax.

With the boys running around the little backyard with Parker, she was free to sit down with her father.

"Tell me everything," he ordered.

"Everything will go straight through brunch, into dinner, and right into breakfast tomorrow."

"Give me the highlights. How do you like Rosalind?"

"I like her a lot. She manages to be straightforward and slippery. I'm never quite sure where I stand with her, but I do like her."

"She's lucky to have you. And being a smart woman, she knows it."

"You might be just a tiny bit biased."

"Just a bit."

He'd always loved her, Stella knew. Even when there had been months between visits. There'd always been phone calls or notes, or surprise presents in the mail.

He'd aged comfortably, she thought now. Whereas her mother waged a bitter and protracted war with the years, Will Dooley had made his truce with them. His red hair was overpowered by the gray now, and his bony frame carried a soft pouch in the middle. There were laugh lines around his eyes and mouth, glasses perched on his nose.

His face was ruddy from the sun. The man loved his gardening and his golf.

"The boys seem happy," he commented.

"They love it there. I can't believe how much I worried about it, then they just slide in like they've lived there all their lives."

"Sweetheart, if you weren't worrying about some such thing, you wouldn't be breathing."

"I hate that you're right about that. Anyway, there are still a few bumps regarding school. It's so hard being the new kids, but they like the house, and all that room. And they're crazy about David. You know David Wentworth?"

"Yeah. You could say he's been part of Roz's household since he was a kid, and now he runs it."

"He's great with the kids. It's a weight off knowing they're with someone they like after school. And I like Harper, though I don't see much of him."

"Boy's always been a loner. Happier with his plants. Good looking," he added.

"He is, Dad, but we'll just stick with discussing leaf-bud cuttings and cleft grafting, okay?"

"Can't blame a father for wanting to see his daughter settled."

"I am settled, for the moment." More, she realized, than she would have believed possible. "At some point, though, I'm going to want my own place. I'm not ready to look yet—too much to do, and I don't want to rock the boat with Roz. But it's on my list. Something in the same school district when the time comes. I don't want the boys to have to change again."

"You'll find what you're after. You always do."

"No point in finding what you're not after. But I've got time. Right now I'm up to my ears in reorganizing. That's probably an exaggeration. I'm up to my ears in organizing. Stock, paperwork, display areas."

"And having the time of your life."

She laughed, stretched out her arms and legs. "I really am. Oh, Dad, it's a terrific place, and there's so much untapped potential yet. I'd like to find somebody who has a real head for sales and customer relations, put him or her in charge of that area while I concentrate on rotating stock, keep ahead of the paperwork, and juggle in some of my ideas. I haven't even touched on the landscape area. Except for a head butt with the guy who runs that."

"Kitridge?" Will smiled. "Met him once or twice, I think. Hear he's a prickly sort."

"I'll say."

"Does good work. Roz wouldn't tolerate less, I can promise you. He did a property for a friend of mine about two years ago. Bought this old house, wanted to concentrate on rehabbing it. Grounds were a holy mess. He hired Kitridge for that. Showplace now. Got written up in a magazine."

"What's his story? Logan's?"

"Local boy. Born and bred. Though it seems to me he moved up north for a while. Got married."

"I didn't realize he's married."

"Was," Will corrected. "Didn't take. Don't know the details. Jo might. She's better at ferreting out and remembering that sort of thing. He's been back here six, eight years. Worked for a big firm out of the city until Roz scooped him up. Jo! What do you know about the Kitridge boy who works for Roz?"

"Logan?" Jolene peeked around the corner. She was wearing an apron that said, JO'S KITCHEN. There was a string of pearls around her neck and fuzzy pink slippers on her feet. "He's sexy."

"I don't think that's what Stella wanted to know."

"Well, she could see that for herself. Got eyes in her head and blood in her veins, doesn't she? His folks moved out to Montana, of all places, two, three years ago."

She cocked a hip, tapped a finger on her cheek as she lined up her data. "Got an older sister lives in Charlotte now. He went out with Marge Peters's girl, Terri, a couple times. You remember Terri, don't you, Will?"

"Can't say as I do."

"'Course you do. She was homecoming and prom queen in her day, then Miss Shelby County. First runner-up for Miss Tennessee. Most agree she missed the crown because her talent wasn't as strong as it could've been. Her voice is a little bit, what you'd call slight, I guess."

As Jo talked, Stella just sat back and enjoyed. Imagine knowing all this, or caring. She doubted she could remember who the homecoming or prom queens were from her own high school days. And here was Jo, casually pumping out the information on events that were surely a decade old.

Had to be a southern thing.

"And Terri? She said Logan was too serious-minded for

her," Jo continued, "but then a turnip would be too serious-minded for that girl."

She turned back into the kitchen, lifting her voice. "He married a Yankee and moved up to Philadelphia or Boston or some place with her. Moved back a couple years later without her. No kids."

She came back with a fresh mimosa for Stella and one for herself. "I heard she liked big-city life and he didn't, so they split up. Probably more to it than that. Always is, but Logan's not one to talk, so information is sketchy. He worked for Fosterly Landscaping for a while. You know, Will, they do mostly commercial stuff. Beautifying office buildings and shopping centers and so on. Word is Roz offered him the moon, most of the stars, and a couple of solar systems to bring him into her operation."

Will winked at his daughter. "Told you she'd have the details."

"And then some."

Jo chuckled, waved a hand. "He bought the old Morris place on the river a couple of years ago. Been fixing it up, or having it fixed up. *And* I heard he was doing a job for Tully Scopes. You don't know Tully, Will, but I'm on the garden committee with his wife, Mary. She'll complain the sky's too blue or the rain's too wet. Never satisfied with anything. You want another Bloody Mary, honey?" she asked Will.

"Can't say as I'd mind."

"So I heard Tully wanted Logan to design some shrubbery, and a garden and so on for this property he wanted to turn over."

Jolene kept on talking as she walked back to the kitchen counter to mix the drink. Stella exchanged a mile-wide grin with her father.

"And every blessed day, Tully was down there complaining, or asking for changes, or saying this, that, or the other. Until Logan told him to screw himself sideways, or words to that effect."

"So much for customer relations," Stella declared.

"Walked off the job, too," Jolene continued. "Wouldn't set foot on the property again or have any of his crew plant a daisy until Tully agreed to stay away. That what you wanted to know?"

"That pretty much covers it," Stella said and toasted Jolene with her mimosa.

"Good. Just about ready here. Why don't you go on and call the boys?"

WITH THE INFORMATION FROM JOLENE ENTERED INTO her mental files, Stella formulated a plan. Bright and early Monday morning, armed with her map and a set of MapQuest directions, she set out for the job site Logan had scheduled.

Or, she corrected, the job Roz thought he had earmarked for that morning.

She was going to be insanely pleasant, cooperative, and flexible. Until he saw things her way.

She cruised the neighborhood that skirted the city proper. Charming old houses, closer to each other than to the road. Lovely sloping lawns. Gorgeous old trees. Oak and maple that would leaf and shade, dogwood and Bradford pear that would celebrate spring with blooms. Of course, it wouldn't be the south without plenty of magnolias along with enormous azaleas and rhododendrons.

She tried to picture herself there, with her boys, living in one of those gracious homes, with her lovely yard to tend. Yes, she could see that, could see them happy in such a place, cozy with the neighbors, organizing dinner parties, play dates, cookouts.

Out of her price range, though. Even with the money she'd saved, the capital from the sale of the house in Michigan, she doubted she could afford real estate here. Besides, it would mean changing schools again for the boys, and she would have to spend time commuting to work.

Still, it made a sweet, if brief, fantasy.

She spotted Logan's truck and a second pickup outside a two-story brick house.

She could see immediately it wasn't as well kept as most of its neighbors. The front lawn was patchy. The foundation plantings desperately needed shaping, and what had been flower beds looked either overgrown or stone dead.

She heard the buzz of chain saws and country music playing too loud as she walked around the side of the house. Ivy was growing madly here, crawling its way up the brick. Should be stripped off, she thought. That maple needs to come down, before it falls down, and that fence line's covered with brambles, overrun with honeysuckle.

In the back, she spotted Logan, harnessed halfway up a dead oak. Wielding the chain saw, he speared through branches. It was cool, but the sun and the labor had a dew of sweat on his face, and a line of it darkening the back of his shirt.

Okay, so he was sexy. Any well-built man doing manual labor looked sexy. Add some sort of dangerous tool to the mix, and the image went straight to the lust bars and played a primal tune.

But sexy, she reminded herself, wasn't the point.

His work and their working dynamics were the point. She stood well out of the way while he worked, and scanned the rest of the backyard.

The space might have been lovely once, but now it was neglected, weedy, overgrown with trash trees and dying shrubs. A sagging garden shed tilted in the far corner of a fence smothered in vines.

Nearly a quarter of an acre, she estimated as she watched a huge black man drag lopped branches toward a short, skinny white man working a splitter. Nearby a burly-looking mulcher waited its turn to chew up the rest.

The beauty here wasn't lost, Stella decided. It was just buried.

It needed vision to bring it to life again.

Since the black man caught her eye, Stella wandered over to the ground crew.

"Help you, Miss?"

She extended her hand and a smile. "I'm Stella Rothchild, Ms. Harper's manager."

"'Meetcha. I'm Sam, this here is Dick."

The little guy had the fresh, freckled face of a twelve-year-old, with a scraggly goatee that looked as if it might have grown there by mistake. "Heard about you." He sent an eyebrow-wiggling grin toward her coworker.

"Really?" She kept her tone friendly, though her teeth came together tight in the smile. "I thought it would be helpful if I dropped by a couple of the jobs, looked at the work." She scanned the yard again, deliberately keeping her gaze below Logan's perch in the tree. "You've certainly got yours cut out for you with this."

"Got a mess of clearing to do," Sam agreed. Covered with work gloves, his enormous hands settled on his hips. "Seen worse, though."

"Is there a projection on man-hours?"

"Pro*jec*tion." Dick sniggered and elbowed Sam.

From his great height, Sam sent down a pitying look.

"You want to know about the plans and, uh, projections," he said, "you need to talk to the boss. He's got all that worked up."

"All right, then. Thanks. I'll let you get back to work."

Walking away, Stella took the little camera out of her bag and began to take what she thought of as "before" pictures.

HE KNEW SHE WAS THERE. STANDING DOWN THERE all pressed and tidy with her wild hair pulled back and shaded glasses hiding her big blue eyes.

He'd wondered when she would come nag him on a job, as it appeared to him she was a woman born to nag. At least she had the sense not to interrupt.

Then again, she seemed to be nothing *but* sense.

Maybe she'd surprise him. He liked surprises, and he'd gotten one when he met her kids. He'd expected to see a couple of polite little robots. The sort that looked to their domineering mother before saying a word. Instead he'd found them normal, interesting, funny kids. Surely it took some imagination to manage two active boys.

Maybe she was only a pain in the ass when it came to work.

Well, he grinned a little as he cut through a branch. So was he.

He let her wait while he finished. It took him another thirty minutes, during which he largely ignored her. Though he did see her take a camera—Jesus—then a notebook out of her purse.

He also noticed she'd gone over to speak to his men and that Dick sent occasional glances in Stella's direction.

Dick was a social moron, Logan thought, particularly when it came to women. But he was a tireless worker, and he would take on the filthiest job with a blissful and idiotic grin. Sam, who had more common sense in his big toe than Dick had in his entire skinny body, was, thank God, a tolerant and patient man.

They went back to high school, and that was the sort of thing that set well with Logan. The continuity of it, and the fact that because they'd known each other around twenty years, they didn't have to gab all the damn time to make themselves understood.

Explaining things half a dozen times just tried his patience. Which he had no problem admitting he had in short supply to begin with.

Between the three of them, they did good work, often exceptional work. And with Sam's brawn and Dick's energy, he rarely had to take on any more laborers.

Which suited him. He preferred small crews to large. It was more personal that way, at least from his point of view. And in Logan's point of view, every job he took was personal.

It was his vision, his sweat, his blood that went into the land. And his name that stood for what he created with it.

The Yankee could harp about forms and systemic bullshit all she wanted. The land didn't give a rat's ass about that. And neither did he.

He called out a warning to his men, then topped the old, dead oak. When he shimmied down, he unhooked his harness and grabbed a bottle of water. He drank half of it down without taking a breath.

"Mr. . . ." No, friendly, Stella remembered. She boosted up her smile, and started over. "Nice job. I didn't realize you did the tree work yourself."

"Depends. Nothing tricky to this one. Out for a drive?"

"No, though I did enjoy looking at the neighborhood. It's beautiful." She looked around the yard, gestured to encompass it. "This must have been, too, once. What happened?"

"Couple lived here fifty years. He died a while back. She couldn't handle the place on her own, and none of their kids still live close by. She got sick, place got rundown. She got sicker. Kids finally got her out and into a nursing home."

"That's hard. It's sad."

"Yeah, a lot of life is. They sold the place. New owners got a bargain and want the grounds done up. We're doing them up."

"What've you got in mind?"

He took another slug from the water bottle. She noticed the mulcher had stopped grinding, and after Logan sent a long, narrowed look over her shoulder, it got going again.

"I've got a lot of things in mind."

"Dealing with this job, specifically?"

"Why?"

"Because it'll help me do my job if I know more about yours. Obviously you're taking out the oak and I assume the maple out front."

"Yeah. Okay, here's the deal. We clear everything out that can't or shouldn't be saved. New sod, new fencing. We knock down the old shed, replace it. New owners want lots of color. So we shape up the azaleas, put a weeping cherry out front, replacing the maple. Lilac over there, and a magnolia on that side. Plot of peonies on that side, rambling roses along the back fence. See they got that rough little hill toward the back there, on the right? Instead of leveling it, we'll plant it."

He outlined the rest of it quickly, rolling out Latin terms and common names, taking long slugs from his water bottle, gesturing.

He could see it, he always could—the finished land. The small details, the big ones, fit together into one attractive whole.

Just as he could see the work that would go into each and every step, as he could look forward to the process nearly as much as the finished job.

He liked having his hands in the dirt. How else could you respect the landscape or the changes you made in it? And as he spoke he glanced down at her hands. Smirked a little at her tidy fingernails with their coat of glossy pink polish.

Paper pusher, he thought. Probably didn't know crabgrass from sumac.

Because he wanted to give her and her clipboard the full treatment and get her off his ass, he switched to the house and talked about the patio they intended to build and the plantings he'd use to accent it.

When he figured he'd done more talking than he normally did in a week, he finished off the water. Shrugged. He didn't expect her to follow everything he'd said, but she couldn't complain that he hadn't cooperated.

"It's wonderful. What about the bed running on the south side out front?"

He frowned a little. "We'll rip out the ivy, then the clients want to try their hand at that themselves."

"Even better. You've got more of an investment if you dig some yourself."

Because he agreed, he said nothing and only jingled some change in his pocket.

"Except I'd rather see winter creeper than yews around the shed. The variegated leaves would show off well, as would the less uniform shape."

"Maybe."

"Do you work from a landscape blueprint or out of your head?"

"Depends."

Should I pull all his teeth at once, or one at a time, she thought, but maintained the smile. "It's just that I'd like to see one of your designs, on paper, at some point. Which leads me to a thought I'd had."

"Bet you got lots of them."

"My boss told me to play nice," she said, coolly now. "How about you?"

He moved his shoulder again. "Just saying."

"My thought was, with some of the reorganizing and transferring I'm doing, I could cull out some office space for you at the center."

He gave her the same look he'd sent his men over her shoulder. A lesser woman, Stella told herself, would wither under it. "I don't work in a frigging office."

"I'm not suggesting that you spend all your time there, just that you'd have a place to deal with your paperwork, make your phone calls, keep your files."

"That's what my truck's for."

"Are you trying to be difficult?"

"Nope. I can do it without any effort at all. How about you?"

"You don't want the office, fine. Forget the office."

"I already have."

"Dandy. But *I* need an office. *I* need to know exactly what stock and equipment, what materials you'll need for this job." She yanked out her notebook again. "One red maple, one magnolia. Which variety of magnolia?"

"Southern. *Grandiflora gloriosa*."

"Good choice for the location. One weeping cherry," she continued, and to his surprise and reluctant admiration, she ran down the entire plan he'd tossed out at her.

Okay, Red, he thought. Maybe you know a thing or two about the horticulture end of things after all.

"Yews or winter creeper?"

He glanced back at the shed, tried both out in his head. Damn if he didn't think she was right, but he didn't see why he had to say so right off. "I'll let you know."

"Do, and I'll want the exact number and specimen type of other stock as you take them."

"I'd be able to find you . . . in your office?"

"Just find me." She turned around, started to march off.

"Hey, Stella."

When she glanced back, he grinned. "Always wanted to say that."

Her eyes lit, and she snapped her head around again and kept going.

"Okay, okay. Jesus. Just a little humor." He strode after her. "Don't go away mad."

"Just go away?"

"Yeah, but there's no point in us being pissed at each other. I don't mind being pissed as a rule."

"I never would've guessed."

"But there's no point, right at the moment." As if he'd just remembered he had them on, he tugged off his work gloves, stuck them finger-first in his back pocket. "I'm doing my job, you're doing yours. Roz thinks she needs you, and I set a lot of store by Roz."

"So do I."

"I get that. Let's try to stay out from under each other's skin, otherwise we're just going to give each other a rash."

She inclined her head, lifted her eyebrows. "Is this you being agreeable?"

"Pretty much, yeah. I'm being agreeable so we can both do what Roz pays us to do. And because your kid has a copy of *Spider-Man* Number 121. If you're mad, you won't let him show it to me."

Now she tipped down her sunglasses, peered at him over the tops. "This isn't you being charming, is it?"

"No, this is me being sincere. I really want to see that issue, firsthand. If I was being charming, I guarantee you'd be in a puddle at my feet. It's a terrible power I have over women, and I try to use it sparingly."

"I just bet."

But she was smiling as she got into her car.

SIX

HAYLEY PHILLIPS WAS RIDING ON FUMES AND A DYING transmission. The radio still worked, thank God, and she had it cranked up with the Dixie Chicks blasting out. It kept her energy flowing.

Everything she owned was jammed into the Pontiac Grandville, which was older than she was and a lot more temperamental. Not that she had much at this point. She'd sold everything that could be sold. No point in being sentimental. Money took you a lot more miles than sentiment.

She wasn't destitute. What she'd banked would get her through the rough spots, and if there were more rough spots than she anticipated, she'd earn more. She wasn't aimless. She knew just where she was going. She just didn't know what would happen when she got there.

But that was fine. If you knew everything, you'd never be surprised.

Maybe she was tired, and maybe she'd pushed the rattling old car farther than it wanted to go that day. But if she and it could just hang on a few more miles, they'd get a break.

She didn't expect to get tossed out on her ear. But, well, if she was, she'd just do what needed to be done next.

She liked the look of the area, especially since she'd skirted around the tangle of highways that surrounded Memphis. On this north edge beyond the city, the land rolled a bit, and she'd seen snatches of the river and the steep bluffs that fell toward it. There were pretty houses—the neat spread of the suburbs that fanned out from the city limits, and now the bigger, richer ones. There were plenty of big old trees, and despite some walls of stone or brick, it *felt* friendly.

She sure could use a friend.

When she saw the sign for In the Garden, she slowed. She was afraid to stop, afraid the old Pontiac would just heave up and die if she did. But she slowed enough to get a look at the main buildings, the space in the security lights.

Then she took a lot of slow breaths as she kept driving. Nearly there. She'd planned out what she would say, but she kept changing her mind. Every new approach gave her a dozen different scenes to play out in her head. It had passed the time, but it hadn't gelled for her.

Maybe some could say that changing her mind was part of her problem. But she didn't think so. If you never changed your mind, what was the point of having one? It seemed to Hayley she'd known too many people who were stuck with one way of thinking, and how could that be using the brain God gave you?

As she headed toward the drive, the car began to buck and sputter.

"Come on, come on. Just a little more. If I'd been paying attention I'd've got you gas at the last place."

Then it conked on her, half in, half out of the entrance between the brick pillars.

She gave the wheel a testy little slap, but it was half-hearted. Nobody's fault but her own, after all. And maybe it was a good thing. Tougher to kick her out if her car was out of gas, and blocking the way.

She opened her purse, took out a brush to tidy her hair. After considerable experimentation, she'd settled back on her own oak-bark brown. At least for now. She was glad she'd gotten it cut and styled before she'd headed out. She liked the longish sweep of side bangs and the careless look of the straight bob with its varying lengths.

It made her look easy, breezy. Confident.

She put on lipstick, powdered off the shine.

"Okay. Let's get going."

She climbed out, hooked her purse over her shoulder, then started the walk up the long drive. It took money—old or new—to plant a house so far from the road. The one she'd grown up in had been so close, people driving by could practically reach out and shake her hand.

But she didn't mind that. It had been a nice house. A good house, and part of her had been sorry to sell it. But that little house outside Little Rock was the past. She was heading toward the future.

Halfway up the drive, she stopped. Blinked. This wasn't just a house, she decided as her jaw dropped. It was a mansion. The sheer size of it was one thing—she'd seen big-ass houses before, but nothing like this. This was the most beautiful house she'd ever laid eyes on outside of a magazine. It was Tara and Manderley all in one. Graceful and *female*, and strong.

Lights gleamed against windows, others flooded the lawn. As if it were welcoming her. Wouldn't that be nice?

Even if it wasn't, even if they booted her out again, she'd had the chance to see it. That alone was worth the trip.

She walked on, smelling the evening, the pine and woodsmoke.

She crossed her fingers on the strap of her purse for luck and walked straight up to the ground-level doors.

Lifting one of the brass knockers, she gave three firm raps.

Inside, Stella came down the steps with Parker. It was her turn to walk him. She called out, "I'll get it."

Parker was already barking as she opened the door.

She saw a girl with straight, fashionably ragged brown hair, a sharply angled face dominated by huge eyes the color of a robin's egg. She smiled, showing a bit of an overbite, and bent down to pet Parker when he sniffed at her shoes.

She said, "Hi."

"Hi." Where the hell had she come from? Stella wondered. There was no car parked outside.

The girl looked to be about twelve. And very pregnant.

"I'm looking for Rosalind Ashby. Rosalind Harper Ashby," she corrected. "Is she home?"

"Yes. She's upstairs. Come in."

"Thanks. I'm Hayley." She held out a hand. "Hayley Phillips. Mrs. Ashby and I are cousins, in a complicated southern sort of way."

"Stella Rothchild. Why don't you come in, sit down. I'll go find Roz."

"That'd be great." Swiveling her head back and forth, Hayley tried to see everything as Stella led her into the parlor. "Wow. You've just got to say wow."

"I did the first time I saw it. Do you want anything? Something to drink?"

"I'm okay. I should probably wait until . . ." She stayed on her feet, wandered to the fireplace. It was like something on a television show, or the movies. "Do you work in the house? Are you, like, the housekeeper?"

"No. I work at Roz's nursery. I'm the manager. I'll just go get Roz. You should sit down."

"It's okay." Hayley rubbed her pregnant belly. "We've been sitting."

"Be right back." With Parker in tow, Stella dashed off.

She hurried up the stairs, turned into Roz's wing. She'd only been in there once, when David had taken her on the grand tour, but she followed the sounds of the television and found Roz in her sitting room.

There was an old black-and-white movie on TV. Not that Roz was watching. She sat at an antique secretary, wearing baggy jeans and a sweatshirt as she sketched on a pad. Her feet were bare, and to Stella's surprise, her toenails were painted a bright candy pink.

She knocked on the doorjamb.

"Hmm? Oh, Stella, good. I was just sketching out an idea I had for a cutting garden along the northwest side of the nursery. Thought it might inspire customers. Come take a look."

"I'd love to, but there's someone downstairs to see you. Hayley Phillips. She says she's your cousin."

"Hayley?" Roz frowned. "I don't have a cousin Hayley. Do I?"

"She's young. Looks like a teenager. Pretty. Brown hair, blue eyes, taller than me. She's pregnant."

"Well, for God's sake." Roz rubbed the back of her neck. "Phillips. Phillips. My first husband's grandmother's sister—or maybe it was cousin—married a Phillips. I think."

"Well, she did say you were cousins in a complicated southern sort of way."

"Phillips." She closed her eyes, tapped a finger in the center of her forehead as if to wake up memory. "She must be Wayne Phillips's girl. He died last year. Well, I'd better go see what this is about."

She got up. "Your boys settled down for the night?"

"Yes, just."

"Then come on with me."

"Don't you think you should—"

"You've got a good level head. So come on, bring it with you."

Stella scooped Parker up and, hoping his bladder would hold, went downstairs with Roz.

Hayley turned as they came in. "I think this is the most completely awesome room. It makes you feel cozy and special just to be in it. I'm Hayley. I'm Wayne Phillips's daughter. My daddy was a connection of your first husband's, on his mother's side. You sent me a very nice note of condolence when he passed last year."

"I remember. I met him once. I liked him."

"So did I. I'm sorry to come this way, without calling or asking, and I didn't mean to get here so late. I had some car trouble earlier."

"That's all right. Sit down, Hayley. How far along are you?"

"Heading toward six months. The baby's due end of May. I should apologize, too, because my car ran out of gas right at the front of your driveway."

"We can take care of that. Are you hungry, Hayley? Would you like a little something to eat?"

"No, ma'am, I'm fine. I stopped to eat earlier. Forgot to feed the car. I have money. I don't want you to think I'm broke or here for a handout."

"Good to know. We should have tea, then. It's a cool night. Hot tea would be good."

"If it's not too much trouble. And if you've got decaffeinated." She stroked her belly. "Hardest thing about being pregnant's been giving up caffeine."

"I'll take care of it. Won't be long."

"Thanks, Stella." Roz turned back to Hayley as Stella went out. "So, did you drive all the way from . . . Little Rock, isn't it?"

"I did. I like to drive. Like to better when the car's not acting up, but you have to do what you have to do." She cleared her throat. "I hope you've been well, Cousin Rosalind."

"I have been, very well. And you? Are you and the baby doing well?"

"We're doing great. Healthy as horses, so the doctor said. And I feel just fine. Feel like I'm getting big as a house, but I don't mind that, or not so much. It's kind of interesting. Um, your children, your sons? They're doing fine?"

"Yes, they are. Grown now. Harper, that's my oldest, lives here in the guest house. He works with me at the nursery."

"I saw it—the nursery—when I was driving in." Hayley

caught herself rubbing her hands on the thighs of her jeans and made herself stop. "It looks so big, bigger than I expected. You must be proud."

"I am. What do you do back in Little Rock?"

"I worked in a bookstore, was helping manage it by the time I left. A small independent bookstore and coffee shop."

"Managed? At your age?"

"I'm twenty-four. I know I don't look it," she said with a hint of a smile. "I don't mind that, either. But I can show you my driver's license. I went to college, on partial scholarship. I've got a good brain. I worked summers there through high school and college. I got the job initially because my daddy was friends with the owner. But I earned it after."

"You said managed. You don't work there now."

"No." She was listening, Hayley thought. She was asking the right questions. That was something. "I resigned a couple of weeks ago. But I have a letter of recommendation from the owner. I'd decided to leave Little Rock."

"It seems a difficult time to leave home, and a job you're secure in."

"It seemed like the right time to me." She looked over as Stella wheeled in a tea cart. "Now *that* is just like the movies. I know saying that makes me sound like a hick or something, but I can't help it."

Stella laughed. "I was thinking exactly the same as I loaded it up. I made chamomile."

"Thanks. Stella, Hayley was just telling me she's left her home and her job. I'm hoping she's going to tell us why she thinks this was the right time to make a couple of drastic moves."

"Not drastic," Hayley corrected. "Just big. And I made them because of the baby. Well, because of both of us. You've probably figured out I'm not married."

"Your family isn't supportive?" Stella asked.

"My mother took off when I was about five. You may not remember that," she said to Roz. "Or you were too polite to mention it. My daddy died last year. I've got aunts and uncles, a pair of grandmothers left, and cousins. Some are still in the Little Rock area. Opinion is . . . mixed about my current situation. Thanks," she added after Roz had poured out and offered her a cup.

"Well, the thing is, I was awfully sad when Daddy passed. He got hit by a car, crossing the street. Just one of those accidents that you can never understand and that, well, just don't seem right. I didn't have time to prepare for it. I guess you never do. But he was just gone, in a minute."

She drank tea and felt it soothe her right down to the bones she hadn't realized were so tired. "I was sad, and mad and lonely. And there was this guy. It wasn't a one-night stand or anything like that. We liked each other. He used to come in the bookstore, flirt with me. I used to flirt back. When I was alone, he was comforting. He was sweet. Anyway, one thing led to another. He's a law student. Then he went back to school, and a few weeks later, I found out I was pregnant. I didn't know what I was going to do. How I was going to tell him. Or anybody. I put it off for a few more weeks. I didn't know what I was going to do."

"And when you did?"

"I thought I should tell him face-to-face. He hadn't been coming into the store like he used to. So I went by the college to look him up. Turned out he'd fallen in love with this girl. He was a little embarrassed to tell me, seeing as we'd been sleeping together. But it wasn't like we'd made each other any promises, or been in love or anything. We'd just liked each other, that's all. And when he talked about this other girl, he got all lit up. You could just see how crazy he was about her. So I didn't tell him about the baby."

She hesitated, then took one of the cookies Stella had arranged on a plate. "I can't resist sweets. After I'd thought about it, I didn't see how telling him would do any of us any good."

"That was a very hard decision," Roz told her.

"I don't know that it was. I don't know what I expected

him to do when I went to tell him, except I thought he had a right to know. I didn't want to marry him or anything. I wasn't even sure, back that far, that I was going to keep the baby."

She nibbled on the cookie while she rubbed a hand gently over the mound of her belly. "I guess that's one of the reasons I went out there, to talk to him. Not just to tell him about it, but to see what he thought we should do. But sitting with him, listening to him go on about this girl—"

She stopped, shook her head. "I needed to decide what to do about it. All telling him would've done was made him feel bad, or resentful or scared. Mess up his life when all he'd really tried to do was help me through a bad time."

"And that left you alone," Stella pointed out.

"If I'd told him, I still would've been alone. The thing is, when I decided I'd keep the baby, I thought about telling him again, and asked some people how he was doing. He was still with that girl, and they were talking about getting married, so I think I did the right thing. Still, once I started to show, there was a lot of gossip and questions, a lot of looks and whispers. And I thought, What we need is a fresh start. So I sold the house and just about everything in it. And here I am."

"Looking for that fresh start," Roz concluded.

"I'm looking for a job." She paused, moistened her lips. "I know how to work. I also know a lot of people would step back from hiring a woman nearly six months along. Family, even distant, through-marriage sort of family, might be a little more obliging."

She cleared her throat when Roz said nothing. "I studied literature and business in college. I graduated with honors. I've got a solid employment record. I've got money—not a lot. My partial scholarship didn't cover everything, and my daddy was a teacher, so he didn't make much. But I've got enough to take care of myself, to pay rent, buy food, pay for this baby. I need a job, any kind of a job for now. You've got your business, you've got this house. It takes a lot of people to help run those. I'm asking for a chance to be one of them."

"Know anything about plants, about gardening?"

"We put in flower beds every year. Daddy and I split the yard work. And what I don't know, I can learn. I learn quick."

"Wouldn't you rather work in a bookstore? Hayley managed an independent bookstore back home," Roz told Stella.

"You don't own a bookstore," Hayley pointed out. "I'll work without pay for two weeks."

"Someone works for me, she gets paid. I'll be hiring the seasonal help in a few weeks. In the meantime . . . Stella, can you use her?"

"Ah . . ." Was she supposed to look at that young face and bulging belly and say no? "What were your responsibilities as manager?"

"I wasn't, like, officially the manager. But that's what I did, when you come down to it. It was a small operation, so I did some of everything. Inventory, buying, customer relations, scheduling, sales, advertising. Just the bookstore end of it. There was a separate staff for the coffee shop."

"What would you say were your strengths?"

She had to take a breath, calm her nerves. She knew it was vital to be clear and concise. And just as vital to her pride not to beg. "Customer relations, which keyed into sales. I'm good with people, and I don't mind taking the extra time you need to take to make sure they get what they want. If your customers are happy, they come back, and they buy. You take the extra steps, personalize service, you get customer loyalty."

Stella nodded. "And your weaknesses?"

"The buying," she said without hesitation. "I'd just want to buy everything if it was up to me. I had to keep reminding myself whose money I was spending. But sometimes I didn't hear myself."

"We're in the process of reorganizing, and some

expanding. I could use some help getting the new system in place. There's still a lot of computer inputting—some of it very tedious—to deal with."

"I can handle a keyboard. PC and Mac."

"We'll go for the two weeks," Roz decided. "You'll get paid, but we'll consider the two weeks a trial balloon for all of us. If it doesn't work out, I'll do what I can to help you find another job."

"Can't say fairer than that. Thanks, Cousin Rosalind."

"Just Roz. We've got some gas out in the shed. I'll go get it, and we'll get your car up here so you can get your things in."

"In? In here?" Shaking her head, Hayley set her cup aside. "I said I wasn't after a handout. I appreciate the job, the chance at the job. I don't expect you to put me up."

"Family, even distant-through-marriage family, is welcome here. And it'll give us all a chance to get to know each other, to see if we're going to suit."

"You live here?" Hayley asked Stella.

"Yes. And my boys—eight and six. They're upstairs asleep."

"Are we cousins?"

"No."

"I'll get the gas." Roz got to her feet and started out.

"I'll pay rent." Hayley rose as well, instinctively laying a hand on her belly. "I pay my way."

"We'll adjust your salary to compensate for it."

When she was alone with Stella, Hayley let out a long, slow breath. "I thought she'd be older. And scarier. Though I bet she can be plenty scary when she needs to. You can't have what she has, and keep it, grow it, without knowing how to be scary."

"You're right. I can be scary, too, when it comes to work."

"I'll remember. Ah, you're from up north?"

"Yes. Michigan."

"That's a long way. Is it just you and your boys?"

"My husband died about two and a half years ago."

"That's hard. It's hard to lose somebody you love. I guess all three of us know about that. I think it can make *you* hard if you don't have something, someone else to love. I've got the baby."

"Do you know if it's a boy or a girl?"

"No. Baby had its back turned during the sonogram." She started to chew on her thumbnail, then tucked the thumb in her fist and lowered it. "I guess I should go out, take the gas Roz is getting."

"I'll go with you. We'll take care of it together."

In an hour they had Hayley settled in one of the guest rooms in the west wing. She knew she gawked. She knew she babbled. But she'd never seen a more beautiful room, had never expected to be in one. Much less to be able to call it her own, even temporarily.

She put away her things, running her fingers over the gleaming wood of the bureau, the armoire, the etched-glass lampshades, the carving of the headboard.

She would earn this. That was a promise she made to herself, and her child, as she indulged in a long, warm bath. She would earn the chance she'd been given and would pay Roz back in labor and in loyalty.

She was good at both.

She dried off, then rubbed oil over her belly, her breasts. She wasn't afraid of childbirth—she knew how to work hard toward a goal. But she was really hoping she could avoid stretch marks.

She felt a little chill and slipped hurriedly into her nightshirt. Just at the edge of the mirror, just at the corner of her vision, she caught a shadow, a movement.

Rubbing her arms warm, she stepped through to the bedroom. There was nothing, and the door was closed, as she'd left it.

Dog-tired, she told herself and rubbed her eyes. It had been a long trip from the past to the verge of the future.

She took one of the books she'd had in her suitcase—the

rest, ones she hadn't been able to bring herself to sell, were still packed in the trunk of her car—and slipped into bed.

She opened it to where she'd left it bookmarked, prepared to settle herself down, as she did most nights, with an hour of reading.

And was asleep with the light burning before she'd finished the first page.

AT ROZ'S REQUEST, STELLA ONCE AGAIN WENT INTO her sitting room and sat. Roz poured them each a glass of wine.

"Honest impression?" she asked.

"Young, bright, proud. Honest. She could have spun us a sob story about being betrayed by the baby's father, begged for a place to stay, used her pregnancy as an excuse for all manner of things. Instead she took responsibility and asked to work. I'll still check her references."

"Of course. She seemed fearless about the baby."

"It's after you have them you learn to be afraid of everything."

"Isn't that the truth?" Roz scooped her fingers through her hair twice. "I'll make a few calls, find out a little more about that part of the Ashby family. I honestly don't remember very well. We never had much contact, even when he was alive. I do remember the scandal when the wife took off, left him with the baby. From the impression she made on me, and you, apparently he managed very well."

"Her managerial experience could be a real asset."

"Another manager." Roz, in a gesture Stella took as only half mocking, cast her eyes to heaven. "Pray for me."

seven

IT DIDN'T TAKE TWO WEEKS. AFTER TWO DAYS, STELLA decided Hayley was going to be the answer to her personal prayer. Here was someone with youth, energy, and enthusiasm who understood and appreciated efficiency in the workplace.

She knew how to read and generate spreadsheets, understood instructions after one telling, and respected color codes. If she was half as good relating to customers as she was with filing systems, she would be a jewel.

When it came to plants, she didn't know much more than the basic this is a geranium, and this is a pansy. But she could be taught.

Stella was already prepared to beg Roz to offer Hayley part-time work when May got closer.

"Hayley?" Stella poked her head in the now efficient and tidy office. "Why don't you come out with me? We've got nearly an hour before we open. We'll have a lesson on shade plants in Greenhouse Number Three."

"Cool. We're input through the H's in perennials. I don't know what half of them are, but I'm doing some reading up at night. I didn't know sunflowers were called Helia . . . wait. Helianthus."

"It's more that Helianthus are called sunflowers. The perennial ones can be divided in spring, or propagated by seeds—in the spring—or cuttings in late spring. Seeds from annual Helianthus can be harvested—from that big brown eye—in late summer or early fall. Though the cultivars hybridize freely, they may not come true from the seeds collected. And I'm lecturing."

"That's okay. I grew up with a teacher. I like to learn."

As they passed through the counter area, Hayley glanced out the window. "Truck just pulled in over by the . . . what do y'all call them? Pavers," she said before Stella could answer. "And, mmmm, just *look* at what's getting out of that truck. Mister tall, dark, and totally *built*. Who's the hunk?"

Struggling not to frown, Stella lifted a shoulder in a shrug. "That would be Logan Kitridge, Roz's landscape designer. I suppose he does score fairly high on the hunk-o-meter."

"Rings my bell." At Stella's expression, Hayley pressed a hand to her belly and laughed. "I'm pregnant. Still have all working parts, though. And just because I'm not looking for a man doesn't mean I don't want to look at one. Especially when he's yummy. He really is all tough and broody-looking, isn't he? What is it about tough, broody-looking men that gives you that tickle down in the belly?"

"I couldn't say. What's he doing over there?"

"Looks like he's loading pavers. If it wasn't so cool, he'd pull off that jacket. Bet we'd get a real muscle show. God, I do love my eye candy."

"That sort'll give you cavities," Stella mumbled. "He's not scheduled for pavers. He hasn't put in the order for pavers. Damn it!"

Hayley's eyebrows shot up as Stella stomped to the door and slammed out. Then she pressed her nose to the window, prepared to watch the show.

"Excuse me?"

"Uh-huh?" Hayley's answer was absent as she tried to get a better look outside. Then she popped back from the window, remembering spying was one thing, getting caught at it another. She turned, put on an innocent smile. And decided she'd gotten a double serving of eye candy.

This one wasn't big and broody, but sort of lanky and dreamy. And hot damn. It took an extra beat for her brain to engage, but she was quick.

"Hey! You must be Harper. You look just like your mama. I didn't get a chance to meet you yet, 'cause you never seemed to be around wherever I was around. Or whenever. I'm Hayley. Cousin Hayley from Little Rock? Maybe your mama told you I was working here now."

"Yeah. Yeah." He couldn't think of anything else. Could barely think at all. He felt lightning-struck and stupid.

"Do you just *love* working here? I do already. There's so much of everything, and the customers are so friendly. And Stella, she's just amazing, that's all. Your mama's like, I don't know, a goddess, for giving me a chance this way."

"Yeah." He winced. Could he *be* any more lame? "They're great. It's great." Apparently he could. And damn it, he was good with women. Usually. But one look at this one had given him some sort of concussion. "You, ah, do you need anything?"

"No." She gave him a puzzled smile. "I thought you did."

"I need something? What?"

"I don't know." She laid a hand on the fascinating mound of her belly and laughed, all throaty and free. "You're the one who came in."

"Right. Right. No, nothing. Now. Later. I've got to get back." Outside, in the air, where he should be able to breathe again.

"It was nice meeting you, Harper."

"You, too." He glanced back as he retreated and saw she was already back at the window.

* * *

OUTSIDE, STELLA SPED ACROSS THE PARKING AREA. She called out twice, and the second time got a quick glance and an absent wave. Building up steam as she went, she pumped it out the minute she reached the stacks of pavers.

"What do you think you're doing?"

"Playing tennis. What does it look like I'm doing?"

"It looks like you're taking material you haven't ordered, that you haven't been authorized to take."

"Really?" He hauled up another stack. "No wonder my backhand is rusty." The truck shuddered as he loaded. "Hey."

Much to her amazement, he leaned toward her, sniffed. "Different shampoo. Nice."

"Stop smelling me." She waved him away by flapping a hand at his chin as she stepped back.

"I can't help it. You're standing right there. I have a nose."

"I need the paperwork on this material."

"Yeah, yeah, yeah. Fine, fine, fine. I'll come in and take care of it after I'm loaded."

"You're supposed to take care of it *before* you load."

He turned, aimed a hot look with those mossy green eyes. "Red, you're a pain in the ass."

"I'm supposed to be. I'm the manager."

He had to smile at that, and he tipped down his sunglasses to look over them at her. "You're real good at it, too. Think of it this way. The pavers are stored on the way to the building. By loading first, then coming in, I'm actually being more efficient."

The smile morphed into a smirk. "That'd be important, I'd think, if we were doing, say, a projection of manhours."

He took a moment to lean against the truck and study her. Then he loaded another stack of pavers. "You standing here watching me means you're wasting time, and likely adding to your own man-hours."

"You don't come in to handle the paperwork, Kitridge, I'll hunt you down."

"Don't tempt me."

He took his time, but he came in.

He was calculating how best to annoy Stella again. Her eyes went the color of Texas bluebonnets when she was pissed off. But when he stepped in, he saw Hayley.

"Hey."

"Hey," she said back and smiled. "I'm Hayley Phillips. A family connection to Roz's first husband? I'm working here now."

"Logan. Nice to meet you. Don't let this Yankee scare you." He nodded toward Stella. "Where are the sacred forms, and the ritual knife so I can slice open a vein and sign them in blood?"

"My office."

"Uh-huh." But he lingered rather than following her. "When's the baby due?" he asked Hayley.

"May."

"Feeling okay?"

"Never better."

"Good. This here's a nice outfit, a good place to work *most* of the time. Welcome aboard." He sauntered into Stella's office, where she was already at her computer, with the form on the screen.

"I'll type this one up to save time. There's a whole stack of them in that folder. Take it. All you have to do is fill them in as needed, date, sign or initial. Drop them off."

"Uh-huh." He looked around the room. The desk was cleared off. There were no cartons, no books sitting on the floor or stacked on chairs.

That was too bad, he thought. He'd liked the workaday chaos of it.

"Where's all the stuff in here?"

"Where it belongs. Those pavers were the eighteen-inch round, number A-23?"

"They were eighteen-inch rounds." He picked up the framed photo on her desk and studied the picture of her boys and their dog. "Cute."

"Yes, they are. Are the pavers for personal use or for a scheduled job?"

"Red, you ever loosen up?"

"No. We Yankees never do."

He ran his tongue over his teeth. "Um-hmm."

"Do you know how *sick* I am of being referred to as 'the Yankee,' as though it were a foreign species, or a disease? Half the customers who come in here look me over like I'm from another planet and may not be coming in peace. Then I have to tell them I was born here, answer all sorts of questions about why I left, why I'm back, who my *people* are, for Christ's sake, before I can get down to any sort of business. I'm from Michigan, not the moon, and the Civil damn War's been over for quite some time."

Yep, just like Texas bluebonnets. "That would be the War Between the damn States this side of the Mason-Dixon, honey. And looks to me like you loosen up just fine when you get riled enough."

"Don't 'honey' me in that southern-fried twang."

"You know, Red, I like you better this way."

"Oh, shut up. Pavers. Personal or professional use?"

"Well, that depends on your point of view." Since there was room now, he edged a hip onto the corner of the desk. "They're for a friend. I'm putting in a walkway for her—my own time, no labor charge. I told her I'd pick up the materials and give her a bill from the center."

"We'll consider that personal use and apply your employee discount." She began tapping keys. "How many pavers?"

"Twenty-two."

She tapped again and gave him the price per paver, before discount, after discount.

Impressed despite himself, he tapped the monitor. "You got a math nerd trapped in there?"

"Just the wonders of the twenty-first century. You'd find it quicker than counting on your fingers."

"I don't know. I've got pretty fast fingers." Drumming them on his thigh, he kept his gaze on her face. "I need three white pine."

"For this same *friend*?"

"No." His grin flashed, fast and crooked. If she wanted to interpret "friend" as "lover," he couldn't see any point in saying the pavers were for Mrs. Kingsley, his tenth-grade English teacher. "Pine's for a client. Roland Guppy. Yes, like the fish. You've probably got him somewhere in your vast and mysterious files. We did a job for him last fall."

Since there was a coffeemaker on the table against the wall, and the pot was half full, he got up, took a mug, and helped himself.

"Make yourself at home," Stella said dryly.

"Thanks. As it happens, I recommended white pine for a windbreak. He hemmed and hawed. Took him this long to decide to go for it. He called me at home yesterday. I said I'd pick them up and work him in."

"We need a different form."

He sampled the coffee. Not bad. "Somehow I knew that."

"Are the pavers all you're taking for personal use?"

"Probably. For today."

She hit Print, then brought up another form. "That's three white pine. What size?"

"We got some nice eight-foot ones."

"Balled and burlapped?"

"Yeah."

Tap, tap, tap, he thought, with wonder, and there you go. Woman had pretty fingers, he noted. Long and tapered, with that glossy polish on them, the delicate pink of the inside of a rose petal.

She wore no rings.

"Anything else?"

He patted his pockets, eventually came up with a scrap of paper. "That's what I told him I could put them in for."

She added the labor, totaled, then printed out three copies while he drank her coffee. "Sign or initial," she told him. "One copy for my files, one for yours, one for the client."

"Gotcha."

When he picked up the pen, Stella waved a hand. "Oh, wait, let me get that knife. Which vein did you plan to open?"

"Cute." He lifted his chin toward the door. "So's she."

"Hayley? Yeah, she is. And entirely too young for you."

"I wouldn't say entirely. Though I do prefer women with a little more . . ." He stopped, smiled again. "We'll just say more, and stay alive."

"Wise."

"Your boys getting a hard time in school?"

"Excuse me?"

"Just considering what you said before. Yankee."

"Oh. A little, maybe, but for the most part the other kids find it interesting that they're from up north, lived near one of the Great Lakes. Both their teachers pulled up a map to show where they came from."

Her face softened as she spoke of it. "Thanks for asking."

"I like your kids."

He signed the forms and found himself amused when she groaned—actually groaned—watching him carelessly fold his and stuff them in his pocket.

"Next time could you wait until you're out of the office to do that? It hurts me."

"No problem." Maybe it was the different tone they were ending on, or maybe it was the way she'd softened up and smiled when she spoke of her children. Later, he might wonder what possessed him, but for now, he went with impulse. "Ever been to Graceland?"

"No. I'm not a big Elvis fan."

"Ssh!" Widening his eyes, he looked toward the door. "Legally, you can't say that around here. You could face fine and imprisonment, or depending on the jury, public flogging."

"I didn't read that in the Memphian handbook."

"Fine print. So, I'll take you. When's your day off?"

"I . . . It depends. You'll take me to Graceland?"

"You can't settle in down here until you've experienced Graceland. Pick a day, I'll work around it."

"I'm trying to understand here. Are you asking me for a date?"

"I wasn't heading into the date arena. I'm thinking of it more as an outing, between associates." He set the empty mug on her desk. "Think about it, let me know."

SHE HAD TOO MUCH TO DO TO THINK ABOUT IT. SHE couldn't just pop off to Graceland. And if she could, and had some strange desire to do so, she certainly wouldn't pop off to Graceland with Logan.

The fact that she'd admired his work—and all right, his build—didn't mean she liked him. It didn't mean she wanted to spend her very valuable off-time in his company.

But she couldn't help thinking about it, or more, wondering why he'd asked her. Maybe it was some sort of a trick, a strange initiation for the Yankee. You take her to Graceland, then abandon her in a forest of Elvis paraphernalia and see if she can find her way out.

Or maybe, in his weird Logan way, he'd decided that hitting on her was an easier away around her new system than arguing with her.

Except he hadn't seemed to be hitting on her. Exactly. It had seemed more friendly, off the cuff, or impulsive. And he'd asked about her children. There was no quicker way to cut through her annoyance, any shield, any defense than a sincere interest in her boys.

And if he was just being friendly, it seemed only polite, and sensible, to be friendly back.

What did people wear to Graceland, anyway?

Not that she was going. She probably wasn't. But it was smart to prepare. Just in case.

In Greenhouse Three, supervising while Hayley watered propagated annuals, Stella pondered on the situation.

"Ever been to Graceland?"

"Oh, sure. These are impatiens, right?"

Stella looked down at the flat. "Yeah. Those are Busy Lizzies. They're doing really well."

"And these are impatiens too. The New Guinea ones."

"Right. You do learn fast."

"Well, I recognize these easier because I've planted them before. Anyway, I went to Graceland with some pals when I was in college. It's pretty cool. I bought this Elvis bookmark. Wonder what ever happened to that? Elvis is a form of Elvin. It means 'elf-wise friend.' Isn't that strange?"

"Stranger to me that you'd know that."

"Just one of those things you pick up somewhere."

"Okay. So, what's the dress code?"

"Hmm?" She was trying to identify another flat by the leaves on the seedlings. And struggling not to peek at the name on the spike. "I don't guess there is one. People just wear whatever. Jeans and stuff."

"Casual, then."

"Right. I like the way it smells in here. All earthy and damp."

"Then you made the right career choice."

"It could be a career, couldn't it?" Those clear blue eyes shifted to Stella. "Something I could learn to be good at. I always thought I'd run my own place one day. Always figured on a bookstore, but this is sort of the same."

"How's that?"

"Well, like you've got your new stuff, and your classics. You've got genres, when it comes down to it. Annuals, biennials, perennials, shrubs and trees and grasses. Water plants and shade plants. That sort of thing."

"You know, you're right. I hadn't thought of it that way."

Encouraged, Hayley walked down the rows. "And

you're learning and exploring, the way you do with books. And we—you know, the staff—we're trying to help people find what suits them, makes them happy or at least satisfied. Planting a flower's like opening a book, because either way you're starting something. And your garden's your library. I could get good at this."

"I don't doubt it."

She turned to see Stella smiling at her. "When I am good at it, it won't just be a job anymore. A job's okay. It's cool for now, but I want more than a paycheck at the end of the week. I don't just mean money—though, okay, I want the money too."

"No, I know what you mean. You want what Roz has here. A place, and the satisfaction of being part of that place. Roots," Stella said, touching the leaves of a seedling. "And bloom. I know, because I want it too."

"But you have it. You're so totally smart, and you know where you're going. You've got two great kids, and a . . . a position here. You worked toward this, this place, this position. I feel like I'm just starting."

"And you're impatient to get on with it. So was I at your age."

Hayley's face beamed good humor. "And, yeah, you're so old and creaky now."

Laughing, Stella pushed back her hair. "I've got about ten years on you. A lot can happen, a lot can change—yourself included—in a decade. In some ways I'm just starting, too—a decade after you. Transplanting myself, and my two precious shoots here."

"Do you get scared?"

"Every day." She laid a hand on Hayley's belly. "It comes with the territory."

"It helps, having you to talk to. I mean, you were married when you went through this, but you—well, both you and Roz had to deal with being a single parent. It helps that you know stuff. Helps having other women around who know stuff I need to know."

With the job complete, Hayley walked over to turn off

the water. "So," she asked, "are you going to Graceland?"

"I don't know. I might."

WITH HIS CREW SPLIT BETWEEN THE WHITE PINES AND the landscape prep on the Guppy job, Logan set to work on the walkway for his old teacher. It wouldn't take him long, and he could hit both the other work sites that afternoon. He liked juggling jobs. He always had.

Going directly start to finish on one too quickly cut out the room for brainstorms or sudden inspiration. There was little he liked better than that *pop*, when he just saw something in his head that he knew he could make with his hands.

He could take what was and make it better, maybe blend some of what was with the new and create a different whole.

He'd grown up respecting the land, and the whims of Nature, but more from a farmer's point of view. When you grew up on a small farm, worked it, fought with it, he thought, you understood what the land meant. Or could mean.

His father had loved the land, too, but in a different way, Logan supposed. It had provided for his family, cost them, and in the end had gifted them with a nice bonanza when his father had opted to sell out.

He couldn't say he missed the farm. He'd wanted more than row crops and worries about market prices. But he'd wanted, needed, to work the land.

Maybe he'd lost some of the magic of it when he'd moved north. Too many buildings, too much concrete, too many limitations for him. He hadn't been able to acclimate to the climate or culture any more than Rae had been able to acclimate here.

It hadn't worked. No matter how much both of them had tried to nurture things along, the marriage had just withered on them.

So he'd come home, and ultimately, with Roz's offer,

he'd found his place—personally, professionally, creatively. And was content.

He ran his lines, then picked up his shovel.

And jabbed the blade into the earth again.

What had he been thinking? He'd asked the woman out. He could call it whatever he liked, but when a guy asked a woman out, it was a frigging date.

He had no intention of dating toe-the-line Stella Rothchild. She wasn't his type.

Okay, sure she was. He set to work turning the soil between his lines to prep for leveling and laying the black plastic. He'd never met a woman, really, who wasn't his type.

He just liked the breed, that's all. Young ones and old ones, country girls and city-slicked. Whip smart or bulb dim, women just appealed to him on most every level.

He'd ended up married to one, hadn't he? And though that had been a mistake, you had to make them along the way.

Maybe he'd never been particularly drawn to the structured, my-way-or-the-highway type before. But there was always a first time. And he liked first times. It was the second times and the third times that could wear on a man.

But he wasn't attracted to Stella.

Okay, shit. Yes, he was. Mildly. She was a good-looking woman, nicely shaped, too. And there was the hair. He was really gone on the hair. Wouldn't mind getting his hands on that hair, just to see if it felt as sexy as it looked.

But it didn't mean he wanted to date her. It was hard enough to deal with her professionally. The woman had a rule or a form or a damn system for everything.

Probably had them in bed, too. Probably had a typed list of bullet points, dos and don'ts, all with a mission statement overview.

What the woman needed was some spontaneity, a little shake of the order of things. Not that he was interested in being the one to provide it.

It was just that she'd looked so pretty that morning, and

her hair had smelled good. Plus she'd had that sexy little smile going for her. Before he knew it, he'd been talking about taking her to Graceland.

Nothing to worry about, he assured himself. She wouldn't go. It wasn't the sort of thing a woman like her did, just for the hell of it. As far as he could tell, she didn't do *anything* for the hell of it.

They'd both forget he'd even brought it up.

BECAUSE SHE FELT IT WAS IMPERATIVE, AT LEAST FOR the first six months of her management, Stella insisted on a weekly progress meeting with Roz.

She'd have preferred a specific time for these meetings, and a specific location. But Roz was hard to pin down.

She'd already held them in the propagation house and in the field. This time she cornered Roz in her own sitting room, where she'd be unlikely to escape.

"I wanted to give you your weekly update."

"Oh. Well, all right." Roz set aside a book on hybridizing that was thick as a railroad tie, and took off her frameless reading glasses. "Time's zipping by. Ground's warming up."

"I know. Daffodils are ready to pop. So much earlier than I'm used to. We've been selling a lot of bulbs. Back north, we'd sell most of those late summer or fall."

"Homesick?"

"Now and then, but less and less already. I can't say I'm sorry to be out of Michigan as we slog through February. They got six inches of snow yesterday, and I'm watching daffodils spearing up."

Roz leaned back in the chair, crossed her sock-covered feet at the ankles. "Is there a problem?"

"So much for the illusion that I conceal my emotions under a composed façade. No, no problem. I did the duty call home to my mother a little while ago. I'm still recovering."

"Ah."

It was a noncommittal sound, and Stella decided she could interpret it as complete non-interest or a tacit invitation to unload. Because she was brimming, she chose to unload.

"I spent the almost fifteen minutes she spared me out of her busy schedule listening to her talk about her current boyfriend. She actually calls these men she sees boyfriends. She's fifty-eight years old, and she just had her fourth divorce two months ago. When she wasn't complaining that Rocky—and he's actually named Rocky—isn't attentive enough and won't take her to the Bahamas for a midwinter getaway, she was talking about her next chemical peel and whining about how her last Botox injection hurt. She never asked about the boys, and the only reference she made to the fact that I was living and working down here was to ask if I was tired of being around the jerk and his bimbo—her usual terms for my father and Jolene."

When she'd run out of steam, Stella rubbed her hands over her face. "Goddamn it."

"That's a lot of bitching, whining, and venom to pack into a quarter of an hour. She sounds like a very talented woman."

It took Stella a minute—a minute where she let her hands slide into her lap so she could stare into Roz's face. Then she let her own head fall back with a peal of laughter.

"Oh, yeah. Oh, yeah, she's loaded with talent. Thanks."

"No problem. My mama spent most of her time—at least the time we were on earth together—sighing wistfully over her health. Not that she meant to complain, so she said. I very nearly put that on her tombstone. 'Not That I Mean to Complain.' "

"I could put 'I Don't Ask for Much' on my mother's."

"There you go. Mine made such an impression on me that I went hell-bent in the opposite direction. I could probably cut off a limb, and you wouldn't hear a whimper out of me."

"God, I guess I've done the same with mine. I'll have to think about that later. Okay, on to business. We're sold out of the mixed-bulb planters we forced. I don't know if you want to do others this late in the season."

"Maybe a few. Some people like to pick them up, already done, for Easter presents and so on."

"All right. How about if I show Hayley how it's done? I know you usually do them yourself, but—"

"No, it's a good job for her. I've been watching her." At Stella's expression, she inclined her head. "I don't like to look like I'm watching, but generally I am. I know what's going on in my place, Stella, even if I do occasionally miss crossing a T."

"And I'm there to cross them, so that's all right."

"Exactly. Still, I've left her primarily to you. She working out for you?"

"More than. You don't have to tell her something twice, and when she claimed she learned fast she wasn't kidding. She's thirsty."

"We've got plenty to drink around here."

"She's personable with customers—friendly, never rushed. And she's not afraid to say she doesn't know, but she'll find out. She's outside right now, poking around your beds and shrubs. She wants to know what she's selling."

She moved to the window as she spoke, to look out. It was nearly twilight, but there was Hayley walking the dog and studying the perennials. "At her age, I was planning my wedding. It seems like a million years ago."

"At her age, I was raising two toddlers and was pregnant with Mason. Now *that* was a million years ago. And five minutes ago."

"It's off topic, again, of the update, but I wanted to ask if you'd thought about what you'll do when we get to May."

"That's still high season for us, and people like to freshen up the summer garden. We sell—"

"No, I meant about Hayley. About the baby."

"Oh. Well, she'll have to decide that, but I expect if she

decides to stay on at the nursery, we'll find her sit-down work."

"She'll need to find child care, when she's ready to go back to work. And speaking of nurseries . . ."

"Hmm. That's thinking ahead."

"Time zips by," Stella repeated.

"We'll figure it out."

Because she was curious, Roz rose to go to the window herself. Standing beside Stella she looked out.

It was a lovely thing, she decided, watching a young woman, blooming with child, wandering a winter garden.

She'd once been that young woman, dreaming in the twilight and waiting for spring to bring life.

Time didn't just zip by, she thought. It damn near evaporated on you.

"She seems happy now, and sure of what she's going to do. But could be after she has the baby, she'll change her mind about having the father involved." Roz watched Hayley lay a hand on her belly and look west, to where the sun was sinking behind the trees and into the river beyond them. "Having a live baby in your arms and the prospect of caring for it single-handed's one hell of a reality check. We'll see when the time comes."

"You're right. And I don't suppose either of us knows her well enough to know what's best. Speaking of babies, it's nearly time to get mine in the tub. I'm going to leave the weekly report with you."

"All right. I'll get to it. I should tell you, Stella, I like what you've done. What shows, like in the customer areas, and what doesn't, in the office management. I see spring coming, and for the first time in years, I'm not frazzled and overworked. I can't say I minded being overworked, but I can't say I mind not being, either."

"Even when I bug you with details?"

"Even when. I haven't heard any complaints about Logan in the past few days. Or from him. Am I living in a fool's paradise, or have you two found your rhythm?"

"There are still a few hitches in it, and I suspect there'll be others, but nothing for you to worry about. In fact, he made a very friendly gesture and offered to take me to Graceland."

"He did?" Roz's eyebrows drew together. "Logan?"

"Would that be out of the ordinary for him?"

"I couldn't say, except I don't know that he's dated anyone from work before."

"It's not a date, it's an outing."

Intrigued, Roz sat again. You never knew what you'd learn from a younger woman, she decided. "What's the difference?"

"Well, a date's dinner and a movie with potential, even probable, romantic overtones. Taking your kids to the zoo is an outing."

Roz leaned back, stretched out her legs. "Things do change, don't they? Still, in my book, when a man and a woman go on an outing, it's a date."

"See, that's my quandary." Since conversation seemed welcomed, Stella walked over again, sat on the arm of the chair facing Roz. "Because that's my first thought. But it seemed like just a friendly gesture, and the 'outing' term was his. Like a kind of olive branch. And if I take it, maybe we'd find that common ground, or that rhythm, whatever it is we need to smooth out the rough spots in our working relationship."

"So, if I'm following this, you'd go to Graceland with Logan for the good of In the Garden."

"Sort of."

"And not because he's a very attractive, dynamic, and downright sexy single man."

"No, those would be bonus points." She waited until Roz stopped laughing. "And I'm not thinking of wading in that pool. Dating's a minefield."

"Tell me about it. I've got more years in that war zone than you."

"I like men." She reached back to tug the band ponytailing her hair a little higher. "I like the company of men. But dating's so complicated and stressful."

"Better complicated and stressful than downright boring, which too many of my experiences in the field have been."

"Complicated, stressful, or downright boring, I like the sound of 'outing' much better. Listen, I know Logan's a friend of yours. But I'd just like to ask if you think, if I went with him, I'd be making a mistake, or giving the wrong impression. The wrong signal. Or maybe crossing that line between coworkers. Or—"

"That's an awful lot of complication and stress you're working up over an outing."

"It is. I irritate myself." Shaking her head, she pushed off the chair. "I'd better get bath time started. Oh, and I'll get Hayley going on those bulbs tomorrow."

"That's fine. Stella—are you going on this outing?"

She paused at the doorway. "Maybe. I'll sleep on it."

eight

SHE WAS DREAMING OF FLOWERS. AN ENCHANTING garden, full of young, vital blooms, flowed around her. It was perfect, tidied and ordered, its edges ruler-straight to form a keen verge against the well-trimmed grass.

Color swept into color, whites and pinks, yellows and silvery greens, all soft and delicate pastels that shimmered in subtle elegance in the golden beams of the sun.

Their fragrance was calming and drew a pretty bevy of busy butterflies, the curiosity of a single shimmery hummingbird. No weed intruded on its flawlessness, and every blossom was full and ripe, with dozens upon dozens of buds waiting their turn to open.

She'd done this. As she circled the bed it was with a sense of pride and satisfaction. She'd turned the earth and fed it, she'd planned and selected and set each plant in exactly the right place. The garden so precisely matched her vision, it was like a photograph.

It had taken her years to plan and toil and create. But now everything she'd wanted to accomplish was here, blooming at her feet.

Yet even as she watched, a stem grew up, sharp and

green, crowding the others, spoiling the symmetry. Out of place, she thought, more annoyed than surprised to see it breaking out of the ground, growing up, unfurling its leaves.

A dahlia? She'd planted no dahlias there. They belonged in the back. She'd specifically planted a trio of tall pink dahlias at the back of the bed, exactly one foot apart.

Puzzled, she tilted her head, studied it as the stems grew and thickened, as buds formed fat and healthy. Fascinating, so fascinating and unexpected.

Even as she started to smile, she heard—felt?—a whisper over the skin, a murmur through her brain.

It's wrong there. Wrong. It has to be removed. *It will take and take until there's nothing left.*

She shivered. The air around her was suddenly cool, with a hint of raw dampness, with bleak clouds creeping in toward that lovely golden sun.

In the pit of her belly was a kind of dread.

Don't let it grow. It will strangle the life out of everything you've done.

That was right. Of course, that was right. It had no business growing there, muscling the others aside, changing the order.

She'd have to dig it out, find another place for it. Reorganize everything, just when she'd thought she was finished. And look at that, she thought, as the buds formed, as they broke open to spread their deep blue petals. It was entirely the wrong color. Too bold, too dark, too bright.

It was beautiful; she couldn't deny it. In fact, she'd never seen a more beautiful specimen. It looked so strong, so vivid. It was already nearly as tall as she, with flowers as wide as dinner plates.

It lies. It lies.

That whisper, somehow female, somehow raging, slithered into her sleeping brain. She whimpered a little, tossed restlessly in her chilly bed.

Kill it! Kill it. Hurry before it's too late.

No, she couldn't kill something so beautiful, so alive, so vivid. But that didn't mean she could just leave it there, out of its place, upsetting the rest of the bed.

All that work, the preparation, the *planning*, and now this. She'd just have to plan another bed and work it in. With a sigh, she reached out, feathered her fingers over those bold blue petals. It would be a lot of work, she thought, a lot of trouble, but—

"Mom."

"Isn't it pretty?" she murmured. "It's so *blue.*"

"Mom, wake up."

"What?" She tumbled out of the dream, shaking off sleep as she saw Luke kneeling in the bed beside her.

God, the room was freezing.

"Luke?" Instinctively she dragged the spread over him. "What's the matter?"

"I don't feel good in my tummy."

"Aw." She sat up, automatically laying a hand on his brow to check for fever. A little warm, she thought. "Does it hurt?"

He shook his head. She could see the gleam of his eyes, the sheen of tears. "It feels sick. Can I sleep in your bed?"

"Okay." She drew the sheets back. "Lie down and bundle up, baby. I don't know why it's so cold in here. I'm going to take your temperature, just to see." She pressed her lips to his forehead as he snuggled onto her pillow. Definitely a little warm.

Switching on the bedside lamp, she rolled out to get the thermometer from the bathroom.

"Let's find out if I can see through your brain." She stroked his hair as she set the gauge to his ear. "Did you feel sick when you went to bed?"

"Nuh-uh, it was . . ." His body tightened, and he made a little groan.

She knew he was going to retch before he did. With a mother's speed, she scooped him up, dashed into the bathroom. They made it, barely, and she murmured and stroked and fretted while he was sick.

Then he turned his pale little face up to hers. "I frew up."

"I know, baby. I'm sorry. We're going to make it all better soon."

She gave him a little water, cooled his face with a cloth, then carried him back to her bed. Strange, she thought, the room felt fine now.

"It doesn't feel as sick in my tummy anymore."

"That's good." Still, she took his temperature—99.1, not too bad—and brought the wastebasket over beside the bed. "Does it hurt anywhere?"

"Nuh-uh, but I don't like to frow up. It makes it taste bad in my throat. And my other tooth is loose, and maybe if I frow up again, it'll come out and I won't have it to put under my pillow."

"Don't you worry about that. You'll absolutely have your tooth for under your pillow, just like the other one. Now, I'll go down and get you some ginger ale. You stay right here, and I'll be back in just a minute. Okay?"

"Okay."

"If you have to be sick again, try to use this." She set the wastebasket beside him on the bed. "I'll be right back, baby."

She hurried out, jogging down the stairs in her nightshirt. One of the disadvantages of a really big house, she realized, was that the kitchen was a mile away from the bedrooms.

She'd see about buying a little fridge, like the one she'd had in her dorm room at college, for the upstairs sitting room.

Low-grade fever, she thought as she rushed into the kitchen. He'd probably be better by tomorrow. If he wasn't, she'd call the doctor.

She hunted up ginger ale, filled a tall glass with ice, grabbed a bottle of water, and dashed back upstairs.

"I get ginger ale," she heard Luke say as she walked back down the hall to her room. "Because I was sick. Even though I feel better, I can still have it. You can have some, too, if you want."

"Thanks, honey, but—" When she swung into the room, she saw Luke was turned away from the door, sitting back against the pillows. And the room was cold again, so cold that she saw the vapor of her own breath.

"She went away," Luke said.

Something that was more than the cold danced up her spine. "Who went away?"

"The lady." His sleepy eyes brightened a bit when he saw the ginger ale. "She stayed with me when you went downstairs."

"What lady, Luke? Miss Roz? Hayley?"

"Nuh-uh. The lady who comes and sings. She's nice. Can I have *all* the ginger ale?"

"You can have some." Her hands shook lightly as she poured. "Where did you see her?"

"Right here." He pointed to the bed, then took the glass in both hands and drank. "This tastes good."

"You've seen her before?"

"Uh-huh. Sometimes I wake up and she's there. She sings the dilly-dilly song."

Lavender's blue, dilly dilly. Lavender's green. That's the song she'd heard, Stella realized with a numb fear. The song she'd caught herself humming.

"Did she—" No, don't frighten him, she warned herself. "What does she look like?"

"She's pretty, I guess. She has yellow hair. I think she's an angel, a lady angel? 'Member the story about the guard angel?"

"Guardian angel."

"But she doesn't have wings. Gavin says she's maybe a witch, but a good one like in *Harry Potter*."

Her throat went desert dry. "Gavin's seen her too?"

"Yeah, when she comes to sing." He handed the glass back to Stella, rubbed his eyes. "My tummy feels better now, but I'm sleepy. Can I still sleep in your bed?"

"Absolutely." But before she got into bed with him, Stella turned on the bathroom light.

She looked in on Gavin, struggled against the urge to pluck him out of his bed and carry him into hers.

Leaving the connecting doors wide open, she walked back into her room.

She turned off the bedside lamp, then slid into bed with her son.

And gathering him close, she held him as he slept.

HE SEEMED FINE THE NEXT MORNING. BRIGHT AND bouncy, and cheerfully told David over breakfast that he'd thrown up and had ginger ale.

She considered keeping him home from school, but there was no fever and, judging by his appetite, no stomach problems.

"No ill effects there," David commented when the boys ran up to get their books. "You, on the other hand, look like you put in a rough one." He poured her another cup of coffee.

"I did. And not all of it because Luke was sick. After he 'frew up,' he settled down and slept like a baby. But before he settled down, he told me something that kept me awake most of the night."

David rested his elbows on the island counter, leaned forward. "Tell Daddy all."

"He says . . ." She glanced around, cocking an ear so she'd hear the boys when they came back down. "There's a lady with yellow hair who comes into his room at night and sings to him."

"Oh." He picked up his dishcloth and began to mop the counter.

"Don't say 'oh' with that silly little smile."

"Hey, I'll have you know this is my amused smirk. Nothing silly about it."

"David."

"Stella," he said with the same stern scowl. "Roz told you we have a ghost, didn't she?"

"She mentioned it. But there's just one little problem with that. There are no such things as ghosts."

"So, what, some blonde sneaks into the house every night, heads to the boys' room, and breaks out in song? *That's* more plausible?"

"I don't know what's going on. I've heard someone singing, and I've felt . . ." Edgy, she twisted the band of her watch. "Regardless, the idea of a ghost is ridiculous. But something's going on with my boys."

"Is he afraid of her?"

"No. I probably just imagined the singing. And Luke, he's six. He can imagine anything."

"Have you asked Gavin?"

"No. Luke said they'd both seen her, but . . ."

"So have I."

"Oh, please."

David rinsed the dishcloth, squeezed out the excess water, then laid it over the lip of the sink to dry. "Not since I was a kid, but I saw her a few times when I'd sleep over. Freaked me out at first, but she'd just sort of *be* there. You can ask Harper. He saw her plenty."

"Okay. Just who is this fictional ghost supposed to be?" She threw up a hand as she heard the thunder of feet on the stairs. "Later."

SHE TRIED TO PUT IT OUT OF HER MIND, AND SUCCEEDED from time to time when the work took over. But it snuck back into her brain, and played there, like the ghostly lullaby.

By midday, she left Hayley working on bulb planters and Ruby at the counter, and grabbing a clipboard, headed toward the grafting house.

Two birds, she thought, one stone.

The music today was Rachmaninoff. Or was it Mozart? Either way, it was a lot of passionate strings and flutes. She passed the staging areas, the tools, the soils and additives and rooting mediums.

She found Harper down at the far end at a worktable with a pile of five-inch pots, several cacti as stock plants, and a tray of rooting medium. She noted the clothespins, the rubber bands, the raffia, the jar of denatured alcohol.

"What do you use on the Christmas cactus?"

He continued to work, using his knife to cut a shoot from the joint of a scion plant. He had beautiful hands, she noted. Long, artistic fingers. "Apical-wedge, then? Tricky, but probably best with that specimen because of the flat stems. Are you creating a standard, or hybridizing?"

He made his vertical slit into the vascular bundle and still didn't answer.

"I'm just wondering because—" She set her hand on his shoulder, and when he jumped and let out a muffled shout, she stumbled back and rammed into the table behind her.

"Shit!" He dropped the knife and stuck the thumb it had nicked in his mouth. "Shit!" he said again, around his thumb, and tugged headphones off with his free hand.

"I'm sorry. I'm so sorry! How bad are you cut? Let me see."

"It's just a scratch." He took it out of his mouth, rubbed it absently on his grimy jeans. "Not nearly as fatal as the *heart attack* you just brought on."

"Let me see the thumb." She grabbed his hand. "You've got dirt in it now."

He saw her gaze slide over toward the alcohol and ripped his hand out of hers. "Don't even think about it."

"Well, it should at least be cleaned. And I really am sorry. I didn't see the headphones. I thought you heard me."

"It's okay. No big. The classical's for the plants. If I listen to it for too long, my eyes get glassy."

"Oh?" She picked up the headphones, held one side to one ear. "Metallica?"

"Yeah. My kind of classical." Now he looked warily at her clipboard. "What's up?"

"I'm hoping to get an idea of what you'll have ready in here to put out for our big spring opening next month. And what you have at the stage you'd want it moved out to the stock greenhouse."

"Oh, well . . ." He looked around. "A lot of stuff. Probably. I keep the staging records on computer."

"Even better. Maybe you could just make me a copy. Floppy disk would be perfect."

"Yeah, okay. Okay, wait." He shifted his stool toward the computer.

"You don't have to do it this minute, when you're in the middle of something else."

"If I don't, I'll probably forget."

With a skill she admired, he tapped keys with somewhat grungy fingers, found what he was after. He dug out a floppy, slid it into the data slot. "Look, I'd rather you didn't take anything out when I'm not here."

"No problem."

"How's, um, Hayley working out?"

"An answer to a prayer."

"Yeah?" He reached for a can of Coke, took a quick drink. "She's not doing anything heavy or working around toxics. Right?"

"Absolutely not. I've got her doing bulb planters right now."

"Here you go." He handed her the floppy.

"Thanks, Harper. This makes my life easier. I've never done a Christmas cactus graft." She clipped the floppy to her board. "Can I watch?"

"Sure. Want to do one? I'll talk you through."

"I'd really like to."

"I'll finish this one up. See, I cut a two-, maybe two-and-a-half-inch shoot, straight through the joint. I've cut the top couple inches from the stem of the stock plant. And on the way to slicing my finger—"

"Sorry."

"Wouldn't be the first time. I made this fine, vertical cut into the vascular bundle."

"I got that far."

"From here, we pare slivers of skin from both sides of the base of the scion, tapering the end, and exposing the central core." Those long, artistic fingers worked cleverly and patiently. "See?"

"Mmm. You've got good hands for this."

"Came by them naturally. Mom showed me how to graft. We did an ornamental cherry when I was about Luke's age. Now we're going to insert the scion into the slit on the stock stem. We want the exposed tissues of both in contact, and match the cut surfaces as close as you can. I like to use a long cactus spine. . . ." He took one from a tray and pushed it straight into the grafted area.

"Neat and organic."

"Uh-huh. I don't like binding with raffia on these. Weakened clothespins are better. Right across the joint, see, so it's held firm but not too tight. The rooting medium's two parts cactus soil mix to one part fine grit. I've already got the mix. We get our new baby in the pot, cover the mix with a little fine gravel."

"So it stays moist but not wet."

"You got it. Then you want to label it and put it in an airy position, out of full sun. The two plants should unite in a couple of days. Want to give it a shot?"

"Yeah." She took the stool when he vacated it, and began, following his directions carefully. "Ah, David was telling me about the house legend this morning."

"That's good." His gaze stayed focused on her hands, and the plant. "Keep the slice really thin. Legend?"

"You know, woo-woo, ghost."

"Oh, yeah, the sad-eyed blonde. Used to sing to me when I was a kid."

"Come on, Harper."

He shrugged, took another sip of Coke. "You want?" He tipped the can from side to side. "I've got more in the cooler under here."

"No, but thanks. You're saying a ghost used to come in your room and sing to you."

"Up until I was about twelve, thirteen. Same with my brothers. You hit puberty, she stops coming around. You need to taper the scion now."

She paused in her work only long enough to slide a glance up at his face. "Harper, don't you consider yourself a scientist?"

He smiled at her with those somewhat dreamy brown eyes. "Not so much. Some of what I do is science, and some of what I do requires knowing some science. But down at it, I'm a gardener."

He two-pointed the Coke can into his waste bin, then bent down to get another out of his cooler. "But if you're asking if I find ghosts at odds with science, not so much either. Science is an exploration, it's experimentation, it's discovery."

"I can't argue with your definition." She went back to the work. "But—"

He popped the top. "Gonna Scully me?"

She had to laugh. "It's one thing for a young boy to believe in ghosts, and Santa Claus, and—"

"You're trying to say there's no Santa Claus?" He looked horrified. "That's just sick."

"But," she continued, ignoring him, "it's entirely another when it's a grown man."

"Who are you calling a grown man? I think I'm going to have to order you out of my house. Stella." He patted her shoulder, transferred soil, then casually brushed it off her shirt. "I saw what I saw, I know what I know. It's just part of growing up in the house. She was always . . . a benign presence, at least to me and my brothers. She gave Mom grief now and then."

"What do you mean, grief?"

"Ask Mom. But I don't know why you'd bother, since you don't believe in ghosts anyway." He smiled. "That's a good graft. According to family lore, she's supposed to be one of the Harper brides, but she's not in any of the paintings or pictures we have." He lifted a shoulder. "Maybe she was a servant who died there. She sure knows her way around the place."

"Luke told me he saw her."

"Yeah?" His gaze sharpened as Stella labeled the pot. "If you're worried that she might hurt him, or Gavin, don't. She's, I don't know, maternal."

"Perfect, then—an unidentified yet maternal ghost who haunts my sons' room at night."

"It's a Harper family tradition."

AFTER A CONVERSATION LIKE THAT, STELLA NEEDED something sensible to occupy her mind. She grabbed a flat of pansies and some trailing vinca from a greenhouse, found a couple of nice free-form concrete planters in storage, loaded them and potting soil onto a flatbed cart. She gathered tools, gloves, mixed up some starter solution, and hauled everything out front.

Pansies didn't mind a bit of chill, she thought, so if they got a few more frosts, they wouldn't be bothered. And their happy faces, their rich colors would splash spring right at the entryway.

Once she'd positioned the planters, she got her clipboard and noted down everything she'd taken from stock. She'd enter it in her computer when she was finished.

Then she knelt down to do something she loved, something that never failed to comfort her. Something that always made sense.

She planted.

When the first was done, the purple and yellow flowers cheerful against the dull gray of the planter, she stepped back to study it. She wanted its mate to be as close to a mirror image as she could manage.

She was half done when she heard the rumble of tires on gravel. Logan, she thought, as she glanced around and identified his truck. She saw him start to turn toward the material area, then swing back and drive toward the building.

He stepped out, worn boots, worn jeans, bad-boy black-lensed sunglasses.

She felt a little itch right between her shoulder blades.

"Hey," he said.

"Hello, Logan."

He stood there, his thumbs hooked in the front pockets of his work pants and a trio of fresh scratches on his forearms just below the rolled-up sleeves of his shirt.

"Picking up some landscape timbers and some more black plastic for the Dawson job."

"You're moving right along there."

"It's cooking." He stepped closer, studied her work. "Those look good. I could use them."

"These are for display."

"You can make more. I take those over to Miz Dawson, the woman's going to snap them up. Sale's a sale, Red."

"Oh, all right." She'd hardly had a *minute* to think of them as her own. "Let me at least finish them. You tell her she'll need to replace these pansies when it gets hot. They won't handle summer. And if she puts perennials in them, she should cover the planters over for winter."

"It happens I know something about plants myself."

"Just want to make sure the customer's satisfied."

He'd been polite, she thought. Even cooperative. Hadn't he come to give her a materials list? The least she could do was reciprocate. "If Graceland's still on, I can take off some time next Thursday." She kept her eyes on the plants, her tone casual as a fistful of daisies. "If that works for you."

"Thursday?" He'd been all prepared with excuses if she happened to bring it up. Work was jamming him up, they'd do it some other time.

But there she was, kneeling on the ground, with that damn hair curling all over the place and the sun hitting it. Those blue eyes, that cool Yankee voice.

"Sure, Thursday's good. You want me to pick you up here or at the house?"

"Here, if that's okay. What time works best for you?"

"Maybe around one. That way I can put the morning in."

"That'll be perfect." She rose, brushed off her gloves and set them neatly on the cart. "Just let me put together a price for these planters, make you up an order form. If she decides against them, just bring them back."

"She won't. Go ahead and do the paperwork." He dug a many folded note out of his pocket. "On these and the materials I've got down here. I'll load up."

"Good. Fine." She started inside. The itch had moved from her shoulder blades to just under her belly button.

It wasn't a date, it wasn't a date, she reminded herself. It wasn't even an outing, really. It was a gesture. A goodwill gesture on both sides.

And now, she thought as she walked into her office, they were both stuck with it.

NINE

"I DON'T KNOW HOW IT GOT TO BE THURSDAY."

"It has something to do with Thor, the Norse god." Hayley hunched her shoulders sheepishly. "I know a lot of stupid things. I don't know why."

"I wasn't looking for the origin of the word, more how it got here so fast. Thor?" Stella repeated, turning from the mirror in the employee bathroom.

"Pretty sure."

"I'll just take your word on that one. Okay." She spread out her arms. "How do I look?"

"You look really nice."

"Too nice? You know, too formal or prepared?"

"No, just right nice." The fact was, she envied the way Stella looked in simple gray pants and black sweater. Sort of tailored, and curvy under it. When she wasn't pregnant, she herself tended to be on the bony side and flat-chested.

"The sweater makes you look really built," she added.

"Oh, God!" Horrified, Stella crossed her arms, pressing them against her breasts. "Too built? Like, hey, look at my boobs?"

"No." Laughing, Hayley tugged Stella's arms down. "Cut it out. You've got really excellent boobs."

"I'm nervous. It's ridiculous, but I'm nervous. I *hate* being nervous, which is why I hardly ever am." She tugged at the sleeve of her sweater, brushed at it. "Why do something you hate?"

"It's just a casual afternoon outing." Hayley avoided the D word. They'd been over that. "Just go and have fun."

"Right. Of course. Stupid." She shook herself off before walking out of the room. "You've got my cell number."

"Everybody has your cell number, Stella." She cast a look at Ruby, who answered it with chuckle. "I think the mayor probably has it on speed dial."

"If there are any problems at all, don't hesitate to use it. And if you're not sure about anything, and can't find Roz or Harper, just call me."

"Yes, Mama. And don't worry, the keg's not coming until three." She slapped a hand over her mouth. "Did I say keg? Peg's what I meant. Yeah, I meant Peg."

"Ha ha."

"And the male strippers aren't a definite." She got a hoot of laughter out of Ruby at that and grinned madly. "So you can chill."

"I don't think chilling's on today's schedule."

"Can I ask how long it's been since you've been on a date—I mean, an outing?"

"Not that long. A few months." When Hayley rolled her eyes, Stella rolled hers right back. "I was busy. There was a lot to do with selling the house, packing up, arranging for storage, researching schools and pediatricians down here. I didn't have time."

"And didn't have anyone who made you want to make time. You're making it today."

"It's not like that. Why is he late?" she demanded, glancing at her watch. "I knew he'd be late. He has 'I'm chronically late for mostly everything' written all over him."

When a customer came in, Hayley patted Stella's shoulder. "That's my cue. Have a good time. May I help you?" she asked, strolling over to the customer.

Stella waited another couple of minutes, assuring herself that Hayley had the new customer in hand. Ruby rang up two more. Work was being done where work needed to be done, and she had nothing to do but wait.

Deciding to do her waiting outside, she grabbed her jacket.

Her planters looked good, and she figured her display of them was directly responsible for the flats of pansies they'd moved in the past few days. That being the case, they could add a few more planters, do a couple of half whiskey barrels, add some hanging pots.

Scribbling, she wandered around, picking out the best spots to place displays, to add other touches that would inspire customers to buy.

When Logan pulled up at quarter after one, she was sitting on the steps, listing the proposed displays and arrangements and dividing up the labor of creating them.

She got up even as he climbed out of the truck. "I got hung up."

"No problem. I kept busy."

"You okay riding in the truck?"

"Wouldn't be the first time." She got in, and as she buckled her seat belt, studied the forest of notes and reminders, sketches and math calculations stuck to his dashboard.

"Your filing system?"

"Most of it." He turned on the CD player, and Elvis rocked out with "Heartbreak Hotel." "Seems only right."

"Are you a big fan?"

"You've got to respect the King."

"How many times have you been to Graceland?"

"Couldn't say. People come in from out of town, they want to see it. You visit Memphis, you want Graceland, Beale Street, ribs, the Peabody's duck walk."

Maybe she could chill, Stella decided. They were just talking, after all. Like normal people. "Then this is the first tic on my list."

He looked over at her. Though his eyes were shielded by the black lenses, she knew, from the angle of his head, that they were narrowed with speculation. "You've been here, what, around a month, and you haven't gone for ribs?"

"No. Will I be arrested?"

"You a vegetarian?"

"No, and I like ribs."

"Honey, you haven't had ribs yet if you haven't had Memphis ribs. Don't your parents live down here? I thought I'd met them once."

"My father and his wife, yeah. Will and Jolene Dooley."

"And no ribs?"

"I guess not. Will *they* be arrested?"

"They might, if it gets out. But I'll give you, and them, a break and keep quiet about it for the time being."

"Guess we'll owe you."

"Heartbreak Hotel" moved into "Shake, Rattle, and Roll." This was her father's music, she thought. It was odd, and kind of sweet, to be driving along, tapping her foot, on the way to Memphis listening to the music her father had listened to as a teenager.

"What you do is you take the kids to the Reunion for ribs," Logan told her. "You can walk over to Beale from there, take in the show. But before you eat, you go by the Peabody so they can see the ducks. Kids gotta see the ducks."

"My father's taken them."

"That might keep him out of the slammer."

"Whew." It was easier than she'd thought it would be, and she felt foolish knowing she'd prepared several avenues for small talk. "Except for the time you moved north, you've always lived in the Memphis area?"

"That's right."

"It's strange for me, knowing I was born here, but having no real memory of it. I like it here, and I like to think—overlooking the lack of ribs to date—that there's a connection for me here. Of course, I haven't been through a summer yet—that I can remember—but I like it. I love working for Roz."

"She's a jewel."

Because she heard the affection in his tone, she shifted toward him a bit. "She thinks the same of you. In fact, initially, I thought the two of you were . . ."

His grin spread. "No kidding?"

"She's beautiful and clever, and you've got a lot in common. You've got a history."

"All true. Probably the history makes anything like that weird. But thanks."

"I admire her so much. I like her, too, but I have such admiration for everything she's accomplished. Single-handedly. Raising her family, maintaining her home, building a business from the ground up. And all the while doing it her own way, calling her own shots."

"Is that what you want?"

"I don't want my own business. I thought about it a couple of years ago. But that sort of leap with no parachute and two kids?" She shook her head. "Roz is gutsier than I am. Besides, I realized it wasn't what I really wanted. I like working for someone else, sort of troubleshooting and coming in with a creative and efficient plan for improvement or expansion. Managing is what I do best."

She waited a beat. "No sarcastic comments to that?"

"Only on the inside. That way I can save them up until you tick me off again."

"I can hardly wait. In any case, it's like, I enjoy planting a garden from scratch—that blank slate. But more, I like taking one that's not planned very well, or needs some shaping up, and turning it around."

She paused, frowned. "Funny, I just remembered. I had a dream about a garden a few nights ago. A really strange dream with . . . I don't know, something spooky about it. I can't quite get it back, but there was something . . . this huge, gorgeous blue dahlia. Dahlias are a particular favorite of mine, and blue's my favorite color. Still, it shouldn't have been there, didn't belong there. I hadn't planted it. But there it was. Strange."

"What did you do with it? The dahlia?"

"Can't remember. Luke woke me up, so my garden and the exotic dahlia went poof." And the room, she thought, the room had been so cold. "He wasn't feeling well, a little tummy distress."

"He okay now?"

"Yeah." Another point for his side, Stella thought. "He's fine, thanks."

"How about the tooth?"

Uh-oh, second point. The man remembered her baby'd had a loose tooth. "Sold to the Tooth Fairy for a crisp dollar bill. Second one's about to wiggle out. He's got the cutest little lisp going on right now."

"His big brother teach him how to spit through the hole yet?"

She grimaced. "Not to my knowledge."

"What you don't know . . . I bet it's still there—the magic dahlia—blooming in dreamland."

"That's a nice thought." *Kill it.* God, where did that come from? she wondered, fighting off a shudder. "It was pretty spectacular, as I recall."

She glanced around as he pulled into a parking lot. "Is this it?"

"It's across the road. This is like the visitors' center, the staging area. We get our tickets inside, and they take groups over in shuttles."

He turned off the engine, shifted to look at her. "Five bucks says you're a convert when we come back out."

"An Elvis convert? I don't have anything against him now."

"Five bucks. You'll be buying an Elvis CD, minimum, after the tour."

"That's a bet."

* * *

IT WAS SO MUCH SMALLER THAN SHE'D IMAGINED. She'd pictured something big and sprawling, something mansionlike, close to the level of Harper House. Instead, it was a relatively modest-sized home, and the rooms—at least the ones the tour encompassed—rather small.

She shuffled along with the rest of the tourists, listening to Lisa Marie Presley's recorded memories and observations through the provided headset.

She puzzled over the pleated fabric in shades of curry, blue, and maroon swagged from the ceiling and covering every inch of wall in the cramped, pool-table-dominated game room. Then wondered at the waterfall, the wild-animal prints and tiki-hut accessories all crowned by a ceiling of green shag carpet in the jungle room.

Someone had lived with this, she thought. Not just someone, but an icon—a man of miraculous talent and fame. And it was sweet to listen to the woman who'd been a child when she'd lost her famous father, talk about the man she remembered, and loved.

The trophy room was astonishing to her, and immediately replaced her style quibbles with awe. It seemed like miles of walls in the meandering hallways were covered, cheek by jowl, with Elvis's gold and platinum records. All that accomplished, all that earned in fewer years, really, than she'd been alive.

And with Elvis singing through her headset, she admired his accomplishments, marveled over his elaborate, splashy, and myriad stage costumes. Then was charmed by his photographs, his movie posters, and the snippets of interviews.

YOU LEARNED A LOT ABOUT SOMEONE WALKING through Graceland with her, Logan discovered. Some snickered over the dated and debatably tacky decor. Some stood glassy-eyed with adoration for the dead King. Others bopped along, rubbernecking or chatting, moving on through so they could get it all in and push on to the souvenir shops. Then they could go home and say, been there, done that.

But Stella looked at everything. And listened. He could tell she was listening carefully to the recording, the way her head would cock just an inch to the right. Listening soberly, he thought, and he'd bet a lot more than five bucks that she followed the instructions on the tape, pressing the correct number for the next segment at exactly the proper time.

It was kind of cute actually.

When they stepped outside to make the short pilgrimage to Elvis's poolside grave, she took off her headphones for the first time.

"I didn't know all that," she began. "Nothing more than the bare basics, really. Over a billion records sold? It's beyond comprehension, really. I certainly can't imagine what it would be like to *do* all that and . . . what are you grinning at?"

"I bet if you had to take an Elvis test right now, you'd ace it."

"Shut up." But she laughed, then sobered again when she walked through the sunlight with him to the Meditation Garden, and the King's grave.

There were flowers, live ones wilting in the sun, plastic ones fading in it. And the little gravesite beside the swimming pool seemed both eccentric and right. Cameras snapped around them now, and she heard someone quietly sobbing.

"People claim to have seen his ghost, you know, back there." Logan gestured. "That is, if he's really dead."

"You don't believe that."

"Oh, yeah, Elvis left the building a long time ago."

"I mean about the ghost."

"Well, if he was going to haunt any place, this would be it."

They wound around toward the shuttle pickup. "People are awfully casual about ghosts around here."

It took him a minute. "Oh, the Harper Bride. Seen her yet?"

"No, I haven't. But that may only be because, you know, she doesn't exist. You're not going to tell me you've seen her."

"Can't say I have. Lot of people claim to, but then some claim to have seen Elvis eating peanut-butter-and-banana sandwiches at some diner ten years after he died."

"Exactly!" She was so pleased with his good sense, she gave him a light punch on the arm. "People see what they want to see, or have been schooled to see, or expect to. Imaginations run wild, especially under the right conditions or atmosphere. They ought to do more with the gardens here, don't you think?"

"Don't get me started."

"You're right. No shop talk. Instead, I'll just thank you for bringing me. I don't know when I'd've gotten around to it on my own."

"What'd you think?"

"Sad and sweet and fascinating." She passed her headphones back to the attendant and stepped on the shuttle. "Some of the rooms were, let's say, unique in decor."

Their arms bumped, brushed, stayed pressed to each other in the narrow confines of the shuttle's seats. Her hair skimmed along his shoulder until she shoved it back. He was sorry when she did.

"I knew this guy, big Elvis fan. He set about duplicating Graceland in his house. Got fabric like you saw in the game room, did his walls and ceilings."

She turned to face him, stared. "You're kidding."

He simply swiped a finger over his heart. "Even put a scar on his pool table to match the one on Elvis's. When he talked about getting those yellow appliances—"

"Harvest gold."

"Whatever. When he starting making noises about putting those in, his wife gave him notice. Her or Elvis."

Her face was alive with humor, and he stopped hearing the chatter of other passengers. There was something about her when she smiled, full out, that blew straight through him.

"And which did he choose?"

"Huh?"

"Which did he choose? His wife or Elvis?"

"Well." He stretched out his legs, but couldn't really shift his body away from hers. The sun was blasting through the window beside her, striking all that curling red hair. "He settled on re-creating it in his basement, and was trying to talk her into letting him put a scale model of the Meditation Garden in their backyard."

She laughed, a delightful roll of sound. When she dropped her head back on the seat, her hair tickled his shoulder again. "If he ever does, I hope we get the job."

"Count on it. He's my uncle."

She laughed again, until she was breathless. "Boy, I can't wait to meet your family." She angled around so she could face him. "I'm going to confess the only reason I came today was because I didn't want to spoil a nice gesture by saying no. I didn't expect to have fun."

"It wasn't a nice gesture so much as a spur of the moment thing. Your hair smelled good, and that clouded my better judgment."

Humor danced over her face as she pushed her hair back. "And? You're supposed to say you had fun, too."

"Actually, I did."

When the shuttle stopped, he got up, stepped back so she could slide out and walk in front of him. "But then, your hair still smells good, so that could be it."

She shot him a grin over her shoulder, and damn it, he felt that clutch in the belly. Usually the clutch meant possibilities of fun and enjoyment. With her, he thought it meant trouble.

But he'd been raised to follow through, and his mama

would be horrified and shocked if he didn't feed a woman he'd spent the afternoon with.

"Hungry?" he asked when he stepped down after her.

"Oh . . . Well, it's too early for dinner, too late for lunch. I really should—"

"Walk on the wild side. Eat between meals." He grabbed her hand, and that was such a surprise she didn't think to protest until he'd pulled her toward one of the on-site eateries.

"I really shouldn't take the time. I told Roz I'd be back around four."

"You know, you stay wrapped that tight for any length of time, you're going to cut your circulation off."

"I'm not wrapped that tight," she objected. "I'm responsible."

"Roz doesn't have a time clock at the nursery, and it doesn't take that long to eat a hot dog."

"No, but . . ." Liking him was so unexpected. As unexpected as the buzz along her skin at the feel of that big, hard hand gripping hers. It had been a long while since she'd enjoyed a man's company. Why cut it short?

"Okay." Though, she realized, her assent was superfluous, as he'd already pulled her inside and up to the counter. "Anyway. Since I'm here, I wouldn't mind looking in the shops for a minute. Or two."

He ordered two dogs, two Cokes and just smiled at her.

"All right, smart guy." She opened her purse, dug out her wallet. And took out a five-dollar bill. "I'm buying the CD. And make mine a Diet Coke."

She ate the hot dog, drank the Coke. She bought the CD. But unlike every other female he knew, she didn't have some religious obligation to look at and paw over everything in the store. She did her business and was done—neat, tidy, and precise.

And as they walked back to his truck, he noticed she glanced at the readout display of her cell phone. Again.

"Problem?"

"No." She slipped the phone back into her bag. "Just

checking to see if I had any messages." But it seemed everyone had managed without her for an afternoon.

Unless something was wrong with the phones. Or they'd lost her number. Or—

"The nursery could've been attacked by psychopaths with a petunia fetish." Logan opened the passenger-side door. "The entire staff could be bound and gagged in the propagation house even as we speak."

Deliberately, Stella zipped her bag closed. "You won't think that's so funny if we get there and that's just what happened."

"Yes, I will."

He walked around the truck, got behind the wheel.

"I have an obsessive, linear, goal-oriented personality with strong organizational tendencies."

He sat for a moment. "I'm glad you told me. I was under the impression you were a scatterbrain."

"Well, enough about me. Why—"

"Why do you keep doing that?"

She paused, her hands up in her hair. "Doing what?"

"Why do you keep jamming those pins in your hair?"

"Because they keep coming out."

To her speechless shock, he reached over, tugged the loosened bobby pins free, then tossed them on the floor of his truck. "So why put them in there in the first place?"

"Well, for God's sake." She scowled down at the pins. "How many times a week does someone tell you you're pushy and overbearing?"

"I don't count." He drove out of the lot and into traffic. "You've got sexy hair. You ought to leave it alone."

"Thanks very much for the style advice."

"Women don't usually sulk when a man tells them they're sexy."

"I'm not sulking, and you didn't say I was sexy. You said my hair was."

He took his eyes off the road long enough to give her an up-and-down glance. "Rest of you works, too."

Okay, something was wrong when that sort of half-assed compliment had heat balling in her belly. Best to return to safe topics. "To return to my question before I was so oddly interrupted, why did you go into landscape design?"

"Summer job that stuck."

She waited a beat, two. Three. "Really, Logan, must you go on and on, boring me with details?"

"Sorry. I never know when to shut up. I grew up on a farm."

"Really? Did you love it or hate it?"

"Was used to it, mostly. I like working outside, and don't mind heavy, sweaty work."

"Blabbermouth," she said when he fell silent again.

"Not that much more to it. I didn't want to farm, and my daddy sold the farm some years back, anyway. But I like working the land. It's what I like, it's what I'm good at. No point in doing something you don't like or you're not good at."

"Let's try this. How did you know you were good at it?"

"Not getting fired was an indication." He didn't see how she could possibly be interested, but since she was pressing, he'd pass the time. "You know how you're in school, say in history, and they're all Battle of Hastings or crossing the Rubicon or Christ knows? In and out," he said, tapping one side of his head, then the other. "I'd jam it in there long enough to skin through the test, then poof. But on the job, the boss would say we're going to put cotoneasters in here, line these barberries over there, and I'd remember. What they were, what they needed. I liked putting them in. It's satisfying, digging the hole, prepping the soil, changing the look of things. Making it more pleasing to the eye."

"It is," she agreed. "Believe it or not, that's the same sort of deal I have with my files."

He slanted her a look that made her lips twitch. "You say. Anyway, sometimes I'd get this idea that, you know, those cotoneasters would look better over there, and instead of barberries, golden mops would set this section off. So I angled off into design."

"I thought about design for a while. Not that good at it," she said. "I realized I had a hard time adjusting my vision to blend with the team's—or the client's. And I'd get too hung up in the math and science of it, and bogged down when it came time to roll over into the art."

"Who did your landscaping up north?"

"I did. If I had something in mind that took machines, or more muscle than Kevin and I could manage, I had a list." She smiled. "A very detailed and specific list, with the design done on graph paper. Then I hovered. I'm a champion hoverer."

"And nobody shoved you into a hole and buried you?"

"No. But then, I'm very personable and pleasant. Maybe, when the time comes and I find my own place, you could consult on the landscaping design."

"I'm not personable and pleasant."

"Already noted."

"And isn't it a leap for an obsessive, linear, detail freak to trust me to consult when you've only seen one of my jobs, and that in its early stages?"

"I object to the term 'freak.' I prefer 'devotee.' And it happens I've seen several of your jobs, complete. I got some of the addresses out of the files and drove around. It's what I do," she said when he braked at a Stop sign and stared at her. "I've spent some time watching Harper work, and Roz, as well as the employees. I made it a point to take a look at some of your completed jobs. I like your work."

"And if you hadn't?"

"If I hadn't, I'd have said nothing. It's Roz's business, and *she* obviously likes your work. But I'd have done some quiet research on other designers, put a file together and presented it to her. That's my job."

"And here I thought your job was to manage the nursery and annoy me with forms."

"It is. Part of that management is to make sure that all

employees and subcontractors, suppliers and equipment are not only suitable for In the Garden but the best Roz can afford. You're pricey," she added, "but your work justifies it."

When he only continued to frown, she poked a finger into his arm. "And men don't usually sulk when a woman compliments their work."

"Huh. Men never sulk, they brood."

But she had a point. Still, it occurred to him that she knew a great deal about him—personal matters. How much he made, for instance. When he asked himself how he felt about that, the answer was, Not entirely comfortable.

"My work, my salary, my prices are between me and Roz."

"Not anymore," she said cheerfully. "She has the last word, no question, but I'm there to manage. I'm saying that, in my opinion, Roz showed foresight and solid business sense in bringing you into her business. She pays you very well because you're worth it. Any reason you can't take that as a compliment and skip the brooding phase?"

"I don't know. What's she paying you?"

"That *is* between her and me, but you're certainly free to ask her." The *Star Wars* theme erupted in her purse. "Gavin's pick," she said as she dug it out. The readout told her the call came from home. "Hello? Hi, baby."

Though he was still a little irked, he watched everything about her light up. "You *did*? You're amazing. Uh-huh. I absolutely will. See you soon."

She closed the phone, put it back in her purse. "Gavin aced his spelling test."

"Yay."

She laughed. "You have *no* idea. I have to pick up pepperoni pizza on the way home. In our family, it's not a carrot at the end of the stick used as motivation—or simple bribery—it's pepperoni pizza."

"You bribe your kids?"

"Often, and without a qualm."

"Smart. So, they're getting along in school?"

"They are. All that worry and guilt wasted. I'll have to set it aside for future use. It was a big move for them—new place, new school, new people. Luke makes friends easily, but Gavin can be a little shy."

"Didn't seem shy to me. Kid's got a spark. Both of them do."

"Comic book connection. Any friend of Spidey's, and so on, so they were easy with you. But they're both sliding right along. So I can scratch traumatizing my sons by ripping them away from their friends off my Things to Worry About list."

"I bet you actually have one."

"Every mother has one." She let out a long, contented sigh as he pulled into the lot at the nursery. "This has been a really good day. Isn't this a great place? Just look at it. Industrious, attractive, efficient, welcoming. I envy Roz her vision, not to mention her guts."

"You don't seem deficient in the guts department."

"Is that a compliment?"

He shrugged. "An observation."

She liked being seen as gutsy, so she didn't tell him she was scared a great deal of the time. Order and routine were solid, defensive walls that kept the fear at bay.

"Well, thanks. For the observation, and the afternoon. I really appreciated both." She opened the door, hopped out. "And I've got a trip into the city for ribs on my list of must-dos."

"You won't be sorry." He got out, walked around to her side. He wasn't sure why. Habit, he supposed. Ingrained manners his mother had carved into him as a boy. But it wasn't the sort of situation where you walked the girl to her door and copped a kiss good night.

She thought about offering her hand to shake, but it seemed stiff *and* ridiculous. So she just smiled. "I'll play the CD for the boys." She shook her bag. "See what they think."

"Okay. See you around."

He started to walk back to his door. Then he cursed under his breath, tossed his sunglasses on the hood, and turned back. "Might as well finish it out."

She wasn't slow, and she wasn't naive. She knew what he intended when he was still a full stride away. But she couldn't seem to move.

She heard herself make some sound—not an actual word—then his hand raked through her hair, his fingers cupping her head with enough pressure to bring her up on her toes. She saw his eyes. There were gold flecks dusted over the green.

Then everything blurred, and his mouth was hard and hot on hers.

Nothing hesitant about it, nothing testing or particularly friendly. It was all demand, with an irritable edge. Like the man, she thought dimly, he was doing what he intended to do, was determined to see it through, but wasn't particularly pleased about it.

And still her heart rammed into her throat, throbbing there to block words, even breath. The fingers of the hand that had lifted to his shoulder in a kind of dazed defense dug in. They slid limply down to his elbow when his head lifted.

With his hand still caught in her hair, he said, "Hell."

He dragged her straight up to her toes again, banded an arm around her so that her body was plastered to his. When his mouth swooped down a second time, any brains that hadn't already been fried drained out of her ears.

He shouldn't have thought of kissing her. But once he had, it didn't seem reasonable to walk away and leave it undone. And now he was in trouble, all wound up in that wild hair, that sexy scent, those soft lips.

And when he deepened the kiss, she let out this sound, this catchy little moan. What the hell was a man supposed to do but want?

Her hair was like a maze of madly coiled silk, and that

pretty, curvy body of hers vibrated against him like a well-tuned machine, revving for action. The longer he held her, the more he tasted her, the dimmer the warning bells sounded to remind him he didn't want to get tangled up with her. On any level.

When he managed to release her, to step back, he saw the flush riding along her cheeks. It made her eyes bluer, bigger. It made him want to toss her over his shoulder and cart her off somewhere, anywhere at all where they could finish what the kiss had started. Because the urge to do so was an ache in the belly, he took another step back.

"Okay." He thought he spoke calmly, but couldn't be sure with the blood roaring in his ears. "See you around."

He walked back to the truck, got in. Managed to turn over the engine and shove into reverse. Then he hit the brakes again when the sun speared into his eyes.

He sat, watching Stella walk forward, retrieve the sunglasses that had bounced off the hood and onto the gravel. He lowered the window as she stepped to it.

His eyes stayed on hers when he reached out to take them from her. "Thanks."

"Sure."

He slipped them on, backed out, turned the wheel and drove out of the lot.

Alone, she let out a long, wheezing breath, sucked in another one; and let that out as she ordered her limp legs to carry her to the porch.

She made it as far as the steps before she simply lowered herself down to sit. "Holy Mother of God," she managed.

She sat, even as a customer came out, as another came in, while everything inside her jumped and jittered. She felt as though she'd fallen off a cliff and was even now, barely—just barely—clinging to a skinny, crumbling ledge by sweaty fingertips.

What was she supposed to do about this? And how could she figure it out when she couldn't think?

So she wouldn't try to figure it out until she could think. Getting to her feet, she rubbed her damp palms on the thighs of her pants. For now, she'd go back to work, she'd order pizza, then go home to her boys. Go home to normal.

She did better with normal.

ten

HARPER SPADED THE DIRT AT THE BASE OF THE clematis that wound its way up the iron trellis. It was quiet on this edge of the garden. The shrubs and ornamental trees, the paths and beds separated what he still thought of as the guest house from the main.

Daffodils were just opening up, with all that bright yellow against the spring green. Tulips would be coming along next. They were one of his favorite things about this leading edge of spring, so he'd planted a bed of bulbs right outside the kitchen door of his place.

It was a small converted carriage house and according to every female he'd ever brought there, it was charming. "Dollhouse" was the usual term. He didn't mind it. Though he thought of it more as a cottage, like a groundskeeper's cottage with its whitewashed cedar shakes and pitched roof. It was comfortable, inside and out, and more than adequate for his needs.

There was a small greenhouse only a few feet out the back door, and that was his personal domain. The cottage was just far enough from the house to be private, so he didn't have to feel weird having overnight guests of the female persuasion. And close enough that he could be at the main house in minutes if his mother needed him.

He didn't like the idea of her being alone, even with David on hand. And thank God for David. It didn't matter that she was self-sufficient, the strongest person he knew. He just didn't like the idea of his mother rattling around in that big old house alone, day after day, night after night.

Though he certainly preferred that to having her stuck in it with that asshole she'd married. Words couldn't describe how he despised Bryce Clerk. He supposed having his mother fall for the guy proved she wasn't infallible, but it had been a hell of a mistake for someone who rarely made one.

Though she'd given him the boot, swiftly and without mercy, Harper had worried how the man would handle being cut off—from Roz, the house, the money, the whole ball.

And damned if he hadn't tried to break in once, the week before the divorce was final. Harper didn't doubt his mother could've handled it, but it hadn't hurt to be at hand.

And having a part in kicking the greedy, cheating, lying bastard out on his ass couldn't be overstated.

But maybe enough time had passed now. And she sure as hell wasn't alone in the house these days. Two women, two kids made for a lot of company. Between them and the business, she was busier than ever.

Maybe he should think about getting a place of his own.

Trouble was, he couldn't think of a good reason. He loved this place, in a way he'd never loved a woman. With a kind of focused passion, respect, and gratitude.

The gardens were home, maybe even more than the house, more than his cottage. Most days he could walk out his front door, take a good, healthy hike, and be at work.

God knew he didn't want to move to the city. All that noise, all those people. Memphis was great for a night out—a club, a date, meeting up with friends. But he'd suffocate there inside a month.

He sure as hell didn't want suburbia. What he wanted was right where he was. A nice little house, extensive gardens, a greenhouse and a short hop to work.

He sat back on his heels, adjusted the ball cap he wore to keep the hair out of his eyes. Spring was coming. There was nothing like spring at home. The way it smelled, the way it looked, even the way it sounded.

The light was soft now with approaching evening. When the sun went down, the air would chill, but it wouldn't have that bite of winter.

When he was done planting here, he'd go in and get himself a beer. And he'd sit out in the dark and the cool, and enjoy the solitude.

He took a bold yellow pansy out of the cell pack and began to plant.

He didn't hear her walk up. Such was his focus that he didn't notice her shadow fall over him. So her friendly "Hey!" nearly had him jumping out of his skin.

"Sorry." With a laugh, Hayley rubbed a hand over her belly. "Guess you were a million miles away."

"Guess." His fingers felt fat and clumsy all of a sudden, and his brain sluggish. She stood with the setting sun at her back, so when he squinted up at her, her head was haloed, her face shadowed.

"I was just walking around. Heard your music." She nodded toward the open windows where REM spilled out. "I saw them in concert once. Excellent. Pansies? They're a hot item right now."

"Well, they like the cool."

"I know. How come you're putting them here? You've got this vine thing happening."

"Clematis. Likes its roots shaded. So you . . . you know, put annuals over them."

"Oh." She squatted down for a closer look. "What color is the clematis?"

"It's purple." He wasn't sure pregnant women should squat. Didn't it crowd things in there? "Ah, you want a chair or something?"

"No, I'm set. I like your house."

"Yeah, me too."

"It's sort of storybook here, with all the gardens. I mean, the big house is amazing. But it's a little intimidating." She grimaced. "I don't mean to sound ungrateful."

"No, I get you." It helped to keep planting. She didn't *smell* pregnant. She smelled sexy. And that had to be wrong. "It's a great place, and you couldn't get my mother out of it with dynamite and wild mules. But it's a lot of house."

"Took me a week to stop walking about on tiptoe and wanting to whisper. Can I plant one?"

"You don't have any gloves. I can get—"

"Hell, I don't mind a little dirt under my nails. A lady was in today? She said it's like good luck for a pregnant woman to plant gardens. Something about fertility, I guess."

He didn't want to think about fertility. There was something terrifying about it. "Go ahead."

"Thanks. I wanted to say . . ." And it was easier with her hands busy. "Well, just that I know how it might look, me coming out of nowhere, landing on your mama's doorstep. But I'm not going to take advantage of her. I don't want you to think I'd try to do that."

"I've only known one person to manage it, and he didn't manage it for long."

"The second husband." She nodded as she patted the dirt around her plant. "I asked David about him so I wouldn't say something stupid. He said how he'd stuck his hand in the till, and cheated on her with another woman." She chose another pansy. "And when Roz got wind of it, she booted him out so hard and fast he didn't land till he was halfway to Memphis. You gotta admire that, because you know even with a mad on, it had to hurt her feelings. Plus, it's just embarrassing when somebody—oops."

She pressed a hand to her side, and had the blood draining out of Harper's face.

"What? What?"

"Nothing. Baby's moving around. Sometimes it gives me a jolt is all."

"You should stand up. You should sit down."

"Let me just finish this one. Back home, when I started to show? People, some people, just figured I'd got myself in trouble and the boy wouldn't stand up for me. I mean, Jesus, are we in the twenty-first century or what? Anyway, that made me mad, but it was embarrassing, too. I guess that's partly why I left. It's hard being embarrassed all the damn time. There." She patted the dirt. "They look really pretty."

He popped up to help her to her feet. "You want to sit for a minute? Want me to walk you back?"

She patted her belly. "This makes you nervous."

"Looks like."

"Me too. But I'm fine. You'll want to get the rest of those planted before it gets dark." She looked down at the flowers again, at the house, at the gardens surrounding it, and those long, lake-colored eyes seemed to take in everything.

Then they zeroed in on his face and made his throat go dry.

"I really like your place. See you at work."

He stood, rooted, as she walked off, gliding along the path, around the curve of it, into the twilight.

He was exhausted, he realized. Like he'd run some sort of crazed race. He'd just have that beer now, settle himself down. Then he'd finish with the pansies.

WITH THE KIDS OUTSIDE TAKING PARKER FOR HIS after-dinner walk, Stella cleaned up the mess two boys and a dog could make in the kitchen over a pepperoni pizza.

"Next pizza night, I buy," Hayley said as she loaded glasses into the dishwasher.

"That's a deal." Stella glanced over. "When I was carrying Luke, all I wanted was Italian. Pizza, spaghetti, manicotti. I was surprised he didn't pop out singing 'That's Amore.' "

"I don't have any specific cravings. I'll just eat anything." In the wash of the outside floodlights, she could see boys and dog racing. "The baby's moving around a lot. That's normal, right?"

"Sure. Gavin just sort of snuggled and snoozed. I'd have to poke him or sip some Coke to get him moving. But Luke did gymnastics in there for months. Is it keeping you up nights?"

"Sometimes, but I don't mind. It feels like we're the only two people in the world. Just me and him—or her."

"I know just what you mean. But Hayley, if you're awake, worried or just not feeling well, whatever, you can come get me."

The tightness in her throat loosened instantly. "Really? You mean it?"

"Sure. Sometimes it helps to talk to somebody who's been there and done that."

"I'm not on my own," she said quietly, with her eyes on the boys outside the window. "Not like I thought I'd be. Was ready to be—I think." When those eyes filled, she blinked them, rubbed at them. "Hormones. God."

"Crying can help, too." Stella rubbed Hayley's shoulders. "And I want you to tell me if you want someone to go with you to your doctor's appointments."

"He said, when I went in, that everything looks good. Right on schedule. And that I should sign up for the classes, you know? Childbirth classes. But they like you to have a partner."

"Pick me!"

Laughing, Hayley turned. "Really? You're sure? It's a lot to ask."

"I would love it. It's almost as good as having another one of my own."

"Would you? If . . ."

"Yes. Two was the plan, but as soon as Luke was born, I thought, how can I not do this again—and wouldn't it be fun to try for a girl? But another boy would be great." She leaned forward on the counter, looked out the window. "They're terrific, aren't they? My boys."

"They are."

"Kevin was so proud, so in love with them. I think he'd have had half a dozen."

Hayley heard the change in tone, and this time, she rubbed a hand on Stella's shoulder. "Does it hurt to talk about him?"

"Not anymore. It did for a while, for a long while." She picked up the dishrag to wipe the counter. "But now it's good to remember. Warm, I guess. I ought to call those boys in."

But she turned at the sound of heels clicking on wood. When Roz breezed in, Stella's mouth dropped open.

She recalled her first impression of Rosalind Harper had been of beauty, but this was the first time she'd seen Roz exploit her natural attributes.

She wore a sleek, form-fitting dress in a muted copper color that made her skin glow. It, along with ice-pick-heeled sandals, showed off lean, toned legs. A necklace of delicate filigree with a teardrop of citrine lay over her breasts.

"David?" Roz scanned the room, then rolled dark, dramatic eyes. "He's going to make me late."

Stella let out an exaggerated breath. "Just let me say, Wow!"

"Yeah." She grinned, did a little half turn. "I must've been insane when I bought the shoes. They're going to kill me. But when I have to drag myself out to one of these charity deals, I like to make a statement."

"If the statement's 'I'm totally hot,' " Hayley put in, "you hit it dead on."

"That was the target."

"You look absolutely amazing. Sex with class. Every

man there's going to wish he was taking you home tonight."

"Well." With a half laugh, Roz shook her head. "It's great having women in the house. Who knew? I'm going to go nag David. He'll primp for another hour if I don't give his ass a kick."

"Have a wonderful time."

"She sure didn't look like anybody's mother," Stella said under her breath.

WHAT WOULD SHE LOOK LIKE IN TWENTY YEARS? Hayley wondered.

She studied herself in the mirror while she rubbed Vitamin E oil over her belly and breasts. Would she still be able to fix herself up and know she looked good?

Of course, she didn't have as much to work with as Roz. She remembered her grandmother saying once that beauty was in the bones. Looking at Roz helped her understand just what that meant.

She'd never be as stunning as Roz, or as eye-catching as Stella, but she looked okay. She took care of her skin, tried out the makeup tricks she read about in magazines.

Guys were attracted.

Obviously, she thought with a self-deprecating smile as she looked down at her belly.

Or had been. Most guys didn't get the hots for pregnant women. And that was fine, because she wasn't interested in men right now. The only thing that mattered was her baby.

"It's all about you now, kid," she said as she pulled on an oversized T-shirt.

After climbing into bed, plumping up her pillows, she reached for one of the books stacked on her nightstand. She had books on childbirth, on pregnancy, on early-childhood development. She read from one of them every night.

When her eyes began to droop, she closed the book.

Switching off the light, she snuggled down. "'Night, baby," she whispered.

And felt it just as she was drifting off. The little chill, the absolute certainty that she wasn't alone. Her heartbeat quickened until she could hear it in her ears. Gathering courage, she let her eyes open to slits.

She saw the figure standing over the bed. The light-colored hair, the lovely sad face. She thought about screaming, just as she did every time she saw the woman. But she bit it back, braced herself, and reached out.

When her hand passed through the woman's arm, Hayley did let out a muffled scream. Then she was alone, shivering in bed and fumbling for the light.

"I'm not imagining it. I'm not!"

STELLA CLIMBED UP THE STEPSTOOL TO HOOK ANOTHER hanging basket for display. After looking over last year's sales, crunching numbers, she'd decided to increase the number offered by 15 percent.

"I could do that," Hayley insisted. "I'm not going to fall off a stupid stepstool."

"No chance. Hand me up that one. The begonias."

"They're really pretty. So lush."

"Roz and Harper started most of these over the winter. Begonias and impatiens are big-volume sellers. With growers like Roz and Harper, we can do them in bulk, and our cost is low. These are bread-and-butter plants for us."

"People could make up their own cheaper."

"Sure." Stella climbed down, moved the ladder, climbed up again. "Ivy geranium," she decided. "But it's tough to resist all this color and bloom. Even avid gardeners, the ones who do some propagating on their own, have a hard time passing up big, beautiful blooms. Blooms, my young apprentice, sell."

"So we're putting these baskets everywhere."

"Seduction. Wait until we move some of the annuals

outside, in front. All that color will draw the customers. Early-blooming perennials too."

She selected another basket. "I've got this. Page Roz, will you? I want her to see these, and get her clearance to hang a couple dozen in Greenhouse Three with the extra stock. And pick out a pot. One of the big ones that didn't move last year. I want to do one up, put it by the counter. I'll move that sucker. In fact, pick out two. Clean off the discount price. When I'm done, they'll not only move, they'll move at a fat profit."

"Gotcha."

"Make sure one of them's that cobalt glaze," she called out. "You know the one? And don't pick it up yourself."

In her mind, Stella began to plan it. White flowers—heliotrope, impatiens, spills of sweet alyssum, silvery accents from dusty miller and sage. Another trail of white petunias. Damn, she should've told Hayley to get one of the stone-gray pots. Good contrast with the cobalt. And she'd do it up hot. Bold red geraniums, lobelia, verbena, red New Guineas.

She added, subtracted plants in her mind, calculated the cost of pots, stock, soil. And smiled to herself as she hung another basket.

"Shouldn't you be doing paperwork?"

She nearly tipped off the stool, might have if a hand hadn't slapped onto her butt to keep her upright.

"It's not all I do." She started to get down, but realized being on the stool kept her at eye level with him. "You can move your hand now, Logan."

"It doesn't mind being there." But he let it fall, slipped it into his pocket. "Nice baskets."

"In the market?"

"Might be. You had a look on your face when I came in."

"I usually do. That's why it's called a face."

"No, the kind of look a woman gets when she's thinking about how to make some guy drool."

"Did I? Mind?" she added, gesturing to a basket. "You're off the mark. I was thinking how I was going to turn two over-stock pots on the discount rack into stupendous displays and considerable profit."

Even as she hung the basket, he was lifting another, and by merely raising his arm, set it in place. "Showoff."

"Shorty."

Hayley came through the doorway, turned briskly on her heel and headed out.

"Hayley."

"Forgot something," she called out and kept going.

Stella blew out a breath and would've asked for another basket, but he'd already picked one up, hung it. "You've been busy," she said.

"Cool, dry weather the last week."

"If you're here to pick up the shrubs for the Pitt job, I can get the paperwork."

"My crew's out loading them. I want to see you again."

"Well. You are."

He kept his eyes on hers. "You're not dim."

"No, I'm not. I'm not sure—"

"Neither am I," he interrupted. "Doesn't seem to stop me from wanting to see you again. It's irritating, thinking about you."

"Thanks. That really makes me want to sigh and fall into your arms."

"I don't want you to fall into them. If I did, I'd just kick your feet out from under you."

She laid a hand on her heart, fluttered her lashes, and did her best woman of the south accent. "My goodness, all this soppy romance is too much for me."

Now he grinned. "I like you, Red. Some of the time. I'll pick you up at seven."

"What? Tonight?" Reluctant amusement turned to outright panic in a fingersnap. "I can't possibly just go out, spur of the moment. I have two kids."

"And three adults in the house. Any reason you can think of why any or all of them can't handle your boys for a few hours tonight?"

"No. But I haven't *asked*, a concept you appear to be

unfamiliar with. And—" She shoved irritably at her hair. "I might have plans."

"Do you?"

She angled her head, looked down her nose. "I always have plans."

"I bet. So flex them. You take the boys for ribs yet?"

"Yes, last week after—"

"Good."

"Do you know how often you interrupt me in the middle of a sentence?"

"No, but I'll start counting. Hey, Roz."

"Logan. Stella, these look great." She stopped in the center of the aisle, scanning, nodding as she absently slapped her dirty gloves against her already dirt-smeared jeans. "I wasn't sure displaying so many would work, but it does. Something about the abundance of bloom."

She took off her ball cap, stuffed it in the back pocket of her work pants, stuffed the gloves in the other. "Am I interrupting?"

"No."

"Yes," Logan corrected. "But it's okay. You up to watching Stella's boys tonight?"

"I haven't said—"

"Absolutely. It'll be fun. You two going out?"

"A little dinner. I'll leave the invoice on your desk," he said to Stella. "See you at seven."

Tired of standing, Stella sat on the stool and scowled at Roz when Logan sauntered out. "You didn't help."

"I think I did." Reaching up, she turned one of the baskets to check the symmetry of the plants. "You'll go out, have a good time. Your boys'll be fine, and I'll enjoy spending some time with them. If you didn't want to go out with Logan, you wouldn't go. You know how to say no loud enough."

"That may be true, but I might've liked a little more notice. A little more . . . something."

"He is what he is." She patted Stella's knee. "And the good thing about that is you don't have to wonder what he's hiding, or what kind of show he's putting on. He's . . . I can't say he's a nice man, because he can be incredibly difficult. But he's an honest one. Take it from me, there's a lot to be said for that."

eLeveN

THIS, STELLA THOUGHT, WAS WHY DATING WAS VERY rarely worth it. In her underwear, she stood in front of her closet, debating, considering, despairing over what to wear.

She didn't even know where she was going. She *hated* not knowing where she was going. How was she supposed to know what to prepare for?

"Dinner" was not enough information. Was it little-black-dress dinner, or dressy-casual on-sale-designer-suit dinner? Was it jeans and a shirt and jacket dinner, or jeans and a silk blouse dinner?

Added to that, by picking her up at seven, he'd barely left her enough time to change, much less decide what to change into.

Dating. How could something that had been so desired, so exciting and so damn much fun in her teens, so easy and natural in her early twenties, have become such a complicated, often irritating chore in her thirties?

It wasn't just that marriage had spoiled her, or rusted her dating tools. Adult dating was complex and exhausting because the people involved in the stupid date had almost certainly been through at least one serious relationship, and breakup, and carried that extra baggage on their backs. They were already set in their ways, had defined their expectations, and had performed this societal dating ritual so often that they really just wanted to cut to the chase—or go home and watch Letterman.

Add to that a man who dropped the date on your head out of the clear blue, then didn't have the sense to give you some guidelines so you knew how to present yourself, and it was just a complete mess before it started.

Fine, then. *Fine*. He'd just get what he got.

She was stepping into the little black dress when the connecting bathroom door burst open and Gavin rushed in. "Mom! I finished my homework. Luke didn't, but I did. Can I go down now? Can I?"

She was glad she'd decided on the open-toed slides and no hose, as Parker was currently trying to climb up her leg. "Did you forget something?" she asked Gavin.

"Nuh-uh. I did all the vocabulary words."

"The knocking something?"

"Oh." He smiled, big and innocent. "You look pretty."

"Smooth talker." She bent down to kiss the top of his head. "But when a door's closed, you knock."

"Okay. Can I go down now?"

"In a minute." She walked over to her dresser to put on the silver hoops she'd laid out. "I want you to promise you'll be good for Miss Roz."

"We're going to have cheeseburgers and play video games. She says she can take us in Smackdown, but I don't think so."

"No fighting with your brother." Hope springs, she thought. "Consider this your night off from your mission in life."

"Can I go *down*?"

"Get." She gave him a light slap on the rump. "Remember, I'll have my phone if you need me."

When he rushed out, she slipped on her shoes and a thin black sweater. After a check in the mirror, she decided the accessories took the dress into the could-be-casual, could-be-more area she'd been shooting for.

She picked up her bag and, checking the contents as she went, walked into the next bedroom. Luke was sprawled belly-down on the floor—his favored position—frowning miserably over his arithmetic book.

"Trouble, handsome?"

He lifted his head, and his face was aggrieved in the way only a young boy could manage. "I hate homework."

"Me too."

"Gavin did the touchdown dance, with his fingers in the air, 'cause he finished first."

Understanding the demoralization, she sat on the floor beside him. "Let's see what you've got."

"How come I have to know two plus three, anyway?"

"How else would you know how many fingers you have on each hand?"

His brow beetled, then cleared with a delighted smile. "Five!"

With the crisis averted, she helped him with the rest of the problems. "There, all done. That wasn't so bad."

"I still hate homework."

"Maybe, but what about the touchdown dance?"

On a giggle, he leaped up and did his strut around the room.

And all, she thought, was right in her little world once more.

"How come you're not going to eat here? We're having cheeseburgers."

"I'm not entirely sure. You'll behave for Miss Roz?"

"Uh-huh. She's nice. Once she came out in the yard and threw the ball for Parker. And she didn't even mind when it got slobbered. Some girls do. I'm going down now, okay? 'Cause I'm hungry."

"You bet."

Alone, she got to her feet, automatically picking up the scatter of toys and clothes that hadn't made it back onto the shelf or into the closet.

She ran her fingers over some of their treasures. Gavin's beloved comic books, his ball glove. Luke's favorite truck, and the battered bear he wasn't yet ashamed to sleep with.

The prickle between her shoulder blades had her stiffening. Even under the light sweater her arms broke out in gooseflesh. Out of the corner of her eye, she saw a shape—a reflection, a shadow—in the mirror over the bureau.

When she spun, Hayley swung around the door and into the room.

"Logan's just pulling up in front of the house," she began, then stopped. "You okay? You look all pale."

"Fine. I'm fine." But she pushed a not-quite-steady hand at her hair. "I just thought . . . nothing. Nothing. Besides pale, how do I look?" And she made herself turn to the mirror again. Saw only herself, with Hayley moving toward her.

"Two thumbs up. I just love your hair."

"Easy to say when you don't wake up with it every morning. I thought about putting it up, but it seemed too formal."

"It's just right." Hayley edged closer, tipping her head toward Stella's. "I did the redhead thing once. Major disaster. Made my skin look yellow."

"That deep, dense brown's what's striking on you." And look at that face, Stella thought with a tiny twist of envy. Not a line on it.

"Yeah, but the red's so now. Anyway, I'm going to go on down. I'll keep Logan busy until. You wait just a few more minutes before you head down, then we'll all be back in the kitchen. Big burger feast."

She didn't intend to make an entrance, for heaven's sake. But Hayley had already gone off, and she did want to check her lipstick. And settle herself down.

At least her nerves over this date—it *was* a date this

time—had taken a backseat to others. It hadn't been Hayley's reflection in the mirror. Even that quick glimpse had shown her the woman who'd stood there had blond hair.

Steadier, she walked out, started down the hall. From the top of the steps, she heard Hayley laugh.

"She'll be right down. I guess you know how to make yourself at home. I'm going on back to the kitchen with the rest of the gang. Let Stella know I'll say bye from her to everyone. Y'all have fun."

Was the girl psychic? Stella wondered. Hayley had timed her exit so adroitly that as she walked down the hall, Stella hit the halfway point on the steps.

And Logan's attention shifted upward.

Good black trousers, she noted. Nice blue shirt, no tie, but with a casual sport coat over it. And still he didn't look quite tame.

"Nice," he said.

"Thanks. You, too."

"Hayley said she'd tell everyone you were leaving. You ready?"

"Sure."

She stepped out with him, then studied the black Mustang. "You own a car."

"This is not merely a car, and to call it such is very female."

"And to say that is very sexist. Okay, if it's not a car, what is it?"

"It's a machine."

"I stand corrected. You never said where we were going."

He opened her door. "Let's find out."

HE DROVE INTO THE CITY, WITH MUSIC SHE DIDN'T recognize on low. She knew it was blues—or supposed it was, but she didn't know anything about that area of music. Mentioning that, casually, not only seemed to shock him but kept conversation going through the trip.

She got a nutshell education on artists like John Lee Hooker and Muddy Waters, B. B. King and Taj Mahal.

And it occurred to her after they'd crossed into the city, that conversation between them never seemed to be a problem. After he parked, he shifted to take a long look at her. "You sure you were born down here?"

"It says so on my birth certificate."

He shook his head and climbed out. "Since you're that ignorant of the blues, you better check it again."

He took her inside a restaurant where the tables were already crowded with patrons and the noise level high with chatter. Once they were seated, he waved the waiter away. "Why don't we just wait on drinks until you know what you want to eat. We'll get a bottle of wine to go with it."

"All right." Since it seemed he'd nixed the pre-dinner conversation, she opened her menu.

"They're known for their catfish here. Ever had it?" he asked.

She lifted her gaze over the top of her menu, met his. "No. And whether or not that makes me a Yankee, I'm thinking I'll go for the chicken."

"Okay. You can have some of mine to give you a sample of what you've been missing. There's a good California Chardonnay on their wine list that'll go with both the fish and the bird. It's got a nice finish."

She set her menu down, leaned forward. "Do you really know that, or are you just making it up?"

"I like wine. I make it a point to know what I like."

She sat back when he motioned the waiter over. Once they'd ordered, she angled her head. "What are we doing here, Logan?"

"Speaking for myself, I'm going to have a really fine catfish dinner and a glass of good wine."

"We've had some conversations, mostly business-oriented."

"We've had some conversations, and some arguments," he corrected.

"True. We had an outing, an enjoyable one, which ended on a surprisingly personal note."

"I do like listening to you talk sometimes, Red. It's almost like listening to a foreign language. Are you laying all those things down like pavers, trying to make some sort of path from one point to the next?"

"Maybe. The fact is, I'm sitting here with you, on a date. That wasn't my intention twenty-four hours ago. We've got a working relationship."

"Uh-huh. And speaking of that, I still find your system mostly annoying."

"Big surprise. And speaking of that, you neglected to put that invoice on my desk this afternoon."

"Did I?" He moved a shoulder. "I've got it somewhere."

"My point is—"

She broke off when the waiter brought the wine to the table, turned the label toward Logan.

"That's the one. Let the lady taste it."

She bided her time, then picked up the glass holding the testing sip. She sampled, lifted her eyebrows. "It's very good . . . has a nice finish."

Logan grinned. "Then let's get started on it."

"The point I was trying to make," she began again, "is that while it's smart and beneficial all around for you and me to develop a friendly relationship, it's probably not either for us to take it to any other level."

"Uh-huh." He sampled the wine himself, kept watching her with those big-cat eyes. "You think I'm not going to kiss you again because it might not be smart or beneficial?"

"I'm in a new place, with a new job. I've taken my kids to a new place. They're first with me."

"I expect they would be. But I don't expect this is your first dinner with a man since you lost your husband."

"I'm careful."

"I never would've guessed. How'd he die?"

"Plane crash. Commuter plane. He was on his way back from a business trip. I had the TV on, and there was a bulletin. They didn't give any names, but I knew it was Kevin's plane. I knew he was gone before they came to tell me."

"You know what you were wearing when you heard the bulletin, what you were doing, where you were standing." His voice was quiet, his eyes were direct. "You know every detail about that day."

"Why do you say that?"

"Because it was the worst day of your life. You'll be hazy on the day before, the day after, but you'll never forget a single detail of that day."

"You're right." And his intuition surprised her, touched her. "Have you lost someone?"

"No, not like what you mean, or how you mean. But a woman like you? She doesn't get married, stay married, unless the man's at the center of her life. Something yanks that center out of you, you never forget."

"No, I won't." It was carved into her heart. "That's the most insightful and accurate, and comforting expression of sympathy anyone's given me. I hope I don't insult you by saying it comes as a surprise."

"I don't insult that easy. You lost their father, but you've built a life—looks like a good one—for your kids. That takes work. You're not the first woman I've been interested in who's had children. I respect motherhood, and its priorities. Doesn't stop me from looking across this table and wondering when I'm going to get you naked."

She opened her mouth, closed it again. Cleared her throat, sipped wine. "Well. Blunt."

"Different sort of woman, I'd just go for the mattress." At her strangled half laugh, he lifted his wine. And waited while their first course was served. "But as it is, you're a . . . since we're having this nice meal together I'll say you're a cautious sort of woman."

"You wanted to say tight-ass."

He grinned, appreciating her. "You'll never know. Added to that, we both work for Roz, and I wouldn't do anything to mess her up. Not intentionally. You've got two kids to worry about. And I don't know how tender you might be yet over losing your husband. So instead of my hauling you off to bed, we're having dinner conversation."

She took a minute to think it through. At the root, she couldn't find anything wrong with his logic. In fact, she agreed with it. "All right. First Roz. I won't do anything to mess her up either. So whatever happens here, we agree to maintain a courteous working relationship."

"Might not always be courteous, but it'll be about the work."

"Fair enough. My boys are my priority, first and last. Not only because they have to be," she added, "but because I want them to be. Nothing will change that."

"Anything did, I wouldn't have much respect for you."

"Well." She waited just a moment because his response had not only been blunt again, but was one she appreciated a great deal. "As for Kevin, I loved him very much. Losing him cut me in two, the part that just wanted to lie down and die, and the part that had to go through the grief and the anger and the motions—and live."

"Takes courage to live."

Her eyes stung, and she took one very careful breath. "Thank you. I had to put myself back together. For the kids, for myself. I'll never feel for another man exactly what I felt for him. I don't think I should. But that doesn't mean I can't be interested in and attracted to someone else. It doesn't mean I'm fated to live my life alone."

He sat for a moment. "How can such a sensible woman have an emotional attachment to forms and invoices?"

"How can such a talented man be so disorganized?" More relaxed than she'd imagined, she enjoyed her salad. "I drove by the Dawson job again."

"Oh, yeah?"

"I realize you still have a few finishing touches that have to wait until all danger of frost is over, but I wanted to tell you it's good work. No, that's wrong. It's not. It's exceptional work."

"Thanks. You take more pictures?"

"I did. We'll be using some of them—before and

after—in the landscaping section of the Web site I'm designing."

"No shit."

"None whatsoever. I'm going to make Roz more money, Logan. She makes more, you make more. The site's going to generate more business for the landscaping arm. I guarantee it."

"It's hard to find a downside on that one."

"You know what I envy you most?"

"My sparkling personality."

"No, you don't sparkle in the least. Your muscle."

"You envy my muscle? I don't think it'd look so good on you, Red."

"Whenever I'd start a project at home—back home—I couldn't do it all myself. I have vision—not as creative as yours, maybe, but I can see what I want, and I've got considerable skill. But when it comes to the heavy, manual labor of it, I'm out. It's frustrating because with some of it, I'd really like to do it all myself. And I can't. So I envy you the muscle that means you can."

"I imagine whether you're doing it or directing it, it's done the way you want."

She smiled into her wine. "Goes without saying. I've heard you've got a place not far from Roz's."

"About two miles out." When their main courses were served, Logan cut a chunk off his catfish, laid it on her plate.

Stella stared at it. "Well. Hmmm."

"I bet you tell your kids they don't know if they like something or not until they've tried it."

"One of the advantages of being a grown-up is being able to say things like that without applying them to yourself. But okay." She forked off a tiny bite, geared herself up for the worst, and ate it. "Interestingly," she said after a moment, "it tastes nothing like cat. Or like what one assumes cat might taste like. It's actually good."

"You might just get back some of your southern. We'll have you eating grits next."

"I don't think so. Those I have tried. Anyway, are you doing the work yourself? On your house."

"Most of it. Land's got some nice gentle rises, good drainage. Some fine old trees on the north side. A couple of pretty sycamores and some hickory, with some wild azalea and mountain laurel scattered around. Some open southern exposure. Plenty of frontage, and a small creek running on the back edge."

"What about the house?"

"What?"

"The house. What kind of house is it?"

"Oh. Two-story frame. It's probably too much space for me, but it came with the land."

"It sounds like the sort of thing I'll be looking for in a few months. Maybe if you hear of anything on the market you could let me know."

"Sure, I can do that. Kids doing all right at Roz's?"

"They're doing great. But at some point we'll need to have our own place. It's important they have their own. I don't want anything elaborate—couldn't afford it, anyway. And I don't mind fixing something up. I'm fairly handy. And I'd really prefer it wasn't haunted."

She stopped herself when he sent her a questioning look. Then shook her head. "Must be the wine because I didn't know *that* was in my head."

"Why is it?"

"I saw—thought I saw," she corrected, "this ghost reputed to haunt the Harper house. In the mirror, in my bedroom, just before you picked me up. It wasn't Hayley. She came in an instant later, and I tried to convince myself it had been her. But it wasn't. And at the same time, it could hardly have been anyone else because . . . it's just not possible."

"Sounds like you're still trying to convince yourself."

"Sensible woman, remember." She tapped a finger on the side of her head. "Sensible women don't see ghosts, or hear them singing lullabies. Or feel them."

"Feel them how?"

"A chill, a . . . *feeling*." She gave a quick shudder and tried to offset it with a quick laugh. "I can't explain it because it's not rational. And tonight, that feeling was very intense. Brief, but intense. And hostile. No, that's not right. 'Hostile' is too strong a word. Disapproving."

"Why don't you talk to Roz about it? She could give you the history, as far as she knows it."

"Maybe. You said you've never seen it?"

"Nope."

"Or felt it?"

"Can't say I have. But sometimes when I've been working a job, walking some land, digging into it, I've felt something. You plant something, even if it dies off, it leaves something in the soil. Why shouldn't a person leave something behind?"

It was something to think about, later, when her mind wasn't so distracted. Right now she had to think about the fact that she was enjoying his company. And there was the basic animal attraction to consider. If she continued to enjoy his company, and the attraction didn't fade off, they were going to end up in bed.

Then there were all the ramifications and complications that would entail. In addition, their universe was finite. They worked for the same person in the same business. It wasn't the sort of atmosphere where two people could have an adult affair without everyone around them knowing they were having it.

So she'd have to think about *that*, and just how uncomfortable it might be to have her private life as public knowledge.

After dinner, they walked over to Beale Street to join the nightly carnival. Tourists, Memphians out on the town, couples, and clutches of young people wandered the street lit by neon signs. Music trickled out of doorways, and people flooded in and out of shops.

"Used to be a club along here called the Monarch. Those shoes going to give you any trouble with this?"

"No."

"Good. Great legs, by the way."

"Thanks. I've had them for years."

"So, the Monarch," he continued. "Happened it shared a back alley with an undertaker. Made it easy for the owners to dispose of gunshot victims."

"That's a pretty piece of Beale Street trivia."

"Oh, there's plenty more. Blues, rock—it's the home of both—voodoo, gambling, sex, scandal, bootleg whiskey, pickpockets, and murder."

Music pumped out of a club as he talked, and struck Stella as southern-fried in the best possible way.

"It's all been right here," he continued. "But you oughta just enjoy the carnival the way it is now."

They joined a crowd lining the sidewalk to watch three boys do running flips and gymnastics up and down the center of the street.

"I can do that." She nodded toward one of the boys as he walked on his hands back to their tip box.

"Uh-huh."

"I can. I'm not going to demonstrate here and now, but I certainly can. Six years of gymnastic lessons. I can bend my body like a pretzel. Well, half a pretzel now, but at one time . . ."

"You trying to get me hot?"

She laughed. "No."

"Just a side effect, then. What does half a pretzel look like?"

"Maybe I'll show you sometime when I'm more appropriately dressed."

"You *are* trying to make me hot."

She laughed again and watched the performers. After Logan dropped money in the tip box, they strolled along the sidewalk. "Who's Betty Paige and why is her face on these shirts?"

He stopped dead. "You've got to be kidding."

"I'm not."

"I guess you didn't just live up north, you lived up north in a cave. Betty Paige, legendary fifties pinup and general sex goddess."

"How do you know? You weren't even born in the fifties."

"I make it a point to learn my cultural history, especially when it involves gorgeous women who strip. Look at that face. The girl next door with the body of Venus."

"She probably couldn't walk on her hands," Stella said, and casually strolled away when he laughed.

They walked off the wine, and the meal, meandering down one side of the street and back up the other. He tempted her with a blues club, but after a brief, internal debate she shook her head.

"I really can't. It's already later than I'd planned. I've got a full day tomorrow, and I've imposed on Roz long enough tonight."

"We'll rain-check it."

"And a blues club will go on my list. Got more checks tonight. Beale Street and catfish. I'm practically a native now."

"Next thing you know you'll be frying up the cat and putting peanuts in your Coke."

"Why in the world would I put peanuts in my Coke? Never mind." She waved him away as he drove out of town. "It's a southern thing. How about if I just say I had a good time tonight?"

"That'll work."

It hadn't been complicated, she realized, or boring, or stressful. At least not after the first few minutes. She'd forgotten, or nearly, what it could be like to be both stimulated and relaxed around a man.

Or to wonder, and there was no point pretending she wasn't wondering, what it would be like to have those hands—those big, work-hardened hands—on her.

Roz had left lights on for her. Front porch, foyer, her own bedroom. She saw the gleam of them as they drove up, and found it a motherly thing to do. Or big sisterly, Stella supposed, as Roz wasn't nearly old enough to be her mother.

Her mother had been too busy with her own life and interests to think about little details like front porch lights. Maybe, Stella thought, that was one of the reasons she herself was so compulsive about them.

"Such a beautiful house," Stella said. "The way it sort of glimmers at night. It's no wonder she loves it."

"No place else quite like it. Spring comes in, the gardens just blow you away."

"She ought to hold a house and garden tour."

"She used to, once a year. Hasn't done it since she peeled off that asshole Clerk. I wouldn't bring it up," he said before Stella spoke. "If she wants to do that kind of thing again, she will."

Knowing his style now, Stella waited for him to come around and open her door. "I'm looking forward to seeing the gardens in their full glory. And I'm grateful for the chance to live here a while and have the kids exposed to this kind of tradition."

"There's another tradition. Kiss the girl good night."

He moved a little slower this time, gave her a chance to anticipate. Those sexy nerves were just beginning to dance over her skin when his mouth met hers.

Then they raced in a shivering path to belly, to throat as his tongue skimmed over her lips to part them. His hands moved through her hair, over her shoulders, and down her body to her hips to take a good, strong hold.

Muscles, she thought dimly. Oh, God. He certainly had them. It was like being pressed against warm, smooth steel. Then he moved in so she swayed back and was trapped between the wall of him and the door. Imprisoned there, her blood sizzling as he devastated her mouth, she felt fragile and giddy, and alive with need.

"Wait a minute," she managed. "Wait."

"Just want to finish this out first."

He wanted a great deal more than that, but already knew he'd have to hold himself at a kiss. So he didn't intend to rush through it. Her mouth was sumptuous, and that slight tremor in her body brutally erotic. He imagined himself gulping her down whole, with violence, with greed. Or savoring her nibble by torturous nibble until he was half mad from the flavor.

When he eased back, the drugged, dreamy look in her eyes told him he could do either. Some other time, some other place.

"Any point in pretending we're going to stop things here?"

"I can't—"

"I don't mean tonight," he said when she glanced back at the door.

"Then, no, there'd be no point in that."

"Good."

"But I can't just jump into something like this. I need to—"

"Plan," he finished. "Organize."

"I'm not good at spontaneity, and spontaneity—this sort—is nearly impossible when you have two children."

"Then plan. Organize. And let me know. I'm good at spontaneity." He kissed her again until she felt her knees dissolve from the knee down.

"You've got my numbers. Give me a call." He stepped back. "Go on inside, Stella. Traditionally, you don't just kiss the girl good night, you wait until she's inside before you walk off wondering when you'll have the chance to do it again."

"Good night then." She went inside, drifted up the stairs, and forgot to turn off the lights.

She was still floating as she started down the hall so the singing didn't register until she was two paces away from her sons' bedroom.

She closed the distance in one leap. And she *saw*, she saw the silhouette, the glint of blond hair in the nightlight, the gleam of eyes that stared into hers.

The cold hit her like a slap, angry and sharp. Then, it, and she, were gone.

On unsteady legs, she rushed between the beds, stroked Gavin's hair, Luke's. Laid her hands on their cheeks, then their backs as she'd done when they were infants. A nervous mother's way to assure herself that her child breathed.

Parker rolled lazily over, gave a little greeting growl, a single thump of his tail, then went back to sleep.

He senses me, smells me, knows me. Is it the same with her? Why doesn't he bark at her?

Or am I just losing my mind?

She readied for bed, then took a blanket and pillow into their room. She laid down between her sons and passed the rest of the night between them, guarding them against the impossible.

twelve

In the greenhouse, Roz watered flats of annuals she'd grown over the winter. It was nearly time to put them out for sale. Part of her was always a little sad to know she wouldn't be the one planting them. And she knew that not all of them would be tended properly.

Some would die of neglect, others would be given too much sun, or not enough. Now they were lush and sweet and full of potential.

And hers.

She had to let them go, the way she'd let her sons go. She had to hope, as with her boys, that they found their potential and bloomed, lavishly.

She missed her little guys. More than she'd realized now that her house had boys in it again with all their chatter and scents and debris. Having Harper close helped, so much at times that it was hard for her not to lean too heavily on him, not to surround him with need.

But he'd passed the stage when he was just hers. Though he lived within shouting distance, and they often worked together side by side, he would never be just hers again.

She had to content herself with occasional visits, with

phone calls and e-mails from her other sons. And with the knowledge that they were happy building their own lives.

She'd rooted them, and tended them, nurtured and trained. And let them go.

She wouldn't be one of those overbearing, smothering mothers. Sons, like plants, needed space and air. But oh, sometimes she wanted to go back ten years, twenty, and just hold on to those precious boys a little bit longer.

And sentiment was only going to make her blue, she reminded herself. She switched off the water just as Stella came into the greenhouse.

Roz drew a deep breath. "Nothing like the smell of damp soil, is there?"

"Not when you're us. Look at these marigolds. They're going to fly out the door. I missed you this morning."

"I wanted to get here early. I've got that Garden Club meeting this afternoon. I want to put together a couple dozen six-inch pots as centerpieces."

"Good advertising. I just wanted to thank you again for watching the boys for me last night."

"I enjoyed it. A lot. Did you have a good time?"

"I really did. Is it going to be a problem for you if Logan and I see each other socially?"

"Why would it be?"

"In a work situation . . ."

"Adults should be able to live their own lives, just like in any situation. You're both unattached adults. I expect you'll figure out for yourself if there's any problem with you socializing."

"And we're both using 'socializing' as a euphemism."

Roz began pinching back some petunias. "Stella, if you didn't want to have sex with a man who looks like Logan, I'd worry about you."

"I guess you've got nothing to worry about, then. Still, I want to say . . . I'm working for you, I'm living in your house, so I want to say I'm not promiscuous."

"I'm sure you aren't." She glanced up briefly from her

work. "You're too careful, too deliberate, and a bit too bound up to be promiscuous."

"Another way of calling me a tight-ass," Stella muttered.

"Not precisely. But if you were promiscuous, it would still be your business and not mine. You don't need my approval."

"I want it—because I'm working for you and living in your house. And because I respect you."

"All right, then." Roz moved on to impatiens. "You have it. One of the reasons I wanted you to live in the house was because I wanted to get to know you, on a personal level. When I hired you, I was giving you a piece of something very important to me, personally important. So if I'd decided, after the first few weeks, that you weren't the sort of person I could like and respect, I'd have fired you." She glanced back. "No matter how competent you were. Competent just isn't that hard to find."

"Thanks. I think."

"I think I'll take in some of these geraniums that are already potted. Saves me time and trouble, and we've got a good supply of them."

"Let me know how many, and I'll adjust the inventory. Roz, there was something else I wanted to talk to you about."

"Talk away," Roz invited as she started to select her plants.

"It's about the ghost."

Roz lifted a salmon-pink geranium, studied it from all sides. "What about her?"

"I feel stupid even talking about this, but . . . have you ever felt threatened by her?"

"Threatened? No. I wouldn't use a word that strong." Roz set the geranium in a plastic tray, chose another. "Why?"

"Because, apparently, I've seen her."

"That's not unexpected. The Harper Bride tends to

show herself to mothers, and young boys. Young girls, occasionally. I saw her myself a few times when I was a girl, then fairly regularly once the boys started coming along."

"Tell me what she looks like."

"About your height." As she spoke, Roz continued to select her geraniums for the Garden Club. "Thin. Very thin. Mid- to late twenties at my guess, though it's hard to tell. She doesn't look well. That is," she added with an absent smile, "even for a ghost. She strikes me as a woman who had a great deal of beauty, but was ill for some time. She's blond, and her eyes are somewhere between green and gray. And very sad. She wears a gray dress—or it looks gray, and it hangs on her as if she'd lost weight."

Stella let out a breath. "That's who I saw. What I saw. It's too fantastic, but I *saw*."

"You should be flattered. She rarely shows herself to anyone outside the family—or so the legend goes. You shouldn't feel threatened, Stella."

"But I did. Last night, when I got home, and went in to check on the boys. I heard her first. She sings some sort of lullaby."

" 'Lavender's Blue.' It's what you could call her trademark." Taking out small clippers, Roz trimmed off a weak side stem. "She's never spoken that I've heard, or heard of, but she sings to the children of the house at night."

" 'Lavender's Blue.' Yes, that's it. I heard her, and rushed in. There she was, standing between their beds. She looked at me. It was only for a second, but she looked at me. Her eyes weren't sad, Roz, they were angry. There was a blast of cold, like she'd thrown something at me in temper. Not like the other times, when I'd just felt a chill."

Interested now, Roz studied Stella's face. "I felt as if I'd annoyed her a few times, on and off. Just a change of tone. Very like you described, I suppose."

"It happened."

"I believe you, but primarily, from most of my experiences, she's always been a benign sort of presence. I always took those temper snaps to be a kind of moodiness. I expect ghosts get moody."

"You expect ghosts get moody," Stella repeated slowly. "I just don't understand a statement like that."

"People do, don't they? Why should that change when they're dead?"

"Okay," Stella said after a moment. "I'm going to try to roll with all this, like it's not insanity. So, maybe she doesn't like me being here."

"Over the last hundred years or so, Harper House has had a lot of people live in it, a lot of houseguests. She ought to be used to it. If you'd feel better moving to the other wing—"

"No. I don't see how that would make a difference. And though I was unnerved enough last night to sleep in the boys' room with them, she wasn't angry with them. It was just me. Who was she?"

"Nobody knows for sure. In polite company, she's referred to as the Harper Bride, but it's assumed she was a servant. A nurse or governess. My theory is one of the men in the house seduced her, maybe cast her off, especially if she got pregnant. There's the attachment to children, so it seemed most logical she had a connection to kids. It's a sure bet she died in or around the house."

"There'd be records, right? A family Bible, birth and death records, photographs, tintypes, whatever."

"Oh, tons."

"I'd like to go through them, if it's all right with you. I'd like to try to find out who she was. I want to know who, or what, I'm dealing with."

"All right." Clippers still in hand, Roz set a fist on her hip. "I guess it's odd no one's ever done it before, including myself. I'll help you with it. It'll be interesting."

"THIS IS SO AWESOME." HAYLEY LOOKED AROUND the library table, where Stella had arranged the photograph albums, the thick Bible, the boxes of old papers, her laptop, and several notebooks. "We're like the Scooby gang."

"I can't believe you saw her, too, and didn't say anything."

Hayley hunched up her shoulders and continued to wander the room. "I figured you'd think I'd wigged. Besides, except for the once, I only caught a glimpse, like over here." She held up a hand at the side of her head. "I've never been around an actual ghost. This is completely cool."

"I'm glad someone's enjoying herself."

She really was. As she and her father had both loved books, they'd used their living room as a kind of library, stuffing the shelves with books, putting in a couple of big, squishy chairs.

It had been nice, cozy and nice.

But this was a *library*. Beautiful bookcases of deep, dark wood flanked long windows, then rose up and around the walls in a kind of platform where the long table stood. There had to be hundreds of books, but it didn't seem overwhelming, not with the dark, restful green of the walls and the warm cream granite of the fireplace. She liked the big black candlesticks and the groupings of family pictures on the mantel.

There were more pictures scattered around here and there, and *things*. Fascinating things like bowls and statues and a dome-shaped crystal clock. Flowers, of course. There were flowers in nearly every room of the house. These were tulips with deep, deep purple cups that sort of spilled out of a wide, clear glass vase.

There were lots of chairs, wide, butter-soft leather chairs, and even a leather sofa. Though a chandelier dripped from the center of the tray ceiling, and even the bookcases lit up, there were lamps with those cool shades that looked like stained glass. The rugs were probably really old, and so interesting with their pattern of exotic birds around the borders.

She couldn't imagine what it must have been like to

have a room like this, much less to know just how to decorate it so it would be—well, gorgeous was the only word she could think of—and yet still be as cozy as the little library she'd had at home.

But Roz knew. Roz, in Hayley's opinion, was the absolute bomb.

"I think this is my favorite room of the house," she decided. "Of course, I think that about every room after I'm in it for five minutes. But I really think this wins the prize. It's like a picture out of *Southern Living* or something, but the accent's on *living*. You wouldn't be afraid to take a nap on the couch."

"I know what you mean." Stella set aside the photo album she'd looked through. "Hayley, you have to remember not to say anything about this to the kids."

"Of course, I won't." She came back to the table, and finally sat. "Hey, maybe we could do a séance. That would be so spooky and great."

"I'm not that far gone yet," Stella replied. She glanced over as David came in.

"Ghost hunter snacks," he announced and set the tray on the table. "Coffee, tea, cookies. I considered angel food cake, but it seemed too obvious."

"Having fun with this?"

"Damn right. But I'm also willing to roll up my sleeves and dive into all this stuff. It'll be nice to put a name to her after all this time." He tapped a finger on Stella's laptop. "And this is for?"

"Notes. Data, facts, speculation. I don't know. It's my first day on the job."

Roz came in, carting a packing box. There was a smudge of dust on her cheek and silky threads of cobwebs in her hair. "Household accounts, from the attic. There's more up there, but this ought to give us a start."

She dumped the box on the table, grinned. "This should be fun. Don't know why I haven't thought of it before. Where do y'all want to start?"

"I was thinking we could have a séance," Hayley began. "Maybe she'll just tell us who she is and why her spirit's, you know, trapped on this plane of existence. That's the thing with ghosts. They get trapped, and sometimes they don't even know they're dead. How creepy is that?"

"A séance." David rubbed his hands together. "Now where did I leave my turban?"

When Hayley burst into throaty laughter, Stella rapped her knuckles on the table. "If we could control the hilarity? I thought we'd start with something a little more mundane. Like trying to date her."

"I've never dated a ghost," David mused, "but I'm up for it."

"Get her time period," Stella said with a slanted look for David. "By what she's wearing. We might be able to pinpoint when she lived, or at least get an estimate."

"Discovery through fashion." Roz nodded as she picked up a cookie. "That's good."

"Smart," Hayley agreed. "But I didn't really notice what she had on. I only got a glimpse."

"A gray dress," Roz put in. "High-necked. Long sleeves."

"Can any of us sketch?" Stella asked. "I'm all right with straight lines and curves, but I'd be hopeless with figures."

"Roz is your girl." David patted Roz on the shoulder.

"Can you draw her, Roz? Your impression of her?"

"I can sure give it a shot."

"I bought notebooks." Stella offered one and made Roz smile.

"Of course you did. And I bet your pencils are all nicely sharpened, too. Just like the first day of school."

"Hard to write with them otherwise. David, while she's doing that, why don't you tell us your experiences with . . . I guess we'll call her the Harper Bride for now."

"Only had a few, and all back when I was a kid, hanging out here with Harper."

"What about the first time?"

"You never forget your first." He winked at her, and

after sitting, poured himself coffee. "I was bunking in with Harper, and we were pretending to be asleep so Roz didn't come in and lower the boom. We were whispering—"

"They always thought they were," Roz said as she sketched.

"I think it was spring. I remember we had the windows open, and there was a breeze. I'd have been around nine. I met Harper in school, and even though he was a year behind me, we hit it off. We hadn't known each other but a few weeks when I came over to spend the night. So we were there, in the dark, thinking we were whispering, and he told me about the ghost. I thought he was making it up to scare me, but he swore all the way up to the needle in his eye that it was true, and he'd seen her lots of times.

"We must've fallen asleep. I remember waking up, thinking somebody had stroked my head. I thought it was Roz, and I was a little embarrassed, so I squinted one eye open to see."

He sipped coffee, narrowing his eyes as he searched for the memory. "And I saw her. She walked over to Harper's bed and bent over him, the way you do when you kiss a child on the top of the head. Then she walked across the room. There was a rocking chair over in the corner. She sat down and started to rock, and sing."

He set the coffee down. "I don't know if I made some sound, or moved, or what, but she looked right at me. She smiled. I thought she was crying, but she smiled. And she put her finger to her lips as if to tell me to hush. Then she disappeared."

"What did you do?" Hayley whispered the question, reverently.

"I pulled the covers over my head, and stayed under till morning."

"You were afraid of her?" Stella prompted.

"Nine-year-old, ghost—and I have a sensitive nature, so sure. But I didn't stay afraid. In the morning it seemed like a dream, but a nice one. She'd stroked my hair and sung to me. And she was pretty. No rattling chains or bloodless howls. She seemed a little like an angel, so I wasn't afraid of her. I told Harper about it in the morning, and he said we must be brothers, because none of his other friends got to see her."

He smiled at the memory. "I felt pretty proud of that, and looked forward to seeing her again. I saw her a few more times when I was over. Then, when I was about thirteen the—we'll say visitations—stopped."

"Did she ever speak to you?"

"No, she'd just sing. That same song."

"Did you only see her in the bedroom, at night?"

"No. There was this time we all camped out back. It was summer, hot and buggy, but we nagged Roz until she let all of us sleep out there in a tent. We didn't make it through the night 'cause Mason cut his foot on a rock. Remember that, Roz?"

"I do. Two o'clock in the morning, and I'm packing four kids in the car so I can take one of them to the ER for stitches."

"We were out there before sunset, out near the west edge of the property. By ten we were all of us half sick on hot dogs and marshmallows, and had spooked ourselves stupid with ghost stories. Lightning bugs were out," he murmured, closing his eyes. "Past midsummer then, and steamy. We'd all stripped down to our underwear. The younger ones fell asleep, but Harper and I stayed up for a while. A long while. I must've conked out, because the next thing I knew, Harper was shaking my shoulder. 'There she is,' he said, and I saw her, walking in the garden."

"Oh, my God," Hayley managed, and edged closer to David as Stella continued to type. "What happened then?"

"Well, Harper's hissing in my ear about how we should go follow her, and I'm trying to talk him out of it without sacrificing my manhood. The other two woke up, and Harper said he was going, and we could stay behind if we were yellow coward dogs."

"I bet that got you moving," Stella commented.

"Being a yellow coward dog isn't an option for a boy in

the company of other boys. We all got moving. Mason couldn't've been but six, but he was trotting along at the rear, trying to keep up. There was moonlight, so we could see her, but Harper said we had to hang back some, so she didn't see us.

"I swear there wasn't a breath of air that night, not a whisper of it to stir a leaf. She didn't make a sound as she walked along the paths, through the shrubs. There was something different about her that night. I didn't realize what it was until long after."

"What?" Breathless, Hayley leaned forward, gripped his arm. "What was different about her that night?"

"Her hair was down. Always before, she'd had it up. Sort of sweet and old-fashioned ringlets spiraling down from the top of her head. But that night it was down, and kind of wild, spilling down her back, over her shoulders. And she was wearing something white and floaty. She looked more like a ghost that night than she ever did otherwise. And I was afraid of her, more than I was the first time, or ever was again. She moved off the path, walked over the flowers without touching them. I could hear my own breath pant in and out, and I must've slowed down because Harper was well ahead. She was going toward the old stables, or maybe the carriage house."

"The carriage house?" Hayley almost squealed it. "Where Harper lives?"

"Yeah. He wasn't living there then," he added with a laugh. "He wasn't more than ten. It seemed like she was heading for the stables, but she'd have to go right by the carriage house. So, she stopped, and she turned around, looking back. I know I stopped dead then, and the blood just drained out of me."

"I guess!" Hayley said, with feeling.

"She looked crazy, and that was worse than dead somehow. Before I could decide whether to run after Harper, or hightail it like a yellow coward dog, Mason screamed. I thought somehow she'd gotten him, and damn near screamed myself. But Harper came flying back. Turned out

Mason had gashed his foot open on a rock. When I looked back toward the old stables, she was gone."

He stopped, shuddered, then let out a weak laugh. "Scared myself."

"Me, too," Hayley managed.

"He needed six stitches." Roz scooted the notebook toward Stella. "That's how she looks to me."

"That's her." Stella studied the sketch of the thin, sad-eyed woman. "Is this how she looked to you, David?"

"Except that one night, yeah."

"Hayley?"

"Best I can tell."

"Same for me. This shows her in fairly simple dress, nipped-in waist, high neck, front buttons. Okay, the sleeves are a little poufed down to the elbow, then snug to the wrist. Skirt's smooth over the hips, then widens out some. Her hair's curly, lots of curls that are scooped up in a kind of topknot. I'm going to do an Internet search on fashion, but it's obviously after the 1860s, right? Scarlett O'Hara hoop skirts were the thing around then. And it'd be before, say, the 1920s and the shorter skirts."

"I think it's near the turn of the century," Hayley put in, then shrugged when gazes shifted to her. "I know a lot of useless stuff. That looks like what they called hourglass style. I mean, even though she's way thin, it looks like that's the style. Gay Nineties stuff."

"That's good. Okay, let's look it up and see." Stella tapped keys, hit Execute.

"I gotta pee. Don't find anything important until I get back." Hayley dashed out, as fast as her condition would allow.

Stella scanned the sites offered, and selected one on women's fashion in the 1890s.

"Late Victorian," she stated as she read and skimmed pictures. "Hourglass. These are all what I'd think of as more stylish, but it seems like the same idea."

She moved to the end of the decade, and over into the early twentieth century. "No, see, these sleeves are a lot bigger at the shoulder. They're calling them leg-o'-mutton, and the bodices on the daywear seem a little sleeker."

She backtracked in the other direction. "No, we're getting into bustles here. I think Hayley may have it. Somewhere in the 1890s."

"Eighteen-nineties?" Hayley hurried back in. "Score one for me."

"Not so fast. If she was a servant," Roz reminded them, "she might not have been dressed fashionably."

"Damn." Hayley mimed erasing a scoreboard.

"But even so, we could say between 1890 and, what, 1910?" Stella suggested. "And if we go with that, and an approximate age of twenty-five, we could estimate that she was born between 1865 and 1885."

She huffed out a breath. "That's too much scope, and too much margin for error."

"Hair," David said. "She may have been a servant, may have had secondhand clothes, but there'd be nothing to stop her from wearing her hair in the latest style."

"Excellent." She typed again, picked through sites. "Okay, the Gibson Girl deal—the smooth pompadour—was popularized after 1895. If we take a leap of faith, and figure our heroine dressed her hair stylishly, we'd narrow this down to between 1890 and 1895, or up to, say '98 if she was a little behind the times. Then we'd figure she died in that decade, anyway, between the ages of . . . oh, let's say between twenty-two and twenty-six."

"Family Bible first," Roz decided. "That should tell us if any of the Harper women, by blood or marriage, and of that age group, died in that decade."

She dragged it in front of her. The binding was black leather, ornately carved. Someone—Stella imagined it was Roz herself—kept it dusted and oiled.

Roz paged through to the family genealogy. "This goes back to 1793 and the marriage of John Andrew Harper to Fiona MacRoy. It lists the births of their eight children."

"Eight?" Hayley widened her eyes and laid a hand on her belly. "Holy God."

"You said it. Six of them lived to adulthood," Roz continued. "Married and begat, begat, begat." She turned the thin pages carefully. "Here we've got several girl children born through Harper marriages between 1865 and 1870. And here, we've got an Alice Harper Doyle, died in childbirth October of 1893, at the age of twenty-two."

"That's awful," Hayley said. "She was younger than me."

"And already gave birth twice," Roz stated. "Tough on women back then, before Margaret Sanger."

"Would she have lived here, in this house?" Stella asked. "Died here?"

"Might have. She married Daniel Francis Doyle, of Natchez, in 1890. We can check the death records on her. I've got three more who died during the period we're using, but the ages are wrong. Let's see here, Alice was Reginald Harper's youngest sister. He had two more, no brothers. He'd have inherited the house, and the estate. A lot of space between Reggie and each of his sisters. Probably miscarriages."

At Hayley's small sound, Roz looked up sharply. "I don't want this to upset you."

"I'm okay. I'm okay," she said again and took a long breath. "So Reginald was the only son on that branch of the family tree?"

"He was. Lots of cousins, and the estate would've passed to one of them after his death, but he had a son—several daughters first, then the boy, in 1892."

"What about his wife?" Stella put in. "Maybe she's the one."

"No, she lived until 1925. Ripe age."

"Then we look at Alice first," Stella decided.

"And see what we can find on servants during that period. Wouldn't be a stretch for Reginald to have diddled around with a nurse or a maid while his wife was breeding. Seeing as he was a man."

"Hey!" David objected.

"Sorry, honey. Let me say he was a Harper man, and

lived during a period where men of a certain station had mistresses and didn't think anything of taking a servant to bed."

"That's some better. But not a lot."

"Are we sure he and his family lived here during that period?"

"A Harper always lived in Harper House," Roz told Stella. "And if I remember my family history, Reginald's the one who converted from gaslight to electricity. He'd have lived here until his death in . . ." She checked the book. "Nineteen-nineteen, and the house passed to his son, Reginald Junior, who'd married Elizabeth Harper McKinnon—fourth cousin—in 1916."

"All right, so we find out if Alice died here, and we go through records to find out if there were any servants of the right age who died during that period." Using her notebook now, Stella wrote down the points of the search. "Roz, do you know when the—let's call them sightings for lack of better. Do you know when they began?"

"I don't, and I'm just realizing that's odd. I should know, and I should know more about her than I do. Harper family history gets passed down, orally and written. But here we have a ghost who as far as I know's been wandering around here for more than a century, and I know next to nothing about her. My daddy just called her the Harper Bride."

"What do you know about her?" Stella readied herself to take notes.

"What she looks like, the song she sings. I saw her when I was a girl, when she came in my room to sing that lullaby, just as she's reputed to have done for generations before. It was . . . comforting. There was a gentleness about her. I tried to talk to her sometimes, but she never talked back. She'd just smile. Sometimes she'd cry. Thanks, sweetie," she said when David poured her more coffee. "I didn't see her through my teenage years, and being a teenage girl I didn't think about her much. I had my mind on other things. But I remember the next time I saw her."

"Don't keep us in suspense," Hayley demanded.

"It was early in the summer, end of June. John and I hadn't been married very long, and we were staying here. It was already hot, one of those hot, still nights where the air's like a wet blanket. But I couldn't sleep, so I left the cool house for the hot garden. I was restless and nervy. I thought I might be pregnant. I wanted it—we wanted it so much, that I couldn't think about anything else. I went out to the garden and sat on this old teak glider, and dreamed up at the moon, praying it was true and we'd started a baby."

She let out a little sigh. "I was barely eighteen. Anyway, while I sat there, she came. I didn't see or hear her come, she was just there, standing on the path. Smiling. Something in the way she smiled at me, something about it, made me know—absolutely know—I had child in me. I sat there, in the midnight heat and cried for the joy of it. When I went to the doctor a couple weeks later, I already knew I was carrying Harper."

"That's so nice." Hayley blinked back tears. "So sweet."

"I saw her off and on for years after, and always saw her at the onset of a pregnancy, before I was sure. I'd see her, and I'd know there was a baby coming. When my youngest hit adolescence, I stopped seeing her regularly."

"It has to be about children," Stella decided, underlining "pregnancy" twice in her notes. "That's the common link. Children see her, women with children, or pregnant women. The died-in-childbirth theory is looking good." Immediately she winced. "Sorry, Hayley, that didn't sound right."

"I know what you mean. Maybe she's Alice. Maybe what she needs to pass over is to be acknowledged by name."

"Well." Stella looked at the cartons and books. "Let's dig in."

* * *

SHE DREAMED AGAIN THAT NIGHT, WITH HER MIND full of ghosts and questions, of her perfect garden with the blue dahlia that grew stubbornly in its midst.

A weed is a flower growing in the wrong place.

She heard the voice inside her head, a voice that wasn't her own.

"It's true. That's true," she murmured. "But it's so beautiful. So strong and vivid."

It seems so now, but it's deceptive. If it stays, it changes everything. It will take over, and spoil everything you've done. Everything you have. Would you risk that, risk all, for one dazzling flower? One that will only die away at the first frost?

"I don't know." Studying the garden, she rubbed her arms as her skin pricked with unease. "Maybe I could change the plan. I might be able to use it as a focal point."

Thunder boomed and the sky went black, as she stood by the garden, just as she'd once stood through a stormy evening in her own kitchen.

And the grief she'd felt then stabbed into her as if someone had plunged a knife into her heart.

Feel it? Would you feel it again? Would you risk that kind of pain, for this?

"I can't breathe." She sank to her knees as the pain radiated. "I can't breathe. What's happening to me?"

Remember it. Think of it. Remember the innocence of your children and hack it down. Dig it out. Before it's too late! Can't you see how it tries to overshadow the rest? Can't you see how it steals the light? Beauty can be poison.

She woke, shivering with cold, with her heart beating against the pain that had ripped awake with her.

And knew she hadn't been alone, not even in dreams.

thirteen

On her day off, Stella took the boys to meet her father and his wife at the zoo. Within an hour, the boys were carting around rubber snakes, balloons, and chowing down on ice cream cones.

Stella had long since accepted that a grandparent's primary job was to spoil, and since fate had given her sons only this one set, she let them have free rein.

When the reptile house became the next objective, she opted out, freely handing the controls of the next stage to Granddad.

"Your mom's always been squeamish about snakes," Will told the boys.

"And I'm not ashamed to admit it. You all just go ahead. I'll wait."

"I'll keep you company." Jolene adjusted her baby-blue ball cap. "I'd rather be with Stella than a boa constrictor any day."

"Girls." Will exchanged a pitying look with each of his grandsons. "Come on, men, into the snake pit!"

On a battle cry, the three of them charged the building.

"He's so good with them," Stella said. "So natural and

easy. I'm so glad we're living close now, and they can see each other regularly."

"You couldn't be happier about it than we are. I swear that man's been like a kid himself the last couple of days, just waiting for today to get here. He couldn't be more proud of the three of you."

"I guess we both missed out on a lot when I was growing up."

"It's good you're making up for it now."

Stella glanced at Jolene as they walked over to a bench. "You never say anything about her. You never criticize."

"Sugar pie, I bit my tongue to ribbons more times than I can count in the last twenty-seven years."

"Why?"

"Well, honey, when you're the second wife, and the stepmama on top of that, it's the smartest thing you can do. Besides, you grew up to be a strong, smart, generous woman raising the two most handsome, brightest, most charming boys on God's green earth. What's the point of criticizing?"

She does you, Stella thought. "Have I ever told you I think you're the best thing that ever happened to my father?"

"Maybe once or twice." Jolene pinked prettily. "But I never mind hearing it repeated."

"Let me add, you're one of the best things that ever happened to me. And the kids."

"Oh, now." This time Jolene's eyes filled. "Now you've got me going." She dug in her purse, dug out a lace hankie. "That's the sweetest thing. The sweetest thing." She sniffled, tried to dab at her eyes and hug Stella at the same time. "I just love you to pieces. I always did."

"I always felt it." Tearing up herself, Stella pushed through her own purse for a more mundane tissue. "God, look at the mess we've made of each other."

"It was worth it. Sometimes a good little cry's as good as some sex. Do I have mascara all down my face?"

"No. Just a little . . ." Stella used the corner of her tissue to wipe away a smear under Jolene's eye. "There. You're fine."

"I feel like a million tax-free dollars. Now, tell me how you're getting on before I start leaking again."

"Work-wise it couldn't be better. It really couldn't. We're about to hit the spring rush dead-on, and I'm so revved for it. The boys are happy, making friends at school. Actually, between you and me, I think Gavin's got a crush on this little curly-headed blond in his class. Her name's Melissa, and the tips of his ears get red when he mentions her."

"That's so sweet. Nothing like your first crush, is there? I remember mine. I was crazy for this boy. He had a face full of freckles and a cowlick. I just about died with joy the day he gave me a little hop-toad in a shoe box."

"A toad."

"Well, honey, I was eight and a country girl, so it was a thoughtful gift all in all. He ended up marrying a friend of mine. I was in the wedding and had to wear the most god-awful pink dress with a hoop skirt wide enough I could've hidden a horse under it and rode to the church. It was covered with ruffles, so I looked like a human wedding cake."

She waved a hand while Stella rolled with laughter. "I don't know why I'm going on about that, except it's the sort of traumatic experience you never forget, even after more than thirty years. Now they live on the other side of the city. We get together every now and then for dinner. He's still got the freckles, but the cowlick went, along with most of his hair."

"I guess you know a lot of the people and the history of the area, since you've lived here all your life."

"I guess I do. Can't go to the Wal-Mart, day or night, without seeing half a dozen people I know."

"What do you know about the Harper ghost?"

"Hmm." Jolene took out a compact and her lipstick and freshened her face. "Just that she's always roamed around there, or at least as far back as anybody can remember. Why?"

"This is going to sound insane, especially coming from me, but . . . I've seen her."

"Oh my goodness." She snapped the compact closed. "Tell me everything."

"There isn't a lot to tell."

But she told her what there was, and what she'd begun to do about it.

"This is so exciting! You're like a detective. Maybe your father and I could help. You know how he loves playing on that computer of his. Stella!" She clamped a hand on Stella's arm. "I bet she was *murdered*, just hacked to death with an ax or something and buried in a shallow grave. Or dumped in the river—pieces of her. I've always thought so."

"Let me just say—ick—and her ghost, at least is whole. Added to that, our biggest lead is the ancestor who died in childbirth," Stella reminded her.

"Oh, that's right." Jolene sulked a moment, obviously disappointed. "Well, if it turns out it's her, that'd be sad, but not nearly as thrilling as murder. You tell your daddy all about this, and we'll see what we can do. We've both got plenty of time on our hands. It'll be fun."

"It's a departure for me," Stella replied. "I seem to be doing a lot of departing from the norm recently."

"Any of that departing have to do with a man? A tall, broad-shouldered sort of man with a wicked grin?"

Stella's eyes narrowed. "And why would you ask?"

"My third cousin, Lucille? You met her once. She happened to be having dinner in the city a couple nights ago and told me she saw you in the same restaurant with a very good-looking young man. She didn't come by your table because she was with her latest beau. And he's not altogether divorced from his second wife. Fact is, he hasn't been altogether divorced for a year and a half now, but that's Lucille for you."

Jolene waved it away. "So, who's the good-looking young man?"

"Logan Kitridge."

"Oh." It came out in three long syllables. "That *is* a good-looking young man. I thought you didn't like him."

"I didn't not like him, I just found him annoying and difficult to work with. We're getting along a little better at work, and somehow we seem to be dating. I've been trying to figure out if I want to see him again."

"What's to work out? You do or you don't."

"I do, but . . . I shouldn't ask you to gossip."

Jolene wiggled closer on the bench. "Honey, if you can't ask me, who can you ask?"

Stella snickered, then glanced toward the reptile house to be sure her boys weren't heading out. "I wondered, before I get too involved, if he sees a lot of women."

"You want to know if he cats around."

"I guess that's the word for it."

"I'd say a man like that gets lucky when he has a mind to, but you don't hear people saying, 'That Logan Kitridge is one randy son of a gun.' Like they do about my sister's boy, Curtis. Most of what you hear about Logan is people—women mostly—wondering how that wife of his let him get loose, or why some other smart woman hasn't scooped him up. You thinking about scooping?"

"No. No, definitely not."

"Maybe he's thinking about scooping you up."

"I'd say we're both just testing the ground." She caught sight of her men. "Here come the Reptile Hunters. Don't say anything about any of this in front of the boys, okay?"

"Lips are sealed."

IN THE GARDEN OPENED AT EIGHT, PREPARED FOR ITS advertised spring opening as for a war. Stella had mustered the troops, supervised with Roz the laying out of supplies. They had backups, seasoned recruits, and the field of combat was—if she said so herself—superbly organized and displayed.

By ten they were swamped, with customers swarming

the showrooms, the outside areas, the public greenhouses. Cash registers rang like church bells.

She marched from area to area, diving in where she felt she was most needed at any given time. She answered questions from staff and from customers, restacked wagons and carts when the staff was too overwhelmed to get to them, and personally helped countless people load purchases in their cars, trucks, or SUVs.

She used the two-way on her belt like a general.

"Miss? Do you work here?"

Stella paused and turned to the woman wearing baggy jeans and a ragged sweatshirt. "Yes, ma'am, I do. I'm Stella. How can I help you?"

"I can't find the columbine, or the foxglove or . . . I can't find half of what's on my list. Everything's changed around."

"We did do some reorganizing. Why don't I help you find what you're looking for?"

"I've got that flat cart there loaded already." She nodded toward it. "I don't want to have to be hauling it all over creation."

"You're going to be busy, aren't you?" Stella said cheerfully. "And what wonderful choices. Steve? Would you take this cart up front and tag it for Mrs . . . I'm sorry?"

"Haggerty." She pursed her lips. "That'd be fine. Don't you let anybody snatch stuff off it, though. I spent a good while picking all that out."

"No, ma'am. How are you doing, Mrs. Haggerty?"

"I'm doing fine. How's your mama and your daddy?"

"Doing fine, too," Steve lifted the handle of her cart. "Mrs. Haggerty's got one of the finest gardens in the county," he told Stella.

"I'm putting in some new beds. You mind my cart, Steve, or I'll come after you. Now where the hell's the columbine?"

"It's out this way. Let me get you another cart, Mrs. Haggerty."

Stella grabbed one on the way.

"You that new girl Rosalind hired?"

"Yes, ma'am."

"From up north."

"Guilty."

She pursed her lips, peered around with obvious irritation. "You sure have shuffled things around."

"I know. I hope the new scheme will save the customer time and trouble."

"Hasn't saved me any today. Hold on a minute." She stopped, adjusting the bill of her frayed straw hat against the sun as she studied pots of yarrow.

"That achillea's good and healthy, isn't it? Does so well in the heat and has a nice long blooming season."

"Wouldn't hurt to pick up a few things for my daughter while I'm here." She chose three of the pots, then moved on. As they did, Stella chatted about the plants, managed to draw Mrs. Haggerty into conversation. They'd filled the second cart and half of a third by the time they'd wound through the perennial area.

"I'll say this, you know your plants."

"I can certainly return the compliment. And I envy you the planting you've got ahead of you."

Mrs. Haggerty stopped, peering around again. But this time with speculation. "You know, the way you got things set up here, I probably bought half again as much as I planned on."

This time Stella offered a wide, wide smile. "Really?"

"Sneaky. I like that. All your people up north?"

"No, actually my father and his wife live in Memphis. They're natives."

"Is that so. Well. Well. You come on by and see my gardens sometime. Roz can tell you where to find me."

"I'd absolutely love to. Thanks."

BY NOON STELLA ESTIMATED SHE'D WALKED TEN miles.

By three, she gave up wondering how many miles she'd walked, how many pounds she'd lifted, how many questions she'd answered.

She began to dream about a long, cool shower and a bottomless glass of wine.

"This is wild," Hayley managed as she dragged wagons away from the parking area.

"When did you take your last break?"

"Don't worry, I've been getting plenty of sit-down time. Working the counter, chatting up the customers. I wanted to stretch my legs, to tell you the truth."

"We're closing in just over an hour, and things are slowing down a bit. Why don't you find Harper or one of the seasonals and see about restocking?"

"Sounds good. Hey, isn't that Mr. Hunky's truck pulling in?"

Stella looked over, spotted Logan's truck. "Mr. Hunky?"

"When it fits, it fits. Back to work for me."

It should have been for her, too. But she watched as Logan drove over the gravel, around the mountains formed by huge bags of mulch and soil. He climbed out one side of the truck, and his two men piled out the other. After a brief conversation, he wandered across the gravel lot toward her.

So she wandered across to him.

"Got a client who's decided on that red cedar mulch. You can put me down for a quarter ton."

"Which client?"

"Jameson. We're going to swing back by and get it down before we knock off. I'll get the paperwork to you tomorrow."

"You could give it to me now."

"Have to work it up. I take time to work it up, we're not going to get the frigging mulch down today. Client won't be happy."

She used her forearm to swipe at her forehead. "Fortunately for you I don't have the energy to nag."

"Been busy."

"There's no word for what we've been. It's great. I'm betting we broke records. My feet feel like a couple of smoked sausages. By the way, I was thinking I'd like to come by, see your house."

His eyes stared into hers until she felt fresh pricks of heat at the base of her spine. "You could do that. I've got time tonight."

"I can't tonight. Maybe Wednesday, after we close? If Roz is willing to watch the boys."

"Wednesday's no problem for me. Can you find the place all right?"

"Yeah, I'll find it. About six-thirty?"

"Fine. See you."

As he walked back to his truck, Stella decided it was the strangest conversation she'd ever had about sex.

THAT EVENING, AFTER HER KIDS WERE FED, AND engaged in their play hour before bed, Stella indulged in that long shower. As the aches and fatigue of the day washed away, her excitement over it grew.

They'd kicked *ass*! she thought.

She was still a little concerned about overstock in some areas, and what she saw as understock in others. But flushed with the day's success, she told herself not to question Roz's instincts as a grower.

If today was any indication, they were in for a rock-solid season.

She pulled on her terry-cloth robe, wrapped her hair in a towel, then did a kind of three-step boogie out of the bathroom.

And let out a short, piping scream at the woman in her bedroom doorway.

"Sorry. Sorry." Roz snorted back a laugh. "Flesh and blood here."

"God!" Since her legs had gone numb, Stella sank onto the side of the bed. "*God!* My heart just about stopped."

"I got something that should start it up again." From behind her back, Roz whipped out a bottle of champagne.

"Dom Perignon? Woo, and two hoos! Yes, I think I detect a beat."

"We're going to celebrate. Hayley's across in the sitting room. And I'm giving her half a glass of this. No lectures."

"In Europe pregnant women are allowed, if not encouraged, to have a glass of wine a week. I'm willing to pretend we're in France if I get a full glass of that."

"Come on over. I sent the boys down to David. They're having a video game contest."

"Oh. Well, I guess that's all right. They've got a half hour before bath and bed. Is that caviar?" she asked when she stepped into the sitting room.

"Roz says I can't have any." Hayley leaned over and sniffed the silver tray with its silver bowl of glossy black caviar. "Because it's not good for the baby. I don't know as I'd like it, anyway."

"Good. More for me. Champagne and caviar. You're a classy boss, Ms. Harper."

"It was a great day. I always start off the first of the season a little blue." She popped the cork. "All my babies going off like that. Then I get too busy to think about it." She poured the glasses. "And by the end I'm reminded that I got into this to sell and to make a profit—while doing something I enjoy doing. Then I come on home and start feeling a little blue again. But not tonight."

She passed the glasses around. "I may not have the figures and the facts and the data right at my fingertips, but I know what I know. We've just had the best single day ever."

"Ten percent over last year." Stella lifted her glass in a toast. "I happen to have facts and data at my fingertips."

"Of course you do." With a laugh, Roz stunned Stella by throwing an arm around her shoulders, squeezing once, then pressing a kiss to her cheek. "Damn right you do. You did a hell of a job. Both of you. Everyone. And it's fair to say, Stella, that I did myself and In the Garden a favor the day I hired you."

"Wow!" She took a sip to open her throat. "I won't argue with that." Then another to let the wine fizz on her tongue before she went for the caviar. "However, as much as I'd love to take full credit for that ten percent increase, I can't. The stock is just amazing. You and Harper are exceptional growers. I'll take credit for five of the ten percent."

"It was fun," Hayley put in. "It was crazy a lot of the time, but fun. All those people, and the noise, and carts sailing out the door. Everybody seemed so happy. I guess being around plants, thinking about having them for yourself, does that."

"Good customer service has a lot to do with those happy faces. And you"—Stella tipped her glass to Hayley—"have that knocked."

"We've got a good team." Roz sat, wiggled her bare toes. They were painted pale peach today. "We'll take a good overview in the morning, see what areas Harper and I should add to." She leaned forward to spread caviar on a toast point. "But tonight we'll just bask."

"This is the best job I've ever had. I just want to say that." Hayley looked at Roz. "And not just because I get to drink fancy champagne and watch y'all eat caviar."

Roz patted her arm. "I should bring up another subject. I've already told David. The calls I've made about Alice Harper Doyle's death certificate? Natchez," she said. "According to official records, she died in Natchez, in the home she shared with her husband and two children."

"Damn." Stella frowned into her wine. "I guess it was too easy."

"We'll just have to keep going through the household records, noting down the names of the female servants during that time period."

"Big job," Stella replied.

"Hey, we're good." Hayley brushed off the amount of work. "We can handle it. And, you know, I was thinking. David said they saw her going toward the old stables, right? So maybe she had a thing going with one of the stablehands. They got into a fight over something, and he killed her. Maybe an accident, maybe not. Violent deaths are supposed to be one of the things that trap spirits."

"Murder," Roz speculated. "It might be."

"You sound like my stepmother. I talked to her about it," Stella told Roz. "She and my father are willing and able to help with any research if we need them. I hope that's all right."

"It's all right with me. I wondered if she'd show herself to one of us, since we started looking into it. Try to point us in the right direction."

"I had a dream." Since it made her feel silly to talk about it, Stella topped off her glass of champagne. "A kind of continuation of one I had a few weeks ago. Neither of them was very clear—or the details of them go foggy on me. But I know it—they—have to do with a garden I've planted, and a blue dahlia."

"Do dahlias come in blue?" Hayley wondered.

"They do. They're not common," Roz explained, "but you can hybridize them in shades of blue."

"This was like nothing I've ever seen. It was . . . electric, intense. This wildly vivid blue, and huge. And she was in the dream. I didn't see her, but I felt her."

"Hey!" Hayley pushed herself forward. "Maybe her name was Dahlia."

"That's a good thought," Roz commented. "If we're researching ghosts, it's not a stretch to consider that a dream's connected in some way."

"Maybe." Frowning, Stella sipped again. "I could hear her, but I couldn't see her. Even more, I could feel her, and there was something dark about it, something frightening. She wanted me to get rid of it. She was insistent, angry, and, I don't know how to explain it, but she was *there*. How could she be in a dream?"

"I don't know," Roz replied. "But I don't care for it."

"Neither do I. It's too . . . intimate. Hearing her inside my head that way, whispering." Even now, she shivered.

"When I woke up, I knew she'd been there, in the room, just as she'd been there, in the dream."

"It's scary," Hayley agreed. "Dreams are supposed to be personal, just for ourselves, unless we want to share them. Do you think the flower had something to do with her? I don't get why she wants you to get rid of it."

"I wish I knew. It could've been symbolic. Of the gardens here, or the nursery. I don't know. But dahlias are a particular favorite of mine, and she wanted it gone."

"Something else to put in the mix." Roz took a long sip of champagne. "Let's give it a rest tonight, before we spook ourselves completely. We can try to carve out some time this week to look for names."

"Ah, I've made some tentative plans for Wednesday after work. If you wouldn't mind watching the boys for a couple of hours."

"I think between us we can manage them," Roz agreed.

"Another date with Mr. Hunky?"

With a laugh, Roz ate more caviar. "I assume that would be Logan."

"According to Hayley," Stella stated. "I was going to go by and see his place. I'd like a firsthand look at how he's landscaping it." She downed more champagne. "And while that's perfectly true, the main reason I'm going is to have sex with him. Probably. Unless I change my mind. Or he changes his. So." She set down her empty glass. "There it is."

"I'm not sure what you'd like us to say," Roz said after a moment.

"Have fun?" Hayley suggested. Then looked down at her belly. "And play safe."

"I'm only telling you because you'd know anyway, or suspect, or wonder. It seems better not to dance around it. And it doesn't seem right for me to ask you to watch my kids while I'm off . . . while I'm off without being honest about it."

"It is your life, Stella," Roz pointed out.

"Yeah." Hayley took the last delicious sip of her champagne. "Not that I wouldn't be willing to hear the details. I think hearing about sex is as close as I'm getting to it for a long time. So if you want to share . . ."

"I'll keep that in mind. Now I'd better go down and round up my boys. Thanks for the celebration, Roz."

"We earned it."

As Stella walked away, she heard Roz's questioning "Mr. Hunky?" And the dual peals of female laughter.

fourteen

GUILT TUGGED AT STELLA AS SHE BUZZED HOME TO clean up before her date with Logan. No, not date, she corrected as she jumped into the shower. It wasn't a date unless there were plans. This was a drop-by.

So now they'd had an outing, a date, and a drop-by. It was the strangest relationship she'd ever had.

But whatever she called it, she felt guilty. She wasn't the one giving her kids their evening meal and listening to their day's adventures while they ate.

It wasn't that she had to be with them every free moment, she thought as she jumped back out of the shower again. That sort of thing wasn't good for them—or for her. It wasn't as if they'd starve if she wasn't the one to put food in front of them.

But still, it seemed awfully selfish of her to give them over to someone else's care just so she could be with a man.

Be intimate with a man, if things went as she expected.

Sorry, kids, Mom can't have dinner with you tonight. She's going to go have some hot, sweaty sex.

God.

She slathered on cream as she struggled between anticipation and guilt.

Maybe she should put it off. Unquestionably she was rushing this step, and that wasn't like her. When she did things that weren't like her, it was usually a mistake.

She was thirty-three years old, and entitled to a physical relationship with a man she liked, a man who stirred her up, a man, who it turned out, she had considerable in common with.

Thirty-three. Thirty-four in August, she reminded herself and winced. Thirty-four wasn't early thirties anymore. It was mid-thirties. Shit.

Okay, she wasn't going to think about that. Forget the numbers. She'd just say she was a grown woman. That was better.

Grown woman, she thought, and tugged on her robe so she could work on her face. Grown, single woman. Grown, single man. Mutual interests between them, reasonable sense of companionship. Intense sexual tension.

How could a woman think straight when she kept imagining what it would be like to have a man's hands—

"Mom!"

She stared at her partially made-up face in the mirror. "Yes?"

The knocking was like machine-gun fire on the bathroom door.

"Mom! Can I come in? Can I? Mom!"

She pulled open the door herself to see Luke, rosy with rage, his fists bunched at his side. "What's the matter?"

"He's *looking* at me."

"Oh, Luke."

"With the face, Mom. With . . . the . . . *face.*"

She knew the face well. It was the squinty-eyed, smirky sneer that Gavin had designed to torment his brother. She knew damn well he practiced it in the mirror.

"Just don't look back at him."

"Then he makes the noise."

The noise was a hissing puff, which Gavin could keep up for hours if called for. Stella was certain that even the most hardened CIA agent would crack under its brutal power.

"All right." How the hell was she supposed to gear herself up for sex when she had to referee? She swung out of the bath, through the boys' room and into the sitting room across the hall, where she'd hoped her sons could spend the twenty minutes it took her to get dressed companionably watching cartoons.

Foolish woman, she thought. Foolish, foolish woman.

Gavin looked up from his sprawl on the floor when she came in. His face was the picture of innocence under his mop of sunny hair.

Haircuts next week, she decided, and noted it in her mental files.

He held a Matchbox car and was absently spinning its wheels while cartoons rampaged on the screen. There were several other cars piled up, lying on their sides or backs as if there'd been a horrendous traffic accident. Unfortunately the miniature ambulance and police car appeared to have had a nasty head-on collision.

Help was not on the way.

"Mom, your face looks crooked."

"Yes, I know. Gavin, I want you to stop it."

"I'm not doing anything."

She felt, actually felt, the sharp edges of the shrill scream razor up her throat. Choke it back, she ordered herself. Choke it back. She would *not* scream at her kids the way her mother had screamed at her.

"Maybe you'd like to not do anything in your room, alone, for the rest of the evening."

"I wasn't—"

"Gavin!" She cut off the denial before it dragged that scream out of her throat. Instead her voice was full of weight and aggravation. "Don't look at your brother. Don't hiss at your brother. You know it annoys him, which is exactly why you do it, and I want you to stop."

Innocence turned into a scowl as Gavin rammed the last car into the tangle of disabled vehicles. "How come I always get in trouble?"

"Yes, how come?" Stella shot back, with equal exasperation.

"He's just being a baby."

"I'm not a baby. You're a dickhead."

"Luke!" Torn between laughter and shock, Stella rounded on Luke. "Where did you hear that word?"

"Somewhere. Is it a swear?"

"Yes, and I don't want you to say it again." Even when it's apt, she thought as she caught Gavin making the face.

"Gavin, I can cancel my plans for this evening. Would you like me to do that, and stay home?" She spoke in calm, almost sweet tones. "We can spend your play hour cleaning your room."

"No." Outgunned, he poked at the pileup. "I won't look at him anymore."

"Then if it's all right with you, I'll go finish getting ready."

She heard Luke whisper, "What's a dickhead?" to Gavin as she walked out. Rolling her eyes to the ceiling, she kept going.

"THEY'RE AT EACH OTHER TONIGHT," STELLA WARNED Roz.

"Wouldn't be brothers if they weren't at each other now and then." She looked over to where the boys, the dog, and Hayley romped in the yard. "They seem all right now."

"It's brewing, under the surface, like a volcano. One of them's just waiting for the right moment to spew over the other."

"We'll see if we can distract them. If not, and they get out of hand, I'll just chain them in separate corners until you get back. I kept the shackles I used on my boys. Sentimental."

Stella laughed, and felt completely reassured. "Okay.

But you'll call me if they decide to be horrible brats. I'll be home in time to put them to bed."

"Go, enjoy yourself. And if you're not back, we can manage it."

"You make it too easy," Stella told her.

"No need for it to be hard. You know how to get there now?"

"Yes. That's the easy part."

She got in her car, gave a little toot of the horn and a wave. They'd be fine, she thought, watching in the rearview as her boys tumbled onto the ground with Parker. She couldn't have driven away if she wasn't sure of that.

It was tougher to be sure she'd be fine.

She could enjoy the drive. The early-spring breeze sang through the windows to play across her face. Tender green leaves hazed the trees, and the redbuds and wild dogwoods teased out blooms to add flashes of color.

She drove past the nursery and felt the quick zip of pride and satisfaction because she was a part of it now.

Spring had come to Tennessee, and she was here to experience it. With her windows down and the wind streaming over her, she thought she could smell the river. Just a hint of something great and powerful, contrasting with the sweet perfume of magnolia.

Contrasts, she supposed, were the order of the day now. The dreamy elegance and underlying strength of the place that was now her home, the warm air that beat the calendar to spring while the world she'd left behind still shoveled snow.

Herself, a careful, practical-natured woman driving to the bed of a man she didn't fully understand.

Nothing seemed completely aligned any longer. Blue dahlias, she decided. Her life, like her dreams, had big blue dahlias cropping up to change the design.

For tonight at least, she was going to let it bloom.

She followed the curve of the road, occupying her mind with how they would handle the weekend rush at the nursery.

Though "rush," she admitted, wasn't precisely the word. No one, staff or customer, seemed to rush—unless she counted herself.

They came, they meandered, browsed, conversed, ambled some more. They were served, with unhurried graciousness and a lot more conversation.

The slower pace sometimes made her want to grab something and just get the job done. But the fact that it often took twice as long to ring up an order than it should—in her opinion—didn't bother anyone.

She had to remind herself that part of her duties as manager was to blend efficiency with the culture of the business she managed.

One more contrast.

In any case, the work schedule she'd set would ensure that there were enough hands and feet to serve the customers. She and Roz had already poured another dozen concrete planters, and would dress them tomorrow. She could have Hayley do a few. The girl had a good eye.

Her father and Jolene were going to take the boys on Saturday, and *that* she couldn't feel guilty about, as all involved were thrilled with the arrangement.

She needed to check on the supply of plastic trays and carrying boxes, oh, and take a look at the field plants, and . . .

Her thoughts trailed off when she saw the house. She couldn't say what she'd been expecting, but it hadn't been this.

It was gorgeous.

A little run-down, perhaps, a little tired around the edges, but beautiful. Bursting with potential.

Two stories of silvered cedar stood on a terraced rise, the weathered wood broken by generous windows. On the wide, covered porch—she supposed it might be called a veranda—were an old rocker, a porch swing, a high-backed bench. Pots and baskets of flowers were arranged among them.

On the side, a deck jutted out, and she could see a short span of steps leading from it to a pretty patio.

More chairs there, more pots—oh, she was falling in love—then the land took over again and spread out to a lovely grove of trees.

He was doing shrubberies in the terraces—Japanese andromeda with its urn-shaped flowers already in bud, glossy-leaved bay laurels, the fountaining old-fashioned weigela, and a sumptuous range of azalea just waiting to explode into bloom.

And clever, she thought, creeping the car forward, clever and creative to put phlox and candytuft and ground junipers on the lowest terrace to base the shrubs and spill over the wall.

He'd planted more above in the yard—a magnolia, still tender with youth, and a dogwood blooming Easter pink. On the far side was a young weeping cherry.

Some of these were the very trees he'd hammered her over moving the first time they'd met. Just what did it say about her feelings for him that it made her smile to remember that?

She pulled into the drive beside his truck and studied the land.

There were stakes, with thin rope riding them in a kind of meandering pattern from drive to porch. Yes, she saw what he had in mind. A lazy walkway to the porch, which he would probably anchor with other shrubs or dwarf trees. Lovely. She spotted a pile of rocks and thought he must be planning to build a rock garden. There, just at the edge of the trees, would be perfect.

The house needed its trim painted, and the fieldstone that rose from its foundation repointed. A cutting garden over there, she thought as she stepped out, naturalized daffodils just inside the trees. And along the road, she'd do ground cover and shrubs, and plant daylilies, maybe some iris.

The porch swing should be painted, too, and there should be a table there—and there. A garden bench near the weeping cherry, maybe another path leading from there to around the back. Flagstone, perhaps. Or pretty stepping-stones with moss or creeping thyme growing between them.

She stopped herself as she stepped onto the porch. He'd have his own plans, she reminded herself. His house, his plans. No matter how much the place called to her, it wasn't hers.

She still had to find hers.

She took a breath, fluffed a hand through her hair, and knocked.

It was a long wait, or it seemed so to her while she twisted her watchband around her finger. Nerves began to tap-dance in her belly as she stood there in the early-evening breeze.

When he opened the door, she had to paint an easy smile on her face. He looked so *male*. The long, muscled length of him clad in faded jeans and a white T-shirt. His hair was mussed; she'd never seen it any other way. There was too much of it, she thought, to be tidy. And tidy would never suit him.

She held out the pot of dahlias she'd put together. "I've had dahlias on the mind," she told him. "I hope you can use them."

"I'm sure I can. Thanks. Come on in."

"I love the house," she began, "and what you're doing with it. I caught myself mentally planting—"

She stopped. The door led directly into what she supposed was a living room, or family room. Whatever it was, it was completely empty. The space consisted of bare drywall, scarred floors, and a smoke-stained brick fireplace with no mantel.

"You were saying?"

"Great views." It was all she could think of, and true enough. Those generous windows brought the outdoors in. It was too bad *in* was so sad.

"I'm not using this space right now."

"Obviously."

"I've got plans for it down the road, when I get the time, and the inclination. Why don't you come on back before you start crying or something."

"Was it like this, when you bought it?"

"Inside?" He shrugged a shoulder as he walked back through a doorway into what might have been a dining room. It, too, was empty, its walls covered with faded, peeling wallpaper. She could see brighter squares on it where pictures must have hung.

"Wall-to-wall carpet over these oak floors," he told her. "Leak upstairs had water stains all over the ceiling. And there was some termite damage. Tore out the walls last winter."

"What's this space?"

"Haven't decided yet."

He went through another door, and Stella let out a whistle of breath.

"Figured you'd be more comfortable in here." He set the flowers on a sand-colored granite counter and just leaned back to let her look.

It was his mark on the kitchen, she had no doubt. It was essentially male and strongly done. The sand tones of the counters were echoed in the tiles on the floor and offset by a deeper taupe on the walls. Cabinets were a dark, rich wood with pebbled-glass doors. There were herbs growing in small terra-cotta pots on the wide sill over the double sinks, and a small stone hearth in the corner.

Plenty of workspace on the long L of the counter, she calculated, plenty of eating space in the diagonal run of the counter that separated the kitchen area from a big, airy sitting space where he'd plopped down a black leather couch and a couple of oversized chairs.

And best of all, he'd opened the back wall with glass. You would sit there, Stella thought, and be a part of the gardens he was creating outside. Step through to the flagstone terrace and wander into flowers and trees.

"This is wonderful. Wonderful. Did you do it yourself?"

Right at the moment, seeing that dreamy look on her

face, he wanted to tell her he'd gathered the sand to make the glass. "Some. Work slows down in the winter, so I can deal with the inside of the place when I get the urge. I know people who do good work. I hire, or I barter. Want a drink?"

"Hmm. Yes. Thanks. The other room has to be your formal dining room, for when you entertain, or have people over for dinner. Of course, everyone's going to end up in here. It's irresistible."

She wandered back into the kitchen and took the glass of wine he offered. "It's going to be fabulous when you're done. Unique, beautiful, and welcoming. I love the colors you've picked in here."

"Last woman I had in here said they seemed dull."

"What did she know?" Stella sipped and shook her head. "No, they're earthy, natural—which suits you and the space."

She glanced toward the counter, where there were vegetables on a cutting board. "And obviously you cook, so the space needs to suit you. Maybe I can get a quick tour along with this wine, then I'll let you get to your dinner."

"Not hungry? I got some yellowfin tuna's going to go to waste, then."

"Oh." Her stomach gave a little bounce. "I didn't intend to invite myself to dinner. I just thought . . ."

"You like grilled tuna?"

"Yes. Yes, I do."

"Fine. You want to eat before or after?"

She felt the blood rush to her cheeks, then drain out again. "Ah . . ."

"Before or after I show you around?"

There was enough humor in his voice to tell her he knew just where her mind had gone. "After." She took a bracing sip of wine. "After. Maybe we could start outside, before we lose the light."

He took her out on the terrace, and her nerves eased back again as they talked about the lay of his land, his plans for it.

She studied the ground he'd tilled and nodded as he spoke of kitchen gardens, rock gardens, water gardens. And her heart yearned.

"I'm getting these old clinker bricks," he told her. "There's a mason I know. I'm having him build a three-sided wall here, about twenty square feet inside it."

"You're doing a walled garden? God, I am going to cry. I always wanted one. The house in Michigan just didn't work for one. I promised myself when I found a new place I'd put one in. With a little pool, and stone benches and secret corners."

She took a slow turn. A lot of hard, sweaty work had already gone into this place, she knew. And a lot of hard, sweaty work was still to come. A man who could do this, would do it, wanted to do this, was worth knowing.

"I envy you—and admire you—every inch of this. If you need some extra hands, give me a call. I miss gardening for the pleasure of it."

"You want to come by sometime, bring those hands and the kids, I'll put them to work." When she just lifted her eyebrows, he added. "Kids don't bother me, if that's what you're thinking. And there's no point planning a yard space where kids aren't welcome."

"Why don't you have any? Kids?"

"Figured I would by now." He reached out to touch her hair, pleased that she hadn't bothered with pins. "Things don't always work out like you figure."

She walked with him back toward the house. "People often say divorce is like death."

"I don't think so." He shook his head, taking his time on the walk back. "It's like an end. You make a mistake, you fix it, end it, start over from there. It was her mistake as well as mine. We just didn't figure that out until we were already married."

"Most men, given the opportunity, will cheerfully trash an ex."

"Waste of energy. We stopped loving each other, then we stopped liking each other. That's the part I'm sorry about," he added, then opened the wide glass door to the kitchen. "Then we stopped being married, which was the best thing for both of us. She stayed where she wanted to be, I came back to where I wanted to be. It was a couple years out of our lives, and it wasn't all bad."

"Sensible." But marriage was a serious business, she thought. Maybe the most serious. The ending of it should leave some scars, shouldn't it?

He poured more wine into their glasses, then took her hand. "I'll show you the rest of the house."

Their footsteps echoed as they moved through empty spaces. "I'm thinking of making a kind of library here, with work space. I could do my designs here."

"Where do you do them now?"

"Out of the bedroom mostly, or in the kitchen. Whatever's handiest. Powder room over there, needs a complete overhaul, eventually. Stairs are sturdy, but need to be sanded and buffed up."

He led her up, and she imagined paint on the walls, some sort of technique, she decided, that blended earthy colors and brought out the tones of wood.

"I'd have files and lists and clippings and dozens of pictures cut out of magazines." She slanted him a look. "I don't imagine you do."

"I've got thoughts, and I don't mind giving them time to stew a while. I grew up on a farm, remember? Farm's got a farmhouse, and my mama loved to buy old furniture and fix it up. Place was packed with tables—she had a weakness for tables. For now, I'm enjoying having nothing much but space around."

"What did she do with all of it when they moved? Ah, someone mentioned your parents moved to Montana," she added when he stopped to give her a speculative look.

"Yeah, got a nice little place in Helena. My daddy goes fly-fishing nearly every damn day, according to my mama, anyway. And she took her favorite pieces with her, filled a frigging moving van with stuff. She sold some, gave some to my sister, dumped some on me. I got it stored. Gotta get around to going through it one of these days, see what I can use."

"If you went through it, you'd be able to decide how you want to paint, decorate, arrange your rooms. You'd have some focal points."

"Focal points." He leaned against the wall, just grinned at her.

"Landscaping and home decorating have the same basic core of using space, focal points, design—and you know that very well or you couldn't have done what you did with your kitchen. So I'll shut up now."

"Don't mind hearing you talk."

"Well, I'm done now, so what's the next stop on the tour?"

"Guess this would be. I'm sort of using this as an office." He gestured to a door. "And I don't think you want to look in there."

"I can take it."

"I'm not sure I can." He tugged her away, moved on to another door. "You'll get all steamed up about filing systems and in and out boxes or whatever, and it'll screw up the rhythm. No point in using the grounds as foreplay if I'm going to break the mood by showing you something that'll insult your sensibilities."

"The grounds are foreplay?"

He just smiled and drew her through a door.

It was his bedroom and, like the kitchen, had been finished in a style that mirrored him. Simple, spacious, and male, with the outdoors blending with the in. The deck she'd seen was outside atrium doors, and beyond it the spring green of trees dominated the view. The walls were a dull, muted yellow, set off by warm wood tones in trim, in floor, in the pitched angles of the ceiling, where a trio of skylights let in the evening glow.

His bed was wide. A man of his size would want room there, she concluded. For sleeping, and for sex. Black iron head- and footboards and a chocolate-brown spread.

There were framed pencil drawings on the walls, gardens in black and white. And when she moved closer, she saw the scrawled signature at the lower corner. "You did these? They're wonderful."

"I like to get a visual of projects, and sometimes I sketch them up. Sometimes the sketches aren't half bad."

"These are a lot better than half bad, and you know it." She couldn't imagine those big, hard hands drawing anything so elegant, so lovely and fresh. "You're a constant surprise to me, Logan. A study of contrasts. I was thinking about contrasts on the way over here tonight, about how things aren't lined up the way I thought they would be. Should be."

She turned back to him, gestured toward his sketches. "These are another blue dahlia."

"Sorry—not following you. Like the one in your dream?"

"Dreams. I've had two now, and neither was entirely comfortable. In fact, they're getting downright scary. But the thing is the dahlia, it's so bold and beautiful, so unexpected. But it's not what I planned. Not what I imagined. Neither is this."

"Planned, imagined, or not, I wanted you here."

She took another sip of wine. "And here I am." She breathed slow in and out. "Maybe we should talk about . . . what we expect and how we'll—"

He moved in, pulled her against him. "Why don't we plant another blue dahlia and just see what happens."

Or we could try that, she thought when his mouth was on hers. The low tickle in her belly spread, and the needy part of her whispered, Thank God, inside her head.

She rose on her toes, all the way up, like a dancer on point, to meet him. And angling her body more truly to his, let him take the glass out of her hand.

Then his hands were in her hair, fingers streaming through it, clutching at it, and her arms were locked around him.

"I feel dizzy," she whispered. "Something about you makes me dizzy."

His blood fired, blasting a bubbling charge of lust straight to his belly. "Then you should get off your feet." In one quick move he scooped her up in his arms. She was, he thought, the sort of woman a man wanted to scoop up. Feminine and slight and curvy and soft. Holding her made him feel impossibly strong, uncommonly tender.

"I want to touch you everywhere. Then start right back at the beginning and touch you everywhere again." When he carried her to the bed, he felt sexy little tremors run through her. "Even when you annoy me, I want my hands on you."

"You must want them on me all the time, then."

"Truer words. Your hair drives me half crazy." He buried his face in it as he lowered the two of them to the bed.

"Me too." Her skin sprang to life with a thousand nerves as his lips wandered down to her throat. "But probably for different reasons."

He bit that sensitive skin, lightly, like a man helping himself to a sample. And the sensation rippled through her in one long, sweet stream. "We're grown-ups," she began.

"Thank God."

A shaky laugh escaped. "What I mean is we . . ." His teeth explored the flesh just above her collarbone in that same testing nibble, and had a lovely fog settling over her brain. "Never mind."

He touched, just as he'd told her he wanted to. A long, smooth stroke from her shoulders down to her fingertips. A lazy pass over her hips, her thigh, as if he were sampling her shape as he'd sampled her flavor.

Then his mouth was on hers again, hot and greedy. Those nerve endings exploded, electric jolts as his hands, his lips ran over her as if he were starved now for each separate taste. Hard hands, rough at the palms, rushed over her with both skill and desperation.

Just as she'd imagined. Just as she'd wanted.

Desires she'd ruthlessly buried broke the surface and screamed into life. Riding on the thrill, she dragged at his shirt until her hands found the hot, bare skin and dug in.

Man and muscle.

He found her breast, had her arching in delicious pleasure as his teeth nipped over shirt and bra to tantalize the flesh beneath, to stir the blood beneath into feverish, pulsing life. Everything inside her went full, and ripe, and ready.

As senses awakened, slashing one against the other in an edgy tangle of needs, she gave herself over to them, to him. And she yearned for him, for that promise of release, in a way she hadn't yearned for in so long. She wanted, craved, the heat that washed through her as the possessive stroke of those labor-scarred hands, the demanding crush of those insatiable lips, electrified her body.

She wanted, craved, all these quivering aches, these madly churning needs and the freedom to meet them.

She rose with him, body to body, moved with him, flesh to flesh. And drove him toward delirium with that creamy skin, those lovely curves. In the softening light, she looked beyond exquisite lying against the dark spread—that bright hair tumbled, those summer-blue eyes clouded with pleasure.

Passion radiated from her, meeting and matching his own. And so he wanted to give her more, and take more, and simply drown himself in what they brought to each other. The scent of her filled him like breath.

He murmured her name, savoring and exploiting as they explored each other. And there was more, he discovered, more than he'd expected.

Her heart lurched as those rugged hands guided her up, over, through the steep rise of desire. The crest rolled through her, a long, endless swell of sultry heat. She arched up again, crying out as she clamped her arms around him, pulses galloping.

Her mouth took his in a kind of ravenous madness, even as her mind screamed—Again!

He held on, held strong while she rode the peak, and the thrill her response brought him made him tremble. He ached, heart, mind, loins, ached to the point of pain.

And when he could bear it no longer, he drove into her.

She cried out once more, a sound of both shock and triumph. And she was already moving with him, a quick piston of hips, as her hands came up to frame his face.

She watched him, those blue eyes swimming, those lush lips trembling with each breath as they rose and fell together.

In the whole of his life, he'd never seen such beauty bloom.

When those eyes went blind, when they closed on a sobbing moan, he let himself go.

HE WAS HEAVY. VERY HEAVY. STELLA LAY STILL beneath Logan and pondered the wonder of being pinned, helplessly, under a man. She felt loose and sleepy and utterly relaxed. She imagined there was probably a nice pink light beaming quietly out of her fingers and toes.

His heart was thundering still. What woman wouldn't feel smug and satisfied knowing she'd caused a big, strong man to lose his breath?

Cat-content, she stroked her hands over his back.

He grunted, and rolled off of her.

She felt immediately exposed and self-conscious. Reaching out, she started to give the spread a little tug, to cover herself at least partially. Then he did something that froze her in place, and had her heart teetering.

He took her hand and kissed her fingers.

He said nothing, nothing at all, and she stayed very still while she tried to swallow her heart back into place.

"Guess I'd better feed you now," he said at length.

"Ah, I should call and make sure the boys are all right."

"Go ahead." He sat up, patting her naked thigh before he rolled out of bed and reached for his jeans. "I'll go get things started in the kitchen."

He didn't bother with his shirt, but started out. Then he stopped, turned and looked at her.

"What?" She lifted an arm, casually, she hoped, over her breasts.

"I just like the way you look there. All mussed and flushed. Makes me want to muss and flush you some more, first chance I get."

"Oh." She tried to formulate a response, but he was already sauntering off. And whistling.

fifteen

THE MAN COULD COOK. WITH LITTLE HELP FROM Stella, Logan put together a meal of delicately grilled tuna, herbed-up brown rice, and chunks of sautéed peppers and mushrooms. He was the sort of cook who dashed and dumped ingredients in by eye, or impulse, and seemed to enjoy it.

The results were marvelous.

She was an adequate cook, a competent one. She measured everything and considered cooking just one of her daily chores.

It was probably a good analogy for who they were, she decided. And another reason why it made little sense for her to be eating in his kitchen or being naked in his bed.

The sex had been . . . incredible. No point in being less than honest about it. And after good, healthy sex she should've been feeling relaxed and loose and comfortable. Instead she felt tense and tight and awkward.

It had been so intense, then he'd just rolled out of bed and started dinner. They might just as easily have finished a rousing match of tennis.

Except he'd kissed her fingers, and that sweet, affectionate gesture had arrowed straight to her heart.

Her problem, her problem, she reminded herself. Over-analyzing, over-compensating, over-something. But if she didn't analyze something how did she know what it was?

"Dinner okay?"

She broke out of her internal debate to see him watching her steadily, with those strong jungle-cat eyes. "It's terrific."

"You're not eating much."

Deliberately she forked off more tuna. "I've never understood people who cook like you, like they do on some of the cooking shows. Tossing things together, shaking a little of this in, pinches of that. How do you know it's right?"

If that was really what she'd been thinking about with her mouth in that sexy sulk, he'd go outside and eat a shovelful of mulch. "I don't know. It usually is, or different enough to be right some other way."

Maybe he couldn't get inside her head, but he had to figure whatever was in there had to do with sex, or the ramifications of having it. But they'd play it her way for the moment. "If I'm going to cook, and since I don't want to spend every night in a restaurant, I'm going to cook, I want to enjoy it. If I regimented it, it'd start to piss me off."

"If I don't regiment it to some extent, I get nervous. Is it going to be too bland, or overly spiced? Overcooked, underdone? I'd be a wreck by the time I had a meal on the table." Worry flickered over her face. "I don't belong here, do I?"

"Define here."

"Here, here." She gestured wide with both arms. "With you, eating this really lovely and inventive meal, in your beautifully designed kitchen in your strangely charming and neglected house after relieving some sort of sexual insanity upstairs in your I'm-a-man-and-I-know-it bedroom."

He sat back and decided to clear the buzz from his head with a long drink of wine. He'd figured her right, he decided, but he just never seemed to figure her enough. "I've never heard that definition of here before. Must come from up north."

"You know what I mean," she fired back. "This isn't . . . It isn't—"

"Efficient? Tidy? Organized?"

"Don't take that placating tone with me."

"That wasn't my placating tone, it was my exasperated tone. What's your problem, Red?"

"You *confuse* me."

"Oh." He shrugged a shoulder. "If that's all." And went back to his meal.

"Do you think that's funny?"

"No, but I think I'm hungry, and that I can't do a hell of a lot about the fact that you're confused. Could be I don't mind all that much confusing you, anyway, since otherwise you'd start lining things up in alphabetical order."

Those bluebell eyes went to slits. "A, you're arrogant and annoying. B, you're bossy and bullheaded. C—"

"C, you're contrary and constricting, but that doesn't bother me the way it once did. I think we've got something interesting between us. Neither one of us was looking for it, but I can roll with that. You pick it apart. Hell if I know why I'm starting to like that about you."

"I've got more to risk than you do."

He sobered. "I'm not going to hurt your kids."

"If I believed you were the sort of man who would, or could, I wouldn't be with you on this level."

"What's 'this level'?"

"Evening sex and kitchen dinners."

"You seemed to handle the sex better than the meal."

"You're exactly right. Because I don't know what you expect from me now, and I'm not entirely sure what I expect from you."

"And this is your equivalent of tossing ingredients in a pot."

She huffed out a breath. "Apparently you understand me better than I do you."

"I'm not that complicated."

"Oh, please. You're a maze, Logan." She leaned forward until she could see the gold flecks on the green of his eyes. "A goddamn maze without any geometric pattern. Professionally, you're one of the most creative, versatile, and knowledgeable landscape designers I've ever worked with, but you do half of your designing and scheduling on the fly, with little scraps of papers stuffed into your truck or your pockets."

He scooped up more rice. "It works for me."

"Apparently, but it shouldn't work for anyone. You thrive in chaos, which this house clearly illustrates. Nobody should thrive in chaos."

"Now wait a minute." This time he gestured with his fork. "Where's the chaos? There's barely a frigging thing in the place."

"Exactly!" She jabbed a finger at him. "You've got a wonderful kitchen, a comfortable and stylish bedroom—"

"Stylish?" Mortification, clear as glass, covered his face. "Jesus."

"And empty rooms. You should be tearing your hair out wondering what you're going to do with them, but you're not. You just—just—" She waved her hand in circles. "Mosey along."

"I've never moseyed in my life. Amble sometimes," he decided. "But I never mosey."

"Whatever. You know wine and you read comic books. What kind of sense does that make?"

"Makes plenty if you consider I *like* wine and comic books."

"You were married, and apparently committed enough to move away from your home."

"What's the damn point in getting married if you're not ready and willing to do what makes the other person happy? Or at least try."

"You loved her," Stella said with a nod. "Yet you walked

away from a divorce unscarred. It was broken, too bad, so you ended it. You're rude and abrupt one minute, and accommodating the next. You knew why I'd come here tonight, yet you went to the trouble to fix a meal—which was considerate and, and civilized—there, put *that* in the C column."

"Christ, Red, you kill me. I'd move on to D, and say you're delicious, but right now it's more like demented."

Despite the fact he was laughing, she was wound up and couldn't stop. "And we have incredible, blow-the-damn-roof-off sex, then you bounce out of bed as if we'd been doing this every night for years. I can't keep up."

Once he decided she'd finished, he picked up his wine, drank thoughtfully. "Let's see if I can work my way back through that. Though I've got to tell you, I didn't detect any geometric pattern."

"Oh, shut up."

His hand clamped over hers before she could shove back from the table. "No, you just sit still. It's my turn. If I didn't work the way I do? I wouldn't be able to do what I do, and I sure as hell wouldn't love it. I found that out up north. My marriage was a failure. Nobody likes to fail, but nobody gets through life without screwing up. We screwed it up, didn't hurt anybody but ourselves. We took our lumps and moved on."

"But—"

"Hush. If I'm rude and abrupt it's because I feel rude and abrupt. If I'm accommodating, it's because I want to be, or figure I have to be at some point."

He thought, What the hell, and topped off his wine. She'd barely touched hers. "What was next? Oh, yeah, you being here tonight. Yeah, I knew why. We're not teenagers, and you're a pretty straightforward woman, in your way. I wanted you, and made that clear. You wouldn't come knocking on my door unless you were ready. As for the meal, there are a couple of reasons for that. One, I like to eat. And two, I wanted you here. I wanted to be with you here, like this. Before, after, in between. However it worked out."

Somewhere, somehow, during his discourse, her temper had ebbed. "How do you make it all sound sane?"

"I'm not done. While I'm going to agree with your take on the sex, I object to the word 'bounce.' I don't bounce anymore than I mosey. I got out of bed because if I'd breathed you in much longer, I'd have asked you to stay. You can't, you won't. And the fact is, I don't know that I'm ready for you to stay anyway. If you're the sort who needs a lot of postcoital chat, like 'Baby, that was amazing'—"

"I'm not." There was something in his aggravated tone that made her lips twitch. "I can judge for myself, and I destroyed you up there."

His hand slid up to her wrist, back down to her fingers. "Any destruction was mutual."

"All right. Mutual destruction. The first time with a man, and I think this holds true for most women, is as nerve-racking as it is exciting. It's more so afterward if what happened between them touched something in her. You touched something in me, and it scares me."

"Straightforward," he commented.

"Straightforward, to your maze. It's a difficult combination. Gives us a lot to think about. I'm sorry I made an issue out of all of this."

"Red, you were born to make issues out of every damn thing. It's kind of interesting now that I'm getting used to it."

"That may be true, and I could say that the fact your drummer certainly bangs a different tune's fairly interesting, too. But right now, I'm going to help you clean up your kitchen. Then I have to get home."

He rose when she did, then simply took her shoulders and backed her into the refrigerator. He kissed her blind and deaf—pent-up temper, needs, frustration, longings all boiled together.

"Something else to think about," he said.

"I'll say."

* * *

ROZ DIDN'T PRY INTO OTHER PEOPLE'S BUSINESS. SHE didn't mind hearing about it when gossip came her way, but she didn't pry. She didn't like—more she didn't permit—others to meddle in her life, and afforded them the same courtesy.

So she didn't ask Stella any questions. She thought of plenty, but she didn't ask them.

She observed.

Her manager conducted business with her usual calm efficiency. Roz imagined Stella could be standing in the whirling funnel of a tornado and would still be able to conduct business efficiently.

An admirable and somewhat terrifying trait.

She'd grown very fond of Stella, and she'd come—unquestionably—to depend on her to handle the details of the business so she herself could focus on the duties, and pleasures, of being the grower. She adored the children. It was impossible for her not to. They were charming and bright, sly and noisy, entertaining and exhausting.

Already, she was so used to them, and Stella and Hayley, being in her house she could hardly imagine them not being there.

But she didn't pry, even when Stella came home from her evening at Logan's with the unmistakable look of a woman who'd been well pleasured.

But she didn't hush Hayley, or brush her aside when the girl chattered about it.

"She won't get specific," Hayley complained while she and Roz weeded a bed at Harper House. "I really like it when people get specific. But she said he cooked for her. I always figure when a man cooks, he's either trying to get you between the sheets, or he's stuck on you."

"Maybe he's just hungry."

"A man's hungry, he sends out for pizza. At least the guys I've known. I think he's stuck on her." She waited, the pause obviously designed for Roz to comment. When there was none, Hayley blew out a breath. "Well? You've known him a long time."

"A few years. I can't tell you what's in his mind. But I can tell you he's never cooked for me."

"Was his wife a real bitch?"

"I couldn't say. I didn't know her."

"I'd like it if she was. A real stone bitch who tore him apart and left him all wounded and resentful of women. Then Stella comes along and gets him all messed up in the head even as she heals him."

Roz sat back on her heels and smiled. "You're awfully young, honey."

"You don't have to be young to like romance. Um . . . your second husband, he was terrible, wasn't he?"

"He was—is—a liar, a cheat, and a thief. Other than that he's charming."

"Did he break your heart?"

"No. He bruised my pride and pissed me off. Which was worse, in my opinion. That's yesterday's news, Hayley. I'm going to plug some *silene armeria* in these pockets," she continued. "They've got a long blooming season, and they'll fill in nice here."

"I'm sorry."

"No need to be sorry."

"It's just that this woman was in this morning, Mrs. Peebles?"

"Oh, yes, Roseanne." After studying the space, Roz picked up her trowel and began to turn the earth in the front of the mixed bed. "Did she actually buy anything?"

"She dithered around for an hour, said she'd come back."

"Typical. What did she want? It wouldn't have been plants."

"I clued in there. She's the nosy sort, and not the kind with what you'd call a benign curiosity. Just comes in for gossip—to spread it or to harvest it. You see her kind most everywhere."

"I suppose you do."

"So, well. She'd gotten word I was living here, and was a family connection, so she was pumping me. I don't pump so easy, but I let her keep at it."

Roz grinned under the brim of her cap as she reached for a plant. "Good for you."

"I figured what she really wanted was for me to pass on to you the news that Bryce Clerk is back in Memphis."

A jerk of her fingers broke off part of the stem. "Is he?" Roz said, very quietly.

"He's living at the Peabody for now and has some sort of venture in the works. She was vague about that. She says he plans to move back permanent, and he's taking office space. Said he looked very prosperous."

"Likely he hosed some other brainless woman."

"You aren't brainless, Roz."

"I was, briefly. Well, it's no matter to me where he is or what he's doing. I don't get burned twice by the same crooked match."

She set the plant, then reached for another. "Common name for these is none-so-pretty. Feel these sticky patches on the stems? They catch flies. Shows that something that looks attractive can be dangerous, or at least a big pain in the ass."

SHE BURIED IT AS SHE CLEANED UP. SHE WASN'T CONcerned with a scoundrel she'd once been foolish enough to marry. A woman was entitled to a few mistakes along the way, even if she made them out of loneliness or foolishness, or—screw it—vanity.

Entitled, Roz thought, as long as she corrected the mistakes and didn't repeat them.

She put on a fresh shirt, skimmed her fingers through her damp hair as she studied herself in the mirror. She could still look good, damn good, if she worked at it. If she wanted a man, she could have one—and not because he assumed she was dim-witted and had a depthless well of money to draw from. Maybe what had happened with Bryce had shaken her confidence and self-esteem for a little while, but she was all right now. Better than all right.

She hadn't needed a man to fill in the pockets of her life before he'd come along. She didn't need one now. Things were back the way she liked them. Her kids were happy and productive, her business was thriving, her home was secure. She had friends she enjoyed and acquaintances she tolerated.

And right now, she had the added interest of researching her family ghost.

Giving her hair another quick rub, she went downstairs to join the rest of the crew in the library. She heard the knock as she came to the base of the stairs, and detoured to the door.

"Logan, what a nice surprise."

"Hayley didn't tell you I was coming?"

"No, but that doesn't matter. Come on in."

"I ran into her at the nursery today, and she asked if I'd come by tonight, give y'all a hand with your research and brainstorming. I had a hard time resisting the idea of being a ghostbuster."

"I see." And she did. "I'd best warn you that our Hayley's got a romantic bent and she currently sees you as Rochester to Stella's Jane Eyre."

"Oh. Uh-oh."

She only smiled. "Jane's still with the boys, getting them settled down for the night. Why don't you go on up to the West wing? Just follow the noise. You can let her know we'll entertain ourselves until she comes down."

She walked away before he could agree or protest.

She didn't pry into other people's business. But that didn't mean she didn't sow the occasional seeds.

Logan stood where he was for a moment, tapping his fingers on the side of his leg. He was still tapping them as he started up the stairs.

Roz was right about the noise. He heard the laughter

and squeals, the stomping feet before he'd hit the top. Following it, he strolled down the hall, then paused in the open doorway.

It was obviously a room occupied by boys. And though it was certainly tidier than his had been at those tender ages, it wasn't static or regimented. A few toys were scattered on the floor, books and other debris littered the desk and shelves. It smelled of soap, shampoo, wild youth, and crayons.

In the midst of it, Stella sat on the floor, mercilessly tickling a pajama-clad Gavin while a blissfully naked Luke scrambled around the room making crazed hooting sounds through his cupped hands.

"What's my name?" Stella demanded as she sent her oldest son into helpless giggles.

"Mom!"

She made a harsh buzzing sound and dug fingers into his ribs. "Try again, small, helpless boy child. What is my name?"

"Mom, Mom, Mom, Mom, Mom!" He tried to wiggle away and was flipped over.

"I can't hear you."

"Empress," he managed on hitching giggles.

"And? The rest, give it all or the torment continues."

"Empress Magnificent of the Entire Universe!"

"And don't you forget it." She gave him a loud, smacking kiss on his cotton-clad butt, and sat back. "And now you, short, frog-faced creature." She got to her feet, rubbing her hands together as Luke screamed in delight.

And stumbled back with a scream of her own when she saw Logan in the doorway. "Oh, my God! You scared me to death!"

"Sorry, just watching the show. Your Highness. Hey, kid." He nodded at Gavin, who lay on the floor. "How's it going?"

"She defeated me. Now I have to go to bed, 'cause that's the law of the land."

"I've heard that." He picked up the bottom half of a pair

of X-Men pj's, lifted an eyebrow at Luke. "These your mom's?"

Luke let out a rolling gut laugh, and danced, happy with his naked state. "Uh-*uh*. They're mine. I don't have to wear them unless she catches me."

Luke started to make a break for the adjoining bath and was scooped up, one-armed, by his mother.

Stronger than she looks, Logan mused as she hoisted her son over her head.

"Foolish boy, you'll never escape me." She lowered him. "Into the pj's, and into bed." She glanced over at Logan. "Is there something . . ."

"I got invited to the . . . get-together downstairs."

"Is it a party?" Luke wanted to know when Logan handed him the pajama bottoms. "Are there cookies?"

"It's a meeting, a grown-up meeting, and if there are cookies," Stella said as she turned down Luke's bed, "you can have some tomorrow."

"David makes really good cookies," Gavin commented. "Better than Mom's."

"If that wasn't true, I'd have to punish you severely." She turned to his bed, where he sat grinning at her, and using the heel of her hand shoved him gently onto his back.

"But you're prettier than he is."

"Clever boy. Logan, could you tell everyone I'll be down shortly? We're just going to read for a bit first."

"Can he read?" Gavin asked.

"I can. What's the book?"

"Tonight we get *Captain Underpants*." Luke grabbed the book and hurried over to shove it into Logan's hands.

"So is he a superhero?"

Luke's eyes widened like saucers. "You don't know about Captain Underpants?"

"Can't say I do." He turned the book over in his hands, but he was looking at the boy. He'd never read to kids before. It might be entertaining. "Maybe I should read it, then I can find out. If that suits the Empress."

"Oh, well, I—"

"Please, Mom! Please!"

At the chorus on either side of her, Stella eased back with the oddest feeling in her gut. "Sure. I'll just go straighten up the bath."

She left them to it, mopping up the wet, gathering bath toys, while Logan's voice, deep and touched with ironic amusement, carried to her.

She hung damp towels, dumped bath toys into a plastic net to dry, fussed. And she felt the chill roll in around her. A hard, needling cold that speared straight to her bones.

Her creams and lotions tumbled over the counter as if an angry hand swept them. The thuds and rattles sent her springing forward to grab at them before they fell to the floor.

And each one was like a cube of ice in her hand.

She'd seen them move. Good God, she'd seen them *move.*

Shoving them back, she swung instinctively to the connecting doorway to shield her sons from the chill, from the fury she felt slapping the air.

There was Logan, with the chair pulled between the beds, as she did herself, reading about the silly adventures of Captain Underpants in that slow, easy voice, while her boys lay tucked in and drifting off.

She stood there, blocking that cold, letting it beat against her back until he finished, until he looked up at her.

"Thanks." She was amazed at how calm her voice sounded. "Boys, say good night to Mr. Kitridge."

She moved into the room as they mumbled it. When the cold didn't follow her, she took the book, managed a smile. "I'll be down in just a minute."

"Okay. See you later, men."

The interlude left him feeling mellow and relaxed. Reading bedtime stories was a kick. Who knew? Captain Underpants. Didn't that beat all.

He wouldn't mind doing it again sometime, especially

if he could talk Mama into letting them read a graphic novel.

He'd liked seeing her wrestling on the floor with her boy. Empress Magnificent, he thought with a half laugh.

Then the breath was knocked out of him. The force of the cold came like a tidal wave at his back, swamping him even as it shoved him forward.

He pitched at the top of the stairs, felt his head go light at the thought of the fall. Flailing out, he managed to grab the rail and, spinning his body, hook his other hand over it while tiny black dots swam in front of his eyes. For another instant he feared he would simply tumble over the railing, pushed by the momentum.

Out of the corner of his eye, he saw a shape, vague but female. And from it he felt a raw and bitter rage.

Then it was gone.

He could hear his own breath heaving in and out, and feel the clamminess of panic sweat down his back. Though his legs wanted to fold on him, he stayed where he was, working to steady himself until Stella came out.

Her half smile faded the minute she saw him. "What is it?" She moved to him quickly. "What happened?"

"She—this ghost of yours—has she ever scared the boys?"

"No. Exactly the opposite. She's . . . comforting, even protective of them."

"All right. Let's go downstairs." He took her hand firmly in his, prepared to drag her to safety if necessary.

"Your hand's cold."

"Yeah, tell me about it."

"You tell me."

"I intend to."

HE TOLD THEM ALL WHEN THEY SAT AROUND THE library table with their folders and books and notes. And he dumped a good shot of brandy in his coffee as he did.

"There's been nothing," Roz began, "in all the years she's been part of this house, that indicates she's a threat. People have been frightened or uneasy, but no one's ever been physically attacked."

"Can ghosts physically attack?" David wondered.

"You wouldn't ask if you'd been standing at the top of the stairs with me."

"Poltergeists can cause stuff to fly around," Hayley commented. "But they usually manifest around adolescent kids. Something about puberty can set them off. Anyway, this isn't that. It might be that an ancestor of Logan's did something to her. So she's paying him back."

"I've been in this house dozens of times. She's never bothered with me before."

"The children." Stella spoke softly as she looked over her own notes. "It centers on them. She's drawn to children, especially little boys. She's protective of them. And she almost, you could say, envies me for having them, but not in an angry way. More sad. But she was angry the night I was going out to dinner with Logan."

"Putting a man ahead of your kids." Roz held up a hand. "I'm not saying that's what I think. We have to think like she does. We talked about this before, Stella, and I've been thinking back on it. The only times I remember feeling anything angry from her was when I went out with men now and again, when my boys were coming up. But I didn't experience anything as direct or upsetting as this. But then, there was nothing to it. I never had any strong feelings for any of them."

"I don't see how she could know what I feel or think."

But the dreams, Stella thought. She's been in my dreams.

"Let's not get irrational now," David interrupted. "Let's follow this line through. Let's say she believes things are serious, or heading that way, between you and Logan. She doesn't like it, that's clear enough. The only people who've felt threatened, or been threatened are the two of you. Why? Does it make her angry? Or is she jealous?"

"A jealous ghost." Hayley drummed her hands on the table. "Oh, that's good. It's like she sympathizes, relates to you being a woman, a single woman, with kids. She'll help you look after them, even sort of look after you. But then you put a man in the picture, and she's all bitchy about it. She's like, you're not supposed to have a nice, standard family—mom, dad, kids—because I didn't."

"Logan and I hardly . . . All he did was read them a story."

"The sort of thing a father might do," Roz pointed out.

"I . . . well, when he was reading to them, I was putting the bathroom back in shape. And she was there. I felt her. Then, well, my things. The things I keep on the counter started to jump. *I* jumped."

"Holy shit," Hayley responded.

"I went to the door, and in the boy's room, everything was calm, normal. I could feel the warmth on the front of me, and this, this raging cold against my back. She didn't want to frighten them. Only me."

But buying a baby monitor went on her list. From now on, she wanted to hear everything that went on in that room when her boys were up there without her.

"This is a good angle, Stella, and you're smart enough to know we should follow it." Roz laid her hands on the library table. "Nothing we've turned up indicates this spirit is one of the Harper women, as has been assumed all these years. Yet someone knew her, knew her when she was alive, knew that she died. So was it hushed up, ignored? Either way, it might explain her being here. If it was hushed up or ignored, it seems most logical she was a servant, a mistress, or a lover."

"I bet she had a child." Hayley laid a hand over her own. "Maybe she died giving birth to it, or had to give it up, and died from a broken heart. It would have been one of the Harper men who got her into trouble, don't you think? Why would she stay here if it wasn't because she lived here or—"

"Died here," Stella finished. "Reginald Harper was head of the house during the period when we think she died. Roz, how the hell do we go about finding out if he had a mistress, a lover, or an illegitimate child?"

sixteen

LOGAN HAD BEEN IN LOVE TWICE IN HIS LIFE. HE'D been in lust a number of times. He'd experienced extreme interest or heavy like, but love had only knocked him down and out twice. The first had been in his late teens, when both he and the girl of his dreams had been too young to handle it.

They'd burned each other and their love out with passion, jealousies, and a kind of crazed energy. He could look back at that time now and think of Lisa Anne Lauer with a sweet nostalgia and affection.

Then there was Rae. He'd been a little older, a little smarter. They'd taken their time, two years of time before heading into marriage. They'd both wanted it, though some who knew him were surprised, not only by the engagement but by his agreement to move north with her.

It hadn't surprised Logan. He'd loved her, and north was where she'd wanted to be. Needed to be, he corrected, and he'd figured, naively as it turned out, that he could plant himself anywhere.

He'd left the wedding plans up to her and her mother,

with some input from his own. He wasn't crazy. But he'd enjoyed the big, splashy, crowded wedding with all its pomp.

He'd had a good job up north. At least in theory. But he'd been restless and dissatisfied in the beehive of it, and out of place in the urban buzz.

The small-town boy, he thought as he and his crew finished setting the treated boards on the roof of a twelve-foot pergola. He was just too small-town, too small-time, to fit into the urban landscape.

He hadn't thrived there, and neither had his marriage. Little things at first, picky things—things he knew in retrospect they should have dealt with, compromised on, overcome. Instead, they'd both let those little things fester and grow until they'd pushed the two of them, not just apart, he thought, but in opposite directions.

She'd been in her element, and he hadn't. At the core he'd been unhappy, and she'd been unhappy he wasn't acclimating. Like any disease, unhappiness spread straight down to the roots when it wasn't treated.

Not all her fault. Not all his. In the end they'd been smart enough, or unhappy enough, to cut their losses.

The failure of it had hurt, and the loss of that once-promising love had hurt. Stella was wrong about the lack of scars. There were just some scars you had to live with.

The client wanted wisteria for the pergola. He instructed his crew where to plant, then took himself off to the small pool the client wanted outfitted with water plants.

He was feeling broody, and when he was feeling broody, he liked to work alone as much as possible. He had the cattails in containers and, dragging on boots, he waded in to sink them. Left to themselves, the cats would spread and choke out everything, but held in containers they'd be a nice pastoral addition to the water feature. He dealt with a trio of water lilies the same way, then dug in the yellow flags. They liked their feet wet, and would dance with color on the edge of the pool.

The work satisfied him, centered him as it always did. It let another part of his mind work out separate problems. Or at least chew on them for a while.

Maybe he'd put a small pool in the walled garden he planned to build at home. No cattails, though. He might try some dwarf lotus, and some water canna as a background plant. It seemed to him it was more the sort of thing Stella would like.

He'd been in love twice before, Logan thought again. And now he could sense those delicate taproots searching inside him for a place to grow. He could probably cut them off. Probably. He probably should.

What was he going to do with a woman like Stella and those two ridiculously appealing kids? They were bound to drive each other crazy in the long term with their different approaches to damn near everything. He doubted they'd burn each other out, though, God, when he'd had her in bed, he'd felt singed. But they might wilt, as he and Rae had wilted. That was more painful, more miserable, he knew, than the quick flash.

And this time there were a couple of young boys to consider.

Wasn't that why the ghost had given him a good kick in the ass? It was hard to believe he was sweating in the steamy air under overcast skies and thinking about an encounter with a ghost. He'd thought he was open-minded about that sort of thing—until he'd come face-to-face, so to speak, with it.

The fact was, Logan realized now, as he hauled mulch over for the skirt of the pool, he hadn't believed in the ghost business. It had all been window dressing or legendary stuff to him. Old houses were supposed to have ghosts because it made a good story, and the south loved a good story. He'd accepted it as part of the culture, and maybe, in some strange way, as something that might happen to someone else. Especially if that someone else was a little drunk, or very susceptible to atmosphere.

He'd been neither. But he'd felt her breath, the ice of it, and her rage, the power of it. She'd wanted to cause him harm, she'd wanted him away. From those children, and their mother.

So he was invested now in helping to find the identity of what walked those halls.

But a part of him wondered if whoever she was was right. Would they all be better off if he stayed away?

The phone on his belt beeped. Since he was nearly done, he answered instead of ignoring, dragging off his filthy work gloves and plucking the phone off his belt.

"Kitridge."

"Logan, it's Stella."

The quick and helpless flutter around his heart irritated him. "Yeah. I've got the frigging forms in my truck."

"What forms?"

"Whatever damn forms you're calling to nag me about."

"It happens I'm not calling to nag you about anything." Her voice had gone crisp and businesslike, which only caused the flutter and the irritation to increase.

"Well, I don't have time to chat, either. I'm on the clock."

"Seeing as you are, I'd like you to schedule in a consult. I have a customer who'd like an on-site consultation. She's here now, so if you could give me a sense of your plans for the day, I could let her know if and when you could meet with her."

"Where?"

She rattled off an address that was twenty minutes away. He glanced around his current job site, calculated. "Two o'clock."

"Fine. I'll tell her. The client's name is Marsha Fields. Do you need any more information?"

"No."

"Fine."

He heard the firm click in his ear and found himself even more annoyed he hadn't thought to hang up first.

* * *

BY THE TIME LOGAN GOT HOME THAT EVENING, HE was tired, sweaty, and in a better mood. Hard physical work usually did the job for him, and he'd had plenty of it that day. He'd worked in the steam, then through the start of a brief spring storm. He and his crew broke for lunch during the worst of it and sat in his overheated truck, rain lashing at the windows, while they ate cold po'boy sandwiches and drank sweet tea.

The Fields job had strong possibilities. The woman ran that roost and had very specific ideas. Since he liked and agreed with most of them, he was eager to put some of them on paper, expand or refine them.

And since it turned out that Marsha's cousin on her mother's side was Logan's second cousin on his father's, the consult had taken longer than it might have, and had progressed cheerfully.

It didn't hurt that she was bound to send more work his way.

He took the last curve of the road to his house in a pleasant frame of mind, which darkened considerably when he saw Stella's car parked behind his.

He didn't want to see her now. He hadn't worked things out in his head, and she'd just muck up whatever progress he'd made. He wanted a shower and a beer, a little quiet. Then he wanted to eat his dinner with ESPN in the background and his work spread out on the kitchen table.

There just wasn't room in that scenario for a woman.

He parked, fully intending to shake her off. She wasn't in the car, or on the porch. He was trying to determine if going to bed with him gave a woman like her the notion that she could waltz into his house when he wasn't there. Even as he'd decided it wouldn't, not for Stella, he heard the watery hiss of his own garden hose.

Shoving his hands in his pockets, he wandered around the side of the house.

She was on the patio, wearing snug gray pants—the sort that stopped several inches above the ankle—and a loose blue shirt. Her hair was drawn back in a bright, curling tail, which for reasons he couldn't explain he found desperately sexy. As the sun had burned its way through the clouds, she'd shaded her eyes with gray-tinted glasses.

She looked neat and tidy, careful to keep her gray canvas shoes out of the wet.

"It rained today," he called out.

She kept on soaking his pots. "Not enough."

She finished the job, released the sprayer on the hose, but continued to hold it as she turned to face him. "I realize you have your own style, and your own moods, and that's your business. But I won't be spoken to the way you spoke to me today. I won't be treated like some silly female who calls her boyfriend in the middle of the workday to coo at him, or like some anal business associate who interrupts you to harangue you about details. I'm neither."

"Not my girlfriend or not my business associate?"

He could see, quite clearly, the way her jaw tightened when she clenched her teeth. "If and when I contact you during the workday, it will be for a reason. As it most certainly was this morning."

She was right, but he didn't have to say so. "We got the Fields job."

"Hooray."

He bit the inside of his cheek to hold back the grin at her sour cheer. "I'll be working up a design for her, with a bid. You'll get a copy of both. That suit you?"

"It does. What doesn't—"

"Where are the kids?"

It threw her off stride. "My father and his wife picked them up from school today. They're having dinner there, and spending the night, as I have a birthing class with Hayley later."

"What time?"

"What time what?"

"Is the class?"

"At eight-thirty. I'm not here for small talk, Logan, or to be placated. I feel very strongly that—" Her eyes widened, then narrowed as she stepped back. He'd stepped forward, and there was no mistaking the tone of that slow smile.

"Don't even think about it. I couldn't be less interested in kissing you at the moment."

"Then I'll kiss you, and maybe you'll get interested."

"I mean it." She aimed the hose like a weapon. "Just keep your distance. I want to make myself perfectly clear."

"I'm getting the message. Go ahead and shoot," he invited. "I sweated out a gallon today, I won't mind a shower."

"Just stop it." She danced back several steps as he advanced. "This isn't a game, this isn't funny."

"I just get stirred right up when your voice takes on that tone."

"I don't have a tone."

"Yankee schoolteacher. I'm going to be sorry if you ever lose it." He made a grab, and instinctively she tightened her fist on the nozzle. And nailed him.

The spray hit him mid-chest and had a giggle bubbling out of her before she could stop it. "I'm not going to play with you now. I'm serious, Logan."

Dripping, he made another grab, feinted left. This time she squealed, dropped the hose, and ran.

He snagged her around the waist, hauled her off her feet at the back end of the patio. Caught somewhere between shock and disbelief, she kicked, wiggled, then lost her breath as she landed on the grass on top of him.

"Let me go, you moron."

"Don't see why I should." God, it felt good to be horizontal. Better yet to have her horizontal with him. "Here you are, trespassing, watering my pots, spouting off lectures." He rolled, pinning her. "I ought to be able to do what I want on my own land."

"Stop it. I haven't finished fighting with you."

"I bet you can pick it up where you left off." He gave her a playful nip on the chin, then another.

"You're wet, you're sweaty, I'm getting grass stains on my—"

The rest of the words were muffled against his mouth, and she would have sworn the water on both of them went to steam.

"I can't—we can't—" But the reasons why were going dim. "In the backyard."

"Wanna bet?"

He couldn't help wanting her, so why was he fighting it? He wanted the solid, sensible core of her, and the sweet edges. He wanted the woman obsessed with forms who would wrestle on the floor with her children. He wanted the woman who watered his pots even while she skinned him with words.

And the one who vibrated beneath him on the grass when he touched her.

He touched her, his hands possessive as they molded her breasts, as they roamed down her to cup her hips. He tasted her, his lips hungry on her throat, her shoulder, her breast.

She melted under him, and even as she went fluid seemed to come alive with heat, with movement.

It was insane. It was rash and it was foolish, but she couldn't stop herself. They rolled over the grass, like two frenzied puppies. He smelled of sweat, of labor and damp. And, God, of man. Pungent and gorgeous and sexy.

She clamped her hands in that mass of waving hair, already showing streaks from the sun, and dragged his mouth back to hers.

She nipped his lip, his tongue.

"Your belt." She had to fight to draw air. "It's digging—"

"Sorry."

He levered up to unbuckle it, then just stopped to look at her.

Her hair had come out of its band; her eyes were sultry, her skin flushed. And he felt those roots take hold.

"Stella."

He didn't know what he might have said, the words were jumbled in his brain and tangled with so much feeling he couldn't translate them.

But she smiled, slow and sultry as her eyes. "Why don't I help you with that?"

She flipped open the button of his jeans, yanked down the zipper. Her hand closed over him, a velvet vise. His body was hard as steel, and his mind and heart powerless.

She arched up to him, her lips skimmed over his bare chest, teeth scoring a hot little line that was a whisper away from pain.

Then she was over him, destroying him. Surrounding him.

She heard birdsong and breeze, smelled grass and damp flesh. And heliotrope that wafted on the air from the pot she'd watered. She felt his muscles, taut ropes, the broad plane of his shoulders, the surprisingly soft waves of his hair.

And she saw, as she looked down, that he was lost in her.

Throwing her head back, she rode, until she was lost as well.

SHE LAY SPRAWLED OVER HIM, DAMP AND NAKED AND muzzy-headed. Part of her brain registered that his arms were clamped around her as if they were two survivors of a shipwreck.

She turned her head to rest it on his chest. Maybe they'd wrecked each other. She'd just made wild love with a man in broad daylight, outside in the yard.

"This is insane," she murmured, but couldn't quite convince herself to move. "What if someone had come by?"

"People come by without an invitation have to take potluck."

There was a lazy drawl to his voice in direct opposition to his grip on her. She lifted her head to study. His eyes were closed. "So this is potluck?"

The corners of his mouth turned up a little. "Seems to me this pot was plenty lucky."

"I feel sixteen. Hell, I never did anything like this when I was sixteen. I need my sanity. I need my clothes."

"Hold on." He nudged her aside, then rose.

Obviously, she thought, it doesn't bother him to walk around outside naked as a deer. "I came here to talk to you, Logan. Seriously."

"You came here to kick my ass," he corrected. "Seriously. You were doing a pretty good job of it."

"I hadn't finished." She turned slightly, reached out for her hairband. "But I will, as soon as I'm dressed and—"

She screamed, the way a woman screams when she's being murdered with a kitchen knife.

Then she gurgled, as the water he'd drenched her with from the hose ran into her astonished mouth.

"Figured we could both use some cooling off."

It simply wasn't in her, even under the circumstances, to run bare-assed over the grass. Instead, she curled herself up, knees to breast, arms around knees, and cursed him with vehemence and creativity.

He laughed until he thought his ribs would crack. "Where'd a nice girl like you learn words like that? How am I supposed to kiss that kind of mouth?"

She seared him with a look even when he held the hose over his own head and took an impromptu shower. "Feels pretty good. Want a beer?"

"No, I don't want a beer. I certainly don't want a damn beer. I want a damn towel. You insane idiot, now my clothes are wet."

"We'll toss 'em into the dryer." He dropped the hose, scooped them up. "Come on inside, I'll get you a towel."

Since he sauntered across the patio to the door, still unconcerned and naked, she had no choice but to follow.

"Do you have a robe?" she asked in cold and vicious tones.

"What would I do with a robe? Hang on, Red."

He left her, dripping and beginning to shiver in his kitchen.

He came back a few minutes later, wearing ratty gym pants and carrying two huge bath sheets. "These ought to do the trick. Dry off, I'll toss these in for you."

He carried her clothes through a door. Laundry room, she assumed as she wrapped one of the towels around her. She used the other to rub at her hair—which would be hopeless, absolutely hopeless now—while she heard the dryer click on.

"Want some wine instead?" he asked as he stepped back in. "Coffee or something."

"Now you listen to me—"

"Red, I swear I've had to listen to you more than any woman I can remember in the whole of my life. It beats the living hell out of me why I seem to be falling in love with you."

"I don't like being . . . Excuse me?"

"It was the hair that started it." He opened the refrigerator, took out a beer. "But that's just attraction. Then the voice." He popped the top and took a long drink from the bottle. "But that's just orneriness on my part. It's a whole bunch of little things, a lot of big ones tossed in. I don't know just what it is, but every time I'm around you I get closer to the edge."

"I—you—you think you're falling in love with me, and your way of showing it is to toss me on the ground and carry on like some sex addict, and when you're done to drench me with a hose?"

He took another sip, slower, more contemplative, rubbed a hand over his bare chest. "Seemed like the thing to do at the time."

"Well, that's very charming."

"Wasn't thinking about charm. I didn't say I wanted to

be in love with you. In fact, thinking about it put me in a lousy mood most of the day."

Her eyes narrowed until the blue of them was a hot, intense light. "Oh, really?"

"Feel better now, though."

"Oh, that's fine. That's lovely. Get me my clothes."

"They're not dry yet."

"I don't care."

"People from up north are always in a hurry." He leaned back comfortably on the counter. "There's this other thing I thought today."

"I don't care about that either."

"The other thing was how I've only been in love—the genuine deal—twice before. And both times it . . . let's not mince words. Both times it went to shit. Could be this'll head the same way."

"Could be we're already there."

"No." His lips curved. "You're pissed and you're scared. I'm not what you were after."

"I wasn't after anything."

"Me either." He set the beer down, then killed her temper by stepping to her, framing her face with his hands. "Maybe I can stop what's going on in me. Maybe I should try. But I look at you, I touch you, and the edge doesn't just get closer, it gets more appealing."

He touched his lips to her forehead, then released her and stepped back.

"Every time I figure some part of you out, you sprout something off in another direction," she said. "I've only been in love once—the genuine deal—and it was everything I wanted. I haven't figured out what I want now, beyond what I have. I don't know, Logan, if I've got the courage to step up to that edge again."

"Things keep going the way they are for me, if you don't step up, you might get pushed."

"I don't push easily. Logan." It was she who stepped to him now, and she took his hand. "I'm so touched that you'd tell me, so churned up inside that you might feel that way about me. I need time to figure out what's going on inside me, too."

"It'd help," he decided after a moment, "if you could work on keeping the pace."

HER CLOTHES WERE DRY BUT IMPOSSIBLY WRINKLED, her hair had frizzed and was now, in Stella's opinion, approximately twice its normal volume.

She dashed out of the car, mortified to see both Hayley and Roz sitting on the glider drinking something out of tall glasses.

"Just have to change," she called out. "I won't be long."

"There's plenty of time," Hayley called back, and pursed her lips as Stella raced into the house. "You know," she began, "what it means when a woman shows up with her clothes all wrinkled to hell and grass stains on the ass of her pants?"

"I assume she went by Logan's."

"Outdoor nookie."

Roz choked on a sip of tea, wheezed in a laugh. "Hayley. Jesus."

"You ever do it outdoors?"

Roz only sighed now. "In the dim, dark past."

STELLA WAS SHARP ENOUGH TO KNOW THEY WERE talking about her. As a result, the flush covered not only her face but most of her body as she ran into the bedroom. She stripped off her clothes, threw them into a hamper.

"No reason to be embarrassed," she muttered to herself as she threw open her armoire. "Absolutely none." She dug out fresh underwear and felt more normal after she put it on.

And reaching for her blouse, felt the chill.

She braced, half expecting a vase or lamp to fly across the room at her this time.

But she gathered her courage and turned, and she saw the Harper Bride. Clearly, for the first time, clearly, though the dusky light slipped through her as if she were smoke. Still, Stella saw her face, her form, the bright ringlets, the shattered eyes.

The Bride stood at the doorway that connected to the bath, then the boys' room.

But it wasn't anger Stella saw on her face. It wasn't disapproval she felt quivering on the air. It was utter and terrible grief.

Her own fear turned to pity. "I wish I could help you. I want to help." With her blouse pressed against her breasts, Stella took a tentative step forward. "I wish I knew who you were, what happened to you. Why you're so sad."

The woman turned her head, looked back with swimming eyes to the room beyond.

"They're not gone," Stella heard herself say. "I'd never let them go. They're my life. They're with my father and his wife—their grandparents. A treat for them, that's all. A night where they can be pampered and spoiled and eat too much ice cream. They'll be back tomorrow."

She took a cautious second step, even as her throat burned dry. "They love being with my father and Jolene. But it's so quiet when they're not around, isn't it?"

Good God, she was talking to a ghost. Trying to draw a ghost into conversation. How had her life become so utterly strange?

"Can't you tell me something, anything that would help? We're all trying to find out, and maybe when we do . . . Can't you tell me your name?"

Though Stella's hand trembled, she lifted it, reached out. Those shattered eyes met hers, and Stella's hand passed through. There was cold, and a kind of snapping shock. Then there was nothing at all.

"You can speak," Stella said to the empty room. "If you can sing, you can speak. Why won't you?"

Shaken, she dressed, fought her hair into a clip. Her heart was still thudding as she did her makeup, half expecting to see that other heartbroken face in the mirror.

Then she slipped on her shoes and went downstairs. She would leave death behind, she thought, and go prepare for new life.

seventeen

THE PACE MIGHT HAVE BEEN SLOW, BUT THE HOURS were the killer. As spring turned lushly green and temperatures rose toward what Stella thought of as high summer, garden-happy customers flocked to the nursery, as much, she thought, to browse for an hour or so and chat with the staff and other customers as for the stock.

Still, every day flats of bedding plants, pots of perennials, forests of shrubs and ornamental trees strolled out the door.

She watched the field stock bagged and burlapped, and scurried to plug holes on tables by adding greenhouse stock. As mixed planters, hanging baskets, and the concrete troughs were snapped up, she created more.

She made countless calls to suppliers for more: more fertilizers, more grass seed, more root starter, more everything.

With her clipboard and careful eye she checked inventory, adjusted, and begged Roz to release some of the younger stock.

"It's not ready. Next year."

"At this rate, we're going to run out of columbine, astilbes, hostas—" She waved the board. "Roz, we've sold out a good thirty percent of our perennial stock already. We'll be lucky to get through May with our current inventory."

"And things will slow down." Roz babied cuttings from a stock dianthus. "If I start putting plants out before they're ready, the customer's not going to be happy."

"But—"

"These dianthus won't bloom till next year. Customers want bloom, Stella, you know that. They want to plug it in while it's flowering or about to. They don't want to wait until next year for the gratification."

"I do know. Still . . ."

"You're caught up." With her gloved hand, Roz scratched an itch under her nose. "So's everyone else. Lord, Ruby's beaming like she's been made a grandmother again, and Steve wants to high-five me every time I see him."

"They love this place."

"So do I. The fact is, this is the best year we've ever had. Weather's part of it. We've had a pretty spring. But we've also got ourselves an efficient and enthusiastic manager to help things along. But end of the day, quality's still the byword here. Quantity's second."

"You're right. Of course you're right. I just can't stand the thought of running out of something and having to send a customer somewhere else."

"Probably won't come to that, especially if we're smart enough to lead them toward a nice substitution."

Stella sighed. "Right again."

"And if we do need to recommend another nursery . . ."

"The customers will be pleased and impressed with our efforts to satisfy them. And this is why you're the owner of a place like this, and I'm the manager."

"It also comes down to being born and bred right here. In a few more weeks, the spring buying and planting season will be over. Anyone who comes in after mid-May's going to be looking mostly for supplies, or sidelines, maybe a basket or planter already made up, or a few plants to replace something that's died or bloomed off. And once that June heat hits, you're going to want to be putting what we've got left of spring and summer bloomers on sale before you start pushing the fall stock."

"And in Michigan, you'd be taking a big risk to put anything in before mid-May."

Roz moved to the next tray of cuttings. "You miss it?"

"I want to say yes, because it seems disloyal otherwise. But no, not really. I didn't leave anything back there except memories."

It was the memories that worried her. She'd had a good life, with a man she'd loved. When she'd lost him that life had shattered—under the surface. It had left her shaky and unstable inside. She'd kept that life together, for her children, but in her heart had been more than grief. There'd been fear.

She'd fought the fear, and embraced the memories.

But she hadn't just lost her husband. Her sons had lost their father. Gavin's memory of him was dimmer—dimmer every year—but sweet. Luke was too young to remember his father clearly. It seemed so unfair. If she moved forward in her relationship with Logan while her boys were still so young . . .

It was a little like no longer missing home, she supposed. It seemed disloyal.

As she walked into the showroom, she spotted a number of customers with wagons, browsing the tables, and Hayley hunkering down to lift a large strawberry pot already planted.

"Don't!"

Her sharp command had heads turning, but she marched right through the curious and, slapping her hands on her hips, glared at Hayley. "Just what do you think you're doing?"

"We sold the point-of-purchase planters. I thought this one here would be good out by the counter."

"I'm sure it would. Do you know how pregnant you are?"

Hayley glanced down at her basketball belly. "Kind of hard to miss."

"You want to move a planter, then you ask somebody to move it for you."

"I'm strong as an ox."

"And eight months pregnant."

"You listen to her, honey." One of the customers patted Hayley on the arm. "You don't want to take chances. Once that baby pops out, you'll never stop hauling things around. Now's the time to take advantage of your condition and let people spoil you a little bit."

"I've got to watch her like a hawk," Stella said. "That lobelia's wonderful, isn't it?"

The woman looked down at her flatbed. "I just love that deep blue color. I was thinking I'd get some of that red salvia to go beside it, maybe back it up with cosmos?"

"Sounds perfect. Charming and colorful, with a whole season of bloom."

"I've got some more room in the back of the bed, but I'm not sure what to put in." She bit her lip as she scanned the tables loaded with options. "I wouldn't mind some suggestions, if you've got the time."

"That's what we're here for. We've got some terrific mixed hollyhocks, tall enough to go behind the cosmos. And if you want to back up the salvia, I think those marigolds there would be fabulous. And have you seen the perilla?"

"I don't even know what it is," the woman said with a laugh.

Stella showed her the deep-purple foliage plant, had Hayley gather up several good marigolds. Between them, they filled another flatbed.

"I'm glad you went with the alyssum, too. See the way

the white pops the rest of your colors? Actually, the arrangement there gives you a pretty good idea what you'll have in your garden." Stella nodded toward the flatbeds. "You can just see the way those plants will complement each other."

"I can't wait to get them in. My neighbors are going to be *green* with envy."

"Just send them to us."

"Wouldn't be the first time. I've been coming here since you opened. Used to live about a mile from here, moved down toward Memphis two years ago. It's fifteen miles or more now, but I always find something special here, so I keep coming back."

"That's so nice to hear. Is there anything else Hayley or I can help you with? Do you need any starter, mulch, fertilizer?"

"Those I can handle on my own. But actually"—she smiled at Hayley—"since this cart's full, if you'd have one of those strong young boys cart that pot out to the counter—and on out to my car after—I'll take it."

"Let me arrange that for you." Stella gave Hayley a last telling look. "And you, behave yourself."

"Y'all sisters?" the woman asked Hayley.

"No. She's my boss. Why?"

"Reminded me of my sister and me, I guess. I still scold my baby sister the way she did you, especially when I'm worried about her."

"Really?" Hayley looked off toward where Stella had gone. "I guess we sort of are, then."

WHILE SHE AGREED THAT EXERCISE WAS GOOD FOR expectant mothers, Stella wasn't willing to have Hayley work all day and then walk close to half a mile home at this stage of her pregnancy. Hayley groused, but every evening Stella herded her to the car and drove her home.

"I *like* walking."

"And after we get home and you have something to eat, you can take a nice walk around the gardens. But you're not walking all that way, and through the woods alone, on my watch, kid."

"Are you going to be pestering me like this for the next four weeks?"

"I absolutely am."

"You know Mrs. Tyler? The lady who bought all those annuals we helped her with?"

"Mmm-hmm."

"She said how she thought we were sisters because you give me grief like she does her baby sister. At the time, I thought that was nice. Now, it's irritating."

"That's a shame."

"I'm taking care of myself."

"Yes, and so am I."

Hayley sighed. "If it's not you giving me the hairy eye, it's Roz. Next thing, people'll start thinking she's my mama."

Stella glanced down to see Hayley slip her feet out of her shoes. "Feet hurt?"

"They're all right."

"I've got this wonderful foot gel. Why don't you use it when we get home, and put your feet up for a few minutes?"

"I can't hardly reach them anymore. I feel . . ."

"Fat and clumsy and sluggish," Stella finished.

"And stupid and bitchy." She pushed back her damp bangs, thought about whacking them off. Thought about whacking all her hair off. "And hot and nasty."

When Stella reached over, bumped up the air-conditioning, Hayley's eyes began to sting with remorse and misery. "You're being so sweet to me—everyone is—and I don't even appreciate it. And I just feel like I've been pregnant my whole life and I'm going to stay pregnant forever."

"I can promise you won't."

"And I . . . Stella, when they showed that video at birthing class and we watched that woman go through it? I don't see how I can do that. I just don't think I can."

"I'll be there with you. You'll be just fine, Hayley. I'm not going to tell you it won't be hard, but it's going to be exciting, too. Thrilling."

She turned into the drive. And there were her boys, racing around the yard with the dog and Harper in what seemed to be a very informal game of Wiffle ball.

"And so worth it," she told her. "The minute you hold your baby in your arms, you'll know."

"I just can't imagine being a mama. Before, I could, but now that it's getting closer, I just can't."

"Of course you can't. Nobody can really imagine a miracle. You're allowed to be nervous. You're supposed to be."

"Then I'm doing a good job."

When she parked, the boys ran over. "Mom, Mom! We're playing Wiffle Olympics, and I hit the ball a *million* times."

"A million?" She widened her eyes at Luke as she climbed out. "That must be a record."

"Come on and play, Mom." Gavin grabbed her hand as Parker leaped up to paw at her legs. "Please!"

"All right, but I don't think I can hit the ball a million times."

Harper skirted the car to get to Hayley's side. His hair curled damply from under his ball cap, and his shirt showed stains from grass and dirt. "Need some help?"

She couldn't get her feet back in her shoes. They felt hot and swollen and no longer hers. Cranky tears flooded her throat. "I'm pregnant," she snapped, "not handicapped."

She left her shoes on the mat as she struggled out. Before she could stop herself, she slapped at Harper's offered hand. "Just leave me be, will you?"

"Sorry." He stuffed his hands in his pockets.

"I can't breathe with everybody hovering around me night and day." She marched toward the house, trying hard not to waddle.

"She's just tired, Harper." Whether it was hovering or not, Stella watched Hayley until she'd gotten inside. "Tired and out of sorts. It's just being pregnant."

"Maybe she shouldn't be working right now."

"If I suggested that, she'd explode. Working keeps her mind busy. We're all keeping an eye on her to make sure she doesn't overdo, which is part of the problem. She feels a little surrounded, I imagine."

"Mom!"

She held up a hand to her impatient boys. "She'd have snapped at anybody who offered her a hand just then. It wasn't personal."

"Sure. Well, I've got to go clean up." He turned back to the boys, who were already squabbling over the plastic bat. "Later. And next time I'm taking you both down."

THE AFTERNOON WAS SULTRY, A SLY HINT OF THE summer that waited just around the corner. Even with the air-conditioning, Stella sweltered in her little office. As a surrender to the weather, she wore a tank top and thin cotton pants. She'd given up on her hair and had bundled it as best she could on top of her head.

She'd just finished outlining the next week's work schedule and was about to update one of her spreadsheets when someone knocked on her door.

"Come in." Automatically, she reached for the thermos of iced coffee she'd begun to make every morning. And her heart gave a little jolt when Logan stepped in. "Hi. I thought you were on the Fields job today."

"Got rained out."

"Oh?" She swiveled around to her tiny window, saw the sheets of rain. "I didn't realize."

"All those numbers and columns can be pretty absorbing."

"To some of us."

"It's a good day to play hookey. Why don't you come out and play in the rain, Red?"

"Can't." She spread her arms to encompass her desk. "Work."

He sat on the corner of it. "Been a busy spring so far. I don't figure Roz would blink if you took a couple hours off on a rainy afternoon."

"Probably not. But I would."

"Figured that, too." He picked up an oddly shaped and obviously child-made pencil holder, examined it. "Gavin or Luke?"

"Gavin, age seven."

"You avoiding me, Stella?"

"No. A little," she admitted. "But not entirely. We've been swamped, here and at home. Hayley's only got three weeks to go, and I like to stick close."

"Do you think you could manage a couple of hours away, say, Friday night? Take in a movie?"

"Well, Friday nights I usually try to take the kids out."

"Good. The new Disney flick's playing. I can pick y'all up at six. We'll go for pizza first."

"Oh, I . . ." She sat back, frowned at him. "That was sneaky."

"Whatever works."

"Logan, have you ever been to the movies with a couple of kids on a Friday night?"

"Nope." He pushed off the desk and grinned. "Should be an experience."

He came around the desk and, cupping his hands under her elbows, lifted her straight out of the chair with a careless strength that had her mouth watering. "I've started to miss you."

He touched his mouth to hers, heating up the contact as he let her slide down his body until her feet hit the floor. Her arms lifted to link around his neck, banding there for a moment until her brain engaged again.

"It looks like I've started to miss you, too," she said as she stepped back. "I've been thinking."

"I just bet you have. You keep on doing that." He tugged at a loose lock of her hair. "See you Friday."

She sat down again when he walked out. "But I have trouble remembering what I'm thinking."

HE WAS RIGHT. IT WAS AN EXPERIENCE. ONE HE HANdled, in Stella's opinion, better than she'd expected. He didn't appear to have a problem with boy-speak. In fact, during the pizza interlude she got the feeling she was odd man out. Normally she could hold her own in intense discussions of comic books and baseball, but this one headed to another level.

At one point she wasn't entirely sure the X-Men's Wolverine hadn't signed on to play third base for the Atlanta Braves.

"I can eat fifty pieces of pizza," Luke announced as the pie was divvied up. "And after, five *gallons* of popcorn."

"Then you'll puke!"

She started to remind Gavin that puke wasn't proper meal conversation, but Logan just plopped a slice on his own plate. "Be smarter to puke after the pizza to make room for the popcorn."

The wisdom and hilarity of this sent the boys off into delighted gagging noises.

"Hey!" Luke's face went mutinous. "Gavin has more pepperoni on his piece. I have two and he has three!"

As Gavin snorted and set his face into the look, Logan nodded. "You know, you're right. Doesn't seem fair. Let's just fix that." He plucked a round of pepperoni off Gavin's piece and popped it into his own mouth. "Now you're even."

More hilarity ensued. The boys ate like stevedores, made an unholy mess, and were so overstimulated by the time they got to the theater, she expected them to start a riot.

"You've got to remember to be quiet during the movie," she warned. "Other people are here to see it."

"I'll try," Logan said solemnly. "But sometimes I just can't help talking."

The boys giggled all the way to the concession counter.

She knew some men who put on a show for a woman's children—to get to the woman. And, she thought as they settled into seats with tubs of popcorn, she knew some who sincerely tried to charm the kids because they were an interesting novelty.

Still, he seemed to be easy with them, and you had to give a man in his thirties points for at least appearing to enjoy a movie with talking monkeys.

Halfway through, as she'd expected, Luke began to squirm in his seat. Two cups of pop, she calculated, one small bladder. He wouldn't want to go, wouldn't want to miss anything. So there'd be a short, whispered argument.

She leaned toward him, prepared for it. And Logan beat her to it. She didn't hear what he said in Luke's ear, but Luke giggled, and the two of them rose.

"Be right back," he murmured to Stella and walked out with his hand over Luke's.

Okay, that was it, she decided as her eyes misted. The man was taking her little boy to pee.

She was a goner.

TWO VERY HAPPY BOYS PILED INTO THE BACK OF Logan's car. As soon as they were strapped in, they were bouncing and chattering about their favorite parts of the movie.

"Hey, guys." Logan slipped behind the wheel, then draped his arm over the seat to look in the back. "You might want to brace yourselves, 'cause I'm gonna kiss your mama."

"How come?" Luke wanted to know.

"Because, as you might have observed yourselves, she's pretty, and she tastes good."

He leaned over, amusement in his eyes. When Stella would have offered him a cheek, he turned her face with one hand and gave her a soft, quick kiss on the mouth.

"You're not pretty." Luke snorted through his nose. "How come she kissed you?"

"Son, that's because I'm one fine-looking hunk of man." He winked into the rearview mirror, noted that Gavin was watching him with quiet speculation, then started the engine.

LUKE WAS NODDING OFF WHEN THEY GOT TO THE house, his head bobbing as he struggled to stay awake.

"Let me cart him up."

"I can get him." Stella leaned in to unbuckle his seat belt. "I'm used to it. And I don't know if you should go upstairs again."

"She'll have to get used to me." He nudged Stella aside and hoisted Luke into his arms. "Come on, pizza king, let's go for a ride."

"I'm not tired."

"'Course not."

Yawning, he laid his head on Logan's shoulder. "You smell different from Mom. And you got harder skin."

"How about that?"

Roz wandered into the foyer as they came in. "Well, it looks like everyone had a good time. Logan, why don't you come down for a drink once you settle those boys down. I'd like to talk to the both of you."

"Sure. We'll be right down."

"I can take them," Stella began, but he was already carrying Luke up the stairs.

"I'll just get us some wine. 'Night, cutie," Roz said to Gavin, and smiled at Stella's back as she followed Logan.

He was already untying Luke's Nikes. "Logan, I'll do that. You go on down with Roz."

He continued to remove the shoes, wondering if the nerves he heard in her voice had to do with the ghost or with him. But it was the boy standing beside her, unusually silent, who had his attention.

"Go ahead and settle him in, then. Gavin and I want to have a little conversation. Don't we, kid?"

Gavin jerked a shoulder. "Maybe. I guess."

"He needs to get ready for bed."

"Won't take long. Why don't you step into my office?" he said to Gavin, and when he gestured toward the bathroom, he saw the boy's lip twitch.

"Logan," Stella began.

"Man talk. Excuse us." And he closed the door in her face.

Figuring it would be easier on them both if they were more eye-to-eye, Logan sat on the edge of the tub. He wasn't sure, but he had to figure the boy was about as nervous as he was himself.

"Did me kissing your mama bother you?"

"I don't know. Maybe. I saw this other guy kiss her once, when I was little. She went out to dinner with him or something, and we had a babysitter, and I woke up and saw him do it. But I didn't like him so much because he smiled *all* the time." He demonstrated, spreading his lips and showing his teeth.

"I don't like him either."

"Do you kiss all the girls because they're pretty?" Gavin blurted out.

"Well, now, I've kissed my share of girls. But your mama's special."

"How come?"

The boy wanted straight answers, Logan decided. So he'd do his best to give them. "Because she makes my heart feel funny, in a good kind of way, I guess. Girls make us feel funny in lots of ways, but when they make your heart feel funny, they're special."

Gavin looked toward the closed door and back again. "My dad kissed her. I remember."

"It's good you do." He had an urge, one that surprised him, to stroke a hand over Gavin's hair. But he didn't think it was the right time, for either of them.

There was more than one ghost in this house, he knew.

"I expect he loved her a lot, and she loved him. She told me how she did."

"He can't come back. I thought maybe he would, even though she said he couldn't. I thought when the lady started coming, he could come, too. But he hasn't."

Could there be anything harder for a child to face, he wondered, than losing a parent? Here he was, a grown man, and he couldn't imagine the grief of losing one of his.

"Doesn't mean he isn't watching over you. I believe stuff like that. When people who love us have to go away, they still look out for us. Your dad's always going to look out for you."

"Then he'd see you kiss Mom, because he'd watch over her, too."

"I expect so." Logan nodded. "I like to think he doesn't mind, because he'd know I want her to be happy. Maybe when we get to know each other some better, you won't mind too much either."

"Do you make Mom's heart feel funny?"

"I sure hope so, because I'd hate to feel like this all by myself. I don't know if I'm saying this right. I never had to say it before, or think about it. But if we decide to be happy together, all of us, your dad's still your dad, Gavin. Always. I want you to understand I know that, and respect that. Man-to-man."

"Okay." He smiled slowly when Logan offered a hand. When he shook it, the smile became a grin. "Anyway, I like you better than the other guy."

"Good to know."

Luke was tucked in and sleeping when they came back in. Logan merely lifted his eyebrows at Stella's questioning look, then stepped back as she readied Gavin for bed.

Deliberately he took her hand as they stepped into the hall. "Ask him if you want to know," he said before she could speak. "It's his business."

"I just don't want him upset."

"He seem upset to you when you tucked him in?"

"No." She sighed. "No."

At the top of the stairs, the cold blew through them. Protectively, Logan's arm came around her waist, pulling her firmly to his side. It passed by, with a little lash, like a flicked whip.

Seconds later, they heard the soft singing.

"She's angry with us," Stella whispered when he turned, prepared to stride back. "But not with them. She won't hurt them. Let's leave her be. I've got a baby monitor downstairs, so I can hear them if they need me."

"How do you sleep up here?"

"Well, strangely enough. First it was because I didn't believe it. Now it's knowing that in some strange way, she loves them. The night they stayed at my parents', she came into my room and cried. It broke my heart."

"Ghost talk?" Roz asked. "That's just what I had in mind." She offered them wine she'd already poured. Then pursed her lips when Stella switched on the monitor. "Strange to hear that again. It's been years since I have."

"I gotta admit," Logan said with his eyes on the monitor, "creeps me out some. More than some, to tell the truth."

"You get used to it. More or less. Where's Hayley?" she asked Roz.

"She was feeling tired—and a little blue, a little cross, I think. She's settled in upstairs with a book and a big tall glass of decaffeinated Coke. I've already talked to her about this, so . . ." She gestured to seats. On the coffee table was a tray of green grapes, thin crackers, and a half round of Brie.

She sat herself, plucked a grape. "I've decided to do something a little more active about our permanent houseguest."

"An exorcism?" Logan asked, sending a sideways glance toward the monitor and the soft voice singing out of it.

"Not quite that active. We want to find out about her history and her connection to this house. Seems to me we're not making any real progress, mostly because we can't really figure out a direction."

"We haven't been able to spend a lot of time on it," Stella pointed out.

"Another reason for outside help. We're busy, and we're amateurs. So why not go to somebody who knows what to do and has the time to do it right?"

"Concert's over for the night." Logan gestured when the monitor went silent.

"Sometimes she comes back two or three times." Stella offered him a cracker. "Do you know somebody, Roz? Someone you want to take this on?"

"I don't know yet. But I've made some inquiries, using the idea that I want to do a formal sort of genealogy search on my ancestry. There's a man in Memphis whose name's come up. Mitchell Carnegie. Dr. Mitchell Carnegie," she added. "He taught at the university in Charlotte, moved here a couple of years ago. I believe he taught at the University of Memphis for a semester or two and may still give the occasional lecture. Primarily, he writes books. Biographies and so on. He's touted as an expert family historian."

"Sounds like he might be our man." Stella spread a little Brie on a cracker for herself. "Having someone who knows what he's doing should be better than us fumbling around."

"That would depend," Logan put in, "on how he feels about ghosts."

"I'm going to make an appointment to see him." Stella lifted her wineglass. "Then I guess we'll find out."

eighteen

Though he felt like he was taking his life in his hands, Harper followed instructions and tracked Hayley down at the checkout counter. She was perched on a stool, a garden of container pots and flats around her, ringing out the last customers. Her shirt—smock? tunic? he didn't know what the hell you called maternity-type clothes—was a bright, bold red.

Funny, it was the color that brought her to mind for him. Vivid, sexy red. Those spiky bangs made her eyes seem enormous, and there were big silver hoops in her ears that peeked and swung through her hair when she moved.

With the high counter blocking the target area, you could hardly tell she was pregnant. Except her eyes looked tired, he thought. And her face was a little puffy—maybe weight gain, maybe lack of sleep. Either way, he didn't figure it was the sort of thing he should mention. The fact was, everything and anything that came out of his mouth these days, at least when he was around her, was the wrong thing.

He didn't expect their next encounter to go well either.

But he'd promised to throw himself on the sword for the cause.

He waited until she'd finished with the customers and, girding his loins, he approached the counter.

"Hey."

She looked at him, and he couldn't say her expression was particularly welcoming. "Hey. What're you doing out of your cave?"

"Finished up for the day. Actually my mother just called. She asked if I'd drive you on home when I finished."

"Well, *I'm* not finished," she said testily. "There are at least two more customers wandering around, and Saturday's my night to close out."

It wasn't the tone she'd used to chat up the customers, he noted. He was beginning to think it was the tone she reserved just for him. "Yeah, but she said she needed you at home for something as soon as you could, and to have Bill and Larry finish up and close out."

"What does she want? Why didn't she call me?"

"I don't know. I'm just the messenger." And he knew what often happened to the messenger. "I told Larry, and he's helping the last couple of stragglers. So he's on it."

She started to lever herself off the stool, and though his hands itched to help her, he imagined she'd chomp them off at the wrists. "I can walk."

"Come on. Jesus." He jammed his hands in his pockets and gave her scowl for scowl. "Why do you want to put me on the spot like that? If I let you walk, my mama's going to come down on me like five tons of bricks. And after she's done flattening me, she'll ream you. Let's just go."

"Fine." The truth was, she didn't know why she was feeling so mean and spiteful, and tired and achy. She was terrified something was wrong with her or with the baby, despite all the doctor's assurances to the contrary.

The baby would be born sick or deformed, because she'd . . .

She didn't know what, but it would be her fault.

She snatched her purse and did her best to sail by Harper and out the door.

"I've got another half hour on the clock," she complained and wrenched open the door of his car. "I don't know what she could want that couldn't wait a half hour."

"I don't know either."

"She hasn't seen that genealogy guy yet."

He got in, started the car. "Nope. She'll get to it when she gets to it."

"You don't seem all that interested, anyway. How come you don't come around when we have our meetings about the Harper Bride?"

"I guess I will, when I can think of something to say about it."

She smelled vivid, too, especially closed up in the car with him like this. Vivid and sexy, and it made him edgy. The best that could be said about the situation was the drive was short.

Amazed he wasn't sweating bullets, he swung in and zipped in front of the house.

"You drive a snooty little car like this that fast, you're just begging for a ticket."

"It's not a snooty little car. It's a well-built and reliable sports car. And I wasn't driving that fast. What the hell is it about me that makes you crawl up my ass?"

"I wasn't crawling up your ass; I was making an observation. At least you didn't go for red." She opened the door, managed to get her legs out. "Most guys go for the red, the flashy. The black's probably why you don't have speeding tickets spilling out of your glove compartment."

"I haven't had a speeding ticket in two years."

She snorted.

"Okay, eighteen months, but—"

"Would you stop arguing for five damn seconds and come over here and help me out of this damn car? I can't get up."

Like a runner off the starting line, he sprinted around

the car. He wasn't sure how to manage it, especially when she was sitting there, red in the face and flashing in the eyes. He started to take her hands and tug, but he thought he might . . . jar something.

So he leaned down, hooked his hands under her armpits, and lifted.

Her belly bumped him, and now sweat did slide down his back.

He felt what was in there move—a couple of hard bumps.

It was . . . extraordinary.

Then she was brushing him aside. "Thanks."

Mortifying, she thought. She just hadn't been able to shift her center of gravity, or dig down enough to get out of a stupid car. Of course, if he hadn't insisted she get in that boy toy in the first place, she wouldn't have been mortified.

She wanted to eat a pint of vanilla fudge ice cream and sit in a cool bath. For the rest of her natural life.

She shoved open the front door, stomped inside.

The shouts of *Surprise!* had her heart jumping into her throat, and she nearly lost control of her increasingly tricky bladder.

In the parlor pink and blue crepe paper curled in artful swags from the ceiling, and fat white balloons danced in the corners. Boxes wrapped in pretty paper and streaming with bows formed a colorful mountain on a high table. The room was full of women. Stella and Roz, all the girls who worked at the nursery, even some of the regular customers.

"Don't look stricken, girl." Roz strolled over to wrap an arm around Hayley's shoulders. "You don't think we'd let you have that baby without throwing you a shower, do you?"

"A baby shower." She could feel the smile blooming on her face, even as tears welled up in her eyes.

"You come on and sit down. You're allowed one glass of David's magical champagne punch before you go to the straight stuff."

"This is . . ." She saw the chair set in the center of the

room, festooned with voile and balloons, like a party throne. "I don't know what to say."

"Then I'm sitting beside you. I'm Jolene, darling, Stella's stepmama." She patted Hayley's hand, then her belly. "And I never run out of things to say."

"Here you go." Stella stepped over with a glass of punch.

"Thanks. Thank you so much. This is the nicest thing anyone's ever done for me. In my whole life."

"You have a good little cry." Jolene handed her a lace-edged hankie. "Then we're going to have us a hell of a time."

They did. Ooohing and awwing over impossibly tiny clothes, soft-as-cloud blankets, hand-knit booties, cooing over rattles and toys and stuffed animals. There were foolish games that only women at a baby shower could enjoy, and plenty of punch and cake to sweeten the evening.

The knot that had been at the center of Hayley's heart for days loosened.

"This was the best time I ever had." Hayley sat, giddy and exhausted, and stared at the piles of gifts Stella had neatly arranged on the table again. "I know it was all about me. I liked that part, but everyone had fun, don't you think?"

"Are you kidding?" From her seat on the floor, Stella continued to meticulously fold discarded wrapping paper into neat, flat squares. "This party rocked."

"Are you going to save all that paper?" Roz asked her.

"She'll want it one day, and I'm just saving what she didn't rip to shreds."

"I couldn't help it. I was so juiced up. I've got to get thank-you cards, and try to remember who gave what."

"I made a list while you were tearing in."

"Of course she did." Roz helped herself to one more glass of punch, then sat and stretched out her legs. "God. I'm whipped."

"Y'all worked so hard. It was all so awesome." Feeling

herself tearing up again, Hayley waved both hands. “Everyone was—I guess I forgot people could be so good, so generous. Man, look at all those wonderful things. Oh, that little yellow gown with the teddy bears on it! The matching hat. And the baby swing. Stella, I just can’t thank you enough for the swing.”

“I’d have been lost without mine.”

“It was so sweet of you, both of you, to do this for me. I just had no idea. I couldn’t’ve been more surprised, or more grateful.”

“You can guess who planned it out,” Roz said with a nod at Stella. “David started calling her General Rothchild.”

“I have to thank him for all the wonderful food. I can’t believe I ate two pieces of cake. I feel like I’m ready to explode.”

“Don’t explode yet, because we’re not quite done. We need to go up, so you can have my gift.”

“But the party was—”

“A joint effort,” Roz finished. “But there’s a gift I hope you’ll like upstairs.”

“I snapped at Harper,” Hayley began as they helped her up and started upstairs.

“He’s been snapped at before.”

“But I wish I hadn’t. He was helping you surprise me, and I gave him a terrible time. He said I was always crawling up his ass, and that’s just what I was doing.”

“You’ll tell him you’re sorry.” Roz turned them toward the west wing, moved passed Stella’s room, and Hayley’s. “Here you are, honey.”

She opened the door and led Hayley inside.

“Oh, God. Oh, my God.” Hayley pressed both hands to her mouth as she stared at the room.

It was painted a soft, quiet yellow, with lace curtains at the windows.

She knew the crib was antique. Nothing was that beautiful, that rich unless it was old and treasured. The wood gleamed, deep with red highlights. She recognized the layette as one she'd dreamed over in a magazine and had known she could never afford.

"The furniture's a loan while you're here. I used it for my children, as my mama did for hers, and hers before her, back more than eighty-five years now. But the linens are yours, and the changing table. Stella added the rug and the lamp. And David and Harper, bless their hearts, painted the room, and hauled the furniture down from the attic."

As emotions swamped her, Hayley could only shake her head.

"Once we bring your gifts up here, you'll have yourself a lovely nursery." Stella rubbed Hayley's back.

"It's so beautiful. More than I ever dreamed of. I—I've been missing my father so much. The closer the baby gets, the more I've been missing him. It's this ache inside. And I've been feeling sad and scared, and mostly just sorry for myself."

She used her hands to rub the tears from her cheeks. "Now today, all this, it just makes me feel . . . It's not the things. I love them, I love everything. But it's that you'd do this, both of you would do this for us."

"You're not alone, Hayley." Roz laid a hand on Hayley's belly. "Neither one of you."

"I know that. I think, well, I think, we'd have been okay on our own. I'd've worked hard to make sure of it. But I never expected to have real family again. I never expected to have people care about me and the baby like this. I've been stupid."

"No," Stella told her. "Just pregnant."

With a half laugh, Hayley blinked back the rest of the tears. "I guess that accounts for a lot of it. I won't be able to use that excuse too much longer. And I'll never, I'll just never be able to thank you, or tell you, or repay you. Never."

"Oh, I think naming the baby after us will clear the decks," Roz said casually. "Especially if it's a boy. Rosalind Stella might be a little hard for him to handle in school, but it's only right."

"Hey, I was thinking Stella Rosalind."

Roz arched a brow at Stella. "This is one of those rare cases when it pays to be the oldest."

THAT NIGHT, HAYLEY TIPTOED INTO THE NURSERY. Just to touch, to smell, to sit in the rocking chair with her hands stroking her belly.

"I'm sorry I've been so nasty lately. I'm better now. We're going to be all right now. You've got two fairy godmothers, baby. The best women I've ever known. I may not be able to pay them back for all they've done for us, not in some ways. But I swear, there's nothing either of them could ask that I wouldn't do. I feel safe here. It was stupid of me to forget that. We're a team, you and me. I shouldn't've been afraid of you. Or for you."

She closed her eyes and rocked. "I want to hold you in my arms so much they hurt. I want to dress you in one of those cute little outfits and hold you, and smell you, and rock you in this chair. Oh, God, I hope I know what I'm doing."

The air turned cold, raising gooseflesh on her arms. But it wasn't fear that had her opening her eyes; it was pity. She stared at the woman who stood beside the crib.

Her hair was down tonight, golden blond and wildly tangled. She wore a white nightgown, muddy at the hem. And there was a look of—Hayley would have said madness—in her eyes.

"You didn't have anyone to help you, did you?" Her hands trembled a bit, but she kept stroking her belly, kept her eyes on the figure, kept talking.

"Maybe you didn't have anyone to be there with you when you were afraid like I've been. I guess I might've gone crazy, too, all on my own. And I don't know what I'd do if anything happened to my baby. Or how I'd stand it, if something happened to take me away from him—her. Even if I were dead I couldn't stand it. So I guess I understand, a little."

At her words, Hayley heard a keening sound, a sound that made her think of a soul, or a mind, shattering.

Then she was alone.

ON MONDAY, HAYLEY SAT PERCHED ON HER STOOL once more. When her back ached, she ignored it. When she had to call for a relief clerk so she could waddle to the bathroom, again, she made a joke out of it.

Her bladder felt squeezed down to the size of a pea.

On the way back, she detoured outside, not only to stretch her legs and back but to see Stella.

"Is it okay if I take my break now? I want to hunt down Harper and apologize." She'd spent all morning dreading the moment, but she couldn't put it off any longer. "He wasn't anywhere to be found on Sunday, but he's probably back in his cave now."

"Go ahead. Oh, I just ran into Roz. She called that professor. Dr. Carnegie? She has an appointment to see him later this week. Maybe we'll make some progress in that area."

Then she narrowed her eyes on Hayley's face. "I tell you what, one of us is going with you to your doctor's appointment tomorrow. I don't want you driving anymore."

"I still fit behind the wheel." Barely.

"That may be, but either Roz or I will take you. And I'm thinking it's time you go part-time."

"You might as well put me in the loony bin as take work away from me now. Come on, Stella, a lot of women work right up to the end. Besides, I'm sitting on my butt most all day. Best thing about finding Harper is walking."

"Walk," Stella agreed. "Don't lift. Anything."

"Nag, nag, nag." But she said it with a laugh as she started toward the grafting house.

Outside the greenhouse she paused. She'd practiced

what she wanted to say. She thought it best to think it all through. He'd accept her apology. His mama had raised him right, and from what she'd seen he had a good heart. But she wanted, very much, for him to understand she'd just been in some sort of mood.

She opened the door. She loved the smell in here. Experimentation, possibilities. One day, she hoped either Harper or Roz would teach her something about this end of the growing.

She could see him down at the end, huddled over his work. He had his headphones on and was tapping one foot to whatever beat played in his ears.

God, he was so cute. If she'd met him in the bookstore, before her life had changed, she'd have hit on him, or worked it around so he'd hit on her. All that dark, messed-up hair, the clean line of jaw, the dreamy eyes. And those artistic hands.

She'd bet he had half a dozen girls dangling on a string, and another half dozen waiting in line for a chance.

She started down toward him and was surprised enough to pull up short when his head snapped up, and he swung around to her.

"Christ on a crutch, Harper! I thought I was going to startle you."

"What? What?" His eyes were dazzled as he dragged off his headset. "What?"

"I didn't think you could hear me."

"I—" He hadn't. He'd smelled her. "Do you need something?"

"I guess I do. I need to say I'm sorry for jumping down your throat every time you opened your mouth the last couple of weeks. I've been an awful bitch."

"No. Well, yeah. It's okay."

She laughed and edged closer to try to see what he was doing. It just looked like he had a bunch of stems tied together. "I guess I had the jumps. What am I going to do, how am I going to do it? Why do I have to feel so fat and ugly all the time?"

"You're not fat. You could never be ugly."

"That's awful nice of you. But being pregnant doesn't affect my eyesight, and I know what I see in the mirror every damn day."

"Then you know you're beautiful."

Her eyes sparkled when she smiled. "I must've been a pitiful case if you're obliged to flirt with a pregnant woman who's got a bad disposition."

"I'm not—I wouldn't." He wanted to, at the very least. "Anyway, I guess you're feeling better."

"So much better. Mostly I was feeling sorry for myself, and I just hate that poor-me crap. Imagine your mama and Stella throwing me a baby shower. I cried all over myself. Got Stella going, too. But then we had the best time. Who knew a baby shower could rock?" She pressed both hands to her belly and laughed. "You ever met Stella's step-mama?"

"No."

"She's just a hoot and a half. I laughed till I thought I'd shoot the baby right out then and there. And Mrs. Haggerty—"

"Mrs. Haggerty? Our Mrs. Haggerty was there?"

"Not only, but she won the song title game. You have to write down the most song titles with 'baby' in it. You'll never guess one she wrote down."

"Okay. I give."

" 'Baby Got Back.' "

Now he grinned. "Get out. Mrs. Haggerty wrote down a rap song?"

"Then rapped it."

"Now you're lying."

"She *did.* Or at least a couple lines. I nearly peed my pants. But I'm forgetting why I'm here. There you were, just trying to help with the best surprise I ever had, and I was bitching and whining. Crawling up your ass, just like you said. I'm really sorry."

"It's no big. I have a friend whose wife had a baby a few

months ago. I swear you could see fangs growing out of her mouth toward the end. And I think her eyes turned red a couple times."

She laughed again, pressed a hand to her side. "I hope I don't get that bad before . . ."

She broke off, a puzzled expression covering her face as she felt a little snap inside. Heard it, she realized. Like a soft, echoing ping.

Then water pooled down between her legs.

Harper made a sound of his own, like that of a man whose words were strangled off somewhere in his throat. He sprang to his feet, babbling as Hayley stared down at the floor.

"Uh-oh," she said.

"Um, that's okay, that's all right. Maybe I should . . . maybe you should . . ."

"Oh, for heaven's sake, Harper, I didn't just pee on the floor. My water broke."

"What water?" He blinked, then went pale as a corpse. "*That* water. Oh, God. Oh, Jesus. Oh, shit. Sit. Sit, or . . . I'll get—"

An ambulance, the marines.

"My mother."

"I think I'd better go with you. We're a little early." She forced a smile so she wouldn't scream. "Just a couple of weeks. I guess the baby's impatient to get out and see what all the fuss is about. Give me a hand, okay? Oh, Jesus, Harper, I'm scared to death."

"It's fine." His arm came around her. "Just lean on me. You hurting anywhere?"

"No. Not yet."

Inside he was still pale, and half sick. But his arm stayed steady around her, and when he turned his head, his smile was easy. "Hey." Very gently, he touched her belly. "Happy birthday, baby."

"Oh, my God." Her face simply illuminated as they stepped outside. "This is *awesome*."

* * *

SHE COULDN'T ACTUALLY HAVE THE BABY, BUT STELLA figured she could do nearly everything else—or delegate it done. Hayley hadn't put a hospital bag together, but Stella had a list. A call to David got that ball rolling even as she drove Hayley to the hospital. She called the doctor to let him know the status of Hayley's labor, left a voice mail on her father's cell phone, and a message on his home answering machine to arrange for her own children, and coached Hayley through her breathing as the first contractions began.

"If I ever get married, or buy a house, or start a war, I hope you'll be in charge of the details."

Stella glanced over as Hayley rubbed her belly. "I'm your girl. Doing okay?"

"Yeah. I'm nervous and excited and . . . Oh, wow, I'm having a baby!"

"You're going to have a fabulous baby."

"The books say things can get pretty tricky during transition, so if I yell at you or call you names—"

"Been there. I won't take it personally."

By the time Roz arrived, Hayley was ensconced in a birthing room. The television was on—an old *Friends* episode. Beneath it on the counter was an arrangement of white roses. Stella's doing, she had no doubt.

"How's Mama doing?"

"They said I'm moving fast." Flushed and bright-eyed, Hayley reached out a hand for Roz's. "And everything's just fine. The contractions are coming closer together, but they don't hurt all that much."

"She doesn't want the epidural," Stella told her.

"Ah." Roz gave Hayley's hand a pat. "That'll be up to you. You can change your mind if it gets to be too much."

"Maybe it's silly, and maybe I'll be sorry, but I want to feel it. Wow! I feel that."

Stella moved in, helped her breathe through it. Hayley

sighed out the last breath, closed her eyes just as David strode in.

"This here the party room?" He set down an overnight case, a tote bag, and a vase of yellow daisies before he leaned over the bed to kiss Hayley's cheek. "You're not going to kick me out 'cause I'm a man, are you?"

"You want to stay?" Delighted color bloomed on Hayley's cheeks. "Really?"

"Are you kidding?" From his pocket he pulled a little digital camera. "I nominate myself official photographer."

"Oh." Biting her lip, Hayley rubbed a hand over her belly. "I don't know as pictures are such a good idea."

"Don't you worry, sugar, I won't take anything that's not G-rated. Give me a big smile."

He took a couple of shots, directed Roz and Stella to stand beside the bed and took a couple more. "By the way, Stella, Logan's taking the boys back to his place after school."

"What?"

"Your parents are at some golf tournament. They were going to come back, but I told them not to worry, I'd take care of the kids. Then apparently Logan came by the nursery, ran into Harper—he's coming by shortly."

"Logan?" Hayley asked. "He's coming here?"

"No, Harper. Logan's taking kid duty. He said he'd take them over to his place, put them to work, and not to worry. We're supposed to keep him updated on baby progress."

"I don't know if—" But Stella broke off as another contraction started.

Her job as labor coach kept her busy, but part of her mind niggled on the idea of Logan riding herd on her boys. What did he mean, 'put them to work'? How would he know what to do if they got into a fight—which, of course, they would at some point. How could he watch them properly if he took them to a job site? They could fall into a ditch, or out of a tree, or cut off an appendage, for God's sake, with some sharp tool.

When the doctor came in to check Hayley's progress, she dashed out to call Logan's cell phone.

"Kitridge."

"It's Stella. My boys—"

"Yeah, they're fine. Got them right here. Hey, Gavin, don't chase your brother with that chain saw." At Stella's horrified squeak, Logan's laughter rolled over the phone. "Just kidding. I've got them digging a hole, and they're happy as pigs in mud and twice as dirty. We got a baby yet?"

"No, they're checking her now. Last check she was at eight centimeters dilated and seventy percent effaced."

"I have no idea what that means, but I'll assume it's a good thing."

"It's very good. She's breezing through it. You'd think she had a baby once a week. Are you sure the kids are all right?"

"Listen."

She assumed he'd held out the phone as she heard giggles and her boys' voices raised in excited argument over just what they could bury in the hole. An elephant. A brontosaurus. Fat Mr. Kelso from the grocery store.

"They shouldn't call Mr. Kelso fat."

"We have no time for women here. Call me when we've got a baby."

He hung up, leaving her scowling at the phone. Then she turned and nearly rammed into Harper. Or into the forest of red lilies he balanced in both hands.

"Harper? Are you in there?"

"She okay? What's going on? Am I too late?"

"She's fine. The doctor's just checking on her. And you're in plenty of time."

"Okay. I thought lilies because they're exotic, and she likes red. I think she likes red."

"They're extremely gorgeous. Let me guide you in."

"Maybe I shouldn't. Maybe you should just take them."

"Don't be silly. We've got a regular party going on. She's a sociable girl, and having people with her is taking her mind off the pain. When I left, David had the Red Hot Chili Peppers on a CD player and a bottle of champagne icing down in the bathroom sink.

She steered him in. It was still the Red Hot Chili Peppers, and David turned his camera to the door to snap a picture of Harper peering nervously through a wonder of red lilies.

"Oh! Oh! Those are the most beautiful things I've ever seen!" A little pale, but beaming, Hayley struggled to sit up in bed.

"They'll make a great focal point, too." Stella helped Harper set them on a table. "You can focus on them during contractions."

"The doctor says I'm nearly there. I can start pushing soon."

He stepped up to the bedside. "You okay?"

"A little tired. It's a lot of work, but not as bad as I thought." Abruptly, her hand clamped down on his. "Oh-oh. Stella."

Roz stood at the foot of the bed. She looked at her son's hand holding Hayley's, looked at his face. She felt something inside her tighten, release painfully. Then she sighed and began to rub Hayley's feet as Stella murmured instructions and encouragement.

The pain increased. Stella watched the arc of contractions on the monitor and felt her own belly tighten in sympathy. The girl was made of iron, she thought. She was pale now, and her skin sheathed in sweat. There were times when Hayley gripped Stella's hand so hard she was surprised her fingers didn't snap. But Hayley stayed focused and rode the contractions out.

An hour passed into another, with the contractions coming fast, coming hard, with Hayley chugging through the breathing like a train. Stella offered ice chips and cool cloths while Roz gave the laboring mother a shoulder massage.

"Harper!" General Rothchild snapped out orders. "Rub her belly."

He goggled at her as if she'd asked him to personally deliver the baby. "Do what?"

"Gently, in circles. It helps. David, the music—"

"No, I like the music." Hayley reached for Stella's hand as she felt the next coming on. "Turn it up, David, in case I start screaming. Oh, oh, fuck! I want to push. I want to push it the hell out, *now*!"

"Not yet. Not yet. Focus, Hayley, you're doing great. Roz, maybe we need the doctor."

"Already on it," she said on her way out the door.

When it was time to push, and the doctor sat between Hayley's legs, Stella noted that both men went a little green. She gave Hayley one end of a towel, and took the other, to help her bear down while she counted to ten.

"Harper! You get behind her, support her back."

"I . . ." He was already edging for the door, but his mother blocked him.

"You don't want to be somewhere else when a miracle happens." She gave him a nudge forward.

"You're doing great," Stella told her. "You're amazing." She nodded when the doctor called for Hayley to push again. "Ready now. Deep breath. Hold it, and push!"

"God almighty." Even with the babble of voices, David's swallow was audible. "I've never seen the like. I've gotta call my mama. Hell, I gotta send her a truckload of flowers."

"Jesus!" Harper sucked in a breath along with Hayley. "There's a head."

Hayley began to laugh, with tears streaming down her face. "Look at all that hair! Oh, God, oh, Lord, can't we get him the rest of the way out?"

"Shoulders next, honey, then that's it. Another good push, okay? Listen! He's already crying. Hayley, that's your baby crying." And Stella was crying herself as with a last desperate push, life rushed into the room.

"It's a girl," Roz said softly as she wiped the dampness from her own cheeks. "You've got a daughter, Hayley. And she's beautiful."

"A girl. A little girl." Hayley's arms were already reaching. When they laid her on her belly so Roz could cut the cord, she kept laughing even as she stroked the baby from head to foot. "Oh, just *look* at you. Look at you. No, don't take her."

"They're just going to clean her up. Two seconds." Stella bent down to kiss the top of Hayley's head. "Congratulations, Mom."

"Listen to her." Hayley reached back, gripped Stella's hand, then Harper's. "She even sounds beautiful."

"Six pounds, eight ounces," the nurse announced and carried the wrapped bundle to the bed. "Eighteen inches. And a full ten on the Apgar."

"Hear that?" Hayley cradled the baby in her arms, kissed her forehead, her cheeks, her tiny mouth. "You aced your first test. She's looking at me! Hi. Hi, I'm your mama. I'm so glad to see you."

"Smile!" David snapped another picture. "What name did you decide on?"

"I picked a new one when I was pushing. She's Lily, because I could see the lilies, and I could smell them when she was being born. So she's Lily Rose Star. Rose for Rosalind, Star for Stella."

NINETEEN

EXHAUSTED AND EXHILARATED, STELLA STEPPED INTO the house. Though it was past their bedtime, she expected her boys to come running, but had to make do with an ecstatic Parker. She picked him up, kissed his nose as he tried to bathe her face.

"Guess what, my furry little pal? We had a baby today. Our first girl."

She shoved at her hair, and immediately got the guilts. Roz had left the hospital before she had, and was probably upstairs dealing with the kids.

She started toward the steps when Logan strolled into the foyer. "Big day."

"The biggest," she agreed. She hadn't considered he'd be there, and was suddenly and acutely aware that her duties as labor coach had sweated off all of her makeup. In addition, she couldn't imagine she was smelling her freshest.

"I can't thank you enough for taking on the boys."

"No problem. I got a couple of good holes out of them. You may need to burn their clothes."

"They've got more. Is Roz up with them?"

"No. She's in the kitchen. David's back there whipping something together, and I heard a rumor about champagne."

"More champagne? We practically swam in it at the hospital. I'd better go up and settle down the troops."

"They're out for the count. Have been since just before nine. Digging holes wears a man out."

"Oh. I know you said you'd bring them back when I called to tell you about the baby, but I didn't expect you to put them to bed."

"They were tuckered. We had ourselves a manly shower, then they crawled into bed and were out in under five seconds."

"Well. I owe you big."

"Pay up."

He crossed to her, slid his arms around her and kissed her until her already spinning head lifted off her shoulders.

"Tired?" he asked.

"Yeah. But in the best possible way."

He danced his fingers over her hair, and kept his other arm around her. "How's the new kid on the block and her mama?"

"They're great. Hayley's a wonder. Steady as a rock through seven hours of labor. And the baby might be a couple weeks early, but she came through like a champ. Only a few ounces shy of Gavin's birth weight, though it took me twice as long to convince him to come out."

"Make you want to have another?"

She went a few shades more pale. "Oh. Well."

"Now I've scared you." Amused, he slung an arm around her shoulder. "Let's go see what's on the menu with that champagne."

HE HADN'T SCARED HER, EXACTLY. BUT HE HAD MADE her vaguely uneasy. She was just getting used to having a relationship, and the man was making subtle hints about babies.

Of course, it could have been just a natural, offhand remark under the circumstances. Or a kind of joke.

Whatever the intent, it got her thinking. Did she want more children? She'd crossed that possibility off her list when Kevin died and had ruthlessly shut down her biological clock. Certainly she was capable, physically, of having another child. But it took more than physical capability, or should, to bring a child into the world.

She had two healthy, active children. And was solely and wholly responsible for them—emotionally, financially, morally. To consider having another meant considering a permanent relationship with a man. Marriage, a future, sharing not only what she had but building more, and in a different direction.

She'd come to Tennessee to visit her own roots, and to plant her family in the soil of her own origins. To be near her father, and to allow her children the pleasure of being close to grandparents who wanted to know them.

Her mother had never been particularly interested, hadn't enjoyed seeing herself as a grandmother. It spoiled the youthful image, Stella thought.

If a man like Logan had blipped onto her mother's radar, he'd have been snapped right up.

And if that's why Stella was hesitating, it was a sad state of affairs. Undoubtedly part of it, though, she decided. Otherwise she wouldn't be thinking it.

She hadn't disliked any of her stepfathers. But she hadn't bonded with them either, or they with her. How old had she been the first time her mother had remarried? Gavin's age, she remembered. Yes, right around eight.

She'd been plucked out of her school and plunked down in a new one, a new house, new neighborhood, and dazed by it all while her mother had been in the adrenaline rush of having a new husband.

That one had lasted, what? Three years, four? Somewhere between, she decided, with another year or so of upheaval while her mother dealt with the battle and debris of divorce, another new place, a new job, a new start.

And another new school for Stella.

After that, her mother had stuck with *boyfriends* for a long stretch. But that itself had been another kind of upheaval, having to survive her mother's mad dashes into love, her eventual bitter exit from it.

And they were always bitter, Stella remembered.

At least she'd been in college, living on her own, when her mother had married yet again. And maybe that was part of the reason that marriage had lasted nearly a decade. There hadn't been a child to crowd things. Yet eventually there'd been another acrimonious divorce, with the split nearly coinciding with her own widowhood.

It had been a horrible year, in every possible way, which her mother had ended with yet one more brief, tumultuous marriage.

Strange that even as an adult, Stella found she couldn't quite forgive being so consistently put into second or even third place behind her mother's needs.

She wasn't doing that with her own children, she assured herself. She wasn't being selfish and careless in her relationship with Logan, or shuffling her kids to the back of her heart because she was falling in love with him.

Still, the fact was it was all moving awfully fast. It would make more sense to slow things down a bit until she had a better picture.

Besides, she was going to be too busy to think about marriage. And she shouldn't forget he hadn't asked her to marry him and have his children, for God's sake. She was blowing an offhand comment way out of proportion.

Time to get back on track. She rose from her desk and started for the door. It opened before she reached it.

"I was just going to find you," she said to Roz. "I'm on my way to pick up the new family and take them home."

"I wish I could go with you. I nearly postponed this

meeting so I could." She glanced at her watch as if considering it again.

"By the time you get back from your meeting with Dr. Carnegie, they'll be all settled in and ready for some quality time with Aunt Roz."

"I have to admit I want my hands on that baby. So, now, what've you been fretting about?"

"Fretting?" Stella opened a desk drawer to retrieve her purse. "Why do you think I've been fretting about anything?"

"Your watch is turned around, which means you've been twisting at it. Which means you've been fretting. Something going on around here I don't know about?"

"No." Annoyed with herself, Stella turned her watch around. "No, it's nothing to do with work. I was thinking about Logan, and I was thinking about my mother."

"What does Logan have to do with your mother?" As she asked, Roz picked up Stella's thermos. After opening it and taking a sniff, she poured a few swallows of iced coffee in the lid.

"Nothing. I don't know. Do you want a mug for that?"

"No, this is fine. Just want a taste."

"I think—I sense—I'm wondering . . . and I already sound like an ass." Stella took a lipstick from the cosmetic bag in her purse, and walking to the mirror she'd hung on the wall, she began to freshen her makeup. "Roz, things are getting serious between me and Logan."

"As I've got eyes, I've seen that for myself. Do you want me to say *and*, or do you want me to mind my own business?"

"And. I don't know if I'm ready for serious. I don't know that he is, either. It's surprising enough it turned out we like each other, much less . . ." She turned back. "I've never felt like this about anyone. Not this churned up and edgy, and, well, fretful."

She replaced the lipstick and zipped the bag shut. "With Kevin, everything was so clear. We were young and in love, and there wasn't a single barrier to get over, not really. It wasn't that we never fought or had problems, but it was all relatively simple for us."

"And the longer you live, the more complicated life gets."

"Yes. I'm afraid of being in love again, and of crossing that line from this is mine to this is ours. That sounds incredibly selfish when I say it out loud."

"Maybe, but I'd say it's pretty normal."

"Maybe. Roz, my mother was—is—a mess. I know, in my head, that a lot of the decisions I've made have been because I knew they were the exact opposite of what she'd have done. That's pathetic."

"I don't know that it is, not if those decisions were right for you."

"They were. They have been. But I don't want to step away from something that might be wonderful just because I know my mother would leap forward without a second thought."

"Honey, I can look at you and remember what it was like, and the both of us can look at Hayley and wonder how she has the courage and fortitude to raise that baby on her own."

Stella let out a little laugh. "God, isn't that the truth?"

"And since it's turned out the three of us have connected as friends, we can give each other all kinds of support and advice and shoulders to cry on. But the fact is, each one of us has to get through what we get through. Me, I expect you'll figure this out soon enough. Figuring out how to make things come out right's what you do."

She set the thermos lid on the desk, gave Stella two light pats on the cheek. "Well, I'm going to scoot home and clean up a bit."

"Thanks, Roz. Really. If Hayley's doing all right once I get them home, I'll leave David in charge. I know we're shorthanded around here today."

"No, you stay home with her and Lily. Harper can handle things here. It's not every day you bring a new baby home."

* * *

AND THAT WAS SOMETHING ROZ CONSIDERED AS SHE hunted for parking near Mitchell Carnegie's downtown apartment. It had been a good many years since there had been an infant in Harper House. Just how would the Harper Bride deal with that?

How would they all deal with it?

How would she herself handle the idea of her firstborn falling for that sweet single mother and her tiny girl? She doubted that Harper knew he was sliding in that direction, and surely Hayley was clueless. But a mother knew such things; a mother could read them on her son's face.

Something else to think about some other time, she decided, and cursed ripely at the lack of parking.

She had to hoof it nearly three blocks and cursed again because she'd felt obliged to wear heels. Now her feet were going to hurt, *and* she'd have to waste more time changing into comfortable clothes once this meeting was done.

She was going to be late, which she deplored, and she was going to arrive hot and sweaty.

She would have loved to have passed the meeting on to Stella. But it wasn't the sort of thing she could ask a manager to do. It dealt with her home, her family. She'd taken this particular aspect of it for granted for far too long.

She paused at the corner to wait for the light.

"Roz!"

The voice on the single syllable had her hackles rising. Her face was cold as hell frozen over as she turned and stared at—stared through—the slim, handsome man striding quickly toward her in glossy Ferragamos.

"I thought that was you. Nobody else could look so lovely and cool on a hot afternoon."

He reached out, this man she'd once been foolish enough to marry, and gripped her hand in both of his. "Don't you look gorgeous!"

"You're going to want to let go of my hand, Bryce, or you're going to find yourself facedown and eating sidewalk. The only one who'll be embarrassed by that eventuality is yourself."

His face, with its smooth tan and clear features, hardened. "I'd hoped, after all this time, we could be friends."

"We're not friends, and never will be." Quite deliberately, she took a tissue out of her purse and wiped the hand he'd touched. "I don't count lying, cheating sons of bitches among my friends."

"A man just can't make a mistake or find forgiveness with a woman like you."

"That's exactly right. I believe that's the first time you've been exactly right in your whole miserable life."

She started across the street, more resigned than surprised when he fell into step beside her. He wore a pale gray suit, Italian in cut. Canali, if she wasn't mistaken. At least that had been his designer of the moment when she'd been footing the bills.

"I don't see why you're still upset, Roz, honey. Unless there are still feelings inside you for me."

"Oh, there are, Bryce, there are. Disgust being paramount. Go away before I call a cop and have you arrested for being a personal annoyance."

"I'd just like another chance to—"

She stopped then. "That will never happen in this lifetime, or a thousand others. Be grateful you're able to walk the streets in your expensive shoes, Bryce, and that you're wearing a tailored suit instead of a prison jumpsuit."

"There's no cause to talk to me that way. You got what you wanted, Roz. You cut me off without a dime."

"Would that include the fifteen thousand, six hundred and fifty-eight dollars and twenty-two cents you transferred out of my account the week before I kicked your sorry ass out of my house? Oh, I knew about that one, too," she said when his face went carefully blank. "But I let that one go, because I decided I deserved to pay something for my own stupidity. Now you go on, and you stay out of my way, you stay out of my sight, and you stay out of my hearing, or I promise you, you'll regret it."

She clipped down the sidewalk, and even the "Frigid bitch" he hurled at her back didn't break her stride.

But she was shaking. By the time she'd reached the right address her knees and hands were trembling. She hated that she'd allowed him to upset her. Hated that the sight of him brought any reaction at all, even if it was rage.

Because there was shame along with it.

She'd taken him into her heart and her home. She'd let herself be charmed and seduced—and lied to and deceived. He'd stolen more than her money, she knew. He'd stolen her pride. And it was a shock to the system to realize, after all this time, that she didn't quite have it back. Not all of it.

She blessed the cool inside the building and rode the elevator to the third floor.

She was too frazzled and annoyed to fuss with her hair or check her makeup before she knocked. Instead she stood impatiently tapping her foot until the door opened.

He was as good-looking as the picture on the back of his books—several of which she'd read or skimmed through before arranging this meeting. He was, perhaps, a bit more rumpled in rolled-up shirtsleeves and jeans. But what she saw was a very long, very lanky individual with a pair of horn-rims sliding down a straight and narrow nose. Behind the lenses, bottle-green eyes seemed distracted. His hair was plentiful, in a tangle of peat-moss brown around a strong, sharp-boned face that showed a black bruise along the jaw.

The fact that he wasn't wearing any shoes made her feel hot and overdressed.

"Dr. Carnegie?"

"That's right. Ms. . . . Harper. I'm sorry. I lost track of time. Come in, please. And don't look at anything." There was a quick, disarming smile. "Part of losing track means I didn't remember to pick up out here. So we'll go straight back to my office, where I can excuse any disorder in the name of the creative process. Can I get you anything?"

His voice was coastal southern, she noted. That easy

drawl that turned vowels into warm liquid. "I'll take something cold, whatever you've got."

Of course, she looked as he scooted her through the living room. There were newspapers and books littering an enormous brown sofa, another pile of them along with a stubby white candle on a coffee table that looked as if it might have been Georgian. There was a basketball and a pair of high-tops so disreputable she doubted even her sons would lay claim to them in the middle of a gorgeous Turkish rug, and the biggest television screen she'd ever seen eating up an entire wall.

Though he was moving her quickly along, she caught sight of the kitchen. From the number of dishes on the counter, she assumed he'd recently had a party.

"I'm in the middle of a book," he explained. "And when I come up for air, domestic chores aren't a priority. My last cleaning team quit. Just like their predecessors."

"I can't imagine why," she said with schooled civility as she stared at his office space.

There wasn't a clean surface to be seen, and the air reeked of cigar smoke. A dieffenbachia sat in a chipped pot on the windowsill, withering. Rising above the chaos of his desk was a flat-screen monitor and an ergonomic keyboard.

He cleaned off the chair, dumping everything unceremoniously on the floor. "Hang on one minute."

As he dashed out, she lifted her brows at the half-eaten sandwich and glass of—maybe it was tea—among the debris on his desk. She was somewhat disappointed when with a crane of her neck she peered around to his monitor. His screen saver was up. But that, she supposed, was interesting enough, as it showed several cartoon figures playing basketball.

"I hope tea's all right," he said as he came back.

"That's fine, thank you." She took the glass and hoped it had been washed sometime in the last decade. "Dr. Carnegie, you're killing that plant."

"What plant?"

"The dieffenbachia in the window."

"Oh? Oh. I didn't know I had a plant." He gave it a baffled look. "Wonder where that came from? It doesn't look very healthy, does it?"

He picked it up, and she saw, with horror, that he intended to dump it in the overflowing wastebasket beside his desk.

"For God's sake, don't just throw it out. Would you bury your cat alive?"

"I don't have a cat."

"Just give it to me." She rose, grabbed the pot out of his hand. "It's dying of thirst and heat, and it's rootbound. This soil's hard as a brick."

She set it beside her chair and sat again. "I'll take care of it," she said, and her legs were an angry slash as she crossed them. "Dr. Carnegie—"

"Mitch. If you're going to take my plant, you ought to call me Mitch."

"As I explained when I contacted you, I'm interested in contracting for a thorough genealogy of my family, with an interest in gathering information on a specific person."

"Yes." All business, he decided, and sat at his desk. "And I told you I only do personal genealogies if something about the family history interests me. I'm—obviously—caught up in a book right now and wouldn't have much time to devote to a genealogical search and report."

"You didn't name your fee."

"Fifty dollars an hour, plus expenses."

She felt a quick clutch in the belly. "That's lawyer steep."

"An average genealogy doesn't take that long, if you know what you're doing and where to look. In most cases, it can be done in about forty hours, depending on how far back you want to go. If it's more complicated, we could arrange a flat fee—reevaluating after that time is used. But as I said—"

"I don't believe you'll have to go back more than a century."

"Chump change in this field. And if you're only dealing with a hundred years, you could probably do this yourself. I'd be happy to direct you down the avenues. No charge."

"I need an expert, which I'm assured you are. And I'm willing to negotiate terms. Since you took the time out of your busy schedule to speak to me, I'd think you'd hear me out before you nudge me out the door."

All business, he thought again, and prickly with it. "That wasn't my intention—the nudging. Of course I'll hear you out. If you're not in any great rush for the search and report, I may be able to help you out in a few weeks."

When she inclined her head, he began to rummage on, through, under the desk. "Just let me . . . how the hell did that get there?"

He unearthed a yellow legal pad, then mined out a pen. "That's Rosalind, right? *As You Like It*?"

A smile whisked over her mouth. "As in Russell. My daddy was a fan."

He wrote her name on the top of the pad. "You said a hundred years back. I'd think a family like yours would have records, journals, documents—and considerable oral family history to cover a century."

"You would, wouldn't you? Actually, I have quite a bit, but certain things have led me to believe some of the oral history is either incorrect or is missing details. I will, however, be glad to have you go through what I do have. We've already been through a lot of it."

"We?"

"Myself, and other members of my household."

"So, you're looking for information on a specific ancestor."

"I don't know as she was an ancestor, but I am certain she was a member of the household. I'm certain she died there."

"You have her death record?"

"No."

He shoved at his glasses as he scribbled. "Her grave?"

"No. Her ghost."

She smiled serenely when he blinked up at her. "Doesn't a man who digs into family histories believe in ghosts?"

"I've never come across one."

"If you take on this job, you will. What might your fee be, Dr. Carnegie, to dig up the history and identity of a family ghost?"

He leaned back in his chair, tapping the pen on his chin. "You're not kidding around."

"I certainly wouldn't kid around to the tune of fifty dollars an hour, plus expenses. I bet you could write a very interesting book on the Harper family ghost, if I were to sign a release and cooperate."

"I just bet I could," he replied.

"And it seems to me that you might consider finding out what I'm after as a kind of research. Maybe I should charge you."

His grin flashed again. "I have to finish this book before I actively take on another project. Despite evidence to the contrary, I finish what I start."

"Then you ought to start washing your dishes."

"Told you not to look. First, let me say that in my opinion the odds of you having an actual ghost in residence are about, oh, one in twenty million."

"I'd be happy to put a dollar down at those odds, if you're willing to risk the twenty million."

"Second, if I take this on, I'd require access to all family papers—personal family papers, and your written consent for me to dig into public records regarding your family."

"Of course."

"I'd be willing to waive my fee for, let's say, the first twenty hours. Until we see what we've got."

"Forty hours."

"Thirty."

"Done."

"And I'd want to see your house."

"Perhaps you'd like to come to dinner. Is there any day next week that would suit you?"

"I don't know. Hold on." He swiveled to his computer, danced his fingers over keys. "Tuesday?"

"Seven o'clock, then. We're not formal, but you will need shoes." She picked up the plant, then rose. "Thank you for your time," she said, extended a hand.

"Are you really going to take that thing?"

"I certainly am. And I have no intention of giving it back and letting you take it to death's door again. Do you need directions to Harper House?"

"I'll find it. Seems to me I drove by it once." He walked her to the door. "You know, sensible women don't usually believe in ghosts. Practical women don't generally agree to pay someone to trace the history of said ghost. And you strike me as a sensible, practical woman."

"Sensible men don't usually live in pigsties and conduct business meetings barefoot. We'll both have to take our chances. You ought to put some ice on that bruise. It looks painful."

"It is. Vicious little . . ." He broke off. "Got clipped going up for a rebound. Basketball."

"So I see. I'll expect you Tuesday, then, at seven."

"I'll be there. Good-bye, Ms. Harper."

"Dr. Carnegie."

He kept the door open long enough to satisfy his curiosity. He was right, he noted. The rear view was just as elegant and sexy as the front side, and both went with that steel-spined southern belle voice.

A class act, top to toe, he decided as he shut the door.

Ghosts. He shook his head and chuckled as he wound his way through the mess back to his office. Wasn't that a kick in the ass.

twenty

LOGAN STUDIED THE TINY FORM BLINKING IN A patch of dappled sunlight. He'd seen babies before, even had his share of personal contact with them. To him, newborns bore a strange resemblance to fish. Something about the eyes, he thought. And this one had all that black hair going for her, so she looked like a human sea creature. Sort of exotic and otherworldly.

If Gavin had been around, and Hayley out of hearing distance, he'd have suggested that this particular baby looked something like the offspring of Aquaman and Wonder Woman.

The kid would've gotten it.

Babies always intimidated him. Something about the way they looked right back at you, as if they knew a hell of a lot more than you did and were going to tolerate you until they got big enough to handle things on their own.

But he figured he had to come up with something better than an encounter between superheros, as the mother was standing beside him, anticipating.

"She looks as if she might've dropped down from Venus, where the grass is sapphire blue and the sky a bowl of gold dust." True enough, Logan decided, and a bit more poetic than the Aquaman theory.

"Aw, listen to you. Go ahead." Hayley gave him a little elbow nudge. "You can pick her up."

"Maybe I'll wait on that until she's more substantial."

With a chuckle, Hayley slipped Lily out of her carrier. "Big guy like you shouldn't be afraid of a tiny baby. Here. Now, make sure you support her head."

"Got long legs for such a little thing." And they kicked a bit in transfer. "She's picture pretty. Got a lot of you in her."

"I can hardly believe she's mine." Hayley fussed with Lily's cotton hat, then made herself stop touching. "Can I open the present now?"

"Sure. She all right in the sun like this?"

"We're baking the baby," Hayley told him as she tugged at the shiny pink ribbon on the box Logan had set on the patio table.

"Sorry?"

"She's got a touch of jaundice. The sun's good for her. Stella said Luke had it too, and they took him out in the sunshine for a little while a few times a day." She went to work on the wrapping paper. "Seems like she and Roz know everything there is to know about babies. I can ask the silliest question and one of them knows the answer. We're blessed, Lily and I."

Three women, one baby. Logan imagined Lily barely got out a burp before one of them was rushing to pick her up.

"Logan, do you think things happen because they're meant to, or because you make them happen?"

"I guess I think you make them happen because they're meant to."

"I've been thinking. There's a lot of thinking time when you're up two or three times in the middle of the night. I just wanted—needed—to get gone when I left Little Rock, and I headed here because I hoped Roz might give me a job. I could just as well have headed to Alabama. I've got closer kin there—blood kin—than Roz. But I came here, and I think I was meant to. I think Lily was supposed to be born here, and have Roz and Stella in her life."

"We'd all be missing out on something if you'd pointed your car in another direction."

"This feels like family. I've missed that since my daddy died. I want Lily to have family. I think—I know—we'd have been all right on our own. But I don't want things to just be all right for her. All right doesn't cut it anymore."

"Kids change everything."

Her smile bloomed. "They do. I'm not the same person I was a year ago, or even a week ago. I'm a mother." She pulled off the rest of the wrapping and let out a sound Logan thought of as distinctly female.

"Oh, what a sweet baby-doll! And it's so soft." She took it out of the box to cradle it much as Logan was cradling Lily.

"Bigger than she is."

"Not for long. Oh, she's so pink and pretty, and look at her little hat!"

"You pull the hat, and it makes music."

"Really?" Delighted, Hayley pulled the peaked pink hat, and "The Cradle Song" tinkled out. "It's perfect." She popped up to give Logan a kiss. "Lily's going to love her. Thank you, Logan."

"I figured a girl can't have too many dolls."

He glanced over as the patio door slammed open. Parker scrambled out a foot ahead of two shouting, racing boys.

They'd been this small once, he realized with a jolt. Small enough to curl in the crook of an arm, as helpless as, well, a fish out of water.

They ran to Logan as Parker sped in circles of delirious freedom.

"We saw your truck," Gavin announced. "Are we going to go work with you?"

"I knocked off for the day." Both faces fell, comically, and the buzz of pleasure it gave him had him adjusting his weekend plans. "But I've got to build me an arbor tomorrow, out in my yard. I could use a couple of Saturday slaves."

"We can be slaves." Luke tugged on Logan's pant leg. "I know what an arbor is, too. It's a thing stuff grows on."

"There you go, then, I've got a couple of expert slaves. We'll see what your mama says."

"She won't mind. She has to work 'cause Hayley's on turnkey."

"Maternity," Hayley explained.

"Got that."

"Can I see her?" Luke gave another tug.

"Sure." Logan crouched down with the baby in his arms. "She sure is tiny, isn't she?"

"She doesn't do anything yet." Gavin frowned thoughtfully as he tapped a gentle finger on Lily's cheek. "She cries and sleeps."

Luke leaned close to Logan's ear. "Hayley feeds her," he said in a conspirator's whisper, "with milk out of her *booby*."

With an admirably straight face, Logan nodded. "I think I heard about that somewhere. It's a little hard to believe."

"It's *true*. That's why they have them. Girls. Guys don't get boobies because they can't make milk, no matter how much they drink."

"Huh. That explains that."

"Fat Mr. Kelso's got boobies," Gavin said and sent his brother into a spasm of hilarity.

Stella stepped to the door and saw Logan holding the baby with her boys flanking him. All three of them had grins from ear-to-ear. The sun was shimmering down through the scarlet leaves of a red maple, falling in a shifting pattern of light and shadow on the stone. Lilies had burst into bloom in a carnival of color and exotic shapes. She could smell them, and the early roses, freshly cut grass, and verbena.

She heard birdsong and the giggling whispers of her boys, the delicate music of the wind chime hung from one of the maple's branches.

Her first clear thought as she froze there, as if she'd walked into an invisible frame of a picture was, Uh-oh.

Maybe she'd said it out loud, as Logan's head turned toward her. When their eyes met, his foolish grin transformed into a smile, easy and warm.

He looked too big crouched there, she thought. Too big, too rough with that tiny child in his arms, too *male* centered between her precious boys.

And so . . . dazzling somehow. Tanned and fit and strong.

He belonged in a forest, beating a path over rocky ground. Not here, in this elegant scene with flowers scenting the air and a baby dozing in the crook of his arm.

He straightened and walked toward her. "Your turn."

"Oh." She reached for Lily. "There you are, beautiful baby girl. There you are." She laid her lips on Lily's brow, and breathed in. "How's she doing today?" she asked Hayley.

"Good as gold. Look here, Stella. Look what Logan bought her."

Yeah, a female thing, Logan mused as Stella made nearly the identical sound Hayley had over the doll. "Isn't that the most precious thing?"

"And watch this." Hayley pulled the hat so the tune played out.

"Mom. Mom." Luke deserted Logan to tug on his mother.

"Just a minute, baby."

They fussed over the doll and Lily while Luke rolled his eyes and danced in place.

"I think Lily and I should go take a nap." Hayley tucked the baby in her carrier, then lifted it and the doll. "Thanks again, Logan. It was awfully sweet of you."

"Glad you like it. You take care now."

"Dolls are lame," Gavin stated, but he was polite enough to wait until Hayley was inside.

"Really?" Stella reached over to flick the bill of his baseball cap over his eyes. "And what are those little people you've got all over your shelves and your desk?"

"Those aren't dolls." Gavin looked as horrified as an eight-year-old boy could manage. "Those are action figures. Come *on*, Mom."

"My mistake."

"We want to be Saturday slaves and build an arbor." Luke pulled on her hand and to get her attention. "Okay?"

"Saturday slaves?"

"I'm building an arbor tomorrow," Logan explained. "Could use some help, and I got these two volunteers. I hear they work for cheese sandwiches and Popsicles."

"Oh. Actually, I was planning to take them to work with me tomorrow."

"An *arbor*, Mom." Luke gazed up pleadingly, as if he'd been given the chance to build the space shuttle and then ride it to Pluto. "I never, ever built one before."

"Well . . ."

"Why don't we split it up?" Logan suggested. "You take them on in with you in the morning, and I'll swing by and get them around noon."

She felt her stomach knot. It sounded normal. Like parenting. Like family. Dimly, she heard her boys begging and pleading over the buzzing in her ears.

"That'll be fine," she managed. "If you're sure they won't be in your way."

He cocked his head at the strained and formal tone. "They get in it, I just kick them out again. Like now. Why don't you boys go find that dog and see what he's up to, so I can talk to your mama a minute?"

Gavin made a disgusted face. "Let's go, Luke. He's probably going to kiss her."

"Why, I'm transparent as glass to that boy," Logan said. He tipped her chin up with his fingers, laid his lips on hers, and watched her watch him. "Hello, Stella."

"Hello, Logan."

"Are you going to tell me what's going on in that head of yours, or do I have to guess?"

"A lot of things. And nothing much."

"You looked poleaxed when you came outside."

" 'Poleaxed.' Now there's a word you don't hear every day."

"Why don't you and I take a little walk?"

"All right."

"You want to know why I came by this afternoon?"

"To bring Lily a doll." She walked along one of the paths with him. She could hear her boys and the dog, then the quick thwack of Luke's Wiffle bat. They'd be fine for a while.

"That, and to see if I could sponge a meal off Roz, which was a roundabout way of having a meal with you. I don't figure I'm going to be able to pry you too far away from the baby for a while yet."

She had to smile. "Apparently I'm transparent, too. It's so much fun having a baby in the house. If I manage to steal her away from Hayley for an hour—and win out over Roz—I can play with her like, well, a doll. All those adorable little clothes. Never having had a girl, I didn't realize how addicting all those little dresses can be."

"When I asked you if Lily made you want another, you panicked."

"I didn't panic."

"Clutched, let's say. Why is that?"

"It's not unusual for a woman of my age with two half-grown children to clutch, let's say, at the idea of another baby."

"Uh-huh. You clutched again when I said I wanted to take the kids to my place tomorrow."

"No, it's just that I'd already planned—"

"Don't bullshit me, Red."

"Things are moving so fast and in a direction I hadn't planned to go."

"If you're going to plan every damn thing, maybe I should draw you a frigging map."

"I can draw my own map, and there's no point in being annoyed. You asked." She stopped by a tower of madly climbing passionflower. "I thought things were supposed to move slow in the south."

"You irritated me the first time I set eyes on you."

"Thanks so much."

"That should've given me a clue," he continued. "You were an itch between my shoulder blades. The one in that spot you can't reach and scratch away no matter how you contort yourself. I'd've been happy to move slow. Generally, I don't see the point in rushing through something. But you know, Stella, you can't schedule how you're going to fall in love. And I fell in love with you."

"Logan."

"I can see that put the fear of God in you. I figure there's one of two reasons for that. One, you don't have feelings for me, and you're afraid you'll hurt me. Or you've got plenty of feelings for me, and they scare you."

He snapped off a passionflower with its white petals and long blue filaments, stuck it in the spiraling curls of her hair. A carelessly romantic gesture at odds with the frustration in his voice. "I'm going with number two, not only because it suits me better, but because I know what happens to both of us when I kiss you."

"That's attraction. It's chemistry."

"I know the frigging difference." He took her shoulders, held her still. "So do you. Because we've both been here before. We've both been in love before, so we know the difference."

"That may be right, that may be true. And it's part of why this is too much, too fast." She curled her hands on his forearms, felt solid strength, solid will. "I knew Kevin a full year before things got serious, and another year before we started talking about the future."

"I had about the same amount of time with Rae. And here we are, Stella. You through tragedy, me through circumstance. We both know there aren't any guarantees, no matter how long or how well you plan it out beforehand."

"No, there aren't. But it's not just me now. I have more than myself to consider."

"You come as a package deal." He rubbed his hands up and down her arms, then stepped away. "I'm not dim, Stella. And I'm not above making friends with your boys to get you. But the fact is, I like them. I enjoy having them around."

"I know that." She gave his arms a squeeze, then eased back. "I know that," she repeated. "I can tell when someone's faking. It's not you. It's me."

"That's the goddamnedest thing to say."

"You're right, but it's also true. I know what it's like to be a child and have my mother swing from man to man. That's not what we're doing here," she said, lifting her hands palms out as fresh fury erupted on his face. "I know that, too. But the fact is, my life centers on those boys now. It has to."

"And you don't think mine can? If you don't think I can be a father to them because they didn't come out of me, then it is you."

"I think it takes time to—"

"You know how you get a strong, healthy plant like this to increase, to fill out strong?" He jerked a thumb toward the passionflower vine. "You can layer it, and you end up with new fruit and flower. By hybridizing it, it gets stronger, maybe you get yourself a new variety out of it."

"Yes. But it takes time."

"You have to start. I don't love those boys the way you do. But I can see how I could, if you gave me the chance. So I want the chance. I want to marry you."

"Oh, God. I can't—we don't—" She had to press the heel of her hand on her heart and gulp in air. But she couldn't seem to suck it all the way into her lungs. "Marriage. Logan. I can't get my breath."

"Good. That means you'll shut up for five minutes. I love you, and I want you and those boys in my life. If anybody had suggested to me, a few months ago, that I'd want to take on some fussy redhead and a couple of noisy kids,

I'd've laughed my ass off. But there you go. I'd say we could live together for a while until you get used to it, but I know you wouldn't. So I don't see why we don't just do it and start living our lives."

"Just do it," she managed. "Like you just go out and buy a new truck?"

"A new truck's got a better warranty than marriage."

"All this romance is making me giddy."

"I could go buy a ring, get down on one knee. I figured that's how I'd deal with this, but I'm into it now. You love me, Stella."

"I'm beginning to wonder why."

"You've always wondered why. It wouldn't bother me if you keep right on wondering. We could make a good life together, you and me. For ourselves." He jerked his head in the direction of the smack of plastic bat on plastic ball. "For the boys. I can't be their daddy, but I could be a good father. I'd never hurt them, or you. Irritate, annoy, but I'd never hurt any of you."

"I know that. I couldn't love you if you weren't a good man. And you are, a very good man. But marriage. I don't know if it's the answer for any of us."

"I'm going to talk you into it sooner or later." He stepped back to her now, twined her hair around his finger in a lightning change of mood. "If it's sooner, you'd be able to decide how you want all those bare rooms done up in that big house. I'm thinking of picking one and getting started on it next rainy day."

She narrowed her eyes. "Low blow."

"Whatever works. Belong to me, Stella." He rubbed his lips over hers. "Let's be a family."

"Logan." Her heart was yearning toward him even as her body eased away. "Let's take a step back a minute. A family's part of it. I saw you with Lily."

"And?"

"I'm heading toward my middle thirties, Logan. I have an eight- and a six-year-old. I have a demanding job. A career, and I'm going to keep it. I don't know if I want to have more children. You've never had a baby of your own, and you deserve to."

"I've thought about this. Making a baby with you, well, that would be a fine thing if we both decide we want it. But it seems to me that right now I'm getting the bonus round. You, and two entertaining boys that are already housebroken. I don't have to know everything that's going to happen, Stella. I don't want to know every damn detail. I just have to know I love you, and I want them."

"Logan." Time for rational thinking, she decided. "We're going to have to sit down and talk this out. We haven't even met each other's family yet."

"We can take care of that easy enough, at least with yours. We can have them over for dinner. Pick a day."

"You don't have any *furniture*." She heard her voice pitch, and deliberately leveled herself again. "That's not important."

"Not to me."

"The point is we're skipping over a lot of the most basic steps." And at the moment, all of them were jumbled and muzzy in her mind.

Marriage, changing things for her boys once more, the possibility of another child. How could she keep up?

"Here you are talking about taking on two children. You don't know what it's like to live in the same house as a couple of young boys."

"Red, I *was* a young boy. I tell you what, you go ahead and make me a list of all those basic steps. We'll take them, in order, if that's what you need to do. But I want you to tell me, here and now, do you love me?"

"You've already told me I do."

He set his hands on her waist, drew her in, drew her up in the way that made her heart stutter. "Tell me."

Did he know, could he know, how huge it was for her to say the words? Words she'd said to no man but the one she'd lost. Here he was, those eyes on hers, waiting for the simple acknowledgment of what he already knew.

"I love you. I do, but—"

"That'll do for now." He closed his mouth over hers and rode out the storm of emotion raging inside him. Then he stepped back. "You make that list, Red. And start thinking what color you want on those living room walls. Tell the boys I'll see them tomorrow."

"But . . . weren't you going to stay for dinner?"

"I've got some things to do," he said as he strode away. "And so do you." He glanced over his shoulder. "You need to worry about me."

ONE OF THE THINGS HE HAD TO DO WAS WORK OFF the frustration. When he'd asked Rae to marry him, it was no surprise for either of them and her acceptance had been instant and enthusiastic.

Of course, look where that had gotten them.

But it was hard on a man's ego when the woman he loved and wanted to spend his life with countered every one of his moves with a block of stubborn, hardheaded *sense*.

He put in an hour on his cross-trainer, sweating, guzzling water, and cursing the day he'd had the misfortune to fall in love with a stiff-necked redhead.

Of course, if she wasn't stiff-necked, stubborn, and sensible, he probably wouldn't have fallen in love with her. That still made the whole mess her fault.

He'd been happy before she'd come along. The house hadn't seemed empty before she'd been in it. Her and those noisy kids. Since when had he voluntarily arranged to spend a precious Saturday off, a solitary Saturday at his own house with a couple of kids running around getting into trouble?

Hell. He was going to have to go out and pick up some Popsicles.

He was a doomed man, he decided as he stepped into the shower. Hadn't he already picked the spot in the backyard for a swing set? Hadn't he already started a rough sketch for a tree house?

He'd started thinking like a father.

Maybe he'd liked the sensation of holding that baby in his arms, but having one wasn't a deal breaker. How was either one of them supposed to know how they'd feel about that a year from now?

Things happen, he thought, remembering Hayley's words, because they're meant to happen.

Because, he corrected as he yanked on fresh jeans, you damn well made them happen.

He was going to start making things happen.

In fifteen minutes, after a quick check of the phone book, he was in his car and heading into Memphis. His hair was still wet.

WILL HAD BARELY STARTED ON HIS AFTER-DINNER decaf and the stingy sliver of lemon meringue pie Jolene allowed him when he heard the knock on the door.

"Now who the devil could that be?"

"I don't know, honey. Maybe you should go find out."

"If they want a damn piece of pie, then I want a bigger one."

"If it's the Bowers boy about cutting the grass, tell him I've got a couple of cans of Coke cold in here."

But when Will opened the door, it wasn't the gangly Bowers boy, but a broad-shouldered man wearing an irritated scowl. Instinctively, Will edged into the opening of the door to block it. "Something I can do for you?"

"Yeah. I'm Logan Kitridge, and I've just asked your daughter to marry me."

"Who is it, honey?" Fussing with her hair, Jolene walked up to the door. "Why it's Logan Kitridge, isn't it? We met you a time or two over at Roz's. Been some time back, though. I know your mama a little. Come on in."

"He says he asked Stella to marry him."

"Is that so!" Her face brightened like the sun, with her

eyes wide and avid with curiosity. "Why, that's just marvelous. You come on back and have some pie."

"He didn't say if she'd said yes," Will pointed out.

"Since when does Stella say anything as simple as yes?" Logan demanded, and had Will grinning.

"That's my girl."

They sat down, ate pie, drank coffee, and circled around the subject at hand with small talk about his mother, Stella, the new baby.

Finally, Will leaned back. "So, am I supposed to ask you how you intend to support my daughter and grandsons?"

"You tell me. Last time I did this, the girl's father'd had a couple of years to grill me. Didn't figure I'd have to go through this part of it again at my age."

"Of course you don't." Jolene gave her husband a little slap on the arm. "He's just teasing. Stella can support herself and those boys just fine. And you wouldn't be here looking so irritated if you didn't love her. I guess one question, if you don't mind me asking, is how you feel about being stepfather to her boys."

"About the same way, I expect, you feel being their stepgrandmother. And if I'm lucky, they'll feel about me the way they do about you. I know they love spending time with you, and I hear their Nana Jo bakes cookies as good as David's. That's some compliment."

"They're precious to us," Will said. "They're precious to Stella. They were precious to Kevin. He was a good man."

"Maybe it'd be easier for me if he hadn't been. If he'd been a son of a bitch and she'd divorced him instead of him being a good man who died too young. I don't know, because that's not the case. I'm glad for her that she had a good man and a good marriage, glad for the boys that they had a good father who loved them. I can live with his ghost, if that's what you're wondering. Fact is, I can be grateful to him."

"Well, I think that's just smart." Jolene patted Logan's hand with approval. "And I think it shows good character, too. Don't you, Will?"

On a noncommittal sound, Will pulled on his bottom lip. "You marry my girl, am I going to get landscaping and such at the family rate?"

Logan's grin spread slowly. "We can make that part of the package."

"I've been toying with redoing the patio."

"First I've heard of it," Jolene muttered.

"I saw them putting on one of those herringbone patterns out of bricks on one of the home shows. I liked the look of it. You know how to handle that sort of thing?"

"Done a few like it. I can take a look at what you've got now if you want."

"That'd be just fine." Will pushed back from the table.

twenty-one

STELLA CHEWED AT IT, STEWED OVER IT, AND WORRIED about it. She was prepared to launch into another discussion regarding the pros and cons of marriage when Logan came to pick up the boys at noon.

She knew he was angry with her. Hurt, too, she imagined. But oddly enough, she knew he'd be by—somewhere in the vicinity of noon—to get the kids. He'd told them he would come, so he would come.

A definite plus on his side of the board, she decided. She could, and did, trust him with her children.

They would argue, she knew. They were both too worked up to have a calm, reasonable discussion over such an emotional issue. But she didn't mind an argument. A good argument usually brought all the facts and feelings out. She needed both if she was going to figure out the best thing to do for all involved.

But when he hunted them down where she had the kids storing discarded wagons—at a quarter a wagon—he was perfectly pleasant. In fact, he was almost sunny.

"Ready for some man work?" he asked.

With shouts of assent, they deserted wagon detail for more interesting activities. Luke proudly showed him the plastic hammer he'd hooked in a loop of his shorts.

"That'll come in handy. I like a man who carries his own tools. I'll drop them off at the house later."

"About what time do you think—"

"Depends on how long they can stand up to the work." He pinched Gavin's biceps. "Ought to be able to get a good day's sweat out of this one."

"Feel mine! Feel mine!" Luke flexed his arm.

After he'd obliged, given an impressed whistle, he nodded to Stella. "See you."

And that was that.

So she chewed at it, stewed over it, and worried about it for the rest of the day. Which, not being a fool, she deduced was exactly what he'd wanted.

THE HOUSE WAS ABNORMALLY QUIET WHEN SHE GOT home from work. She wasn't sure she liked it. She showered off the day, played with the baby, drank a glass of wine, and paced until the phone rang.

"Hello?"

"Hi there, is this Stella?"

"Yes, who—"

"This is Trudy Kitridge. Logan's mama? Logan said I should give you a call, that you'd be home from work about this time of day."

"I . . . oh." Oh, God, oh, God. Logan's *mother*?

"Logan told me and his daddy he asked you to marry him. Could've knocked me over with a feather."

"Yes, me, too. Mrs. Kitridge, we haven't decided . . . or I haven't decided . . . anything."

"Woman's entitled to some time to make up her mind, isn't she? I'd better warn you, honey, when that boy sets his mind on something, he's like a damn bulldog. He said you wanted to meet his family before you said yes or no. I think that's a sweet thing. Of course, with us living out here now, it's not so easy, is it? But we'll be coming back sometime during the holidays. Probably see Logan for Thanksgiving, then our girl for Christmas. Got grandchildren in Charlotte, you know, so we want to be there for Christmas."

"Of course." She had no idea, no idea whatsoever what to say. How could she with no time to prepare?

"Then again, Logan tells me you've got two little boys. Said they're both just pistols. So maybe we'll have ourselves a couple of grandchildren back in Tennessee, too."

"Oh." Nothing could have touched her heart more truly. "That's a lovely thing to say. You haven't even met them yet, or me, and—"

"Logan has, and I raised my son to know his own mind. He loves you and those boys, then we will, too. You're working for Rosalind Harper, I hear."

"Yes. Mrs. Kitridge—"

"Now, you just call me Trudy. How you getting along down there?"

Stella found herself having a twenty-minute conversation with Logan's mother that left her baffled, amused, touched, and exhausted.

When it was done, she sat limply on the sofa, like, she thought, the dazed victim of an ambush.

Then she heard Logan's truck rumble up.

She had to force herself not to dash to the door. He'd be expecting that. Instead she settled herself in the front parlor with a gardening magazine and the dog snoozing at her feet as if she didn't have a care in the world.

Maybe she'd mention, oh so casually, that she'd had a conversation with his mother. Maybe she wouldn't, and let him stew over it.

And all right, it had been sensitive and sweet for him to arrange the phone call, but for God's *sake*, couldn't he have given her some warning so she wouldn't have spent the first five minutes babbling like an idiot?

The kids came in with all the elegance of an army battalion on a forced march.

"We built a *whole* arbor." Grimy with sweat and dirt,

Gavin rushed to scoop up Parker. "And we planted the stuff to grow on it."

"Carol Jessmint."

Carolina Jessamine, Stella interpreted from Luke's garbled pronunciation. Nice choice.

"And I got a splinter." Luke held out a dirty hand to show off the Band-Aid on his index finger. "A *big* one. We thought we might have to hack it out with a *knife*. But we didn't."

"Whew, that was close. We'll go put some antiseptic on it."

"Logan did already. And I didn't cry. And we had submarines, except he says they're poor boys down here, but I don't see why they're poor because they have *lots* of stuff in them. And we had Popsicles."

"And we got to ride in the wheelbarrow," Gavin took over the play-by-play. "And I used a real hammer."

"Wow. You had a busy day. Isn't Logan coming in?"

"No, he said he had other stuff. And look." Gavin dug in his pocket and pulled out a wrinkled five-dollar bill. "We each got one, because he said we worked so good we get to be cheap labor instead of slaves."

She couldn't help it, she had to laugh. "That's quite a promotion. Congratulations. I guess we'd better go clean up."

"Then we can eat like a bunch of barnyard pigs." Luke put his hand in hers. "That's what Logan said when it was time for lunch."

"Maybe we'll save the pig-eating for when you're on the job."

They were full of Logan and their day through bathtime, through dinner. And then were too tuckered out from it all to take advantage of the extra hour she generally allowed them on Saturday nights.

They were sound asleep by nine, and for the first time in her memory, Stella felt she had nothing to do. She tried to read, she tried to work, but couldn't settle into either.

She was thrilled when she heard Lily fussing.

When she stepped into the hall, she saw Hayley heading down, trying to comfort a squalling Lily. "She's hungry. I thought I'd curl up in the sitting room, maybe watch some TV while I feed her."

"Mind company?"

"Twist my arm. It was lonely around here today with David off at the lake for the weekend, and you and Roz at work, the boys away." She sat, opened her shirt and settled Lily on her breast. "There. That's better, isn't it? I put her in that baby sling I got at the shower, and we took a nice walk."

"It's good for both of you. What did you want to watch?"

"Nothing, really. I just wanted the voices."

"How about one more?" Roz slipped in, walked over to Lily to smile. "I wanted to take a peek at her. Look at her go!"

"Nothing wrong with her appetite," Hayley confirmed. "She smiled at me today. I know they say it's just gas, but—"

"What do they know?" Roz sprawled in a chair. "They inside that baby's head?"

"Logan asked me to marry him."

She didn't know why she blurted it out—hadn't known it was pushing from her brain to her tongue.

"Holy cow!" Hayley exploded, then immediately soothed Lily and lowered her voice. "When? How? Where? This is just awesome. This is the biggest of the big news. Tell us everything."

"There's not a lot of every anything. He asked me yesterday."

"After I went inside to put the baby down? I just knew something was up."

"I don't think he meant to. I think it just sort of happened, then he was irritated when I tried to point out the very rational reasons we shouldn't rush into anything."

"What are they?" Hayley wondered.

"You've only known each other since January," Roz began, watching Stella. "You have two children. You've each been married before and bring a certain amount of baggage from those marriages."

"Yes." Stella let out a long sigh. "Exactly."

"When you know you know, don't you?" Hayley argued. "Whether it's five months or five years. And he's great with your kids. They're nuts about him. Being married before ought to make both of you understand the pitfalls or whatever. I don't get it. You love him, don't you?"

"Yes. And yes to the rest, to a point, but . . . it's different when you're young and unencumbered. You can take more chances. Well, if you're not me you can take more chances. And what if he wants children and I don't? I have to think about that. I have to know if I'm going to be able to consider having another child at this stage, or if the children I do have would be happy and secure with him in the long term. Kevin and I had a game plan."

"And your game was called," Roz said. "It isn't an easy thing to walk into another marriage. I waited a long time to do it, then it was the wrong decision. But I think, if I could have fallen, just tumbled into love with a man at your age, one who made me happy, who cheerfully spent his Saturday with my children, and who excited me in bed, I'd have walked into it, and gladly."

"But you just said, before, you gave the exact reasons why it's too soon."

"No, I gave the reasons you'd give—and ones I understand, Stella. But there's something else you and I understand, or should. And that is that love is precious, and too often stolen away. You've got a chance to grab hold of it again. And I say lucky you."

SHE DREAMED AGAIN OF THE GARDEN, AND THE BLUE dahlia. It was ladened with buds, fat and ripe and ready to burst into bloom. At the top, a single stunning flower swayed electric in the quiet breeze. Her garden, though no longer tidy and ordered, spread out from its feet in waves and flows and charming bumps of color and shape.

Then Logan was beside her, and his hands were warm and rough as he drew her close. His mouth was strong and exciting as it feasted on hers. In the distance she could hear her children's laughter, and the cheerful bark of the dog.

She lay on the green grass at the garden's edge, her senses full of the color and scent, full of the man.

There was such heat, such pleasure as they loved in the sunlight. She felt the shape of his face with her hands. Not fairy-tale handsome, not perfect, but beloved. Her skin shivered as their bodies moved, flesh against flesh, hard against soft, curve against angle.

How could they fit, how could they make such a glorious whole, when there were so many differences?

But her body merged with his, joined, and thrived.

She lay in the sunlight with him, on the green grass at the edge of her garden, and hearing the thunder of her own heartbeat, knew bliss.

The buds on the dahlia burst open. There were so many of them. Too many. Other plants were being shaded, crowded. The garden was a jumble now, anyone could see it. The blue dahlia was too aggressive and prolific.

It's fine where it is. It's just a different plan.

But before she could answer Logan, there was another voice, cold and hard in her mind.

His plan. Not yours. His wants. Not yours. Cut it down, before it spreads.

No, it wasn't her plan. Of course it wasn't. This garden was meant to be a charming spot, a quiet spot.

There was a spade in her hand, and she began to dig.

That's right. Dig it out, dig it up.

The air was cold now, cold as winter, so that Stella shuddered as she plunged the spade into the ground.

Logan was gone, and she was alone in the garden with the Harper Bride, who stood in her white gown and tangled hair, nodding. And her eyes were mad.

"I don't want to be alone. I don't want to give it up."

Dig! Hurry. Do you want the pain, the poison? Do you want it to infect your children? Hurry! It will spoil everything, kill everything, if you let it stay.

She'd get it out. It was best to get it out. She'd just plant it somewhere else, she thought, somewhere better.

But as she lifted it out, taking care with the roots, the flowers went black, and the blue dahlia withered and went to dust in her hands.

KEEPING BUSY WAS THE BEST WAY NOT TO BROOD. And keeping busy was no problem for Stella with the school year winding down, the perennial sale at the nursery about to begin, and her best saleswoman on maternity leave.

She didn't have time to pick apart strange, disturbing dreams or worry about a man who proposed one minute, then vanished the next. She had a business to run, a family to tend, a ghost to identify.

She sold the last three bay laurels, then put her mind and her back into reordering the shrub area.

"Shouldn't you be pushing papers instead of camellias?"

She straightened, knowing very well she'd worked up a sweat, that there was soil on her pants, and that her hair was frizzing out of the ball cap she'd stuck on. And faced Logan.

"I manage, and part of managing is making sure our stock is properly displayed. What do you want?"

"Got a new job worked up." He waved the paperwork, and the breeze from it made her want to moan out loud. "I'm in for supplies."

"Fine. You can put the paperwork on my desk."

"This is as far as I'm going." He shoved it into her hand. "Crew's loading up some of it now. I'm going to take that Japanese red maple, and five of the hardy pink oleanders."

He dragged the flatbed over and started to load.

"Fine," she repeated, under her breath. Annoyed, she glanced at the bid, blinked, then reread the client information.

"This is my father."

"Uh-huh."

"What are you doing planting oleander for my father?"

"My job. Putting in a new patio, too. Your stepmama's already talking about getting new furniture for out there. And a fountain. Seems to me a woman can't see a flat surface without wanting to buy something to put on it. They were still talking about it when I left the other night."

"You—what were *you* doing there?"

"Having pie. Gotta get on. We need to get started on this if I'm going to make it home and clean up before this dinner with the professor guy tonight. See you later, Red."

"Hold it. You just hold it. You had your mother call me, right out of the blue."

"How's it out of the blue when you said you wanted us to meet each other's families? Mine's a couple thousand miles away right now, so the phone call seemed the best way."

"I'd just like you to explain . . ." Now she waved the papers. "All this."

"I know. You're a demon for explanations." He stopped long enough to grab her hair, crush his mouth to hers. "If that doesn't make it clear enough, I'm doing something wrong. Later."

"THEN HE JUST WALKED AWAY, LEAVING ME STANDING there like an idiot." Still stewing hours later, Stella changed Lily's diaper while Hayley finished dressing for dinner.

"You said you thought you should meet each other's families and stuff," Hayley pointed out. "So now you talked to his mama, and he talked to your daddy."

"I know what I said, but he just went tromping over

there. And he had her call me without letting me know first. He just goes off, at the drop of a hat." She picked up Lily, cuddled her. "He gets me stirred up."

"I kinda miss getting stirred up that way." She turned sideways in the mirror, sighed a little over the post-birth pudge she was carrying. "I guess I thought, even though the books said different, that everything would just spring back where it was after Lily came out."

"Nothing much springs after having a baby. But you're young and active. You'll get your body back."

"I hope." She reached for her favorite silver hoops while Stella nuzzled Lily. "Stella, I'm going to tell you something, because you're my best friend and I love you."

"Oh, sweetie."

"Well, it's true. Last week, when Logan came by to bring Lily her doll, and you and the boys came outside? Before I went in and he popped the big Q? You know what the four of you looked like?"

"No."

"A family. And I think whatever your head's running around with, in your heart you know that. And that that's the way it's going to be."

"You're awfully young to be such a know-it-all."

"It's not the years, it's the miles." Hayley tossed a cloth over her shoulder. "Come here, baby girl. Mama's going to show you off to the dinner guests before you go to sleep. You ready?" she asked Stella.

"I guess we'll find out."

They started toward the stairs, with Stella gathering her boys on the way, and met Roz on the landing.

"Well, don't we all look fine."

"We had to wear new shirts," Luke complained.

"And you look so handsome in them. I wonder if I can be greedy and steal both these well-dressed young men as my escorts." She held out both her hands for theirs. "It's going to storm," she said with a glance out the window. "And look here, I believe that must be our Dr. Carnegie, and right on time. What in the world is that man driving? It looks like a rusty red box on wheels."

"I think it's a Volvo." Hayley moved in to spy over Roz's shoulder. "A really old Volvo. They're like one of the safest cars, and so dopey-looking, they're cool. Oh, my, look at that!" Her eyebrows lifted when Mitch got out of the car. "Serious hottie alert."

"Good God, Hayley, he's old enough to be your daddy."

Hayley just smiled at Roz. "Hot's hot. And he's hot."

"Maybe he needs a drink of water," Luke suggested.

"And we'll get one for Hayley, too." Amused, Roz walked down to greet her first guest.

He brought a good white wine as a hostess gift, which she approved of, but he opted for mineral water when she offered him a drink. She supposed a man who drove a car manufactured about the same time he'd been born needed to keep his wits about him. He made appropriate noises over the baby, shook hands soberly with the boys.

She gave him points for tact when he settled into small talk rather than asking more about the reason she wanted to hire him.

By the time Logan arrived, they were comfortable enough.

"I don't think we'll wait for Harper." Roz got to her feet. "My son is chronically late, and often missing in action."

"I've got one of my own," Mitch said. "I know how it goes."

"Oh, I didn't realize you had children."

"Just the one. Josh is twenty. He goes to college here. You really do have a beautiful home, Ms. Harper."

"Roz, and thank you. It's one of my great loves. And here," she added as Harper dashed in from the kitchen, "is another."

"Late. Sorry. Almost forgot. Hey, Logan, Stella. Hi, guys." He kissed his mother, then looked at Hayley. "Hi. Where's Lily?"

"Sleeping."

"Dr. Carnegie, my tardy son, Harper."

"Sorry. I hope I didn't hold you up."

"Not at all," Mitch said as they shook hands. "Happy to meet you."

"Why don't we sit down? It looks like David's outdone himself."

An arrangement of summer flowers in a long, low bowl centered the table. Candles burned, slim white tapers in gleaming silver, on the sideboard. David had used her white-on-white china with pale yellow and green linens for casual elegance. A cool and artful lobster salad was already arranged on each plate. David sailed in with wine.

"Who can I interest in this very nice Pinot Grigio?"

The doctor, Roz noted, stuck with mineral water.

"You know," Harper began as they enjoyed the main course of stuffed pork, "you look awfully familiar." He narrowed his eyes on Mitch's face. "I've been trying to figure it out. You didn't teach at the U of M while I was there, did you?"

"I might have, but I don't recall you being in any of my classes."

"No. I don't think that's it anyway. Maybe I went to one of your lectures or something. Wait. Wait. I've got it. Josh Carnegie. Power forward for the Memphis Tigers."

"My son."

"Strong resemblance. Man, he's a killer. I was at the game last spring, against South Carolina, when he scored thirty-eight points. He's got moves."

Mitch smiled, rubbed a thumb over the fading bruise on his jaw. "Tell me."

Conversation turned to basketball, boisterously, and gave Logan the opportunity to lean toward Stella. "Your daddy says he's looking forward to seeing you and the boys on Sunday. I'll drive you in, as I've got an invitation to Sunday dinner, too."

"Is that so?"

"He likes me." He picked up her free hand, brushed his lips over his fingers. "We're bonding over oleanders."

She didn't try to stop the smile. "You hit him where it counts."

"You, the kids, his garden. Yeah, I'd say I got it covered. You write that list for me yet, Red?"

"Apparently you're doing fine crossing things off without consulting me."

His grin flashed. "Jolene thinks we should go traditional and have a June wedding."

When Stella's mouth dropped open, he turned away to talk to her kids about the latest issues of Marvel Comics.

Over dessert, a rustling, then a long, shrill cry sounded from the baby monitor standing on the buffet. Hayley popped up as if she were on springs. "That's my cue. I'll be back down after she's fed and settled again."

"Speaking of cues." Stella rose as well. "Time for bed, guys. School night," she added even before the protests could be voiced.

"Going to bed before it's dark is a gyp," Gavin complained.

"I know. Life is full of them. What comes next?"

Gavin heaved a sigh. "Thanks for dinner, it was really good, and now we have to go to bed because of stupid school."

"Close enough," Stella decided.

"'Night. I liked the finger potatoes 'specially," Luke said to David.

"Want a hand?" Logan called out.

"No." But she stopped at the doorway, turned back and just looked at him a moment. "But thanks."

She herded them up, beginning the nightly ritual as thunder rumbled in. And Parker scooted under Luke's bed to hide from it. Rain splatted, fat juicy drops, against the windows as she tucked them in.

"Parker's a scaredy-cat." Luke snuggled his head in the pillow. "Can he sleep up here tonight?"

"All right, just for tonight, so he isn't afraid." She lured him out from under the bed, and stroking him as he trembled, laid him in with Luke. "Is that better now?"

"Uh-huh. Mom?" He broke off, petting the dog, and exchanging a long look with his brother.

"What? What are you two cooking up?"

"You ask her," Luke hissed.

"Nuh-uh. You."

"You."

"Ask me what? If you've spent all your allowances and work money on comics, I—"

"Are you going to marry Logan?" Gavin blurted out.

"Am I—where did you get an idea like that?"

"We heard Roz and Hayley talking about how he asked you to." Luke yawned, blinked sleepily at her. "So are you?"

She sat on the side of Gavin's bed. "I've been thinking about it. But I wouldn't decide something that important without talking to both of you. It's a lot to think about, for all of us, a lot to discuss."

"He's nice, and he plays with us, so it's okay if you do."

Stella let out a laugh at Luke's rundown. All right, she thought, maybe not such a lot to discuss from certain points of view.

"Marriage is a very big deal. It's a really big promise."

"Would we go live in his house?" Luke wondered.

"Yes, I suppose we would if . . ."

"We like it there. And I like when he holds me upside down. And he got the splinter out of my finger, and it hardly hurt at all. He even kissed it after, just like he's supposed to."

"Did he?" she murmured.

"He'd be our stepdad." Gavin drew lazy circles with his finger on top of his sheet. "Like we have Nana Jo for a stepgrandmother. She loves us."

"She certainly does."

"So we decided it'd be okay to have a stepdad, if it's Logan."

"I can see you've given this a lot of thought," Stella managed. "And I'm going to think about it, too. Maybe we'll talk about it more tomorrow." She kissed Gavin's cheek.

"Logan said Dad's always watching out for us."

Tears burned the back of her eyes. "Yes. Oh, yes, he is, baby."

She hugged him, hard, then turned to hug Luke. "Good night. I'll be right downstairs."

But she walked through to her room first to catch her breath, compose herself. Treasures, she thought. She had the most precious treasures. She pressed her fingers to her eyes and thought of Kevin. A treasure she'd lost.

Logan said Dad's always watching out for us.

A man who would know that, would accept that and say those words to a young boy was another kind of treasure.

He'd changed the pattern on her. He'd planted a bold blue dahlia in the middle of her quiet garden. And she wasn't digging it out.

"I'm going to marry him," she heard herself say, and laughed at the thrill of it.

Through the next boom of thunder, she heard the singing. Instinctively, she stepped into the bath, to look into her sons' room. She was there, ghostly in billowing white, her hair a tangle of dull gold. She stood between the beds, her voice calm and sweet, her eyes insane as she stared through the flash of lightning at Stella.

Fear trickled down Stella's back. She stepped forward, and was shoved back by a blast of cold.

"No." She raced forward again, and hit a solid wall. "No!" She battered at it. "You won't keep me from my babies." She flung herself against the frigid shield, screaming for her children who slept on, undisturbed.

"You bitch! Don't you touch them."

She ran out of the room, ignoring Hayley, who raced down toward her, ignoring the clatter of feet on the stairs. She knew only one thing. She had to get to her children, she had to get through the barrier and get to her boys.

At a full run she hit the open doorway, and was knocked back against the far wall.

"What the hell's going on?" Logan grabbed her, pushing her aside as he rushed the room himself.

"She won't let me in." Desperate, Stella beat her fists against the cold until her hands were raw and numb. "She's got my babies. Help me."

Logan rammed his shoulder against the opening. "It's like fucking steel." Rammed it again as Harper and David hit it with him.

Behind them, Mitch stared into the room, at the figure in white, who glowed now with a wild light. "Name of God."

"There has to be another way. The other door." Roz grabbed Mitch's arm and pulled him down the hall.

"This ever happen before?"

"No. Dear God. Hayley, keep the baby away."

Frantic, her hands throbbing from pounding, Stella ran. Another way, she thought. Force wouldn't work. She could beat against that invisible ice, rage and threaten, but it wouldn't crack.

Oh, please, God, her babies.

Reason. She would try reason and begging and promises. She dashed out into the rain, yanked open the terrace doors. And though she knew better, hurled herself at the opening.

"You can't have them!" she shouted over the storm. "They're mine. Those are my children. My life." She went down on her knees, ill with fear. She could see her boys sleeping still, and the hard, white light pulsing from the woman between them.

She thought of the dream. She thought of what she and her boys had talked about shortly before the singing. "It's not your business what I do." She struggled to keep her voice firm. "Those are my children, and I'll do what's best for them. You're not their mother."

The light seemed to waver, and when the figure turned, there was as much sorrow as madness in her eyes. "They're not yours. They need me. They need their mother. Flesh and blood."

She held up her hands, scraped and bruised from the beating. "You want me to bleed for them? I will. I am." On her knees, she pressed her palms to the cold while the rain sluiced over her.

"They belong to me, and there's nothing I won't do to keep them safe, to keep them happy. I'm sorry for what happened to you. Whatever it was, whoever you lost, I'm sorry. But you can't have what's mine. You can't take my children from me. You can't take me from my children."

Stella pushed her hand out, and it slid through as if slipping through ice water. Without hesitation, she shoved into the room.

She could see beyond her, Logan still fighting to get through, Stella pressed against the other doorway. She couldn't hear them, but she could see the anguish on Logan's face, and that his hands were bleeding.

"He loves them. He might not have known until tonight, but he loves them. He'll protect them. He'll be a father to them, one they deserve. This is my choice, our choice. Don't ever try to keep me from my children again."

There were tears now as the figure flowed across the room toward the terrace doors. Stella laid a trembling hand on Gavin's head, on Luke's. Safe, she thought as her knees began to shake. Safe and warm.

"I'll help you," she stated firmly, meeting the grieving eyes again. "We all will. If you want our help, give us something. Your name, at least. Tell me your name."

The Bride began to fade, but she lifted a hand to the glass of the door. There, written in rain that dripped like tears, was a single word.

Amelia

When Logan burst through the door behind her, Stella spun toward him, laid a hand quickly on his lips. "Ssh. You'll wake them."

Then she buried her face against his chest and wept.

epilogue

"AMELIA." STELLA SHIVERED, DESPITE THE DRY clothes and the brandy Roz had insisted on. "Her name. I saw it written on the glass of the door just before she vanished. She wasn't going to hurt them. She was furious with me, was protecting them from me. She's not altogether sane."

"You're all right?" Logan stayed crouched in front of her. "You're sure?"

She nodded, but she drank more brandy. "It's going to take a little while to come down from it, but yes, I'm okay."

"I've never been so scared." Hayley looked toward the stairs. "Are you sure all the kids are safe?"

"She would never hurt them." Stella laid a reassuring hand on Hayley's. "Something broke her heart, and her mind, I think. But children are her only joy."

"You'll excuse me if I find this absolutely fascinating, and completely crazy." Mitch paced back and forth across the floor. "If I hadn't seen it with my own eyes—" He shook his head. "I'm going to need all the data you can put together, once I'm able to get started on this."

He stopped pacing, stared at Roz. "I can't rationalize it. I saw it, but I can't rationalize it. An . . . I'll call it an entity, for lack of better. An entity was in that room. The room was sealed off." Absently he rubbed his shoulder where he'd rammed against the solid air. "And she was inside it."

"It was more of a show than we expected to give you on

your first visit," Roz said, and poured him another cup of coffee.

"You're very cool about it," he replied.

"Of all of us here, I've lived with her the longest."

"How?" Mitch asked.

"Because this is my house." She looked tired, and pale, but there was a battle light in her eyes. "Her being here doesn't change that. This is my house." She took a little breath and a sip of brandy herself. "Though I'll admit that what happened tonight shook me, shook all of us. I've never seen anything like what happened upstairs."

"I have to finish the project I'm working on, then I'm going to want to know everything you have seen." Mitch's eyes scanned the room. "All of you."

"All right, we'll see about arranging that."

"Stella ought to lie down," Logan said.

"No, I'm fine, really." She glanced toward the monitor, listened to the quiet hum. "I feel like what happened tonight changed something. In her, in me. The dreams, the blue dahlia."

"Blue dahlia?" Mitch interrupted, but Stella shook her head.

"I'll explain when I feel a little steadier. But I don't think I'll be having them anymore. I think she'll let it alone, let it grow there because I got through to her. And I believe, absolutely, it was because I got through mother to mother."

"My children grew up in this house. She never tried to block me from them."

"You hadn't decided to get married when your sons were still children," Stella announced, and watched Logan's eyes narrow.

"Haven't you missed some steps?" he asked.

She managed a weary smile. "Not any important ones, apparently. As for the Bride, maybe her husband left her, or she was pregnant by a lover who deserted her, or . . . I don't know. I can't think very clearly."

"None of us can, and whether or not you think you're

fine, you're still pale." Roz got to her feet. "I'm going to take you upstairs and put you to bed."

She shook her head when Logan started to protest. "You're all welcome to stay as long as you like. Harper?"

"Right." Understanding his cue, and his duty, he got to his feet. "Can I get anyone another drink?"

Because she was still unsteady, Stella let Roz take her upstairs. "I guess I am tired, but you don't have to come up."

"After a trauma like that, you deserve a little pampering. I imagine Logan would like the job, but tonight I think a woman's the better option. Go on, get undressed now," Roz told her as she turned down the bed.

As the shock eased and made room for fatigue, Stella did what she was told, then slipped through the bathroom to take a last look at her children for the night. "I was so afraid. So afraid I wouldn't get to my boys."

"You were stronger than she was. You've always been stronger."

"Nothing's ever ripped at me like that. Not even . . ." Stella moved back to her room, slipped into bed. "The night Kevin died, there was nothing I could do. I couldn't get to him, bring him back, stop what had already happened, no matter how much I wanted to."

"And tonight you could do something, and did. Women, women like us at any rate, we do what has to be done. I want you to rest now. I'll check on you and the boys myself before I go to bed. Do you want me to leave the light on?"

"No, I'll be fine. Thanks."

"We're right downstairs."

In the quiet dark, Stella sighed. She lay still, listening, waiting. But she heard nothing but the sound of her own breathing.

For tonight—at least for tonight—it was over.

When she closed her eyes, she drifted to sleep.

Dreamlessly.

* * *

SHE EXPECTED LOGAN TO COME BY THE NURSERY THE next day. But he didn't. She was certain he would come by the house before dinner. But he didn't.

Nor did he call.

She decided that after the night before he'd needed a break. From her, from the house, from any sort of drama. How could she blame him?

He'd pounded his hands, his big, hard hands, bloody from trying to get to her boys, then to her. She knew all she needed to know about him now, about the man she'd grown to love and respect.

Knew enough to trust him with everything that was hers. Loved him enough to wait until he came to her.

And when her children were in bed, and the moon began to rise, his truck rumbled up the drive to Harper House.

This time she didn't hesitate, but dashed to the door to meet him.

"I'm glad you're here." She threw her arms around him first, held tight when his wrapped around her. "So glad. We really need to talk."

"Come on out first. I got something in the truck for you."

"Can't it wait?" She eased back. "If we could just sit down and get some things aired out. I'm not sure I made any sense last night."

"You made plenty of sense." To settle it, he gripped her hand, pulled her outside. "Seeing as after you scared ten years off my life, you said you were going to marry me. Didn't have the opportunity to follow through on that then, the way things were. I've got something to give you before you start talking me to death."

"Maybe you don't want to hear that I love you."

"I can take time for that." Grabbing her, he lifted her off her feet and circled them both to the truck. "You going to organize my life, Red?"

"I'm going to try. Are you going to disorganize mine?"

"No question about it." He lowered her until her lips met his.

"Hell of a storm last night—in every possible sense," she said as she rested her cheek against his. "It's over now."

"This one is. There'll be others." He took her hands, kissed them, then just looked down at her in the dusky light of the moon.

"I love you, Stella. I'm going to make you happy even when I irritate the living hell out of you. And the boys . . . Last night, when I saw her in there with them, when I couldn't get to them—"

"I know." Now she lifted his hands to kiss his raw, swollen knuckles. "One day, when they're older, they'll fully appreciate how lucky they are to have had two such good men for fathers. I know how lucky I am to love and be loved by two such good men."

"I figured that out when I started falling for you."

"When was that?"

"On the way to Graceland."

"You don't waste time."

"That's when you told me about the dream you'd had."

Her heart fluttered. "The garden. The blue dahlia."

"Then later, when you said you'd had another, told me about it, it just got me thinking. So . . ." He reached into the cab of the truck, took out a small pot with a grafted plant. "I asked Harper if he'd work on this."

"A dahlia," she whispered. "A blue dahlia."

"He's pretty sure it'll bloom blue when it matures. Kid's got a knack."

Tears burned into her eyes and smeared her voice. "I was going to dig it up, Logan. She kept pushing me to, and it seemed she was right. It wasn't what I'd put there, wasn't what I'd planned, no matter how beautiful it was. And when I did, when I dug it up, it died. It was so stupid of me."

"We'll dig this one in instead. We can plant this, you and me, and the four of us can plant a garden around it. That suit you?"

She lifted her hands, cupped his face. "It suits me."

"That's good, because Harper worked like a mad scientist on it, shooting for a deep, true blue. I guess we'll wait and see what we get when it blooms."

"You're right." She looked up at him. "We'll see what we get."

"He gave me the go-ahead to name it. So it'll be Stella's Dream."

Now her heart swirled into her eyes. "I was wrong about you, Logan. You're perfect after all."

She cradled the pot in her arm as if it were a child, precious and new. Then taking his hand, she linked fingers so they could walk in the moon-drenched garden together.

In the house, in the air perfumed with flowers, another walked. And wept.

Turn the page for a look at

BLACK ROSE

the second book in the
IN THE GARDEN TRILOGY.
Coming soon from Piatkus Books.

chapter one

Harper House

December, 2004

DAWN, THE AWAKENING PROMISE OF IT, WAS HER favorite time to run. The running itself was just something that had to be done, three days a week, like any other chore or responsibility. Rosalind Harper did what had to be done.

She ran for her health. A woman who'd just had—she could hardly say *celebrated* at this stage of her life—her forty-fifth birthday had to mind her health. She ran to keep strong, as she desired and needed strength. And she ran for vanity. Her body would never again be what it had been at twenty, or even thirty, but by God, it would be the best body she could manage at forty-five.

She had no husband, no lover, but she did have an image to uphold. She was a Harper, and Harpers had their pride.

But, Jesus, maintenance was a bitch.

Wearing sweats against the dawn chill, she slipped out of her bedroom by the terrace door. The house was still sleeping. Her house that had been too empty was now occupied again, and rarely completely quiet any longer.

There was David, her surrogate son, who kept her house in order, kept her entertained when she needed entertaining, and stayed out of her way when she needed solitude.

No one knew her moods quite like David.

And there was Stella and her two precious boys. It had been a good day, Roz thought as she limbered up on the terrace, when she'd hired Stella Rothchild to manage her nursery.

Of course, Stella would be moving before much longer and taking those sweet boys with her. Still, once Stella was married to Logan—and wasn't that a fine match—they'd only be a few miles away.

Hayley would still be here, infusing the house with all that youth and energy. It had been another stroke of luck, and a vague and distant family connection, that had Hayley, then six months pregnant, landing on her doorstep. In Hayley she had the daughter she'd secretly longed for, and the bonus of an honorary grandchild with the darling little Lily.

She hadn't realized how lonely she'd been, Roz thought, until those girls had come along to fill the void. With two of her own three sons moved away, the house had become too big, too quiet. And a part of her dreaded the day when Harper, her firstborn, her rock, would leave the guest house a stone's throw from the main.

But that was life. No one knew better than a gardener that life never stayed static. Cycles were necessary, for without them there was no bloom.

She took the stairs down at an easy jog, enjoying the way the early mists shrouded her winter gardens. Look how pretty her lambs ear was with its soft silvery foliage covered in dew. And the birds had yet to bother the bright fruit on her red chokeberry.

Walking to give her muscles time to warm, and to give herself the pleasure of the gardens, she skirted around the side of the house to the front.

She increased to a jog on the way down the drive, a tall, willowy woman with a short, careless cap of black hair. Her eyes, a honeyed whisky brown, scanned the grounds—the towering magnolias, the delicate dogwoods, the placement of ornamental shrubs, the flood of pansies she'd planted only weeks before, and the beds that would wait a bit longer to break into bloom.

To her mind, there were no grounds in western Tennessee that could compete with Harper House. Just as there was no house that could compare with its dignified elegance.

Out of habit, she turned at the end of the drive and jogged in place to study it in the pearly mists.

It stood grandly, she thought, with its melding of Greek Revival and Gothic styles, the warm yellow stone mellow against the clean white trim. Its double staircase rose up to the balcony wrapping the second level, and served as a crown for the covered entryway on the ground level.

She loved the tall windows, the lacy woodwork on the rail of the third floor, the sheer space of it, and the heritage it stood for.

She had prized it, cared for it, and worked for it since it had come into her hands at her parents' death. She had raised her sons there, and when she'd lost her husband, she'd grieved there.

One day she would pass it to Harper as it had passed to her. And she thanked God for the absolute knowledge that he would tend it and love it just as she did.

What it had cost her was nothing compared with what it gave, even in this single moment, standing at the end of the drive, looking back through the morning mists.

But standing there wasn't going to get her three miles done. She headed west, keeping close to the side of the road though there'd be little to no traffic this early.

To take her mind off the annoyance of exercise, she started reviewing her list of things to do that day.

She had some good seedlings going for annuals that should be ready to have their seed leaves removed. She needed to check all the seedlings for signs of damping off. Some of the older stock would be ready for pricking off.

And, she remembered, Stella had asked for more amaryllis, more forced bulb planters, more wreaths and poinsettia for the holiday sales. Hayley could handle the wreaths. The girl had a good hand at crafting.

Then there were the field-grown Christmas trees and hollies to deal with. Thank God she could leave that end to Logan.

She had to check with Harper, to see if he had any more of the Christmas cacti he'd grafted ready to go. She wanted a couple for herself.

She juggled all the nursery business in her mind even as she passed In the Garden. It was tempting—it always was—to veer off the road onto that crushed stone entryway, to take an indulgent solo tour of what she'd built from the ground up.

Stella had gone all out for the holidays, Roz noted with pleasure, grouping green, pink, white, and red poinsettias into a pool of seasonal color in front of the low-slung house that served as the entrance to the retail space. She'd hung yet another wreath on the door, tiny white lights around it, and the small white pine she'd dug from the field stood decorated on the front porch.

White-faced pansies, glossy hollies, and hardy sage added more interest and would help ring up those holiday sales.

Resisting temptation, Roz continued down the road.

She had to carve out some time, if not today then certainly later this week, to finish up her Christmas shopping. Or at least put a bigger dent in it. There were holiday parties to attend, and the one she'd decided to give. It had been awhile since she'd opened the house to entertain in a big way.

The divorce, she admitted, was at least partially to blame for that. She'd hardly felt like hosting parties when she'd felt stupid and stung and more than a bit mortified by her foolish, and mercifully brief, union to a liar and a cheat.

But it was time to put that aside now, she reminded herself, just as she'd put him aside. The fact that Bryce Clerk was back in Memphis made it only more important that she live her life, publically and privately, exactly as she chose.

At the mile-and-a-half mark, a point she judged by an old, lightning-struck hickory, she started back. The thin fog had dampened her hair and sweatshirt, but her muscles felt warm and loose. It was a bitch, she mused, that everything they said about exercise was true.

She spotted a deer meandering across the road, her coat thickened for winter, her eyes on alert at the intrusion of a human.

You're beautiful, Roz thought, puffing a little on the last half mile. Now stay the hell out of my gardens. Another note went in her file to give her gardens another treatment of repellant before the deer and its pals decided to come around for a snack.

She was just making the turn into the drive when she heard muffled footsteps, then saw the figure coming her way. Even with the mists she had no trouble identifying the other early riser.

They both stopped and jogged in place, and she grinned at her son.

"Up with the worms this morning."

"Thought I'd be up and out early enough to catch you." He scooped a hand through his dark hair. "All that celebrating for Thanksgiving, then your birthday, I figured I'd better work off the excess before Christmas hits."

"You never gain an ounce. It's annoying."

"Feel soft." He rolled his shoulders, then his eyes, whiskey brown like hers, and laughed. "Besides, I gotta keep up with my mama."

He looked like her. There was no denying her stamp was on his face. But when he smiled, she saw his father. "That'll be the day, pal of mine. How far you going?"

"How far'd you?"

"Three miles."

He flashed a grin. "Then I'll do four." He gave her a light pat on the cheek as he passed.

"Should've told him five, just to get his goat," she chuckled, and slowing to a cool-down walk, she started down the drive.

The house shimmered out of the mists. She thought, Thank God that's over for another day. And she circled around to go in as she'd left.

The house was still quiet, and lovely. And haunted.

She'd showered and changed for work, and had started down the central stairs that bisected the wings when she heard the first stirrings.

Stella's boys getting ready for school, Lily fussing for her breakfast—good sounds, Roz thought. Busy, family sounds she'd missed.

Of course, she'd had the house full only a couple weeks earlier, with all her boys home for Thanksgiving and her birthday. Austin and Mason would be back for Christmas. A mother of grown sons couldn't ask for better.

God knew there'd been plenty of times when they'd been growing up that she'd yearned for some quiet. Just an hour of absolute peace where she had nothing more exciting to do than soak in a hot tub.

Then she'd had too much time on her hands, hadn't she? Too much quiet, too much empty space. So she'd ended up marrying some slick son of a bitch who'd helped himself to her money so he could impress the bimbos he'd cheated on her with.

Spilled milk, Roz reminded herself. And it wasn't constructive to dwell on it.

She walked into the kitchen where David was already whipping something in a bowl, and the seductive fragrance of fresh coffee filled the air.

"Morning, gorgeous. How's my best girl?"

"Up and at 'em anyway." She went to a cupboard for a mug. "How was the date last night?"

"Promising. He likes Gray Goose martinis and John Waters movies. We'll try for a second round this weekend. Sit yourself down. I'm making French toast."

"French toast?" It was a personal weakness. "Damn it, David, I just ran three miles to keep my ass from falling all the way to the back of my knees, then you hit me with French toast."

"You have a beautiful ass, and it's nowhere near the back of your knees."

"Yet," she muttered, but she sat. "I passed Harper at the end of the drive. He finds out what's on the menu, he'll be sniffing at the back door."

"I'm making plenty."

She sipped her coffee while he heated up the skillet.

He was movie-star handsome, only a year older than her own Harper, and one of the delights of her life. As a boy he'd run tame in her house, and now he all but ran it.

"David . . . I caught myself thinking about Bryce twice this morning. What do you think that means?"

"Means you need this French toast," he said while he soaked thick slices of bread in his magic batter. "And you've probably got yourself a case of the mid-holiday blues."

"I kicked him out right before Christmas. I guess that's it."

"And a merry one it was, with that bastard out in the cold. I wish it *had* been cold," he added. "Raining ice and frogs and pestilence."

"I'm going to ask you something I never did while it was going on. Why didn't you ever tell me how much you disliked him?"

"Probably the same reason you didn't tell me how much you disliked that out-of-work actor with the fake Brit accent I thought I was crazy about a few years back. I love you."

"It's a good reason."

He'd started a fire in the little kitchen hearth, so she angled her body toward it, sipped coffee, felt steady and solid.

"You know if you could just age twenty years and go straight, we could live with each other in sin. I think that would be just fine."

"Sugar-pie." He slid the bread into the skillet. "You're the only girl in the world who'd tempt me."

She smiled, and resting her elbow on the table, set her

chin on her fist. "Sun's breaking through," she stated. "It's going to be a pretty day."

A PRETTY DAY IN EARLY DECEMBER MEANT A BUSY ONE for a garden center. Roz had so much to do she was grateful she hadn't resisted the breakfast David had heaped on her. She missed lunch.

In her propagation house, she had a full table covered with seed trays. She'd already separated out specimens too young for pricking off. And now began the first transplanting with those she deemed ready.

She lined up her containers, the cell packs, the individual pots or peat cubes. It was one of her favorite tasks, even more than sowing, this placing of a strong seedling in the home it would occupy until planting time.

Until planting time, they were all hers.

And this year, she was experimenting with her own potting soil. She'd been trying out recipes for more than two years now, and believed she'd found a winner, both for indoor and outdoor use. The outdoor recipe should serve very well for her greenhouse purposes.

From the bag she'd carefully mixed, she filled her containers, tested the moisture and approved. With care, she lifted out the young plants, holding them by their seed leaves. Transplanting, she made certain the soil line on the stem was at the same level it had been in the seed tray, then firmed the soil around the roots with experienced fingers.

She filled pot after pot, labeling as she went and humming absently to the Enya music playing gently from the portable CD player she considered essential equipment in a greenhouse.

Using a weak fertilizer solution, she watered them.

Pleased with the progress, she moved through the back opening and into the perennial area. She checked the section—plants recently started from cuttings, those started more than a year before that would be ready for sale in a few months. She watered, and tended, then moved to stock plants to take more cuttings. She had a tray of anemones begun when Stella stepped in.

"You've been busy." Stella, with her curling red hair bundled back in a ponytail, scanned the tables. "Really busy."

"And optimistic. We had a banner season, and I'm expecting we'll have another. If Nature doesn't screw around with us."

"I thought you might want to take a look at the new stock of wreaths. Hayley's worked on them all morning. I think she outdid herself."

"I'll take a look before I leave."

"I let her go early, I hope that's all right. She's still getting used to having Lily with a sitter, even if the sitter is a customer and only a half mile away."

"That's fine." She moved on to the catananche. "You know you don't have to check every little thing with me, Stella. You've been managing this ship for nearly a year now."

"They were excuses to come back here."

Roz paused, her knife suspended above the plant roots, primed for cutting. "Is there a problem?"

"No. I've been wanting to ask, and I know this is your domain, but I wondered if when things slow down a bit after the holidays, if I can spend some time with the propagation. I'm missing it."

"All right."

Stella's bright blue eyes twinkled when she laughed. "I can see you're worried I'll try to change your routine, organize everything my way. I promise I won't. And I won't get in your way."

"You try, I'll just boot you out."

"Got that."

"Meanwhile, I've been wanting to talk to you. I need you to find me a supplier for good, inexpensive soil bags. One-, five-, ten-, and twenty-five-pound to start."

"For?" Stella asked as she pulled a notebook out of her back pocket.

"I'm going to start making and selling my own potting soil. I've got mixes I like for indoor and outdoor use, and I want to private label it."

"That's a great idea. Good profit in that. And customers will like having Rosalind Harper's gardening secrets. There are some considerations, though."

"I thought of them. I'm not going to go hog-wild right off. We'll keep it small." With soil on her hands still, she plucked a bottle of water from a shelf. Then, absently wiping her hand on her shirt, twisted the cap. "I want the staff to learn how to bag, but the recipe's my secret. I'll give you and Harper the ingredients and the amounts, but it doesn't go out to the general staff. For right now, we'll set up the procedure in the main storage shed. It takes off, we'll build one for it."

"Government regulations—"

"I've studied on that. We won't be using any pesticides, and I'm keeping the nutrient content to below the regulatory levels." Noting Stella continue to scribble on her pad, Roz took a long drink. "I've applied for the license to manufacture and sell."

"You didn't mention it."

"Don't get your feelings hurt." Roz set the bottle aside, dipped a cutting in rooting medium. "I wasn't sure I'd go on and do the thing, but I wanted the red tape out of the way. It's kind of a pet project of mine I've been playing with for awhile now. But I've grown some specimens in these mixes, and so far I like what I see. I got some more going now, and if I keep liking it, we're going for it. So I want an idea how much the bags are going to run us, and the printing. I want classy. I thought you could fiddle around with some logos and such. You're good at that. In the Garden needs to be prominent."

"No question."

"And you know what I'd really like?" She paused for a minute, seeing it in her head. "I'd like brown bags. Something that looks like burlap. Old-fashioned, if you follow me. So we're saying, This is good, old-fashioned, dirt, southern soil. And I'm thinking I want cottage garden flowers on the bag. Simple flowers."

"That says, This is simple to use, and it'll make your garden simple to grow. I'll get on it."

"I can count on you, can't I, to work out the costs, profits, marketing angles with me?"

"I'm your girl."

"I know you are. I'm going to finish up these cuttings, then take off early myself if nothing's up. I want to get some shopping in."

"Roz, it's already nearly five."

"Five? It can't be five." She held up an arm, turned her wrist and frowned at her watch. "Well, shit. Time got away from me again. Tell you what, I'm going to take off at noon tomorrow. If I don't, you hunt me down and push me out."

"No problem. I'd better get back. See you back at the house."

THE REEF

Nora Roberts

The *New York Times* bestseller

Tate Beaumont, a beautiful student of marine archaeology, and Matthew Lassiter, a sea-scarred young man, share a dream of finding Angelique's Curse, the jewelled amulet surrounded by legend and said to be long lost at the bottom of the Caribbean.

Forced into a reluctant partnership with Matthew and his uncle, Tate soon learns that her arrogant but attractive fellow diver holds as many secrets as the sea itself. And when the truth emerges about the mysterious death of Matthew's father eight years earlier, desire – and danger – begin to rise to the surface.

'Nora Roberts is at the top of her game'
People

'A consistently entertaining writer'
USA Today

'The publishing world might be hard-pressed to find an author with a more diverse style or fertile imagination than Roberts'
Publishers Weekly

978-0-7499-3159-9

HIGH NOON

Nora Roberts

Those closest to you can do the most harm

Phoebe MacNamara first comes face to face with Duncan Swift high up on a rooftop, as she tries to stop one of his ex-employees from jumping. As Savannah's chief hostage negotiator, Phoebe is talented, courageous and willing to risk her life to save others – and Duncan is determined to keep this intriguing woman in his life.

But Phoebe has made enemies too. When she is viciously assaulted and sent threatening messages, she realises that someone is out to destroy her – both professionally and personally. With Duncan by her side, Phoebe must discover just who is pursuing her, before it's too late . . .

'Women are addicted to her contemporary novels as chocoholics are to Godiva . . . Roberts is a superstar'
New York Times

978-0-7499-3898-7

Other bestselling titles available by mail:

☐ High Noon	Nora Roberts	£6.99
☐ Sanctuary	Nora Roberts	£6.99
☐ Montana Sky	Nora Roberts	£6.99
☐ Northern Lights	Nora Roberts	£6.99
☐ Tribute	Nora Roberts	£11.99

The prices shown above are correct at time of going to press. However, the publishers reserve the right to increase prices on covers from those previously advertised, without further notice.

PIATKUS

Please allow for postage and packing: **Free UK delivery.**
Europe; add 25% of retail price; Rest of World; 45% of retail price.

To order any of the above or any other Piatkus titles, please call our credit card orderline or fill in this coupon and send/fax it to:

Piatkus Books, P.O. Box 121, Kettering, Northants NN14 4ZQ
Fax: 01832 733076 Tel: 01832 737526
Email: aspenhouse@FSBDial.co.uk

☐ I enclose a UK bank cheque made payable to Piatkus for £ . . . .
☐ Please charge £ . . . . . . to my Visa, Delta, Maestro.

☐☐☐☐☐☐☐☐☐☐☐☐☐☐☐☐

Expiry Date ☐☐☐☐ Maestro Issue No. ☐☐

NAME (BLOCK LETTERS please) . . . .

ADDRESS . . . .

. . . .

. . . .

Postcode . . . . Telephone . . . .

Signature . . . .

Please allow 28 days for delivery within the UK. Offer subject to price and availability.